A Dictionary of Stage Directions in English Drama, 1580–1642

This dictionary, the first of its kind, defines and explains over 900 terms found in the stage directions of English professional plays from the 1580s to the early 1640s. The terms are taken primarily from surviving printed and manuscript sources, and from the plays performed on the London stage, by both minor and major dramatists. The authors draw on a database of over 22,000 stage directions culled from around 500 such plays. Each entry offers a definition, gives examples of how the term is used, cites additional instances, and gives cross-references to other relevant entries. Terms defined range from the obvious and common to the obscure and rare, including actions, places, objects, sounds, and descriptions. The authors have also provided a user's guide and an introduction which describes the scope and rationale of the volume. This will be an indispensable work of reference for scholars, historians, directors, and actors.

ALAN C. DESSEN is Peter G. Phialas Professor of English, University of North Carolina, Chapel Hill. His previous books include *Elizabethan Stage Conventions and Modern Interpreters* (1984) and *Recovering Shakespeare's Theatrical Vocabulary* (1995).

LESLIE THOMSON is Associate Professor of English, University of Toronto. She edited Middleton and Webster's *Anything for a Quiet Life* for the Oxford edition of Thomas Middleton, and has published articles on original staging and stage directions.

A Dictionary of
Stage Directions in English Drama
1580–1642

ALAN C. DESSEN and LESLIE THOMSON

CAMBRIDGE
UNIVERSITY PRESS

PUBLISHED BY THE PRESS SYNDICATE OF THE UNIVERSITY OF CAMBRIDGE
The Pitt Building, Trumpington Street, Cambridge CB2 1RP, United Kingdom

CAMBRIDGE UNIVERSITY PRESS
The Edinburgh Building, Cambridge CB2 2RU, UK   http://www.cup.cam.ac.uk
40 West 20th Street, New York, NY 10011–4211, USA   http://www.cup.org
10 Stamford Road, Oakleigh, Melbourne 3166, Australia

First published 1999

Printed in United Kingdom at the University Press, Cambridge

Typeface Lexicon (*The Enschede Font Foundry*) in 8.5 and 10.5 on 12pt   *System* QuarkXPress™   [SE]

A catalogue record for this book is available from the British Library

Library of Congress cataloguing in publication data

Dessen, Alan C., 1935–
    A dictionary of stage directions in English drama, 1580–1642 /
Alan C. Dessen and Leslie Thomson.
        p.   cm.
    Includes bibliographical references (p. 285).
    ISBN 0 521 55250 8
    1. English drama – Early modern and Elizabethan, 1500–1600 –
Dictionaries.   2. Stage directions – History – 16th century –
Dictionaries.   3. Theater – England – Production and direction –
History – 17th century – Dictionaries.   4. Theater – England –
Production and direction – History – 16th century – Dictionaries.
    5. Stage directions – History – 17th century – Dictionaries.
    6. English drama – 17th century – Dictionaries.   I. Thomson, Leslie.
    II. Title.
    PR658.S59D47   1999
    822′.3003–dc21   98-44871
                                                             CIP

ISBN 0 521 55250 8   hardback

Contents

Acknowledgments

This dictionary, and the database on which it relies, could hardly have been compiled without the resources of the Folger Shakespeare Library. Its collection of original and later editions of the plays, as well as of other relevant material, is second to none. But it is the librarians and the atmosphere of the place that have made the often tedious work a pleasure to do. We especially want to thank Reading Room Supervisor Betsy Walsh, Rosalind Larry, Camille Seerattan, LuEllen DeHaven, Harold Batie, and Susan Sehulster. All the effort compiling the database of stage directions would have been next to useless without the contribution of David Thomson, who wrote the program enabling us to search a term to discover how often and where it is used, and who was always ready to give assistance even when he did not really have the time. Numerous colleagues offered comments and suggestions which helped us to establish the format of the entries, the kinds of information to be included, and the range to cover. In addition to the many who responded to our questionnaires, we have especially appreciated the help of R. A. Foakes, Andrew Gurr, William Ingram, Rosalyn Knutson, Richard Kuhta, James Lusardi, Paul Nelsen, Lena Cowen Orlin, Bruce Smith, Stanley Wells, and those who, early in the project, attended and contributed to a lunchtime presentation by us at the Folger. Most particularly, for the list of Plays and Editions Cited and for his many useful ideas for improvements and solutions to problems, we thank Peter W. M. Blayney. To Sarah Stanton, whose advice, patience, and encouragement helped make the task easier than it might have been, we are most grateful.

Introduction

The purpose of this volume is to define and provide examples of terms
found in the stage directions of English professional plays that date from
the 1580s to the early 1640s. By providing such definitions we hope to make
readily available information about English Renaissance theatrical termi-
nology already known to specialists but not to other readers of Shakespeare
and his contemporaries, and to present information and documentation
unfamiliar even to theatre historians and editors. This reference work is
therefore designed to serve as both a handbook for the generalist and a
scholarly tool for the specialist.

To accomplish such goals requires a large number of decisions, some of
which (the sparing use of evidence from dialogue, the exclusion of evidence
from masques) may seem arbitrary or puzzling to readers. The primary
function of this Introduction is therefore to explain our procedures and the
rationale behind them.

In preparing what we hope will be a useful and usable resource, our focus
is on the terms – what we conceive of as the *theatrical vocabulary* – actually
used by the playwrights, bookkeepers, and scribes of the period as reflected
primarily in the stage directions to be found in the surviving manuscripts
and printed texts of plays. Behind this phrase lies our postulation of the
presence then of a language of the theatre shared by playwrights, players,
and playgoers that can easily be blurred or eclipsed in modern editions,
stage productions, and on-the-page interpretations. In some instances, to
re-establish such meanings is easy, no more than translating a Latin word
(*exiturus, manet, rustici*). In other situations, to recover such meanings is
more challenging but nonetheless possible, a process analogous to the
work of an iconographer who ranges widely in the available literature so as
to explicate an image appropriately (see *booted, hair, rosemary*). Elsewhere
the meaning or implementation of a theatrical signal remains very much in
doubt, a matter of scholarly controversy (see *shop, study, trees, vanish*). Our
goal has been to isolate terms and then gloss them as best we can by referring principally to other stage directions rather than to the OED (which we
have, however, regularly consulted).

With few exceptions, the entries in this dictionary are therefore keyed to
words or phrases actually found in the stage directions of this period.
Modern scholarly terms will occasionally be defined (*fictional stage directions,
permissive stage directions*); inevitably, some use must be made of information
provided in the dialogue. The emphasis, however, is on that theatrical
vocabulary found in the tens of thousands of stage directions that consti-
tute the primary evidence for what we know (or think we know) about the
presentation of such plays to their original audiences.

The significance of stage directions

For the reader not familiar with the underpinnings of English Renaissance theatre scholarship, such heavy emphasis on stage directions may seem curious. Why not give equal weight to other kinds of evidence? After all, no account of English Restoration staging would be complete without reference to the playgoing accounts of Samuel Pepys, so why not build here as well on eye-witness accounts? What about theatrical documents such as Henslowe's papers? Most tellingly, why relegate to a lesser status references in play dialogue to actions, costume, properties, and parts of the stage?

What most readers do not realize is how little evidence has actually survived about the staging of plays in this period – the norm is silence. A few eye-witness accounts from playgoers are available (including several for Shakespeare plays), but these accounts can be singularly unrevealing, often amounting to no more than partial plot summaries. Similarly, scraps of useful information do turn up in Henslowe's inventory of costumes and properties (and are cited here when appropriate), but again surprisingly little can be gleaned about theatrical practice from these and comparable documents.

Dialogue evidence is far more plentiful, but this material represents shifting sands, not bedrock. Even when dealing with seemingly concrete stage directions (Q1's "*Romeo opens the tomb*," *The Tempest*'s "*they heavily vanish*") the interpreter today cannot be certain whether the original playgoer saw a verisimilar effect (an elaborate tomb property, a disappearance by means of theatrical trickery) or whether the "tomb" or the "vanishing" was generated by a combination of dialogue, mimed action from the players, and the spectator's imaginative participation. If stage directions can be opaque rather than transparent, dialogue evidence is far trickier to interpret. At least one scholar has argued that a verisimilar "wall" property was necessary for *Richard II* because Hotspur refers to Flint Castle as "yon lime and stone" (3.3.26). Similarly, consider Brutus's reaction to Caesar's ghost: "Art thou some god, some angel, or some devil, / That mak'st my blood cold, and my hair to stare?" (4.3.279–80) or Gertrude's description of Hamlet in the closet scene: "Forth at your eyes your spirits wildly peep, / And as the sleeping soldiers in th' alarm, / Your bedded hair, like life in excrements, / Start up and stand an end" (3.4.119–22). Are we to conclude from these two passages that Richard Burbage had a fright wig or that he had the ability to make his hair stand on end? Or are such descriptions substitutes for what cannot be physically displayed to a playgoer? To tease out stage practice from dialogue is repeatedly to encounter this problem.

To rely almost exclusively on stage directions is, by contrast, to stay within the realm of what was or could have been done in the original productions, particularly when the play in question is linked to a professional company or to an experienced playwright (as distinct from university players and amateur authors). The exigencies of the playhouse are reflected in so-called "permissive" signals, as with the use of *or*, *as many as may be*, or "*Exit Venus. Or if you can conveniently, let a chair come down from the top of the stage, and draw her up*" (*Alphonsus of Aragon*, 2109–10). Scholars rightly observe that these and comparable stage directions may more reflect the playwright's original conception than the actual staging (we are assuming that most stage directions are authorial in origin). But who would be a better judge of what could or could not be accomplished by the players than an experienced writer who had seen many of his plays move from script to stage? When documenting our entries we have therefore made plentiful use of evidence from the canons of such seasoned (and prolific) playwrights as Dekker, Shakespeare, Heywood, Middleton, Fletcher, Massinger, Brome, and Shirley. The thousands of extant stage directions provide the only substantive clues to the language shared by these and other theatrical professionals.

Drawing upon stage directions as evidence, however, is not without its problems. First, editors and theatre historians rightly point to the importance of provenance (place of origin, derivation) in dealing with these signals. Thus, a theatre historian seeking to reconstruct the physical features of a particular building such as the Globe will draw only upon evidence from plays known to have been performed in that building. For an editor, a different question of origins is also crucial: did the manuscript from which the text was printed preserve the pre-production concept of the author(s); had it been annotated for performance (and if so, by whom) or recopied and perhaps "improved" by a scribe; or was it compiled by one or more of the players who had acted in it?

When widely scattered stage directions are used as evidence, the provenance of individual plays cannot be completely ignored (as when Marston, writing with a particular theatre in mind, refers to a *music house*), but in practice we have found this distinction less important than other variables. Indeed, the study of thousands of stage directions does not elicit a technical backstage vocabulary that is the exclusive property of one or another group of theatrical professionals or is linked to specific venues. Some usages are more likely to turn up in texts annotated for performance – e.g., *ready*, *clear* – but examples of the former are sprinkled throughout printed texts of the period, and examples of the latter, although plentiful in the manuscript of Heywood's *The Captives*, are to be found in only two other texts. The language used by a professional dramatist may not be exactly the same as that used by a bookkeeper, a scribe, an amateur writer, an academic, or a Ben Jonson refashioning his play for a reader, nor is there an exact correlation among varying venues or during disparate decades. Nonetheless, by proceeding carefully (and by not building edifices upon unique or highly idiosyncratic usages) we hope to isolate and define a range of terms that would have made excellent sense to Marlowe, Shakespeare, Dekker, Heywood, Jonson, Marston, Chapman, Middleton, Massinger, Brome, Ford, and Shirley.

Similar questions of chronology (when a play and its theatrical signals were composed) can sometimes be relevant to the entries, but with a few exceptions we have not attempted to trace the evolution of terms in the manner of the *OED*. Some locutions found in the 1580s and early 1590s are superseded or simplified in the playtexts that follow (see *let, proffer*); the earlier signals are often longer, without the shorthand forms that later become commonplace. For the bulk of the period up through the 1630s, however, continuity rather than evolution appears to be the norm. To minimize the importance of chronology is not to argue that staging procedures and the terms used to signal those procedures stayed the same in all theatres between the 1580s and the early 1640s. Nonetheless, the fact that a host of playwrights in many theatres over many decades appear to be using the same shared language strikes us as significant. In compiling dictionary entries some account of changes in usage can be instructive as can identifying any distinctive terms or procedures limited largely to Peele, Greene, and the 1580s. But if (as is often the case) Shakespeare/Heywood and Brome/Shirley make use of much the same theatrical vocabulary, the importance of chronological distinctions is greatly diminished. Of greater significance for an investigation of the original stage practice are those signifiers that remain useful and meaningful over the full stretch of Elizabethan–Jacobean–Caroline drama.

When provenance and chronology are invoked, what needs stressing is that there is indeed a widely shared theatrical vocabulary, especially from the 1590s on, and that the major variations in that vocabulary arise less often from different venues or different decades than from authorial idiosyncrasy. For example, Chapman is more likely than any other professional dramatist to use Latin terms, but it is Massinger who is particularly fond of "*exeunt praeter* . . ." where another dramatist would use *manet* or "*exeunt all saving* . . ." Similarly, Massinger and others regularly use *aside* to mean *speak aside*, but Shakespeare, for one, prefers other locutions (e.g., *to himself*) and uses *aside* primarily to denote onstage positioning. In short, there are variations aplenty which, whenever possible, are signaled in our entries.

Inclusions and exclusions

The origins of this dictionary project are to be found in the work of Alan Dessen, who for over twenty years has been collecting materials from medieval, Tudor, Elizabethan, Jacobean, and Caroline playtexts – a selective rather than inclusive process that most recently produced *Recovering Shakespeare's Theatrical Vocabulary* (Cambridge University Press, 1995). Leslie Thomson has also considered problems related to stage directions and original staging in a number of articles. The writing of the entries has been divided more or less evenly, with each of us working on various subject areas.

Our primary tool in constructing entries is a database compiled by

Professor Thomson that consists of over 22,000 stage directions culled from roughly 500 plays (some of them in more than one version). Although we make occasional reference to early Elizabethan troupe plays from the 1560s and 1570s, the database itself does *not* include items from before 1581 (the date of Robert Wilson's *The Three Ladies of London*, the first extant play linked to the London professional theatre); plays with academic auspices; translations; or masques, pageants, and other theatrical events not linked to the professional repertory theatre. The database does, however, include a few plays of uncertain origin that seem to us to be "professional" (e.g., *Tom a Lincoln*); a few of late but uncertain date that seem likely to antedate the closing of the theatres (*The Platonic Lovers*); and some not published until the 1650s or later but certainly written earlier (*The Thracian Wonder*).

As noted at the outset, our primary focus is on the shared theatrical language linked to the professional theatre in London. The moral interludes and other forms of Tudor and early Elizabethan professional drama are not without interest, but are geared to performance by smaller troupes on the road who lacked the resources of the larger companies that developed when permanent theatres were built in London. Some academic plays (e.g., the tragedies of Thomas Goffe written for students at Oxford) include theatrical signals very much in tune with the professional drama, but most of these plays are scripted with very different circumstances in mind.

To sidestep completely the plentiful evidence about the presentation of masques at court may puzzle some readers, especially since their authors are responsible for many of the plays in our database. Masques, however, were no-expense-spared productions with one-time-only effects and therefore tell us little about the exigencies of professional repertory theatre where any onstage devices or choices had to be practicable and repeatable – although masques or pageants included within professional plays often provide suggestive evidence about special effects that could be achieved with the same resources (and the same limitations) as everything else presented in a particular theatre. In dealing with a shared theatrical vocabulary the issue of what is feasible within the constraints of time, budget, and available facilities is of some importance.

In constructing entries, the two most difficult questions have proven to be which items should be glossed and how much documentation should be provided. As to the former, we have heeded the responses to questionnaires distributed to scholars and theatrical professionals and have been as comprehensive as possible. Included, therefore, are a number of unique items (see *astringer, helter skelter, pewter, pot birds*) along with other terms that recur only once or twice in our database. At the other extreme, we have also included items that might not seem to need explanation (verbs such as *bring, carry, lead*; adverbs or prepositions such as *before, behind, forth, in, off, out*) when we have found usages that we consider theatrically significant or suggestive.

Given the wealth of material available in our database, the question of how much documentation to provide has presented a particularly difficult set of choices. Some theatre historians who responded to our queries wanted everything – in essence, a complete concordance of usages of each term. For the non-specialist, however, such massive documentation can drown a reader in a sea of italics and citations (how does one present roughly 375 examples of *sword* or 600 examples of *door*?). At the risk of disappointing everyone, we have sought to satisfy both constituencies. As a general practice – but especially in complex, heavily documented entries – we have placed the essential information or distinctions at the beginning. When the number of examples is within manageable limits, we include everything. When the number proliferates (as is often the case with verbs and widely used properties such as swords and crowns), we quote representative examples and then offer a sampling of citations that can epitomize the rest of the evidence, with the plays in such series placed in roughly chronological order so as to suggest the range of that evidence. As noted earlier, when singling out specific examples we rely more heavily upon signals from veteran professionals such as Heywood, Dekker, Fletcher, Middleton, Massinger, Brome, Shirley, and especially Shakespeare, and draw less upon material from figures such as Killigrew, Glapthorne, and Carlell. We have not sought to "privilege" Shakespeare over his contemporaries, but we recognize that most users of this volume will be more familiar with his plays than with those of Massinger or Brome.

Several omissions should be noted. Even though the names of actors do occasionally appear in stage directions (most notably in Webster's Induction to Marston's *The Malcontent*), we do not include entries for proper names. Similarly, with few exceptions we do not include the many professions or social types regularly cited in these signals. To avoid making our documentation even more unwieldy we have made no attempt to incorporate into our entries information about the dimensions and configurations of theatre buildings, the history and composition of theatre companies, and the economics of the playhouses and playgoing – important topics but beyond the range of this dictionary. Some terms familiar to theatre historians are not among our entries because they do not appear in stage directions, so a reader will encounter *discover* but not *discovery space, hell* but not *hellmouth*. Again, our goal is to isolate and define the terms actually used by playwrights and theatrical personnel in this period as reflected in our database.

A comment is needed about the stage directions provided by Ben Jonson. The first printed version of *Volpone* (the 1607 Quarto) contains no stage directions at all, not even an *enter*; the first printed version of *The Alchemist* (the 1612 Quarto) has only one ("*Dol is seen*" at 2.3.210). The various signals in these two plays now familiar to readers (e.g., the entrance of Volpone in Act 4 "*as impotent*") were added later for the 1616 Folio. Jonson was a professional dramatist highly knowledgeable about his theatre, but throughout his career and especially in the plays that follow *Bartholomew Fair* he often chose to augment his texts with a reader in mind. We have incorporated some of these signals when we have found them instructive or provocative (e.g., "*This Scene is acted at two windows, as out of two contiguous buildings,*" "*He grows more familiar in his Courtship, plays with her paps, kisseth her hands, etc.,*" *The Devil Is an Ass*, 2.6.37, 71) but have been sparing in our use of what we deem to be "literary" stage directions from the Jonson canon.

Texts, documentation, and procedures

In choosing texts from which to draw our citations we have tried to combine accuracy, efficiency, and accessibility. The editorial tradition that started with Shakespeare's plays in the early eighteenth century has not been kind to the original stage directions, so that these theatrical signals have been regularly omitted, rewritten, rearranged, and moved. Thanks to the resources of the Folger Shakespeare Library and microfilm, our database has been compiled from the early printed texts, not from modern editions, so that the documentation within the entries *could* have been linked exclusively to those most authoritative first versions of the plays. To have done so, however, would have made it difficult for users of this dictionary (many of whom will not have access either to the originals or to reproductions of them) to find items they might wish to pursue. We have therefore sought when possible to draw citations from editions that reproduce accurately the original stage directions and are accessible in many libraries (e.g., the Bowers *Dekker*, the Edwards–Gibson *Massinger*, the Revels Plays, Malone Society Reprints, and Tudor Facsimile Texts). Some nineteenth-century collections of plays (of Heywood, Day, Davenport, Brome, Davenant, and Glapthorne) are more reliable on stage directions than are the critical editions produced by the "New Bibliography." See the User's Guide for a summary of our citation practices.

Since Shakespeare is almost always read in modern spelling, we have modernized the spelling of all passages drawn from old-spelling texts. In addition, to avoid obvious inconsistencies we have regularized the use of italic and roman type in the presentation of stage directions and have also expanded abbreviations and contractions – although for the most part we have retained the original capitalization, punctuation, and spelling of proper names. Any minor distortions caused by such changes are offset by the added ease for readers and, in symbolic terms, by the presentation of Shakespeare and his contemporaries as orthographic equals – as opposed to "modern" Shakespeare versus "primitive" Heywood.

To sidestep a host of scholarly controversies and to economize on what can be massive documentation we have for the most part omitted authors' names from our entries. In the attempt to reconstruct a theatrical vocabulary the authorship of specific plays or parts of plays is usually not of major importance. Since an index to plays and topics would be very unwieldy, we have provided plentiful cross-references within the entries by means of bold type and also a list of Terms by Category. References to scholarly works do not appear in entries, but our Select Bibliography includes relevant studies.

A final word is needed about accuracy. In constructing entries from a database various generalizations are inevitable, as with "this term occurs only twice." These claims are subject to the limitations of the compiler of the database (whose eye may have skipped over a stage direction or two, or even an entire page) or to unusual variations in the original spelling (*hood-winked/hudwincked, malcontent/male-content, panting for breath/painting for breth*). Such generalizations should therefore be understood as "to the best of our knowledge and according to the information in our database." In addition, some items will inevitably be omitted or skewed in any attempt at amassing such entries, whereas terms not found in stage directions may be commonplace elsewhere (and therefore may be conspicuous by their absence here). We welcome additions, corrections, and comments from our readers.

Alan C. Dessen and Leslie Thomson
Chapel Hill, Toronto, and Washington DC, 1998

User's guide

Terms in bold italic within entries are cross-references to other entries (e.g., *rapier* in the *sword* entry).

Play titles in lists of citations are in roughly chronological order; examples for quotation are not necessarily chronological.

For plays in the Shakespeare canon, citations include not only reference to a quarto and/or the First Folio, but also act–scene–line reference to the Riverside edition. For the occasional item found in the Riverside textual notes but not in the text, the reference in square brackets indicates where the term belongs (e.g., *breast* in Quarto *2 Henry VI*, E2r, [3.2.0]). In a few cases where even the Riverside notes do not include the entry term, this fact is indicated in the square brackets.

Square brackets are also used for a few non-Shakespearean plays when the edition cited does not include the original term.

For directions found in the textual notes but not in the text of the Glover–Waller *Beaumont and Fletcher*, citations give the page number where the stage direction belongs and the page number of the note, separated by a slash (e.g., *ambo* in *Philaster*, 95/406).

All references are to stage directions, so *s.d.* is not included. Because many editions do not provide line numbers for stage directions, the line cited is the one preceding the direction in question. When line numbers are not available, page numbers or signatures are given. References to a play in multi-volume works of an author (e.g., Heywood, Fletcher, Brome, Davenant) give page numbers but not volume numbers, which can be found in the List of Plays and Editions Cited.

The source for play titles, authorship attributions, and dates is the third edition of the *Annals of English Drama 975–1700*. In citations the initial articles are omitted from play titles, and longer titles have been shortened. See the List of Plays and Editions Cited for complete information.

For citations within parentheses, "also" is used to refer to a similar usage in the play being quoted, whereas "see also" is for similar usages in a different play or plays. The absence of either "also" or "see also" from a parenthetical list following a quotation means that the uses are the same; "see also" outside parenthetical references generally indicates that the examples cited are broadly similar in their use of the relevant term or phrase. In addition, "see also" is used to cite related terms, usually at the end of an entry.

There are no entries for proper names, and with few exceptions professions and social roles are not glossed (so there are no entries for *friar*, *nurse*, *merchant*, etc.). The reference work to be consulted for this information is *An Index of Characters in Early Modern English Drama*, compiled by Thomas Berger, Sidney Sondergard and William Bradford. With two exceptions (*fictional stage directions* and *permissive stage directions*) entries are only for terms found in stage directions.

Generalizations such as "this term is found only twice" or "there are roughly 600 examples of *door*" should be understood as implying "in our database" and "in stage directions of the period." References to the use of a term are only to its use in stage directions.

The following abbreviations are used in the *Dictionary*:

DS	dumb show	Riv.	*The Riverside Shakespeare*, ed.
F	First Folio		G. Blakemore Evans. Boston, 1974.
Q1	first quarto	r	recto (right page)
Q2	second quarto	v	verso (left page)

Dictionary of stage directions

A

abed

of the many signals for a figure in a **bed** only three use this term: "*King abed*" (*Maid's Tragedy*, 61), "*Livia discovered abed, and Moroso by her*" (*Woman's Prize*, 80), "*Son abed*" (added by the bookkeeper in the manuscript of *Barnavelt*, 1656).

above

by far the most common term (occurring roughly 300 times in over 150 plays) for the performance area over the main platform elsewhere designated **walls** or **window**, which also functioned as the **music room**; typically one or two figures appear *above*, or **aloft**, five being the maximum in all but a few plays, with the more figures *above*, the more minimal the action and shorter the scene; for a sampling of the usual direction, **enter** *above*, see *Battle of Alcazar* plot, 25, 56; *Jew of Malta*, 658; *Locrine*, 309; *Englishmen for My Money*, 1706; *Antonio and Mellida*, 1.1.98; *Family of Love*, D3r, E2r; *1 If You Know Not Me*, 240; *Gentleman Usher*, 5.1.0; *Woman Is a Weathercock*, 3.1.17; *Humour out of Breath*, 469; *Dutch Courtesan*, 2.1.8; *Miseries of Enforced Marriage*, 1867; *Ram Alley*, H3v; *Puritan*, H2r; *2 Iron Age*, 379; *More Dissemblers*, B6v; *Changeling*, 3.3.176; *Barnavelt*, 2144–5; *Chances*, 228; *Queen of Corinth*, 56; *False One*, 340; *Loyal Subject*, 153; *Maid in the Mill*, 11; *Dick of Devonshire*, 264–5; *Believe as You List*, 1960–3; *Love's Sacrifice*, 691; *Cunning Lovers*, D4v; *Seven Champions*, G3r; *Messalina*, 1415; *Rebellion*, 83; *Claracilla*, F9v, F12v; *Distresses*, 301; *Obstinate Lady*, B1v; *Noble Stranger*, C4r; sometimes the signal is simply *above* (*Spanish Tragedy*, [2.2.17]; *Merchant of Venice*, D2r, 2.6.25; *Lust's Dominion*, 3.2.188; *Blurt*, 3.1.135; Folio *Othello*, 89, 1.1.81; *Michaelmas Term*, 2.3.96; *Philaster*, 100; *Revenge of Bussy*, 5.5.85; *Witch*, 1345; *Maid of Honour*, 2.4.0; *Duchess of Suffolk*, D1r; *Vow Breaker*, 2.4.73–4; *Example*, D2v; *Court Beggar*, 233; *Lady's Trial*, 1189; *Lost Lady*, 589); some figures **appear** *above* (*Edmond Ironside*, 873; *Poetaster*, 4.9.0; *Brazen Age*, 237; *Prophetess*, 388; *Antipodes*, 311), which may involve the use of an upper-level **curtain** specified in several directions: "*The curtains drawn*

above, Theodosius, and his Eunuchs discovered" (*Emperor of the East*, 1.2.288); see also *Thracian Wonder*, D1v; *Eastward Ho*, E3v; *Epicœne*, 4.6.0; *Unnatural Combat*, 5.2.238; *Goblins*, 5.5.19; less common is **exit** *above* (Quarto *2 Henry VI*, C1r, 1.4.52; *Death of Huntingdon*, 2214; Q2 *Bussy D'Ambois*, 5.4.186; *Woman's Prize*, 20; *Women Beware Women*, 2.2.387; *'Tis Pity*, 3.2.64; *Just Italian*, 241; *Bashful Lover*, 5.3.89; *Love and Honour*, 175; *Princess*, D1r).

Signals for **music/song** *above* imply the use of a music room: "*Music and a Song, above, and Cupid enters*" (*Tragedy of Byron*, 2.2), "*Musicians show themselves above*" (*Late Lancashire Witches*, 216), "*Trumpets small above*" (*Four Plays in One*, 359), "*Corporal and Watch above singing*" (*Knight of Malta*, 116), "*Still music above*" (*Cruel Brother*, 183); see also *Sophonisba*, 4.1.210; *Roman Actor*, 2.1.215; *Fatal Dowry*, 4.2.50; *Fatal Contract*, G3v; *Money Is an Ass*, E3r; *Novella*, 129; *Parson's Wedding*, 494; **fictional** designations include *above* on the walls (*Blind Beggar of Alexandria*, 2.0; *1 Iron Age*, 298), in/at a window (*Christian Turned Turk*, F3v; *Doctor Faustus*, B 1205–6; *Henry VIII*, 3015, 5.2.19; *Devil's Law Case*, 5.5.0; *Widow*, E3v; *Wizard*, 2143; *Princess*, C3v), "*at the grate*" (*New Wonder*, 174), "*in a Gallery*" (*Second Maiden's Tragedy*, 2004), "*in a cloud*" (*Silver Age*, 130), "*upon a Balcony*" (*Weeding of Covent Garden*, 8); other examples of action *above* are "*sits above*" (*David and Bethsabe*, 23), "*speaks from above*" (*Epicœne*, 4.2.70; see also *David and Bethsabe*, 212; *Heir*, 583; *Wizard*, 2398), "*with Lavall's body, above*" (*Four Plays in One*, 353), "*looks from above*" (*Jack Drum's Entertainment*, D3r), "*ready above*" (*Knight of Malta*, 85/387; see also *Welsh Ambassador*, 796–8), "*Peep above*" (*Little French Lawyer*, 440; see also *New Trick*, 232), "*Lights above*" (*Little French Lawyer*, 421), "*Callibeus above drops a Letter*" (*Osmond*, B1r), "*climbs the tree, and is received above*" (*Fawn*, 5.0), "*a great noise above*" (*Picture*, 4.2.144), "*from above a Willow garland is flung down*" (*What You Will*, B1v); in a few signals *above* denotes something other than the upper platform: "*Medea with strange fiery works, hangs above in the Air*" (*Brazen Age*, 217), "*Sink down, above flames*" (*If This Be Not a Good Play*, 5.3.149), "*Medlay appears above the Curtain*" (*Tale of a Tub*, 5.10.9); see also *Island Princess*, 107.

abscondit se

the seldom used Latin for "hides himself" found in *All Fools*, 1.1.240, *Nero*, 39.

act

can refer to (1) the *entr'acte* entertainment, (2) one of the five segments of a play, (3) performing an *action*; differentiating between the first two usages is not always possible, but instances of *act* for *music* between the *acts* are "*They sleep all the Act*" (Folio *Midsummer Night's Dream*, 1507, [3.2.463]), "*the cornets and organs playing loud full music for the Act*" (*Sophonisba*, 1.2.236, also 2.1.0, 2.3.114, 3.2.84, 4.1.218), "*In the act-time De Flores hides a naked rapier*" (*Changeling*, 3.1.0), "*Whilst the Act plays, the Footstep, little Table, and Arras hung up for the Musicians*" (*City Madam*, 4.4.160), "*a passage over the Stage, while the Act is playing*" (*Fatal Dowry*, 2.2.359), "*Act Ready*" (annotated *Two Merry Milkmaids*, E2r, H1v, and more), "*Knock Act*" (annotated *Two Merry Milkmaids*, E2r), "*long Act 4*" (*Believe as You List*, 1791; see also *James IV*, 1165; *1 Fair Maid of the West*, 320); for more see *Antonio's Revenge*, 3.1.0, 4.2.118; *Malcontent*, 2.1.0; *Fawn*, 5.0; one of the five *acts* is meant in "*The first Act being ended, the Consort of Music soundeth a pleasant Galliard*" (*Fedele and Fortunio*, 387–8, also 863, 1095, 1487, 1807), "*all awake, and begin the following Act*" (*Histriomastix*, E2r), "*after the first act*" (*James IV*, 633, 651), "*Finis Actus primi*" (*Knight of the Burning Pestle*, 178, also 193, 209); see also *Antonio's Revenge*, 5.1.0; *Charlemagne*, 575; *Faithful Friends*, 2816; *Landgartha*, H4r; behavior is signaled in "*Acts furiously*" (*Ladies' Privilege*, 107), "*acting the postures*" (*Nice Valour*, 188), "*This Scene is acted at two windows*" (*Devil Is an Ass*, 2.6.37); see also *Poetaster*, 3.4.345; MS *Poor Man's Comfort*, 1270; *Court Beggar*, 247, 263.

action

used occasionally to signal a distinctive movement or *gesture*: "*Walks by, and uses action to his Rapier*" (Quarto *Every Man Out*, 2110), "*gentle actions of saluta-tions*" (*Tempest*, 1537, 3.3.19), "*Whispers, and uses vehe-ment actions*" (*Renegado*, 2.1.68), "*depart in a little whisper and wanton action*" (*Your Five Gallants*, A2r), "*A Spirit (over the door) does some action to the dishes as they enter*" (*Late Lancashire Witches*, 206); the term is usually found in *dumb shows* and other mimed *actions*: "*meeting them with action of wonderment*" (*Changeling*, 4.1.0), "*with mute action*" (*Queen and Concubine*, 46), "*makes passionate action*" (*Hamlet*, Q2 H1v, Folio 1998, 3.2.135), "*Silent actions of passions, kiss her hand*" (*2 Arviragus and Philicia*, F11v), Chastity "*in*

dumb action uttering her grief to Mercy" (*Warning for Fair Women*, G3r), "*They Dance an Antic in which they use action of Mockery and derision to the three Gentlemen*" (*English Moor*, 67); atypical are "*the first scene Consisting more in action than speech*" (*Launching of the Mary*, 2669–70), a group dancing like fools and "*acting the postures*" (*Nice Valour*, 188); see also *Your Five Gallants*, I3r.

afar off, far off, afar

widely used (with *afar* sometimes spelled *a far*) (1) usually for offstage *sounds* but (2) occasionally for onstage actions; most commonly *afar off* are the sounds of a *march* (Folio *3 Henry VI*, 389, 1.2.68; Q2 *Hamlet*, O1v, 5.2.349; *All's Well*, 1648, 3.5.37; *Blind Beggar of Bednal Green*, 4; *Sophonisba*, 5.2.29; *Timon of Athens*, 1647, 4.3.45; *If This Be Not a Good Play*, 5.2.43; *Prophetess*, 389; *Love and Honour*, 106) and *drums*; for a sampling of roughly thirty-five examples of drums *afar off* see *Edmond Ironside*, 963, 1560, 1771; *Woodstock*, 2152; *1 Henry VI*, 1614, 3.3.28; 1989, 4.2.38; Folio *Richard III*, 3807, 5.3.337; *King Lear*, K1v, 2737, 4.6.284; *Antony and Cleopatra*, 2731, 4.9.29; *Coriolanus*, 503, 1.4.15; *Sophonisba*, 5.1.71; *Knight of Malta*, 109; *If This Be Not a Good Play*, 4.3.7, 5.1.4, 5.1.76, 5.2.43; *Valiant Welshman*, B2r, B2v, D1v; *Two Noble Ladies*, 1664; *Sisters*, C5v; *Unfortunate Lovers*, 43, 44; *Bonduca* provides "*Drums within at one place afar off*," "*Drums in another place afar off*," "*Alarms, Drums and Trumpets in several places afar off, as at a main Battle*" (116–18, also 90); also heard *afar off* are a *tucket* (*All's Well*, 1602, 3.5.0), *battle* (*Edward III*, E3r), *charge* (*King John and Matilda*, 44), *retreat* (*Antony and Cleopatra*, 2630, 4.7.8), *flourish* (*Love and Honour*, 111; *Platonic Lovers*, 14), *trumpets/cornets* (*Spanish Tragedy*, 1.2.99; *Look about You*, 1002; *Sophonisba*, 5.2.29, 5.3.0; *2 If You Know Not Me*, 316; *Virgin Martyr*, 1.1.108), *alarms* (Folio *2 Henry VI*, 3304, 5.2.77; *Coriolanus*, 509, 1.4.19; 573, 1.5.3; *If This Be Not a Good Play*, 5.1.4, 5.1.76; *Birth of Merlin*, G2v), *music* (*Pilgrim*, 221), "*Singing within*" (*Tottenham Court*, 105); sometimes the signal is pre-sented in terms of *as* [*if*]: "*A Bell rings as far off*" (*Messalina*, 691), "*Here the Alarums sound as afar off*" (*Landgartha*, H4r), "*A retreat being sounded as from far*" (*Love and Honour*, 101), "*Alarum afar off, as at a Sea fight*" (*Antony and Cleopatra*, 2752, 4.12.3); a useful distinc-tion is provided by Folio *Hamlet*'s "*March afar off, and shout within*" (3836, 5.2.349) where "*afar off*" denotes a sound in the distance as distinct from the *shout* that presumably occurs just offstage.

Afar off is also used for onstage action; an example is "*Enter Hamlet and Horatio afar off*" (Folio *Hamlet*,

3245, 5.1.55) where the term means "on the stage but at a distance" as made explicit in *"Stand at distance"* (*News from Plymouth*, 193); other examples include *"riseth, and stands afar off"* (*Thomas Lord Cromwell*, E1v), *"She sits far off from him"* (*Wisdom of Doctor Dodypoll*, 1311), *"Enter two Citizens at both doors, saluting afar off"* (*Double Marriage*, 360), *"Nobles afar off"* when the Tyrant enters (*Second Maiden's Tragedy*, 1656), an entrance *"While they are fighting afar off"* (*Country Girl*, I4v); an abbess in a **dumb show** puts down a baby, then *"standing afar off"* watches a shepherd pick it up, but the more familiar usage is found later in the same manuscript when *"a trumpet sounds afar off"* (*Tom a Lincoln*, 167, 801–3).

affrighted, frighted

the most common terms for "frightened, afraid" usually as adjectives or adverbs linked to an **as** [**if**] construction, an action, or both; *as* [*if*] locutions include *"starting as something affright"* (*David and Bethsabe*, 93), *"Enter, as affrighted and amazed"* (*Wise Woman of Hogsdon*, 309), *"Into this Tumult Enter Calisto as affrighted"* and *"as affright run in"* (*Escapes of Jupiter*, 109, 2392–3), *"Enter King with his Rapier drawn in one hand, leading Maria seeming affrighted in the other"* (*Lust's Dominion*, 3.2.0); *affrighted* is often used when figures **enter**/**exit**: *"Exeunt omnes, as fast as may be, frighted"* (*Comedy of Errors*, 1447, 4.4.146), *"Thunder and lightning. All the servants run out of the house affrighted"* (*Silver Age*, 122), *"it Thunders and Lightens: all affrightedly – Exeunt"* (*Match Me in London*, 5.3.0); *affrighted* figures also **start** or otherwise react instinctively: *"affrightedly starts up"* (*Lovesick Court*, 129), *"he frighted, sits upright"* (*Witch of Edmonton*, 4.2.69), *"Reads to herself. Starts as if affrighted, shakes with fear"* (*Launching of the Mary*, 2129–30); occasionally *fright* is used as a verb, adjective, or noun: *"Charlemont rises in the disguise and frights D'Amville away"* (*Atheist's Tragedy*, 4.3.174; see also *Epicœne*, 4.5.220; *Conspiracy*, K2v), *"some spirit in a frightful shape"* (*If This Be Not a Good Play*, 4.4.38), enter *"undressed, and in a fright"* (*Andromana*, 261); see also **fearful**.

afore
see **before**

again

in the locution **enter** *again* a widely used equivalent to today's *re-enter* (a term not found): *"Enter Ghost again"* (Folio *Hamlet*, 125, [1.1.125]), *"enter presently again"* (*Queen and Concubine*, 28), *"Exeunt, and come in again"* (*Humorous Day's Mirth*, 4.2.26), *"Enter*

Roderique again at another door" (*All's Lost by Lust*, 5.2.0), *"Exit. And straight enters again"* (*Famous Victories*, B4v), *"enter again in a maze"* (*Locrine*, 2064); at the climax of *Taming of a Shrew* first Valeria, then a boy are sent off to call the wives to their husbands and then *"Enter Valeria again"* and *"Enter the Boy again"* with the refusals (F4r, F4v, also D3r); for Shakespeare figures who *enter again* see *Comedy of Errors*, 1476, 5.1.9; Folio *2 Henry VI*, 2773, 4.8.0; Q2 *Romeo and Juliet*, D4r, 2.2.157; Folio *Hamlet*, 1999, 3.2.135; *Antony and Cleopatra*, 1132, 2.5.84; *Coriolanus*, 1993, 3.1.262; *Cymbeline*, 2895, 5.2.0; *Tempest*, 1616–17, 3.3.82; for representative examples from the Fletcher canon see *Captain*, 314; *Maid's Tragedy*, 42; *Nice Valour*, 157; *Maid in the Mill*, 59; *Bloody Brother*, 295; *Faithful Shepherdess*, 405, 428; *again* can also be attached to **exits**: *"Virolet and they off again"* (*Double Marriage*, 362), *"she sees Jolas and goes in again"* (*Aglaura*, 1.1.22), enter *"dancing a hornpipe, and dance out again"* (*James IV*, 1179–80).

alarm, alarum

two spellings of the widely used signal (roughly 400 examples) for a call to **arms** in the form of **sound** produced offstage before and during a **battle** helping to create an atmosphere of conflict and confusion; at Richard III's call for "A flourish, trumpets! strike alarum, drums!" is *"Flourish. Alarums"* (Folio *Richard III*, 2926, 4.4.151) and evidence indicates that a **drum** was usually used, although occasionally a **trumpet** or another instrument is indicated; the signal is most commonly simply *alarum* – the predominant spelling – with numerous examples in stage plots and playhouse manuscripts (*Battle of Alcazar* plot, 22; *Troilus and Cressida* plot, 11, 14, 30, 32, 33, 45; *2 Seven Deadly Sins*, 34, 63, 67; *1 Tamar Cham*, 15, 17, 41; *Edmond Ironside*, 956; *Two Noble Ladies*, 1, 2029); *alarum* occurs regularly in Shakespeare plays with military business (*1 Henry VI*, 586, 1.4.111; Folio *Henry V*, 2483, 4.6.0; *Macbeth*, 2415, 5.7.13; *Antony and Cleopatra*, 2621, 4.7.0); for typical uses of *alarum* in the Heywood canon see *Rape of Lucrece*, 242; *Golden Age*, 50, 74; *1 Iron Age*, 309; *2 Iron Age*, 361; for other *alarums* see *2 Tamburlaine*, 3724; *Orlando Furioso*, 1342; *Trial of Chivalry*, H4v; *All's Lost by Lust*, 2.3.0; for the more specific *alarum* **within** see *Battle of Alcazar*, 362, 1300; *Death of Huntingdon*, 1926; *Revenge of Bussy*, 4.1.0; *All's Well*, 1977, 4.1.64; Folio *King Lear*, 2918, 5.2.0; *Macbeth*, 15, 1.2.0; *Two Noble Ladies*, 2016, 2022; *Amorous War*, G4r; *Brennoralt*, 1.1.18, 5.2.0; probably a call for reduced volume is *alarum* **afar off** (Folio *2*

Henry VI, 3304, 5.2.77; *Birth of Merlin*, G2v; *Antony and Cleopatra*, 2752, 4.12.3; *If This Be Not a Good Play*, 5.1.4); the signal for continuing sound is *alarum still*: "*Alarum continues still afar off*" (*Coriolanus*, 573, 1.5.3), "*Alarum, still afar off*" (*If This Be Not a Good Play*, 5.1.76); see also Octavo *3 Henry VI*, C2v, [2.5.0; not in Riv.]; *Death of Huntingdon*, 1943; *Julius Caesar*, 2674, 5.5.29; *Revenge of Bussy*, 4.1.6, 10; *Two Noble Ladies*, 66, 1212; commonly combined signals are *alarum excursions* (*1 Henry VI*, 1541, 3.2.103; *Richard III*, M3r, 3824, 5.4.0; *David and Bethsabe*, 814; *Guy of Warwick*, C4r; *1 Henry IV*, K1v, 5.4.0; *Caesar and Pompey*, 4.2.0; *All's Lost by Lust*, 2.5.0; *1 Iron Age*, 295) and *alarum retreat* (*1 Henry VI*, 638, 1.5.39; Folio *2 Henry VI*, 2773, 4.8.0; Folio *3 Henry VI*, 1311, 2.6.30; *Alphonsus of Germany*, I1r; *Julius Caesar*, 2699, 5.5.51; *King Lear*, K4r, 2926, 5.2.4; *Imposture*, B3v); other uses of *alarum* include "*Alarums to the fight*" (*2 Henry VI*, F4v, 2511, 4.3.0), "*Alarum, and Chambers go off*" (Folio *Henry V*, 1118, 3.1.34), "*Alarums continued*" (*Macbeth*, 2393, 5.6.10), "*Loud alarum*" (*Julius Caesar*, 2473, 5.2.2), "*A great Alarum and shot*" (*Fortune by Land and Sea*, 410), "*After a long alarum*" (*Hieronimo*, 11.0, 11.111; see also *Weakest Goeth*, 2), "*A short Alarum*" (*1 Henry VI*, 608, 1.5.14; *All's Well*, 2007, 4.1.88), "*Soft Alarum*" (*Doubtful Heir*, F3r), "*Strike up alarum a while*" (*Alphonsus of Aragon*, 373), "*Sound alarum*" (*King Leir*, 2614; *Locrine*, 801, 821).

ale
see *beer*

alias
used in *disguise* plots to mean "now known as": *enter* "*Shore alias Flood*" (*2 Edward IV*, 155), "*Leverduce, alias Lugier*" (*Wild Goose Chase*, 356), "*Shortyard, alias Blastfield*" (*Michaelmas Term*, 2.1.0); see also *Edward I*, 267; *Thracian Wonder*, C4r; *2 If You Know Not Me*, 320; *Insatiate Countess*, [5.1.0]; *Knight of Malta*, 83; *Weeding of Covent Garden*, 12; *Queen and Concubine*, 90; atypical are "*Belphagor, terming himself Castiliano*" (*Grim the Collier*, G7r), and "*Enter Filenio now called Niofell, and his servant Goffo, now called Foggo*" (*Wit of a Woman*, 361–2); these ten examples that range from Peele to Brome may shed some light on Shakespeare's one usage, "*Enter Rosalind for Ganymede, Celia for Aliena, and Clown, alias Touchstone*" (*As You Like It*, 782–3, 2.4.0); since Touchstone is not named in Act 1, the direction for this, his first appearance in Arden, could be read to mean that "Touchstone," like "Ganymede" and "Aliena," is an assumed name.

aliis
in the locution *cum aliis* Latin for "with others" (an alternative to *caeteri/cum caeteris*) found when figures *enter* and *exit*; see Q2 *Hamlet*, B3v, 1.2.0; Folio *Hamlet*, 1020, 2.2.0; *Wisdom of Doctor Dodypoll*, 1312; *2 If You Know Not Me*, 313; *Coriolanus*, 2424, 3.3.135; *Noble Stranger*, I1r; usages are inconsistent, as in *Tragedy of Byron* where an entrance "*cum aliis*" is followed by another entrance "*with others*" (5.1.0, 25).

aloft
a seldom used synonym for *above* that designates the performance level over the main platform; *aloft* is the more usual term in the Shakespeare canon: "*Enter aloft the drunkard with attendants*" (*Taming of the Shrew*, 151, Induction.2.0), "*Enter Richard aloft, between two Bishops*" (*Richard III*, H1v, 2313, 3.7.94), "*They heave Antony aloft to Cleopatra*" (*Antony and Cleopatra*, 3045, 4.15.37, also 2996, 4.15.0); see also *Titus Andronicus*, A3r, 1.1.0; *1 Henry VI*, 1952, 4.2.2; Folio *2 Henry VI*, 632, 1.4.12; Q2 *Romeo and Juliet*, H2v, 3.5.0; for more entrances *aloft* see *Charlemagne*, 2132–3; *Greene's Tu Quoque*, C4v, F1r; *Turk*, 83, 210, 1785; *Dumb Knight*, 116, 128, 186, 189; *Seven Champions*, K3v, K4r; *Herod and Antipater*, D1r; *Messalina*, 2230; other uses of *aloft* are "*opens the door, and finds Lorenzo asleep aloft*" (*Alphonsus of Germany*, B1v), "*music aloft*" and "*there must appear aloft, as many gallants and ladies as the room Can well hold*" (*Launching of the Mary*, 245, 2677–8), "*gloriously crowned in an Arch-glittering Cloud aloft*" (*Messalina*, 2208–9).

alone
widely used (over 100 examples) (1) usually to direct an actor to *enter alone* onto an empty stage to deliver a speech but (2) occasionally to mean "unaccompanied but not alone on stage"; figures who appear *alone* sometimes deliver weighty speeches: Friar Laurence "*alone with a basket*" (Q2 *Romeo and Juliet*, D4v, 2.3.0), Juliet for her "Gallop apace, you fiery-footed steeds" (Q2 *Romeo and Juliet*, G1r, 3.2.0), Richard II in prison (*Richard II*, I3v, 5.5.0), the sleepless Henry IV "*in his nightgown alone*" (*2 Henry IV*, E3v, 3.1.0), Lady Macbeth "*alone with a Letter*" (*Macbeth*, 348, 1.5.0); entrances *alone* may also be linked to comedy: Launcelot Gobbo (*Merchant of Venice*, C1r, 2.2.0), Benedick (*Much Ado*, C4v, 2.3.0), Berowne "*with a paper in his hand, alone*" (*Love's Labour's Lost*, E2v, 4.3.0); for plays with multiple examples of such entrances *alone* see *Gallathea* (2.1.0, 2.3.0, 2.4.0, 2.5.0, 3.1.0, 4.3.0, 5.1.0, 5.3.9), *Cymbeline* (592, 1.6.0; 2081,

3.6.0; 2218, 4.1.0; 2857, 5.1.0), *Two Noble Kinsmen* (E4r, 2.4.0; F1v, 2.6.0; F2r, 3.1.0; F4r, 3.2.0; I3v, 4.2.0); Romeo appears *alone* at *Romeo and Juliet*, 2.1.0 in both Q1 (C4v) and Q2 (D1r), but for his molehill speech Henry VI appears at *3 Henry VI*, 2.5.0 *alone* in the Folio (1134) but *solus* in the Octavo (C2v); figures can appear *alone* in the midst of *battle* sequences: "*Abdelmelech alone in the battle*" (*Captain Thomas Stukeley*, 2773–4), "*Alarm again, and enter the Earl of Warwick alone*" (*2 Henry VI*, H2v, [5.2.0; not in Riv.]); see also *1 Tamburlaine*, 663; Quarto *2 Henry VI*, H3r, [5.2.30]; *alone* can be linked to *exits* as well as entrances: "*They all march off and leave Saturn alone*" (*Golden Age*, 52), "*Vortiger left alone*" (*Hengist*, DS before 4.3, 7), "*Here they all steal away from Wyatt and leave him alone*" (*Sir Thomas Wyatt*, 4.3.51).

As with *solus*, however, *alone* does not always signify "alone on stage," for occasionally the entering figure joins others already present; examples are a *melancholy* Paris complaining of being "all solitary" who enters *alone* to join three goddesses already onstage (*Arraignment of Paris*, 416), Envy who enters "*alone to all the Actors sleeping on the Stage*" (*Histriomastix*, E1v), Grissil who enters *alone* with her husband and others onstage and with a large group "*after her*" (*Patient Grissil*, 5.2.105); see also *1 Troublesome Reign*, E4r; *Taming of a Shrew*, E4v; *Titus Andronicus* includes several examples of the typical use of *alone* (Quarto D1v, 2.3.0; Folio 554, [2.1.0]) but also provides an entrance of an unattended Tamora "*alone to the Moor*" and an appearance of Aaron *alone* to address Titus (D1v, 2.3.9; F1r, 3.1.149); Falstaff begins his first scene in *2 Henry IV* "*alone, with his page bearing his sword and buckler*" (B1r, 1.2.0); when applied to a figure who is part of a large entering group, *alone* apparently means either "unaccompanied" or "set apart from others onstage"; a group entrance for the trial of the queen in *Henry VIII* starts with two vergers, then two scribes, "*after them, the Bishop of Canterbury alone*" (1334–5, 2.4.0) followed by four other bishops as a unit and a host of others; a comparable group entrance has "*Cardinal alone*" in the middle (*Lust's Dominion*, 5.1.0), and another large entrance after a *wedding* includes "*Baltazar alone*" (*Noble Spanish Soldier*, 5.4.0); some figures enter *alone* with others trailing behind or observing: "*Cupid alone, in Nymph's apparel, and Neptune listening*" (*Gallathea*, 2.2.0), "*Isabella alone, Gniaca following her*" (*Insatiate Countess*, 4.2.0); other variations include a short scene that starts with "*Medice after the song, whispers alone with his servant*" (*Gentleman Usher*,

3.1.0), "*aside alone*" (*Captain Thomas Stukeley*, 1071), a usurper who in an ensemble scene "*ascends alone*" to the throne (*Bloody Banquet*, 55).

aloof, aloof off

a number of figures are directed to *stand* or *enter aloof/aloof off*, an equivalent to *aside*, *afar off*, or "*Stand at distance*" (*News from Plymouth*, 193); typical is Folio *3 Henry VI* where the French king asks a group "*to stand aside*" and "*They stand aloof*" (1847, 3.3.111); for others who *stand aloof* see *Satiromastix*, 2.1.156; *Lust's Dominion*, 4.3.48; *Whore of Babylon*, 2.1.24, 4.2.0; *Two Noble Kinsmen*, L1v, 5.1.136; *Witch of Edmonton*, 5.1.76; *stand aloof* can be linked to an entrance: "*enter and stand aloof beholding all*" (*Whore of Babylon*, 4.1.0), "*Roger comes in sadly behind them, with a pottle-pot, and stands aloof off*" (*1 Honest Whore*, 2.1.117), "*Enter Jane in a Seamster's shop working, and Hammond muffled at another door, he stands aloof*" (*Shoemakers' Holiday*, 3.4.0); see also *2 Edward IV*, 173; *English Moor*, 76; entrances in which one figure is *aloof/aloof off* include *James IV*, 118–19; *John a Kent*, 648, 1605; *Patient Grissil*, 4.2.108; *Escapes of Jupiter*, 2280; *No Wit*, 4.1.0; *Captives*, 2985; *Virgin Martyr*, 3.3.100; *Sparagus Garden*, 160; *Young Admiral*, H3v; *Gamester*, E3v; *Hyde Park*, C4r; *Sisters*, D6r; *Changes*, H3r; *School of Compliment*, C4v; *Distresses*, 303; figures who enter *aloof* often are spying, eavesdropping, "*following aloof*" (*John a Kent*, 605; *Whore of Babylon*, 2.2.185), "*muffled aloof off*" (*Roaring Girl*, 4.2.219); typical is Horace who enters *aloof* (*Satiromastix*, 4.2.24) so as to elicit the comment "Captain, captain, Horace stands sneaking here"; comparable is "*She espies her husband, walking aloof off, and takes him for another Suitor*" (*1 Edward IV*, 83); *aloof* can be combined with *retire*: "*Enter Stukeley and his Italian band: who keeping aloof, Sebastian sends Antonio to him, with whom Stukeley draws near toward the king, and having awhile conferred, at last retires to his soldiers*" (*Captain Thomas Stukeley*, 2450–3); a variation is for a figure to enter *followed* by another who *listens* (*Roaring Girl*, 2.2.3; *Old Fortunatus*, 3.1.186); see also *Captives*, 2984–5; *Traitor*, 4.2.92.

altar

used for various *ceremonies*, most often in *dumb shows* of a *funeral*, *sacrifice*, or *wedding*; uses in funerals include when the dead Ithocles is placed "*on one side of the Altar*," "*Calantha goes and kneels before the altar*," then she and "*the rest rise, doing obeisance to the altar*" (*Broken Heart*, 5.3.0); altars for a sacrifice include "*Busyris with his Guard and Priests to sacrifice; to* them two strangers, Busyris takes them and kills them upon the Altar," then "Hercules discovering himself beats the Guard, kills Busyris and sacrificeth him upon the Altar" (Brazen Age, 183, also 247, 248), "the solemnity of a sacrifice; which being entered, whilst the attendants furnish the altar" (Sophonisba, 3.1.116, also 5.1.26; see also Bonduca, 112; 2 Iron Age, 390; Amyntas, 2Cr); altars for weddings include "An Altar set forth. Enter Pyrrhus Leading Hermione as a bride," then "Pyrrhus and Hermione kneel at the altar" (2 Iron Age, 426); see also Match Me in London, 5.3.0; elsewhere an altar is used for various forms of worship: "An Altar to be set forth with the Image of Mars" (Faithful Friends, 2822–3), "Fortune is discovered upon an altar" (Hengist, DS before 1.2, 1), "the high Priest with attendants, Guards, and Choristers: they sing. An Altar and Tapers set" (Jews' Tragedy, 2147–8), "sprinkleth upon the altar, milk; then imposeth the honey, and kindleth his gums, and after censing about the altar placeth his censer thereon" (Sejanus, 5.177); see also Two Noble Kinsmen, K4v, 5.1.61; L1v, 5.1.136; Women Beware Women, 5.2.72; that the altar was a specific property is indicated in some directions already quoted and by "an Altar discovered and Statues" (Game at Chess, 2038–9), "Altar ready," then "An Altar discovered, with Tapers, and a Book on it" and a figure "ascends up the Altar" (Knight of Malta, 152, 161), "An Altar prepared" (Pilgrim, 225; Sea Voyage, 62), "An Altar raised" (2 Arviragus and Philicia, E12r); unique locutions are "Here the Hind vanishes under the Altar: and in the place ascends a Rose Tree" (Two Noble Kinsmen, L2r, 5.1.162), "Out of the altar the ghost of Asdruball ariseth" (Sophonisba, 5.1.38); Henslowe's inventory lists "one little altar" (Diary, App. 2, 70).

amazed

frequently used (roughly 50 examples) to denote visible confusion or shock: "Enter as affrighted and amazed" (Wise Woman of Hogsdon, 309), "the Lords rise, all amazed" (Queen and Concubine, 25; see also Maid of Honour, 4.4.108), "Enter Ariel, with the Master and Boatswain amazedly following" (Tempest, 2200–1, 5.1.215), Francis the drawer who befuddled by Prince Hal's trick "stands amazed not knowing which way to go" (1 Henry IV, D2v, 2.4.79); the term is sometimes linked to specific stage business: "suddenly riseth up a great tree between them, whereat amazedly they step back" (Warning for Fair Women, E3v), "Amazed lets fall the Daggers" (Alphonsus of Germany, I3v), "He kneels amazed, and forgets to speak" (Mad Lover, 5); usually amazed is not reinforced by other details; for a sampling of the many figures who enter/stand amazed

see Cobbler's Prophecy, 1335; John a Kent, 1147; Richard II, I1v, 5.3.22; Phoenix, H2v; Sophonisba, 2.2.58; Two Maids of More-Clacke, E3r; Fair Maid of Bristow, D3r; Faithful Shepherdess, 373; Henry VIII, 2273, 3.2.372; Night Walker, 381; Wife for a Month, 53; Renegado, 2.4.9; Fatal Contract, F1r, K1r; Late Lancashire Witches, 221; Court Beggar, 264; Rebellion, 37; Bloody Banquet, 56; Prisoners, B11r; variations include amazedly (Woman Is a Weathercock, 3.4.16; Silver Age, 122; Tom a Lincoln, 2105; Herod and Antipater, B1r; Conspiracy, D3v), "in amazement" (Honest Man's Fortune, 217; Hengist, DS before 4.3, 11), "seems amazed" (Blurt, 4.2.0; Antipodes, 335), "stand in amaze" (No Wit, 4.3.148), "The Giant in a maze lets fall his Club" (Seven Champions, I4r; see also Rare Triumphs, 1740; Locrine, 2064); an alternative is "They are all in a muse" (James IV, 941); see also **wonder**.

ambo

Latin for "both" found in the locution **exeunt** ambo, so presumably **together** as opposed to **severally**, at different stage **doors**; three sets of Shakespeare figures are directed to exeunt ambo: Hortensio and Gremio (Taming of the Shrew, 448, 1.1.145), Leonato and Antonio (Much Ado, H2v, 5.1.109), Oxford and Somerset (Octavo 3 Henry VI, E3r, [5.2.50]); the signal is found six times in Edward I (267, 1212, 1404, 1927, 2175, 2303) and is used for roughly twenty other pairs: Three Ladies of London, C2v; Gallathea, 5.3.9; Arraignment of Paris, 536; Captain Thomas Stukeley, 1170; 2 If You Know Not Me, 310; Two Maids of More-Clacke, D2r; Greene's Tu Quoque, D2r; Law Tricks, 161; Maid's Metamorphosis, E2v; Philaster, 95/406; Queen and Concubine, 43; Queen's Exchange, 523; Sparagus Garden, 186; Weeding of Covent Garden, 60; 1 Arviragus and Philicia, A11r; Landgartha, C3r, E2r; two examples in Insatiate Countess are linked to **prisoners** ("Exeunt ambo guarded," "Exeunt ambo with Officers," 4.1.112, 5.2.116), but such is not the case for two other instances in this play (4.2.111, 251) and for most of the examples above; what is not clear (as with **solus/alone**) is why this term is attached to a relatively small group of pairs and not to hundreds of others that undoubtedly are to **depart** in the same fashion.

ambush

an infrequently used term that (1) may be **fictional** but (2) in the phrase in ambush may indicate a specific onstage effect; clearly fictional are "Enter the ambushed Soldiers" (Doctor Faustus, B 1473), "Enter all the ambush" (George a Greene, 536); examples of in ambush are "Enter one of the Frenchmen, with five or six

other soldiers in ambush" (All's Well, 1911–12, 4.1.0),
"Those in ambush rusheth forth and take him" (Dutch
Courtesan, 5.1.49), "Enter Pheander again, and two Lords
in ambush" (Thracian Wonder, F2v).

and others, and the rest, and his train, and attendants, and an army, and followers
see *permissive stage directions*

angel
a supernatural figure found in a few plays, usually
as a divine messenger or guide; an *angel* appears
most often in *Martyred Soldier*: "As he is writing an
Angel comes and stands before him," "the Angel writes, and
vanishes," "An Angel ascends from the cave, singing,"
"Two Angels descend," "two Angels about the bed" (209,
241, 247, 248, also 188, 242, 243); *Looking Glass for
London* provides "brought in by an Angel, Oseas the
Prophet," "An Angel appeareth to Jonas," "the Angel van-
isheth" (159, 974, 985) and in the annotated quarto of
this play the bookkeeper wrote "Enter Angel" in the
margin just above "The Angel appeareth" (F2v, 1490);
Two Noble Ladies offers "an Angel shaped like a patriarch,
upon his breast a blue table full of silver letters, in his right
hand a red crosier staff, on his shoulders large wings"
(1101–3) and at the second entrance of this figure is a
bookkeeper's "Enter Angel" (1854–5 for 1846–8); only
Doctor Faustus specifies two kinds: "the good Angel and
the evil Angel" (A 101; at B 96 this is "the Angel and
Spirit"; and compare "good Angel, and Evil," A 452,
640, 706, with "the two Angels," B 402, 581, 647, also B
1995–6); *angels* appear with prophecies in *Guy of
Warwick*, E4v, F1v; *Landgartha* I1r; see also *Three Lords
of London*, A2v; *1 If You Know Not Me*, 228; *Shoemaker a
Gentleman*, 1.3.101; *Night Walker*, 365; *Messalina*, 2170;
Battle of Alcazar has "Fame like an Angel" (1268).

anger, angry, angrily
to display *anger* figures are directed to **enter** angry
(*1 Edward IV*, 20; *Princess*, C1v), angrily (*2 Edward IV*,
130; *Fair Em*, 955), provide *angry* looks: "look angrily
on Fausta" (Alphonsus of Aragon, 1784–5), enter
"looking angrily each on other with Rapiers drawn" (Fair
Em, 813–14), "exit with an angry look upon Valerio" (Jews'
Tragedy, 2428–9); *angry* figures also **rage**, **stamp** their
feet, **storm**, and enter **chafing**, "in choler" (Parson's
Wedding, 377), "in a fury" (Mad World, 5.2.41).

answer
can signal (1) a **sound** from **within**, usually in a military context, (2) various onstage business; offstage

answers include "Parle without, and answer within"
(Folio *Richard II*, 1646, 3.3.61; see also *Trial of Chivalry*,
B1v; *Faithful Friends*, 1366; *Jews' Tragedy*, 798),
"Trumpet answers within" (Folio *King Lear*, 3066,
5.3.117), "Sound drum answer a trumpet" (Devil's
Charter, D1v, also D2r, D3v, H3r); other offstage uses
are "Doyt knocks within, Frisco answers within" (Blurt,
2.2.65; see also *Merry Devil of Edmonton*, D2v;
Captives, 758), "Clerk Calls: answer within" (Launching
of the Mary, 1143–4); signals for onstage *answers*
include "Glendower speaks to her in Welsh, and she
answers him in the same" (1 Henry IV, F3r, 3.1.195; see
also *Edward I*, 630), a figure "answers with shaking his
head" (Folio *Every Man In*, 4.2.50), one "who had before
counterfeited death, riseth up, and answereth" (2 Iron Age,
428) and another "answers with fear and interruptions"
(Catiline, 5.140); atypical are "The Queen makes no
answer" (Henry VIII, 1363, 2.4.12; see also *Parson's
Wedding*, 426), "the dance of eight madmen, with music
answerable thereunto" (Duchess of Malfi, 4.2.114).

antic, antique
since the meanings are undifferentiated by spelling
in the original texts, either word can mean (1)
"grotesque, fantastic, incongruous, ludicrous" –
here spelled *antic* or (2) "old" – here *antique*; the first
is by far the most common as noun/adjective/
adverb; sometimes a kind of **dance** is meant, but few
details are given: "dance an Antic" (Messalina, 846–7),
"like Fairies, dancing antics" (Honest Lawyer, G2v); see
also *Devil's Charter*, L2v; *English Moor*, 67; *Landgartha*,
E4v; the term can also describe a way of dancing:
"dance anticly" (Martyred Soldier, 238; see also *Thracian
Wonder*, E4r); several times *antic* is linked to the
supernatural: "Clown, Merlin, and a little antic Spirit"
(Birth of Merlin, E4v), "an Antic of little Fairies enter"
(MS *Humorous Lieutenant*, 2329–31), "three antic fairies
dancing" (Dead Man's Fortune, 53–4); *antic* denotes one
or more figures in *James IV*: "Enter after Oberon, King of
Fairies, an Antic, who dance about a Tomb" (2–3, also
1725, 1732); for other figures see *John a Kent*, 780–1,
798, 819; *Old Wives Tale*, 0; *New Trick*, 250; the term
can describe a grotesque pageant or entertainment:
"the Antic Masque consisting of eight Bacchanalians enter
girt with Vine leaves" (Messalina, 2200–2); in *Woodstock*
a bookkeeper wrote "Antic" in the left margin (2093)
for the entrance of "country gentlemen" to entertain Woodstock with their "sports"; a **masque** in
Perkin Warbeck has "four Scotch Antics, accordingly
habited" (3.2.111) and in *Love's Sacrifice* masquers enter
"in an Antic fashion" (1845) described as "outlandish

feminine Antics"; Ford also uses the term in another context: "*a crown of feathers on, anticly rich*" (*Lover's Melancholy*, 3.3.26); other locutions are interesting if uninformative about specific actions: "*Makes Antic curtsies*" (*Great Duke of Florence*, 2.1.53), "*carried in Antic state, with Ceremony*" and "*dances an antic mockway*" (*Soddered Citizen*, 995, 1918), "*anticly attired, with bows and quivers*" (*Sophonisba*, 1.2.35), "*anticly attired in brave Clothes*" (*Thracian Wonder*, F2v); Henslowe's inventory lists "antics' coats" (*Diary*, App. 2, 26, 52); only twice does *antique* probably mean "old": "*on the top, in an antique Scutcheon, is written Honor*" (*Four Plays in One*, 311), "*with a long white hair and beard, in an antique armor*" (*Picture*, 2.1.85).

apart
an equivalent to *aside* that can mean either (1) "speak aside" or (2) "elsewhere on the stage"; signals for speaking *apart* include "*Apart to herself*" (*Maidenhead Well Lost*, 145), "*apart to himself*" and "*apart to his own people*" (*Four Prentices*, 187, 193); see also *Four Prentices*, 192, 193; *Jews' Tragedy*, 648, 677, 1730; signals for stage movement include "*takes him apart*" (*Looking Glass for London*, 1183; *Wits*, 149), "*prays apart*" (*Jews' Tragedy*, 976), "*walking apart with a Book*" (*Bussy D'Ambois*, 2.2.0); for *enter apart* see *Bussy D'Ambois*, 4.2.79; atypical is "*They both look strangely upon her, apart each from other*" (*Maid's Metamorphosis*, F2v).

apparel, appareled
used regularly (roughly eighty examples) as alternatives to *attire, clothes, garment, habit*: "*Some with apparel*" (*Taming of the Shrew*, 151–2, Induction.2.0), "*a pack full of apparel*" (*Famous Victories*, F4v), "*a fair suit of apparel on his back*" (*Rare Triumphs*, 1374); most common is the locution *in X's apparel* used for *disguise*: "*Alenso in Falleria's apparel and beard*" (*Two Lamentable Tragedies*, H4r), "*the whores in boy's apparel*" (*Your Five Gallants*, I2v), "*two wenches in boy's apparel*" (*Fleer*, 2.1.436); for figures who *enter* in another's *apparel* see *Fedele and Fortunio*, 390–1; *Friar Bacon*, 513; *George a Greene*, 659; *Knack to Know a Knave*, 1504; *Sir John Oldcastle*, 2195, 2223–4, 2238–9, 2266, 2506–7; *Blurt*, 3.2.0; *Wisdom of Doctor Dodypoll*, 1365, 1575; *School of Compliment*, G3r; disguises include a woman "*in man's apparel*" (*Solimon and Perseda*, H4r; *James IV*, 1743; *Maid's Tragedy*, 67; *Two Noble Ladies*, 271; *Swaggering Damsel*, F3r), a man "*in woman's apparel*" (*Wars of Cyrus*, C3v; *Woman in the Moon*, E4r; *Scornful*

Lady, 289; *Noble Gentleman*, 218; *Vow Breaker*, 2.1.0; *Obstinate Lady*, I1r; *Swaggering Damsel*, F4r), Amazons in woman's *apparel* (*Landgartha*, D1v, G4r, I2r), a woman in woman's *apparel* (*Wise Woman of Hogsden*, 305; *Obstinate Lady*, H4r; *Wizard*, 1289), along with figures in pilgrim's (*Alphonsus of Aragon*, 1387), **nun's** (*Friar Bacon*, 1895), nymph's (*Gallathea*, 2.2.0), page's *apparel* (*Hog Hath Lost His Pearl*, 980), and *appareled like* Fortune (*Alphonsus of Germany*, C4r).

Figures also appear *with/put on* another's *apparel* (*Dead Man's Fortune*, 24; *Dumb Knight*, 167), "*shift apparel*" (*Edmond Ironside*, 1226; *May Day*, 4.3.53); changes in costume are signaled by "*altered in Apparel*" (*Trick to Catch the Old One*, F4v), "*changed in apparel*" (*Puritan*, H3r; *No Wit*, 4.3.0), "*in fresh apparel*" (*Queen*, 950), "*in her own apparel*" (*Night Walker*, 380), "*in their stolen Apparel*" (*Tempest*, 2248, 5.1.255); figures appear richly *appareled* (*Taming of a Shrew*, A3v; *Antipodes*, 246; *Traitor*, 3.2.8) or are given **rich** apparel (*Doctor Faustus*, A 525–6, B 472–3; *Michaelmas Term*, Induction.29) and enter *in apparel* described as *gorgeous* (*City Wit*, 328), *gay* (*Hog Hath Lost His Pearl*, 689), *glistering* (*Tempest*, 1868, 4.1.193), **night** (*Antonio and Mellida*, 5.2.0), **mean** (*Coriolanus*, 2621–2, 4.4.0), **poor** (*John of Bordeaux*, 753), **mourning** (*Puritan*, A3r); other locutions include "*disguised in country apparel*" (*Friar Bacon*, 355–6), "*appareled youthfully*" (*School of Compliment*, C3v), "*rudely, and carelessly appareled*" (*Nice Valour*, 170), "*like a Negro in strange Apparel*" (*Obstinate Lady*, F2v), "*appareled in a Canvas suit*" (*Jews' Tragedy*, 1997–8), actors to deliver a **prologue** "*having cloaks cast over their apparel*" (*Antonio and Mellida*, Induction.0); see also *Alphonsus of Germany*, E3r; *Histriomastix*, G1r; *Knave in Grain*, 2464; *Obstinate Lady*, F2r; *apparel* rarely appears as a verb: "*sitting on his bed, appareling himself, his trunk of apparel standing by him*" (*What You Will*, B3v).

apparition
a supernatural figure called for in three plays: "*First Apparition, an Armed Head*," "*Second Apparition, a Bloody Child*," "*Third Apparition, a Child Crowned*" (*Macbeth*, 1604, 4.1.68; 1616, 4.1.76; 1628, 4.1.86), "*the Jesuit in rich attire like an Apparition*" (*Game at Chess*, 1576–7; Malone MS "*The Black Bishop's Pawn (as in an Apparition)*," 927–8; see also *Cymbeline*, 3065, 5.4.29).

appear
typically suggests an unexpected, surprising event commonly linked to supernatural business: "*Bungay conjures and the tree appears with the dragon*

shooting fire" (*Friar Bacon*, 1197–8, also 1208, 1635–7),
"*Three suns appear in the air*" (Octavo *3 Henry VI*, B3v,
2.1.20), "*Alonzo's Ghost appears to De Flores*"
(*Changeling*, 4.1.0), "*appear exhalations of lightning and
sulphurous smoke in midst whereof a devil*" (*Devil's
Charter*, A2v), "*The Spirit appears*" (*Late Lancashire
Witches*, 204, also 199), "*The Angel appeareth*" (*Looking
Glass for London*, 1490, also 974, 1230–1), "*Thunder
and lightning, two Dragons appear*" and "*Blazing star
appears*" (*Birth of Merlin*, F3r, F4r); a **blazing star** also
appears in *Captain Thomas Stukeley*, 2457–8; *Revenger's
Tragedy*, I2v; *Bloody Banquet*, 1859; for other uses of
appear linked to supernatural figures or events see
1 Troublesome Reign, G2v; *Maid's Metamorphosis*, G2v;
Silver Age, 122, 159; *Brazen Age*, 176, 237; *Catiline*,
1.318; *Hog Hath Lost His Pearl*, 1663; *Second Maiden's
Tragedy*, 1928; *Prophetess*, 367, 388; *Wasp*, 2220–1;
sometimes *appear* is linked to the drawing of a
curtain for a **discovery**: "*The Curtains being drawn
there appears in his bed King Phillip*" (*Lust's Dominion*,
1.2.0), "*The Curtain is drawn, Clorin appears sitting in
the Cabin*" (*Faithful Shepherdess*, 437), "*strikes ope a
curtain where appears a body*" (*Hoffman*, 8–10); the use
of *appear* in directions that do not refer to a curtain
may therefore imply a discovery: "*Ignatius Loyola
appearing, Error at his foot as asleep*" (*Game at Chess*,
13–14), "*Candido and his wife appear in the Shop*"
(*2 Honest Whore*, 3.3.0); see also *Old Law*, K1v; *English
Traveller*, 81; in *Antonio's Revenge* "*The curtain's drawn,
and the body of Feliche, stabbed thick with wounds,
appears hung up*" (1.2.207) on the upper level; figures
also *appear* **above** (*Novella*, 129; *Antipodes*, 311), at a
window (Quarto *Every Man Out*, 1018; *Poetaster*, 4.9.0;
Jack Drum's Entertainment, C2v; *Princess*, C3v), and on
the **walls** (*1 Troublesome Reign*, C3v; *Richard II*, F4v,
3.3.61; *Edmond Ironside*, 873; *Timon of Athens*, 2512,
5.4.2); see also *Launching of the Mary*, 2677; when
appear is equivalent to **enter** the circumstances are
unusual: "*King appears laden with chains, his head, and
arms only above*" (*Island Princess*, 107), "*Hector and Ajax
appear betwixt the two Armies*" (*1 Iron Age*, 299),
"*Medlay appears above the Curtain*" (*Tale of a Tub*,
5.10.9); occasionally *appear* describes how objects or
figures **seem**: "*the artificial figures of Antonio and his
children, appearing as if they were dead*" (*Duchess of
Malfi*, 4.1.55), "*Appears passionate*" (*King John and
Matilda*, 70), "*Pulcheria appears troubled*" (*Emperor of
the East*, 3.2.0); see also *White Devil*, 5.3.82; *Court
Beggar*, 268; *Princess*, F2r, H1r; once *appear* signals a
change of identity: "*throw off his cloak, Appear disguised as the wasp*" (*Wasp*, 1072–3).

apricock
cited only in *Wisdom of Doctor Dodypoll*: "*a basket of
Apricocks*" (1437).

apron
can be a woman's **garment** but can also be used by a
man; women's *aprons* include "*Maid with an Apron*"
(*How a Man May Choose*, F4r), "*Marian, with a white
apron*" (*Death of Huntingdon*, 457), "*Susan with something in her Apron*" – wheat and barley for the hens
(*Fortune by Land and Sea*, 394); male servants are
directed to enter "*in white sleeves and apron*" (*Two
Maids of More-Clacke*, H1v), "*his apron on, Basin of water,
Scissors, Comb, Towels, Razor, etc.*" (*Fancies Chaste and
Noble*, 2372–3).

arbor
the few relevant directions are unusually inconsistent; the opening of *Faithful Shepherdess*, "*Enter Clorin
a shepherdess, having buried her Love in an Arbor*" (372), is
clearly **fictional**; *Escapes of Jupiter* calls for a **discovery**:
"*An Arbor discovered shepherds and shepherdesses discovered*" (1061); in *Looking Glass for London* as with other
tree signals an *arbor* is part of a special effect: "*The
Magi with their rods beat the ground, and from under the
same riseth a brave Arbor*" (522–3); the **dumb show** in Q1
Hamlet includes "*he sits down in an Arbor*" (F3r,
3.2.135) as opposed to "*a bank of flowers*" in Q2/Folio
(H1v, 1994); *Spanish Tragedy* would seem to demand a
substantial property, for to murder Horatio "*They
hang him in the arbor*" and to revenge herself upon
the place where her son was murdered Isabella "*cuts
down the arbor*" (2.4.53, 4.2.5) commenting "Down
with these branches and these loathsome boughs, /
Of this unfortunate and fatal pine"; in contrast, two
Caroline plays seem to dispense with such a property: in *Witty Fair One* a figure "*comes from the Arbor*"
(B4r), and *Deserving Favourite* clearly invokes **as in**
with an entrance "*(as in an Arbor) in the night*" (E1v).

arise
see **rise**

arm
cited in a variety of locutions and contexts such as
(1) items **carried** on/under/in the arms, (2) **arm in arm**,
(3) **wounded**/**bloody** arms, (4) a range of actions such
as holding, **pulling**, **binding** arms; objects carried *on
the arm* are a **cloak** (*Dick of Devonshire*, 715), **robe** (*Fedele
and Fortunio*, 945), **basket** (*Three Ladies of London*, C4v,
E4r), **papers** (*Amends for Ladies*, 1.1.392), **chains**

(*Princess*, C3r), **napkins** (*Woodstock*, 3–4), *shoes* (*Shoemaker a Gentleman*, 2.1.61); *under the arm* are found a **box** (*Devil's Charter*, I3v; *Fedele and Fortunio*, 273), *basket* (*Fedele and Fortunio*, 1245), **crown** (*Jews' Tragedy*, 2995), **habit** (*Novella*, 118), **cloak** (*Warning for Fair Women*, D2v), **books** (*Rare Triumphs*, 1332–3; *Friar Bacon*, 172–3; *Titus Andronicus*, F3v, 4.1.0), "*rich attires*" (*Whore of Babylon*, 2.2.149), "*Cassandra half dead under his arm*" (*Young Admiral*, D4v); usually carried *in the arms* are either a child (*Titus Andronicus*, H4v, 5.1.19; *Edmond Ironside*, 1509; *Patient Grissil*, 4.1.0; *Thracian Wonder*, B1r; *Yorkshire Tragedy*, 527; *Tom a Lincoln*, 166, 2700; *Four Plays in One*, 321; *Cure for a Cuckold*, C3v; *Love's Sacrifice*, 1866–7) or a woman (*Charlemagne*, 1024–5; *Northward Ho*, 3.2.61; Quarto *King Lear*, L3v, 5.3.257; *Cymbeline*, 2496, 4.2.195; *Faithful Shepherdess*, 409; *Golden Age*, 35; *Bashful Lover*, 3.1.28; *Love's Mistress*, 101; *Prisoners*, C8r) but occasionally a man (*Queen's Exchange*, 491) and items of clothing (*Eastward Ho*, A4r; *Wizard*, 2204); atypical is "*with a bundle of Osiers in one arm and a child in another*" (*Patient Grissil*, 4.2.20).

Figures **enter**/**exit** *arm in arm* (*Shoemakers' Holiday*, 4.3.0; *Blurt*, 5.2.0; *Revenger's Tragedy*, H1v; *Caesar and Pompey*, 4.6.155; *Honest Man's Fortune*, 270; *No Wit*, 4.3.0; *Soddered Citizen*, 539); variations include a woman "*armed in*" by a man (*Country Girl*, C1r, also G1r), "*hanging on Planet's arms*" (*Jack Drum's Entertainment*, G4r), "*leaning on his arm*" (*Rebellion*, 72); *bloody arms* are common, sometimes **bare**/**naked**/**stripped** (*Locrine*, 1574; *Antonio's Revenge*, 3.2.86; *2 Edward IV*, 155; *Devil's Charter*, A2v; *Just Italian*, 255); detailed examples are "*unbraced, his arms bare, smeared in blood*" (*Antonio's Revenge*, 1.1.0), "*his arms stripped up to the elbows all bloody*" (*Appius and Virginia*, H1r), "*his arms naked besmeared with blood*" (*Mucedorus*, A2r); figures are **stabbed**/**hurt** *in the arm* (*Edward I*, 894; *Amends for Ladies*, 4.4.73–4; *Fair Maid of Bristow*, D2v; *Hollander*, 101); a wounded figure may enter "*with his Arm in a scarf*" (*Widow's Tears*, 4.1.0; *Humorous Day's Mirth*, 4.3.0; *Coriolanus*, 746–7, 1.9.0; *Lovers' Progress*, 85; *Sparagus Garden*, 192), and a **prisoner** with "*her arms in a scarf pinioned*" (*Love and Honour*, 103); for the *binding*/*unbinding* of *arms* see *Two Lamentable Tragedies*, E2r; *Maid's Tragedy*, 61; *Bashful Lover*, 2.8.138; *Gentleman of Venice*, D4v, K3v; *Parson's Wedding*, 482; *Unfortunate Lovers*, 46; the many other actions include *take*/*hold*/*support*/**catch** *in one's arms*/*by the arm* (*2 Edward IV*, 182; *1 Honest Whore*, 1.1.70; *Coriolanus*, 695–6, 1.6.75; *Lovesick King*, 1791; *Bloody Banquet*, 558; *Goblins*, 2.6.20; *Amorous War*,

K4v; *Princess*, B4v; *Just Italian*, 240; *Parson's Wedding*, 479, 511), **sink**/**fall** *in his arms* (*Downfall of Huntingdon*, 213; *Sophonisba*, 5.3.34; *Seven Champions*, G4r), *pull*/*take*/**lead** *by the arm* (*Warning for Fair Women*, D1r; *Wise Woman of Hogsdon*, 329; *Court Beggar*, 234; *Albovine*, 78), **wreathe** *arms* (*Antonio's Revenge*, 4.2.110, 118), *fold arms* (*Death of Huntingdon*, 964–5), "*spreads his arms*" (Q2 *Hamlet*, B3r, 1.1.126; *Hengist*, DS before 2.2, 6); other actions include "*strips up his arm*" (*King Leir*, 2125), "*cuts his arm*" (*2 Tamburlaine*, 3304; see also *Traitor*, 3.3.95), "*Shows his arm*" (*Travels of Three English Brothers*, 362), "*holds his arm and stays him*" (*Antonio's Revenge*, 1.2.217), "*takes his scarf and ties it about his arm*" as a silent message (*Hieronimo*, 11.163), "*Stabs at the child in her arms*" (*Yorkshire Tragedy*, 556–7), "*Tybalt under Romeo's arm thrusts Mercutio in*" (Q1 *Romeo and Juliet*, F1v, 3.1.90), "*They espy one another draw, and pass at each other, instantly both spread their arms to receive the wound*" (*Lovesick Court*, 141); atypical are "*Sucks her arm*" (*Witch of Edmonton*, 2.1.142), "*Bites Blood by the arm*" (*Two Noble Ladies*, 1504), "*his arm transfixed with a dart*" (*Sophonisba*, 2.2.0), a prisoner "*laden with chains, his head, and arms only above*" (*Island Princess*, 107), "*three soldiers: one without an arm*" (*Maidenhead Well Lost*, 114).

arm in arm

usually describes how a man and woman **enter**: "*the Duchess arm in arm with the Bastard: he seemeth lasciviously to her*" (*Revenger's Tragedy*, H1v); for comparable entrances see *Shoemakers' Holiday*, 4.3.0; *Blurt*, 5.2.0; *Honest Man's Fortune*, 270; *No Wit*, 4.3.0; for an **exit**: "*Exeunt, arm in arm embracing*" (*Soddered Citizen*, 539); an exception is "*Exeunt, Cato going out arm in arm betwixt Athenodorus and Statilius*" (*Caesar and Pompey*, 4.6.155) where the three male figures are off to dinner; although Marston does not use this locution, he does have Antonio and Andrugio united in their grief enter "*wreathed together*" (*Antonio and Mellida*, 4.2.0) and, after Antonio says "We must be still and steady in resolve. / Let's thus our hands, our hearts, our arms involve," has three revengers "*wreathe their arms*," "*Exeunt, their arms wreathed*" and in a later scene "*Exeunt twined together*" (*Antonio's Revenge*, 4.2.110, 118, 5.2.97).

armed

although distinctions are sometimes difficult, typically *armed* means "wearing **armor**" rather than "carrying a **weapon**"; in *Antony and Cleopatra* "*an Armed Soldier*" (2526, 4.4.18) speaks of "riveted trim," which suggests armor, as does the context of "*Enter Edgar armed*" (Folio *King Lear*, 3067, 5.3.117), "*Enter Ajax armed*" (*Troilus and Cressida*, I1r, 2547, 4.5.0); other directions implying armor include "*armed from top to toe*" (*Sophonisba*, Prologue.0, also 1.2.185, 5.2.0, 32), "*armed all save the head*" and "*armed head and all*" (*Queen*, 3307, 3433, 3515–16), "*armed Cap-a-pe*" (*Seven Champions*, G2v, also C2r, C4v, G4v, L1r), "*all armed, save the beaver*" (*White Devil*, 5.2.44, also 2.2.37); for similar usages see *Woodstock*, 2847; *Sir Thomas More*, 410; *Trial of Chivalry*, F2v; *Soliman and Perseda*, E1v; *Four Plays in One*, 311; *Bloody Brother*, 273; *Captives*, 2727; *Maid's Revenge*, F3v; *Perkin Warbeck*, 3.4.3; *2 Arviragus and Philicia*, G1or; *Traitor*, 4.1.73; *Gentleman of Venice*, K3r; *Sisters*, C6r; *Landgartha*, H1v; *Princess*, C3v; sometimes specific armor is cited: "*armed like a Champion*" (*Fedele and Fortunio*, 1337), "*armed after the Trojan manner*" (*Birth of Merlin*, C3r), "*like a Soldier armed*" (*Constant Maid*, H1r); an attendant in charge of serving a meal is "*an armed Sewer*" (*Satiromastix*, 5.2.0; *Wonder of a Kingdom*, 3.1.148; *Case Is Altered*, 1.3.0); *armed* occasionally seems to refer to weapons: "*armed with petronels*" (*Antonio and Mellida*, 1.1.34), "*armed with shields and swords*" (*Martyred Soldier*, 250); see also *Dick of Devonshire*, 771–2; unique locutions include "*First Apparition, an Armed Head*" (*Macbeth*, 1604, 4.1.68), "*Queen Elizabeth, completely armed*" (*2 If You Know Not Me*, 337), "*Philippo half armed, and two soldiers following him with the rest of the armor*" (*Lust's Dominion*, 4.4.0, also 4.3.39), "*like Merchants, armed underneath*" (*Island Princess*, 110).

armor

used in roughly twenty-five plays, most often when figures *enter* in armor: "*Mowbray in armor*" (Folio *Richard II*, 301–2, 1.3.6), "*Duke of Herford appellant in armor*" (*Richard II*, B2r, 1.3.25), "*Duke of Gloucester and Buckingham in armor*" (Quarto *Richard III*, G2v; Folio "*Richard and Buckingham, in rotten Armor, marvellous illfavored,*" 2082–3, 3.5.0), "*one in Armor*" (*Troilus and Cressida*, L4r, 3462, 5.6.26); for more examples of *in armor* see *Antonio and Mellida*, 1.1.34, 3.1.0, 5.2.166; *Birth of Merlin*, G4r; *Noble Gentleman*, 234; *Two Noble Ladies*, 1945–6; *Picture*, 1.1.0; *Unnatural Combat*, 3.3.36; *Seven Champions*, E4v; figures also enter *with armor* (*Woodstock*, 2673; *Histriomastix*, G1r; *Two Noble Kinsmen*, G4r, 3.6.16; *Vow Breaker*, 4.1.24); more detailed locutions are "*rusty armor*" (*Cobbler's Prophecy*, 734–5), "*all black in armor*" (*Locrine*, 435), "*the Armor of Achilles*" (*1 Iron Age*, 335), "*in an old Armor*" (*Faithful Friends*, 1046), "*as in the Prince's Armor*" (*Fatal Contract*, E1r), "*an antique armor*" (*Picture*, 2.1.85); stage business related to *armor* includes the logistically daunting "*nine knights in armor, treading a warlike Almain*" (*Arraignment of Paris*, 478), "*disrobeth himself and appeareth in armor*" (*Devil's Charter*, G3r), "*Philippo half armed, and two soldiers following him with the rest of the armor*" (*Lust's Dominion*, 4.4.0), "*Puts on Armor*" (*Brennoralt*, 1.1.53), "*remove the Armor off the Table*" (*Conspiracy*, I4r), "*the pieces of Armor hung upon several trees*" (*Gentleman of Venice*, I1r), "*carrying his armor piecemeal*" (*Loyal Subject*, 83); see also **armed**, **arms**.

arms

when used to designate something other than the part of the **body** this can mean **armor**, **weapons**, or a heraldic coat of *arms*; typically figures **enter** *in arms*, suggesting armor: "*Duke of Norfolk in arms defendant*" (Quarto *Richard II*, B2r; Folio "*Mowbray in armor,*" 301–2, 1.3.6), "*Richard in arms*" (Folio *Richard III*, 3431, 5.3.0), "*in Complete Arms*" (*Jews' Tragedy*, 2742); see also *King John*, 2250, 5.2.0; *Valiant Welshman*, B2v, F1v, I1v; *Travels of Three English Brothers*, 329; *Golden Age*, 36; *1 Iron Age*, 293, 341; *Atheist's Tragedy*, 2.6.0; *Dumb Knight*, 115; less often the locution and/or context implies weapons: "*flings down his Arms*" (*Valiant Welshman*, I1r), "*weapons and arms are brought forth*" (*Catiline*, 5.151), "*Soldiers running over the Stage, one throwing away his arms*" (*Brennoralt*, 2.1.41); in Folio *Every Man In* a figure calls for "my armor, my sword" and "*arms himself*" (5.1.48); heraldic *arms* identify allegiance: "*Soldiers led in by their Captains, distinguished severally by their Arms and Ensigns*" (*Hannibal and Scipio*, 256), "*A Coat of Arms is hung out*" (*Caesar and Pompey*, 3.2.107).

army

a collective noun (roughly fifty examples) usually found when a figure **enters** *and/with* an *army*; for a sampling see *Battle of Alcazar* plot, 77; *1 Henry VI*, 2064, 4.4.0; *King Leir*, 2389, 2549; *Julius Caesar*, 1908, 4.2.0; 2328, 5.1.0; 2351, 5.1.20; 2700, 5.5.51; Folio *Hamlet*, 2734, 4.4.0; *Valiant Welshman*, H4v; *Herod and Antipater*, F4r; *Shoemaker a Gentleman*, 2.2.45, 3.3.0; for the **exeunt** of armies see *King Leir*, 2613; *Julius Caesar*, 2402, 5.1.66; Folio *King Lear*, 2879, 5.1.37; *1 Iron Age* provides "*A parley. Both Armies have an interview,*" "*Both the Armies make ready to join battle, but Hector steps betwixt them,*" two combatants who "*appear betwixt the two Armies*" (see also *Vow Breaker*, 4.1.75–6) and "*are parted by both armies*" (294, 296, 299, 300); variations include "*the whole Army*" (*All's*

Well, 1696, 3.5.74), "*with Drums and an Army*" (*Alphonsus of Germany*, G2r; see also *Titus Andronicus*, H4r, 5.1.0; Folio *2 Henry VI*, 2990–1, 5.1.0), "*with his Army, marching*" (*Antony and Cleopatra*, 1960, 3.8.0, also 1973, 3.10.0), "*with his Army over the stage*" (Q2 *Hamlet*, K3r, 4.4.0), "*Lucius, Iachimo, and the Roman Army at one door: and the Britain Army at another*" (*Cymbeline*, 2892–3, 5.2.0), "*The Armies make towards one another*" (*Edmond Ironside*, 1860, also 1977–8), "*Enter the English Army, and encompass them*" (*Valiant Scot*, H2r), "*both armies meeting embrace*" (*Captain Thomas Stukeley*, 2456); atypical is an entrance "*as in the Army*" (*1 Arviragus and Philicia*, D3v).

arras

an alternative term for the *curtain*/*hangings* suspended in front of the tiring-house wall which, like *hangings*, usually occurs in conjunction with *behind*: "*peeps fearfully forth from behind the arras*" (*Atheist's Tragedy*, 2.5.110), "*they withdraw behind the Arras*" (*English Traveller*, 79), "*Enter Lamira behind the Arras*" (*Honest Man's Fortune*, 246), "*stands behind the Arras*" (*Jews' Tragedy*, 1899–1900, also 2798), "*takes from behind the arras a bottle and bag*" (*Love and Honour*, 149), "*speaks as behind the Arras*" (*Wizard*, 427); for similar locutions see *1 If You Know Not Me*, 235, 236; *Philaster*, 93, 95; *Women Pleased*, 293; *Spanish Gypsy*, H4r; *Noble Stranger*, E1r, F1r; *Albovine*, 101; *Faithful Friends*, 2621–3; *Unfortunate Lovers*, 66; the phrase *from the arras is rare* (*Honest Man's Fortune*, 247; *Country Girl*, K4v); other references to the *arras* include "*Boy ready for the song at the Arras*" (*Believe as You List*, 1970–1), "*wraps herself in the Arras*" (Q2 *Bussy D'Ambois*, 5.1.193), "*Arras hung up for the Musicians*" and "*Musicians come down to make ready for the song at the Arras*" (*City Madam*, 4.4.160, 5.1.7), "*Chair at the Arras*" (*Cruel Brother*, 155, 179), "*Six Chairs placed at the Arras*" (*Maid in the Mill*, 14/386), "*A hand is thrust out between the Arras*" (*Albovine*, 63), "*takes up the Arras*" (*Revenge of Bussy*, 5.4.35); signals to *draw* the *arras* include "*The Arras is drawn, and Zenocrate lies in her bed of state*" (*2 Tamburlaine*, 2968, also 3110; see also *Sir Thomas More*, 104–6; *Lover's Melancholy*, 2.2.10; *Distresses*, 338), "*Arras spread*" (*Bloody Banquet*, 1051), "*opens the arras*" (*Albovine*, 101).

arrow

regularly cited with bows and quivers; an example is *Titus Andronicus* where Titus enters bearing "*the arrows with letters on the ends of them*" and subsequently "*the Emperor brings the Arrows in his hand that

Titus shot at them" (G4v, 4.3.0; H2r, 4.4.0); sometimes the *shooting* is threatened but not carried out: "*Zenocia with Bow and Quiver, an Arrow bent*" (*Custom of the Country*, 315), "*Cupid's bow bent all the way towards them*" (*Nice Valour*, 157); usually the playgoer does not see the shooting of the *arrow* but does see the results: "*Enter Clifford wounded, with an arrow in his neck*" (Octavo *3 Henry VI*, C3v, 2.6.0), "*Enter Ralph, with a forked arrow through his head*" (*Knight of the Burning Pestle*, 229); similarly Tarquin enters "*with an arrow in his breast*" (*Rape of Lucrece*, 249), Achilles "*with an arrow through his heel*" (*1 Iron Age*, 332), Vespatian "*wounded in the Leg with an Arrow*" (*Jews' Tragedy*, 862–3), Strozza "*with an arrow in his side*" (*Gentleman Usher*, 4.1.10); he later reappears "*having the Arrow head,*" 5.2.0); a more complex effect can be seen in *Brazen Age* where "*Hercules shoots, and goes in: Enter Nessus with an arrow through him, and Dejanira*" (181); an assortment of bows, *arrows*, and quivers is frequently found in *hunting* scenes: "*two Ladies with bows and arrows in their hands and quivers athwart their backs*" (*Tom a Lincoln*, 1183–7, also 1252), "*Bows, Arrows, and Quivers by their sides*" (*Seven Champions*, D3v); for various combinations of bows, *arrows*, quivers see Octavo *3 Henry VI*, C5v, 3.1.0; *Downfall of Huntingdon*, 1261, 2506; *Histriomastix*, C2r; *Sophonisba*, 1.2.35; *Golden Age*, 11, 27; *1 Iron Age*, 332; *Landgartha*, E4v; Henslowe's inventory includes "*Cupid's bow and quiver*" (*Diary*, App. 2, 72); atypical are six dancing Moors with "*Erect Arrows stuck round their heads*" (*Amorous War*, E2v).

as at

an infrequently used *as* [*if*] signal that can be linked to (1) a *sound* effect, (2) a specific place, (3) an ongoing activity; examples are "*Alarum afar off, as at a Sea fight*" (*Antony and Cleopatra*, 2752, 4.12.3; see also *Bonduca*, 118), "*marching as being at Mile End*" (*1 Edward IV*, 25), "*as at Dice*" (*Valentinian*, 17), "*Queen and her Women as at work*" (*Henry VIII*, 1615, 3.1.0), "*Knock within, as at dresser*" (*Late Lancashire Witches*, 206).

as at first
see *as before*

as before

indicates that a costume or stage effect should reproduce what has been previously displayed; examples are *Locrine* where Ate's appearance is described in the opening *dumb show* and each of the four subsequent dumb shows calls for "*Ate as before*"

(2–4, 431, 961, 1353, 1771), Q1 *Hamlet* where the mad Ophelia first appears *"playing on a Lute, and her hair down singing"* and reappears *"as before"* (G4v, 4.5.20; H1v, [4.5.154]), *Coriolanus* (1121, 2.1.204), and *Queen's Exchange* (530) where figures *"Exeunt in State, as before"*; for examples see *Warning for Fair Women*, E3v, H4r; *Hieronimo*, 1.0; *Blurt*, 2.2.335; *Antony and Cleopatra*, 1624, 3.3.2; *Tom a Lincoln*, 171; *Anything for a Quiet Life*, D1v, G3v; *Cure for a Cuckold*, D2v; *Picture*, 5.3.127; *Lover's Melancholy*, 2.1.233, 2.2.60, 3.2.0; *Lady's Trial*, 1593; *Country Girl*, G2r; *Dick of Devonshire*, 1821; *Late Lancashire Witches*, 240; *Telltale*, 1799; *Just Italian*, 225; sometimes a costume or action is specified: *"as before in man's habit, sword and pistol"* (*English Moor*, 75), *"hermit-like, as before"* (*John a Kent*, 406), *"with the state of Persia as before"* (*Travels of Three English Brothers*, 404), *"upon the walls as before"* (*Devil's Charter*, D3v), *"blind him, and bind him as before"* (*Gentleman of Venice*, K3v), *"in the chair as before"* (*Court Beggar*, 257), *"her hair dishevelled as before"* (*Unfortunate Lovers*, 80); for a Latin version, *ut antea*, see *Wonder of a Kingdom*, 3.2.0, *Ladies' Privilege*, 107; comparable locutions include *"calling the Friar, as afore"* (*Death of Huntingdon*, 106), *"all that were in before"* (*Humorous Day's Mirth*, 5.2.0), *"the Kings before named"* (*2 Iron Age*, 356), *"as at first"* (*Antonio's Revenge*, 1.2.213; *All's Well*, 1730–1, [3.6.0]), *"in their first Habits"* (*Late Lancashire Witches*, 252), *"in his former disguise"* (*1 Edward IV*, 75), an Epilogue *"appareled as in the last Scene"* (*Landgartha*, K2r), *"He doth as he did before"* and *"Doing as before"* (*Spanish Tragedy*, 1.4.151, 162).

as from

a large sub-category of *as [if]* signals used to denote recently completed offstage actions or events that (1) pose significant staging problems or (2) have been sidestepped in order to speed up the narrative; the result can be a sense of actions, places, or a "world" just offstage to be imagined by the playgoer; to avoid onstage torture figures are directed to **enter** *"in their shirts, as from Torments"* (*Shoemaker a Gentleman*, 4.2.0), *"as from the Rack"* (*Sophy*, 5.593); for a completed journey figures enter *"as from horse"* (*City Nightcap*, 107), *"as new come out of the Country"* (*Wise Woman of Hogsdon*, 340), and for a forest/**woods** *"as out of the woods, with Bow and Arrows, and a Cony at his girdle"* (*Promos and Cassandra*, K4r), *"as out of a Bush"* (*Two Noble Kinsmen*, F2v, 3.1.30); other places include *"as from prison"* (*City Madam*, 5.3.59), *"as out of the house"* (*How a Man May Choose*, B4r), *"in his gown as from his study"* (*Witty Fair One*, E1v; see also *Goblins*,

4.1.32), *"as coming from a Tavern"* (*Example*, E4v).

Elsewhere **banquet** scenes are plentiful but so too are scenes that start just after such a meal and are keyed to signals such as *"as from dinner"* (*New Way to Pay*, 3.3.0; *Wise Woman of Hogsdon*, 336), *"as from table"* (*Roaring Girl*, 1.1.0), *"as from supper"* (*Roaring Girl*, 3.2.0; *Love's Sacrifice*, 1823), with figures often carrying **napkins** or other items: *"as it were brushing the Crumbs from his clothes with a Napkin, as newly risen from supper"* (*Woman Killed*, 118), *"having his napkin on his shoulder, as if he were suddenly raised from dinner"* (*Downfall of Huntingdon*, 166–8); similarly a **bed** can be brought onstage when needed but also common are variations of entrances *"as from bed"* (*Woman Killed*, 141; *Lovers' Progress*, 128; *Thierry and Theodoret*, 30; *2 Iron Age*, 381; *Royal King*, 77; *Aglaura*, 5.3.141), *"as from his chamber"* (*Bashful Lover*, 5.1.71; *'Tis Pity*, 2.1.0), *"as from sleep"* (*Andromana*, 238) usually keyed to figures in **nightgowns** or **unready**; since shipwrecks and immersions in **water** are difficult to display directly, water is suggested just offstage as seen in Triton *"with his Trump, as from the sea"* (*Silver Age*, 138), *"wet from sea"* (*Looking Glass for London*, 1369); for **weddings** and other church scenes figures are directed to enter *"as from church"* (*Insatiate Countess*, 1.1.141), *"as newly come from the Wedding"* (*Fortune by Land and Sea*, 371), *"as from a wedding"* (*Woman's Prize*, 2), *"in black scurvy mourning coats, and Books at their Girdles, as coming from Church"* (*Puritan*, B2v); related is *"all in mourning apparel, Edmond in a Cypress Hat. The Widow wringing her hands, and bursting out into passion, as newly come from the Burial of her husband"* (*Puritan*, A3r); also to be imagined just offstage are various recreational activities so that figures are directed to enter *"as from Walking"* (*English Traveller*, 44), *"as newly come from play"* (*Wise Woman of Hogsdon*, 279), *"with a spear in his Rest as from the tilt"* (*Tom a Lincoln*, 798–9), *"her head and face bleeding, and many women, as from a Prize"* (*Antipodes*, 300), *"as from hunting"* (*Late Lancashire Witches*, 171), *"as from Hawking"* (*Queen's Exchange*, 506), *"with her Hawk on her fist … as if they came from hawking"* (*Quarto 2 Henry VI*, C1v, 2.1.0).

Shakespeare's plays provide few *as from* directions, but make plentiful use of *from* constructions (where *as [if]* may be implicit): *"from dinner"* (*Quarto Merry Wives*, B1r, 1.2.0), *"from the Courtesan's"* and *"from the Bay"* (*Comedy of Errors*, 995, 4.1.13; 1073, 4.1.84), *"from hunting"* (*Taming of the Shrew*, 18, Induction.1.15; *Titus Andronicus*, E2r, 2.4.10), *"from his Arraignment"* (*Henry VIII*, 889, 2.1.53), *"from the Murder of Duke Humphrey"* (*Folio 2 Henry VI*, 1690–1, 3.2.0), "from the Pursuit" (*Coriolanus*, 759, 1.9.11), "from tilting" (*Pericles*, D1r, 2.3.0), "from the Cave" (*Cymbeline*, 2245, 4.2.0), "from his Cave" and "out of his Cave" (*Timon of Athens*, 2233, 5.1.30; 2360, 5.1.130).

as [if]

a large family of directions distinctive to the drama of this period; variations include *as in*, *as from*, *as at*, *as to*, *make as though*, and by extension *seem*, *make signs*, *make show*; explicit use of *as if/as though* is evident in earlier drama up through the early 1590s, often attached to the imperative *make*: "Make as if she swoons" (*Cobbler's Prophecy*, 970), "Make as if ye would fight" (*Edward I*, 432); Quarto 2 *Henry VI* provides "*Alarms within, and the chambers be discharged, like as it were a fight at sea*," "*the Cardinal is discovered in his bed, raving and staring as if he were mad*," "*Enter the King and Queen with her Hawk on her fist . . . as if they came from hawking*" (F1v, [4.1.0]; F1v, [3.3.0]; C1v, [2.1.0]; not in Riv.]); subsequent explicit use of *if/though* is sparse; after his bout with Douglas, Falstaff "*falls down as if he were dead*" (1 *Henry IV*, K2v, 5.4.76; see also *Bride*, 62); elsewhere figures *enter* "*having his napkin on his shoulder, as if he were suddenly raised from dinner*" (*Downfall of Huntingdon*, 166–8), "*with riding wands in their hands, as if they had been new lighted*" (*Look about You*, 1–3); actions include "*This spoke as if she studied an evasion*" (*Great Duke of Florence*, 4.1.106), "*tolls the bell, as if he pulled the rope*" (*Two Maids of More-Clacke*, B4v), "*tears off his doublet, making strange faces as if compelled to it*" (*Fair Maid of the Inn*, 201), "*as he offers to touch her, she starts as if he plucked up her coats*" (*Parson's Wedding*, L4v).

Far more plentiful are constructions where the *if/though* has dropped out to create what can be termed *as [if]*; this change can best be seen when *as* is directly followed by a participle or adjective: "*as affrighted and amazed*" (*Wise Woman of Hogsdon*, 309), "*as not being minded*" (*English Traveller*, 87), "*as being conducted by them into the City*" (1 *Iron Age*, 302), "*as newly shipwrecked*" (*Captives*, 653; see also *Thracian Wonder*, B4v), "*as peeping if my Lord were gone*" (*Example*, G1v), "*as desirous to speak with him*" (*Cardinal*, 3.2.85), "*as taking opportunity to go to her chamber*" (*Example*, D1r); other examples include entrances "*as walking*" (*Sir Thomas More*, 1282), "*as distracted*" (*White Devil*, 3.3.0), "*as robbed*" (*Love's Pilgrimage*, 262), "*as newly ravished*" (*Queen of Corinth*, 17), "*with Sergeants as arrested*" (*City Madam*, 5.3.59), "*as conferring by two and two*" (*Damoiselle*, 407), "*as being hard pursued*" (*Bloody Banquet*, 229), "*led by two of*

the guard, as not yet fully recovered" (*Double Marriage*, 364), "*as being thrown off his horse, And falls*" and "*as going by his house*" (*Yorkshire Tragedy*, 632, 715); a figure can be borne off "*as being swooned*" (*Antonio's Revenge*, 4.1.230), and a *fight* can conclude "*both fall down as dead*" (*Trial of Chivalry*, E3r), "*fall as killed*" (*Captain*, 290).

In addition to the widely used *as from/as in* locutions, *as [if]* signals can be used for *sound* effects and to provide a sense of place: "*A noise within, as the fall of a Horse*" (*Guardian*, 4.1.0), "*as before the City Corioles*" and "*two Officers, to lay Cushions, as it were, in the Capitol*" (*Coriolanus*, 479–80, 1.4.0; 1203–4, 2.2.0), "*as upon the Exchange*" (*How a Man May Choose*, A2r); atypical is "*Exeunt, fall as into the sea*" (2 *Passionate Lovers*, L5r); of particular interest are the *as* signals linked to **night** scenes where, lacking variable lighting, the players could not change the onstage illumination throughout the course of a performance; signals such as "*as in the dark*" (*Mad Couple*, 76), "*as if groping in the dark*" (2 *Iron Age*, 380), "*(as in an Arbor) in the night*" (*Deserving Favourite*, E1v), "*softly as by night*" (*Captain Thomas Stukeley*, 924–5) suggest how onstage "darkness" was generated by a combination of suitable acting (groping in the **dark**, tiptoeing), a shared theatrical vocabulary (the use of lighting implements and appropriate costumes such as **nightgowns**), and the imaginative participation (and acquiescence) of the playgoer – all in the spirit of *as if*.

as in

of the various *as [if]* signals *as in* is the most revealing as to what distinguishes pre-1660 from later staging; **prison** scenes are common (as are *enter in prison* signals), but four Caroline plays provide "*as in prison*" (*Brennoralt*, 1.4.0; *Queen and Concubine*, 35; *City Nightcap*, 176; 2 *Arviragus and Philicia*, F4v); although *in prison* may conjure up a familiar image to today's reader, *as in prison* suggests that this distinctive locale could be generated by means of the behavior of the entering actor in conjunction with the playgoer's imagination; similarly, a reader's expectations about onstage **rooms** should be tested against "*as in his house at Chelsea*" and "*as in his chamber in the Tower*" (*Sir Thomas More*, 1412, 1730), "*as in his Chamber in a morning, half ready*" (*Woman Is a Weathercock*, 1.1.1–2), "*Bould putting on his doublet, Fee-Simple on a bed, as in Bould's chamber*" (*Amends for Ladies*, 4.2.1–2; see also *Sir John Oldcastle*, 2086; *Twins*, G1r); *Conspiracy* twice directs figures to enter "*as in their Tent*" (H3r, I3r), and *Amorous War* twice calls for entrances "*as in a Wood*" (C2v, C3v); other examples include "*as in sessions*" (*Sir Thomas More*, 104), "*working as in their shop*" (*Amends for Ladies*, 2.1.1), "*as in a Tavern*" (*Gamester*, C3r; *Wit in a Constable*, 231), "*as in the Duke's garden*" (*Gentleman of Venice*, B2v), "*as in his Study*" (*Fair Maid of the Inn*, 193; *Aglaura*, 1.2.6), "*as in his study reading*" (*Greene's Tu Quoque*, B4v).

Other *as in* signals are less revealing; some call attention to a specific locale: "*as in Baynard's Castle*" (*King John and Matilda*, 11), "*Two Devonshire Merchants, as being in Sherris*" (*Dick of Devonshire*, 93); some set up an activity: "*as in the Army*" (1 *Arviragus and Philicia*, D3v), "*Two soldiers meet as in the watch*" (*Rape of Lucrece*, 204), "*enter the Satyrs as in the chase*" (*Golden Age*, 32); one locution directs one or more figures awaiting a duel to appear "*as in the field*" (*Little French Lawyer*, 391; *Country Girl*, H1r), "*as in a Grove*" (*Knave in Grain*, 905); atypical are "*as in haste*" (*Sophy*, 3.318), "*speaks this as in scorn*" (*White Devil*, 3.2.46), "*falls down as in a swoon*" (*Alchemist*, 4.5.62).

as many as may be
see *permissive stage directions*

as to
this sub-category of *as* [*if*] signals (1) occasionally serves as the opposite of the more common *as from* but (2) is usually linked to a specific place or event; for the former compare the widely used *as from bed* with "*as though to bed*" (*Queen's Exchange*, 507), "*in her nightclothes, as going to bed*" (*Match at Midnight*, 77); *White Devil* provides "*in her nightgown as to bed-ward,*" "*kneels down as to prayers,*" "*go as 'twere to apprehend Vittoria*" (2.2.23, 37); typical places, events, and actions include "*as to the Parliament*" (Folio *Richard II*, 1921, 4.1.0), "*as to her Trial*" (*Winter's Tale*, 1174–5, 3.2.0), "*as to revels*" (*Golden Age*, 53), "*in solemnity as to marriage*" (*Four Plays in One*, 338), "*as to see the Execution*" (*Witch of Edmonton*, 5.3.0), "*as to the Wedding with Rosemary*" (*City Wit*, 358), "*as to a Duel*" (*Goblins*, 1.1.0).

ascend
roughly sixty directions have figures *ascend* (1) from *under the stage*, (2) to a *chair of state* or dais, (3) to the level *above* the main platform; examples of *rising* from *below* include "*Pluto ascendeth from below in his chair*" (*Arraignment of Paris*, 819), "*ascends another devil*" (*Devil's Charter*, A2v, also G1v, G2r), "*A flash of fire and Lightfoot ascends like a spirit*" (*Hog Hath Lost His Pearl*, 1616–18, also 1710), "*An Angel ascends from the*

cave" (*Martyred Soldier*, 241, also 243); see also Q2 *Bussy D'Ambois*, 2.2.132, 3.1.50, 4.2.60, 5.1.154; *Revenge of Bussy*, 5.1.0; *Caesar and Pompey*, 2.1.24; *Shoemaker a Gentleman*, 1.3.101; *If This Be Not a Good Play*, 2.3.75, 3.2.139; *Two Noble Kinsmen*, L2r, 5.1.162; *Atheist's Tragedy*, 2.4.83; *Julia Agrippina*, Prologue.1; elsewhere figures *ascend* to a raised platform: "*Here he ascendeth the throne*" (Quarto *Richard III*, H4v, 4.2.3; see also *Prophetess*, 346), "*Ely ascends the chair*" (*Downfall of Huntingdon*, 45), "*coming near the chair of state, Ferdinand Ascends*" (*Hoffman*, 483–4); for similar examples see *Death of Huntingdon*, 958–9; *Doctor Faustus*, B 905; *Caesar and Pompey*, 1.2.14; *Christian Turned Turk*, F2v; *Atheist's Tragedy*, 5.2.98; MS *Poor Man's Comfort*, 1270; *Heir*, 577; *Jews' Tragedy*, 7, 355, 1107–8; *Bloody Banquet*, 54–5; signals to *ascend* either to the upper level or to the **heavens** include "*Cupid ascends*" (*Love's Mistress*, 130), "*Venus ascends*" (*Mad Lover*, 62), "*Jupiter, the Gods and Planets ascend to heaven*" (*Silver Age*, 164); see also *Woman in the Moon*, A4r, C3v; *Family of Love*, A3r; *Cymbeline*, 3149, 5.4.113; *Golden Age*, 78; *Four Plays in One*, 311, 360; *More Dissemblers*, B8r; *World Tossed at Tennis*, F2v; *Maid in the Mill*, 59; *Prophetess*, 345; *Wife for a Month*, 26; other locutions include "*ascends the Scaffold*" (*Insatiate Countess*, 5.1.128, also 154), *ascends a* **ladder** (*Insatiate Countess*, 3.1.42; *Hog Hath Lost His Pearl*, 265–6), "*ascends up the Altar*" (*Knight of Malta*, 161).

aside
the more than 550 examples fall into two groups: (1) *to stand* or move *aside* so as to observe other figures or carry on some surreptitious activity, (2) *to speak aside* so as to maintain the fiction that the speaker's words can be heard only by the playgoer or by some but not all of the other figures onstage (*aside* as a noun is not found); the various meanings can be seen in *News from Plymouth* which signals one speech *aside* (188) but also provides *take aside* (152, 153), *step aside* (182, 195), "*beckons Topsail aside*" (152).

For stage movement, locutions include *pull* aside (*City Wit*, 315; *Fatal Contract*, C2r), **lead** aside (*Humorous Courtier*, I3v; *Love and Honour*, 144; *Platonic Lovers*, 14), **walk** aside (*Albovine*, 26; *Love and Honour*, 167), *slip* aside (*Three Lords of London*, H3r; *Herod and Antipater*, C3r), **call** aside (Folio *Every Man Out*, 3.6.99), **read** aside (*Jovial Crew*, 421), **confer** aside (*Old Fortunatus*, 3.1.240, 249; *Lovesick Court*, 92); most common are *stand aside* (*Alphonsus of Aragon*, 57, 1910; *Locrine*, 2021; *Love's Labour's Lost*, E2v, 4.3.20; *Patient Grissil*, 4.1.111; *Histriomastix*, F3v; *Wily Beguiled*, 1003;

Wise Woman of Hogsdon, 292; *2 Edward IV*, 171; *Thracian Wonder*, E4r; *Ram Alley*, F4v; *Turk*, 369; *Faithful Friends*, 1223; *King John and Matilda*, 76; *Damoiselle*, 420; *Weeding of Covent Garden*, 21), take aside (*Warning for Fair Women*, A4v; *Alarum for London*, 396; *Widow's Tears*, 1.3.117; *Fair Maid of the Inn*, 214; *King John and Matilda*, 54; *Court Beggar*, 253; *New Academy*, 77; *City Wit*, 356; *Mad Couple*, 66; *English Moor*, 25; *Bloody Banquet*, 1075; *Love and Honour*, 184; *Fair Favourite*, 240, 245; *Distresses*, 311, 320, 344, 355, 362; *Just Italian*, 267; *Albovine*, 79; *Platonic Lovers*, 16, 73; *Unfortunate Lovers*, 25; *Wits*, 153, 186, 223), step aside (*Fedele and Fortunio*, 75; *Love's Labour's Lost*, E3r, 4.3.42; *Renegado*, 4.2.43; *Maid of Honour*, 1.2.73; *New Way to Pay*, 5.1.93; *Picture*, 3.6.66, 83; *Staple of News*, 2.4.17; *Heir*, 524; *Soddered Citizen*, 1901; *Andromana*, 269; *Prisoners*, C4r; *News from Plymouth*, 182, 195; *Wits*, 124), **go** aside (*Famous Victories*, F4r; *Bashful Lover*, 1.2.95; *Emperor of the East*, 4.4.61; *Mad Couple*, 91; *Damoiselle*, 424; *City Wit*, 307; *Swaggering Damsel*, F4r; *Bride*, 60; *Conspiracy*, H1v; *Landgartha*, D4r); occasionally *aside* carries with it an implicit "stand or move aside" (*Coriolanus*, 992, 2.1.96), as in the few examples of **enter** aside (*Launching of the Mary*, 1832; *Law Tricks*, 147; *Sparagus Garden*, 195), presumably an elliptical version of "enter and stand aside"; *Wizard* provides enter "*aside talking*" (1827); atypical is **exit** aside (*Fair Maid of the Exchange*, 34; *Virgin Martyr*, 4.1.84); in the first a figure says "I'll step aside, and hear their conference," exits, and re-enters; in *Virgin Martyr* Sapritius and another "*Exeunt aside*" but he hears and comments upon what follows and then "*breaks in*" (108); variations include "*Let him put her aside*" (*Three Ladies of London*, F2v), "*takes Memnon aside and talks with him*" (*Mad Lover*, 4), "*takes Amy aside, and courts her in a gentle way*" (*Jovial Crew*, 426), "*takes Clack aside, and gives him a Paper*" (*Jovial Crew*, 442), "*takes him aside and whispers*" (*Weakest Goeth*, 470), "*takes him aside, and persuades him*" (*Staple of News*, 2.5.116), "*walks aside full of strange gestures*" (*Mad Lover*, 14), "*The Moors stand aside with the Crown*" (*Lust's Dominion*, 5.1.7), "*Parthenius goes off, the rest stand aside*" (*Roman Actor*, 5.2.19), "*They draw her aside to rifle her*" (*Duchess of Suffolk*, F1v), "*draws his sword, and runs at him when he turns aside*" (*Cupid's Revenge*, 286).

The large majority of designated *asides* are linked to speech not movement and contain only the single word; *Money Is an Ass* provides twenty-eight examples (all simply *aside*), *Jew of Malta* twenty-five (one is an "*aside to her*"), *Two Noble Ladies* twenty-five (with seven *to* someone), *Obstinate Lady* eighteen, *Queen and Concubine* fifteen, *Maid's Tragedy* twelve (all simply *aside*); the majority of *asides* signaled in today's editions are not marked as such in the original manuscripts and printed editions, particularly in the Shakespeare canon where the only designated spoken *asides* are Quarto *Merry Wives*, E1r, 3.3.139 and *Pericles*, D4v, 2.5.74, 78; in addition to *aside to* someone figures are directed to **whisper** aside (*Amends for Ladies*, 5.2.83), **talk** aside (*Fatal Contract*, C2v; *Jovial Crew*, 446; *New Academy*, 18, 101; *Novella*, 173; *Queen's Exchange*, 464), speak aside (*Selimus*, 1726; *Two Maids of More-Clacke*, A3r, B1r, G3r; *Devil's Law Case*, [5.2.16]; *New Academy*, 8; *Prisoners*, B4r, B4v); variations are "*Ticket talks aside with Toby*" (*City Wit*, 307), "*She goes aside, and speaks as followeth*" (*Famous Victories*, F4r), "*all this aside*" (*2 Edward IV*, 99; see also *Devil's Law Case*, 2.1.135), "*Close aside to Bunch*" (*Weakest Goeth*, 1261); that a spoken *aside* may have involved some distinctive stage movement is suggested by "*She turns aside and speaks*" (*Taming of a Shrew*, B3r); alternatives to *aside* are **apart**, **to himself**, and actions such as **privately**, speak *in* someone's *ear* and "*speaketh this secretly at one end of the stage*" (*Fair Em*, 235).

asleep
see *sleep*

asp
see *snake*

ass, mule
the *ass* like the **horse** occasionally appears onstage; Bacchus **enters** "*riding upon an Ass*" (*Summer's Last Will*, 967), and as part of a ceremony Ward enters "*on an Ass*," two knights "*pull him off the Ass*," he **exits** "*mounted on the Ass*" (*Christian Turned Turk*, F2v); ass and mule are equated in *Soliman and Perseda* where Basilisco enters "*riding of a Mule*" but "*Piston getteth up on his Ass, and rideth with him to the door*" (B4r–v); figures playing *asses* include "*Pyramus with the Ass head*" (Folio *Midsummer Night's Dream*, 927, 3.1.102), "*Apuleius, with a pair of Ass ears in his hand*" (*Love's Mistress*, 91); also in *Love's Mistress* Apuleius presents a display for Midas that includes "*A Proud Ass with ears,*" "*a Prodigal Ass,*" "*a Drunken Ass,*" "*An Ignorant Ass*" (104–5); a *mule driver* appears as part of a group in *Fair Maid of the Inn*, 175.

assail
occurs three times in the context of **battle**: "*assail the walls*" (*Edmond Ironside*, 914), "*they offer to assail*

Antipater" (*Herod and Antipater*, F4r), "*Hector takes up a great piece of a Rock, and casts at Ajax, who tears a young Tree up by the roots, and assails Hector*" (*1 Iron Age*, 300).

assault

seldom used, usually to signal an onstage action of **battle**: "*Here is a very fierce assault on all sides*" (*1 Edward IV*, 20), "*Assault, and they win the Tower*" (*David and Bethsabe*, 212), "*The shepherds give the first assault, and beat off some of the Sicilian Lords*" (*Thracian Wonder*, G3v), "*They assault him and he kills them*" (*Conspiracy*, B4r, also G2v); twice *assault* denotes offstage **sound**: "*Alarum, a charge, after long skirmish, assault, flourish*" (*Edward I*, 2207; see also *David and Bethsabe*, 814); two other uses establish a context for the visual or audible: "*Enter Martius bleeding, assaulted by the Enemy*" (*Coriolanus*, 564, 1.4.61), "*A flourish, as to an assault*" (*Maid of Honour*, 2.3.0).

astringer

unique to *All's Well*: "*Enter a gentle Astringer*" (2601, 5.1.6); editors often emend this direction to "*enter a gentleman*" or "*enter a gentleman, a stranger*," but the *OED* cites *astringer/austringer/ostringer* as "a keeper of goshawks," hence, a falconer; such falconers are called for in Folio *2 Henry VI* where a **hunting** party includes "*Falconers hallooing*" (716, 2.1.0); the equivalent signal in the Quarto (C1v) calls for the same group to enter "*as if they came from hawking*" and specifies that Queen Margaret is to enter "*with her Hawk on her fist*"; *Perkin Warbeck* provides "*Lambert Simnel like a falconer*" (5.3.0).

attendants

see *permissive stage directions*

attire, attired

widely used (roughly ninety examples) typically in the locutions *in X's attire* or *attired like a* (a form of the ubiquitous *like a*); such locutions can be used for **disguise**: "*Alfrida in the kitchen maid's attire*" (*Knack to Know a Knave*, 1532), a lady "*in Merchant's wives' attire*" (*Look about You*, 1851), Sir Thomas More's man "*attired like him*" (*Sir Thomas More*, 737), "*Francisco in a parson's habit, and a true Parson otherwise attired*" (*Heir*, 572), a figure out of disguise "*in his true attire*" (*Satiromastix*, 2.2.0); the term is regularly used for gender reversals: a "*boy in Woman's attire*" (*Taming of a Shrew*, A4r), a man "*in woman's attire*" (*Wars of Cyrus*, E2r; *Englishmen for My Money*, 2255, 2654; *Wonder of a Kingdom*, 3.3.0), a woman "*in page's attire*" (*Antonio*

and Mellida, 3.2.271) or "*in man's attire*" (*Gallathea*, 2.1.12; *Twelfth Night*, 250, 1.4.0; *Revenge of Bussy*, 5.3.0; *Lover's Melancholy*, 1.3.49 – the same figure reappears "*in woman's attire*," 4.3.44), "*Laurentia in Anthony's attire*" (*Englishmen for My Money*, 2426), "*attired like his wife masked*" (*Westward Ho*, 4.2.52), "*Hercules attired like a woman, with a distaff and a spindle*" (*Brazen Age*, 241), "*Philocles in Mariana's attire, and Mariana in his*" (*Dumb Knight*, 192).

For examples of costumes rather than disguises, signals for **night** attire are common (*Lust's Dominion*, 2.3.91; *Sophonisba*, 1.2.0; *Tom a Lincoln*, 1564; *Fatal Contract*, D4v; *Love's Sacrifice*, 2350–1; *Mad Couple*, 76; *City Wit*, 358; *Messalina*, 676), with the term sometimes distinguished from the **nightgown**: "*in her nightgown and night attire*" (*Two Maids of More-Clacke*, E3v), "*in her smock, Nightgown, and night attire*" (*Woman Killed*, 139), "*Robin Hood in the Lady Falconbridge's gown, night attire on his head*" (*Look about You*, 1747–8) where *attire* uncharacteristically is linked to **tire**/headdress (see also *Eastward Ho*, A4r); widely used are variations of **rich** attire/richly attired (*Summer's Last Will*, 443; *Three Lords of London*, A2v; *James IV*, 2444; *Woodstock*, 1130; *Looking Glass for London*, 1509; *Devil's Charter*, G4v; *Birth of Merlin*, D2v; *Shoemaker a Gentleman*, 5.1.59; *Faithful Friends*, 2481; *Lovesick King*, 1711; *Women Beware Women*, 4.3.0; *Game at Chess*, 1576–7; *Grateful Servant*, I2r; *Unfortunate Lovers*, 31); examples include "*in her richest attire*" (*Perkin Warbeck*, 5.2.137), "*with rich attires under his arm*" (*Whore of Babylon*, 2.2.149), "*in her best attire*" (*Humorous Day's Mirth*, 2.1.0), "*gorgeously attired*" (*Wonder of a Kingdom*, 3.1.0), "*gallantly attired*" (*Your Five Gallants*, A2r); at the other extreme are figures "*in poor attire*" (MS *Humorous Lieutenant*, 46–7), "*in base mourning attire*" (*Malcontent*, 4.5.0), "*meanly attired*" (*Old Fortunatus*, 1.1.0), "*basely attired*" (*Taming of a Shrew*, C3v); figures are directed to enter *attired like* a warrior (*Cymbeline*, 3066–7, 5.4.29), physician (*Grim the Collier*, G5v), woodman (*Isle of Gulls*, 232), gentleman (*Trial of Chivalry*, K1v), merchant's wife (*What You Will*, G4v), madman (*Orlando Furioso*, 842), satyrs (*Isle of Gulls*, 239), devils (*Old Fortunatus*, 1.3.0), "*one like a poor soldier, the other like a poor scholar*" (*Isle of Gulls*, 222); more detailed are "*attired in a gown and cap like a Schoolmaster*" (*Fedele and Fortunio*, 77–8), "*attired like a waterbearing woman with her Tankard*" (*Three Lords of London*, C2v), "*attired like Amazons, with Battleaxes in their hands, and Swords on*" (*Landgartha*, B2v – these figures reappear "*attired like women only*," E4r); other directions include "*oddly attired*"

(*Downfall of Huntingdon*, 457), "*quaintly attired like Masquers*" (*Whore of Babylon*, 1.2.81), "*carelessly attired*" (*Lover's Melancholy*, 1.2.0), "*new attired*" (*Eastward Ho*, F2r), "*ladylike attired*" (*1 Edward IV*, 81; *Staple of News*, Induction.0) and in "*devil's attire*" (*Looking Glass for London*, 1667), "*masquing attire*" (*Antonio's Revenge*, 5.2.19, 31), "*Welsh attire*" (*Two Maids of More-Clacke*, G2v), "*broom-man's attire*" (*Gentleman Usher*, 2.2.129), "*her Own Amazonian attire*" (*Two Noble Ladies*, 1971), a *devil* "*in man's habit, richly attired*" (*Birth of Merlin*, D2v); atypical is *attire* as a verb, when Ariel "*helps to attire*" Prospero (*Tempest*, 2044, 5.1.87).

awake

see *wake*

ax, battleax

can refer to (1) a *battleax*, the sword-like equivalent of a *halberd* or *bill*, (2) an executioner's *ax*, and perhaps the same thing, (3) an *ax* for chopping; two plays specify a *battleax*: "*armed after the Trojan manner, with Target, Sword, and Battleax*" (*Birth of Merlin*, C3r), "*Prologue delivered by an Amazon with a Battleax in her hand*" (*Landgartha*, A4v, also B2v, H3v, H4r); *rods* and *axes* are paired in three Roman plays: "*the Senators, and Rods and Axes borne before them*" (*Valentinian*, 88; see also *Wounds of Civil War*, 5; *Caesar and Pompey*, 1.2.0), and *Landgartha* provides "*Soldiers with Axes*" (B3v, also B4r); elsewhere "*They must have axes for the nonce to fight withal*" (*Alphonsus of Germany*, E1v); an *ax* for beheading most famously appears in *Atheist's Tragedy*: "*As he raises up the ax, strikes out his own brains*" (5.2.241) and less spectacularly: "*Buckingham from his Arraignment, Tipstaves before him, the Ax with the edge towards him*" (*Henry VIII*, 889–90, 2.1.53), "*Falconbridge bound, the Headsman bearing the ax before him*" (*1 Edward IV*, 53; see also *Edmond Ironside*, 644; *Swetnam*, G2r; *Queen*, 230–2); directions in *Dumb Knight* differentiate between "*one with poleaxes, the other with hand axes*" (128, also 129), and in *Warning for Fair Women* an *ax* is used to cut down a *tree* (E3v).

B

bag

most often a small *bag* for *money*: "*a Table is furnished with diverse bags of money*" (*Devil's Charter*, A2r), "*Show a bag of money*" (*King Leir*, 1683), a figure "*with money Bags, and this Motto, I am an Usurer*" (*New Trick*, 251, also 265), "*Throat the Lawyer from his study, books and bags of money on a Table*" (*Ram Alley*, B3v), "*two or three with bags of money*" (*Queen*, 3787–8); sometimes *gold* is specified: "*a post with a letter and a bag of gold*" (*Friar Bacon*, 1494–5); for other instances where a *bag* contains either money or gold see *Jew of Malta*, 686, 695; *Woodstock*, 1751; *Captain Thomas Stukeley*, 583, 2266, 2273, 2281; *Wise Woman of Hogsdon*, 317; *Thomas Lord Cromwell*, B1v; *Weakest Goeth*, 252; *1 Fair Maid of the West*, 272, 275; *Dutch Courtesan*, 2.3.0, 45; *Miseries of Enforced Marriage*, 1538; *Wit at Several Weapons*, 94; *Two Merry Milkmaids*, E1v; *Cruel Brother*, 164; *Just Italian*, 217; *Renegado*, 2.4.0; *City Wit*, 279, 368; *Love's Mistress*, 109; *Fatal Contract*, B2v; *Wits*, 224; other signals for a *bag* include "*his Staff, with a Sandbag fastened to it*" (*2 Henry VI*, D1v, 1117–18, 2.3.58), "*a bag of Nuts*" (*Grim the Collier*, I2v), "*puts the Bills and Bonds into a Bag*" (*City Wit*, 280), "*They seize upon him, bind his arms and feet, and blind him with a bag*" (*Gentleman of Venice*, D4v); in *Two Lamentable Tragedies* a large *bag* holds parts of a *body* in a sequence that ends when a figure "*falls over the bag*" (F4v, also E2r, F3v); for more see *Old Fortunatus*, 3.1.389; *Warning for Fair Women*, G2r; *Sir Thomas Wyatt*, 2.3.8; *If This Be Not a Good Play*, 2.2.16; *New Wonder*, 153; *Guardian*, 5.4.110; *Novella*, 110; *Challenge for Beauty*, 26; *Love and Honour*, 149; *Sisters*, B5v; *Parson's Wedding*, 494.

balcony

a term for the performance level *above* in two plays: "*Enter Dorothy and Susan, in the Balcony*" (*Covent Garden*, 41, also 20, 21, 47), "*Enter Dorcas above upon a Balcony*" (*Weeding of Covent Garden*, 8); the coincidence of play titles and setting perhaps suggests an allusion to an actual *balcony* in Covent Garden.

ball

the only examples are "*a Tun of Tennis balls*" presented to Henry V (*Famous Victories*, D3r) and three *golden* balls: in *Ball* "*A golden Ball descends*" (I2v); in a *masque* in *Constant Maid* a figure enters "*dancing, with a Golden Ball in his hand*," "*The Goddesses dance, and court Paris for his Ball*," Paris "*gives Venus the Ball*" (H1r–v); in *Arraignment of Paris* "*Ate having trundled the ball into place … Juno taketh the ball up*," Paris "*giveth the golden Ball to Venus*," Diana "*delivereth the ball of gold*" to Queen Elizabeth (355, 524, 1240).

ballad

used rarely for a *song*: "*Enter a Ballad singer, and sings a Ballad*" (*Histriomastix*, C1r), "*places all things in order and a candle by them, singing with the ends of old Ballads*

as he does it" (1 Honest Whore, 2.1.0), "Sings a mock-song to
a ballad tune" (Distresses, 305); see also Antipodes, 304.

bank

three uses of this property come in **dumb shows**: "lies
him down upon a bank of flowers" (Hamlet, Q2 H1v, Folio
1994, 3.2.135), "the old Queen weeping, with both her
Infants, the one dead; she lays down the other on a bank,
and goes to bury the dead" (Bloody Banquet, 847–9), "A
Crocodile sitting on a river's bank" (Locrine, 961–2); the
two other uses are also in the context of mimed
action: "Curtains open, Robin Hood sleeps on a green
bank, and Marian strewing flowers on him" (Downfall of
Huntingdon, 1490–1), "Enter Enchanter, leading Lucilla
and Lassingbergh bound by spirits, who being laid down on
a green bank, the spirits fetch in a banquet" (Wisdom of
Doctor Dodypoll, 1063–4); Henslowe's inventory lists
"two moss banks" (Diary, App. 2, 74).

banner

each usage indicates a symbolic inscription or
picture on the banner; in one **dumb show** Falsehood
"sticks up her banner" and Truth enters "with her
banner" (Whore of Babylon, 4.1.0), and in another "an
armed Knight bearing a Crimson Banneret in hand, with
the inscription Valor: by his side a Lady, bearing a Watchet
Banneret, the inscription Clemency: . . . two Ladies, one
bearing a white Banneret, the inscription Chastity: the
other a black, the inscription Constancy" (Four Plays in
One, 311, also 334, 355); a banner is twice linked to
medicine: "a Banner of Cures and Diseases hung out"
(Widow, G1v), "Achitophel and Disease, with a Banner full
of ruptures" (Herod and Antipater, C4r).

banquet

specified in roughly 100 directions most of which
deal with how banquets are to be brought onstage;
banquets can be **discovered** by means of a **curtain**
(Westward Ho, 4.2.52), **prepared** (Macbeth, 1254, 3.4.0;
Loyal Subject, 147; Rape of Lucrece, 205; Valentinian, 88;
Women Beware Women, 3.3.0; Court Secret, D1r), mentioned with no verb attached (1 Tamburlaine, 1638;
Folio Titus Andronicus, 1451, 3.2.0; Maid's Tragedy, 51;
Atheist's Tragedy, 2.1.0; Brazen Age, 198; Bloody Brother,
267; 'Tis Pity, 4.1.0, 5.6.0; Messalina, 1508; Cunning
Lovers, G3v; Wasp, 2164); representative are "two ser-
vants preparing for a Banquet" (Conspiracy, B1r), "A long
table, and a banquet in state" (1 Iron Age, 302); most
common are directions for a banquet to be **fetched** in
(Wisdom of Doctor Dodypoll, 1064), served in (Wisdom of
Doctor Dodypoll, 330; Timon of Athens, 338, 1.2.0; 2 If

You Know Not Me, 297; Honest Man's Fortune, 269),
set/set **out**/**forth** (Satiromastix, 4.1.0; Bloody Brother,
306; Thierry and Theodoret, 24; Custom of the Country,
334; English Traveller, 66; Love's Mistress, 149; Duke of
Milan, 1.3.0; Unnatural Combat, 3.2.136; Great Duke of
Florence, 4.2.153; Noble Spanish Soldier, 5.4.0; Rebellion,
65; Soddered Citizen, 1802; Obstinate Lady, H3v),
brought in/on/out/forth (Battle of Alcazar plot, 91;
Doctor Faustus, B 1012; Taming of the Shrew, 2536–7,
5.2.0; Thomas Lord Cromwell, D2r; Lust's Dominion,
3.2.33; Escapes of Jupiter, 1614; Timon of Athens, 1424,
3.6.41; Silver Age, 101; 1 Iron Age, 280; Tempest, 1536,
3.3.19; Captain, 295; Hengist, 4.2.0; Grateful Servant,
I2r; Bloody Banquet, 1901; Goblins, 3.7.58; News from
Plymouth, 173); variations include "They bring forth a
table, and serve in the banquet" (1 Edward IV, 58), "They
bring in water, wine, and oil, Music, and a banquet"
(David and Bethsabe, 712), "A Banquet first plain, and
presently set out with all Delicates" (Love's Mistress, 101),
"A Banquet brought in. Enter Zephyrus with Psyche, and
places her at the Banquet" (Love's Mistress, 101), "enter two
banquets brought forth, at one the King and the Prince in
their State, at the other the Lords" (Royal King, 25).

Figures also **enter** at a banquet (Silver Age, 141;
Politician, F3r), to a banquet (Battle of Alcazar, 1067;
Doctor Faustus, A 878–9; Looking Glass for London, 1848;
Women Pleased, 270; Valiant Welshman, C2r), most
commonly with a banquet (Edmond Ironside, 384–6;
Blind Beggar of Alexandria, 3.54; Grim the Collier, H9v;
Antony and Cleopatra, 1334, 2.7.0; Travels of Three
English Brothers, 375; Wit at Several Weapons, 124;
Swetnam, H4v; New Trick, 281; Bloody Banquet, 1073;
Deserving Favourite, D3v; Albovine, 31); detailed exam-
ples are entrances "with a rich Banquet" (City Madam,
5.3.7; Guardian, 3.6.0), "with a table and a banquet on it"
(Taming of a Shrew, A3v), "with a Banquet, Wine, and two
Tapers" (Late Lancashire Witches, 237), "Enter all the
nobles, with covered dishes, to the banquet" (Hieronimo,
1.0), "A furnished Table is brought forth: then enters the
Duke and his Nobles to the banquet" (Revenger's Tragedy,
I2v); Spanish Tragedy provides "Enter the Banquet" and
"Sit to the banquet" (1.4.115, 127), the plot of Battle of
Alcazar provides "Enter a banquet brought in by Mr. Hunt
and W. Cartwright: to the banquet enter Sebastian" and
others (91–3), City Madam provides "The Banquet ready.
One Chair, and Wine" (5.1.95); occasionally the removal
of the banquet is signaled: "takes off the Banquet" (Love's
Mistress, 103), exeunt "with spirits and banquets"
(Wisdom of Doctor Dodypoll, 1122), "the Banquet vanishes"
(Tempest, 1584–5, 3.3.52); atypical are "Lights, and a
Banquet follow" (Amorous War, G2v), "Enter an armed

Sewer, after him the service of a Banquet" (*Satiromastix*,
5.2.0), "*Enter the spirit with banqueting stuff*" (*Wisdom of
Doctor Dodypoll*, 951), "*A banquet brought in, with limbs of
a Man in the service*" (*Golden Age*, 21).

bar

a portable railing or barrier at which a ***prisoner*** is
placed in ***trial***/courtroom scenes: "*The Prisoners
brought to the Bar by a Guard*" (*Swetnam*, D3r), "*A Bar set
out*" and "*Audley and Bonvile bring him to the Bar as out
of his bed, then take their seats*" (*Royal King*, 77); three
playhouse annotations are instructive: in the manuscript of *Captives* the bookkeeper has added "*Bar
ready*" (2834), in the manuscript of *Barnavelt* the
order "Let him be sent for presently" is accompanied by both a direction ("*A Bar brought in*") and a
bookkeeper's marginal annotation ("*Bar*" and
"*Table*," 2159–60), in the annotated *Two Merry
Milkmaids* the bookkeeper added "*A Table A Bar*" to
the quarto's "*the form of a court*" (I3r); a printed text
provides both an anticipatory signal "*The Bar and
Book ready on a Table*" and then "*A Bar, Tablebook, two
Chairs and Paper, standish set out*" (*Spanish Curate*,
96/501, 98); *bars* can be *set* (*Jews' Tragedy*, 356), set
forth (*Lovers' Progress*, 144, *Parliament of Love*, 5.1.32),
set out (*City Nightcap*, 119, 133; *Dick of Devonshire*, 1626;
Arcadia, H4r), ***brought*** in (*Queen of Corinth*, 72); other
usages include figures "*At a Bar*" (MS *Poor Man's
Comfort*, 2034), "*at the bar*" (*Sir Thomas More*, 106),
"*placed at the Bar*" (*Chabot*, 3.2.0, 5.2.0; *Two Merry
Milkmaids*, I3r), "*stands to the bar*" (*Tragedy of Byron*,
5.2.42); atypically *Devil's Law Case* calls for two *bars*:
"*Enter Crispiano like a judge, with another judge;
Contilupo and another lawyer at one bar; Romelio, Ariosto,
at another*" (4.2.52).

bare, bareheaded

(1) widely used to signal a man's removal of his ***hat***
as a token of respect or deference, whereas (2) *bare*
occasionally refers to the ***arms*** or ***feet***; for examples
of respect, a group of lords enter "*doing courtesy to
each other, Clerk of the Council waiting bareheaded*" (*Sir
Thomas More*, 1159–60), "*at his entrance they all stand
bare*" (*Conspiracy*, F4v), to show their appreciation
for Coriolanus the Roman soldiers "*cast up their Caps
and Lances: Cominius and Lartius stand bare*"
(*Coriolanus*, 795–6, 1.9.40; see also *Shoemaker a
Gentleman*, 4.1.240); many of the roughly sixty
examples are linked to ***ushers*** (*Gentleman Usher*,
1.2.0; *Widow's Tears*, 1.2.32, 2.2.10, 3.2.0; *Tragedy of
Byron*, 5.3.83; *Henry VIII*, 1339–40, 2.4.0; *Queen's*

Exchange, 530), or other figures who appear ***before***
(*Captain Thomas Stukeley*, 2046; *Caesar and Pompey*,
1.2.0; *Queen and Concubine*, 1; *Shoemaker a Gentleman*,
5.2.78); typical are "*Enter an Usher bare, perfuming a
room*" (*Wonder of a Kingdom*, 3.1.0), "*two bareheaded
before them*" (*Lust's Dominion*, 5.1.0), "*Dorilus bare before
her*" (*Two Merry Milkmaids*, H1v), "*Enter first, barehead*"
(*Downfall of Huntingdon*, 2698), "*Enter Grimundo bare
leading Belinda*" (*Grateful Servant*, I2r), two lords
"*bareheaded; Philip and Mary after them*" (*1 If You Know
Not Me*, 216); occasionally the *bare* figure comes *after*
(*Widow's Tears*, 5.5.150), ***following*** (*Caesar and Pompey*,
4.6.0); other entrances include an ***unready*** figure
who appears "*bareheaded in his shirt: a pair of Pantofles
on*" (*Blurt*, 4.2.0), a father going to ***execution*** "*bare
head, with the Headsman, and other Officers*" (*Comedy of
Errors*, 1600–1, 5.1.129), a Christian forsaking his religion "*on an Ass, in his Christian habit, bareheaded*"
(*Christian Turned Turk*, F2v), a ***poor*** figure "*Bare and
ragged*" (*Wonder of a Kingdom*, 3.1.67), an impostor
showing respect "*booted and bareheaded*" (*Taming of
the Shrew*, 2200–1, 4.4.0); see also *Edward I*, 40; *Look
about You*, 1464, 2823; *Eastward Ho*, F1r; *Antonio's
Revenge*, 4.1.70, 5.1.0, 5.3.0; *What You Will*, H1v; *Bussy
D'Ambois*, 2.1.137; *Caesar and Pompey*, 5.2.22;
Gentleman Usher, 2.2.0; *Whore of Babylon*, 1.2.81;
Wonder of a Kingdom, 5.2.0; *Humour out of Breath*, 473;
Queen of Corinth, 60; *Honest Man's Fortune*, 245; *Women
Beware Women*, 1.3.101; *Queen*, 637; *Dick of Devonshire*,
1555; *Country Girl*, G1r; other usages of *bare* include
"*Piero, unbraced, his arms bare, smeared in blood*"
(*Antonio's Revenge*, 1.1.0; see also *Bussy D'Ambois*, 5.1.0),
"*Sir Charles in prison, with Irons, his feet bare, his gar-
ments all ragged and torn*" (*Woman Killed*, 127); see also
barefoot; atypical is "*Simplicity in bare black, like a poor
Citizen*" (*Three Lords of London*, B3v).

barefoot

specified for a ***mourning*** King David "*barefoot, with
some loose covering over his head*" (*David and Bethsabe*,
972), six abject citizens "*in their Shirts, barefoot, with
halters about their necks*" (*Edward III*, I3v), two women
undergoing a ritual of public penance: Jane Shore
"*in a white sheet barefooted with her hair about her ears,
and in her hand a wax taper*" (*2 Edward IV*, 165), Dame
Elinor "*barefoot, and a white sheet about her, with a wax
candle in her hand*" (Quarto *2 Henry VI*, D2r, 2.4.16).

basin

a property cited in various contexts: "*a Beadle beating
a basin*" (*2 Honest Whore*, 5.2.366), "*A great Hubbub and*

noise, a ringing of basins" (Knave in Grain, 2882), "Titus Andronicus, with a knife, and Lavinia, with a Basin" (Titus Andronicus, K1r, 5.2.165), "Secco, his apron on, Basin of water, Scissors, Comb, Towels, Razor, etc." (Fancies Chaste and Noble, 2372–3), "Cough up in a Basin" (City Wit, 311); for more see Taming of the Shrew, 151–2, Induction.2.0; Knight of the Burning Pestle, 203; Match at Midnight, 81; Court Beggar, 244; Challenge for Beauty, 37, 38; Country Girl, F4v.

basket

used to carry various items onstage: "Marina with a Basket of flowers" (Pericles, F2r, 4.1.12), "a Man with meat in a basket" and "a Wench with a basket, and a child in it under a loin of mutton" (Chaste Maid, 2.2.96, 127, also 114); other signals similarly link a basket with figures from the country: "with a basket, disguised like Country folk" (King Leir, 2091–2; see also Downfall of Huntingdon, 2096–7), "a Country Wench, with a Basket of Eggs" (Jack Drum's Entertainment, G2v) or to other poor and simple figures: "the Clown with a basket and two pigeons in it" (Titus Andronicus, H1v, 4.3.77), "Friar alone with a basket" (Q2 Romeo and Juliet, D4v, 2.3.0), "old Gobbo with a basket" (Merchant of Venice, C1v, 2.2.32), an old woman "very poorly a begging, with her basket and clap-dish" (2 Edward IV, 169), "an Hermit and Servant with a Basket" (Queen's Exchange, 489), "a Groom with a basket" (Quarto Every Man Out, 3490); kinds of basket include a "Peddler's Basket" (Fedele and Fortunio, 1245), "Baker's Basket" (Jovial Crew, 362), "handbasket with a cross bottom of thread" (Weakest Goeth, 205); a larger property is the "great buck basket" in which Falstaff hides (Quarto Merry Wives, D4r, 3.3.4, also 3.3.142); for other baskets see Three Ladies of London, C4v; Histriomastix, B4v; Wisdom of Doctor Dodypoll, 1437; Patient Grissil, 1.2.0, 4.2.108; Greene's Tu Quoque, B1r, I2v; Bartholomew Fair, 4.2.31, 5.3.72; Lovesick King, 942; Virgin Martyr, 5.1.38; Martyred Soldier, 222.

bastinado

"to hit with a stick or cudgel"; the term occurs once: "He bastinadoes Simpliticius" (What You Will, E2v).

battle

(1) usually a call for sound produced within but (2) occasionally a direction for onstage action; typically the sound is instrumental: "The cornets sound a battle within" (Antonio and Mellida, 1.1.0; see also Dick of Devonshire, 434–5), "Drums and Trumpets in several places afar off, as at a main Battle" (Bonduca, 118), "Sound trumpets to the battle," then "sound the battle within" (1 Tamburlaine, 705, 1286; see also Captain Thomas Stukeley, 2770), "A Battle struck within" and "a short Thunder as the burst of a Battle" (Two Noble Kinsmen, C4r, 1.4.0; K4v, 5.1.61), "A Battle beaten within" (Amorous War, K2r, also K2v), "The battle short" (1 Tamburlaine, 1309); also found is to the battle: "Alarums to the battle" (Quarto 2 Henry VI, F4v; Folio "alarums to the fight," 2511, 4.3.0, also Quarto H2r, 5.2.0), "Sound to the battle" (2 Tamburlaine, 2921; see also 1 Tamburlaine, 2184), "Alarum, as in Battle" (Coriolanus, 722, 1.8.0); elsewhere either the sounds of instruments or of "fighting" within are signaled: "Exeunt, Alarum, battle within" (Rape of Lucrece, 248), "The battle continued within" (Caesar and Pompey, 4.2.0), "The battle hard [heard?], afar off" (Edward III, E3r), "The Battle" (Famous Victories, F1r); several directions suggest a **fictional** offstage destination: "Exeunt, to the battle" (Soliman and Perseda, F1v), "To the Battle, and Mycetes comes out alone" (1 Tamburlaine, 663, also 1298).

Sometimes part or all of the battle is onstage: "The Battle continues, the Britains fly, Cymbeline is taken" (Cymbeline, 2908–9, 5.2.10), "enter to the battle" (Battle of Alcazar, 1301, also 1366), "Join Battle: The Christians are beaten off" (Four Prentices, 244), "Alarum, and a Battle, the Moor prevails: All exeunt" (Lust's Dominion, 4.1.41), "The battle enters, Richard wounded" and "Enters Richmond to battle again, and kills Richard" (True Tragedy of Richard III, 1984, 2001), "A Christian battle shown between the two Brothers" (Travels of Three English Brothers, 324, also 323); see also David and Bethsabe, 1469; Captain Thomas Stukeley, 2773–4; in 1 Tamburlaine "Enter to the Battle, and after the battle, enter Cosroe wounded" (851) probably means that the **armies** come onstage to represent the **fight**; several times the term seems to denote the armies themselves: "Enter two battles strongly fighting" and "both the battles offer to meet, and as the Kings are joining battle, Enter Sir Cuthbert" (James IV, 655, 2442–3), "The battles join" (Golden Age, 50, 74); in a very different context and usage during a wedding celebration "Fiddlers pass through, and play the battle" (Late Lancashire Witches, 204), a tune called "The Sack of Troy."

battleax

see **ax**

battledore

a small racquet used in playing shuttlecock, as the only instance indicates: "Enter Ward and Sordido, one with a shuttlecock the other a battledore" (Women Beware Women, 2.2.79).

bear

the animal pursues a figure in three plays: "*Exit pursued by a bear*" (Winter's Tale, 1500, 3.3.58), "*Enter a Nymph, pursued by a wild Bear*" (Conspiracy, D3v; see also Mucedorus, A3v); in Mucedorus the consequences are shown: "*Enter Mucedorus like a shepherd with a sword drawn and a bear's head in his hand*" (A3v, also C2r); see also Locrine, 4–5.

bear, bearing, borne

roughly 200 directions call for figures to *enter* or *exit bearing* (1) *ceremonial* properties and/or *weapons*, (2) a *train*, (3) other properties, (4) a *body* usually *dead* but sometimes *sick*; the various formal entrances include "*a Gentleman bearing the Purse, with the great Seal, and a Cardinal's Hat: Then two Priests, bearing each a Silver Cross: Then a Gentleman Usher bareheaded, accompanied with a Sergeant at Arms, bearing a Silver Mace: Then two Gentleman bearing two great Silver Pillars*" (Henry VIII, 1337–42, 2.4.0, also 175–6, 1.1.114; 3356–9, 5.4.0), "*Queen Elinor in her litter borne by four Negro Moors*" (Edward I, 1015), "*the Cardinals and Bishops, some bearing Crosiers, some the Pillars*" (Doctor Faustus, B 891–2), "*King Agrippa; two of his Attendants go before him, bearing his Crown between them*" (Jews' Tragedy, 57–8), "*bearing two tapers lighted*" (Women Beware Women, 5.2.72), "*bearing Bannerets inscribed*" (Four Plays in One, 334), "*Abbot bearing a Cross*" (Lovesick King, 164), "*bearing the Crown on a cushion*" (Lust's Dominion, 5.1.0); see also 1 Tamburlaine, 143; Richard III, M3r, 3843–4, 5.5.0; Sir Thomas More, 1174; 2 Edward IV, 136; Look about You, 2823; 1 If You Know Not Me, 195; Birth of Merlin, G3v; If This Be Not a Good Play, 1.2.0; Quarto King Lear, B1v, 1.1.33; MS Poor Man's Comfort, 1093; Herod and Antipater, L2r; Antipodes, 246.

Signals for weapons to be *borne* on include "*Sir John alone, with his page bearing his sword and buckler*" (2 Henry IV, B1r, 1.2.0), "*a Herald bearing Andrugio's helm and sword*" (Antonio's Revenge, 2.1.0), "*bearing in his hand his shivered Lance*" (Edward III, G1v), "*the Headsman bearing the ax before him*" (1 Edward IV, 53); see also Downfall of Huntingdon, 2699; Jack Straw, 876–7; Caesar and Pompey, 1.2.0; Devil's Charter, D2r; Four Plays in One, 295; Faithful Friends, 2823–4; Queen, 231; figures also enter *bearing* another's train: "*Ferneze ushering Aurelia, Emilia and Maquerelle bearing up her train*" (Malcontent, 1.6.0), "*the Mufty, or chief Priest: two meaner Priests bearing his train*" (Christian

Turned Turk, F2v), "*her train with all state borne up*" (Roman Actor, 2.1.246); see also Sophonisba, Prologue.0; Gentleman Usher, 2.2.0; Widow's Tears, 1.2.32; 1 If You Know Not Me, 244; Bondman, 3.3.0; Faithful Friends, 2481–2; Duchess of Suffolk, A3r; Emperor of the East, 3.2.0; Picture, 1.2.128; Antipodes, 313; Queen's Exchange, 530; directions to *bear* other properties onstage include "*his boy bearing a Lute and Books*" (Taming of the Shrew, 898–9, 2.1.38), "*Ferdinand (bearing a Log)*" (Tempest, 1235, 3.1.0), "*one bearing Bags sealed*" (Captain Thomas Stukeley, 2266), "*Hercules bearing his two brazen pillars*" (Brazen Age, 247), "*One bearing light, a standish and paper, which sets a Table*" (Bussy D'Ambois, 5.1.0, also 4.2.0), "*two Footmen, bearing the frame of a great picture*" (City Match, 308), "*bearing an offering for the King*" (Faithful Friends, 2477–8); see also 1 Edward IV, 81; Jack Drum's Entertainment, C3r; Nice Valour, 188.

A *funeral* procession sometimes includes the bearing of a body or *coffin*: "*two men bearing a Coffin covered with black*" (Titus Andronicus, A4r, 1.1.69), "*Ventidius as it were in triumph, the dead body of Pacorus borne before him*" (Antony and Cleopatra, 1494–5, 3.1.0), "*Matilda's Hearse, borne by Virgins*" (King John and Matilda, 83), "*four bearing Ithocles on a hearse, or in a chair*" (Broken Heart, 5.3.0), "*two bearing a Coffin, Jasper in it*" (Knight of the Burning Pestle, 216); see also Law Tricks, 183; Atheist's Tragedy, 5.2.67; 1 Iron Age, 345; Devil's Law Case, 5.4.125; Double Marriage, 406; Duchess of Suffolk, G2r; a concern for getting an immobile "body" or figure offstage (or on) is reflected in "*Exeunt, bearing off Antony's body*" (Antony and Cleopatra, 3107, 4.15.91, also 2995, 4.14.140), "*They stop his mouth and bear him in*" (Hieronimo, 8.55), "*bearing a Child*" (Cobbler's Prophecy, 1199–1200), "*bearing Sophonisba in a chair*" (Sophonisba, 5.3.115), "*Dies, the guard run and bear up his body*" (Conspiracy, I2r), "*bearing the Queen to Prison*" (Shoemaker a Gentleman, 1.2.106), "*bearing away the Corpse*" (Fatal Contract, D3v); for more see Spanish Tragedy, 4.4.217; Death of Huntingdon, 944; Quarto 2 Henry VI, H3v, [5.2.65]; Folio 3 Henry VI, 1216, 2.5.78; Massacre at Paris, 206; Caesar and Pompey, 5.1.272; Coriolanus, 3837, 5.6.154; Valiant Welshman, G1v; Brazen Age, 197; 1 Iron Age, 334; 2 Iron Age, 414, 427; Nero, 56; Roman Actor, 4.2.308, 5.1.131; Wizard, 716; Court Beggar, 257; see also *bring, carry*.

beard

an essential part of theatrical presentation, as is made clear when the absence of an actor's *beard* provides an opportunity for Sir Thomas More to step in and play a role in an interlude (belatedly "*Enter Luggins with the beard*," *Sir Thomas More*, 1135); *beards* are usually linked to **disguise**; sometimes the *beard* is one of several items specified: "*Gown, Beard, and Constable's staff*" (*Night Walker*, 357), "*hermit's gown and beard*" (*Malcontent*, 3.5.28), "*a sheet, a hair, and a beard*" (*Atheist's Tragedy*, 4.3.55), "*Alenso in Falleria's apparel and beard*" (*Two Lamentable Tragedies*, H4r); a figure out of disguise can appear "*without hair or beard*" (*Wit of a Woman*, 1662); the **putting** on of *beards* is occasionally signaled but more common is the **pulling** off: "*puts on the beard*" (*English Moor*, 4), "*Enter Gloster in the Hermit's gown, putting on the beard*" (*Look about You*, 2071–2), "*Pulls his Beard and hair off*" (*Island Princess*, 169), "*pulls off their beards, and disguise*" (*Epicœne*, 5.4.211), "*pulls off his beard and discovers himself*" (*Claracilla*, F11v), "*unbeard*" (*Lovesick Court*, 143); from the Brome canon alone comes "*Off his beard and gown*" (*Court Beggar*, 247), "*Off his Beard, etc.*" (*Damoiselle*, 387), "*Pull off Matho's beard*" (*Lovesick Court*, 147), "*casts off his Peruke, and Beard*" (*Novella*, 177); see also *John a Kent*, 298–9; *Wit at Several Weapons*, 82; *Example*, H3v; *Deserving Favourite*, M3v; *Fool Hath Lost His Favourite*, F2v; the phrase *false beard* is widely used: "*in his false beard, leading in Millicent veiled*" (*English Moor*, 76), "*disguised like a Captain with a patch on his eye and a false beard*" (*Wizard*, 343–5); in *Challenge for Beauty* a man enters "*with a false beard in his hand*" and re-enters "*disguised*" (41–2); for examples of *pulling off/putting on/taking up/in false beards* see *Phoenix*, F3v; *Bloody Banquet*, 313–14; *English Moor*, 8; *Lovesick Court*, 145; *Novella*, 157; *Weeding of Covent Garden*, 10; *Love and Honour*, 181.

When *beards* are not linked to disguise the emphasis can be upon age or a disheveled state: "*all ragged in an overgrown red Beard*" (*Caesar and Pompey*, 2.1.0), "*with hair and beard overgrown*" (*Golden Age*, 38), "*a long white hair and beard, in an antique armor*" (*Picture*, 2.1.85), "*a white Beard and Hair*" (*Thracian Wonder*, C4v), "*Makes signs of his white head and beard*" (*Captain*, 296); occasionally the focus is upon grooming, as in entrances "*looking in a glass, trimming his Beard; Giacopo brushing him*" (*Love's Sacrifice*, 676–7), "*his hair and beard trimmed, habit and gown changed*" (*Lover's Melancholy*, 5.2.0); unusual effects include the first appearance of Dissimulation in "*a Farmer's long coat, and a cap, and his poll and beard painted motley*" (*Three Ladies of London*, A2v), the humiliation of Edward II where his tormentors "*wash him with puddle water, and shave his beard away*" (*Edward II*, 2301); in the

earlier troupe plays in which a small number of actors played many parts in rapid succession *beards* were attached by strings, as seen in *Like Will to Like* where two figures enter with "*no Cap nor Hat on their head, saving a night Cap, because the strings of the beards may not be seen*" (D4v), but in *Antonio's Revenge* Balurdo enters "*with a beard half off, half on*" (2.1.20) and states "the tiring-man hath not glued on my beard half fast enough."

beat

the roughly 200 examples include (1) one figure *beating* another, often **off/in/out/away**, and less commonly (2) *beating* on **doors**, (3) *beating* of **drums**; for a sampling of roughly sixty figures who *beat* someone see *Orlando Furioso*, 863, 877, 919; *Doctor Faustus*, A 928; *Comedy of Errors*, 1327, 4.4.44; *Taming of the Shrew*, 2010, 4.3.32; 2434, 5.1.57; Quarto *Merry Wives*, F2v, 4.2.186; *Sir John Oldcastle*, 580; *Wily Beguiled*, 2007, 2015, 2020, 2063, 2073, 2109; *Gentleman Usher*, 5.4.278; *Epicœne*, 4.2.103; *King and No King*, 215; *Silver Age*, 104, 142, 158; *Bartholomew Fair*, 2.6.146, 4.5.60; *Valiant Welshman*, I1r; *Love's Mistress*, 131; *Virgin Martyr*, 4.2.107, 110; *Bondman*, 3.3.132; *City Madam*, 2.2.209; *Two Noble Ladies*, 483; *Late Lancashire Witches*, 199; *City Wit*, 359; *English Moor*, 45; *Traitor*, 3.1.165; figures are also *beaten out* (*Taming of a Shrew*, A2r; *1 Henry VI*, 425, 1.3.56; *Escapes of Jupiter*, 2115; *Sea Voyage*, 13), *away* (*Woodstock*, 2874; *Greene's Tu Quoque*, C3r; *Woman Killed*, 100; *Hieronimo*, 11.73; *Four Prentices*, 176, 187; *Volpone*, 2.3.1; *Fair Maid of the Exchange*, 8; *Coriolanus*, 2703, 4.5.49; *Golden Age*, 53; *Silver Age*, 94; *Alchemist*, 5.5.116), **before** (*Escapes of Jupiter*, 2197–8; *Silver Age*, 116; *1 Iron Age*, 320; *Maid's Revenge*, F2r), "*about the stage*" (*Edmond Ironside*, 562–4), *in* (*Orlando Furioso*, 770; *Spanish Tragedy*, Fourth Addition, 169; *Selimus*, 657, 2461–2; *Lust's Dominion*, 4.2.56, 4.4.74; *Hieronimo*, 11.28, 90; *Coriolanus*, 1949–50, 3.1.227; *Silver Age*, 114; *Brazen Age*, 175; *Tom a Lincoln*, 924, 939; *Valiant Welshman*, B3v, G4v, I2v; *Bride*, 37; *Prisoners*, A6r; *Princess*, A3r), most commonly *off*; for a sampling of the latter see *Thracian Wonder*, G3v; *Escapes of Jupiter*, 72; *Silver Age*, 160; *2 Iron Age*, 368, 389; *Sea Voyage*, 13; *Love's Cure*, 175; *1 Fair Maid of the West*, 298; *Shoemaker a Gentleman*, 3.4.17; *Valiant Scot*, H1v, H3r; *Late Lancashire Witches*, 245; *New Trick*, 270; *Queen's Exchange*, 487; sometimes the means of *beating* is specified: a **cudgel** (Folio *Every Man In*, 3.5.117), potlid (*Famous Victories*, D4v), flail (*Grim the Collier*, I3v), **stone** (*Jews' Tragedy*, 2762), **fiddle** (*Orlando Furioso*, 1225), "*beats and kicks him*" (*New Way* to Pay, 1.1.72; *Queen*, 1749; *Landgartha*, C4r); a **blow** or **army** can be *beat back*: "*Stabs at him, he beats it back, and wounds her*" (*Christian Turned Turk*, H3r), "*the Romans are beat back to their Trenches*" (*Coriolanus*, 523, 1.4.29; see also *1 Henry VI*, 216–17, 1.2.21); variations include "*beats his breast*" (*Jovial Crew*, 445), *beats* his **head** (*Mad Couple*, 47), "*beats out his own brains*" (*Seven Champions*, L1r), enter "*with dry sticks and straw, beating two flints*" (*Valiant Scot*, G3r), "*The Magi with their rods beat the ground, and from under the same riseth a brave Arbor*" (*Looking Glass for London*, 522–3).

Signals that refer to doors include *beat "at the door*" (*Alchemist*, 5.3.44; *Noble Spanish Soldier*, 2.1.105), "*beats to come in*" (*Noble Spanish Soldier*, 5.2.32), "*beat against the gates*" (*Silver Age*, 157), "*A beating within*" (*Spanish Gypsy*, C3v); typical signals for drums are "*Drums beat A March within*" (MS *Bonduca*, 644–5, also 1408, 1848–9, 2149–51), "*beat a March softly within*" (*Fatal Contract*, I4v); for more see *1 Henry VI*, 684–5, 2.2.0; *King John*, 372, 2.1.77; *Coriolanus*, 3621, 5.4.48; MS *Humorous Lieutenant*, 535, 1727; *Loyal Subject*, 163; *Revenge of Bussy*, 3.1.59; *Birth of Merlin*, C3r, F2r; *Valiant Welshman*, B2v; *Jews' Tragedy*, 841, 860, 2010, and more; atypical is "*Here within they must beat with their hammers*" (*Thomas Lord Cromwell*, A2v); see also **bounce, knock**.

beaver
can denote the lower part of the faceguard on a **helmet** or the visor as well; in *Two Noble Ladies* first Miranda enters "*in her Own Amazonian attire, an helmet on and the beaver down,*" then "*lets him take off her helmet. She puts up her beaver*" (1971–3, 1985–6); in *Sophonisba* a figure enters with his "*beaver shut,*" then reveals his identity by removing it (5.3.6, 28); in *White Devil* Bracciano is "*all armed, save the beaver*" and "*Lodovico sprinkles Bracciano's beaver with a poison*" (5.2.44, 76); in *Faithful Friends* a figure enters with "*a Capon's tail in his Beaver*" (1047).

beckon
typically occurs in a context of secrecy and/or seduction: "*Ghost beckons Hamlet*" (Folio *Hamlet*, 643, 1.4.57; see also *Valiant Scot*, I4r), "*Herod whispers with Joseph, and beckons all the rest unto them, but Mariam, and Antipater*" (*Herod and Antipater*, B3v), "*Beckons Douze, she steals after*" (*Twins*, D4r), "*Young Pallantine beckons Lucy from between the hangings, as she is going*" (*Wits*, 143), "*Lady Vanity singing, and beckoning with her hand*" (*Sir Thomas More*, 1080); for other examples see *Look about You*, 668–9; *Hog Hath Lost His Pearl*, 256–7;

Two Merry Milkmaids, E3r; *Country Girl*, G3v; *Example*, G1v; *Seven Champions*, C3r; *Goblins*, 1.1.54; *News from Plymouth*, 150, 152; not surprisingly, *beckon* occurs as part of lengthy mimed actions, including **dumb shows** (*Four Plays in One*, 326; *Second Maiden's Tragedy*, 2228; *Two Noble Ladies*, 1547; *Bloody Banquet*, 854; *Cardinal*, 3.2.85).

bed
widely cited (roughly 150 examples); *beds* or figures in *beds* are (1) **discovered**, (2) **thrust/drawn in/out/forth**, (3) mentioned in **as [if]** signals, (4) specified in a variety of actions, and (5) a substantial number of figures **enter** *in/on* their *beds*; owing to the presence of **curtains** on Elizabethan *beds* a discovery can be effected by the parting of either the **arras** or the **bed** curtains; sometimes a stage curtain is specified or a *bed* rather than a figure is discovered: "*The Arras is drawn, and Zenocrate lies in her bed of state, Tamburlaine sitting by her*" (*2 Tamburlaine*, 2968), "*a Bed discovered with a Blackamoor in it*" (*Monsieur Thomas*, 159), "*Porcius discovers a bed, and a sword hanging by it*" (*Caesar and Pompey*, 4.6.0), "*A curtain drawn, a bed discovered*" (*Amends for Ladies*, 5.2.180), "*Tent opens, she is discovered in her bed*" (*Edward I*, 1453); many directions can be read either way: "*Enter Livia discovered abed, and Moroso by her*" (*Woman's Prize*, 80), "*discovered in her bed*" (*Rape of Lucrece*, 222; *Traitor*, 5.3.0), "*The Curtains being drawn there appears in his bed King Philip*" (*Lust's Dominion*, 1.2.0), "*draweth the curtain: and the Ghost of Andrugio is displayed sitting on the bed*" and "*Exit Maria to her bed, Andrugio drawing the curtains*" (*Antonio's Revenge*, 3.2.72, 103); Quarto 2 *Henry VI* provides "*Then the Curtains being drawn, Duke Humphrey is discovered in his bed, and two men lying on his breast and smothering him in his bed*," "*Warwick draws the curtains and shows Duke Humphrey in his bed*," "*then the Curtains be drawn, and the Cardinal is discovered in his bed, raving and staring as if he were mad*" (E2r, [3.2.0]; E3r, [3.2.146]; F1v, [3.3.0]); for other discoveries of *beds/*figures in *beds* see *What You Will*, B3v; *Tom a Lincoln*, 169–70; *Wonder of a Kingdom*, 3.2.0; *All's Lost by Lust*, 4.2.0; *Love's Mistress*, 121; *Love's Sacrifice*, 1270–1; *Brennoralt*, 3.4.18; *Parson's Wedding*, 477.

Most signals are for *beds* to be brought onstage; figures regularly enter *in* (*Massacre at Paris*, 256; *Woman Killed*, 154; *1 If You Know Not Me*, 200; *Trick to Catch the Old One*, G3r; *Cymbeline*, 903, 2.2.0; *Cupid's Revenge*, 245; *White Devil*, 5.3.81; *Four Plays in One*, 322; *New Trick*, 291), *on* their *beds* (*Wild Goose Chase*, 372; *Martyred Soldier*, 216; *'Tis Pity*, 5.5.0; *Court Beggar*, 245;

Love's Cruelty, F3r; *Lost Lady*, 606; *Princess*, D2r); representative are "*Enter Othello, and Desdemona in her bed*" (Folio *Othello*, 3239, 5.2.0), "*Enter Thierry, on a bed, with Doctors and attendants*" (*Thierry and Theodoret*, 64), enter "*on a bed, as in Bould's chamber*" (*Amends for Ladies*, 4.2.2); atypical is "*Enter Theodosia and Phillipo on several Beds*" (*Love's Pilgrimage*, 246); sometimes figures appear *on a bed* and especially *in a bed* but are not directed to enter: "*Enter into the Admiral's house, and he in his bed*" (*Massacre at Paris*, 301), "*Enter the King, Salisbury, and Warwick, to the Cardinal in bed*" (Folio *2 Henry VI*, 2132–3, 3.3.0); see also *Sappho and Phao*, 3.3.0; *Mad World*, 3.2.0; *Devil's Law Case*, 3.2.68; *Vow Breaker*, 4.2.0; *Country Captain*, B8r; *beds*/figures on *beds* are *drawn forth* (*Atheist's Tragedy*, 5.1.59); *Very Woman*, 4.2.19; *Cruel Brother*, 191), *drawn out* (*Maidenhead Well Lost*, 154; *Messalina*, 1100), *thrust out/forth* (*Escapes of Jupiter*, 1368; *Faithful Friends*, 2613–14; *Witch of Edmonton*, 4.2.0; *Late Lancashire Witches*, 249; *Lost Lady*, 606), **put** *forth* (Folio *2 Henry VI*, 1849, 3.2.146; *Mad Couple*, 73; *Queen's Exchange*, 524; *Weeding of Covent Garden*, 87; *Obstinate Lady*, E2v): "*A Bed thrust out: Lodovico sleeping in his clothes; Dorothea in Bed*" (*City Nightcap*, 111), "*The bed thrust forth with Aphelia asleep*" (*Fatal Contract*, G1r), "*A bed thrust out upon the stage, Allwit's Wife in it*" (*Chaste Maid*, 3.2.0), "*Enter the four old Beldams, drawing out Danae's bed: she in it*" (*Golden Age*, 67); a few directions require the removal of a *bed*: "*The bed is drawn in*" (*Golden Age*, 70; *Escapes of Jupiter*, 989), "*The Bed pulled in*" (*New Trick*, 293), "*Puts in the bed*" (*Mad Couple*, 76; *City Wit*, 319); several plays call for *beds* to be **ready** (*Spanish Curate*, 117/501, 118; annotated *Two Merry Milkmaids*, K3r; *Wasp*, 41; see also *Woodstock*, 2377–8); Henslowe's inventory includes "one bedstead" (*Diary*, App. 2, 57).

Figures who enter *in/on beds* are often **sick**: "*A bed thrust out, Antoninus upon it sick, with Physicians about him*" (*Virgin Martyr*, 4.1.0); see also *Two Lamentable Tragedies*, B1r; *Martyred Soldier*, 175; *Princess*, E1r; *as [if]* signals can be used in lieu of an onstage *bed*, so that figures are directed to enter **as from** bed (*Lovers' Progress*, 128; *Thierry and Theodoret*, 30; *2 Iron Age*, 381; *Tom a Lincoln*, 2406–7), *as out of bed* (*Woman Killed*, 141; *Coxcomb*, 325; *Royal King*, 77; *Aglaura*, 5.3.141), "*as going to bed*" (*Fatal Contract*, F4v; *Match at Midnight*, 77), "*as though to bed*" (*Queen's Exchange*, 507), "*in his shirt, as started from bed*" (*Amends for Ladies*, 4.1.2), "*Dalavill in a Nightgown: Wife in a night-tire, as coming from Bed*" (*English Traveller*, 70), "*half unready, as newly started from their Beds*" (*2 Iron Age*, 413), "*unbuttoned as*

out of bed" (*Swaggering Damsel*, H2v), "*in her nightgown as to bed-ward*" (*White Devil*, 2.2.23); actions include *lying on a bed* (*Devil's Charter*, I3r; *Golden Age*, 68), "*leaps into the bed*" (*Tom a Lincoln*, 1647), "*falls on the bed*" (Quarto *Othello*, M3v, 5.2.198), "*throws herself upon a bed*" (*White Devil*, 4.2.128), "*takes her and puts her into the Bed*" (*Maidenhead Well Lost*, 152), "*leads her to stand at the bed's feet*" and "*riseth from the bed*" (*Cruel Brother*, 191, 194), "*Ties his arms to the bed*" (*Maid's Tragedy*, 61), "*dies in his bed*" (*True Tragedy of Richard III*, 192), "*falls upon her bed within the Curtains*" (Q1 *Romeo and Juliet*, I1r, 4.3.58), "*draw the curtains and smother the young princes in the bed*" (*Battle of Alcazar*, 37–8), "*They tumble Marcus over the bed, and take her away*" (*Valiant Welshman*, H4v, also H4r); see also *Edward I*, 2607; *Dumb Knight*, 166; *Silver Age*, 155; *2 Iron Age*, 411; *Fatal Contract*, G2r, G2v; *Hog Hath Lost His Pearl*, 1567–8; *Sophonisba* provides "*ready for bed*" (1.2.62, 3.1.169), "*lay Vangue in Syphax's bed and draw the curtains*" (3.1.161), "*Offering to leap into bed, he discovers Vangue*" (3.1.182), "*hasteth in the bed of Syphax*" (4.1.213), "*hasteneth within the canopy, as to Sophonisba's bed*" (4.1.218), "*They leap out of the bed*" (5.1.3); see also **abed**.

beer, ale

rarely specified **drinks**; beer can be in a **jack** (*1 If You Know Not Me*, 209; *Bloody Brother*, 262), a **bottle** (*Looking Glass for London*, 2237), or a **bowl** (*Wise Woman of Hogsdon*, 336; *Match at Midnight*, 26); see also *Two Lamentable Tragedies*, A4r; *Mad Couple*, 22; two directions cite *ale*: "*a bottle of ale, cheese, and halfpenny loaves*" (*2 Edward IV*, 173), "*bring out the stand of ale, and fall a drinking*" (*George a Greene*, 1183); see also **wine**.

before, afore

widely used (roughly 300 examples) (1) most often in signals that deal with the positioning of **entering** figures but also as (2) "previously, previous to," frequently as part of the locution **as before**, (3) "in front of"; for examples of entrances, twenty directions use *before* in conjunction with *after*: "*two Angels before her, and two after her*" (*Three Lords of London*, A4v), "*Disanius before a hearse, Philocles after*" (*Lovesick Court*, 162); for a sampling see *Malcontent*, 4.5.0; *Devil's Charter*, A4r, D2r; *Tom a Lincoln*, 1721–2; *Shoemaker a Gentleman*, 5.2.78; *Queen*, 3115–17; more plentiful are signals without *after* in which one or more figures are directed to enter *before*; such figures can be **ushers** or other attendants designated as **bare**/bareheaded: "*a Gentleman Usher before Clermont*" (*Revenge of Bussy*, 3.2.0), "*Dorilus bare before her*" (*Two Merry*

Milkmaids, H1v); for a sampling see *Caesar and Pompey*, 5.1.0; *Royal King*, 65; *Queen and Concubine*, 1; other figures who appear *before/afore* a higher ranking figure include officers (*Chabot*, 3.2.0, 5.2.0), lictors (*Wounds of Civil War*, 4–5; *Coriolanus*, 1240, 2.2.36; *Appius and Virginia*, D2v), senators (*Rape of Lucrece*, 165), a tipstaff (*Queen and Concubine*, 115), a sergeant at arms (*Henry VIII*, 175–6, 1.1.197), "*the Sheriff and his Bailiffs*" (*Sir John Oldcastle*, 59); *before* is often used for entrances in **state** or in ceremonial fashion: "*in all state and royalty, the Purse and Mace before him*" (*When You See Me*, 1–2), "*in full state, triumphal ornaments carried before him*" (*Sophonisba*, 5.4.0, also 3.2.0); for a sampling see *Henry VIII*, 175–9, 1.1.114; *If This Be Not a Good Play*, 1.2.0; *Royal King*, 25; *Old Law*, I1v; in addition to **purse/mace** (*Sir Thomas More*, 1174), other objects borne *before* include a **crown** (*Jews' Tragedy*, 57–60), "*Swords of State, Maces, &c.*" (*If This Be Not a Good Play*, 1.2.0), "*Rods and Axes*" (*Wounds of Civil War*, 5; *Caesar and Pompey*, 1.2.0; *Valentinian*, 88), a Roman eagle (*Shoemaker a Gentleman*, 3.3.0), "*with his Staff and Key, and other offices borne before him to wait on the King*" (*Royal King*, 25); also entering *before* are a servant (*Wise Woman of Hogsdon*, 312), fiddler (*Country Girl*, D3r), prentice (*City Match*, 249), pages (*Three Lords of London*, B1r; *What You Will*, A4r; *Malcontent*, 2.1.0, 5.4.0; *Henry VIII*, 2769–70, 5.1.0; *Coronation*, 262), heralds (*Three Lords of London*, F4r; *When You See Me*, 2883–4; *Whore of Babylon*, 4.3.25; *Queen*, 3308–9), figures bearing **weapons/armor** (*James IV*, 2406–7; *Sophonisba*, 5.2.32; *1 Iron Age*, 341; *Noble Gentleman*, 234); dead **bodies** can come *before* (*Edward III*, G1v; *Antony and Cleopatra*, 1494–5, 3.1.0), as can a **drum**/drummer (Quarto *2 Henry VI*, D1v, 2.3.58; *2 If You Know Not Me*, 342; *Trial of Chivalry*, A4v), **trumpet**/trumpeter (Folio *Midsummer Night's Dream*, 1924, 5.1.126; Quarto *King Lear*, L1v, 5.3.117; *Caesar and Pompey*, 3.1.63; *Swetnam*, E2v; *Birth of Merlin*, C3r; *Politician*, K1v), **music**/musicians (*Summer's Last Will*, 443; *Edward I*, 746; *Cymbeline*, 3068, 5.4.29; *Late Lancashire Witches*, 206); most commonly placed *before* are a **torch/light/link** (*Woodstock*, 117; *Warning for Fair Women*, D2v; *Satiromastix*, 1.1.113, 138, 5.1.160; *Jack Drum's Entertainment*, C3r; *What You Will*, A4r; *Family of Love*, D4r; *London Prodigal*, F4r; *Sophonisba*, 5.3.0; *Second Maiden's Tragedy*, 1878; *Macbeth*, 569–70, 2.1.0; *Henry VIII*, 2769–70, 5.1.0); *before* the condemned going to **execution** may appear a headsman/hangman/executioner/tipstaves: "*the Headsman bearing the ax before him*" (*1 Edward IV*, 53); see also *2 Edward IV*, 136; *Insatiate Countess*, 5.1.66;

Henry VIII, 889, 2.1.53; *Virgin Martyr*, 4.3.32; *Queen*, 230–1, 3115.

The most common usage of *before* as "previously, previous to" is in the locution *as before* which calls for a costume or stage effect that had been displayed earlier; typical is Q1 *Hamlet* where the mad Ophelia first appears "*playing on a Lute, and her hair down singing*" and reappears "*as before*" (G4v, 4.5.20; H1v, [4.5.154]); variations include "*Enter one of the Soldiers sent out before*" (*Widow's Tears*, 5.4.0), "*Enter the Queen, and all that were in before*" (*Humorous Day's Mirth*, 5.2.0); presenters enter *before* **masques/dumb shows**: "*Enter Tragedy afore the show*" (*Warning for Fair Women*, G2v); see also *Battle of Alcazar*, 1256; *Women Pleased*, 308.

For examples of *before* as "in front of," figures are directed to enter **beating/driving/thrusting** others *before* them: "*Amphitrio, beating before him his servants*" (*Silver Age*, 116), Joan "*driving Englishmen before her*" (*1 Henry VI*, 589, 1.5.0); see also *Orlando Furioso*, 770; *Taming of a Shrew*, G1r; *Whore of Babylon*, DS before Act 1, 47; MS *Humorous Lieutenant*, 1805–6; *1 Iron Age*, 320; *New Way to Pay*, 5.1.88; *Herod and Antipater*, G2v; *Hog Hath Lost His Pearl*, 812; *Birth of Merlin*, F4r; *Maid's Revenge*, F2r; *Bride*, 37; atypical is a pursued figure "*flying before him with a Child in her arms*" (*Thracian Wonder*, B1r); also common are figures who **kneel** *before* (*Selimus*, 1469; *Rape of Lucrece*, 184; *Broken Heart*, 5.3.0), **fall** down *before* a person/object (*Three Lords of London*, I3r; *Two Noble Kinsmen*, B1v, 1.1.24; C4r, 1.4.0): "*Kneel all down before the brazen Head*" (*Alphonsus of Aragon*, 1307), "*falls down on her knees before the Queen fearful and weeping*" (*2 Edward IV*, 126); *before* can be used to signal action in front of the tiring-house wall/**discovery** space: "*Enter Mr. Ricot again walking before the gate*" (*English Traveller*, 62), "*Enter Golding discovering a Goldsmith's shop, and walking short turns before it*" (*Eastward Ho*, A2r), "*They draw the Curtains from before Nature's shop*" (*Woman in the Moon*, A2v); Shakespeare uses *before* for action in front of the **walls** of a **city** (represented by the tiring-house), so that combatants enter "*before the Gates*" of Harfleur (Folio *Henry V*, 1259, 3.3.0), "*before Bordeaux*" (*1 Henry VI*, 1949, 4.2.0), "*before Angiers*" (*King John*, 292, 2.1.0), "*before Athens*" (*Timon of Athens*, 2507–8, 5.4.0), invoking *as* [*if*] "*as before the City Corioles*" (*Coriolanus*, 479–80, 1.4.0); other uses of *before* as "in front of" include "*a scarf before his face*" (*Orlando Furioso*, 1350–1, 1475), "*with heaps of gold before him*" (*Jew of Malta*, 35; *Thomas Lord Cromwell*, B1v), a killing "*before the Altar*" (*2 Iron Age*, 390), "*on a bier before the bar*"

(*Parliament of Love*, 5.1.32), "*an Angel comes and stands before him*" (*Martyred Soldier*, 209), "*pass directly before the Cardinal, and gracefully salute him*" (*Henry VIII*, 755–6, 1.4.63), "*Nightingale sets his foot afore him, and he falls with his basket*" (*Bartholomew Fair*, 4.2.31), "*Timantus runs at him, and Urania steps before*" (*Cupid's Revenge*, 285).

begin

used in a variety of locutions to initiate an action (with that action sometimes interrupted); figures *begin* to *sing* (*Old Wives Tale*, 534), **dance** (*Late Lancashire Witches*, 215), **rise** (*Andromana*, 261), **retire** (*Trial of Chivalry*, I2v), **draw** a **sword** (*Sophonisba*, 2.2.44), **strip** another (*Alarum for London*, 748; *Princess*, H3r), "*paint her*" (*English Moor*, 38), "*cut the body*" of a murder victim (*Two Lamentable Tragedies*, E2r); variations include "*soft music begins*" (*Dick of Devonshire*, 433), "*The Drum begins to march*" (Folio 3 *Henry VI*, 2556, 4.7.50), "*Begin again*" to **fight** (1 *Henry VI*, 1318, 3.1.103; see also *Birth of Merlin*, C3r), "*Here he begins to break the branches*" (*Friar Bacon*, 1214), "*begin to sing, and presently cease*" (*Histriomastix*, H2r); see also *Launching of the Mary*, 2794–5; *begin* can signal the beginning of a **scene**, **act**, **song**, speech: "*All forsake the stage, saving Andrugio, who, speaking, begins the Act*" (*Antonio's Revenge*, 5.1.0; see also *Antonio and Mellida*, 3.2.123), "*They all awake, and begin the following Act*" (*Histriomastix*, E2r); for examples of *begin* as shorthand for *begin to sing/speak* see *Summer's Last Will*, 1064; *Wounds of Civil War*, 5–6.

behind

roughly 100 occurrences (1) most commonly in versions of *behind* a **curtain** but also for (2) figures who **enter**/**come**/**stay** *behind*, (3) various other actions; examples of *behind the curtain* include "*lying behind the Curtains*" and "*from behind the Curtains*" (*Battle of Alcazar* plot, 27, 84), "*sitting in a study behind a Curtain*" (*Satiromastix*, 1.2.0), "*Draws a curtain; behind it Timothy asleep*" (*City Match*, 252); see also *Thracian Wonder*, D1v; *What You Will*, C4r; *Dutch Courtesan*, 5.1.13; *If This Be Not a Good Play*, 5.4.0; 2 *Iron Age*, 411; *Guardian*, 3.6.0; *Lovers' Progress*, 104; *Princess*, C2r; examples of *behind the **arras*** include "*Falstaff stands behind the arras*" (Quarto *Merry Wives*, E1r, 3.3.91), "*peeps fearfully forth from behind the arras*" (*Atheist's Tragedy*, 2.5.110), "*withdraw behind the Arras*" (*English Traveller*, 79), "*puts him behind the arras*" (*Albovine*, 101); see also *Sir Thomas More*, 104; 1 *If You Know Not Me*, 235, 236; *Honest Man's Fortune*, 246; *Faithful*

Friends, 2622–3; *Women Pleased*, 293; *Spanish Gypsy*, H4r; *Jews' Tragedy*, 1899–1900, 2798; *Love and Honour*, 149; *Noble Stranger*, E1r, F2r; *Unfortunate Lovers*, 66; examples of *behind the **hangings*** are "*Goes behind the hangings*" (*Duke's Mistress*, I1r), "*Exit and stays behind the hangings*" (*Grateful Servant*, F2r), "*comes from behind the hangings*" (*Maid's Revenge*, E2v, F1v), "*stirs behind the hangings*" (*Andromana*, 261); see also *Philaster*, 93, 95; *Northern Lass*, 75; *Jews' Tragedy*, 1887–9; *Rebellion*, 17, 18; *Traitor*, 3.3.8; *News from Plymouth*, 178; an alternative is "*Here is discovered, behind a traverse, the artificial figures of Antonio and his children*" (*Duchess of Malfi*, 4.1.55), "*peeps from behind a traverse*" (*Volpone*, 5.3.9).

Various locutions direct figures to enter after or *behind* others: "*Enter Celia, and Ladies behind her*" (*Humorous Lieutenant*, 333), "*stealing behind*" (*Woman's Prize*, 85), "*behind laughing*" (*Fancies Chaste and Noble*, 1785), "*behind to observe*" (*Telltale*, 368–9), "*comes in sadly behind*" (1 *Honest Whore*, 2.1.118); see also *Three Ladies of London*, F1v; *Midsummer Night's Dream*, F2v, 4.1.0; *Sophonisba*, 4.1.42; *Cymbeline*, 3332, 5.5.68; *Humorous Day's Mirth*, 5.1.6; *Whore of Babylon*, 1.1.0; *Novella*, 164; *Court Beggar*, 264; *Love's Sacrifice*, 2737–8; *Swaggering Damsel*, H1r; figures also **remain** onstage or stay *behind* others: "*Parolles and Lafew stay behind commenting of this wedding*" (*All's Well*, 1089–90, 2.3.183), "*Thersites only stays behind and concludes*" (1 *Iron Age*, 345); see also *Arraignment of Paris*, 721; 2 *Iron Age*, 408; *Aglaura*, 1.3.50; elsewhere a figure is *behind* another: "*the scholar stands behind, gives him the first word*" (*No Wit*, 4.3.40), "*comes behind him, and pulls him by the arm*" (*Albovine*, 78); for more see *Fool Would Be a Favourite*, C8r; *Just Italian*, 221; *Goblins*, 2.6.20; *Aglaura*, 5.1.24; *Landgartha*, I3v; properties are also left *behind*: "*all run away…leaving the booty behind them*" (1 *Henry IV*, C4v, 2.2.101), "*they fly, leaving their Clothes behind*" (1 *Henry VI*, 766, 2.1.77; see also *Dutch Courtesan*, 4.5.20); for more see *Jack Straw*, 488; *Two Maids of More-Clacke*, G1r; in *Julia Agrippina* one figure "*lets fall a poniard behind*" another (5.522–3); other locutions include "*the place behind the Stage*" and "*bound with their hands behind them*" (*Alphonsus of Aragon*, 1246–7, 1783–4; see also *Two Lamentable Tragedies*, E2r), "*the women kneeling behind*" (*Broken Heart*, 5.3.0), "*pinches behind*" (*Cupid's Whirligig*, 3.1.119), "*stands behind the post*" (*Devil's Charter*, F3v), "*taking gifts of the Prior behind, and his master before*" (*Downfall of Huntingdon*, 49–50), "*her garment painted behind with fools' faces and devils' heads*" (*Old Fortunatus*, 1.3.0; see also *Three Lords of London*, F4r,

G1v), "*Behind the State stabs Theodoret*" (*Thierry and Theodoret*, 38), "*with the scabbard thrusts him behind*" (*Young Admiral*, K2v); for more see *City Madam*, 5.3.44; *Messalina*, 1282–3; *School of Compliment*, I3r; *Tottenham Court*, 136.

bell

several kinds of *bells* are represented: (1) a tower *bell* that sounds an **alarm**, announces a death, or gives the time, (2) a **door** or **gate** *bell*, (3) a hand*bell* used to call servants; the first two are an offstage **sound** but the third *bell* sometimes appears onstage; these different sounds suggest that the *bells* used to create them were correspondingly different in size and type; a large loud *bell* seems called for in Quarto *Othello* when after the fight between Roderigo and Cassio comes "*A bell rung*" (F1r, 2.3.160) and Iago asks "Who's that that rings the bell? . . . / The town will rise"; in *Massacre at Paris* the massacre begins when "*the bell tolls*" (338); in *Macbeth* a "*Bell rings*" (836, 2.3.80) at Macduff's "Ring the alarum bell" when he discovers Duncan murdered; and in *Michaelmas Term* at Quomodo's supposed death "*A bell tolls; a confused cry within*" (4.3.0); in *Changeling* "*ring a bell*" (5.1.73) is acknowledged with De Flores's "The fire-bell rings"; for similar instances see *Jew of Malta*, 1508; *Weakest Goeth*, 1774; *Two Maids of More-Clacke*, B4v; *Macbeth*, 642, 2.1.61; *Island Princess*, 92, 113; *Night Walker*, 360; *Fatal Contract*, D2v; *Cardinal*, 5.3.180; *Queen's Exchange*, 478; *Arcadia*, E2r; a *bell* that gives the time is called for in *Roaring Girl* where it is a signal to shut up shop and eat (2.1.354); in *Shoemakers' Holiday* the "*Bell rings*" (5.2.176) on Shrove Tuesday and "when the pancake bell rings . . . we may shut up our shops, and make holiday"; for other *bells* linked to telling time see Quarto *Every Man In*, 1.4.146; *Englishmen for My Money*, 677; *Wit of a Woman*, 1527; *Captives*, 869; *Launching of the Mary*, 42, 1135; a *bell* is rung to request entry at a door or gate in *Golden Age*, 57, 61; *Bloody Brother*, 295; *Novella*, 114, 149, 170; *Bird in a Cage*, F3r, H2v; *Messalina*, 691, 712; see also **strike**.

A smaller, hand-held *bell* seems required in *Devil's Charter* when Alexander "*tinketh a bell*" to call Bernardo (B3r, E3r, G1r, G2r); a direction for properties in *Barnavelt* – "*Table: Bell*" (1184) – suggests a conventional setting most apparent in *News from Plymouth* where the *bell* is never actually rung: "*A curtain drawn by Dash (his clerk) Trifle discovered in his study. Papers, taper, seal and wax before him, bell*" (167) and Trifle asks "O, are you come? 'Tis well! I was

about / To ring for you"; a *bell* is used by a vintner to call his drawers (*Weeding of Covent Garden*, 33); atypical signals for a hand*bell* are "*Bell, Book, and Candle, for the Dirge*" (*Doctor Faustus*, B 1111–12), "*a coffin, cords and a bell*" (*Duchess of Malfi*, 4.2.165), "*Coxcomb, Bauble, Bells, and Coat*" (*Queen and Concubine*, 34), "*a bell ringing*" (*Faithful Shepherdess*, 387), "*rings a bell, and draws a curtain*" (*Histriomastix*, B4v).

belonging

synonymous with "suitable" in two directions for supernatural business: "*Medea do ceremonies belonging to conjuring*" (*Alphonsus of Aragon*, 939), "*Here do the Ceremonies belonging, and make the Circle, Bullingbrooke or Southwell reads, Conjuro te, etc.*" (Folio *2 Henry VI*, 643–5, 1.4.22).

below

this locator usually designates either (1) *below* the upper playing level, on the main platform or (2) *below* the main platform; when it means "*below* the gallery" the term is often used in apposition to **above** or to one of the other terms for the upper playing space: "*Lord Scales upon the Tower walls walking. Enter three or four Citizens below*" (*2 Henry VI*, G1r, 2598–9, 4.5.0), "*King, and Lords below, old Bruce, Leister, Oxford and Fitzwater above*" (*King John and Matilda*, 80), "*Whilst she plays and sings above, Paulo waits below*" (*Novella*, 129); figures on the upper level sometimes overhear or watch those *below* (*Antonio and Mellida*, 1.1.98; *Chances*, 233; *Virgin Martyr*, 2.3.56; *Dick of Devonshire*, 1611; *Love's Sacrifice*, 2350; *Rebellion*, 83); figures recently on the gallery **enter** below (*Englishmen for My Money*, 2049; *Ram Alley*, C4v; *Greene's Tu Quoque*, F2r; *Philaster*, 100; *Widow*, F1r; *Monsieur Thomas*, 139; *Duke of Milan*, 2.1.182); other instances where *below* denotes the main platform are Q2 *Bussy D'Ambois*, 5.4.186; *Devil's Charter*, D3v; *Brazen Age*, 206; *1 Iron Age*, 298, 319; *Devil Is an Ass*, 2.7.23; *More Dissemblers*, B8r; *Virgin Martyr*, 2.3.134; *Custom of the Country*, 355; *Fatal Dowry*, 4.2.70; *Knight of Malta*, 117; *Queen of Corinth*, 57; *Claracilla*, F10v; *Goblins*, 5.5.111.

Below can also be synonymous with **under the stage** or **beneath** the stage, as in the annotated manuscript of *Believe as You List*: "*Gascoine and Hubert below, ready to open the Trapdoor for Mr. Taylor*" (1825, also 1931); other examples are "*Music below*" (*Prophetess*, 385), "*Noise below*" (*Rule a Wife*, 229, 231), "*Pluto ascendeth from below in his chair*" (*Arraignment of Paris*, 819); see also *If This Be Not a Good Play*, 5.4.68;

New Wonder, 121; *Bloody Banquet*, 1613, 1687; *Weeding of Covent Garden*, 33; *Aglaura*, 5.1.118; for a problematic usage of *below* see *Double Marriage*, 339.

Atypical uses of *below* include one linked to the **chair of state**, which seems to have been on a dais on the main platform: "*the High Priest ascends the Chair, the other three sit below*" for a trial (*Jews' Tragedy*, 354–5) and a direction in *Look about You* which is less clear but perhaps describes a similar physical relationship between Henry and his newly crowned son: "*Henry the elder places his Son, the two Queens on either hand, himself at his* [*son's*] *feet, Leicester and Lancaster below him*" (2825–7); in *Knight of the Burning Pestle* "*Wife below, Rafe below*" (162) means "below the main platform among the audience."

beneath

a seldom used alternative to **below**, usually to mean *beneath* the upper playing level on the main platform, as in "*Enter Cusay beneath*" (*David and Bethsabe*, 214); see also *Widow's Tears*, 3.2.78; *Fawn*, 5.0; *Miseries of Enforced Marriage*, 2002; *Knight of Malta*, 87; *Messalina*, 2228–9; twice *beneath* is a version of **under the stage**: "*a flame of fire appeareth from beneath, and Radagon is swallowed*" (*Looking Glass for London*, 1230–1; see also *Antonio's Revenge*, 3.1.127); atypical is "*Two fiery Bulls are discovered, the Fleece hanging over them, and the Dragon sleeping beneath them*" (217).

betting

a **noise** specified twice: "*Confused noise of betting within*" (*Hyde Park*, G4r), "*A noise below in the bowling-alley of betting and wrangling*" (*New Wonder*, 121).

between, betwixt

interchangeable terms (with *between* by far the most common) used (1) typically to establish the physical relationship of entering figures, (2) sometimes to direct that one figure be controlled by others but also (3) to describe the action of one figure separating others; usually *between* is linked to **enter**: "*Antony, Caesar, Octavia between them*" (*Antony and Cleopatra*, 963, 2.3.0), "*Richard aloft, between two Bishops*" (Folio *Richard III*, 2313, 3.7.94), "*Helen again, passing over between two Cupids*" (*Doctor Faustus*, B 1872), "*Then Galeatzo betwixt two Senators, reading a paper to them*" (*Antonio's Revenge*, 5.1.0), "*Bride between Frankford and another*" (*Cure for a Cuckold*, H4r), "*a Guard making a lane. Enter between them, King John … and all the King's party*" (*King John and Matilda*, 29), "*Iacomo bare betwixt the two Dukes*" (*Wonder of a*

Kingdom, 5.2.0, also 4.1.0); for similar entrances see *2 Seven Deadly Sins*, 33; *Histriomastix*, F2v; *Northward Ho*, 5.1.477; *Trial of Chivalry*, G2v; *Roaring Girl*, 5.2.168; *Your Five Gallants*, I2v; *Devil's Charter*, A2r, D2r; *Two Noble Kinsmen*, B1r, 1.1.0; MS *Poor Man's Comfort*, 1093; *Bloody Brother*, 267; *Herod and Antipater*, F4r, L3v; *Antipodes*, 313; *New Academy*, 45; *Cardinal*, 3.2.85; figures enter/exit **led** between others: "*Katherine Dowager, sick, led between Griffith, her Gentleman Usher, and Patience her Woman*" (*Henry VIII*, 2548–50, 4.2.0), "*pinioned and led betwixt two Officers*" (*2 Edward IV*, 175), "*led off betwixt them*" (*1 Arviragus and Philicia*, A8v); see also *Cobbler's Prophecy*, 1629–30; *Caesar and Pompey*, 2.4.90; *Northward Ho*, 1.2.0; *Puritan*, H3r; *Devil's Law Case*, 2.4.0; *Queen and Concubine*, 22; *Swaggering Damsel*, I2v; the same implication of a figure in others' control is present in "*bearing the man between two in a Chair*" (*2 Henry VI*, C2r, 796, 2.1.65), "*Balthazar between Lorenzo and Horatio, captive*" (*Spanish Tragedy*, 1.2.109); see also *2 Troublesome Reign*, D2v; *1 Iron Age*, 307.

The other common usage of *between/betwixt* describes the action of one figure separating others, usually to prevent or stop a **fight**: "*Let Fraud make as though he would strike him, but let Dissimulation step between them*" (*Three Ladies of London*, A3v), "*stand between the two factions*" (*Brazen Age*, 196), "*runs betwixt them and parts them*" (*Four Prentices*, 189, also 191), "*they draw, Blunt and the Doctor comes between them*" (*Fair Maid of Bristow*, C2v), "*kneels between the Armies*" (*Hoffman*, 1203), and with more extreme consequences "*They make a dangerous pass at one another the Lady purposely runs between, and is killed by them both*" (*Second Maiden's Tragedy*, 2133–5), "*They fight, Elgina goes between, Erkinwald kills her*" (*Lovesick King*, 826); for other uses of *between/betwixt* for separation see *2 Seven Deadly Sins*, 23; *Histriomastix*, F3r; *Edmond Ironside*, 1860–1; *Sir John Oldcastle*, 1593; *Insatiate Countess*, 1.1.141; *Trick to Catch the Old One*, B2r; *Birth of Merlin*, C3r; *Christian Turned Turk*, H1v; *Honest Man's Fortune*, 226; *Amends for Ladies*, 4.4.95; *1 Iron Age*, 296, 299; *2 Iron Age*, 361; *Bloody Brother*, 253; *Knave in Grain*, 1323–4; *Herod and Antipater*, G2v; *Welsh Ambassador*, 2223; *2 Passionate Lovers*, L5v; *Unfortunate Lovers*, 67; *Vow Breaker*, 3.4.84, 4.1.75; *Claracilla*, F2r; other locutions include "*Embraces between them*" (*Country Girl*, E4v), "*between every couple a torch carried*" (*Changes*, K2v), "*Andrugio's ghost is placed betwixt the music houses*" (*Antonio's Revenge*, 5.3.49), "*bearing his Crown between them*" (*Jews' Tragedy*, 58), "*Papers this while being offered and subscribed between either*" (*Look about*

You, 200–1), "*suddenly riseth up a great tree between them*" (*Warning for Fair Women*, E3v), "*calls between the hangings*" (*Wits*, 124, also 143), "*an excursion betwixt Herbert and O'Hanlon*" (*Captain Thomas Stukeley*, 1174), "*thrusts his dagger betwixt Alphonso's doublet and shirt*" (*Twins*, D3r); see also *Edward I*, 630; Folio *Every Man Out*, 3.9.65, 80; *Thracian Wonder*, C4v; *Sophonisba*, Prologue.0; *Nobody and Somebody*, D4r; *Caesar and Pompey*, 1.2.20, 4.6.155; *Charlemagne*, 2544–6; *Devil's Charter*, L3r; *Miseries of Enforced Marriage*, 1855; *1 Iron Age*, 335; *Two Noble Ladies*, 2090; *Fatal Contract*, E3v; *Landgartha*, I3v; *Aglaura*, 1.6.49; *Albovine*, 63.

bier

used occasionally for a ***coffin*** that could be ***carried*** or ***placed*** on a stand: "*Montross on a bier before the bar*" (*Parliament of Love*, 5.1.32), "*with the bodies of Ferdinand and Violanta on a bier*" and "*they lament over the bier*" (*Four Plays In One*, 333); *Death of Huntingdon* provides "*A Bier is brought in*," "*Bier brought, he sits*," with the comment "*on my deathbed I may here sit down*," and later "*A march for burial*," "*The Queen following the Bier*," "*set it in the midst of the Stage*" (755–7, 2908, 2911–13); see also *Costly Whore*, 290.

bilboes

see ***prison***

bill

either (1) a ***paper*** or (2) a ***weapon***; calls for paper *bills* include "*Gloster offers to put up a Bill: Winchester snatches it, tears it*" (*1 Henry VI*, 1203–4, 3.1.0), "*Men to and fro bring in Bags, and have Bills*" (*If This Be Not a Good Play*, 2.2.16), "*with their bills ready written in their hands*" (*James IV*, 409–10), "*Tapwell kneeling delivers his bill of debt*" (*New Way to Pay*, 4.2.33), "*takes the bills, and puts them up in his pockets*" (*Staple of News*, 1.3.20), "*with bills on his back*" (*When You See Me*, 1018), "*A Table set forth with empty Moneybags, Bills, Bonds, and Books of accounts, etc.*" (*City Wit*, 279, also 280), "*an Antic habited in Parchment Indentures. Bills, Bonds, Wax, Seals, and Pen and Inkhorns: on his breast writ, I am a Scrivener*" (*New Trick*, 250); in *Histriomastix* a figure "*setting up bills*" calls them "Text bills for Plays" (F2r); for more examples see *Captain Thomas Stukeley*, 595; *1 Edward IV*, 82; *Old Fortunatus*, 3.1.389; Quarto *Every Man Out*, 1899, 1972; *May Day*, 2.4.206; *Thomas Lord Cromwell*, C2v; *Timon of Athens*, 656, 2.2.0; *Volpone*, 2.2.110; *New Wonder*, 149; *Fair Quarrel*, 4.1.31; *Chabot*, 2.1.0; calls for the *bill* that is a ***sword***-like weapon are "*with bills and halberds*" (Quarto *2 Henry VI*, D2r, [2.4.16; not in

Riv.]), "*Watchmen with Bills*" (*Fedele and Fortunio*, 1309), "*with Bills and staves*" (*Nobody and Somebody*, H3v), "*with bills and a hangman*" (*2 Edward IV*, 136, also 172), "*lame Porter in rusty armor, and a broken bill*" (*Cobbler's Prophecy*, 734–5); see also *Captain Thomas Stukeley*, 1371; *How a Man May Choose*, E1r.

bind, bound

widely used in the many scenes involving ***prisoners*** and captures; figures are ***led***/***dragged*** in *bound* (*Sophonisba*, 2.3.47; *Silver Age*, 87; *Two Noble Ladies*, 1149), sometimes with their ***hands***/***arms*** bound: "*all bound with their hands behind them*" (*Alphonsus of Aragon*, 1783–4); see also *Island Princess*, 160; *2 Passionate Lovers*, L3r, L4v; *Unfortunate Lovers*, 46; variations include "*gagged and bound*" (*Lust's Dominion*, 2.3.34; *Night Walker*, 349), "*bound and halters about their necks*" (*Little French Lawyer*, 441), "*bound and hoodwinked*" (*Valiant Scot*, C4v; *Court Beggar*, 218; *Just Italian*, 273), "*bound back to back*" (*Roman Actor*, 3.2.46), "*bound in a Chair*" (*Queen's Exchange*, 546), "*upon a Bed bound, and held down by servants*" (*Court Beggar*, 245; see also *Queen's Exchange*, 524); most common is for prisoners to enter simply *bound*; for a sampling of the forty-five examples see *Woodstock*, 2972; *Spanish Tragedy*, 3.6.16; *Titus Andronicus*, E3r, 3.1.0; *Knack to Know an Honest Man*, 1294, 1327, 1469; *Nobody and Somebody*, D1v; *King Leir*, 2508; *Downfall of Huntingdon*, 910; *Sir John Oldcastle*, 2060; *Puritan*, G4v; *Wisdom of Doctor Dodypoll*, 1063; *Insatiate Countess*, 5.2.15; *Sophonisba*, 5.4.0; *Fortune by Land and Sea*, 410; *Four Prentices*, 183, 232; *Dumb Knight*, 154, 193; *Brazen Age*, 203; *2 Iron Age*, 373; *Little French Lawyer*, 438; *Prophetess*, 369; *Bashful Lover*, 2.8.0; *Two Noble Ladies*, 1240–1; *Virgin Martyr*, 1.1.118; *Gentleman of Venice*, B2v; *Just Italian*, 267.

Also common is for figures to *bind* someone onstage (*Three Lords of London*, I3v; *1 Tamburlaine*, 1365; *1 Henry IV*, C4r, 2.2.92; *Antonio's Revenge*, 5.3.62; *Humour out of Breath*, 443; *Custom of the Country*, 381; *Duchess of Suffolk*, F2r; *Bride*, 50; *Love and Honour*, 162; *Goblins*, 1.1.89); less common are ***enter*** binding (*Wit at Several Weapons*, 94; *Sisters*, B5v), ***offer*** to bind (*Comedy of Errors*, 1394, 4.4.105); variations include "*bind him with scarfs*" (*Just Italian*, 263), "*bind him to a tree*" (*Distresses*, 322), "*Bind him to the post*" (*Greene's Tu Quoque*, L1v), "*bind him to the stake*" (*Spanish Tragedy*, 3.1.48; *Martyred Soldier*, 222), "*bind her to the Chair*" (*Fatal Contract*, I3r), "*bind his arms and feet, and blind him with a bag*" (*Gentleman of Venice*, D4v, also K3v), "*Hercules beats Cerberus, and binds him in chains*" (*Silver*

Age, 158), after a body is cut in pieces "*binds the arms behind his back with Beech's garters*" (*Two Lamentable Tragedies*, E2r); figures also *unbind* another onstage: "*Unbinds his arms*" (*Bashful Lover*, 2.8.138), "*Cupid being bound the Graces unbind him*" (*Wife for a Month*, 25), "*cuts Dondolo's bonds*" (*Just Italian*, 268); see also *Spanish Tragedy*, 3.1.79; *Dead Man's Fortune*, 58; *Lust's Dominion*, 5.2.68; *Devil's Charter*, C3r; *Match Me in London*, 5.2.62; *Bashful Lover*, 3.3.104; *Rebellion*, 62; *Gentleman of Venice*, F2r; *Goblins*, 3.7.57, 4.2.5, 4.6.0; *Just Italian*, 277; *Distresses*, 324; *Unfortunate Lovers*, 48, 57, 66; *2 Arviragus and Philicia*, E12r; *Princess*, A4r; for entrances of figures *unbound* see *Mad World*, 2.6.6; *Unfortunate Lovers*, 61; for the *binding up* of a **wound** see *Distresses*, 285.

bird

refers to a **sound** in five plays: "*An artificial charm of birds being heard within*" (*Arraignment of Paris*, 164), "*Music suddenly plays, and Birds sing*" (*Blurt*, 4.2.0; see also *Jovial Crew*, 381), "*Birds chirp*" (*Queen and Concubine*, 45), "*Pot Birds*" (*Pilgrim*, 221).

bite, bit

the few examples are Hieronimo who "*bites out his tongue*" (*Spanish Tragedy*, 4.4.191), "*exit, biting his thumbs*" (*Dick of Devonshire*, 1713–14), a spirit that "*bites*" three figures in sequence to drive them **mad** (*Two Noble Ladies*, 1521, 1527, 1537); the only reference to a *bit* in the **mouth** is Tamburlaine's entrance "*drawn in his chariot by Trebizon and Soria with bits in their mouths, reins in his left hand, in his right hand a whip, with which he scourgeth them*" (*2 Tamburlaine*, 3979).

black

usually associated with **mourning** and death: "*three Queens in Black, with veils stained*" (*Two Noble Kinsmen*, B1v, 1.1.24), "*Tamburlaine all in black, and very melancholy*" (*1 Tamburlaine*, 1844), "*sitting at a table covered with black, on which stands two black tapers lighted, she in mourning*" (*Insatiate Countess*, 1.1.0), a "*Body in a Chair dressed up in black velvet which sets out the paleness of the hands and face*" (*Second Maiden's Tragedy*, 2225–6), an entrance "*in black scurvy mourning coats, and Books at their Girdles, as coming from Church*" (*Puritan* B2v); for figures (most of them in mourning) who **enter** in black see *Three Lords of London*, B1r; *Edmond Ironside*, 964 (a **chorus**); *Death of Huntingdon*, 886; *Antonio's Revenge*, 2.2.0; *All's Well*, 3, 1.1.0; *Whore of Babylon*, DS before Act 1, 29;

Sophonisba, 5.4.20; *Second Maiden's Tragedy*, 117–18, 1877; *Chaste Maid*, 5.4.0; *Woman's Prize*, 87; *Queen of Corinth*, 72; *Bondman*, 1.3.81; *Duke of Milan*, 2.1.121; *Renegado*, 4.2.70; *Swetnam*, A1v; *Very Woman*, 2.3.23; *Queen and Concubine*, 22; *Deserving Favourite*, L1v; more specific costume signals include a *black* **safeguard** (*Roaring Girl*, 2.1.154), **habit** (*Conspiracy*, G1r), **veil** (*Warning for Fair Women*, D1r; *Devil's Law Case*, 4.2.52; *Welsh Ambassador*, 774; *Shoemaker a Gentleman*, 1.3.0), **robes** (*Caesar and Pompey*, 4.4.0; *Devil's Charter*, A2v; *Costly Whore*, 287), "*a black velvet cap and a white feather*" and "*black rags, a copper chain on, an old gown half off*" (*Lover's Melancholy*, 3.1.0, 3.3.38), "*in his black doublet and round cap*" (*What You Will*, D3r), "*Their eyes blinded with black patches*" (*Amorous War*, H2r), "*in bare black, like a poor Citizen*" (*Three Lords of London*, B3v), "*Enter three in black cloaks, at three doors*" as a **prologue** (*Four Prentices*, 165).

Objects **covered** in *black* include a **horse** (*Alarum for London*, 261–2), **coffin** (*Titus Andronicus*, A4r, 1.1.69), **drum** (*Jews' Tragedy*, 3044), "*A Table and a Chair covered with black*" (*Rape of Lucrece*, 234; see also *Noble Spanish Soldier*, 1.2.0); to indicate an unwanted **wedding** "*servants in blacks*" enter "*Covering the place with blacks*" (*Custom of the Country*, 313; see also *Soddered Citizen*, 1184, 1500, 2726); *black* objects include a **box** (*Renegado*, 4.2.57; *Fine Companion*, B3v), **hourglass** (*Summer's Last Will*, 360), **banneret** (*Four Plays in One*, 311), **jack** (*Summer's Last Will*, 1070; *Jovial Crew*, 362), **pots** (*Soddered Citizen*, 994), a **bodkin** "*tied in a piece of black bobbin*" (*Parson's Wedding*, 411), "*a great black bowl with a posset in it*" (*Summer's Last Will*, 803); *black* can be associated with the supernatural: "*two Furies, with black Tapers*" (*Night Walker*, 364), "*a Spirit in black*" (*Birth of Merlin*, C3r), "*a Ghost, coal-black*" (*If This Be Not a Good Play*, 5.4.261), "*Ate with thunder and lightning all in black*" (*Locrine*, 2); *black* is occasionally linked to a figure's makeup or coloring: "*all ragged, in an overgrown red Beard, black head*" (*Caesar and Pompey*, 2.1.0), "*Phineas, all black in armor, with Aethiopians after him, driving in Perseus*" (*Locrine*, 435–6), "*He draws the Curtains and finds her struck with Thunder, black*" (*Looking Glass for London*, 552–3), a madman with "*his face whited, black shag hair, long nails, a piece of raw meat*" (*Lover's Melancholy*, 3.3.19); *English Moor* provides "*A box of black painting*," an entrance with "*her face black*," "*Inductor like a Moor leading Phillis (black and) gorgeously decked with jewels*" (37, 51, 65); *blackamoors* are specified in *Titus Andronicus*, G2v, 4.2.51; *Love's Labour's Lost*, G3v, 5.2.157; *Monsieur Thomas*, 159.

blazing star

an effect with supernatural implications, usually linked to *thunder*; perhaps fireworks were used, but directions give no indication; in *Bloody Banquet* "*a blazing Star*" (1859) elicits "I like not thy prodigious bearded fire"; see also *Battle of Alcazar*, 1276; *Captain Thomas Stukeley*, 2457–9; *2 If You Know Not Me*, 292; *Birth of Merlin*, F4r; *Revenger's Tragedy*, I2v; for a *star* see *Brazen Age*, 254.

blind, blindfold

blind can mean either (1) "sightless, unable to see" or, especially when used as a verb, (2) "blindfold, blindfolded"; for examples of blindness, figures *enter* "*like a blind Aqua vitae man*" (*Beggar's Bush*, 238), "*being blind*" (*Revenge of Bussy*, 5.3.18; *Sophy*, 4.194), simply *blind* (*Maid in the Mill*, 18; *Valiant Scot*, E1v); alternatively figures enter/are *led in* blindfold (*Witch*, 946; *Four Plays in One*, 321), blinded (*Lady of Pleasure*, 4.1.0); examples of *blind* as a transitive verb that means *blindfold* include "*blind him with a rag*" (*Alchemist*, 3.5.14), "*seize upon him, bind his arms and feet, and blind him with a bag*" (*Gentleman of Venice*, D4v, also K3v), "*blind Simplicity, turn him thrice about, set his face towards the contrary post, at which he runs*" (*Three Lords of London*, I3v); *Amorous War* provides "*They blind them,*" "*Their eyes blinded with black patches,*" "*They unblind them*" (G4v, H2r, I3r); see also *Phoenix*, I1r; as a variation *blindfolded* figures are directed to enter *hoodwinked* (*Bloody Banquet*, 1430), "*bound and hoodwinked*" (*Valiant Scot*, C4v; *Just Italian*, 273); for a reference to "*Blind man's Buff*" see *Humour out of Breath*, 467; atypical is "*Enter a Trumpet blinded*" (*Brennoralt*, 2.3.90).

blindfold

see *blind*

block

cited in three *execution* scenes where a scheduled beheading is interrupted: "*the executioner with his sword and block*" (*Dead Man's Fortune*, 50–1), "*Lies on the Block*" (*Two Noble Kinsmen*, M3r, 5.4.38), "*She mounts the Scaffold, submits her head to the block*" (*Messalina*, 2592–3).

bloody, bleeding

bloody is widely used for (1) properties, (2) people; most of the *bloody* properties are *weapons* such as *swords* (*Locrine*, 3–4; *Roman Actor*, 5.1.180; *Fair Favourite*, 256; *Osmond*, A2r), *daggers/poniards/*
knives (Quarto *King Lear*, L3r, 5.3.222; *Challenge for Beauty*, 60; *Love's Sacrifice*, 2585), but also specified are a *bloody handkerchief* (*Warning for Fair Women*, F3r; *Cupid's Revenge*, 283), *napkin* (*Spanish Tragedy*, 3.13.85), *shirt* (*Woman in the Moon*, B4v), *banquet* (*Battle of Alcazar*, 1067), "*bowl of blood*" (*Warning for Fair Women*, C4v; *Golden Age*, 20), "*Letter written in blood*" (Q2 *Bussy D'Ambois*, 5.3.84), "*skull all bloody*" (*Bloody Banquet*, 1921), "*javelins bloodied*" after a *hunt* (*Brazen Age*, 194); when applied to people *bloody* can describe the *mouth* (*Albovine*, 102), forehead (*Brazen Age*, 176), *head*/pate (*1 Henry VI*, 1298, 3.1.85; *Fair Maid of the Inn*, 173), *face* (*King John and Matilda*, 26), most often the *arms/hands*: "*their heads and faces bloody, and besmeared with mud and dirt*" (*Doctor Faustus*, B 1490–1), "*Envy, his arms naked besmeared with blood*" (*Mucedorus*, A2r), "*his arms bare, smeared in blood, a poniard in one hand, bloody*" (*Antonio's Revenge*, 1.1.0, also 3.2.86), "*his arms stripped up to the elbows all bloody*" (*Appius and Virginia*, H1r), "*his hands and face scratched, and bloody*" (*Late Lancashire Witches*, 195); see also *Locrine*, 1574; *Faithful Shepherdess*, 437; *Maid's Tragedy*, 70; *Just Italian*, 255; figures *enter* "*bloody and wounded*" (*Alarum for London*, 1570), "*all bloody*" (*Tom a Lincoln*, 2231; *Rape of Lucrece*, 249; *Valiant Scot*, D2v), simply *bloody* (*Two Lamentable Tragedies*, C3r; *Coriolanus*, 858, 1.10.0; *Seven Champions*, B2v; *Rebellion*, 42; *Young Admiral*, H2r; *Country Girl*, G4r); Macbeth's second *apparition* is "*a Bloody Child*" (*Macbeth*, 1616, 4.1.76); variations include "*Friar stoops and looks on the blood and weapons*" (Q1 *Romeo and Juliet*, K2r, 5.3.139), "*bloodies himself with Sueno's blood, and falls down as dead*" (*Politician*, I2v), "*puts his hand to his eye, with a bloody sponge and the blood runs down*" (*Princess*, F4v); see also *Two Lamentable Tragedies*, B4r; *Warning for Fair Women*, D1v; *Devil's Charter*, A2v.

Bleeding is usually an equivalent to *wounded/hurt*: "*a bleeding Captain*" (*Macbeth*, 17, 1.2.0), "*Achilles discovered in his Tent, about him his bleeding Myrmidons, himself wounded*" (*1 Iron Age*, 324); for figures who enter *bleeding* see *Yorkshire Tragedy*, 536; *Look about You*, 1165; *Miseries of Enforced Marriage*, 1395; *Caesar and Pompey*, 5.1.261, 268; *Coriolanus*, 564, 1.4.61; *2 Fair Maid of the West*, 394; *Goblins*, 2.5.0; *Wasp*, 1442; other locutions include "*her head and face bleeding*" (*Antipodes*, 300), "*find Alvarez bleeding*" (*Cardinal*, 3.2.94), "*his arm bleeding apace*" (*2 Edward IV*, 155), "*a bleeding heart upon a knife's point*" (*Golden Age*, 20), "*his wounds gaping and after him Lucrece undressed, holding a dagger fixed in his bleeding bosom*" (*Devil's Charter*, G2r);

bleed as a verb is rare: "*Smite him, he bleeds*" (*Downfall of Huntingdon*, 674).

blow

an alternative to *wind* that typically describes a *horn blown* onstage or *within*: "*Post blowing a horn Within*" (Folio *3 Henry VI*, 1901, 3.3.161), "*Jack blowing of his horn*" (*George a Greene*, 454), "*Horns blow*" (*Death of Huntingdon*, 503), "*A sowgelder's horn blown*" (*English Moor*, 14; see also *Picture*, 2.1.82); for similar signals see *Summer's Last Will*, 634, 775; *When You See Me*, 198–9; *1 Arviragus and Philicia*, D1r; *Guardian*, 2.4.60; *Goblins*, 3.7.41; twice *blow* means "breathing hard": "*Enter one blowing*" (Folio *3 Henry VI*, 697, 2.1.42), "*Enter Nice blowing*" (*Honest Lawyer*, F1v) – he says "I have lost my wind"; a figure in *Puritan* "*blows a pipe*" of *tobacco* (B4r).

blue

occasionally specified for (1) *blue coats* worn by the *followers* of a lord or other dignitary, (2) a *blue gown* as part of the punishment for a prostitute; for *blue* coats, figures are directed to enter "*in his lord's attire with Bluecoats after him*" (*Edmond Ironside*, 1243–4), "*like a lord with his comrades in blue coats*" (*Mad World*, 2.1.82), "*as new come out of the Country*" with servants "*with blue Coats to attend him*" (*Wise Woman of Hogsdon*, 340); see also *Taming of a Shrew*, B2r; *Two Maids of More-Clacke*, B4r; *Wonder of a Kingdom*, 4.2.0; *Two Maids of More-Clacke* also provides a figure in hospital "*and a bluecoat boy with him*" (C3r) and another "*in blue like nurse*" (H3v); in *2 Honest Whore* two women in Bridewell being punished as whores appear in *blue* gowns (5.2.265, 311; see also *City Madam*, 5.3.59) along with the comment "Being stripped out of her wanton loose attire, / That Garment she puts on, base to the eye, / Only to clothe her in humility"; in *Three Lords of London* Fraud appears "*in a blue gown, red cap and red sleeves*" (I2v, also I3r); other uses of *blue* include Scottish "*Soldiers with blue Caps*" (*Valiant Scot*, G3r), *blue satin* worn by six Moors (*Amorous War*, E2v), Ganymede in a *masque* wearing "*a blue robe powdered with stars*" (*Women Beware Women*, 5.2.50), an *angel* "*upon his breast a blue table full of silver letters*" (*Two Noble Ladies*, 1101–2); see also *2 Honest Whore*, 5.2.366; *World Tossed at Tennis*, D2r.

bodkin

used twice to denote a small instrument used by women: "*pulls her bodkin, that is tied in a piece of black*

bobbin" (*Parson's Wedding*, 411), "*with her bodkin curls her hair*" (*1 Honest Whore*, 2.1.12).

body

most of the 100 examples are concerned with the introduction and removal of *corpses*: "*Ventidius as it were in triumph, the dead body of Pacorus borne before him*" (*Antony and Cleopatra*, 1494–5, 3.1.0), "*The dead body is carried away*" (*Hamlet*, Q2 H1v, Folio 2000, 3.2.135); for entrances the most common locution is the simple *enter* with a body; for a sampling see *Battle of Alcazar*, 1544; *Massacre at Paris*, 486; *Julius Caesar*, 1570, 3.2.40; *Cymbeline*, 2601, 4.2.281; *Atheist's Tragedy*, 2.4.23; 5.1.47; *Duchess of Malfi*, 5.5.7; *Custom of the Country*, 331; *Duke of Milan*, 5.2.47; *Fatal Dowry*, 4.4.91; *All's Lost by Lust*, 5.5.51; *Prisoners*, C2r, C9v; in *1 Iron Age* one group enters "*with the body of Hector borne by Grecian soldiers*" and another "*with the body of Achilles borne by Trojan soldiers, they interchange them*" (345); other locutions include *bring* in (Quarto *King Lear*, L3r, 5.3.238; *Second Maiden's Tragedy*, 2225; *Bird in a Cage*, K2v), bring *out* (Folio *King Lear*, 3184, 5.3.238), *bear* in a body: "*then is brought in the Body of Vortimer in a Chair dead*" (*Hengist*, DS before 4.3, 9–10), "*to them a mariner bearing in a dead body*" (*Tom a Lincoln*, 2861–2); for *exits* as with entrances *exeunt* with a body is the most common usage: "*Exit Hamlet with the dead body*" (Q1 *Hamlet*, G3v, [3.4.217]); for a sampling see *Woodstock*, 2633, 2655; *Death of Huntingdon*, 2676; *Blind Beggar of Bednal Green*, 48; *Hoffman*, 1664; *Coriolanus*, 3837–8, 5.6.154; *Custom of the Country*, 332; *Thierry and Theodoret*, 40; *Changeling*, 3.2.26; *'Tis Pity*, 5.5.106; the many variations include *bear in/out/off/away* (Folio *3 Henry VI*, 2854, 5.2.50; Q2 *Bussy D'Ambois*, 5.4.186; *Tom a Lincoln*, 2865; *Roman Actor*, 4.2.308; *Unnatural Combat*, 2.1.263), *carry away/carrying* (*Massacre at Paris*, 504; *Captain Thomas Stukeley*, 2827; *Hoffman*, 1069), *hurry* away (*Hengist*, DS before 2.2, 8–9); typical are "*they bear the body into the fields*" (*Arden of Faversham*, 2387), "*mournfully bear in the body*" (*Death of Huntingdon*, 944), "*some bear out Ennius's body*" (*Cobbler's Prophecy*, 1361), "*Exeunt, bearing off Antony's body*" (*Antony and Cleopatra*, 3107, 4.15.91); more elaborate are "*They march out with the body of the King, lying on four men's shoulders with a dead march, drawing weapons on the ground*" (*Massacre at Paris*, 1263), "*The trumpets sound a dead march, the King of Spain mourning after his brother's body, and the King of Portugal bearing the body of his son*" (*Spanish Tragedy*, 4.4.217).

Bodies can be *discovered*: "*the body of Feliche, stabbed* thick with wounds, appears hung up" (Antonio's Revenge, 1.2.207), "strikes open a curtain where appears a body" (Hoffman, 8–10; see also Revenger's Tragedy, C1v); for **funerals** bodies are carried on **hearses** (Double Marriage, 401, 406; Seven Champions, E4v), **biers** (Four Plays In One, 333), in **coffins**, or simply borne: "The Body of Matilda lying on the Hearse" (King John and Matilda, 84), "they put the body of young Aire into a Coffin" (2 Edward IV, 183; see also Selimus, 1257), "Enter Funeral. Body borne by four Captains and Soldiers" (Fatal Dowry, 2.1.47); actions include "bestrides the wounded body of Ferneze and seems to save him" (Malcontent, 2.5.9), "mistakes the body of Borachio for Soquette" (Atheist's Tragedy, 4.3.205), "Jupiter above strikes him with a thunderbolt, his body sinks" (Brazen Age, 254), **ghosts** that enter, "dance about the dead body, and Exeunt" (Revenge of Bussy, 5.5.119); after a **fight** in which all are apparently **killed** "Cethus riseth up from the dead bodies and speaks" (2 Iron Age, 427), and after a murder "Bring down the body, and cover it over with Faggots" (Two Lamentable Tragedies, D2v); uses of body not linked to corpses include "his sword drawn, his body wounded, his shield struck full of darts" (Sophonisba, 1.2.62), "Robin Goodfellow in a suit of Leather close to his body" (Grim the Collier, I2r), and from Devil's Charter: "He boweth his body," "She looketh in two glasses and beholdeth her body," barbers who "trimmed and rubbed their bodies" (G1r, H1v, I3r); a direction in Country Girl describes "white stitched Bodies" or bodices (D3r).

bolt
see **thunderbolt**

bonds
(1) linked with **bills** in calls for "business papers" but (2) occasionally the restraints that **bind** a prisoner; examples of **papers** are an entrance "with bills and bonds" (New Wonder, 149), "an Antic habited in Parchment Indentures. Bills, Bonds, Wax, Seals, and Pen, and Inkhorns" (New Trick, 250); City Wit provides "A Table set forth with empty Moneybags, Bills, Bonds, and Books of accounts, etc." and "puts the Bills and Bonds into a Bag" (279–80); an example of restraints is "cuts Dondolo's bonds" (Just Italian, 268).

book, tablebook
a widely used property (roughly 130 examples) linked to (1) contemplation, (2) learning, (3) the supernatural, (4) a **study**, and sometimes (5) a table-book or notebook for recording thoughts; a book fre-

quently conveys a state of contemplation, prayer, or melancholy in the figure who **enters** with it, most famously in "Enter Hamlet reading on a Book" (Folio Hamlet, 1203, 2.2.168); similar entrances include "Hieronimo with a book in his hand" (Spanish Tragedy, 3.13.0), "Matilda, in mourning veil, reading on a book" (Death of Huntingdon, 961–2), "Doctor Shaw, pensively reading on his book" (2 Edward IV, 162), "the King with a Prayer book" (Folio 3 Henry VI, 1410, 3.1.12), "Protestants with books, and kneel together" (Massacre at Paris, 532), "Queen Mary with a Prayer Book in her hand, like a Nun" (Sir Thomas Wyatt, 1.3.0), "Books at their Girdles, as coming from Church" (Puritan, B2v), "Constantius in private meditation, they rudely Come to him, strike down his Book and Draw their swords upon him" (Hengist, DS before 2.2, 3–5, also 3.2.0); for more see Antonio's Revenge, 2.2.0; Wit of a Woman, 1531; Caesar and Pompey, 4.4.15, 5.2.0; Mad World, 4.1.0; Second Maiden's Tragedy, 1877; White Devil, 5.6.0; Duchess of Malfi, 5.5.0; Maid of Honour, 4.3.0; Game at Chess, 469–70; Picture, 4.2.0; Bashful Lover, 3.1.0; Lovers' Progress, 122; Messalina, 238, 676–7; Bloody Banquet, 388, 1013–14; Twins, F2v; similarly books can represent learning: "disguised like a Schoolmaster, in the apparel of Pedante, with a book in his hand" (Fedele and Fortunio, 390–1), "school boys, sitting with books in their hands" (What You Will, C4r), "Philosopher in black rags, a copper chain on, an old gown half off, and book" (Lover's Melancholy, 3.3.38, also 2.1.47), "like a scholar, with two books" (Antiquary, 475); see also Friar Bacon, 172–4; How a Man May Choose, C3r; Law Tricks, 125; More Dissemblers, B3v; Monsieur Thomas, 112; occasionally a book is linked to the supernatural: "with a magical book and rod" (Devil's Charter, A2v, also L3v), "looks in a book, strikes with his wand" (Fair Maid of the Inn, 201), "Throws his charmed rod, and his books under the stage. A flame riseth" (Two Noble Ladies, 1899–1901, also 1856–8).

A book is a conventional property for a **study** scene: "in his study with books, coffers, his triple Crown upon a cushion before him" (Devil's Charter, B2v, also G1r, L3r), "from his study, books and bags of money on a Table, a chair and cushions" (Ram Alley, B3v), "sitting in a study behind a Curtain, a candle by him burning, books lying confusedly" (Satiromastix, 1.2.0), "in his Study. A Taper, Bags, Books, etc." (Novella, 110); see also Two Merry Milkmaids, B1r; 'Tis Pity, 2.2.0; Virgin Martyr, 5.1.0; Doubtful Heir, E5r; other calls for a book and related properties to set a scene include "a servant setting out a Table, on which he places a skull, a picture, a book and a Taper" (1 Honest Whore, 4.1.0), "An Altar discovered, with

Tapers, and a Book on it" (*Knight of Malta*, 161, also 152),
"*The Bar and Book ready on a Table*" (*Spanish Curate*,
96/501), "*A Table, Count book, Standish, Chair and stools
set out*" (*City Madam*, 1.2.143), "*A Table set forth with
empty Money bags, Bills, Bonds, and Books of accounts,
etc.*" (*City Wit*, 279), "*bring a little table, and a paper book:
for Clerk of the Check*" (*Launching of the Mary*, 1141–2);
see also *If This Be Not a Good Play*, 2.2.0; *Devil's Law
Case*, 3.3.0; *Cunning Lovers*, H2r; *Fair Favourite*, 228;
other examples include "*the Friars with Bell, Book, and
Candle, for the Dirge*" (*Doctor Faustus*, B 1111–12), "*Saint
Dunstan with his Beads, Book, and Crosier staff, etc.*"
(*Grim the Collier*, G2r), "*walking apart with a Book*"
(*Bussy D'Ambois*, 2.2.0), "*turns over a Book*" (MS
Humorous Lieutenant, 787–8), "*Throws away the book*"
(*Maid of Honour*, 4.3.20), "*Lays the book under his
Pillow*" (*Roman Actor*, 5.1.159), "*one like a Soldier armed,
with a Book in his hand*" (*Constant Maid*, H1r), "*strikes
down her book*" (*Antipodes*, 295), "*kiss the Bishops' Books*"
(*Queen and Concubine*, 22); in *Distresses* a figure "*discovered
sleeping on her book, her glass by*" elicits "Her glass
and book! the mirrors that / Reflect her face and
mind" (338); a figure who forgets the lines of a part
he is playing "*Takes out a book and holds it in his hand,
and looks on it at the breaches*," or breaks in the action
(*Noble Stranger*, E3v); in *Two Noble Ladies* first a figure
is "*in a chair asleep, in her hands a prayer book, devils
about her*" and awaking "*looks in her book, and the
Spirits fly from her*" (1752–4, 1796–7); see also *Titus
Andronicus*, F3v, 4.1.0; *Taming of the Shrew*, 899, 2.1.38;
Sir John Oldcastle, 1944–5; *Whore of Babylon*, DS before
Act 1, 42–6, 49–52; *New Way to Pay*, 4.3.123; *Bondman*,
2.2.121; *Believe as You List*, 982–4, 1115–18; *Very Woman*,
4.2.19; *Parson's Wedding*, 413; although sometimes
book means *tablebook*, only seven directions specify
such a note*book* or commonplace *book*, as when
Nathaniel is directed to "*Draw out his Tablebook*" and
record a "most singular and choice epithet" (*Love's
Labour's Lost*, F4r, 5.1.15); for more examples see *Blurt*,
3.3.11; *Maidenhead Well Lost*, 142; *Spanish Curate*, 98;
Roman Actor, 5.1.94; *Variety*, B3v; *News from
Plymouth*, 132.

booted

to *enter* booted is to imply a recently completed
journey or one about to be undertaken and by
extension to suggest weariness or *haste*; typical is
Friar Bacon where the gentlemen arrive "*booted and
spurred*" (1935) with Lacy announcing "we have hied
and posted all this night to Fressingfield"; see also
When You See Me, 198; *Tale of a Tub*, 2.2.0; *boots* are
often linked to other related items: "*booted and
spurred, a riding wand*" (*King Leir*, 398–9, 408–9; see
also *Eastward Ho*, C2r), "*in a shirt of mail and Booted*"
(*Captain Thomas Stukeley*, 1114), "*the men booted, the gentlewomen
in cloaks and safeguards*" (*Merry Devil of
Edmonton*, B1r); for figures who simply *enter booted*
see *Edward I*, 1435; *Taming of the Shrew*, 2200, 4.4.0;
Q1 *Romeo and Juliet*, I3r, 5.1.11; *1 Edward IV*, 48; *Two
Lamentable Tragedies*, D4r; *Northward Ho*, 1.1.0,
4.1.207, 4.3.0, 5.1.454; *Fair Maid of the Exchange*, 41;
Widow's Tears, 3.1.0; *Ram Alley*, C1v; *City Wit*, 289;
other uses include a clown's entrance "*with one boot
on*" (*Wit without Money*, 166), Bracciano's **ghost** "*in his
leather cassock and breeches, boots*" (*White Devil*, 5.4.123),
"*Whilst they are saluting, Sir Owen gets to Emulo's leg and
pulls down his Boot*" (*Patient Grissil*, 2.1.140); see also
Richard II, I1r, 5.2.84; *Woman Killed*, 133; *Staple of News*,
1.1.0; *Country Captain*, B8r.

bosom

used for (1) a man or woman's chest or **breast**, (2) a
garment that covers that part of the **body**, with the
two senses sometimes hard to distinguish; references
to the part of the body include "*sleeps on her
bosom*" (*Charlemagne*, 1071), "*Tormiella flies to his
bosom*" (*Match Me in London*, 5.3.0), "*She falls upon his
bosom*" (*Soddered Citizen*, 2299–2300), "*draws his sword
and runs it on his bosom*" (*Two Merry Milkmaids*, H2r),
"*a dagger fixed in his bleeding bosom*" (*Devil's Charter*,
G2r); for examples of a garment, objects are taken
out of a figure's bosom: "*He plucks it out of his bosom and
reads it*" (*Richard II*, H4v, 5.2.71), "*she pulls a letter out of
her bosom*" (*Tom a Lincoln*, 2757–8), "*Pulls his
Indentures out of Mamon's bosom*" (*Jack Drum's
Entertainment*, F3r); see also *2 Arviragus and Philicia*,
F3r; *Prisoners*, C1or; *bosoms* can be **opened**: "*He stirreth
and moveth them opening both their bosoms*" (*Devil's
Charter*, I3v), "*Opens his bosom, and puts them in*"
(severed **hands**) and "*opens his bosom and takes out his
hands*" (*Selimus*, 1436, 1487–8); a figure appears with
"*a white Rose in her bosom*" (*Warning for Fair Women*,
I1r); atypical is "*He searches the queen's pockets, hands,
neck, Bosom and Hair*" (*Charlemagne*, 1094–6); see also
Parson's Wedding, 479.

bottle

a container linked to **sack** (*1 Henry IV*, K1v, 5.3.54;
Lady Mother, 573–4, 618), to **beer**: "*a bottle of beer in one
slop*" (*Looking Glass for London*, 2237), or to **wine**: "*a
bottle of wine, and Manchets*" (*New Trick*, 230); see also
Chances, 186, 227; *Two Noble Ladies*, 560; *Sparagus*

Garden, 158; Variety, D6v; for other *bottles* of liquor
see *2 Edward IV*, 173; *Woman Is a Weathercock*, 5.2.6–7;
Fortune by Land and Sea, 393; *Bonduca*, 152; *Bondman*,
2.3.17; *Antiquary*, 493; *Bashful Lover*, 3.1.39, 73;
Soddered Citizen, 993–4; *Gentleman of Venice*, F4v, G2r;
Lovesick Court, 99, 101, 120; *Very Woman*, 3.5.44;
Weeding of Covent Garden, 13, 15; *Princess*, C1v, E1v, G4r;
two directions cite a "*casting bottle*" (*Antonio and
Mellida*, 3.2.24; *Fancies Chaste and Noble*, 234); for
more *bottles* see *Sir John Oldcastle*, 2398–9; *Death of
Huntingdon*, 2403; *Sir Thomas Wyatt*, 2.3.8; *Devil's
Charter*, K3r, K4r, L1r, L1v; *Love and Honour*, 149; see
also **can**, **flagon**, **jack**.

boughs
see **branches**

bounce
meaning "**knock** loudly," as in "*bounce at the gate,
within*" (*Doctor Faustus*, B 1675), "*Bounces at the door*"
(*Jews' Tragedy*, 2839), "*bounces thrice at the door; it flies
open*" (*Goblins*, 2.6.11).

bow
see **arrow**

bow
called for in relatively few directions although in
social practice a widely used gesture of respect by
men (as distinct from the **curtsy** by women); *bowing*
is most common as an expression of duty to figures
of rank: "*all bow as the Pope marcheth solemnly through*"
(*Devil's Charter*, E1r, also G1r), "*Enter Plutus, with a
troop of Indians, singing and dancing wildly about him,
and bowing to him*" (*Four Plays in One*, 360); figures in
masques enter "*bowing to the Duke*" (*Women Beware
Women*, 5.2.50), "*bow to her she rises and shows the like*"
(*Your Five Gallants*, I2v); in *Two Noble Kinsmen*
Palamon and Arcite preparing to fight "*bow several
ways: then advance and stand*" and later "*all rise and bow
to the Altar*" (H1v, 3.6.93; K4v, 5.1.61, also L1v, 5.1.136);
for other examples see *Miseries of Enforced Marriage*,
2862; *Bondman*, 3.2.72; *Grateful Servant*, K4v; *Goblins*,
3.7.57; see also **conge**, **make a leg**.

bower
a seldom used term that may or may not refer to a
distinctive property; in *Arraignment of Paris* a **trial**
configuration is likely when the gods sitting as a tribunal are "*set in Diana's bower*" while Paris and the
three goddesses "*stand on sides before them*" (827); in

Faithful Shepherdess a **discovery** is likely when, after
the command "bring him to the Bower," "*The Satyr
leadeth him to the Bower, where he spieth Amoret*" (438);
in *Isle of Gulls* the signal "*Enter the duke, at Adonis's
bower*" (300) is followed by a long descriptive speech
that starts "But here's the place: upon this crystal
stream"; see also **arbor**, **trees**.

bowl
(1) usually a container linked to **wine**, sometimes to
beer or **ale**, but (2) a few signals refer to the game of
bowls; calls for a *bowl* in the context of **drinking**
include "*The Lord Mayor brings a bowl of wine, and
humbly on his knees offers it to the King*" (*1 Edward IV*, 61),
"*singeth, holding a Bowl of drink in his hand*" (*Jack
Drum's Entertainment*, I1v), "*a bowl of Beer*" (*Wise
Woman of Hogsdon*, 336; *Match at Midnight*, 26), "*a great
black bowl with a posset in it*" (*Summer's Last Will*, 803);
see also *Sophonisba*, 5.3.88, 92; *Fawn*, 5.152; *Devil's
Charter*, I2v; *Witch of Edmonton*, 3.4.30; *Cardinal*,
5.3.234; for examples in the Brome canon see
Antipodes, 255; *City Wit*, 367; *Jovial Crew*, 390, 391;
Lovesick Court, 155; two plays have the reminder
"*Bowl of wine ready*" (*Custom of the Country*, 313/455;
Chances, 210/398); various ceremonial *bowls* include
"*great standing Bowls for the Christening Guests*" (*Henry
VIII*, 3356–7, 5.4.0), "*harvest-folks with a bowl*"
(*Histriomastix*, B3r), "*a Magician with a Bowl*"
(*Humorous Lieutenant*, 342, MS 2315–17); two plays
call for "*a bowl of blood*" (*Warning for Fair Women*, C4v;
Golden Age, 20); other examples are "*a rich bowl*"
(*Devil's Charter*, H1r), "*A confused fray with stools, cups
and bowls*" (*Silver Age*, 142), "*a skull made into a drinking
bowl*" (*Albovine*, 38), "*a silver bowl*" (*Swaggering Damsel*,
B1r); a figure enters "*a Hatchet in one hand, and a Bowl
in the other*" (*Thracian Wonder*, C4v); Henslowe's
inventory lists "*one elm bowl*" (*Diary*, App. 2, 81);
bowls for the game include "*Sir Abraham throwing
down his Bowls*" (*Woman Is a Weathercock*, 3.3.1), "*Porter
with bowls*" (*Look about You*, 872), figures who enter
"*to play at bowls*" (*2 Edward IV*, 173), and "*a noise below
in the bowling alley*" followed by the entrance of "*the
bowlers*" (*New Wonder*, 121, 124).

box
a container linked to a variety of items and stage
business: "*boxes for Presents*" (*Battle of Alcazar* plot,
33–4), "*draweth out of his boxes aspics*" (*Devil's Charter*,
I4r, also I3v), "*a black Box at his girdle*" (*Fine
Companion*, B3v), "*opens the Box, and falls asleep*" (*Love's
Mistress*, 152, also 153), "*like a Peddler Woman with her

Box" (*Novella*, 145; see also *Queen and Concubine*, 31); elsewhere a *box* is said to contain **poison** (*Aglaura*, 5.3.120; *Politician*, H4v) and **painting** (*1 Honest Whore*, 2.1.0; *English Moor*, 37); for other uses of a *box* see *Three Ladies of London*, E1v; *Fedele and Fortunio*, 273; *Spanish Tragedy*, 3.5.0; *Warning for Fair Women*, G1r; *Whore of Babylon*, 4.1.0; *Chaste Maid*, 2.3.8; *Devil's Charter*, A2v, H1r, I2v; *Two Maids of More-Clacke*, H1v; *New Wonder*, 174; *Staple of News*, 1.3.52; *Match at Midnight*, 74; *New Way to Pay*, 5.1.182; *Renegado*, 4.2.57; *Duchess of Suffolk*, I3v; *Damoiselle*, 406; *Hollander*, 93.

brains

used as a noun or verb linked to violent death, usually suicide; in *Seven Champions* a figure "*beats out his own brains*" (L1r), and in *1 Tamburlaine* Bajazeth "*brains himself against the cage*" and his wife then "*runs against the Cage and brains herself*" (2085, 2100); in *Atheist's Tragedy* D'Amville is prepared to **execute** Charlemont and Castabella but "*As he raises up the ax, strikes out his own brains*" (5.2.241) so that the executioner comments "In lifting up the ax, I think he has knocked / His brains out"; *Alphonsus of Germany* provides a murder rather than a self-inflicted death: "*He dashes out the Child's brains*" (H4r).

branches, boughs

usually indicate the people's welcome or favor: "*Men with boughs of Laurel*" who meet another group "*in Triumph*" (*Imposture*, B3v), "*Citizens carrying boughs, boys singing after them*" who welcome home their king (*Island Princess*, 121), "*Soldiers (unarmed, with olive branches)*" who welcome the triumphant Matilda (*Bashful Lover*, 4.3.68), citizens favoring Barnavelt who enter "*with Boughs and flowers*" (*Barnavelt*, 2113–15) saying "strew, strew: more Garlands, and more, flowers, / Up with the boughs"; see also *Faithful Friends*, 2098–2100; Virtue's attendants are "*crowned with Olive branches and laurels*" (*Old Fortunatus*, 5.2.260), the personages in Queen Katherine's vision have "*Branches of Bays or Palm in their hands*" (*Henry VIII*, 2645–6, 4.2.82), four virgins who appeal for mercy enter "*with branches of Laurel in their hands*" (*1 Tamburlaine*, 1781); atypical are Malcolm's army "*with Boughs*" from Birnam (*Macbeth*, 2380, 5.6.0), a contest among magicians where Hercules "*begins to break the branches*" of a *tree* (*Friar Bacon*, 1214), a *ceremony* where priests "*put several branches of poppy*" into a *censer* (*Sejanus*, 5.177); see also **triumph**, **victory**.

brand

similar to a **torch**, this property is rarely cited: "*Althea with the brand*" and "*fires the brand*" (*Brazen Age*, 199); see also *Battle of Alcazar* plot, 28; a variant is "*comes out with a firebrand*" (*Bartholomew Fair*, 2.5.59).

brave

widely used for costly, fashionable, extravagant clothing (often equivalent to **gallant**); typical are Tranio's first appearance *brave* as "Lucentio" (*Taming of the Shrew*, 786, 1.2.217), "*Torrenti very brave, between the two Dukes, attended by all the Courtiers, wondering at his costly habit*" (*Wonder of a Kingdom*, 4.1.0); for other figures who appear *very brave* see *Woodstock*, 352; *Match at Midnight*, 54; *Knave in Grain*, 571; *Fatal Contract*, C1r; *Country Girl*, H4r; in *2 Honest Whore* Matheo enters *brave* (4.1.0) and asks "How am I suited, Front? am I not gallant, ha?" with the response "Exceeding passing well, and to the time"; when a previously **poor** soldier is transformed he enters "*in all his bravery, and his man in a new livery*" (*Royal King*, 58); for other figures who **enter** *brave* see *Patient Grissil*, 4.3.230; *2 Honest Whore*, 5.2.265; *Honest Man's Fortune*, 270; *Welsh Ambassador*, 1068–9; *Match at Midnight*, 95; *Country Girl*, H3r, H3v; *Novella*, 129; *Bird in a Cage*, F4r; *Gentleman of Venice*, H2r; variations include "*gallant and brave*" (*Two Maids of More-Clacke*, H1v), "*disguised in bravery*" (*New Academy*, 56), "*in her bravery*" (*Arraignment of Paris*, 496), "*in brave Apparel*" (*Obstinate Lady*, F2r), "*Antimon brave, anticly attired in brave Clothes*" (*Thracian Wonder*, F2v); *James IV* provides "*March over bravely first the English host, the sword carried before the King by Percy. The Scottish on the other side, with all their pomp bravely*" (2406–8; see also *Lust's Dominion*, 4.1.39); atypical is "*The Magi with their rods beat the ground, and from under the same riseth a brave Arbor*" (*Looking Glass for London*, 522–3); this usage is to be distinguished from the verbal form (where *brave* means "quarrel") that is found only once: "*Enter Chiron and Demetrius braving*" (*Titus Andronicus*, C3r, 2.1.25).

bread

(1) most commonly found in combination with **wine** or **meat** but also specified (2) as part of the **setting** of a **table**, (3) as food for a **prisoner**; figures are directed to **enter** with "Bread and a Bottle" (*Fortune by Land and Sea*, 393), "Bread and Wine" (*Guy of Warwick*, E1v; *Launching of the Mary*, 1935–7), "bread and meat in his hand" (*Seven Champions*, I3r), "bread and cheese and a bottle" (*Sir John Oldcastle*, 2398–9); see also *Princess*, E1v; *Siege*, 385;

examples of tables are "*a Tablecloth, Bread, Trenchers and salt*" (*Woman Killed*, 132, also 117), "*A Table ready covered with Cloth Napkins Salt Trenchers and Bread*" (*Spanish Curate*, 129/501); prisoners are given "*a piece of brown bread and a Carrot root*" (*Martyred Soldier*, 206), "*brown bread, and a wooden dish of water*" (*Believe as You List*, 1987–90; the bookkeeper adds in the margin "*bread and water,*" 1986–7); actions include "*Overthrows the gingerbread*" (*Bartholomew Fair*, 3.6.98), "*They play still towards her, and Jockey often breaks bread and cheese, and gives her, till Jeffrey being called away, and he then gives her all, and is apprehended*" (*2 Edward IV*, 173); atypical are "*a woman, with Diet-bread and Drink*" (*Knight of the Burning Pestle*, 205), "*Enter Bread and Meatman*" (*Knave in Grain*, 1698).

break

the roughly forty-five examples include (1) *break* an object, (2) *break open* a *trunk* or *door*, (3) *enter* by *breaking in*, (4) *break off* an action or conversation, (5) *break* someone's *head*; objects *broken* include a *pitcher* (*Old Wives Tale*, 624, 645), *ring* (*Fatal Contract*, F2r), *chain* (*Look about You*, 1303–4), *branches* (*Friar Bacon*, 1214), "*bread and cheese*" (*2 Edward IV*, 173), most commonly a *glass*/*glasses* (*Old Wives Tale*, 838; *Friar Bacon*, 1869; *Alchemist*, 1.1.115; *Wonder of a Kingdom*, 3.1.192; *Renegado*, 1.3.145); atypical is "*a hand appears that breaketh down the Head with a hammer*" (*Friar Bacon*, 1636–7); figures *break open* a trunk (*Two Maids of More-Clacke*, G2r; *Herod and Antipater*, B3v), *letter* (*Very Woman*, 5.2.4), *door* (*Island Princess*, 115; *Jews' Tragedy*, 2231; *Traitor*, 5.1.165), and come onstage by *breaking in* (*Spanish Tragedy*, 4.4.156; Folio *2 Henry VI*, 670, 1.4.40; *Virgin Martyr*, 4.1.108): "*Break open door; rush in*" (*No Wit*, 5.1.150), "*They break with violence into the Chamber*" (*Alphonsus of Germany*, F4v); figures *break off* various actions (*Histriomastix*, G1v; *Amends for Ladies*, 3.4.137; *Match Me in London*, 5.3.0; *Women Beware Women*, 4.3.0; *Court Beggar*, 266) and *break from* someone (*Rape of Lucrece*, 189; *Fool Would Be a Favourite*, F3r; *Landgartha*, B1v): "*they dance a strain*" and "*Violetta on a sudden breaks off*" (*Blurt*, 1.1.158, 169), "*break off their private talk*" (*Lost Lady*, 592), "*breaks violently from them*" (*Noble Stranger*, G4r), "*They break asunder*" (*Look about You*, 200); to *break a head* is to *wound* with a *blow* (*Arden of Faversham*, 840, 1682; *Sisters*, D2r), as in "*She breaks his head, and beats him*" (*City Madam*, 2.2.209); a variation is "*Breaks the can over his head*" (*News from Plymouth*, 143; see also *Orlando Furioso*, 1232); *break* occasionally appears in offstage cries: "*Within, break open door*" (*Honest*

Lawyer, G2r; see also *Conspiracy*, K2v); atypical are *break down trees* (*Brazen Age*, 253), "*The boy runs a note; Antonio breaks it*" (*Antonio and Mellida*, 4.1.147), "*A cave suddenly breaks open*" (*Whore of Babylon*, 4.1.0).

breast

used in roughly thirty directions to denote a man's or woman's *bosom*/chest; exceptions where the reference is to a woman's *breasts* are a Caroline *dumb show* where "*they return her child, she points to her breasts, as meaning she should nurse it*" (*Bloody Banquet*, 855–6) and possibly "*they bind her to the Chair, the Eunuch much fears her breast*" (*Fatal Contract*, I3r), "*Rash whispers with her; her hand after at her breast*" (*Country Girl*, G2v); other examples involving women include "*Sets the Garland on her breast*" (*King John and Matilda*, 87), "*with Jewels and a great crucifix on her breast*" (*Second Maiden's Tragedy*, 1930–1, also 2226); unique and probably *fictional* is Jonson's "*He grows more familiar in his Courtship, plays with her paps, kisseth her hands, etc.*" (*Devil Is an Ass*, 2.6.71); most of the signals are for a variety of actions involving men: "*walks sadly, beats his breast*" (*Jovial Crew*, 445; see also *Two Merry Milkmaids*, H4r), "*tears open his breast*" (*Antonio's Revenge*, 3.1.0), "*Toucheth his breast with his cross*" (*Two Noble Ladies*, 1869–70), "*sets his breast unto his sword*" (*Spanish Tragedy*, 2.5.67), "*he snatches away her knife, and sets it to his own breast*" (*Fair Maid of the Inn*, 215), "*He lays his breast open, she offers at with his sword*" (Folio *Richard III*, 371, 1.2.178); see also *Antonio's Revenge*, 4.2.68; *Cruel Brother*, 189; *Soddered Citizen*, 145; *Goblins*, 3.2.13; *Prisoners*, A9r; *Claracilla*, F11v; *Deserving Favourite*, N2v; sometimes *writing* is found on a *breast*: "*upon his breast a blue table full of silver letters*" (*Two Noble Ladies*, 1102, also 1082; see also *New Trick*, 250, 251); atypical are a corpse placed "*thwart Antonio's breast,*" (*Antonio's Revenge*, 4.2.23), "*His foot on the Doctor's breast*" (*Bashful Lover*, 5.1.135), "*Enter Tarquin with an arrow in his breast*" (*Rape of Lucrece*, 249), "*He putteth to either of their breasts an Aspic*" to murder two boys (*Devil's Charter*, I4r), "*Duke Humphrey is discovered in his bed, and two men lying on his breast and smothering him*" (Quarto *2 Henry VI*, E2r, [3.2.0]).

breath, breathe

linked to (1) figures *out of breath*, (2) *pauses* in *fights*, (3) occasional stage business; figures enter "*Panting for breath*" (*Captain Thomas Stukeley*, 2799; *Rape of Lucrece*, 252), "*out of breath*" (*Maid in the Mill*, 34) with the latter saying "I have recovered breath, I'll speak unto him presently"; in *Coriolanus* "*Martius fights till* they be driven in breathless" (741, 1.8.13); examples related to fights include "*They fight and breathe afresh*" (*Hieronimo*, 11.121), "*They fight a good while and then breathe*" (*Orlando Furioso*, 1536), "*a fierce fight with sword and target, then after pause and breathe*" (*Rape of Lucrece*, 252); see also *Look about You*, 2507, 2518; *Goblins*, 1.1.59; atypical are "*He cries hup, and holds his breath*" (*Princess*, H2v), "*Corporal breathes upon Frailty*" (*Puritan*, B3r), "*Enter Envy alone to all the Actors sleeping on the Stage: the music sounding: she breathes amongst them*" (*Histriomastix*, E1v, also F2v); see also **blow**, **panting**.

bring, brought

a majority of the roughly 280 examples call for figures to be *brought* onstage; some are **prisoners**: "*The Prisoners are brought in well guarded*" (*Sir Thomas More*, 606–7), "*The Prisoners brought to the Bar by a Guard*" (*Swetnam*, D3r); see also *Sir John Oldcastle*, 1640–1; *Revenger's Tragedy*, A4r; *Silver Age*, 86; *Fortune by Land and Sea*, 410, 418; *Jews' Tragedy*, 356–8; also *brought* in are **bodies** (*King Lear*, L3r, 3184, 5.3.238; *Michaelmas Term*, 4.4.51; *Second Maiden's Tragedy*, 2225; *Hengist*, DS before 4.3, 10; *Aglaura*, 5.1.184; *Bird in a Cage*, K2v); over twenty figures are *brought* in **sick/sleeping/bound** in a **chair**; for a sampling see *1 Henry VI*, 1069, 2.5.0; 1469–70, 3.2.40; Folio *3 Henry VI*, 2257–8, 4.3.27; *Warning for Fair Women*, G4r; *Englishmen for My Money*, 2434; *Yorkshire Tragedy*, 720; *Gentleman Usher*, 4.3.0, 5.4.39; *Emperor of the East*, 4.3.0; *Broken Heart*, 4.4.0; *Antipodes*, 263; *Queen's Exchange*, 546; variations include "*brought forth to execution*" (*2 Edward IV*, 180), they "*bring away the Ensigns*" (*Four Prentices*, 234), "*Nobles bring him to the door and return*" (*1 If You Know Not Me*, 239; see also *Histriomastix*, B4r), "*He goes in and brings him out*" (*2 Tamburlaine*, 3764), "*She offers to go, he brings her back*" (*Swaggering Damsel*, D3v); the many objects *brought* in include a **bar**, **bier**, **chair**, **chest/trunk**, **coffin**, **hearse**, **throne**, **tree**, food, **garments**, **irons**, **letters/papers**, severed **limbs**, **stocks**, **weapons**, most commonly a **table**, **banquet**, **wine**; atypical is *bring* as an imperative: "*Bring down the body*" and "*Bring forth the boy*" (*Two Lamentable Tragedies*, D2v, G3r).

buckler

a small **shield** held by a handle at the back and used to ward off blows, always cited with a **sword**: "*Sampson and Gregory, with Swords and Bucklers*" (Q2 *Romeo and Juliet*, A3r, 1.1.0), "*Sir John alone, with his page bearing his sword and buckler*" (*2 Henry IV*, B1r,

1.2.0); for more see *Three Ladies of London*, A3r; *Edward I*, 267; *Sir Thomas More*, 411; *Satiromastix*, 4.2.0; *Histriomastix*, D2v; *Jews' Tragedy*, 1996; see also **target**.

buffet

to "exchange blows"; the term occurs once: "*They buffet*" (*Antipodes*, 303).

bull

signaled twice in the same play; at the outset of the golden fleece episode "*Two fiery Bulls are discovered, the Fleece hanging over them, and the Dragon sleeping beneath them*" (*Brazen Age*, 217); in Hercules's fight with Achelous the shape-shifter "*When the Fury sinks, a Bull's head appears*" so "*He tugs with the Bull, and plucks off one of his horns*" (*Brazen Age*, 176); elsewhere a group of **masquers** includes "*a Stag, a Ram, a Bull and a Goat*" (*City Nightcap*, 156); Henslowe's inventory lists "one bull's head" (*Diary*, App. 2, 83).

burn, burning

in the roughly thirty uses the modifier is more common than the verb; examples of *burn* include "*burns his Club and Lion's skin*" (*Brazen Age*, 254), "*burn perfumes*" (*White Devil*, 2.2.23); see also *Jack Straw*, 775; *Three Lords of London*, I3v; *Witch of Edmonton*, 4.1.20; in *If This Be Not a Good Play* a hand is "*burnt off*" (5.4.41) suggesting an action, but in *Nero* "*a Woman with a burnt Child*" (56) describes appearance after the "event"; sometimes *burning* indicates either actual **fire** or a representation of it; the annotated quarto of *Looking Glass for London* has a bookkeeper's "*burning sword*" just before the printed "*A hand from out a cloud, threateneth a burning sword*" (F4v, 1636; see also *Locrine*, 3); other *burning* properties are **staves** (*1 Iron Age*, 314), **crown** and **weapons** (*Silver Age*, 159), **thunderbolt** (*Silver Age*, 154), as well as the more expected **torch** (*1 Henry VI*, 1452, 3.2.25), **taper** (Folio *2 Henry VI*, 1188–9, 2.4.16), **lamp** (*Martyred Soldier*, 206); for similar examples see *Hoffman*, 1413; *Satiromastix*, 1.2.0; *If This Be Not a Good Play*, 4.4.0; *Two Noble Kinsmen*, B1r, 1.1.0; *Messalina*, 2252–3; *2 Tamburlaine* signals "*the Town burning*" (3190), and Tamburlaine says "So, burn the turrets of this cursed town / Flame to the highest region of the air" suggesting some kind of special effect.

bush

the five relevant directions may or may not direct the bringing onstage of a property *bush* but do require a real or imagined place of concealment:

"*Thirsty climbing up into a tree. Robin into a bush*" (*Honest Lawyer*, I2r), "*Enter Cranwell staggering, and falls near the Bush where the Child is*" (*Duchess of Suffolk*, F2v); three scenes direct figures to enter *out of/from a bush*: "*Philaster creeps out of a bush*" (*Philaster*, 129), "*Enter Palemon as out of a Bush, with his Shackles*" and "*Enter Palemon from the Bush*" (*Two Noble Kinsmen*, F2v, 3.1.30; G4r, 3.6.0).

bustle

used for various impromptu *scuffles* or tussles: the plebeians "*all bustle about Coriolanus*" (*Coriolanus*, 1893, 3.1.184); in *Insatiate Countess* the term twice describes a short unarmed *fight* between two figures (4.1.88, 5.2.184); in *Edward I* a "*Bustling*" (1822) Friar and Farmer are told to stop "brawling" and later there is "*Bustling on both sides*" (2016); in *Goblins* bustle is used when soldiers make arrests (4.3.42); *King John and Matilda* has a forced unmasking and "*In the bustle, Fitzwater drops one of his Gloves*" (52); only once does the term describe a confrontation in which a figure is killed: "*They bustle. Caroll slain*" (*1 Fair Maid of the West*, 270).

busy

used to signal engagement in some ongoing activity: "*Enter with a Hammer above, very busy*" (*Jew of Malta*, 2281), "*in busy talk one to the other*" (*Warning for Fair Women*, D2v), "*Landrey, and two or three insinuating Lords, busy in conference*" (*Fatal Contract*, B1v), "*Howlet busy Amongst them*" (*Wasp*, 477); see also *Staple of News*, 1.2.129; *Fatal Contract*, D4v; *Soddered Citizen*, 2690–2; *Prisoners*, C9v, C1or; *busy* is frequently linked to *about*: "*busy about his hair*" (*Lady of Pleasure*, 4.3.11), "*a tirewoman, busy about her head*" (*Michaelmas Term*, 3.1.0), "*busy about fastening Hortenzo*" (*Lust's Dominion*, 5.2.0), "*busy themselves about Herbert*" who is *wounded* (*Sir John Oldcastle*, 57–8).

button, unbutton

button (1) is usually found as a participle linked to figures who are *unready* but (2) occasionally appears as a noun; typical are entrances "*above at a window, in his nightcap: buttoning*" (*Doctor Faustus*, B 1205–6), "*undressed, and buttoning themselves as they go*" (*Parson's Wedding*, 517), "*new and richly clothed, buttoning themselves*" (*Wits*, 130); comparable uses of *unbutton* include "*unbuttoning himself*" (*City Match*, 284), "*unbuttoned as out of bed*" (*Swaggering Damsel*, H2v); atypical is "*Flings down his hat, unbuttons himself, draws*" (*Goblins*, 1.2.4); use as a noun includes "*cuts off*

the Cutpurse's ear, for cutting of the gold buttons off his cloak*" (*Massacre at Paris*, 622) and calls for a *button-monger* (*Hengist*, 1.2.0, 3.3.121).

C

cabin

found in only two directions, both in *Faithful Shepherdess*: first Clorin enters "*in her Cabin, Alexis, with her*" and later "*The Curtain is drawn, Clorin appears sitting in the Cabin, Amoret sitting on the one side of her, Alexis and Cloe on the other, the Satyr standing by*" (429, 437).

cabinet

a case for jewels, documents, and other valuable objects; representative are entrances "*with a Cabinet of Jewels*" (*Wedding*, E4v), "*a Cabinet, Paper in it*" (*Deserving Favourite*, M3v); in *Fair Favourite* "*She reaches a cabinet*" that "*doth contain in jewels, / Enough to ransom you as oft as fortune can / Betray you to the foe*" and "*He takes the cabinet*" (217–18, also 228); a sequence in *Novella* includes "*She lets the Cabinet fall out of the Window,*" "*Enter a Zaffie, taking up the Cabinet,*" "*He gives the Cabinet to Nan, who knocks at door*" (151–3); see also *Revenge of Bussy*, 4.5.49; *Gentleman of Venice*, G1r; *Prisoners*, B3v.

caeteri, cum caeteris

Latin for "others, with others" found occasionally in *exits*: "*Exeunt caeterae*" (*Law Tricks*, 164), "*Exit cum Caeteris*" (*Wit in a Constable*, 229), "*Exit King cum caeteris suis*" (*Young Admiral*, C3v), "*Exit Balia, manent caeteri*" (*Wit of a Woman*, 72); an alternative is *cum aliis* (Q2 *Hamlet*, B3v, 1020, 1.2.0; Folio *Hamlet*, 1019, 2.2.0).

call

occurs frequently in the *sound* signal *call within* when figures offstage *call* to others either off or onstage: "*Emilia calls within*" (Quarto *Othello*, M2r, [5.2.85]), "*Knocking and calling within*" (*Hoffman*, 548), "*Within call Iacamo*" (*Royal Master*, D2v), "*Goes from the window, and calls within*" (*Distresses*, 302); see also *Fair Em*, 157–8, 185, 188; *Death of Huntingdon*, 102; *When You See Me*, 577; *Bartholomew Fair*, 2.5.45; *Knave in Grain*, 1985; *Inconstant Lady*, 2.2.49; another signal is *enter* calling: "*Enter Mouse the clown calling his master*" (*Mucedorus*, D1r), "*Enter the Black Knight in his Litter; calls*" (*Game at Chess*, 2002–3); see also *Look about You*, 782; *Caesar and Pompey*, 2.3.0; *Devil's Charter*, L2v; *Your*

Five Gallants, F3v; *Conspiracy*, E3v; other examples of *call* are "*Paris offers to go in, and Capulet calls him again*" and "*Boy whistles and calls*" (Q1 *Romeo and Juliet*, G2v, 3.4.11; I4v, [5.3.17]), "*both call him, the Drawer stands amazed, not knowing which way to go*" (*1 Henry IV*, D2v, 2.4.79), "*knock again, and call out to talk with Faustus*" (*Doctor Faustus*, B 1679), "*goes in and out calling*" (Folio *Every Man In*, 3.5.65), "*call Shift aside*" (Quarto *Every Man Out*, 2200), "*calls him back*" (*Poetaster*, 4.9.80, also 88), "*going out, he calls*" (*Two Merry Milkmaids*, L3v); see also *2 Tamburlaine*, 3045; *Wounds of Civil War*, 259; *Sir John Oldcastle*, 2247; *Thomas Lord Cromwell*, D1r; *Warning for Fair Women*, A4r; *Revenger's Tragedy*, I3v; *Launching of the Mary*, 1143; *Princess*, C3v; a unique usage in the annotated manuscript of *Believe as You List* also names a player: "*Mr. Hobs: called up*" (661–2).

can

a container for *sack*: "*a silver Can of Sack*" (*Jovial Crew*, 418; see also *New Academy*, 19), or for *wine* or other liquor (MS *Humorous Lieutenant*, 1711–12; *Bartholomew Fair*, 4.6.141; *Soddered Citizen* 1063; *News from Plymouth*, 141, 143); see also **bottle**.

candle

a *light* that (1) by convention can indicate *night*/darkness on a *stage* with no variable lighting and is linked to (2) religious rites, (3) the *study* and *reading*; *candles*/**tapers** are found in scenes located indoors as opposed to *torches*/**links** that usually indicate outdoor locales; an exception is the shaming of Dame Elinor who must show herself in public "*barefoot, and a white sheet about her, with a wax candle in her hand*" (Quarto *2 Henry VI*, D2r, 2.4.16; "*wax candles*" are also specified in *Amyntas*, Z1v); for figures who **enter** with a candle see *Old Wives Tale*, 27; *Antonio and Mellida*, 3.2.123; *Monsieur D'Olive*, 2.1.64; *Chances*, 190; *Coxcomb*, 318; *Valiant Welshman*, H3v; *Hog Hath Lost His Pearl*, 1804; *Duchess of Suffolk*, D1r; *Mad Couple*, 31; *Parson's Wedding*, 455; *Wits*, 209; see also *Amends for Ladies*, 2.1.71; *1 Honest Whore*, 2.1.0, 64; *Parson's Wedding*, 479.

For examples of religious rites, the fake Capuchins present the dying Bracciano "*with a crucifix and hallowed candle*" (*White Devil*, 5.3.129), friars appear "*with Bell, Book, and Candle, for the Dirge*" (*Doctor Faustus*, B 1111–12); examples of study/reading are "*in his Study, Candle and Books about him*" (*Two Merry Milkmaids*, B1r), "*sits down having a candle by her, and reads*" (*Hoffman*, 1728–9), "*Horace sitting in a study behind a Curtain, a candle by him burning, books lying confusedly*" (*Satiromastix*, 1.2.0); *tables* can be **set**

"*with a candle burning, a death's head, a cloak and a cross*" (*If This Be Not a Good Play*, 4.4.0), "*with Jewels and Money upon it, an Egg roasting by a Candle*" (*Women Pleased*, 242); in *Fedele and Fortunio* figures "*throw their candles into the Tomb where Crackstone lieth*" and "*Crackstone riseth out of the Tomb with one candle in his mouth, and in each hand one*" (590–1, 598–9); with reference to the *candle*lit indoor theatres *What You Will* directs figures in an induction to "*sit a good while on the Stage before the Candles are lighted, talking together*" (A2r); to **put** out a *candle* is to indicate onstage darkness, so that to masquerade successfully as another man "*Albert ascends, and being on the top of the ladder, puts out the candle*" (*Hog Hath Lost His Pearl*, 265–6; see also *Country Captain*, C12r).

canopy

a cover or hanging either suspended over a *chair*/**state** or held over noble figures in a procession; Henslowe's inventory lists "one wooden canopy" (*Diary*, App. 2, 65), but sometimes it was made of fabric; calls for a *canopy* are "*four Noblemen bearing a Canopy, under which the Duchess of Norfolk*" (*Henry VIII*, 3357–9, 5.4.0; see also *1 If You Know Not Me*, 244), "*Empress of Babylon: her Canopy supported by four Cardinals*" (*Whore of Babylon*, 1.1.0); for other entrances *under a canopy* see *Alphonsus of Aragon*, 1582–5; *Edward I*, 630; *Seven Champions*, G1r; *Fair Favourite*, 228; sometimes it is difficult to be certain if the *canopy* is already suspended over figures seated onstage or is carried onstage over them: "*Loud music, Honoria in state under a Canopy, her train borne up by Silvia and Acanthe*" (*Picture*, 1.2.128), "*Aurelia (under a Canopy), Astutio presents her with letters*" (*Maid of Honour*, 4.2.0); see also *Just Italian*, 254; *Humorous Courtier*, I3r; the *canopy* is more clearly part of the stage furnishings in *Satiromastix*: "*chair is set under a Canopy*" (5.2.22); see also *Landgartha*, E4r; on several occasions the *canopy* is opened to reveal seated or reclining figures: "*solemnly draws the Canopy, where the Queen sits at one end*" of a *table* (*Fatal Contract*, H3r); see also *Albovine*, 95; *Platonic Lovers*, 33; such examples suggest that *canopy* is here an alternative for *curtain*/**arras** and that the action described is a *discovery*; some instances suggest the use of a recessed space in the tiring-house wall: "*Scudmore passeth one door, and entereth the other, where Bellafront sits in a Chair, under a Taffeta Canopy*" (*Woman Is a Weathercock*, 3.2.68–70), music plays "*within the canopy*" and "*Syphax hasteneth within the canopy, as to Sophonisba's bed*" (*Sophonisba*, 4.1.200, 218).

cantat, cantant

these Latin terms for *sings*/**sing** appear randomly, almost always in boys' company plays and most often from Marston; his two *Antonio* plays use the Latin exclusively when giving a basic direction for singing (*Antonio and Mellida*, 2.1.61, 3.1.108, 3.2.36, 4.1.149, 5.2.8, 18, 25; *Antonio's Revenge*, 1.2.165, 2.2.136, 3.2.52, 5.2.19, 5.3.32, 185); sometimes the word is part of a phrase: "*Exeunt cum Choro cantantium*" (*Amyntas*, 2C3v), "*Cantat saltatque cum cithera*" (*Dutch Courtesan*, 5.1.20), "*Cantant et Saltant*" (*Love's Metamorphosis*, B2v), "*Chorus Juvenum cantantes et saltantes*" (*May Day*, 1.1.0); see also *Mother Bombie*, 1121; *Love's Metamorphosis*, C4v; *Dutch Courtesan*, 2.1.8, 2.2.69, 2.3.104; *Sophonisba*, 4.1.212; *Gentleman Usher*, 5.1.48; *Law Tricks*, 164; *Sir Giles Goosecap*, 3.2.23, 30, 38, 5.2.387; *Amends for Ladies*, 4.2.124; *Fatal Dowry*, 2.2.124; *Nero*, 57.

canvas

the few examples are "*throws off his Gown, discovering his doublet with a satin forepart and a Canvas back*" (*Hengist*, 5.1.286–9) and entrances "*in a Canvas suit*" (*Jews' Tragedy*, 1998), "*in canvas coats like Sailors*" (*Three Lords of London*, F3r).

cap

often cited as (1) a **nightcap**, (2) any one of a number of distinctive *caps*, and (3) found in a variety of actions; for examples of *nightcaps*, figures enter "*unready, in his nightcap, garterless*" (*Two Maids of More-Clacke*, E3v), "*his Arm in a scarf, a nightcap on his head*" (*Widow's Tears*, 4.1.0), "*in his nightcap: buttoning*" (*Doctor Faustus*, B 1205–6); other *caps* specified are a *corner cap* (*Friar Bacon*, 2021–2; *Devil's Charter*, A2v), *Scotch cap* (*Locrine*, 1596), *flat cap/prentice's cap* (*Eastward Ho*, B3r, B4r), "*fool's Cap and Coat*" (*City Wit*, 367), **sea** cap (*King Leir*, 1992), "*Cap of Maintenance*" for royalty (*1 If You Know Not Me*, 244; MS *Poor Man's Comfort*, 1094); more detailed signals include "*a rich Cap and Mantle*" (*Double Marriage*, 350), "*a black velvet cap, and a white feather*" (*Lover's Melancholy*, 3.1.0), "*basely attired, and a red cap on his head*" (*Taming of a Shrew*, C3v), "*Fraud in a blue gown, red cap and red sleeves*" (*Three Lords of London*, I2v), Scottish "*Soldiers with blue Caps*" (*Valiant Scot*, G3r), "*rich Cap, the Tunicle, and the triple Crown set upon Alexander's head*" (*Devil's Charter*, A2v); see also *Three Ladies of London*, A2v; *Three Lords of London*, I2r; *Fedele and Fortunio*, 77–8; *What You Will*, D3r; *Thracian Wonder*, C1v; *Chabot*, 5.3.0; *Wonder of a Kingdom*, 1.4.0; *Late Lancashire Witches*, 241; *Changes*,

I3v; the **casting/flinging/throwing** up of *caps* is an expression of popular acclaim: "*They all shout and wave their swords, take him up in their Arms, and cast up their Caps*" (*Coriolanus*, 695–6, 1.6.75, also 794–6, 1.9.40; 2424–5, 3.3.137); see also *Sir Thomas More*, 710; *Shoemakers' Holiday*, 5.2.201; *Hoffman*, 1187–8; other actions include "*gives him his cap*" (*Sir Thomas More*, 1651), "*puts off his cap*" (*Antonio's Revenge*, 4.2.11), "*Throws his nightcap away*" (*Two Lamentable Tragedies*, I2r), "*a prentice brushing his Master's cloak and Cap*" (*Westward Ho*, 2.1.0).

caper

"to **dance** or behave in a frolicsome or fantastic way"; the few directions include "*Bowdler capers and sings*" (*Fair Maid of the Exchange*, 71), "*untrusses and capers*" (*All Fools*, 2.1.398); see also *Charlemagne*, 1560, 1587; *Northward Ho*, 2.1.249; *Chaste Maid*, 3.3.116; *Cupid's Whirligig*, 4.5.74; *Fatal Dowry*, 4.1.71; *Bondman*, 5.3.258; *Queen and Concubine*, 56; *Bride*, 8; *School of Compliment*, G4r.

captive

a seldom used alternative to **prisoner**: "*Balthazar between Lorenzo and Horatio captive*" (*Spanish Tragedy*, 1.2.109, also 1.4.137), "*like Amazon Captives, shackled with Golden Fetters, and pinioned with silken cords*" (*Amorous War*, C2v); see also *Hieronimo*, 12.0; *Edward II*, 1528; *Cymbeline*, 3030, 5.3.94; *Tom a Lincoln*, 1014; *1 Arviragus and Philicia*, A8v; *Sophy*, 1.2.121.

cards

items seen when figures enter "*with Cards, Carpet, stools, and other necessaries*" then "*spread a Carpet, set down lights and Cards*" (*Woman Killed*, 121), and referred to in "*Enter aloft to cards*" (*Dumb Knight*, 186), "*A noise above at cards*" (*New Wonder*, 123).

carelessly

linked to disorderly **clothes**; figures are directed to enter "*carelessly attired*" (*Lover's Melancholy*, 1.2.0), "*in black, carelessly habited*" (*Very Woman*, 2.3.23), "*unbraced and careless dressed*" (*What You Will*, A4r), "*rudely, and carelessly appareled, unbraced, and untrussed*" (*Nice Valour*, 170).

carpet

occasionally used to help establish a sense of place and/or occasion: "*brings out a carpet, spreads it and lays on it two fair cushions*" (*White Devil*, 1.2.204), "*with Cards, Carpet, stools, and other necessaries*" (*Woman*

Killed, 121, also 117), "*A Table being covered with a green Carpet, a state Cushion on it*" (*Sir Thomas More*, 735); see also *Gentleman Usher*, 2.1.71; *Conspiracy of Byron*, 1.2.14; *Bird in a Cage*, K2v.

carry, carrying, carried

of the roughly 100 uses of this verb and modifier (1) more than half describe the transportation of a "dead" *body*, a captive, or a figure in a *chair* because *sick* or *wounded*, (2) the rest refer to properties alone; examples of *carried* bodies/figures include "*Bedford dies, and is carried in by two in his Chair*" (*1 Henry VI*, 1558, 3.2.114), "*the dead body is carried away*" (*Hamlet*, Q2 H1v, Folio 2000, 3.2.135; see also *Hoffman*, 1069; *Charlemagne*, 1138–9), "*Enter Lear in a chair carried by Servants*" (Folio *King Lear*, 2771, 4.7.23), "*Exit Horatio carrying Andrea on his back*" (*Hieronimo*, 11.170; see also *Friar Bacon*, 807), "*all help carry Feliche to his grave*" (*Antonio's Revenge*, 4.2.96), "*Alinda entranced carried out*" (*Queen and Concubine*, 114), "*Enter Marinel, throwing down one he carries*" (*Brennoralt*, 1.2.0), "*carried in as sick in a couch*" (*Wits*, 183); elsewhere figures who are prisoners or otherwise under others' control are *carried*: "*Enter Sir Richard Ratcliffe, with Halberds, carrying the Nobles to death at Pomfret*" (Folio *Richard III*, 1933–4, 3.3.0), "*hale Edmund away, and carry him to be beheaded*" (*Edward II*, 2440), "*carries her away in his arms*" (*Golden Age*, 35), "*One draws and stands at the door, whilst the other carry her away*" (*Bride*, 36), "*tosses off her Bowl, falls back, and is carried out*" (*Jovial Crew*, 391); for more figures *carried* see *Alphonsus of Aragon*, 1676–7; *Arraignment of Paris*, 742; *Battle of Alcazar* plot, 63–5; *Four Prentices*, 246; *Soliman and Perseda*, I2r; *Alarum for London*, 261; *Weakest Goeth*, 1366, 1782, 2081; *Pericles*, E4v, 3.2.110; *Captives*, 2462; *Valiant Welshman*, G1v; *Love's Pilgrimage*, 297; *Picture*, 3.5.2; *Queen's Exchange*, 491; *Traitor*, 3.2.44.

Properties are *carried* onstage or off: "*carrying out the Table*" (*Tempest*, 1618, 3.3.82), "*the sword carried before the King*" (*James IV*, 2406–7), "*a boy carrying a gilt harp*" (*Antonio and Mellida*, 5.2.0), "*A Dinner carried over the Stage in covered Dishes*" (*City Wit*, 279), "*carries in the Pistols and returns*" (*Gentleman of Venice*, F2v), "*between every couple a torch carried*" (*Changes*, K2v); see also *Death of Huntingdon*, 333–4; *Looking Glass for London*, 1618; *Two Noble Kinsmen*, L1v, 5.1.136; *Henry VIII*, 2656, 4.2.82; *Second Maiden's Tragedy*, 1878; *Old Law*, I1v; *Island Princess*, 121; *Virgin Martyr*, 1.1.118; *Wonder of a Kingdom*, 5.2.0; *Soddered Citizen*, 994–5; *Faithful Friends*, 1049; see also *bear*, **bring**.

casement

a rarely used synonym for **window**: "*Victoria setteth open the Casement of her window*" (*Fedele and Fortunio*, 192), "*The Casement opens, and Katherine appears*" (*Jack Drum's Entertainment*, C2v), "*Alexander out of a Casement*" (*Devil's Charter*, E2r).

casket

usually holds something of value, as when "*Bassanio comments on the caskets to himself*" (*Merchant of Venice*, E4r, 3.2.62); some *caskets* contain **jewels** (*Knight of the Burning Pestle*, 182; *Picture*, 3.2.30; *Loyal Subject*, 134; *Guardian*, 5.4.118); *caskets* with a variety of contents appear in *Coxcomb*, 317; *No Wit*, 5.1.251; *Silver Age*, 97; *Honest Man's Fortune*, 204; *Rule a Wife*, 208, 222; *Laws of Candy*, 284; *Spanish Gypsy*, I4v; *English Traveller*, 37; *2 Passionate Lovers*, L4r; *Renegado*, 3.5.48; there is one "*caskinet*" (*Country Girl*, F2r); a larger property is called for in *Fatal Dowry* where the *casket* holds a body (4.4.0).

cast

an alternative to **throw** used roughly thirty-five times in almost as many contexts; one of the few repeated usages is for figures to "*cast up their caps*" in celebration (*Coriolanus*, 696, 1.6.75; 795, 1.9.40; *Shoemakers' Holiday*, 5.2.201; *Hoffman*, 1187–8); *cast* is also linked to a **cloak**: "*cloaks cast over their apparel*" (*Antonio and Mellida*, Induction.0), "*gently casts his cloak*" (*Soddered Citizen*, 1304–5); see also *Three Lords of London*, D4r; *Warning for Fair Women*, D2v; clothing is cited in other locutions: "*Casts off his gown*" (*Lover's Melancholy*, 1.2.112; see also *Wounds of Civil War*, 252), "*casts a scarf over his face*" (*Sophy*, 3.356), "*casts off his Peruke, and Beard*" (*Novella*, 177); elsewhere figures variously *cast* a **sword** (*Bloody Brother*, 257; *Love's Sacrifice*, 2534–5), **knife** (*2 Edward IV*, 129), **stone** (*Captives*, 2434), **rock** (*1 Iron Age*, 300), **purse** (*2 Edward IV*, 123), **jewel** (*2 Fair Maid of the West*, 399), **pot** (*Mucedorus*, D3v), **weapons** (*Herod and Antipater*, F4r), **bags** (*Captain Thomas Stukeley*, 2281); notable signals are "*all but the Nurse go forth, casting Rosemary on her and shutting the Curtains*" (Q1 *Romeo and Juliet*, I2v, 4.5.95), "*casts herself from the rock*" (*Tom a Lincoln*, 2827–30), "*Cast flames of fire forth of the brazen Head*" (*Alphonsus of Aragon*, 1254, also 1246–7), "*Cast Comfits*" and "*all rise and cast incense into the fire*" (*Cobbler's Prophecy*, 42, 1589), "*a Friar with a holy water-pot casting water*" (*Devil's Charter*, E1r), "*cast their Warders between them, and part them*" (*Four Prentices*, 204), "*Pride casts a mist*" (*Histriomastix*, D1r), "*Jonas the Prophet cast out of* the Whale's belly upon the Stage" (Looking Glass for London, 1460–1).

castle

a **fictional** location represented by the tiring house, as in "exit into the castle" (John a Kent, 811, 827, 847, 850, 1329, also 1187), "he summons from the Castle with a trumpet" (Devil's Charter, D3v); the term can also suggest an onstage location: "as in Baynard's Castle" (King John and Matilda, 11).

cat

one is brought onstage in Vow Breaker where Joshua enters with "his Cat in a string" (3.2.0) ready to hang it for killing a mouse; supernatural cats appear twice in Witch: "she Conjures: And Enter a Cat (playing on a Fiddle,) and Spirits (with Meat)," "A Spirit like a Cat descends" (437–40, 1345–6).

catch

occurs either (1) as a noun for a **song** or round for three or more voices singing in **parts** or (2) as a verb usually meaning "to grasp, lay hold of" but occasionally "to trap"; in a catch the second singer begins the first line as the first goes on to the second and so on, so that one singer "catches" and repeats the words of another; sometimes the lyrics are given but more often not; in Twelfth Night "Catch sung" (769, 2.3.71) refers to the singing of "Hold thy peace" by Andrew Aguecheek, Toby Belch, and Feste; Country Captain gives the lyrics for "A Catch Sung" (C5v); in Rape of Lucrece "Valerius, Horatius and the Clown their Catch" (232) is followed by a long and clear example of the form for three singers; singing in parts is also called for in Swetnam, G2r; Women Beware Women, 5.2.72; King John and Matilda, 84; Court Beggar, 209; Jovial Crew, 419; Landgartha, F1r; Princess, G3v, H1v; Wallenstein, 77; Wits, 209; in Messalina the lyrics to a catch are given followed by the note that it "was left out of the Play in regard there was none could sing in Parts" (2542–3).

For examples of the verb, figures catch/catch up **swords** (Alchemist, 1.1.115; rev. Aglaura, 5.1.66) or other figures (Yorkshire Tragedy, 546; Phoenix, H2v; Late Lancashire Witches, 200; Goblins, 2.6.20; Parson's Wedding, 511); representative are "catches her up in his arms" (Lovesick King, 1791), "catches at her throat" (Widow's Tears, 5.5.69), "They catch one another's Rapiers, and both are wounded" (Q1 Hamlet, I3v, [5.2.302]); for catch as trap, to expose Mars and Venus "Vulcan catcheth them fast in his net" (Brazen Age, 237),

and in a successful murder plot "Ithocles sits down, and is catched in the engine" (Broken Heart, 4.4.20).

cave

usually an offstage **fictional** place from/**out** of which figures **enter**; a visible onstage cave is likely in Whore of Babylon where a **dumb show** begins "A cave suddenly breaks open, and out of it comes Falsehood" and "she sticks up her banner on the top of the Cave" (4.1.0); in two plays the cave is a **prison** designated **below**: "An Angel ascends from the cave, singing" and "Victoria rises out of the cave, white" (Martyred Soldier, 241, 244; see also Woman in the Moon, D4r), "They put Evandra down into the cave," "Descends the cave," "open the cave" (Love and Honour, 124, 148, 149); other signals could be either verisimilar or fictional (with an implicit as [if]): "Enter Guy being in his Cave" (Guy of Warwick, F1v), "Enter the Cave" and "Goes to the mouth of the Cave" (Aglaura, 5.1.3, 15), "Enter Aeneas and Dido in the Cave at several times" and "Exeunt to the Cave" (Dido, 995, 1059); most common are entrances out of the cave (Timon of Athens, 2360, 5.1.30), from the cave (Timon of Athens, 2233, 5.1.130; Cymbeline, 2245, 4.2.0; Valiant Welshman, E4r), "Alphonso creeps out of a cave" (Twins, E1r); atypical is "Fire flashes out of the Cave, and hideous noise" (1 Arviragus and Philicia, D8v); Jews' Tragedy provides the most elaborate cave sequence wherein figures defeated in **battle** "enter the cave" (906, 1002, 1037), emerge "out of the Cave" (930), "Groan in the Cave" (1009), and a survivor "Speaks in the Cave" (1060–1), "Opens the Cave" (1079); that many of these usages are fictional is suggested by Marston's as [if] entrance for two figures "as out of a cave's mouth" (Sophonisba, 4.1.0).

cease

linked to the timing of **music** or other **sound** usually produced **within**; most of the roughly thirty examples are versions of cease music (Old Fortunatus, 3.1.460; Thracian Wonder, C4r; Henry VIII, 2673, 4.2.95; Late Lancashire Witches, 215; Custom of the Country, 335; Lover's Melancholy, 5.2.23; Cruel Brother, 137; City Madam, 4.2.66; Love's Sacrifice, 1856, 2741; Lady Mother, 755; Antipodes, 335); more specific directions illustrate the desire to control the timing of sounds, especially in relation to other sounds and/or events: "Then trumpets cease, and Music sounds" (Doctor Faustus, B 1301), "The day clears, enchantments cease: Sweet Music" (Seven Champions, G4r), "Infernal music plays softly whilst Erictho enters, and when she speaks ceaseth" (Sophonisba, 4.1.101), "They begin to sing, and presently cease" (Histriomastix, H2r), "Cease recorders during her devotions" and "Last change. Cease music" (Broken Heart, 5.3.0, 5.2.19, also 5.2.0), "Salutations ended: cease music" (Perkin Warbeck, 2.1.39), "suddenly the Hoboys cease, and a sad Music of Flutes heard" (King John and Matilda, 83), "Hoboys cease, and solemn Music plays during his speech" (Messalina, 1510–12, also 2200); for more see King Leir, 2614–15; Thracian Wonder, B4v; Old Fortunatus, 4.1.114; Antonio and Mellida, 1.1.29; Antonio's Revenge, 2.1.0; What You Will, B1v; Troilus and Cressida, I2v, 2678–9, 4.5.116; Timon of Athens, 490–3, 1.2.145; Queen and Concubine, 22, 128; see also **done**, **end**, **stop**.

cense, censer
the verb cense ("to perfume with incense") and the noun censer ("an incense vessel, thurible") are found occasionally; censing can be part of preparations for **conjuring** (Devil's Charter, G1v) or the **perfuming** of a **room**, as when a servant enters "with two Censers" (Quarto Every Man Out, 1425); religious **ceremonies** include "after censing about the altar placeth his censer thereon" (Sejanus, 5.177), an entrance "bearing a censer with fire in it" followed by "set the censer and tapers on Juno's altar with much reverence" (Women Beware Women, 5.2.72).

ceremony
linked to a variety of activities including (1) **conjuring**, (2) religion, (3) the court; for examples of conjuring, directions call for "ceremonies belonging to conjuring" (Alphonsus of Aragon, 939), "Here do the Ceremonies belonging, and make the Circle" (Folio 2 Henry VI, 643, 1.4.22), "Music sounds ceremoniously" (Wizard, 1818); signals for religious and political ceremony include "Ceremonies ended, the Priest speaks" (Thracian Wonder, D1v), "Coming near the Tomb they all kneel, making show of Ceremony" (Love's Sacrifice, 2738–9), "conges with great reverence and ceremony to the Queen" (Fatal Contract, H4r); in Women Beware Women after the duke and others "pass solemnly over" the **stage** the Cardinal enters "in a rage, seeming to break off the ceremony" (4.3.0); in Perkin Warbeck Perkin enters, is presented to the king, then "in state retires some few paces back: During which ceremony the Noblemen slightly salute" Perkin's **followers** (2.1.39); sometimes a specific ceremony is signaled: "the ceremony of the Cardinal's instalment in the habit of a soldier" (Duchess of Malfi, 3.4.7); see also Devil's Law Case, 5.2.14; in Soddered Citizen figures carry in **bottles**, **cans**, **pots**, **tobacco pipes** "in Antic state, with Ceremony" and

Miniona and Brainsick "salute with ceremony" (994–5, 1610).

certain
a **permissive** term (comparable to **diverse**) usually used to leave unspecified the exact number of actors needed; typical are "certain grave learned men, that had been banished" (Whore of Babylon, DS before Act 1, 49–50), "Enter with a Drum on one side certain Spaniards, on the other side certain Citizens of Bullen" (Four Prentices, 176), "certain Romans with spoils" and "certain Volsces come in the aid of Aufidius" (Coriolanus, 569, 1.5.0; 740–1, 1.8.13); directions call for certain soldiers (1 Edward IV, 30), "Noblemen and Soldiers" (2 Edward IV, 108), lords (Revenger's Tragedy, C1v), senators (Timon of Athens, 54, 1.1.38; Faithful Friends, 2488), priests (Whore of Babylon, 1.1.115), monks (2 Troublesome Reign, D3v; Hengist, 1.1.28), huntsmen (James IV, 1548–9, 1587), commoners (Julius Caesar, 2, 1.1.0), merchants (Looking Glass for London, 1008), townsmen (Love's Pilgrimage, 291), singers (Four Plays in One, 334), nymphs and reapers (Tempest, 1799, 4.1.133; 1805, 4.1.138), outlaws (Two Gentlemen of Verona, 1544, 4.1.0), "certain of the Guard" (Henry VIII, 175–6, 1.1.114); certain is occasionally applied to objects: "searcheth his pocket, and findeth certain papers" (1 Henry IV, E4r, 2.4.531); see also Devil's Charter, C3r; atypical is "at certain Changes" of the **dance** (Henry VIII, 2647, 4.2.82).

chafe, chafing
to complain, fume, display irritation; typical are Franceschina, rejected by her lover, who enters "with her hair loose, chafing" (Dutch Courtesan, 2.2.0), a figure who announces "I am discovered and undone" then "chafes" (Mad Couple, 96); in Downfall of Huntingdon "John rises, all compass Fitzwater, Fitzwater chafes" (1227); other figures are directed to **enter** "chafing and stamping" (Swaggering Damsel, G1v), simply "chafing" (2 Edward IV, 110; Grim the Collier, H7v, I6v; Love's Sacrifice, 1387); atypical is to **exit** "in a chafe" (Grim the Collier, G9r); see also **anger**, **rage**, **stamp**, **storm**.

chain
refers to either (1) a restraint for **prisoners** comparable to **fetters**, **gyves**, **irons**, **manacles**, **shackles** or (2) a valuable object; prisoners appear "chained by the necks" (Lust's Dominion, 5.2.0), "led in chains" (Doctor Faustus, B 894; Martyred Soldier, 179), "laden with chains, his head, and arms only above" (Island Princess,

107), "*an Iron about his neck, two Chains manacling his wrists; a great Chain at his heels*" (*Dick of Devonshire*, 1624–5, also 1531), simply *chained* (*Princess*, G3r); Fortune is attended by kings "*chained in silver Gyves*" (*Old Fortunatus*, 1.1.63), "*the Fates bring the four winds in a chain*" (*Golden Age*, 79), "*Hercules beats Cerberus, and binds him in chains*" (*Silver Age*, 158); see also *Renegado*, 4.3.50; *Claracilla*, F1v; for examples of a *chain* of value, figures appear *with a chain* (*Comedy of Errors*, 955, 3.2.164; *Puritan*, D3r, G4r; *Chaste Maid*, 1.1.90), a **gold** chain (*Shoemakers' Holiday*, 3.2.127; *Wonder of a Kingdom*, 4.1.0), "*a chain of Pearl*" (*Your Five Gallants*, I3r; Q2 *Bussy D'Ambois*, 3.1.0; *No Wit*, 4.3.40; *Second Maiden's Tragedy*, 2226; *Hyde Park*, B4r), wearing a *chain* (*Satiromastix*, 5.2.158; *Wonder of a Kingdom*, 1.4.0), and *give chains* (*Spanish Tragedy*, 1.2.87; *Prisoners*, B3v), gamble for a *chain* (*Soliman and Perseda*, D3r–E1r); variations include "*a copper chain on*" (*Lover's Melancholy*, 3.3.38), "*breaks the chain*" (*Look about You*, 1303–4), "*puts the chain about his neck*" (*Alphonsus of Germany*, E1v), "*puts her chains upon his arm*" (*Princess*, C3r), "*in an Ape's habit, with a chain about his neck*" (*Bondman*, 3.3.0), "*all hung with Chains, Jewels, Bags of Money, etc.*" (*City Wit*, 368).

chair

found as (1) a widely used piece of stage furniture, (2) the **throne** or raised *chair* of **state**, (3) the *sick-chair* used to transport **sick**, **wounded**, or dying figures; signals call for *chairs* along with **tables**, **stools**, and **lights** to be **set** out on the **stage**: "*two Chairs set out*" (*Lovers' Progress*, 104; *Love's Pilgrimage*, 265), "*Table ready: and six chairs to set out*" (*Believe as You List*, 654–6, also 1794–5), "*A Table, Count book, Standish, Chair and stools set out*" (*City Madam*, 1.2.143, also 2.2.10), "*Enter two or three setting three or four Chairs, and four or five stools*" (*Woman Is a Weathercock*, 5.2.1), "*Six Chairs placed at the Arras*" (*Maid in the Mill*, 14/386); actions involving the *chair* of state include "*Rises and resigns his chair*" (*Great Duke of Florence*, 4.2.208), "*the High Priest ascends the Chair, the other three sit below*" (*Jews' Tragedy*, 354–5), "*he raises Herod and sets him in his Chair, makes Alexander and Aristobulus kiss his feet*" (*Herod and Antipater*, F4r, also I4v), Tamburlaine using Bajazet as a footstool so that he "*gets up upon him to his chair*" (1 *Tamburlaine*, 1473), "*Fortune takes her Chair, the Kings lying at her feet, she treading on them as she goes up*" (*Old Fortunatus*, 1.1.63), "*coming near the chair of state, Ferdinand Ascends, places Hoffman at his feet, sets a Coronet on his head*" (*Hoffman*, 483–5).

Although **beds** could be **thrust** on/**off** the **stage**, the portable *chair* carried by the arms or on poles is the most widely used signal that a figure is sick/wounded/dying (comparable terms such as **litter**/**sedan** are rarely found in stage directions); in *Othello* after "finding" the wounded Cassio, Iago cries "O for a chair / To bear him easily hence" and the quarto directs that Cassio re-enter "*in a Chair*" (N1r, 5.2.282); variations include "*Garullo brought in a Chair with a doctor*" (*Telltale*, 2231–3), "*Bedford brought in sick in a Chair*" (1 *Henry VI*, 1469–70, 3.2.40); for other *sick-chairs* see *Edward I*, 40; *Battle of Alcazar*, 1302; *Locrine*, 33; 1 *Henry VI*, 1069, 2.5.0; 2 *Henry VI*, C2r, 796, 2.1.65; 2 *Edward IV*, 155; *Warning for Fair Women*, G4r; *Yorkshire Tragedy*, 720; *Englishmen for My Money*, 2434; *Weakest Goeth*, 1366, 1782, 2081; *Satiromastix*, 5.2.37; *Sophonisba*, 5.3.115; *Gentleman Usher*, 4.3.0; 5.4.39; Folio *King Lear*, 2771, 4.7.23; *Two Noble Kinsmen*, M4r, 5.4.85; *Custom of the Country*, 374, 378; *Valentinian*, 76; *Love's Pilgrimage*, 254; *Emperor of the East*, 4.3.0; *Broken Heart*, 4.4.0; *Court Beggar*, 218, 257; *Queen and Concubine*, 127; *Sparagus Garden*, 180; *Antipodes*, 263; *Queen's Exchange*, 546; *Old Couple*, 43, 76; *Soddered Citizen*, 2215.

chamber

refers (like the less often used **room**) to (1) a **fictional** space that can be represented by the main **stage** but (2) is usually to be imagined offstage and (3) is often linked to the **discovery** space or a stage **door**; examples are a group "*ushered to their several chambers*" (2 *Iron Age*, 411), "*discover a chamber*" (*Parson's Wedding*, 506), "*Enter one and opens the Chamber door*" (*Little French Lawyer*, 440), "*seems to open a chamber door*" (*Love's Cruelty*, G2v); onstage effects are likely when figures **enter in**/**as in** a *chamber*; such entrances include *in a chamber* (*Witch*, 1633; *Hog Hath Lost His Pearl*, 1567), "*in his chamber out of his study*" (*Mad World*, 4.1.0), "*as in her chamber*" (*Twins*, G1r), "*as in Bould's chamber*" (*Amends for Ladies*, 4.2.2), "*as in a chamber, and set down at a table*" (*Sir John Oldcastle*, 2086–7), "*as in his chamber in the Tower*" (*Sir Thomas More*, 1729), "*as in his Chamber in a morning, half ready*" (*Woman Is a Weathercock*, 1.1.1–2); more common are offstage *chambers*: "*they all march to the Chamber*" (*Edward I*, 1940), "*gives Freshwater access to the Chamber and returns*" (*Ball*, E1v), an entrance "*towards the Ladies' chamber*" (*Monsieur D'Olive*, 5.2.0), "*Mendoza with his sword drawn, standing ready to murder Ferneze as he flies from the Duchess's chamber*" (*Malcontent*, 2.5.0); entrances *into* an offstage *chamber* include "*They* break with violence into the Chamber" (*Alphonsus of Germany*, F4v), "*goes into the Queen's Chamber*" (*Edward I*, 1453; see also *Atheist's Tragedy*, 2.5.0), "*hideth himself in the chamber behind the Bed-curtains*" (*2 Iron Age*, 411); see also *Goblins*, 5.2.18; *Aglaura*, 5.1.120; offstage **sounds** are sometimes associated with a *chamber*: "*speaks out of his chamber*" (*True Tragedy of Richard III*, 588), "*Sings In her Chamber*" (*Jews' Tragedy*, 2213–14), a **voice** from **within** "*out of his chamber*" (*Malcontent*, 1.2.5); other **as [if]** signals include entrances **as from** a chamber (*Bashful Lover*, 5.1.71; *'Tis Pity*, 2.1.0), "*as taking opportunity to go to her chamber*" (*Example*, D1r; see also *Game at Chess*, 1941–3; *Brennoralt*, 3.3.0); atypical are "*the bed chamber on fire*" (*Fatal Contract*, D4r), "*appeareth above, as at her chamber window*" (*Poetaster*, 4.9.0), "*Empty a chamber pot on his head*" (*Fedele and Fortunio*, 1424–6).

chambers

short cannon fired **within** to produce the **sound** of a salute or to indicate a **battle** and to replace or supplement onstage action: "*Alarums within, and the chambers be discharged, like as it were a fight at sea*" (Quarto *2 Henry VI*, F1v, [4.1.0]), "*Alarum, and Chambers go off*" (Folio *Henry V*, 1078, 3.Chorus.33; 1118, 3.1.34), "*Drum and Trumpet, Chambers discharged*" (*Henry VIII*, 731, 1.4.49) – which caused the fire that destroyed the first Globe; in *Battle of Alcazar* "*The Trumpets sound, the chambers are discharged*" precedes the entrance of the King of Portugal, then a battle is signaled with "*Alarums within, let the chambers be discharged, then enter to the battle, and the Moors fly*" (977, 1300–1); for other examples see *Travels of Three English Brothers*, 325; *2 If You Know Not Me*, 345; *World Tossed at Tennis*, E2r; *Maid of Honour*, 2.3.0; *Renegado*, 5.8.16; twice an alternative term, *guns*, is used: "*sound Trumpets, Drums, Cornets and Guns*" (*Rare Triumphs*, 1523–4), "*a health to the good success of the Mary: which must be Continued with shooting of guns to the last man: which orderly discharged will be about eleven or thirteen guns*" (*Launching of the Mary*, 2794–8); as practicality would suggest and these plays confirm, *chambers* were shot off in outdoor theatres; an apparent exception is "*Chambers shot off*" in *Revenge of Bussy* (4.1.10), an indoor theatre play; see also **ordnance**.

change

one **round** or figure of a **dance**, as in "*Dance the first change*" (*Broken Heart*, 5.2.12, also 15), "*dance together sundry changes*" (*Love's Sacrifice*, 1849); see also

Malcontent, 5.5.85; *Henry VIII*, 2647, 2651, 4.2.82; *Soddered Citizen*, 1917; *change* is the source of puns about changing sexual partners in *Insatiate Countess* when "*They take the women, and dance the first change*" then "*The second change. Isabella falls in love with [Guido] when the changers speak*" (2.1.79, 105, also 148); see also *Satiromastix*, 2.1.135, 140.

charge

most often denotes an offstage **sound** – a military signal usually played on a **trumpet** – but can also refer to an onstage action of **attack**; calls for the sound from **within** include "*A charge sounded*" (Folio *Richard II*, 413, 1.3.117), "*Trumpets sound as to a charge*" (*Two Noble Kinsmen*, M1r, 5.3.55), "*A charge with a peal of Ordnance*" (*Devil's Charter*, I1v), "*Charges and shouts*" (*White Devil*, 5.3.0), "*Charge Trumpets and shot within*" (*Double Marriage*, 343); see also *Edward I*, 2207; *Jew of Malta*, 2346; *Thracian Wonder*, G3r; *Birth of Merlin*, C3r; *Maid of Honour*, 2.5.0; *Osmond*, A2r; *King John and Matilda*, 26, 27, 44, 80; *Seven Champions*, E3v; *Claracilla*, D2v; *Fool Would Be a Favourite*, C7v; *Sophonisba* calls for a quieter instrument: "*The cornets afar off sounding a charge*" (5.3.0, also 2.2.0, 5.2.43); an onstage action is implied in "*Brennoralt charges through*" (*Brennoralt*, 1.2.27), "*Virgilius charges him*" (*Princess*, H2r), "*The King charges*" (*Prisoners*, B10v); one direction refers to loading a **weapon**: "*charging a Pistol*" (*Jack Drum's Entertainment*, H1v).

chariot

a large property **drawn** onto the **stage**, usually carrying a victor in **battle**: "*Captains with Laurels, Domitian, in his Triumphant Chariot*" (*Roman Actor*, 1.4.13), "*Matilda (a wreath of laurel on her head, in her chariot drawn through them)*" (*Bashful Lover*, 4.3.68); particularly well known is Tamburlaine's entrance "*drawn in his chariot by Trebizon and Soria with bits in their mouths, reins in his left hand, in his right hand a whip, with which he scourgeth them*" (*2 Tamburlaine*, 3979; see also *Wounds of Civil War*, 1070–1, 1074); variations include "*Enter Pluto, his Chariot drawn in by Devils*" (*Silver Age*, 135) and as part of a **masque** "*Cupid and the Graces ascend in the Chariot*" (*Wife for a Month*, 26); *Four Plays in One* provides four **triumphs**, each climaxing with chariots "*drawn by two Moors,*" "*drawn by two Cupids, and a Cupid sitting in it,*" "*with Death drawn by the Destinies,*" "*with the person of Time sitting in it, drawn by four persons, representing Hours, singing*" (311, 334, 355, 363); see also *Battle of Alcazar*, 212; *Captain Thomas Stukeley*, 2493–4, 2509;

Henslowe's inventory includes "Phaeton's chariot" (*Diary*, App. 2, 66).

charm, charmed

cast a spell or be spellbound in plays with supernatural figures and related stage business: "*draws, and is charmed from moving*" and "*all enter the circle which Prospero had made, and there stand charmed*" (*Tempest*, 623, 1.2.467; 2011–13, 5.1.57), "*charms him dumb*" (*Doctor Faustus*, B 1758), "*Charms him with his rod asleep*" (*Cobbler's Prophecy*, 137, also 91), "*Witches charm together*" (*Late Lancashire Witches*, 256); see also *Orlando Furioso*, 1252–3; *Faithful Shepherdess*, 408; *Witch*, 1998; *Two Noble Ladies*, 1899; *Love's Mistress*, 152.

chase

usually appears as a verb equivalent to **pursue**: "*chasing the Protestants*" (*Massacre at Paris*, 339), "*Mumford must chase Cambria away*" (*King Leir*, 2614–15), "*chaseth them off the Stage*" (*Honest Man's Fortune*, 234), "*let young Marius chase Pompey over the stage, and old Marius chase Lucretius*" (*Wounds of Civil War*, 333–4); see also *Trial of Chivalry*, I1v, I2v; *chase/pursue* are sometimes interchangeable, as seen in *1 Troublesome Reign* where "*The Bastard pursues Austria*" but earlier "*The Bastard chaseth Limoges*" (E2r, C4r) and *Captain Thomas Stukeley* where in the same direction Stukeley *pursues* two Irishman and then is **rescued** by his **followers** who "*chase the Irish out*" (1171–3); *chase* as *pursuit* can appear as a noun, as when the British flee and the Romans enter "*upon the chase*" (MS *Bonduca*, 1654) with their leader saying "soft, soft, pursue it soft"; once *in the chase* signals **hunting** (*Golden Age*, 32).

cheek

the few uses are linked to (1) cosmetics/facial **color**, (2) a **kiss**; after bringing on cosmetics a servant "*rubs his cheek with the colors*" (*1 Honest Whore*, 2.1.0), and as part of an application of cosmetics that proves poisonous a servant "*rubbeth her cheeks with a cloth*" (*Devil's Charter*, H1v); in a **masque** the West Wind has "*one cheek red and another white*" (*No Wit*, 4.3.148); in *Devil's Charter* a figure "*being presented unto the Pope, kisseth his foot, and then advancing two degrees higher, kisseth his cheek*" (E1r).

chess, chessboard

a seldom cited game: "*Here Prospero discovers Ferdinand and Miranda, playing at Chess*" (*Tempest*, 2141–2, 5.1.171), "*Table and Chess*" (*Women Beware Women*, 2.2.203), "*Chessboard and men set ready*" and "*Play at chess*" (*Spanish Curate*, 102/501, 106), "*Table, Chessboard, and Tapers*" (Q2 *Bussy D'Ambois*, 1.2.0), "*sets down a Chessboard*" (*Love's Sacrifice*, 1125).

chest

(1) a container for **money** or **treasure** but also (2) an alternative to **trunk** and large enough to conceal a person; examples include "*the chest or trunk to be brought forth*" (*Dead Man's Fortune*, 66), "*A chest brought in*" (*Roman Actor*, 2.1.330), "*Enter Jaques, Pedro, and Porters, with Chest and Hampers*" (*Woman's Prize*, 83); the use of a *chest* for concealment is best seen in an extended sequence in *Wits*: "*They draw in a chest*," "*He enters the chest*," "*knocks at the chest*," "*Opens a wicket at the end of the chest*," "*Exeunt, carrying out the chest*," "*opens the chest and lets him out*" (189–90, 194, 197, 206, 212–14).

chime

probably an abbreviation of "bell chimes" – small **bells** arranged by size, suspended on a bar, and played with a hammer; Henslowe's inventory lists a "chime of bells" (*Diary*, App. 2, 59); each signal is for a **sound** to accompany a supernatural event; the *John of Bordeaux* manuscript has "*here a Chime*" at Bacon's call to Morpheus to charm the Emperor asleep and later "*Chime*" at the entry of a "spirit" (436–7, 652); similarly in *John a Kent* "*Music Chime*" is signaled as figures are charmed to sleep (1138; also 1145–8), and later when others depart under a spell "*The Chime plays, and Gosselen with the Countess goes turning out*" (1158; also 1161, 1164); in *Merry Devil of Edmonton* the Prologue describes Fabell with "His fatal chime prepared at his head" and as the action begins "*The Chime goes*" (A3v), he asks "What means the tolling of this fatal chime?" and a devil enters.

choir

a rarely called for group of singers for a **ceremony**: "*The choir and music: the friars make a Lane with ducks and obeisance*" (*Captives*, 879–83), "*A choir within and without*" (*Arraignment of Paris*, 167); see also *Jews' Tragedy*, 2147–8; *Love's Sacrifice*, 1820.

choler

see **anger**

chorus

(1) usually the designation for a figure, elsewhere called a **presenter**, who gives a narrative summary of

events but (2) occasionally a group of singers; most often the *chorus* is an expedient method of presenting plot information that would be difficult or time-consuming to stage, as in *David and Bethsabe*, 551, 1573; Folio *Henry V*, 462, 2.Chorus.o; 1044, 3.Chorus.o; *Thomas Lord Cromwell*, B1v, D1v, D3v; *Philotas*, B8r, C5r, D4v, E8r; *1 Fair Maid of the West*, 319; *Seven Champions*, F2v; the *chorus* is called Time in *Winter's Tale*, 1579, 4.1.0, and also in *Tom a Lincoln* where he explicates a *dumb show* (1006, 1113, 1681, 2846); a *chorus* figure also introduces or explains a dumb show in *Captain Thomas Stukeley*, 2418; *Thracian Wonder*, B4v; *Travels of Three English Brothers*, 348, 350; *2 Fair Maid of the West*, 386; *Christian Turned Turk*, F2v; *Valiant Welshman*, C4v, G3v; *Prophetess*, 362; *Bloody Banquet*, 19, 860; sometimes *chorus* is the term for a segment in which more than one figure comments on the action (*Soliman and Perseda*, C3r, E2r, F2r, G3r, I2r; *James IV*, 1922; *Magnetic Lady*, end of each act); groups include "Chorus of shepherds and shepherdesses" (*Shepherds' Holiday*, 403), "Chorus of Swains" (*Amyntas*, 2B2v), "Chorus of Musicians" (*Sejanus*, 1.581, 2.500, 3.749, 4.523), "Chorus Juvenum cantantes et saltantes" (*May Day*, 1.1.0); for similar examples see *1 Tamar Cham*, 3, 24, 44, 73, 91; *Sophonisba*, 1.2.42, 57, 62; *City Madam*, 5.3.42; see also *prologue*.

circle

occurs as noun and verb, usually in a supernatural context: "Here do the Ceremonies belonging, and make the Circle, Bullingbrooke or Southwell reads, Conjuro te etc." (Folio *2 Henry VI*, 643–5, 1.4.22), "all enter the circle which Prospero had made and there stand charmed" (*Tempest*, 2011–13, 5.1.57), "another Circle, into which (after semblance of reading with exorcisms) appear exhalations of lightning and sulphurous smoke in the midst whereof a devil" (*Devil's Charter*, A2v, also G1v); in *Bartholomew Fair* the game of vapors involves the drawing of "a circle on the ground" (4.4.136); directions describing an action include "They circle Posthumus round as he lies sleeping" (*Cymbeline*, 3071, 5.4.29), "Enter Persephone with the three furies, they Circle him about" (*Jews' Tragedy*, 2381); see also *Devil's Charter*, A2v; *Prophetess*, 363; *Variety*, D9r.

city

this *fictional* term probably designates the tiring-house wall and *doors* when Coriolanus and soldiers are located "as before the City Corioles," then "They fight, and all enter the city" (*Coriolanus*, 478–80, 1.4.0;

568, 1.4.62); see also *1 Iron Age*, 302; elsewhere a "plot" or map is called for: "with a paper in his hand, drawing the platform of the city" (*Dido*, 1408), and Henslowe's inventory lists "the city of Rome" (*Diary*, App. 2, 62).

clamor

the contexts of the three occurrences indicate a loud and cacophonous *noise* produced *within*: "A clamor of ravens" (*Edward III*, H4r), "Within a clamor" (*Honest Man's Fortune*, 226), "shrieks and clamors are heard within" (*2 Iron Age*, 394).

clap

(1) found in several locutions as a verb but (2) less common as a noun; to take someone into custody the figure in authority *claps* the individual "on the shoulder" (*2 Edward IV*, 123; *Great Duke of Florence*, 4.1.43; *Lady Mother*, 1302), with a *devil* sometimes doing the *clapping* (*Mad World*, 4.1.29; *New Trick*, 270); *clapping* is also linked to the *shutting* of a *window* (*Blurt*, 4.1.68) or *door*: "Claps to the door" (Quarto *Every Man In*, 5.1.15), "Enter Fallace running, at another door, and claps it to" (Quarto *Every Man Out*, 2724), "noise of clapping a door" (*Picture*, 4.2.130); other usages include "Claps his Sword over the Table" (*Amends for Ladies*, 3.4.54–5), "claps his hands" to strike a *blow* (*Soddered Citizen*, 1759–60), "Clap hands" to confirm a wager (*Herod and Antipater*, C1r); for a special effect "Enter Ariel (like a Harpy) claps his wings upon the Table, and with a quaint device the Banquet vanishes" (*Tempest*, 1583–5, 3.3.52); as a noun, *clap* is found only in "a sudden Thunderclap" (*Captain Thomas Stukeley*, 2456–7; see also *Faithful Friends*, 2833) and a figure who enters "very poorly a begging, with her basket and a clap-dish" (*2 Edward IV*, 169).

clear

a bookkeeper's signal to *clear* the *stage* found in three playtexts: *Captives*, 293, 1248, 1428, 1719, 2464–5, 2573–4, 2724, 2826, and more; *King and No King*, 216, 222; and the annotated quarto of *Looking Glass for London*, A4r, A4v, B1v, and throughout.

climb

a seldom used verb most often linked to a *tree*, as when a figure "climbs the tree" (*Fawn*, 5.0) or "Climbs up" (*Old Fortunatus*, 4.1.75) on "apple trees"; for similar stage business see *Thracian Wonder*, D1r; *Duchess of Suffolk*, H1r; *Honest Lawyer*, I2r; elsewhere a figure *climbs* a *rock* (MS *Bonduca*, 2567–8; *Love's*

Mistress, 100) and **walls** (*Four Prentices*, 234); in
Downfall of Huntingdon a figure "*offers to climb*" a **rope**
suspended as a noose (2435).

cloak

a basic item of costume cited in a variety of contexts
(roughly sixty-five examples); figures appear "*in
mourning cloaks*" (2 *Henry VI*, D2r, 1169–70, 2.4.0;
Selimus, 1748), "*in a Livery cloak*" (*Trick to Catch the Old
One*, H1v), "*in his cloak and broom man's attire*"
(*Gentleman Usher*, 2.2.129), "*in a whitish cloak, new come
up out of the country*" (*Michaelmas Term*, Induction.0);
cloaks can be associated with journeys/arrivals so
that entrances include "*the men booted, the gentlewomen in cloaks and safeguards*" (*Merry Devil of
Edmonton*, B1r), "*Jane, in haste, in her riding cloak and
safeguard, with a pardon in her hand*" (2 *Edward IV*, 139);
cloaks are worn by actors presenting **prologues**/epi-
logues: **enter** "*in a cloak for the prologue*" (*Rebellion*, 91;
see also *Antonio and Mellida*, Induction.0), "*Enter three
in black cloaks, at three doors*" as a prologue (*Four
Prentices*, 165), "*Captain puts on his Cloak*" to speak the
Epilogue and two women "*pull him by the cloak*"
(*Parson's Wedding*, 533); *cloaks* are regularly linked to
swords/rapiers (*Woodstock*, 5; *Eastward Ho*, B4r; *Knight
of Malta*, 155; *Match Me in London*, 3.1.12; *Country
Captain*, C5v; *Dick of Devonshire*, 1288–90; *Mad Couple*,
38; *Parson's Wedding*, 495) and swordplay: "*puts off her
cloak and draws*" (*Roaring Girl*, 3.1.54), "*his sword in his
hand, a Cloak on his Arm*" and "*draws and wraps his
Cloak about his arm*" (*Dick of Devonshire*, 715, 772–4),
"*throws his cloak on the other's point; gets within him and
takes away his sword*" (*Bride*, 36); also linked to *cloaks*
are **hats**: "*Cloaks and Hats brought in*" (*Antipodes*, 263;
see also *What You Will*, D3r), "*meets them with the
Prince's cloak and hat*" (*When You See Me*, 1773–4), "*puts
on Hat, Feather, and Cloak*" (*Queen's Exchange*, 529; see
also *Antipodes*, 295).

For examples of actions, signals call for the dis-
position of *cloaks* such as **putting** on (*Two Lamentable
Tragedies*, F3v), **pulling** off (*King Leir*, 2018; *Court
Beggar*, 268), "*Throws off his cloak*" (*Renegado*, 3.5.50;
Wasp, 1072), "*lays down his Cloak*" (*Soddered Citizen*,
1361–2), "*steal away their cloaks*" (*New Wonder*, 124),
enter "*running with Cocledemoy's cloak*" and "*leaving
his cloak behind him*" (*Dutch Courtesan*, 4.5.37, 4.5.20);
for examples of concealment/**disguise**, **plate**,
swords, a **racket**, and **pictures** are hidden *under a cloak*
(*Bride*, 21; *Court Beggar*, 245; *Eastward Ho*, A2r;
Satiromastix, 5.2.158), and figures "*shift cloaks*" (*Fine
Companion*, G3r), appear "*in their petticoats, cloaks over*

them, with hats over their headtires" (*Gentleman Usher*,
2.1.153), most commonly "*muffled in his cloak*" (*May
Day*, 3.3.145; *Second Maiden's Tragedy*, 589–91; *Look
about You*, 1810; *Faithful Friends*, 2837–8; *Goblins*,
4.3.35); typical is "*muffled in a cloak steals off the Stage*"
(*Maid's Revenge*, F1v); see also *Thomas Lord Cromwell*,
C4v; *Lost Lady*, 593; other actions include "*a prentice
brushing his Master's cloak and Cap*" (*Westward Ho*,
2.1.0), "*gently casts his Cloak about her*" (*Soddered
Citizen*, 1304–6), "*cuts off the Cutpurse's ear, for cutting
of the gold buttons off his cloak*" (*Massacre at Paris*, 622),
"*in Alphonso's clothes*" and "*trying several ways to wear
his cloak and hat*" (*Twins*, E1v); for other *cloaks* see
Three Lords of London, D4r; *Two Lamentable Tragedies*,
D3v; *Warning for Fair Women*, D2v; *Greene's Tu Quoque*,
H1r, L4r; *Satiromastix*, 2.2.0; *Amends for Ladies*,
4.1.144; *If This Be Not a Good Play*, 4.4.0; *Loyal Subject*,
148; *Weeding of Covent Garden*, 57; Henslowe's inventory provides a number of *cloaks* (see especially
Diary, App. 2, 115–19, 124–8) that include "one red
cloak with white copper lace" (115), "one short cloak
of black satin with sleeves" (118), "one red scarlet
cloak with silver buttons" (132), "one long black
velvet cloak" (133).

clock

always occurs with the verb **strikes**, sometimes with
a number, to call for **sound** produced **within** to simulate a bell-tower *clock*: "*Clock strikes*" (*Cymbeline*,
958, 2.2.50), "*The clock strikes twelve*" (*Atheist's Tragedy*,
4.3.0); see also *Looking Glass for London*, 337; *Richard
III*, M2r, 3743, 5.3.275; *Twelfth Night*, 1344, 3.1.129;
Julius Caesar, 826, 2.1.191; *Devil's Charter*, F3v;
Christian Turned Turk, F3v; *Roaring Girl*, 3.1.27;
Changeling, 5.1.0, 11, 67.

close

an elastic term that can vary widely in meaning as a
noun, verb, adjective, or adverb; *close* as **end** appears
rarely as a noun and verb: "*Toward the close of the
music*" (*Phoenix*, F3r), "*closes with this Song below*" (*More
Dissemblers*, B8r); *close* as **shut** appears in "*close the
Tent*" (*Edward I*, 1517, 1686), "*close the curtains*"
(*Sophonisba*, 1.2.32; see also *Mad Lover*, 59, *Parson's
Wedding*, 495), **dancers** who "*close Ferentes in*" (*Love's
Sacrifice*, 1850); *close* as "secret, apart" appears in "*close
in conference*" (*Devil's Charter*, A2r), "*sits close a while*"
(*David and Bethsabe*, 1826, 1842), "*in close mourning*"
(*Albovine*, 83), "*stealing from them closely away*"
(*Selimus*, 2079–80); examples of *close* as near include
"*close by*" (*Virgin Martyr*, 2.3.133), "*a suit of Leather close*

to his body" (*Grim the Collier*, I2r), two who "*sit close to keep out*" a third (*Herod and Antipater*, F3v), but this usage is sometimes hard to distinguish from *secret*, as in such locutions as **stand** *close* (*May Day*, 3.3.199; *Revenge of Bussy*, 5.1.32; *Mad Lover*, 47; *Claracilla*, F9v), **follow** *closely* (*All Fools*, 3.1.0; *Gentleman Usher*, 2.1.0; *Revenge of Bussy*, 3.4.0), enter "*closely observing their drunkenness*" (*Atheist's Tragedy*, 2.2.17, also 4.4.14); *close* as a verb meaning "draw near" ("*meets Maria and closeth with her; the rest fall back*," *Malcontent*, 5.5.0) is found regularly in Caroline **fight** scenes: "*They fight, and close*" (*Cardinal*, 4.3.75; *Goblins*, 1.1.82, 2.3.15), "*closes with, and disarms him*" (*City Wit*, 360), "*They draw, fight, close*" (*Cruel Brother*, 125); see also *Lovesick Court*, 142; *Swisser*, 5.2.117; *Twins*, D2v; *Princess*, I1v; also found occasionally are verbs such as *enclose* ("*The Rock encloses him*," *Birth of Merlin*, G2v) and *disclose* (to **discover** one's identity, take off a **disguise**) so that figures *disclose* (*Country Girl*, K1r), *disclose* themselves (*Four Prentices*, 176; *Valiant Welshman*, D3r; *Obstinate Lady*, F1r); atypical are dancers "*At every close, expressing a cheerful Adoration of their Gods*" (*Amorous War*, E2v).

closet

of the six uses four probably refer to a **door** in the tiring-house wall: "*A closet discovered*" (*Atheist's Tragedy*, 5.1.0), "*locks him into a closet*" (*Devil's Law Case*, 5.4.167; see also *Goblins*, 2.6.6), "*Anvile out of the Closet*" (*Northern Lass*, 33), and two may be **fictional**: "*Enter Lord Cardinal in his Closet*" (*More Dissemblers*, B2r), "*Antonio disguised, sitting in a closet*" (*Rebellion*, 51).

cloth

used for (1) *tablecloth*, (2) *sackcloth* for **mourning** or penitence, (3) the *cloth of state*, (4) a variety of other *cloths*; for *tablecloths*, figures enter "*laying a Cloth*" (*2 Troublesome Reign*, E1v), "*bringing in cloth and napkins*" (*Humorous Day's Mirth*, 3.1.0), with "*a Tablecloth, Bread, Trenchers and salt*" (*Woman Killed*, 132, also 117; see also *Friar Bacon*, 1325), simply "*with a Tablecloth*" (*Thracian Wonder*, C4v); *Spanish Curate* calls for "*A Table ready covered with Cloth Napkins Salt Trenchers and Bread*" (129/501); signals for mourning/penitence are "*sits him down in sackclothes, his hands and eyes reared to heaven*" (*Looking Glass for London*, 2078–9, also 2105), "*Pericles makes lamentation, puts on sackcloth*" (*Pericles*, G3r, 4.4.22; see also *Emperor of the East*, 5.3.0); other directions include "*The King takes place under the Cloth of State*" (*Henry*

VIII, 1343–4, 2.4.0), "*rubbeth her cheeks with a cloth*" (*Devil's Charter*, H1v), "*a Piece of painted Cloth, like a Herald's Coat*" (*Thracian Wonder*, G1r), "*some relief in a cloth for mistress Shore*" (*2 Edward IV*, 166), "*Ely, with a yard in his hand, and linen cloth, dressed like a woman*" (*Downfall of Huntingdon*, 1111–12); see also *Michaelmas Term*, 2.3.355; Henslowe's inventory includes "the cloth of the Sun and Moon" (*Diary*, App. 2, 72), "one pair of French hose, cloth of gold" (111, also 112), "one woman's gown of cloth of gold" (167).

clothes, clothed

found in a variety of locutions: "*anticly attired in brave Clothes*" (*Thracian Wonder*, F2v), "*A bed thrust out: Lodovico sleeping in his clothes*" (*City Nightcap*, 111), "*fantastically clothed in Dondolo's habit*" (*Just Italian*, 280), "*new and richly clothed, buttoning themselves*" (*Wits*, 130, also 151, 179); figures appear "*in new clothes*" (*Albovine*, 93), "*in his Pilgrim's clothes*" (*Alphonsus of Aragon*, 1911–12), "*in woman's clothes*" (*Sparagus Garden*, 208; *Antiquary*, 503; *Hollander*, 141), "*in disguised clothes*" (*Hollander*, 131), "*in riding clothes*" (*Variety*, C2r), and *clothed* "*in white*" (*Unfortunate Lovers*, 24), "*in a robe spotted with Stars*" (*Whore of Babylon*, DS before Act 1, 37–8); figures **enter** with clothes (*Night Walker*, 362; *Constant Maid*, E2v), "*a flasket of clothes*" (*Dead Man's Fortune*, 46–7), "*bloody clothes*" (*Battle of Alcazar* plot, 101), "*rich clothes*" (*Hoffman*, 1930), "*very brave, with Jarvis's clothes in his hand*" (*Match at Midnight*, 54); one locution directs X to appear in Y's *clothes*: "*Zanthia, in Corsica's Clothes*" (*Bondman*, 3.3.0), "*Alphonso in the Orator's clothes*" (*Dumb Knight*, 182); see also *Twins*, E1v, F3r; *Constant Maid*, E4r; *Tottenham Court*, 125; references to **night**-clothes include "*pass over the Stage with Pillows, Nightclothes, and such things*" (*Little French Lawyer*, 416), "*in her nightclothes, as going to bed*" (*Match at Midnight*, 77; see also *Parson's Wedding*, 387, 494); actions include "*Tailor sets his clothes*" (*Fatal Dowry*, 4.1.0), "*rich clothes are put about him*" (*Four Prentices*, 177), "*Moll above lacing of her clothes*" (*Puritan*, H2r), "*Beadle put off his clothes*" (*Three Ladies of London*, F2r), "*as it were brushing the Crumbs from his clothes with a Napkin*" (*Woman Killed*, 118), "*they fly, leaving their Clothes behind*" (*1 Henry VI*, 766, 2.1.77), Falstaff "*goes into the basket, they put clothes over him*" (*Quarto Merry Wives*, E1v, 3.3.142); see also *Woman in the Moon*, A2v; *Wedding*, H3r; *Goblins*, 3.7.58; *Amorous War*, H2r; *clothe* occasionally appears as a transitive verb: "*they clothe Francisco*" (*What You Will*, D3r), "*help to unclothe him*" (*Wits*, 160, also 164).

cloud

probably a property located in the upper regions of the tiring house/**heavens** that could be attached to descent machinery: "*Cupid descending in a cloud*" (*Love's Mistress*, 87), "*Jupiter descends in a cloud*" and "*ascends in his cloud*" (*Silver Age*, 98, 155); figures who appear "*in an Arch-glittering Cloud aloft*" (*Messalina*, 2208–9) later descend, and "*Air comes down hanging by a cloud*" (*No Wit*, 4.3.40); *Silver Age* provides figures **above** "*in a cloud*" (130, 152); elsewhere "*from the heavens descends a hand in a cloud*" (*Brazen Age*, 254), and "*A hand from out a cloud, threateneth a burning sword*" (*Looking Glass for London*, 1636); that a painted **curtain** was sometimes used is suggested by "*One half of a cloud drawn. Singers are discovered: then the other half drawn. Jupiter seen in glory*" (*Four Plays in One*, 363).

club

a property used for actual or threatened violence, usually by commoners: "*three or four Citizens with Clubs or partisans*" (Q2 *Romeo and Juliet*, A4r, 1.1.72), "*a Company of Mutinous Citizens, with Staves, Clubs, and other weapons*" (*Coriolanus*, 2–3, 1.1.0), "*two Vintner's boys, with Clubs*" (*Miseries of Enforced Marriage*, 1349–50), "*Townsmen with clubs*" (*Sir John Oldcastle*, 31, also 56); see also *Ram Alley*, E3r; *Tom a Lincoln*, 941; atypical examples are "*Spirits with fiery Clubs*" and "*The Giant in a maze lets fall his Club*" (*Seven Champions*, G3v, I4r); see also *Silver Age*, 159; for the *club* of Hercules see *Locrine*, 1354–5; *Brazen Age*, 254; Henslowe's inventory lists "three clubs" (*Diary*, App. 2, 61).

coals

cited occasionally as fuel along with **wood** and **logs**: "*Janicola and Babulo carrying coals, Laureo with wood, Grissil with wood*" (*Patient Grissil*, 5.2.51), "*Servingman with Logs and Coals*" (Q1 *Romeo and Juliet*, I1r, [4.4.13]); Mephostophilis brings Faustus "*a chafer of coals*" to make his congealed **blood** flow (*Doctor Faustus*, A 510), and *coals* form part of the preparation for **conjuring** in *Devil's Charter*, G1v; atypical is "*a Ghost, coal-black*" (*If This Be Not a Good Play*, 5.4.261), a Puritan in **hell** who has been "smoked out of our own Country."

coat

a distinctive item of clothing often linked to rank or profession: "*a Farmer's long coat*" (*Three Ladies of London*, A2v), "*in canvas coats like Sailors*" (*Three Lords of London*, F3r), "*in a tawny coat like a tinker*" (*Two Maids of More-Clacke*, C3v), "*in a fool's coat*" (*Antiquary*, 502; *City Wit*, 367), "*with a Piece of painted Cloth, like a Herald's Coat*" (*Thracian Wonder*, G1r; see also *Perkin Warbeck*, 4.1.19), "*in his prentice's Coat and Cap*" (*Eastward Ho*, B4r), Mayor and citizens "*in their velvet coats*" (*1 Edward IV*, 11; see also *Shoemakers' Holiday*, 2.3.93); servants or members of a retinue appear in **tawny** coats (*Grim the Collier*, G5v), "*livery coats*" (*Sir John Oldcastle*, 1962; *Histriomastix*, C2v), most commonly **blue** coats (*Taming of a Shrew*, B2r; *Two Maids of More-Clacke*, B4r, C3r; *Wonder of a Kingdom*, 4.2.0); typical are "*Winchester and his men in Tawny Coats*" (*1 Henry VI*, 391–2, 1.3.28), "*servingmen with blue Coats to attend him*" (*Wise Woman of Hogsdon*, 340), "*in his lord's attire with Bluecoats after him*" (*Edmond Ironside*, 1243–4), "*like a lord with his comrades in blue coats*" (*Mad World*, 2.1.82); other distinctive *coats* include "*a Florentine soldier's coat*" (*Bashful Lover*, 2.7.0), "*black scurvy mourning coats*" (*Puritan*, B2v; see also *Case Is Altered*, 1.3.0), a **devil** with "*a skin coat all speckled on the throat*" (*Caesar and Pompey*, 2.1.24), "*every man with his red Cross on his coat*" (*Edward I*, 40), "*a coat made like an almanac*" in a **masque** (*No Wit*, 4.3.40), heralds' *coats* "*having the arms of London before, and an Olive tree behind*" and "*the arms of Spain before, and a burning ship behind*" (*Three Lords of London*, F4r, G1v); actions include "*offers to lay his Coat under the king*" (*Valiant Scot*, H3v), "*Pulls the coats up, and shows the breeches*" to demonstrate a she is really a he (*City Wit*, 371), "*takes up the child by the skirts of his long coat in one hand and draws his dagger with the other*" (*Yorkshire Tragedy*, 506–8); a traitor enters "*with his coat turned*" (*David and Bethsabe*, 1083), and the comforter of a shipwrecked figure "*puts off his Hat and Coat, and puts on him*" (*Thracian Wonder*, B4v; see also *Knave in Grain*, 2276); for other *coats* see *Orlando Furioso*, 442; *Charlemagne*, 2025; *Thracian Wonder*, C4v; *1 If You Know Not Me*, 209; *Queen and Concubine*, 34; *Parson's Wedding*, 410, 480; for a *coat of* **arms** see *Edward II*, 1459; *Caesar and Pompey*, 3.2.107; Henslowe's inventory provides a number of *coats* that includes "six green coats for Robin Hood" (*Diary*, App. 2, 21), "three soldiers' coats" (20), "two leather antics' coats" (52), "one black satin coat" (103), "Juno's coat" (122), "Tamburlaine's coat with copper lace" (115).

cock

the few references are (1) an offstage **sound**, "*The cock crows*" (Q2 *Hamlet*, B3r, 1.1.139), (2) an unusual action in which Mars transforms a figure into a *cock*: "*Gallus sinks, and in his place riseth a Cock and crows*"

(*Brazen Age*, 231, also 233), (3) soldiers in a late Caroline play who enter with "*Cockfeathers in their Hats*" (*Amorous War*, F2r).

coffin

called for in *funeral*, *mourning*, and *execution* scenes: "*they put the body of young Aire into a Coffin, and then he sits down on the one side of it, and she on the other*" (*2 Edward IV*, 183), "*the coffin of the Gentleman, solemnly decked, his sword upon it, attended by many in black, his brother being the chief mourner; at the other door the coffin of the virgin, with a garland of flowers, with epitaphs pinned on it*" (*Chaste Maid*, 5.4.0), "*the coffin set down, helm, sword, and streamers hung up, placed by the Herald, whilst Antonio and Maria wet their handkerchiefs with their tears, kiss them, and lay them on the hearse, kneeling*" (*Antonio's Revenge*, 2.1.0); occasionally *coffin* (like *drum*, *trumpet*, *halberd*) stands alone so that those *bearing* it are implied: a group enters "*after the coffin*" (Q1 *Hamlet*, I1v, [5.1.217]), "*The still flutes sound a mournful sennet. Enter a coffin*" (*Antonio and Mellida*, 5.2.208); but usually the bearers or process of carrying is specified: "*Petruchio borne in a Coffin*" (*Woman's Prize*, 87), "*Enter two bearing a Coffin, Jasper in it*" (*Knight of the Burning Pestle*, 216), "*Father with her in a Coffin*" (*Witch of Edmonton*, 4.2.142), "*Leonora, with two coffins borne by her servants, and two winding sheets stuck with flowers*" (*Devil's Law Case*, 5.4.125); *Titus Andronicus* provides a group "*bearing a Coffin covered with black*," "*set down the Coffin*," "*lay the Coffin in the Tomb*" (A4r–v, 1.1.69; B1v, 1.1.149); a *coffin* can be brought on in advance of an execution, as in signals for "*a Coffin and a Gibbet*" (*Barnavelt*, 2811–12), "*a coffin, cords and a bell*" (*Duchess of Malfi*, 4.2.165); actions include "*Pointing after the coffin*" (*Michaelmas Term*, 4.4.67), "*He rises out of the coffin*" (*Swisser*, 3.2.123), "*Heaves up the Coffin*" to show it is empty (*Knight of the Burning Pestle*, 227), "*Ero opens, and he sees her head laid on the coffin, etc.*" (*Widow's Tears*, 5.3.137), "*goes into the Coffin*" to fake a death and "*They see the Prince, throw down the Coffin, and run to kneel and embrace him*" (*Politician*, I3v, K1v); for more *coffins* see *Selimus*, 1257; *Richard II*, K1v, 5.6.29; Folio *Hamlet*, 3405–6, 5.1.217; *Puritan*, G4v; *Knight of the Burning Pestle*, 226; *Swisser*, 3.1.60, 137, 3.2.94; *Wedding*, I4r; *Politician*, K1v; Henslowe's inventory includes "two coffins" (*Diary*, App. 2, 83).

colors

(1) usually a *flag*, *ensign*, or *standard* of a regiment or ship called for in approximately 100 directions, (2)

occasionally *paint*; usually in the military context the phrase is *drum* and *colors*, which can mean not only the instrument and property but also the players bringing them onstage; typically these items indicate readiness for *battle* and are part of a show of power: "*Fortinbras and English Ambassador, with Drum, Colors, and Attendants*" (Folio *Hamlet*, 3852–3, 5.2.361), "*Enter with Drum and Colors, Cordelia, Gentleman, and Soldiers*" (Folio *King Lear*, 2349–50, 4.4.0, also 2918, 5.2.0; 2938–9, 5.3.0), "*Ralph and his company with Drums and Colors*" (*Knight of the Burning Pestle*, 224), "*Enter at one door the Portugal army with drum and Colors*" (*Battle of Alcazar* plot, 78–9, also 103), "*Enter from wars with drums and Colors*" (*Travels of Three English Brothers*, 322); see also *Woodstock*, 2716–17, 2773–4; Folio *Titus Andronicus*, 5, 1.1.0; *1 Tamar Cham*, 103; Folio *2 Henry VI*, 2990–1, 5.1.0; Folio *3 Henry VI*, 2737, 5.1.57, and more; Folio *Richard III*, 3404–5, 5.2.0; *Four Prentices*, 200; Folio *Richard II*, 1359, 3.2.0; 1582, 3.3.0; Folio *Henry V*, 1534, 3.6.86; *Alarum for London*, 1609–10; *Thracian Wonder*, G2v; *Lust's Dominion*, 4.2.135; *All's Well*, 1695, 3.5.74; *Hieronimo*, 10.0, 30; *2 If You Know Not Me*, 337; *Macbeth*, 2174, 5.2.0; 2378, 5.6.0; *Rape of Lucrece*, 240; *Coriolanus*, 478–80, 1.4.0; 3734, 5.6.69; *Birth of Merlin*, G3v; *If This Be Not a Good Play*, L1r; *Bonduca*, 96; *Four Plays in One*, 293; *Hengist*, 2.3.8–12; *Faithful Friends*, 163–5; in *Two Noble Ladies* the bookkeeper twice added *drum and colors* (1644, 1911–12); a few directions call for *colors* only: "*the Lieutenant with Colors in his hand, pursuing three or four Soldiers*" (*Humorous Lieutenant*, 328, MS 1802–6), "*with colors and soldiers*" (*Valiant Welshman*, E1v, E2v), "*Flourish Colors*" (*Double Marriage*, 361); see also *Wounds of Civil War*, 334–5, 1070–1; *Vow Breaker*, 1.3.128; *Siege*, 429; in *1 Iron Age* the bodies of Hector and Achilles are accompanied by soldiers "*trailing the Colors on both sides*" (345), in *Loyal Subject* a figure with no more wars to fight enters "*carrying his armor piecemeal, his Colors wound up, and his Drums in Cases*" (83), and in *Faithful Friends* peace is signaled by figures with "*Olive Branches in their hands, Colors wrapt up, and slow march*" (2098–100); occasionally *colors* denotes paint: "*a pencil and colors*" (*Cobbler's Prophecy*, 736), "*several pots of colors*" (*Two Merry Milkmaids*, L4r), "*a vial with white color in it*," "*he rubs his cheek with the colors*," and as a verb "*colors her lips*" (*1 Honest Whore*, 2.1.0, 12).

combat

a one-on-one *fight* or duel, usually a noun: "*They fight a Combat, the Moor is struck down*" (*Lust's*

Dominion, 4.2.135), "*in this combat both having lost their swords and Shields, Hector takes up a great piece of a Rock, and casts it at Ajax*" (*1 Iron Age*, 300); in *Dumb Knight* one figure then another enters "*like a combatant,*" then "*the combat being fought, Philocles overcomes the Duke*" (195, 196); for more see *Devil's Law Case*, 5.6.16; *Seven Champions*, L1r; twice the term is a verb: "*Massinissa and Syphax combat. Syphax falls*" (*Sophonisba*, 5.2.43), "*They combat with javelins first, after with swords and targets*" (*Golden Age*, 51).

come

the roughly 200 examples include (1) most commonly entrances where figures are directed to *come in/out/forth/down/up/again* but also (2) actions in which figures *come to/near/after/behind/between/toward* others or *come forth/back*, (3) *come to* oneself (to recover from a *faint*); directions for figures to *enter* include *come up* (*Old Wives Tale*, 777; *If This Be Not a Good Play*, 1.1.49, 50, 53; *Queen's Exchange*, 536), *come down* (*Frederick and Basilea*, 36; Folio *Titus Andronicus*, 264, 1.1.233; Folio *3 Henry VI*, 233, 1.1.205; *Soliman and Perseda*, H4v; *Two Lamentable Tragedies*, C4v, I1v; *2 Edward IV*, 139; *Old Fortunatus*, 1.1.140; *Philaster*, 101/407; *Devil Is an Ass*, 2.7.28; *No Wit*, 4.3.40; *Tale of a Tub*, 1.1.22; *City Wit*, 362; *Claracilla*, F12v), *come out* (*Cobbler's Prophecy*, 1325; *1 Tamburlaine*, 663; *2 Tamburlaine*, 2921; *Locrine*, 434; *George a Greene*, 795; *Sir John Oldcastle*, 2210; *Old Fortunatus*, 1.1.63; *Merry Devil of Edmonton*, E3v; *Timon of Athens*, 1117–18, 3.4.0; *Epicœne*, 1.1.0; *Bartholomew Fair*, 2.5.59; *Jews' Tragedy*, 945–7, 1079–80; *City Match*, 310), most commonly *come in/forth* (*Summer's Last Will*, 420, 775, 967; *Edward I*, 1015, 2175; *Humorous Day's Mirth*, 4.2.26; *Old Fortunatus*, 4.1.111; *Hamlet*, Q2 H1v, Folio 1995, 3.2.135; *1 Honest Whore*, 2.1.117; *Poetaster*, 3.4.345; *Four Prentices*, 226; *Merry Devil of Edmonton*, B1r; *Miseries of Enforced Marriage*, 1351, 2289; *2 Iron Age*, 411; *White Devil*, 2.2.37; *Bartholomew Fair*, 2.3.43, 2.5.155, 4.1.67, 5.2.1; *World Tossed at Tennis*, D2r; *Martyred Soldier*, 242; *Staple of News*, 1.2.143; *Seven Champions*, C3r; *Andromana*, 209; *Arcadia*, E2r; *Hyde Park*, H1v; *Bride*, 50; *Parson's Wedding*, 402; *Princess*, C3r); for a sampling of *come* by itself see *Three Ladies of London*, F3r; Folio *3 Henry VI*, 1131, 2.4.11; *Two Lamentable Tragedies*, G1r; *Warning for Fair Women*, D1r; Folio *Every Man In*, 4.8.42; Quarto *Every Man Out*, 1122; *Merry Devil of Edmonton*, B2v; *Timon of Athens*, 340, 1.2.0; atypical is *come on* (*Sir John Oldcastle*, 423); detailed examples include "*goes in,*

and comes out again with all the rest" (*2 Tamburlaine*, 4507), "*run in, and come out again straight*" (*Three Ladies of London*, B1r), "*Musicians come down*" (*City Madam*, 5.1.7, also 3.1.4), "*let a chair come down from the top of the stage*" (*Alphonsus of Aragon*, 2109–10), "*He goes in at one door, and comes out at another*" (*English Traveller*, 69; *Spanish Tragedy*, 3.11.8).

For examples of actions, *come forth* can be directed either at those already onstage (*All Fools*, 1.1.345; *Epicœne*, 4.5.129, 298; *Alchemist*, 5.5.58, 90) or those who are to *enter* (*John a Kent*, 581; *Locrine*, 5–6, 432; Q2 *Romeo and Juliet*, C2v, 1.5.0; *Fair Maid of Bristow*, A3r; *Humour out of Breath*, 479; *Renegado*, 2.5.120; *Grateful Servant*, F4r; *Bride*, 34); of the various onstage actions most common are *come between* (*Fair Maid of Bristow*, C2v; *2 Iron Age*, 361; *Knave in Grain*, 1323–4), *come toward* (*Alphonsus of Aragon*, 192; Quarto *Every Man Out*, 1217; *Roaring Girl*, 3.1.155; *Soddered Citizen*, 1609; *Witty Fair One*, C2r); to *come again/back again* is usually to *re-enter* (*Humorous Day's Mirth*, 4.2.26; *Bartholomew Fair*, 2.3.43, 4.1.19, 47, 104; *Herod and Antipater*, F3v; *Andromana*, 211); for *come to* oneself see *Alchemist*, 4.5.77; *Aglaura*, 5.3.161.

compliment

(1) usually a noun or verb that requires some formal act of civility, courtesy, or respect but can mean (2) *complement* (the usual spelling), "accoutrement"; typical are "*The King and Queen with Courtly Compliments salute and part*" (*Noble Spanish Soldier*, 1.1.0), "*Enter Alphonso; Pynto and Muretto complimenting on either side of him*" (*Queen*, 1028–9), "*they embrace, making a mutual show of compliment*" (*Conspiracy*, G1v; see also *Anything for a Quiet Life*, E1v); *Love's Sacrifice* provides "*Exit Giacopo going backward with the glass, Maurucio complimenting*" and "*The women hold hands and dance about Ferentes in diverse complimental offers of Courtship*" (799–800, 1851–3); variations include "*After their salute. All the rest compliment as strangers*" (*2 Iron Age*, 406), "*They two stand, using seeming compliments*" (*Antonio and Mellida*, 1.1.115), "*Callow stroking up his hair, compliments with Faces and Legs*" (*Two Merry Milkmaids*, C3r), "*While they talk, Corbo and Douze are sometime dancing, sometime complimenting, and sometimes laughing to one another*" (*Twins*, D4r); see also *Two Maids of More-Clacke*, H2v; *2 Iron Age*, 411; *White Devil*, 2.2.37; *Noble Spanish Soldier*, 5.4.46; *Staple of News*, 2.5.77; *Perkin Warbeck*, 2.3.71; *Changes*, C1v; an example of the alternative meaning is enter "*with the complements of a Roman General before them*" (*Sophonisba*, 3.2.0).

conceal

a rarely used alternative to **hide**: "*conceals them behind the curtain*" (*Dutch Courtesan*, 5.1.13), "*conceals himself*" (*Woman Is a Weathercock*, 2.2.1–2).

conduct

a seldom used alternative to **lead**; figures are *conducted in* (*Edward I*, 927; *2 Iron Age*, 420) and are seen "*conducting the General and his Queen to their Lodging*" (*2 Iron Age*, 411); *as* [*if*] examples are entrances "*as Conducting the White to a Chamber*" (*Game at Chess*, 1941–3), "*march two and two, discoursing, as being conducted by them into the City*" (*1 Iron Age*, 302); see also *Lovesick King*, 140.

confer, conference

used regularly when onstage figures **consult** each other, often in a **dumb show** or **aside**; sometimes additional stage action is spelled out: "*All this while, she stands conferring privately with her Suitors, and looking on their bills*" (*1 Edward IV*, 82), "*draws near to the king, and having awhile conferred, at last retires to his soldiers*" (*Captain Thomas Stukeley*, 2452–3), "*Lawyers and others pass over the Stage as conferring by two and two*" (*Damoiselle*, 407); examples of *conferring* that take place *aside* include "*takes her aside. And that while the young men and maids court and confer at the other side*" (*New Academy*, 77), "*confer aside*" (*Old Fortunatus*, 3.1.240, 249; *Lovesick Court*, 92), and in a related action "*Walk and confer*" (*Challenge for Beauty*, 23); for a sampling of two or more figures who confer/**enter** conferring see *John a Kent*, 412–13; *Family of Love*, C1v; *1 If You Know Not Me*, 239; *Four Prentices*, 176; *Four Plays in One*, 326; *Costly Whore*, 237; *Jews' Tragedy*, 1103; *New Way to Pay*, 3.2.278; *Two Noble Ladies*, 616; *Dick of Devonshire*, 1615; *Court Beggar*, 268; *Queen's Exchange*, 530; *Cardinal*, 2.3.58; *News from Plymouth*, 195; in *Death of Huntingdon* "*All stand in Council*" is followed shortly by "*Again confer*" (2971, 2987); in a display of her linguistic skills Queen Elizabeth entertains the French and Florentine ambassadors and "*in their several languages confers with them*" (*2 If You Know Not Me*, 317); atypical are "*They confer their letters*" (*Sejanus*, 5.268), "*Bawd and Gabriel confer devoutly the while*" (*Weeding of Covent Garden*, 67); examples of the less common noun form include "*Landrey, and two or three insinuating Lords, busy in conference*" (*Fatal Contract*, B1v), enter "*betwixt two other Cardinals, Roderigo in his purple habit close in conference with them*" (*Devil's Charter*, A2r); other locutions include "*in private conference*" (*Weakest Goeth*, 1314; *Swetnam*, A1r; *Hengist*, DS before 2.2, 9–10), "*in conference with*" (*1 Henry VI*, 2820, 5.5.0), "*joins in conference with*" (*Novella*, 174); see also **whisper**.

confused

most often describes a **sound** produced **within** linked to various kinds of **noise**: "*a strange, hollow and confused noise*" (*Tempest*, 1808, 4.1.138, also 70, 1.1.60), "*Confused noise of betting within*" (*Hyde Park*, G4r), "*A confused noise within of laughing and singing*" (*Jovial Crew*, 386); see also *Michaelmas Term*, 4.3.0; *If This Be Not a Good Play*, 5.4.260; *Christian Turned Turk*, F2v; *Rebellion*, 41; signals for onstage actions include "*Enter confusedly*" (*No Wit*, 5.1.153), "*A confused fray with stools, cups and bowls*" (*Silver Age*, 142; see also *Golden Age*, 22; *Brazen Age*, 196; *Escapes of Jupiter*, 72), "*fight all in a confused manner*" (*Rebellion*, 33), "*books lying confusedly*" (*Satiromastix*, 1.2.0); see also *Histriomastix*, F3v, G1r; *2 Iron Age*, 361, 427; *Parson's Wedding*, 511.

conge

both as verb and noun an equivalent to **bow**, an act of courtesy/**obeisance** by men (as distinct from the **curtsy** by women); examples are "*he conges with great reverence and ceremony to the Queen*" (*Fatal Contract*, H4r), "*They pass with many strange Conges*" (*Silver Age*, 116), "*march over the stage, and conge to the King and Queen*" (*Rape of Lucrece*, 203); as part of an elaborate **ceremony** in *Thracian Wonder* "*The men all pass by the two old Shepherds with obeisance, Radagon last; as he makes Conge, they put the Crown upon his head*" (C4r–v); several directions set up comic/satiric effects: "*makes a conge or two to nothing*" (*Nice Valour*, 149), "*They all make ridiculous conges to Bianca: rank themselves, and dance in several postures*" (*Fair Maid of the Inn*, 175), a figure "*trying several ways to wear his cloak and hat, congeing to the Post as to a Gentlewoman, kissing her, and offering to lead her in gentle manner*" (*Twins*, E1v); see also *Escapes of Jupiter*, 2195–6; *Henry VIII*, 2646, 4.2.82; *Country Girl*, B2v.

conjure, conjurer

(1) the action of calling up supernatural figures or objects, (2) a figure, more commonly a **magician**, linked to supernatural events; examples of the action and its consequences include "*Bullingbrooke or Southwell reads, Conjuro te, etc. It Thunders and Lightens terribly: then the Spirit riseth*" (Folio *2 Henry VI*, 644–7, 1.4.22), "*Here Bungay conjures and the tree appears with the dragon shooting fire*" (*Friar Bacon*, 1197–8, also 291), "*she Conjures; and Enter a Cat (playing on a Fiddle) and*

Spirits (with Meat)" (*Witch*, 437–40); for similar locutions see *Doctor Faustus*, A 243; *Humorous Lieutenant*, 342, MS 2328; *Devil's Charter*, A2v; the figure is specified in one set of signals: "*Enter the Conjurer; it lightens and thunders*" and "*Enter the Conjurer, and strike Corebus blind*" (*Old Wives Tale*, 415, 559, also 629, 803), but typically the term describes a **habit**: "*one in the habit of a Conjurer*" (*White Devil*, 2.2.0; see also *Wizard*, 2305), "*in the strange habit of a Conjuress*" (*Brazen Age*, 217); see also *Maid's Revenge*, E3v; other locutions similarly imply specific garb: "*in a conjuring robe*" (*Bussy D'Ambois*, 4.2.7), "*like a Conjurer*" (*Changes*, K2r), "*disguised as a Conjurer*" (*Wizard*, 2456, also 2541).

consort

denotes either a "whole consort" – several instruments of the same family, or a "broken consort" – instruments of different families, string and wind; on the few occasions when *consort* is used, neither directions nor dialogue specify the instruments: "*A strain played by the consort*" (*Mad World*, 2.1.143), "*Consort a Lesson*" (*Thracian Wonder*, D1v), "*Consort of Music*" (*Fawn*, 1.2.102); see also *John a Kent*, 554; in *Fedele and Fortunio* the *consort* plays at the end of each act (387–8, 863–4, 1095–6, 1487–8, 1807–8); *Virgin Martyr* provides "*Consort, enter Angelo with a Basket filled with fruit and flowers*," then "*Music*" (5.1.38, 45) which signals the entrance of a spirit (Angelo) and the visited figure seems to locate the music *above*: "'*tis in the Air, / Or from some better place.*"

consult

an alternative to the more widely used **confer**; three conspirators enter "*as in a chamber, and sit down at a table, consulting about their treason: King Harry and Suffolk listening at the door*" (*Sir John Oldcastle*, 2086–8), and another group enters "*at the one door: After they consult a little while, enter at the other door*" a second party (*Valiant Welshman*, C4v); the verb is found in a plot: "*After Gorboduc hath Consulted with his Lords he brings his two sons to two several seats*" (*2 Seven Deadly Sins*, 19–20); see also *Four Plays in One*, 326; *Jews' Tragedy*, 1110; *Court Beggar*, 260; *Dick of Devonshire*, 1677.

continue

a timing indicator, usually for **sound** produced **within**: "*Alarm continues*" and "*Alarm continues still afar off*" (*Coriolanus*, 546, 1.4.47; 573, 1.5.3; see also *Macbeth*, 2393, 5.6.10; *2 Iron Age*, 394; *Lust's Dominion*,

4.2.135; *Prophetess*, 373; *Lovesick King*, 46), "*The Music continues*" (*Henry VIII*, 2657, 4.2.82; see also *Northern Lass*, 88), "*Thunder continued*" and "*The battle continued within*" (*Caesar and Pompey*, 2.5.0, 4.2.0), "*the cry continued*" (*Shoemaker a Gentleman*, 5.1.30); see also *Cymbeline*, 2908, 5.2.10; *Devil's Law Case*, 5.6.16; *Escapes of Jupiter*, 430; signals to *continue* onstage action are "*the fight continued*" (*Trial of Chivalry*, I1r), "*continues in her discontent*" (*Silver Age*, 156).

convenient

a rarely used **permissive** term for "appropriate, suitable to the circumstances": "*a Tomb, placed conveniently on the Stage*" (*James IV*, 3), attendants who "*stand in convenient order about the Stage*" (*Henry VIII*, 1349, 2.4.0), "*Exit Venus. Or if you can conveniently, let a chair come down from the top of the stage, and draw her up*" (*Alphonsus of Aragon*, 2109–10).

coranto

a "courante" or lively **dance** with tripping steps and light hops: "*Music: and, Enter Egystus and Clytemnestra dancing a Coranto*" (*Herod and Antipater*, C3r), "*running a coranto pace*" (*Antonio and Mellida*, 2.1.61); see also *Messalina*, 1017; *Duke's Mistress*, F4r.

cord, cords

an equivalent to **rope** used (1) as a **strangling** cord, (2) as a **ladder** in romantic situations, (3) for the **binding** of **prisoners**; the strangling *cord/**halter*** is called for in *Antonio's Revenge* where Strotzo enters "*a cord about his neck*" and subsequently "*Piero comes from his chair, snatcheth the cord's end, and Castilio aideth him; both strangle Strotzo*" (4.1.162, 195) and in *Custom of the Country* which has "*some ready with a cord to strangle Zenocia*" (357); "*a Hangman with Cords*" is specified in *Virgin Martyr* (4.2.61), and comparable *cords* are cited in *Antonio's Revenge*, 1.1.0; *Duchess of Malfi*, 4.2.165; *Novella*, 155; for examples of ladders, Q1 *Romeo and Juliet* has the nurse enter "*with the ladder of cords in her lap*" (F3r, 3.2.31) whereas Q2 has "*Enter Nurse with cords*" (G1v); more explicit is *Insatiate Countess* which provides "*He throws up a ladder of cords, which she makes fast to some part of the window; he ascends, and at top falls*" (3.1.42); calls for binding *cords* include "*Plays with the cord that binds his arms*" (*Parson's Wedding*, 482) and entrances "*with a cord, half unbound*" (*Mad World*, 2.6.6), "*in a Cord*" (*Alarum for London*, 1467), "*with Cords and Shackles*" (*English Traveller*, 81), "*like Amazon Captives, shackled with Golden Fetters, and pinioned with silken cords*" (*Amorous War*, C2v).

corner

refers to a part of the *stage*, although probably not always the same location; "*place themselves in every corner of the Stage*" (Antony and Cleopatra, 2477, 4.3.8) is perhaps made clearer by "*Enter four at several corners*" (No Wit, 4.3.148), "*Enter at four several corners*" (Golden Age, 78), "*the Devils appear at every corner of the stage*" (Silver Age, 159); several directions refer to a single location: "*when he hath laid the Child in a Corner, he departs in haste*" and "*Stroza hides Julia in a corner, and stands before her*" (Maidenhead Well Lost, 127, 152), "*The boy in a corner*" (Your Five Gallants, B3r); elsewhere a hiding figure "*steps to a corner*" and speaks an *aside* (Warning for Fair Women, D2v); in Knave in Grain use of the upper level is implied but not certain: "*Tomaso in a corner of the Gallery*" and "*Lodwicke in another corner*" (2908, 2915).

cornet

a versatile wooden wind instrument which could be played loud or soft cited in over 120 directions; the most common signal is simply *cornets* or *flourish* cornets for a fanfare played *within* when a king, duke or other important figure *enters* or *exits*, often in a military context; in All's Well "*Flourish Cornets*" announces the entrance of the King of France and his party (237, 1.2.0, also 594–6, 2.1.0), and the *sound* conveys Coriolanus's status: "*Cornets. Enter Coriolanus, Menenius, all the Gentry, Cominius, Titus Latius, and other Senators*" (1672–3, 3.1.0, also 1120, 2.1.204; 1378, 2.2.154); for a selection of similar examples see Fawn, 4.587; Malcontent, 4.1.77, 4.3.54; Henry VIII, 317–20, 1.2.0; 1332, 2.4.0; Birth of Merlin, A4r; Wit at Several Weapons, 134; Two Merry Milkmaids, D3r; Women Beware Women, 3.3.20, 240; Faithful Friends, 773–5, 2925; Guardian, 5.4.28; Messalina, 1858–9, 2199; the military context is apparent in "*The cornets sound a battle within*" (Antonio and Mellida, 1.1.0, also 29, 34; see also Dick of Devonshire, 434–5), "*Here the cornets sound thrice, and at the third sound enters Philocles, disguised like a combatant*" (Dumb Knight, 195, also 128, 129); *cornets* sometimes precede festivities or entertainments: "*A Banquet set out, Cornets sounding*" (Noble Spanish Soldier, 5.4.0, also 57), "*The Cornets sound a Lavolta which the Masquers are to dance*" (Blurt, 2.2.239), "*Cornets for a dumb show*" (Quarto Poor Man's Comfort, E1v), "*Fortune's Triumph, sound Trumpets, Drums, Cornets and Guns*" (Rare Triumphs, 1523–4), "*flourish Cornets: Dance and music: cornets*" (Woodstock, 2093–4); see also Malcontent, 5.5.66, 85; Two Merry

Milkmaids, P4r; English Moor, 16; probably the most signals for the sound of *cornets* are in Two Noble Kinsmen, among them "*Cornets in sundry places. Noise and hallooing as people a-Maying*" (F2r, 3.1.0), "*Cornets. Trumpets sound as to a charge*" (M1r, 5.3.55), "*Cornets. A great cry and noise within crying a Palamon*" (M1v, 5.3.66, also 71, 77, 89, 93, 104) punctuating the offstage combat between Palamon and Arcite; the Marston canon has the most calls for *cornets*, especially in Sophonisba: "*Four Boys, anticly attired, with bows and quivers, dancing to the cornets a fantastic measure,*" "*Cornets, a march,*" "*the cornets and organs playing loud full music for the Act,*" "*With a full flourish of cornets, they depart*" (1.2.35, 185, 236, 3.2.84, also 2.2.0, 3.1.116, 5.4.59); two indoor theatre plays have a signal suggesting the substitution of quieter *cornets* for *horns*: "*Cornets like horns*" (Malcontent, 3.4.1), "*Wind horns of Cornets*" (Two Noble Kinsmen, F3v, 3.1.96); for other *cornets* see What You Will, G4v; Antonio's Revenge, 1.2.193, 2.1.0, 3.1.0; Blind Beggar of Bednal Green, 102; More Dissemblers, B7v, E5r; Virgin Martyr, 1.1.118; Love and Honour, 111.

coronet

a small *crown* often denoting a status inferior to that of the sovereign; typical are a *funeral* for a duke's daughter that includes "*a Coronet lying on the Hearse*" (1 Honest Whore, 1.1.0), the designation of an heir wherein a monarch *ascends* his *throne*, "*places Hoffman at his feet, sets a Coronet on his head*" (Hoffman, 484–5); in Quarto King Lear the first entrance of Lear and his daughters includes "*one bearing a Coronet*" (B1v, 1.1.33), and an entertainment in Messalina includes "*three Courtesans in the habit of Queens with Coronets of state*" (2228–9); atypical is "*Enter an armed sewer, after him a company with covered dishes: Coronets on their heads*" (Wonder of a Kingdom, 3.1.148); see also Edward III, G2v; Look about You, 2831, 2868, 2879; Four Plays in One, 311.

corpse

an alternative to the more widely used *body* (usually spelled *corse*) found primarily in *funerals* and related *ceremonies*: ladies "*winding Marcello's corpse*" (White Devil, 5.4.65), "*the corpses of Mustaffa and Aga, with funeral pomp*" (Selimus, 1996–7), "*A counterfeit corpse brought in, Tomasin, and all the Mourners equally counterfeit*" (Michaelmas Term, 4.4.51), "*Enter the Corpse of Henry the sixth with Halberds to guard it, Lady Anne being the Mourner*" (Folio Richard III, 173–4, 1.2.0); as with *drum*, *trumpet*, or *halberd*, this term standing alone can include those **carrying** the *corpse*: "*Exit Corpse*" (Folio *Richard III*, 423, 1.2.226), "*Enter a Corpse, after it Irishmen mourning, in a dead March: To them enters Eustace, and talks with the chief Mourner, who makes signs of consent, after burial of the Corpse, and so Exeunt*" (*Four Prentices*, 178); see also *Selimus*, 2007; Q2 *Hamlet*, M4r, 5.1.217; *Every Woman In*, G1r; *Fatal Contract*, D3v.

couch

an alternative to the widely used **bed**; figures **enter** "*with couch*" (*Roman Actor*, 5.1.154), "*carried in the Couch*" (*Alphonsus of Germany*, H1r), "*carried in as sick in a couch*" (*Wits*, 183); two late Caroline plays call for *couches* to be **discovered**: "*discovered on a Couch*" (*Landgartha*, D2v), "*Draws a canopy. Eurithea is found sleeping on a couch*" (*Platonic Lovers*, 33); actions include "*Falls on her Couch*" (*Court Beggar*, 207), "*leaps off from his couch*" (*Volpone*, 3.7.139), "*stabs him upon his couch*" (*Maid's Revenge*, I3r).

council, parliament

either **fictional** terms directed at a reader or coded terms for a specific onstage effect linked to a **table**, **chairs**, and distinctive costumes and therefore comparable to a generic locution such as "*the form of a court*" (*Two Merry Milkmaids*, I3r); uses of *parliament* are rare: *2 Henry VI* signals the entrance of the king and his entourage "*to the Parliament*" (Quarto D3r, Folio 1292–4, 3.1.0), Quarto *Richard II* provides "*Enter Bullingbrook with the Lords to parliament*" (G4r, 4.1.0); Folio *Richard II*, however, directs "*Enter as to the Parliament*" (1921), and this use of *as* [*if*] is echoed in two Caroline directions: enter "*as at a council of war*" (*Cardinal*, 2.1.0), "*Enter Lords as to Council*" (*Sophy*, 3.42); most of the relevant directions provide few details; typical are entrances "*with his Council of War*" (*Antony and Cleopatra*, 3108–9, 5.1.0), "*with all his Council*" (*Philotas*, D7r), "*In council together*" (*Captain Thomas Stukeley*, 2687–8), and "*All stand in Council*" (*Death of Huntingdon*, 2971), "*set in Council*" (*Grim the Collier*, G2v), "*place themselves to council*" (*Sophonisba*, 2.1.0), "*the Emperor disposing their affairs to the Council, Exeunt*" (*Travels of Three English Brothers*, 349); when Talbot and his allies "*whisper together in council*" (*1 Henry VI*, 1495, 3.2.59) Joan comments "God speed the parliament! Who shall be the speaker?"; advisors or courtiers can be termed *councillors* (*Mucedorus*, B2v; *2 Seven Deadly Sins*, 15, 30; *Whore of Babylon*, DS before Act 1, 32, 43); related are "*Jolas a Lord of the Council*" (*Aglaura*, 2.1.0), "*Clerk of the Council waiting bareheaded*" (*Sir Thomas More*, 1159–60); atypical is Q2

Hamlet's use of *as*: "*Enter Claudius, King of Denmark, Gertrude the Queen, Council: as Polonius, and his Son Laertes, Hamlet Cum Aliis*" (B3v, 1.2.0).

Sometimes further details are provided; Quarto *Richard III* (G1r, 3.4.0) signals "*Enter the Lords to Council*" but the Folio (1964–6) has the same group enter "*at a Table*"; similarly a scene in *Rebellion* begins with a call for "*A table and chairs*" and a group then "*sit in council*" (28–9), the Venetian *council* scene in Quarto *Othello* begins "*Enter Duke and Senators, set at a Table with lights and Attendants*" (C1r, 1.3.0), *Sir Thomas Wyatt* has "*the Lord Treasurer kneeling at the Council Table*" (1.6.0); *King John and Matilda* provides "*A Chair of state discovered, Tables and Chairs responsible, a Guard making a lane*" so that King John, Pandulph, and the lords "*enter between them*" (29), and after "*A Table and Chairs set out*" a later scene instructs "*Sit to Council*" (47); especially elaborate is the situation in *Henry VIII*: "*A Council Table brought in with Chairs and Stools, and placed under the State. Enter Lord Chancellor, places himself at the upper end of the Table, on the left hand: a Seat being left void above him, as for Canterbury's Seat*"; five figures "*seat themselves in Order on each side. Cromwell at lower end, as Secretary*"; a few lines later "*Cranmer approaches the Council Table*" (3035–41, 3055, 5.2.35, 42).

counterfeit

used occasionally as (1) a verb ("to feign"), (2) an adjective ("feigned"); examples of the verb include figures who *counterfeit* **sleep** (*2 Fair Maid of the West*, 350), devotion (*Virgin Martyr*, 2.1.86), another's **voice** (*Witty Fair One*, E1r), "*a sick voice*" (*Albovine*, 102), death (*Prisoners*, B7r, C8r); more detailed are "*Sinon who had before counterfeited death, riseth up*" (*2 Iron Age*, 428), "*Here let him counterfeit the passion of love by looks and gesture*" (*Fedele and Fortunio*, 795–6), "*Enter Charlemont; D'Amville counterfeits to take him for a ghost*" (*Atheist's Tragedy*, 3.2.17); examples of the adjective include a *counterfeit* **box** (*Love's Mistress*, 152), **head** (*Travels of Three English Brothers*, 386), **letters**-patent (*2 Edward IV*, 171), physician (*Rare Triumphs*, 1046), "*The Courtesan on a bed for her counterfeit fit*" (*Mad World*, 3.2.0), "*A counterfeit corpse brought in, Tomasin, and all the Mourners equally counterfeit*" (*Michaelmas Term*, 4.4.51), "*with counterfeit passion present the King a bleeding heart upon a knife's point*" (*Golden Age*, 20).

court

see **woo**

courtroom

see *trial*

cover, covered

used for (1) the *covering* of a *table* with a *cloth* for a meal, (2) *covered dishes*, (3) objects *covered* in *black*, (4) concealment; to *prepare* for a meal servants "*come to cover*" (*Warning for Fair Women*, D1r), enter "*with a table covered*" (*1 Edward IV*, 50), "*cover the board and fetch in the meat*" (*Taming of a Shrew*, D3r), "*cover a Table, two bottles of wine, Dishes of Sugar, and a dish of Sparagus*" (*Sparagus Garden*, 158); *Spanish Curate* provides "*A Table ready covered with Cloth Napkins Salt Trenchers and Bread*" (129/501), and *Match at Midnight* "*A table set out*" and two figures "*as to cover it for dinner*" (27); tables can also be *covered* "*with treasure*" (*Antipodes*, 324), "*with a green Carpet*" (*Sir Thomas More*, 735); often specified as *covered* are dishes for a meal/ *banquet*/special effect: "*A Dinner carried over the Stage in covered Dishes*" (*City Wit*, 279), "*with covered dishes, to the banquet*" (*Hieronimo*, 1.0), "*a child in a covered Dish*" (*Maidenhead Well Lost*, 158), "*Dishes covered with papers in each ready*" (*Spanish Curate*, 132/501); see also *Doctor Faustus*, B 1775; *Mad World*, 2.1.151; *White Devil*, 4.3.19; *Wonder of a Kingdom*, 3.1.148, 5.2.0; objects *covered* in black include a *horse* (*Alarum for London*, 261–2), *coffin* (*Titus Andronicus*, A4r, 1.1.69), "*a Drum covered with black, beating a sad Retreat*" (*Jews' Tragedy*, 3044), but most commonly a table: "*A Table and a Chair covered with black*" (*Rape of Lucrece*, 234), "*a table covered with black, on which stands two black tapers lighted, she in mourning*" (*Insatiate Countess*, 1.1.0); see also *Noble Spanish Soldier*, 1.2.0; to indicate an unwanted *wedding* "*servants in blacks*" enter "*Covering the place with blacks*" (*Custom of the Country*, 313); occasionally objects are *covered* in *white*: "*an altar covered with white*" (*Broken Heart*, 5.3.0), "*A bed covered with white*" (*Vow Breaker*, 4.2.0); for examples of concealment, a figure who is *dead* not sick is hidden by "*a Litter covered*" (*Prophetess*, 336), and a murderer is directed to "*Bring down the body, and cover it over with Faggots*" (*Two Lamentable Tragedies*, D2v, also E2r); *Costly Whore* has "*the hearse with Frederick on, covered with a black robe*" (287, also 290); in *Old Wives Tale* a figure digs a *hole*, then "*covers it again*" (606); *heads/faces* can be *covered*: "*covered with a black veil*" (*Warning for Fair Women*, D1r), "*David barefoot, with some loose covering over his head, and all mourning*" (*David and Bethsabe*, 972, also 1083), "*dragged off, his head covered*" (*Renegado*, 2.5.92); atypical are *masquers* "*with covered cups in their hands*" (*Women Beware*

Women, 5.2.50) and poisoners who "*put on spectacles of glass, which cover their eyes and noses*" (*White Devil*, 2.2.23).

coxcomb

a distinctive *cap* associated with a fool and by extension with folly; in *Queen and Concubine* a fool's costume consists of "*Coxcomb, Bauble, Bells, and Coat*" (34), to play a practical joke a trickster "*puts a coxcomb on Mulligrub's head*" (*Dutch Courtesan*, 2.3.93), a madwoman appears "*in a rich gown, great farthingale, great ruff, muff, fan, and coxcomb on her head*" (*Lover's Melancholy*, 3.3.48), Virtue enters with "*a coxcomb on her head*" accompanied by "*other Nymphs all in white with coxcombs on their heads*" (*Old Fortunatus*, 1.3.0); in two plays a foolish figure who makes a brief appearance is designated *Coxcomb* (*Fair Maid of the Inn*, 192; *Match Me in London*, 4.2.0).

cradle

to present a baby to his king a figure enters "*with a rich Cradle borne after him by two Servants*" (*Royal King*, 67); to set up his *strangling* of two *snakes* "*The Nurses bring young Hercules in his Cradle, and leave him*" (*Silver Age*, 126); see also *Patient Grissil*, 4.2.91.

creep

associated with (1) surreptitious activity, (2) feebleness, (3) cowardice, abject behavior; figures *enter creeping in* (*Night Walker*, 365), *exit creeping* (*Eastward Ho*, E4r; *Duchess of Suffolk*, H1v), and are directed to creep "*under the stool*" (*Cobbler's Prophecy*, 75), "*under the Table*" (*Variety*, D10r), "*out of a bush*" (*Philaster*, 129), "*out of a cave*" (*Twins*, E1r), "*upon his hands*" (*Valiant Welshman*, D4v); other variations include "*creeps in and observes them*" (*What You Will*, D3r), "*creeping in, as he were sick*" (*Platonic Lovers*, 100), "*left wounded, and for dead, stirs and creeps*" (*Warning for Fair Women*, F1v, also F2r).

crocodile

see *snake*

crosier

an episcopal *staff* or crook (often spelled *crozier*): enter "*St. Dunstan with his Beads, Book, and Crosier staff, etc.*" (*Grim the Collier*, G2r), an *angel* "*with his crosier staff in one hand, and a book in the other*" who "*Toucheth his breast with his cross*" (*Two Noble Ladies*, 1857–8, 1869–70); see also *Doctor Faustus*, B 891; *Whore of Babylon*, DS before Act 1, 48–9.

cross

(1) usually denotes the symbolic *cross*, ***crucifix*** but can occasionally be (2) a verb, (3) "across," (4) a *cross-road*; examples of *cross* as crucifix are "*A cross of Flowers*" provided by an ***angel*** (*Virgin Martyr*, 5.1.139), "*The white cross*" as symbol of a Knight of Malta (*Maid of Honour*, 5.2.289), ***wounded*** soldiers who enter "*every man with his red Cross on his coat*" (*Edward I*, 40), a ***table*** "*set out with a candle burning, a death's head, a cloak and a cross*" (*If This Be Not a Good Play*, 4.4.0); for examples of making the sign of the *cross*, a figure "*crosseth himself*" (*Doctor Faustus*, A 899, 902, 905; *Devil's Charter*, L3v), "*Makes a cross on Clifford's face with his finger*" (*Perkin Warbeck*, 2.2.83); a *cross* can be part of a ***ceremony***: "*Enter Abbot bearing a Cross*" (*Lovesick King*, 164), "*two Priests, bearing each a Silver Cross*" (*Henry VIII*, 1338–9, 2.4.0); see also *Duchess of Malfi*, 3.4.7; atypical are papal *cross* ***keys*** (*Devil's Charter*, A2v, E1r); see also *Two Noble Ladies*, 1869–70; other usages include "*cross the stage*" (*Histriomastix*, G1r; *Jews' Tragedy*, 2428), "*lays her finger cross her mouth*" (*Captain*, 297; see also *Second Maiden's Tragedy*, 2226), an entrance "*at the Cross*" described as "a cross that parts three several ways" (*Old Wives Tale*, 140, 431, 872; see also *Histriomastix*, B4v).

crow

a crowbar, used for prying open a ***door*** or ***tomb***: "*Romeo and Balthasar, with a torch, a mattock, and a crow of iron*" (Q1 *Romeo and Juliet*, I4v, 5.3.21), "*Friar with Lantern, Crow* [i.e. *Crow*], *and Spade*" (Q2 *Romeo and Juliet*, L3v, 5.3.120), "*Lysander solus with a crow of iron*" (*Widow's Tears*, 5.5.0, also 68), "*an iron crow and dark lantern*" (*Wits*, 210, also 211).

crowd

another name for a ***viol***: "*Enter Assistance and Hortensio bareheaded with his crowd*" (*Humour out of Breath*, 473).

crown, crowned

of the roughly 150 examples (1) the largest group consists of figures who enter *crowned/with a crown* but also common are (2) various locutions for *crowning*, removing a *crown*, (3) *crowns* in ***ceremonies***, pageants, and symbolic actions, (4) *crowns* not linked to royalty; for a sampling of the many figures who enter *crowned/with a crown* see *2 Tamburlaine*, 3110; *Orlando Furioso*, 1343; *Titus Andronicus*, A3v, [1.1.18]; Quarto *Richard III*, H4v, 4.2.0; *2 Seven Deadly Sins*, 26; *Woodstock*, 350–1; *Nobody and Somebody*, E3v, E4v;

Downfall of Huntingdon, 1629, 2700; *Old Fortunatus*, 1.1.63, 5.2.260; *Look about You*, 77–8; *Hoffman*, 2584; *If This Be Not a Good Play*, 1.2.0; *Macbeth*, 1628, 4.1.86; *Royal King*, 65; *Golden Age*, 68; *Broken Heart*, 5.3.0; *Queen*, 638; *Queen and Concubine*, 22; *Traitor*, 3.2.25; *Coronation*, 285; for a sampling of *crowning/***setting*** a *crown* on a figure's ***head*** see *Spanish Tragedy*, 1.3.86; *Alphonsus of Aragon*, 786, 794, 836; *Locrine*, 227; *Doctor Faustus*, B 1296; *Selimus*, 1664; *Alphonsus of Germany*, F1r; *Thracian Wonder*, C4r; *Hoffman*, 484–5; *Four Prentices*, 234; *Devil's Charter*, A2v; *Wonder of a Kingdom*, 3.1.148; *Valiant Welshman*, C4v, E3v, F3r; *Virgin Martyr*, 5.2.219; *Jews' Tragedy*, 3028; *Herod and Antipater*, I4v; *Valiant Scot*, K3v; *Bloody Banquet*, 55–6; typical are "*takes the Crown and puts it on*" (*1 Tamburlaine*, 903), "*Install and Crown her*" (*James IV*, 153), "*they Crown him, and accept him for their Prince*" (*Four Prentices*, 176), "*takes the Crown off of Flaminius's head, and puts it on Alphonsus*" (*Alphonsus of Aragon*, 501–2, also 806); for the removing of a *crown* see *Doctor Faustus*, B 1294–5; Folio *3 Henry VI*, 2285, 4.3.48; *Selimus*, 1659; figures *give/***offer***/present crowns*: "*the Priests offer Hercules the Crown of Egypt which he refuseth*" (*Brazen Age*, 183), "*present their Crowns to him at his feet, and do him homage*" (*Birth of Merlin*, G4r); see also *Herod and Antipater*, F3v; *Shoemaker a Gentleman*, 5.2.182.

Special or symbolic *crowns* include an *imperial crown* (*2 Tamburlaine*, 3110; *Alphonsus of Germany*, E3r; *Devil's Charter*, G1v; *Look about You*, 2822; *Two Noble Kinsmen*, B1v, 1.1.24), a papal *triple crown* (*Devil's Charter*, A2v, B2v), Pluto's "*burning crown*" (*Golden Age*, 79; *Silver Age*, 159), the spirit of the martyred Dorothea "*in a white robe, crowns upon her robe, a Crown upon her head*" (*Virgin Martyr*, 5.2.219), "*a Tree of gold laden with Diadems and Crowns of gold*" (*Arraignment of Paris*, 456; see also *Battle of Alcazar*, 1268–9); Henslowe's inventory includes "three Imperial crowns; one plain crown" (*Diary*, App. 2, 89), "one ghost's crown; one crown with a sun" (90); *crowns* can be ***carried*** "*on a cushion*" (*Look about You*, 2822; *Lust's Dominion*, 5.1.0), "*upon laurel wreaths*" (*Malcontent*, 5.5.66); *crowns* are often linked to the ***scepter*** (*Friar Bacon*, 2077; *2 Tamburlaine*, 3110; *Look about You*, 2821–2; *Golden Age*, 78; *Four Plays in One*, 311; *Queen's Exchange*, 505; *Constant Maid*, H1r) or other attributes of royalty: "*Sussex bearing the Crown, Howard bearing the Scepter, the Constable the Mace, Tame the Purse, Shandoyse the Sword*" (*1 If You Know Not Me*, 239, also 195, 244); actions include "*comes out alone with his Crown in his hand, offering to* hide it" (*1 Tamburlaine*, 663), "*each of them kill a Pagan King, take off their Crowns, and exeunt*" (*Four Prentices*, 247, also 234), "*takes off his Crown, kisses it, and pours poison in the King's ears*" (*Hamlet*, Q2 H1v, Folio 1995–6, 3.2.135), "*take the Crown of them, and present it kneeling to Vespatian, he refuseth twice, they draw and force him to ascend and take it*" (*Jews' Tragedy*, 1106–8), "*The Bishops take her Crown and Wand, give her a Wreath of Cypress, and a white Wand*" (*Queen and Concubine*, 22); crowns not linked to royalty include "*A crown of thorns*" (*Four Prentices*, 249), "*A crown of feathers*" (*Lover's Melancholy*, 3.3.26), and figures crowned with bays (*Queen and Concubine*, 124), **garlands** (*Herod and Antipater*, F4r; *1 Arviragus and Philicia*, A8v), "*an Oaken Garland*" (*Coriolanus*, 1061–2, 2.1.161), "*Olive branches and laurels*" (*Old Fortunatus*, 5.2.260), "*a Laurel Wreath*" (*Jews' Tragedy*, 6; see also *Rape of Lucrece*, 253); atypical are **prisoners** "*bearing crowns of gold, and manacled*" (*Wounds of Civil War*, 1073–4), "*brings in the head of a crowned King*" (*Silver Age*, 97), Fortune followed by "*four Kings with broken Crowns and Scepters*" (*Old Fortunatus*, 1.1.63), a **banquet** followed by "*a second course of Crowns*" (*1 Tamburlaine*, 1746).

crucifix

Matilda "*Draws a Crucifix*" to defend herself against tempters (*Death of Huntingdon*, 2536), a **spirit** appears "*Stuck with Jewels and a great crucifix on her breast*" (*Second Maiden's Tragedy*, 1930–1, also 2227), the fake Capuchins present the dying Bracciano "*with a crucifix and hallowed candle*" (*White Devil*, 5.3.129, also 135); *Noble Spanish Soldier* provides "*A Table set out covered with black: two waxen Tapers: the King's Picture at one end, a Crucifix at the other, Onelia walking discontentedly weeping to the Crucifix*" (1.2.0).

cry, crying

usually occurs in the call for **sound**, *cry **within***: "*A Cry within of Women*" (*Macbeth*, 2328, 5.5.7), "*a confused cry within*" (*Michaelmas Term*, 4.3.0), "*Dapper cries out within*" (*Alchemist*, 5.3.63), "*A cry of hounds within*" (Quarto *Every Man Out*, 1002–3), "*An alarum, noise and cries within, a flourish*" (*Unnatural Combat*, 5.2.324); for more see *Comedy of Errors*, 1657, 5.1.183; *Philaster*, 127; *Revenge of Bussy*, 4.1.39; *Charlemagne*, 72–3; *Two Maids of More-Clacke*, G1r; *Knight of the Burning Pestle*, 204; *Yorkshire Tragedy*, 640; *Tempest*, 45, 1.1.35; *1 Iron Age*, 332; *2 Iron Age*, 381; *Fair Maid of the Inn*, 173; *Night Walker*, 348; frequently the call for offstage sound also gives the *cry*: "*Cry within, Fly, fly, fly*" (*Julius*

Caesar, 2688, 5.5.42), "*a great cry within, Charon, a boat, a boat*" (*Hieronimo*, 12.0), "*Cry within follow, follow*" (*Bloody Banquet*, 240), "*A cry within help, murder, murder*" (*Cobbler's Prophecy*, 1324–5), "*crying liberty and freedom within*" (*Double Marriage*, 395), "*A shout, and a general cry within, whores, whores*" (*Maid of Honour*, 4.1.23), "*Some cry treason within*" (*Duke's Mistress*, I1v), "*Cry within, Kill Kill Kill*" (*Two Noble Ladies*, 67, also 249–51, 1146); for more see *Mucedorus*, A2v, D3r, F2v; *Isle of Gulls*, 243; *Famous Victories*, F1r; *Shoemaker a Gentleman*, 1.1.106, 5.1.0; *Rule a Wife*, 224; *Fortune by Land and Sea*, 389; *Tom a Lincoln*, 798; *Jews' Tragedy*, 897–8; similar directions describe an onstage *cry*: "*Enter a Soldier, crying, a Talbot, a Talbot*" (*1 Henry VI*, 765, 2.1.77), "*Enter one crying a Miracle*" (*2 Henry VI*, C2r, 784, 2.1.56), "*all cry, Martius, Martius, cast up their Caps and Lances*" (*Coriolanus*, 794–5, 1.9.40), "*Exit crying Murder*" (*Macbeth*, 1811, 4.1.85), "*Enter the Nobles and crown King John, and then cry God save the King*" (*1 Troublesome Reign*, G1v), "*Enter a Collier, crying a monster*" (*Downfall of Huntingdon*, 1100, also 26–7, 991); see also *Edward I*, 682; *Jack Straw*, 1114; *Shoemakers' Holiday*, 1.1.235; *Sir John Oldcastle*, 56; *Histriomastix*, G1r; *Swetnam*, F1r, F2r–v, F3r; *Hoffman*, 1188; *Honest Lawyer*, B2r; *Traitor*, 5.3.137; *Princess*, G4r; occasionally *crying* is combined with **noise** or **shout**: "*A noise within crying room for the Queen*" (*Henry VIII*, 329, 1.2.8), "*A great noise within crying run, save, hold*" (*Two Noble Kinsmen*, M3v, 5.4.39; see also *Miseries of Enforced Marriage*, 1537), "*A shout within, crying Antonio*" and "*A noise within, crying Rescue, rescue*" (*Rebellion*, 34, 39); see also *2 If You Know Not Me*, 347; *Puritan*, F2v; other uses of *cries* and *crying* are "*a Cry of hounds*" (*Titus Andronicus*, D1r, 2.2.10), "*Ghost cries under the stage*" (Q2 *Hamlet*, D4v, 1.5.148), "*Horsecourser all wet, crying*" (*Doctor Faustus*, A 1175), "*on the walls cries to them*" (*1 Edward IV*, 19), "*two Pages, the one laughing, the other crying*" (*Jack Drum's Entertainment*, B4v), "*crying Hoboys*" (*When You See Me*, 1525); in *Family of Love* a Town Crier *cries* for silence (H3v); in *Loyal Subject* "*Ancient, crying Brooms*" is selling them (128).

cudgel

a short, thick stick or **club** used as a **weapon**: "*beats him with a cudgel*" (Folio *Every Man In*, 3.5.117), "*Bridget beating Rufflit: Crasy takes Bridget's Cudgel, and lays on*" and "*Rufflit cudgels him*" (*City Wit*, 359, 362); for other *cudgels* see *Sir Thomas More*, 453; *Look about You*, 2601; *Case Is Altered*, 2.7.83; *Woman Is a Weathercock*, 5.1.48–9; *New Way to Pay*, 1.1.92, 2.3.28.

cum

Latin for "with" found in locutions when figures
enter and especially *exit*; most common is *cum suis*
(literally "with his own"), an equivalent for "with his
followers, men, *train*, attendants"; *Bussy D'Ambois*
provides "*Descendit cum suis*" and "*Surgit Spiritus cum
suis*" (4.2.138, 5.2.51); comparable are *cum
caeteris/cum aliis* (both meaning "with others"), *cum
servis* ("with servants," *Insatiate Countess*, 2.4.57;
Wisdom of Doctor Dodypoll, 1218), *cum filio/filia/filiabus*
("with son/daughter/daughters," *May Day*, 2.4.243;
No Wit, 4.1.258; *Humour out of Breath*, 448), *cum puero*
("with the boy," *Humour out of Breath*, 419), *cum mil-
itibus* ("with soldiers," *Downfall of Huntingdon*, 70; *If
This Be Not a Good Play*, 5.2.79), *cum* a named figure
(*Death of Huntingdon*, 1765; *Widow's Tears*, 5.5.86; *Bussy
D'Ambois*, 2.1.206, 3.2.283) as in "*Exit cum Montsurry*"
(*Bussy D'Ambois*, 5.2.98); not surprisingly *cum*
appears occasionally in longer Latin directions:
"*Redit cum lumine*" ("he returns with a light,"
Monsieur D'Olive, 5.1.35), "*Cantat saltatque cum cithera*"
("she sings and dances with a lute," *Dutch Courtesan*,
5.1.20); see also *Arraignment of Paris*, 51; *Amyntas*, 2C3v.

cup

a drinking vessel usually linked to *wine*: "*Rose takes a
cup of wine*" (*Shoemakers' Holiday*, 3.3.58), "*a drawer with
a cup of wine and a towel*" (*May Day*, 3.3.188), "*stirring
and mingling a cup of wine*" (*Satiromastix*, 5.1.0, also 50),
"*Diego ready in bed, wine, cup*" (*Spanish Curate*, 117/501);
see also *Christian Turned Turk*, F2v; *Conspiracy*, I4r;
Bloody Banquet, 417, 431; once the beverage is *sack*
(*Gentleman Usher*, 2.1.0); sometimes *poison* is added:
"*they offer a cup of wine unto Octavian, and he is poisoned*"
(*Valiant Welshman*, C4v), "*Brand solus, with cup, bottle of
poison*" (*Death of Huntingdon*, 2403); see also *Four Plays
in One*, 326, 327, 333; *Hoffman*, 1527; in *Alphonsus of
Germany* "*Alphonsus takes the Cup*" and "*drinks to the
King of Bohemia*," then "*puts poison into the Beaker*"
(F1v); other examples are "*a standing cup*" (*Dutch
Courtesan*, 3.2.0), "*Caudle cup*" (*Mad Couple*, 34), "*A con-
fused fray with stools, cups and bowls*" (*Silver Age*, 142, also
113), "*sets the two cups asunder*" (Quarto *Every Man Out*,
3838); see also *Alphonsus of Germany*, C4r; *Death of
Huntingdon*, 518; *Selimus*, 1749; *Mad Lover*, 40;
Messalina, 2203; *Princess*, E2r.

curtain

can designate (1) fabric suspended in front of an
opening in the tiring-house wall where figures or
scenes were *discovered*, (2) *bed* curtains, (3) the material which hung just in front of the tiring-house wall;

roughly sixty plays have about ninety directions for
a *curtain* of which seventy-eight call for the *curtain* to
be *opened* or *closed*; typically several figures and
often properties are revealed when a *curtain* is
drawn: "*Bethsabe with her maid bathing over a spring*"
(*David and Bethsabe*, 23), "*the king sits sleeping, his sword
by his side*" (*Death of Huntingdon*, 925–6), "*Jupiter dandling Ganymede upon his knee, and Mercury lying asleep*"
(*Dido*, 0), "*Clorin appears sitting in the Cabin, Amoret
sitting on the one side of her, Alexis and Cloe on the other, the
Satyr standing by*" (*Faithful Shepherdess*, 437), "*Bianca in
her night attire, leaning on a Cushion at a Table, holding
Fernando by the hand*" (*Love's Sacrifice*, 2350–2); see also
Woman in the Moon, A2v; *Antonio's Revenge*, 1.2.207,
3.2.72; *Downfall of Huntingdon*, 51–6; *Friar Bacon*,
1561–3; *Old Wives Tale*, 843; *Looking Glass for London*,
552–3; *Grim the Collier*, G2v; *Histriomastix*, B4v; *What
You Will*, C4r, G3r; *Sophonisba*, 1.2.35; *Lust's Dominion*,
1.1.0; *Old Fortunatus*, 3.1.356; *Westward Ho*, 4.2.52;
Whore of Babylon, DS before Act 1, 27; *Wisdom of Doctor
Dodypoll*, 2–4; *Hoffman*, 8–10, 1411–13; *Henry VIII*, 1100,
2.2.61; *City Match*, 252, 309; *Wife for a Month*, 25; *Fatal
Dowry*, 2.2.255; *Twins*, G2r; *Valiant Welshman*, H4v;
elsewhere a *curtain* is opened to reveal a *study*:
"*Alexander draweth the Curtain of his study where he discovereth the devil sitting in his pontificals*" (*Devil's
Charter*, L3v, also L3r); see also *Woman Hater*, 128; *News
from Plymouth*, 167; several directions use *behind* the
curtain: "*Enter Iolante (with a rich banquet and tapers) (in
a chair, behind a curtain)*" (*Guardian*, 3.6.0), "*Horace
sitting in a study behind a Curtain*" (*Satiromastix*, 1.2.0);
see also *If This Be Not a Good Play*, 5.4.0; *What You Will*,
C4r; *Lovers' Progress*, 104.

Sometimes the phrasing suggests bed *curtains*:
"*Then the Curtains being drawn, Duke Humphrey is discovered in his bed, and two men lying on his breast and
smothering him*" (Quarto 2 *Henry VI*, E2r [3.2.0], also
E3r, [3.2.146], F1v, [3.3.0]), "*they draw the curtains and
smother the young princes in the bed*" (*Battle of Alcazar*,
37–8), "*draws a Curtain, where Fernando is discovered in
bed*" (*Love's Sacrifice*, 1269–70), "*Time draws a curtain
and discovers Angellica in her bed asleep*" (*Tom a Lincoln*,
150–1), "*lay the Princess in a fair bed and close the
curtains*" (*Sophonisba*, 1.2.32, also 1.2.35, 3.1.161, 5.1.0),
"*Laverdure draws the Curtains sitting on his bed appareling himself, his trunk of apparel standing by him*" (*What
You Will*, B3v); see also *Sappho and Phao*, 3.3.37; *Mad
World*, 2.6.92; *Merry Devil of Edmonton*, A3v;
Brennoralt, 3.4.18, 5.3.155; other directions imply
that the bed is within a *curtained* space: "*A curtain
drawn, a bed discovered, Ingen with his sword in his hand,
and a Pistol, the Lady in a petticoat, the Parson*" (*Amends

for Ladies, 5.2.180–3), "*The Curtains being drawn there appears in his bed King Phillip, with his Lords*" (*Lust's Dominion*, 1.2.0).

Other signals for a *curtain* include "*falls upon her bed within the Curtains*" (Q1 *Romeo and Juliet*, I1r, 4.3.58), "*knocks up the curtain*" (*Spanish Tragedy*, 4.3.0), "*conceals them behind the curtain*" (*Dutch Courtesan*, 5.1.13), "*hideth himself in the chamber behind the Bed curtains*" (*2 Iron Age*, 411), "*appears above the Curtain*" (*Tale of a Tub*, 5.10.9); for the few directions for a *curtain* to be closed see *Downfall of Huntingdon*, 56; *If This Be Not a Good Play*, 5.4.53; *Looking Glass for London*, 510; *Sir Giles Goosecap*, 5.2.132; *Tom a Lincoln*, 155, 171; *Mad Lover*, 59; *Picture*, 4.2.206; *City Match*, 258; occasionally the phrasing indicates that the *curtain* is **above**: "*The curtains drawn above, Theodosius, and his Eunuchs discovered*" (*Emperor of the East*, 1.2.288), "*draws her window curtain*" (*Jews' Tragedy*, 2225, 2941–2); see also *Thracian Wonder*, D1v; *Unnatural Combat*, 5.2.238; a *curtain* is drawn to reveal a **picture** in *White Devil*, 2.2.23; *Fatal Contract*, B3v, I1r; *City Match*, 308; see also **arras, hangings, traverse**.

curtsy

a gesture of respect or reverence usually linked to women (as distinct from the primarily male **bow/conge**) made by bending the **knees** with one **foot** forward and lowering the **body**: "*she makes a Curtsy to the Table*" (*Bloody Banquet*, 1920), "*Makes a low curtsy, as she goes off*" (*Bondman*, 3.2.111); in *Fair Favourite* two women "*curtsy to Thorello, very low; then bow to the others, they to them*" and a third woman "*curtsies to all, but Saladine, they to her*" (250–1); in *Two Noble Kinsmen* after Emilia and her maids have set their offering on the **altar** "*she sets fire to it, then they curtsy and kneel*" (L1v, 5.1.136, also L2r, 5.1.173); in Queen Katherine's vision in *Henry VIII* "*the first two*" personages "*hold a spare Garland over her Head, at which the other four make reverend Curtsies*" (2647–9, 4.2.82); occasionally a man is directed to *curtsy* (probably a version of **make a leg**); examples are Isabella and Hippolito's dance for the duke which includes "*curtsy to themselves, both before and after*" (*Women Beware Women*, 3.3.200), "*Warman ever flattering and making curtsy*" (*Downfall of Huntingdon*, 48–9); see also *Epicœne*, 2.5.23, 29, 44; *Two Merry Milkmaids*, C4r; *Mad Couple*, 22; *Twins*, E1v; *2 Cid*, B4r.

cushion

used for a variety of purposes including (1) to help establish a sense of "place," (2) to **carry** a **crown**, (3) to provide the padding for a fake pregnancy; to estab-

lish a location the final sequence in Q2 *Hamlet* begins with "*A table prepared, Trumpets, Drums and officers with Cushions, King, Queen, and all the state, Foils, daggers, and Laertes*" (N3v, 5.2.224), and the first Senate scene in *Coriolanus* begins: "*Enter two Officers, to lay Cushions, as it were, in the Capitol*" (1203–4, 2.2.0); for similar introductions of *cushions* see *Widow's Tears*, 3.2.1; *Ram Alley*, B3v; *White Devil*, 1.2.204; in *Lust's Dominion* figures enter "*bearing the Crown on a cushion*" (5.1.0); see also *Look about You*, 2822; *Devil's Charter*, B2v; *Coronation*, 287; for an example of a *cushion* to fake pregnancy, when the supposedly pregnant Luce is revealed to be "*yet an untouched Virgin*," another figure states "*Cushion come forth, here signior Shallow, take your child unto you*" and "*flings the cushion at him*" (*Heir*, 575); see also **with child**.

cut

the roughly twenty examples include (1) the *cutting* of a variety of objects, (2) onstage violence such as the *cutting* off of a **hand, nose**, or **ear**; figures are directed to *cut* a **cable** (*Jew of Malta*, 2346), **tree** (*Warning for Fair Women*, E3v), **ruffs** (*Dead Man's Fortune*, 20); more detailed are "*Enter Boy in a Shop cutting up square parchments*" (*Fair Maid of the Exchange*, 40), "*cuts Dondolo's bonds, and gives him the knife*" (*Just Italian*, 268); *Spanish Tragedy* calls for the *cutting down* of a hanged figure and an **arbor** (2.5.12, 4.2.5); examples of *cutting* of people are "*cuts his arm*" (*2 Tamburlaine*, 3304), "*offers to cut her face*" (*Telltale*, 1051), "*begins to cut the body*" of a murder victim (*Two Lamentable Tragedies*, E2r), "*cuts off one hand*" and "*cuts off the other hand*" (*Edmond Ironside*, 700, 702, also 717; see also *Selimus*, 1431), "*Cuts off his Nose*" (*Edmond Ironside*, 708, also 717; *Edward I*, 903), "*cuts off the Cutpurse's ear, for cutting of the gold buttons off his cloak*" (*Massacre at Paris*, 622); *Titus Andronicus* provides "*her hands cut off, and her tongue cut out, and ravished,*" "*He cuts off Titus's hand,*" "*He cuts their throats*" (E2r, 2.4.0; F2r, 3.1.191; K1v, 5.2.203); atypical are "*cut away the Goose while he talketh, and leave the head behind him with them*" (*Jack Straw*, 487–8), *cut off* as "interrupt" ("*Here Em cuts him off,*" *Fair Em*, 485).

D

dag

a seldom used term for a heavy **pistol** or handgun: "*points to his chains and shows his dags*" (*Claracilla*, F1v); in *Spanish Tragedy* Pedringano enters "*with a pistol*" but then "*Shoots the dag*" (3.3.0, 32), and in *Rule a Wife*

Estifania enters *"with a Pistol, and a Dagge"* (227) wherein *Dagge* could be either a second pistol or a misprint for *dagger*; the other undisputed use is as a concealed *weapon*: *"Draws a pocket dag"* (*Fatal Dowry*, 4.1.164); for concealed weapons carried by revengers Marston calls not for *dags* but for *"pistolets and short swords under their robes"* (*Malcontent*, 5.5.66).

dagger

widely used along with the *poniard* for (1) violence and threats of violence, (2) suicide, (3) other distinctive actions; for figures who enter *with a dagger* (often *in his hand*/*drawn*) see *Rare Triumphs*, 1607; *Cobbler's Prophecy*, 1326–7; *Edward I*, 830; *Famous Victories*, C2v; *True Tragedy of Richard III*, 1331–2; *2 Troublesome Reign*, E3v; *King Leir*, 1453–4; *Second Maiden's Tragedy*, 991; *Queen's Exchange*, 540; figures are directed to *pull* out (*Devil's Charter*, C2v), *show* (*Massacre at Paris*, 355; *Whore of Babylon*, 5.2.157), *flourish* daggers (*Sir Thomas More*, 1068); most common is the *drawing* of daggers (*Antonio's Revenge*, 2.2.215; *Trick to Catch the Old One*, H1r; *Queen of Corinth*, 18; *Fatal Contract*, D1v, G2v; *Claracilla*, F12r; *Distresses*, 315; *Princess*, H3v; *Royal Master*, H4r); other actions with a *dagger* include *snatch*/*hold*/*take away* (*Cobbler's Prophecy*, 1328–9; *Sparagus Garden*, 164; *Antipodes*, 321), *let fall* (*Alphonsus of Germany*, I3v; *King Leir*, 1739, 1743), *"offereth to throw his dagger"* (*Massacre at Paris*, 1063), *"holding a dagger fixed in his bleeding bosom"* (*Devil's Charter*, G2r), *"Alberto draws out his dagger, Maria her knife, aiming to menace the Duke"* (*Antonio's Revenge*, 5.1.0), *"She takes Plangus's Dagger, flings it at Ephorbas, and kills him"* (*Andromana*, 270); daggers can be paired with other *weapons* such as a short *sword* (*Eastward Ho*, A2r), *rapier* (*Friar Bacon*, 1819), *foils* (Q2 *Hamlet*, N3v, 5.2.224); to denote off-stage violence a figure can enter *"his Sword in one hand, and in the other a bloody Dagger"* (*Love's Sacrifice*, 2584–5), *"with his dagger in him"* (*Valentinian*, 74); menacing actions include *"sets a dagger to his breast"* (*Claracilla*, F11v; see also *Goblins*, 3.2.13), *"bringing out their Mother one by one shoulder, and the other by the other, with daggers in their hands"* (*Revenger's Tragedy*, H1v), *"Syphax, his dagger twon about her hair, drags in Sophonisba in her nightgown petticoat"* (*Sophonisba*, 3.1.0; see also *Rebellion*, 61), *"takes up the child by the skirts of his long coat in one hand and draws his dagger with the other"* (*Yorkshire Tragedy*, 506–8); in *'Tis Pity* Giovanni first *"Offers his dagger"* to his sister, saying "And here's my breast, strike home!" and in the final scene enters *"with a heart upon his dagger"* (1.2.209;

5.6.9); the *dagger's* association with violence is spelled out by a villain who *"lays his finger on his mouth, and draws his dagger"* (*Antonio's Revenge*, 2.2.215) saying "Look, here's a trope: a true rogue's lips are mute; / I do not use to speak, but execute."

For examples of *daggers* linked to suicide, Hieronimo enters *"with a poniard in one hand, and a rope in the other"* and subsequently *"flings away the dagger and halter"* (*Spanish Tragedy*, 3.12.0, 19; see also *Looking Glass for London*, 2041–2); to encourage suicide Mephostophilis gives a *dagger* to Faustus (*Doctor Faustus*, A 1317–18, B 1831–3), and Techelles offers *"a naked dagger"* to Agydas (*1 Tamburlaine*, 1072); for an interrupted suicide Romeo *"offers to stab himself, and Nurse snatches the dagger away"* (Q1 *Romeo and Juliet*, G1v, 3.3.108); other distinctive actions are *"sweareth him on his Dagger"* (*Soliman and Perseda*, B2v), *"diggeth with his dagger"* in a fit of madness (*Spanish Tragedy*, 3.12.71), *"strike the stage with their daggers, and the grave openeth"* (*Antonio's Revenge*, 4.2.87), enter *"with a piece of meat upon his dagger's point"* (*Taming of a Shrew*, D4v); see also *Soliman and Perseda*, H3r; *Christian Turned Turk*, C2v.

dance, dancing

widely used (almost 350 examples) usually to signal the formal activity but sometimes to describe a way of moving; most common is simply *dance* (*Doctor Faustus*, B 473; *Woodstock*, 2149; *Old Fortunatus*, 3.1.300; Quarto *Every Man Out*, 3909; *Birth of Merlin*, E1r; *Revenger's Tragedy*, I3v; *Pericles*, D2r, 2.3.98, 106; *Changeling*, 4.3.212; MS *Poor Man's Comfort*, 385; *Barnavelt*, 2156; *Great Duke of Florence*, 4.2.209; *City Madam*, 3.1.71; *Humorous Courtier*, E1r; *Love's Mistress*, 104, 105, 119, 133, 146, 159; *Lady Mother*, 2601; *Mad Couple*, 98; *Antipodes*, 337; *Ball*, C2v, G3v, I3v); more detailed directions are *"a Dance of Shepherds and Shepherdesses"* (*Winter's Tale*, 1988–9, 4.4.165, also 2164, 4.4.342), *"here they Dance the witches' Dance"* (*Witch*, 2022–4; see also *Macbeth*, 1680, 4.1.132), *"In the dance they discover themselves"* (*Hannibal and Scipio*, 221); see also *Thracian Wonder*, D1v; *Duchess of Malfi*, 4.2.114; *World Tossed at Tennis*, F1r; *Women Beware Women*, 3.3.200; *Northern Lass*, 41; *Love's Mistress*, 119, 133; *Landgartha*, F3r; sometimes *music* is also called for: *"Enter Music, dance"* (*Swetnam*, K3r–v), *"Music, and a dance"* (*'Tis Pity*, 4.1.35) or instruments specified: *"dancing to the cornets"* (*Sophonisba*, 1.2.35), *"dance to music of Cornets and Violins"* (*English Moor*, 16); see also *Cobbler's Prophecy*, 1021; *Malcontent*, 5.5.118; the basic signal frequently comes in the context of a *masque*:

"*Music, Dance*" (*Henry VIII*, 773, 1.4.76), "*Music plays and they dance*" (Q2 *Romeo and Juliet*, C3r, 1.5.25), "*Enter the Masquers, they dance*" (*Dutch Courtesan*, 4.1.6); see also *Death of Huntingdon*, 1325; *Much Ado*, C1r, 2.1.154; *Timon of Athens*, 455–6, 1.2.130; *Every Woman In*, H4v; *Cupid's Whirligig*, 5.8.28; *Wife for a Month*, 26; *Wonder of a Kingdom*, 4.1.0; *Changes*, K2v; *Jovial Crew*, 366; *Cardinal*, 3.2.85; *Constant Maid*, H1r.

Frequently *dance* is explained or elaborated, as when it is linked to **antic**: "*dances an antic mockway*" (*Soddered Citizen*, 1918), "*dance anticly*" (*Martyred Soldier*, 238), "*dance a short nimble antic to no Music*" (*Landgartha*, E4v), "*three antic fairies dancing*" (*Dead Man's Fortune*, 53–4); see also *Devil's Charter*, L2v; *Honest Lawyer*, G2v; *Messalina*, 846–7; *English Moor*, 67; elsewhere the name of the *dance* or a technical term is given: "*The two dance a jig devised for the nonce*" (*James IV*, 95), "*While the measure is dancing*" (*Antonio's Revenge*, 5.3.49), "*dance a strain*" and "*dances the Spanish pavin*" (*Blurt*, 1.1.158, 4.2.32; see also *New Trick*, 250–1), "*Dance the first change*" (*Broken Heart*, 5.2.12; see also *Love's Sacrifice*, 1849), "*Dances Sellenger's round, or the like*" (*Court Beggar*, 262), "*dancing a Coranto*" (*Duke's Mistress*, F4r; see also *Herod and Antipater*, C3r; *Messalina*, 1017), "*The Morris sing and dance*" (*Jack Drum's Entertainment*, A4r); frequently figures *dance about* someone or something, as in *Tempest* when the spirits bring in the banquet and "*dance about it with gentle actions of salutations*" (1537, 3.3.19); other examples are "*dance about a Tomb*" (*James IV*, 2–3), "*they dance about the dead body*" (*Revenge of Bussy*, 5.5.119); see also *Guy of Warwick*, B4r; *Love's Sacrifice*, 1846; similar phrasing occurs when figures *dance* and *sing*: "*the four Dancing and singing practice about him*" (*Court Beggar*, 262), "*sing and dance about him*" (*Bride*, 51); see also *Four Plays in One*, 360; *Goblins*, 3.1.2; for more *dancing* and singing see *Maid's Metamorphosis*, C4r; *Queen of Corinth*, 18; *English Moor*, 67; detailed directions include "*dance (with mocks and mows)*" and "*in a graceful dance*" (*Tempest*, 1617, 3.3.82; 1806, 4.1.138), "*dance the drunken round*" (*Eastward Ho*, E3r), "*dance in several postures*" (*Fair Maid of the Inn*, 175, also 201), "*takes his wife to dance*" (*Malcontent*, 5.5.67, 75), "*place themselves in a figure for a dance*" and "*The dance expressing a fight*" (*Hannibal and Scipio*, 220, 256, also 221), "*all dance in a Ring*" (*Maid's Metamorphosis*, D1r), "*mingle in the dance*" (*Antipodes*, 338), "*dance after the ancient Ethiopian manner*" (*Amorous War*, E2v), "*dance together*" (*Grateful Servant*, I2r), "*Dances looking on his Feet*" (*Court Beggar*, 261), "*dances vilely*" (*English Moor*, 67); see also **change**.

dark

used for (1) figures who **enter** in the dark, (2) a *dark lantern* equipped with a sliding panel to dim the *light*; the two instances of the former invoke **as [if]**: "*as in the dark*" (*Mad Couple*, 76), "*as if groping in the dark*" (*2 Iron Age*, 380); related is "*softly as by night*" (*Captain Thomas Stukeley*, 924–5); the lantern (along with other **lights** such as **candle/taper/torch**) indicates **night**/darkness, with the *dark* lantern regularly associated with clandestine activity; examples are a figure waiting in the *dark* to commit a murder ('*Tis Pity*, 3.7.0), figures secretly visiting a **tomb**/graveyard at **night** (*Knight of Malta*, 142; *Wits*, 210); for comparable uses of *dark* lanterns see *Novella*, 106; *Queen's Exchange*, 535; *Wizard*, 2203; *Distresses* both calls for this property and later directs "*shuts the lantern*" (292–3), and a clandestine visit to a tomb in *Law Tricks* calls for "*a Thieves' Lantern*" (185).

dart

a rarely cited small **spear** or **javelin**: "*Maid like an Irish footboy with a dart*" (*Amends for Ladies*, 2.3.10–11, also 113–14), "*his arm transfixed with a dart*" (*Sophonisba*, 2.2.0, also 1.2.62, 5.2.32), "*a dart in one hand*" (*Locrine*, 1574–5).

dead

used regularly (roughly seventy-five examples) (1) primarily to describe *dead* figures, bodies, and **body** parts but also in (2) **dead march**, (3) other locutions and actions; *dead* is most often linked to **body** for entrances, **exits**, **discoveries**, stage business; signals to **enter**/exit include "*Ventidius as it were in triumph, the dead body of Pacorus borne before him*" (*Antony and Cleopatra*, 1494–5, 3.1.0), "*then is brought in the Body of Vortimer in a Chair dead*" (*Hengist*, DS before 4.3, 9–10), "*Exeunt carrying the dead bodies*" (*Hoffman*, 1069); see also *Wars of Cyrus*, G2v; *Massacre at Paris*, 504; *Philotas*, D7r; *Cymbeline*, 2495–6, 4.2.195; *Tom a Lincoln*, 2861–2; *Nero*, 56; *Aglaura*, 5.1.33, 5.3.72; the three versions of *Hamlet* provide "*finds the King dead*" (Q1 F3r, Q2 H1v, Folio 1997, 3.2.135), "*The dead body is carried away*" (Q2 H1v, Folio 2000, 3.2.135), "*Exit Hamlet with the dead body*" (Q1 G3v, [3.4.217]); examples of body parts are "*Gives her a dead man's hand*" (*Duchess of Malfi*, 4.1.43), "*takes a dead man's head upon his sword's point holding it up*" (*Edmond Ironside*, 989–90), "*one with Dead men's heads in dishes: another with Dead men's bones*" (*Battle of Alcazar* plot, 97–9); discoveries are "*Discovering the body of her dead to certain Lords*" (*Revenger's Tragedy*, C1v), three discovered "*dead in* chairs" (*Albovine*, 105), "*Shows his dead son*" (*Spanish Tragedy*, 4.4.88).

Dead is found in a variety of locutions: "*shoots him dead*" (*Bloody Banquet*, 1522), "*stabs Ennius, and he falls dead*" (*Cobbler's Prophecy*, 1334), "*strikes him down dead*" (*Mucedorus*, E4v), "*falls over the dead man*" (*Looking Glass for London*, 796), "*left wounded, and for dead, stirs and creeps*" (*Warning for Fair Women*, F1v), *ghosts* who enter, "*dance about the dead body, and Exeunt*" (*Revenge of Bussy*, 5.5.119), a queen who enters "*with both her Infants, the one dead; she lays down the other on a bank, and goes to bury the dead*" (*Bloody Banquet*, 847–9); after a *fight* in which all are apparently killed "*Cethus riseth up from the dead bodies and speaks*" (*2 Iron Age*, 427); *counterfeit* deaths often invoke *as* [*if*]/*seems*: "*falls down as if he were dead*" (*1 Henry IV*, K2v, 5.4.76; *Bride*, 62), "*lies down, and feigns himself dead*" (*Jack Drum's Entertainment*, D2r; *Prisoners*, C8r), "*lying on a Table, seeming dead*" (*Humour out of Breath*, 452), "*bloodies himself with Sueno's blood, and falls down as dead*" (*Politician*, I2v; see also *Trial of Chivalry*, E2r); the Duchess is shown "*the artificial figures of Antonio, and his children, appearing as if they were dead*" (*Duchess of Malfi*, 4.1.55); atypical is "*Cassandra half dead under his arm*" (*Young Admiral*, D4v); *deadly* is found only in "*supporting Doron deadly wounded*" (*Two Noble Ladies*, 222), "*deadly wounded and panting for breath*" (*Rape of Lucrece*, 252).

dead march

a *march* for a *funeral* usually played by a muffled military *drum* or drums, probably in an established pattern: "*A sennet sounded, enter two with mourning pennons: a Drum sounding a dead march*" (*Alarum for London*, 260–1), "*Exeunt: Drums beating a Dead March*" (MS *Bonduca*, 2149–51; Folio "*Exeunt with a dead march,*" 137); typically instruments are not specified: "*Exeunt with a dead March*" (Folio *King Lear*, 3302, 5.3.327), "*Exeunt bearing the Body of Martius. A dead March Sounded*" (*Coriolanus*, 3837–8, 5.6.154), "*A dead march, and pass round the stage*" (*Sir Thomas Wyatt*, 1.2.58), "*a dead march within*" (*Hieronimo*, 8.0); rarely another instrument is cited: "*A Dead March within of Drum and Sackbuts*" (*Mad Lover*, 40); given that drums were the usual instrument, perhaps the direction in *Spanish Tragedy* beginning "*The trumpets sound a dead march*" (4.4.217) should read "*The trumpets sound, a dead march*"; atypical is a cue for covert action: "*Talbot, Bedford, and Burgundy, with scaling Ladders: Their Drums beating a Dead March*" (*1 Henry VI*, 683–5, 2.1.7); when linked to a funeral, *dead march* may

imply some distinctive movement or gestures: "*a Corpse, after it Irishmen mourning, in a dead March*" (*Four Prentices*, 178), "*They march out with the body of the King, lying on four men's shoulders with a dead march, drawing weapons on the ground*" (*Massacre at Paris*, 1263); *Charlemagne* has a bookkeeper's "*dead march*" at the entrance of a funeral (2721); see also **afar off**, **doleful**, **march**, **soft**.

death's head

a seldom used alternative to *skull*: "*To get into the charnel house he takes hold of a death's head,*" "*They lie down with either of them a death's head for a pillow,*" "*starts at the sight of a death's head*" (*Atheist's Tragedy*, 4.3.77, 204, 210), and more symbolically "*A table set forth with two tapers, a death's head, a book. Jolenta in mourning*" (*Devil's Law Case*, 3.3.0), "*A table is set out with a candle burning, a death's head, a cloak and a cross*" (*If This Be Not a Good Play*, 4.4.0).

deformed

rarely used for "ugly, misshapen"; in *Muses' Looking Glass* "*a deformed fellow*" is forced to see himself in a mirror (A4v) and in *Women Pleased* Belvidere enters in *disguise* "*deformed*" (286) with Silvio commenting "What Beldam's this? how old she is, and ugly" and describing her as "old, and of a crooked carcass."

degrees

twice refers to *stairs* or levels: "*The Consuls enter the degrees*" and later "*ascend*" (*Caesar and Pompey*, 1.2.0, 14), "*Alexander being set in state, Caesar Borgia and Caraffa advance to fetch King Charles, who being presented unto the Pope, kisseth his foot, and then advancing two degrees higher, kisseth his cheek*" (*Devil's Charter*, E1r), and twice indicates that something should be done slowly or in stages: "*Enter Empress by degrees, gazing at him*" (*Messalina*, 1524), "*Enter people passing over by degrees, (talking)*" (*1 Passionate Lovers*, D8r).

deliver

in the roughly sixty examples a few figures are *delivered* to someone onstage: a child (*Golden Age*, 20), *prisoners* (*Cymbeline*, 3031, 5.3.94; *Claracilla*, F9v; *Distresses*, 323); usually objects are *delivered*, most commonly *letters*, *petitions*, *papers*, or other *writings*; for a sampling see *Cobbler's Prophecy*, 884; *Wounds of Civil War*, 1106; *Captain Thomas Stukeley*, 595, 1056; *Warning for Fair Women*, H3r; *Look about You*, 22; *What You Will*, B3r; *Sophonisba*, 2.2.41, 3.1.60; *1 If You Know Not Me*, 216; *Woman Hater*, 129;

Maidenhead Well Lost, 108; *More Dissemblers*, B8r; *Two Noble Ladies*, 1544; *Emperor of the East*, 1.2.114, 5.2.36; *New Way to Pay*, 4.2.33; *Politician*, C4r; other items *delivered* include a *garland* (*Henry VIII*, 2649–50, 4.2.82), *cup* (*Four Plays in One*, 326), *purse* (*Devil's Charter*, E4r), *chain* (*Soliman and Perseda*, E1r), *shields* (*Your Five Gallants*, I2v; *Insatiate Countess*, 2.1.48), *coronets* (*Look about You*, 2831), the trophies of Hercules (*Brazen Age*, 239), papal cross *keys* (*Devil's Charter*, E1r), "*A Tun of Tennis balls*" (*Famous Victories*, D3r); actions include "*delivering a Packet upon his knee*" (*Aglaura*, 1.3.27), "*having delivered his dish makes low obeisance*" (*Bloody Banquet*, 1095), "*They subscribe, seal, and deliver interchangeably*" (*City Match*, 312; see also *Old Couple*, 60); only in a late Caroline play is a speech *delivered*: "*Prologue delivered by an Amazon*" (*Landgartha*, A4v, also K1r).

depart

widely used (roughly eighty examples) as an alternative to *exit*: "*take their leaves and depart*" (*1 If You Know Not Me*, 216), "*makes a curtsy and departs*" (*Warning for Fair Women*, A4r), "*as they entered so they depart*" (*Dead Man's Fortune*, 59), "*The King departs one way in great sorrow, the Ladies the other way in great joy*" (*Golden Age*, 20); over half the relevant signals provide *depart* with no such details; for a sampling see *Locrine*, 7–8, 437, 1358, 1774; *James IV*, 1732; *Doctor Faustus*, A 526, B 473; *1 Henry VI*, 2453, 5.3.23; *Looking Glass for London*, 1230; *Death of Huntingdon*, 961; *Captain Thomas Stukeley*, 2447, 2458–9; *Warning for Fair Women*, D1r, G3r; *Antonio's Revenge*, 5.3.153; *Sophonisba*, Prologue.29, 2.1.153, 2.3.88, 3.2.84; *Devil's Charter*, A2v, I3r; Quarto *Every Man Out*, 1160; *1 Edward IV*, 64, 75; *Pericles*, E1r, 3.Chorus.14; *Tempest*, 1538, 3.3.19; *Silver Age*, 96, 126; *Tom a Lincoln*, 153, 169, 1704; *White Devil*, 5.3.150; *Herod and Antipater*, C3r, F3v, F4r; *Twins*, E1v; *Bloody Banquet*, 1074; locutions include *offers* to depart (*Fedele and Fortunio*, 244–5; *Edmond Ironside*, 841–2, 1495, 1501; *Sir Thomas More*, 1086, 1824; *Blurt*, 2.2.239; *Henry VIII*, 1481, 2.4.121; *Duke's Mistress*, D2v; *Parson's Wedding*, 496), *depart severally* (*Case Is Altered*, 1.9.93; *Herod and Antipater*, I4v; *Lovesick Court*, 129), *all save* or *all but X depart* (*Eastward Ho*, B1v; *Dutch Courtesan*, 5.1.63; *Malcontent*, 4.3.71, 5.4.14; *Fawn*, 4.423; *Sophonisba*, 3.1.117); figures *depart suddenly* (*Three Lords of London*, G4v; *Four Prentices*, 222), *heavily* (*2 Seven Deadly Sins*, 25), *laughing* (*White Devil*, 2.2.23), *weeping* (*Hengist*, DS before 1.2, 9), *in haste* (*Maidenhead Well Lost*, 127), "*in a mighty passion*" (*Pericles*, G3r, 4.4.22), "*after a little pause*" (*Fatal*

Contract, B2v), "*All with doing duty*" (*Hoffman*, 1728), "*trailing the Colors on both sides*" (*1 Iron Age*, 345), "*wringing her hands, in tears*" (*Warning for Fair Women*, E3v), "*in a little whisper and wanton action*" (*Your Five Gallants*, A2r); atypical is "*The Herald departeth from the king to the walls sounding his trumpet*" (*Edmond Ironside*, 872–3).

descend

occurs roughly ninety times in sixty plays (1) most often in a signal to *descend* from *above* either by lowering from the *heavens* or from the upper platform and less often (2) to *descend* through the *trapdoor* or (3) from a *state*; of *descents* from above, the more detailed are for those seeming to require mechanical means: "*Jupiter descends in Thunder and Lightning, sitting upon an Eagle*" (*Cymbeline*, 3126–7, 5.4.92), "*Cupid descending in a cloud*" (*Love's Mistress*, 87, also 129), "*Music while the Throne descends*" (*Doctor Faustus*, B 2006; see also *Variety*, D11r), "*Fortune descends down from heaven to the Stage*" (*Valiant Welshman*, A4r), "*Love descends half-way, then speaks*" (*Rebellion*, 52); for less explicit directions probably indicating similar *descents* see *Woman in the Moon*, B1v, B4r, C1r; *Widow's Tears*, 3.2.78; *Whore of Babylon*, 5.6.88; *Cupid's Revenge*, 227, 235; *If This Be Not a Good Play*, 2.3.83; *Witch*, 1345–6; *Tempest*, 1730–1, 4.1.74; *Four Plays in One*, 311, 312, 359; *Golden Age*, 78; *Silver Age*, 98, 121, 154; *Brazen Age*, 254; *Women Beware Women*, 5.2.97; *World Tossed at Tennis*, C2r; *Mad Lover*, 61; *Wife for a Month*, 25; *Seven Champions*, B2r; *Ball*, I2v; *Messalina*, 2227; typically when a figure is to come down from the upper level, usually within the tiring house, the signal is simply *descend* with little or no elaboration (*John a Kent*, 980; Folio *3 Henry VI*, 2528, 4.7.29; *Turk*, 265, 1793; *Love's Cure*, 212; *Second Maiden's Tragedy*, 2021; *Renegado*, 3.5.85; *Roman Actor*, 4.2.106; *Great Duke of Florence*, 2.3.162; *Picture*, 4.4.86; *Unnatural Combat*, 2.1.203, 5.2.257; *Wizard*, 2178; *Obstinate Lady*, H1v, H2v); more explicit directions are "*They descend down, open the gates, and humble them*" (*James IV*, 2128), "*Hoboys sound, whilst the Barons descend*" (*King John and Matilda*, 83), "*Morose descends with a long sword*" (*Epicœne*, 4.2.120), "*Albert descending from Maria*" (*Hog Hath Lost His Pearl*, 341, also 352, 419), "*A Cupid descending, sings this*" (*More Dissemblers*, B7v).

Figures *descend* or *sink* through the trapdoor, often in a supernatural context: "*The devil descendeth with thunder and lightning*" (*Devil's Charter*, G2r), "*The Angel descends*" (*Martyred Soldier*, 242, 243, 247), "*she stamps: the chair and dog descends*" (*Rebellion*, 66); see also Q2 *Bussy D'Ambois*, 2.2.246, 3.1.61, 4.2.159; *Shoemaker a Gentleman*, 1.3.101, 119; *Sophonisba*, 3.1.169, 199, 205; *Macbeth*, 1611, 4.1.72; 1622, 4.1.81; 1637, 4.1.94; *Revenge of Bussy*, 5.5.161; *Atheist's Tragedy*, 2.4.2, 5.2.105; *Maid's Tragedy*, 13; *Love and Honour*, 148, 149; elsewhere dialogue establishes that a figure *descends* from a raised dais or state on the main platform, often from a **throne** on it: "*Aratus brings Clearchus to the King, and seems to inform him who he is, he descends, and they embrace*" (*Conspiracy*, G1v), "*The Ladies descend from the State*" (*Great Duke of Florence*, 5.2.157), "*Descends his throne*" (*Jews' Tragedy*, 3252–3), "*The King descends, takes her up: the Lords rise, all amazed*" (*Queen and Concubine*, 25); for less explicit signals see *Death of Huntingdon*, 960–1; Folio *3 Henry VI*, 1779, 3.3.46; *Edward I*, 1015; *Maid of Honour*, 4.4.59; *Just Italian*, 277; *Picture*, 1.2.232, 2.2.248; *Humorous Courtier*, I3v; see also **down, fall**.

devil

a demonic figure who appears frequently in a supernatural context, although the generic term does not include a number of named *devils*; directions sometimes call for a *devil* to impersonate a non-demonic figure – or for a non-demonic figure to assume the **disguise** of a *devil*, but there are few indications of their appearance; for undisguised, unnamed *devils* – the most common – see *Friar Bacon*, 294, 807, 2010; *Battle of Alcazar* plot, 59; *Doctor Faustus*, B 225, 250, 374, 472, 1485–6, 1775–6, 2088; *Histriomastix*, C4r; *Knack to Know a Knave*, 373, 1583, 1717; *Devil's Charter*, L1v, L2v, L3v, M1v, M2r, M2v; *If This Be Not A Good Play*, 4.2.33, 51; *Silver Age*, 135, 156, 159; *Prophetess*, 355; *Two Noble Ladies*, 1752–4, 1860–1; *Seven Champions*, H1r; in *Grim the Collier* Belphagor who has been disguised as a human reappears "*like a Devil, with Horns on his head*" (K2r) and in *Doctor Faustus* the A text calls for "*a devil dressed like a woman*" (595), the B text for "*a woman devil*" (536); *Birth of Merlin* provides "*the Devil in man's habit*" with his "*feet and his head horrid*" (D2v), and the Clown says "even though he hide his horns with his Hat and Feather, I spied his cloven foot for all his cunning" (the disguised *devil* also appears at E1r, E2r, G2r); for other *devils* in disguise see *Devil's Charter*, A2v, G1v, M2r; *Grim the Collier*, H8r; *Mad World*, 4.1.29; *New Trick*, 252; elsewhere figures disguise themselves as *devils*: "*one clad in devil's attire*" (*Looking Glass for London*, 1667), "*Madge with a Devil's vizard*" (*Monsieur Thomas*, 138); for more see *Old Fortunatus*, 1.3.0; *New Trick*, 282; *Queen's Exchange*, 535; *Goblins*, 1.1.84; see also **spirit**.

dice

the game is occasionally cited: "*The Friar spreads the lappet of his gown and falls to dice*" (*Edward I*, 1733), "*the play at dice*" (*Sir John Oldcastle*, 1497); see also *Michaelmas Term*, 2.1.0; *Costly Whore*, 255; *Valentinian*, 17.

dies, dying

typically the action is indicated by the words of the dying figure, eliminating the need to specify who *dies*; for a sampling from across the period often with more than one example in a play, see *1 Henry VI*, 1185, 2.5.114; 2263, 4.7.32; *Captain Thomas Stukeley*, 2982; *Battle of Alcazar*, 1335, 1504; *Julius Caesar*, 1288, 3.1.77; 2576, 5.3.90; 2698, 5.5.51; Quarto *Othello*, M3r, 5.2.125; M4v, 5.2.251; N2r, 5.2.359; *Hieronimo*, 11.111; *Charlemagne*, 2240, 2548, 2550; *Antony and Cleopatra*, 3567, 5.2.313; 3587, 5.2.328; Folio *King Lear*, 3283, 5.3.312; *Atheist's Tragedy*, 4.5.60, 5.1.98, 5.2.268; *Maid's Tragedy*, 71; *Bonduca*, 142, 143, 157; *Bloody Brother*, 274; *Duchess of Malfi*, 4.2.353; *Changeling*, 5.3.177, 179; '*Tis Pity*, 3.7.33, 4.1.100, 5.5.93, 5.6.61, 92, 107; *Two Noble Ladies*, 264; *Broken Heart*, 5.2.155; *Messalina*, 2353, 2356, 2366, 2424, 2434; *Brennoralt*, 5.3.169, 265; more elaborate directions include "*Bedford dies, and is carried in by two in his Chair*" (*1 Henry VI*, 1558, 3.2.114), "*the Queen falls down and dies*" (Q1 *Hamlet*, I3v, [5.2.302]), "*Here the Executioner strikes, and Herod dies*" (*Herod and Antipater*, L4r), "*She suddenly dies at the Queen's bed's feet*" (*Edward I*, 2607), "*The music sounds, and she dies*" (*2 Tamburlaine*, 3063), "*She dies, King wake*" and "*Pieces go off, Friars die*" (*Lust's Dominion*, 3.2.116, 3.3.88), "*The King dies in his bed*" (*True Tragedy of Richard III*, 192), "*Falls and dies*" (Q2 *Bussy D'Ambois*, 5.1.156), "*She dies. Still music above*" (*Cruel Brother*, 183), "*Die both*" (*Thierry and Theodoret*, 69), "*feigns to die*" (*Turk*, 1837), "*Brings up the body, she swoons and dies*" (*Aglaura*, 5.1.184); *dying* is rarely signaled: a figure "*at last dying, laid in a marble tomb*" (*James IV*, 676), "*Enter Eugenia dying as she goes*" (*Conspiracy*, D3v), "*Enter Diomed wounded, bringing in Patroclus dying*" (*1 Iron Age*, 312), "*Groans of dying men heard within*" (*Thracian Wonder*, C1r); see also **moritur**.

dig

in *2 If You Know Not Me* a figure reduced to poverty enters "*with a spade*" and "*digs*" (302–3), and in *Spanish Tragedy* Hieronimo in his distraction says "Away! I'll rip the bowels of the earth" and "*diggeth with his dagger*" (3.12.71); *Old Wives Tale*, where unearthing a buried object is central to the plot, provides *"the two Brothers in their shirts with spades digging," "Here they dig and descry the light under a little hill," "digs and spies a light"* (587, 603, 825).

disarm

the roughly twenty examples typically come during a *fight*: *"enter again in Skirmish Iachimo and Posthumus; he vanquisheth and disarmeth Iachimo"* (*Cymbeline*, 2895–6, 5.2.0), *"They fight, one is killed, the other two disarmed"* (*Dick of Devonshire*, 1737–8, also 775, 1711–12), *"beats him and disarms him"* (Quarto *Every Man In*, 4.2.115), *"draws his Sword from under his Gown. Crasy closes with, and disarms him"* (*City Wit*, 360); see also *Vow Breaker*, 2.3.18; *Albovine*, 107; *Claracilla*, E10v; *Cruel Brother*, 125; *Queen's Exchange*, 487; *Young Admiral*, E1v; *Distresses*, 340; *Hollander*, 101; *Prisoners*, A9v, B9r; *Lovesick Court*, 142; *Variety*, E1v; as this list indicates, *disarm* occurs primarily in plays written well into the seventeenth century, but a unique exception and usage is when *"Massinissa disarms his head"* by removing **armor** (*Sophonisba*, 5.3.28); see also *Jews' Tragedy*, 2143; a variant is *"set upon him, get him down and disweapon him"* (*Blurt*, 2.1.85).

discharge

either (1) an offstage **sound** representing the firing of **chambers** or (2) a signal for the onstage firing of a handgun; calls for the sound **within** linked to **battle** are the "warlike voice" of *"Drum and Trumpet, Chambers discharged"* (*Henry VIII*, 731, 1.4.49), *"The Trumpets sound, the chambers are discharged"* (*Battle of Alcazar*, 977), *"a health to the good success of the Mary: which must be Continued with shooting of guns to the last man: which orderly discharged will be about eleven or thirteen guns"* (*Launching of the Mary*, 2794–8); see also *Alarum for London*, 203; *Maid of Honour*, 2.3.0; *Dick of Devonshire*, 31; examples of the onstage **shooting** of a handgun are *"the Soldier dischargeth his Musket at the Lord Admiral"* (*Massacre at Paris*, 199), *"Enter Govianus discharging a Pistol"* (*Second Maiden's Tragedy*, 748–50); see also *Atheist's Tragedy*, 4.3.23; *Bloody Banquet*, 1995; a noteworthy combination of offstage sound and onstage action is *"As the Prince is going forth, a Pistol is discharged within, he falls"* (*Politician*, H1v).

disclose

unlike the widely used **discover**, this synonym occurs only four times when a figure *discloses himself* (*Valiant Welshman*, D3r); see also *Four Prentices*, 176; *Country Girl*, K1r; *Obstinate Lady*, F1r.

discontented

only two figures are designated **malcontented**, but a larger number appear *discontented*: Apemantus *"discontentedly like himself"* (*Timon of Athens*, 341, 1.2.0), *"Shore looks earnestly and perceives it is the King, whereat he seemeth greatly discontented"* (*1 Edward IV*, 67); in *Silver Age* Pluto attempts to cheer up Proserpine *"but she continues in her discontent"* (156); other locutions include *"in discontented appearance"* (*1 Honest Whore*, 1.1.0), *"wondrous discontentedly"* (*Second Maiden's Tragedy*, 1655), *"makes discontented signs"* (*Captain*, 297), *"expressing great fury and discontent"* (*Hengist*, DS before 4.3, 4), a figure in **mourning** *"walking discontentedly weeping to the Crucifix"* (*Noble Spanish Soldier*, 1.2.0); see also *Hieronimo*, 3.0; *Revenger's Tragedy*, C1v; *Prophetess*, 363; *Royal King*, 72; *Four Plays in One*, 326.

discover

an action signaled roughly 200 times in a variety of contexts, always with the idea of revelation ("reveal" does not occur in directions), either (1) of true identity by removing a **disguise** or (2) of a hidden scene; most of the over seventy directions for a disguised figure to *discover* or for another to remove the disguise are a basic direction: *"Discovers"* (*Match at Midnight*, 88), *"they discover"* (*Money Is an Ass*, H1v), *"Discovers himself"* (*Old Couple*, 81), *"Duke is discovered"* (*Witch*, 2125–6), *"Lodovico discovers him"* (*Queen*, 3545); for other examples see *Blind Beggar of Bednal Green*, 114; *Family of Love*, I3v; *Dutch Courtesan*, 5.2.50, 5.3.36; *2 Honest Whore*, 5.2.178; *Isle of Gulls*, 224; *Bartholomew Fair*, 5.5.120; *Devil's Law Case*, 5.6.33; *City Nightcap*, 183; *Damoiselle*, 464; *Guardian*, 5.4.189; *Heir*, 574, 583; *Bloody Banquet*, 1979, 2011; *Lady Mother*, 2560–1; *Aglaura*, 1.6.58; more detailed signals to *discover* by removing a disguise include *"Hercules discovering himself beats the Guard"* (*Brazen Age*, 183), *"kills Egistus, first discovering himself"* (*2 Iron Age*, 421), *"throws off his Gown, discovering his doublet with a satin forepart and a Canvas back"* (*Hengist*, 5.1.286–9), *"In the dance they discover themselves in order"* (*Hannibal and Scipio*, 221), *"Kneels to Leon, and discovers her hair"* (*Philaster*, 144/416), *"discovers himself to his mother"* (*Two Maids of More-Clacke*, G3v), *"the rest being departed Lodovico and Gasparo discover themselves"* (*White Devil*, 5.3.150), *"pull off the shell and discover him"* (*Volpone*, 5.4.73), *"Pulls off Lovering's periwigs, he is discovered to be Martha"* (*Hollander*, 152), *"pulls off his vizard and discovers himself to be Altamont"* (*Just Italian*, 277), *"pulls off his beard and discovers himself"*

(*Claracilla*, F11v); see also ***disclose***, ***display***, ***pull off***, ***undisguise***.

In more than ninety directions *discover* signals the ***opening*** of a ***curtain*** or ***door*** to reveal scenes ranging from the simple to the complex, such as a ***shop***, ***study***, ***tomb***, or ***altar***; examples of shops include "*Enter Maudline and Moll, a shop being discovered*" (*Chaste Maid*, 1.1.0), "*A Mercer's Shop discovered, Gartred working in it*" (*Greene's Tu Quoque*, B1r), "*Enter (a Shop being discovered) Walter Chamlet, his wife Rachel, two Prentices*" (*Anything for a Quiet Life*, C3r), "*Juniper a Cobbler is discovered, sitting at work in his shop*" (*Case Is Altered*, 1.1.0); for more see *Shoemaker a Gentleman*, 1.2.0; *Mad Couple*, 55; *Renegado*, 1.3.0; some *discoveries* of study scenes are "*Discovers Catiline in his study*" (*Catiline*, 1.1.15; see also *Law Tricks*, 180), "*Alexander draweth the Curtain of his study where he discovereth the devil sitting in his pontificals*" (*Devil's Charter*, L3v), "*A curtain drawn by Dash (his clerk) Trifle discovered in his study*" (*News from Plymouth*, 167), "*The Countess of Swevia discovered sitting at a table covered with black*" (*Insatiate Countess*, 1.1.0), "*Ciprian discovered at his book*" (*Two Noble Ladies*, 83), "*A canopy is drawn, the king is discovered sleeping over papers*" (*Albovine*, 95; see also *Distresses*, 338); examples of tombs *discovered* include "*The Tomb here discovered richly set forth*" (*Second Maiden's Tragedy*, 1726–7), "*discovers the Tomb, looks in and wonders*" (*Widow's Tears*, 4.2.0); see also *Knight of Malta*, 138/388; *Wife for a Month*, 26; *Love's Sacrifice*, 2734; *Lost Lady*, 549; altars *discovered* include "*King Priam discovered kneeling at the Altar*" (*2 Iron Age*, 390), "*Fortune is discovered upon an Altar*" (*Hengist*, DS before 1.2, 1), "*an Altar discovered and Statues*" (*Game at Chess*, 2038–9); see also *Knight of Malta*, 161; occasionally *discover* is linked to a ***tent***: "*The Queen's Tent opens, she is discovered in her bed*" (*Edward I*, 1453), "*He discovereth his Tent where her two sons were at Cards*" (*Devil's Charter*, I1v); see also *1 Iron Age*, 390.

A ***bed*** is usually *discovered* by ***drawing*** open a curtain, as in one of only three uses of the term in the Shakespeare canon: "*the Curtains being drawn, Duke Humphrey is discovered in his bed, and two men lying on his breast and smothering him*" (Quarto *2 Henry VI*, E2r, [3.2.0], also F1v, [3.2.146]); other locutions include "*A curtain drawn, a bed discovered, Ingen with his sword in his hand, and a Pistol, the Lady in a petticoat, the parson*" (*Amends for Ladies*, 5.2.180–3), "*Offering to leap into bed, he discovers Vangue*" (*Sophonisba*, 3.1.182, also 1.2.35, 5.1.0), "*draws a Curtain where Fernando is discovered in bed*" (*Love's Sacrifice*, 1269–70), "*A Bed discovered with a Blackamoor in it*" (*Monsieur Thomas*, 159), "*Enter*

Livia discovered abed, and Moroso by her*" (*Woman's Prize*, 80); see also *Tom a Lincoln*, 150–1, 169–70; *All's Lost by Lust*, 4.2.0; *Traitor*, 5.3.0; *Wonder of a Kingdom*, 3.2.0; *Love's Mistress*, 121; *Wasp*, 62; *Lovesick King*, 1201; *Parson's Wedding*, 477.

The variety of other signals for *discovered* scenes includes the other use of the term in a Shakespeare play: "*Here Prospero discovers Ferdinand and Miranda, playing at Chess*" (*Tempest*, 2141–2, 5.1.171); some notable directions are "*Hell is discovered*" (*Doctor Faustus*, B 2017), "*He draws a curtain, and discovers Bethsabe with her maid bathing over a spring*" (*David and Bethsabe*, 23), "*the Curtains draw, there is discovered Jupiter dandling Ganymede upon his knee, and Mercury lying asleep*" (*Dido*, 0), "*A Chair of state discovered, Tables and Chairs responsible*" (*King John and Matilda*, 29), "*draws a Curtain, discovering Truth in sad habiliments*" (*Whore of Babylon*, DS before Act 1, 27), "*Two fiery Bulls are discovered, the Fleece hanging over them, and the Dragon sleeping beneath them*" (*Brazen Age*, 217), "*Here is discovered, behind a traverse, the artificial figures of Antonio and his children, appearing as if they were dead*" (*Duchess of Malfi*, 4.1.55), "*Eugenius discovered sitting laden with many Irons, a Lamp burning by him*" (*Martyred Soldier*, 206; see also *Epicœne*, 4.6.0; *Four Plays in One*, 363; *Emperor of the East*, 1.2.288); for more see *Jew of Malta*, 2346; *Wisdom of Doctor Dodypoll*, 2–4; *Atheist's Tragedy*, 5.1.0; *If This Be Not a Good Play*, 5.4.0; *White Devil*, 5.4.65; *Broken Heart*, 3.2.32; *Double Marriage*, 346; *Jovial Crew*, 365, 388; the anomalous "*Bobadilla discovers himself: on a bench*" (Quarto *Every Man In*, 1.3.84) becomes "*is discovered lying on his bench*" (Folio *Every Man In*, 1.5.0); several directions have figures *discovered* ***above***: "*Tiberio and Ducimel above are discovered, hand in hand*" (*Fawn*, 5.457), "*discovering Cuckold's-Haven above*" (*Eastward Ho*, E3v), "*discovered on the upper Stage*" (*World Tossed at Tennis*, C4r); see also ***appear***.

disguise, disguised

from the thousands of scenes that involve *disguise* roughly 230 directions specify that figures appear *disguised*/*in disguise*; over half of these signals stipulate only ***enter*** *disguised*; typical is "*Enter the Prince and Poins disguised*" (Folio *2 Henry IV*, 1256, 2.4.233); for plays with more than two examples see *George a Greene*, 448–9, 680, 1106–7, 1138; *Fair Em*, 277, 291, 302; *Dead Man's Fortune*, 22, 30, 45; *Blind Beggar of Bednal Green*, 16, 53, 72; *Fleer*, 1.3.225, 4.1.54, 4.2.15; *Honest Lawyer*, C3v, G4v, H1v; *Bloody Banquet*, 243, 743, 2006; a related locution calls for entrances *dis-*

guised like a: "Enter Falstaff disguised like an old woman" (Quarto Merry Wives, F2v, 4.2.181); a sampling includes disguised like a soldier (Quarto Every Man In, 2.1.0; Sophonisba, 2.2.41; Welsh Ambassador, 3), servingman (Fair Maid of Bristow, B1v; Anything for a Quiet Life, F4r; Damoiselle, 385), Priest of Faery (Alchemist, 3.5.0), Amazon (Antonio and Mellida, 1.1.0; Swetnam, E1r), scholar (Broken Heart, 1.3.0), seamster (Roaring Girl, 1.1.0), schoolmaster/pedant (Fedele and Fortunio, 390; Wise Woman of Hogsdon, 320), priest (Captain Thomas Stukeley, 2838), conjurer (Wizard, 2456), hermit (Malcontent, 4.3.0), physician/doctor (Two Merry Milkmaids, D3v; Rebellion, 72), Italian (Spanish Gypsy, D3v), country folk (King Leir, 2092); included in this category are a man "disguised like a woman" (George a Greene, 612–13), a woman "disguised like a man" (Fair Maid of Bristow, E4v); occasionally the stock components of a disguise (beard, false hair, mask, patch, scarf, vizard) or other details (muffled) are provided: "disguised like a Captain with a patch on his eye and a false beard" (Wizard, 343–5), "Blanch disguised, with a mask over her face" (Fair Em, 855–6; see also Northern Lass, 98), "disguised, and in a Vizard" (Wise Woman of Hogsdon, 308; see also Distresses, 322), "in mean Apparel, Disguised, and muffled" (Coriolanus, 2621–2, 4.4.0), "like a Soldier disguised at all parts, a half Pike, gorget, etc." (Widow's Tears, 4.2.0); figures appear disguised "in a Soldier's habit" (Valiant Welshman, G4v), "in country apparel" (Friar Bacon, 355–6), "in the Habits of Friars" (1 Honest Whore, 5.2.314), "in bravery" (New Academy, 56); a figure who re-appears as before/in the same disguise may be "still disguised" (Malcontent, 4.4.0; Two Maids of More-Clacke, I1v), whereas when some but not all have shed disguises an entrance can be "as themselves, Vaster disguised" (Honest Lawyer, H1v); atypical are "a little disguised" (Distresses, 332), "an antic quaintly disguised" (John a Kent, 780); alternatives to disguised include dressed like, attired like, in the habit of, in the shape of, simply like a.

When disguise appears as a noun the most common locution is enter in disguise; for typical instances see May Day, 4.5.97; Monsieur D'Olive, 5.2.0; Michaelmas Term, 3.1.35; Revenger's Tragedy, B2v; Fair Quarrel, 1.1.258; Goblins 3.2.0; sometimes other details are supplied: "Marius in disguise and Lelia, like a post boy" (Faithful Friends, 2414–15), two "like shepherds, Octavio in disguise" (Humour out of Breath, 431); variations include "in courtesan's disguise, and masked" (Mad World, 4.3.0), "in quaint disguises" (Sisters, C3v), "in some odd disguise" (Wasp, 745), "in other disguises" (Bird in the Cage, D3r); less common are with a disguise

(Cunning Lovers, B4v; Honest Man's Fortune, 231), "with his disguise in his hand" (Bloody Banquet, 877), "without disguise" (Dead Man's Fortune, 58–9); a sequence in Atheist's Tragedy starts with a specified disguise ("a sheet, a hair, and a beard"), then "They run out diverse ways and leave the disguise," then "Charlemont rises in the disguise and frights D'Amville away" (4.3.55, 69, 174); another widely used locution attaches disguise to a verb so that figures put off (John a Kent, 472–3; Volpone, 5.12.84; Golden Age, 67; Valiant Welshman, H2v; Fine Companion, H4r, K2r), shove off (No Wit, 4.3.148), throw off (Northern Lass, 106, Aglaura, 3.1.22), pluck off (Bondman, 5.3.154), most commonly pull off disguises (Two Lamentable Tragedies, I3v; Fair Favourite, 224; Holland's Leaguer, L4v; Soddered Citizen, 2210; Sophy, 5.65); the latter category includes such signals as "pulls off their beards, and disguise" (Epicœne, 5.4.211), "pulls off his patches and disguise" (Distresses, 339), "pulls off his disguised Hair" (Two Merry Milkmaids, L2v); other locutions include "putting on a disguise" (City Nightcap, 175), "puts on his disguise again" (Widow's Tears, 5.5.0), "out of his disguise" (Revenger's Tragedy, G2r), "in his former disguise" (1 Edward IV, 75); disguise as a verb is rare, occurring only as "he disguiseth himself" (Mucedorus, D4r, D4v, F1r), "They disguise themselves" (Caesar and Pompey, 4.4.87).

dish, dishes

usually associated with meals: "All sit: dishes brought in before" (If This Be Not a Good Play, 1.3.18), "with Dishes and Service over the Stage" (Macbeth, 473–4, 1.7.0); dishes can contain water (Bashful Lover, 3.3.200), meat (Wit without Money, 193), "sweet meats" (Bloody Banquet, 1094), eggs (Match at Midnight, 28); figures enter with "a court dish" (Warning for Fair Women, F2v), "Dishes of Sugar, and a dish of Sparagus" (Sparagus Garden, 158), "Dishes of Apples, Nuts, and Cheesecakes" (Thracian Wonder, C4v), simply with a dish/dishes (Folio Richard II, 2763, [5.5.94]; 1 If You Know Not Me, 215; Bloody Brother, 262; Spanish Curate, 135; Late Lancashire Witches, 206); covered dishes are specified for banquets and other occasions: "with covered dishes, to the banquet" (Hieronimo, 1.0), "A Dinner carried over the Stage in covered Dishes" (City Wit, 279), "covered dishes march over the stage" (Mad World, 2.1.151); see also Doctor Faustus, B 1775; White Devil, 4.3.19; Wonder of a Kingdom, 3.1.148; some covered dishes do not contain food: "with a child in a covered Dish" (Maidenhead Well Lost, 158), "Dishes covered with papers in each ready" (Spanish Curate, 132/501); Titus

Andronicus provides "*strikes the dish with a knife*" (Folio 1504, 3.2.51), "*Titus like a Cook, placing the dishes*" (Quarto K2r, 5.3.25); *dishes* not linked to meals include "*a wooden dish of water*" for a **prisoner** (*Believe as You List*, 1989–90), a beggar with a *clap-dish* (*2 Edward IV*, 169), "*a chafing-dish: a perfume in it*" (*Antonio's Revenge*, 3.1.0; see also *1 Honest Whore*, 2.1.0), "*Itis's head in a dish*" (*2 Seven Deadly Sins*, 83).

disperse

either (1) "to scatter in various directions" or (2) "to dispel, cause to disappear"; an example of the former is "*Upon Subtle's entry they disperse*" (*Alchemist*, 4.5.33) and of the latter "*Enter a Masquerado of several shapes, and Dances, after which enter Belvidere and disperses them*" (*Women Pleased*, 308); either or both meanings may be pertinent to two **battle** scenes where after onstage **combat** "*the Rebels are dispersed*" (*1 Edward IV*, 31), "*They fight, the Centaurs are all dispersed and slain*" (*Silver Age*, 143); atypical is "*Burden dispersedly*" (*Tempest*, 525, 1.2.382) in the midst of Ariel's "Come unto these yellow sands," which presumably means that offstage barking **sounds** come from several directions or are not in unison.

displayed

of the three uses in directions two, both in the Marston canon, are equivalent to **discover**: "*Maria draweth the curtain, and the Ghost of Andrugio is displayed*" (*Antonio's Revenge*, 3.2.72), "*The Curtains are drawn by a Page*" and a group is "*displayed sitting at Dinner*" (*What You Will*, G3r); the other usage describes a figure who "*Looks on her hair displayed*" – or hanging loose – before her husband strangles her with it (*Turk*, 2098).

distaff

a tool used in **spinning**, conventionally symbolic of women and women's work, as in the two similar occurrences: "*Hercules attired like a woman, with a distaff and a spindle*" (*Brazen Age*, 241), "*Hercules following with a distaff*" (*Locrine*, 1355–6).

distracted

see **mad**

ditty

used several times for a **song**: "*this ditty being sung in parts*" (*Women Beware Women*, 5.2.72), "*this ditty is sung, to very solemn music*" (*Duchess of Malfi*, 3.4.7); see also *Fedele and Fortunio*, 192–3.

diverse

a **permissive** term (spelled *divers* and comparable to **several**) by which the number of actors, objects, or actions is left indeterminate: "*diverse Spirits in shape of Dogs and Hounds*" (*Tempest*, 1929–30, 4.1.254), "*Music in diverse places*" (*Women Pleased*, 307); of the roughly forty examples, thirty are linked to people, so that signals call for *diverse* attendants, servants, lords, gentlemen, noblemen, courtiers, musicians, citizens, senators; for a sampling see Folio *Richard III*, 3844, 5.5.0; *All's Well*, 239, 1.2.0; 594, 2.1.0; *Wit of a Woman*, 394; *When You See Me*, 1820; *Macbeth*, 473, 1.7.0; *Timon of Athens*, 1383, 3.6.0; *Duchess of Malfi*, 3.4.7; *Love's Pilgrimage*, 289; *Wife for a Month*, 26; *Birth of Merlin*, G4r; *Maid of Honour*, 3.3.0; *Herod and Antipater*, C3r; *Very Woman*, 3.1.0; *Novella*, 106; *Traitor*, 4.1.73; *diverse* is also linked to **excursions** (*Captain Thomas Stukeley*, 1170), **bags** of **money** (*Devil's Charter*, A2r), **muskets** (*Dick of Devonshire*, 1623), supplications (*1 Edward IV*, 81), "*diverse complimental offers of Courtship*" (*Love's Sacrifice*, 1852–3); figures who **enter/exit** are directed to "*enter at diverse doors*" (*Selimus*, 658), "*Exeunt diverse ways*" (*Golden Age*, 71; *1 Iron Age*, 309; *Atheist's Tragedy*, 4.3.69; *Royal King*, 74; *Brennoralt*, 4.3.13); *diverse* can be used as a noun: "*diverse like Merchants*" (*Christian Turned Turk*, H1v), "*diverse with weapons*" (*Doctor Faustus*, B 1486), "*Diverse within cry*" (*Doubtful Heir*, F3v).

dog, dogging

the noun occurs more often than the verb; the animal, or an actor dressed as one, is brought onstage in several plays; examples include figures "*leading the Dog*" (Quarto *Every Man Out*, 1868, also 3293, 3473, 3551; see also *Downfall of Huntingdon*, 2293), "*takes a dog and ties it to the chair: she stamps: the chair and dog, descend*" (*Rebellion*, 66); other examples are "*a brace of greyhounds*" and "*the Boy upon the dogs*" (*Late Lancashire Witches*, 196, 199), "*servants with water Spaniels and a duck*" and "*Spits in the dog's mouth*" (*Roaring Girl*, 2.1.361, 371); Henslowe's inventory lists "one black dog" (*Diary*, App. 2, 92); costumed actors are "*diverse Spirits in shape of Dogs and Hounds*" (*Tempest*, 1929–30, 4.1.254); in *Witch of Edmonton* the figure "*Dog*" listed in the *Dramatis Personae* as a "familiar" appears repeatedly (2.1.227, 3.1.76, 3.3.0, and more); the variant *hound* also occurs: "*Brian with his man, and his hound*" (*Merry Devil of Edmonton*, E1v), "*A cry of hounds within*" and "*a Huntsman with a greyhound*" (Quarto *Every Man Out*, 1002–3, 1010); the verbal form signals close pursuit: "*Enter Charlemont,*

Borachio dogging him in the churchyard" (*Atheist's Tragedy*, 4.3.0), "*Stroza goes to hide [the Child], and Parma dogs him*" (*Maidenhead Well Lost*, 127), "*Enter dogging of them, Ariaspes, Jolas*" (*Aglaura*, 1.4.2); see also **spaniel**.

doleful, dolefully

a modifier sometimes linked to **music** played at a **funeral**, as in *2 Tamburlaine* for the death of Zenocrate: "*the drums sounding a doleful march*" (3190); *Chaste Maid* provides "*Recorders dolefully playing*" (5.4.0) for the supposed deaths of Moll and Touchwood Junior; see also **dead march**, **sad**, **solemn**.

done

the roughly thirty uses of this timing indicator are linked to either (1) action, often in a **dumb show** or (2) **sound**, especially a **song**; the desire to control the sequence of a series of actions is apparent in "*After the Christening and marriage done, the Heralds having attended, they pass over*" (*Edward I*, 1927, also 2076), "*The fifth Act being done, let the Consort sound a cheerful Galliard*" (*Fedele and Fortunio*, 1807–8), "*he discloseth himself unto them; which done, they Crown him*" (*Four Prentices*, 176), "*burn perfumes afore the picture, and wash the lips of the picture, that done, quenching the fire, and putting off their spectacles they depart laughing*" (*White Devil*, 2.2.23), "*They dance, which done, a Bell Rings*" (*Bird in a Cage*, F3r); for comparable signals in sequences of mimed action see *Battle of Alcazar*, 36–40; *Battle of Alcazar* plot, 63; *John a Kent*, 1257–9; *Captain Thomas Stukeley*, 2443–5; *Warning for Fair Women*, D1v; *Sir John Oldcastle*, 603; *Sejanus*, 5.177; *Hieronimo*, 1.0; *Whore of Babylon*, DS before Act 1, 40–3, 1.2.81; *2 Iron Age*, 423, 427; *Henry VIII*, 2651–3, 4.2.82; *Tom a Lincoln*, 168–9; *Herod and Antipater*, F4r; *done* is sometimes an alternative to the more common **cease** for the timing of a song or other sounds: "*The song being done, Juno speaks*" (*Arraignment of Paris*, 185, also 813), "*When they have done singing, Vice and Virtue hold Apples out to him*" (*Old Fortunatus*, 4.1.136), "*in dumb signs, Courts him, till the song be done*" (*Westward Ho*, 4.2.52), "*Cupid joins their hands, and sings; Which done, Exeunt Masquers*" (*Constant Maid*, H1v); for more see *Orlando Furioso*, 1257–9; *Patient Grissil*, 1.2.0; *Sophonisba*, 3.1.116; *Tragedy of Byron*, 2.65; *Little French Lawyer*, 418; *Love's Cruelty*, E4v; *Lovesick Court*, 163; see also **end**, **stop**.

door

of the nearly 600 examples (1) the majority are entrances, most commonly variations on **enter** at

several doors, **enter at one door and at another door**, but also widely used are (2) actions *at the door/to the door*, (3) **open/shut/lock** a door; for a sampling of *enter at several doors* see *Doctor Faustus*, B 1181, 1489, 1995–6; *Woodstock*, 2; *Dead Man's Fortune*, 8, 29; *King John*, 646–7, 2.1.333; *Twelfth Night*, 656, 2.2.0; *1 Honest Whore*, 5.2.86; *Insatiate Countess*, 1.1.288, 2.2.0, 2.4.0, 3.3.0; *Timon of Athens*, 2–3, 1.1.0; 1383, 3.6.0; *Woman's Prize*, 20, 29; *Four Prentices*, 234; *Maid of Honour*, 4.5.0; *Shoemaker a Gentleman*, 5.1.0; *Lady's Trial*, 80; *Match at Midnight*, 75; *Late Lancashire Witches*, 218, 244; *Imposture*, B1r; variations include entrances/**exits** "*severally at several doors*" (*Lust's Dominion*, 3.1.20), "*at several doors opposite*" (*Malcontent*, 5.1.0), "*at three several doors*" (*Maid's Metamorphosis*, D4v; *World Tossed at Tennis*, C4v), "*at both doors*" (*Custom of the Country*, 363; *Double Marriage*, 360), "*at two sundry doors*" (*Fair Em*, 813), "*at diverse doors*" (*Selimus*, 657); atypical is "*Enter three in black cloaks, at three doors*" as **prologue** (*Four Prentices*, 165).

For a small sampling of hundreds of entrances/exits *at one door/at another door* see *Battle of Alcazar* plot, 68–71, 78–83; *2 Seven Deadly Sins*, 7–8, 39; *Midsummer Night's Dream*, B3r, 2.1.0; B3v, 2.1.59; *Captain Thomas Stukeley*, 355–6, 970–1, 2440–1; *2 Edward IV*, 110, 167; *2 Honest Whore*, 1.1.0, 3.3.0, 5.1.0; *Trial of Chivalry*, A2r, A4v, G2v, I3v; *Antony and Cleopatra*, 1175–6, 2.6.0; 1538, 3.2.0; *Cymbeline*, 1374–6, 3.1.0; 2892–3, 5.2.0; *Four Prentices*, 235; *2 Iron Age*, 382, 386, 405; *Four Plays in One*, 309, 321, 326; for a small sampling of *at one door/at the other door* see *Locrine*, 1278–9, 2022, 2062–3, 2022–4; *Edmond Ironside*, 813–14, 986–7, 1569; *Jack Drum's Entertainment*, B3v, E4v; *Sophonisba*, Prologue.0, 5.3.0; *Silver Age*, 100, 131; *1 Iron Age*, 289, 331; *Prophetess*, 363; *Mad Lover*, 2, 29; *Captives*, 1496–8, 2726–7, 2984; *Renegado*, 5.3.45; *City Madam*, 4.4.155; atypical are two figures "*at one door*," two "*at the other*," a fifth "*In the midst*" (*English Traveller*, 49), "*At the middle door, Enter Golding discovering a Goldsmith's shop*" (*Eastward Ho*, A2r); the initial *one door* in the locution can be left implicit: "*Enter Freevill, speaking to some within; Malheureux at the other door*" (*Dutch Courtesan*, 4.2.0, also 3.2.0); for some examples see *Fair Em*, 291; *Shoemakers' Holiday*, 3.4.0; *Antonio and Mellida*, 4.1.220; *Satiromastix*, 5.2.0; *Sophonisba*, 3.2.0; *Nice Valour*, 172; *Mad Lover*, 65; *Birth of Merlin*, C3r, E3v, G4r; variations include "*Enter Alberdure at one door, and meets with the Peasant at the other door*" (*Wisdom of Doctor Dodypoll*, 1005–6), "*Enter Livia at one door, and Moroso at another, hearkening*" (*Woman's Prize*, 22), enter *"passing over the stage and knocks at the other door"* (*Hog Hath Lost His Pearl*, 2–3); *another/the other door* can be used for an exit and then entry of different figures (*Antonio's Revenge*, 5.1.0; *Satiromastix*, 3.1.272) or the re-entry of the same figures (*Woman Is a Weathercock*, 3.2.68; *Caesar and Pompey*, 4.3.0; *Distresses*, 305); typical are *"Exeunt at one door: Enter Dorcas at another"* (*Tom a Lincoln*, 386), *"goes off; then at the other door enter Eunuch"* (*Fatal Contract*, E1r), *"goes in at one door, and comes out at another"* (*English Traveller*, 69; *Spanish Tragedy*, 3.11.8), *"They march softly in at one door, and presently in at another"* (*2 Iron Age*, 379; see also *Spanish Gypsy*, I3r); atypical is Grissil's exit, then *"Enter at the same door Mario and Lepido"* (*Patient Grissil*, 2.2.122) so that the Marquess asks them *"what was she that passed by you?"*; two directions are for entrances *"at the farther door"* (*Your Five Gallants*, B2r; *Second Maiden's Tragedy*, 1725; see also *Captain Thomas Stukeley*, 260–1); see also **end**, **side**, **way**.

For a sampling of *at the door/enter at the door* see Folio *Othello*, 3343, 5.2.84; *Caesar and Pompey*, 4.2.0; *Custom of the Country*, 376; *Mad Lover*, 47; *Loyal Subject*, 122; *Little French Lawyer*, 409; *Lovers' Progress*, 104; *Woman's Prize*, 46; *Barnavelt*, 384; *City Madam*, 5.3.4; actions include *"speaks at the door"* (*Guardian*, 3.6.104; *Bondman*, 3.2.38), *"listening at the door"* (*Sir John Oldcastle*, 2088), *"At the door Francis kisses her"* (*City Nightcap*, 131), *"meets Crasy at the door"* (*City Wit*, 332), *"puts out the candle at the door and returns"* (*Country Captain*, C12r), *"sit at her door"* (*Warning for Fair Women*, B2v; see also *Two Lamentable Tragedies*, C4r), *"stays at the door with his sword drawn"* (*Unnatural Combat*, 4.2.25), *"lays a Suit and Letter at the door"* (*Wit without Money*, 180); the manuscript of *Bonduca* provides *"shows herself but at the Door,"* *"peeping at the Door,"* *"stopping the Soldiers at the Door"* (1048–9, 1850–2, 2108); *at the door* is most often linked to **knocking**: *"they knock at the door with a Knocker with inside"* (*Puritan*, E2v), *"knocks at the door and crieth"* (*Richard II*, I2r, 5.3.38), *"One knocks within at the door"* (*Spanish Tragedy*, Fourth Addition, 71); for some examples of *knocking at the door* see *Massacre at Paris*, 349; *George a Greene*, 622; *Two Lamentable Tragedies*, C4v, G1r, G3r; *2 Henry IV*, E3r, 2.4.351; K2v, 5.3.70; *Malcontent*, 4.1.0; *Grim the Collier*, H12r, I9v; *Devil's Charter*, C3r, K3r; *Gentleman Usher*, 4.1.0; *Woman Is a Weathercock*, 3.1.1; *Atheist's Tragedy*, 4.5.50; *Alchemist*, 5.3.44; *New Trick*, 233; *City Match*, 258; *Novella*, 153; *Humorous Courtier*, I2v; *Gentleman of Venice*, A4r; *Maid's Revenge*, F1r.

For a sampling of *opening doors* see *Titus Andronicus*, I3r, 5.2.8; *Arden of Faversham*, 2359–60; *Alphonsus of Germany*, B1v; *Grim the Collier*, I9v; *Little French Lawyer*, 440; *Duke's Mistress*, I1r, K2r; detailed examples are *"breaking open a Door"* (*Island Princess*, 115; *No Wit*, 5.1.150; *Jews' Tragedy*, 2231–2; *Traitor*, 5.1.165), *"throwing open the doors violently"* (*Guardian*, 3.6.142), *"Opens a door, Paulina discovered comes forth"* (*Renegado*, 2.5.119), *"The Mayor opens the door, and brings the keys in his hand"* (Octavo *3 Henry VI*, D7r, [4.7.34]); figures *shut doors* (*Thomas Lord Cromwell*, C4r; Quarto *Every Man In*, 5.1.15; Quarto *Every Man Out*, 3825–6; *Amends for Ladies*, 5.2.130), *lock doors* (*Death of Huntingdon*, 1921; *Lust's Dominion*, 3.2.55; *Island Princess*, 137; *Captain*, 297, 299; *Fatal Dowry*, 3.1.401, 4.1.154; *Gentleman of Venice*, I1r); variations include *"Unlocks the door"* (*Renegado*, 4.2.0), *"makes fast the door"* (*Traitor*, 5.3.137; *Weeding of Covent Garden*, 55), *"bolts the door"* (*Twins*, F2v), *"Puts to the door and locks it"* (*Renegado*, 2.5.158); *John a Kent* provides *"opens the door,"* *"makes fast the door,"* *"tries the door"* (778, 848, 893); actions *to the door* include *enter* (Folio *Richard III*, 1794, 3.2.0; *Second Maiden's Tragedy*, 2081–3; *Bonduca*, 128; *Captain*, 273), **follow** (*King Leir*, 2625), **bring** (*Three Lords of London*, H2r; *Satiromastix*, 3.1.272; *1 If You Know Not Me*, 239), **go** (*Warning for Fair Women*, D1r; *Valiant Welshman*, F3v; *Staple of News*, 1.1.23; *Distresses*, 304, 305), **ride** (*Soliman and Perseda*, B4v); more detailed are *"runs to the door and holds it"* (*Weeding of Covent Garden*, 24), *"go to the door, and meet the King"* (*Satiromastix*, 2.1.83); atypical are *"perfuming the door"* (*Two Maids of More-Clacke*, A1r), *"looks through the door"* (*Cupid's Whirligig*, 4.5.31, 53, 66), *"Jars the Ring of the Door, the Maid enters catches him"* (*Phoenix*, H2v).

doublet

a man's close-fitting jacket, with or without **sleeves**; **unready** figures **enter** in **hose** and doublet (*Look about You*, 2745; *Histriomastix*, D2v; *May Day*, 3.3.165), *"without doublets"* (*King Leir*, 2477), *"putting on his doublet"* (*Amends for Ladies*, 4.2.1), *"half dressed, in his black doublet and round cap"* (*What You Will*, D3r); a figure in **prison** enters *"with a Torch, a Nightcap, and his Doublet open"* (*Fleer*, 5.3.0); actions include *"Unbuttons his doublet"* (*Andromana*, 235), *"Opens his doublet"* to find a **wound** (*Just Italian*, 264), *"Throws off his cloak and doublet"* (*Renegado*, 3.5.50), *"throws off his Gown, discovering his doublet with a satin forepart and a Canvas back"* (*Hengist*, 5.1.286–9), *"thrusts his dagger betwixt Alphonso's doublet and shirt"* (*Twins*, D3r); see also *King Leir*, 2213; *Eastward Ho*, B4r; *Amorous War*,

H2r, H2v; Henslowe's inventory provides a number of *doublets* that includes "one little doublet for boy" (*Diary*, App. 2, 13), "one yellow leather doublet for a clown" (35), "one ash color satin doublet, laid with gold lace" (97), "one great peachcolor doublet, with silver lace" (107), "one black satin doublet, laid thick with black and gold lace" (147), "Harry the fifth satin doublet, laid with gold lace" (177).

down

(1) most often used in directions for figures to *descend* from *above* but can also describe (2) descent from a *chair of state* on a dais, (3) descent through the *trapdoor*, (4) a *fall* in a *fight* or *faint*; *down* describes movement from the upper level of the stage to the main platform in Q1 *Romeo and Juliet*: "*He goeth down*" and "*She goeth down from the window*" (G3v, 3.5.42, 67) and Folio *Titus Andronicus*: "*A long Flourish till they come down*" (264, 1.1.234); figures also *come down* in *Two Lamentable Tragedies*, C4r, C4v, I1v; *James IV*, 2128; *Tale of a Tub*, 1.1.22; *Soliman and Perseda*, H4v; *Revenge of Bussy*, 5.5.87; *Devil Is an Ass*, 2.7.28; *City Madam*, 3.1.4, 5.1.7; *down* can also mean that a figure is to be lowered from above mechanically: "*let Venus be let down from the top of the Stage*" and "*Exit Venus. Or if you can conveniently, let a chair come down from the top of the stage, and draw her up*" (*Alphonsus of Aragon*, 2–3, 2109–10), "*Air comes down hanging by a cloud*" (*No Wit*, 4.3.40), "*Fortune descends down from heaven to the Stage*" (*Valiant Welshman*, A4r); twice figures *leap* down from above (*Fortune by Land and Sea*, 395; *Turk*, 1792) and twice the stage *post* probably represents a *tree* climbed by a figure who then *leaps/comes down*" (*Old Fortunatus*, 4.1.90; *Thracian Wonder*, D1r); in *Blurt* a thief climbs to the upper level on a *ladder* and others "*take him down*" (4.3.34), and in *City Wit* a figure "*lets down a Rope*," then "*comes down*" (361–2); for properties *thrown* down from above see *Thracian Wonder*, D1v; *Dutch Courtesan*, 2.1.56; *Great Duke of Florence*, 5.1.47; other usages related to the upper level are "*Bring down the body*" (*Two Lamentable Tragedies*, D2v), "*bringeth her down*" (*Devil's Charter*, I1v).

Figures *go* or *come* down from the *chair of state* on its raised platform in Folio *3 Henry VI*, 233, 1.1.205; *Old Fortunatus*, 1.1.140; *Lust's Dominion*, 5.1.81; *Jews' Tragedy*, 80–1; rev. *Aglaura*, 5.3.178; see also MS *Poor Man's Comfort*, 1382; in *Edward IV* a figure comes *down* from a *scaffold* (139), and in *Messalina* one on a scaffold about to be executed "*suddenly rising up leaps down*" (2592–4); for signals to go *down* through the trapdoor see *Alphonsus of Aragon*, 970; *Old Wives Tale*, 909; *Alarum for London*, 1311; *Grim the Collier*, I12v; *Atheist's Tragedy*, 2.4.13; *Devil's Charter*, A2v; *If This Be Not a Good Play*, 3.2.179, 5.3.149; *Silver Age*, 164; *Love and Honour*, 124; those *down* in a *fight* are usually defeated but not killed (*Doctor Faustus*, B 1294; *Blind Beggar of Bednal Green*, 82; Q2 *Bussy D'Ambois*, 5.4.69; *Blurt*, 2.1.85; *Dick of Devonshire*, 775, 1711–12; *Hannibal and Scipio*, 246); in *English Traveller* a figure "*Sinks down*" in a faint (91); atypical is "*rises and throws down the table*" (*Knave in Grain*, 1857–8); see also *sink*.

drag

typically one figure *drags* another, usually a male who *enters* with a female: "*the Greeks dragging in Cassandra*" (2 *Iron Age*, 389), "*Soranzo unbraced, and Annabella dragged in*" ('*Tis Pity*, 4.3.0), "*two Soldiers dragging Justina bound*" (*Two Noble Ladies*, 1149, also 914); several directions have a woman *dragged* on by the *hair*: "*dragging The Lady by the hair*" (*Jews' Tragedy*, 2240–1), "*the Bandit dragging Evadne by the hair*" (*Rebellion*, 60; see also *Virgin Martyr*, 4.1.59; *Goblins*, 2.6.7; *Brennoralt*, 5.3.162), "*Syphax, his dagger twon about her hair, drags in Sophonisba in her nightgown*" (*Sophonisba*, 3.1.0); two signals for a figure to be *dragged* that mention hair might indicate the same actions: "*Enter the Queen, dragging in Matilda, her hair loose, and Face bloody*" (*King John and Matilda*, 26), "*Enter Aphelia dragged by two Ruffians in her petticoat and hair*" (*Fatal Contract*, I1v, also I2v); elsewhere a female is *dragged* offstage: "*Exit dragging her*" (*All's Lost by Lust*, 2.1.145); see also *Argalus and Parthenia*, 23; *Captain*, 301; signals for male figures to be *dragged* on or off are "*dragging the old Earl violently, and rifling him*" (*Four Prentices*, 186), "*two dragging in the Cardinal*" (*Massacre at Paris*, 1102), "*drags the Magician out by the heels*" (*Valiant Welshman*, G1r), "*Grimaldi dragged off, his head covered*" (*Renegado*, 2.5.92), "*Hangmen dragging in*" two *prisoners* (*Roman Actor*, 3.2.46), "*drag him to a chair and hold him down in it*" (*Captain*, 310); see also *Dutch Courtesan*, 4.5.146; *Silver Age*, 164; *Jews' Tragedy*, 2009; one direction cites a property: "*Enter two, dragging of ensigns; then the funeral of Andrea*" (*Hieronimo*, 12.0).

dragon

occasionally part of magical or supernatural business; a *devil* ascends "*riding upon a Lion, or dragon*" (*Devil's Charter*, G1v), and a magician enters "*in a Throne drawn by Dragons*" (*Prophetess*, 341); as part of a magical contest "*Bungay conjures and the tree appears*

with the dragon shooting fire" (*Friar Bacon*, 1197–8);
Achelous the shape-changer in his fight with
Hercules "*is beaten in, and immediately enters in the
shape of a Dragon*" so that Hercules "*beats away the
dragon*" (*Brazen Age*, 175); at the outset of the golden
fleece episode "*Two fiery Bulls are discovered, the Fleece
hanging over them, and the Dragon sleeping beneath
them*" (*Brazen Age*, 217); the **head** of a defeated *dragon*
is brought in by Tom a Lincoln (*Tom a Lincoln*,
2231–2), and a devil appears "*with the face, wing, and
tail of a Dragon; a skin coat all speckled on the throat*"
(*Caesar and Pompey*, 2.1.24); Henslowe's inventory
includes "one dragon in Faustus" (*Diary*, App. 2, 84),
"one chain of dragons" (82).

draw, drawn

this very widely used verb and modifier (over 600
examples) can refer to (1) a *weapon*, (2) a *curtain*, (3) a
property such as a *bed*, (4) various smaller items
taken from a *pocket*; there are also assorted unique
usages; typically *draw* signals the action with an
unspecified weapon (*Titus Andronicus*, C3v, 2.1.45;
Comedy of Errors, 1497, 5.1.32; *All Fools*, 3.1.332; *Amends
for Ladies*, 1.1.244; *Four Prentices*, 210; *Parliament of
Love*, 4.2.53; 2 *Passionate Lovers*, H2v; *Lady Mother*, 435;
Lost Lady, 617; *Country Girl*, I4v; *Aglaura*, 1.6.49); more
detailed signals include "*They draw, to them enters
Tybalt, they fight*" (Q1 *Romeo and Juliet*, A4v, 1.1.72),
"*Draw both the conspirators, and kills Martius*"
(*Coriolanus*, 3805, 5.4.130), "*draws, and is charmed from
moving*" (*Tempest*, 624, 1.2.467), "*see one another and
draw*" (*Insatiate Countess*, 1.1.141, 4.2.38), "*They draw
all, and fight*" (*Bartholomew Fair*, 4.4.145), "*puts off her
cloak and draws*" (*Roaring Girl*, 3.1.54), "*Draw and fall
down*" (*Coxcomb*, 322), "*draws and wraps his Cloak about
his arm*" (*Dick of Devonshire*, 772–3), "*Retires and draws,
runs at him*" and "*Another pass, they close*" (*Goblins*,
2.3.14, 15); for more see Folio 2 *Henry VI*, 1944–5,
3.2.236; *Fair Maid of the Inn*, 157; *Messalina*, 1411–12;
Bride, 36, 61; *Princess*, G1r; when specified the
weapon is usually a *sword*: "*Coriolanus draws his
Sword*" (*Coriolanus*, 1939, 3.1.222), "*Mendoza with his
sword drawn, standing ready to murder Ferneze*"
(*Malcontent*, 2.5.0), "*Enter Charlemont doubtfully, with
his sword drawn, is upon them before they are aware*"
(*Atheist's Tragedy*, 4.3.69), "*then Vortiger left alone draws
his sword and offers to run himself thereon*" (*Hengist*, DS
before 4.3, 7–8), "*draws his Sword from under his Gown*"
(*City Wit*, 360), "*all start up, and draw their Swords*"
(*Conspiracy*, K1r), "*draws his sword and runs up and down
crying sa sa sa tarararara*" (*Two Noble Ladies*, 1523–4); a

rapier is also frequently produced: "*Enter Edmund
with his rapier drawn*" (Quarto *King Lear*, E1r, 2.2.43;
see also *Comedy of Errors*, 1440–1, 4.4.143), "*Exit
drawing his rapier*" (*All Fools*, 3.1.250), "*draws his rapier,
offers to run at Piero*" (*Antonio's Revenge*, 1.2.217),
"*looking angrily each on other with Rapiers drawn*" (*Fair
Em*, 813–14); and a *knife*: "*Draw a knife*" (*Antony and
Cleopatra*, 1118, 2.5.73), "*He offers to force her, and she
draws her knife*" (*Catiline*, 2.278), "*runs to Flamineo with
her knife drawn*" (*White Devil*, 5.2.52), "*She draws her
knife. Ramble his sword*" (*City Madam*, 3.1.46), "*Draw
two knives*" (*Match Me in London*, 3.3.33); other
weapons *drawn* include a *pistol* (*Amends for Ladies*,
5.2.174–6), *dag* (*Fatal Dowry*, 4.1.164), *poniard*
(*Guardian*, 3.6.40), *stiletto* (*Just Italian*, 238), *daggers*
(*Goblins*, 3.2.13); sometimes a different action, *offers
to draw*, is specified: "*Offers to draw and is held*"
(*Philaster*, 105), "*Hiempsall offers to draw, and Jugurth
stabs him*" (*Herod and Antipater*, F3v); for examples of
the basic *offers to draw* see *Humorous Day's Mirth*,
1.5.100–1; *Thomas Lord Cromwell*, F3v; *Charlemagne*,
2129; *Launching of the Mary*, 2613; *Prisoners*, B9v;
Platonic Lovers, 101; *Swaggering Damsel*, C2v;
Landgartha, F4r; *Variety*, D5r .

The numerous directions to *draw* a curtain/*arras*
include "*draws the curtains and shows Duke Humphrey
in his bed*" (Quarto 2 *Henry VI*, E3r, [3.2.146]), "*they
draw the curtains and smother the young princes in the
bed*" (*Battle of Alcazar*, 37–8), "*Enter Friar Bacon drawing
the curtains with a white stick*" (*Friar Bacon*, 1561),
"*Draws the Curtain, within are discovered Bright and
Newcut*" (*City Match*, 309), "*Here the Curtains draw*"
(*Dido*, 0), "*The curtains drawn above*" (*Emperor of the
East*, 1.2.288), "*Draw the curtain and show the picture*"
(*Fatal Contract*, B3v), "*They stand aside while the cur-
tains are drawn*" (*Selimus*, 864), "*The Arras is drawn, and
Zenocrate lies in her bed of state*" (2 *Tamburlaine*, 2968),
"*Draws the arras; Melander discovered in a chair sleeping*"
(*Lover's Melancholy*, 2.2.10); for more examples of
drawing these or less often a *canopy*/*hangings* see
Looking Glass for London, 510–11; *Woodstock*, 2432; *Sir
Thomas More*, 104; *David and Bethsabe*, 23; *Downfall of
Huntingdon*, 54–5; *Death of Huntingdon*, 925; *Old
Fortunatus*, 3.1.356; *Antonio's Revenge*, 1.2.207; *Whore of
Babylon*, DS before Act 1, 27; *Grim the Collier*, G2v;
Henry VIII, 1100, 2.2.61; *Tom a Lincoln*, 150, and more;
Distresses, 338; *Fatal Contract*, H3r; *Platonic Lovers*, 33;
Unfortunate Lovers, 79.

Figures or properties are also *drawn* onstage: "*A
bed drawn forth with Rousard*" (*Atheist's Tragedy*, 5.1.59),
"*The Duke (on his Bed) is drawn forth*" (*Cruel Brother*, 191;

see also *Golden Age*, 67; *Maidenhead Well Lost*, 154; *Lost Lady*, 613; *Very Woman*, 4.2.19; *Messalina*, 1100; "*Last, a Chariot drawn by two Moors*" (*Four Plays in One*, 311, also 334, 355, 363), "*Pluto, his Chariot drawn in by Devils*" (*Silver Age*, 135; see also *2 Tamburlaine*, 3979; *Wounds of Civil War*, 1070–1; *Captain Thomas Stukeley*, 2493–4; *Bashful Lover*, 4.3.69), "*David drawn on a hurdle*" (*Edward I*, 2361), "*Julio drawn in a Cart*" (2883), "*two Moors drawing Bajazeth in his cage*" (*1 Tamburlaine*, 1444), "*a Throne drawn by Dragons*" (*Prophetess*, 341), "*They draw in a chest*" (*Wits*, 189), "*Maudline drawing Moll by the hair*" (*Chaste Maid*, 4.4.18), "*three Servants, drunk, drawing in Fresco*" (*Atheist's Tragedy*, 2.2.0), "*draws him in by the leg*" (*Orlando Furioso*, 751); elsewhere smaller properties are *drawn out* of clothing or a container: "*The Prince draws it out, and finds it to be a bottle of Sack*" (*1 Henry IV*, K1v, 5.3.54), "*Balurdo draws out his writing tables*" (*Antonio's Revenge*, 1.2.92; see also *Court Beggar*, 260), "*Draw out his Tablebook*" (*Love's Labour's Lost*, F4r, 5.1.15), "*draweth out a bloody napkin*" (*Spanish Tragedy*, 3.13.85), "*Draws a Crucifix*" (*Death of Huntingdon*, 2536), "*draweth out of his boxes aspics*" (*Devil's Charter*, I4r), "*draws forth his watch*" and "*draws out his pockets*" (*Staple of News*, 1.1.10, 1.2.98), "*Draw Lots and hang them up with Joy*" (*Hengist*, DS before 1.2, 3–4; see also *King Leir*, 551; *Jews' Tragedy*, 560–1; *Lovesick Court*, 155), "*Draws a letter*" (*Love's Sacrifice*, 874–5), "*Drawing out her husband's Picture*" (*Puritan*, A4v), "*Draws out a paper, pen, and ink*" (*Platonic Lovers*, 91), "*draws out his Fiddle*" (*Variety*, D3v); different or unique locutions reflecting the range of meanings of *draw* include "*let a chair come down from the top of the stage, and draw her up*" (*Alphonsus of Aragon*, 2109–10), "*draws a circle on the ground*" (*Bartholomew Fair*, 4.4.136; see also *Dido*, 1408), "*As the King draws near, Eudora offers to kneel*" (*Conspiracy*, N1r), "*draw themselves aside*" (*Devil's Charter*, E1v), "*Offers to go out, and suddenly draws back*" (*Dutch Courtesan*, 2.1.145), "*drawing weapons on the ground*" (*Massacre at Paris*, 1263), "*draw wine and carouse*" (*Messalina*, 2205–6), "*draws off her ring and offers it to him*" (*Wizard*, 1857–8).

drawer

this figure together with such properties as **wine**, **glasses**, **cups**, and **towels** establishes a **tavern** setting; frequently called "boy," although probably not always played by one, the *drawer* typically appears at the start of a scene or is summoned when customers want to **drink**, usually bringing wine then leaving: "*Drawer with Wine, Plate, and Tobacco*" (*Amends for Ladies*, 3.4.36), "*Drawer with Wine and a Cup*" (*All Fools*, 5.2.52, also 5.2.0), "*Drawer enters with wine and exit*" (*Bride*, 31, also 23, 27, 49), "*Drawer with four quarts of wine*" (*Coxcomb*, 318), "*a drawer with a cup of wine and a towel*" (*May Day*, 3.3.188), "*drawer with wine and bread*" (*Launching of the Mary*, 1935–7, also 1958–9), "*A Table, Stools, Bottles of wine, and Glasses, set out by two Drawers*" (*Variety*, D6v); for a selection of other *drawers* who help to create the world in which they function see *2 Henry IV*, D2v, 2.4.0; *Look about You*, 1497; *1 Fair Maid of the West*, 265; *Greene's Tu Quoque*, C1v; *London Prodigal*, B2v; *Trick to Catch the Old One*, E2r; *Eastward Ho*, E1r; *Northward Ho*, 1.2.13; *Match at Midnight*, 40; *Knave in Grain*, 1568; *Cure for a Cuckold*, E4r; *Weeding of Covent Garden*, 57; *Imposture*, E5v; *Gamester*, C3r.

dreadful

a rarely used description for discordant **sound/noise**: "*the Spirits come about him with a dreadful noise*" (*Late Lancashire Witches*, 245), "*A dreadful music*" (*Renegado*, 5.3.45; *Roman Actor*, 5.1.180); see also **horrid**.

dress, dressed

various verb forms of *dress* are linked to (1) the act of *dressing* or the state of being *dressed*, (2) descriptions of costume, (3) **disguise**; in the first category, a figure can enter "*preparing to be dressed*" (*Sophonisba*, 2.2.41), "*as newly dressed*" (*Fatal Dowry*, 4.1.0), "*dressing himself*" (*Albovine*, 62; *Distresses*, 345), "*as dressing her*" or "*as nastily dressed as they can dress her*" (*Parson's Wedding*, 387, 479), simply *dressed* (*2 Arviragus and Philicia*, E4v); atypical is "*dressing his weapon*" (*Hollander*, 109); as to costume, **unready** figures can be "*unbraced and careless dressed*" (*What You Will*, A4r), "*half dressed*" (*What You Will*, D3r; *Gentleman Usher*, 2.1.123); comparable signals include "*fantastically dressed*" (*City Match*, 277), "*richly dressed*" (*Constant Maid*, H1r), "*neatly dressed*" (*Country Girl*, C3v); more specific are "*dressed like a Bride*" (*Amends for Ladies*, 5.2.1–2), "*loosely dressed like a Courtesan*" (*City Wit*, 367), "*dressed with Ribbons and Scarfs*" (*Thracian Wonder*, C4r), a **corpse** "*dressed up in black velvet*" (*Second Maiden's Tragedy*, 2225), Bacchus "*dressed in Vine leaves*" (*Summer's Last Will*, 967), "*with a new fashion gown dressed gentlewoman-like*" (*Michaelmas Term*, 3.1.0).

"*Dressed*" is often linked to disguise; for a figure to **enter** *dressed like* is equivalent to the widely used *enter **like** a* or *disguised like a*: "*the Pedant dressed like Vincentio*" (*Taming of the Shrew*, 2180, 4.4.0), "*one* *dressed like a Moor"* (*John a Kent*, 369); many of these usages involve men *dressed* as women: *"the Clown dressed like Angelica"* (*Orlando Furioso*, 1027–8), *"dressed like a woman"* (*Downfall of Huntingdon*, 1112), *"Snip like a Wench dressed up"* (*Blind Beggar of Bednal Green*, 71), *"a Boy dressed for a Lady"* (*Roman Actor*, 4.2.222); for other men *dressed* as women see *Doctor Faustus*, A 595–6; *Queen and Concubine*, 124; *Telltale*, 1209; *Deserving Favourite*, I4v; *Noble Stranger*, G4v; other examples include *"boys dressed like Fairies"* (Quarto *Merry Wives*, G2r, 5.5.36), *"dressed like two trumpeters"* (*City Match*, 249), *"his maid dressed like Queen Fortune"* (*Humorous Day's Mirth*, 5.2.128); a murderous deception involves *"the skull of his love dressed up in Tires"* (*Revenger's Tragedy*, F1r); atypical is *dress* as a noun: enter *"out of her Puritan dress"* (*City Match*, 279), *"lets fall a Jewel from her dress"* (*Court Secret*, B1r); unique is *"Knock within, as at dresser"* with reference to offstage **meat** being *dressed* for a feast (*Late Lancashire Witches*, 206).

drink, drinking

the frequency of directions to *drink* – over 140 in more than eighty plays – indicates both the popularity of this stage business and the regular practice of signaling it; besides a wide variety of specific situations, figures (1) *drink* in a **tavern** or other convivial scene, (2) *drink* a **health** or **pledge**, (3) *drink* **poison** in **wine** and (4) sometimes *drink* is a noun; typically the signal is simply *"drink"* or a variant (*1 Henry IV*, D3v, 2.4.155; *Sophonisba*, 3.1.145; *Volpone*, 5.1.12, 16; *Atheist's Tragedy*, 2.1.22; *Tempest*, 1084, 2.2.45; 1095, 2.2.55; *Chaste Maid*, 3.3.110; *Great Duke of Florence*, 2.2.21, 30, 4.2.167, 193; *Messalina*, 336, 499, 506; *Launching of the Mary*, 1973–4, 1977–9; *Sophy*, 4.180, 181, 188); more elaborate directions indicate a context: *"bring out the stand of ale, and fall a drinking"* (*George a Greene*, 1183), *"dance the drunken round, and drink carouses"* (*Eastward Ho*, E3r), *"drinks and falls over the stool"* (*Look about You*, 1503), *"drinks and then falls asleep"* (*Taming of a Shrew*, F2r), *"As soon as she is set, she drinks of her bottle"* (*Woman Is a Weathercock*, 5.2.6–7), *"Tomazo was drinking and here sets down the bottle"* (*Gentleman of Venice*, G2r), *"drink round"* (*Valiant Welshman*, C2r), *"drinks and gives Varillus the bowl"* (*Lovesick Court*, 155, also 166), *"Drinks and spits"* (*Brennoralt*, 2.2.44); for more see *Two Lamentable Tragedies*, A4r; *King Leir*, 2187–8, 2182, 2492; *Knave in Grain*, 1853–4; *Novella*, 121; *Bloody Banquet*, 417; figures *drink to* each other or in celebration: *"Drinks to Hortensio"* (*Taming of the Shrew*, 2579, 5.2.37; see

also *Two Merry Milkmaids*, D3r), *"Lust drinks to Brown, he to Mistress Sanders, she pledgeth him"* (*Warning for Fair Women*, D1r), *"drinks a health"* (*Fawn*, 5.157, also 2.43), *"sets the two cups asunder, and first drinks with the one, and pledges with the other"* (Quarto *Every Man Out*, 3838–9), *"drink healths and dance"* (*White Devil*, 2.2.37), *"The King drinks, they all stand"* (*Royal King*, 26); see also *2 Henry VI*, D1v, 1115–16, 2.3.58; *City Wit*, 368; *Conspiracy*, I4v; *Goblins*, 3.2.2; *News from Plymouth*, 174; *Parson's Wedding*, 488, 457, 460; examples of drinking poisoned wine are *"Drinks the poison"* (*Herod and Antipater*, I4r, I4v), *"drinks off a Vial of poison"* (*Love's Sacrifice*, 2797–8), *"offers to drink poison"* (*Swisser*, 5.2.47); see also *Alphonsus of Germany*, F1v; Q1 *Hamlet*, I3r, [5.2; not in Riv.]; *Sophonisba*, 5.3.100; *Noble Spanish Soldier*, 5.4.57; *'Tis Pity*, 4.1.62; *Hannibal and Scipio*, 237; *drink* is occasionally a noun: *"Hostess with drink"* (*Doctor Faustus*, B 1745), *"holding a bowl of drink in his hand"* (*Jack Drum's Entertainment*, I1v), *"Diet-bread and Drink"* (*Knight of the Burning Pestle*, 205); see also, *Love's Mistress*, 102; *Jovial Crew*, 390; for additional uses of the verb see *Summer's Last Will*, 1064; *1 Edward IV*, 61; *Mucedorus*, D3v; *Two Maids of More-Clacke*, C3v; *Bartholomew Fair*, 2.5.81, 4.4.75; *Yorkshire Tragedy*, 450; *Albovine*, 36; *Wallenstein*, 77; *Landgartha*, G1r; *Siege*, 386, 426; *Princess*, E2r, E3r, G4r.

drive

found in **fight** and **battle** scenes; many of the roughly forty examples are attached to an adverb, most commonly **in** (*Locrine*, 436; *Battle of Alcazar*, 1385; *Blind Beggar of Bednal Green*, 93; *Histriomastix*, G1r; *Trial of Chivalry*, I1r; *Lust's Dominion*, 4.2.135; Quarto *Othello*, F1r, [2.3.144]; *Revenge of Bussy*, 1.2.138; *Tempest*, 2247, 5.1.255; *New Way to Pay*, 5.1.88; *Lady's Trial*, 2608–9) but also **over** (*Thracian Wonder*, G3v), about (*Edmond Ironside*, 1981), **out** (*Doctor Faustus*, B 1488; *Miseries of Enforced Marriage*, 2296–7; *Travels of Three English Brothers*, 323, 324), away (*Fair Maid of the Exchange*, 9; *Trial of Chivalry*, H4v; *Costly Whore*, 270), back (*Locrine*, 2063; *Death of Huntingdon*, 2005; *1 Edward IV*, 29; *1 If You Know Not Me*, 228), **off** (*Edmond Ironside*, 962–3; *Prophetess*, 373; *Shoemaker a Gentleman*, 3.4.0, 3.5.16; *2 Passionate Lovers*, L6r), **before** (*Whore of Babylon*, DS before Act 1, 47; MS *Humorous Lieutenant*, 1805–6; *Herod and Antipater*, G2v; *Birth of Merlin*, F4r; *Hog Hath Lost His Pearl*, 812); representative are *"fights till they be driven in breathless"* (*Coriolanus*, 741, 1.8.13), *"the White Dragon drives off the Red"* (*Birth of Merlin*, F3r), *"driving*

Englishmen before her" (*1 Henry VI*, 589, 1.5.0), "*offers to follow, he drives her back*" (*Cobbler's Prophecy*, 1539), "*drives Canute back about the Stage*" (*Edmond Ironside*, 1996–7), "*The five Kings driven over the Stage*" (*Caesar and Pompey*, 4.2.0); atypical is "*a noise within of driving beasts*" (*Captain Thomas Stukeley*, 1202).

drop

in eleven directions for various actions *drop* twice describes "body language": "*Then comes dropping after all Apemantus discontentedly like himself*" (*Timon of Athens*, 340–1, 1.2.0), "*Ursla comes in again dropping*" (*Bartholomew Fair*, 2.3.43); elsewhere *drop* signals an action: "*drops one of his Gloves*" (*King John and Matilda*, 52), "*above drops a Letter*" (*Osmond*, B1r; see also *Wizard*, 883), "*drops a scarf*" (*Rebellion*, 60); other locutions are "*Drops down in his chair*" (*Albovine*, 73, 77), "*Soldiers drop away*" (*Two Noble Ladies*, 1382); perhaps most memorable is when a figure in *Two Lamentable Tragedies* picks up a sack of **body** parts and "*one of the legs and head drops out*" (F4v).

drown

used only when Sabren says "And that which Locrine's sword could not perform, / This pleasant stream shall present bring to pass" and "*She drowneth herself*" (*Locrine*, 2248).

drum

widely used (roughly 360 examples in about 100 plays) to denote the instrument or the drummer or both; sometimes the *drum* is called for alone, but more often in one of several conventional combinations especially *drum* and **trumpet**/*fife*, and *drum* and *colors*/*ensign*; usually a *drum* is linked to military or other ceremonial events and is sounded from **within**; basic signals include "*Drum. Enter Brutus, Lucillus, and the Army*" (*Julius Caesar*, 1908, 4.2.0, also 2351, 5.1.20), "*Drum beats*" (*King John*, 372, 2.1.77), "*Drums again*" (MS *Humorous Lieutenant*, 551); see also Folio *2 Henry VI*, 2350, 4.2.30; *Death of Huntingdon*, 2735, 2756; *Blind Beggar of Bednal Green*, 3; *King Leir*, 2546; *Revenge of Bussy*, 3.1.59; *Dick of Devonshire*, 1737; more specific and more common is **sound** *drum*: "*Sound drum, enter Lord Mayor*" (*Shoemakers' Holiday*, 1.1.235), "*The drum sounds a parley*" (*Soliman and Perseda*, H4r, also D3r), "*The Drums sound Enter Edmond with Edricus*" (*Edmond Ironside*, 1565–6); see also *Cobbler's Prophecy*, 1485; *Downfall of Huntingdon*, 1942; *Jews' Tragedy*, 568–9, 2062; some directions specify that the *drum* is played offstage: "*Drum*

within" (*Macbeth*, 127, 1.3.29; see also *Knight of the Burning Pestle*, 224; *Loyal Subject*, 163; *Humorous Lieutenant*, 316, MS 1365), "*Within Drums beat Marches*" (*Birth of Merlin*, C3r, also F2r), "*Drum softly within*" (*Bonduca*, 96), "*Sound Drum within*" (*Edmond Ironside*, 955; see also *Four Prentices*, 173; *Mucedorus*, A2v); for *drum* **afar off**, which probably requires a decrease in volume, see *1 Tamar Cham*, 58–9; Folio *Richard III*, 3807, 5.3.337; *Woodstock*, 2152; *Edmond Ironside*, 1560; *Blind Beggar of Bednal Green*, 4; *King Lear*, K1v, 2737, 4.6.284; *Antony and Cleopatra*, 2731, 4.9.29; *Coriolanus*, 503, 1.4.15; *If This Be Not a Good Play*, 4.3.7; *Valiant Welshman*, B2r, B2v, D1v; *Bonduca*, 90, 117, 118; *Knight of Malta*, 109; *Jews' Tragedy*, 841; *Unfortunate Lovers*, 44.

Over sixty signals are for *drum and trumpet*: "*Drum and Trumpet, Chambers discharged*" (*Henry VIII*, 731, 1.4.49), "*Sound Drums and Trumpets, and then enter two of Titus's sons, and then two men bearing a Coffin*" (*Titus Andronicus*, A4r, 1.1.69), "*Alarum, Drums and Trumpets*" (*Antony and Cleopatra*, 2621, 4.7.0, also 1175, 2.6.0), "*the Drum playing, and Trumpet sounding*" (Folio *3 Henry VI*, 2256, 4.3.27), "*The Drum and Trumpets sound Enter with a banquet*" (*Edmond Ironside*, 383–4); for more of this combination see *2 Tamburlaine*, 2325, 2402, 2680, 4333; *Battle of Alcazar*, 68; *1 Henry VI*, 1948–9, 4.2.0; Quarto *Richard III*, I4v, 4.4.135; L1v, [5.2.0]; *King Leir*, 2388, 2665; *2 Troublesome Reign*, C4v; *Alphonsus of Germany*, F1r; *All's Well*, 1539–40, 3.3.0; *Devil's Charter*, A3r, D1r, D1v; *Coriolanus*, 710–12, 1.7.0; 3648, 5.5.7; 3705–6, 5.6.48; *Antipodes*, 313; unique is "*Trumpets and Kettle Drums*" (Q2 *Hamlet*, G4v, 3.2.89); several directions are for *drum and fife*: "*Alcibiades with Drum and fife in warlike manner*" (*Timon of Athens*, 1652, 4.3.48), "*A march for burial, with drum and fife*" (*Death of Huntingdon*, 2908); see also *Arraignment of Paris*, 478; *Edward II*, 1306.

Occurring in over ninety plays, the most frequent signal is *drum and colors*, a combination requiring the musician to bring his instrument onstage: "*Enter with Drum and Colors, Cordelia, Gentleman, and Soldiers*" (Folio *King Lear*, 2349–50, 4.4.0), "*Enter Macbeth, Seyton, and Soldiers, with Drum and Colors*" (*Macbeth*, 2319–20, 5.5.0), "*Drum and Colors. Enter the King and his poor Soldiers*" (Folio *Henry V*, 1534–5, 3.6.86), "*Enter Ralph and his company with Drums and colors*" (*Knight of the Burning Pestle*, 224), "*Spaniards and Moors with drums and colors fly over the stage*" (*Lust's Dominion*, 4.2.135); for this combination in playhouse plots and manuscripts see *Battle of Alcazar* plot, 103; *1 Tamar Cham*, 103; *2 Seven Deadly Sins*, 28;

Faithful Friends, 163–5; *Two Noble Ladies*, 1644, 1911–12; for more *drum and colors* see Folio *2 Henry VI*, 2990–1, 5.1.0; Folio *3 Henry VI*, 2737, 5.1.57; Folio *Richard II*, 1582–3, 3.3.0; *Alarum for London*, 1609; *Coriolanus*, 478–9, 1.4.0; 3734, 5.6.69; *Whore of Babylon*, 5.3.0; *Bonduca*, 90, 96; *Perkin Warbeck*, 4.1.0; *Jews' Tragedy*, 821, 846; in *Loyal Subject* a figure enters followed by "*Soldiers carrying his armor piecemeal, his Colors wound up, and his Drums in Cases*" (83); the drummer also frequently enters with an ***army*** or soldiers: "*Lucius with an Army of Goths with Drums and Soldiers*" (*Titus Andronicus*, H4r, 5.1.0), "*Oxford with drum and soldiers and all cry*" (Octavo *3 Henry VI*, E1v, 5.1.57), "*Collen with Drums and an Army*" (*Alphonsus of Germany*, G2r), "*certain Noblemen and Soldiers, with drums*" (*2 Edward IV*, 108); see also *1 Henry VI*, 193–4, 1.2.0; *Four Prentices*, 175; *Birth of Merlin*, F2r; similarly the player of the *drum* sometimes enters with an ensign – a flag with an identifying insignia and also the bearer of it: "*Enter in triumph with drum and ensign*" (*David and Bethsabe*, 1561, also 156, 767), "*King Richard with drum and Ensign*" (*Downfall of Huntingdon*, 59), "*at one door, History with Drum and Ensign*" (*Warning for Fair Women*, A2r); see also *Blind Beggar of Alexandria*, 8.0; two notable uses are "*a devil playing on a Drum, after him another bearing an Ensign*" (*Doctor Faustus*, B 1485–6), "*the King of Thrace and Lords, his Drum unbraced, Ensigns folded up*" (*Thracian Wonder*, E1r).

drunk

describes certain recognizable behavior in figures who ***drink***: "*Caliban sings drunkenly*" (*Tempest*, 1223, 2.2.178), "*Enter a Tapster, beating out of his doors Sly drunken*" (*Taming of a Shrew*, A2r), "*A drunken feast, they quarrel and grow drunk*" (*Patient Grissil*, 4.3.38), "*dance the drunken round*" (*Eastward Ho*, E3r), "*The drunken mirth*" (*Fair Maid of Bristow*, C3r), "*fall both drunk*" (*Launching of the Mary*, 1981), "*drunk and quarreling*" (*Bondman*, 3.3.119); for *drunk* figures see *1 Tamar Cham*, 36; *King Leir*, 2489; *Looking Glass for London*, 771; *Trick to Catch the Old One*, E3v; *Atheist's Tragedy*, 2.2.0, 2.4.2; *Eastward Ho*, B3r; *Queen*, 1678–9; *Swisser*, 5.1.48; *Love's Mistress*, 105; *Antiquary*, 494; *News from Plymouth*, 145; *Princess*, C1v, E3r; *Obstinate Lady*, E4r; *Brothers*, E6r; *Jovial Crew*, 390; figures are "*half drunk*" in *Wise Woman of Hogsdon*, 295; *Wit of a Woman*, 1643–4; *Soddered Citizen*, 3; once the quality is personified: "*Drunkenness, Sloth, Pride, and Plenty lead Cupid to his state, who is followed by Folly, War, Beggary, and Slaughter*" (*Fawn*, 5.139).

duck

the six examples are evenly divided between (1) a ***bird***, (2) a quick lowering of the ***head*** and ***body***; for examples of the bird, in two plays groups enter "*with water Spaniels and a duck*" (*Roaring Girl*, 2.1.361; *Histriomastix*, C2r) with a figure in the former anticipating "*the bravest sport at Parlous pond*" and one in the latter saying "*Let's Duck it with our Dogs to make us sport*"; in *More Dissemblers* gypsies enter "*with Booties of Hens, and Ducks, etc.*" (E1r); for examples of the action, a comical figure "*lifts up his head out of the Tomb, and ducks down again*" (*Fedele and Fortunio*, 494–5), an ***antic*** exits with "*a ducking curtsy*" (*John a Kent*, 791), to pay respect to the entering nobles "*the friars make a Lane with ducks and obeisance*" (*Captives*, 880–3).

duel
see ***field***

dumb show

sometimes abbreviated to *show*, this term refers to mimed performances of various lengths in about forty-five plays (in more than fifty other plays with a *dumb show* the terms are not used in directions); (1) many *dumb shows* are simply or primarily an expedient means of summarizing events not presented due to time and/or staging constraints, (2) others are more complex, often revealing information to the audience in order to create dramatic irony, (3) still others are overtly allegorical, requiring explication; staging conventions that for other actions made specific directions unnecessary did not exist for *dumb shows*, so that virtually all are described in detail too great to reproduce here; the few *dumb shows* not described usually represent well-known stories or events: "*the show of Lucrece*" (*John of Bordeaux*, 1267), "*the show of Troilus and Cressida*" (*Rare Triumphs*, 219, also 225, 231, 237, 243), "*the solemn show of the marriage*" (*Two Maids of More-Clacke*, A1v), or the description is supplied by a ***chorus***/***prologue***/***presenter*** (*Spanish Tragedy*, 3.15.28; *2 Fair Maid of the West*, 387); the following roughly chronological list of those plays which use *dumb show* (or the abbreviation *show*) in directions demonstrates its continuous popularity and usefulness: *Arraignment of Paris*, 456, 478, 494, 496; *Three Lords of London*, I2r–I3v; *Battle of Alcazar*, 24–8, 35–40, 1256–7; *Battle of Alcazar* plot, 5–10, 24–30, 55–65, 90–101; *2 Seven Deadly Sins*, 14, 80; *Edward I*, 1964; *Locrine*, 2–8, 431–8, 961–4; *Warning for Fair Women*, D1r–v, G2v–G3r; *Weakest*

Goeth, 1–8; *Thracian Wonder*, B4v; *Antonio's Revenge*, 3.1.0, 5.1.0; *Satiromastix*, 2.1.83; *Whore of Babylon*, before 1.1, 27–52, 1.2.81, 2.2.185, 4.1.0, 4.4.0; *Hamlet*, Q1 F3r, Q2 H1v, Folio 1990–2002, 3.2.135; *1 Fair Maid of the West*, 275; *1 If You Know Not Me*, 216, 228, 239; *Revenger's Tragedy*, I2v; *Macbeth*, 1657–8, 4.1.111; *Travels of Three English Brothers*, 351, 403; *Pericles*, C1v, 2.Chorus.16; *Christian Turned Turk*, F2v; *Valiant Welshman*, C4v; *Henry VIII*, 2642–57, 4.2.82; *Four Plays in One*, 321, 326; *Golden Age*, 19–20, 35, 53, 72, 78–9; *Silver Age*, 96–7, 146, 156; *Brazen Age*, 239; *White Devil*, 2.2.23, 37; *Tom a Lincoln*, 149–55, 165–71, 1701–6, 2860–5; *Swetnam*, G2r; *Hengist*, before 1.2, 1–12, before 2.3, 1–22, before 4.3, 1–17; *Prophetess*, 363; *Herod and Antipater*, C3r, F3v, F4r, I4v; *Two Noble Ladies*, 1543–9; *Faithful Friends*, 2476–84; *Game at Chess*, Malone MS 1187–90; *Jews' Tragedy*, 1102–10; *Maidenhead Well Lost*, 127, 144, 151–2; *Bloody Banquet*, 846–59; *Queen and Concubine*, 46; *Cunning Lovers*, I2v; *Landgartha*, F1r.

during

used to call for an action to take place *during* another activity such as a *song*, speech, *ceremony*, or *dance*: "*A Song, during which, she washes*" (*Challenge for Beauty*, 37), "*during their silent congratulation, Narcissus enters aloft with a Torch*" (*Messalina*, 2229–31), "*privately feeds Maquerelle's hands with jewels during this speech*" (*Malcontent*, 1.6.10; see also *Messalina*, 1511–12), "*During these Songs, Andrugio peruses a Letter*" (*More Dissemblers*, B8r), "*The Song is sung, during which a Page whispers with Simplicius*" (*What You Will*, G3r; see also *Queen of Aragon*, 357); *Broken Heart* signals actions "*During which time,*" "*during her devotions,*" simply "*during which*" (3.2.16, 5.3.0, 5.2.12); other actions take place *during* a ceremony (*Duchess of Malfi*, 3.4.7; *Perkin Warbeck*, 2.1.39), dance (*Fair Maid of the Inn*, 175), *music* (*Messalina*, 2203–4); see also *Messalina*, 2519–20; *Lovesick Court*, 163.

E

ear

used for (1) *hair* about the *ears*, (2) speaking or making *sounds* in someone's *ear*, (3) acts of violence, most commonly a *box* on the *ear*, (4) various actions or special effects; female figures appear with their hair about their *ears*: "*Mistress Shore in a white sheet barefooted with her hair about her ears, and in her hand a wax taper*" (*2 Edward IV*, 165); see also Folio *Richard III*,

1306, 2.2.33; *Antonio's Revenge*, 3.1.51; Folio *Troilus and Cressida*, 1082–3, 2.2.100; *1 Iron Age*, 269; *Tom a Lincoln*, 2252; *Swisser*, 4.1.0; *Broken Heart*, 4.2.57; *Love's Sacrifice*, 1268; roughly a dozen figures are directed to *whisper* in someone's *ear*; for a sampling see *Spanish Tragedy*, 3.10.77; *Friar Bacon*, 391; *Edmond Ironside*, 96; Quarto *Richard III*, F4v, 3.2.111; I1v, 4.2.79; Q1 *Romeo and Juliet*, C4r, 1.5.122; *Antony and Cleopatra*, 1378, 2.7.38; *Grim the Collier*, H9r; *Monsieur D'Olive*, 5.2.9; *Appius and Virginia*, B3r; other signals include "*speaketh in her ear*" (*Locrine*, 374; *Humorous Day's Mirth*, 3.1.232; *Grim the Collier*, H1r), "*round in his ear*" (*John a Kent*, 551), "*aloud in her ear*" (*Three Lords of London*, D4v), "*Sings in Gonzalo's ear*" (*Tempest*, 1003, 2.1.299), "*Halloo in his ear*" (*Doctor Faustus*, A1204; *Guy of Warwick*, E2v), "*The Devil windeth his horn in his ear*" (*Devil's Charter*, M2v; see also *Arraignment of Paris*, 813), simply *in* someone's *ear* (*Hieronimo*, 8.50; *Puritan*, G1v; *Broken Heart*, 5.2.12; *Money Is an Ass*, H1v; *Brennoralt*, 1.2.42).

For examples of violence, a box on the *ear* is most common (*Friar Bacon*, 575; *Doctor Faustus*, A 905; *Famous Victories*, B3v; *2 Henry VI*, B4r, 529, 1.3.138; *Alphonsus of Germany*, D1r; *Grim the Collier*, H3v; *Revenger's Tragedy*, C3r; *Captain*, 310; *Woman's Prize*, 23; *Antipodes*, 303; *Landgartha*, D2r; *News from Plymouth*, 145), but also signaled are *fall by the ears* (*Mucedorus*, D3v; *Bartholomew Fair*, 4.4.115, 5.4.335), "*strikes him on the ear*" (*James IV*, 327), "*wrings him by the ears*" (*Taming of the Shrew*, 584, 1.2.17), "*pulls him by the ears*" (*Midas*, 5.2.157; *Tottenham Court*, 164); other actions include "*pulls the Wool out of his ears*" (*Old Wives Tale*, 822), "*Stops his ears, shows he is troubled with the Music*" (*Captain*, 297), "*pours poison in the sleeper's ears*" (*Hamlet*, Q2 H1v, Q1 F3r, Folio, 1996, 3.2.135, also Folio 2131, 3.2.261), "*cuts off the Cutpurse's ear, for cutting of the gold buttons off his cloak*" (*Massacre at Paris*, 622), a cutpurse who "*tickles him in the ear with a straw twice to draw his hand out of his pocket*" (*Bartholomew Fair*, 3.5.145); atypical are six *dancing* Moors who enter with "*Great pendants of Pearl at their ears*" (*Amorous War*, E2v), "*The ears fall off*" (*Midas*, 5.3.121), "*Apuleius, with a pair of Ass ears in his hand*" and "*a Proud Ass with ears*" (*Love's Mistress*, 91, 104); see also *Guy of Warwick*, F3r.

earnest

used occasionally to denote *looks* or demeanors that are "intent, serious": "*looks earnestly and perceives it is the King, whereat he seemeth greatly discontented*" (*1 Edward IV*, 67; see also *Devil's Charter*, F2r), "*reading* very earnestly on a Letter" (*Weakest Goeth*, 980–1), "*as the bride goes by, she beholds James the citizen with earnest eye*" (*Two Maids of More-Clacke*, A3r), "*She must be earnest in her looks all the time he speaks*" (*Parson's Wedding*, 414).

earth

a rarely used *fictional* term for the main platform of the *stage*: "*Falls on the earth*" (*English Traveller*, 48; *Martyred Soldier*, 209), "*Kiss the earth*" (*Messalina*, 2130); sometimes the *trapdoor* is involved: "*set trees into the earth*" (*Old Fortunatus*, 1.3.19), "*with her foot in several places strikes the earth, and up riseth Campeius*" (*Whore of Babylon*, 4.1.0), "*Earth gapes and swallows the three murderers by degrees*" (*Messalina*, 2149–51).

echo

sometimes occurs as a speech heading when a figure *within* repeats the last word or words of an onstage speaker; the circumstances vary but usually the speaker is surprised and disconcerted, as in *Duchess of Malfi* where the *echo* picks up Antonio's last words so as to confirm the Duchess's death (5.3.0); in *Anything for a Quiet Life* a hiding figure helps to prove the loudness of a woman's voice by echoing it (G4r); in *Hog Hath Lost His Pearl* the echo repeats all or part of the speaker's last words, seeming to answer his questions (1350); for other examples of this most common use of the device see *Old Wives Tale*, 402; *Maid's Metamorphosis*, E3r; *Amyntas*, 2D3v; *Launching of the Mary*, 1232–40; *Queen's Exchange*, 495; an *echo* confuses or comforts by repeating all or part of the ends of a figure's speeches in *Wounds of Civil War*, 1229; *Cobbler's Prophecy*, 502; *Old Fortunatus*, 1.1.2; *Turk*, 2003–17; *Love's Mistress*, 101–2; *Arraignment of Paris* provides "*An Echo to their song*" (166, also 742); a figure named *Echo* appears in *Cynthia's Revels*, 1.2.3 where she first repeats from below then comes up to the main stage, has an extended exchange with Mercury not limited to repetitions, and sings "Slow, slow, fresh fount."

embrace

widely used (roughly 120 examples), usually with no additional details; *embrace* can be combined with *kiss* (*Two Lamentable Tragedies*, A2v; *Antonio's Revenge*, 3.1.0; *Maid of Honour*, 5.1.17; *Queen and Concubine*, 4), *compliment* (*Anything for a Quiet Life*, E1v), *whisper* (*Cardinal*, 3.2.86; *Platonic Lovers*, 14); typical are "*they kiss her hand and embrace*" (*Queen of Corinth*, 60), "*Embracing and kissing mutually*" (*Roman Actor*,

3.2.128), "*they embrace, making a mutual show of compliment*" (*Conspiracy*, G1v), "*they whisper, kindly embracing*" (*Two Noble Ladies*, 2077–9); figures also *offer* to embrace (*Fedele and Fortunio*, 793; *Doctor Faustus*, B 1299–1300; *Prophetess*, 363; *Travels of Three English Brothers*, 404; *Maid of Honour*, 5.1.17; *1 Passionate Lovers*, E6r); variations include "*Embrace his neck*" (*Looking Glass for London*, 1564), "*Embrace fantastically*" (*Devil's Charter*, F2v), "*embrace affectionately*" (*Lovesick Court*, 128–9), "*runs cheerfully to embrace*" (*Platonic Lovers*, 16), "*runs and embraces him*" (*Thomas Lord Cromwell*, E2v; *Tom a Lincoln*, 2968), "*Exeunt, arm in arm embracing*" (*Soddered Citizen*, 539); noteworthy is an allegorical *dumb show* in which a wife agrees to murder her husband: "*Lust embraceth her, she thrusteth Chastity from her, Chastity wrings her hands, and departs: Drury and Roger embrace one another: the Furies leap and embrace one another*" (*Warning for Fair Women*, D1r).

enchanter, enchantments

the figure, elsewhere called a *magician*, is linked to supernatural events and *spirits*: "*Enter Enchanter, leading Lucilla and Lassingbergh bound by spirits*" who "*fetch in a banquet*" (*Wisdom of Doctor Dodypoll*, 1063–4, also 951–3), "*the Enchanter Ormandine with some selected friends that live with him in his Magic Arts, with his spirits*" (*Seven Champions*, G1r); see also *Guy of Warwick*, B3v; *Gentleman Usher*, 1.2.47; once this figure is specifically female: "*Medusa the Enchantress with her box of enchantments under her arm*" (*Fedele and Fortunio*, 272–3); the other use of *enchantments* is "*The day clears, enchantments cease*" (*Seven Champions*, G4r).

encompass, compass

equivalent terms used in a variety of contexts: "*more devils enter with a noise encompassing him*" (*Devil's Charter*, M2v), "*Enter the English Army, and encompass them*" (*Valiant Scot*, H2r), "*a Nymph, encompassed in her Tresses*" (*Two Noble Kinsmen*, B1r, 1.1.0), "*compass the stage*" (*Cobbler's Prophecy*, 1565), "*They compass in Winifred, dance the drunken round*" (*Eastward Ho*, E3r), "*Ganymede compassed in with soldiers*" (*Golden Age*, 75); for more see *Edmond Ironside*, 1977–8; *Four Prentices*, 223; *Downfall of Huntingdon*, 1227; the synonym *surround* occurs once (*Messalina*, 2546).

encounter

a seldom used alternative to *meet*: "*As he is going out Stump encounters him*" (*Alarum for London*, 501); see also *Devil's Charter*, A3r; *Herod and Antipater*, F4r; *Landgartha*, F1r.

end

indicates either (1) the timing of *sounds* and actions or (2) location; signals for the *end* of a *song* are typically linked to other action: "*The song ended, the cornets sound a sennet*" (*Antonio's Revenge*, 5.3.32), "*the song ended, the Hearse is set down*" (*Fatal Contract*, E3v); see also *Arraignment of Paris*, 313, 508, 621; *Edward I*, 1246; *Woman in the Moon*, B1r; *Honest Man's Fortune*, 239; *Martyred Soldier*, 209; *Fatal Dowry*, 4.2.86; *Roman Actor*, 2.1.221; *Unnatural Combat*, 3.3.36; *Picture*, 2.2.200; *School of Compliment*, L2r; *Novella*, 129; *Country Girl*, K4v; *Messalina*, 2205; *Lost Lady*, 599; *Lovesick Court*, 129, 163; *Fair Favourite*, 228; *Queen of Aragon*, 378; *Landgartha*, F1v; other signals for sounds *ended* are "*Cornets sound a Battle, which ended, Enter Captain*" (*Dick of Devonshire*, 434–5), "*The first strain ends*" (*Dumb Knight*, 177), "*shooting of guns … which ended (a loud shout within)*" (*Launching of the Mary*, 2796–8), "*Music ends*" (*Little French Lawyer*, 418, 430); the *end* of a *dance* is also signaled: "*a graceful dance, towards the end whereof, Prospero starts suddenly and speaks*" (*Tempest*, 1806–7, 4.1.138), "*The dance: – which ended, they all run out in couples*" (*Lover's Melancholy*, 3.3.91), "*At this third change they end, and she meets the King*" (*Satiromastix*, 2.1.140), "*The furies join in the dance, and in the end carry the young man away*" (*Traitor*, 3.2.44); see also *Thracian Wonder*, C4r; *Two Maids of More-Clacke*, B4r; *Fair Maid of Bristow*, A2v; *Your Five Gallants*, I3r; *Insatiate Countess*, 2.1.148; *Woman Is a Weathercock*, 5.2.31; *Witch of Edmonton*, 3.4.49; *No Wit*, 4.3.148; *Four Plays in One*, 360; Quarto *Poor Man's Comfort*, C1r; *Faithful Friends*, 2579–80; *Northern Lass*, 41; *Bondman*, 3.3.52; *Court Beggar*, 268; *Late Lancashire Witches*, 217; *Shepherds' Holiday*, 405; *Messalina*, 2278–9; *Twins*, G2v; *Opportunity*, E3v; *Landgartha*, E4v; directions for the *end* of other actions are "*the poisoner woos the Queen with gifts, she seems harsh awhile, but in the end accepts love*" (*Hamlet*, Q2 H1v, Folio 2000–2, 3.2.135), "*The first Act being ended, the Consort of Music soundeth a pleasant Galliard*" (*Fedele and Fortunio*, 387–8, also 863–4, 1487–8), "*looks forth, and at the end sits close again*" (*David and Bethsabe*, 1842), "*the Masque ended, Time presents the Prisoners*" (*Jews' Tragedy*, 3105–6), "*Salutations ended, cease music*" (*Perkin Warbeck*, 2.1.39); see also *Histriomastix*, H3r; *If This Be Not a Good Play*, 5.4.0; *Revenger's Tragedy*, I3v.

The location most often cited is the *end of the stage*, which can denote a *side* of the stage or a *door*:

"*sit at the other end of the stage*" (*Antipodes*, 264), "*cornets sound; and enter at one end of the stage a Herald*" (*Dumb Knight*, 128, 129, 176), "*speaketh this secretly at one end of the stage*" (*Fair Em*, 235), "*a chair is placed at either end of the Stage*" (*1 Iron Age*, 335), "*standing at several ends of the Stage*" (*Love's Sacrifice*, 1851), "*Enter Stukeley at the further end of the stage*" (*Captain Thomas Stukeley*, 260–1); see also *John a Kent*, 780, 798; *Histriomastix*, F4r; *Fair Maid of the Exchange*, 41; *2 If You Know Not Me*, 309; *Witch of Edmonton*, 4.2.109; *Queen*, 2506–8; similar directions refer simply to an *end*: "*Exit at one end*" and "*Exit at the other end*" (*Country Girl*, K1v), "*the Queen sits at one end bound with Landrey at the other*" (*Fatal Contract*, H3r, also E3v), "*from under the stage, at both ends, arises Water and Earth*" (*No Wit*, 4.3.40); see also *Cobbler's Prophecy*, 3–4; *Sir Thomas More*, 1–2; *Captain Thomas Stukeley*, 2575; *Thomas Lord Cromwell*, C2v; *Warning for Fair Women*, A2r, E3v; *Your Five Gallants*, I2v; *Virgin Martyr*, 5.1.94, 96; *Queen and Concubine*, 46; *Wizard*, 1017–18; other locators using *end* are "*the other end of the Shop*" (*Amends for Ladies*, 2.1.71–2), "*sit down at each end of one Table*" (*Faithful Friends*, 2486–7; see also *Henry VIII*, 3037, 5.2.35; *Noble Spanish Soldier*, 1.2.0); some directions refer to the *end* of a property: "*snatcheth the cord's end*" (*Antonio's Revenge*, 4.1.195; see also *Comedy of Errors*, 1288, 4.4.7; *Northern Lass*, 33), "*Kisses the end of his cudgel*" (*New Way to Pay*, 2.3.28), "*arrows with letters on the ends of them*" (*Titus Andronicus*, G4v, 4.3.0), "*reaches it to him on the end of his Lance*" (*Jews' Tragedy*, 1076–8); atypical is "*singing with the ends of old Ballads*" (*1 Honest Whore*, 2.1.0).

engine

of the two examples, one is a trick *chair* "*with an engine*" so that a figure who sits "*is catcht in the engine*" (*Broken Heart*, 4.4.0, 20), and the other is "*an Engine fastened to a Post,*" a mechanism to lower figures through the *trapdoor* (*Queen's Exchange*, 535).

ensign

a military or naval *standard* (a *banner* or *flag*) and also the soldier who carries the *ensign*, which is usually called for with *drum* and soldiers in the context of *armies* going to *battle* or returning victorious: "*Enter David with Joab, Abussus, Cusay, with drum and ensign against Rabba,*" then "*Enter in triumph with drum and ensign*" (*David and Bethsabe*, 767, 1561, also 156); for more see *Edward III*, I2v; *Downfall of Huntingdon*, 59–62; *Warning for Fair Women*, A2r; *Captain Thomas Stukeley*, 722, 2442–59; *Blind Beggar of*

Alexandria, 8.0; *Four Prentices*, 217; *Weakest Goeth*, 353; *2 If You Know* Not Me, 342; *Devil's Charter*, A4r, D1r, D1v, K1r; *Prophetess*, 374; the visual symbolism is apparent in "*Enter two, dragging of ensigns; then the funeral of And*rea" (*Hieronimo*, 12.0), "*a devil playing on a Drum, after him another bearing an Ensign*" (*Doctor Faustus*, B 1485–6), "*beat the Pagans, take away the Crowns on their heads, and in the stead hang up the contrary Shields, and bring away the Ensigns, flourishing them, several ways*" (*Four Prentices*, 234), "*Soldiers led in by their Captains, distinguished severally by their Arms and Ensigns*" (*Hannibal and Scipio*, 256), "*the King of Thrace and Lords, his Drum unbraced, Ensigns folded up*" (*Thracian Wonder*, E1r); the figure is meant in "*the king sitteth in the midst mounted highest, and at his feet the Ensign underneath him*" (*Edward I*, 101, also 40, 111).

enter

by far the most widely used term in directions; a **large** majority of the thousands of signals consist of (1) *enter* and some combination of (a) proper names (**Ham**let, Faustus, Hieronimo), (b) titles or professions (*queen, bishop, merchant*), (c) generic types or collective nouns (***army***, *citizens*, ***followers***, *men, others, rest, servants, soldiers, train, women*); also plentiful are **signals** that specify (2) the place where/from which the entrance is to be made (with much reference to **doors**) and the subsequent onstage positioning, (3) the costume, demeanor, or actions of the entering figure; as to place, figures are directed to enter **above, aloft, below, severally**/*at several doors, at one door/side* and *at the other, one way/the other way*, and also *on the walls, in/as [if] in a field, garden, prison, shop, study, tavern, tent, woods*; entrances can specify stage positioning (*enter **afar off**, **aloof**, at the door*) or relationships (*enter alone, before, behind, solus, to him/her/them*); figures enter **bearing** X or **being** *borne*, **carrying** or being *carried*, **leading** or **being** *led*, and also **bleeding, chafing, conferring, creeping, crying, dancing, marching, mourning, musing**, panting, **raging**, raving, **reading, running, sleeping, striving, sweating, talking, trussing, weeping, wringing** their **hands**; the many descriptive terms attached to *enter*/entering figures include **affrighted, amazed, angry, armed, bare, booted, bound, brave, crowned, discontented, disguised, fearful, gallant, guarded** (often with **halberds**), **mad, masked, muffled, ravished, secretly, sick, softly, unready, wet, wounded**, with **hair** disheveled, in **haste**, in someone's **hand**, in a **halter/nightgown/veil/vizard**; figures *enter from*/**as from** hunting, bed, a meal, other

activities and *enter with* a **banquet, body, keys, letters, lights** (**candle, lantern, taper, torch**), **money, table, weapons** (**dagger, pistol, rapier, sword**), **wine**, a variety of other objects and *in/on* a bed, **bier, chair, chariot, coffin, hearse**; shorthand terms include *enter as before* and (for re-entries) *enter again*; atypical are Jonson and a few other dramatists who list figures' names at the outset of a scene without an *enter*; see also **come, forth, in, intrat** (the seldom used Latin term), **issue, out, return, rush**.

entertain

a cryptic and probably **permissive** term: "*the Queen entertains the Ambassadors, and in their several languages confers with them*" (*2 If You Know Not Me*, 317), "*brings in Perkin at the door where Crawford entertains him, and from Crawford, Huntley salutes him*" (*Perkin Warbeck*, 2.1.39); see also *Woman Is a Weathercock*, 2.1.116–17; *Wit of a Woman*, 395; *Four Plays in One*, 326.

excursions

from the Latin *excurrere* ("the action of running out"), this military term for "an issuing forth against an enemy, a sortie" and the related **skirmish** are examples of a staging code now difficult to explicate since neither term is made clearer by dialogue; most common in the roughly fifty-five examples is *excursions* with **alarum**, probably signaling both offstage **sounds** and onstage action together representing a larger **fictional** conflict; given that the direction almost invariably comes when the stage has just been cleared, probably as many soldiers as were available entered, performed some representative action, and exited; possibly they merely crossed **over the stage** as if going to **battle**.

The basic formula appears frequently in the Shakespeare history plays, as when the stage is cleared before the signal and figures come on to give the results of battle: "*Alarum, excursions. Enter the King, the Prince, Lord John of Lancaster, Earl of Westmorland*" (*1 Henry IV*, K1v, 5.4.0), "*Alarum, excursions. Enter Catesby*" (*Richard III*, M3r, 3824, 5.4.0); but onstage action is called for with "*An Alarum. Talbot in an Excursion*" and "*Alarum: Excursions, wherein Talbot's Son is hemmed about, and Talbot rescues him*" (*1 Henry VI*, 1463, 3.2.35; 2169–71, 4.6.0); several non-Shakespearean examples also provide evidence of onstage action: "*Alarm, excursions of all: The five Kings driven over the Stage, Crassinius chiefly pursuing: At the door enter again the five Kings. The battle con-*

tinued within" (*Caesar and Pompey*, 4.2.0), *"an excursion betwixt Herbert and O'Hanlon"* (*Captain Thomas Stukeley*, 1173), *"Shore and his Soldiers issue forth and repulse him. After excursions, wherein the Rebels are dispersed, enter Mayor"* (*1 Edward IV*, 31), *"Alarum, excursions, Mumford after them, and some half naked"* (*King Leir*, 2506), *"A Battle presented; Excursion, the one half drive out the other; then enter with heads on their swords"* (*Travels of Three English Brothers*, 323); in some cases it is impossible to know if *excursions* is being elaborated or separate actions described: *"Alarum within: Excursions over the Stage. The Soldiers disguised like Lackies running, Maillard following them"* (*Revenge of Bussy*, 4.1.0), *"Excursions. The Bastard chaseth Limoges the Austrich Duke, and maketh him leave the Lion's skin"* and *"Excursions. The Bastard pursues Austria, and kills him"* (*1 Troublesome Reign*, C4r, E2r, also E3r); only rarely is the stage not cleared in advance: in *1 Henry VI* the dying Bedford is onstage in a chair at *"Retreat. Excursions. Pucell, Alanson, and Charles fly"* (1551–2, 3.2.109), and in Folio *3 Henry VI* *"Alarums. Excursions. Enter the Queen, the Prince, and Exeter"* (1263–4, 2.5.124) comes when Henry is still onstage and those who enter tell him to *"fly"*; for more of the typical signal see Folio *2 Henry VI*, 3296, 5.2.71; Folio *3 Henry VI*, 1056, 2.3.0; 1119, 2.4.0; 2799–2800, 5.2.0; *2 Troublesome Reign*, D1v; *King Leir*, 2614–15, 2631–2; *King John*, 608–9, 2.1.299; 1282–3, 3.2.0; 1297–8, 3.3.0; *Edward II*, 1493; *David and Bethsabe*, 814; *Alarum for London*, 1569–70; *Death of Huntingdon*, 1926; Folio *Henry V*, 2384, 4.4.0; *Nobody and Somebody*, H1r; *Captain Thomas Stukeley*, 2686; *Thracian Wonder*, H2r; *Trial of Chivalry*, I2r; *1 Iron Age*, 295.

execution, executioner

enter to execution can be either a ***fictional*** telling of the story or a coded term that means *as [if] to execution*; clearly fictional is *"Enter the Judges and Senators with Titus's two sons bound, passing on the Stage to the place of execution"* (*Titus Andronicus*, E3r, 3.1.0), but *as [if]* is explicit in *"hurried away as to execution"* (*Hengist*, DS before 2.2, 14–15); some figures ***enter*** simply *"to execution"* (*Bloody Brother*, 283), *"to the execution"* (*Fair Maid of Bristow*, E4r), but most of the relevant signals include a distinctive figure (sheriff, justice, *executioner*, hangman), a distinctive ***weapon*** (***ax***, ***halberd***), or both: *"Enter master Browne to execution with the Sheriff and Officers"* (*Warning for Fair Women*, I2v), *"Enter the Sheriffs, the silver Oar, Purser and Clinton going to Execution"* (*Fortune by Land and Sea*, 427); *Witch of*

Edmonton provides enter *"as to see the Execution,"* *"Enter Sawyer to Execution, Officers with Halberds, country people,"* *"Enter Frank to Execution, Officers, Justice, Sir Arthur, Warbeck, Somerton"* (5.3.0, 20, 52); at *Richard III*, 5.1.0 the quarto provides the simple formula *"Enter Buckingham to execution"* (L1v) but the Folio has *"Enter Buckingham with Halberds, led to Execution"* (3371–2); *2 Edward IV* directs *"Then is young Aire brought forth to execution by the Sheriff and Officers"* and *"Here he is executed"* (180, 181); if the *execution* is to be onstage, a ***scaffold***, ***ladder*** or ***block*** may be specified: *"Enter Merry and Rachel to execution with Officers with Halberds, the Hangman with a ladder, etc."* (*Two Lamentable Tragedies*, K1v), *"Enter King Egereon Allgerius Tesephon with lords the executioner with his sword and block and officers with halberds"* (*Dead Man's Fortune*, 49–51); if the condemned is a woman, a change in coiffure may be signaled: *"Enter Isabella, with her hair hanging down, a chaplet of flowers on her head, a nosegay in her hand, Executioner before her, and with her a Cardinal"* (*Insatiate Countess*, 5.1.66), *"Enter executioner before Salassa, her Hair loose, after her, Almada, Collumello and officers"* (*Queen*, 3115–17); atypical is *"ready for execution"* (*Atheist's Tragedy*, 5.2.238); only one play calls for a figure to be ***brought*** in *"on a hurdle"* (*Edward I*, 2361), a common fate for condemned figures in this period.

Executioners appear frequently: *"Don Sago guarded, Executioner, scaffold"* (*Insatiate Countess*, 5.1.0), *"Executioners, with a Rack"* (*Double Marriage*, 334), *"Executioners with a Coffin a Gibbet"* (*Barnavelt*, 2810–12), figures *"bound, a guard of halberds, and an executioner"* (*Dumb Knight*, 154, 193); for a sampling see *King John*, 1570, 4.1.0; Quarto *Richard III*, C4r, 1.3.337; *Two Noble Kinsmen*, M2v, 5.4.0; *Duchess of Malfi*, 4.2.165; *Queen of Corinth*, 76; *Knight of Malta*, 110; *Barnavelt*, 2713, 2854; *Old Law*, C4r, L2r; *Emperor of the East*, 5.1.0; *Herod and Antipater*, L2v; *Perkin Warbeck*, 2.2.52; actions include *"The King takes the sword from the Executioner"* (*Fatal Contract*, E4r), *"Here the Executioner strikes, and Herod dies"* (*Herod and Antipater*, L4r).

exit, exeunt

often not specified in the manuscripts and early printed texts, particularly *exits **during*** as opposed to at the end of a scene; unlike ***enter***, *exit* and the plural *exeunt* regularly stand alone rather than being supplemented by designated figures, actions, and other details; of the more specific directions the largest group consists of *exit/exeunt* some figures but *manet/stay/remain* others or *exeunt all/omnes but/saving/praeter* others; other signals for group movement include *exeunt ambo, arm in arm*, omnes, *together, severally, at several doors, several ways, at one door/side* and *at the other*; interrupted *exits* are common, usually indicated by *offers to go* but also *going, exiturus*; figures are directed to *exit from above, from the walls, from the window, behind* the *arras/curtains/hangings, to/into/toward* a *battle, castle, cave, house, priory, study, temple*, and with a *body, coffin, dance, dead march, drum, train, trumpet*, other *sounds* and instruments, *torches*; variations include *exit "to Death"* (*Sir Thomas Wyatt*, 5.2.181), *"with the horse"* (*Woodstock*, 1480), *"Exit and stays behind the hangings"* (*Grateful Servant*, F2r), *"Exit up"* (*Two Lamentable Tragedies*, B4r), *"Exit. And Enter above"* (*Sea Voyage*, 18; *Westward Ho*, 4.1.126); re-entrances are signaled by *exit* and *enter/come again/return*, sometimes *presently*; shorthand terms include *exits as before*, "*in manner as they entered*" (*Henry VIII*, 1613, 2.4.242; *Fortune by Land and Sea*, 430, *Soddered Citizen*, 1108), *"Exit corpse"* (Folio *Richard III*, 423, 1.2.226).

For examples of actions, figures *exit leading out* others/being *led, carrying out*/being *carried, bearing, beating, dragging* someone, *on* someone's *back, with/cum/after* another, *drawing* a *weapon*, and *arming, chafing, creeping, crying, dancing, fighting, flourishing, hallooing, hugging, marching*, neighing (*Late Lancashire Witches*, 211), *pursuing, reeling*, roaring (*Friar Bacon*, 2073), *running, singing, staggering, striving, weeping, whistling*, "*winding their horns*" (*Downfall of Huntingdon*, 1365), "*pushing in the corpses*" (*Puritan*, H1r), "*biting his thumbs*" (*Dick of Devonshire*, 1713–14), "*shaking his head, and shoulders*" (*Example*, G1r), "*hiding her face*" (*Philaster*, 147/417), "*looking back*" (*Swaggering Damsel*, D4v), "*inviting him to follow*" (*Renegado*, 2.4.134; see also *Valiant Scot*, I4r), "*tearing her hair*" (*Jack Drum's Entertainment*, D3v), "*going backward with the glass*" (*Love's Sacrifice*, 799–800), "*Exit King, frowning upon the Cardinal, the Nobles throng after him smiling, and whispering*" (*Henry VIII*, 2080–1, 3.2.203); adverbs and other locutions attached to *exit* include *affrightedly, aside, hastily, jocundly* (*Soddered Citizen*, 2016), *jeeringly* (*Landgartha*, D2r), *presently*, (*1 Honest Whore*, 4.3.25), *warily* (*Soddered Citizen*, 1363), *in state*, in *pomp, guarded*/with a guard, "*as fast as may be*" (*Comedy of Errors*, 1447, 4.4.146; *Taming of the Shrew*, 2490, 5.1.111), "*with Conges*" (*Country Girl*, B2v), "*with an angry look upon Valerio*" (*Jews' Tragedy*, 2428–9), "*saying

nothing as displeased*" (*Swaggering Damsel*, F1v), "*Exit, where he entered*" (*Country Girl*, I2r); figures *exit for* someone/for a purpose, as in *exits "for wine"* (*Yorkshire Tragedy*, 442–3), "*for a candle*" (*1 Honest Whore*, 2.1.64), "*to fetch Officers*" (*Witch of Edmonton*, 4.2.134); other distinctive *exits* include "*stares upon the Cardinal in his exit*" (*Cardinal*, 4.2.202), "*Exit with a resolve not to do it*" (*Fatal Contract*, D1r), "*Exit Eunuch busy to quench the fire*" (*Fatal Contract*, D4v), "*Exit pursued by a Bear*" (*Winter's Tale*, 1500, 3.3.58), "*Exeunt, fall as into the sea*" (*2 Passionate Lovers*, L5r); see also *clear, depart, forth, fly, go, in, off, out*.

exiturus

Latin for *offers to go, going*; see *Woman Is a Weathercock*, 1.1.50; *Anything for a Quiet Life*, D3r; *Soddered Citizen*, 121, 1238; *Telltale*, 567; most of the examples are from Chapman's plays: Q2 *Bussy D'Ambois*, 3.2.317; *Conspiracy of Byron*, 2.1.96; *May Day*, 2.2.74; *Monsieur D'Olive*, 5.2.59; *Widow's Tears*, 2.1.15, 4.2.177, 5.3.81, 5.5.125.

eyes

found in (1) a covering for the *eyes*, (2) a *glance*, or *look*, (3) a variety of actions; the most common covering is a *patch*: "*like a poor Soldier with a patch over one eye*" (*Roaring Girl*, 5.1.55), "*Their eyes blinded with black patches*" (*Amorous War*, H2r); see also *Wizard*, 343–5; *Claracilla*, D5r; *Princess*, F1r; *Whore of Babylon* provides "*scarfs before their eyes*" and "*pulling the veils from the Councillors' eyes*" (DS before Act 1, 33, 38–9); *glass* coverings for the *eyes* are required for "*the Devil like a Gentleman, with glass eyes*" (*New Trick*, 252), poisoners who "*put on spectacles of glass, which cover their eyes and noses*" (*White Devil*, 2.2.23); figures *fix* their *eyes* upon someone or something: "*stands with his eyes fixed upon the ground*" (*Prisoners*, A6r), "*fixeth his eye on Buckingham, and Buckingham on him, both full of disdain*" (*Henry VIII*, 177–9, 1.1.114); see also *Jack Drum's Entertainment*, H4v; *Two Noble Ladies*, 1011; a figure courts one woman while "*glancing his eye on Julia*" (*Turk*, 935), another "*sits him down in sackclothes, his hands and eyes reared to heaven*" (*Looking Glass for London*, 2078–9), a bride "*beholds James the citizen with earnest eye*" (*Two Maids of More-Clacke*, A3r); actions include "*Dries her eyes*" (*Queen's Exchange*, 467), "*wipes his eyes*" of *tears* (*Wise Woman of Hogsdon*, 316), an entrance "*yawning and rubbing his eyes*" (*Swaggering Damsel*, H2v), "*put out one eye*" (*Osmond*, C7r), "*Pulls out his eyes*" (*Selimus*, 1415), "*draws his handkerchief (as to wipe his eyes) just before the Country fellow, and scatters some small money" (Knave in Grain, 2968–9), "puts his hand to his eye, with a bloody sponge and the blood runs down" (Princess, F4v).

F

face

the roughly seventy-five examples consist of (1) items on/over/**covering**/**hiding** the *face*, (2) colors on the *face*, (3) **bloody**, **wounded** faces, (4) a wide variety of actions; *Caesar and Pompey* provides "*hides his face with his robe*," a **devil** "*with the face, wings, and tail of a Dragon*," "*a sword, as thrust through his face*" (5.1.266, 2.1.24, 4.3.0); items *on/over/covering* the *face* include a **patch** (*Edmond Ironside*, 1313; *Look about You*, 2008; *Amends for Ladies*, 3.4.3), **mask** (*Fair Em*, 855–6), **veil** (*Titus Andronicus*, K2r, 5.3.25; *Sophonisba*, 4.1.213; *King John and Matilda*, 85; *Inconstant Lady*. 5.3.0; *Unfortunate Lovers*, 39), **cloak** (*Lost Lady*, 593), **scarf** (*Orlando Furioso*, 1350–1, 1475; *Trial of Chivalry*, K1v; *Sophy*, 3.356; *Albovine*, 96), plasters (*Dick of Devonshire*, 941), golden **vizards** (*Henry VIII*, 2645, 4.2.82); detailed examples include "*Covers her face with her white veil*" (*Cruel Brother*, 139), "*in mourning, with a hood over her face*" (*Andromana*, 221), "*in his winding sheet, only his face discovered*" (*Love's Sacrifice*, 2763–4); for colors and comparable details, *faces* are **black** (*English Moor*, 51), **white** (*English Moor*, 63), whited (*Lover's Melancholy*, 3.3.19), "*russet-color*" (*Grim the Collier*, I2r), **mealed** (*Knight of the Burning Pestle*, 222), pale (*Second Maiden's Tragedy*, 2225–6), **gilded** (*Old Fortunatus*, 1.3.0), spotted (*Whore of Babylon*, 4.1.0; see also *Three Ladies of London*, E1v), leprous (*Unnatural Combat*, 5.2.271); more specific are a devil "*like a King, with a red face*" (*Devil's Charter*, G1v; see also *No Wit*, 4.3.40), "*her face colored like a Moor*" (*Devil's Law Case*, 5.6.29), "*like Amazons; Their faces discolored to a comely Brown*" (*Amorous War*, E1v, also K4v); bloody/bleeding/wounded faces include "*their heads and faces bloody, and besmeared with mud and dirt*" (*Doctor Faustus*, B 1490–1), "*his hands and face scratched, and bloody*" (*Late Lancashire Witches*, 195); see also *Two Lamentable Tragedies*, B4r; *King John and Matilda*, 26; *Dick of Devonshire*, 865; *Antipodes*, 300.

For examples of actions, most common are figures who **fall** on their *faces* (*Two Noble Kinsmen*, C4r, 1.4.0; K4v, 5.1.76; L1v, 5.1.129; *Maid of Honour*, 2.2.63; *Roman Actor*, 4.2.113), lie on their *faces* (Quarto *2 Henry VI*, B4v, 1.4.11; *Maid of Honour*, 4.3.34; *Damoiselle*, 409), **fling**/**throw** in someone's *face* **meal**

(*Hengist*, 5.1.319), **water** (*Renegado*, 5.3.115), **wine** (*Fortune by Land and Sea*, 368; *Miseries of Enforced Marriage*, 1076–7; *Politician*, F4r); other distinctive actions include "*looks full in his face*" (*Late Lancashire Witches*, 238; see also *Spanish Tragedy*, 3.13.132), "*sprinkling water on her face*" (*Queen of Corinth*, 18; see also *Fancies Chaste and Noble*, 234–5), "*offers to cut her face*" and "*umbers her face*" (*Telltale*, 1051, 1053), "*blows tobacco in their faces*" (*Roaring Girl*, 2.1.66), "*Makes a cross on Clifford's face with his finger*" (*Perkin Warbeck*, 2.2.83), "*stabs his arm, and bloodies Sentloe's face*" (*Fair Maid of Bristow*, D2v), four Cupids "*each having his fan in his hand to fan fresh air in her face*" (*Arraignment of Paris*, 496), "*draws forth a knife, and making as though she meant to spoil her face, runs to her*" (*2 Edward IV*, 129), "*tears off his doublet, making strange faces as if compelled to do it*" (*Fair Maid of the Inn*, 201), "*blind Simplicity, turn him thrice about, set his face towards the contrary post, at which he runs*" (*Three Lords of London*, I3v); see also *Antonio and Mellida*, 3.2.123; *Devil's Charter*, A2v, M1v; *Philaster*, 147/417; *Two Merry Milkmaids*, C3r.

faint

an alternative to **swoon** and its variant **sound** and like them generally signaled without embellishment (*Looking Glass for London*, 1576; *Wise Woman of Hogsdon*, 329; *Old Law*, K2v; *Conspiracy*, K4v; *Gamester*, D2r; *Example*, D2v; *School of Compliment*, K1v; *Traitor*, 4.2.8; rev. *Aglaura*, 5.1.188; *Fatal Contract*, K2r; *Obstinate Lady*, D3r; *Brennoralt*, 5.3.69; *Rebellion*, 23; *Andromana*, 227, 230, 270); several figures enter fainting (*Grim the Collier*, I12r; *Weakest Goeth*, 959; *Honest Man's Fortune*, 239); see also **fall**, **sink**.

fairy

calls for these supernatural figures give little indication of their appearance: "*A Bevy of Fairies*" (*Amyntas*, X2v), "*the Fairies, singing and dancing*" (*Maid's Metamorphosis*, C4r; see also *Endymion*, G3r; *Gallathea*, 2.3.5); **antic** sometimes describes *fairies*: "*an Antic of little Fairies enter*" (MS *Humorous Lieutenant*, 2329–31), "*three antic fairies dancing*" (*Dead Man's Fortune*, 53–4), "*like Fairies, dancing antics*" (*Honest Lawyer*, G2v); these help clarify "*Enter after Oberon, King of Fairies, an Antic, who dance about a Tomb*" (*James IV*, 2–3, also 633–4); Oberon and his fairies, best known from *Midsummer Night's Dream* (B3v, 2.1.59; H4r, 5.1.390), appear as well in *Lust's Dominion*, 3.2.74 and *Guy of Warwick*, B4r; there is also a figure "*like the King of Fairies*" (*Amyntas*, 2Dr); besides Titania in *Midsummer Night's Dream*, 650,

2.2.0; 1509–10, 4.1.0, a *queen of fairies* appears in *Tom a Lincoln*, 1251–2, 1564, 1702; *Valiant Welshman*, C2v, D4v; Quarto *Merry Wives* provides "*boys dressed like Fairies, Mistress Quickly, like the Queen of Fairies*" (G2r, 5.5.36).

fall

widely used (over 300 examples) (1) to indicate when a figure *falls* to (or into) the stage, (2) for properties that *fall*, (3) idiomatically in the phrases *fall to* or "begin" and *fall asleep*; frequently when *fall* is the equivalent of *swoon/sound* both terms are used: "*the King falls in a sound*" (Quarto *2 Henry VI*, E2v; Folio "*King sounds*," 1729, 3.2.32), "*then she falls and sounds*" (*Edward I*, 41), "*Falls down in a feigned swoon*" (*Michaelmas Term*, 4.4.55), "*falls down as in a swoon*" (*Alchemist*, 4.5.62), "*Runs at her and falls by the way in a Sound*" (*Second Maiden's Tragedy*, 1339–41); see also *1 Edward IV*, 88; *Grim the Collier*, K1r; *Atheist's Tragedy*, 3.1.73; *Lovers' Progress*, 127, 130; for other examples where *fall* means *faint* see *Blind Beggar of Bednal Green*, 8; *Damoiselle*, 459; *Novella*, 151; *Arcadia*, G3v; *falls* is also used when a figure *dies*, particularly as a result of violence: "*Fight, Tybalt falls*" and "*stabs herself and falls*" (Q1 *Romeo and Juliet*, F2r, 3.1.131; K2v, [5.3.170]), "*They catch one another's Rapiers, and both are wounded, Laertes falls down, the Queen falls down and dies*" (Q1 *Hamlet*, I3v, [5.2.302]), "*Strike him, he falls*" (*Jew of Malta*, 1682), "*a sword, as thrust through his face; he falls*" (*Caesar and Pompey*, 4.3.0), "*As the Prince is going forth, a Pistol is discharged within, he falls*" (*Politician*, H1v, also I2v); see also *1 Henry VI*, 539–40, 1.4.69; *Blind Beggar of Bednal Green*, 47; Q2 *Bussy D'Ambois*, 5.1.156; *Coriolanus*, 3805–6, 5.6.130; *1 Iron Age*, 322; *Hengist*, 5.2.179; *Nero*, 76; *Island Princess*, 150; *Roman Actor*, 5.2.72; *Conspiracy*, K4v; *Aglaura*, 3.1.18, 5.1.59; *Argalus and Parthenia*, 34; *Unfortunate Lovers*, 69; *Unfortunate Mother*, 151; figures also *fall distracted* or otherwise incapacitated: "*Falls in a Trance*" (Folio *Othello*, 2420, 4.1.43; Quarto "*falls down*," I3v), "*falleth in an ecstasy upon the ground*" (*Devil's Charter*, M2r), "*Falls distracted*" (*Messalina*, 1080); for more see *Antonio and Mellida*, 4.1.155; *Sir Thomas Wyatt*, 5.2.150; *Volpone*, 5.12.23; *Devil's Law Case*, 3.3.302; elsewhere figures *fall drunk*: "*Reels and falls*" (*Chaste Maid*, 3.2.164), "*drinks and falls over the stool*" (*Look about You*, 1503), "*tosses off her bowl, falls back, and is carried out*" (*Jovial Crew*, 391); see also *English Traveller*, 34; *Great Duke of Florence*, 4.2.211; *Launching of the Mary*, 1981; other signals for a figure to *fall* to the stage include "*The Ghosts fall on their knees*" (*Cymbeline*, 3128, 5.4.92;

see also *2 Edward IV*, 126), "*falls groveling on the ground*" (*Edward I*, 2587), "*falls over the dead man*" (*Looking Glass for London*, 796), "*Moll trips up his heels, he falls*" (*Roaring Girl*, 2.1.331), "*Enter Clem falling for haste*" (*1 Fair Maid of the West*, 315), "*Enter Husband as being thrown off his horse, And falls*" (*Yorkshire Tragedy*, 632, also 272), "*Falls on his face*" (*Roman Actor*, 4.2.113); see also Q1 *Romeo and Juliet*, K1v, 5.3.72; Quarto *King Lear*, I3r, 4.6.41; *Insatiate Countess*, 3.1.84; *Rape of Lucrece*, 185; *Fortune by Land and Sea*, 386; *Bartholomew Fair*, 4.2.31; *Two Noble Kinsmen*, B1v, 1.1.24; C4r, 1.4.0; *Martyred Soldier*, 209; *Maid of Honour*, 2.2.63; *Duchess of Suffolk*, F2r, F2v; *Queen's Exchange*, 506; *Fool Would Be a Favourite*, C8r; *Swisser*, 5.2.117; *Cardinal*, Epilogue.2; several figures *fall* on a *sword* (*Caesar and Pompey*, 5.2.161; *Nero*, 97; *Albovine*, 99; *Unfortunate Lovers*, 70); *fall* is also part of an idiom signaling *beating*: "*They fall by the ears*" (*Bartholomew Fair*, 4.4.115, also 5.4.335; see also *Mucedorus*, D3v), "*She falls upon him and beats him*" (*Epicœne*, 4.2.103; see also Folio *Every Man In*, 4.10.72; *Rebellion*, 46), "*The Guard fall on him and he falls*" (*Fatal Contract*, D3v); see also *Guy of Warwick*, C1r; *Devil's Law Case*, 2.2.26; *Swaggering Damsel*, D1r.

Sometimes a figure *falls* through the *trapdoor*: "*The Ground opens, and he falls down into it*" (*Grim the Collier*, I12v), "*falls in the Pit*" (*Bloody Banquet*, 683), "*falls into the Stage*" (*Duke's Mistress*, I1v); see also Folio *Titus Andronicus*, 999, 2.3.245; *Hog Hath Lost His Pearl*, 1790; *Valiant Welshman*, D4v; there are two *falls* from *above*: "*ascends, and at top falls*" (*Insatiate Countess*, 3.1.42); see also *Monsieur Thomas*, 138; other directions for a figure to *fall* are "*falls upon her bed within the Curtains*" (Q1 *Romeo and Juliet*, I1r, 4.3.58), "*falls on the bed*" (Quarto *Othello*, M3v, 5.2.198), "*Falls passionately upon the Hearse*" (*King John and Matilda*, 85), "*both of them fall into the water*" (*Locrine*, 963–4), "*Exeunt, fall as into the sea*" (*2 Passionate Lovers*, L5r), "*Falls, hangs*" (*Vow Breaker*, 2.3.41).

Properties also *fall* in a variety of contexts; some literally *fall*: "*A stone falls and kills Proximus*" (*Birth of Merlin*, F2v), "*A letter falleth*" (*Spanish Tragedy*, 3.2.23), "*Lets fall her glove*" (*Two Maids of More-Clacke*, A3r; *Spanish Tragedy*, 1.4.99), "*his hat falls off*" (*Wonder of a Kingdom*, 3.1.67), "*lets the Cabinet fall out of the Window*" (*Novella*, 151), "*lets fall a Jewel from her dress*" (*Court Secret*, B1r); see also *Fedele and Fortunio*, 600; *Midas*, 5.3.121; *Miseries of Enforced Marriage*, 780; *Queen's Exchange*, 474; *Maid's Revenge*, E1r; *Twins*, D2v; elsewhere a raised *weapon* is lowered or *let fall*: "*Here she lets fall the sword*" (*Richard III*, B2v, 376, 1.2.182),

"Offers to stab, lets the poniard fall" (*Herod and Antipater*, B4v), *"quakes and lets fall the Dagger"* (*King Leir*, 1739–40, also 1743), *"runs to Flamineo with her knife drawn and coming to him lets it fall"* (*White Devil*, 5.2.52), *"The Giant in a maze lets fall his Club"* (*Seven Champions*, I4r), *"Pulls off her veil, lets fall his sword"* (*Thierry and Theodoret*, 47); see also *Alphonsus of Germany*, I3v; *Christian Turned Turk*, C2r; *Love's Sacrifice*, 2609; *Wizard*, 2112; *Conspiracy*, I2r.

The idiom *fall to* for "begin" occurs frequently: *"fall to the Dance"* (*King John and Matilda*, 51; see also *If This Be Not a Good Play*, 4.4.7; *Fair Maid of the Inn*, 201), *"fall a drinking"* (*George a Greene*, 1183), *"falleth to eat"* (*Grim the Collier*, I10r), *"falls a strewing of flowers"* (Quarto *Every Man Out*, 1406), *"fall to their vapors again"* (*Bartholomew Fair*, 4.4.17, also 4.2.36), *"fall to writing"* (*Thracian Wonder*, C2r); see also *Edward I*, 630; *Alchemist*, 4.6.25; related to this usage is *fall asleep*: *"drinks and then falls asleep"* (*Taming of a Shrew*, F2r, also A2r), *"They both fall asleep"* (*Old Fortunatus*, 2.2.328); for more see *Alphonsus of Aragon*, 926; *Endymion*, D3r, G3r; *Taming of the Shrew*, 17, Induction.1.15; *Friar Bacon*, 1601; *King Leir*, 1452; *Tom a Lincoln*, 1466; *Queen and Concubine*, 45; *Antiquary*, 496; another *fall* idiom signals the action of moving away, pulling back from, or joining others: *"They fall off, she beckons Mr. William, whisper"* (*Country Girl*, G3v), *"He turns to her. She falls off"* (*Great Duke of Florence*, 2.3.141), *"The third change ended, Ladies fall off"* (*Insatiate Countess*, 2.1.148), *"Another change; they fall in"* (*Satiromastix*, 2.1.135), *"Puntarvolo falls in with Sordido, and his son"* (Quarto *Every Man Out*, 1160–1, also 2362), *"the shield boys fall at one end"* (*Your Five Gallants*, I2v); see also *Shoemakers' Holiday*, 1.1.235; *Malcontent*, 5.5.0; *Perkin Warbeck*, 3.2.85; *Soddered Citizen*, 1287–9; *Unnatural Combat*, 1.1.63; in *Roaring Girl* "Fall from them to the other" (2.1.271) marks a shift of focus from one group to another.

fan, fanning

a *fan* is occasionally specified as a property for a woman; in two Caroline plays a servant brings in a "Mask and Fan" for his mistress (*Northern Lass*, 23), and a madwoman afflicted with pride enters *"in a rich gown, great farthingale, great ruff, muff, fan, and coxcomb on her head"* (*Lover's Melancholy*, 3.3.48); for examples of *fanning*, Cleopatra makes her first entrance *"with Eunuchs fanning her"* (*Antony and Cleopatra*, 16, 1.1.10), and Helen enters with four Cupids *"each having his fan in his hand to fan fresh air in her face"* (*Arraignment of Paris*, 496); Henslowe's

inventory includes "two fans of feathers" (*Diary*, App. 2, 75).

fantastic, fantastically

used in a variety of locutions with little helpful detail, although several directions refer to clothing or appearance: *"a fantastical shape"* (*Antipodes*, 316), *"fantastically dressed"* (*City Match*, 277; see also *Just Italian*, 280; *Love and Honour*, 137), *"enters fantastical"* (*Look about You*, 80); other signals describe actions: *"singing fantastically"* (*Antonio and Mellida*, 2.1.61), *"Embrace fantastically"* (*Devil's Charter*, F2v), *"walking fantastically"* (*Maid of Honour*, 1.2.0); atypical is *"Music striking up a light fantastic Air"* (*World Tossed at Tennis*, D2r).

fearful, fear

linked to a variety of actions and situations; examples of *fearful/fearfully* are *"falls down on her knees before the Queen fearful and weeping"* (*2 Edward IV*, 126) and entrances *"fearfully, the Devil following her"* (*Birth of Merlin*, G2r), *"running fearfully"* (*Silver Age*, 119), *"fearfully looking about him"* (*Captain Thomas Stukeley*, 2838–9); figures *speak* (*Swisser*, 1.1.71) and **walk** about fearfully (*Woman in the Moon*, A3r), a **devil** enters *"in a fearful shape"* (*Virgin Martyr*, 5.1.122), and a figure **charmed** by **magic** *"Kneels with a fearful countenance and so is fixed"* (*Two Noble Ladies*, 497–8); *fearful* can be used with **seems**: *"seeming fearful to come forward"* (*Wisdom of Doctor Dodypoll*, 1615), *"seems fearful, and flies"* (*Family of Love*, D1r; see also *Four Plays in One*, 333); *Atheist's Tragedy* provides *"peeps fearfully forth from behind the arras"* and *"avoids him fearfully"* (2.5.111, 3.2.19, also 2.6.67), and *Devil's Charter* *"more thunder and fearful fire"* and *"Thunder and lightning with fearful noise"* (A2v, M2v); locutions using *fear* include *"shakes with fear"* (*Launching of the Mary*, 2130), *"in a fear"* (*Yorkshire Tragedy*, 373), *"in all fear"* (*Little French Lawyer*, 440), *"enter suddenly and in fear"* (*Blurt*, 3.2.0; see also *Hengist*, 5.2.141), *"her fear makes her fall"* (*Fool Would Be a Favourite*, C8r), *"answers with fear and interruptions"* (*Catiline*, 5.140); atypical is *fear* as a verb: *"much fears her breast"* (*Fatal Contract*, I3r).

feather

usually linked to men's **hats** or **caps**: *"Cockfeathers in their Hats"* (*Amorous War*, F2r), *"a black velvet cap and a white feather"* (*Lover's Melancholy*, 3.1.0), *"puts on Hat, Feather, and Cloak"* (*Queen's Exchange*, 529); a king enters with a *"plume of feathers"* (*Perkin Warbeck*, 3.1.0), a madman enters *"A crown of feathers on, anticly* rich" (*Lover's Melancholy*, 3.3.26), a playgoer "*Puts his feather in his pocket*" to avoid jests (*Malcontent*, Induction.46); see also *What You Will*, D3r; Henslowe's inventory includes "two fans of feathers" (*Diary*, App. 2, 75); related are "*a Feather shop*" (*Roaring Girl*, 2.1.0), a *featherman* who has "*brought feathers to the Playhouse*" (*Muses' Looking Glass*, A2r).

feel

either (1) to ***search*** or (2) less specifically "examine by means of touch"; compare "*He feels his pockets*" (*Alchemist*, 4.3.42; see also *Siege*, 397) to "*Feels about, and Enters the cave*" (*Jews' Tragedy*, 3008–9), "*takes a Dagger and feels upon the point of it*" (*Soliman and Perseda*, H3r); to determine whether figures are men or ***devils*** Matilda "*Feels them all*" (*Death of Huntingdon*, 2549).

feign

a rarely used term for dissembling: "*He feigns, as if one were present, to fright the other*" (*Epicœne*, 4.5.220), "*lies down, and feigns himself dead*" (*Jack Drum's Entertainment*, D2r; see also *Turk*, 1837), "*Falls down in a feigned swoon*" (*Michaelmas Term*, 4.4.55), "*He feigns to weep*" (*City Match*, 263), "*Feigns sleeping*" (*Country Captain*, B1or); see also ***counterfeit***, ***seems***.

fetch

an alternative to ***bring*** used mostly to bring figures and less commonly objects onstage; for figures who are *fetched/fetched in* see *Spanish Tragedy*, 1.4.137; *Doctor Faustus*, B 536; *Two Lamentable Tragedies*, I3r; *Warning for Fair Women*, G3r; *Death of Huntingdon*, 959–60; *Captain Thomas Stukeley*, 1473; *Antonio's Revenge*, 4.1.92; *1 Honest Whore*, 2.1.57; *Whore of Babylon*, 1.2.81; *Devil's Charter*, E1r; *Game at Chess*, 1943–4; *Witch of Edmonton*, 4.2.134; *New Trick*, 281, 296; *Dick of Devonshire*, 1897–8; *Twins*, F3v; *Aglaura*, 1.6.116; *Cunning Lovers*, I2v; *Andromana*, 261; variations include "*Enter two Keepers to fetch them off*" (*Pilgrim*, 196), "*fetches Florelli to kiss the Duke's hand*" (*Gentleman of Venice*, B2r); objects *fetched* are a ***crown*** (*Lust's Dominion*, 5.1.31), ***candle*** (*Amends for Ladies*, 2.1.71), ***head*** (*2 Arviragus and Philicia*, F11r), ***cabinet*** (*Prisoners*, B3v), ***banquet*** (*Wisdom of Doctor Dodypoll*, 1064), "*Bow and arrows*" (*1 Iron Age*, 332); more detailed are "*They cover the board and fetch in the meat*" (*Taming of a Shrew*, D3r), "*They bind him to a stake, and fetch stones in baskets*" (*Martyred Soldier*, 222), "*fetcheth out the Hobby horse and the morris dance, who dance about*" (*Summer's Last Will*, 193).

fetters

a restraint for ***prisoners*** comparable to ***chains***, ***gyves***, ***irons***, ***manacles***, ***shackles***: "*in fetters*" (*Maid of Honour*, 4.3.0), "*three more fettered*" (*2 Edward IV*, 121), "*in prison, fettered and gyved*" (*Appius and Virginia*, I1r), "*undoes his Fetters*" (*Goblins*, 3.3.3); in *Love's Mistress* "*Cupid in fetters*" (136) elicits the question "what shackled runaway is this?"; atypical is an entrance "*like Amazon Captives, shackled with Golden Fetters, and pinioned with silken cords*" (*Amorous War*, C2v).

fictional stage directions

a scholarly term (coined by Richard Hosley) to distinguish between *fictional* directions (that "usually refer not to theatrical structure or equipment but rather to dramatic fiction") and *theatrical* directions (that "usually refer not to dramatic fiction but rather to theatrical structure or equipment"); examples of the former are *on shipboard*, *within the* ***prison***, ***enter*** *the city* as opposed to theatrical signals such as ***within***, *at another* ***door***, ***scaffold thrust out***; the same onstage event can therefore be signaled by both *enter* ***above*** and *enter upon the* ***walls*** [of a city], with the second locution the *fictional* version of the first; the clearest *theatrical* signals are practical directions about properties and personnel in the tiring house; an example is the bookkeeper's annotations in the playhouse manuscript of *Believe as You List* that include "*Table ready: and six chairs to set out*," "*Gascoine and Hubert below: ready to open the Trapdoor for Mr. Taylor*," "*Antiochus – ready: under the stage*" (654–6, 1825–31, 1877–9); in contrast, in *fictional* directions a dramatist sometimes slips into a narrative, descriptive style seemingly more suited to a reader facing a page than an actor on the stage so as to conjure up a vivid image more appropriate to a cinematic scene than an onstage effect at the Globe: "*the Romans are beat back to their Trenches*" (*Coriolanus*, 523, 1.4.29), Jonas "*cast out of the Whale's belly upon the Stage*" (*Looking Glass for London*, 1460–1); some *fictional* signals show the dramatist thinking out loud in the process of writing (so that the details anticipate what will be evident in the forthcoming action): "*Parolles and Lafew stay behind, commenting of this wedding*" (*All's Well*, 1089–90, 2.3.183), "*Enter two sergeants to arrest the Scholar George Pyeboard*" (*Puritan*, E1r).

    Complications can arise when a reader cannot be certain if a direction is *theatrical* (and therefore calls for a significant property such as a ***tomb*** or ***tree***) or *fictional* (so that a sense of a tomb, ***tavern***, ***ship***, or forest is to be generated by means of language, costume, hand-held properties, or appropriate actions in conjunction with the imagination of the playgoer); representative are the differing interpretations of "*Romeo opens the tomb*" (Q1, K1r, 5.3.48), a signal that may or may not require an elaborate tomb property; such complications are further compounded by the presence of an explicit or implicit *as* [*if*]; "*Enter Marius solus from the Numidian mountains, feeding on roots*" (*Wounds of Civil War*, 1189–90) initially may appear to be a *fictional* direction that tells the story, but a starving Marius who has been alone in exile could enter "[*as if*] *from the Numidian mountains*" so that the actor will use "*feeding on roots*" along with disheveled costume and *hair* to convey his mental and physical state; similarly, "*Enter Sanders's young son, and another boy coming from school*" (*Warning for Fair Women*, F4r) may be merely a *fictional* telling of the story, but if construed as "[*as if*] *coming from school*," the two boys could be dressed in distinctive costumes and carrying *books*; a *fictional* signal such as *enter on the walls* requires only that the figure enter *above*/*aloft*; other seemingly *fictional* signals ("*coming from school*," Jonas "[*as if*] *out of the Whale's belly*") may in contrast convey some practical instructions albeit in an Elizabethan code.

fiddle, fiddler

the five-stringed instrument or the musician who plays it, typically linked to *tavern* scenes and rustic *dancing* but also used in *window* wooing scenes; *fiddlers* appear onstage more often than other musicians to create a festive – sometimes raucous – atmosphere associated with commoners: "*Enter six Country Wenches, all red Petticoats, white stitched Bodies, in their Smock-sleeves, the Fiddler before them*" (*Country Girl*, D3r); see also *Old Wives Tale*, 734; *Mother Bombie*, 1715; *May Day*, 4.1.18; *Wit of a Woman*, 388; *Westward Ho*, 5.2.0, 5.3.16; *Northward Ho*, 5.1.196; *Ram Alley*, H3r; *Monsieur Thomas*, 136, 139; *Witch of Edmonton*, 3.4.13, 66; *Duke of Milan*, 2.1.50; *Knave in Grain*, 1785; *Love's Cruelty*, D4v; *Gamester*, C3r; *Wit in a Constable*, 232; *Late Lancashire Witches*, 204; *Goblins*, 4.1.35, 93, 96, 4.3.29; *Parson's Wedding*, 506, 510, 519; *Distresses*, 303; *Variety*, D3v; for three uses in the Brome canon see *Court Beggar*, 262, 263; *Queen and Concubine*, 124; *Weeding of Covent Garden*, 33; as these examples indicate, *fiddlers* and their music are more common in later plays; stage business is often initiated by the fiddlers' entrance but two plays make notable use of the instrument itself: in *Orlando Furioso* a fiddler's

music awakens the mad Orlando who "*takes away his fiddle*," "*strikes and beats him with the fiddle*," "*breaks it about his head*" upon which the *fiddler*, not surprisingly, departs (1192, 1213–14, 1220, 1225, 1232); in *Witch* Hecate "*conjures, and Enter a Cat (playing on a Fiddle)*" (437–9).

field

used occasionally in (1) the locution *enter in the field*, (2) *fictional* directions; figures preparing to *fight* a duel enter "*in the field*" (*Siege*, 409), "*as in the field*" (*Little French Lawyer*, 391; *Country Girl*, H1r), "*as in a Grove*" (*Knave in Grain*, 905); an alternative is an entrance "*as to a Duel*" (*Goblins*, 1.1.0); *field*/*fields* can appear in fictional signals: "*Then they bear the body into the fields*" (*Arden of Faversham*, 2387), "*Enter Laxton in Gray's Inn fields with the Coachman*" (*Roaring Girl*, 3.1.0).

fiend

a synonym for *devil* or *spirit*; in *1 Henry VI* when Joan calls up her "familiar spirits," "*Enter Fiends*" (2433, 5.3.7), and in *Two Noble Ladies* "*The fiends roar and fly back*" (1847).

fife

a wind instrument played like a modern flute, usually accompanied by a military *drum* (as distinct from the smaller *tabor*); the connotations of *drum and fife* are almost always martial, in contrast to the festive associations of *tabor and pipe*; only once is the *fife* cited in a non-military context: "*Folly with a Fife, Niceness, Newfangle, Dalliance, and Jealousy with Instruments, they play while Venus sings*" (*Cobbler's Prophecy*, 999–1000, also 1025); in *1 Henry IV* the military connotations are ironic: "*Enter the prince marching, and Falstaff meets him playing upon his truncheon like a fife*" (G3r, 3.3.87); in *Timon of Athens* a fife and drum occur in a martial context: "*with Drum and Fife in warlike manner*" (1652–3, 4.3.48) and in *Arraignment of Paris* Pallas's show begins with "*nine knights in armor, treading a warlike Almain, by drum and fife*" (478); see also *Death of Huntingdon*, 2908; *Edward II*, 1306; *Devil's Charter*, E1r, L1r.

fight

widely used (roughly 380 examples) usually as a verb and often simply as *fight*/*they fight*; *Dick of Devonshire* provides "*They fight*" (772, 1409), "*They fight. Pike disarms and trips him down*" (1711–12), "*They fight, one is killed, the other two disarmed*" (1737–8); *Trial of Chivalry* provides fifteen examples ranging from a simple *fight* to such actions as "*Fight, and hurt each other, both fall down as dead*" (E3r), "*Alarum, they fight, France put to the worst, enters Rodorick and Peter, the fight continued, and Navarre driven in*" (I1r); see also C2v, G3r, G3v, H1r, H3v, I1v, I2r, I2v, I3r, I3v; *Valiant Welshman* provides ten examples that include "*They fight, and are both slain*" (I3r), "*they fight: Monmouth beats them in*" (B3v, also I2v), "*They fight at Poleax, Codigune is conquered*" (E3r), "*They fight, and Caradoc beats and overthrows many of them*" (I1r), "*They fight, and Constantine winneth the Eagle, and waveth it about*" (I3r); see also B4r, G4v, I3r; of the many *fight* locutions the two most common are **draw** *and fight* (Quarto *King Lear*, H1v, 3.7.78; *Chaste Maid*, 4.4.55; *Jews' Tragedy*, 1226; *English Moor*, 8; *Love and Honour*, 167) and **offers** *to fight* (Quarto *2 Henry VI*, H2v, [5.2; not in Riv.]; *Sir John Oldcastle*, 7; Quarto *Merry Wives*, D3r, 3.1.72; Folio *Every Man In*, 4.2.133; *Hieronimo*, 10.112; *Landgartha*, C1r); variations include "*Make as if ye would fight*" (*Edward I*, 432), "*Draw and fight, throw pots and stools*" (*Amends for Ladies*, 3.4.133–4), "*He fighteth first with one, and then with another, and overcomes them both*" (*Orlando Furioso*, 1526–7), "*Alarum, a fierce fight with sword and target, then after pause and breathe*" and "*Alarum, fight with single swords, and being deadly wounded and panting for breath, making a stroke at each other with their gauntlets they fall*" (*Rape of Lucrece*, 252), "*Here they fight; Sir Thomas being weaponless defends himself with stones*" (*Travels of Three English Brothers*, 360).

fillip
see *finger*

find
an equivalent to **discover** both (1) in the theatrical sense of **parting** a **curtain** and (2) the more general sense of "come upon, see"; examples of the former include "*draws the Curtains, and finds Caradoc a reading*" (*Valiant Welshman*, H4v), "*draws the Curtains and finds her struck with Thunder, black*" (*Looking Glass for London*, 552–3); more general are "*finds his father's monument*" (*Atheist's Tragedy*, 3.1.126), "*searcheth his pocket, and findeth certain papers*" (*1 Henry IV*, E4r, 2.4.531), "*unlacing her, finds her great belly, and shows it to Diana*" (*Golden Age*, 35); what is *found* is often a person, **dead** or alive: "*break open the trunks, and find Alexandra, and Aristobulus*" (*Herod and Antipater*, B3v), "*the Queen returns, finds the King dead*" (*Hamlet*, Q1 F3r, Q2 H1v, Folio 1997, 3.2.135), "*findeth Viselli murdered*

upon the ground and starteth" (*Devil's Charter*, C3r); atypical is "*finds a louse*" (*Cupid's Whirligig*, 2.3.64); see also *Two Lamentable Tragedies*, C4r; *Alphonsus of Germany*, B1v; *Yorkshire Tragedy*, 651; *Histriomastix*, B1v; *Woman Is a Weathercock*, 5.2.5; *Wit at Several Weapons*, 94; *Fatal Contract*, H1r; *Late Lancashire Witches*, 248; *Bloody Banquet*, 852–3; *Duchess of Suffolk*, C3v; *Cardinal*, 3.2.94; *Lost Lady*, 591; *Princess*, C2r; *Wits*, 210; *Wizard*, 2286.

finger
the fifteen examples are linked to a wide variety of actions; to lay a *finger* on one's **mouth** is to signal **silence** (*Captain*, 297), as when a villain "*lays his finger on his mouth, and draws his dagger*" (*Antonio's Revenge*, 2.2.215) saying "Look, here's a trope: a true rogue's lips are mute; / I do not use to speak, but execute"; *fingers* are used to make the **sign** of the **cross** ("*Makes a cross on Clifford's face with his finger*," *Perkin Warbeck*, 2.2.83; see also *Devil's Charter*, E1r) and are associated with **rings** ("*plays with the wedding ring upon her finger*," *Parson's Wedding*, 417; see also *Four Plays in One*, 321; *Soddered Citizen*, 2784–6); other actions include "*Fillips all the while with his fingers*" (*Country Captain*, C6v), "*Beats his fingers against his sides*" (*Duchess of Suffolk*, C3v), "*with his Finger menaces Eulalia*" (*Queen and Concubine*, 22), "*They put the Tapers to his fingers, and he starts*" (Quarto *Merry Wives*, G3r, 5.5.88), a **ceremony** where a priest "*takes of the honey, with his finger, and tastes*" (*Sejanus*, 5.177), "*open the box and dip her finger in it, and spot Conscience's face*" (*Three Ladies of London*, E1v); see also *Launching of the Mary*, 1937; *Princess*, H3r.

fire
usually a noun (or adjective *fiery*), less often a verb meaning "ignite"; directions are often very descriptive but do not indicate exactly what is meant or how the effects were achieved: "*Let there be a Brazen Head … out of which cast flames of fire*" (*Alphonsus of Aragon*, 1246–7, also 1254), "*Bungay conjures and the tree appears with the dragon shooting fire*" (*Friar Bacon*, 1197–8); in the annotated quarto of *Looking Glass for London* the bookkeeper's "*lightning and bolt*" precedes the printed "*a flame of fire appeareth from beneath, and Radagon is swallowed*" (E2v, 1230–1), which suggests that at least in some instances *fire* and **lightning** were synonymous, as does "*with a sudden Thunderclap the sky is one* [or *on?*] *fire*" (*Captain Thomas Stukeley*, 2456–7); see also *Devil's Charter*, A2v, G1v; *flame of fire* also occurs in *Old Wives Tale*, 555; *Two Noble Ladies*,

1860; for *flash* of fire see *No Wit*, 4.3.40; *Silver Age*, 159; *Virgin Martyr*, 5.1.122; *Hog Hath Lost His Pearl*, 1616; *1 Arviragus and Philicia*, D8v; in the B text of *Doctor Faustus* Mephostophilis enters "*with the Chafer of Fire*" (457) which in the A text is "*a chafer of coals*" (510); for other examples of ritual or domestic *fire* see *Cobbler's Prophecy*, 1589; *Pericles*, E4r, 3.2.86; *Women Beware Women*, 5.2.72; *Launching of the Mary*, 76; *Amyntas*, 2Cr; sometimes *fires* are ignited: "*a silver Hind, in which is conveyed Incense and sweet odors, which being set upon the Altar . . . she sets fire to it*" (*Two Noble Kinsmen*, L1v, 5.1.136), "*break down the trees, and make a fire, in which Hercules places himself*" (*Brazen Age*, 253); in *Locrine* Medea "*hath a garland in her hand, and putting it on Creon's daughter's head, setteth it on fire*" (1772–4); there is one signal for "*quenching the fire*" (*White Devil*, 2.2.23); the verbal form also occurs: "*Fires the barrel tops*" (*If This Be Not a Good Play*, 5.4.64), "*As he toucheth the bed it fires*" (*Silver Age*, 155), "*fires the brand*" (*Brazen Age*, 200); elsewhere *fire* denotes a *torch* or *brand*: "*a three-forked fire in his hand*" (*No Wit*, 4.3.40), "*Pluto with a club of fire*" (*Silver Age*, 159), "*Spirits with fiery Clubs*" (*Seven Champions*, G3v), "*A fiery light*" described as "*A bloody arm . . . that holds a pine / Lighted*" (*Catiline*, 1.318); atypical is "*Two fiery Bulls are discovered*" (*Brazen Age*, 217); a unique usage occurs in *Roaring Girl* when a figure puts a pipe of tobacco "*to the fire*" (2.1.42); see also *burn*.

fireball

this graphic but undefined term occurs once: "*Hector, Paris, Troilus, Aeneas, with burning staves and fireballs*" (*1 Iron Age*, 314).

firebrand

see *brand*

fireworks

pyrotechnic devices or effects linked to supernatural events and figures, especially *devils*: "*a devil dress[ed] like a woman, with fireworks*" and "*Mephostophilis with fireworks*" (*Doctor Faustus*, A 595–6, B 1487), "*Devils dancing, with Fireworks and Crackers*" (*New Trick*, 280); a more spectacular effect is suggested by "*the Devils appear at every corner of the stage with several fireworks. . . fireworks all over the house*" (*Silver Age*, 159); "*Fireworks on Lines*" (*If This Be Not a Good Play*, 2.1.192) refers to *squibs* on strings; for other *fireworks* see *Battle of Alcazar*, 1279; *Doctor Faustus*, B 1125–6; *If This Be Not a Good Play*, 4.2.125; *Silver Age*, 160.

flag

a property called for twice: "*Valerio with a white Flag; the Herald summons the town to a parley*" (*Jews' Tragedy*, 797–8) and quite differently in a *masque*: "*Water with green flags upon his head standing up instead of hair*" (*No Wit*, 4.3.40); see also *ensign*, *standard*.

flagon

a large vessel for holding *wine*: "*a Table and Flagons of Wine on it*" (Folio *Hamlet*, 3675–6, 5.2.224), "*a flagon of wine and a bowl*" (*Devil's Charter*, I2v); see also *David and Bethsabe*, 491; *Duke of Milan*, 1.1.0; *Match at Midnight*, 81; *Lady Mother*, 620; see also *bottle*, *bowl*, *can*, *pitcher*.

flame

an effect linked to supernatural events, evidently produced from *under the stage*, through the *trapdoor*: "*Thunder, and the Gulf opens, flames issuing*" (*Caesar and Pompey*, 2.1.24), "*Plutus strikes the Rock, and flames fly out*" (*Four Plays in One*, 362), "*Throws his charmed rod, and his books under the stage. A flame riseth*" (*Two Noble Ladies*, 1899–1901); for more see *Bonduca*, 113; *If This Be Not a Good Play*, 5.3.149; see also *fire*.

flash

typically linked to *fire*, with supernatural implications: "*A thing like a globe opens of one side of the stage and flashes out fire*" (*No Wit*, 4.3.40), "*A flash of fire and Lightfoot ascends like a spirit*" (*Hog Hath Lost His Pearl*, 1616–18), "*Harpax in a fearful shape, fire flashing out of the study*" (*Virgin Martyr*, 5.1.122); see also *Friar Bacon*, 1635; *Silver Age*, 159; *1 Arviragus and Philicia*, D8v; in *Honest Lawyer* a figure pretending to be a *spirit* "*flashes powder*" (I2v).

fling

signals an action done (1) by or to a figure, (2) to properties; examples of *fling*, sometimes as part of another action, include "*Dance again: and in the first course Matilda flings from him*" (*Death of Huntingdon*, 1341–2; see also *Rape of Lucrece*, 226), "*flings and tumbles him over: pulls him up again*" (MS *Bonduca*, 2508–10), "*He flings her into the well*" (*Faithful Shepherdess*, 409), "*Flings himself into the river*" (*Locrine*, 1756), a figure "*Flings down*" another and "*disarms him*" (*Cruel Brother*, 125); more commonly figures *fling* or *fling down*/*away* a *hat* (*Downfall of Huntingdon*, 172; *Goblins*, 1.2.4), *bottle* (*Lady Mother*, 618), *bag* (*Cruel Brother*, 164), *letter* (*Fawn*, 4.57), *sword* (*Cruel Brother*, 189; *Christian Turned Turk*, C2v), *purse* (*King Leir*, 1018;

Just Italian, 265; *Brennoralt*, 2.4.89; *Wits*, 128), **weapons** (*Lust's Dominion*, 4.4.85; *Messalina*, 1329); other examples include "*Flings away the dagger and halter*" (*Spanish Tragedy*, 3.12.19), "*flinging up caps*" (*Sir Thomas More*, 710), "*Flings wine in his face*" (*Fortune by Land and Sea*, 368), "*fling firework among them*" (*Doctor Faustus*, B 1125), "*flings the cushion at him*" (*Heir*, 575); see also *Wise Woman of Hogsdon*, 281; *Valiant Welshman*, I1r; MS *Humorous Lieutenant*, 2332; *Just Italian*, 249; *flung* occurs once: "*from above a Willow garland is flung down*" (*What You Will*, B1v); see also **throw**, **toss**.

flourish

a widely used signal (over 500 examples) for either (1) a fanfare usually played **within** on a **trumpet** or **cornet**, primarily when important figures **enter** and **exit** but also at such events as the reading of **proclamations** and the start of entertainments or rarely (2) a verb meaning "brandish or wave about"; theatrical fanfares were likely the same patterned sounds as those used in the real world and probably varied little from play to play; the most common signal for the **sound** is simply *flourish*, many from bookkeepers in manuscripts (*John of Bordeaux*, 71; *Charlemagne*, 72, 2620; *Second Maiden's Tragedy*, 256, 1028, 1168; *Believe as You List*, 1336, 1361, 2894; *Two Noble Ladies*, 557, 924; *Wasp*, 239, 471, 743) or quartos annotated for performance (*Looking Glass for London*, A2r, A4r, C4v, and more; *Two Merry Milkmaids*, D3r, D3v, E2v, E4v, H1v); Q2 *Hamlet* provides examples of the basic usages: "*Flourish. Enter Claudius, King of Denmark, Gertrude the Queen, Council*" and "*Flourish. Exeunt all, but Hamlet*" (B3v, 1.2.0; C1r, 1.2.128); other examples of the basic signal are Folio *3 Henry VI*, 870–2, 2.2.0; Folio *Henry V*, 462, 2.Chorus.0; 1044, 3.Chorus.0; *All's Well*, 327, 1.2.76; *1 Fair Maid of the West*, 307; *Antony and Cleopatra*, 15, 1.1.10; *Coriolanus*, 744, 1.10.0; *Four Plays in One*, 291, 292; *Mad Lover*, 3; *Virgin Martyr*, 5.2.242; *Queen and Concubine*, 32, 33; *Antipodes*, 266, 274; sometimes the direction is *sound a flourish* (*Edward III*, K2r; *1 Tamar Cham*, 10; *1 Henry VI*, 192, 1.2.0; Folio *2 Henry VI*, 1168, 2.3.105; *Hieronimo*, 10.32, 13.0; *Sophonisba*, 5.2.49); instruments are often specified: *flourish* **cornet** (*Woodstock*, 2093; *All's Well*, 237, 1.2.0; *Coriolanus*, 1120, 2.1.204; *Birth of Merlin*, A4r; *Two Noble Kinsmen*, K3v, 5.1.7; *Laws of Candy*, 250; *Two Noble Ladies*, 367), "*The cornets sound a flourish*" (*Antonio and Mellida*, 1.1.98, 139), "*a full flourish of cornets*" (*Sophonisba*, 3.2.84), *flourish* **trumpet** (Folio *2 Henry VI*, 2, 1.1.0; Folio *Midsummer*

Night's Dream, 1904, 5.1.107; Q2 *Hamlet*, D1r, 1.4.6; *Thracian Wonder*, E2r, G1r; *Birth of Merlin*, F4r; *Henry VIII*, 2445, 4.1.36); some signals are for a **drum** to accompany the *flourish*: "*Sound a Flourish with Drums*" (*Antony and Cleopatra*, 1491, 2.7.133), "*A Flourish with Drums and Trumpets*" (*Coriolanus*, 3648, 5.5.7); see also *Devil's Charter*, K1r; *Rape of Lucrece*, 240; another recurring combination is *flourish and* **shout** (*Julius Caesar*, 174, 1.2.78; *Sir Thomas Wyatt*, 2.2.53; *Sophonisba*, 2.3.30; *Rape of Lucrece*, 245; *Silver Age*, 94; *Hengist*, 2.3.167; *Faithful Friends*, 632–3); a few directions specify *flourish* **afar off** (*Love and Honour*, 111; *Platonic Lovers*, 14) or *flourish within* (*Spanish Gypsy*, G4r; *Fatal Contract*, B2r; *Jews' Tragedy*, 3062); there is a **long** *flourish* (Folio *Titus Andronicus*, 264, 1.1.233; Folio *Richard II*, 420, 1.3.122; *Shoemakers' Holiday*, 5.5.0) and a **short** *flourish* (*Sophonisba*, 5.4.59; *Turk*, 286; *Two Noble Kinsmen*, E4v, 2.5.0; *Bonduca*, 127; *Roman Actor*, 3.2.148; *Faithful Friends*, 775); unusual or unique locutions are "*Retreat, and Flourish*" (*Macbeth*, 2478, 5.9.0), "*Exeunt, the cornets flourishing*" (*Sophonisba*, 5.2.100), "*all go off with a flourish*" (*1 Iron Age*, 277), "*A flourish, as to an assault*" (*Maid of Honour*, 2.3.0), "*A most untunable flourish*" (*Antipodes*, 336).

Occasionally *flourish* signals the action of brandishing or waving: "*flourishes over him with his longsword*" (Folio *Every Man In*, 5.3.35), "*Flourishing his sword ensheathed*" (*New Way to Pay*, 5.1.360; see also *Court Beggar*, 233), "*flourishing his dagger*" (*Sir Thomas More*, 1068), "*bring away the Ensigns, flourishing them*" (*Four Prentices*, 234), "*Flourish Colors*" (*Double Marriage*, 361).

flowers

called for on a wide variety of occasions: Isabella "*dressed with flowers and garlands*" for a **ceremony** in a **masque** (*Women Beware Women*, 5.2.72), citizens supporting Barnavelt who enter "*with Boughs and flowers*" (*Barnavelt*, 2113–15), a figure going to her **execution** "*her hair hanging down, a chaplet of flowers on her head, a nosegay in her hand*" (*Insatiate Countess*, 5.1.66), Paris at the Capulet monument "*with flowers and sweet water*" who "*strews the Tomb with flowers*" (Q1 *Romeo and Juliet*, I4v, 5.3.0, 11); other **strewings** of flowers are "*Enter a maid strewing flowers, and a serving-man perfuming the door*" (*Two Maids of More-Clacke*, A1r), "*Enter Hymen with a Torch burning: a Boy, in a white Robe before singing, and strewing Flowers*" (*Two Noble Kinsmen*, B1r, 1.1.0), "*Curtains open, Robin Hood sleeps on a green bank, and Marian strewing flowers on* him" (*Downfall of Huntingdon*, 1490–1); ***funeral*** scenes include "*a garland of flowers*" on the ***coffin*** of a virgin (*Chaste Maid*, 5.4.0), "*The Queen following the Bier, carrying a Garland of flowers*" (*Death of Huntingdon*, 2911–12), two coffins and "*two winding-sheets stuck with flowers*" (*Devil's Law Case*, 5.4.125); heavenly *flowers* are important for a sequence in *Virgin Martyr* (5.1.38, 135, 139); variations include Marina "*with a Basket of flowers*" (*Pericles*, F2r, 4.1.12), the maid holding up Emilia's ***train*** with "*her hair stuck with flowers*" (*Two Noble Kinsmen*, L1v, 5.1.136), an entrance "*gathering of Flowers*" (*Wily Beguiled*, 147), nymphs "*with flowers in their laps*" (*Brazen Age*, 235), a ***dumb show*** in which a king "*lies him down upon a bank of flowers*" (*Hamlet*, Q2 H1v, Folio 1994, 3.2.135), a ***ghost*** that shows a guilty figure "*a pot of lily-flowers with a skull in't*" (*White Devil*, 5.4.123), "*The Queen looking upon a flower in one of the Ladies' heads*" (*Aglaura*, 1.3.28).

flute

a wooden wind instrument played from the end rather than along the side and usually called a ***recorder***, linked to ***funerals*** or other solemn occasions: "*The still flutes sound a mournful sennet*" (*Antonio and Mellida*, 5.2.208), "*a sad Music of Flutes heard*" (*King John and Matilda*, 83); see also *Antonio's Revenge*, 4.1.130; *Fedele and Fortunio*, 434.

fly

widely used (eighty examples) for "enter or exit rapidly, flee" usually linked to ***battles*** or ***fights***: "*fly over the stage*" (*Lust's Dominion*, 4.2.135; see also *Edward II*, 1777), "*Ariadne flying before him with a Child in her arms*" (*Thracian Wonder*, B1r), "*The Battle continues, the Britains fly, Cymbeline is taken*" (*Cymbeline*, 2908–9, 5.2.10); for figures who ***enter*** *flying* see *Titus Andronicus*, F3v, 4.1.0; *Edmond Ironside*, 976; *Edward III*, F4v; *Guy of Warwick*, C4r; *Four Prentices*, 226; *Woman Hater*, 95; *Two Noble Ladies*, 4; *Dick of Devonshire*, 300–1; *Bloody Banquet*, 16–17; for a sampling of the roughly forty examples of ***exit*** *flying* see *Battle of Alcazar*, 1366–7, 1386; *Orlando Furioso*, 441, 982; *Edmond Ironside*, 988, 991, 1592; *Two Lamentable Tragedies*, C4r; *2 Seven Deadly Sins*, 65; *Captain Thomas Stukeley*, 1352; *1 Henry VI*, 766, 2.1.77; 1552, 3.2.109; 2461, 5.3.29; Quarto *2 Henry VI*, H3r, [5.2.65]; Folio *3 Henry VI*, 1131, 2.4.11; 2254, 2259, 4.3.27; Q1 *Romeo and Juliet*, F1v, [3.1.90]; *1 Henry IV*, K2r, 5.4.43; *Death of Huntingdon*, 943; *Alarum for London*, 781, 1511; *Fair Maid of Bristow*, A3r; *Brazen Age*, 224; *Travels of Three English Brothers*, 360; *Valiant Welshman*, G1r; *Herod and*

Antipater, F3v; *Bloody Banquet*, 15; *Gentleman of Venice*, D3v; other aggressive actions include "*Flies after Bianca*" (*Taming of the Shrew*, 887, 2.1.29), *fly at/upon* (*Sir John Oldcastle*, 701; *Court Beggar*, 252; MS *Poor Man's Comfort*, 1920; *Northern Lass*, 65).

Examples not linked to battles/fights include "*flies to his bosom*" (*Match Me in London*, 5.3.0), "*seemeth to reject his suit, flies to the tomb, kneels and kisseth it*" (*Antonio's Revenge*, 3.1.0), "*Gerardine rising out of the Trunk, she seems fearful, and flies*" (*Family of Love*, D1r), "*She looks in her book, and the Spirits fly from her*" and "*The fiends roar and fly back*" (*Two Noble Ladies*, 1796–7, 1847); see also *Fedele and Fortunio*, 599; *James IV*, 5; occasionally *fly* is an offstage shout: "*Cry within, Fly, fly, fly*" (*Julius Caesar*, 2688, 5.5.42); see also *Thracian Wonder*, G4r; *Woman Is a Weathercock*, 3.3.5; *Claracilla*, D2v; variations include "*the Tombstone flies open*" (*Second Maiden's Tragedy*, 1927; see also *Goblins*, 2.6.11), "*Plutus strikes the Rock, and flames fly out*" (*Four Plays in One*, 362), "*Pots fly clink*" (*Weeding of Covent Garden*, 33); atypical are "*Mercury flies from above*," "*As he toucheth the bed it fires, and all flies up*" (*Silver Age*, 138, 155) and the noun *flight*: "*is wounded, and put to flight*" (*Weakest Goeth*, 592–3).

fog

see ***mist***

foil

a light ***sword*** with a blunt edge used in fencing: "*Enter King, Queen, Laertes and Lords, with other Attendants with Foils, and Gauntlets*" (Folio *Hamlet*, 3674–5, 5.2.224), "*foils in their hands*" (*London Prodigal*, D1r), "*[foil] and target*" (MS *Poor Man's Comfort*, 2220); Henslowe's inventory lists "*seventeen foils*" (*Diary*, App. 2, 77).

follow, following, followers

widely used (roughly 300 examples), particularly for entrances when a figure *follows* another onto the ***stage*** or ***enters*** *following*: "*Enter Balurdo, backward; Dildo following him . . . ; Flavia following him backward . . . ; Rossaline following her*" (*Antonio and Mellida*, 3.2.123); most of the signals provide no details though occasionally actors are directed to *follow* ***closely*** (*All Fools*, 3.1.0; *Gentleman Usher*, 2.1.0; *Revenge of Bussy*, 3.4.0), ***amazedly*** (*Tempest*, 2201, 5.1.215), ***aloof*** (*John a Kent*, 605; *Whore of Babylon*, 2.2.185), ***unseen*** (*Conspiracy of Byron*, 3.1.0, 5.2.0); sometimes onstage figures ***offer*** *to follow* (*Cobbler's Prophecy*, 1539; *1 Edward IV*, 21; *Bride*, 18; *Wits*, 145); for plays with multiple examples of *follow* see *Wisdom of Doctor Dodypoll*, 87, 329, 855, 1292, 1772; *Caesar and Pompey*, 1.2.0, 2.1.89, 2.3.0, 4.1.0, 4.3.0, 4.6.0, 5.1.0, 258; *Sophonisba*, Prologue.0, 1.2.0, 35, 2.2.0, 25, 3.1.0; *Jews' Tragedy*, 1038, 1103, 2085, 2242, 2659, 3044, 3131; variations include "*Exit Ghost beckoning him to follow*" (*Valiant Scot*, I4r; see also *Renegado*, 2.4.134), "*follows him to the door, and returns*" (*King Leir*, 2625), "*Enter Contempt, Venus following him, he pushing her from him twice or thrice*" (*Cobbler's Prophecy*, 1486–7), "*Enter Don Zuccone, following Dona Zoya on his knees*" (*Fawn*, 5.89), "*following in disguise*" (*Costly Whore*, 278); also common are offstage **cries** of *follow*: "*A noise within, Follow, follow, follow*" (*Merry Devil of Edmonton*, E2v); for a sampling see *Nobody and Somebody*, D3v; *Miseries of Enforced Marriage*, 1537; *Two Noble Ladies*, 248–51; *Shoemaker a Gentleman*, 1.1.106, 131; *Jews' Tragedy*, 897–8; *Messalina*, 2132–3; *Lovesick King*, 98–9; roughly twenty-five plays have entering figures accompanied by *followers*, as in Morocco's first appearance in *Merchant of Venice* with "*three or four followers accordingly*" (B4v, 2.1.0, also C2v, 2.2.113; I3v, 5.1.126); for a sampling see *Locrine*, 2024, 2063; *1 Tamburlaine*, 1261, 1263; *Titus Andronicus*, A3r, 1.1.0; *Eastward Ho*, E1v; *Hoffman*, 529; Quarto *King Lear*, B1v, 1.1.33; *Pericles*, A2v, 1.1.0; *Silver Age*, 97; *Captives*, 1306; *Perkin Warbeck*, 2.1.39, 5.1.74; *Jews' Tragedy*, 59; *Queen's Exchange*, 506; *Deserving Favourite*, B2v, C2v, C4v.

foot, feet

found in such locutions and actions as (1) **stamps** with his foot, (2) **barefoot**, (3) **kisses** her foot, (4) footman, footboy, (5) at the feet of a figure/**bed**; several figures stamp with their *foot* as a signal (*stamp* by itself is more common): "*He stamps with his foot, and the Soldiers show themselves*" (Folio *3 Henry VI*, 189–90, 1.1.169), "*stamps with his foot: to him a Servant*" (*Amends for Ladies*, 2.3.2); see also *Four Plays in One*, 326; *Osmond*, C7r; *barefoot* is usually associated with **mourning**/penance: "*barefoot, with some loose covering over his head*" (*David and Bethsabe*, 972), "*barefoot, and a white sheet about her, with a wax candle in her hand*" (Quarto *2 Henry VI*, D2r, 2.4.16); see also *Edward III*, I3v; *2 Edward IV*, 165; as a sign of homage/abasement a figure may kiss a *foot*: "*Offers to kiss her foot*" (*New Way to Pay*, 2.2.85), "*being presented unto the Pope, kisseth his foot, and then advancing two degrees higher, kisseth his cheek*" (*Devil's Charter*, E1r); see also *Travels of Three English Brothers*, 322; *Herod and Antipater*, F4r; related are "*offers to stoop to his foot*" (*Travels of Three English Brothers*, 322), "*falls down at the foot of Theseus*"

(*Two Noble Kinsmen*, B1v, 1.1.24), "*Error at his foot as asleep*" (*Game at Chess*, 13–14); to *foot* can be to **dance/caper**: "*Practice footing*" (*Court Beggar*, 261, also 263), "*seems to foot the tune*" (*Mad World*, 2.1.143), "*seems to caper and hurt his foot*" (*Bride*, 8); other usages include "*kicks it by with his foot*" (*Andromana*, 237), "*His foot on the Doctor's breast*" (*Bashful Lover*, 5.1.135), "*sets his foot afore him, and he falls with his basket*" (*Bartholomew Fair*, 4.2.32), "*with his foot he overturneth them*" and "*with his foot overthroweth the child*" (*Death of Huntingdon*, 938–9, 942); see also *Whore of Babylon*, 4.1.0; *footmen* can be found in *Edward I*, 1015, 1098; *2 Honest Whore*, 1.1.13; *Mad World*, 2.1.6, 2.6.7; *No Wit*, 1.2.64; *City Match*, 235, 276, 277, and more; *Country Captain*, D7r; *Parson's Wedding*, 394; and *footboys* in *Amends for Ladies*, 2.3.10, 4.3.1, 4.4.59, 94; *Wild Goose Chase*, 315; *Magnetic Lady*, 4.8.0; atypical are a *footstep* as an item of furniture (*City Madam*, 4.4.160) and *footed* **stools** (*Launching of the Mary*, 77).

The plural *feet* is found primarily in variations of *at his/her feet*; examples of laying objects at another's *feet* are "*present their Crowns to him at his feet, and do him homage*" (*Birth of Merlin*, G4r), "*lay down their properties at the Queen's feet*" (*Arraignment of Paris*, 1213), "*kneels, and lays the sword at Aphelia's feet*" (*Fatal Contract*, E4v; see also *Prophetess*, 363; *Queen of Corinth*, 60); figures *sit*, **lie**, **kneel** (*Henry VIII*, 1364–5, 2.4.12; *Revenge of Bussy*, 4.3.96; *Sparagus Garden*, 191; *Grateful Servant*, K4r) at someone's *feet*: typical are "*lieth all this while dead at his feet*" and "*sit down at Amurack's feet*" (*Alphonsus of Aragon*, 492–3, 935), "*The maids sit down at her feet mourning*" (*Broken Heart*, 4.4.0), "*the Kings lying at her feet, she treading on them as she goes up*" (*Old Fortunatus*, 1.1.63); variations include "*cast down their weapons at his feet*" (*Herod and Antipater*, F4r), "*She lays her hand under her husband's feet*" (*Taming of a Shrew*, G1v), "*the Cardinal places himself under the King's feet on his right side*" (*Henry VIII*, 318–20, 1.2.0; see also *Hoffman*, 484; *Look about You*, 2826); for more see *Edward I*, 101; *Sophonisba*, 5.2.49; references to a *bed's feet* include "*stands at his Bed's feet sadly*" (*Witch of Edmonton*, 4.2.69), "*She suddenly dies at the Queen's bed's feet*" (*Edward I*, 2607); see also *Lust's Dominion*, 1.2.0; *Cruel Brother*, 191; other directions call for a **devil** "*his feet and his head horrid*" (*Birth of Merlin*, D2v), "*bind his arms and feet*" (*Gentleman of Venice*, D4v), "*Dances looking on his Feet, etc.*" (*Court Beggar*, 261), "*He writes his name with his staff and guides it with feet and mouth*" (*Titus Andronicus*, F4v, 4.1.68); see also *Herod and Antipater*, C3r, F3v; *Fool Would Be a Favourite*, C8r; *Landgartha*, E3r.

for

can serve as an equivalent to *disguised* as, *like*, *alias*, or (for a play-within-a-play) "in the role of"; disguises include "*Cupid for Ascanius*" (Dido, 1371), "*Portia for Balthazar*" (Merchant of Venice, H1r, 4.1.166), "*Rosalind for Ganymede, Celia for Aliena*" (As You Like It, 782, 2.4.0); see also Michaelmas Term, 2.3.423; examples of roles played are "*a Boy dressed for a Lady*" (Roman Actor, 4.2.222, also 3.2.228), "*Enter Pedant for Judas, and the Boy for Hercules*" (Love's Labour's Lost, I1v, 5.2.587, also 561); a related usage combines *for* with *take*/*mistake*: "*they take him for Duke Humphrey*" (Quarto 2 Henry VI, B2r, [1.3.5]), "*counterfeits to take him for a ghost*" and "*mistakes the body of Borachio for Soquette*" (Atheist's Tragedy, 3.2.17, 4.3.205), "*taking Chorebus for a Grecian by reason of his habit, fights with him and kills him*" (2 Iron Age, 390).

forth

(1) usually used with a variety of verbs to indicate figures or objects being brought onto and less commonly *off* the *stage* but also found in such locutions as (2) *stand*/*step*/*come forth*, (3) *pull*/*draw forth* a *weapon*; more than 100 figures *come*/*issue forth* or *bring*/*carry*/*set*/*thrust*/*draw*/*lead forth* objects/people; in the majority of instances *forth* indicates "onto the stage" but exceptions include "*Then Soliman dies, and they carry him forth with silence*" (Soliman and Perseda, I2r), "*They all but the Nurse go forth*" (Q1 Romeo and Juliet, I2v, 4.5.95; see also Duke's Mistress, G2r), "*Puts forth the Drawer and shuts the door*" (Quarto Every Man Out, 3825–6), "*the Attendants go forth with the hearse*" (Lovesick Court, 163), "*Scilla offers to go forth and Anthony calls him back*" (Wounds of Civil War, 258–9), "*Here the noblemen go forth, and bring in the Duke of Epire like a combatant*" (Dumb Knight, 195); see also Alphonsus of Aragon, 1871; 1 Edward IV, 56, 67; Sophonisba, 1.2.236; Bondman, 5.1.57; Sparagus Garden, 193; Court Beggar, 268.

Regularly *brought*/*led*/*carried forth* onto the stage are *prisoners* and figures *sick*/*wounded*/*sleeping*; for a sampling see Folio 3 Henry VI, 2799–2800, 5.2.0; Sir Thomas Wyatt, 3.2.44; Warning for Fair Women, H3v; Sir John Oldcastle, 1640–1, 2541; Four Prentices, 232; Roman Actor, 2.1.287; Renegado, 4.2.0; servants and soldiers are more likely to *come*/*issue forth*; for a sampling see 1 Troublesome Reign, F2v; 1 Edward IV, 31; Jovial Crew, 365; variations include "*Servingmen come forth with Napkins*" (Q2 Romeo and Juliet, C2v, 1.5.0), "*Then is young Aire brought forth to execution by*

the Sheriff and Officers" (2 Edward IV, 180), "*Those in ambush rusheth forth and take him*" (Dutch Courtesan, 5.1.49), "*The Soldiers thrust forth Theocrine, her garments loose, her hair disheveled*" (Unnatural Combat, 5.2.185); objects *set*/*thrust*/*drawn forth* include a *scaffold* (Virgin Martyr, 4.3.4), *altar* (2 Iron Age, 426), *bar* (Lovers' Progress, 144; Parliament of Love, 5.1.32), *banquet* (Westward Ho, 4.2.52; Royal King, 25; Custom of the Country, 334; Faithful Friends, 2485; Unnatural Combat, 3.2.136; Great Duke of Florence, 4.2.153; Obstinate Lady, H3v; Rebellion, 65), *table* (Revenger's Tragedy, I2v; Fortune by Land and Sea, 420; Bondman, 2.3.0; Renegado, 2.4.0; Antipodes, 324; Wedding, I1r; Noble Stranger, G3r), most commonly a *bed* (2 Henry VI, 1849, 3.2.146; Atheist's Tragedy, 5.1.59; Witch of Edmonton, 4.2.0; Fatal Contract, G1r; Very Woman, 4.2.19; Queen's Exchange, 524; Weeding of Covent Garden, 87; Mad Couple, 73; Obstinate Lady, E2v; Cruel Brother, 191); atypical are "*let there come forth this show*" (Locrine, 432), "*Here the Head speaks and a lightning flasheth forth*" (Friar Bacon, 1635).

For figures who *stand forth* see Midsummer Night's Dream, A2v, [1.1.24, 26]; Julius Caesar, 2407, 5.1.69; examples of *step forth* are "*Berowne steps forth*" (Love's Labour's Lost, I2v, 5.2.664), "*step both forth and restrain her*" (Isle of Gulls, 308); comparable is "*holds forth her right hand*" (Bondman, 3.2.59); occasionally figures already onstage *come forth* (All Fools, 1.1.345; Epicœne, 4.5.129, 298; Alchemist, 5.5.58, 90); usage with weapons includes "*draws forth a knife*" (2 Edward IV, 129; Tom a Lincoln, 35–6), "*Whips forth his Sword*" (Herod and Antipater, K2r); see also Arden of Faversham, 320; Just Italian, 233.

fray

the term for a disturbance or brawl found only in three Heywood directions, each for "*A confused fray*" (Golden Age, 22; Silver Age, 142; Brazen Age, 196).

frighted

see *affrighted*

frown

a rarely signaled silent action: "*Exit King, frowning upon the Cardinal*" (Henry VIII, 2080, 3.2.203, also 3181, 5.2.148), "*winks and frowns*" (Woman in the Moon, B1r); several examples link a *frown* to *reading*: "*reads privately and frowns*" (Fair Maid of the Exchange, 59), "*reads the letter, frowns and stamps*" (King Leir, 1172); see also Four Plays in One, 326; Politician, A4v.

funeral

refers to a public procession involving a *hearse/bier*, *mourning* figures, and appropriate accoutrements and *music*: "*Enter Funeral. Body borne by four Captains and Soldiers. Mourners. Scutcheons, and very good order*" along with "*Solemn Music*" (*Fatal Dowry*, 2.1.47), "*a Funeral, a Coronet lying on the Hearse, Scutcheons and Garlands hanging on the sides*" (*1 Honest Whore*, 1.1.0); the *funeral* of a warrior may be preceded by a *dead march* or may include other elements: "*Enter two, dragging of ensigns; then the funeral of Andrea*" (*Hieronimo*, 12.0); comparable are "*They bear him off with a sad and funeral march, etc.*" (*2 Iron Age*, 414), "*Solemn Music, to a funeral song the Hearse borne over the stage*" (*Law Tricks*, 183); some signals provide only *enter* the funeral (*Atheist's Tragedy*, 3.1.0; *Mad Lover*, 70; *Duchess of Suffolk*, G2v), but others contain additional details: enter "*with funeral pomp*" (*Selimus*, 1996–7), "*Enter the Queens with the Hearses of their Knights, in a Funeral Solemnity, etc.*" (*Two Noble Kinsmen*, C4v, 1.5.0), "*Enter a Friar, after him a funeral in white, and bearers in white*" (*Turk*, 585–6) "*A dead march. Enter the funeral of Charlemont as a soldier*" (*Atheist's Tragedy*, 3.1.6), "*Dead March. Enter the Funeral of King Henry the Fifth*" (*1 Henry VI*, 2–3, 1.1.0).

furnished, furniture

in a variety of locutions *furnished* means "having, supplied with": sailors "*furnished with Sea devices fitting for a fight*" (*Fortune by Land and Sea*, 416), "*in his study furnished with glasses, vials, pictures of wax characters, wands, conjuring habit, Powders paintings*" (*Maid's Revenge*, E3v), "*Furnished with things from London*" (*Yorkshire Tragedy*, 27); "*A Table furnished*" (*Sea Voyage*, 56; *Wasp*, 2185) is signaled for *banquets* and other special events: "*A furnished Table is brought forth*" (*Revenger's Tragedy*, I2v), a *table* is "*furnished with diverse bags of money*" (*Devil's Charter*, A2r); *furnish* as a transitive verb is rare: a *sacrifice* enters "*whilst the attendants furnish the altar*" (*Sophonisba*. 3.1.116); two of the three uses of *furniture* clearly mean "costume and accoutrements": Cockledemoy *disguised* "*in his barber's furniture*" (*Dutch Courtesan*, 2.1.244), a jeweller, tire-women, tailor "*with everyone their several furniture*" (*Histriomastix*, D3r); the third, an entrance "*with Servants and furniture for the table*" (*Dutch Courtesan*, 3.3.60), presumably sets up a *furnished* table.

fury

either (1) an alternative to *spirit* or (2) a synonym for *anger*; the supernatural *devil*-figure is called for in

"*a Fury all fireworks*" (*Brazen Age*, 175, also 176), "*Malbecco his Ghost guarded with Furies*" (*Grim the Collier*, G2v, also G4r, K1v), "*Persephone with the three furies*" (*Jews' Tragedy*, 2381), "*Enter two Furies out of the Conjurer's Cell*" (*Old Wives Tale*, 629, also 417), "*the Fates and Furies down to hell*" (*Silver Age*, 164), "*Death: Grimes: and furies*" (*Lady Mother*, 2474); *furies* also appear in *Battle of Alcazar* plot, 28, 57, 95; *Rare Triumphs*, 2–6; *Warning for Fair Women*, D1r; *If This Be Not a Good Play*, 1.1.49; *Night Walker*, 364; *Four Plays in One*, 355; *Herod and Antipater*, L3v; *Traitor*, 3.2.44; *Messalina*, 832–3, 846–7; a *masque* in *Faithful Friends* provides "*three young lords like furies*" (2561–2); elsewhere figures enter "*in a fury*" (*Alphonsus of Aragon*, 1027; *Mad World*, 5.2.41; *Nice Valour*, 173; *Seven Champions*, C2r); in *Hengist* Constantius "*fairly spreads his arms and yields to their furies*," and Roxena expresses "*great fury and discontent*" (DS before 2.2, 6, DS before 4.3, 4); in *Histriomastix* the idea is personified: "*Enter War, Ambition, Fury, Horror, Ruin*" (F1r, also F3v).

G

gallant

used to describe costly, fashionable, extravagant clothing (hence comparable to *brave*), often linked to a rise in status: "*Mother and the young Lady gallant*" (*Maidenhead Well Lost*, 131, also 130), enter "*in a gallant habit*" (*Unnatural Combat*, 4.2.25), "*three wenches gallantly attired*" (*Your Five Gallants*, A2r), "*a Cutpurse very gallant, with four or five men after him, one with a wand*" (*Roaring Girl*, 5.1.241), "*Chartley very gallant, in his hand a Lady*" (*Wise Woman of Hogsdon*, 325); for other uses of *very gallant* see *Old Fortunatus*, 2.2.0, 3.1.389; *Anything for a Quiet Life*, H1r; in *Eastward Ho* Quicksilver appears "*in his prentice's Coat and Cap, his gallant breeches and Stockings*" (B4r), and for a *disguise* a woman enters "*as a gallant gentleman, her husband like a serving-man after her*" (*No Wit*, 2.1.169); see also *Old Fortunatus*, 1.2.131; *Blind Beggar of Bednal Green*, 34; MS *Poor Man's Comfort*, 971; *Honest Lawyer*, C3r; *Challenge for Beauty*, 33; *New Trick*, 265; *Wasp*, 1887; atypical is "*Enter Bubble gallanted*" (*Greene's Tu Quoque*, I3v).

gallery

a rarely used term for the playing area *above* the main platform: "*in a corner of the Gallery*" (*Knave in Grain*, 2908), "*above in a Gallery*" (*Second Maiden's Tragedy*, 2004).

galliard

a quick and lively *dance*, twice called for as *entr'acte music* in *Fedele and Fortunio*: "*a pleasant Galliard*" and "*a cheerful Galliard*" (388, 1807–8); for other examples see *Jack Drum's Entertainment*, H4r; *Insatiate Countess*, 2.1.154; *Renegado*, 1.2.51.

gallows

see *gibbet*

garden

used rarely to designate a location: "*Enter Morosa and Oriana in the garden*" (*Traitor*, 2.2.0; see also *Heir*, 526), "*Iphigene (as in a Garden)*" (*Brennoralt*, 3.1.0; see also *Gentleman of Venice*, B2v); this location is similarly established with "*Enter Gardeners*" (*Richard II*, G2v, 3.4.23); an alternative also occurs: "*Enter Brutus in his Orchard*" (*Julius Caesar*, 615, 2.1.0; see also *Amyntas*, X2v); see also *arbor*.

garland

called for in a wide variety of contexts: "*Clown with Garlands upon his Hook*" at a shepherds' *dance* (*Thracian Wonder*, C4r), Diana's nymphs with "*garlands on their heads, and javelins in their hands*" (*Golden Age*, 27), Bacchus "*dressed in Vine leaves, and a garland of grapes on his head*" and his companions with "*Ivy garlands on their heads*" (*Summer's Last Will*, 967); a victorious Coriolanus is "*crowned with an Oaken Garland*" (1061–2, 2.1.161; see also *Guardian*, 5.1.0), and a group returning from war includes "*maimed Soldiers with headpieces and Garlands on them*" and "*the Ancient borne in a Chair, his Garland and his plumes on his headpiece*" (*Edward I*, 40); *funerals* include "*a garland of flowers*" (*Chaste Maid*, 5.4.0; *Death of Huntingdon*, 2911–12), a figure "*with a Garland on her head*" (*Fatal Contract*, E3v), "*Hearse, Scutcheons and Garlands hanging on the sides*" (*1 Honest Whore*, 1.1.0); Matilda's *hearse* is "*attended by the Queen, bearing in her hand a Garland, composed of Roses and Lilies*" so that the king "*takes the Garland from the Queen*" and "*sets the Garland on her breast*" (*King John and Matilda*, 84, 86, 87); most often specified are *willow garlands*: masquers "*in white robes, with garlands of willows*" ('*Tis Pity*, 4.1.35; see also *Northern Lass*, 41), "*from above a Willow garland is flung down and the song ceaseth*" (*What You Will*, B1v); see also *Wisdom of Doctor Dodypoll*, 1312; *Woman Is a Weathercock*, 1.2.233, 5.1.22; also specified are *laurel garlands* (*Old Fortunatus*, 1.3.0), a "*garland of Red Roses*" (*Tom a Lincoln*, 404), "*on their heads Garlands of Bays*" for the personages in Queen Katherine's vision (*Henry VIII*, 2644–5, 4.2.82) and for

Comedy (*Mucedorus*, A2r); a *wedding* has a nymph "*bearing a wheaten Garland*" and an attendant "*holding a Garland over her head*" (*Two Noble Kinsmen*, B1r, 1.1.0), the *triumph* of Love has "*Garlands of Roses*" (*Four Plays in One*, 334), a *masque* has "*Isabella dressed with flowers and garlands*" (*Women Beware Women*, 5.2.72); see also *Amends for Ladies*, 5.2.298; *Philaster*, 133/412; *Silver Age*, 127; *Two Noble Kinsmen*, E4v, 2.5.0; *Four Plays in One*, 292; *Herod and Antipater*, F4r; *Amyntas*, T2v, Z1v; *1 Arviragus and Philicia*, A8v; atypical is a *dumb show* where Medea "*hath a garland in her hand, and putting it on Creon's daughter's head, setteth it on fire*" (*Locrine*, 1772–4); Henslowe's inventory includes a *garland* (*Diary*, App. 2, 68).

garment

a seldom used alternative to *clothes*, *apparel*: nobles "*bringing out the King's garments*" (*George a Greene*, 1191), a *disguised* figure "*masked, and in other Garments*" (*Match Me in London*, 2.4.86), a *ravished* woman "*her garments loose, her hair disheveled*" (*Unnatural Combat*, 5.2.185), a figure in *prison* "*his garments all ragged and torn*" (*Woman Killed*, 127), Earth in a *masque* with "*his garment of a clay color*" (*No Wit*, 4.3.40); see also *Cobbler's Prophecy*, 1624; *Old Fortunatus*, 1.3.0; *Bartholomew Fair*, 5.5.106.

gate

a *fictional* term that refers to (1) the *stage doors* as the gates to a *house* or *city*, (2) offstage *sounds*; figures are directed to *open gates* (*James IV*, 2128) and *enter* to the gates (*King John*, 608–9, 2.1.299), "*before the Gates*" (Folio *Henry V*, 1259, 3.3.0), "*walking before the gate*" (*English Traveller*, 62); Coriolanus provides "*Martius follows them to gates, and is shut in*" and "*Enter the Gates*" (538–9, 543, 1.4.42, 45); actions include "*They beat against the gates*" (*Silver Age*, 157), "*at the Entrance of the Gate Marius is stabbed*" (*Faithful Friends*, 2159–61), "*Beg at Virginia's gate*" (*Fedele and Fortunio*, 1036, 1052), "*Gloucester's men rush at the Tower Gates*" (*1 Henry VI*, 374, 1.3.14, also 391, 1.3.28), "*goes soft to the Gate*" (*Jews' Tragedy*, 1339); offstage sounds include "*Knocking at the gate*" *within* (*New Way to Pay*, 2.2.31; *Doctor Faustus*, B 1675; *Example*, A3r), "*A noise is heard as if the gates were broken*" (*Conspiracy*, K2v).

gauntlet

a long protective *glove* cited in four plays: "*Enter King, Queen, Laertes and Lords, with other Attendants with Foils, and Gauntlets, a Table and Flagons of Wine on it*" (Folio *Hamlet*, 3674–6, 5.2.224), "*Throws down his*

Gauntlet" (Folio *3 Henry VI*, 2585, 4.7.75); see also *Rape of Lucrece*, 252; *Wasp*, 474.

gaze
a seldom used synonym for **look**: "*They first gaze on one another, then walk up and down*" (*Humorous Courtier*, C1r); for other examples see *Alphonsus of Aragon*, 425; *1 Henry VI*, 2482, 5.3.45; Quarto *Poor Man's Comfort*, H3r; *Love's Sacrifice*, 1848; *Weeding of Covent Garden*, 8; *Goblins*, 4.2.41; *Prisoners*, C9v; *Princess*, B3v, I1v; *Distresses*, 359.

gesture
used occasionally for some distinctive action or sign; two figures **charmed** to **sleep** lie down "*using very sluggish gestures*" (*John a Kent*, 1147), to rebuke a villain two **ghosts** remain **silent** but "*use several gestures*" (*Unnatural Combat*, 5.2.278), Alonso enters Prospero's magic circle "*with a frantic gesture, attended by Gonzalo, Sebastian, and Antonio in like manner*" (*Tempest*, 2009–11, 5.1.57); *Fedele and Fortunio* directs "*Here let him counterfeit the passion of love by looks and gesture*" (795–6), and the title figure of *Mad Lover* "*walks aside full of strange gestures*" (14) so that an observer comments "What face, and what postures he puts on."

ghost
found in a number of plays and linked to a variety of effects which help to confirm or augment its supernatural nature; in *Atheist's Tragedy* a figure wearing "*a sheet, a hair, and a beard*" (4.3.55) disguised as "the ghost of old Montferrers" is told he looks "so like a ghost that, notwithstanding I have some foreknowledge of you, you make my hair stand almost on end"; probably some of the *ghosts* in other plays also appeared in this archetypal dress–Henslowe's inventory lists a "ghost's suit" and "ghosts' bodies" (*Diary*, App. 2, 37)–but the only other direction suggesting such a costume is "*his Father's Ghost in white*" (*Jews' Tragedy*, 2722); **white** is also linked to *ghosts* in *Second Maiden's Tragedy* where one is "*all in white*" (1930), and in a unique but suggestive direction in *Knight of the Burning Pestle* which calls for Jasper, pretending to be a *ghost*, to enter "*his face mealed*" (222); typically, however, the implication is that a *ghost* is dressed like the figure when alive, as the dialogue indicates at "*Enter Ghost*" in Q2 *Hamlet* (B1v, 1.1.39); the phrasing of numerous other directions indicates a recognizable appearance: "*the Ghost of Caesar*" (*Julius Caesar*, 2287, 4.3.274), "*the Ghost of*

Banquo" (*Macbeth*, 1299, 3.4.36; 1363, 3.4.87), "*the Ghost of Andrugio*" (*Antonio's Revenge*, 3.2.72, 5.1.0, 5.3.49), "*Malbecco his Ghost*" (*Grim the Collier*, G2v, K1v), "*The ghost of Montferrers*" (*Atheist's Tragedy*, 2.6.19, 3.2.30, 5.1.26), "*six Saxon Kings' ghosts crowned, with Scepters in their hands, etc.*" (*Queen's Exchange*, 505); for similar locutions see *Battle of Alcazar* plot, 26, 61; *Richard III*, L3v, 3561, 5.3.117, and more; *Locrine*, 1088, 1331, 1671, 1757, 1989; *Woodstock*, 2439, 2461–2; *2 Edward IV*, 162; *Hieronimo*, 12.0; *Sophonisba*, 5.1.38; *Devil's Charter*, G2r, M2r; *Revenge of Bussy*, 5.5.119; *White Devil*, 4.1.102; *Catiline*, 1.0; *Julia Agrippina*, Prologue.37; *Seven Champions*, C1v; in *Second Maiden's Tragedy* both **body** and **ghost** are present: "*the Ghost in the same form as the lady is dressed in the Chair*" (2383–7); the supernatural element is most apparent when a *ghost* is visible to only one character, usually his or her murderer–as in *Richard III* and *Macbeth*, or would-be avenger–as in Q2 *Hamlet*, I3v, 3.4.101; examples of one or both are "*the Ghost of Andrea, and with him Revenge*" (*Spanish Tragedy*, 1.1.0, also 3.15.0, 4.5.0), "*Alonzo's ghost appears to De Flores*" (*Changeling*, 4.1.0, also 5.1.57), "*the Ghost of Agamemnon, pointing unto his wounds: and then to Egistus and the Queen, who were his murderers*" (*2 Iron Age*, 423); for other examples see *2 Edward IV*, 162; *Herod and Antipater*, L1r, L1v; *Unnatural Combat*, 5.2.271; *Valiant Scot*, I3v, I4r; *Messalina*, 2544; *Vow Breaker*, 3.1.56, 3.4.57, 4.2.176; in *Cymbeline* the *ghosts* of Posthumus's parents and brothers appear to him in a dream (3127, 5.4.92); sometimes the living pretend to be dead: "*Milesia riseth like a ghost*" (*Lost Lady*, 595), "*Timoclea like a Ghost*" (*Turk*, 1255, 1624), "*Montecelso as a Ghost*" (*Cunning Lovers*, I2r); for more see *Atheist's Tragedy*, 3.2.17, 30, 4.3.174; *Fatal Contract*, E1r; *Fool Would Be a Favourite*, F8r; see also **apparition**, **spirit**.

gibbet, gallows
found occasionally in **execution** scenes; figures "*set up the Gibbet*" (*Sir Thomas More*, 584), enter "*with a Coffin and a Gibbet*" (*Barnavelt*, 2811–12), enter "*to the Gallows, with the Hangman, and Officers*" (*Blind Beggar of Bednal Green*, 58); atypical is a **cudgel** described as "*an ashen Gibbet*" (*Blind Beggar of Bednal Green*, 109).

gilded
see **gold**

gilt
see **gold**

glance

the two uses suggest surreptitious behavior: "*seems to read the letters, but glances on Mistress Shore in his reading*" (*1 Edward IV*, 61), "*Borgias courts Julia, and Mulleasses, Amada, glancing his eye on Julia*" (*Turk*, 934–5).

glass, looking glass

glass refers to several distinctly different properties: (1) a *looking-glass* or mirror, (2) a **drinking** *glass*, (3) other assorted items; most common is the *looking glass*: "*A show of eight Kings, and Banquo last, with a glass in his hand*" (*Macbeth*, 1657–8, 4.1.111), "*sleeping on her book, her glass by*" (*Distresses*, 338), "*with a Casting bottle, sprinkling his Hat and Face, and a little looking glass at his Girdle, setting his Countenance*" (*Fancies Chaste and Noble*, 234–6), "*the Jesuit in rich attire like an Apparition presents himself before the Glass*" (*Game at Chess*, 1576–9), "*Haircut preparing his periwig, table, and looking glass*" (*Lady of Pleasure*, 3.1.0), "*with a Glass in her hand and a Comb*" (*Love's Metamorphosis*, E2r), "*looking in a glass, trimming his Beard*" (*Love's Sacrifice*, 676–7, also 799–800); see also *Dead Man's Fortune*, 38; Folio *Richard II*, 2198, 4.1.275; *Antonio and Mellida*, 3.2.123; *May Day*, 3.1.77; *Widow's Tears*, 1.1.0, 14; *1 Honest Whore*, 2.1.0; *Cupid's Revenge*, 244; *Cupid's Whirligig*, 4.4.0; *2 Iron Age*, 429; *Bloody Brother*, 302; *Muses' Looking Glass*, A2r; *City Madam*, 1.1.46; *2 Fair Maid of the West*, 376; *Novella*, 125; *Parson's Wedding*, 387; in *Devil's Charter* a figure looks in two magical "*glasses and beholdeth her body*" (H1v, also F4v).

Examples of a *glass* for drinking are "*a glass of wine*" and "*a Glass of water*" (*Atheist's Tragedy*, 5.2.200, 209), "*Fills two glasses, gives her one*" (*Two Maids of More-Clacke*, H3r), "*drink, break the glass*" (*Wonder of a Kingdom*, 3.1.192), "*a Jug and glass*" (*Fine Companion*, K3r), "*Glasses and a Napkin*" (*Jovial Crew*, 416); for more see *Orlando Furioso*, 1234; *David and Bethsabe*, 527; *Alphonsus of Germany*, F1r; Quarto *Every Man Out*, 340; *Volpone*, 2.2.110; *Captain*, 281; *Love's Pilgrimage*, 235; *Old Law*, F4v; *Weeding of Covent Garden*, 35, 41; *Variety*, D6v.

Other kinds of *glass* cited are "*perspective glass*" (*Travels of Three English Brothers*, 404; see also *Friar Bacon*, 1869; *John a Kent*, 736), "*king Edward in his suit of Glass*" (*Edward I*, 630), "*shows a light in a glass*" (*Old Wives Tale*, 424), "*a pane of glass*" (*Great Duke of Florence*, 5.1.37), "*a glass of Lotion*" (*Knight of the Burning Pestle*, 205), "*a broken Glass*" (*Coxcomb*, 359; see also *Alchemist*, 1.1.115; *Renegado*, 1.3.145), "*glass eyes*" (presumably eyeglasses, *New Trick*, 252).

globe

called for nine times, always in the context of a **dumb show**; in several signals a *globe* is linked to Fortune and the drawing of **lots**: a figure "*appareled like Fortune, drawn on a Globe, with a Cup in her hand, wherein are Bay leaves, whereupon are written the lots*" (*Alphonsus of Germany*, C4r), "*a Nymph with a Globe, another with Fortune's wheel, then Fortune*" (*Old Fortunatus*, 1.1.63, also 1.3.0), "*the three fatal sisters, with a rock, a thread, and a pair of shears; bringing in a Globe, in which they put three lots*" (*Golden Age*, 78); a *globe* can also symbolize worldly power: "*Henry the elder bareheaded, bearing a sword and a Globe*" (*Look about You*, 2823), a Turk with "*a Globe in one hand, an Arrow in the other*" (*Christian Turned Turk*, F2v); see also *Friar Bacon*, 2075–6; other examples are "*a thing like a Globe opens of one side of the Stage, and flashes out fire*" (*No Wit*, 4.3.40), "*a Globe seated in a ship*" (*Looking Glass for London*, 59); see also *Maid's Metamorphosis*, E2r; Henslowe's inventory lists "one globe" (*Diary*, App. 2, 61).

glove

the few examples are "*Pulls off his Glove*" (*Bird in a Cage*, E3v), enter "*with Gloves, Ring, Purse, etc.*" (*Wise Woman of Hogsdon*, 286; see also *Costly Whore*, 242), and three signals from *King John and Matilda*: "*In the bustle Fitzwater drops one of his Gloves, Hubert takes it up*," "*He looks towards the Garden door, and whilst she turns herself that way, he changes the Glove, and gives her the other poisoned*," "*Kisses the poisoned Glove*" (52, 74); Henslowe's inventory includes "*one pair of wrought gloves*" (*Diary*, App. 2, 87).

go

widely used (over 400 examples) in a range of locutions that include (1) most commonly **exits** where figures *go in, out, forth, away* but also (2) **weapons** that *go off*, (3) **going/offers** to go, (4) onstage actions such as *go up, **down**, **before**, **aside**, away, to the **door**, to/toward* someone; a sampling of the roughly 150 exits or *offered* exits includes *go forth* (*Battle of Alcazar*, 39; Q1 *Romeo and Juliet*, I2v, 4.5.95; *1 Edward IV*, 67; *Grim the Collier*, G4v; *Devil's Charter*, K4r; *Bondman*, 5.1.57; *Lovesick Court*, 163; *Politician*, H1v), *go away* (*Shoemakers' Holiday*, 2.2.34; *Sir John Oldcastle*, 56; *Wily Beguiled*, 1587; Q1 *Hamlet*, F3r, [3.2.135]; *Woman Is a Weathercock*, 5.2.29; *Coriolanus*, 1275, 2.2.66; *Royal King*, 72; *Fair Quarrel*, 3.1.111; '*Tis Pity*, 2.2.106; *Court Beggar*, 209), *go in* (*Spanish Tragedy*, 1.4.99; *Old Wives Tale*, 196, 838; *Downfall of Huntingdon*, 44, 62, 372; *Old*

Fortunatus, 4.2.28, 5.2.358; *Thomas Lord Cromwell*, D3v; Folio *Every Man In*, 3.5.65; *Brazen Age*, 181; *Antony and Cleopatra*, 1975, 3.10.0; *Women Pleased*, 293; *Captives*, 755; *Valiant Welshman*, B3r; *Late Lancashire Witches*, 199; *Court Secret*, B3r, B5r), most commonly *go out* (*Three Ladies of London*, C2v; *Summer's Last Will*, 116, 420, 775, 934, 1115; *Doctor Faustus*, B 1295; *Massacre at Paris*, 206, 569, 635; *Captain Thomas Stukeley*, 2812–13, 2888; *Look about You*, 663; *Shoemakers' Holiday*, 5.1.35; *Mucedorus*, D3v; *What You Will*, B3r; *King Leir*, 1547; *Lust's Dominion*, 4.3.39; *Greene's Tu Quoque*, D2v; *Fawn*, 4.57; *Malcontent*, 2.2.37; *Widow's Tears*, 1.3.118; *Cymbeline*, 2894–5, 5.2.0; *Second Maiden's Tragedy*, 2446–50; *Alchemist*, 2.3.225; *Fatal Contract*, E2r, G1r; *Love's Sacrifice*, 803, 1153, 1819; *Broken Heart*, 4.4.0; *City Wit*, 341; *Wedding*, E1v, G1r, G4r); *go off* is common in the Massinger canon (*Emperor of the East*, 2.1.405; *City Madam*, 4.4.155; *Unnatural Combat*, 1.1.342, 2.3.130; *Very Woman*, 4.2.165; *Bashful Lover*, 1.1.172; *New Way to Pay*, 1.1.98, 2.2.33; *Bondman*, 3.2.112; *Roman Actor*, 2.1.140, 5.2.19) but less so elsewhere (*1 Iron Age*, 277; *If This Be Not a Good Play*, 5.2.85, 5.4.0; *1 Fair Maid of the West*, 275; *Two Noble Ladies*, 1549; *Fatal Contract*, E1r; *Seven Champions*, C3r; *Lady of Pleasure*, 4.1.0; *Twins*, D2v); *Orlando Furioso* provides *go out, in, forth* (573, 852, 1286).

Weapons that *go off* include *pieces* (Q2 *Hamlet*, D1r, 1.4.6; *Lust's Dominion*, 3.3.88; *Double Marriage*, 343, 353; *Fortune by Land and Sea*, 416; *Changeling*, 5.1.93), **ordnance** (Folio *2 Henry VI*, 2168, 4.1.0; *Devil's Charter*, D3v; *Dick of Devonshire*, 433), **chambers** (Folio *Henry V*, 1078, 3.Chorus.33; 1118, 3.1.34; *Travels of Three English Brothers*, 325; see also Folio *Hamlet*, 3751, [5.2.283]); *Whore of Babylon*, 5.6.14; examples of exits forestalled include "*Going*" (*Jovial Crew*, 416), "*Going out*" (*Puritan*, C4v; *Queen*, 3817), "*She is going*" (*1 Henry VI*, 2496, 5.3.59; 2618, 5.3.174), "*As they are going out, Antonio stays Mellida*" (*Antonio and Mellida*, 2.1.292), "*Make as though you were a going out*" (*Alphonsus of Aragon*, 1094), "*Nurse offers to go in and turns again*" (Q1 *Romeo and Juliet* G2r, 3.3.162, also G2v, 3.4.11); related are entrances/exits "*as going to bed*" (*Match at Midnight*, 77; *Fatal Contract*, F4v), "*as going to milking*" (*Tottenham Court*, 106), "*going to Execution*" (*Fortune by Land and Sea*, 427), "*going to be Married*" (*Scornful Lady*, 281), "*go as 'twere to apprehend Vittoria*" (*White Devil*, 2.2.37); for *go aside* see *Famous Victories*, F4r; *Bashful Lover*, 1.2.95; *Emperor of the East*, 4.4.61; *Mad Couple*, 91; *Damoiselle*, 424; *City Wit*, 307; *Swaggering Damsel*, F4r; *Bride*, 60; *Conspiracy*, H1v; *Landgartha*, D4r; atypical are *go backward* (*Night Walker*, 338; *Love's Sacrifice*,

799), "*He goes up the rope*" (*Christian Turned Turk*, F4r), "*They go off on their hands, and knees*" (*New Way to Pay*, 1.1.98).

goat

as a joke on Princess Elizabeth's jailer a clown enters "*leading a goat*" (*1 If You Know Not Me*, 230); four **masquers** enter "*with horns on their heads: a Stag, a Ram, a Goat, and an Ox*" (*English Moor*, 15; see also *City Nightcap*, 156).

goblet

specified in only a few directions: "*a silver Goblet*" (*Doctor Faustus*, A 985), "*a gilt goblet*" (*Insatiate Countess*, 2.1.184); for others see *Dutch Courtesan*, 3.3.0; *Conspiracy*, D1r, I4v; see also **cup**.

going

an alternative to the widely used **offers** *to go* wherein a figure starts to **exit** but is forestalled; occasionally the term stands alone: "*Going*" (*Jovial Crew*, 416), "*Going out*" (*Puritan*, C4v; *Queen*, 3817); more commonly a pronoun/proper name is provided: "*She is going*" (*1 Henry VI*, 2496, 5.3.59; 2618, 5.3.174), "*She is going out*" (*Love's Sacrifice*, 803); sometimes the full sequence is specified: "*As they are going out, Antonio stays Mellida*" (*Antonio and Mellida*, 2.1.292), "*The brothers going out, Octavio stays them*" (*Humour out of Breath*, 448); for representative examples of "*as he/she/they are going in/out/forth*" see *Massacre at Paris*, 199; *Death of Huntingdon*, 128–9; *Alarum for London*, 501, 1117; *Old Fortunatus*, 4.2.28; *Politician*, H1v; *Wits*, 143; *Andromana*, 211, 214, 250; *Alphonsus of Aragon* spells out the effect for the actor: "*Make as though you were a going out*" (1094).

gold, golden, gilded, gilt

the roughly sixty examples include mostly (1) *golden* objects, (2) **money**, **treasure**; the many objects include a *gold/golden* **chain** (*Shoemakers' Holiday*, 3.2.127; *Wonder of a Kingdom*, 4.1.0), **wand** (*Queen and Concubine*, 22), *sprig* (*Tom a Lincoln*, 2232), **viol** (*Arcadia*, F1r), *wedges* (*Golden Age*, 11; *No Wit*, 4.3.40), **rings** (*Amorous War*, E2v), **vizards** (*Old Fortunatus*, 1.3.0; *Henry VIII*, 2645, 4.2.82), *fetters* (*Amorous War*, C2v), "*a rod of gold with a dove on it*" (*Friar Bacon*, 2076), "*a gilded rapier*" (*1 Edward IV*, 57), "*a golden round full of Lots*" carried by Fortune (*Hengist*, DS before 1.2, 2), "*A golden Head*" that ascends (*If This Be Not a Good Play*, 2.3.75, 3.2.139), "*Vice with a gilded face*" (*Old Fortunatus*, 1.3.0), "*a white robe with golden stars*"

(*Women Beware Women*, 5.2.50), "*Scilla in triumph in his chair triumphant of gold*" and **prisoners** "*bearing crowns of gold*" (*Wounds of Civil War*, 1070, 1073); *gilt* objects include a **harp** (*Antonio and Mellida*, 5.2.0), **goblet** (*Insatiate Countess*, 2.1.184), **key** (*Renegado*, 2.5.104), **laurel** (*Virgin Martyr*, 1.1.118), "*gilt spurs and Gauntlet*" (*Wasp*, 474); *Old Fortunatus* provides "*a fair tree of Gold with apples on it*" (1.3.0), and *Arraignment of Paris* "*A Tree of gold laden with Diadems and Crowns of gold*" (456); also distinctive are *golden* **balls** (*Ball*, I2v; *Constant Maid*, H1r), as in *Arraignment of Paris* where Paris "*giveth the golden Ball to Venus*" and Diana "*delivereth the ball of gold*" to Queen Elizabeth (524, 1240); *golden* **writing** includes "*words writ in gold*" on a **pendant** (*Death of Huntingdon*, 2910), "*the table of the writing in golden Letters*" (*Lovesick King*, 1539), "*a sable shield written on with Golden letters*" (*Two Noble Ladies*, 1082).

Gold as money/treasure can be found in a **purse** (*May Day*, [1.2.1]) or in heaps: "*Barabas in his Countinghouse, with heaps of gold before him*" (*Jew of Malta*, 35), "*Plenty in Majesty, upon a Throne, heaps of gold*" (*Histriomastix*, B3v); figures enter with "*a bag of gold*" (*Friar Bacon*, 1494–5; *Fatal Contract*, B2v), "*with a paper with gold in it*" (*Distresses*, 305), "*with ingots of gold*" (*Histriomastix*, B3r), "*with a ladle full of molten gold*" (*If This Be Not a Good Play*, 5.4.34), "*with as many Jewels robes and Gold as he can carry*" (*2 Seven Deadly Sins*, 66–7), "*with his gold and a scuttle full of horsedung*" (*Case Is Altered*, 3.5.0); figures are directed to **show** gold (*Mad Couple*, 31), most commonly *give gold* (*Spanish Tragedy*, 3.2.80; *Insatiate Countess*, 4.2.98; *Wonder of a Kingdom*, 4.2.0; *Hengist*, DS before 2.2, 2; *Bashful Lover*, 1.1.84; Quarto *Poor Man's Comfort*, F3v; *Jews' Tragedy*, 695–6; *King John and Matilda*, 78; *Maid's Revenge*, I2r; *Cruel Brother*, 172); other actions include "*discovers his gold*" (*Hog Hath Lost His Pearl*, 1578), "*handles the gold*" and "*Unpurses the gold*" (*Atheist's Tragedy*, 5.1.7, 21), "*A head comes up full of gold, she combs it into her lap*" (*Old Wives Tale*, 782), "*cuts off the Cutpurse's ear, for cutting of the gold buttons off his cloak*" (*Massacre at Paris*, 622), "*they seem to be overcome with pity, But looking on the gold kill him, as he turns his Back*" (*Hengist*, DS before 2.2, 7–8); see also *Soliman and Perseda*, D3r; *1 Troublesome Reign*, E4v; *Bashful Lover*, 3.3.192.

gorget

a piece of **armor** for the throat specified in a few directions: "*in their velvet coats and gorgets, and leading staves*" (*1 Edward IV*, 11), "*in his gorget and shirt, shield,*" sword" (*Sophonisba*, 2.2.0), "*like a Soldier disguised at all parts, a half Pike, gorget, etc.*" (*Widow's Tears*, 4.2.0), "*his gorget on, his sword, plume of feathers, leading staff*" (*Perkin Warbeck*, 3.1.0); see also *Wasp*, 495.

gown

a basic item of costume for men and women found as (1) a **nightgown**, (2) part of a **disguise**, (3) a sign of office, rank or profession, (4) a call for other distinctive individuals and effects; *gown* can be a shortened form of *nightgown*, as when a **sleeping** Edward IV is captured and brought onstage "*in his Gown*" (Folio *3 Henry VI*, 2257–8, 4.3.27); disguises include "*a Hermit's gown and beard*" (*Malcontent*, 3.5.28), "*Gown, Beard, and Constable's staff*" (*Night Walker*, 357); in *Look about You* Robin Hood enters "*in the Lady Falconbridge's gown, night attire on his head*" (1747–8), "*Gloster in the Hermit's gown, putting on the beard*" (2071–2), and after Gloster enters in a distinctive *gown* (77–81, 782) John appears twice "*in Gloster's gown*" (929, 1063); *gowns* for various members of society include "*a gown and cap like a Schoolmaster*" (*Fedele and Fortunio*, 77–8), "*the Waits in Sergeants' gowns*" (*2 If You Know Not Me*, 297), "*a velvet coat, and an Alderman's gown*" (*Shoemakers' Holiday*, 2.3.93), a "*Citizen's gown*" (*Eastward Ho*, A4r), "*a shepherd gown*" (*Antonio and Mellida*, 3.1.0), "*hat, staff, and Pilgrim's gown*" (*Weakest Goeth*, 32; see also *Thracian Wonder*, E1r), "*sea gowns and sea caps*" (*King Leir*, 1991–2; see also *Antonio and Mellida*, 4.1.0), "*Lord Mayor, in his scarlet gown, with a gilded rapier by his side*" (*1 Edward IV*, 57), "*scarlet gowns*" for "*officers of state*" (*Tragedy of Byron*, 5.2.0), a "*blue gown*" for a prostitute (*2 Honest Whore*, 5.2.265, 311; *City Madam*, 5.3.59), "*Tutor in his gown as from his study*" (*Witty Fair One*, E1v); other references to identifiable *gowns* include "*his Father's Gown and Robes*" (*Fatal Contract*, G4v), "*his Master's Gown*" (*Grim the Collier*, H3r), "*his wife's Gown*" (*Eastward Ho*, D4v), "*in her first gown*" (*Guardian*, 3.2.0); a cured madman appears "*habit and gown changed*" (*Lover's Melancholy*, 5.2.0).

Other special *gowns* include a **malcontent** "*in some frieze gown*" (*Malcontent*, 3.2.0), "*Fraud in a blue gown, red cap and red sleeves*" (*Three Lords of London*, I2v), "*an old rug gown, muffled with clouts*" (*Albovine*, 70), a "*gown of Humility*" (*Coriolanus*, 1426–7, 2.3.39), "*an Irish Gown tucked up to mid-leg*" for an Amazon (*Landgartha*, E3r, also F2v, H4r, I2r), a madwoman in "*a rich gown, great farthingale, great ruff, muff, fan, and coxcomb on her head*" (*Lover's Melancholy*, 3.3.48), "*the Country Wench coming in with a new fashion gown dressed gentlewoman-*

like" (*Michaelmas Term*, 3.1.0); stage business includes "*plucks Aurelia by the gown*" (*Changes*, D3r), "*draws his Sword from under his Gown*" (*City Wit*, 360), "*The Friar spreads the lappet of his gown and falls to dice*" (*Edward I*, 1733), and before being executed Sir Thomas More "*gives* [the hangman] *his gown*" (*Sir Thomas More*, 1932–3); for the **casting/throwing** off of gowns see *Staple of News*, 1.1.15; *Lover's Melancholy*, 1.2.112; *Court Beggar*, 247; detailed examples are "*Here let the Senate rise and cast away their Gowns, having their swords by their sides*" (*Wounds of Civil War*, 252–3), "*He throws off his Gown, discovering his doublet with a satin forepart and a Canvas back*" (*Hengist*, 5.1.286–9); as an uninvited observer at Vittoria's trial Bracciano "*Lays a rich gown under him*" as his seat (*White Devil*, 3.2.3); variations include "*not full ready, without a gown*" (*1 Honest Whore*, 2.1.12), a madman with "*an old Gown half off*" (*Lover's Melancholy*, 3.3.38); gowns can be linked to **slippers** (*2 If You Know Not Me*, 302, 309), **caps** (*Chabot*, 5.3.0; *Changes*, I3v; *Thracian Wonder*, C1v), as in "*Miles with a gown and a corner cap*" (*Friar Bacon*, 2021–2); for a sampling of figures who appear simply *in a gown* see *David and Bethsabe*, 601; *Locrine*, 309; *Sir John Oldcastle*, 2210; Q2 *Romeo and Juliet*, A4r, 1.1.74; *Much Ado*, G3v, 4.2.0; *Julius Caesar*, 2240, 4.3.236; *Chabot*, 3.1.0; *Rule a Wife*, 229; Henslowe's inventory includes "a damask gown" (*Diary*, App. 2, 102), "one man's gown" (129), "one woman's gown of cloth of gold" (167), "one senator's gown" (16), "one green gown for Marian" (20), "one friar's gown of gray" (182), "Harry the fifth's velvet gown" (11, 172).

grate

may refer to actual bars in two **prison** scenes but is likely **fictional**: "*Mellida goes from the grate*" (*Antonio's Revenge*, 2.2.125), "*above at the grate, a box hanging down*" (*New Wonder*, 174).

grave

a **fictional** designation for the **trapdoor** in the main platform: "*Laertes leaps into the grave*" (Q1 *Hamlet*, I1v; Folio "*Leaps in the grave*," 3444, 5.1.250), "*They strike the stage with their daggers, and the grave openeth*" (*Antonio's Revenge*, 4.2.87).

great

a widely used intensifier (over 100 examples) (1) most often used to describe **sound** but also linked to (2) **pomp** and **state**, (3) great-bellied, (4) a wide variety of objects, emotions, and actions; when used to characterize the volume of sound, *great* most often

describes offstage **noise** (*Three Lords of London*, F4v; *Friar Bacon*, 1614; *Alarum for London*, 1117; *Sir John Oldcastle*, 2193; *Sir Thomas Wyatt*, 4.4.23; *Spanish Curate*, 124; *Captives*, 1429; *Late Lancashire Witches*, 222); more detailed signals include "*A great noise within crying, run, save, hold*" (*Two Noble Kinsmen*, M3v, 5.4.39), "*Horns winded, a great noise of hunting*" (*Golden Age*, 32), "*A great noise within of rude Music, Laughing, Singing, etc.*" (*Jovial Crew*, 423), "*A great Hubbub and noise, a ringing of basins*" (*Knave in Grain*, 2882), "*with a great noise above, as fallen*" (*Picture*, 4.2.144), "*A greater noise of Mutiny is heard*" (*Conspiracy*, H4v); elsewhere *great* modifies **shout** (*Woodstock*, 2095; *Sir Thomas More*, 689; *Hieronimo*, 4.0; *Coriolanus*, 3705–6, 5.6.48; *Pericles*, C4v, 2.2.59; *Two Noble Kinsmen*, M2r, 5.3.92; *Silver Age*, 126; *Brazen Age*, 192, 205; *Humorous Lieutenant*, 306; *Rape of Lucrece*, 240; *Swisser*, 5.3.147), **cry** (Quarto *Every Man In*, 3.4.148; *Hieronimo*, 12.0; *Two Noble Kinsmen*, M1v, 5.3.66; *1 Iron Age*, 332; *2 Iron Age*, 381; *Seven Champions*, H1r); *great* can modify **alarum** alone (*Wounds of Civil War*, 333; *1 Iron Age*, 311; *Thracian Wonder*, G4r) and *alarum* with other terms: "*A great Alarum and shot*" and "*A great Alarum, and Flourish*" (*Fortune by Land and Sea*, 410, 418), "*A great alarum and excursions*" (*1 Iron Age*, 295); *great* also describes **flourish**: "*A great flourish of Trumpets*" (*Henry VIII*, 2445, 4.1.36), "*a great flourish of Trumpets and Drums within*" (*Four Plays in One*, 311); other *great* sounds include a **fight** (*Edward II*, 1493), **voice** (*Cobbler's Prophecy*, 632), **knocking** (*Second Maiden's Tragedy*, 1357–8), "*screek*" (*Alarum for London*, 207), "*winding of horns*" (*Brazen Age*, 190), "*crack and noise within*" (*Alchemist*, 4.5.55), "*thunder crack*" (*2 Iron Age*, 412), "*Tempestuous storm*" (*Captives*, 456); see also **loud**.

Great is also used to describe entrances *in great state* (*David and Bethsabe*, 1106; *Woodstock*, 350–1; *Escapes of Jupiter*, 1154; *Changeling*, 4.1.0; *Women Beware Women*, 4.3.0), pomp (*1 Tamburlaine*, 918; *James IV*, 684; *Looking Glass for London*, 516), **solemnity** (*Women Beware Women*, 1.3.101) and is found in locutions for **with child** such as "*great with child*" (*Birth of Merlin*, B3r), "*great-bellied*" (*Devil's Law Case*, 5.1.0; *Antipodes*, 269; see also *Golden Age*, 35); the many objects described as *great* include a **tree** (*Warning for Fair Women*, E3v), **ruff** (*Lover's Melancholy*, 3.3.48), **cup** (MS *Bonduca*, 2260), **bowl** (*Summer's Last Will*, 803), **rock** (*1 Iron Age*, 300), buck **basket** (Quarto *Merry Wives*, D4r, 3.3.4), "*the great book of Accompts*" (*Believe as You List*, 982–3), "*the great Seal*" (*Henry VIII*, 1337–8, 2.4.0), "*a great piece of beef*" (*Looking Glass for London*, 2238); Henslowe's inventory includes "one great horse with his legs" (*Diary*, App.

2, 85); emotions exhibited include *great sorrow* (*Tom a Lincoln*, 2863; *Bloody Banquet*, 859), *grief* (*Tom a Lincoln*, 1704), *displeasure* (*Captain Thomas Stukeley*, 2448), *joy* (*Golden Age*, 20; *If This Be Not a Good Play*, 5.4.0), and figures are seen *"greatly discontented"* (*1 Edward IV*, 67), *"greatly rejoicing"* (*Tom a Lincoln*, 168) and making *"great lamentation"* (*Tom a Lincoln*, 2865), *"great passion and submission"* (*Hengist*, DS before 4.3, 3); also described as *great* are a *banquet* (*Timon of Athens*, 338, 1.2.0), *train* of *followers* (*2 Iron Age*, 426; *Challenge for Beauty*, 5), *rabble* (*Swetnam*, E2v), *"the great Turk"* (*Alphonsus of Aragon*, 848; *Travels of Three English Brothers*, 328, 392); actions include *"the prentices do great service"* (*1 Edward IV*, 20), *"conges with great reverence and ceremony"* (*Fatal Contract*, H4r), a *"show of great pain"* (*Four Plays in One*, 321).

great-bellied
see *with child*

green
usually associated with the *woods* or *hunt*: *"in green, bow and arrows"* (*Downfall of Huntingdon*, 2506), *"Jupiter like a woodman in green"* (*Silver Age*, 146), hunters *"with Javelins, and in green"* (*Brazen Age*, 187), masquers *"like Diana's knights led In by four other knights: (In Green) with horns about their necks and boars-spears in their hands"* (*Woodstock*, 2119–20); for comparable figures *in green* see *Edward I*, 1246; *Downfall of Huntingdon*, 1260; *1 Edward IV*, 40; Henslowe's inventory lists *green hose*, "one green gown for Marian," "six green coats for *Robin Hood*" (*Diary*, App. 2, 20–2); for examples not linked to hunting, *"Robin Hood sleeps on a green bank"* (*Downfall of Huntingdon*, 1490–1), two figures are *"laid down on a green bank"* (*Wisdom of Doctor Dodypoll*, 1063–4), Spring enters *"with his train, overlaid with suits of green moss, representing short grass"* (*Summer's Last Will*, 160); other examples are a *table* "covered with a green Carpet" (*Sir Thomas More*, 735), *"a tree with green and withered leaves mingled together"* (*Old Fortunatus*, 1.3.0), a *masque* that includes *"Water with green flags upon his head standing up instead of hair"* (*No Wit*, 4.3.40); see also *Downfall of Huntingdon*, 2700; Quarto *Merry Wives*, G3r, 5.5.102; *World Tossed at Tennis*, D2r.

greyhound
Quarto *Every Man Out* calls for *"a Huntsman with a greyhound"* (1010), and a sequence in *Late Lancashire Witches* starts with *"a brace of greyhounds"* (196) that when beaten turn into a woman and a boy.

groan
a *sound* either produced *within* or made by a figure onstage; examples of offstage *groans* are *"From under the stage a groan"* (*Antonio's Revenge*, 3.1.195; see also *Catiline*, 1.315), *"Groans of dying men heard within"* (*Thracian Wonder*, C1r; see also *Turk*, 1442), *"Groan in the Cave"* (*Jews' Tragedy*, 1009, also 1012); see also *Seven Champions*, C1r; *Prisoners*, C5v, C8r; signals for *groans* from an onstage figure are *"lifteth himself up, and groans"* (*1 Henry VI*, 577, 1.4.103), *"in extreme torment and groaneth whilst the devil laugheth at him"* (*Devil's Charter*, M1v, also K4v), *"recovers a little in voice, and groans"* (*Revenger's Tragedy*, I3v); see also Folio *3 Henry VI*, 1323, 2.6.41; *Guy of Warwick*, F2r; *Two Lamentable Tragedies*, C4r; *Insatiate Countess*, 3.1.107; *Albovine*, 71, 72, 74; *Princess*, D1v.

ground
a *fictional* designation for the main platform; figures or objects are *on the ground* (*Arden of Faversham*, 380–1; *Woman in the Moon*, B4v; *Captain Thomas Stukeley*, 2281; *Thracian Wonder*, C4v; *Devil's Charter*, C3r, M2r; Quarto *Poor Man's Comfort*, F4r) or *fall* on/to the ground (*Spanish Tragedy*, 1.3.9; *Edward I*, 2587; *Sir John Oldcastle*, 55; *Antonio and Mellida*, 4.1.155; *Two Noble Ladies*, 245; *Prisoners*, A6r; *Princess*, D3r, G1v, I1v; *Claracilla*, E12r); elsewhere a funeral procession exits *"drawing weapons on the ground"* (*Massacre at Paris*, 1263), a figure *"draws a circle on the ground"* (*Bartholomew Fair* 4.4.136), another *"Kisseth the ground"* (*Queen of Aragon*, 405), and one with a dagger *"sticks it in the ground"* (*Rebellion*, 61); *ground* is also linked to the area *under the stage*: "A groan of many people is heard under ground" (*Catiline*, 1.315) or is more specifically equated with the *trapdoor* through which figures *descend*: "The Ground opens, and he falls down into it" (*Grim the Collier*, I12v; see also *Sophonisba*, 5.1.21; *Old Wives Tale*, 909) or from which figures *rise*: *"from under the ground in several places, rise up spirits"* (*If This Be Not a Good Play*, 5.4.0), "The Magi with their rods beat the ground, and from under the same riseth a brave Arbor" (*Looking Glass for London*, 522–4); atypical is *"throws the ground in"* (*George a Greene*, 795).

grove
see *field*

guarded
in addition to several hundred references to *guards*, figures *enter/exit* "*guarded forth*" (*Sir Thomas*

Wyatt, 3.2.44), "*guarded off*" (*Court Secret*, C1v), most commonly simply *guarded*; for entrances *guarded* see Folio *Richard III*, 44, 1.1.41; *Insatiate Countess*, 4.1.112, 5.1.0; *White Devil*, 3.1.10; *Swetnam*, E3r; *City Nightcap*, 133, 172; *Duchess of Suffolk*, D2v; *Arcadia*, H4r; *Young Admiral*, D1r; *Duke's Mistress*, K1r; for exits see *Insatiate Countess*, 4.1.112; *Sophonisba*, 2.3.88; *Believe as You List*, 1772; *Court Secret*, E5v; variations include "*Bound and Guarded*" (*Woodstock*, 2972), "*prisoner and guarded*" (*Captives*, 2804–5), a figure in **hell** "*guarded with Furies*" (*Grim the Collier*, G2v), "*guarded by Corporal and Soldiers*" (*Knight of Malta*, 155), "*The Prisoners are brought in well guarded*" (*Sir Thomas More*, 606–7); *Duchess of Suffolk* provides entrances "*to the Tower guarded*" and "*guarded to prison*" (A3v); atypical is a **blue** headdress for a prostitute "*guarded with yellow*" (*2 Honest Whore*, 5.2.366).

gulf
a **fictional** term for the **trapdoor** used only by Chapman: "*the Gulf opens*" (*Caesar and Pompey*, 2.1.24); see also *Bussy D'Ambois*, 5.3.74; *Revenge of Bussy*, 5.5.5.

guns
see **chambers**

gyves
a restraint for **prisoners** comparable to **chains**, **fetters**, **irons**, **manacles**, **shackles**; figures appear "*in Gyves*" (*Captain Thomas Stukeley*, 1935), "*in prison, fettered and gyved*" (*Appius and Virginia*, I1r); kings who are prisoners of Fortune enter "*chained in silver Gyves*" (*Old Fortunatus*, 1.1.63).

H

habiliment
a seldom used equivalent to **habit**/**attire**/**apparel**; figures enter "*in his habiliments*" (*Chances*, 235), "*in their night habiliments*" (*Tom a Lincoln*, 2494–5), "*in shepherd's habiliments*" (*Two Lamentable Tragedies*, H4r); in *Whore of Babylon* Truth is **discovered** "*in sad habiliments; uncrowned: her hair disheveled*" (DS before Act 1, 27–8).

habit
widely used (over 100 examples) for "clothing," "costume," by extension "disguise," most com-

monly as part of a locution wherein a figure **enters** *in the habit of X, in Y's habit, habited like Z*: "*in the strange habit of a Conjuress*" (*Brazen Age*, 217), "*in Friar's habit*" (*Lovers' Progress*, 134), "*habited like Shepherds*" (*Henry VIII*, 753–4, 1.4.63); other figures attached to such locutions include a page (*Wise Woman of Hogsdon*, 289), churchman (*Challenge for Beauty*, 56), slave (*Believe as You List*, 2322–3), merchant (*Two Maids of More-Clacke*, F1r), madman (*Bartholomew Fair*, 5.2.14), Jew (*Devil's Law Case*, 3.2.0), **conjurer** (*White Devil*, 2.2.0), fool (*Antonio's Revenge*, 4.1.0, 4.2.0), doctor (*Henry VIII*, 1334, 2.4.0; *Court Beggar*, 257), a **mean** man (*Taming of the Shrew*, 897, 2.1.38; *Honest Man's Fortune*, 250), a Commendatore and a Clarissimo (*Volpone*, 5.5.0); examples of *habit* as **disguise** include Iris entering "*with a habit*" (a beldam's disguise) for Juno (*Silver Age*, 122), a figure entering with "*a Zaffie's habit under his arm*" (*Novella*, 118), the wooer of the jailer's daughter "*in habit of Palamon*" (*Two Noble Kinsmen*, L2r, 5.2.0), a woman "*in man's habit, sword and pistol*" (*English Moor*, 75), a figure "*disguised in a Soldier's habit*" (*Valiant Welshman*, G4v); in *2 Iron Age* a group of Trojans enters "*in Greekish habits*" followed by Aeneas "*who taking Chorebus for a Grecian by reason of his habit, fights with him and kills him*" (389–90); when figures who have changed costume revert to their original status **as before**, they enter "*in his own habit*" (*John a Kent*, 1031, 1447), "*in her own habit*" (*English Moor*, 63), "*in their first Habits*" (*Late Lancashire Witches*, 252), "*having thrown off the habit*" (*Gentleman of Venice*, K1r); other usages include "*in a rich habit*" (*New Way to Pay*, 4.2.33; *Traitor*, 3.2.25), "*in a poor habit*" (*Telltale*, 1030; *Jovial Crew*, 408), "*in mourning habit*" (*Malcontent*, 5.5.43; *King John and Matilda*, 84), with a "*conjuring habit*" (*Maid's Revenge*, E3v); examples of *habited* as "clothed, costumed" include "*richly habited*" (*Guardian*, 3.2.0; *Maid of Honour*, 4.4.48), "*carelessly habited*" (*Very Woman*, 2.3.23), "*Habited like a king*" (*Believe as You List*, 881), a newly wealthy figure who enters "*well habited*" (*Fortune by Land and Sea*, 424); the baby Princess Elizabeth is "*richly habited in a Mantle*" (*Henry VIII*, 3359–60, 5.4.0), the reapers in Prospero's **masque** are "*properly habited*" (*Tempest*, 1805, 4.1.138), "*four Scotch Antics*" and "*four wild Irish*" are "*accordingly habited*" (*Perkin Warbeck*, 3.2.111), the five Starches are "*all properly habited to express their affected colors*" (*World Tossed at Tennis*, D2r), an **antic** enters "*habited in Parchment Indentures. Bills, Bonds, Wax, Seals, and Pen, and Inkhorns*" (*New Trick*, 250).

hair

widely cited, most commonly when a female figure *enters* with *her hair loose, disheveled*, or *about her ears* to convey that she is distraught with **madness**, shame, **rage**, extreme grief, or the effects of recent violence; in the latter category, disheveled *hair* is one way of signaling enter **ravished**: "*The Soldiers thrust forth Theocrine, her garments loose, her hair disheveled*" (*Unnatural Combat*, 5.2.185); see also *Dick of Devonshire*, 687–9; *Swisser*, 4.1.0; for examples of **anger**, in *Dutch Courtesan* Franceschina enters "*with her hair loose, chafing*" (2.2.0; see also *Northward Ho*, 5.1.194); for examples from Shakespeare's plays see, for grief, Folio *Richard III* (1306, 2.2.33) and, for madness, Q1 *Hamlet* where Ophelia appears "*playing on a Lute, and her hair down singing*" (G4v, 4.5.20; see also Folio *Troilus and Cressida*, 1082–3, 2.2.100); loosened *hair* is also linked to women undergoing public penance or condemned to death: "*Mistress Shore in a white sheet barefooted with her hair about her ears, and in her hand a wax taper*" (2 *Edward IV*, 165), "*Isabella, with her hair hanging down, a chaplet of flowers on her head, a nosegay in her hand*" (*Insatiate Countess*, 5.1.66), "*Salassa her hair loose, a white rod in her hand*" (*Queen*, 3786–7); atypical is Emilia's entrance to devotion "*in white, her hair about her shoulders*" (*Two Noble Kinsmen*, L1v, 5.1.136); to gain this effect a boy actor playing the role need only have changed his wig; other examples are *loose hair* (*Antonio's Revenge*, 3.2.0; *Swetnam*, G2r; *Emperor of the East*, 5.3.0; *Bloody Banquet*, 1919–20; *King John and Matilda*, 26; *Unfortunate Lovers*, 72), *disheveled hair* (*Warning for Fair Women*, E3v; *Whore of Babylon*, DS before Act 1, 28; *Messalina*, 1861; *Unfortunate Lovers*, 80; *Landgartha*, E3r), *hair about the ears* (*Antonio's Revenge*, 3.1.51; 1 *Iron Age*, 269; *Tom a Lincoln*, 2252; *Broken Heart*, 4.2.57; *Love's Sacrifice*, 1268); male figures with disheveled *hair* include the fugitive Humber with "*his hair hanging over his shoulders*" (*Locrine*, 1573–4), Saturn "*with hair and beard overgrown*" (*Golden Age*, 38), a madman "*his face whited, black shag hair, long nails, a piece of raw meat*" (*Lover's Melancholy*, 3.3.19), "*four wild Irish*" who are "*long haired*" (*Perkin Warbeck*, 3.2.111).

For examples of actions, female figures are **drawn**, **pulled**, **dragged**, **led**, and trailed by their *hair*: "*she draws one of the ladies by the hair of the head along the stage*" (*Tom a Lincoln*, 2620–1), enter "*dragging in Dorothea by the Hair*" (*Virgin Martyr*, 4.1.59), enter "*drawing Moll by the hair*" (*Chaste Maid*, 4.4.18); see also *Death of Huntingdon*, 1715; *Alphonsus of Germany*, F4v; Q2 *Bussy D'Ambois*, 5.1.0; *Fatal Contract*, I1v, I2v;

Jews' Tragedy, 2240–1; *Maid's Revenge*, I3r; *Rebellion*, 60; less common is the use of a **dagger**: "*Syphax, his dagger twon about her hair, drags in Sophonisba in her nightgown petticoat*" (*Sophonisba*, 3.1.0), "*takes his dagger and winds it about her hair, and sticks it in the ground*" (*Rebellion*, 61); as a sign of vexation a figure "*Tears his hair*" (*Yorkshire Tragedy*, 487), exits "*tearing her hair*" (*Jack Drum's Entertainment*, D3v); an **unready** Bellafront "*with her bodkin curls her hair, colors her lips*" (1 *Honest Whore*, 2.1.12), but onstage grooming can also be performed by men: enter "*curling his hair*" (*Humorous Courtier*, H2v), "*Novall sits in a chair, Barber orders his hair, Perfumer gives powder, Tailor sets his clothes*" (*Fatal Dowry*, 4.1.0); a previously disheveled figure enters "*his hair and beard trimmed, habit and gown changed*" (*Lover's Melancholy*, 5.2.0); "*a white Beard and Hair*" are a sign of age (*Thracian Wonder*, C4v; *Captain*, 296; *Picture*, 2.1.85); along with **beards**, false *hair* is used for male **disguise**: "*Pulls his Beard and hair off*" (*Island Princess*, 169), "*Pulls off his disguised Hair*" (*Two Merry Milkmaids*, L2v), whereas a figure who has lost his disguise enters "*without hair or beard*" (*Wit of a Woman*, 1662); in contrast, a woman who has been disguised as a man reveals her identity when she "*discovers her hair*" (*Philaster*, 144/416); unusual effects include "*Absalon hangs by the hair*" (*David and Bethsabe*, 1469), "*He strangles her with her own hair*" (*Turk*, 2106–7).

halberd

a **weapon** with an **ax**-like blade and a steel spike mounted on a shaft; *halberds* are sometimes found in ceremonial occasions, as when the guards accompanying a **hearse** enter with "*their Halberds reversed*" (*Fatal Contract*, E3v), but more often are linked to figures under arrest or being **led** to **execution**; Folio *Richard III* provides examples of both uses: "*Enter the Corpse of Henry the sixth with Halberds to guard it, Lady Anne being the Mourner*" (173–4, 1.2.0), "*Enter Sir Richard Ratcliffe, with Halberds, carrying the Nobles to death at Pomfret*" (1933–4, 3.3.0), "*Enter Buckingham with Halberds, led to Execution*" (3371–2, 5.1.0); as seen in these three examples **enter** with halberds is an elliptical signal that a figure is to be accompanied by officers **carrying** halberds (or *halberts*); sometimes the figures carrying the weapons are specified: "*Officers, with bills and halberds*" (Quarto 2 *Henry VI*, D2r, [2.4.16; not in Riv.]); see also *Downfall of Huntingdon*, 911; *Two Lamentable Tragedies*, I1v, K1v; *Dead Man's Fortune*, 51; *Antonio's Revenge*, 5.1.0; *Dutch Courtesan*, 4.5.0; more representative is the situation in *Henry VIII* where the bearers of various weapons are implied: "*Enter Buckingham from his Arraignment, Tipstaves before him, the Ax with the edge towards him, Halberds on each side*" (889–91, 2.1.53); that *halberds* were included in many scenes where they are not actually specified is suggested in *Match Me in London* where the "*Guard*" enters and a condemned figure "*Snatches a Halberd*" (4.3.66, 76); for other *halberds* see *Spanish Tragedy*, 3.1.30; *Sir Thomas More*, 1603, 1862; *Captain Thomas Stukeley*, 1371–2; *Thomas Lord Cromwell*, D1r, F3r, F3v; *Warning for Fair Women*, K3r; *Dumb Knight*, 154, 193; *Witch of Edmonton*, 5.3.0, 20; '*Tis Pity*, 3.7.20; *Dick of Devonshire*, 1625; *Duchess of Suffolk*, G3v; for a different but comparable term: "*Enter with Welsh hooks, Rice ap Howell, a Mower, and the Earl of Leicester*" (*Edward II*, 1912).

hale
to *drag* someone forcefully usually off the stage: "*hale them out*" (*Caesar and Pompey*, 5.2.200), "*hale Edmund away*" (*Edward II*, 2440), "*Hale him in*" (*Three Ladies of London*, D1v); in her *anger* at the messenger Cleopatra says "I'll unhair thy head" and "*hales him up and down*" (*Antony and Cleopatra*, 1107, 2.5.64).

half
used (1) in several locutions for someone who is *unready*, surprised, or partly clothed, (2) in other locutions such as *half way, half drunk*; figures are directed to *enter* "*half ready*" (*Woman Is a Weathercock*, 1.1.1–2; *Wise Woman of Hogsdon*, 311), "*half unready*" (*Fedele and Fortunio*, 1614; *Captives*, 2464, 2512), "*half naked*" (*King Leir*, 2476, 2506; *Four Prentices*, 176), "*half dressed*" (*Gentleman Usher*, 2.1.123), "*with a beard half off, half on*" (*Antonio's Revenge*, 2.1.20); in *1 Henry VI* after the suddenly awakened soldiers "*leap over the walls in their shirts*" the French leaders enter "*half ready, and half unready*" (720–2, 2.1.38); variations include "*in his fool's coat but half on*" (*Summer's Last Will*, 0), in "*an old gown half off*" (*Lover's Melancholy*, 3.3.38), "*half unready, as newly started from their Beds*" (*2 Iron Age*, 413), "*half armed, and two soldiers following him with the rest of the armor*" (*Lust's Dominion*, 4.4.0), "*Enter Francisco half dressed, in his black doublet and round cap, the rest rich, Jacomo bearing his hat and feather. Adrian his doublet and band, Randolfo his cloak and staff, they clothe Francisco*" (*What You Will*, D3r); other locutions include "*half drunk*" (*Wit of a Woman*, 1643–4; *Wise Woman of Hogsdon*, 295; *Soddered Citizen*, 3), "*half Reeling*" (*Conspiracy*, C4v), "*with a cord, half unbound*" (*Mad World*, 2.6.6), "*Cassandra half dead under his arm*"

(*Young Admiral*, D4v), "*They march half the Stage*" (*1 Arviragus and Philicia*, A8v), "*draws his sword out half way*" (*Twins*, D2v), "*Love descends half way, then speaks*" (*Rebellion*, 52).

halloo
a *shout* to call someone or get attention typically linked to *hunting* as the *sound* signal *hallooing within* (*Death of Huntingdon*, 37; *Look about You*, 2583; *Patient Grissil*, 1.2.0; *Shoemakers' Holiday*, 2.1.0; *Two Angry Women*, 2093, 2444–5; *Tottenham Court*, 103); other examples are "*Halloo in his ear*" (*Doctor Faustus*, A 1204; see also *Guy of Warwick*, E2v), "*blowing their horns, and hallooing*" (*Summer's Last Will*, 775, also 634), "*Noise and hallooing as people a-Maying*" (*Two Noble Kinsmen*, F2r, 3.1.0), "*Enter Huntsmen hallooing and whooping*" (*Aglaura*, 1.4.0, also 5.1.74).

halter
to *enter* with a *halter* or wearing such a hanging *cord/rope* around the *neck* is to indicate that a figure is (1) contemplating suicide, (2) facing *execution*, (3) calling attention to his abject position as if to say "my life is in your hands"; signals for *halters* linked to suicide are *enter* "*with a halter ready to hang himself*" (*Edward I*, 2108, also 2135), "*with a Halter in his hand, looking about*" and "*offers to hang himself*" (*Caesar and Pompey*, 2.1.0, 24), "*with a Halter about his neck*" and then "*strangles himself*" (*Sir Thomas Wyatt*, 2.3.70, 84); see also *David and Bethsabe*, 1415; *Humorous Day's Mirth*, 5.2.108; Folio *Every Man Out*, 3.7.0; *All's Lost by Lust*, 5.3.0; *Vow Breaker*, 2.4.0; sometimes one figure offers a *halter* so as to suggest another commit suicide, as in *Epicæne* where to taunt Morose Truewit "*shows him a halter*" (2.2.27); see also *Believe as You List*, 1915; *Novella*, 146; occasionally the figure carries both a *halter* and a *dagger* (*Spanish Tragedy*, 3.12.19; *Looking Glass for London*, 2041–2); in both these scenes, moreover, another direction refers to the *halter* as a *rope* (*Spanish Tragedy*, 3.12.0; *Looking Glass for London*, 2065).

Figures facing execution enter "*bound and halters about their necks*" (*Little French Lawyer*, 441; *Bonduca*, 102); see also *Bondman*, 5.3.239; *Believe as You List*, 2199–2200; *Perkin Warbeck*, 5.3.184; for other *halters* linked to executions/murders see *Old Fortunatus*, 5.2.156; *Guy of Warwick*, C4r–v; *All's Lost by Lust*, 4.2.0; *Jews' Tragedy*, 1996–7, 2012, 3131–2; for examples of abject figures, the former *followers* of Jack Cade appear before Henry VI "*with halters about their necks*" (*2 Henry VI*, G3v, 2860–1, 4.9.9) so that Clifford glosses the gesture "all his powers do yield, / And humbly thus, with halters on their necks, / Expect your highness's doom of life or death"; similarly, a messenger bearing a rebel's defiance to a king enters *"with a halter about his neck"* (*Edward I*, 1965), a group of nobles pleading for forgiveness from their ruler enters *"in shirts nightcaps and Halters"* (*Wasp*, 534–5), a group enters to deliver a **petition** *"with ropes about their necks, their weapons with the points towards them"* (*Christian Turned Turk*, H1v), a repentant rebel enters *"with a halter about his neck"* (*Captain Thomas Stukeley*, 1279–80) announcing that "I bear this hateful cord in sign of true Repentance, of my treasons past" and "on humble knees will sue for pardon"; see also *Edward III*, I3v.

hammer

the few references to this tool are noteworthy: Barabas enters *"with a Hammer above, very busy"* (*Jew of Malta*, 2281) and a figure *"hangs up his sword and takes his hammer vowing to God Vulcan never to Use other Weapon"* (*Faithful Friends*, 2827–9); in *Friar Bacon* a brazen **head** appears, then *"a hand appears that breaketh down the Head with a hammer"* (1636–7), and elsewhere offstage blacksmiths *"must beat with their hammers"* (*Thomas Lord Cromwell*, A2v); the most striking use comes in *Two Lamentable Tragedies*: *"When the boy goeth into the shop Merry striketh six blows on his head and with the seventh leaves the hammer sticking in his head,"* then the boy is brought *"forth in a chair, with a hammer sticking in his head"* (C4r, D3v).

hand

of the nearly 500 examples (1) the most common locution is to **enter** with an object *in one's hand* but also signaled are (2) **kissing** a hand, (3) **wringing** hands, (4) *hand in hand*, (5) a variety of actions such as *holding, taking, joining,* **offering** hands, (6) severed hands, (7) a *hand* as a manifestation of heaven; of the several hundred entrances with an object *in one's hand Alphonsus of Germany* provides a **torch**, **cup**, *"glass of Wine in their hands"* (B1r, C4r, F1r), *Caesar and Pompey* a **paper**, a **halter**, **robes**, a **book**, (1.2.0, 2.1.0, 4.4.0, 4.6.15, 5.2.0), *Devil's Charter* **keys**, libels, a **dagger**, **linstock**, **book**, **vial**, **ensign**, **letters** (A2v, A4r, C3r, C4v, G1r, G4v, I1v, K1v); less commonly a figure enters **in** someone's hand: *"Cordelia with her father in her hand"* (Quarto *King Lear*, K3v, 5.2.0); see also *Old Fortunatus*, 4.1.0; *Wise Woman of Hogsdon*, 325; *Roaring Girl*, 5.2.128; *Old Couple*, 69; more than forty figures are directed to *kiss a hand*; typical are *"The Duke*

extends his hand, Iacomo kisses it"* (*Grateful Servant*, F4r, also H2v), *"Give him her hand to kiss"* (*Maid of Honour*, 3.3.81; *Renegado*, 1.2.100; see also *Osmond*, A4r); the *wringing of hands* is done by **mourning/weeping** women: *"she looks for her Babe and finding it gone, wrings her hands"* (*Bloody Banquet*, 852–3), *"The Widow wringing her hands, and bursting out into passion, as newly come from the Burial of her husband"* (*Puritan*, A3r); for entrances/actions *hand in hand* see *Three Ladies of London*, A3v; *Three Lords of London*, I2v; *Edward I*, 1504; *Locrine*, 433; *Dead Man's Fortune*, 61; *Edmond Ironside*, 2062; *Fawn*, 5.457; *Chabot*, 1.1.115; *Antony and Cleopatra*, 1464, 2.7.112.

Of the many other actions and gestures the most common are *taking of/by* a hand, *joining* of hands, *holding/staying/holding up* of hands, *offering* of a hand, *laying* of a hand on a person/**sword**; examples include *"takes her away lovingly by the hand"* (1 *Tamburlaine*, 1050), *"They all take hands, and dance round"* (*Northern Lass*, 64), *"Holds her by the hand silent"* (*Coriolanus*, 3539, 5.3.182), *"he offers to stab himself, and she holds his hand"* (*Tom a Lincoln*, 38–41), *"Lays his Hand on his Head"* (Folio 3 *Henry VI*, 2453, 4.6.68), *"pulls off her Glove, and offers her hand to Pisander"* (*Bondman*, 3.2.104), *"kneels down and holds up his hands to heaven"* (*Arden of Faversham*, 1475–6; see also *Looking Glass for London*, 2078–9; *City Madam*, 5.3.59; *Love's Sacrifice*, 2663–4; *Lost Lady*, 593); other actions include *"creeps upon his hands"* (*Valiant Welshman*, D4v; see also *New Way to Pay*, 1.1.98), *"beckoning with her hand"* (*Sir Thomas More*, 1080), *"fight hand to hand"* (1 *Henry VI*, 2460–1, 5.3.29), *"She lays her hand under her husband's feet"* (*Taming of a Shrew*, G1v), *"with her hand puts him back"* (1 *Iron Age*, 277), *"takes their hands and makes signs to marry them"* (*Maidenhead Well Lost*, 144), *"privately feeds Maquerelle's hands with jewels during this speech"* (*Malcontent*, 1.6.10), *"puts his hand to his eye, with a bloody sponge and the blood runs down"* (*Princess*, F4v); for *hands* in **pockets** see *Woman in the Moon*, B1r; *Yorkshire Tragedy*, 189–90; *Bartholomew Fair* provides a cutpurse who *"tickles him in the ear with a straw twice to draw his hand out of his pocket"* and *"As they open the stocks, Wasp puts his shoe on his hand, and slips it in for his leg"* (3.5.145, 4.6.77); signals for severed *hands* include *"a dead man's hand"* (*Duchess of Malfi*, 4.1.43), *"He cuts off one hand"* and *"Cuts off the other hand"* (*Edmond Ironside*, 700, 702, also 717; see also *Selimus*, 1431, 1487–8); *Titus Andronicus* provides *"her hands cut off, and her tongue cut out, and ravished"* (E2r, 2.4.0), *"He cuts off Titus's hand"* (F2r, 3.1.191, also F2v, 3.1.233); a torment in **hell** includes *"Hand burnt off"* (*If This Be*

Not a Good Play, 5.4.41); for **bloody** hands see *Faithful Shepherdess*, 437; *Maid's Tragedy*, 70; *Late Lancashire Witches*, 195; supernatural *hands* include "*A hand from out a cloud, threateneth a burning sword*" (*Looking Glass for London*, 1636), "*A hand with a Bolt appears above*" and "*The hand taken in*" (*Prophetess*, 388), "*from the heavens descends a hand in a cloud, that from the place where Hercules was burnt, brings up a star, and fixeth it in the firmament*" (*Brazen Age*, 254; see also *Friar Bacon*, 1636–7); occasionally *hand* can mean **side**: "*on the one hand of him Queen Elinor, on the other Leicester*" (*Look about You*, 968–9, also 2826), "*on either hand*" (*Whore of Babylon*, 1.1.0), "*on the left hand*" of a **table** (*Henry VIII*, 3037, 5.2.35); for a *handbasket* see *Histriomastix*, B4v; *Weakest Goeth*, 205; *Launching of the Mary*, 925, 1828; atypical are "*a handful of Snakes*" (*If This Be Not a Good Play*, 5.4.34), a "*two hand sword*" (*Old Wives Tale*, 253), "*two-handed*" (*Noble Gentleman*, 234), "*as near at hand*" (*Messalina*, 712).

handkerchief, kerchief

used in a variety of actions: "*at the window throws down her handkerchief*" (*Volpone*, 2.2.220), "*in a Seamster's shop, at work upon a laced Handkerchief*" (*Wise Woman of Hogsdon*, 284), "*draws his handkerchief (as to wipe his eyes) just before the Country fellow, and scatters some small money*" (*Knave in Grain*, 2968–9), **mourners** who "*wet their handkerchiefs with their tears, kiss them, and lay them on the hearse*" (*Antonio's Revenge*, 2.1.0); a **bloody** handkerchief is specified in *Warning for Fair Women*, F3r; *Cupid's Revenge*, 283; see also *Amends for Ladies*, 2.3.11; *Cupid's Revenge*, 235; *Captives*, 2316; figures with *kerchiefs* (usually spelled *kercher*) are either **sick** (*Shoemaker a Gentleman*, 3.2.10) or **unready**, as in entrances "*a kerchief on his head, and an Urinal in his hand*" (*Fair Em*, 350–1), "*in their nightgowns and kerchiefs on their heads*" (*John a Kent*, 582).

hang, hanging

used for (1) onstage suicides and **executions**, (2) the *hanging up/out* of objects, (3) *hanging on, hanging her* **head**, or other stage business; for figures who are *hanged*, *hang* themselves, or **offer** *to* do so see *David and Bethsabe*, 1469; *Massacre at Paris*, 498; *Alarum for London*, 1291; *Caesar and Pompey*, 2.1.24; *Ram Alley*, I1r; *Vow Breaker*, 2.4.41, 3.2.68; more detailed are "*hang him in the arbor*" (*Spanish Tragedy*, 2.4.52), "*with a halter ready to hang himself*" (*Edward I*, 2108); objects that are *hung* for display include a **head** (*Vow Breaker*, 2.1.113), **body** (*Antonio's Revenge*, 1.2.207), **table** *of laws* (*If This Be Not a Good Play*, 2.1.12), **lance, shield**, and

sword (*Faithful Friends*, 2824–5, 2827–8), **coat** *of* **arms** and *sword* (*Caesar and Pompey*, 3.2.107, 4.6.0), *shields* (*Three Lords of London*, H1r; *Four Prentices*, 234), **helm**, *sword*, and *streamers* (*Antonio's Revenge*, 2.1.0), "*a box hanging down*" (*New Wonder*, 174), "*her husband's picture hanging on the wall*" (*Warning for Fair Women*, E3v; see also *Wit of a Woman*, 389), "*a Banner of Cures and Diseases*" (*Widow*, G1v), "*the picture of a strange fish*" (*City Match*, 248); also *hanging* are a **harp** (*Grim the Collier*, G7r), *roundelays* (*Orlando Furioso*, 572), "*Scutcheons and Garlands hanging on the sides*" of a **hearse** (*1 Honest Whore*, 1.1.0), **crowns** (*Battle of Alcazar*, 1268–9), "*pieces of Armor*" upon **trees** (*Gentleman of Venice*, I1r); stage business includes figures *hanging on* another/*about his* **neck** (*Alarum for London*, 1139; *Jack Drum's Entertainment*, G4r; *Queen's Exchange*, 537; *News from Plymouth*, 193; *Albovine*, 66; *Prisoners*, B9r), *hanging* their *heads* (*Alphonsus of Aragon*, 46; *1 Henry VI*, 2445, 5.3.17; *Aglaura*, 5.3.108); variations are "*Besha hanging upon Martia's sleeve*" (*Humorous Day's Mirth*, 1.5.0), "*hanging about his neck lasciviously*" (*Insatiate Countess*, 3.4.82); disheveled **hair** can be *hanging* down (*Locrine*, 1573–4; *Insatiate Countess*, 5.1.66; *Two Noble Kinsmen*, B1r, 1.1.0; *Swetnam*, G2r; *Unfortunate Lovers*, 72); atypical are "*Shows a Knife hanging by her side*" (*Woman Is a Weathercock*, 5.1.13), "*his sword which hung by his Bed side*" (*Alphonsus of Germany*, B2r), "*Two fiery Bulls are discovered, the Fleece hanging over them*" (*Brazen Age*, 217), "*Air comes down hanging by a cloud*" (*No Wit*, 4.3.40).

hangings

an infrequently used alternative for the **curtain** or **arras** that hung just in front of the tiring-house wall; typically figures are **behind** the *hangings*: "*Goes behind the hangings*" and "*wounds Valerio behind the hangings*" (*Duke's Mistress*, I1r), "*stands behind the hangings*" (*Jews' Tragedy*, 1887–9), "*comes from behind the Hangings*" (*Maid's Revenge*, F1v), "*Withdraws behind the hangings*" (*Traitor*, 3.3.8); see also *Philaster*, 93, 95; *Grateful Servant*, F2r; *Rebellion*, 17, 18; *News from Plymouth*, 178; *Andromana*, 261; elsewhere a figure hides "*at the hangings*" (*City Wit*, 328), "*appears under the Hanging*" (*Princess*, D1v), "*Draws the hangings*" (*Unfortunate Lovers*, 79, 80; see also *Gentleman of Venice*, F3v), "*calls between the hangings*" (*Wits*, 124, also 143, 156).

harp, harper

a rarely cited instrument and musician: "*a boy carrying a gilt harp*" (*Antonio and Mellida*, 5.2.0), "*hangs his*

Harp on the wall" and "Harp sounds on the wall" (*Grim the Collier*, G7r, G8r), "Harpers play, and the Bardh riseth from his Tomb" (*Valiant Welshman*, A4v, also A4r, C2v), "Enter the Harper, and sing to the tune" (*Edward I*, 455, also 1015, 2361).

hastily, in haste

linked to over 100 figures who enter "*running in haste*" (*Selimus*, 1877; *Captain Thomas Stukeley*, 2784), "*running hastily*" (*Tom a Lincoln*, 699; *Valiant Welshman*, F4r), "*falling for haste*" (*1 Fair Maid of the West*, 315), "*posting in haste*" (*Wounds of Civil War*, 747); usually no additional details are provided; for a sampling of the roughly seventy figures who enter *hastily/in haste* see *Three Lords of London*, F1v, H3r; *Thomas Lord Cromwell*, D4r; Q1 *Romeo and Juliet*, G3v, 3.5.36; *Puritan*, H1v; *Roaring Girl*, 3.2.68; *Hoffman*, 1567; *When You See Me*, 1322, 1678; *Amends for Ladies*, 1.1.391; *Fawn*, 4.590; *Mad World*, 2.1.5; *Gentleman Usher*, 1.2.151, 3.2.212; *Coriolanus*, 238, 1.1.222; *Two Noble Kinsmen*, M3v, 5.4.39, 40; *Tom a Lincoln*, 166, 360, 809; *Captives*, 3116; *Honest Man's Fortune*, 227; *Valiant Welshman*, G4r; *Honest Lawyer*, H3r; *Appius and Virginia*, H1r; *Fatal Contract*, I3r; *City Wit*, 329; *Wedding*, F3r, F4v; entrances are signaled "*very hastily*" (*Woodstock*, 1558; *Yorkshire Tragedy*, 371), "*hastily, in a sweat*" (*Soddered Citizen*, 1122), "*hastily at several doors*" and "*meets them In haste*" (*Woodstock*, 2, 796), "*clothing himself in haste*" (*Wits*, 164), "*as it were in haste*" (*Downfall of Huntingdon*, 142; see also *Sophy*, 3.318), "*Jane, in haste, in her riding cloak and safeguard, with a pardon in her hand*" (*2 Edward IV*, 139); variations include "*exit in haste*" (*Soddered Citizen*, 439), "*departs in haste*" (*Maidenhead Well Lost*, 127), "*warily and hastily over the stage*" (*Atheist's Tragedy*, 2.4.0), "*Passes hastily*" (*Goblins*, 4.6.13), "*goes out, enters hastily again*" (*Aglaura*, 5.1.137; *Brennoralt*, 2.4.25), "*frowns upon them, they return hastily*" (*Politician*, A4v); haste occasionally appears as a verb: "*hasteth in the bed of Syphax*" and "*hasteneth within the canopy, as to Sophonisba's bed*" (*Sophonisba*, 4.1.213, 218); for other actions done *hastily/in haste* see *Cobbler's Prophecy*, 641; *Mucedorus*, D2r; *Captain Thomas Stukeley*, 2805; *Traitor*, 3.3.121; *Vow Breaker*, 3.1.0; *Parson's Wedding*, 533.

hat

important (along with *caps*) for costume and social protocol (as seen in the many figures directed to enter *bare*, bareheaded) and stage business (as witnessed by Hamlet's exchange with Osric); occa-

sionally *hats* are carried in rather than worn: "*Hats brought in three or four*" (*Wonder of a Kingdom*, 3.1.71), "*meets them with the Prince's cloak and hat*" (*When You See Me*, 1773–4), enter "*half dressed, in his black doublet and round cap, the rest rich, Iacomo bearing his hat and feather, Adrian his doublet and band, Randolfo his cloak and staff*" (*What You Will*, D3r); see also *Antipodes*, 263; *Caesar and Pompey*, 4.4.0; the absence of a *hat* is sometimes noted (*Westward Ho*, 5.1.0) as are the *putting* on (*Antipodes*, 295; *Queen's Exchange*, 529) and especially the putting/taking off of *hats* (*Anything for a Quiet Life*, D3v; *Thracian Wonder*, B4v); variations are "*without his hat, in a Nightcap*" (*Eastward Ho*, E4r), "*in their shirts, and without Hats*" (*Thomas Lord Cromwell*, C2r), "*Snatches off his hat and makes legs to him*" (*Revenger's Tragedy*, G3r), "*Flings away his napkin, hat, and sitteth down*" (*Downfall of Huntingdon*, 172), "*She strikes off Eustace's hat*" (*Elder Brother*, 41), "*Flings down his hat, unbuttons himself, draws*" (*Goblins*, 1.2.4); in *Roaring Girl* "*Turn his hat*" is a means for Moll to pick a *fight* (3.1.162); distinctive *hats* include a magical "*wishing Hat*" (*Old Fortunatus*, 4.1.0, also 2.1.70, 5.1.154), "*a Cardinal's Hat*" (*Henry VIII*, 1338, 2.4.0; see also *Duchess of Malfi*, 3.4.7), "*all in mourning apparel, Edmond in a Cypress Hat*" (*Puritan*, A3r), "*a Palmer's Gown, Hat, and Staff*" (*Thracian Wonder*, E1r), "*a Masked Gentlewoman in a broad hat, and scarfed*" (*Wit at Several Weapons*, 122); Henslowe's inventory lists various *hats* including "one white hat" (*Diary*, App. 2, 40), "one hat for Robin Hood" (41); *hats* as part of a *disguise* include women "*in their petticoats, cloaks over them, with hats over their headtires*" (*Gentleman Usher*, 2.1.153), "*Bedford like the clown, and Hodge in his cloak and his Hat*" (*Thomas Lord Cromwell*, C4v); sometimes attention is called to objects carried in a *hat* such as *rosemary* (*Noble Spanish Soldier*, 5.2.0), *money* (*Princess*, C2v), *roses* (*Tom a Lincoln*, 404), *points* (*Parson's Wedding*, 514), "*as returning from war, every one with a Glove in his hat*" (*Blurt*, 1.1.0); Octavo 3 *Henry VI* calls for "*white Roses in their hats*" for the Yorkists (A2r, 1.1.0), "*red Roses in their hats*" for the Lancastrians (A3r, 1.1.49), and in a climactic moment "*Clarence takes his red Rose out of his hat, and throws it at Warwick*" (E2r, 5.1.82); other actions include "*starts, his hat falls off, offer it him*" (*Wonder of a Kingdom*, 3.1.67), enter "*in Alphonso's clothes*" and "*trying several ways to wear his cloak and hat*" (*Twins*, E1v), "*Scilla after them with his hat in his hand, they offer to fly away*" (*Wounds of Civil War*, 336), "*He guards himself, and puts by with his hat, slips, the other running falls over* him, and Forrest kills him" (Fortune by Land and Sea, 386); see also Eastward Ho, A2r; Fancies Chaste and Noble, 234; Goblins, 3.7.64; Wits, 161, 166.

hatchet

a small *ax* for use with one hand, cited twice: "*snatcheth up the fellow's hatchet that was slain*" (Alphonsus of Germany, E1v), "*a Hatchet in one hand, and a Bowl in the other*" (Thracian Wonder, C4v); Henslowe's inventory lists "one wooden hatchet, one leather hatchet" (Diary, App. 2, 64).

head

the many references (roughly 220) consist of (1) severed *heads* (mostly human but also of animals killed in a *hunt*), (2) locutions in which objects are *placed* on the head, (3) *bloody*, broken, and *bare* heads, (4) a wide variety of actions; severed *heads* are specified in Edward I, 2673; Old Wives Tale, 863; Wounds of Civil War, 565; 1 Tamar Cham, 62–4; Titus Andronicus, F2v, 3.1.233; 2 Henry VI, F4v, 2530–1, 4.4.0; G3r, 2763, 4.7.129; H1r, 3057, 5.1.63; Richard III, G3r, 2106, 3.5.20; King John, 1282–3, 3.2.0; Two Lamentable Tragedies, F4v; Sir Thomas Wyatt, 5.2.155; Captain Thomas Stukeley, 1359; Thomas Lord Cromwell, G3r; Silver Age, 97; Escapes of Jupiter, 1442–4; Caesar and Pompey, 5.2.188; False One, 315, 371; Double Marriage, 405; Bonduca, 130; Bloody Brother, 281; Hengist, DS before 2.2, 11; Vow Breaker, 2.1.113; 2 Arviragus and Philicia, F11r; variations are a "*head on a spear*" (Edward I, 2361), "*heads on their swords*" (Travels of Three English Brothers, 323), "*Dead men's heads in dishes*" (Battle of Alcazar plot, 98); false/**counterfeit** heads are called for in Doctor Faustus, B 1412; Travels of Three English Brothers, 386; related actions include "*Her head struck off*" (Virgin Martyr, 4.3.179), "*offers to strike off Albinius's head*" (Alphonsus of Aragon, 622), "*submits her head to the block*" (Messalina, 2592–3), "*takes a dead man's head upon his sword's point holding it up to Edmond's soldiers they fly*" (Edmond Ironside, 989–91), "*cut away the Goose while he talketh, and leave the head behind him with them*" (Jack Straw, 487–8); other *heads* include a *death's head* (Atheist's Tragedy, 4.3.77, 204, 210; If This Be Not a Good Play, 4.4.0; Devil's Law Case, 3.3.0), brazen head (Alphonsus of Aragon, 1246, 1254, 1268, 1307; Friar Bacon, 1563, 1615, 1635–7), head in a *well* (Old Wives Tale, 634, 645, 782), *golden* head (If This Be Not a Good Play, 2.3.75, 3.2.139), and the heads of a *bull* (Brazen Age, 176), boar (Woman in the Moon, B4v; Brazen Age, 194), **stag** (Death of Huntingdon, 333–4), buck (Merry Wives, G1v, G3r, 5.5.0, 102), *ass* (Folio

Midsummer Night's Dream, 927, 3.1.102), **bear** (Mucedorus, A3v, C2r), **lion** (Silver Age, 131), **dragon** (Tom a Lincoln, 2231); Henslowe's inventory includes "one bull's head" (Diary, App. 2, 83), "two lion heads" (85), "one boar's head and Cerberus's three heads" (73), "Argus's head" (67), "Iris's head" (70), "old Mahomet's head" (65), "one frame for the heading in Black Joan" (91).

Of the many objects on or *set*/placed on *heads* the most common are a **crown/coronet** (for a sampling see Alphonsus of Aragon, 501–2, 786, 794, 806, 836, 1582–5; Locrine, 227; Doctor Faustus, B 1296; Four Prentices, 234; Devil's Charter, A2v; Virgin Martyr, 5.2.219; Jews' Tragedy, 3028; Broken Heart, 5.3.0) and **garland** (Locrine, 945, 1772–4; Summer's Last Will, 967; Mucedorus, A2r; Amends for Ladies, 5.2.298–9; Golden Age, 27; Philaster, 133/412; Henry VIII, 2644–5, 4.2.82; Two Noble Kinsmen, B1r, 1.1.0; Fatal Contract, E3v; Amyntas, T2v, Z1v); also on *heads* are a **coxcomb** (Old Fortunatus, 1.3.0; Dutch Courtesan, 2.3.93; Lover's Melancholy, 3.3.48), chaplet of **flowers** (Insatiate Countess, 5.1.66), **wreath** (Old Wives Tale, 808; Arraignment of Paris, 578; Noble Stranger, B1r), **kerchief** (John a Kent, 582; Fair Em, 350–1), **windmill** (Court Beggar, 267), **cap** (Taming of a Shrew, C3v), **nightcap** (Widow's Tears, 4.1.0), **attire** (Look about You, 1748), **laurel** (Bashful Lover, 4.3.68; Virgin Martyr, 1.1.118), mitres (Looking Glass for London, 1617–18), **arrows** (Amorous War, E2v); see also David and Bethsabe, 972, 1083; No Wit, 4.3.40; **horns** are sometimes specified on *heads*: "*like a Devil, with Horns on his head*" (Grim the Collier, K2r), a **devil** "*his feet and his head horrid*" (Birth of Merlin, D2v); see also Doctor Faustus, A 1111, B 1491; Old Fortunatus, 1.3.0; English Moor, 15; a *head* can be *armed* with a *helmet* (Macbeth, 1604, 4.1.68) as seen in "*armed all save the head*" and "*armed head and all*" (Queen, 3307, 3434, 3515–16), "*disarms his head*" (Sophonisba, 5.3.28).

Heads are described as *black* (Caesar and Pompey, 2.1.0), *white* (Captain, 296), *bloody*/bleeding (Doctor Faustus, B 1490; Fair Maid of the Inn, 173; Antipodes, 300), most commonly **broken** (Arden of Faversham, 840, 1682; Grim the Collier, H7r; Monsieur Thomas, 138; City Madam, 2.2.209; Jews' Tragedy, 2232; Sisters, D2r); to show respect or humility figures appear **bareheaded**: "*Clerk of the Council waiting bareheaded*" (Sir Thomas More, 1159–60); for a sampling see Edward I, 40; Comedy of Errors, 1599–1600, 5.1.129; Taming of the Shrew, 2200–1, 4.4.0; Downfall of Huntingdon, 2698; Widow's Tears, 1.2.32, 3.2.0; Henry VIII, 1339–40, 2.4.0; Queen of Corinth, 60; Honest

Man's Fortune, 245; *Women Beware Women*, 1.3.101;
Shoemaker a Gentleman, 5.2.78; the most common
action is the **shaking** of heads (*1 Henry VI*, 2448,
5.3.19; Folio *Every Man In*, 4.2.50; *Royal King*, 51;
Queen and Concubine, 36; *Country Girl*, G2v; *Example*,
G1r); figures are also directed to *scratch* (*Court Beggar*,
261; *Sophy*, 2.183; *Aglaura*, 1.1.9, 1.3.55), **hang**
(*Alphonsus of Aragon*, 46; *1 Henry VI*, 2445, 5.3.17;
Aglaura, 5.3.108), **raise** (*Death of Huntingdon*, 2647),
nod (*Caesar and Pompey*, 5.1.255) their *heads*; blows to
the *head* are common (*Friar Bacon*, 1612–14; *Locrine*,
1357–8; Quarto *2 Henry VI*, D2r, 2.3.92; *Mad Couple*,
47; *Queen's Exchange*, 487) as are other violent
actions: "*Hercules swings Lychas about his head, and
kills him*" (*Brazen Age*, 252; see also *2 Iron Age*, 393),
"*Breaks the can over his head*" (*News from Plymouth*,
143), "*striketh six blows on his head and with the seventh
leaves the hammer sticking in his head*" (*Two Lamentable
Tragedies*, C4r, also B4r, D3v); other actions include
"*declines his head upon her neck*" (*Hamlet*, Q2 H1v, Folio
1993, 3.2.135), "*holds his head down as fast asleep*" (*If
This Be Not a Good Play*, 4.4.16), "*Sneakup's head in the
Lady's lap*" (*City Wit*, 347), "*Lays his Hand on his Head*"
(Folio *3 Henry VI*, 2453, 4.6.68), "*a tirewoman, busy
about her head*" (*Michaelmas Term*, 3.1.0), a **ghost**
"*tossing his torch about his head in triumph*" (*Antonio's
Revenge*, 5.1.0), "*lifts up his head out of the Tomb, and
ducks down again*" and "*Empty a chamber pot on his
head*" (*Fedele and Fortunio*, 494–5, 1424–6); see also
Renegado, 2.5.92; *Roman Actor*, 5.1.180; atypical are
"*his head shaved in the habit of a slave*" (*Believe as You
List*, 2322–3), a **shield** "*having a Maidenhead with a
Crown in it*" (*Four Prentices*, 229), an **arrow** head
(*Gentleman Usher*, 5.2.0), entrances "*laden with chains,
his head, and arms only above*" (*Island Princess*, 107) and
"*with a forked arrow through his head*" (*Knight of the
Burning Pestle*, 229); **make head** meaning "advance in
battle" is found in *Golden Age*, 23.

headpiece

a **helmet** or protection for the **head**; figures enter
"*with a bill and headpiece*" (*How a Man May Choose*,
E1r), "*with a Headpiece and a long sword*" (*Fine
Companion*, I1v), "*in a shirt of Mail, a headpiece, sword
and Buckler*" (*Sir Thomas More*, 410–11); in *Edward I*
wounded soldiers appear "*with headpieces and
Garlands on them*" and with "*his Garland and his
plumes on his headpiece*" (40).

headtire

see **tire**

health

a term for **drinking** a toast: "*they drink healths and
dance*" (*White Devil*, 2.2.37), "*a health to the good success
of the Mary*" (*Launching of the Mary*, 2794–5), "*Music
and healthing within*" (*2 Iron Age*, 409), "*The health goes
about*" (*Faithful Friends*, 2519–20), "*Sound a health*"
(*Opportunity*, E3v); for more see *Wars of Cyrus*, E4r;
Fawn, 5.157; *Parson's Wedding*, 488; see also **pledge**.

heard

linked to **sound** in roughly thirty-five directions:
"*After their going in, is heard the noise of a Sea fight*"
(*Antony and Cleopatra*, 1975–6, 3.10.0), "*A tempestuous
noise of Thunder and Lightning heard*" (*Tempest*, 2, 1.1.0,
also 1039, 2.2.0; 1929, 4.1.254), "*A groan of many people
is heard under ground*" (*Catiline*, 1.315), "*A march far off is
heard*" (*Sophonisba*, 5.1.71), "*Voices are heard within*"
(*Conspiracy*, G3r, also H4r, H4v, I1r, I3r, K2v), "*sweet
Music is heard*" (MS *Humorous Lieutenant*, 2328–9), "*A
trampling of horses heard*" (*Insatiate Countess*, 2.4.0),
"*shrieks and clamors are heard within*" (*2 Iron Age*, 394);
for more of the most common signal for **music** or a
specific instrument to be *heard* see *Warning for Fair
Women*, D1r; *Malcontent*, 1.1.0; *Westward Ho*, 4.2.52;
Two Noble Kinsmen, L1v, 5.1.129; L2r, 5.1.168; *Four Plays
in One*, 363; *Martyred Soldier*, 209; *King John and
Matilda*, 83; *Unfortunate Lovers*, 43, 78; *Cardinal*,
5.3.91; *Landgartha*, I1r; for more of other sounds
heard see *Two Lamentable Tragedies*, C4r; *Alarum for
London*, 207; *Sir John Oldcastle*, 2193, 2222; *Thracian
Wonder*, C1r; Q2 *Bussy D'Ambois*, 5.3.82; *Two Noble
Kinsmen*, K4v, 5.1.61; *Unfortunate Lovers*, 28.

hearse

a means for **carrying** the **dead** comparable to a **coffin**
or **bier**: "*Enter the Queens with the Hearses of their
Knights, in a Funeral Solemnity, etc.*" (*Two Noble
Kinsmen*, C4v, 1.5.0), enter "*distractedly, with the
hearses of his two sons borne after him*" (*Atheist's Tragedy*,
5.2.67); a *hearse* may perhaps be distinguished from
a simpler *coffin* by objects lying/**hanging** on it: "*a
Funeral, a Coronet lying on the Hearse, Scutcheons and
Garlands hanging on the sides*" (*1 Honest Whore*, 1.1.0),
"*four with the hearse of Winchester, with the scepter and
purse lying on it*" (*1 If You Know Not Me*, 239), "*a rich
Hearse with five pendants, Armor plumed Helmet and
sword upon it*" (*Wasp*, 474–5); only in *Antonio's Revenge*
does the *hearse* appear to be a framework around a
coffin upon which objects can be **placed**: "*the coffin
set down, helm, sword and streamers hung up, placed by the
Herald, whilst Antonio and Maria wet their handkerchiefs*

with their tears, kiss them, and lay them on the hearse, kneeling" (2.1.0); locutions include figures who **enter** in a hearse (*Alarum for London*, 300; *Seven Champions*, E4v), *with a hearse* (Quarto *Richard III*, A4r, 1.2.0; *Old Law*, D2r), and **bring** in (*Arraignment of Paris*, 709; *2 Tamburlaine*, 4616; *Witty Fair One*, I2v; *Cleopatra*, E1v; *Julia Agrippina*, 5.152), are borne on/upon a hearse (*Double Marriage*, 401, 406); more detailed is "*enter four bearing Ithocles on a hearse, or in a chair, in a rich robe, and a crown on his head*" (*Broken Heart*, 5.3.0); several marginal directions call for *hearses* to be **ready** (*Mad Lover*, 69; *Two Noble Kinsmen*, C3v, [1.3.58]; C4v, [1.4.26]); in *Lovesick Court* figures enter **before** and after a hearse, then "*the hearse set down, Eudina kneels to it. Philocles kneels on the other side*" and "*Attendants go forth with the hearse*" (162–3); for other uses of before/after see *Whore of Babylon*, DS before Act 1, 32; *Wasp*, 478; hearses can be accompanied by appropriate **music**: "*Solemn Music, to a funeral song the Hearse borne over the stage*" (*Law Tricks*, 183), Tamburlaine "*bearing the hearse of Zenocrate, and the drums sounding a doleful march*" (*2 Tamburlaine*, 3190), "*a sad Music of Flutes heard*," then enter figures "*ushering Matilda's Hearse, borne by Virgins*" (*King John and Matilda*, 83); see also *Bonduca*, 144; actions include "*He comes from under the hearse*" (*Alarum for London*, 303), "*the song ended, the Hearse is set down between both companies*" (*Fatal Contract*, E3v), "*Falls passionately upon the Hearse*" and "*peruses the Motto of the Hearse*" (*King John and Matilda*, 85, 86).

heart

in *Golden Age* Saturn, who has ordered his son killed, is presented with "*a bleeding heart upon a knife's point, and a bowl of blood*" (20), for "a young Kid's heart" has been substituted to save the child's life; at the climax of *'Tis Pity* Giovanni enters with Annabella's "*heart upon his dagger*" (5.6.9).

heave

a seldom used alternative to **lift/raise**: "*They heave Antony aloft to Cleopatra*" (*Antony and Cleopatra*, 3045, 4.15.37), "*Heaves up the Coffin*" (*Knight of the Burning Pestle*, 227), "*heaving up their hands for mercy*" (*City Madam*, 5.3.59); see also *Launching of the Mary*, 2670–2).

heavens

a rarely used term for the roof over the **stage** and/or the space just below the roof where machinery for **ascents** and **descents** was located: "*from the heavens*

descends a hand in a cloud*" (*Brazen Age*, 254), "*Juno and Iris descend from the heavens*" and "*the Gods and Planets ascend to heaven*" (*Silver Age*, 121, 164), "*Fortune descends down from heaven to the Stage*" (*Valiant Welshman*, A4r).

heels

of the roughly twenty examples (1) a majority are found in the locution **trip** up/**strike** up his heels ("to cause to fall") but (2) figures are also **pulled** onto/**off** the **stage** by the heels; for trip up his heels see *Look about You*, 2630; *Roaring Girl*, 2.1.331; *Devil's Charter*, F4r; *Sisters*, B6r; and for strike up see *Warning for Fair Women*, F1r; *Poetaster*, 3.4.18; *Little French Lawyer*, 396; *Tale of a Tub*, 4.2.37; *Hollander*, 141; *Fool Would Be a Favourite*, C7v; variations include "*trips up his heels and holds him*" (*Eastward Ho*, A3v), "*tripped up his heels in scuffle and sits on him*" (*Fatal Contract*, H4v), "*He leads him a Lavolta, and strikes up his heels, and there leaves him*" (*Wit of a Woman*, 1024); each of the four examples of by the heels is attached to a different verb: "*draweth in Rotsi by the heels groaning*" (*Devil's Charter*, K4v), "*pulls him by the heels off the Stage*" (*Princess*, H3v), "*drags the Magician out by the heels*" and "*plucks the Witch out by the heels*" (*Valiant Welshman*, G1r, G1v); other examples are **spurs** on the heels (*Landgartha*, E3r), "*Achilles with an arrow through his heel*" (*1 Iron Age*, 332), a **prisoner** with "*an Iron about his neck, two Chains manacling his wrists; a great Chain at his heels*" (*Dick of Devonshire*, 1624–5), a botcher who "*hangs three or four pair of hose upon a stick, and falls to sewing one hose heel*" (*Weakest Goeth*, 227–8).

hell

the one use indicates an exit through the **trapdoor**: "*the Fates and Furies down to hell*" (*Silver Age*, 164); Henslowe's inventory lists "one Hell mouth" (*Diary*, App. 2, 56); see also **below, beneath, under the stage**.

hellish

occurs once: "*Enter (at the sound of hellish music) Pluto, and Charon*" (*If This Be Not a Good Play*, 1.1.0); see also **hideous, horrid, infernal**.

helmet

specified (1) before, during, and after **battles**, (2) at **funerals** and other **ceremonies**; signals for battles include enter "*with Helmets on, plumed*" (*Amorous War*, L1r), "*take off their Helmets*" (*Trial of Chivalry*, I4v; *Amorous War*, L2r), "*loseth his Helmet*" (*1 Iron Age*, 310), "*Fight, Her Helmet falls off*" (*Argalus and Parthenia*, 64); *Two Noble Ladies* provides "*in her Own Amazonian* attire, an helmet on and the beaver down" and "She lets him take off her helmet. She puts up her beaver" (1971–3, 1985–6); see also *White Devil*, 5.1.43; *Gentleman of Venice*, I1v; *Landgartha*, F1r; signals for funerals provide "*a Herald bearing Andrugio's helm and sword*" (*Antonio's Revenge*, 2.1.0), a **hearse** with "*Armor plumed Helmet and sword upon it*" (*Wasp*, 475); the ceremony that transforms the Cardinal into a warrior involves "*delivering up his cross, hat, robes, and ring at the shrine, and investing him with sword, helmet, shield and spurs*" (*Duchess of Malfi*, 3.4.7); Henslowe's inventory includes "one helmet with a dragon" (*Diary*, App. 2, 80); see also **headpiece**.

helter skelter

"in chaos or confusion"; an extended fight sequence includes "*In the fight, enter the Sheriff and two of his men,*" "*Proffer to fight again,*" finally "*Helter skelter again*" (*Sir John Oldcastle*, 1, 7, 20).

here

of the roughly forty-five examples about half call attention to timing or placement: "*Fight here*" (*Cupid's Revenge*, 286), "*sings here*" (*Looking Glass for London*, 1687), "*Kent here set at liberty*" (Folio *King Lear*, 1405, 2.4.127), "*The Tomb here discovered*" (*Second Maiden's Tragedy*, 1726–7); the remainder are found in a variety of locutions especially prevalent up through the early 1590s that begin with *here*: "*Here enters the Mayor and the Watch*" (*Arden of Faversham*, 2401, also 1233–4; see also *David and Bethsabe*, 753; *Dead Man's Fortune*, 25–6), "*Here fight,*" "*Here pinch him,*" "*Here open the door*" (*Knack to Know an Honest Man*, 44, 507, 1081), "*here the ladies speak in prison*" (*Dead Man's Fortune*, 25–6), "*Here she runs about the stage*" (*Cobbler's Prophecy*, 107), "*Here he begins to break the branches*" and "*Here the Head speaks*" (*Friar Bacon*, 1214, 1635); for a sampling of the latter group see *John of Bordeaux*, 436–7; *Fedele and Fortunio*, 795–6; *Edward I*, 1723; *Titus Andronicus*, D1r, 2.2.10; *1 Henry VI*, 629, 1.5.32; Folio *3 Henry VI*, 233, 1.1.205; *Looking Glass for London*, 796; uses of *hereupon* are rare: "*Hereupon did rise a Tree of gold*" (*Arraignment of Paris*, 456, also 478).

hide

an action signaled roughly twenty times; a figure "*hides himself*" behind an **arras** and another "*Hides himself in the charnel house*" (*Atheist's Tragedy*, 2.5.55, 4.3.79); elsewhere a figure "*hideth himself in the chamber behind the Bed curtains*" (*2 Iron Age*, 411), "*hides himself*" in a **tomb** (*Law Tricks*, 186), "*is run in to hide*

himself*" (*Epicœne*, 4.5.220), "*Hides him under the table*" (*Two Noble Ladies*, 98–9); see also *Charlemagne*, 2215; other directions include "*Stroza hides Julia in a corner, and stands before her*" (*Maidenhead Well Lost*, 152), "*Brusor hides her with a Lawn*" (*Soliman and Perseda*, F4r), "*Hide the women under their habits*" (*Queen's Exchange*, 540); for more figures who *hide* themselves see *Three Lords of London*, F3v; *Christian Turned Turk*, E1v; *Fleer*, 4.1.54; *Duchess of Suffolk*, D2r; *Arcadia*, E2r; *Swisser*, 4.2.6; atypical is "*muffled and hid*" (*Love and Honour*, 143); only one direction has a property hidden: "*In the act-time De Flores hides a naked rapier*" (*Changeling*, 3.1.0).

hideous

describes **music** (*Love's Mistress*, 151) and **noise** (*1 Arviragus and Philicia*, D8v); see also **hellish**, **horrid**, **infernal**.

hoboy

or "hautboy," a wooden reed instrument similar to the modern oboe, sometimes called a **shawm**; the sound of *hoboys*–always plural in directions–can accompany (1) supernatural or sinister events, (2) an entrance of nobility or royalty, (3) a **banquet**, **wedding** procession or other **ceremony**, (4) a **masque** or **dumb show**; *hoboy* can also refer to the musician; in *Macbeth* a direction for *hoboys* comes at the beginning of the **witches'** "show" of eight kings (1651, 4.1.106); the supernatural is also a factor in *Antony and Cleopatra* where "*Music of the Hoboys is under the Stage*" (2482, 4.3.12) with the ominous interpretation: "'tis the god Hercules, whom Antony loved, now leaves him"; in *Double Marriage* "*Strange Music within, Hoboys*" (348) prompts fear–"what horrid noise is the Sea pleased to sing. / A hideous Dirge"; *hoboys* play when royalty/nobility **enter**/**exit** in *Cardinal* (3.2.83) where "This music speaks the king upon entrance"; for similar examples see Folio *2 Henry VI*, 2, 1.1.0; *Charlemagne*, 154; *1 Fair Maid of the West*, 326; *Macbeth*, 431, 1.6.0; *Bloody Brother*, 267; *Welsh Ambassador*, 1068; *Game at Chess*, 2013–15; *Queen's Exchange*, 457; *Perkin Warbeck*, 2.1.39; *Messalina*, 518–20; *Queen and Concubine*, 1; *Osmond*, C7v; the instrument is frequently required for a combined grand entrance and banquet: "*Hoboys. A small Table under a State for the Cardinal, a longer Table for the Guests*" (*Henry VIII*, 661–2, 1.4.0), "*Hoboys Playing loud Music. A great Banquet served in*" (*Timon of Athens*, 337–8, 1.2.0); see also Folio *Titus Andronicus*, 2523, [5.3.25]; *Macbeth*, 472, 1.7.0; *Maid's Tragedy*, 8;

Valentinian, 88; *Hengist*, 4.2.0; *'Tis Pity*, 4.1.0;
Messalina, 1508–12; *Cunning Lovers*, G3v; *Antipodes*,
246; *hoboys* are also linked to marriage (*Two Maids of
More-Clacke*, A1v; *Fatal Dowry*, 2.2.359; *Women Beware
Women*, 4.3.0, 71) and to other public ceremonies
(*Hoffman*, 480; *1 Fair Maid of the West*, 312–13, 321; *King
John and Matilda*, 83; *Antipodes*, 313, 315) and are
sometimes played at the beginning of a *masque*:
"*Hoboys. Enter King and others as Masquers*" (*Henry VIII*,
753–4, 1.4.63; see also *Welsh Ambassador*, 2198; *'Tis
Pity*, 4.1.28; *Antipodes*, 264) or at the start of a *dumb
show*: "*Hoboys play. The dumb show enters*" (Folio
Hamlet, 1990, [3.2.135]); see also *1 Fair Maid of the West*,
274–5; *Birth of Merlin*, G4r; *Whore of Babylon*, 1.2.81,
2.2.185; *Match Me in London*, 5.3.0; *Hengist*, DS before
2.2, 1, DS before 4.3, 1; *Cunning Lovers*, I2v; the instrument is part of the sound of Roman victory in
Coriolanus (3621, 5.4.48) and accompanies dancing in
Timon of Athens (490–3, 1.2.145); the meaning of
"*Enter Compton, crying Hoboys*" (*When You See Me*, 1525)
is unclear; see also *waits*.

hole

a rarely used *fictional* term for the *trapdoor* in the
main platform: "*Peter falls into the hole*" (*Hog Hath Lost
His Pearl*, 1790), "*They throw all the bottles in at a hole
upon the Stage*" (*Princess*, G4r); see also *gulf, pit, well*.

honor

a verb or noun that signals an act of respect and *reverence* (typically a *bow, conge, curtsy, making a leg*):
"*doing honor to Letoy as they pass*" (*Antipodes*, 246),
"*makes a courtly honor*" (*Mad World*, 2.1.143), "*makes a
low honor to the body and kisses the hand*" (*Second
Maiden's Tragedy*, 2229), "*kisses the Bride, and honors the
Bridegroom*" (*Satiromastix*, 2.1.83), "*A dance, making
honors to the Duke and curtsy to themselves, both before
and after*" (*Women Beware Women*, 3.3.200); see also
Cobbler's Prophecy, 1664; *Whore of Babylon*, 1.2.81; *Four
Prentices*, 176; *Woman Is a Weathercock*, 5.2.31.

hood, hoodwinked

hoods are used primarily to *blindfold*, as when
figures enter "*bound and hooded*" (*Court Beggar*, 218),
"*bound and hoodwinked*" (*Valiant Scot*, C4v; *Just Italian*,
273); in *Andromana* a figure enters "*with a hood over
her face, which she throws up when she sees the King*" (221),
and in *Bloody Banquet* Tymethes voluntarily "*puts on
the hood*," "*Pulls off the hood*," and later enters *hoodwinked* (1001, 1060, 1430); an item of costume, "*a
French hood*," is specified in *Shoemakers' Holiday*

(3.3.0); Henslowe's inventory includes two *hoods*
(*Diary*, App. 2, 16, 123).

horn

occurs in roughly 130 directions for specific signals
and *flourishes* usually *winded* offstage; the several
kinds of *horn* include (1) a *hunting* horn, (2) a *post
horn*, (3) a *horn* blown as a summons, as well as (4) a
property animal *horn*, often symbolic of cuckoldry;
when linked to hunting the *sounds* probably con-
sisted of one note blown in various rhythmical pat-
terns depending on the stage of the hunt so as to
create a considerable and specific aural effect; in
Folio *Titus Andronicus* the direction "*Wind Horns*" is
followed by "*Here a cry of hounds, and wind horns in a
peal*" and later "*Wind Horns. Enter Marcus from
hunting*" (711, 712, 2.2.10; 1082–3, 2.4.10; also
699–700, 2.2.0); at the entrance of hunters in the
manuscript of *Barnavelt* the bookkeeper added
"*Horns*" in both margins (1726–7); for more exam-
ples of *horns* linked to hunting see *James IV*, 1548;
Woodstock, 2095; *Taming of the Shrew*, 18,
Induction.1.15; Quarto *Merry Wives*, G2r, 5.5.29;
Midsummer Night's Dream, F4r, 4.1.102; F4v, 4.1.138;
Blind Beggar of Alexandria, 3.26; *Downfall of
Huntingdon*, 1365; *Death of Huntingdon*, 331–4, 503;
Shoemakers' Holiday, 2.2.9; *Woman Killed*, 98; *Patient
Grissil*, 1.1.0, 1.2.0; Folio *King Lear*, 538, 1.4.10; *Golden
Age*, 32; *Silver Age*, 130; *Brazen Age*, 186, 187, 189–92;
Two Noble Kinsmen, H2r–v, 3.6.106, 131; *Thierry and
Theodoret*, 19, 21; *Old Law*, H2r–v; *Martyred Soldier*,
204; *Sea Voyage*, 17; *Maidenhead Well Lost*, 122;
1 Passionate Lovers, E4v.

The sound of the *horn* announcing the arrival of a
post was probably equally distinctive but different:
"*Post blowing a horn Within*" (Folio *3 Henry VI*, 1901,
3.3.161), "*Sound a Horn within, enter a Devil like a Post*"
(*Devil's Charter*, M2r); in the manuscript of *Wasp* the
bookkeeper noted "*Horn*" at the entry of a messenger (1469); see also *Edward III*, A3v; *Summer's Last Will*,
634, 775; *Woodstock*, 584–5; *When You See Me*, 198–9;
1 If You Know Not Me, 198; *Epicœne*, 2.1.38; Quarto *Poor
Man's Comfort*, E4r, G1v; *Thierry and Theodoret*, 16;
Duke of Milan, 1.3.136; *Picture*, 1.2.304; *Queen's
Exchange*, 529; *1 Arviragus and Philicia*, D1r; *Sophy*,
[3.153]; "*Post Horn*" occurs once (*Queen and Concubine*,
106).

Occasionally an onstage figure is directed to *wind
a horn* as a summons (*John a Kent*, 469; *1 Henry VI*, 902,
2.3.60; *Old Wives Tale*, 838, 872; *Downfall of
Huntingdon*, 1613; *Two Noble Kinsmen*, F3v, 3.1.96, 108;

G3r, 3.5.92; *English Traveller*, 79, 82; *Guardian*, 2.4.60; *Princess*, H2r); for other signals for a *horn* see *Downfall of Huntingdon*, 986, 1258; *Duchess of Suffolk*, D4r; *Cunning Lovers*, B4v; *Goblins*, 1.3.0, 3.7.41; *Andromana*, 230; atypical is "*she windeth a horn in Vulcan's ear and runneth out*" (*Arraignment of Paris*, 813); directions in two indoor theatre plays suggest that quieter **cornets** substituted for *horns*: "*Cornets like horns*" (*Malcontent*, 3.4.1), "*Wind horns of cornets*" (*Two Noble Kinsmen*, F3v, 3.1.96); see also **sowgelder's horn**.

Various uses of an animal's *horn* include "*the Knight with a pair of horns on his head*" (*Doctor Faustus*, A 1111, also B 1491), "*Slitgut, with a pair of Ox horns, discovering Cuckold's-Haven above*" (*Eastward Ho*, E3v), "*He tugs with the Bull, and plucks off one of his horns. Enter from the same place Achelous with his forehead all bloody*" (*Brazen Age*, 176), "*Belphagor like a Devil, with Horns on his head*" (*Grim the Collier*, K2r), "*Horace and Bubo pulled in by the horns bound, both like Satyrs*" (*Satiromastix*, 5.2.158); for other examples see *Old Fortunatus*, 1.3.0, 93, 5.1.0, 128; *English Moor*, 15; cuckoldry is implied when a figure taunts Mars by "*making horns at every turn*" (*Cobbler's Prophecy*, 1021–2); see also *Massacre at Paris*, 759.

horrid

describes a horrible, offensive **sound** of **music** or **noise**, usually linked to fear-inducing events associated with death and the supernatural; in *Messalina* "*Horrid Music*" is signaled when "*Two Spirits dreadfully enter and (to the Treble Violin and Lute) sing a song of despair*" (2514, 2518–19); *horrid* occurs most often in the Fletcher canon: "*A Horrid noise of Music within*" (*Little French Lawyer*, 440), "*six disguised, singing and dancing to a horrid Music*" (*Queen of Corinth*, 18), "*Within strange cries, horrid noise, Trumpets*" (*Double Marriage*, 348); for similar locutions see *Sea Voyage*, 61; *Lady Mother*, 2474–5; *Unfortunate Lovers*, 78; see also **dreadful**, **hellish**, **infernal**.

horse

three onstage *horses* are called for: in a military **funeral** in which the dead figure is "*carried upon a horse covered with black*" (*Alarum for London*, 261–2), in a skimmington that includes the "*wife on a horse*" (*Late Lancashire Witches*, 234), in a comic sequence with "*Enter a spruce courtier a horseback*" and "*Exit servant with the horse*" (*Woodstock*, 1424–5, 1480); unusual *horses* are specified when Neptune is awarded the **sea** as his kingdom and "*is mounted upon a seahorse*" (*Golden Age*, 78), in the Trojan *horse* sequence when

"*The Horse is discovered*" and "*Pyrrhus, Diomed, and the rest, leap from out the Horse*" (*2 Iron Age*, 372, 380); Henslowe's inventory includes "*one great horse with his legs*" (*Diary*, App. 2, 85); more common are **as [if]** signals/**sounds** that suggest *horses* offstage; figures enter "*as from horse*" (*City Nightcap*, 107), "*as seeking the horses*" (*Goblins*, 3.4.9), "*as being thrown off his horse, And falls*" (*Yorkshire Tragedy*, 632); sound effects are "*A noise within like horses*" (*Chances*, 223), "*A Noise within Trampling of Horses*" (*Captives*, 2743–4; *Insatiate Countess*, 2.4.0), "*A noise within, as the fall of a Horse*" (*Guardian*, 4.1.0); atypical are "*a vaulting horse*" used for the murder of Camillo (*White Devil*, 2.2.37), "*fetcheth out the Hobby horse and the morris dance*" (*Summer's Last Will*, 193), "*a scuttle full of horsedung*" (*Case Is Altered*, 3.5.0).

hose

a man's tights that are fastened to a **doublet**; of the few examples three call for figures to enter *in hose and doublet* (*Look about You*, 2745; *Histriomastix*, D2v; *May Day*, 3.3.165); variations include an entrance carrying "*a pair of large hose, and a codpiece*" (*Humorous Day's Mirth*, 2.2.49), a clown "*with one hose off the other on, without any britches*" (*Tom a Lincoln*, 2419), a botcher who "*hangs three or four pair of hose upon a stick, and falls to sewing one hose heel*" (*Weakest Goeth*, 227–8); Henslowe's inventory lists various *hose* that include "*three pair of canvas hose*" (*Diary*, App. 2, 35), "*one pair of French hose, cloth of gold*" (111), "*a pair of hose for the clown*" (33), "*one pair of hose for the Dauphin*" (48).

hound

see **dog**

hourglass

used to set a scene: "*Vials, gallipots, plate, and an hourglass by her. The Courtesan on a bed, for her counterfeit fit*" (*Mad World*, 3.2.0), "*like an aged Hermit, carrying a pair of balances, with an hourglass in either of them; one hourglass white, the other black*" (*Summer's Last Will*, 360), "*Time . . . and all his properties, as Scythe, Hourglass and Wings*" (*Whore of Babylon*, DS before Act 1, 28–30; see also *Thracian Wonder*, C1r), "*three or four young Gentlewomen sewing by an hourglass*" (*Law Tricks*, 163).

house

(1) usually a **fictional** locale **behind** a stage **door** but occasionally (2) a household, (3) other distinctive *houses* including the playhouse itself; *Wit of a Woman*

provides a sequence in which figures set up *tables* in front of their *houses* to advertise their wares so that the subsequent signals include "*Exit to his house*," an entrance "*from Balia's house*," "*Exeunt into his house*," "*Exeunt Ladies to Balia's house*" (386–7, 421–2, 547, 864); comparable directions include "*Enter Crackstone out of Victoria's house*" and "*Enter Pedante disguised, coming forth of Victoria's house*" (*Fedele and Fortunio*, 1156–7), "*enter from the widow's house a service*" (*James IV*, 2051–2), "*All the servants run out of the house affrighted*" (*Silver Age*, 122), "*Paulo takes fees of all as they enter the house*" (*Novella*, 129), "*Enter into the Admiral's house, and he in his bed*" (*Massacre at Paris*, 301), "*She puts Alphonso into the orator's house*" (*Dumb Knight*, 164), "*Go to one house, and knock at door*" (*Two Lamentable Tragedies*, G3r); *Insatiate Countess* provides a pair of linked moments where first Claridiana and Rogero "*are received in at one another's houses by their Maids*" and later are "*taken in one another's houses, in their shirts and nightgowns*" (3.1.0, 121); see also *Sir John Oldcastle*, 2222; *Hieronimo*, 1.0; *No Wit*, 4.1.0; such signals may include an implicit *as [if]* that is sometimes made explicit, as in entrances "*as out of the house*" (*How a Man May Choose*, B4r), "*as going by his house*" (*Yorkshire Tragedy*, 714–15), "*as in his house at Chelsea*" (*Sir Thomas More*, 1412).

For examples of other usages, *Game at Chess* provides "*Enter from the Black house, the Black Queen's pawn, from the white house the white Queen's pawn*" (99–101), but elsewhere in this manuscript *house* is used for a group rather than a place, as seen in enter "*both the houses*" (1231); *house* denotes "household" in the entrance of two "*of the house of Capulet*" (Q2 *Romeo and Juliet*, A3r, 1.1.0), "*They all draw, enter Piso and some more of the house to part them*" (*Every Man In*, Quarto 3.4.148; Folio 4.2.127), "*three household Servants*" (1 *If You Know Not Me*, 204) and in a related sense "*Enter the house of York*" (Octavo 3 *Henry VI*, B7v, [2.2.80; not in Riv.]); *house* as playhouse is found in "*fireworks all over the house*" (*Silver Age*, 159), "*A Boy of the house*" who meets "*Two Gentlemen entering upon the Stage*" (*Magnetic Lady*, Induction.0); other *houses* include "*They go up into the Senate house*" (*Titus Andronicus*, A4r, 1.1.63), "*Andrugio's ghost is placed betwixt the music houses*" (*Antonio's Revenge*, 5.3.49), "*Hides himself in the charnel house*" (*Atheist's Tragedy*, 4.3.79); see also *Thomas Lord Cromwell*, B4v; *English Traveller*, 73.

hug

used occasionally as an alternative to *embrace*: "*King is very merry, hugging Medina very lovingly*" (*Noble Spanish Soldier*, 5.4.0), "*hugs and shakes him*" (*City Wit*,

363); see also *Money Is an Ass*, C2v; *Virgin Martyr*, 3.2.124; *Princess*, C2v; two other examples involve inanimate objects: "*Hugs his bags*" (*Jew of Malta*, 695), "*hugs the quart-pot*" (*Parson's Wedding*, 458).

hunt, hunting

hunt scenes are keyed to (1) generic signals, most commonly *enter from hunting*, (2) the presence of huntsmen, woodmen, falconers often in *green*, (3) distinctive *sound* effects, (4) appropriate properties, especially *weapons* such as bows and *javelins*; for entrances "*from hunting*" see *Taming of a Shrew*, A2r; *Taming of the Shrew*, 18, Induction.1.15; *Titus Andronicus*, E2r, 2.4.10; 2 *Seven Deadly Sins*, 82; MS *Humorous Lieutenant*, 187; other generic signals include "*as from hunting*" (*Late Lancashire Witches*, 171), "*in the chase*" (*Golden Age*, 32), "*as if they came from hawking*" (Quarto 2 *Henry VI*, C1v, [2.1.0; not in Riv.]); although *huntsmen* appear frequently their costumes are rarely specified, with the few directions general rather than specific: "*in his hunting weeds*" (*Insatiate Countess*, 3.4.34, 116), "*like a Huntsman*" (*Isle of Gulls*, 239), "*like a huntress*" (*Silver Age*, 146; *Brazen Age*, 184), "*like hunters*" (*Patient Grissil*, 1.1.0; *Shoemakers' Holiday*, 2.1.0); for *hunters* dressed in green see *Edward I*, 1246; *Downfall of Huntingdon*, 1260, 2506; 1 *Edward IV*, 40; *Silver Age*, 146; *Brazen Age*, 187; Henslowe's inventory includes green garments for Robin Hood and Marian (*Diary*, App. 2, 20–1).

As to sound effects, some signals are generic: "*a noise of hunting is made within*" (Quarto *Merry Wives*, G3r, 5.5.102), "*A noise of Hunters heard*" (*Tempest*, 1929, 4.1.254); more common are directions to *wind* horns and signals for *horns*, *shouts*, or *hallooing*: "*Huntsmen hallooing and whooping*" (*Aglaura*, 1.4.0), "*Horns winded, a great noise of hunting*" (*Golden Age*, 32); as to properties, a wide variety of weapons are cited, most commonly bows, quivers, and javelins, but also live or dead animals; examples include entrances "*with her Hawk on her fist*" (Quarto 2 *Henry VI*, C1v, 2.1.0), with "*Bow and Arrows, and a Cony at his girdle*" (*Promos and Cassandra*, K4r), "*(In green) with horns about their necks and boarspears in their hands*" (*Woodstock*, 2120), "*Orion like a hunter, with a horn about his neck, all his men after the same sort hallooing and blowing their horns*" (*Summer's Last Will*, 634), "*a Huntsman with a greyhound*" (Quarto *Every Man Out*, 1010); at the climax of a successful *hunt* appear a stag's *head* (*Death of Huntingdon*, 333–4), a boar (*Prophetess*, 325), "*the Lion's head and skin*" (*Silver Age*, 131); most elaborate is the *hunt* for the Caledonian boar in *Brazen Age* which starts with horns winded offstage, a group *"with Javelins, and in green"* and Atlanta *"with a Javelin,"* then includes *"Adonis winding his horn,"* *"a great winding of horns, and shouts,"* further horns, cries, and *"great shouts,"* and finally the entrance of the successful *hunters* *"with the head of the Boar"* and *"with their javelins bloodied"* (184–94).

hurly-burly

an alternative to **skirmish**, denoting an onstage **scuffle** or **fight**: *"Here Gloster's men beat out the Cardinal's men, and enter in the hurly-burly the Mayor of London, and his Officers"* (*1 Henry VI*, 425–7, 1.3.56), *"Enter Captain and seeing the hurly-burly, runs away"* (*Ram Alley*, G1r), *"In the tumult enter Acrisius to pacify them, and in the hurly-burly is slain by Perseus, who laments his death"* (*Silver Age*, 96); see also **fray**.

hurry

found occasionally (1) in the locution *in a hurry*, a less common version of **hastily**, **in haste**, (2) as a verb, usually *hurry away* someone; figures enter *"in a hurry with weapons drawn"* (*Golden Age*, 24; see also *Spanish Gypsy*, H2r; *Martyred Soldier*, 205); examples of the verb include *"knock him down, hurry him away in a sound"* (*Valiant Scot*, K1r), *"hurry away his body"* (*Hengist*, DS before 2.2, 8–9); see also *Alarum for London*, 730; *Two Noble Ladies*, 403–4.

hurt

an alternative to the more widely used **wound/ wounded** and linked primarily to swordplay: *"Hurts the King"* (Folio *Hamlet*, 3804, 5.2.322), *"hurts him in the arm"* (*Hollander*, 101), *"led in hurt"* (*Chaste Maid*, 5.1.6), *"They fight and he's hurt"* (*Landgartha*, C1v); figures *hurt* someone in *Faithful Shepherdess*, 424; *1 If You Know Not Me*, 225; *Revenge of Bussy*, 5.5.85; *Inconstant Lady*, 3.1.76; *English Moor*, 8; and enter *hurt* in *Sir Thomas More*, addition 2, 67; *Faithful Shepherdess*, 414; *Miseries of Enforced Marriage*, 1372; *1 Fair Maid of the West*, 317; action sequences include *"They fight and the Husband's hurt"* (*Yorkshire Tragedy*, 262–3), *"Fight, and hurt each other, both fall down as dead"* (*Trial of Chivalry*, E3r); atypical is *"seems to caper and hurt his foot"* (*Bride*, 8).

I

image, statue

image usually denotes a representation of a Roman deity: *"An Altar to be set forth with the Image of Mars"* (*Faithful Friends*, 2822–3), *"A priest with the image of Cupid"* (*Parliament of Love*, 5.1.32; see also *Cupid's Revenge*, 225), *"Enter a Priest with the image of Jupiter"* (*Virgin Martyr*, 1.1.23); in *Conspiracy* a Flamen enters *"with the Images of some of the gods"* and *"Here they all seem to take an oath by touching of the Image"* (F4r–v), in *Roman Actor* *"Caesar, in his sleep troubled, seems to pray to the Image* [Minerva], *they scornfully take it away"* (5.1.180), in *Virgin Martyr* Christians *"spit at the Image, throw it down, and spurn it"* (3.2.53); Catholic *images* are called for in *Whore of Babylon* where Cardinals and friars enter *"with Images, Crosier staves etc."* (DS before Act 1, 48–9); see also *Fedele and Fortunio*, 600–1; an early atypical play provides the most extended use of an *image*: *"They draw the Curtains from before Nature's shop, where stands an Image clad and some unclad, they bring forth the clothed image,"* *"Concord fast embraceth the Image,"* *"The Image walks about fearfully,"* *"Image speaks"* (*Woman in the Moon*, A2v–A3r); the less common *statue* is used in *Winter's Tale* where the massed entry for the final scene includes *"Hermione (like a Statue)"* (3184–5, 5.3.0) and in *Game at Chess* where the Trinity manuscript has *"Music an Altar discovered and Statues"* (2038–9) but the Malone manuscript provides *"An Altar discovered with Tapers on it: and Images about it"* and *"The Images move in a Dance"* (1317–20).

in

widely used in many locutions, most notably (1) an entrance with an object *in* one's **hand**, (2) an entrance *in/as* [*if*] *in* a **shop**, **study**, **prison**, **garden**, (3) the movement of figures and objects on and **off** the **stage**; as with the comparable use of **out/forth**, *in* can signal either an entrance or an **exit** and therefore does not serve as a firm equivalent to today's sense of onstage and offstage; rather, to **go** *in* is to exit but to **come** *in* is to **enter**; **beat** *in* can denote an entrance (*"Theophilus beating in the Blades before him,"* *Bride*, 37), but usually signals an exit (*Orlando Furioso*, 770; *Spanish Tragedy*, Fourth Addition, 169; *Selimus*, 657, 2461–2; *Silver Age*, 114; *Brazen Age*, 175; *Lust's Dominion*, 4.2.56, 4.4.74; *Hieronimo*, 11.28, 90; *Coriolanus*, 1949–50, 3.1.227; *Tom a Lincoln*, 924, 939; *Valiant Welshman*, B3v, G4v, I2v); other examples of *in* for movement off the stage include **carry** *in* (*1 Henry VI*, 1558, 3.2.114; *English Traveller*, 35; *Virgin Martyr*, 4.1.160), **follow** *in* (*Late Lancashire Witches*, 245), **run** *in* (*1 Tamburlaine*, 705), **shut** *in* (*Lust's Dominion*, 1.1.145; *Coriolanus*, 538–9, 1.4.46; *Messalina*, 754), most commonly *go in*; for a sampling of the latter see *Spanish Tragedy*, 1.4.99; *Orlando Furioso*, 852; *Old Wives Tale*, 196, 838; *Downfall of Huntingdon*, 44, 62, 372; *Old*

Fortunatus, 4.2.28, 5.2.358; *Thomas Lord Cromwell*, D3v; Folio *Every Man In*, 3.5.65; *Antony and Cleopatra*, 1975, 3.10.0; *Brazen Age*, 181; *Mad Lover*, 62; *Captives*, 755; *Valiant Welshman*, B3r; *Late Lancashire Witches*, 199; *Court Secret*, B3r, B5r; **beds** taken off the stage are **drawn** in (*Golden Age*, 70; *Lost Lady*, 613; rev. *Aglaura*, 5.3.34), **put** in (*Mad Couple*, 76; *City Wit*, 319), **pulled** in (*New Trick*, 293); various uses of in include "The hand taken in" (*Prophetess*, 388), "*Exit Hamlet tugging in Polonius*" (Folio *Hamlet*, 2585, 3.4.217), "*Violanta makes show of great pain, is instantly conveyed in by the Women*" (*Four Plays in One*, 321), "*Nurse offers to go in and turns again*" (Q1 *Romeo and Juliet*, G2r, 3.3.162, also G2v, 3.4.11), "*goes in, and comes out again with all the rest*" (2 *Tamburlaine*, 4507; see also *Three Ladies of London*, B1r), "*Boy goes in behind the Arras*" (*Women Pleased*, 293), "*He goes in at one door, and comes out at another*" (*English Traveller*, 69; *Spanish Tragedy*, 3.11.8).

More common are entrances that combine *in* with a verb; typical are **rush** (*Downfall of Huntingdon*, 1624; *Richard II*, K1r, 5.5.104; *Volpone*, 5.4.61; *Turk*, 1446; *Christian Turned Turk*, H1v; *No Wit*, 5.1.150; *Country Girl*, E2v; *Wizard*, 2290; *Conspiracy*, K2v), **fetch** (*Doctor Faustus*, B 536; *Taming of a Shrew*, D4r; *Captain Thomas Stukeley*, 1473; 1 *Honest Whore*, 2.1.57; *Whore of Babylon*, 1.2.81; *Game at Chess*, 1943–4; *New Trick*, 281, 296; *Dick of Devonshire*, 1897–8; *Twins*, F3v), **lead** (*Lust's Dominion*, 5.1.162; *Sophonisba*, 2.3.47; *Chaste Maid*, 5.1.6; *If This Be Not a Good Play*, 4.4.0; *Virgin Martyr*, 1.1.118, 5.2.219; *Believe as You List*, 2199–2200, 2322–3; *Renegado*, 4.2.70; *Bondman*, 1.3.81, 4.3.63; *Unnatural Combat*, 2.1.78), but a sampling includes **carry** (*Wits*, 183), **conduct** (*Edward I*, 927; 2 *Iron Age*, 420), **creep** (*What You Will*, D3r; *Night Walker*, 365; *Platonic Lovers*, 100), **drag** (*Massacre at Paris*, 1102; *Sophonisba*, 3.1.0; 2 *Iron Age*, 389; *Virgin Martyr*, 4.1.59; *Roman Actor*, 3.2.46; *'Tis Pity*, 4.3.0), **drive** (*Locrine*, 436; *Trial of Chivalry*, I1r, I2r), **march** (*Brazen Age*, 203; 2 *Iron Age*, 379), **pluck** (*Lover's Melancholy*, 5.1.118), **pull** (*Satiromastix*, 5.2.158), **usher** (*Captives*, 2168; *Roman Actor*, 2.1.246; *Great Duke of Florence*, 4.2.153); most common are **come in** (for a sampling see *Summer's Last Will*, 420, 775, 967; *Edward I*, 1015, 2175; *Humorous Day's Mirth*, 4.2.26; *Hamlet*, Q2 H1v, Folio 1995, 3.2.135; 1 *Honest Whore*, 2.1.117; *Miseries of Enforced Marriage*, 1351, 2289; *Four Prentices*, 226; 2 *Iron Age*, 411; *White Devil*, 2.2.37; *Bartholomew Fair*, 2.3.43, 2.5.155, 4.1.67, 5.2.0; *Herod and Antipater*, F3v; *Martyred Soldier*, 242; *Seven Champions*, C3r; *Hyde Park*, H1v), **bring in** (for a sampling see 1 *Tamburlaine*, 1983; 2 *Tamburlaine*, 4045; *Sir Thomas More*, 606–7; *King John*,

2634, 5.7.27; *Volpone*, 4.6.21; *If This Be Not a Good Play*, 5.4.161; *Changeling*, 5.3.142; *Virgin Martyr*, 1.1.118, 4.3.32; *Broken Heart*, 4.4.0; *Herod and Antipater*, I2v; *Soddered Citizen*, 1809); **banquets** are *fetched in* (*Wisdom of Doctor Dodypoll*, 1063–4), *served in* (*Timon of Athens*, 338, 1.2.0; *Wisdom of Doctor Dodypoll*, 330; *Honest Man's Fortune*, 269), *brought in* (*Taming of the Shrew*, 2536–7, 5.2.0; *Lust's Dominion*, 3.2.33; *Wisdom of Doctor Dodypoll*, 944; *Timon of Athens*, 1424, 3.6.40; *Tempest*, 1536, 3.3.19; *Golden Age*, 21; *Silver Age*, 101; 1 *Iron Age*, 280; *Love's Mistress*, 101); also *brought in* are **tables**, **chairs**, **bars**; variations include "*Enter Pluto, his Chariot drawn in by Devils*" (*Silver Age*, 135), "*Enter Master Gresham, leading in the Ambassador. Music, and a banquet served in*" (2 *If You Know Not Me*, 297), "*Men to and fro bring in Bags, and have Bills*" (*If This Be Not a Good Play*, 2.2.16), "*Stukeley brought in with Bills and halberds*" (*Captain Thomas Stukeley*, 1371–2), "*Satyrs with Music, playing as they come in before Fortune*" (*Old Fortunatus*, 4.1.111).

In/out often do correspond to today's use of *onstage/offstage*, as in *Old Couple* where two figures are "*brought in in chairs*" and later "*Enter Servants, and carry them out*" (43, 46), but inconsistencies are readily documented; in *Bartholomew Fair* Ursula first "*Comes out with a firebrand*" but later "*comes in, with the scalding pan*" (2.5.59, 155); from the same scene in 1 *Henry VI* comes "*Bedford brought in sick in a Chair*" and "*Bedford dies, and is carried in by two in his Chair*" (1469–70, 1558, 3.2.40, 114) so that he is "*brought in*" for his entrance and is "*carried in*" for his exit; for the same action in *King Lear* the quarto signals "*The bodies of Goneril and Regan are brought in*" (see also H1r, 3.7.27), but the Folio provides "*Goneril and Regan's bodies brought out*" (L3r, 3184, 5.3.238); in *Golden Age* a scene begins with "*Enter the four old Beldams, drawing out Danae's bed*" and ends with "*The bed is drawn in*" (67, 70), so that *out* corresponds to today's *in*/onstage and *in* corresponds to *out*/offstage.

indenture

a **paper** property cited in three directions (*Jack Drum's Entertainment*, F3r; *Anything for a Quiet Life*, F4v; *New Trick*, 250); see also **bills**, **bonds**.

infernal

describes a kind of **music**, but in the only instance may also mean that the **sound** comes from under the stage: "*Infernal music plays softly whilst Erictho enters, and when she speaks ceaseth*" (*Sophonisba*, 4.1.101); see also **hellish**.

ink

an abbreviation of "inkhorn," a property almost always linked to *paper* and/or *pen*: "*Ink: paper ready*" (*Captives*, 1341, also 1361), "*with ink and paper in his hand*" (*Locrine*, 309–10), "*with a Lute, pen, ink and paper being placed before her*" (*1 Honest Whore*, 3.3.0), "*Taper: pen and ink Table*" (*Barnavelt*, 1610–11), "*Deed, seal, Ink*" (*Old Couple*, E2r, [60]); see also *Massacre at Paris*, 670, 888; *Sir John Oldcastle*, 876–7; *Hieronimo*, 6.0; *Revenge of Bussy*, 4.4.0; *Nero*, 39; *Northern Lass*, 12; *Lady Mother*, 43–4; *Country Captain*, D1r; *Brennoralt*, 2.1.29; an *inkhorn* is also cited: "*Draws Inkhorn and paper*" (*Fatal Dowry*, 4.1.176), "*a parchment writing, and pocket inkhorn*" and "*Draws out a paper, pen, and ink*" (*Platonic Lovers*, 90–1), "*an Antic habited in Parchment Indentures. Bills, Bonds, Wax, Seals, and Pen, and Inkhorns: on his breast writ, I am a Scrivener*" (*New Trick*, 250); the only directions actually for *ink* are the marginal notation "*Red ink*" (*Spanish Tragedy*, 3.2.25) and "*a painted box of ink in his hand*" for Usury to "spot" the face of Conscience (*Three Ladies of London*, E1v).

instrument

a general term seldom made specific in dialogue, although it almost always refers to a *music*-making instrument: "*Here is heard a sudden twang of Instruments, and the Rose falls from the Tree*" (*Two Noble Kinsmen*, L2r, 5.1.168), "*Folly with a Fife, Niceness, Newfangle, Dalliance, and Jealousy with Instruments, they play while Venus sings*" (*Cobbler's Prophecy*, 999–1000), "*satyrs playing on their Instruments*" (*Dead Man's Fortune*, 38–9); see also *Alphonsus of Aragon*, 44–7, 980, 994, 1007, 1020, 2116; *Wit at Several Weapons*, 133; a page "*with an Instrument*" has a "Theorbo," a kind of lute (*All Fools*, 2.1.401), and a figure "*playing on some instrument*" has a "chime" (*John a Kent*, 1098); non-musical *instruments* are cited twice: "*the Barber, with a Case of Instruments*" (*Herod and Antipater*, G1v), "*Table, two looking glasses, a box with Combs and instruments*" (*Devil's Charter*, H1r).

intrat, intrant

the seldom used Latin terms for *enter*; see *Campaspe*, 4.1.22; *All Fools*, 4.1.74; *Bussy D'Ambois*, 5.3.56; *Woman Is a Weathercock*, 2.1.179; *Wit in a Constable*, 171; of the few uses by professional playwrights one occurs as part of a sequence of Latin directions that begins a Chapman play (*May Day*, 1.1.0) and four occur in a brief section of *2 If You Know Not Me* (309–13) in which all the directions are in Latin.

invisible

although invisibility plays a significant role in a range of plays, the term *invisible* is found only five times, three of them in *Tempest*: "*Enter Ferdinand and Ariel, invisible playing and singing,*" "*Enter Ariel invisible,*" "*Prosper on the top (invisible)*" (519, 1.2.374; 1392, 3.2.41; 1535–6, 3.3.17); *Old Wives Tale* provides "*Enter Jack invisible, and taketh off Sacrapant's wreath from his head, and his sword out of his hand*" (808) with the response "What hand invades the head of Sacrapant?"; *Late Lancashire Witches* (a play rich in magical effects) offers "*Enter an invisible spirit*" (196); Henslowe records the purchase of "a robe for to go invisible" (*Diary*, App. 2, 208), but no such property is to be found in directions or dialogue; rather, most of the relevant scenes depend upon appropriate action (with one actor demonstrably unable to "see" another actor onstage) and dialogue; typical is Sinew's comment about an *invisible* **spirit** in *Two Noble Ladies*: "I hear him though I see him not" (655); see also **vanish**.

iron, irons

in the plural a restraint for **prisoners** comparable to **chains**, **fetters**, **gyves**, **manacles**, **shackles**: "*in prison, with Irons*" (*Woman Killed*, 127), "*sitting laden with many Irons*" (*Martyred Soldier*, 206), "*in irons*" and "*His irons taken off*" (*Maid of Honour*, 3.1.74, 4.3.47); a madhouse scene calls twice for an off-stage **sound** ("*Shake Irons within*") followed by "*Irons brought in*" (*Pilgrim*, 208, 213, 214); in the singular, *iron* can be a restraint or a tool: "*an Iron about his neck, two Chains manacling his wrists; a great Chain at his heels*" (*Dick of Devonshire*, 1624–5), "*a wrenching Iron*" (*Jews' Tragedy*, 1336–7, also 1338), a "*marking iron*" (*Three Lords of London*, H2v); as a modifier *iron* appears only as an "*iron crow*" (*Wits*, 210, 211), "*a crow of iron*" (*Widow's Tears*, 5.5.0), "*a mattock, and a crow of iron*" used by Romeo to force open the Capulet **tomb** (Q1 *Romeo and Juliet*, I4v, 5.3.21); atypical is "*Enter man with pan and irons*" to elicit a confession (*Fatal Contract*, I2r).

issue

an alternative to **enter** often combined with **forth**, as when a rebel approaches the city **walls** and "*Shore and his Soldiers issue forth and repulse him*" (*1 Edward IV*, 31); see also *1 Troublesome Reign*, F2v; *No Wit*, 4.3.40; *Jovial Crew*, 365; variations are "*issues from the tent*" (*2 Tamburlaine*, 3673), two onstage abductors who "*issue out and bear them away*" (*Isle of Gulls*, 242); for the appearance of a **devil** "*the Gulf opens, flames issuing*" (*Caesar and Pompey*, 2.1.24).

J

jack, blackjack
a large leather jug for **beer** coated with tar, hence **black**: "*three or four servants with a great Kettle, and blackjacks*" (*Jovial Crew*, 362); usually the modifier is omitted: "*Yeoman of the Cellar, with a Jack of Beer and a Dish*" (*Bloody Brother*, 262); see also *Summer's Last Will*, 967; *Warning for Fair Women*, F2v; *1 If You Know Not Me*, 209; *Vow Breaker*, 5.1.84.

javelin
either (1) a light **spear** linked to **hunting** or (2) a pointed **weapon** with a long shaft like a **pike** or **lance** used for **thrusting** in **battle**; in *Brazen Age* a large hunting party enters "*with Javelins, and in green*" and "*with their javelins bloodied*" (187, 194), and in *Golden Age* Diana and her nymphs enter "*garlands on their heads, and javelins in their hands, their Bows and Quivers*" (27); see also *Humorous Lieutenant*, 285; javelins for **fighting** are called for in "*two Pages with targets and javelins*" (*Sophonisba*, Prologue.0, 1.2.185, 5.2.0, 5.3.6); see also *Golden Age*, 51; *2 Iron Age*, 373.

jewel
mostly found when figures **enter**, often simply *with a jewel/jewels*; see *Humorous Day's Mirth*, 1.1.0; *Old Fortunatus*, 3.1.217; *Scornful Lady*, 237; *Guardian*, 2.2.0, 2.3.45; *Birth of Merlin*, C4v; *Variety*, C10r; variations include entrances with "*a Jewel and a Ring*" (*Cupid's Revenge*, 247), "*with a Cabinet of Jewels*" (*Wedding*, E4v), "*Looking upon their Jewels*" (*Escapes of Jupiter*, 727; see also *Golden Age*, 62), "*every one holding a Jewel*" (*If This Be Not a Good Play*, 4.4.0), "*gorgeously decked with jewels*" (*English Moor*, 65), "*richly attired and decked with Jewels*" (*Lovesick King*, 1711–12); a **spirit** appears "*all in white, Stuck with Jewels and a great crucifix on her breast*" (*Second Maiden's Tragedy*, 1930–1); jewels can be part of a larger **treasure**: "*all hung with Chains, Jewels, Bags of Money, etc.*" (*City Wit*, 368), "*with as many Jewels robes and Gold as he can carry*" (*2 Seven Deadly Sins*, 66–7), "*at a Table with Jewels and Money upon it*" (*Women Pleased*, 242), "*A Table set forth, Jewels and Bags upon it*" (*Renegado*, 2.4.0); figures are directed to **show** jewels (*Valentinian*, 31; *Soddered Citizen*, 1229–31), *give jewels* (*Renegado*, 3.1.87; *Just Italian*, 230; *Unfortunate Mother*, 126); more detailed is "*gives jewels, and ropes of pearl to

the Duke; and a chain of gold to every Courtier*" (*Wonder of a Kingdom*, 4.1.0); other actions include "*casts a jewel*" (*2 Fair Maid of the West*, 399), "*lets fall a Jewel from her dress, he takes it up, and offers it to her*" (*Court Secret*, B1r), "*Ferneze privately feeds Maquerelle's hands with jewels during this speech*" (*Malcontent*, 1.6.10); atypical is "*looking upon the picture of Alberdure in a little Jewel*" (*Wisdom of Doctor Dodypoll*, 85–6); see also *Your Five Gallants*, C1r; *Island Princess*, 135; *Queen and Concubine*, 73.

jig
since this lively **dance** is signaled only once the phrasing is apposite: "*The two dance a jig devised for the nonce*" (*James IV*, 95).

join
of the roughly fifteen uses (1) most signal *joining hands*, (2) others describe the coming together of several figures; some hands are *joined* at a **wedding**: "*joins them hand in hand, takes a Ring from Gerrard, puts it on Violanta's finger*" (*Four Plays in One*, 321), "*Bride and Bridegroom kiss, and by the Cardinal are joined hand in hand*" (*Noble Spanish Soldier*, 5.4.0); see also *Devil's Charter*, A2r; *Nice Valour*, 197; *Challenge for Beauty*, 56; *Queen's Exchange*, 530; *Constant Maid*, H1v; directions for figures to *join* together are "*The rest join and drive in the Moors*" and "*joins them together, they embrace*" (*Lust's Dominion*, 4.2.135, 4.3.48), "*joins in conference with*" (*Novella*, 174), "*join in the dance*" (*Traitor*, 3.2.44); see also *No Wit*, 3.1.0; *Bloody Brother*, 253; *Sophy*, 5.99.

justle
to shove or elbow someone, often to provoke a quarrel: "*As Virgilius comes in, he meets Bragadine going out, they justle, and look scurvily at one another*" (*Princess*, C3r); two figures "*meet and justle*" (*Cupid's Whirligig*, 1.2.76) with the non-belligerent one reacting "*I cry ye mercy sir, I did not see ye*"; most uses of this verb are transitive so that one figure *justles* another: "*takes the Wall and justles Strowd*" (*Blind Beggar of Bednal Green*, 36); see also *Puritan*, G3v; *Roaring Girl*, 3.1.151; *Law Tricks*, 133; *Fine Companion*, F1v; *Wedding*, F4v; *2 Passionate Lovers*, H2r.

K

keep, keeper
the sixty examples include (1) widely varying uses of the verb but (2) mostly *keepers* who accompany

prisoners, (3) a few other *keepers*; as a verb *keep* is most often linked to violence: "*keeps in the midst*" for protection (*Welsh Ambassador*, 2222), "*they fight and keep them back*" (*Trial of Chivalry*, I3r; see also *Seven Champions*, C2r), "*They fight, Brand falls, young Bruce keeps him down*" (*King John and Matilda*, 78), "*Diocles draws his Sword, keeps off Maximinian*" (*Prophetess*, 363); elsewhere figures "*sit close to keep out*" a third (*Herod and Antipater*, F3v), enter "*keeping the door*" (*City Match*, 249), "*keep the Stage*" when others depart (*1 Iron Age*, 277), "*dance a strain, and whilst the others keep on, the King and Celestine stay*" (*Satiromastix*, 2.1.131); occasionally *keep* is linked to music: "*The song, and he keeps time*" (*Your Five Gallants*, C1r), a figure "*Sings and his crew Keeps the Burden*" (*Soddered Citizen*, 2700).

For a sampling of roughly forty *keepers* who serve as jailers see Folio *Richard III*, 836, 1.4.0; *2 Seven Deadly Sins*, 2; *Northward Ho*, 4.3.162; *Puritan*, F3v; *Atheist's Tragedy*, 3.3.24; *Fair Maid of Bristow*, E3r; *Island Princess*, 106; *Fatal Dowry*, 2.2.161; more detailed examples include "*the Keeper of Ludgate*" (*New Wonder*, 171, also 177, 184), "*Enter Keeper with a Dish*" (Folio *Richard II*, 2763, 5.5.94), "*Enter Anne Sanders and her keeper following her*" (*Warning for Fair Women*, K1r), "*Enter Keeper, Stranguidge, Shore disguised, and three more fettered*" (*2 Edward IV*, 121, also 135), "*two Keepers to fetch them off*" (*Pilgrim*, 196, also 190, 208–9), "*Enter Sforza and Keeper, as in Prison*" (*Queen and Concubine*, 35, also 37–8, 42); other *keepers* include "*Stagekeepers as a guard*" (*Captives*, 2805), a *game keeper* (*Friar Bacon*, 1389, 1895), "*a Boxkeeper*" (*Gamester*, E4r), "*an old Innkeeper*" (*True Tragedy of Richard III*, 542), a "*tennis keeper*" (*Captain Thomas Stukeley*, 585).

kerchief
see *handkerchief*

keyhole
a seldom used *fictional* term in signals for lines to be spoken at a stage *door*; in *Alchemist* an onstage Face "*speaks through the keyhole*" to an offstage Mammon knocking at the door (3.5.58), and *Puritan* calls for speeches from "*Sir Godfrey through the keyhole within*" and "*Edmund at keyhole*" (G2v, G3r).

keys
linked to (1) *prison*/prisoners, (2) the *house*/household, (3) the control of wealth, (4) the papacy or other high office; in *Knack to Know an Honest Man* the escape of two prisoners is connected with two

entrances of "*Phillida with the keys*" (1071, 1153), and others who control prisoners carry "*a gilt key*" (*Renegado*, 2.5.104), "*a key and lights*" (*Love and Honour*, 120, 130); the countess thinks Talbot is her prisoner when her porter enters "*with keys*" (*1 Henry VI*, 870, 2.3.32); figures who have control of a house enter "*with Keys*" (*Woman Killed*, 131), "*with a Key in his hand*" (*English Traveller*, 71); in *Coxcomb* an escaping Viola enters "*with a Key, and a little Casket*" (317), throws the key "*Back through a window*," and then cannot return to the house; similarly, *keys* are used to control access when "*Montsurry turns a key*" to be alone with Tamyra (*Bussy D'Ambois*, 5.1.40) and Clarinda enters "*with a Key*" to facilitate passage within the house (*Lovers Progress*, 102; see also *Charlemagne*, 2270); *keys* are important for many intrigues, as seen in "*Enter Hog in his chamber with Rebecca laying down his bed, and seeming to put the keys under his bolster conveyeth them into her pocket*" (*Hog Hath Lost His Pearl*, 1567–9); to let loose the Greeks from the Trojan *horse* "*Enter Synon with a stealing pace, holding the key in his hand*" (*2 Iron Age*, 379); for *keys* that control wealth/possessions, in *City Madam* Luke Frugal gains control of his brother's fortune when he gets the *key* of his counting house and re-enters "*with a key*" (3.3.0) that later he must relinquish; in *Old Couple* control of a miser's wealth is passed on when he "*Gives Theodore the keys*" (25); see also *Honest Lawyer*, B3v; *Roman Actor*, 2.1.287; elsewhere *cross* or *golden* keys are linked to the papacy: Pope Alexander under siege "*throws his keys*" (*Devil's Charter*, D4r, also A2v, E1r), the Empress of Babylon is accompanied by "*the one bearing a sword, the other the keys*" (*Whore of Babylon*, 1.1.0); the Lord Martial's office is symbolized by "*his Staff and Key, and other offices borne before him to wait on the King*" (*Royal King*, 25); in *3 Henry VI* Edward gains control of the city of York from the Mayor when he "*Takes his keys*" (Folio 2538, 4.7.37) or "*The Mayor opens the door, and brings the keys in his hand*" (Octavo D7r, [4.7.34]).

kick
the roughly forty uses include (1) humiliation of a coward, (2) punishment of a servant or social inferior, (3) comic business; Aspatia disguised as a man provokes Amintor into a duel when she strikes and then "*kicks him*" (*Maid's Tragedy*, 69) so that he responds "A man can bear / No more and keep his flesh"; locutions include "*kicks her out*" (*Widow's Tears*, 1.3.151), "*Kicks him and thrust him out*" (*Country Girl*, E3r, also E3v), enter "*kicking the Lieutenant*"

(*Doubtful Heir*, C8v), "*beats, and kicks him*" (*New Way to Pay*, 1.1.72; *Queen*, 1749; *Landgartha*, C4r), "*Strike him soundly, and kick him*" (*Northward Ho*, 4.3.180; *Queen's Exchange*, 527); most signals provide only *kicks*/*kicks him*; for a sampling see *Epicœne*, 4.5.298; *Nice Valour*, 168; *Bashful Lover*, 5.1.122; *Great Duke of Florence*, 3.1.382; *Fatal Dowry*, 4.1.133; *City Nightcap*, 96, 109, 151, 167; *Damoiselle*, 435; *City Wit*, 368; *Antipodes*, 298; *Sparagus Garden*, 184, 199; *Tottenham Court*, 146; *Politician*, E2r; *Example*, G1r; *Wedding*, L3v; *Princess*, H3r; *Just Italian*, 252; atypical is "*kicks down their pots*" of **ale** when soldiers surprise a **drunken** watch (*King Leir*, 2497).

kill

of the 180 examples (1) most call for one figure to *kill* another with no further details supplied; variations include (2) *kill* oneself, (3) **offers** to kill another, (4) *offers to kill* oneself; for *kill* oneself see *Locrine*, 2131; *1 Iron Age*, 344; *Antony and Cleopatra*, 2934, 4.14.94; *Rape of Lucrece*, 238; *Second Maiden's Tragedy*, 1356; *Revenge of Bussy*, 5.5.193; *Maid's Tragedy*, 71; *Valentinian*, 69, 71; *Cleopatra*, D7v; for *offers to kill* see *Spanish Tragedy*, 2.1.77; Folio *3 Henry VI*, 3020, 5.5.42; *Poetaster*, 4.6.12; *1 If You Know Not Me*, 228; *New Way to Pay*, 5.1.293; *1 Arviragus and Philicia*, B5v; *2 Passionate Lovers*, L4r, L5v; *Unfortunate Mother*, 150; *Conspiracy*, I1v; *Prisoners*, A10v; for *offers to kill* oneself see *Locrine*, 2153; *Hoffman*, 921–2; *Amends for Ladies*, 3.2.23–4; *Philaster*, 144; *Double Marriage*, 398; *Fair Maid of the Inn*, 215; *Appius and Virginia*, H2v; MS *Poor Man's Comfort*, 1906; *Parliament of Love*, 3.3.106; *Lovesick Court*, 142; *Fool Would Be a Favourite*, B6v; *1 Passionate Lovers*, E7v; *Obstinate Lady*, I2v; *Conspiracy*, K4v; a variation is "*he snatcheth at some weapon to kill himself, is prevented, and led away*" (*Whore of Babylon*, 2.2.185); sometimes a place for the *killing* is specified: "*kills them upon the Altar*" (*Brazen Age*, 183; see also *2 Iron Age*, 390), "*kills him under the sign of the Castle in Saint Albans*" (Quarto *2 Henry VI*, H2r, 5.2.65), "*these four kill the four at the Table, in their Chairs*" (*Revenger's Tragedy*, I3v); when not a **sword**/**dagger** the means of *killing* may be given: "*Kills him with his fist*" (*Valiant Scot*, K2v), "*shoots at him and kills him*" (*Massacre at Paris*, 823; see also *Locrine*, 6–7), "*kills Judas with a stone*" (*Bonduca*, 156; see also *Brazen Age*, 253; *Birth of Merlin*, F2v); **as** [**if**] signals include "*Fall as killed*" (*Captain*, 290), "*as ready to kill him*" (*Sophonisba*, 5.2.43); the spoken word *kill* can be a **sound** effect: "*Cry within, Kill Kill Kill*" (*Two Noble Ladies*, 67, 77, 81; see also *Queen and Concubine*, 99; *Lovesick King*, 98–9);

actions include "*They fight and kill one another*" (*2 Iron Age*, 429; *Two Lamentable Tragedies*, E4v), "*He stabs the King with a knife as he readeth the letter, and then the King getteth the knife and kills him*" (*Massacre at Paris*, 1185), "*They make a dangerous pass at one another the Lady purposely runs between, and is killed by them both*" (*Second Maiden's Tragedy*, 2133–5).

kiss

roughly 360 signals direct figures to *kiss* (a small percentage of the actual onstage *kisses*), with a majority consisting of simply *kiss*/*kisses her*; more than forty figures are directed to *kiss* a **hand**, sometimes with **kneeling** involved: "*The Duke extends his hand, Iacomo kisses it*" (*Grateful Servant*, F4r, also H2v), "*Give him her hand to kiss*" (*Maid of Honour*, 3.3.81; *Renegado*, 1.2.100; *Osmond*, A4r), the barons "*each on his knee kissing the King's hand*" (*King John and Matilda*, 83); *Humorous Courtier* alone provides seven examples of hands being *kissed* (D2v, D3r, I4r, I4v, K1r), including "*They kneel, kiss his hand by turns*" (K1v); for a sampling of the *kissing* of hands see *Edward III*, G2r; *Wily Beguiled*, 912; *Wisdom of Doctor Dodypoll*, 45; *Antonio and Mellida*, 1.1.178; *Travels of Three English Brothers*, 344; *Second Maiden's Tragedy*, 2229; *Queen of Corinth*, 60; *Mad Lover*, 65; *Valiant Welshman*, C4r; *Herod and Antipater*, G2v; *Love's Sacrifice*, 1227; *Queen's Exchange*, 465; *Gentleman of Venice*, B2r; *Imposture*, D2r; *Swaggering Damsel*, B4r; also common are figures who **offer** to kiss (*Fair Em*, 373; *Death of Huntingdon*, 3037; *Travels of Three English Brothers*, 372; *Spanish Gypsy*, F3v, F4v; *Believe as You List*, 2118; *Tale of a Tub*, 2.4.76; *Bride*, 18, 51; *1 Passionate Lovers*, B8v; *Platonic Lovers*, 19); sometimes that offer is rejected: "*He offers to kiss her, she strikes him*" (*English Moor*, 32), "*offering to kiss his hand is disgraced and Haly accepted*" (*Travels of Three English Brothers*, 348–9); variations include "*address to kiss them, and are thrust back*" (*Wits*, 146), "*He offers to Kiss and she starts, wakes, and falls on her knees*" (*Two Noble Ladies*, 1793–4); *kiss* is also linked to **embrace**: "*Embracing and kissing mutually*" (*Roman Actor*, 3.2.128), "*Offers to kiss and embrace her*" (*Maid of Honour*, 5.1.17); see also *Two Lamentable Tragedies*, A2v; *2 Edward IV*, 129; *Antonio's Revenge*, 3.1.0; *Queen and Concubine*, 4.

The nature of the *kiss* is sometimes specified: "*Kiss long*" (*Court Beggar*, 200; see also *Country Girl*, I3v), "*Kiss again double*" (*Messalina*, 870), "*Kiss mutually*" and "*She Kisses him vehemently*" (*Soddered Citizen*, 1326–7, 2233–4); as a sign of homage/abasement a figure may *kiss* a **foot**: "*Offers to kiss her foot*"

(*New Way to Pay*, 2.2.85), "*being presented unto the Pope, kisseth his foot, and then advancing two degrees higher, kisseth his cheek*" (*Devil's Charter*, E1r); see also *Travels of Three English Brothers*, 322; *Herod and Antipater*, F4r; figures are directed to *kiss* a **letter** (*Great Duke of Florence*, 4.1.69; *Landgartha*, H3r), **crown** (*Hamlet*, Q2 H1v, Folio 1996, 3.2.135), poisoned **glove** (*King John and Matilda*, 74), **handkerchief** (*Antonio's Revenge*, 2.1.0), **slipper** (*Humour out of Breath*, 464), **paper** (*King Leir*, 1058; *Two Noble Ladies*, 1546; *New Academy*, 8), **book** (*Whore of Babylon*, DS before Act 1, 44; *Messalina*, 256; *Queen and Concubine*, 22), **picture** (*White Devil*, 2.2.23; *Picture*, 2.2.327), shoe (*Maid of Honour*, 5.1.24), **tomb** (*Antonio's Revenge*, 3.1.0), **cudgel** (*New Way to Pay*, 2.3.28), **sword** (*Famous Victories*, G2r; *Jews' Tragedy*, 940; *Love's Sacrifice*, 2644) or its **hilt** (*Fair Favourite*, 224; *Just Italian*, 236; *Wits*, 214), the **earth** (*Messalina*, 2130); actions include Paris "*kisseth Helen*" but "*she with her hand puts him back*" (*1 Iron Age*, 277), "*as he kisses his hand, he snatches out his sword*" (*Fatal Contract*, I4r), "*Celestine and all the Ladies doing obeisance to the King, who only kisses her*" (*Satiromastix*, 2.1.156), "*Madge with a Devil's vizard roaring, offers to kiss him, and he falls down*" (*Monsieur Thomas*, 138).

kneel, knee

over 300 figures are directed to *kneel/kneel down* (a small percentage of the actual onstage *kneelings*), usually with no further details; *kneeling* can be combined with other actions, especially the **kissing** of a **hand** (*Edward III*, G2r; *Maid of Honour*, 4.4.57; *Antipodes*, 293, 313; *Love and Honour*, 107; *Prisoners*, C8v; *Conspiracy*, M1v; *Doubtful Heir*, D8v; *Humorous Courtier*, D2v, K1v) but also **whispering** (*Roman Actor*, 2.1.161; *'Tis Pity*, 3.6.0); typical are the barons "*each on his knee kissing the King's hand*" (*King John and Matilda*, 83); various figures **offer** to kneel (*Fair Maid of the Inn*, 218; *2 Arviragus and Philicia*, G3r; *Conspiracy*, N1r); a variation is "*About to Kneel he prevents*" (*Soddered Citizen*, 1307–9).

Kneeling is linked specifically to **hearses/tombs** (*Antonio's Revenge*, 3.1.0; *Second Maiden's Tragedy*, 1891–2; *Lovesick Court*, 163; *Lost Lady*, 553), **altars** (*Sophonisba*, 5.1.26; *Brazen Age*, 248; *Two Noble Kinsmen*, L1v, 5.1.136; *Broken Heart*, 5.3.0), prayer/religious rites (*Guy of Warwick*, E1v); representative are "*Coming near the Tomb they all kneel, making show of Ceremony*" (*Love's Sacrifice*, 2738–9), "*discovered kneeling at the Altar*" (*2 Iron Age*, 390, also 426), "*kneels down as to prayers*" (*White Devil*, 2.2.23), "*kneels down and*

holds up his hands to heaven*" (*Arden of Faversham*, 1475–6); in reaction to a **sign** from the gods figures "*fall again upon their faces, then on their knees*" (*Two Noble Kinsmen*, L1v, 5.1.129), in reaction to Jupiter's thunderbolt "*The Ghosts fall on their knees*" (*Cymbeline*, 3127–8, 5.4.92; see also *Silver Age*, 122), a victim of magic "*Kneels with a fearful countenance and so is fixed*" (*Two Noble Ladies*, 497–8); actions involving *kneeling* can include **swords**, other objects, or various appeals: "*kneels, and lays the sword at Aphelia's feet*" (*Fatal Contract*, E4v; see also *Goblins*, 2.3.71), "*kneeling delivers his bill of debt*" (*New Way to Pay*, 4.2.33), "*kneels for mercy*" (*Whore of Babylon*, 2.2.185), "*kneels down for pardon*" (*Four Plays in One*, 321), "*kneels, sues, weeps*" (*Match Me in London*, 5.3.0), "*Kneels down, holds up his hands speaks a little and riseth*" (*Love's Sacrifice*, 2663–4), "*kneeling before Bajazet, and holding his legs*" (*Selimus*, 1469–70), "*the Lord Treasurer kneeling at the Council Table*" (*Sir Thomas Wyatt*, 1.6.0); *kneeling* is linked to formal occasions such as knighting, the elevation to an office, and the reaction to royalty: "*Hieronimo kneels down, and the King creates him Marshal of Spain*" (*Hieronimo*, 1.0), guards "*make a lane kneeling*" for a **mourning** duchess to pass through (*Hoffman*, 1682–4); in response to a legal summons Queen Katherine "*makes no answer, rises out of her Chair, goes about the Court, comes to the King, and kneels at his Feet*" (*Henry VIII*, 1363–5, 2.4.12); other actions include "*kneels amazed, and forgets to speak*" (*Mad Lover*, 5), "*kneels; he takes her up*" (*Queen's Exchange*, 545), "*She Kneels and will not be raised*" (*Soddered Citizen*, 2306–7).

References to *knees* are less common (roughly twenty-five); locutions include bend/**fall** on one's *knees* (*Hoffman*, 1691; *Woman Killed*, 141; *Two Noble Ladies*, 1794; *King John and Matilda*, 63; *Messalina*, 492; *Bride*, 63), on one's *knees* or messengers on their *knees* (*Bashful Lover*, 5.3.169; *Aglaura* 1.3.27); typical are "*They all bend their knees to Caesar, except Caradoc*" (*Valiant Welshman*, I3v; see also *Jews' Tragedy*, 1161), "*brings a bowl of wine, and humbly on his knees offers it to the King*" (*1 Edward IV*, 61), "*falls down on her knees before the Queen fearful and weeping*" (*2 Edward IV*, 126, also 129); abject figures "*go off on their hands, and knees*" (*New Way to Pay*, 1.1.98), and *Fawn* provides "*Zuccone, pursued by Zoya on her knees*" (4.280, also 5.89 for the situation reversed); children can be placed *on* one's *knee*: "*Jupiter dandling Ganymede upon his knee*" (*Dido*, 0), "*She sits down and setting Edward on her knee and Alfred in her arm*" (*Edmond Ironside*, 1507–9); a woman teasing a misogynist "*sits on his knee*" and "*rises from* his knee" (*Woman Hater*, 141); atypical is "*She lies down and leans her elbow on his Knee*" (*Soddered Citizen*, 2244–6).

knife

of the roughly forty calls for a *knife* (1) most refer to a small ***weapon*** concealed until needed, more than half of which are used by female figures, (2) a few cite an implement for eating or other actions; Lucrece is the model for females who either use a *knife* to defend themselves against rape or threaten suicide once ***ravished***, as in "*Offers violence, she draws a knife*" (*King John and Matilda*, 9), "*snatcheth out her knife*" (*Sophonisba*, 4.1.51), "*He offers to force her, and she draws her knife*" (*Catiline*, 2.278), "*with a knife in her hand*" (*Jews' Tragedy*, 2580), "*Throws her and takes her Knife*" (*Little French Lawyer*, 437), "*offers to kill herself with a knife, he holds her*" (*Lovesick Court*, 146); for other *knives* linked to women and violence see *2 Edward IV*, 129; *Antonio's Revenge*, 5.1.0; *Woman Is a Weathercock*, 5.1.13; *Antony and Cleopatra*, 1118, 2.5.73; *Maid's Tragedy*, 70; *Match Me in London*, 3.3.33; *Cupid's Revenge*, 288; *White Devil*, 5.2.52; *Thierry and Theodoret*, 49; *Fair Maid of the Inn*, 215; Quarto *Poor Man's Comfort*, G1r; *City Madam*, 3.1.46; *Novella*, 166; *Messalina*, 752–3; *Sisters*, B6v; other examples of a *knife* linked more generally to violence are "*Titus Andronicus, with a knife*" to cut ***throats*** (*Titus Andronicus*, K1r, 5.2.165; also Folio 1504, 3.2.51), Hieronimo "*with a knife stabs the Duke and himself*" (*Spanish Tragedy*, 4.4.201); see also *Massacre at Paris*, 1185; *Appius and Virginia*, H1r; the kind of *knife* is sometimes specified: "*Chopping knife*" (*Battle of Alcazar* plot, 30), "*wooden Knife*" (*Woman Killed*, 117), "*penknife*" (*Cobbler's Prophecy*, 449), "*pruning knives*" and "*a long knife*" (*If This Be Not a Good Play*, 2.3.0, 5.4.34), "*three Shoemakers' Knives*" (*Soddered Citizen*, 2153), "*sacrificing knife*" (*Amyntas*, 2C1r), "*a bloody knife*" (Quarto *King Lear*, L3r, 5.3.222); the temptation to commit suicide is symbolized in "*The evil angel tempteth him, offering the knife and rope*" (*Looking Glass for London*, 2064–5), "*A Halter, a Knife, a Vial*" (*Novella*, 146); examples of a *knife* linked to eating are "*with Napkins on their arms and knives in their hands*" (*Woodstock*, 3–4), "*a table and knives ready for oysters*" (*Parson's Wedding*, 432); notable uses of a *knife* include "*a bleeding heart upon a knife's point*" (*Golden Age*, 20), a "Gelder" who "*whets his knife*" for a threatened castration (*Court Beggar*, 244), a figure who "*shows a keen knife which he pulls out of his sleeve*" (*Fatal Contract*, H4v); for more *knives* see *Warning for Fair Women*, A2r;

Tom a Lincoln, 35–6; *Witch of Edmonton*, 4.2.69; *Just Italian*, 268; *Guardian*, 3.6.142; see also ***dagger***, ***poniard***.

knock, knocking

a common signal (roughly 280 examples) used (1) mostly for an offstage ***sound***, (2) occasionally for an onstage action, and (3) in several atypical directions; perhaps not surprising but nevertheless significant, the sound of a *knock* from ***within*** is virtually always acknowledged onstage; typically the context is provided by the response and the signal is simply *knock*, with some plays using the device a number of times; for a sampling of this basic direction see *1 Henry VI*, 1435, 3.2.12; Q2 *Romeo and Juliet*, G4v, 3.3.70, 73, 75, 77; *Englishmen for My Money*, 1334, 1464, 1500, 2546; *Julius Caesar*, 946, 2.1.303; *Family of Love*, E1v, F1v; *Troilus and Cressida*, H1v, 2293, 4.2.34; H2r, 2300, 4.2.39; *Westward Ho*, 5.4.103, 125, 148, 158; *Macbeth*, 727, 2.2.262; 732, 2.2.66; 737, 2.2.70; 754, 2.3.3; 761, 2.3.19, and more; *Volpone*, 1.3.67, 1.4.158; *Alchemist*, 2.4.18, 3.3.75, 4.5.66, 5.1.32, 5.4.137, and more; *Ram Alley*, E2r, H1v; *Cymbeline*, 1043, 2.3.76; *Night Walker*, 315, 357; *Faithful Friends*, 1038; *Captives*, 1030; *Inconstant Lady*, 4.2.7, 10; *Traitor*, 3.1.170, 5.1.162; *Weeding of Covent Garden*, 12, 33; in *Second Maiden's Tragedy* the bookkeeper noted *Knock* (1355, 1359) and *Knock within* (1378–9); *knock within* is also very common (*Julius Caesar*, 680, 2.1.59; *Hoffman*, 548; *Macbeth*, 717, 2.2.54; 743, 2.3.0; *Greene's Tu Quoque*, K4v; *Atheist's Tragedy*, 2.5.74; *Women Beware Women*, 3.2.92; *Anything for a Quiet Life*, C2r; *Spanish Curate*, 88, 106; *Welsh Ambassador*, 1962, 2009; *Inconstant Lady*, 3.4.131; *Launching of the Mary*, 2056, 2127, 2154); *knock **without*** (i.e., within) also occurs (*Volpone*, 1.1.82, 3.8.15, 5.4.47; *Alchemist*, 1.2.162, 3.2.159; *Inconstant Lady*, 4.2.4; *Emperor of the East*, 3.4.39); *knock at the **door*** sometimes signals a sound within, as in *Atheist's Tragedy* when a "*Knock at the door*" (4.5.50) is acknowledged "what bouncing's that?"; elsewhere "*The Duke of York knocks at the door and crieth*" (*Richard II*, I2r, 5.3.38), "*Peto knocks at door*" (*2 Henry IV*, E3r, 2.4.351, also K2v, 5.3.70); see also *New Way to Pay*, 2.2.31; *Maid's Revenge*, F1r; *Humorous Courtier*, I2v; *City Match*, 258; *Example*, A3r; *Conspiracy*, L2r; *Fair Favourite*, 244.

Sometimes the figure *knocking* is onstage: "*Enter Maquarelle, knocking at the Lady's door*" (*Malcontent*, 4.1.0), "*Bernardo knocketh at the study*" (*Devil's Charter*, I3r), "*Enter Merry knocking at the door, and Rachel comes down*" (*Two Lamentable Tragedies*, C4v, also G1r), "*Enter*

Malipiero, who knocks at a Door, to him a Servant" (*Gentleman of Venice*, A4r); see also *Fedele and Fortunio*, 1186; *Gentleman Usher*, 4.1.0; *Hog Hath Lost His Pearl*, 2–3; more than one *knock* is sometimes required: "*They knock again, and call out to talk with Faustus*" (*Doctor Faustus*, B 1679); see also *Lust's Dominion*, 1.1.138; *Messalina*, 697; other signals for a *knock* include "*They knock and Titus opens his study door*" (*Titus Andronicus*, I3r, 5.2.8), "*He speaks through the keyhole, the other knocking*" (*Alchemist*, 3.5.58), "*Knocks heard*" (Q2 *Bussy D'Ambois*, 5.3.82), "*Knocks, and Clarislona looks out at the window*" (*Knave in Grain*, 313), "*knocks, and enters*" (*New Way to Pay*, 1.2.47), "*knocks violently*" (*Wizard*, 2233), "*knocks hastily*" (*Aglaura*, 1.6.31); see also *Mad World*, 4.4.0; *Puritan*, E2v; *Silver Age*, 117; *Queen's Exchange*, 510; *Weeding of Covent Garden*, 33.

 Knock occurs in some unusual contexts, each different; a figure pretending to be blind "*Goes knocking with his staff*" (*Downfall of Huntingdon*, 1498), another is directed to "*Sit down and knock your head*" (*Friar Bacon*, 1612–14); Hieronimo famously "*knocks up the curtain*" (*Spanish Tragedy*, 4.3.0); in the annotated quarto of *Two Merry Milkmaids* a bookkeeper wrote "*Knock Act*" (E2r) before the first *entr'acte* entertainment, probably as a reminder to call up the performers; "*Knock for School. Enter the Dance*" in *Two Noble Kinsmen* (G3v, 3.5.137) may carry a similar meaning.

knock down

the consequence of a *fight*: "*Set upon him. He knocks some down*" (*Downfall of Huntingdon*, 474, also 990), "*They fight. Anthynus knock down one Outlaw*" (*Queen's Exchange*, 487), "*Enter Soldiers, knock him down, hurry him away in a sound*" (*Valiant Scot*, K1r); see also *Sir John Oldcastle*, 23; *Fatal Contract*, H1r.

L

ladder

cited infrequently but may have been used in a large number of scenes, particularly (1) romantic trysts (where the *ladders* are made of *rope/cords*), (2) sieges, (3) *executions*; romantic situations call for "*the ladder of cords*" (Q1 *Romeo and Juliet*, F3r, 3.2.31; Q2 provides only "*cords,*" G1v), "*a ladder of ropes*" (*May Day*, 3.3.0); more elaborate are "*He throws up a ladder of cords, which she makes fast to some part of the window; he ascends, and at top falls*" (*Insatiate Countess*, 3.1.42),

"*Albert ascends, and being on the top of the ladder, puts out the candle*" (*Hog Hath Lost His Pearl*, 265–6); "*scaling ladders*" are specified in two siege scenes (*1 Henry VI*, 683–4, 2.1.7; Folio *Henry V*, 1082, 3.1.0); execution scenes provide a condemned man who "*mounts up the ladder*" (*2 Edward IV*, 136), another who "*on the ladder*" gives a farewell **kiss** to his wife (*Sir Thomas More*, 680); *Two Lamentable Tragedies* signals an entrance "*to execution with Officers with Halberds, the Hangman with a ladder, etc.,*" "*Go up the ladder,*" "*Turn off the Ladder*" (K1v–K2r); to observe a tournament two figures "*go up the ladders*" (*Soliman and Perseda*, B2v), and for the haughty Queen Elinor's **descent** an attendant sets "*a ladder to the side of the litter*" (*Edward I*, 1015); the most elaborate *ladder* sequence is in *Duchess of Suffolk* where two tilers enter "*going to work with a tray of Tiles and a Ladder,*" one "*Goeth up the Ladder and works,*" a fugitive subsequently "*Shakes the Ladder*" and "*Gets up the Ladder*" (C3r–v, C4r, H1v).

lame

linked to soldiers back from the wars: "*Enter Rafe being lame*" (*Shoemakers' Holiday*, 3.2.54), "*Enter lame legged Soldier*" (*Wonder of a Kingdom*, 4.2.41); see also *False One*, 337; *City Wit*, 295; *Cobbler's Prophecy* calls for Mars's "*lame Porter*" to enter "*in rusty armor, and a broken bill*" (734–5); see also **stump**.

lament

a seldom called for demonstration of sorrow, with every occurrence but one (*1 Edward IV*, 84) in a **dumb show**: "*Cleon shows Pericles the tomb, whereat Pericles makes lamentation*" (*Pericles*, G3r, 4.4.22), "*The Poisoner, with some two or three Mutes comes in again, seeming to lament with her*" (Folio *Hamlet*, 1998–9; Q2 "*condole,*" H1v, 3.2.135), "*they lament over the bier*" (*Four Plays in One*, 333); for more see *Tom a Lincoln*, 170; *White Devil*, 2.2.37; *Silver Age*, 96; see also **mourning**.

lamp

a seldom cited source of **light**, as opposed to the widely used **candle**, **taper**, and **torch** or the less common **lantern**; a figure **reads** a **letter** "*at the lamp which burneth in the Temple*" (*Fedele and Fortunio*, 436–7), Friar Bacon appears with "*a book in his hand, and a lamp lighted by him*" (*Friar Bacon*, 1562) for his scene with the brazen **head**, a figure in **prison** is "*laden with many Irons, a Lamp burning by him*" (*Martyred Soldier*, 206); a *lamp* is central to the action in *Love's Mistress* where to **discover** the identity of her lover (Cupid) Psyche enters "*in night attire, with a*

Lamp and a Razor" (120) but inadvertently awakens him with drops of "scalding oil."

lance

either a horseman's long wooden shaft with an iron or steel head or a somewhat shorter *spear*; given the difficulty of maneuvering the longer *weapon*, perhaps the shorter one is usually called for: "*all cry, Martius, Martius, cast up their Caps and Lances*" (*Coriolanus*, 794–5, 1.10.40), "*Both the Armies make ready to join battle, but Hector steps betwixt them holding up his Lance*" (*1 Iron Age*, 296, also 322), "*the Dwarf bearing Sir Pergamus's lance and shield*" (*Faithful Friends*, 2823–4, also 1049); see also *Three Lords of London*, G1v, G2v, I2v; *Edward III*, G1v; *Jews' Tragedy*, 1076–8; Henslowe's inventory lists eight *lances* (*Diary*, App. 2, 56).

lane

see *make a lane*

lantern

used to indicate *night*/darkness on a *stage* with no variable lighting (along with the *taper*, *candle*, and *torch*); the *lantern* can appear in any night scene, as when carried by the watch in *When You See Me* (945–7) or a carrier in *1 Henry IV* (C2r, 2.1.0), but is often linked to surreptitious activity such as clandestine visits at night to a graveyard or *tomb*; in both quartos of *Romeo and Juliet* Friar Laurence arrives at the Capulet tomb with a *lantern* (Q1, K2r, Q2, L3v, 5.3.120); for comparable uses of *lanterns* see *Old Wives Tale*, 27; *Atheist's Tragedy*, 2.3.14, 62; *Night Walker*, 341; *Greene's Tu Quoque*, L2r; *If This Be Not a Good Play*, 3.2.0; a *dark* lantern (with a sliding panel to dim the light) or "*a Thieves' Lantern*" (*Law Tricks*, 185) is even more likely to be linked to clandestine activity, as when carried by a figure waiting in the dark to commit a murder (*'Tis Pity*, 3.7.0); see also *Knight of Malta*, 142; *Wits*, 210; *Novella*, 106; *Queen's Exchange*, 535; *Wizard*, 2202–4; *Distresses* calls for a *dark lantern* and later directs "*shuts the lantern*" (292–3).

lap

figures (1) lie, *sleep*, *fall* in another's *lap*, (2) *enter* with objects in their *laps*; locutions include "*Lies down on her Lap*" (*Guardian*, 5.2.38), "*They sit: Sneakup's head in the Lady's lap*" (*City Wit*, 347), "*sits down with Wanton in his lap*" (*Parson's Wedding*, 481); in *Insatiate Countess* a figure "*dances a Lavolta, or a Galliard, and in*

the midst of it falleth into the bride's lap, but straight leaps up, and danceth it out*" (2.1.154); twice a man is *discovered* sleeping in a woman's *lap* (*Old Fortunatus*, 3.1.356; *Rebellion*, 67); entrances include nymphs "*with flowers in their laps*" (*Brazen Age*, 235), a maid "*with her lap full of things*" (*Parson's Wedding*, 455), the nurse "*with the ladder of cords in her lap*" (Q1 *Romeo and Juliet*, F3r, 3.2.31); *Costly Whore* provides "*Flings down her lap full of Petitions*" (280), and in *Old Wives Tale* "*A head comes up full of gold, she combs it into her lap*" (782); atypical is a *lappet* (the loose fold of a *garment*): "*The Friar spreads the lappet of his gown and falls to dice*" (*Edward I*, 1733).

laugh, laughing

signaled roughly forty times, often with no more than the basic term (*Taming of a Shrew*, B3v; *Patient Grissil*, 3.2.100; *Fawn*, 5.25; *Wit without Money*, 170; *Mad Lover*, 27; *Virgin Martyr*, 3.2.124; *Dick of Devonshire*, 1680; *Jews' Tragedy*, 1454; *English Traveller*, 27; *Country Girl*, G3r; *Hollander*, 101; *Bride*, 22; *Parson's Wedding*, 515); more detailed examples are "*they point at her, and laugh*" (*Woman Is a Weathercock*, 5.2.5–6), "*laughs having read the letter*" (Folio *Every Man In*, 1.3.56), "*runs up and down laughing*" (*Two Noble Ladies*, 1538), "*laughs and looks off*" (*English Moor*, 67), "*A confused noise within of laughing and singing*" (*Jovial Crew*, 386, also 423), "*laughing to himself*" (*Selimus*, 1878), "*aside and laugh*" (*Sparagus Garden*, 146), "*falls into a laughter*" (*Swaggering Damsel*, H1r); see also *Blurt*, 4.2.36; *Jack Drum's Entertainment*, B4v; *Satiromastix*, 3.1.236; *Silver Age*, 124; *Brazen Age*, 237; *Herod and Antipater*, K1r; *Fancies Chaste and Noble*, 1785; *Twins*, D4r; some directions link *laughter* to *devils*/evil: "*Alexander is in extreme torment and groaneth whilst the devil laugheth at him*" (*Devil's Charter*, M1v, also L3v), "*Devils run laughing over the stage*" (*Seven Champions*, H1r, also C1r, G3v), "*Vice laughing*" (*Old Fortunatus*, 4.1.136); see also *If This Be Not a Good Play*, 3.2.175, 5.4.34; *Match Me in London*, 5.3.0; *White Devil*, 2.2.23.

laurel

a sign of honor or achievement, usually for victors in *battle*: "*Men with boughs of Laurel singing before the Duke*" (*Imposture*, B3v), "*Captains with Laurels, Domitian, in his Triumphant Chariot*" (*Roman Actor*, 1.4.13), "*Matilda (a wreath of laurel on her head, in her chariot drawn through them)*" (*Bashful Lover*, 4.3.68); "*Crown him with Laurel*" is the reward for a dead hero (*Rape of Lucrece*, 253); variations include "*dukes' crowns upon laurel wreaths*" as part of a *masque* (*Malcontent*,

5.5.66), "*four Virgins with branches of Laurel in their hands*" to appeal for mercy (*1 Tamburlaine*, 1781); see also *Old Fortunatus*, 1.3.0, 5.2.260; *Virgin Martyr*, 1.1.118; *Jews' Tragedy*, 6.

lavolta

a lively *dance* with much jumping: "*a Lavolta which the Masquers are to dance*" (*Blurt*, 2.2.239), "*He leads him a Lavolta*" (*Wit of a Woman*, 1024); see also *Insatiate Countess*, 2.1.154.

lead, leading, led

widely used (roughly 250 examples) when figures *exit* and especially *enter*: "*Enter Master Gresham, leading in the Ambassador*" (*2 If You Know Not Me*, 297), "*the Prologue leads Massinissa's troops over the stage, and departs*" (*Sophonisba*, Prologue.29), "*Enter Dorothea in a white robe, crowns upon her robe, a Crown upon her head, led in by the Angel*" (*Virgin Martyr*, 5.2.219), "*Enter Squire leading a man with a glass of Lotion in his hand, and the Dwarf leading a woman, with Diet-bread and Drink*" (*Knight of the Burning Pestle*, 205, also 203, 204); many of the figures being *led* are *prisoners*: "*led Prisoner*" (*Virgin Martyr*, 4.2.61), "*led in chains*" (*Doctor Faustus*, B 894; *Martyred Soldier*, 179), "*led by two holding pistols*" (*If This Be Not a Good Play*, 5.3.44), "*with Halberds, led to Execution*" (Folio *Richard III*, 3371–2, 5.1.0); for a sampling see *Titus Andronicus*, H4v, 5.1.19; *Trial of Chivalry*, I2r; *Old Fortunatus*, 1.1.63; *2 Edward IV*, 180; *Alarum for London*, 1467; *Puritan*, G4v; *Sophonisba*, 2.3.47; *Silver Age*, 87; *Philaster*, 138/413; *Double Marriage*, 364; *Roman Actor*, 1.4.13; *Believe as You List*, 2199–2200, 2322–3; *Hengist*, 2.3.11–12, 5.2.210–11; *Two Noble Ladies*, 1240–1; *Dick of Devonshire*, 1957; *Just Italian*, 273; also *led* are the weak/*wounded*/dying: "*Enter old Talbot led*" (*1 Henry VI*, 2229–30, 4.7.0), "*led in hurt*" (*Chaste Maid*, 5.1.6), "*wounded and led*" (*Love and Honour*, 112), "*Enter Katherine Dowager, sick, led between Griffith, her Gentleman Usher, and Patience her Woman*" (*Henry VIII*, 2448–50, 4.2.0, also 2767, 4.2.173); see also *Death of Huntingdon*, 1749–50; *Look about You*, 1615; Quarto *King Lear*, H2r, 4.1.9; *Antony and Cleopatra*, 2049, 3.11.24; *Imposture*, B3v; figures in *dances*, *weddings*, and other *ceremonies* often are *led*: "*A dance of Shepherds and Shepherdesses; Pan leading the men, Ceres the maids*" (*Prophetess*, 386; see also *Nice Valour*, 157, 188), "*Hippolita the Bride, led by Theseus*" (*Two Noble Kinsmen*, B1r, 1.1.0), "*leading Hermione as a bride*" (*2 Iron Age*, 426; *Noble Spanish Soldier*, 5.4.0), "*Ostorius leading Artesia Crowned*" (*Birth of Merlin*, C1r); see also *Edward*

I, 1927; *Fawn*, 5.139; *Faithful Friends*, 2817–18; *Fatal Contract*, E3v; *Wasp*, 478; figures enter *leading* an animal such as a *dog* (*Downfall of Huntingdon*, 2293; Quarto *Every Man Out*, 1868), *goat* (*1 If You Know Not Me*, 230), *monkey* (*Eastward Ho*, A4r).

The most common locution is *lead in*: "*soldiers leading in three kings bound*" and Dioclesian "*leading in Artemia*" (*Virgin Martyr*, 1.1.118); see also *Lust's Dominion*, 5.1.162; *Sophonisba*, 2.3.47; *Chaste Maid*, 5.1.6; *If This Be Not a Good Play*, 4.4.0; *Virgin Martyr*, 1.1.118, 5.2.219; *Believe as You List*, 2199–2200, 2322–3; *Renegado*, 4.2.70; *Bondman*, 1.3.81, 4.3.63; *Unnatural Combat*, 2.1.78; also to be found are *lead off* (*Edmond Ironside*, 2063; *Four Prentices*, 244; *Renegado*, 3.5.110; *Roman Actor*, 2.1.239; *Conspiracy*, K4v), *forth* (*1 Edward IV*, 56; *Renegado*, 4.2.0; *Sparagus Garden*, 193), *away* (*Sir Thomas More*, 502; *Sir John Oldcastle*, 2142–3; *2 Edward IV*, 173; *Malcontent*, 4.3.67; *Whore of Babylon*, 2.2.185; *Match Me in London*, 2.4.86; *Swetnam*, F3r; *Parson's Wedding*, 480), *out* (Folio *3 Henry VI*, 2295, 4.3.57; *Sir Thomas More*, 818; *Warning for Fair Women*, I1r; *2 Edward IV*, 176, 178; *Bussy D'Ambois*, 4.2.127; *Revenge of Bussy*, 4.3.107; *Bloody Brother*, 312, 313; *Hengist*, DS before 4.3, 4–5; *Jews' Tragedy*, 865; *Country Captain*, D10v; *Damoiselle*, 459; *English Moor*, 44); the manner of *leading* is rarely specified; one figure is "*led by the hair by two Soldiers*" (*Death of Huntingdon*, 1715–16) and several are *led* by the *hand*: "*leading in his hand an ancient Matron*" (*Cymbeline*, 3065–8, 5.4.29), "*leading their ladies hand in hand*" (*Dead Man's Fortune*, 61), "*Chartley leading Gratiana by the Arm*" (*Wise Woman of Hogsdon*, 329), "*with his Rapier drawn in one hand, leading Maria seeming affrighted in the other*" (*Lust's Dominion*, 3.2.0); see also *Custom of the Country*, 385; figures can be *led between*/betwixt others: "*pinioned and led betwixt two Officers*" (*2 Edward IV*, 175), two consuls as an escort "*leading Brutus betwixt them*" (*Caesar and Pompey*, 2.4.90), "*led off betwixt them*" (*1 Arviragus and Philicia*, A8v); see also *Cobbler's Prophecy*, 1629–30; *Puritan*, H3r; *Northward Ho*, 1.2.0; *Devil's Law Case*, 2.4.0; *Queen and Concubine*, 22; *Swaggering Damsel*, I2v; examples that do not involve an entrance/exit include "*Lead him once or twice about, whipping him, and so Exit*" (*Three Ladies of London*, F2r), "*leads him aside*" (*Humorous Courtier*, I3v; *Love and Honour*, 144; *Platonic Lovers*, 14).

leaf, leaves

(1) most often *leaves* from a *tree* or vine but also (2) pages of *paper*; examples of the former are "*Oaken-leaved garlands*" (*Guardian*, 5.1.0), "*a tree with green and*

withered leaves mingled together" (*Old Fortunatus*, 1.3.0),
a ***cup*** with "*Bay leaves, whereupon are written the lots*"
(*Alphonsus of Germany*, C4r), Bacchus "*dressed in Vine
leaves*" (*Summer's Last Will*, 967), a **masque** of
Bacchanalians "*girt with Vine leaves*" (*Messalina*,
2201–2); *leaves* of paper are required for a poet who
enters "*with leaves in his hand*" (*Northward Ho*, 4.1.0), a
figure who "*turns over the leaves and reads these entries*"
(*Conspiracy*, D3v).

leap

occurs in a variety of contexts to describe a wide
range of actions; figures *leap over* (*Cobbler's Prophecy*,
1021), *leap in/into* (*Prisoners*, C7v), *leap **off/down** from
above* (*Old Fortunatus*, 4.1.90; *Turk*, 1792), through
the **trapdoor** (*Old Wives Tale*, 909; *Fortune by Land and
Sea*, 395), and from a **scaffold** (*Sir Thomas More*, 635);
examples include "*The French leap over the walls in
their shirts*" (*1 Henry VI*, 720, 2.1.38), "*leaps over the stool
and runs away*" (*2 Henry VI*, C3r, 903, 2.1.150), "*Laertes
leaps into the grave*" and "*Hamlet leaps in after Laertes*"
(Q1 *Hamlet*, I1v, 5.1.250, 258), "*the Duchess of Burgundy
with young Frederick in her hand, who being pursued of the
French, leaps into a River, leaving the child upon the bank*"
(*Weakest Goeth*, 4–6), "*mounts the Scaffold, submits her
head to the block, and suddenly rising up leaps down*"
(*Messalina*, 2592–4), "*Leaps up the scaffold. Castabella
leaps after him*" (*Atheist's Tragedy*, 5.2.130); other locutions are "*leap out of the bed*" (*Sophonisba*, 5.1.3), "*leaps
from whispering with the boy*" (Folio *Every Man Out*,
2.1.143), "*leaps off from his couch*" and "*leaps out from
where Mosca had placed him*" (*Volpone*, 3.7.139, 267),
"*leaping in great joy*" (*If This Be Not a Good Play*, 5.4.0),
"*leap from out the Horse*" (*2 Iron Age*, 380), "*leaps from his
Chariot*" (*Captain Thomas Stukeley*, 2509); see also
2 Troublesome Reign, A3r; *Warning for Fair Women*, D1r,
I4r; *Insatiate Countess*, 2.1.154; *Witch of Edmonton*,
2.1.227; *Staple of News*, 1.2.87, 2.2.62; *Wits*, 175.

leave

most of the roughly sixty uses involve figures who
(1) *leave **behind*** or **part** from another figure/object,
(2) take their *leave*; figures often simply *leave*
another: "*vanquisheth and disarmeth Iachimo, and then
leaves him*" (*Cymbeline*, 2896–7, 5.2.0); in all three versions of the **dumb show** in *Hamlet* (3.2.135) the queen
leaves the **sleeping** king (Q1 F3r, Q2 H1r, Folio 1995);
see also *Cobbler's Prophecy*, 1022; *Sir Thomas Wyatt*,
4.3.51; *Wit of a Woman*, 1025; *Histriomastix*, B4r, G1r;
Golden Age, 35, 52; *2 Iron Age*, 411; *Maid's Tragedy*, 71;
Jews' Tragedy, 1109; *Queen's Exchange*, 505; *Grateful

Servant, I2r; *Prisoners*, B5r, B7r; an alternative is **exit**
leaving someone *behind* (*Fedele and Fortunio*, 1368;
Summer's Last Will, 116; *Antonio and Mellida*, 4.1.128;
Travels of Three English Brothers, 391; *Whore of Babylon*,
DS before Act 1, 41); occasionally the *leaving* does not
involve an exit: "*leaves Clara, and goes to Maria*" (*Court
Secret*, B5v), "*leaves Tullius and runs to Melintus and
parts them*" (*Claracilla*, F2r); objects *left* behind
include a **disguise** (*Atheist's Tragedy*, 4.3.69), **cloak**
(*Dutch Courtesan*, 4.5.20), **scroll** of **paper** (*Herod and
Antipater*, C3r, F3v), child (*Duchess of Suffolk*, F2v), **lion**
skin (*1 Troublesome Reign*, C4r), with the *leaving* often a
result of **haste** or **pursuit**: "*leave the pickax and spades
behind*" (*Two Maids of More-Clacke*, G1r), "*They all run
away … leaving the booty behind them*" (*1 Henry IV*, C4v,
2.2.101), "*they fly, leaving their Clothes behind*" (*1 Henry
VI*, 766, 2.1.77); variations include "*leaving her bed*"
(*Vow Breaker*, 4.2.208), an emperor who "*leaving his
State, offers to embrace* **spirits** (*Doctor Faustus*, B
1298–9), "*Leaves the Torch burning*" (*Messalina*,
2252–3), "*leaves the hammer sticking in his head*" (*Two
Lamentable Tragedies*, C4r); for figures who take *leave*
of others see *Battle of Alcazar*, 26–7; *Edward I*, 2146;
Satiromastix, 3.1.266; *Wit of a Woman*, 855–6, 862;
Pericles, E1r, 3.Chorus.14; *1 If You Know Not Me*, 216,
239; *Travels of Three English Brothers*, 320; *Revenge of
Bussy*, 1.1.144; *Silver Age*, 96; *Four Plays in One*, 321;
Hengist, DS before 1.2, 7; *Herod and Antipater*, I4v;
Unnatural Combat, 2.1.114; *Love's Sacrifice*, 1152; *City
Wit*, 358; typical is "*young Lords, taking leave for the
Florentine war*" (*All's Well*, 594–5, 2.1.0); atypical are
"*leave open the stocks*" (*Bartholomew Fair*, 4.6.163),
"*gives the Tailor leave to talk*" (*Staple of News*, 1.2.53).

leg

found in (1) **make a leg**, a male version of **curtsy**, (2)
property *legs*, (3) a scattering of other actions and
usages; examples of *legs* for acts of courtesy include
"*Snatches off his hat and makes legs to him*" (*Revenger's
Tragedy*, G3r), "*legging and scraping*" (*Swaggering
Damsel*, F2v), "*compliments with Faces and Legs*" (*Two
Merry Milkmaids*, C3r); *legs* as stage properties are
found in "*He pulls off his leg*" (*Doctor Faustus*, B 1561, A
1206), "*He draws him in by the leg*" and re-enters "*with
a leg*" (*Orlando Furioso*, 751, 758), "*gnawing on a Capon's
Leg*" (*Woman Is a Weathercock*, 5.1.65–6); Henslowe's
inventory includes "*Kent's wooden leg*" (*Diary*, App.
2, 69), "*one great horse with his legs*" (85); see also
Two Lamentable Tragedies, E2r, F3v, F4v; actions
include "*Pointing to his leg*" (*Alarum for London*, 775),
"*Shakes his legs*" (*Inconstant Lady*, 3.4.4), "*kneeling

before Bajazet, and holding his legs" (Selimus, 1469–70),
"Whilst they are saluting, Sir Owen gets to Emulo's leg and
pulls down his Boot" (Patient Grissil, 2.1.140), "As they
open the stocks, Wasp puts his shoe on his hand, and slips it
in for his leg" (Bartholomew Fair, 4.6.77); variations
include "a swaddled leg" (Damoiselle, 457), "a great
bumbasted leg" (Gentleman Usher, 2.1.28), a "lame legged
Soldier" (Wonder of a Kingdom, 4.2.41), "wet on his legs"
(Merry Devil of Edmonton, E3r), "wounded in the Leg with
an Arrow" (Jews' Tragedy, 862–3); see also Amorous War,
E2v; Landgartha, E3r.

lesson

a piece of **music** to be performed, as in "Consort a
Lesson" (Thracian Wonder, D1v); **recorders** or especially
cornets are usually specified: "A solemn lesson upon the
Recorders" (Antipodes, 335); see also Faithful Friends,
2925; Virgin Martyr, 1.1.118; Two Noble Ladies, 1541.

let

appears as (1) an auxiliary verb or an equivalent to
"permit, allow," usually in constructions such as lets
go, lets **in**, lets **down**, most commonly lets **fall**, (2) in
the imperative, a usage not to be found after the
early 1590s; examples of the former include "She lets
him take off her helmet" (Two Noble Ladies, 1985), "lets
her go" (Princess, A3v), "He lets in Angelo, and locks the
Door" (Captain, 299), "Hoist him up and let him down
again" (Alarum for London, 1007), "lets down a Rope"
(City Wit, 361); more plentiful are examples of let fall,
usually linked to **weapons**: "Amazed lets fall the
Daggers" (Alphonsus of Germany, I3v); see also Quarto
Richard III, B2v, [1.2.182]; King Leir, 1739, 1743; Thierry
and Theodoret, 47; White Devil, 5.2.52; Herod and
Antipater, B4v; Love's Sacrifice, 2609; Seven Champions,
I4r; Conspiracy, I2r; other objects let fall are a **paper**
(Quarto 2 Henry VI, A2v, 1.1.52), **scarf** (Wit at Several
Weapons, 102), **jewel** (Court Secret, B1r), **image** (Fedele
and Fortunio, 600), **gloves** (Spanish Tragedy, 1.4.99;
Quarto 2 Henry VI, B4r, 1.3.137), "lets the Cabinet fall
out of the Window" (Novella, 151).

The imperative let is found regularly in the 1580s
and early 1590s but not thereafter; Locrine provides
thirteen examples: "let there come forth a Lion running
after a Bear" (4–5), "Let him write a little and then read"
(341), "Let them fight" (797, 832), "Let her offer to kill
herself" (2153); see also 432, 833–4, 963–4, 1353–8,
1629–30, 1669–70, 2064; other multiple uses are
found in Three Ladies of London (B1r, B4v, E1v, E3r,
F2v), Wounds of Civil War (120, 252, 258, 333–5), and
include "Let Fraud make as though he would strike him,

but let Dissimulation step between them" (Three Ladies of
London, A3v), "Let young Marius chase Pompey over the
stage" (Wounds of Civil War, 333–4); other examples
are "let a smoke arise" (Cobbler's Prophecy, 1565), "let the
chambers be discharged" (Battle of Alcazar, 1300), "let
Venus be let down from the top of the Stage" and "let a
chair come down from the top of the stage, and draw her up"
(Alphonsus of Aragon, 2–3, 2109–10); see also Fedele and
Fortunio, 1807–8; Orlando Furioso, 1285–6; occasionally the imperative let is preceded by **here**: "Here let
the Potter's wife go to the Queen" (Edward I, 2281), "Here
let him counterfeit the passion of love by looks and gesture"
(Fedele and Fortunio, 795–6).

letter

a widely used property and plot device cited in over
400 directions, typically **enter** with a letter: "Macbeth's
Wife alone with a Letter" (Macbeth, 348, 1.5.0), "the King
of France with Letters, and diverse Attendants" (All's Well,
238–9, 1.2.0), "Hangman with a letter" (Spanish
Tragedy, 3.7.18), "with a Letter in each hand" (2 Arviragus
and Philicia, F5v), "sad, with a Letter in his hand" (Cure
for a Cuckold, B3r), "an open letter in his hands" (New
Academy, 8); see also Love's Labour's Lost, A4v, 1.1.180;
Michaelmas Term, 2.3.0; Cupid's Whirligig, 2.1.0;
Amends for Ladies, 2.1.16; News from Plymouth, 182; two
playhouse manuscripts have a bookkeeper's call for
a player to enter "with a letter" (Believe as You List,
1223–5; John of Bordeaux, 466–7); elsewhere a figure
enters to **deliver** a letter: "Clown with a Letter, and
Fabian" (Twelfth Night, 2448, 5.1.280), "a Messenger,
booted, with letters, and kneeling gives them to the King"
(1 Edward IV, 48; see also Q2 Hamlet, L3v, 4.7.35;
Antony and Cleopatra, 211, 1.2.117), "a post with a letter
and a bag of gold" (Friar Bacon, 1494–5), "Deliver letters"
(Look about You, 22); for similar locutions see Warning
for Fair Women, H3r; Knight of the Burning Pestle, 214;
Ram Alley, A3r; Coxcomb, 357; Revenge of Bussy, 3.2.60;
More Dissemblers, B4v; Duchess of Suffolk, A3r; Soddered
Citizen, 2646–7; Telltale, 978–9; Politician, C4r; Sophy,
1.2.30, 3.155; figures enter **reading** a letter: "Hotspur
solus reading a Letter" (1 Henry IV, C4v, 2.3.0; see also
Jew of Malta, 1302), "Mister Flower at one door reading a
letter from Ferdinand, at the other Mistress Flower, with a
Letter from Anthony" (Fair Maid of the Exchange, 58); for
more see Edmond Ironside, 1739; Quarto 2 Henry VI,
F4v, [4.4.0]; Warning for Fair Women, E4r;
Charlemagne, 1765; Antony and Cleopatra, 428, 1.4.0;
Pericles, D3r, 2.5.0; Cymbeline, 1468, 3.2.0; Amends for
Ladies, 2.3.1–2; Captives, 1251–2; King John and Matilda,
37; Queen, 788; sometimes a letter is read onstage:

"*Opens the Letter, and reads*" (*Julius Caesar*, 664, 2.1.45),
"*a Page, delivering a letter to Sophonisba which she privately reads*" (*Sophonisba*, 3.1.60), "*reads the letter,
frowns and stamps*" (*King Leir*, 1172), "*reads the letter to
himself*" (*Cruel Brother*, 121); see also Folio *3 Henry VI*,
1911, 3.3.166; *Alphonsus of Germany*, E1r; *Love's Labour's
Lost*, F1r, 4.3.193; Quarto *Merry Wives*, B4r, 2.1.0;
Romeo and Juliet, Q1 B3r, Q2 B3v, 1.2.64; *Soddered
Citizen*, 1301–6; in some of these cases and elsewhere
the reading is done aloud, signaled either by "*Letter*"
before the text (*Edmond Ironside*, 1275; Q2 *Hamlet*,
E4r, 2.2.115; *Measure for Measure*, 1985, 4.2.119; *All's
Well*, 1420, 3.2.19; 1559, 3.4.3; Folio *King Lear*, 2715,
4.6.262) or by *read the letter* (*Friar Bacon*, 1515; *Thomas
Lord Cromwell*, G1r; *2 If You Know Not Me*, 294; *Roaring
Girl*, 3.2.49; *White Devil*, [4.2.25]; *New Way to Pay*,
4.3.73); sometimes a *letter* is **thrown** or **dropped**:
"*Victoria comes to the window, and throws out a letter,
which Fedele taketh up, and reads it*" (*Fedele and Fortunio*,
435–6), "*Callibeus above drops a Letter*" (*Osmond*, B1r),
"*A letter falleth*" (*Spanish Tragedy*, 3.2.23); see also *'Tis
Pity*, 5.1.45; *Wizard*, 883.

The popularity of *letters* yields a wide variety of
stage business; a sampling includes "*seems to read
the letters, but glances on Mistress Shore in his reading*"
(*1 Edward IV*, 61), "*He stabs the King with a knife as he
readeth the letter*" (*Massacre at Paris*, 1185), "*As Puttota
goes out, she flings away the letter. The Page puts it up, and
as he is talking, Hercules steals it out of his pocket*" (*Fawn*,
4.57), "*Blanche snatcheth the letter from him*" (*Fair Em*,
577), "*Give them the letters and they stamp and storm*"
(*Fair Maid of the Exchange*, 70), "*Enter Montsurry like
the Friar, with a Letter written in blood*" (Q2 *Bussy
D'Ambois*, 5.3.84), "*They confer their letters*" (*Sejanus*,
5.268), "*Kissing the letter*" (*Great Duke of Florence*,
4.1.69; see also *Landgartha*, H3r), "*Change letters*"
(*Fleer*, 3.1.0), "*tears the letter*" (*Launching of the Mary*,
2031), "*Letters upon a Table*" (*Gentleman of Venice*, H1r),
"*throws away the Letter*" (*Lovesick Court*, 114), "*Secretly
gives her a Letter*" (*Maid's Revenge*, D4v, also E1r), "*pulls
a letter out of her bosom*" (*Tom a Lincoln*, 2757–8); for
more see *Titus Andronicus*, G4v, 4.3.0; *Merchant of
Venice*, F2v, 3.2.236; *Charlemagne*, 1801–2; *Pericles*,
C1v, 2. Induction.16; *Cupid's Revenge*, 284, 285;
Roaring Girl, 3.2.73; *Silver Age*, 97; *Herod and Antipater*,
G2v; *Love's Sacrifice*, 874–5; *Mad Couple*, 31; *Politician*,
F2v.

levet

a **trumpet** call to awaken soldiers in the morning as
the only use makes clear: "*Trumpet a Levet*" (*Double

Marriage, 338) termed "a quaint levet to waken our
brave General."

lift

the roughly twenty-five signals refer to a range of
actions; figures are *lifted* from **kneeling** (*Captain*, 309;
Fair Favourite, 238), from **sitting** (*Albovine*, 78), and
"*the Soldiers lift up Euphanes, and shout*" (*Queen of
Corinth*, 60), "*The stage opens, Prospero lifts Evandra up*"
(*Love and Honour*, 121); see also *Endymion*, G2v; *Woman
in the Moon*, A3r; elsewhere a figure *lifts* himself or a
part of his body: "*lifteth himself up, and groans*"
(*1 Henry VI*, 577, 1.4.103), "*lifts up his head out of the
Tomb, and ducks down again*" (*Fedele and Fortunio*,
494–5), "*lifts his hand up, subscribes*" (*Christian Turned
Turk*, F2v); see also *Inconstant Lady*, 3.1.101; other
detailed directions are "*Lifts up his drawn sword*"
(*Downfall of Huntingdon*, 755), "*As they lift up the Cake,
the Spirit snatches it, and pours down bran*" (*Late
Lancashire Witches*, 205), "*As they are lifting their
weapons, enter the Mayor of Hereford, and his officers and
Townsmen with clubs*" (*Sir John Oldcastle*, 30–1); for
another example see *Two Maids of More-Clacke*, G2r;
see also **heave**, **raise**.

light

portable *lights* (usually **candles**, **links**, **lanterns**,
tapers, **torches**) are widely cited (1) often to indicate
by convention **night**/darkness on a **stage** with no
variable lighting but also for (2) the setting of a
banquet, **council**, or **writing table**, (3) various distinctive onstage effects and actions; over sixty signals
call for entrances *with light* (*Mad Couple*, 73; *Witty Fair
One*, H1r), "*with a light in his hand*" (*Antipodes*, 318),
most commonly *with a light/lights*; for a sampling of
the large latter group see *Jew of Malta*, 639; *Sir John
Oldcastle*, 1454–5; *Satiromastix*, 1.1.58, 143; *Dutch
Courtesan*, 1.1.0, 4.1.0; *Malcontent*, 2.1.0, 5.3.0, 5.5.0;
Hoffman, 1682; Quarto *Othello*, B4r, [1.2.28]; B4v,
[1.2.54; not in Riv.]; M1r, 5.2.0; Folio *Troilus and
Cressida*, 2934, 5.1.66; Quarto *King Lear*, F4v, 3.3.0;
Fair Maid of Bristow, A3r; *Fair Maid of the Inn*, 148;
Women Pleased, 251, 272; *Picture*, 3.4.0; *Fatal Contract*,
F4v, G2r; *Love's Sacrifice*, 1124, 1239, 1830; *Lady of
Pleasure*, 4.1.17; *Bloody Banquet*, 1073, 1416; *Cruel
Brother*, 187, 196; figures **enter** with "*lights before*"
(*Satiromastix*, 1.1.113, 138, 5.1.161; *Woodstock*, 117; *Jack
Drum's Entertainment*, C3r) and "*lights after*"
(*Woodstock*, 2385; *Woman Killed*, 117; *White Devil*,
2.2.23); a few signals call only for *a light* (*Mad Couple*,
77), *lights* (*Insatiate Countess*, 2.1.0; *Perkin Warbeck*,

1.3.0; *'Tis Pity*, 3.7.20; *City Wit*, 363), "*Lights ready*" (*Custom of the Country*, 328/455); only *Little French Lawyer* calls for "*A light within*" and "*Lights above*" (419, 421), and only in *Catiline* "*A fiery light appears*" (1.318).

Lights are regularly linked to the setting of a banquet/council/writing table: "*A Table with lights set out*" (*Bloody Banquet*, 1051), "*set at a Table with lights and Attendants*" (Quarto *Othello*, C1r, 1.3.0), "*One bearing light, a standish and paper, which sets a Table*" (*Bussy D'Ambois*, 5.1.0); see also *Northward Ho*, 4.1.0; *Rape of Lucrece*, 245; *English Traveller*, 66; *Love's Sacrifice*, 1124; *New Trick*, 281; *Doubtful Heir*, D7r; *Platonic Lovers*, 81; *Weeding of Covent Garden*, 13; two Ford plays call for "*Two lights of virgin wax*" for a **funeral** ceremony (*Broken Heart*, 5.3.0), "*wax lights*" for the friar's preaching to Annabella (*'Tis Pity*, 3.6.0); elsewhere are references to *torchlight* (*Revenger's Tragedy*, A2r; *Double Marriage*, 352), "*a Taper light*" (*Rape of Lucrece*, 221); for *lighted* tapers/torches/**lamps** see *Fedele and Fortunio*, 493; *Friar Bacon*, 1562; *Sir Thomas More*, 956; *2 Edward IV*, 162; *Insatiate Countess*, 1.1.0; *Virgin Martyr*, 2.1.86; *Women Beware Women*, 5.2.72; *Messalina*, 677; a few figures are directed to **put** out a *light* (*Golden Age*, 69; *Game at Chess*, 1946; *Aglaura*, 5.1.110); *light* is occasionally used as a verb: "*lights the link*" (*Knave in Grain*, 1908), "*lights away the Ladies*" (*Court Secret*, F4r), "*lighted in with Torches*" (*Escapes of Jupiter*, 1669), "*Exit, his Page lighting him*" (*Dutch Courtesan*, 1.2.161); atypical is "*The Petition is delivered up by Randolfo, the Duke lights his tobacco pipe with it and goes out dancing*" (*What You Will*, B3r); the verb can also mean "alight, dismount": "*riding wands in their hands, as if they had been new lighted*" (*Look about You*, 2–3), "*alighting into an Inn*" (*Phoenix*, B3v).

Lights are regularly included in descriptions of stage action: "*Syphax setteth away his light, and prepareth to embrace Sophonisba*" (*Sophonisba*, 4.1.51), "*They discover one another by the light, throw away their weapons, and embrace*" (*Goblins*, 2.3.18), "*The Tombstone flies open, and a great light appears in the midst of the Tomb*" (*Second Maiden's Tragedy*, 1927–9); *lights* can be linked to **pursuit** or to the **masque**, as in entrances "*with lights, as pursuing them*" (*Tottenham Court*, 103), "*hastily, pursuing Ursula, with lights*" (*Vow Breaker*, 3.1.0), "*all masked, two and two with lights like masquers*" (*Satiromastix*, 5.2.37); *Novella* sets up some distinctions among different *lights*: "*diverse Gentlemen pass to and fro with lights, at last enter Pantaloni, lighted by Nicolo, with dark Lanterns*" (106); "*a*

light in a glass" is the basis of Sacrapant's power in *Old Wives Tale* (424, 603, 825, 838); two plays take into account the *lighting* of candles in an indoor theatre: "*Tiremen enter to mend the lights*" (*Staple of News*, Induction.48), "*they sit a good while on the Stage before the Candles are lighted, talking together*," then "*enter Tireman with lights*" (*What You Will*, A2r).

lightning

the uses of this term alone–rather than in **thunder and lightning**–are few: "*a lightning flasheth forth*" (*Friar Bacon*, 1635), "*exhalations of lightning*" (*Devil's Charter*, A2v), "*He is killed with a flash of lightning*" (*Unnatural Combat*, 5.2.306), "*the devil sinks with lightning*" (*Virgin Martyr*, 5.2.238); see also **fire**, **flash**.

like

widely used in entrances (over 300 examples) in the locution *like a* (1) usually to mean *enter* **disguised** *as a* (wherein a figure already seen is to take on a different costume/persona) but also (2) *enter* **attired** or **habited** *as a* (wherein the actor is directed to appear in the costume appropriate for a specific figure/role); although the *like a* locution is the norm, the full sense is sometimes spelled out; of the thousands of disguised figures relatively few are directed to **enter** *disguised like a*: "*disguised like an Amazon*" (*Antonio and Mellida*, 1.1.0; *Swetnam*, E1r), Falstaff "*disguised like an old woman*" (Quarto *Merry Wives*, F2v, 4.2.181); other entrances include *disguised like a* seamster (*Roaring Girl*, 1.1.0), hermit (*Malcontent*, 4.3.0), man (*Fair Maid of Bristow*, E4v), scholar (*Broken Heart*, 1.3.0), "*an old Servingman*" (*Anything for a Quiet Life*, F4r); *Alchemist* provides both "*Subtle disguised like a Priest of Faery*" and the more typical "*Surly like a Spaniard*" (3.5.0, 4.3.20).

Examples of the more economical *like a* locution number over two hundred and include just about every conceivable disguise; several plays include four to six examples with *Amends for Ladies* providing ten (1.1.189, 2.3.10, 2.3.76, 3.2.2, 4.3.1, 4.4.2, 5.2.2–3, 117) including eight disguises ("*like a waiting Gentlewoman*," "*like an Irish footboy*" four times, "*like a woman*" twice, "*like a Doctor*") and two non-disguises ("*like a Man*" without the woman's disguise, "*like a Bride*"); *Blind Beggar of Bednal Green* provides six (along with four instances of simple *enter disguised*) including *like a* soldier, servingman, beggar, "*like a Wench dressed up*" (25, 82, 85, 71); the many disguises in *Dutch Courtesan* include Cocledemoy *like a* barber, bellman, sergeant and Frevill *like a* pander (2.3.16,

4.5.75, 5.3.0, 4.4.40); *City Wit* provides *like a **lame*** soldier, a physician, court messenger, citizen, dancer, doctor, "*dressed like a Courtesan*" (295, 300, 320, 328, 332, 358, 367); *Downfall of Huntingdon* provides disguises "*like an old man*" twice (950, 1468) and *like* a citizen, peddler, "*dressed like a woman*," "*like a country man with a basket*," (557, 1571, 1112, 2096–7); the Shakespeare canon includes "*Ariel like a water Nymph*" and "*like a Harpy*" (*Tempest*, 453–4, 1.2.316; 1583, 3.3.52), Posthumus "*like a poor Soldier*" (*Cymbeline*, 2894, 5.2.0), "*Hermione (like a Statue)*" (*Winter's Tale*, 3185, 5.3.0); gender shifts include a woman *like a* page (*Wars of Cyrus*, C3v; *1 Honest Whore*, 4.1.109; *Roaring Girl*, 4.1.37; *Hog Hath Lost His Pearl*, 1204; *Maid's Revenge*, H4v), a woman "*like a Page*" then "*like a Woman*" (*Doubtful Heir*, C1v, E3v), a woman "*like a man*" (*Roaring Girl*, 3.1.33), a page "*like a Woman*" (*Honest Man's Fortune*, 277), a man *like a* woman (*2 Seven Deadly Sins*, 56–7) and "*like a Lady*" (*Bird in a Cage*, E3r); most widely used are *like a* doctor/physician, shepherd, soldier, hermit, friar; in the Heywood canon Jupiter appears "*like a Nymph, or a Virago*" and "*like a Peddler*" (*Golden Age*, 29, 60), "*like a woodman*" (*Silver Age*, 150); atypical are multiple uses such as "*Goldwire like a Justice of Peace, Dingem like a Constable, the Musicians like watchmen*" (*City Madam*, 3.1.55).

For examples of situations not involving disguise, the father of Posthumus is "*attired like a warrior*" (*Cymbeline*, 3066–7, 5.4.29), Antiochus is "*Habited like a king*" (*Believe As You List*, 881), other figures are *attired like* a madman (*Orlando Furioso*, 842), gentleman (*Trial of Chivalry*, K1v), "*woman, with a distaff and a spindle*" (Hercules in *Brazen Age*, 241); more typical are "*like a Victor*" (*More Dissembers*, B7v), "*like a Captain of a ship*" (*Fortune by Land and Sea*, 413), "*like a civil Merchant*" (*English Traveller*, 37), "*like a mourner*" (*Hoffman*, 1683), "*like a combatant*" (*Dumb Knight*, 195), "*like a King*" and "*like a Soldier armed*" (*Constant Maid*, H1r), "*like a Bridegroom leading Flavia his Bride*" (*Faithful Friends*, 2817–18), "*like a Miller all mealy with a wand in his hand*," "*like an Italian Merchant*," "*like a Parson*" (*Three Ladies of London*, A3r, B2r, C4r); related locutions include "*Orlando like himself*" (*2 Honest Whore*, 4.1.28), "*her Maid page-like*" (*Challenge for Beauty*, 63), "*lady-like attired*" (*1 Edward IV*, 81; *Staple of News*, Induction.0), "*with a new fashion gown dressed gentlewoman-like*" (*Michaelmas Term*, 3.1.0); other usages include "*Speak like a crier*" (*Atheist's Tragedy*, 4.4.44), "*speaks in a vile tone like a Player*" (*Court Beggar*, 262), "*scents after it like a Hound*"

(*Bartholomew Fair*, 3.2.80), "*playing upon his truncheon like a fife*" (*1 Henry IV*, G3r, 3.3.87), "*her face colored like a Moor*" (*Devil's Law Case*, 5.6.29).

limbs

found only twice, both times as part of a ***banquet*** course composed of human parts; *Golden Age* provides "*A banquet brought in, with limbs of a Man in the service*" (21), an Epyrian hostage, with the host commenting "This is the Epyre's head, and these his limbs"; *Bloody Banquet* calls for a servant "*bringing in Tymethes's limbs*" (1715–16) with the Tyrant directing "Before her eyes lay the divided limbs" and "hang those quarters up"; Henslowe's inventory includes "Phaeton's limbs" (*Diary*, App. 2, 66), "The Moor's limbs, and Hercules's limbs" (25).

link

a ***torch*** used to ***light*** people along the streets: "*lights the link*" (*Knave in Grain*, 1908), enter "*before her with a Link*" (*Family of Love*, D4r); see also *Witch of Edmonton*, 4.1.14; *Wit in a Constable*, 230; an alternative meaning for *links* as "a chain of sausages" occurs in one direction that calls for "*a gammon of raw bacon, and links or puddings in a platter*" (*Alphonsus of Germany*, F1r).

linstock

a long forked ***stick*** for holding a match used to *fire* a cannon; a gunner's boy appears "*with a Linstock*" (*1 Henry VI*, 524, 1.4.56), and the pope enters "*with a Linstock in his hand*" and "*delivereth his Linstock*" to his appointed "master of our Ordinance" (*Devil's Charter*, C4v, D1r); in *Whore of Babylon* Florimell enters "*followed by Captains, Mariners and Gunners with Linstocks*" (5.5.0) exhorting "Shoot, shoot, they answer; brave: more Linstocks: shoot."

lion

onstage *lions* are called for twice: a ***devil*** ascends "*with a red face crowned imperial riding upon a Lion, or dragon*" (*Devil's Charter*, G1v), a ***dumb show*** specifies "*let there come forth a Lion running after a Bear or any other beast, then come forth an Archer who must kill the Lion in a dumb show*" (*Locrine*, 4–7); *Lion* is part of the Pyramus and Thisby story when "*The Lion roars. Thisby runs off*" (Folio *Midsummer Night's Dream*, 2065, 5.1.264); a figure desperate for food enters "*with lion's flesh upon his sword*" (*Battle of Alcazar*, 582–3); the *lion's skin* is associated with Hercules who enters "*with the Lion's head and skin*" after defeating the Nemean *lion* (*Silver Age*, 131), "*appears in his Lion's skin*"

(*Friar Bacon*, 1208), before dying "*burns his Club, and Lion's skin*" (*Brazen Age*, 254); in a dumb show Omphale has "*a club in her hand, and a lion's skin on her back, Hercules following with a distaff*" (*Locrine*, 1354–6); in *1 Troublesome Reign* the Bastard chases Austria "*and maketh him leave the Lion's skin*" (C4r); Henslowe's inventory includes "one lion skin" (*Diary*, App. 2, 66), "one lion, two lion heads" (85).

listen

used primarily for eavesdropping: "*Cupid alone, in nymph's apparel, and Neptune listening*" (*Gallathea*, 2.2.0), two figures who "*enter again softly, stealing to several stands, and listen*" (*Broken Heart*, 3.2.16), three figures "*consulting about their treason: King Harry and Suffolk listening at the door*" (*Sir John Oldcastle*, 2086–8); for other figures who *listen*/**enter** *listening* see *Rare Triumphs*, 308; *John a Kent*, 1050–1; *Warning for Fair Women*, G3r; *Old Fortunatus*, 3.1.186, 4.2.28; *Roaring Girl*, 2.2.3; *Mad World*, 3.2.174; *Fawn*, 2.350; *Nice Valour*, 153; *Herod and Antipater*, C2r; *Lover's Melancholy*, 4.3.44; *Love's Sacrifice*, 1189; *New Academy*, 8; *Hyde Park*, C3v; *Humorous Courtier*, E1r; *Wizard*, 1017–18, 1660–1; *Andromana*, 209; *Love and Honour*, 157.

litter

found in dialogue as a possible equivalent to the modern *stretcher* (e.g., *King John*, 5.3.16) but rarely in directions where the call is consistently for a **chair**; Gloucester tells Kent "There is a litter ready; lay him in't" (3.6.90) but later Lear is directed to enter "*in a chair carried by Servants*" (Folio *King Lear*, 2771, 4.7.23); such references to *litter*/*stretcher* and *chair* may refer to the same portable property (probably a chair that could be carried either on poles or by the arms); *Edward I* calls for a far more elaborate *litter* so that Queen Elinor enters "*in her litter borne by four Negro Moors*" and "*one having set a ladder to the side of the litter, she descendeth*" (1015); "*a Litter covered*" is specified for the supposedly **sick** but actually **dead** emperor in *Prophetess* (336, also 342) and is linked to the Black Knight (Gondomar) in *Game at Chess* who enters "*in his Litter*" (2002–3).

little

used primarily to describe (1) timing and/or distance, (2) properties; uses of *little* to characterize action are "*To them Raven, and a little after him Monsieur Kickshaw*" (*Bride*, 9; see also *Tottenham Court*, 143), "*after a little skirmish within*" and "*advanceth a little*" (*Devil's Charter*, D3v, M2r, also I3r), "*after a little*

pause*" (*Fatal Contract*, B2v; *Maid's Metamorphosis*, C2r), "*after a little dancing*" (*Shoemakers' Holiday*, 3.3.51; *Love's Sacrifice*, 1846), "*consult a little while*" (*Valiant Welshman*, C4v), "*writes a little*" (*Law Tricks*, 204; *Locrine*, 341), "*whispers a little*" (*1 If You Know Not Me*, 216; see also *Your Five Gallants*, A2r), "*making a little show to rescue*" (*Three Lords of London*, H1r), "*Sinks a little*" (*Virgin Martyr*, 5.1.152); for more examples see *Tom a Lincoln*, 153; *Love's Sacrifice*, 2664; *Launching of the Mary*, 2794; *Hannibal and Scipio*, 216, 225; *Platonic Lovers*, 16; *Fair Favourite*, 216; properties are a *little* **bottle** (*Princess*, C1v), **casket** (*Coxcomb*, 317), **looking glass** (*Fancies Chaste and Noble*, 235), **table** (*City Madam*, 4.4.160; *Launching of the Mary*, 1141; *Variety*, D12r), "*a little piece of fine parchment*" (*Devil's Charter*, A2v), "*a little hill*" (*Old Wives Tale*, 603), "*a little glass vial*" (*Wife for a Month*, 39); see also *Locrine*, 962; *Antonio's Revenge*, 4.1.0; *Wisdom of Doctor Dodypoll*, 86; *Noble Stranger*, G3r; other uses of *little* are "*a little noise below*" (rev. *Aglaura*, 5.1.105), "*a little antic Spirit*" (*Birth of Merlin*, E4v; see also MS *Humorous Lieutenant*, 2330), "*a little disguised*" (*Distresses*, 332), "*recovers a little in voice*" (*Revenger's Tragedy*, I3v); see also **small**.

lock

used as a verb linked to action involving a stage **door**; figures are directed to "*lock the door*" (*Island Princess*, 137; *Captain*, 297, 299; *Fatal Dowry*, 3.1.401, 4.1.154; *Gentleman of Venice*, I1r), and in one instance "*the doors*" (*Lust's Dominion*, 3.2.55); variations are "*locks himself in*" (*Second Maiden's Tragedy*, 2030), "*Puts to the door and locks it*" and "*Unlocks the door*" (*Renegado*, 2.5.158, 4.2.0), "*locks him into a closet*" (*Devil's Law Case*, 5.4.167; *Goblins*, 2.6.6); that a figure may turn a **key** but never actually *lock* a stage door is reflected in such signals as "*seems to lock a door*" (*Death of Huntingdon*, 1921), "*seems to lock her in*" (*Platonic Lovers*, 47), along with the practical direction "*turns a key*" (*Bussy D'Ambois*, 5.1.40); the only example of *lock* not linked to a door is a victor in battle who is presented "*with a standing bowl, which he locks in a Casket*" (*Silver Age*, 97); *lock* is not found as a noun, although "*a bunch of Picklocks*" (*Queen's Exchange*, 535) is brought in by thieves who comment "lay down your Picklocks, they have done well their office in our passage hither."

logs

appear only in two Shakespeare plays; in *Romeo and Juliet*, 4.4.13 servants enter "*with Logs and Coals*" (Q1, I1r) or "*with spits and logs, and Baskets*" (Q2, K1v), and in *Tempest* Ferdinand enters "*bearing a Log*" whereas earlier Caliban had appeared "*with a burden of Wood*" (1235, 3.1.0; 1038, 2.2.0).

long

a modifier used (1) to indicate the timing of *sounds* or actions, (2) to describe the size of a property; examples of timing are "*A long Flourish till they come down*" (Folio *Titus Andronicus*, 264, 1.1.233), "*A long flourish. They all cry, Martius, Martius*" (*Coriolanus*, 794, 1.10.40) which comes between two directions for a simple *flourish*; for other *long*-lasting sounds see *Battle of Alcazar*, 1336; Folio *Richard II*, 420, 1.3.122; *Shoemakers' Holiday*, 5.5.0; *Hieronimo*, 1.0, 11.0; *1 Fair Maid of the West*, 312; *Maid of Honour*, 2.5.0; *long* actions are a *kiss* (*Country Girl*, I3v; *Court Beggar*, 200) and a *whisper* (*Lost Lady*, 592); three examples have *long* used by a bookkeeper in a practical, theatrical sense almost certainly to indicate the length of the *entr'acte* entertainment: in the manuscript of *Believe as You List* at the end of the first and fourth acts "*long*" appears in the left margin (575, 1791), in *1 Fair Maid of the West* "*Act long*" appears at the end of the fourth act (320), and in the annotated copy of *Two Merry Milkmaids* a bookkeeper wrote "*Long*" in the left margin at the end of Act 1 (E2v); *long* properties are a *coat* (*Three Ladies of London*, A2v; *Yorkshire Tragedy*, 506–7), *knife* (*If This Be Not a Good Play*, 5.4.34), nails (*Lover's Melancholy*, 3.3.19), *rapier* (*Roaring Girl*, 2.1.217), *scroll* (*If This Be Not a Good Play*, 2.2.34; *Soddered Citizen*, 2376), *sword* (Folio *Every Man In*, 5.3.35; *Epicœne*, 4.2.120; *Faithful Friends*, 1047–8; *Fine Companion*, I1v), *table* (*Henry VIII*, 662, 1.4.0; *1 Iron Age*, 302), *hair* (*Picture*, 2.1.85; *Perkin Warbeck*, 3.2.111), *staves* (Quarto *2 Henry VI*, F3r, 4.2.0, 30).

look, looking

(1) usually signals the action of *looking* at someone or something but can also denote (2) *reading*, (3) telling time; given the extensive use of the direction (roughly 130 examples) it is worth noting that as a silent action *looking* does warrant a direction; one locution has a figure simply *look on/at* something or someone (Folio *Richard III*, 362, 1.2.170; Q1 *Romeo and Juliet*, K2r, 5.3.139; *Downfall of Huntingdon*, 2578; *King Leir*, 420; *Turk*, 2098; *Amends for Ladies*, 4.4.1; *Golden Age*, 62; *Hengist*, DS before 2.2, 7–8; *Valiant Welshman*, H4r; *Picture*, 3.5.187; *Conspiracy*, D4r; *Aglaura*, 1.3.28; *Fatal Contract*, I3v; *Queen of Aragon*, 393); more specific signals are *look wrathfully* (*1 Tamburlaine*, 1050), *angrily* (*Alphonsus of Aragon*, 1784; *Fair Em*, 813–14), *earnestly* (*1 Edward IV*, 67; *Devil's Charter*, F2r),

strangely (*Greene's Tu Quoque*, K3r; *Maid's Metamorphosis*, F2v), *ghostly* (*Just Italian*, 254), *scurvily* (*Your Five Gallants*, B3r; *Princess*, C3r), *sadly* (*Weakest Goeth*, 808; *Princess*, D3r); elsewhere a figure *looks about* (*Mucedorus*, D2r; *Captain Thomas Stukeley*, 2839; *Caesar and Pompey*, 2.1.0; *Woman Is a Weathercock*, 1.2.145; *Duchess of Suffolk*, C3v; *Love's Sacrifice*, 1165–6; *Late Lancashire Witches*, 248; *Queen and Concubine*, 30), *looks in/out* (*Fedele and Fortunio*, 1414–15; *Mother Bombie*, 1745; *Westward Ho*, 5.4.164; *Widow's Tears*, 4.2.0; *Monsieur D'Olive*, 5.1.27; *Amends for Ladies*, 5.2.163–5; *New Academy*, 77; *Albovine*, 63; *Wits*, 156; *Country Captain*, B10r) or *back*: "*Piero's going out, looks back*" (*Antonio's Revenge*, 2.1.180), "*Looks backwards*" (*Great Duke of Florence*, 5.1.27); see also *Golden Age*, 64; *1 If You Know Not Me*, 225; *Swaggering Damsel*, D4v; others *look/look out* from *above* (*Jack Drum's Entertainment*, D3r; *Court Beggar*, 233), "*looks out of the window*" (*Taming of the Shrew*, 2397, 5.1.15; see also *Knave in Grain*, 313; *Woman Hater*, 123; *Lost Lady*, 590; *Parson's Wedding*, 402); elsewhere figures *look in* a *looking glass* (*Devil's Charter*, H1r; *Novella*, 125); for other locutions see *David and Bethsabe*, 1842; Q1 *Romeo and Juliet*, H2r, 3.5.235; *Wisdom of Doctor Dodypoll*, 85; *2 Edward IV*, 155; *Cupid's Whirligig*, 4.5.31, 53; *Faithful Shepherdess*, 420; *Jews' Tragedy*, 1392; *Late Lancashire Witches*, 238; *English Moor*, 66; *Bloody Banquet*, 852–3; *Distresses*, 358.

Look can signal reading: "*looketh upon a book*" (*Devil's Charter*, L3r), "*looking on their bills*" (*1 Edward IV*, 82; see also Quarto *Every Man Out*, 1899), "*Looks in an Almanac*" (*Fair Quarrel*, 5.1.127); see also *Spanish Tragedy*, 3.1.69; *Death of Huntingdon*, 2819; *King Leir*, 410–12; *Caesar and Pompey*, 5.1.38; *1 If You Know Not Me*, 228; *Bondman*, 2.2.121; *Two Noble Ladies*, 1796; *Fair Maid of the Inn*, 201; *Great Duke of Florence*, 2.1.39; *Noble Stranger*, E3v; figures also *look on/in* a *watch* (*Devil's Charter*, G1r; *New Academy*, 48; *Sophy*, 5.176); atypical is *look* as a noun: "*let him counterfeit the passion of love by looks and gesture*" (*Fedele and Fortunio*, 795–6), "*exit with an angry look*" (*Jews' Tragedy*, 2428–9), "*with distracted looks*" (*New Way to Pay*, 5.1.88).

looking glass
see *glass*

lots

these symbols of chance are *drawn* on six occasions: "*Fortune is discovered upon an altar, in her hand a golden round full of Lots; Enter Hengist and Hersus with others, they Draw Lots and hang them up with joy*" (*Hengist*, DS before 1.2, 1–4), "*the three fatal sisters, with a rock, a* thread, and a pair of shears; bringing in a Globe, in which they put three lots; Jupiter draws heaven" (*Golden Age*, 78), a figure "*appareled like Fortune, drawn on a Globe, with a Cup in her hand, wherein are Bay leaves, whereupon are written the lots*" (*Alphonsus of Germany*, C4r); for other examples see *King Leir*, 551; *Amorous War*, G4r; *Lovesick Court*, 154.

loud

always modifies *music*, typically for a **ceremonial** entrance or special occasion: "*Loud Music, and Enter Ushers before, the Secretary, Treasurer, Chancellor; Admiral, Constable hand in hand, the King following, others attend*" (*Chabot*, 1.1.115), "*Loud music. They possess the Stage all in state*" (*2 Iron Age*, 408, also 405, 411), "*Loud music, Honoria in state under a Canopy*" (*Picture*, 1.2.128, also 2.2.122); see also *Sophonisba*, 1.2.236; *Charlemagne*, 151; *Timon of Athens*, 337, 1.2.0; *No Wit*, 4.3.0, 40; *1 Iron Age*, 302; *Maid of Honour*, 4.2.0, 28, 5.2.0; *Prophetess*, 363; *Emperor of the East*, 1.1.82, 3.2.0; *King John and Matilda*, 51; *Young Admiral*, K3r; *Bloody Banquet*, 1093; a signal in *Love's Mistress* specifies volume: "*Loud Music, and still Music*" (108).

low

typically modifies a **sound**: "*Low March within*" and "*Low Alarums*" (*Julius Caesar*, 1936, 4.2.24; 2585, 5.3.96; 2667, 5.5.23); for other examples of both these *low* sounds see *Birth of Merlin*, F2r; *Shoemaker a Gentleman*, 5.1.54; *Knight of Malta*, 109; *Two Noble Ladies*, 1216, 1662–3; atypical is "*makes low obeisance*" (*Bloody Banquet*, 1095).

lower stage

the main platform, cited twice when the upper level is also in use: "*Exeunt all on the lower stage*" (*Antonio and Mellida*, 1.1.139), "*They renew Blindman's Buff on the Lower stage*" (*Humour out of Breath*, 467).

lute

a stringed instrument plucked like a guitar or mandolin, sometimes played solo but usually for a **song** often under sad circumstances, as in "*Ophelia playing on a Lute, and her hair down singing*" (Q1 *Hamlet*, G4v, 4.5.20); for similar uses of the *lute* to accompany **singing** see *Fedele and Fortunio*, 193; *Midas*, 4.1.89; *What You Will*, A4r; *Dutch Courtesan*, 1.2.135, 145; *Chances*, 198; *Spanish Curate*, 89; *Believe as You List*, 2022–3; *Picture*, 2.2.200; *Weeding of Covent Garden*, 10; *Messalina*, 2518–19; *Cardinal*, 5.3.91; the instrument is put to notable use when a figure enters "*with a Lute and Kate with him*" and after singing she "*offers to

strike him with the lute*" (*Taming of a Shrew*, C1v, C2r); the *lute* is played alone or called for as a property in *Jew of Malta*, 1949; *Taming of the Shrew*, 899, 2.1.38; *Old Fortunatus*, 3.1.0; *1 Honest Whore*, 3.3.0; *Sophonisba*, 4.1.200, 218; *Timon of Athens*, 455–6, 1.2.130; *Witch of Edmonton*, 4.2.60; *Lovers' Progress*, 114; *City Wit*, 352; *'Tis Pity*, 2.1.55; *Platonic Lovers*, 33; *Arcadia*, F1r; *Argalus and Parthenia*, 23; *Aglaura*, 3.2.0.

M

mace

a ceremonial **staff** borne as a symbol of authority and often accompanied by a **purse** and **sword**: "*A table being covered with a green Carpet, a state Cushion on it, and the Purse and Mace lying thereon*" (*Sir Thomas More*, 735–6), "*Enter Byplay the Governor, Macebearer, Swordbearer, Officer, the Mace and Sword laid on the Table, the Governor sits*" (*Antipodes*, 287); the *mace*, purse, sword are often borne **before** high-ranking figures; representative examples are a king "*Crowned, wearing Robes Imperial, Swords of State, Maces, etc. being borne before him*" (*If This Be Not a Good Play*, 1.2.0), "*Sir Thomas More, with Purse and Mace borne before him*" (*Sir Thomas More*, 1174); see also *Thomas Lord Cromwell*, E1v; *When You See Me*, 2; *Old Law*, I1v; the *mace* is part of a coronation or other royal **ceremonies** (*1 If You Know Not Me*, 195, 239, 244; *Birth of Merlin*, C1r) and is sometimes carried by a sergeant, as in "*A Sergeant at Arms, bearing a Silver Mace*" (*Henry VIII*, 1340–1, 2.4.0; see also *Devil's Charter*, A2v); when awarded hell as his kingdom Pluto is presented "*with a Mace, and burning crown*" (*Golden Age*, 79); for other *maces* both with and without purse and sword see *Woodstock*, 115, 790, 901–2; *Sir Thomas More*, 1530; *Sir Thomas Wyatt*, 1.2.40; *When You See Me*, 2915.

mad, distracted, raving

few of the plentiful *mad* scenes provide specific signals; typical is "*Enter Lear*" (Folio *King Lear*, 2526, 4.6.80); more detailed directions are usually generic, most commonly **enter** mad (*Old Wives Tale*, 196; *Dead Man's Fortune*, 40; *Jack Drum's Entertainment*, H4r; *Phoenix*, K1v; *1 Honest Whore*, 5.2.299; *Hoffman*, 1429; *Wisdom of Doctor Dodypoll*, 855; Quarto *King Lear*, I3v, 4.6.80; *Witch of Edmonton*, 4.1.172; *Rebellion*, 58, 86), enter distracted/distractedly (Folio *Hamlet*, 2766, 4.5.20; *Atheist's Tragedy*, 4.3.210, 5.2.67; *White Devil*, 3.3.0; *Bondman*, 5.1.97; *Queen and Concubine*, 99; *Wizard*, 591; *School of Compliment*, H3r); variations include enter raving (Quarto *Troilus and Cressida*, D2v,

2.2.100; *Insatiate Countess*, 4.2.111), *"runs raving"* (*Cobbler's Prophecy*, 1329–30), *"with distracted looks"* (*New Way to Pay*, 5.1.88), *"Rises distractedly"* (*Roman Actor*, 5.1.187); such generalized signals that leave the implementation to the actor are best seen in *White Devil* where the speeches of the dying Bracciano *"are several kinds of distractions and in the action should appear so"* and later *"Cornelia doth this in several forms of distraction"* (5.3.82, 5.4.82); comparable signals include *"Sings part of the old Song, and acts it madly"* (*Court Beggar*, 247), *"attired like a madman"* (*Orlando Furioso*, 842), *"raving and staring as if he were mad"* (Quarto *2 Henry VI*, F1v, 3.3.0); *mad* women are directed to enter with disheveled **hair**, usually *"with her hair about her ears"* (Q1 *Hamlet*, G4r, 4.5.20; Folio *Troilus and Cressida*, 1082–3, 2.2.100; *Tom a Lincoln*, 2252; *1 Iron Age*, 269; *Broken Heart*, 4.2.57); unusually elaborate is the sequence in *Lover's Melancholy* where a series of specific maladies is displayed, so that a victim of lycanthropia enters *"his face whited, black shag hair, long nails, a piece of raw meat"* and a philosopher subject to dotage and delirium enters *"in black rags, a copper chain on, an old gown half off, and book"* (3.3.19, 38); the possible variations can be seen in the three versions of Ophelia's first *mad* appearance in *Hamlet* (4.5.20): *"Enter Ophelia"* (Q2, K4r), *"Enter Ophelia distracted"* (Folio, 2766), *"Enter Ophelia playing on a Lute, and her hair down singing"* (Q1, G4v).

magic, magician

magic/magical describe the actions of a *magician* and supernatural effects; examples of the modifier are *"Prospero (in his Magic robes)"* (*Tempest*, 1946, 5.1.0), *"a magical book"* and *"a Magical glass"* (*Devil's Charter*, A2v, F4v), *"her Magic rod"* (*Prophetess*, 363), *"his Magic Arts"* (*Seven Champions*, G1r); appearances of the figure are *"Magician with a Bowl"* to **conjure** (*Humorous Lieutenant*, 342, MS 2315–17), *"The Magi with their rods beat the ground, and from under the same riseth a brave Arbor"* (*Looking Glass for London*, 522–4, also 514–15); for other *magicians* see *Wars of Cyrus*, D2r; *Birth of Merlin*, C1r; *Valiant Welshman*, G1r, H1r; see also **enchanter**.

make a lane

a signal to set up a distinctive entrance for a special occasion such as a **funeral** or a state visit: *"Enter as many as may be spared, with lights, and make a lane kneeling while Martha the Duchess like a mourner with her train passeth through"* (*Hoffman*, 1682–4), *"A Chair of state discovered, Tables and Chairs responsible, a Guard*

making a lane," so that King John, Pandulph, and the lords *"enter between them"* (*King John and Matilda*, 29); to arrest an entering Cromwell figures *"make a lane with their Halberds"* so that when *"Cromwell's men offer to draw"* their leader says "Make a lane there, the traitor's at hand, / Keep back Cromwell's men" (*Thomas Lord Cromwell*, F3v); a comparable locution has courtiers *"make a rank for the Duke to pass through"* (*Antonio and Mellida*, 2.1.183).

make a leg, make legs

to show respect by a bending of the **knee** and extending backward of the **leg** (a male version of the **curtsy**), as in *"Snatches off his hat and makes legs to him"* (*Revenger's Tragedy*, G3r); when a jailer *"makes legs"* and refuses to speak his prisoner responds: "You're very civil, Hell take your courtesy" (*Queen and Concubine*, 36), and after Brand is directed to *"Make legs"* (*Death of Huntingdon*, 1818) the king responds "Less of your curtsy" (here too *curtsy* could be *courtesy*); see also *How a Man May Choose*, C4r; *Epicœne*, 2.1.10; *Twins*, E1v; a variation is an entrance *"legging and scraping"* (*Swaggering Damsel*, F2v); see also **obeisance**.

make a stand

(1) in a battlefield context to **fight** or to take up a combative position, (2) in a non-military context to take up some formal **posture**; battlefield examples include *"the soldiers march and make a stand"* (*Hoffman*, 1186–7), *"Enter Enceladus leading his Army, Jupiter leading his. They make a stand"* (*Golden Age*, 50), *"In their march they are met by Ulysses and King Diomed, at which they make a stand"* (*1 Iron Age*, 292); see also *Captain Thomas Stukeley*, 2441–3; *Rape of Lucrece*, 240; after a combat a group of entering figures *"make a stand in divided files"* (*Antonio and Mellida*, 1.1.34); for an individual rather than a group, after *"coming into the midst of the soldiers"* a bloody Virginius (who has just murdered his daughter) *"makes a stand"* and asks for death (*Appius and Virginia*, H1r); for examples not linked to combat, three devils enter with implements to torture sinners and *"All three make a stand, laughing"* (*If This Be Not a Good Play*, 5.4.34), and for marriage revels *"Enter Groneas and Lemophil leading Euphrania; Chrystalla and Philema leading Prophilus; Nearchus supporting Calantha; Crotolon, Amelus. Cease loud music; all make a stand"* (*Broken Heart*, 5.2.0).

make as though, make as if

used frequently up through about 1590 but rarely found thereafter; these phrases can be combined with **let**: "*Let him make as though he would give him some*" (*Locrine*, 1669–70), "*Let Fraud make as though he would strike him*" and "*Let Simplicity make as though he read it*" (*Three Ladies of London*, A3v, B4v); more common is the imperative: "*Make as though ye read it*" (*Three Ladies of London*, F2v), "*Make as if she swoons*" (*Cobbler's Prophecy*, 970), "*Make as if ye would fight*" (*Edward I*, 432), "*make as though thou goest out*" (*Alphonsus of Aragon*, 187, also 1094, 1507–8); later examples when they do occur are descriptive rather than imperative: "*makes as though he would speak to him*" (*Thomas Lord Cromwell*, F2v), "*making as if he helped the Sheriff, knocks down his men*" (*Downfall of Huntingdon*, 990–1), "*She draws forth a knife, and making as though she meant to spoil her face, runs to her, and falling on her knees, embraces and kisses her, casting away the knife*" (*2 Edward IV*, 129).

make signs, make show

locutions comparable to **seem** regularly found in **dumb shows** and other mimed actions; examples from dumb shows include "*makes signs of consent*" (*Four Prentices*, 178), "*makes shows to call for help*" (*White Devil*, 2.2.37), "*makes show of sorrow to the Queen*" (*Queen of Corinth*, 60), "*makes show of persuading them to join with the Portuguese*" (*Captain Thomas Stukeley*, 2453–4), "*takes their hands and makes signs to marry them*" (*Maidenhead Well Lost*, 144, also 152), "*he kneels for mercy, but they making signs of refusal, he snatcheth at some weapon to kill himself, is prevented*" (*Whore of Babylon*, 2.2.185); see also *Death of Huntingdon*, 928; *Captain*, 296–7; *Four Plays in One*, 321; during the dumb show in *Hamlet* the queen "*makes passionate action*" (Q2 H1v, Folio 1998, 3.2.135), and during her vision in *Henry VIII* Katherine "*makes (in her sleep) signs of rejoicing*" (2654–5, 4.2.82); for examples of comparable actions not in dumb shows, after **biting** out his **tongue** Hieronimo "*makes signs for a knife to mend his pen*" (*Spanish Tragedy*, 4.4.198), and figures at a **tomb** "*all kneel, making show of Ceremony*" (*Love's Sacrifice*, 2738–9); see also *Captain Thomas Stukeley*, 2448; *Epicœne*, 2.1.10; *Martyred Soldier*, 197; *Example*, G1r, H2v; *Conspiracy*, I1v.

make show

see **make signs**

malcontented

found only twice (as opposed to the more widely used **discontented**) with both examples early in the period: "*Edward the first malcontented*" (*Friar Bacon*, 1),

"*the King of Paphlagonia, malcontent*" (*Looking Glass for London*, 863).

manacles

a seldom cited restraint for prisoners comparable to **chains**, **fetters**, **gyves**, **irons**, **shackles**: "*Varillus manacled, and led by Tersulus*" (*Lovesick Court*, 162), "*an Iron about his neck, two Chains manacling his wrists; a great Chain at his heels*" (*Dick of Devonshire*, 1624–5); see also *Wounds of Civil War*, 1073–4.

manet, manent

literally "he/she remains" and "they remain," a signal that a figure is to **stay**/**remain** onstage when others **depart**, as in Folio *Hamlet* where Claudius, Gertrude, and others *exeunt* and "*Manet Hamlet*" (2142, 3.2.270); the distinction between singular and plural is not always observed, as in "*Manet Tranio and Lucentio*" (*Taming of the Shrew*, 448, 1.1.145); many of the 150 examples combine *manet* with an **exeunt**: "*Exeunt, manet Greedy*" (*New Way to Pay*, 3.2.288), "*Exeunt, manent Novall and Perigot*" (*Parliament of Love*, 3.1.32); for a sampling see *James IV*, 1613; *Comedy of Errors*, 1426, 4.4.130; 1898–9, 5.1.408; *Edmond Ironside*, 1127; *Fair Em*, 451, 500; *Trial of Chivalry*, A3v; *Weakest Goeth*, 1150, 1292; *Old Fortunatus*, 1.1.314, 3.1.183, 3.1.336; *If This Be Not a Good Play*, 1.3.191, 2.3.62, 3.1.30; *Amends for Ladies*, 1.1.408–9; *Revenge of Bussy*, 2.1.130, 4.4.56; *Gentleman Usher*, 1.2.140, 2.1.176, 3.2.296; *Monsieur D'Olive*, 3.1.81, 3.2.133, 5.1.226; *Coriolanus*, 1379, 2.2.154; *Maid's Tragedy*, 57; *Brazen Age*, 197, 246; *Little French Lawyer*, 433, 447; *Fair Maid of the Inn*, 151, 164, 183; *Lovers' Progress*, 101, 103; *English Traveller*, 14, 88; *Rape of Lucrece*, 167, 182, 200; *Welsh Ambassador*, 618–19; for a sampling of *manet* without a preceding *exeunt* see *Orlando Furioso*, 770; *Whore of Babylon*, 5.2.109; *Custom of the Country*, 327; *Captives*, 437, 885; alternatives to *manet* are locutions with stay/remain/only/save/**praeter**, most commonly all but: "*Thersites only stays behind*" and "*They all go off with a flourish, only Paris and Helen keep the Stage*" (*1 Iron Age*, 345, 277), "*All save Freevill depart*" (*Dutch Courtesan*, 5.1.63), "*Exeunt omnes praeter Shore*" (*2 Edward IV*, 125), "*Exeunt all, but Hamlet*" (Q2 *Hamlet*, C1r, 1.2.128).

manner

used in a variety of locutions usually in the sense of "fashion"; figures **enter** "*in mourning manner*" (*Love's Sacrifice*, 2736), "*in warlike manner*" (*Antony and Cleopatra*, 614–15, 2.1.0; *Timon of Athens*, 1652, 4.3.48), "*attired and armed after the Trojan manner*" (*Birth of Merlin*, C3r; see also *Amorous War*, E2v); examples of "*in like manner*" are enter "*with his sword drawn, D'avolos in like manner*" (*Love's Sacrifice*, 2380–1), "*The chime again, and they turn out in like manner*" (*John a Kent*, 1161), "*Exeunt, in manner as they entered*" (*Henry VIII*, 1613, 2.4.242; *Soddered Citizen*, 1108); see also *Antonio and Mellida*, 2.1.183; *Tempest*, 2010–11, 5.1.57; actions include "*offering to lead her in gentle manner*" (*Twins*, E1v), "*fight all in a confused manner*" (*Rebellion*, 33), "*addresses him in most humble manner to Miniona*" (*Soddered Citizen*, 671–3), "*The Bishops place themselves on each side the Court in manner of a Consistory*" (*Henry VIII*, 1346–7, 2.4.0); see also *Lovesick Court*, 163.

map

called for twice: "*One brings a Map*" (*2 Tamburlaine*, 4518); see also *Anything for a Quiet Life*, F1r.

march, marching

can signal either an action or an offstage *sound*; the terms occur roughly 200 times, an indication of the military nature of numerous plays; *march/marching* frequently describe how figures *enter*: "*King Richard marching with Drums and Trumpets*" (Quarto *Richard III*, I4v, 4.4.135), "*the prince marching, and Falstaff meets him, playing upon his truncheon like a fife*" (*1 Henry IV*, G3r, 3.3.87), "*Caesar with his Army, marching*" (*Antony and Cleopatra*, 1960, 3.8.0, also 1177, 2.6.0; 2647–8, 4.8.0; 3595, 5.2.332), "*To them march in all the Argonauts*" (*Brazen Age*, 203), "*all the Greeks on one side, all the Trojans on the other: Every Trojan Prince entertains a Greek, and so march two and two*" (*1 Iron Age*, 302), "*march softly in at one door, and presently in at another*" (*2 Iron Age*, 379, also 378); for entrances of other figures, usually *marching* and often with soldiers, see *Alphonsus of Aragon*, 284–5; *2 Seven Deadly Sins*, 49; *Four Prentices*, 175, 200; *1 Edward IV*, 8, 25; *Lust's Dominion*, 4.1.39; *Troilus and Cressida*, L4v, 3521–2, 5.9.0; *Hieronimo*, 13.0; *Macbeth*, 2288–90, 5.4.0; *Coriolanus*, 3734–5, 5.6.69; for figures who *exit marching* see Folio *Hamlet*, 3905, 5.2.403; *2 If You Know Not Me*, 348; *Macbeth*, 2212, 5.2.31; 2317, 5.4.21; examples of *march over the stage* and variants are "*A march of Captains over the Stage*" (*Revenge of Bussy*, 3.1.0), "*As they march over the Stage, enter Lychas with the shirt*" (*Brazen Age*, 247), "*The organs play, and covered dishes march over the stage*" (*Mad World*, 2.1.151), "*They march over, and go out*" (*Cymbeline*, 2894–5, 5.2.0), "*March over bravely*" (*James IV*, 2406), "*They march about the Stage*" (Q2 *Romeo and Juliet*, C2v, 1.4.114; see

also *Woodstock*, 2772, 2774), "*They march along the stage one an other*" (*Edmond Ironside*, 1785–6).

A common direction for sound is *march afar off*, signaling a *drum* played *within* to create an impression of distance, as in "*Drums afar off marching*" (*If This Be Not a Good Play*, 4.3.7, also 5.2.43), "*Low March within*" (*Julius Caesar*, 1936, 4.2.24), "*Drums March within*" (*Woodstock*, 2673); in *1 Henry VI* "*A March afar off*" is acknowledged with "*I hear their drums*" (389, 1.2.68; see also *Birth of Merlin*, F2r; *Two Noble Ladies*, 1662–4); for more see Folio *Hamlet*, 3836, 5.2.349; *Blind Beggar of Bednal Green*, 4; *All's Well*, 1648, 3.5.37; *Timon of Athens*, 1647, 4.3.44; *Knight of Malta*, 109; a sound linked to a *funeral* is *dead march*: "*Exeunt bearing the Body of Martius. A dead March Sounded*" (*Coriolanus*, 3837–8, 5.6.154; see also Folio *King Lear*, 3302, 5.3.327), "*A dead march. Enter the funeral of Charlemont as a soldier*" (*Atheist's Tragedy*, 3.1.6); see also *Massacre at Paris*, 1263; *Charlemagne*, 2721; *Bonduca*, 137; similar phrases are "*doleful march*" (*2 Tamburlaine*, 3190), "*sad and funeral march*" (*2 Iron Age*, 414), "*still march*" (*King Leir*, 2464), "*solemn march*" (*Turk*, 644), "*soft March*" (*Duchess of Suffolk*, F4v), "*slow march*" (*Faithful Friends*, 2100); atypical are "*A scurvy march*" (*Hoffman*, 1126–7), "*English March*" and "*French March*" (Folio *3 Henry VI*, 1617, 3.3.30; 1620, 3.3.32), "*Danish March*" (Folio *Hamlet*, 1944–5, 3.2.89).

marriage

see *wedding*

mask, masked

masks are worn (1) as an article of women's clothing, (2) as part of a woman's *disguise*, (3) by masquers in a *masque*; after a *hunt* or journey female figures enter "*with their riding rods, unpinning their masks*" (*1 Edward IV*, 39, also 81), a courtesan appears as "*a Masked Gentlewoman in a broad hat, and scarfed*" (*Wit at Several Weapons*, 122), a servant brings in a "*Mask and Fan*" for his mistress (*Northern Lass*, 23), citizen wives meeting men at a *tavern* enter "*masked*" (*Westward Ho*, 2.3.0), both men and women sit as observers "*in Masks*" (*Antipodes*, 264); *masks* for disguise are more common; examples include entrances "*disguised, with a mask over her face*" (*Fair Em*, 855–6), "*in courtesan's disguise, and masked*" (*Mad World*, 4.3.0), "*half ready and masked*" (*Wise Woman of Hogsdon*, 311), "*masked, and in other Garments*" (*Match Me in London*, 2.4.86); for other women who appear *masked* see *Blurt*, 2.2.239, 5.3.84; *Roaring Girl*, 5.2.128; *Wit at Several Weapons*, 133; *Maidenhead Well Lost*, 151; *Changes*, K2v; *Bloody Banquet*,

1141; the distinction between female and male disguise (the latter usually involves a *beard*, false *hair*, *patch*, *scarf*, *vizard*) can be seen in "*Boyster vizarded, and Luce masked*" (*Wise Woman of Hogsdon*, 308), whereas a man disguised as a woman appears "*attired like his wife masked*" (*Westward Ho*, 4.2.52), "*like a woman masked*" and "*like a Lady masked*" (*Amends for Ladies*, 2.3.76; 5.2.3); signals for the removing of masks include "*pulls off her mask*" (*Picture*, 3.5.57; *Guardian*, 4.2.58), "*unpins her mask*" (*Swaggering Damsel*, I2v); the link between *masks* and the masque/masquing (usually spelled *mask/masking*) can be seen in "*The Dance of old women masked*" (*Old Law*, G4v), the *service* offered by allegorical figures "*dancing (and Masked)*" (*Four Plays in One*, 363), the entrance of a group "*all masked, two and two with lights like masquers*" (*Satiromastix*, 5.2.37), the appearance of three men "*Masked*" after a *dance* has begun who "*take them to Dance*" (*Wit at Several Weapons*, 134).

masque, masquers, masquing, masquery

the term *masque* (often spelled *mask*) is used loosely in directions to refer to performances or entertainments that can include spectacle, *dance*, *music*, *song*, and mime; detailed descriptions are seldom given (in contrast to directions for *dumb shows*) and sometimes a *masque* is signaled with no elaboration (*Death of Huntingdon*, 1319; *Histriomastix*, E1v; *Cynthia's Revels*, 5.7.0, 5.9.0, 5.10.0; *May Day*, 5.1.101; *Every Woman In*, H2v; *Costly Whore*, 255; *2 Arviragus and Philicia*, E9r; *Osmond*, B3v); occasionally an indication of subject matter is given: "*a Masque of Beasts*" (*Mad Lover*, 49), "*A masque of Soldiers*" (*Maid's Revenge*, H3r), "*the Masque of the Fairy Queen*" (*Valiant Welshman*, C2v), "*The Masque, wherein all the Virtues dance together*" (*Muses' Looking Glass*, M2r), "*a Masquerado of several shapes, and Dances*" (*Women Pleased*, 308); some directions are more detailed: "*Enter in the masque the Count of Arsena, Mendosa, Claridiana, Torchbearers. They deliver the shields to their several mistresses*" (*Insatiate Countess*, 2.1.48), "*The Masque. Enter Time bearing an Escutcheon, six Roman Champions crowned with Laurel follow, each bears an Escutcheon: Jehochanan and Simeon follow guarded: Time presents his Escutcheon to the General*" (*Jews' Tragedy*, 3068–71), "*Enter the Masque in which is young Tullius Marius and Arman and Lelia in Lady's habit; they follow the three young lords like furies, after dance with the Ladies*" (*Faithful Friends*, 2556–64); see also *Malcontent*, 5.5.66; *Revenger's Tragedy*, I3v; *Timon of Athens*, 465, 1.2.130; *Landgartha*, E4v.

Other directions refer to *masquers* (usually spelled *maskers*) dressed for a *masque* and typically *masked*: "*King and others as Masquers, habited like Shepherds*" (*Henry VIII*, 753–4, 1.4.63), "*the Masquers of Amazons, with Lutes in their hands, dancing and playing*" (*Timon of Athens*, 455–6, 1.2.130), "*The Masquers take the Ladies and fall to the Dance*" (*King John and Matilda*, 51), "*the Masquers, Fancy, Desire, Delight, Hope, Fear, Distrust, Jealousy, Care, Ire, Despair, they dance, after which Cupid speaks*" (*Wife for a Month*, 26), "*seven Masquers all in Shrouds*" (*Soddered Citizen*, 1916), "*four Masquers with horns on their heads: a Stag, a Ram, a Goat, and an Ox followed by four persons, a Courtier, a Captain, a Scholar and a Butcher*" (*English Moor*, 15), "*The Masquers enter. All in willow Garlands, Four Men, Four Women*" (*Northern Lass*, 41); for more see Q2 *Romeo and Juliet*, C1r, 1.4.0; *Merchant of Venice*, D1v, 2.6.0; Folio *Much Ado*, 493–4, 2.1.85; *Death of Huntingdon*, 1325; *Blurt*, 2.2.239, 335; *Dutch Courtesan*, 4.1.6; *Whore of Babylon*, 1.2.81; *Your Five Gallants*, I2v; *Cupid's Whirligig*, 5.8.28; *Nice Valour*, 157; *City Nightcap*, 156; *Perkin Warbeck*, 3.2.111; *Changes*, K2v; *Constant Maid*, H1v; *Obstinate Lady*, G4r; *Cardinal*, 3.2.91; occasionally clothing for a *masque* is specified: "*in masquery*" (*Antonio and Mellida*, 5.2.87; *Antonio's Revenge*, 5.3.32), "*in masquing attire*" (*Antonio's Revenge*, 5.2.19, 31), "*in their Masquing Robes*" (*Woman Is a Weathercock*, 5.1.64–5, 128), "*in a masquing suit with a vizard in his hand*" (*Mad World*, 2.4.1); the one reference to an *antimasque* is perhaps informative about the meaning of *antic* in other directions: "*the Antic Masque consisting of eight Bacchanalians enter girt with Vine leaves, and shaped in the middle with Tun Vessels, each bearing a Cup in their hands, who during the first strain of Music played four times over, enter by two at a time, at the Tune's end, make stand; draw wine and carouse, then dance all: The Antimasque gone off: and solemn Music playing: Messalina and Silius gloriously crowned in an Arch-glittering Cloud aloft*" (*Messalina*, 2200–9).

mattock

a tool used for loosening earth cited twice: "*Romeo and Balthasar, with a torch, a mattock, and a crow of iron*" (Q1 *Romeo and Juliet*, I4v, 5.3.21), "*Dametas, with a mattock and spade*" (*Isle of Gulls*, 294); Henslowe's inventory lists "*one wooden mattock*" (*Diary*, App. 2, 71).

meal

used in two special cases as *white* makeup: in *Three Ladies of London* Simplicity enters "*like a Miller all* mealy with a wand in his hand" (A3r), and in *Knight of the Burning Pestle* to impersonate a *ghost* Jasper enters "*his face mealed*" (222); for a different purpose, a robber "*Throws meal in his face, takes his purse*" (*Hengist*, 5.1.319).

mean

roughly equivalent to *poor* and used to describe *apparel* or a *habit*: "*Coriolanus in mean Apparel, Disguised, and muffled*" (*Coriolanus*, 2621–2, 4.4.0), '*Lucentio, in the habit of a mean man*" (*Taming of the Shrew*, 897, 2.1.38); see also *Old Fortunatus*, 1.1.0; *Patient Grissil*, 4.3.0; *Pericles*, C4v, 2.2.59; *Honest Man's Fortune*, 250; *Just Italian*, 210.

measure

either (1) a grave or stately *dance* or (2) in *sword*-fighting the action of determining the required distance between opponents by the length of a fencer's reach when lunging or thrusting; uses for dancing are "*dance a measure*" (*Two Maids of More-Clacke*, B3v), "*tread a measure*" and "*Cornets sound the measure over again*" (*Malcontent*, 4.2.0; 5.5.118), "*tread a solemn measure with changes*" (*Soddered Citizen*, 1916–17); see also *Antonio's Revenge*, 5.3.49; *Blurt*, 1.1.158; *Sir Giles Goosecap*, 5.2.386; *Malcontent*, 5.5.85; *Sophonisba*, 1.2.35; *Cupid's Revenge*, 226; *Maid's Tragedy*, 12; *School of Compliment*, L2v; twice the reference is to weapons: "*They measure, and Fabricio gets his Sword*" (*Captain*, 279), "*They measure and Device gets both weapons*" (*Country Captain*, C11r).

meat

either (1) food as distinct from *drink* or (2) an actual piece of *meat*, with the two senses sometimes hard to distinguish; for examples of *meat* as food, figures *enter* "*with meat and a bottle*" (*Bonduca*, 152), "*with wine and Meat*" (MS *Bonduca*, 963–4; *Downfall of Huntingdon*, 1516; *Two Noble Kinsmen*, F4v, 3.3.0; *Two Noble Ladies*, 559; *Fatal Contract*, H4r), simply *with meat* (*Dead Man's Fortune*, 30; *Taming of the Shrew*, 2015, 4.3.35; *Richard II*, K1r, 5.5.94; *Downfall of Huntingdon*, 2394; *Love's Pilgrimage*, 241; *Witch*, 440); actual *meat* may be required when a madman enters with "*a piece of raw meat*" (*Lover's Melancholy*, 3.3.19) and for entrances "*with meat in a basket*" (*Chaste Maid*, 2.2.96; *Three Ladies of London*, E4r), "*with bread and meat in his hand*" (*Seven Champions*, I3r), "*with a piece of meat upon his dagger's point*" (*Taming of a Shrew*, D4v), "*with a Trencher, with broken meat and a Napkin*" (*Wise Woman of Hogsdon*, 335); figures also enter "*with dishes*

of meat" (*Wit without Money*, 193), "*with napkins in their hands, followed by pages with stools and meat*" (*Fawn*, 2.0), "*like a Cook, placing the meat on the Table*" (Folio *Titus Andronicus*, 2425–6, 5.3.25); other actions include "*They cover the board and fetch in the meat*" and "*eat up all the meat*" (*Taming of a Shrew*, D4r), "*the meat goes over the Stage*" (*Thomas Lord Cromwell*, E3v), "*Strumbo hearing his voice shall start up and put meat in his pocket, seeking to hide himself*" (*Locrine*, 1648–9; see also *Selimus*, 1943), a hostess "*setting meat on the table*" but "*Eumenides walketh up and down, and will eat no meat*" (*Old Wives Tale*, 734); after "*a Table is set with meat*" for beggars "*they quarrel and grow drunk, and pocket up the meat*" (*Patient Grissil*, 4.3.11, 38); see also *Epicœne*, 3.7.16.

meditating

the few examples call for a visible display of thought or contemplation but do not indicate how to achieve the effect; *meditation* in *Hengist* is linked to a *book*, presumably a prayerbook: "*Enter to them Constantius in private meditation, they rudely Come to him, strike down his Book and Draw their swords upon him*" (DS before 2.2, 3–5); *meditation* in *Four Plays in One* is definitely linked to *prayer* when a man awaiting the birth of a child "*walks in meditation, seeming to pray*" (321); in contrast, a foolish figure "*walks off, meditating*" (Quarto *Every Man Out*, 3544); for figures who are directed to *enter* meditating see *Humour out of Breath*, 440; *Law Tricks*, 122; *Lost Lady*, 613.

meet

widely used (roughly 170 examples) mostly in entrances when (1) figures already onstage are *met* by those entering, (2) figures *enter* at different *doors* and *meet*; examples of the former are "*Enter Trumpets sounding, they go to the door, and meet the King and his Train*" (*Satiromastix*, 2.1.83), "*Enter the prince marching, and Falstaff meets him playing upon his truncheon like a fife*" (*1 Henry IV*, G3r, 3.3.87), and of the latter "*Enter Alberdure at one door, and meets with the Peasant at the other door*" (*Wisdom of Doctor Dodypoll*, 1005–6), "*Enter at one Door Mariam and Alexandra; at another Kiparim and Salumith, they meet and pass disdainfully*" (*Herod and Antipater*, D3r); most signals supply no additional details: "*Enter the three Witches, meeting Hecate*" (*Macbeth*, 1429–30, 3.5.0, also 16–17, 1.2.0), "*Enter Chartley and his man, meeting Luce*" (*Wise Woman of Hogsdon*, 312), "*They march about the stage. Then enter King Lewis and his train, and meet with King Edward*" (*2 Edward IV*, 108); variations include "*meet and justle*"

(*Cupid's Whirligig*, 1.2.76), "*meet and salute*" (*Love's Sacrifice*, 1818; see also Quarto *Every Man Out*, 2033–4; *Politician*, F4v), "*meets her and strikes her*" (*Maidenhead Well Lost*, 107), "*meeting them with action of wonderment*" (*Changeling*, 4.1.0), "*meets them, and they look strangely upon him*" (*Greene's Tu Quoque*, K3r), "*Two soldiers meet as in the watch*" (*Rape of Lucrece*, 204; see also *Antony and Cleopatra*, 2474, 4.3.6), "*the Duke meets Maria and closeth with her; the rest fall back*" (*Malcontent*, 5.5.0), "*Enter Theseus (victor) the three Queens meet him, and fall on their faces before him*" (*Two Noble Kinsmen*, C4r, 1.4.0); most common is *meet* linked to **embrace**: "*meet and embrace affectionately*" (*Lovesick Court*, 128–9); see also *Captain Thomas Stukeley*, 2456; *Warning for Fair Women*, E3v; *Antonio and Mellida*, 1.1.98, 115; *2 Edward IV*, 108; *Devil's Charter*, L2v; *2 Iron Age*, 380; *Appius and Virginia*, H3v; occasionally the *meeting* is linked to an **exit** or to a **battle/fight**: "*Make as though you were a going out, Medea meet her*" (*Alphonsus of Aragon*, 1094–5), "*Enter Dalavill meeting Young Geraldine going out*" (*English Traveller*, 91; see also *Broken Heart*, 4.4.0), "*Alarum sounded, both the battles offer to meet*" (*James IV*, 2442; see also *Trial of Chivalry*, I2v).

melancholy

the fourteen examples provide no indication of how the actor is to achieve the effect; figures are directed to **enter** melancholic (*Old Fortunatus*, 3.1.0), very melancholy (*1 Tamburlaine*, 1844; *Wounds of Civil War*, 604–5; *Devil's Law Case*, 5.4.43), most often *melancholy* (*Blurt*, 1.2.0; *Woman Killed*, 108; *Dutch Courtesan*, 4.3.0; *Woman Is a Weathercock*, 2.1.119; *No Wit*, 4.3.0; *Appius and Virginia*, B3v, F3r; *Fatal Contract*, I1r; *Duke's Mistress*, I1v); Saturn enters *melancholy* and after receiving supposed evidence that his son is dead **departs** "*in great sorrow*" (*Golden Age*, 20).

menace

an action occasionally signaled as part of a **dumb show** or other extended stage business: "*Alberto draws out his dagger, Maria her knife, aiming to menace the Duke*" (*Antonio's Revenge*, 5.1.0), "*draw their swords: menace each other, and severally depart*" (*Lovesick Court*, 129); see also *2 Seven Deadly Sins*, 3; *Death of Huntingdon*, 940; *Queen and Concubine*, 22.

midst, middle

these terms–typically *in the midst*–(1) usually indicate a location but (2) several times describe an intervention; directions for figures to **enter**/**exit** by

the *middle **door**/in the midst* are "*At the middle door, Enter Golding discovering a Goldsmith's shop*" (*Eastward Ho*, A2r), "*Enter Inguar in the middle*" and "*Exit in the middle*" (*Landgartha*, D1r, I4v), "*Gorboduc entering in The midst between*" (*2 Seven Deadly Sins*, 32–3); see also *Trial of Chivalry*, I4r; *English Traveller*, 49; *Covent Garden*, 21, 24, and more; *Parson's Wedding*, 402; another location is *in the midst of the **stage***, which can mean simply "on the stage": "*The Queen following the Bier, carrying a Garland of flowers: set it in the midst of the Stage*" (*Death of Huntingdon*, 2911–13), "*sets up a Pillar in the middle of the stage*" (*Virgin Martyr*, 4.2.61), or into the **trapdoor**: "*Arising in the midst of the stage*" (*Poetaster*, 0); see also *Devil's Charter*, A2v; *Turk*, 114–16; *World Tossed at Tennis*, D3r; other signals of location are "*Let there be a brazen Head set in the middle of the place behind the Stage*" (*Alphonsus of Aragon*, 1246–7), "*then the shieldboys fall at one end, the torch-bearers at the other; the masquers in the middle*" (*Your Five Gallants*, I2v), "*the King sitteth in the midst mounted highest*" (*Edward I*, 101), "*in the midst of the Tomb*" (*Second Maiden's Tragedy*, 1928–9), "*coming into the midst of the soldiers*" (*Appius and Virginia*, H1r); for more see *Edmond Ironside*, 1978; *Old Fortunatus*, 1.3.0; *Trial of Chivalry*, I3r; *Brazen Age*, 247; *Double Marriage*, 361; *Herod and Antipater*, F4r; *Welsh Ambassador*, 2222; *Northern Lass*, 64; *Country Girl*, D3r; an interrupted action is signaled in "*Alonzo's ghost appears to De Flores in the midst of his smile*" (*Changeling*, 4.1.0), "*Guido dances a Lavolta, or a Galliard, and in the midst of it falleth into the bride's lap*" (*Insatiate Countess*, 2.1.154); see also *Your Five Gallants*, F2r; *Royal King*, 72; *Landgartha*, F1v.

milk, milkmaid

"*milk, in an earthen vessel*" is part of a ritual in *Sejanus* (5.177) but otherwise is not specified; *milkmaids* appear in several plays usually with no other details (*Hyde Park*, G3r) or with a generic signal such as **enter** "*like Milkmaids*" (*Two Merry Milkmaids*, C2v), "*as going to milking*" (*Tottenham Court*, 106); the one item that is specified is the milk **pail**: "*Enter two Milkmaids with pails*" (*Coxcomb*, 348, 368, 370), "*The Pail goes*" when a country witch makes her pail move on its own (*Late Lancashire Witches*, 202).

mist, fog

most of the *mists* or *fogs* referred to in various plays appear to be **fictional** rather than linked to a special onstage effect; for representative scenes (without *mist* called for in a direction) see *Edward III*, H4v;

Arden of Faversham, 1721–1805; *2 If You Know Not Me*, 302–3; exceptions might include the **dumb show** in *Prophetess* in which "*Delphia raises a mist*" (363), a bogus supernatural effect in *Four Plays in One* (307), the **masque** in *Maid's Tragedy* in which "*Night rises in mists*" (8), the situation in *Histriomastix* where "*Pride casts a mist*" and then five or more figures "*vanish off the Stage*" (D1r); however, in the final sequence of the latter play (H2r) five figures are again directed to **vanish**, but no *mist* is specified.

mistake, take for

mistake is occasionally found as a verb: "*mistakes in upon them*" (*Conspiracy*, D3v), "*mistakes the body of Borachio for Soquette*" (*Atheist's Tragedy*, 4.3.205), "*Quarlous in the habit of the madman is mistaken by Mrs. Purecraft*" (*Bartholomew Fair*, 5.2.14), "*She mistaking as she moved, put up the Letter, it falls down*" (*Maid's Revenge*, E1r); when combined with *for*, *take* serves as *mistake*: "*they take him for Duke Humphrey*" (Quarto *2 Henry VI*, B2r, [1.3.5]), "*counterfeits to take him for a ghost*" (*Atheist's Tragedy*, 3.2.17), "*taking Chorebus for a Grecian by reason of his habit, fights with him and kills him*" (*2 Iron Age*, 390).

mock

used as a verb and in various noun forms, primarily for *mockery* in **song**, **dance**, or mimed **action**: "*Sings a mock-song to a ballad tune*" (*Distresses*, 305), "*Dance an Antic in which they use action of Mockery and derision to the three Gentlemen*" (*English Moor*, 67); in *Soddered Citizen* **masquers** "*tread a solemn measure with changes, the whilst Wittworth dances an antic mockway, then retires to his chair and sleeps*" (1916–19); in *Bonduca* Junius sings a song with Petillius "*after him in mockage*" (100) at which point Junius complains "Must I be thus abused?"; see also *1 Arviragus and Philicia*, D4v; the spirits in *Tempest* who bring in the banquet re-enter "*and dance (with mocks and mows) and carrying out the Table*" (1616–18, 3.3.82).

money

occurs regularly in a variety of locutions; a figure appears "*laden with Money*" (*Fatal Dowry*, 2.2.274; *Soddered Citizen*, 2725–6), "*with lights and money before him*" (*Atheist's Tragedy*, 5.1.0), "*at a Table with Jewels and Money upon it*" (*Women Pleased*, 242); most common is the *giving* of *money* (*Two Lamentable Tragedies*, E3v; *Jack Drum's Entertainment*, A3v; *Wily Beguiled*, 707; *Charlemagne*, 1801–2; *Insatiate Countess*, 5.1.91; *Fair Quarrel*, 3.2.15, 17, 22; *Two Noble Ladies*, 610;

Jovial Crew, 392; *City Wit*, 359; *Northern Lass*, 72; *Bloody Banquet*, 856; *Swaggering Damsel*, G1r; *Bird in a Cage*, F2v; *Gentleman of Venice*, E4r; *Wedding*, E4r; *Noble Stranger*, C1r), but figures also *take* (*Alchemist*, 1.2.70), *take away* (*James IV*, 1731; *Bride*, 51), *take out* (*Bird in a Cage*, E3r), **offer** (*Antipodes*, 277; *Princess*, D1r, F2v), **enter** with money (*If This Be Not a Good Play*, 2.2.53; *Loyal Subject*, 103; *Honest Lawyer*, H3r); **bags** of money are common: "*from his study, books and bags of money on a Table*" (*Ram Alley*, B3v), "*with bags of money before him casting of account*" (*Thomas Lord Cromwell*, B1v); see also *Woodstock*, 1751; *King Leir*, 1683; *Captain Thomas Stukeley*, 583; *Devil's Charter*, A2r; *Dutch Courtesan*, 2.3.0; *1 Fair Maid of the West*, 275; *Miseries of Enforced Marriage*, 1538; *New Trick*, 251; *Queen*, 3787–8; *City Wit*, 279, 368; *Wits*, 224; other locutions are "*puts money in his pocket*" (*Weeding of Covent Garden*, 38; see also *New Wonder*, 175), "*showing him press money*" (*Locrine*, 616), "*throws money among them*" (*Thomas Lord Cromwell*, A2v; see also *Distresses*, 305), "*scatters some small money*" (*Knave in Grain*, 2969), "*with his money in his hat*" (*Princess*, C2v).

monkey

called for once: "*Beatrice leading a Monkey after her*" (*Eastward Ho*, A4r).

monument

rarely used with no indication of what is meant: "*Enter Castabella mourning, to the monument of Charlemont*" and "*Charlemont finds his father's monument*" (*Atheist's Tragedy*, 3.1.52, 126); see also *Argalus and Parthenia*, 41.

moritur

Latin for "he/she **dies**" found intermittently from the early 1600s on; see *Hoffman*, 997, 1598; *Christian Turned Turk*, D4v, I3r; Q2 *Bussy D'Ambois*, 5.4.145; *Turk*, 1699, 1958, 2380, 2385; *Witch of Edmonton*, 3.3.64; *Noble Spanish Soldier*, 5.4.137; *All's Lost by Lust*, 5.5.123, 193; *Broken Heart*, [4.4.70]; *Duke's Mistress*, I1v; *Politician*, L2r.

morris

a grotesque country **dance** performed by dancers often dressed as Robin Hood and his followers: "*Iocastus with a Morris, himself maid Marian, Bromius the Clown*" (*Amyntas*, 2C4v; see also *Witch of Edmonton*, 3.1.0, 3.4.13, 49); in *Summer's Last Will* a figure "*fetcheth out the Hobby horse and the morris dance*" (193); the *morris* is conventionally accompanied by a **tabor** and *pipe* (*Shoemakers' Holiday*, 3.3.47, 51); in *Jack Drum's Entertainment* the term denotes both dancers and dance: "*The Tabor and Pipe strike up a Morris*," "*Enter the Morris*," then "*The Morris sing and dance, and Exeunt*" (A3v, A4r); "*Morris dancers*" are cited twice (*Histriomastix*, C2v; *Women Pleased*, 281).

mount

a seldom used direction for a figure to *mount* an onstage dais and/or a property on it: "*mounts unto the Throne*" (*Histriomastix*, H2v), "*mounting the tribunal*" (*Herod and Antipater*, F3v), "*mounts the Scaffold*" (*Messalina*, 2592); similar are "*mounts up the ladder*" (*2 Edward IV*, 136), "*mounts the walls*" (*Brazen Age*, 224); elsewhere a figure is *mounted* "*on the Ass*" (*Christian Turned Turk*, F2v) and "*upon a seahorse*" (*Golden Age*, 78), and "*the king sitteth in the midst mounted highest*" (*Edward I*, 101); atypical is "*leads his train up to the mount*" (*Sophonisba*, 5.2.22).

mourning

associated with the color **black** and with distinctive **sounds**, **music**, **attire**, behavior: "*David barefoot, with some loose covering over his head, and all mourning*" (*David and Bethsabe*, 972), "*two with mourning pennons: a Drum sounding a dead march: Dalva carried upon a horse covered with black: Soldiers after, trailing their Pikes*" (*Alarum for London*, 260–3; see also *Hieronimo*, 12.0), "*A table set forth with two tapers, a death's head, a book. Jolenta in mourning*" (*Devil's Law Case*, 3.3.0), "*sitting at a table covered with black, on which stands two black tapers lighted, she in mourning*" (*Insatiate Countess*, 1.1.0); *Puritan* provides entrances "*all in mourning apparel, Edmond in a Cypress Hat. The Widow wringing her hands, and bursting out into passion, as newly come from the Burial of her husband*," "*in black scurvy mourning coats, and Books at their Girdles, as coming from Church*" (A3r, B2v); costume descriptions are often generic rather than specific: "*in mourning coats*" (*Case Is Altered*, 1.3.0), "*in mourning habit*" (*Malcontent*, 5.5.43; *Faithful Friends*, 969), "*in mourning cloaks*" (*2 Henry VI*, D2r, 1169–70, 2.4.0; *Selimus*, 1748), "*in mourning manner*" (*Love's Sacrifice*, 2736), "*in base mourning attire*" (*Malcontent*, 4.5.0), "*in mourning veil*" (*Death of Huntingdon*, 962; see also *Country Girl*, B3r; *Young Admiral*, C1r; *Love and Honour*, 152); sounds/music include "*Enter a Corpse, after it Irishmen mourning, in a dead March*" (*Four Prentices*, 178), "*The still flutes sound a mournful sennet. Enter a coffin*" (*Antonio and Mellida*, 5.2.208), "*a sad Music of Flutes heard*," then the entrance of a **hearse** attended

by figures "*all in mourning habits*" (*King John and Matilda*, 84), "*while all the company seem to weep and mourn, there is a sad song in the music room*" (*Chaste Maid*, 5.4.0); figures **enter/exit** in mourning (*Anything for a Quiet Life*, F4r; *Fatal Contract*, E3v; *Cleopatra*, D10r; *Coronation*, 287; *Lovesick King*, 1360; *Argalus and Parthenia*, 62; *2 Arviragus and Philicia*, E10v; *Andromana*, 221; *Albovine*, 25), simply *mourning*: "*the King of Spain mourning after his brother's body*" (*Spanish Tragedy*, 4.4.217), "*they bear the king over the stage mourning*" (*Tom a Lincoln*, 2699), "*Castabella mourning, to the monument of Charlemont*" (*Atheist's Tragedy*, 3.1.52), "*The maids sit down at her feet mourning*" (*Broken Heart*, 4.4.0); see also *Sir Thomas More*, 1793–4; *Edward II*, 601, 1286; *How a Man May Choose*, H1r; *Mad Lover*, 40; variations include "*disguised like mourners*" (*Selimus*, 1909; see also *Hoffman*, 1683), "*he sits by her and mourns*" (*Whore of Babylon*, DS before Act 1, 31), "*they mournfully bear in the body*" (*Death of Huntingdon*, 944), "*the mournful solemnity of Massinissa's presenting Sophonisba's body*" (*Sophonisba*, 5.4.36), "*the song ended, the Hearse is set down between both companies, Aphelia mourning at one end, and the King at the other*" (*Fatal Contract*, E3v); for *mourners* see Folio *Richard III*, 174, 1.2.0; *Antonio's Revenge*, 2.1.0; *Law Tricks*, 183; *Michaelmas Term*, 4.4.51; *Chaste Maid*, 5.4.0; *Swetnam*, G2r; *Fatal Dowry*, 2.1.47; *Duchess of Suffolk*, G2r; *Wasp*, 476; atypical is "*the Crown upon a mourning Cushion*" (*Coronation*, 287).

mouth

found in a variety of locutions and actions (1) most commonly **stopping**/laying a **finger** on one's *mouth* but also (2) the *mouth* of a **cave**/**vault**, (3) objects placed in the *mouth*; to *stop* a figure's *mouth* is to silence him: "*The Guard lead off Lamia stopping his mouth*" (*Roman Actor*, 2.1.239); see also *Grim the Collier*, H10r; *Hieronimo*, 8.55; *Devil's Charter*, C2v; to *lay a finger* on the *mouth* is to signal silence (*Captain*, 297; *Virgin Martyr*, 4.3.187), as when a villain "*lays his finger on his mouth, and draws his dagger*" (*Antonio's Revenge*, 2.2.215) saying "Look, here's a trope: a true rogue's lips are mute; / I do not use to speak, but execute"; related is "*touches the Clown's mouth with his wand*" (*Birth of Merlin*, G1v); *Sophonisba* provides entrances "*as out of a cave's mouth*" and "*Through the vault's mouth*" (4.1.0, 4.1.42); see also *Aglaura*, 5.1.15; objects in the *mouth* include a **ring** (*Rare Triumphs*, 1373), **key** (*Roman Actor*, 2.1.287), knot (*Prisoners*, C7r), captive kings drawing Tamburlaine's **chariot** "*with bits in their mouths*" (*2 Tamburlaine*, 3979), a figure who "*riseth out of the Tomb with one candle in his mouth, and in each hand one*" (*Fedele and Fortunio*, 598–9); atypical are "*He writes his name with his staff and guides it with feet and mouth*" and "*She takes the staff in her mouth, and guides it with her stumps and writes*" (*Titus Andronicus*, F4v, G1r, 4.1.68, 76); other locutions are "*bloody about their mouths*" (*Albovine*, 102), "*makes a mouth at him*" (*Staple of News*, 2.2.59); actions include "*pulls the Beaker from his mouth*" (*Alphonsus of Germany*, F1v; see also *Fatal Contract*, H4v), "*kisses her, and she shoves him away with her mouth*" (*Parson's Wedding*, 409), "*Spits in the dog's mouth*" (*Roaring Girl*, 2.1.371).

muffled

specified in roughly twenty-five directions; to **enter** *muffled* is to appear with one's **face** concealed by a **garment**, hence surreptitiously or in conspiratorial fashion, as when Coriolanus enters "*in mean Apparel, Disguised and muffled*" (2621–2, 4.4.0); Lucius describes the offstage conspirators: "Their hats are plucked about their ears / And half their faces buried in their cloaks, / That by no means I may discover them / By any mark of favor" (*Julius Caesar*, 2.1.73–6); the item regularly specified is the **cloak** so that a figure can appear "*muffled in his cloak*" (*1 Edward IV*, 67; *Second Maiden's Tragedy*, 589–91), "*in a cloak, muffled*" (*Timon of Athens*, 1169, 3.4.40); see also *Look about You*, 1810; *May Day*, 3.3.145; *Faithful Friends*, 2837–9; *Goblins*, 4.3.35; *Maid's Revenge*, F1v; occasionally the emphasis falls upon the verb/action: "*muffles himself in his cloak*" (*May Day*, 3.3.113), "*Muffles himself*" (*Queen*, 3114); but most common is *muffled* with no further details; for representative examples see *Puritan*, F1r; *Satiromastix*, 4.3.68; *Shoemakers' Holiday*, 3.4.0; *1 Honest Whore*, 5.2.86; *Roaring Girl*, 3.2.190, 4.2.78, 219; *Brazen Age*, 220; *Devil's Law Case*, 4.2.0; *Guardian*, 1.1.80; *Spanish Gypsy*, C4v; *Valiant Scot*, K1r; *Knave in Grain*, 2542; *Aglaura*, 1.4.1.

mule

see *ass*

multitudes

a rarely used *permissive* term: "*Multitudes with Halters about their Necks*" (Folio *2 Henry VI*, 2860–1, 4.9.9; Quarto "*Rebels,*" G3v), "*Sir Thomas being weaponless defends himself with stones; at last being oppressed with multitudes his servant flies and he is taken*" (*Travels of Three English Brothers*, 360).

music

this common direction for **sound** occurs more than 630 times in over 220 plays usually with context the only indication of the instrument(s); *music* can accompany a **song**, **banquet**, **dumb show**, or other set piece, and is sometimes signaled for *entr'acte* entertainment; the basic signal, *music*, is found in the margins of stage plots and playhouse manuscripts (*Dead Man's Fortune*, 24, 34, 49; *John a Kent*, 777, 916; *Woodstock*, 2117, 2436; *Second Maiden's Tragedy*, 2224; *Captives*, 1480; *Two Noble Ladies*, 1099, 1771, 1854; *Launching of the Mary*, 244, 622, 1215, 2014, 2668); other examples include "*Music an Altar discovered and Statues, with a Song*" (*Game at Chess*, 2038–9, also 1576–9, 2002–3), "*Music Dumb show: Fortune is discovered upon an altar*" (*Hengist*, DS before 1.2, 1, also 1.1.28), "*Music. A banquet*" and "*Music. A closet discovered*" (*Atheist's Tragedy*, 2.1.0, 5.1.0), "*Boy danceth, Music. Finis Actus primi*" (*Knight of the Burning Pestle*, 178, also 193, 209); the basic call for *music* recurs in the Shakespeare canon (*Taming of the Shrew*, 187, Induction.2.35; *Twelfth Night*, 939, 2.4.50, for "Come away Death"; *Macbeth*, 1679, 4.1.132; *Two Noble Kinsmen*, B1r, 1.1.0; C4v, 1.5.0), in the Middleton canon (*Michaelmas Term*, 3.5.71; *Trick to Catch the Old One*, B4r, D2r; *Hengist*, 2.1.0; *Women Beware Women*, 3.3.133, 200, 227, 5.2.48, 71), and in the Fletcher canon (*Maid's Tragedy*, 11; *Chances*, 227; *Captain*, 295; *Bonduca*, 100); sometimes the signal is *music* **sounds**: "*Music sounds a short strain*" (*Antonio's Revenge*, 1.2.64), "*Then trumpets cease, and Music sounds*" (*Doctor Faustus*, B 1301), "*The music sounds, and she dies*" (*2 Tamburlaine*, 3063), "*The Music sounds, and Pasquil's Eye is fixed upon Catherine*" (*Jack Drum's Entertainment*, H4v), "*Music sounds: Enter Vice with a gilded face, and horns on her head*" (*Old Fortunatus*, 1.3.0); see also *Histriomastix*, E1v; *Patient Grissil*, 5.2.105; *Cupid's Whirligig*, 3.3.181; *Knave in Grain*, 592, 1212; *Challenge for Beauty*, 56; an alternate locution, frequent in Shakespeare, is *music* **plays**: "*Music plays and they dance*" (Q2 *Romeo and Juliet*, C3r, 1.5.25), "*Music plays. Enter two or three Servants with a Banquet*" (*Antony and Cleopatra*, 1333–4, 2.7.0, also 1464, 2.7.112); see also *Taming of the Shrew*, 1564, 3.2.183; *Richard II*, I4r, 5.5.41; *1 Henry IV*, F3v, 3.1.228; *Twelfth Night*, 898, 2.4.14; *Coriolanus*, 2653, 4.5.0; examples elsewhere are "*The Music plays, they bring out the banquet*" (*Thomas Lord Cromwell*, D2r, also D2v, D3v), "*Music plays, they dance*" (*Cobbler's Prophecy*, 1021); see also *Insatiate Countess*, 3.1.14; *Michaelmas Term*, Induction.29; *Woman Is a Weathercock*, 1.2.393; *Hengist*, 4.2.0; *Fair Maid of the Inn*, 201; *Goblins*, 2.2.2.

An elaboration of the basic term is **loud** *music*, usually for a grand entrance or special occasion: "*Loud Music, and Enter Ushers before, the Secretary, Treasurer, Chancellor; Admiral, Constable hand in hand, the King following, others attend*" (*Chabot*, 1.1.115), "*Loud music. They possess the Stage in all state*" (*2 Iron Age*, 408, also 405, 411); see also *Sophonisba*, 1.2.236; *Timon of Athens*, 337, 1.2.0; *No Wit*, 4.3.0, 40; *Maid of Honour*, 4.2.0, 28, 5.2.0; *Prophetess*, 363; *Picture*, 1.2.128, 2.2.122; *Emperor of the East*, 1.1.82, 3.2.0; *King John and Matilda*, 51; *Bloody Banquet*, 1093; also found is **soft** *music*, typically for solemn or supernatural business: "*He vanishes in Thunder; then (to soft Music) Enter the shapes again, and dance (with mocks and mows)*" (*Tempest*, 1616–17, 3.3.82, also 1716, 4.1.59), "*A sad sound of soft music. The Tomb is discovered*" (*Love's Sacrifice*, 2733–4), "*Soft music, enter seven Masquers all in Shrouds, and tread a solemn measure*" (*Soddered Citizen*, 1916–17); see also *Birth of Merlin*, D3v; *Faithful Friends*, 2485; *Broken Heart*, 4.3.141; *Constant Maid*, E2r; *Wasp*, 2183, 2321 (where the signal is added by the bookkeeper at **magic** business); *Antipodes*, 313; similar are **sad** *music* and **solemn** *music*: "*Solemn Music. Enter (as in an Apparition) Sicilius Leonatus, Father to Posthumus*" (*Cymbeline*, 3065–6, 5.4.29, also 2482, 4.2.186), "*Solemn and strange Music: and Prosper on the top invisible*" (*Tempest*, 1535–6, 3.3.17, also 2008, 5.1.57), "*A sad music, the Players bearing off Paris's body*" (*Roman Actor*, 4.2.308), "*during all which ceremony, this ditty is sung, to very solemn music, by diverse Churchmen*" (*Duchess of Malfi*, 3.4.7); see also *Warning for Fair Women*, D1r; *Law Tricks*, 183; *Second Maiden's Tragedy*, 2454–5; *City Madam*, 5.3.59; *Fatal Contract*, E3v; another related term is **still** or soft *music*: "*A noise of still music; and Enter the high Priest with attendants*" (*Jews' Tragedy*, 2147); see also *As You Like It*, 2682, 5.4.107; *Double Marriage*, 331; *Love's Mistress*, 108; quite different is the timing signal *music still* or continuing, as in "*Music still: Enter Shadow … singing*" (*Old Fortunatus*, 3.1.389); at Titania's call for "*music, such as charmeth sleep*" in Folio *Midsummer Night's Dream* "*Music still*" (1600, 4.1.83) might mean that the musicians continue playing from earlier in the scene, although possibly it should be "*still music*"; conversely, in *Little French Lawyer* "*Still Music within*" (431) is a direction for it to continue; other signals are for *music to* **cease**: "*Salutations ended, cease music*" (*Perkin Warbeck*, 2.1.39), "*Cease loud music, all make a stand*" (*Broken Heart*, 5.2.0, also 5.2.19); see also Folio *Merchant of Venice*, 2525, 5.1.110; *Old Fortunatus*, 3.1.460, 4.1.114;

Thracian Wonder, C4r; *Henry VIII*, 2673, 4.2.95; *Custom of the Country*, 335; *Cruel Brother*, 137; *City Madam*, 4.2.66; *Lady Mother*, 755; *Queen and Concubine*, 128.

Of the numerous combined signals most common are those for *music* and **song**/*music* and **dance**; for examples of the former see *Blurt*, 1.2.208; *Chaste Maid*, 4.1.151; *Honest Man's Fortune*, 239; *More Dissemblers*, B1r, C2r, E1r, F2r; *Custom of the Country*, 336; *False One*, 341; *Roman Actor*, 5.1.159; *Broken Heart*, 3.2.0; typical are "*Music, Song*" (*As You Like It*, 2136, 4.2.9), "*Music, and a Song*" (*Macbeth*, 1464, 3.5.33; see also *Julius Caesar*, 2278, 4.3.266); for *music* and dance see *Woodstock*, 2093–4; Folio *Much Ado*, 561, 2.1.150; *Tragedy of Byron*, 2.65; *Two Noble Kinsmen*, G3v, 3.5.137; *Swetnam*, K3r–v; *Little French Lawyer*, 431; *'Tis Pity*, 4.1.35; *English Moor*, 16; *Jovial Crew*, 366; other directions include "*the dance consisting of eight Madmen, with music answerable thereunto*" (*Duchess of Malfi*, 4.2.114), "*Music of all sorts*" (*Epicœne*, 3.7.3), "*Music sounds ceremoniously*" (*Wizard*, 1818), "*Music in diverse places*" (*Women Pleased*, 307); the instrument is seldom named: "*Music of the Hoboys is under the Stage*" (*Antony and Cleopatra*, 2482, 4.3.12; see also *Double Marriage*, 348), "*Still Music of Records*" (*Two Noble Kinsmen*, L1v, 5.1.136; see also *Landgartha*, B1v), "*Music Chime*" (*John a Kent*, 1138), "*Music. Cornet*" (*Blind Beggar of Bednal Green*, 102), "*Music of Bells etc.*" (*Isle of Gulls*, 266).

Although typically *music* is played **within**, only rarely is this location specified: "*Music sounds within*" (Folio *Troilus and Cressida*, 1477, 3.1.0), "*Music within: the Fiddlers*" (*Westward Ho*, 5.3.16), "*Song, to the Music within*" (*John a Kent*, 1149), "*A Horrid noise of Music within*" (*Little French Lawyer*, 440, also 429); see also *Alphonsus of Aragon*, 922; *James IV*, 1; *Selimus*, 866; *Lust's Dominion*, 1.1.0, 3.2.0; *1 Iron Age*, 274; *Pilgrim*, 221, 223; some directions also spell out what might have been common practice–that the musicians are located **above** in a **music room**–as implied by "*Music and a Song, above*" (*Tragedy of Byron*, 2.2), "*Still music above*" (*Cruel Brother*, 183), "*music aloft*" (*Launching of the Mary*, 2793, also 245); see also *Woman's Prize*, 35; *Roman Actor*, 2.1.215; *Picture*, 3.5.25; *Fatal Contract*, G3v; occasionally *music* clearly means the musicians: in *2 Henry IV* "*Enter Music*" (E1v, 2.4.225) is acknowledged "The music is come sir" and Falstaff replies "Let them play"; similarly "*Enter Prince Richard with music*," then "*Exeunt Music*" (*Look about You*, 2170, 2184), "*Music come down*" (*City Madam*, 3.1.4); see also *Edward I*, 746; *Shoemaker a Gentleman*,

1.3.119; *Old Law*, K3r; *Love and Honour*, 156; *Sophy*, 5.260.

music room
by inference from directions and other evidence a location *above* on the upper playing level, which given the number of signals for music above is probably used more often than indicated by the few actual directions: *"there is a sad song in the music room"* (*Chaste Maid*, 5.4.0), *"speaks in the Music room behind the Curtains"* (*Thracian Wonder*, D1v), *"Music, and a Song from the music room"* (*Country Girl*, K4v); see also *Money Is an Ass*, E3r; *Parson's Wedding*, 387.

musing
indicates that a figure is to be visibly pondering/thinking: *"walks up and down musing"* (*Lust's Dominion*, 4.3.92); for directions to *enter*/*walk*/walk by/*stand* musing see *2 Fortune's Tennis*, 15; *Maid of Honour*, 4.4.133; *New Way to Pay*, 2.3.60; *Bloody Banquet*, 887; *City Wit*, 333; *Aglaura*, 4.3.53; *Landgartha*, F3r; an alternative is *"They are all in a muse"* (*James IV*, 941); *Court Beggar* provides a comic version with some possible stage business attached: *"He writes in his tables, sometimes scratching his head, as pumping his Muse"* (261).

musket, musketeer
as with *halberd*, *drum*, *trumpet* and other portable objects, *musket* can refer either to the *weapon* (a smoothbore shoulder gun) or to the figure carrying it; of the few references four are found in the same play, *Dick of Devonshire*, which calls for an entrance *"with muskets,"* *"a Guard of muskets,"* *"twelve Musketeers,"* *"Diverse muskets"* (435–6, 864–6, 787–8, 1623–4); soldiers with *muskets* are cited in two plays (*Tragedy of Byron*, 5.4.17; *Unnatural Combat*, 5.2.43), a *musketeer* and a sergeant enter with Charlemont in *Atheist's Tragedy* (2.6.0), an assassination attempt includes *"As they are going, the Soldier dischargeth his Musket at the Lord Admiral"* (*Massacre at Paris*, 199).

mute
figures identified as *mutes* are brought onstage in *Epicœne* where *"The Mute is stealing away"* (2.2.88), in *Just Italian* where one of them *"pulls off his vizard and discovers himself to be Altamont"* (277), in the *dumb show* in Folio *Hamlet* where the poisoner is accompanied by *"some two or three Mutes"* (1998–9, 3.2.135); instances of *mute* as an adjective are *"Enter Sforza at the other end raging, and the Jailer, with mute action"*

(*Queen and Concubine*, 46), and after Friar Bacon strikes Friar Bungay dumb, *"Bungay is mute, crying Hud hud"* (*Friar Bacon*, 787); see also *2 Fortune's Tennis*, 6.

N

naked
used to describe (1) partial undress, unreadiness (but not the total absence of clothing), (2) less commonly an unsheathed *weapon*; for examples of partial undress, a *shipwrecked* figure appears *"as newly landed and half naked"* (*Four Prentices*, 176), and *sleeping* figures surprised by an attack enter *"half naked"* (*King Leir*, 2476, also 2506); half naked becomes more specific in *"the Ghost of young Malefort, naked from the waist, full of wounds"* (*Unnatural Combat*, 5.2.271), *"Offers his naked breast"* (*Cruel Brother*, 189); atypical is *"Enter Envy, his arms naked besmeared with blood"* (*Mucedorus*, A2r); see also *half*, *unready*; for naked *daggers*/*poniards* see *Twins*, E1v, E2v; *Messalina*, 951; *Cruel Brother*, 122; in *Changeling* De Flores *"hides a naked rapier"* (3.1.0).

napkin
linked to onstage or offstage eating and *drinking*; the *napkin* is a regular part of the *as from* dinner formula so that figures *enter* *"with napkins, as from supper"* (*Love's Sacrifice*, 1823), *"having his napkin on his shoulder, as if he were suddenly raised from dinner"* (*Downfall of Huntingdon*, 166–8), *"as it were brushing the Crumbs from his clothes with a Napkin, as newly risen from supper"* (*Woman Killed*, 118); *Wise Woman of Hogsdon* provides entrances of a figure *"with a Trencher, with broken meat and a Napkin,"* a second *"with a Bowl of Beer and a Napkin,"* a third *"with his Napkin as from Dinner"* (335–6); see also *Woodstock*, 3–5; *Shoemakers' Holiday*, 5.4.0; *napkins* are also introduced when meals or other refreshments are to be consumed onstage: after entering *"with Wine and a napkin"* a boy *"fills the wine and gives them the napkin"* (*Wily Beguiled*, 351–2, 354–5), two figures enter *"with napkins in their hands, followed by pages with stools and meat"* (*Fawn*, 2.0); see also *Humorous Day's Mirth*, 3.1.0; *Woman Is a Weathercock*, 3.2.1; *Jovial Crew*, 416; *New Academy*, 19; in Q2 *Romeo and Juliet* the shift from 1.4 (the Queen Mab scene) to 1.5 (the Capulets' ball) is effected when the masquers *"march about the Stage, and Servingmen come forth with Napkins"* (C2v, 1.5.0); *napkins* not linked to food/drink include the *"bloody*

napkin" associated with the murdered Horatio (*Spanish Tragedy*, 3.13.85), the "*Napkins and Fire*" introduced for Cerimon's resuscitation of Thaisa (*Pericles*, E4r, 3.2.86).

neck
usually cited (1) for objects *about the neck*, (2) **embraces**/**hanging** about the neck but also (3) found in a variety of other actions and contexts; the most common object cited as *about the neck* is the **halter**/**rope**/**cord**, whether for suicide or **execution**: "*bound and halters about their necks*" (*Little French Lawyer*, 441), "*with ropes about their necks, their weapons with the points towards them*" (*Christian Turned Turk*, H1v), "*in their Shirts, barefoot, with halters about their necks*" (*Edward III*, I3v); see also *Edward I*, 1965; *2 Henry VI*, G3v, 2860–1, 4.9.9; *Captain Thomas Stukeley*, 1279–80; *Sir Thomas Wyatt*, 2.3.70; *Every Man Out*, Quarto 2300, Folio 3.7.0; *Antonio's Revenge*, 4.1.162; *Bonduca*, 102; *Vow Breaker*, 2.4.0; *Perkin Warbeck*, 5.3.184; *Jews' Tragedy*, 1997, 3131–2; comparable are "*a chain about his neck*" (*Bondman*, 3.3.0; *Alphonsus of Germany*, E1v), "*an Iron about his neck*" (*Dick of Devonshire*, 1624), "*chained by the necks*" (*Lust's Dominion*, 5.2.0); other objects specified *about the neck* are a **scythe** (*Summer's Last Will*, 803), string (*Tom a Lincoln*, 2864), **towel** (*Eastward Ho*, B3r), **horns** (*Woodstock*, 2120; *Summer's Last Will*, 634), "*a foul napkin*" (*Inconstant Lady*, 3.4.0), "*a Table written*" (*Tragedy of Byron*, 2.2); **embraces** or comparable actions include "*Embrace his neck*" (*Looking Glass for London*, 1564), "*hanging about his neck lasciviously*" (*Insatiate Countess*, 3.4.82), "*hangs about his neck whispering*" (*Albovine*, 66), "*taketh Em about the neck*" (*Fair Em*, 168–70), "*takes her up, and declines his head upon her neck*" (*Hamlet*, Q2 H1v, Folio 1993, 3.2.135), "*hanging about Hiparcus's neck wounded and fainting*" (*Prisoners*, B9r); other actions are "*The Pagan takes the Halter from his own Neck, and puts it about Sparrow's neck, and runs away*" (*Guy of Warwick*, C4v), "*as Camillo is about to vault, Flamineo pitcheth him upon his neck, and with the help of the rest, writhes his neck about, seems to see if it be broke, and lays him folded double as 'twere under the horse*" (*White Devil*, 2.2.37); atypical is "*Clifford wounded, with an arrow in his neck*" (*Octavo 3 Henry VI*, C3v, 2.6.0).

net
used for (1) catching fish, (2) trapping people; for examples of fishing, *Pericles* provides "*two Fishermen, drawing up a Net*" (C3r, 2.1.115), and *Humour out of*

Breath supplies an entrance "*they with angles, and he with a net*" (415, also 444); one of the madmen on display in *1 Honest Whore* is "*an old man, wrapped in a Net*" (5.2.176) who, when he states he is not a fisherman, is asked "What do you with that net then?"; for examples of trapping people, in *Brazen Age* Vulcan appears "*with his net of wire*," then catches Venus and Mars "*fast in his net*" (236–7), and a sequence in *Fedele and Fortunio* includes "*Here Crackstone runs into the net, Fedele after him*," "*leading Crackstone in the net*," "*Let him out of the net*," "*Exit with them that held the net*" (1367–8, 1373–4, 1446, 1474–5).

night
(1) appears regularly in signals for costume, particularly the widely used **nightgown**, (2) occasionally stands alone as an indicator of the time of day; in addition to the *nightgown*/**nightcap**, directions call for a *night mantle* (*Love's Sacrifice*, 1268), *night* **apparel** (*Antonio and Mellida*, 5.2.0), *night* **clothes** (*Parson's Wedding*, 387, 494), *night* **habiliments** (*Tom a Lincoln*, 2494–5), *night* **attire** (*Look about You*, 1748; *Lust's Dominion*, 2.3.91; *Sophonisba*, 1.2.0; *Coxcomb*, 361; *Love's Mistress*, 120; *Fatal Contract*, D4v; *Love's Sacrifice*, 2350–1; *Messalina*, 676; *Mad Couple*, 76; *City Wit*, 358); several figures are directed to wear both *nightgown* and *night attire* (*Two Maids of More-Clacke*, E3v; *Woman Killed*, 139); variations include "*in her nightclothes, as going to bed*" (*Match at Midnight*, 77), "*pass over the Stage with Pillows, Nightclothes, and such things*" (*Little French Lawyer*, 416), "*Dalavill in a Nightgown: Wife in a Nighttire, as coming from Bed*" (*English Traveller*, 70); for examples of *night* not linked to clothing, *Atheist's Tragedy* calls for "*A banquet. In the night*" (2.1.0), and *Platonic Lovers* signals "*A table with Nightlinen set out*" (28); two plays invoke *as* [*if*] for entrances "(*as in an Arbor*) *in the night*" (*Deserving Favourite*, E1v), "*softly as by night*" (*Captain Thomas Stukeley*, 924–5).

nightcap
like the **nightgown** can indicate (1) **night**/early morning, (2) unreadiness/vulnerability, (3) **sickness**/debility; **unready** or newly awakened figures **enter** "*in his nightcap: buttoning*" (*Doctor Faustus*, B 1206), "*in his nightcap trussing himself*" (*Westward Ho*, 2.1.0; see also *Devil's Charter*, C1v, I3v), "*unready, in his nightcap, garterless*" (*Two Maids of More-Clacke*, E3v); a prisoner in **prison** enters "*with a Torch, a Nightcap, and his Doublet open*" (*Fleer*, 5.3.0), and a **wounded** figure enters "*his Arm in a scarf, a nightcap on his head*" (*Widow's Tears*, 4.1.0); several directions call for both

a *nightcap* and a nightgown (*Antonio's Revenge*, 3.1.0, 131; *Insatiate Countess*, 2.4.14, 4.1.112); see also *Two Lamentable Tragedies*, I2r; *Eastward Ho*, E4r; *Northward Ho*, 4.1.0; *Custom of the Country*, 363–4; *Dick of Devonshire*, 941; *Wasp*, 535; *Soddered Citizen*, 2414.

nightgown

widely used (roughly forty examples) to signal (1) the time as *night* or early morning, (2) the place as a bedroom or other domestic space, (3) more generally *unreadiness*, a troubled conscience, or sleeplessness; a sense of place is made explicit in an entrance "*in her nightgown as to bed-ward*" (*White Devil*, 2.2.23); examples of unreadiness/troubled *sleep* include the sleepless Henry IV in his *nightgown* (*2 Henry IV*, E3v, 3.1.0), "*in his nightgown all unready*" (*2 Iron Age*, 381; see also *Platonic Lovers*, 86); *nightgowns* are regularly combined with other items of costume such as a *shirt* (*Alphonsus of Germany*, B1r, F2r, G1r; *Humorous Day's Mirth*, 1.1.0; *Insatiate Countess*, 3.1.121; *Parson's Wedding*, 500), *slippers* (*2 Iron Age*, 385; *Captain*, 296; *Parson's Wedding*, 500), night *attire* (*Woman Killed*, 139; *Two Maids of More-Clacke*, E3v), "*in their nightgowns and kerchers on their heads*" (*John a Kent*, 582); for some of the many figures who *enter* in nightgowns see *John a Kent*, 604; *James IV*, 1941; *Julius Caesar*, 984, 2.2.0; Q1 *Hamlet*, G2v, 3.4.101; Quarto *Othello*, B3r, 1.1.159; *Woman Killed*, 138; *Sophonisba*, 1.2.35, 4.1.42; *Devil's Charter*, C1r; *Mad World*, 2.4.14; *Golden Age*, 70; *English Traveller*, 70; *Great Duke of Florence*, 2.2.43; *Martyred Soldier*, 199; *Jews' Tragedy*, 1360; *Twins*, F2v; *Bloody Banquet*, 1141–2; *Brennoralt*, 5.2.0; *Country Girl*, K1v; *Just Italian*, 264; atypical is "*drags in Sophonisba in her nightgown petticoat*" (*Sophonisba*, 3.1.0).

nisi

Latin for "except" used twice in the locution *exeunt omnes nisi* ("exeunt all except"), an alternative to *manet* (*Vow Breaker*, 5.1.69; *All's Lost by Lust*, 1.1.116), and once in "*Enter Omnes nisi Bateman, Anne*" (*Vow Breaker*, 1.2.48).

noise

the roughly 130 examples are typically linked to *sound* from *within*; *noise* can refer to (1) voices *crying* or *shouting*, (2) actions difficult to stage such as a *battle* or *hunt*, (3) sounds establishing the context for an entrance, (4) *music* or other sounds from instruments, (5) sounds creating a mysterious atmosphere; the signal can be merely *noise* or *noise within*, and subsequent events or dialogue provide

specifics: in Q2 *Hamlet* "*A noise within*" (L1r, 4.5.96, 109; L1v, 4.5.153) precedes the entrances of a messenger, Laertes, and Ophelia; in *Antony and Cleopatra* this signal represents the disturbance caused by the "rural fellow" wanting entry (3479, 5.2.232), and in *Coriolanus* is the *noise* of the "rabble" (1987, 3.1.259); elsewhere "*A Noise*" precedes the entrance of a ghost (*If This Be Not a Good Play*, 5.4.261), and "*Noise within*" induces fear (*1 Edward IV*, 14; *Lovers' Progress*, 108, 109); a call for *noise* occurs in playhouse manuscripts (*John of Bordeaux*, 121; *Two Noble Ladies*, 1147; *Captives*, 1428, 2032–3, 2036, 2758, 2772; *Wasp*, 2113); for more examples of the basic signal in various contexts see *Spanish Tragedy*, 3.13.44; Folio *2 Henry VI*, 1942, 3.2.235; *Downfall of Huntingdon*, 1099; *Hieronimo*, 12.23; MS *Bonduca*, 2104; *Game at Chess*, 634; *Duchess of Suffolk*, E1v; *Aglaura*, 3.2.65; more detailed directions give words shouted or cried: "*A noise within, Down with the Tawny-Coats*" and "*A noise again, Stones, Stones*" (*1 Henry VI*, 1281–2, 3.1.73; 1286, 3.1.75), "*A great noise within crying, run, save, hold*" (*Two Noble Kinsmen*, M3v, 5.4.39; M1v, 5.3.66), "*Make a noise, Westward ho*" (*Edward I*, 2287), "*A noise within crying, Liberty, liberty*" (*Histriomastix*, F3v), "*A noise within, crying down with your swords*" (*Honest Man's Fortune*, 259), "*A noise within of, Diablo Englese*" (*Dick of Devonshire*, 1740), "*A noise within, Follow, follow, follow*" (*Merry Devil of Edmonton*, E2v; see also *Sir Thomas Wyatt*, 4.4.23; *Nobody and Somebody*, D3v; *Miseries of Enforced Marriage*, 1537; *Two Noble Kinsmen*, M1v, 5.3.66; *Messalina*, 2132–3; *Prisoners*, A5v); for more see *Henry VIII*, 329, 1.2.8; *Duchess of Suffolk*, F2r; *Rebellion*, 39; *Princess*, I1v.

Examples of *noise* for hunting include "*Enter Titus Andronicus, and his three sons, making a noise with hounds and horns*" (*Titus Andronicus*, D1r, 2.2.0), "*A noise of Hunters heard, Enter diverse Spirits in shape of Dogs and Hounds*" (*Tempest*, 1929–30, 4.1.254), "*After a noise of horns and shoutings, enter certain Huntsmen*" (*James IV*, 1548–9), "*Horns winded, a great noise of hunting, Enter Diana, all her Nymphs in the chase*" (*Golden Age*, 32); see also Quarto *Merry Wives*, G3r, 5.5.102; *Shoemakers' Holiday*, 2.1.9; *Patient Grissil*, 1.1.0; *Martyred Soldier*, 205; *noise* indicative of an offstage disturbance is variously described: "*Noise and Tumult within; Enter Porter and his men*" (*Henry VIII*, 3257–8, 5.3.0), "*Tumult and noise within*" (*Valentinian*, 22; see also *Golden Age*, 7; *Captives*, 1496, 2037), "*the noise of a Sea fight*" (*Antony and Cleopatra*, 1975, 3.10.0), "*A noise of fighting within*" (*Princess*, B4v), "*A great crack and noise within*" (*Alchemist*, 4.5.55), "*A mutinous noise* is heard" and "A noise is heard as if the gates were broken" (*Conspiracy*, H4r, K2v), "*Thunder and lightning with fearful noise the devils thrust him down and go Triumphing*" (*Devil's Charter*, M2v), "*A confused noise to come pressing in*" (*If This Be Not a Good Play*, 5.4.260), "*Within strange cries, horrid noise, Trumpets*" (*Double Marriage*, 348); see also *Edward III*, H4v; *Sir Thomas More*, 689; *Rape of Lucrece*, 243; *2 Iron Age*, 413; *Late Lancashire Witches*, 245; *Unnatural Combat*, 5.2.324; *Rebellion*, 41; several directions link *noise* to **horses**: "*A Noise within Trampling of Horses*" (*Captives*, 2743–4), "*A noise within, as the fall of a Horse*," followed by "*The Horse hath broke his neck*" (*Guardian*, 4.1.0), "*Noise within as of a coach*" (*New Way to Pay*, 3.2.241); see also *Chances*, 223; some *noise* comes from **below**: "*A noise below in the bowling-alley of betting and wrangling*" (*New Wonder*, 121), "*Carafogo makes a noise below*" (*Rule a Wife*, 229, also 231); see also *Aglaura*, 5.1.118; and some from **above**: "*Friar John makes a noise in the Garret*" (*New Trick*, 235), "*A noise above at cards*" (*New Wonder*, 123), "*Ricardo entering with a great noise above, as fallen*" (*Picture*, 4.2.144).

Sometimes *noise* is linked to music: "*A noise of still music*" (*Jews' Tragedy*, 2147), "*A great noise within of rude Music, Laughing, Singing, etc.*" (*Jovial Crew*, 423, also 364, 386), "*A Horrid noise of Music within*" (*Little French Lawyer*, 440), "*Strike up a noise of Viols*" (*Rare Triumphs*, 968), "*A Noise within of a Tabor and a Pipe*" (*Shoemakers' Holiday*, 3.3.47), "*Enter a noise of Fiddlers*" (*Westward Ho*, 5.2.0), "*a confused noise of music*" (*Christian Turned Turk*, F2v); other noteworthy directions for *noise* include "*A tempestuous noise of Thunder and Lightning heard*" and "*a strange hollow and confused noise*" (*Tempest*, 2, 1.1.0; 1807–8, 4.1.138), "*Noise and hallooing as people a-Maying*" (*Two Noble Kinsmen*, F2r, 3.1.0), "*Enter a Company of countrymen making a noise*" (*Edmond Ironside*, 104–5), "*A great Hubbub and noise, a ringing of basins*" (*Knave in Grain*, 2882), "*On a sudden in a kind of Noise like a Wind, the doors clattering, the Tombstone flies open*" (*Second Maiden's Tragedy*, 1926–7), "*A confused noise of betting within*" (*Hyde Park*, G4r), "*The noise of clapping a door*" (*Picture*, 4.2.130), "*a noise of a mill*" (*Rebellion*, 66); in *Spanish Curate* "*Pewter ready for noise*" is followed by "*A great noise within*" and "*Noise still*" (123/501, 124).

nose

linked to (1) a **patch** on the *nose*, (2) various actions; in *Knight of the Burning Pestle* Sir Pockhole is led in "*with a patch over his Nose*" (204) and reveals that Barbarossa (the barber) has "cut the gristle of my

Nose away, / And in the place this velvet plaster stands"; see also *Parson's Wedding*, 405; actions include "*blows his nose*" (*Lady Mother*, 794), "*Pulls him by the Nose*" (*Puritan*, G4r; *1 Passionate Lovers*, B2r), "*wrings him by the nose*" (*Woman's Prize*, 23), "*cuts his nose*" (*Edward I*, 903), "*Cuts off his Nose*" (*Edmond Ironside*, 708, also 717); in *Staple of News* a figure "*holds up his nose*" (2.4.7) followed by the comment "You snuff the air now, as the scent displeased you?"; the poisoners in *White Devil* "*put on spectacles of glass, which cover their eyes and noses*" (2.2.23).

nosegay

a small bunch of **flowers** carried by **hand**: "*a Boy with a nosegay*" for Princess Elizabeth (*1 If You Know Not Me*, 219), "*many School Boys with Scarfs and Nosegays*" for an entertainment (*Queen and Concubine*, 124), "*servants with Nosegays, cakes and wine*" (*Wit of a Woman*, 1611–12); a figure going to **execution** enters "*with her hair hanging down, a chaplet of flowers on her head, a nosegay in her hand*" (*Insatiate Countess*, 5.1.66).

note

used rarely to indicate a piece of **writing**: "*with written notes in their hands*" (*Captain Thomas Stukeley*, 586–7), "*reads a note which he finds among his Books*" (*Alphonsus of Germany*, B1v), "*Sophia sola with a book and a note*" (*Picture*, 4.2.0), "*with a note*" (*Spanish Curate*, 114).

now

a seldom used signal usually for the timing of actions: "*Now sound up the Drum*" (Quarto *2 Henry VI*, F4r, [4.2.121]), "*Now they strangle him*" (*Massacre at Paris*, 1115), "*She weeps now*" (*Night Walker*, 380), "*At the Feather shop now*" (*Roaring Girl*, 2.1.147, also 157, 171); see also *Three Lords of London*, I3r; *Captain Thomas Stukeley*, 1934; *Warning for Fair Women*, E3v; *No Wit*, 4.3.40; *Weeding of Covent Garden*, 43; more general are "*Enter Filenio now called Niofell, and his servant Goffo, now called Foggo*" (*Wit of a Woman*, 361–2), "*he married now*" (*Trick to Catch the Old One*, E4r); see also *World Tossed at Tennis*, F1r–v; *Landgartha*, K2r.

nun

nuns appear in small or supernumerary roles in a variety of plays (*Jew of Malta*; *Death of Huntingdon*; *Measure for Measure*; *Mad Lover*; *Fatal Contract*; *Lovesick King*; *Imposture*); how a *nun* is to be costumed is assumed rather than specified, so that signals call for entrances "*in Nun's apparel*" (*Friar Bacon*, 1895), "*in* a nun's habit" (Fair Favourite, 237), "with a Prayer Book in her hand, like a Nun" (Sir Thomas Wyatt, 1.3.0), "disguised like Nuns, with lighted Tapers in their hands" (Fedele and Fortunio, 492–3).

O

oar
twice a *silver* oar is linked to pirates (who have violated the laws of the *sea*) being *led* to *execution*; in *Fortune by Land and Sea* two figures "*going to Execution*" are accompanied by "*the Sheriffs, the silver Oar*" (427), and in *2 Edward IV* two comparable figures are preceded by "*one bearing a silver oar*" (136).

obeisance
to *make obeisance* is to *bow*, *kneel*, *conge*, or otherwise show respect or *reverence* usually to high-ranking figures; in *Captives* "*the friars make a Lane with ducks and obeisance*" for the entering nobles (880–3), and in *Bloody Banquet* servants bringing in a *banquet* to the king first "*depart, making obeisance*" and later "*each having delivered his dish makes low obeisance*" (1074, 1094–6); a victor in *battle* can *swear* others to *obeisance* (Golden Age, 53; Silver Age, 97); for other *obeisance* to monarchs see *Satiromastix*, 2.1.156; *Captain Thomas Stukeley*, 2444; for other objects of *obeisance*, in *Second Maiden's Tragedy* the Tyrant directs the soldiers "*to make obeisance*" to the *dead* Lady "*and he himself makes a low honor to the body and kisses the hand*" (2228–9); after her devotions "*Calantha and the rest rise, doing obeisance to the altar*" (Broken Heart, 5.3.0); *Thracian Wonder* provides an elaborate *ceremony* in which "*The men all pass by the two old Shepherds with obeisance, Radagon last; as he makes Conge, they put the Crown upon his head . . . The rest of the Shepherds pass by him with obeisance . . . The wenches come with obeisance to Ariadne, crown her Queen of the Shepherdesses, they lead her to Radagon their King; she and they make obeisance to him, he rises and kisses her*" (C4r–v).

observe
typically indicates that the observer is *unseen* by those being watched: "*all enter the circle which Prospero had made, and there stand charmed; which Prospero observing, speaks*" (Tempest, 2011–13, 5.1.57), "*D'Amville and Borachio, closely observing their drunkenness*" (Atheist's Tragedy, 2.2.17), "*shroud and observe*" (Isle of Gulls, 234); see also *Malcontent*, 2.1.0; *Queen of Corinth*, 60; *Loyal Subject*, 128; *Bloody Banquet*, 210; *Cardinal*, 5.3.125.

odd
a cryptic term probably meaning *strange* in the sense of "unusual, fantastic, or grotesque"; none of the four uses is the same: "*oddly attired*" (Downfall of Huntingdon, 457), "*in odd shapes*" (Love's Sacrifice, 1847), "*sings any odd toy*" (Orlando Furioso, 1213), "*some odd disguise*" (Wasp, 745).

off
widely used in a variety of locutions (1) most commonly *bear*, *beat*, *bring*, *carry*, *chase*, *drive*, *fly*, *go*, *run*, *steal*, *take*, *thrust* off the *stage* but also (2) *afar off*, *aloof off*, (3) *cast*, *throw*, *pull*, *tear*, *put*, *pluck* off items of clothing, a *disguise*, *chains*, (4) *cut*, *strike* off a *head*, *hand*, *hat*, (5) *shoot* off a *piece/chamber/weapon*; *Renegado* provides "*Grimaldi dragged off*," "*Throws off his cloak and doublet*," "*leads off Donusa*," "*The chain taken off*," "*The chamber shot off*" (2.5.92, 3.5.50, 3.5.110, 4.3.50, 5.8.16); the sense of "the stage" implicit in *bring off/go off* is occasionally made explicit: "*Alarum they fight Edmond drives Canutus off the stage*" (Edmond Ironside, 962–3).

offer
(1) widely used in the locution *offers to* to denote an action that is started but is then interrupted or otherwise not completed, and also found as (2) *offers at*, (3) the *offering* of objects; before the 1590s alternatives to *offers to* are also common, such as *proffer*, *make as though*: "*Orgalio proffers to go in*" (Orlando Furioso, 852), "*Make as though you were a going out*" (Alphonsus of Aragon, 1094); from the 1590s on *offers to* is the term of choice; of the more than 200 examples the largest category is *offers to go* (less often *going/exiturus*) wherein figures make a movement/*gesture* as if to *exit* but change their minds or are prevented: "*Nurse offers to go in and turns again*" and "*Paris offers to go in, and Capulet calls him again*" (Q1 Romeo and Juliet, G2r, 3.3.162; G2v, 3.4.11); for a sampling see *Wily Beguiled*, 1587; *Shoemakers' Holiday*, 1.4.56, 2.2.34; *Antonio's Revenge*, 3.1.0; *Blind Beggar of Alexandria*, 5.133; *Fair Quarrel*, 3.1.111; *Bashful Lover*, 1.1.172; 'Tis Pity, 2.2.106.

Of other actions *offered*, most prevalent are threatened suicides: figures *offer to stab* themselves (as in Q1 Romeo and Juliet, G1v, 3.3.108), *kill* themselves (the most common usage), *hang* themselves; also regularly *offered* are other acts of violence, most often *offer to fight* (as in Quarto Merry Wives, D3r, 3.1.72), *draw*, *strike* but also *offer to shoot*, *run* at him, "*come near and stab*" (Antonio's Revenge, 3.1.139), "*bind him*"

(*Comedy of Errors*, 1394, 4.4.105); other examples include *offer to* **follow**, **drink**, **kneel**, **embrace**, **kiss**; atypical is "*offers to discloak him*" (*Devil Is an Ass*, 1.6.111); sometimes the reason for the interruption is spelled out: "*draws his rapier, offers to run at Piero, but Maria holds his arm and stays him*" (*Antonio's Revenge*, 1.2.217), "*As she turns back, he offers to shoot, but returning he withdraws his hand*" (*2 If You Know Not Me*, 326); more detailed signals include "*one like a Cupid*" who enters "*offering to shoot*" and then re-enters with his "*Bow bent all the way towards them*" (*Nice Valour*, 156–7), "*offers to Kiss and she starts, wakes, and falls on her knees*" (*Two Noble Ladies*, 1793–4); other distinctive actions are "*Gloster offers to put up a Bill: Winchester snatches it, tears it*" (*1 Henry VI*, 1203–4, 3.1.0), "*offers to strike him with the lute*" (*Taming of a Shrew*, C2r), "*Offering to leap into bed, he discovers Vangue*" (*Sophonisba*, 3.1.182), "*takes the rope, and offers to climb*" (*Downfall of Huntingdon*, 2435), "*Offers to kiss her foot*" (*New Way to Pay*, 2.2.85), "*The Sophy gives Sir Anthony his hand as he offers to stoop to his foot*" (*Travels of Three English Brothers*, 322), "*Bolt offers to lay his Coat under the king*" (*Valiant Scot*, H3v).

Offer at is most commonly linked to a **sword**: "*He lays his breast open, she offers at with his sword*" (Folio *Richard III*, 371, 1.2.178); see also *Alarum for London*, 716; *Look about You*, 2518; *Bloody Brother*, 253; *1 Passionate Lovers*, C8r; *Lady Mother*, 2451; a variation is "*offers his sword to her*" (*Sophonisba*, 5.1.21); other examples include "*Offers at her hand*" (*Platonic Lovers*, 31), "*offers at two or three Chairs; at last finds the great one*" (*Woman Is a Weathercock*, 5.2.4–5); for the *offering* of an object such as a **crown, ring, money, wine** see *Looking Glass for London*, 561, 2064–5; *1 Edward IV*, 61; *Sophonisba*, 2.1.0; *Brazen Age*, 183; *Wonder of a Kingdom*, 3.1.67, 192; *Christian Turned Turk*, F2v; *Valiant Welshman*, C4v; *Herod and Antipater*, C3r; *Bloody Banquet*, 422; *Court Secret*, B1r; *Constant Maid*, H1r; *Wizard*, 1857–8; *1 Passionate Lovers*, G1r; *Princess*, F2v; *Prisoners*, B3v; figures *offer* a **hand** (*Bondman*, 3.2.104), **service** (*Four Plays in One*, 363), violence (*Osmond*, A8r); examples of *offer* as a noun include "*one bearing an offering for the King*" (*Faithful Friends*, 2477–8), "*diverse complemental offers of Courtship*" (*Love's Sacrifice*, 1852–3); see also *Conspiracy*, I1v, K4v.

omnes

Latin for "all" found regularly in group departures as **exeunt** *omnes*; variations of this widely used locution include *exeunt omnes saving* X (*Antonio's Revenge*, 4.1.67), *but* X (*Knack to Know a Knave*, 1278; Quarto

Merry Wives, F1r, [3.4; not in Riv.]; *Faithful Shepherdess*, 376; *Love's Sacrifice*, 2408), most commonly **manet** X (*Knack to Know an Honest Man*, 1284; *King Leir*, 576; *Lust's Dominion*, 4.2.56; *Maid's Tragedy*, 57; *1 Iron Age*, 271; *Custom of the Country*, 332; *Swetnam*, A3v; *Faithful Friends*, 231–2, 797–8), **praeter** X; for a sampling of the latter see *Alphonsus of Aragon*, 908; *2 Edward IV*, 125; *1 If You Know Not Me*, 215, 218, 229, 239; *Thierry and Theodoret*, 17; *Bondman*, 5.2.91; *City Madam*, 1.2.103; *City Wit*, 287; *Damoiselle*, 407; *exeunt omnes* is also linked to **severally** (*Landgartha*, H1v), "*at several doors*" (*1 Arviragus and Philicia*, C7v), "*several ways*" (*Doctor Faustus*, B 742); for a sampling of simply *exeunt omnes* see *Alphonsus of Aragon*, 2116; *Doctor Faustus*, A 808; *Woodstock*, 1013; *Edmond Ironside*, 218; *Famous Victories*, D1r, F1r, G2v; *Mucedorus*, F4r; *Sir Thomas Wyatt*, 1.4.49; *Four Prentices*, 177; *Antony and Cleopatra*, 880, 2.2.170; *Pericles*, E4v, 3.2.110; *Two Noble Kinsmen*, F1v, 2.5.64; *Tom a Lincoln*, 1474; *Court Beggar*, 256; examples of *exeunt omnes* as the final direction in a play include *Antonio's Revenge*, 5.3.185; *Malcontent*, 5.5.174; *Insatiate Countess*, 5.2.242; *Macbeth*, 2529, 5.9.41; *Changeling*, 5.3.227; atypical is *omnes* in an entrance in *Vow Breaker*, 1.2.48.

open

widely used (roughly 120 directions) (1) most often for a **door** but also frequently for (2) the **trapdoor**, (3) a **letter**, (4) various other properties; the door can be *opened* by a figure onstage to reveal or admit others: "*She openeth the door, enter Shorthose and Robin after him*" (*Grim the Collier*, I9v), or to leave: "*Breaks ope the door, and goes in*" (*Jews' Tragedy*, 2231–2) or it can be *opened* from the tiring house: "*Enter Severino (throwing open the doors violently)*" (*Guardian*, 3.6.142); for a representative selection of the most common locution, *open the door*, and variations, see *Arden of Faversham*, 2359; *Knack to Know an Honest Man*, 1081; *Alphonsus of Germany*, B1v; Quarto *Merry Wives*, B3v, [1.4; not in Riv.]; *Downfall of Huntingdon*, 4; *Second Maiden's Tragedy*, 1725; *No Wit*, 5.1.150; *Little French Lawyer*, 440; *Island Princess*, 115; *Albovine*, 101; *Renegado*, 2.5.119; *Messalina*, 700; *Duke's Mistress*, I1r, K2r; *Brennoralt*, 5.3.19; *Fair Favourite*, 244; *Distresses*, 345, 346; occasionally a **shop** opens: "*Three shops open in a rank*" (*Roaring Girl*, 2.1.0); see also *2 If You Know Not Me*, 283; *Match Me in London*, 2.1.0; directions to *open* the trapdoor, under various **fictional** designations, occur in *Antonio's Revenge*, 4.2.87; *Grim the Collier*, I12v; Q2 *Bussy D'Ambois*, 2.2.126; *Caesar and Pompey*, 2.1.24; *Queen's Exchange*, 536; *Love and Honour*,

121; another signal is to *open* a **tomb**: "*Romeo opens the tomb*" (Q1 *Romeo and Juliet*, K1r, 5.3.48); see also *Titus Andronicus*, A4v, 1.1.89; *Widow's Tears*, 4.3.0, 5.2.0, 5.3.0, 137, 5.5.18; *Second Maiden's Tragedy*, 1927; *Knight of Malta*, 145; *Love's Sacrifice*, 2763; atypical is "*Strikes ope a curtain where appears a body*" (*Hoffman*, 8–10).

Frequently figures *open* and **read** a **letter**: "*Opens the Letter, and reads*" (*Julius Caesar*, 664, 2.1.45), "*an open letter in his hands*" (*New Academy*, 8); see also *King Leir*, 995, 1169; *Merchant of Venice*, F2v, 3.2.236; *Warning for Fair Women*, H3r; *Cupid's Revenge*, 285; *Great Duke of Florence*, 4.1.81; *Very Woman*, 5.2.4; *Platonic Lovers*, 92; *News from Plymouth*, 182; *Landgartha*, H3r; *Country Captain*, D7r; *Sophy*, 3.157; a comparable action is "*opens the Box, and falls asleep*" (*Love's Mistress*, 152; see also *Three Ladies of London*, E1v; *Devil's Charter*, I2v; *New Way to Pay*, 5.1.182; *Queen and Concubine*, 34; *Aglaura*, 5.3.120); other items *opened* include a *bible* (*1 If You Know Not Me*, 228), *cage* (*Bird in a Cage*, H3r), **casement** (*Fedele and Fortunio*, 192), **casket** (*Picture*, 3.2.30), **curtain** (*Mad Lover*, 60; *Hoffman*, 1411), **dark lantern** (*Bloody Banquet*, 1455; *Cruel Brother*, 191), **study** (*Staple of News*, 2.5.44), **tent** (*Edward I*, 1453, 1587), **trunk** (*Two Maids of More-Clacke*, G2r; *Herod and Antipater*, B3v), *wicket* (*Wits*, 194, 213), **gates** (*James IV*, 2128), **hangings** (*Gentleman of Venice*, F3v), **lots** and a **cave** (*Jews' Tragedy*, 560–1, 1079), **stocks** (*Bartholomew Fair*, 4.6.77, 163); somewhat different are "*He lays his breast open*" (Folio *Richard III*, 371, 1.2.178), "*a Nightcap, and his Doublet open*" (*Fleer*, 5.3.0); for similar examples see *Selimus*, 1436, 1487; *Antonio's Revenge*, 3.1.0; *Devil's Charter*, I3v; *Just Italian*, 264.

or

used regularly (roughly 230 examples) in **permissive** signals so as to leave indefinite the number of figures who **enter** or other details linked to **sounds**, properties, and actions; most of these uses of *or* leave indeterminate the number of entering figures, as in "*an Officer to whip him, or two if you can*" (*Three Ladies of London*, F1v); two Shakespeare plays provide "*an Officer or two,*" "*a Drawer or two,*" "*three or four officers*" (*2 Henry IV*, C1r, 2.1.0; D2v, 2.4.0; K3v, 5.4.0), "*three or four with tapers,*" "*two or three other*" (*Much Ado*, I2v, 5.3.0; I3r, 5.4.33); comparable locutions are used for the repetition of actions/sounds: "*A pass or two*" (*Amends for Ladies*, 4.4.89–90; *Tottenham Court*, 173), "*Fight and part once or twice*" (*Look about You*, 2504), "*Capers three or four times*" (*Cupid's Whirligig*, 4.5.74), "*makes a conge or two to nothing*" (*Nice Valour*, 149), "*a strain or two*" (*Antipodes*, 338; *Lovesick Court*, 128; *Timon of Athens*, 492, 1.2.145),

"*a piece or two go off*" (*Double Marriage*, 353), "*A long flourish or two*" (*Shoemakers' Holiday*, 5.5.0), "*cry vive le Roi two or three times*" (*Massacre at Paris*, 592); see also *Three Ladies of London*, F2r; *Cobbler's Prophecy*, 1486–7; *Old Fortunatus*, 1.1.0; *Alphonsus of Germany*, D1r; *Woman Is a Weathercock*, 5.2.4–5; *Wonder of a Kingdom*, 1.3.21; *Aglaura*, 5.1.120; *Parson's Wedding*, 469.

Less plentiful are uses of *or* with reference to alternative actions, sounds, or properties; examples of actions are "*makes legs: or signs*" (*Epicœne*, 2.1.10), "*dances a Lavolta, or a Galliard*" (*Insatiate Countess*, 2.1.154), "*a round of Fairies, or some pretty dance*" (*James IV*, 634, also 1936); alternative sounds include "*a Flute or whistle*" (*Fedele and Fortunio*, 434), "*a noise or tumult*" (*Captives*, 2037), "*Recorders or other solemn Music*" (*Second Maiden's Tragedy*, 2454–5), "*whistles and Dances Sellenger's round, or the like*" (*Court Beggar*, 262), "*a strange wild fashioned dance to the Hoboys or Cornets*" (*More Dissemblers*, E5r), "*dance a short nimble antic to no Music, or at most to a single Violin*" (*Landgartha*, E4v); alternative properties include "*links or puddings in a platter*" (*Alphonsus of Germany*, F1r), the dead Ithocles brought in "*on a hearse, or in a chair*" (*Broken Heart*, 5.3.0), "*three or four Citizens with Clubs or partisans*" (Q2 *Romeo and Juliet*, A4r, 1.1.72); as to costume or **disguise**, Jupiter enters "*in the habit of a nymph or shepherdess*" (*Escapes of Jupiter*, 334–5), "*like a Nymph, or a Virago*" (*Golden Age*, 29); sometimes at issue is the availability of a particular property or resource: "*Exit Venus. Or if you can conveniently, let a chair come down from the top of the stage, and draw her up*" (*Alphonsus of Aragon*, 2109–10); other distinctive alternatives include "*let there come forth a Lion running after a Bear or any other beast*" (*Locrine*, 4–6; see also *Devil's Charter*, G1v), "*After a solemn service, enter from the widow's house a service, musical songs of marriages, or a masque, or what pretty triumph you list*" (*James IV*, 2051–3); such locutions can be found in a playhouse manuscript and even in a plot: "*Either strikes him with a staff or Casts a stone*" (*Captives*, 2432–4), "*causeth the chest or trunk to be brought forth*" (*Dead Man's Fortune*, 65–6); *Woman Is a Weathercock* repeats *or* an unusual number of times in one signal: "*Enter two or three setting three or four Chairs, and four or five stools*" (5.2.1).

oration

in *Game at Chess* "*The Oration*" (2016) in Latin is described as a "short Congratulatory Speech" and in *John a Kent* "*Turnop speaketh the Oration*" (371), an explanation of figures in a "country merriment"; in Folio *Richard III* Richmond's pre-battle speech is described as "*His Oration to his Soldiers*" (3702,

5.3.236), but Richard III's comparable *oration* receives no such designation.

orchard
see *garden*

order
usually associated with the appropriate forms, procedures, and rankings for *ceremonies* and other public occasions; for *funerals* "*Heralds Lead the rest in order after the Hearse*" (*Wasp*, 478), "*Body borne by four Captains and Soldiers. Mourners. Scutcheons, and very good order*" (*Fatal Dowry*, 2.1.47); in *Henry VIII* a long direction ends with "*The rest of the Attendants stand in convenient order about the Stage*" (1348–9, 2.4.0), and another long signal begins with the heading "*The Order of the Coronation*" and includes "*passing over the Stage in Order and State*" (2420, 2444, 4.1.36); also in *Henry VIII* the personages in Queen Katherine's vision "*observe the same order*" as previously and the *council* members "*seat themselves in Order on each side*" of the *table* (2650–1, 2653, 4.2.82; 3040, 5.2.35); comparable signals include "*Sennet about the Stage in order*" (*1 If You Know Not Me*, 246), "*Then all pass in their order to the king's pavilion*" (*Edward I*, 1932), "*the duke duchess and the rest take a new state in order*" (*Telltale*, 2149–50), "*In the dance they discover themselves in order, Sophonisba last*" (*Hannibal and Scipio*, 221), "*Enter the solemn order of the Bridegroom's return from Church*" (*Two Maids of More-Clacke*, A3r); see also *Your Five Gallants*, I2v; examples of *order* not linked to public occasions are "*Novall sits in a chair, Barber orders his hair*" (*Fatal Dowry*, 4.1.0), a figure setting up cosmetics who "*places all things in order*" (*1 Honest Whore*, 2.1.0); atypical is "*receives the Order of Saint Iago*" (*Travels of Three English Brothers*, 404).

ordnance
refers to the offstage *sound* of a *cannon* being *discharged*: "*Exeunt Marching, after which a Peal of Ordnance are shot off*" (Folio *Hamlet*, 3905–6, 5.2.403), "*Alarum. Fight at Sea. Ordnance goes off*" (Folio *2 Henry VI*, 2168, 4.1.0), "*A charge with a peal of Ordnance*" (*Devil's Charter*, I1v, also D3v); see also *Massacre at Paris*, 338; *1 Henry VI*, 902–3, 2.3.60; *Hieronimo*, 4.0, 12.19; *Dick of Devonshire*, 433.

organ
an instrument cited in two plays, both performed at Paul's playhouse, which is known to have had an *organ*; in *Sophonisba* "*Chorus with cornets, organ, and voices*" (1.2.42) is followed by five more uses, mostly

at *entr'acte* breaks (1.2.236, 2.3.113, 3.1.116, 3.2.84, 5.4.36); two directions in *Mad World* call for *organs* (2.1.151, 155), the plural denoting the multiple pipes in the instrument.

others
see *permissive stage directions*

out
widely used (roughly 550 examples) in many locutions, most revealingly in the movement of figures and objects onto and off the *stage*; as with the comparable use of *in*, *out* can signal either an entrance or an *exit* with the key being the verb used rather than any firm equivalent to today's sense of onstage and offstage; to *go out* is to exit, but to *come out* is to *enter*; although usages are not consistent, usually *bring out* is to move onstage, but to *take/bear out* is to move offstage; for a sampling of *go out* see *Summer's Last Will*, 116, 420, 775, 934, 1115; *Massacre at Paris*, 206, 569, 635; *Taming of a Shrew*, G2r; *Edmond Ironside*, 2062; *Captain Thomas Stukeley*, 2812–13, 2889–90; *Shoemakers' Holiday*, 5.1.35; *Lust's Dominion*, 4.3.39; *Blind Beggar of Alexandria*, 5.133; *Cymbeline*, 2894–5, 5.2.0; *Second Maiden's Tragedy*, 2446–50; *Broken Heart*, 4.4.0; *Perkin Warbeck*, 2.1.39; *City Wit*, 340; for *come out* see *Cobbler's Prophecy*, 1325; *1 Tamburlaine*, 663; *2 Tamburlaine*, 2921; *Locrine*, 434; *George a Greene*, 795; *Sir John Oldcastle*, 2210; *Old Fortunatus*, 1.1.63; *Merry Devil of Edmonton*, E3v; *Timon of Athens*, 1117–18, 3.4.0; *Epicæne*, 1.1.0; *Bartholomew Fair*, 2.5.59; *Jews' Tragedy*, 945–7, 1079–80; *City Match*, 310; for figures' movement off the stage *out* is linked to a variety of other verbs including *steal* (*Lover's Melancholy*, 2.1.125), *carry* (*Broken Heart*, 4.3.97; *Jovial Crew*, 391), *run* (*Locrine*, 1672; *Comedy of Errors*, 1445, [4.4.146]), *beat* (*1 Henry VI*, 425, 1.3.56; *Taming of a Shrew*, D3r; *1 If You Know Not Me*, 224), *bear* (*James IV*, 1820; *Antonio's Revenge*, 1.2.270; *Caesar and Pompey*, 5.1.272), *hale* (*Caesar and Pompey*, 5.2.200), *pursue* (*Maid in the Mill*, 59), *lead* (*2 Edward IV*, 176, 178; *Bloody Brother*, 313; *Damoiselle*, 459), *thrust* (*Match Me in London*, 5.3.0; *Four Plays in One*, 326), *send* (*Four Plays in One*, 321), *march* (*Massacre at Paris*, 1263), *pull* (Quarto *2 Henry VI*, E3v, [3.2.231]); especially for large objects (*altar*, *banquet*, *bar*, *bed*, *chairs*, *scaffold*, *stocks*, *table*) *out* usually indicates onto the stage and is often attached to verbs such as *put*, *draw*, *thrust*, most commonly *set*, *bring*: "*Stocks brought out*" (Folio *King Lear*, 1217, 2.2.139), "*A Table, Count book, Standish, Chair and stools set out*" (*City Madam*, 1.2.143), "*The Scaffold set out, and the stairs*" (*Knight of Malta*, 109), "*A*

bed thrust out upon the stage, Allwit's Wife in it" (*Chaste Maid*, 3.2.0), *"Table ready: and six chairs to set out"* (*Believe as You List*, 654–6, also 1794–5), *"She's drawn out upon a Bed"* (*Maidenhead Well Lost*, 154); *out* can appear by itself with the verb left implicit: *"Chair and stools out"* (*Two Noble Kinsmen*, G2v, [3.5.64]; *Spanish Curate*, 128), *"A Table out, two stools"* (*Knight of Malta*, 129), *"Enter Biondello, Lucentio and Bianca, Gremio is out before"* (*Taming of the Shrew*, 2379–80, 5.1.0); both senses of *out* can be found in the same scene in Folio *3 Henry VI*: *"Enter Warwick, Somerset, and the rest, bringing the King out in his Gown"* and *"They lead him out forcibly"* (2257–8, 2295, 4.3.27, 57), so that to bring the king onto the stage is to bring him *out* but to lead him off the stage is also to take him *out*.

overcome

a seldom used term linked to a **fight**: *"Here they fight, and Joan de Puzel overcomes"* (*1 Henry VI*, 306, 1.2.103), *"fighteth first with one, and then with another, and overcomes them both"* (*Orlando Furioso*, 1526–7); for more see *Soliman and Perseda*, E4r; *Dumb Knight*, 132, 196; *Maidenhead Well Lost*, 161; *Seven Champions*, L1r; see also **overthrow**.

overhear

signals surreptitious **listening**: *"Cocledemoy stands at the other door, disguised like a French Peddler, and overhears them"* (*Dutch Courtesan*, 3.2.0, also 1.2.161), *"Enter Lisander privately and overhears them"* (*Isle of Gulls*, 234); see also *James IV*, 1953; *Gentleman Usher*, 1.1.254; *Family of Love*, E1r; *Hieronimo*, 3.38; *Wise Woman of Hogsdon*, 289; *Claracilla*, E3r.

overthrow

signaled six times: *"with his foot overthroweth the child"* (*Death of Huntingdon*, 942), *"Overthrows the table"* (*Rebellion*, 87), *"Overthrows the gingerbread"* (*Bartholomew Fair*, 3.6.98), *"beats and overthrows many of them"* (*Valiant Welshman*, I1r); for more see *Dumb Knight*, 131; *Roman Actor*, 5.2.71; see also **overcome**.

over the stage

see **pass**, **stage**

P

painted, painting

(1) usually equivalent to "colored, color" and associated with **disguise** and cosmetics, (2) less commonly

linked to *paintings* of figures/**images**; examples of *painted* as *colored* include *"a Piece of painted Cloth, like a Herald's Coat"* (*Thracian Wonder*, G1r; see also *Launching of the Mary*, 1831, 1986, 2015), *Dissimulation "his poll and beard painted motley"* and *"Usury with a painted box of ink in his hand"* (*Three Ladies of London*, A2v, E1v), *"a Tun painted with yellow ochre"* (*John a Kent*, 369–70) described as "the golden Tun," *"a box of black painting"* and *"He begins to paint her"* (*English Moor*, 37–8); in *Love's Mistress* "The Box is full of ugly Painting" (152) which the clown thinks will make him fair-faced so "Daub on, daub on"; to set up a disguise as a chimney sweep *"Enter Lorenzo with his glass in his hand, and Angelo with a pot of painting"* (*May Day*, 3.1.77); in an elaborate cosmetics scene in *1 Honest Whore* Roger *"pulls out of his pocket, a vial with white color in it, and two boxes, one with white, another red painting"* and *"rubs his cheeks with the colors"* (2.1.0); see also *Variety*, D1r; *Maid's Revenge*, E3v; examples of *painted* garments are *"Rumor painted full of Tongues"* (*2 Henry IV*, A2r, Induction.0), Vice *"her garment painted behind with fools' faces and devils' heads"* and Virtue *"her attire behind painted with Crowns, and Laurel garlands, stuck full of stars, held out by hands, thrust out of bright clouds"* (*Old Fortunatus*, 1.3.0); in *Wisdom of Doctor Dodypoll* a figure is *"discovered (like a Painter) painting Lucilia"* (2–4); see also **colors**.

panting

used occasionally as an equivalent to *out of* **breath**; figures are directed to *pant* (rev. *Aglaura*, 5.1.66) and **enter** *panting* (*Honest Lawyer*, B3v), *"Panting for breath"* (*Captain Thomas Stukeley*, 2799); stage combats include *"They go off the Stage grappling together: . . . they enter again panting"* (*Twins*, D2v), *"fight with single swords, and being deadly wounded and panting for breath, making a stroke at each other with their gauntlets they fall"* (*Rape of Lucrece*, 252); see also **blow**.

pantoffles

see **slippers**

paper

used in over 160 directions for properties variously described in dialogue; usually the direction itself indicates little more than that *paper* is required, as when Hal *"findeth certain papers"* in Falstaff's pockets (*1 Henry IV*, E4r, 2.4.531) or when Berowne enters *"with a paper in his hand, alone"* (*Love's Labour's Lost*, E2v, 4.3.0); similar examples include *"a Scrivener with a paper in his hand"* (Quarto *Richard III*, G4r, 3.6.0;

see also *Henry VIII*, 176, 1.1.114), *"folds the paper the contrary way"* (*Hieronimo*, 6.3), *"all look on the Paper"* (*Woman Is a Weathercock*, 5.2.110), *"put up their papers"* (*Isle of Gulls*, 222), *"Tear the papers"* (*Spanish Tragedy*, 3.13.123), *"kiss the paper"* (*King Leir*, 1058), *"Throws down a paper"* (*Thracian Wonder*, D1v), *"reading a Paper"* (*Doubtful Heir*, B3v; see also *Epicœne*, 5.2.57; *Distresses*, 358), *"secretly gives him a paper"* (*Women Pleased*, 299; see also *Grateful Servant*, L1r), *"All hold up papers"* (*Satiromastix*, 3.1.239), *"show a Paper"* (*Fatal Contract*, F3v); elsewhere a *paper* is part of more elaborate stage business, often a **dumb show**: *"a Doctor of Physic, a Midwife, two Soldiers; the King points them to the Bishops, they each deliver Papers, kiss the Bishops' Books, and are dismissed. The Paper given to the King. He with his Finger menaces Eulalia, and sends her the Papers; she looks meekly…All the Lords peruse the Papers. They show various countenances"* (*Queen and Concubine*, 22); for other extended actions with *papers* see *Antonio's Revenge*, 5.1.0; *Sophonisba*, 2.1.103; *Devil's Charter*, C3r; *1 Fair Maid of the West*, 275; *Night Walker*, 381; *Four Plays in One*, 326; *Two Noble Ladies*, 1544–7.

Frequently *paper* is one of several related properties (**ink**, a **standish**, **table**, and **light**), brought onstage to set a scene and initiate certain stage business: *"Enter Bellamont in his Nightcap, with leaves in his hand, his man after him with lights, Standish and Paper"* (*Northward Ho*, 4.1.0), *"the Maid with Ink and Paper"* (*Massacre at Paris*, 670), *"One bearing light, a standish and paper, which sets a Table"* (*Bussy D'Ambois*, 5.1.0), *"three of the Guard (with paper and Ink)"* (*Brennoralt*, 2.1.29), *"Draws Inkhorn and paper"* (*Fatal Dowry*, 4.1.176); see also *Revenge of Bussy*, 4.4.0; *Nero*, 39; *Northern Lass*, 12; *Platonic Lovers*, 91; such properties are called for in several playhouse manuscripts and a playtext with evidence of bookkeeper annotation: *"Ink: paper ready"* and *"with pen Ink and paper"* (*Captives*, 1341, 1361), *"A Table out, sword and papers"* (*Dick of Devonshire*, 1549–50), *"Here bring a little table, and a paper book: for the Clerk of the Check"* (*Launching of the Mary*, 1141–2), *"A Bar, Tablebook, two Chairs, and Paper, standish set out"* and *"Bed ready, wine, table, Standish and Paper"* (*Spanish Curate*, 98, 113/501); see also *Woodstock*, 858; *Believe as You List*, 300–2; some of the many other signals for *paper* are *"writes a little, throws down the paper and departs"* (*Law Tricks*, 204), *"Papers this while being offered and subscribed between either"* (*Look about You*, 200–1), *"departs, leaving at Antipater's feet two Scrolls of paper"* (*Herod and Antipater*, C3r), *"a Box, in which are little pieces of paper rolled up"* (*Noble Stranger*, G3r), *"he lays her the paper folded double*

and she writes on the nether side above"* (*Soddered Citizen*, 961–3), *"eating paper"* (*Wizard*, 134), *"with Books and Papers, he lays them on the Table"* (*Jovial Crew*, 357), *"three or four Projectors with bundles of papers"* (*Antipodes*, 308), *"the king is discovered sleeping over papers"* (*Albovine*, 95); see also *Dido*, 1408; *Three Lords of London*, H2r, H2v; *Locrine*, 309–10; *Woman Hater*, 129; *1 Honest Whore*, 3.3.0; *Amends for Ladies*, 1.1.391–2; *Chabot*, 5.2.0; *Anything for a Quiet Life*, F2r; *Staple of News*, 5.4.0; *Fair Maid of the Inn*, 175; *Lover's Melancholy*, 3.1.0; *Emperor of the East*, 5.2.36; *Princess*, C1v; *Fair Favourite*, 223; *Cunning Lovers*, H2r; *Lovesick Court*, 150; see also **bills**, **letter**, **parchment**, **scroll**, **write**.

paps
see **breast**

parchment
of the ten calls for this property, four specify only *a parchment* (*1 Fair Maid of the West*, 308; *Cruel Brother*, 159; *Brothers*, F1r; *Cardinal*, 5.1.46); somewhat more specific are *"a parchment roll"* (*Emperor of the East*, 4.3.27), *"a long Scroll of Parchment"* (*Soddered Citizen*, 2376), *"a parchment writing"* (*Platonic Lovers*, 90); although there is no indication how or if *parchment* denotes a property visually different from **paper** or other similar items, the remaining directions are slightly more detailed: *"a little piece of fine parchment in his hand"* and *"subscribeth to the parchment"* (*Devil's Charter*, A2v), *"Boy in a Shop cutting up square parchments"* (*Fair Maid of the Exchange*, 308), *"an Antic habited in Parchment Indentures. Bills, Bonds, Wax, Seals, and Pen and Inkhorns: on his breast writ, I am a Scrivener"* (*New Trick*, 250); see also **scroll**.

parley
denotes either (1) a **conference** between enemies or (2) the aural signal for such a *parley* (often spelled *parle*); the term can stand by itself (*Edmond Ironside*, 977; *Alphonsus of Germany*, I1v; Folio *Henry V*, 1253, 3.2.136; *Thracian Wonder*, H2v; *Brazen Age*, 223; *1 Iron Age*, 294; *Perkin Warbeck*, 3.4.3) or can be linked to the verb **sound**: *"Sound a parley"* (Folio *2 Henry VI*, 2777, 4.8.3; *2 Troublesome Reign*, E4r; *Double Marriage*, 403; *Timon of Athens*, 2511, 5.4.2), *"The Drum sounds a parley"* (*Soliman and Perseda*, H4r), *"Trumpets sound a Parley"* (*1 Henry VI*, 1624, 3.3.35; *Sir Thomas Wyatt*, 2.2.51), *"The trumpet sounds a parley. Enter Sir Walter Blunt"* (*1 Henry IV*, H4r, 4.3.29); sometimes the *parley* is **answered**: *"Parley without, and answer within"* (Folio *Richard II*,

1646, 3.3.61; see also *Trial of Chivalry*, B1v; *Faithful Friends*, 1366) and once not answered: "*the Herald sounds a parley, and none answers*" (*Sir Thomas Wyatt*, 2.2.19); when the *parley* is sounded by a group besieging a *city*, the inhabitants usually appear *above*/*on the walls*: "*They Sound a Parley: Enter two Senators with others on the Walls of Corioles*" (*Coriolanus*, 499–500, 1.4.12), "*the Herald summons the town to a parley, is answered; and enter Joseph and Captains upon the wall*" (*Jews' Tragedy*, 797–9); see also *Orlando Furioso*, 394; *Selimus*, 1165–6, 2361–2; *Four Prentices*, 230; *Guy of Warwick*, C2r; stage business linked to the *parley* includes "*The two Kings parley, and change hostages for peace*" (*Bloody Banquet*, 6–7), "*Hengist amazed, sends one to entreat a peaceable parley, which seeming to be granted by laying down their weapons*" (*Hengist*, DS before 4.3, 15–17), "*Sound a Parley, and Richard and Clarence whisper together, and then Clarence takes his red Rose out of his hat, and throws it at Warwick*" (Octavo *3 Henry VI*, E2r, [5.1.79]).

parliament
see *council*

part, parts
as a verb usually (1) to separate figures in a *fight*, (2) to *depart*/*go* away from someone, and as a noun (3) one of the melodic lines in a *song*/*catch*, (4) *part* of the *stage*; for *parting* combatants see Q1 *Romeo and Juliet*, A4v, [1.1.72]; Quarto *Every Man In*, 3.4.148; *1 Iron Age*, 300, 310; *Christian Turned Turk*, E1v; *Two Noble Ladies*, 279; *Unfortunate Lovers*, 68; *Claracilla*, E1ov, F2r; typical are "*They wrestle and are parted*" (*Nobody and Somebody*, G3r), "*laboring to part them*" (*City Match*, 239), "*Fight and part once or twice*" (*Look about You*, 2504); *Four Prentices* provides "*she runs betwixt them and parts them*" (189, also 202), "*cast their Warders between them, and part them*" (204), "*They fight and are parted*" (213, also 236); see also *Travels of Three English Brothers*, 404; *part* as "depart" often is hard to distinguish from "move apart": "*salute and part*" (*Noble Spanish Soldier*, 1.1.0), "*With courtesy they part*" (*Two Noble Ladies*, 1548), "*They part several ways*" (*Brazen Age*, 239), "*Embrace and part several ways*" (*Timon of Athens*, 1579, 4.2.29); atypical are "*A great noise within at their parting*" (*Late Lancashire Witches*, 222), "*parts from Modestina and addresses him in most humble manner to Miniona*" (*Soddered Citizen*, 670–3); see also *Edmond Ironside*, 978; *Downfall of Huntingdon*, 46, 72; *Golden Age*, 20.

For a song/catch "*in parts*" see *Swetnam*, G2r;

Women Beware Women, 5.2.72; *King John and Matilda*, 84; *Messalina*, 2542–3; *Landgartha*, F1r; *Princess*, G3v; *Wits*, 209; *part* can be used in various theatrical senses, most commonly as *part* of the stage: "*withdraw at the other part of the stage*" (Quarto *Every Man Out*, 1121), "*Enter on the one part . . . On the other part*" (*1 Iron Age*, 345); see also *Cobbler's Prophecy*, 1565–6; *Look about You*, 76–8; *Woman Is a Weathercock*, 5.2.180–3; also theatrical are "*presents the part*" (*No Wit*, 4.3.40), *part* of a *scene* (*Epicœne*, 4.6.0), enter "*with parts in their hands*" (*Antonio and Mellida*, Induction.0); other locutions include "*like a Soldier disguised at all parts*" (*Widow's Tears*, 4.2.0), "*their upper parts naked*" (*Amorous War*, E2v), take part: "*They fight, and David takes his brother's part*" (*Edward I*, 1885), "*stands by, sees them fight takes part with neither*" (*Miseries of Enforced Marriage*, 1351–2); see also *Insatiate Countess*, 3.1.42; *Travels of Three English Brothers*, 324; *Court Beggar*, 247; *Aglaura*, 3.1.24; *Prisoners*, A6r.

pass, passing, passage
(1) most commonly describes the action of crossing the *stage* from one *door* to another, variously signaled with *pass over*, *pass over the stage* and sometimes *pass by* (the latter can also refer to other actions, as can *pass through*), but also (2) a *pass* made with a *weapon*; examples of *pass over* are "*They pass over in great solemnity*" (*Changeling*, 4.1.0, also 5.1.73, 5.2.8), "*As they pass over, Diana ascends*" (*Four Plays in One*, 311, also 338), "*Enter Corax, passing over*" (*Lover's Melancholy*, 1.2.101), "*Enter people passing over by degrees, (talking)*" (*1 Passionate Lovers*, D8r); for more see *Edward I*, 1927; *2 Seven Deadly Sins*, 45; *Doctor Faustus*, B 1872; *Blurt*, 1.2.31; *Every Woman In*, B4r; *Epicœne*, 3.7.16; *Thierry and Theodoret*, 44; *Double Marriage*, 361; *Match at Midnight*, 81; *Wife for a Month*, 22; *Broken Heart*, 1.3.43; *Antipodes*, 300; *Goblins*, 4.6.11; examples of the more specific *pass over the stage* are "*Enter two Senators, with Ladies, passing over the Stage, with other Lords*" (*Coriolanus*, 3639–40, 5.5.0), "*Music sound, Mephostophilis brings in Helen, she passeth over the stage*" (*Doctor Faustus*, B 1802–3), "*speaking as they pass over the Stage*" (Quarto *Every Man Out*, 2747–8), "*Here pass over the stage a physician, a gentleman usher, and a waiting maid*" (*Dumb Knight*, 140), "*Pass softly over the stage*" (*Swetnam*, G2r), "*A service as for dinner, pass over the stage*" (*Antipodes*, 246), "*Lawyers and others pass over the Stage as conferring by two and two*" (*Damoiselle*, 407); for more see *2 Henry IV*, K4r, 5.5.4; *Sir John Oldcastle*, 2601–2; *Shoemakers' Holiday*, 1.1.235; *Sejanus*, 5.460; *Hieronimo*, 1.0; *Puritan*, B2v; *Revenger's Tragedy*, A2r;

Your Five Gallants, A2r; *Birth of Merlin*, C1r; *Match Me in London*, 2.4.35; *Henry VIII*, 2444, 4.1.36; *Hog Hath Lost His Pearl*, 2; *Two Merry Milkmaids*, O1v; *Little French Lawyer*, 416; *Loyal Subject*, 136; *Novella*, 129; *Mad Couple*, 76; *Messalina*, 1859–60; *Doubtful Heir*, D5r; *Goblins*, 2.6.6; *Broken Heart*, 3.2.16; *Cardinal*, 4.1.33; the locution *passage over the stage* is seldom used: "*Here a passage over the Stage, while the Act is playing for the Marriage*" (*Fatal Dowry*, 2.2.359), "*Here is a passage of the lieger Ambassadors over the stage severally*" (*White Devil*, 3.1.64, also 5.1.0); see also *Henry VIII*, 175–9, 1.1.114; *Opportunity*, F4r.

Pass by or simply *pass* can be the equivalent of *pass over the stage*: "*pass by, quaking, and trembling*" (*Catiline*, 4.0), "*Enter Courtier and passes by, half Reeling*" (*Conspiracy*, C4v, also D1r), "*Enter Courtiers, who pass by neglectfully*" (*Duke's Mistress*, B4r), "*They pass with many strange Conges*" (*Silver Age*, 116), "*Loud music as they pass*" (*Picture*, 2.2.122), "*as she passeth by, he smiles and folds his arms, as if he did embrace her*" (*Death of Huntingdon*, 963–5), "*Enter an armed Sewer: some half dozen in mourning coats following, and pass by with service*" (*Case Is Altered*, 1.3.0, also 1.4.0, 1.9.93); see also *Spanish Tragedy*, 1.2.110; *Cobbler's Prophecy*, 1–4; Folio *Every Man In*, 2.3.4; *Cynthia's Revels*, 2.3.122, 161; *Pericles*, C4r, 2.2.16; *Maid's Tragedy*, 3; *Chances*, 237; *Custom of the Country*, 347; *City Wit*, 358; *Holland's Leaguer*, H4v, I1r; *Twins*, E1v; *Princess*, D3r; elsewhere figures *pass by* each other: "*enters the Ghost of Andrugio, who passeth by them tossing his torch about his head in triumph*" (*Antonio's Revenge*, 5.1.0), "*passeth by them with disdain*" (*Changes*, H3v), "*both Troops pass by each other*" (*Fatal Contract*, E3v), "*They pass directly before the Cardinal*" (*Henry VIII*, 754–5, 1.4.63), "*pinching Gripe, as they pass by him*" (*Honest Lawyer*, G2v), "*The men all pass by the two old Shepherds with obeisance*" (*Thracian Wonder*, C4r, also C4v), "*Dorilus kneels as the Duchess passeth by*" (*Two Merry Milkmaids*, E3r, also K2v); see also *Sejanus*, 5.430; sometimes figures **make a lane** or a **rank** for others to *pass through*: "*make a rank for the Duke to pass through*" (*Antonio and Mellida*, 2.1.183), "*Piero passeth through his guard*" (*Antonio's Revenge*, 3.1.0), "*Enter as many as may be spared, with lights, and make a lane kneeling while Martha the Duchess like a mourner with her train passeth through*" (*Hoffman*, 1682–4); see also *Maid of Honour*, 4.2.28; atypical is "*Fiddlers pass through, and play the battle*" (*Late Lancashire Witches*, 204); less common locutions are "*passing on the Stage to the place of execution*" (*Titus Andronicus*, E3r, 3.1.0), "*passeth one door, and entereth the other*" (*Woman Is a Weathercock*, 3.2.68), "*passeth to

his throne*" (*Sophonisba*, 5.2.49), "*all pass in their order to the king's pavilion*" (*Edward I*, 1932), "*they meet and pass disdainfully*" (*Herod and Antipater*, D3r), "*pass to and fro with lights*" (*Novella*, 106), "*passing in they knock at the door*" (*Puritan*, E2v), "*pass round the stage*" (*Sir Thomas Wyatt*, 1.2.58), "*Pass to his seat*" (*Swetnam*, E3v); see also *Three Lords of London*, G4v; *Two Lamentable Tragedies*, B3v; *Captain Thomas Stukeley*, 2772–3; *Late Lancashire Witches*, 234; a unique usage is "*whilst the scene passeth above*" (*Antonio and Mellida*, 1.1.115).

A *pass* is made with a weapon in *Goblins* when first a figure "*Retires and draws, runs at him,*" then makes "*Another pass, they close*" (2.3.14, 15); comparable examples are "*they see one another and draw and make a pass*" (*Insatiate Countess*, 4.2.38, 52), "*They make a dangerous pass at one another the Lady purposely runs between, and is killed by them both*" (*Second Maiden's Tragedy*, 2133–5); see also *Amends for Ladies*, 4.4.89–90, 92; *Miseries of Enforced Marriage*, 2288–9; *Tottenham Court*, 173; *Lovesick Court*, 141.

passion

can refer to love, sorrow, **anger**, or some combination of mimed emotions; demonstrations of love are "*Colin the enamored shepherd singeth his passion of love*" (*Arraignment of Paris*, 536), "*Silent actions of passions, kiss her hand*" (*2 Arviragus and Philicia*, F11v), "*let him counterfeit the passion of love by looks and gesture*" (*Fedele and Fortunio*, 795–6); of sorrow: "*Falls passionately upon the Hearse*" (*King John and Matilda*, 85, also 70), "*The Widow wringing her hands, and bursting out into passion, as newly come from the Burial of her husband*" (*Puritan*, A3r), "*kneels at the Tomb wondrous passionately*" (*Second Maiden's Tragedy*, 1891–3), "*with counterfeit passion present the King a bleeding heart upon a knife's point*" (*Golden Age*, 20); of anger: "*(with much seeming passion) swears him; then stamps with his foot*" (*Four Plays in One*, 326), "*She in passion interrupts him and in disdain speaks*" (*Prisoners*, B5r, also B11r); see also *Antonio's Revenge*, 1.2.254; *Devil's Charter*, C1v; *Hengist*, DS before 4.3, 3; other examples of mimed *passion* include "*the Queen returns, finds the King dead, makes passionate action*" (*Hamlet*, Q2 H1v, Folio 1997–8, 3.2.135), "*Cleon shows Pericles the tomb, whereat Pericles makes lamentation, puts on sackcloth, and in a mighty passion departs*" (*Pericles*, G3r, 4.4.22).

patch

a covering for the *face* linked to (1) *disguise*, usually that of a *wounded* soldier, (2) venereal disease; *patches* linked to disguise include "*pulls off his patches and disguise" (*Distresses*, 339), "*disguised like a Captain with a patch on his eye and a false beard*" (*Wizard*, 343–5); for comparable *patches* linked to the **eye**/face see *Edmond Ironside*, 1313; *Look about You*, 2008; *Claracilla*, D5r; *Princess*, F1r; in *Roaring Girl* the deceitful Trapdoor enters "*like a poor Soldier with a patch over one eye*" but Moll reacts: "Soldier? thou deserv'st to be hang'd up by that tongue which dishonors so noble a profession" and is directed to "*Pull off his patch*" (5.1.55, 105), after which another figure adds: "I did not think there had been such knavery in black patches as now I see"; similarly in *Amends for Ladies* a group of blustering pretenders enters with "*several patches on their faces*" (3.4.2–3) and an innocent figure asks "if they be not very valiant or dare not fight, how come they by such Cuts and gashes, and such broken faces?"; for an example of disease, in *Knight of the Burning Pestle* Sir Pockhole is led in "*with a patch over his Nose*" (204) and reveals that Barbarossa (the barber) has "cut the gristle of my Nose away, / And in the place this velvet plaster stands"; in *Parson's Wedding* "*The Captain has a patch over his nose*" (405).

pause

a verb or noun linked to (1) **fights** and violence, (2) **exits** and other stage business; signals for fights include "*fight and pause*" (*Fortune by Land and Sea*, 386; *Brennoralt*, 5.3.213; *Aglaura*, 5.1.55), two **dragons** that "*fight a while and pause*" (*Birth of Merlin*, F3r), "*a fierce fight with sword and target, then after pause and breathe*" (*Rape of Lucrece*, 252); in *Woman Killed* Frankford pursues Wendoll "*with his sword drawn, the maid in her smock stays his hand, and clasps hold on him. He pauses for a while*" (138); other pauses are "*Pauses a little*" from knocking on a **door** (*Maid's Metamorphosis*, C2r), "*after a little pause speaks*" (*Fatal Contract*, E3v), "*at his entrance they all stand bare, and after some pause, Aratus speaks to him*" (*Conspiracy*, F4v), "*Enter the Eunuch with bags of Gold, gives to each of them one, and after a little pause departs*" (*Fatal Contract*, B2v); in *Captain Thomas Stukeley* two groups enter at separate doors and "*After some pause Antonio is sent forth to Phillip*" (2443–4), and in *Cunning Lovers* "*Mantua makes some strange pauses, viewing the Lady exactly, at length (recalling his hand once or twice) troth-plights them*" (I2v); see also *Andromana*, 249.

pavilion

a synonym for **tent** used only in the Peele canon: "*Then all pass in their order to the king's pavilion, the king sits in his Tent with his pages about him*" (*Edward I*,

1932), "*goes to his pavilion, and sits close a while*" and "*unfolds the pavilion*" (*David and Bethsabe*, 1826, 1846).

peal

a **discharge** of guns or **cannon** producing a volley of loud **sound**; the *peal* is used especially as an expression of joy or for a **salute**, usually in a military context, as when Fortinbras commands "Go, bid the soldiers shoot" and "*a Peal of Ordnance are shot off*" (Folio *Hamlet*, 3906, 5.2.403) or to indicate victory (*1 Henry VI*, 902–3, 2.3.60); for similar examples see *Hieronimo*, 4.0, 12.19; *2 If You Know Not Me*, 338; *Devil's Charter*, I1v; *Whore of Babylon*, 5.6.14; *Dick of Devonshire*, 433; a different usage occurs in *Antonio and Mellida* where "*a peal of shot is given*" (1.1.139) to mark the end of a "triumph"; the idea of a series of sounds seems to be the point of Titus's reference to "a hunter's peal" at the unusual direction "*Here a cry of hounds, and wind horns in a peal*" (Folio *Titus Andronicus*, 712, 2.2.10); see also **chambers**, **ordnance**.

pearl

found most commonly in a **chain** of *pearls* (*Your Five Gallants*, I3r; Q2 *Bussy D'Ambois*, 3.1.0; *No Wit*, 4.3.40; *Hyde Park*, B4r); in *Amorous War* six **dancing** Moors enter with "*Great pendants of Pearl at their ears*" (E2v), and in *Wonder of a Kingdom* a figure "*gives jewels, and ropes of pearl to the Duke; and a chain of gold to every Courtier*" (4.1.0); especially elaborate is a **corpse** "*dressed up in black velvet which sets out the paleness of the hands and face, And a fair Chain of pearl cross her breast and the Crucifix above it*" (*Second Maiden's Tragedy*, 2225–7); for a single *pearl* see *Parson's Wedding*, 424.

peep

used in the sense of "peek" (which does not occur): "*peeps fearfully forth from behind the arras*" (*Atheist's Tragedy*, 2.5.110; see also *Volpone*, 5.3.9), "*peeps out above*" (*New Trick*, 232; see also *Little French Lawyer*, 440), "*peeps from under the Table*" (*Variety*, D11r), "*peeps over his shoulder*" (*Brennoralt*, 2.1.36, also 4.1.18), "*Peeps into the pot*" (*Landgartha*, G1r); see also *Chances*, 199; *Spanish Curate*, 90; *Inconstant Lady*, 3.1.78; *Example*, G1v; *Bride*, 34; *Sophy*, 3.187; *Parson's Wedding*, 426.

pen

a property almost always called for with **ink** and/or **paper**: "*with pen Ink and paper*" (*Captives*, 1361), "*a Lute, pen, ink and paper being placed before her*" (*1 Honest Whore*, 3.3.0), "*one ready with pen and ink*" (*Sir John Oldcastle*, 876–7); see also *Massacre at Paris*, 888;

Hieronimo, 6.0; *Revenge of Bussy*, 4.4.0; *Lady Mother*, 41–4; *Platonic Lovers*, 91; other calls for a *pen* are "*Taper: pen and ink Table*" (*Barnavelt*, 1610–11), "*with a writing and pen*" (*Believe as You List*, 1), "*a Porringer full of water and a pen in it*" (*John a Kent*, 370–1), "*an Antic habited in Parchment Indentures. Bills, Bonds, Wax, Seals, and Pen, and Inkhorns: on his breast writ, I am a Scrivener*" (*New Trick*, 250); in *Spanish Tragedy* Hieronimo "*makes signs for a knife to mend his pen*" (4.4.198); a related term occurs once: "*the Herald with a pencil and colors*" (*Cobbler's Prophecy*, 735–6).

pendant

called for occasionally as (1) part of an earring, (2) a *flag*, (3) an ornamental hanging *shield* or cloth at a *funeral*; for an example of earrings, six *dancing* Moors enter with "*Great pendants of Pearl at their ears*" (*Amorous War*, E2v), and for flags, *black* pendants are carried in a *retreat* (*Jews' Tragedy*, 3044–5); found in funerals are "*a white pendant*" with "*words writ in gold*" (*Death of Huntingdon*, 2909–10), "*a rich Hearse with five pendants*" (*Wasp*, 474–5).

people

used (1) as a collective noun comparable to *followers*, *men*, *others*, *train*, and more specifically for (2) off-stage *sounds*, (3) the locution *to the people*; for entrances and exits of *people*/*with the people* see *1 Troublesome Reign*, F2r; *Caesar and Pompey*, 1.2.0; *Coriolanus*, 1950, 3.1.228; *Bonduca*, 128; *Tom a Lincoln*, 2230; *Goblins*, 1.4.28; *1 Passionate Lovers*, D5v; *Unfortunate Lovers*, 24; variations include "*two Tribunes of the people*" (*Coriolanus*, 896–7, 2.1.0; 1239–40, 2.2.36), "*Country people*" (*Two Noble Kinsmen*, E3r, 2.3.23; *Shoemaker a Gentleman*, 5.1.0; *Witch of Edmonton*, 5.3.20), "*poor people*" (*Sir John Oldcastle*, 324), "*common people*" (*Henry VIII*, 892, 2.1.53), "*the Doctor's people*" (*Soddered Citizen*, 1809), "*people passing over by degrees*" (*1 Passionate Lovers*, D8r), "*people running over the Stage*" (*Osmond*, A2r); signals for sounds are "*A groan of many people is heard under ground*" (*Catiline*, 1.315), "*great shouts of the people*" (*Coriolanus*, 3705–6, 5.6.48; *Hieronimo*, 4.0), "*People talking without*" (*Parson's Wedding*, 393), "*Noise and hallooing as people a-Maying*" (*Two Noble Kinsmen*, F2r, 3.1.0); see also *Cupid's Revenge*, 277; *to the people* means either *aside* or "to the playgoer" (as with a choric speech); examples of *asides* are "*apart to his own people*" (*Four Prentices*, 193), "*He speaks to the people*" (*Maid's Metamorphosis*, B4v; see also *Locrine*, 406); twice in *Warning for Fair Women* Tragedy "*Turning to*

the people" serves as a *chorus* (A3r, D1v); *Two Lamentable Tragedies* provides fifteen *asides* marked "*To the people*," "*to people*," or merely "*People*" (B1r, B1v, B2v, B4r, C3v, C4v, D2r, D4v, G4v, H1r, H3r, I3r).

perfume

usually found as a noun, as when figures appear "*with herbs and perfumes*" (Quarto *Every Man Out*, 1394), "*with a chafing-dish, a perfume in it*" (*Antonio's Revenge*, 3.1.0); *Humorous Lieutenant* calls for "*two Ushers, and Grooms with perfumes*" (282) with one *usher* ordering "Round, round, perfume it round, quick"; for other maids, servants, and attendants with *perfumes* see *Blurt*, 2.2.0; *Malcontent*, 1.1.7; MS *Humorous Lieutenant*, 3; *Picture*, 1.2.81; *Ball*, H3r; *Constant Maid*, E1r; for perfumer, a figure enters "*as newly dressed, a Tailor, Barber, Perfumer*" and "*sits in a chair, Barber orders his hair, Perfumer gives powder, Tailor sets his clothes*" (*Fatal Dowry*, 4.1.0); uses of *perfume* as a verb are "*an Usher bare, perfuming a room*" (*Wonder of a Kingdom*, 3.1.0; see also *Launching of the Mary*, 2018–19), "*a maid strewing flowers, and a servingman perfuming the door*" (*Two Maids of More-Clacke*, A1r); for examples of other uses, when a devil ascends in response to his conjuring "*Alexander putteth on more perfume*" (*Devil's Charter*, G1v), and to *poison* a portrait two poisoners "*put on spectacles of glass, which cover their eyes and noses, and then burn perfumes afore the picture, and wash the lips of the picture*" (*White Devil*, 2.2.23).

periwig

although *wig* is not called for in directions, *periwig* is found in three Caroline plays: "*Enter Lord unready; Haircut preparing his periwig, table, and looking glass*" (*Lady of Pleasure*, 3.1.0), "*pulls off his periwig*" (*Wit in a Constable*, 208), "*Pulls off Lovering's Periwigs, he is discovered to be Martha*" (*Hollander*, 152); see also *hair*, *peruke*.

permissive stage directions

a category that includes the many signals that leave key details indeterminate (1) most commonly the specific number of actors required for an entrance but also (2) a variety of actions; the number of figures to *enter* is usually left open by means of a collective noun (*army*, *attendants*, *followers*, *lords*, *men*, *others*, *train*, *and the rest*), but alternatives include the use of *or* and a variety of other locutions; typical of hundreds of examples is *Midsummer Night's Dream* which provides "*Enter Theseus, Hippolita, with others*,"

"*Enter the King of Fairies, at one door, with his train; and the Queen, at another, with hers*" (A2r, 1.1.0; B3v, 2.1.59); variations include "*an Officer to whip him, or two if you can*" (*Three Ladies of London*, F1v), a lady "*and some other women for show*" (*Two Maids of More-Clacke*, A1v); Folio *2 Henry VI* provides entrances for "*Multitudes with Halters about their Necks*" and for Cade "*with infinite numbers*" with "*all his rabblement*" (2860–1, 4.9.9; 2350–1, 4.2.30; 2773–4, 4.8.0); also *permissive* are locutions such as "*as many as may be*" (*Edward I*, 40; *Double Marriage*, 400), "*as many as can be*" (*Titus Andronicus*, A4v, 1.1.69), "*so many Alderman as may*" (*Sir Thomas More*, 954), "*as many as may be spared*" (*Hoffman*, 1682), "*as many Pages with Torches as you can*" (*What You Will*, H1v); in such scenes a stage replete with personnel is desirable (*as many as may be*), but *permissive* terms allow for the limitations of personnel, budget, and other exigencies, as when early in a performance those responsible for collecting tickets may not be available as supernumeraries.

Such open signals are also used for onstage actions/choices; sometimes a direction calls for an effect but leaves the specific words or melody to the performers: "*He plays and sings any odd toy, and Orlando wakes*" (*Orlando Furioso*, 1213–14), "*speaks anything, and Exit*" (*Trial of Chivalry*, E4r), "*Jockey is led to whipping over the stage, speaking some words, but of no importance*" (*2 Edward IV*, 180), "*Here they two talk and rail what they list*" (*Greene's Tu Quoque*, I1r), "*whistles and Dances Sellenger's round, or the like*" (*Court Beggar*, 262); more common are terms such as a **while**, a **pretty** while, a good while that leave open the duration of an action: "*A noise heard about the house, a pretty while, then enter the Constable*" (*Sir John Oldcastle*, 2222–3), "*they sit a good while on the Stage before the Candles are lighted, talking together*" (*What You Will*, A2r), "*They fight a good while and then breathe*" (*Orlando Furioso*, 1536); some signals leave open special effects or significant bits of stage business: "*A Spirit (over the door) does some action to the dishes as they enter*" (*Late Lancashire Witches*, 206), "*enter from the widow's house a service, musical songs of marriages, or a masque, or what pretty triumph you list*" (*James IV*, 2051–3), "*let there come forth a Lion running after a Bear or any other beast*" (*Locrine* 4–6), "*Exit Venus. Or if you can conveniently, let a chair come down from the top of the stage, and draw her up*" (*Alphonsus of Aragon*, 2109–10); such *permissive* directions can be found even in playhouse books and plots: **descend** "*out of a tree, if possible it may be*" (*John a Kent*, 836), "*Either strikes him with a staff or Casts a stone*" (*Captives*, 2432–4), "*causeth the chest or trunk to be*

brought forth" (*Dead Man's Fortune*, 65–6), "*with as many Jewels robes and Gold as he can carry*" (*2 Seven Deadly Sins*, 66–7); see also **belonging**, **certain**, **convenient**, **diverse**, **during**, **several**, **sundry**.

peruke

rarely used for *wig*/**hair**; to reveal that the supposed she is a he, Dauphine "*takes off Epicœne's peruke*" (*Epicœne*, 5.4.204); a male figure reveals his true identity when he "*casts off his Peruke and Beard*" (*Novella*, 177); see also **periwig**.

peruse

a synonym for **read** in eight directions, all of which simply describe a figure or figures who *peruse* various written materials: "*Andrugio peruses a Letter*" (*More Dissemblers*, B8r), "*takes the scroll and peruses it*" (*Court Beggar*, 191), "*at a table perusing some papers*" (*Wizard*, 2221–2), "*peruses the Motto of the Hearse*" (*King John and Matilda*, 86); see also *James IV*, 767; *Sophonisba*, 2.1.103; *Queen and Concubine*, 22; *Distresses*, 358.

petition

a **fictional** term, more common in later plays, for a **paper** with which figures **enter** (*2 Honest Whore*, 1.1.68; *If This Be Not a Good Play*, 3.3.63; *Prophetess*, 347; *Great Duke of Florence*, 1.2.0; *Emperor of the East*, 1.2.32, 3.2.181; *Doubtful Heir*, C8r; *Fair Favourite*, 235; *Lovesick Court*, 160; *Politician*, A4v); elsewhere a *petition* is **delivered** (*Cobbler's Prophecy*, 884; *What You Will*, B3r; *Christian Turned Turk*, H1v; *Roman Actor*, 4.1.112; *Maidenhead Well Lost*, 108; *Guardian*, 2.1.53) and presented (*Emperor of the East*, 3.2.0; *Fair Favourite*, 235); atypical is "*her lap full of Petitions*" (*Costly Whore*, 280).

petticoat

an undergarment that usually indicates that a female figure is **unready**, vulnerable, or surprised: "*a bed discovered*" with "*the Lady in a petticoat*" (*Amends for Ladies*, 5.2.180–2), a figure **dragged in** "*in her petticoat and hair*" (*Fatal Contract*, I1v), "*Syphax, his dagger twon about her hair, drags in Sophonisba in her nightgown petticoat*" (*Sophonisba*, 3.1.0); *Herod and Antipater* distinguishes the female *petticoat* from the male **waistcoat** by having Alexandra enter "*in her petticoat*" and Aristobulus "*in his waistcoat or shirt, both amazedly*" (B1r); other uses include country wenches wearing "*all red Petticoats*" (*Country Girl*, D3r), a figure "*in her smock and a tattered petticoat*" (*Soddered Citizen*, 1268), servants **disguised** "*in their petticoats, cloaks over them,* with hats over their headtires" (*Gentleman Usher*, 2.1.153); see also *Jack Drum's Entertainment*, F1r.

pewter
used in a unique signal for a distinctive **sound** effect when "*A great noise within*" is preceded by an anticipatory "*Pewter ready for noise*" at which a figure says "The Ladles, Dishes, Kettles, how they fly all! / And how the Glasses, through the Rooms!" (*Spanish Curate*, 123/501, 124–5).

pick, picking
of the ten directions all but two are for *picking* a **pocket/purse**: "*They pick his pocket*" (*Hengist*, 5.1.250), "*Cocledemoy picks Malheureux's pocket of his purse*" (*Dutch Courtesan*, 5.3.16), "*He picketh his purse*" (*Bartholomew Fair*, 2.6.58), "*Crabb, picks his pocket as he leans on him, he finds his hand in his pocket*" (*Princess*, C2r); see also *Alchemist*, 4.6.25; *Bride*, 51; *Sisters*, C4r–v; the two unique uses are "*Jack Cade lies down picking of herbs and eating them*" (Quarto *2 Henry VI*, G4r, 4.10.15), "*Enter Old Courtiers, picking their teeth, and striking off crumbs from their shirts*" (*Fair Favourite*, 250).

pickax
a tool cited twice: "*two sailors with a trunk, wherein is Mistress Mary in her winding sheet, others with pickax and spades, as on the sands*" (*Two Maids of More-Clacke*, F4r, also G1r), "*Carpenter, Mason, Smith, in Devils' habits; two dark Lanterns, a Pickax and a Rope*" (*Queen's Exchange*, 535).

picture
of the thirty-five examples some of the more notable are "*Enter a servant setting out a Table, on which he places a skull, a picture, a book and a Taper*" (*1 Honest Whore*, 4.1.0), "*A Table set out covered with black: two waxen Tapers: the King's Picture at one end, a Crucifix at the other*" (*Noble Spanish Soldier*, 1.2.0), "*Show Tarlton's picture*" (*Three Lords of London*, C2r), "*brings her to her husband's picture hanging on the wall*" (*Warning for Fair Women*, E3v), "*burn perfumes afore the picture, and wash the lips of the picture*" (*White Devil*, 2.2.23), "*kiss the picture*" (*Picture*, 2.2.327, also 3.5.187, 4.1.27), "*Takes a Picture out of her bosom*" (*2 Arviragus and Philicia*, F3r), "*hanging out the picture of a strange fish*" (*City Match*, 248), "*Draw the curtain and show the picture*" and "*Stabs the picture*" (*Fatal Contract*, B3v, B4r), "*discovers the duke's picture, a poniard sticking in it*" (*Traitor*, 5.3.22); for other *pictures* see *Fair Em*, 2; *Antonio and Mellida*,

5.1.0; *Wisdom of Doctor Dodypoll*, 85; *Blind Beggar of Alexandria*, 3.0; *Blurt*, 2.2.81; *Satiromastix*, 5.2.158; *Humorous Day's Mirth*, 2.2.49; *Fawn*, 1.2.108; *Wit of a Woman*, 389; *1 Fair Maid of the West*, 302; *Conspiracy of Byron*, 3.2.138; *Puritan*, A4v; *Whore of Babylon*, 2.2.185; *Two Noble Kinsmen*, I3v, 4.2.0; *Devil's Law Case*, 3.3.374, 4.2.473; *Spanish Gypsy*, H1v; *Vow Breaker*, 3.4.0, 77, 84, 4.2.247; *Maid's Revenge*, E3v; *Siege*, 400; *Novella*, 147; *Emperor of the East*, 2.1.243; *Love's Sacrifice*, 876; *1 Passionate Lovers*, C2r, C3r; *Aglaura*, 1.3.34; *Gentleman of Venice*, F2r.

piece
either (1) a **weapon** brought on by a player or (2) the **sound** of a **cannon** or gun fired offstage; a hand-held property is called for in "*De Flores with a piece*" which is later fired **within** (*Changeling*, 5.1.87, 93), "*shows a piece*" (*Staple of News*, 2.4.107), "*a fowling piece*" (*Honest Lawyer*, F3v); see also *Shoemakers' Holiday*, 1.1.116; *Devil's Charter*, K3r; *Woman's Prize*, 56; sound signals are "*A flourish of trumpets and two pieces go off*" (Q2 *Hamlet*, D1r, 1.4.6), "*Charge Trumpets, Pieces go off*" (*Double Marriage*, 343, also 353); see also *Alarum for London*, 203; *Lust's Dominion*, 3.3.88; *1 Fair Maid of the West*, 315; *Fortune by Land and Sea*, 416; *Dick of Devonshire*, 31.

pike
a **staff** with an iron point or spike used as a **weapon**: "*Enter Tarquin, Porsenna, and Aruns with their pikes and Targeters*" (*Rape of Lucrece*, 243); see also *Widow's Tears*, 4.2.0; in *Alarum for London* a military **funeral** has soldiers "*trailing their pikes*" (262–3) and in *Four Prentices* "*They toss their pikes*" (203); also found is *pikestaff*: "*Luellen is slain with a Pikestaff*" (*Edward I*, 2128, also 2146).

pillar
a term used once for a stage **post**: "*Rolliardo comes from the Pillar*" (*Bird in a Cage*, H3r) and once for a portable property: "*sets up a Pillar in the middle of the stage*" (*Virgin Martyr*, 4.2.61).

pinch
a seldom signaled action usually linked to **fairies**: "*The Fairies dance, and with a song pinch him, and he falleth asleep*" (*Endymion*, G3r); see also *Guy of Warwick*, C1r; Quarto *Merry Wives*, G3r, 5.5.102; *Alchemist*, 3.5.31; *Honest Lawyer*, G2v; for other directions to *pinch* see *Knack to Know an Honest Man*, 507; *Grateful Servant*, D3r; *Goblins*, 1.3.22, 64.

pinioned

used seldom for "tied"; **prisoners** enter "*pinioned and led betwixt two Officers*" (2 *Edward IV*, 175), "*pinioned, and with a guard of Officers*" (*Puritan*, B2v), "*her arms in a scarf pinioned*" (*Love and Honour*, 103); for others who enter *pinioned* see 2 *Edward IV*, 136; *Dutch Courtesan*, 5.3.8; *Two Noble Kinsmen*, M2v, 5.4.0; unusually elaborate is an entrance "*like Amazon Captives, shackled with Golden Fetters, and pinioned with silken cords*" (*Amorous War*, C2v, also H2v).

pipe

denotes two different kinds of *pipe*: (1) a wind instrument, commonly the three-hole, eighteen-note **flute** or **recorder** played with one hand and usually accompanied by a **tabor**, but also a *bagpipe*, (2) a *pipe* for **tobacco**; calls for the instrument are "*Ariel plays the tune on a Tabor and Pipe*" (*Tempest*, 1481, 3.2.124), "*Tabor and Pipe strike up a Morris*" (*Jack Drum's Entertainment*, A3v, also A2v; see also *Shoemakers' Holiday*, 3.3.47); for more see *Midas*, 4.1.108; *World Tossed at Tennis*, E3r; *Amyntas*, 2C4v; a *bagpipe* is called for twice: "*Drum soundeth and a Bagpipe*" (*Captain Thomas Stukeley*, 1166; see also *Hyde Park*, H1r); *Arraignment of Paris* provides "*he pipeth*" (287); uses of the *pipe* for smoking are "*Servants with wine, Plate, Tobacco and pipes*" (*Woman Is a Weathercock*, 3.2.4–5), "*The Petition is delivered up by Randolfo, the Duke lights his tobacco pipe with it*" (*What You Will*, B3r); see also *Amends for Ladies*, 2.1.69; *Blurt*, 4.2.0; *Puritan*, B4r; *Soddered Citizen*, 994.

pistol

more than sixty directions call specifically for a *pistol* or **dag**, with a large number of figures directed to **enter** with one or more *pistols*; such entrances are common in the Fletcher canon (see MS *Humorous Lieutenant*, 2387–8; *Honest Man's Fortune*, 258; *Knight of Malta*, 148; *Love's Cure*, 233; *Lovers' Progress*, 104; *Rule a Wife*, 227); for a sampling from other dramatists see *Spanish Tragedy*, 3.3.0; *Satiromastix*, 4.2.0; *Woman Is a Weathercock*, 5.2.37; *Duchess of Malfi*, 3.2.141; *City Nightcap*, 175; *Novella*, 164; *Politician*, I1r; *Imposture*, E1r; *Bloody Banquet*, 1513; other entrances call for a **sword** and a *pistol* (*Amends for Ladies*, 5.2.180–1; *Noble Spanish Soldier*, 4.1.0; *English Moor*, 75; *Gentleman of Venice*, I3v), a crossbow and a *pistol* (*Malcontent*, 3.5.0), "*pistolets and short swords under their robes*" (*Malcontent*, 5.5.66); also specified are *cases of pistols* (*Insatiate Countess*, 4.4.0; *White Devil*, 5.6.23; *Gentleman of Venice*, F2v; *Just Italian*, 245; *Siege*, 431), the **drawing** of

pistols (*Amends for Ladies*, 5.2.174–6; *Novella*, 142), the **showing**/presenting of pistols (*White Devil*, 5.6.104; *Rule a Wife*, 228; *Guardian*, 5.2.130; *City Nightcap*, 179; *Duke's Mistress*, H4v; *English Moor*, 78), the **charging**/loading of a *pistol* (*Jack Drum's Entertainment*, H1v), **prisoners** "*led by two holding pistols*" (*If This Be Not a Good Play*, 5.3.44), revengers who "*environ Mendoza, bending their pistols on him*" (*Malcontent*, 5.5.118); occasionally the *pistols* are fired onstage: enter "*discharging a Pistol*" (*Second Maiden's Tragedy*, 749–50), "*Shoots her with a Pistol*" (*Alarum for London*, 1078), simply **shoot** (*White Devil*, 5.6.118); more common is to have the *pistol* fired offstage: "*A Pistol shot within*" (*Lovers' Progress*, 109; Q2 *Bussy D'Ambois*, 5.4.72; *Rebellion*, 66; 1 *Arviragus and Philicia*, A10r), the anticipatory warning "*John Bacon ready to shoot off a Pistol*" (*Love's Pilgrimage*, 290/417); a signal in *Politician* makes clear the link between offstage **sound** and onstage action: "*As the Prince is going forth, a Pistol is discharged within, he falls*" (H1v).

pistolet

see **dag**, **pistol**

pit

a rare **fictional** designation for the **trapdoor** and area under the **stage**: "*falls in the Pit*" (*Bloody Banquet*, 683), "*D'Amville thrusts him down into the gravel pit*" (*Atheist's Tragedy*, 2.4.13).

pitcher

associated with the drawing of **water**; in *Patient Grissil* Grissil enters "*running with a Pitcher*" (1.2.169) announcing she had been "running to fetch water"; although rarely cited elsewhere the *pitcher* is basic to the stage action in *Old Wives Tale*: "*Here she strikes her Pitcher against her sister's, and breaks them both*," "*Enter Zantippa with a Pitcher to the Well*," "*Here she offers to dip her Pitcher in, and a head speaks in the Well*," "*She breaks her Pitcher upon his head*" (624, 629, 634, 645).

pitchfork

found only when a newly prosperous Strumbo enters "*with a pitchfork, and a Scotch cap*" (*Locrine*, 1596).

place

of the roughly 100 examples (1) more than half direct figures to be *placed*/*place* themselves, take their *places* onstage, *place* objects (most commonly **chairs** and **lights**), but *place* as a noun is also linked

to (2) offstage *sounds*, (3) entrances, (4) areas of the
stage; for a sampling of the *placing* of figures (often
at a *table*) see *Wounds of Civil War*, 4; *Downfall of
Huntingdon*, 2697; *Look about You*, 2825–6;
Satiromastix, 4.3.68; *Chabot*, 3.2.0; *Henry VIII*, 332–3,
1.2.8; *City Madam*, 1.3.5; *Herod and Antipater*, B4v, F4r;
Love's Mistress, 101; *Queen*, 3424; *New Trick*, 281;
Messalina, 1509, 2199; *Goblins*, 2.6.1; for *taking* one's
place see *Sir John Oldcastle*, 2575; *Chabot*, 3.2.0, 5.2.0;
Coriolanus, 1242, 2.2.36; *Devil's Charter*, L1r; *Silver Age*,
161; *1 Iron Age*, 307; *Henry VIII*, 1343–6, 2.4.0; *'Tis Pity*,
5.6.0; *Valiant Scot*, A3v; *Landgartha*, E4r; figures who
place themselves are found in *Sophonisba*, 2.1.0;
Henry VIII, 319–20, 1.2.0; 1346–7, 2.4.0; 3036–7,
5.2.35; *Custom of the Country*, 355; *Welsh Ambassador*,
1070; *Vow Breaker*, 2.1.113; *Hannibal and Scipio*, 220;
variations include: "*places Hoffman at his feet*"
(*Hoffman*, 484), "*placing them in secret*" (*Spanish
Tragedy*, 2.2.6), "*place him on one side of the altar*"
(*Broken Heart*, 5.3.0), "*Andrugio's ghost is placed betwixt
the music houses*" (*Antonio's Revenge*, 5.3.49), "*They
place themselves in every corner of the Stage*" (*Antony and
Cleopatra*, 2477, 4.3.8, also 1464, 2.7.112); *place* can be
linked to *shift*: "*The Senators shift their places*"
(*Sejanus*, 5.609); see also Folio *Midsummer Night's
Dream*, 1460, [3.2.416]; *Look about You*, 2630–1; for the
substitution of one object *in the place of* another see
Wily Beguiled, Prologue.46–7; *Old Fortunatus*,
3.1.356; *Brazen Age*, 231; *Two Noble Kinsmen*, L2r,
5.1.162; for *placing* a chair or a figure in a chair see
Westward Ho, 4.2.52; *Devil's Charter*, L3r; *Laws of
Candy*, 271; *Broken Heart*, 4.3.0, 4.4.0; unusual is "*Six
Chairs placed at the Arras*" (*Maid in the Mill*, 14/386); for
the *placing* of other objects (a *table*, *tent*, *boxes*,
dishes, *tapers*) see *Titus Andronicus*, K2r, 5.3.25;
2 Seven Deadly Sins, 1; *1 Honest Whore*, 2.1.0, 4.1.0;
Sejanus, 5.177; *Escapes of Jupiter*, 904; *Golden Age*, 67;
Henry VIII, 3035–6, 5.2.35; *No Wit*, 4.2.0; *World Tossed
at Tennis*, D3r; *Love's Sacrifice*, 1124; *Bloody Banquet*,
1094; *Lovesick King*, 165–6; *Wedding*, I1r.

Sounds linked to *place* include "*Alarms, Drums and
Trumpets at several places afar off*" (*Bonduca*, 118, also
116, 117; see also *Histriomastix*, G1v), "*Cornets in sundry
places*" (*Two Noble Kinsmen*, F2r, 3.1.0; see also *Women
Pleased*, 307); *place* is associated with entrances in
locutions such as "*Enter from the same place*" (*Brazen
Age*, 176), enter "*from another place*" and "*at two several
places*" (*Devil's Charter*, A2v, A3r), "*from under the
ground in several places, rise up spirits*" (*If This Be Not a
Good Play*, 5.4.0); see also *Wise Woman of Hogsdon*, 308;
Rape of Lucrece, 243; atypical is "*Let there be a brazen

Head set in the middle of the place behind the Stage*"
(*Alphonsus of Aragon*, 1246–7); more general are "*she
makes them survey the place*" (*Golden Age*, 35), "*steals in,
and stands in some by place*" (*Match Me in London*, 5.3.0);
see also *Three Lords of London*, G1v, G4v; *Cobbler's
Prophecy*, 1565–6; *Grim the Collier*, G2r; *Whore of
Babylon*, 4.1.0; *Brazen Age*, 254; *Obstinate Lady*, F1r;
other uses include "*wounded in several places*" (*Lovers'
Progress*, 86), "*Enter the Ghost of Banquo, and sits in
Macbeth's place*" (*Macbeth*, 1299, 3.4.36).

plate

utensils for the *table* or domestic use; servants or
drawers **bring in** "*a cupboard of plate*" (*Devil's Charter*,
L1r), "*wine, Plate, Tobacco and pipes*" (*Woman Is a
Weathercock*, 3.2.4–5; see also *Amends for Ladies*,
3.4.36); a courtesan counterfeiting sickness has
"*Vials, gallipots, plate, and an hourglass by her*" (*Mad
World*, 3.2.0), and a visitor brings "*two spoons and
plate*" (*Chaste Maid*, 3.2.24) as a christening gift with
the *plate* described as "*a fair high standing cup*";
gold and *silver* plate are valued items, as indicated by
"*two prentices, preparing the Goldsmith's Shop with plate*"
(*1 Edward IV*, 63), a surreptitious figure who enters
"*with plate under his cloak*" (*Bride*, 21), "*a great quantity
of rich Plate*" used as a bribe (*Devil's Charter*, A2r);
Weakest Goeth provides citizens "*with Bags and Plate,
and things to hide*" and "*He seeks up and down for a place
to hide his Plate*" (252–3, 261–2); see also *Wonder of a
Kingdom*, 3.1.192.

play, playing

(1) usually linked to *music*, sometimes a specific
instrument but can also refer to *playing* (2) by a
musician, (3) of music for an *act* (i.e., *entr'acte*), (4) a
game; a common call for *sound* is *music plays* (*Taming
of the Shrew*, 1564, 3.2.183; *1 Henry IV*, F3v, 3.1.228;
Merchant of Venice, I2v, 5.1.68; *Antony and Cleopatra*,
1333, 2.7.0; 1464, 2.7.12; *Coriolanus*, 2653, 4.5.0; *Fair
Maid of the Inn*, 201); some signals provide a context:
"*Music plays and they dance*" (Q2 *Romeo and Juliet*, C3r,
1.5.25), "*the music plays and there Enters three antic
fairies dancing*" (*Dead Man's Fortune*, 53–4), "*let the
music play before him, and so go forth*" (*Orlando Furioso*,
1285–6), "*while the Banquet is Brought forth Music
plays*" (*Hengist*, 4.2.0; see also *Thomas Lord Cromwell*,
D2r), "*Hoboys cease, and solemn Music plays during his
speech*" (*Messalina*, 1510–12); see also *John a Kent*, 918;
Fawn, 4.408; *Lust's Dominion*, 3.2.30; *Your Five
Gallants*, F2v; *Second Maiden's Tragedy*, 2227–8,
2454–5; *Witty Fair One*, E1r; *Jews' Tragedy*, 2215–17;

English Moor, 67; *Wizard*, 2390–1; directions to *play* specific instruments include "*Ophelia playing on a Lute*" (Q1 *Hamlet*, G4v, 4.5.20), "*Ariel plays the tune on a Tabor and Pipe*" (*Tempest*, 1481, 3.2.124), "*Hoboys playing loud Music*" (*Timon of Athens*, 337, 1.2.0), "*a devil playing on a Drum*" (*Doctor Faustus*, B 1485), "*The chime plays*" (*John a Kent*, 1158), "*Cornets and organs playing full music*" (*Sophonisba*, 3.1.116, also 4.1.200, 5.4.36), "*Recorders dolefully playing*" (*Chaste Maid*, 5.4.0), "*A Bagpipe playing*" (*Hyde Park*, H1r), "*playing on a Fiddle*" (*Queen and Concubine*, 124), "*A Treble plays within*" (*Country Girl*, D1r); for more see *Fedele and Fortunio*, 193; *Alphonsus of Aragon*, 2116; *John a Kent*, 1098; *Cobbler's Prophecy*, 1000; Folio *3 Henry VI*, 2256, 4.2.27; *Summer's Last Will*, 360; Folio *Every Man Out*, 3.9.80; *Malcontent*, 5.5.66; *Fawn*, 5.139; *Mad World*, 2.1.151; *Two Maids of More-Clacke*, A1v; *Maid's Tragedy*, 8; *Valiant Welshman*, A4v; *Witch*, 438–9; *Witch of Edmonton*, 4.2.60; *Two Noble Ladies*, 1099; *Lovesick Court*, 163; sometimes the signal for music is simply *play* (*Rare Triumphs*, 1621; *John a Kent*, 572, 581; *Taming of a Shrew*, C2r; *Old Fortunatus*, 4.1.111; *Law Tricks*, 152; *Wit of a Woman*, 393; *Lady Mother*, 734; *Court Beggar*, 262).

Directions referring primarily to the musicians' actions are "*the waits play softly*" (*Fatal Contract*, H3r; see also *Sir Thomas More*, 758, 954–5), "*Fiddlers pass through, and play the battle*" (*Late Lancashire Witches*, 204; see also *Parson's Wedding*, 519), "*a strain played by the consort*" (*Mad World*, 2.1.143); see also *Late Lancashire Witches*, 206; signals to *play* music for an *entr'acte* are "*a base lute and a treble viol play for the Act*" (*Sophonisba*, 4.1.218, also 1.2.236, 4.1.218), "*Whilst the Act plays*" (*City Madam*, 4.4.160); see also *Malcontent*, 2.1.0; *Fawn*, 5.0; *Fatal Dowry*, 2.2.359; combined signals are for *singing* and *playing* (*Orlando Furioso*, 1213–14; *Tempest*, 519, 1.2.374; *Nice Valour*, 157; *Novella*, 129), *dancing* and *playing* (*Gallathea*, 2.3.5; *Timon of Athens*, 451, 1.2.130), "*enter with music and play round about him*" (*Orlando Furioso*, 1258; see also *Old Fortunatus*, 2.2.328); atypical usages are "*She plays the vixen*" (*Woman in the Moon*, A4v), "*Dog plays the Morris*" (*Witch of Edmonton*, 3.4.49), "*Plays with the cord that binds his arms*" (*Parson's Wedding*, 482, also 417).

In non-musical contexts, the *playing* of games includes "*Ferdinand and Miranda, playing at Chess*" (*Tempest*, 2141–2, 5.1.171), "*play at bowls*" (*2 Edward IV*, 173), "*play at dice*" (*Sir John Oldcastle*, 1497; see also *Costly Whore*, 255); for more see *2 Tamburlaine*, 3739; *Soliman and Perseda*, D3r; *Wise Woman of Hogsdon*, 279; *Love's Sacrifice*, 1146; *Fool Would Be a Favourite*, B5r;

Hamlet provides *sword*play (Folio 3725, 5.2.265; Q1 I3r, Folio 3742, 5.2.280; Q1 I3r, Folio 3774, 5.2.300).

pledge

a *salute* or toast: "*drinks, and they all pledge him*" (*Conspiracy*, I4v), "*sets the two cups asunder, and first drinks with the one, and pledges with the other*" (Quarto *Every Man Out*, 3838–9), "*break the glass, they pledge it in plate*" (*Wonder of a Kingdom*, 3.1.192); for other examples see *Warning for Fair Women*, D1r; *News from Plymouth*, 174; see also *health*.

plot

a theatrical property cited twice: "*The Plot of a Scene of mirth, to conclude this fourth Act*" (*Faithful Friends*, 2815–16), "*Corax with a paper plot*" for the "Masque of Melancholy" (*Lover's Melancholy*, 3.3.0).

pluck

used for a variety of actions: "*plucks her back*" (*1 Iron Age*, 271), "*plucks Aurelia by the gown*" (*Changes*, D3r), "*Grilla plucked in by them*" (*Lover's Melancholy*, 5.1.118), "*Pluck him down*" (MS *Poor Man's Comfort*, 1382), "*plucked up*" from under the *stage* (*Renegado*, 4.3.6); figures *pluck off* a *headtire* (*Amends for Ladies*, 3.2.41–3), *disguise* (*Bondman*, 5.3.154), and Hercules "*tugs with the Bull, and plucks off one of his horns*" (*Brazen Age*, 176); the most common locution is *pluck out*: "*pluck out his tongue*" (*Antonio's Revenge*, 5.3.62), "*plucks out a gilt key*" (*Renegado*, 2.5.104), "*plucks out his entrails*" (*Caesar and Pompey*, 5.2.175), "*plucks out Vallinger's sword*" (*Fair Maid of Bristow*, D2v), "*plucks the Witch out by the heels*" (*Valiant Welshman*, G1v), "*plucks it out of his bosom and reads it*" (*Richard II*, H4v, 5.2.71); see also *Mad Lover*, 40; *Launching of the Mary*, 1982, 1986.

pocket

most of the roughly forty *pockets* belong to men and are linked to (1) the *picking* of a *pocket*, (2) *carrying/putting* an item *in a pocket*; for picking *pockets* see *Your Five Gallants*, C1r; *Hengist*, 5.1.250; *Sisters*, C4r–v; *Bride*, 51, 78; *Princess*, C2r; more specific are "*picks Malheureux's pocket of his purse*" (*Dutch Courtesan*, 5.3.16), "*as he is talking, Hercules steals it* [a letter] *out of his pocket*" (*Fawn*, 4.57); to set up a successful theft a cutpurse "*tickles him in the ear with a straw twice to draw his hand out of his pocket*" (*Bartholomew Fair*, 3.5.145); in a related locution a figure *searches/feels* another's *pockets*: "*He searcheth his pocket, and findeth certain papers*" (*1 Henry IV*, E4r, 2.4.531), "*searches first*

one, then the other Pocket" (Witch of Edmonton, 4.2.69);
see also Alchemist, 4.3.42; Bride, 65; Brennoralt, 1.2.11;
Siege, 397; Wits, 166; figures put in their pockets a
feather (Malcontent, Induction.46), **letter** (Thomas
Lord Cromwell, F3r), **bills** (Staple of News, 1.3.20), **purses**
(King Leir, 1528), **money** (Weeding of Covent Garden, 38),
meat (Locrine, 1648–9; Patient Grissil, 4.3.38), their
hands (Woman in the Moon, B1r; Yorkshire Tragedy,
189–90); items carried in pockets are a **horn** (English
Traveller, 79), **vial** (1 Honest Whore, 2.1.0), **gloves**
(Amends for Ladies, 2.3.11); actions include "taking
certain papers out of his pocket putteth in others in their
stead" (Devil's Charter, C3r), "seeming to put the keys
under his bolster conveyeth them into her pocket" (Hog
Hath Lost His Pearl, 1568–9); atypical are "a pocket
inkhorn" (Platonic Lovers, 91), "a pocket dag" (Fatal
Dowry, 4.1.163), "the pocket-Gallant" (Your Five
Gallants, A2r, B3r); see also Bashful Lover, 3.3.187, 189;
Staple of News, 1.2.98; Conspiracy, L3r; Wits, 161.

point
(1) as a verb, typically linked to a dialogue reference
to an object or figure, sometimes as part of a **dumb
show**, and as a noun either (2) the strings and laces
on a man's clothing, particularly those that tie **hose**
to **doublet** or (3) the point of a **weapon**; examples of
pointing to explain dialogue are "point to the
hangman" (2 Edward IV, 139), "the Ghost points to his
wounds" (Fatal Contract, E1r), "laughing, and pointing
scornfully" (Herod and Antipater, K1r), "Points to the
ring" (Insatiate Countess, 2.2.50), "Pointing first to the
head on the ground: and then to his wound" (Woman in the
Moon, B4v), "Pointing to his brows" (Cupid's Whirligig,
1.2.80), "Points to Matilda's Corpse" (King John and
Matilda, 79), "they whisper, and point" (Twins, G4r, also
C1r, C3v), "Points to his Crown" (Rebellion, 89); for
more see Alphonsus of Aragon, 328; Looking Glass for
London, 1576; Massacre at Paris, 153; Shoemakers'
Holiday, 4.4.73; Sir John Oldcastle, 363–5; Volpone,
2.2.110; Captain, 297; Two Merry Milkmaids, D1v;
Broken Heart, 4.2.116; Late Lancashire Witches, 238, 239;
Cardinal, 3.2.94; dumb shows offer "they return her
child, she points to her breasts, as meaning she should nurse
it" (Bloody Banquet, 855–6), "Disanius seems to acquaint
the King with the manner of Philargus's death, pointing at
Varillus" (Lovesick Court, 163); see also Soliman and
Perseda, D3r; Warning for Fair Women, E3v; Woman Is a
Weathercock, 5.2.5–6; Queen and Concubine, 22.

For examples of the noun, points on clothing are
most often associated with **trussing**, the fastening or
tying of points, so that figures are directed to **enter**

with themselves or attendants "trussing his points"
(Hieronimo, 6.1; Merry Devil of Edmonton, F2r; Hog
Hath Lost His Pearl, 457), "trussing their points as new
up" (Merry Devil of Edmonton, E4r), "untrussed in his
Nightcap, tying his points" (Devil's Charter, C1v); after a
group in a dumb show brings a figure to his wedding
bed "They cheer him on, and others snatch his Points, and
so Exit" (Maidenhead Well Lost, 152); atypical are a
group "with rosemary in their hands, and points in their
hats" (Parson's Wedding, 514), a woman "with a new
fashion gown, dressed gentlewoman-like, the Tailor points
it" (Michaelmas Term, 3.1.0); examples of points on
weapons include "takes a Dagger and feels upon the
point of it" (Soliman and Perseda, H3r), "throws his cloak
on the other's point" (Bride, 36), **prisoners** with "their
weapons with the points towards them" (Christian Turned
Turk, H1v), a **ceremony** that includes "a pointless
sword" and "a sword with a point" (Friar Bacon,
2074–5); objects placed on points include "a piece of
meat upon his dagger's point" (Taming of a Shrew, D4v),
"a dead man's head upon his sword's point" (Edmond
Ironside, 989–90), "present the King a bleeding heart upon
a knife's point" (Golden Age, 20), "bearing in one hand his
sword with the Dragon's head on the points" (Tom a
Lincoln, 2231–2); see also Three Lords of London, G1v.

poison
directions cite only a few of the many uses and
kinds of poison in plays of the period; Hamlet provides the best known: "pours poison in the King's ears"
(Q1 F3r, Q2 H1v, Folio 1996, 3.2.135; Folio 2131,
3.2.260); equally inventive are "Lodovico sprinkles
Bracciano's beaver with a poison" (White Devil, 5.2.76),
"he changes the Glove, and gives her the other poisoned"
and "Kisses the poisoned Glove" (King John and Matilda,
74); most often poison is administered in **wine**
(Alphonsus of Germany, F1v; Death of Huntingdon, 2403;
Sophonisba, 5.3.92; Valiant Welshman, C4v; Herod and
Antipater, H2v, I4r, I4v; Swisser, 5.2.47; 'Tis Pity,
4.1.62; Conspiracy, M2v, M4r; Bloody Banquet, 1826);
also called for is poison in a **vial** (Love's Sacrifice, 2798)
and **box** (Aglaura, 5.3.120; Politician, H4v); for other
atypical locutions see Malcontent, 5.3.35; Valentinian,
74; Maid's Revenge, I3r; Hannibal and Scipio, 267.

pole
occurs once as an alternative to **spear**: "Enter two with
the Lord Say's head, and Sir James Cromer's, upon two
poles" (Quarto 2 Henry VI, G3r, 4.7.129), and once a
barber "takes down his pole" (Knight of the Burning
Pestle, 202).

poleax

a *weapon* cited twice for an onstage *fight*: "*They fight at Poleax, Codigune is conquered*" (*Valiant Welshman*, E3r; see also *Hieronimo*, 11.85); elsewhere a *poleax* is a property in a formal entrance: "*cornets sound; and enter at the other end of the stage a Herald, two Pages with axes and poleaxes; then the King of Cyprus and Philocles, like combatants, and their army*" (*Dumb Knight*, 129, also 128); see also *Four Prentices*, 222; *Antonio's Revenge*, 4.1.70; *Lover's Melancholy*, 4.2.49.

pomp

to *enter in pomp* is to enter in *state* accompanied by a large retinue and the full panoply of power; examples are Richard III's entrance "*in pomp*" for his coronation (Folio *Richard III*, 2588, 4.2.0), "*Rasni with his Lords in pomp, who make a ward about him, with him the Magi in great pomp*" (*Looking Glass for London*, 514–16); other figures are directed to enter "*in great pomp*" (*James IV*, 684; *1 Tamburlaine*, 918), "*with funeral pomp*" (*Selimus*, 1997) and to "*Exeunt in pomp*" (*Four Plays in One*, 311); *pomp* is linked to *bravely* at the climax of *James IV*: "*March over bravely first the English host, the sword carried before the King by Percy. The Scottish on the other side, with all their pomp bravely*" (2406–8).

poniard

apparently interchangeable with *dagger*, as suggested in *Spanish Tragedy* where Hieronimo contemplating suicide enters "*with a poniard in one hand, and a rope in the other*" and subsequently "*flings away the dagger and halter*" (3.12.0, 19); elsewhere the *poniard* is associated with suicide when a jailer brings Antiochus a "*poniard and halter*" (*Believe as You List*, 1915; see also *Duchess of Malfi*, 3.2.71); figures are directed to *draw* (*Guardian*, 3.6.40; *Example*, D2v), *show* (*Fair Maid of the Inn*, 208; *Traitor*, 3.3.76), *stab* with *poniards* (*Traitor*, 4.2.111; *Albovine*, 86, 102); *Love's Sacrifice* provides "*draws his poniard and stabs her*" (2544–5); for figures who enter *with a poniard* see *Friar Bacon*, 945; *Noble Spanish Soldier*, 4.1.0; *Match Me in London*, 4.5.0; *Broken Heart*, 3.2.118; Piero enters "*unbraced, his arms bare, smeared in blood, a poniard in one hand, bloody, and a torch in the other*" (*Antonio's Revenge*, 1.1.0, also 3.2.86); two plays specify a *naked poniard* (*Messalina*, 951; *Cruel Brother*, 122); variations include: "*Offers to stab, lets the poniard fall*" (*Herod and Antipater*, B4v; see also *Julia Agrippina*, 5.522–3), "*Pretending a violent stab he flings away the Poniard*" (*Messalina*, 1181–2), "*discovers the duke's picture, a poniard sticking in it*" (*Traitor*, 5.2.22).

poor, poorly

used to signal poverty, *poor* is sometimes linked to soldiers: "*Leonatus Posthumus following like a poor Soldier*" (*Cymbeline*, 2892–4, 5.2.0), "*the King and his poor Soldiers*" (*Henry V*, 1534–5, 3.6.86), "*a rabble of poor soldiers*" (*Hoffman*, 1125); see also *Sir John Oldcastle*, 324; *Roaring Girl*, 5.1.55; also designated as *poor* are scholars (*Friar Bacon*, 172; *2 Honest Whore*, 1.1.24; *Isle of Gulls*, 222; *Two Noble Ladies*, 67), men (*Looking Glass for London*, 291, 600; *Edward II*, 24; *Knack to Know a Knave*, 986), women (*Sir Thomas More*, 1617; *Country Girl*, F1v); figures enter *like* a poor woman (*Orlando Furioso*, 927), shepherd (*Seven Champions*, F3r), citizen (*Three Lords of London*, B3v); elsewhere figures appear in *poor habits* (*Queen*, 4; see also *Seven Champions*, F4v), *attire* (MS *Humorous Lieutenant*, 46–7), array (*Hog Hath Lost His Pearl*, 46); other examples include "*Enter Bussy D'Ambois poor*" (Q2 *Bussy D'Ambois*, 1.1.0), "*very poorly a begging*" (*2 Edward IV*, 169), "*in scorn causeth her to be thrust out poorly*" (*Four Plays in One*, 326), "*miserably poor*" (*Valiant Scot*, F4v); for more see *Three Lords of London*, B3v; *Thomas Lord Cromwell*, E1r; *How a Man May Choose*, I4v; *Michaelmas Term*, Induction. 29; *Knave in Grain*, 117, 2190; *Love's Sacrifice*, 2055; see also *ragged*.

post

either (1) one of the two *posts* or *pillars* supporting the *heavens* or (2) a *messenger* whose arrival is frequently announced with a *horn*; signals citing the stage *post* are "*set his face towards the contrary post*" (*Three Lords of London*, I3v), "*Bind him to the post*" (*Greene's Tu Quoque*, L1v), "*fastens the glove to a post*" (*Humour out of Breath*, 468), "*stands behind the post*" (*Devil's Charter*, F3v), "*practising, to the post*" (Folio *Every Man In*, 3.5.141, also 4.7.12), "*an Engine fastened to a Post*" (*Queen's Exchange*, 535), "*congeing to the Post as to a Gentlewoman*" (*Twins*, E1v); see also *tree*; calls for a messenger are "*Post blowing a horn Within,*" then "*Enter the Post*" (Folio *3 Henry VI*, 1901, 3.3.161; 1904, 3.3.162; Octavo "*Sound for a post within,*" D2r), "*Enter a post with a letter and a bag of gold*" (*Friar Bacon*, 1494–5); see also *Thomas Lord Cromwell*, B1v; *Tom a Lincoln*, 2952–3; *Thierry and Theodoret*, 16; MS *Poor Man's Comfort*, 1325; *Lovesick King*, 1774; *Captives*, 2429; *Picture*, 1.2.304; *Perkin Warbeck*, 4.4.63; *Queen and Concubine*, 106; *Sophy*, 1.2.30; several directions are for more than one *post* (*2 If You Know Not Me*, 339, 340, 341; *Loyal Subject*, 89, 90; *Landgartha*, B2v); occasionally a figure is *disguised* as a *post*: "*Sound a Horn within, enter a Devil like a Post*" (*Devil's Charter*, M2r),

"*Marius in disguise and Lelia, like a post boy*" (*Faithful Friends*, 2414–15); see also *1 Tamar Cham*, 52; *Coxcomb*, 357.

posting

an alternative to the more common **hastily/in haste**: "*posting in haste*" (*Wounds of Civil War*, 747), "*posting over the stage*" (*Two Maids of More-Clacke*, H1v), and "*in post*" for the entrance of a "*hasty Doctor*" (*Wisdom of Doctor Dodypoll*, 1771).

posture

refers primarily to various undefined but distinctive movements or **gestures**: "*dance in several postures*" (*Fair Maid of the Inn*, 175), "*walking by, and practising his postures*" (*Maid of Honour*, 1.2.7; see also *Northern Lass*, 71), "*the Beggars are discovered in their postures*" (*Jovial Crew*, 365); figures enter "*in several postures*" (*City Madam*, 1.1.46) and "*in a sad posture*" (*City Match*, 212), a figure frozen by **magic** "*stands fixed in a posture of running at him with his sword*" (*Two Noble Ladies*, 488–9), to mock Mother Sawyer a group "*Exeunt in strange posture*" (*Witch of Edmonton*, 2.1.93); see also *Nice Valour*, 188; *Late Lancashire Witches*, 239; *Parson's Wedding*, 403.

pot

most often a vessel linked to a beverage, especially **wine**: "*a Friar with a chine of Beef and a pot of wine*" (*Old Wives Tale*, 373), "*the watchmen drunk, with each a pot*" (*King Leir*, 2489, also 2497), "*Overturns Wine, Pot, Cups and all*" (*Quarto Every Man Out*, 3876), "*Jaques with a pot of Wine*" (*Woman's Prize*, 4); *pots* are also properties in **tavern** or **drinking** scenes: "*Enter Clem with his pots*" (*2 Fair Maid of the West*, 414), "*Draw and fight, throw pots and stools*" (*Amends for Ladies*, 3.4.133–4), "*in a guesthouse…every one pots in their hand*" (*Faithful Friends*, 319–21), "*Vintner's boys with bottles, Cans, Blackpots, wine pots, Temple pots*" (*Soddered Citizen*, 993–4), "*Drawer, A Table, Pot and Glasses*" (*Weeding of Covent Garden*, 35, also 33, 43); other locutions are "*a holy water-pot*" (*Devil's Charter*, E1r), "*his maid dressed like Queen Fortune, with two pots in her hand*" containing **lots** to be drawn (*Humorous Day's Mirth*, 5.2.128), "*Angelo with a pot of painting*" for a **disguise** (*May Day*, 3.1.77; see also *Two Merry Milkmaids*, L4r), "*a pot of lily-flowers with a skull in it*" (*White Devil*, 5.4.123); a *pot* can also hold *honey* (*Old Wives Tale*, 199), *rice* (*Jew of Malta*, 1356), **water** (*Old Wives Tale*, 352, also 610, 614; *If It Be Not Good*, 3.2.0); for other *pots* see *Mucedorus*, D3r, D3v; *Launching of the Mary*, 76; *Landgartha*, G1r;

the term *pottle-pot* (*1 Honest Whore*, 2.1.117) indicates the quantity of wine it holds, as does *quart pot* (*Parson's Wedding*, 458); other combination forms include "*Pot Birds*" (*Pilgrim*, 221), "*beateth him with her potlid*" (*Famous Victories*, D4v), "*Empty a chamber pot on his head*" (*Fedele and Fortunio*, 1424–6), "*Viols, gallipots, plate, and an hourglass by her*" (*Mad World*, 3.2.0).

pot birds

found only in *Pilgrim* where to enhance a sense of the forest directions call first for "*Music and Birds*," then "*Music afar off. Pot Birds*" (221); the signal may allude to the creation of warbling **sounds** by blowing into a bowl of water through a pipe.

powder

the few examples point to a variety of uses; *powder* can be a potion to induce **sleep** (*Devil's Charter*, I2v) or gunpowder, as when a figure pretending to be a **spirit** "*flashes powder*" (*Honest Lawyer*, I2v); a man being dressed "*sits in a chair, Barber orders his hair, Perfumer gives powder, Tailor sets his clothes*" (*Fatal Dowry*, 4.1.0), and an elaborate description of a **study** includes "*glasses, vials, pictures of wax characters, wands, conjuring habit, Powders paintings*" (*Maid's Revenge*, E3v); atypical is *powdered* as a participle: "*Ganymede in a blue robe powdered with stars*" (*Women Beware Women*, 5.2.50).

power

used in both the singular and the plural as an equivalent to **army**; most of the examples are from the Shakespeare canon: "*Enter Titus with his Power, from the Pursuit*" (*Coriolanus*, 759, 1.9.11), "*Enter the two Kings with their powers, at several doors*" (*King John*, 646–7, 2.1.333), "*Alarum. Enter the powers of France over the stage, Cordelia with her father in her hand*" (*Quarto King Lear*, K3v, 5.2.0), "*to them Ferrex and Porrex several ways with Drums and Powers*" (*2 Seven Deadly Sins*, 31–2); for other entrances *with his/their power(s)* see Folio *3 Henry VI*, 651–2, 2.1.0; Octavo *3 Henry VI*, E1r, [5.1.15; not in Riv.]; *1 Henry IV*, K1r, 5.3.0; *Alarum for London*, 322; *Julius Caesar*, 1943, 4.2.30; Quarto *King Lear*, K3r, [5.1.0; not in Riv.]; *Timon of Athens*, 2507–8, 5.4.0; atypical is "*Enter the French Power and the English Lords*" (Folio *Henry V*, 3269–70, 5.2.280) where *power* designates the French court rather than an army.

praeter

Latin for "except" (often spelled *preter*) used as part of a locution that serves as an equivalent to **manet**:

"*Exeunt omnes praeter Shore*" (*2 Edward IV*, 125), "*Exeunt omnes praeter Savil*" (*Scornful Lady*, 271); see also *Alphonsus of Aragon*, 908; *1 If You Know Not Me*, 215, 218, 229, 239; *Nero*, 36, 65, 93; *City Wit*, 287; *Damoiselle*, 407; *Queen and Concubine*, 34; *Lovesick Court*, 100; *2 Cid*, B4r; *Ladies' Privilege*, 96; use of this Latin formula is by no means consistent within a given play, so that *Thierry and Theodoret* provides both "*Exeunt omnes, praeter*" and "*Exeunt all but*" (17, 28); the locution is found regularly in the Massinger canon; see *Bondman*, 5.2.91; *City Madam*, 1.2.103; *Duke of Milan*, 2.1.242; *Fatal Dowry*, 1.2.288, 2.2.149; *New Way to Pay*, 3.2.170; *Picture*, 2.2.80; *Roman Actor*, 1.2.102.

pray, prayer
the few signals for *praying* include "*kneel and pray*" (*Guy of Warwick*, E1v), "*prays apart*" (*Jews' Tragedy*, 976), "*sits weeping and praying*" (*2 Edward IV*, 167), "*walks in meditation, seeming to pray*" (*Four Plays in One*, 321), "*kneels down as to prayers*" (*White Devil*, 2.2.23), "*Caesar, in his sleep troubled, seems to pray to the Image*" (*Roman Actor*, 5.1.180); see also *Looking Glass for London*, 1230; atypical is "*holds up his hands instead of praying*" (*Ram Alley*, G2r); for *prayer* **books** see Folio *3 Henry VI*, 1410, 3.1.12; *2 Edward IV*, 166; *Two Noble Ladies*, 1753; *Twins*, F2v; more detailed is an entrance "*with a Prayer Book in her hand, like a Nun*" (*Sir Thomas Wyatt*, 1.3.0); see also **kneel**).

prepare
linked to a wide variety of actions: "*Prepare to play*" for the fencing in Folio *Hamlet* (3725, 5.2.265), "*Prepares for death*" at an **execution** (*Challenge for Beauty*, 68), "*the Justice's three men prepare for a robbery*" (*Phoenix*, F3r); the verb is regularly used for onstage effects that demand special properties or attention: "*An Altar prepared*" (*Sea Voyage*, 62; *Pilgrim*, 225), "*two prentices, preparing the Goldsmith's Shop with plate*" (*1 Edward IV*, 63), "*The while the Hangman prepares, Shore at this speech mounts up the ladder*" (*2 Edward IV*, 136); several **trial** scenes warrant *preparing*: "*Officers preparing seats for the Judges*" (*Devil's Law Case*, 4.2.0), "*some to prepare the judgment seat*" (*Warning for Fair Women*, H3v), "*Treasurer and Secretary who take their places prepared on one side of the Court*" (*Chabot*, 3.2.0); most common are versions of "*A banquet prepared*" (*Macbeth*, 1253, 3.4.0; *Rape of Lucrece*, 205; *Loyal Subject*, 147; *Valentinian*, 88; *Women Beware Women*, 3.3.0; *Conspiracy*, B1r; *Court Secret*, D1r); also *prepared* are familiar objects such as **tables**, **chairs**, **tapers**, a **bed** (Q2 *Hamlet*, N3v, 5.2.224; *Rape of Lucrece*, 187;

Gentleman of Venice, D8v; *Grateful Servant*, K3v; *Country Captain*, C11v; *Traitor*, 5.3.0); other examples include "*Lord unready; Haircut preparing his periwig, table, and looking glass*" (*Lady of Pleasure*, 3.1.0), "*Masquers preparing to dance*" (*Two Merry Milkmaids*, O1v), "*preparing to be dressed*" and "*prepareth to embrace*" (*Sophonisba*, 2.2.41, 4.1.51); atypical is a supposed sowgelder who for a threatened castration "*whets his knife and all in preparation, Linen, Basin, etc.*" (*Court Beggar*, 244); exactly how to *prepare* a **banquet**, **altar**, **trial**, **shop**, **execution** is not specified but is left to the implementation of the players.

presenter
a rarely used alternative for the **chorus** that introduces or summarizes events or explicates a **dumb show**; in *Battle of Alcazar* the *presenter* appears and speaks throughout the play (1, 28, 40, 307, 797, 1059), then "*Enter the Presenter before the last dumb show, and speaketh*" (1255–6); see also *Battle of Alcazar* plot, 23, 54, 89; *Four Prentices*, 175; a "*Presenter or prologue*" begins *Your Five Gallants* (A2r), and in *Taming of the Shrew* "*The Presenters above speaks*" (557, 1.1.248) refers to three figures.

presently
"immediately" (rather than today's meaning of "soon"), most commonly found when figures re-**enter**; one or more figures exit and "*enter presently*" (*Westward Ho*, 4.2.52; *Queen and Concubine*, 28; *Grateful Servant*, K4r), "*returns presently*" (*What You Will*, B3v; *Whore of Babylon*, DS before Act 1, 47), "*They march softly in at one door, and presently in at another*" (*2 Iron Age*, 379; *Spanish Gypsy*, I3r); the term is also found in **exits**: "*Enter Candido, and Exit presently*" (*1 Honest Whore*, 4.3.25), "*presently slips out*" (*Witty Fair One*, H2v), "*Antonio offers to come near and stab; Piero presently withdraws*" (*Antonio's Revenge*, 3.1.139); atypical is sheathes a **sword** "*and draws it again presently*" (*Young Admiral*, K2v).

pretty
occasionally used in **permissive** signals to modify such terms as **way**, **while**, **fight**: "*A noise again heard about the house, a pretty while, then enter the Constable*" (*Sir John Oldcastle*, 2222–3), two figures who "*have all this while talked together a pretty way*" (*Gentleman Usher*, 3.2.276; see also *John a Kent*, 1098), "*enter from the widow's house a service, musical songs of marriages, or a masque, or what pretty triumph you list*" (*James IV*, 2051–3), "*after a good pretty fight his Lieutenant and*

Ancient rescue Stukeley" (*Captain Thomas Stukeley*, 1172–3).

prevent

a seldom used alternative to *stay* wherein a figure is *prevented* from completing an action; most examples are linked to threatened violence: *"offereth to stab herself Barbarossa preventeth her"* (*Devil's Charter*, C4r), *"draws his sword and offers to run himself thereon Enter Hersus and prevents him"* (*Hengist*, DS before 4.3, 7–9), *"snatcheth at some weapon to kill himself, is prevented, and led away"* (*Whore of Babylon*, 2.2.185); not linked to violence is *"About to Kneel he prevents"* (*Soddered Citizen*, 1307–9).

prison, prisoner

a number of plays call for figures to *enter* "*in prison*" (*Puritan*, F1r; *Revenger's Tragedy*, E3v; *Fleer*, 5.3.0; *When You See Me*, 1231; *King and No King*, 198; *Philaster*, 131/411; *Atheist's Tragedy*, 3.3.0; *Two Noble Kinsmen*, D2r, [2.2.0]; *Brennoralt*, 2.1.0; *Court Secret*, C6v; *Doubtful Heir*, C1v); more detailed are "*in prison, fettered and gyved*" (*Appius and Virginia*, I1r), "*in prison, with Irons, his feet bare, his garments all ragged and torn*" (*Woman Killed*, 127); variations include "*They take Guiniver and Voda, and put them in prison*" (*Valiant Welshman*, C4v), "*retires to his Prison*" (*Court Secret*, F4r), "*A shout in the prison*" (*Eastward Ho*, H3v), "*Exeunt some of them with him to prison*" (*Four Prentices*, 177), "*here the ladies speak in prison*" (*Dead Man's Fortune*, 25–6); other figures enter "*guarded to prison*" (*Duchess of Suffolk*, A3v), "*bearing the Queen to Prison*" (*Shoemaker a Gentleman*, 1.2.106), "*from prison*" (*Revenger's Tragedy*, E3r); atypical are a place heading "*The Prison, Marshalsea*" (*Puritan*, B3v), "*the master of the Prison*" (*Greene's Tu Quoque*, I1r), two *prisoners* "*in the Bilboes*" of a ship (*Double Marriage*, 346); although two directions mention a *grate* (*Antonio's Revenge*, 2.2.125; *New Wonder*, 174), a sense of *prison* was probably generated by one or more *prisoners* in *chains/fetters/gyves/irons/manacles/shackles* accompanied by a jailer/*keeper* with *keys*; such a staging of this locale is suggested by such *as* [*if*] signals as "*as from prison*" (*City Madam*, 5.3.59) and entrances in four Caroline plays "*as in prison*" (*Brennoralt*, 1.4.0; *Queen and Concubine*, 35; *City Nightcap*, 176; *2 Arviragus and Philicia*, F4v).

Prisoners are regularly cited, most commonly as part of a group entrance or in the locution *with/and* X *prisoner*; for a sampling of *prisoners* as part of an entrance see *Alphonsus of Germany*, I1v, K1v; Folio

Henry V, 2483–4, 4.6.0; 2578–9, 4.7.54; *Cymbeline*, 3331–2, 5.5.68; *Eastward Ho*, H1r, H2v; *Prophetess*, 363; *All's Lost by Lust*, 2.5.0, 4.1.149; for a sampling of *with/and* X *prisoner* see *George a Greene*, 367, 870; *Edward I*, 2207; *Edward II*, 2412; *Mucedorus*, B2v; *Selimus*, 692–3, 2392–3, 2478–9; *Woodstock*, 2956–7; Quarto *Richard III*, G1r, 3.3.0; *Richard II*, E4v, 3.1.0; *1 Henry IV*, K4r, 5.5.0; *Thracian Wonder*, G3v, H2r, H2v; Quarto *King Lear*, K4r, 5.3.0; *Four Prentices*, 177; *Fortune by Land and Sea*, 418; *Lovesick King*, 1904–5; *King John and Matilda*, 25; *Rebellion*, 43, 46; other locutions are "*take him prisoner*" in *battle* (*Alphonsus of Aragon*, 1676–7; *Famous Victories*, F2v; *George a Greene*, 742; *1 Troublesome Reign*, E2r, E3r; *Travels of Three English Brothers*, 331; *Guy of Warwick*, C4r; *Tom a Lincoln*, 940, 954–60; *Lovesick King*, 1902; *Shoemaker a Gentleman*, 3.5.16; *Princess*, H2r), *leading* X *prisoner/led prisoner* (*Philaster*, 138/413; *Hengist*, 5.2.210–11; *Tom a Lincoln*, 970–1; *Roman Actor*, 1.4.13; *Virgin Martyr*, 4.2.61; *Jews' Tragedy*, 3130), as *prisoners* (Folio *King Lear*, 2939, 5.3.0; *Travels of Three English Brothers*, 361; *Prophetess*, 374; *Ladies' Privilege*, 138), *bound* prisoner (*Four Prentices*, 232; *Fortune by Land and Sea*, 410), *bringing* in X *prisoner* (*Sir John Oldcastle*, 1641; *Silver Age*, 86), "*Spencer prisoner and wounded*" (*2 Fair Maid of the West*, 367); linked to *prisoners* are *guards* and in *trial* scenes a *bar*: "*prisoner and guarded*" (*Captives*, 2804–5), "*The Prisoners are brought in well guarded*" (*Sir Thomas More*, 606–7), "*The Prisoners brought to the Bar by a Guard*" (*Swetnam*, D3r), "*Lifter the prisoner at the bar*" (*Sir Thomas More*, 106), "*A Bar set, and the Prisoners brought in*" (*Jews' Tragedy*, 356–8); see also *captive*.

private, privately

used for (1) speeches *aside* not heard by onstage figures, (2) *private* conversations not heard by the playgoer, (3) a variety of actions *apart/aside*; an *aside* can be designated "*private to himself*" (*Four Prentices*, 179, also 180, 209); more common are figures who *talk/whisper* privately/in private (*Devil's Charter*, A2v; *Fair Maid of the Exchange*, 68, 69, 71; *Lovesick Court*, 93; *Lost Lady*, Folio 592, MS 1656–7, 1677; *Knave in Grain*, 2769–70; *Cardinal*, 2.1.35; *Imposture*, E7v), "*discourse privately*" (*James IV*, 896), "*confer privately*" (*Fawn*, 1.2.148), speak "*in private conference*" (*Weakest Goeth*, 1314; *Swetnam*, A1r); one or more figures can *enter* privately or *stand* private so as to be separate from others onstage: enter "*privately and overhears them*" (*Isle of Gulls*, 234), "*standing privately to hear the passages, chafing and stamping*" (*Swaggering Damsel*, G1v), "*All this while, she stands conferring privately with her*

Suitors, and looking on their bills" (*1 Edward IV*, 82); see also *Prophetess*, 374; *Little French Lawyer*, 416; *Loyal Subject*, 124; *Four Plays in One*, 325; variations include "*courts her again in private*" (*Fair Maid of the Exchange*, 69), "*They dissuade her, privately*" (*Epicœne*, 2.3.4), "*reads privately and frowns*" (*Fair Maid of the Exchange*, 59), "*Ferneze privately feeds Maquerelle's hands with jewels during this speech*" (*Malcontent*, 1.6.10); see also *Sophonisba*, 3.1.60.

proclamation

a *paper* property brought on for *reading* aloud by a herald or similar figure: "*a Gentleman reading a Proclamation*" (Quarto *Othello*, E3r; Folio "*Othello's Herald with a Proclamation*," 1097, 2.2.0), "*Enter after a Drum, a Captain with a Proclamation*" (*Four Prentices*, 173), "*a Woman with a Proclamation*" (*Swetnam*, E2v); see also *Women Pleased*, 279; *Queen*, 2340; the action of reading is signaled in "*make the proclamation upon the walls*" (*Edward I*, 2070).

proffer

occurs mostly in *proffers to*, a less common version of the widely used *offer to* locution which signals an action that is started but not completed; with one exception ("*Pandulph proffers to descend*," *King John and Matilda*, 31) examples are limited to the 1580s and 1590s: "*They proffer to go in*" (*Cobbler's Prophecy*, 415), "*Proffer to embrace her*" (*Fedele and Fortunio*, 793), "*Orgalio proffers to go in*" (*Orlando Furioso*, 852), "*Proffer to fight again*" (*Sir John Oldcastle*, 7); *King Leir* provides three examples: "*Proffer to go*" (1532, 1537), "*Proffer to go out*" (1547); occasionally a figure will *proffer* an object to another: "*Perillus proffers his doublet*" (*King Leir*, 2213), "*Proffers him a naked poniard*" (*Cruel Brother*, 122).

prologue

sometimes a heading/segment at the start of a play but also the figure usually called the *chorus* who provides a narrative summary of events preceding the action; such a *prologue* appears and speaks at *David and Bethsabe*, 0; Folio *Henry V*, 1, Prologue.0; *What You Will*, A3v; *Weakest Goeth*, 9; *Isle of Gulls*, 210, 215; *Every Woman In*, A2r; *Your Five Gallants*, A2r; *Staple of News*, Induction.0; in *Four Prentices* the heading *Prologue* is elaborated: "*Enter three in black cloaks, at three doors*" (165); the heading is also in *Old Fortunatus* before 1.1; *Cynthia's Revels* before 1.1; *Sophonisba*, Prologue.0; *Whore of Babylon* before 1.1; *Nice Valour*, 144; for a *prologue* accompanying a play-within-a-play see *Sir Thomas More*, 1028; *Midsummer*

Night's Dream, G4r, 5.1.107; *Hamlet*, Q1 F3r, Q2 H1v, Folio 2016, 3.2.140; *Four Plays in One*, 334, 355; *Spanish Gypsy*, G4r; *Antipodes*, 265; a few directions add details: "*Enter, for a Prologue, Follywit*" (*Mad World*, 5.2.15), "*reads the Prologue, they sit to hear it*" (*Histriomastix*, C1r), "*Prologue attired like Fame*" (*Travels of Three English Brothers*, 319), "*Enter Poet for Prologue*" (*Jovial Crew*, 443), "*Prologue delivered by an amazon with a Battleax in her hand*" and "*Scania (that spoke the Prologue) now delivers the Epilogue*" (*Landgartha*, A4v, K1r).

proper, properly

appear occasionally as "fitting, appropriate" usually linked to costume: "*certain Reapers (properly habited)*" (*Tempest*, 1805, 4.1.138), the five Starches "*all properly habited to express their affected colors*" (*World Tossed at Tennis*, D2r), a "*Marshall, with his Marshall's staff, and all the rest in their proper apparel*" (*Alphonsus of Germany*, E3r); related are "*four Scotch Antics*" and "*four wild Irish*" who are "*accordingly habited*" (*Perkin Warbeck*, 3.2.111); in *World Tossed at Tennis* the Worthies "*descend, each one led by a Muse, the most proper and pertinent to the person of the Worthy*" (C4r).

property

the three uses denote objects that are attributes *proper* or appropriate to distinctive figures: Time appears "*in black, and all his properties (as Scythe, Hourglass and Wings) of the same Color*" (*Whore of Babylon*, DS before Act 1, 29–30), the three Fates "*lay down their properties* [distaff, spindle, and knife] *at the Queen's feet*" (*Arraignment of Paris*, 1213), "*Enter Hecate and other witches: (with Properties, and Habits fitting)*" (*Witch*, 181–2).

pull

widely used (roughly 120 examples) primarily when figures (1) *pull off* a *disguise*, (2) *pull out* a *weapon* or other object, (3) *pull* someone; for examples of disguise, figures *pull* off a visor (*Aglaura*, 3.1.34), **vizard** (*King John and Matilda*, 52; *Just Italian*, 277), **mask** (*Picture*, 3.5.57; *Guardian*, 4.2.58), **veil** (*Thierry and Theodoret*, 47), **hood** (*Bloody Banquet*, 1060), **patch** (*Edmond Ironside*, 1313; *Roaring Girl*, 5.1.105; *Princess*, F1r; *Claracilla*, D5r), **periwig** (*Hollander*, 152; *Wit in a Constable*, 208), **beard** (*Island Princess*, 169; *Wit at Several Weapons*, 82; *Lovesick Court*, 147; *Bloody Banquet*, 313–14; *Fool Would Be a Favourite*, F2v; *Deserving Favourite*, M3v; *Example*, H3v; *Claracilla*, F11v; *Love and Honour*, 181), disguise (*Two Lamentable Tragedies*, I3v; *Sophy*, 5.65; *Fair Favourite*, 224; *Soddered*

Citizen, 2210; *Holland's Leaguer*, L4v), *buck's* **head** (Quarto *Merry Wives*, G3r, 5.5.102), *tortoise shell* (*Volpone*, 5.4.73); typical are "*pulls off his disguised Hair*" (*Two Merry Milkmaids*, L2v), "*pulls off their beards, and disguise*" (*Epicœne*, 5.4.211), "*pulls off his patches, and disguise*" (*Distresses*, 339); weapons *pulled out* are a **dagger** (*Devil's Charter*, C2v), **sword** (*Seven Champions*, H1r; *Tom a Lincoln*, 1592–3; *Osmond*, B8r; *Distresses*, 337), **knife** (*Tom a Lincoln*, 35–6; *Fatal Contract*, H4v), **pistol** (*Just Italian*, 245); other objects *pulled out/off/on/in* include a **letter** (*Tom a Lincoln*, 2757–8; *News from Plymouth*, 185), **book** (*King Leir*, 1440; *Roman Actor*, 5.1.94), **purse** (*Mad Lover*, 67; *Bashful Lover*, 3.3.188), **glove** (*Bird in a Cage*, E3v), **bodkin** (*Parson's Wedding*, 411), **string** (*Tom a Lincoln*, 2864), **vial** (*1 Honest Whore*, 2.1.0), **cloak** (*King Leir*, 2018), *syringe* (*Knight of the Burning Pestle*, 206), **bed** (*New Trick*, 293), *patents* (*Court Beggar*, 268), **papers** (*Cure for a Cuckold*, E4r; *Princess*, C1r), **indentures** (*Jack Drum's Entertainment*, F3r), **napkins** (*Fine Companion*, I2r), *victuals* (*Locrine*, 1629–30), **boots** (*Patient Grissil*, 2.1.140; *Staple of News*, 1.1.0), "*a red herring*" (*Every Man In*, Quarto 3.1.188, Folio 3.4.53), "*a sheet, a hair, and a beard*" (*Atheist's Tragedy*, 4.3.55); see also *Whore of Babylon*, DS before Act 1, 38–9; *Two Maids of More-Clacke*, B4v, D1v; *Fatal Contract*, H4v; *City Wit*, 371; *Bride*, 78.

For examples of onstage interactions, figures *pull* another figure **out** (Quarto *2 Henry VI*, E3v, [3.2.231]), **down** (*Soliman and Perseda*, B2r; *Guy of Warwick*, C1r; *Hannibal and Scipio*, 246), up (MS *Bonduca*, 2509–10; *Queen's Exchange*, 537), in (*Bussy D'Ambois*, 5.1.0; *English Moor*, 70; *Albovine*, 63), **aside** (*Fatal Contract*, C2r; *City Wit*, 315), *after* (*Grim the Collier*, I3v; *Damoiselle*, 434), most commonly *back* (*Edmond Ironside*, 1383; *Warning for Fair Women*, D1r; *Grim the Collier*, H8v; *Golden Age*, 32; *Tom a Lincoln*, 1915; *Court Beggar*, 242; *Brennoralt*, 3.3.39; *Bird in a Cage*, E2r; *Wedding*, G1r; *Bride*, 27; *Lost Lady*, 593), and *pull* someone *by the arm* (*Albovine*, 78), **hair** (*Maid's Revenge*, I3r), *ears* (*Midas*, 5.2.157; *Tottenham Court*, 164), *nose* (*Puritan*, G4r; *1 Passionate Lovers*, B2r), **sleeve** (*Edmond Ironside*, 219; *2 Edward IV*, 147; *Woman Is a Weathercock*, 1.2.156; *Wedding*, H3v), *skirt* (*Goblins*, 4.1.96), **cloak** (*Parson's Wedding*, 533); for a sampling of figures who simply *pull* another see *Downfall of Huntingdon*, 51; *Death of Huntingdon*, 128–9, 519, 1346; *Westward Ho*, 5.3.0; *Fatal Contract*, F2r; *King John and Matilda*, 52; *Northern Lass*, 64; *Brennoralt*, 3.2.13; *Distresses*, 361; *Parson's Wedding*, 411, 479, 483; distinctive actions include "*Pulls out his eyes*" (*Selimus*, 1415), "*pulls his beard*" (*John a Kent*, 299–300), "*pull him off*

the Ass" (*Christian Turned Turk*, F2v), "*pulls Skimmington off the horse*" (*Late Lancashire Witches*, 234), "*pulls off his leg*" (*Doctor Faustus*, B 1561, A 1206), "*pulls the Beaker from his mouth*" (*Alphonsus of Germany*, F1v), "*pulls off her Glove, and offers her hand to Pisander*" (*Bondman*, 3.2.104), "*pulls the chair from under him*" (*1 If You Know Not Me*, 224), "*pulls the Wool out of his ears*" (*Old Wives Tale*, 822), "*pulls him by the heels off the Stage*" (*Princess*, H3v), "*Horace and Bubo pulled in by the horns bound, both like Satyrs*" (*Satiromastix*, 5.2.158).

purse

widely used (seventy examples) in a variety of actions; most common is to *give*/**deliver** a purse (*Three Lords of London*, H4v; Quarto *Richard III*, F4v, [3.2.106]; *Sir John Oldcastle*, 2697–8; *King Leir*, 1327; *2 Edward IV*, 174; *Malcontent*, 3.3.78; *Ram Alley*, D1v; *Devil's Charter*, E4r; *Two Noble Kinsmen*, M3r, 5.4.35; *Wife for a Month*, 44; *Four Plays in One*, 321; *Fatal Contract*, E2r; *City Match*, 237; *Launching of the Mary*, 906, 2628), but figures also **offer** (*Sir John Oldcastle*, 197), **shake** (*Royal King*, 47; *Princess*, A4r), **pull** out (*Mad Lover*, 67; *Bashful Lover*, 3.3.188), **throw**/**cast**/**fling** (Folio *Richard III*, 1910, 3.2.106; *Death of Huntingdon*, 411; *King Leir*, 1018; *2 Edward IV*, 123, 169; *Lady's Trial*, 1253; *Brennoralt*, 2.4.89; *Just Italian*, 265; *Wits*, 128), **enter** with purses (*Wise Woman of Hogsdon*, 286; *Lovers' Progress*, 85, 95; *Bashful Lover*, 5.1.0; *Launching of the Mary*, 1257–8; *Sparagus Garden*, 214); see also *Captain Thomas Stukeley*, 1268; *King Leir*, 1350, 1521; *Old Fortunatus*, 3.1.356; *Woman Is a Weathercock*, 4.3.2; *Honest Man's Fortune*, 204; *Guardian*, 2.2.0; *City Wit*, 295; *Jovial Crew*, 381; *Soddered Citizen*, 2198–9; several plays display the theft of a *purse* (*Dutch Courtesan*, 5.3.16; *Bartholomew Fair*, 2.6.58; *Honest Lawyer*, B3v); actions include "*Throws meal in his face, takes his purse*" (*Hengist*, 5.1.319), "*Hold a purse ready*" (*Custom of the Country*, 331/455), "*shows his purse boastingly*" (*Bartholomew Fair*, 3.5.36, 115, 137); along with the **sword**, **scepter**, and **mace** the *purse* can be part of a royal procession: "*Sussex bearing the crown, Howard bearing the Scepter, the Constable the Mace, Tame the purse, Shandoyse the sword*" (*1 If You Know Not Me*, 239, also 195, 244); see also *Downfall of Huntingdon*, 42, 59–60; *Sir Thomas Wyatt*, 1.2.40; *Henry VIII*, 1337, 2.4.0; atypical is "*Unpurses the gold*" (*Atheist's Tragedy*, 5.1.21).

pursue

used mostly when a figure **enters** pursuing/pursued by another: "*Enter Loreine running, the Guise and the rest* pursuing him" (*Massacre at Paris*, 342); for a sampling of over thirty examples see *Edward I*, 2067; *Orlando Furioso*, 1343–4; *2 Seven Deadly Sins*, 64; *1 Henry VI*, 587, 1.5.0; *Edmond Ironside*, 988–9; *Alarum for London*, 637–8, 698, 796; *Weakest Goeth*, 5–6, 1795–6, 1807; Folio *Othello*, 1261, 2.3.144; *Trial of Chivalry*, I2v; *Four Prentices*, 189, 226; *Valentinian*, 22; *Love's Cure*, 175; *Rape of Lucrece*, 240, 249; *Birth of Merlin*, F4r; *Vow Breaker*, 3.1.0; *Valiant Scot*, H2r; *Bloody Banquet*, 250; *Example*, E3v; *Grateful Servant*, I2r; variations include a figure who enters alone *pursued* (*Edward II*, 1167) and several *as [if]* entrances "*as pursued*" (*Rebellion*, 37), "*as being hard pursued*" (*Bloody Banquet*, 229), "*Uncle, servants and tenants, with lights, as pursuing them*" (*Tottenham Court*, 103); less common are **exits** that involve *pursuing*: "*pursuing her with his drawn sword*" (*Bloody Banquet*, 17–18), "*pursues him out*" (*Captain Thomas Stukeley*, 1352–3); see also *Maid in the Mill*, 59; *Bloody Banquet*, 15–16; *Prisoners*, B7r; in a **dumb show** Jupiter "*being hotly pursued, draws his sword, beats away Saturn*" (*Golden Age*, 53); a few signals call for a *pursuit* **over the stage**: "*The five Kings driven over the Stage, Crassinius chiefly pursuing*" (*Caesar and Pompey*, 4.2.0; see also *Lust's Dominion*, 4.2.135; *Costly Whore*, 270); three figures are *pursued* by a **bear**, most famously in *Winter's Tale* (1500, 3.3.58) but also in *Conspiracy*, D3v and "*Enter Segasto running and Amadine after him, being pursued with a bear*" (*Mucedorus*, A3v); atypical are "*Enter Zuccone, pursued by Zoya on her knees*" (*Fawn*, 4.280), "*he bringeth the Ghost of Candie ghastly haunted by Caesar pursuing and stabbing it*" (*Devil's Charter*, G2r), "*Enter Titus with his Power, from the Pursuit*" (*Coriolanus*, 759, 1.9.11).

put

the nearly 150 examples include a range of locutions, most commonly either (1) *put on/off* items of **clothing** or (2) *put on/off* a **disguise** but also (3) *put* something in a **pocket**, (4) *put* a figure *by/in/back*, (5) *put* a **sword** *up/by*, (6) *put out* a **light**, (7) *put on* a **crown**, (8) *put* a **bed** *out/forth/in*; for a sampling of clothing and other items *put on/off* see *Three Ladies of London*, F2r; *1 Edward IV*, 88; *Shoemakers' Holiday*, 2.3.93; *Antonio's Revenge*, 4.2.11; *Thracian Wonder*, B4v; *Roaring Girl*, 3.1.54; *Amends for Ladies*, 4.2.1, 5.2.235; Q2 *Bussy D'Ambois*, 4.2.51; *Four Prentices*, 177; *Pericles*, G3r, 4.4.22; *Brazen Age*, 248; *Anything for a Quiet Life*, D3v; *Christian Turned Turk*, F2v; *Renegado*, 1.2.58; *Fatal Contract*, H1r; *Herod and Antipater*, C3r; *Bloody Banquet*, 1001; for disguises *put on/off* see *John a Kent*, 472–3; *Look about You*, 2072; *Fair Maid of Bristow*, F2r;

Dumb Knight, 167; *Volpone*, 5.12.84; *Widow's Tears*, 5.5.0; *Woman Is a Weathercock*, 5.2.70; *Golden Age*, 67; *Christian Turned Turk*, B2v; *Valiant Welshman*, H2v; *City Nightcap*, 175; *English Moor*, 4; *Sisters*, B2v; *Fine Companion*, H4r, K2r; exiting figures can be *put in* (*Knack to Know an Honest Man*, 739; *Dumb Knight*, 164), **down** (*Love and Honour*, 124), "*in a tomb*" (*Titus Andronicus*, C1r, 1.1.386), "*in prison*" (*Valiant Welshman*, C4v); for *swords put up/by* see *All Fools*. 2.1.296; *Fortune by Land and Sea*, 386; *Christian Turned Turk*, H1v; *Jovial Crew*, 400; *Goblins*, 1.1.73, 78; *Lady Mother*, 475; *Princess*, A3v; for the *putting out* of **torches/tapers/** other lights see *Escapes of Jupiter*, 979–80; *Golden Age*, 69; *Devil's Charter*, F3v; *Faithful Friends*, 2621; *Hog Hath Lost His Pearl*, 266; *Game at Chess*, 1946; *Country Captain*, C12r; crowns are *put on* in *Spanish Tragedy*, 1.3.86; *Alphonsus of Aragon*, 501–2; *Thracian Wonder*, C4r–v; *Jews' Tragedy*, 65–7; *1 Passionate Lovers*, F8r; for *beds put out/forth/in* see Folio *2 Henry VI*, 1849, 3.2.146; *Mad Couple*, 73, 76; *Weeding of Covent Garden*, 87; *City Wit*, 319; *Obstinate Lady*, E2v; for "*a Scaffold put out*" see *Barnavelt*, 2852–3; other actions include "*put him on the Rack*" (*Messalina*, 651), "*put him in the stocks*" (*Bartholomew Fair*, 4.1.34), "*puts poison into the Beaker*" (*Alphonsus of Germany*, F1v), "*puts his pantoffle to his lips; he kisses it*" (*Humour out of Breath*, 464), "*They put out one eye*" (*Osmond*, C7r).

Q

quaint

describes a distinctive but unspecified costume or **disguise**: "*in quaint disguises*" (*Sisters*, C3v), "*an antic quaintly disguised*" (*John a Kent*, 780), "*three Kings quaintly attired like Masquers*" (*Whore of Babylon*, 1.2.81); only in *Tempest* is the term applied to an onstage effect: "*Enter Ariel (like a Harpy) claps his wings upon the Table, and with a quaint device the Banquet vanishes*" (1583–5, 3.3.52).

quiver

see **arrow**

R

rabble

a disorderly group or mob, usually of the lower classes: "*a rabble of Plebeians with the Aediles*" (*Coriolanus*, 1886, 3.1.179), "*Cade, and all his* rabblement" (Folio 2 Henry VI, 2773–4, 4.8.0), "Quince, Flute, Thisby and the rabble" (Midsummer Night's Dream, G2r, 4.2.0), "a Herald with a Proclamation, a Trumpet before him, a great rabble of men following him" (Swetnam, E2v), "A Rabble of rude Fellows" (Damoiselle, 434), "a rabble of poor soldiers" (Hoffman, 1125; see also Queen and Concubine, 101).

rack

used for onstage torture/**torment**: "They rack Adda" (Herod and Antipater, I3r), "enter Manuell to be racked" (Dick of Devonshire, 1928–30), "Gorion brought out and put on the rack" (Jews' Tragedy, 2748–50; see also Q2 Bussy D'Ambois, 5.1.144; Messalina, 651), "Enter Ronvere, Guard, Executioners, with a Rack" and "Put on the rack" (Double Marriage, 334), "Some go for the rack" (Virgin Martyr, 5.2.188); an alternative is to have the torture offstage and use an **as from** signal so that figures **enter** "as from the Rack" (Sophy, 5.593), "in their shirts, as from Torments" (Shoemaker a Gentleman, 4.2.0).

rackets

occasionally called for in entrances **as from** an off-stage game of tennis; figures enter "in their waistcoats with rackets" (Devil's Charter, I2v), "with their Rackets, diverse attending" (When You See Me, 1819–20), accompanied by "a boy with Rackets" (Greene's Tu Quoque, D4r); the dutiful Golding is set off from the frivolous Quicksilver when the latter appears "with his hat, pumps, short sword and dagger, and a racket trussed up under his cloak" (Eastward Ho, A2r); Henslowe's inventory includes "two rackets" (Diary, App. 2, 63).

rage, raging, in a rage

angry figures **enter**/**exit** in a rage (Fair Em, 451; Timon of Athens, 1210, 3.4.78; Escapes of Jupiter, 2217; Puritan, D4r; Women Beware Women, 4.3.0), in rage (Woodstock, 225; Princess, C4r), raging (Queen and Concubine, 46; Wizard, 2000); during the course of a scene figures are directed to rage (Edward II, 2071; Noble Spanish Soldier, 5.4.53), "rise in a rage from thy chair" (Alphonsus of Aragon, 1051), so that "Mars rises in a rage" (Cobbler's Prophecy, 958); see also **anger, chafing, fury, stamp, storm**.

rags, ragged

three plays call for figures to appear in rags: "Philosopher in black rags" (Lover's Melancholy, 3.3.38); see also Renegado, 3.2.26; Jovial Crew, 393, 395; ragged occurs about twice as often: figures appear ragged

(Virgin Martyr, 3.3.0), "Bare and ragged" (Wonder of a Kingdom, 3.1.67), "extreme ragged" (Royal King, 14, also 13); other locutions include "a ragged Courtier" (Fool Would Be a Favourite, C2v), "Sir Charles in prison with irons, his face bare, his garments all ragged and torn" (Woman Killed, 127), a figure in despair "all ragged, in an overgrown red Beard, black head, with a Halter in his hand" (Caesar and Pompey, 2.1.0).

rain

whether this requires only a **sound** or actual falling water is not clear from the contexts of the three uses: "Rain, Thunder and lightning" (If This Be Not a Good Play, 4.2.33), "at which there falls a shower of rain" (Brazen Age, 183), "It snows, and rains, thunders" (Duchess of Suffolk, F2v).

raise

usually linked to **kneeling**: "He raises her, and leads her out" (Revenge of Bussy, 4.3.107), "he raises Herod and sets him in his Chair" (Herod and Antipater, F4r, also I4v); for comparable actions see Cobbler's Prophecy, 1188; 1 If You Know Not Me, 216; Jews' Tragedy, 124–5; Great Duke of Florence, 4.2.328; Lovesick Court, 163; other uses of raise are "Raise her head" (Death of Huntingdon, 2647), "As he raises up the ax, strikes out his own brains" (Atheist's Tragedy, 5.2.241), "She knocks, and raises the Court" out of **bed** (Aglaura, 5.3.141); see also **heave, lift**.

rank

occasionally found as (1) a noun meaning "row, orderly line," (2) a verb used for courtiers who arrange themselves in the proper **order** for a **dance** or other action; examples of the noun are "The three shops open in a rank" (Roaring Girl, 2.1.0), "make a rank for the Duke to pass through" (Antonio and Mellida, 2.1.183), "stand in rank for the measure" (Antonio's Revenge, 5.3.36); for examples of the verb, "all make ridiculous conges to Bianca: rank themselves, and dance in several postures" (Fair Maid of the Inn, 175), "salute, and are saluted; they rank themselves, and go out the Quire singing" (Love's Sacrifice, 1819–20); see also **make a lane**.

rapier

a slender two-edged **sword** found in (1) entrances with a rapier, (2) the **drawing** of rapiers or entrances with a rapier drawn, (3) a variety of related actions; figures **enter** with rapiers (Alphonsus of Aragon, 1781; Lust's Dominion, 3.2.89; Jews' Tragedy, 1336–7) and with a rapier and **dagger** (Friar Bacon, 1819), **pistol**

(*Gentleman of Venice*, I3v), ***cloak*** (*Woodstock*, 5; *Eastward Ho*, B4r; *Match Me in London*, 3.1.12; *Dick of Devonshire*, 1287–89); most common are entrances with a *rapier drawn* (*Comedy of Errors*, 1440–1, 4.4.143; *Fair Em*, 814; *Alarum for London*, 800–1; *Lust's Dominion*, 3.1.20, 3.2.0, 151; Quarto *King Lear*, E1r, 2.2.43; *Jews' Tragedy*, 2113, 2120, 2994; *Two Merry Milkmaids*, N2r; *'Tis Pity*, 3.7.0), "*in his hand*" (*Blurt*, 4.2.0); variations include entrances "*with Rapiers fighting*" (*May Day*, 4.3.0), "*running with a rapier*" (*Revenger's Tragedy*, H1v), "*with a long rapier by his side*" (*Roaring Girl*, 2.1.217), "*the Lord Mayor, in his scarlet gown, with a gilded rapier by his side*" (*1 Edward IV*, 57), ***angels*** "*with bright Rapiers in their hands*" (*Three Lords of London*, A2v); for the onstage drawing of *rapiers* see *Antonio's Revenge*, 1.2.217, 5.2.19; *Jack Drum's Entertainment*, H2v; *All Fools*, 3.1.250; *Lust's Dominion*, 5.3.47; *Woman Hater*, 110; atypical is an entrance "*all weaponed, their Rapiers' sheaths in their hands*" (*Blurt*, 5.1.0); actions include the ***putting*** up of rapiers (*Jews' Tragedy*, 2114–15, 2121–2), "*Offers to strike her with his Rapier*" (*Maid's Metamorphosis*, A4r), "*run all at Piero with their rapiers*" (*Antonio's Revenge*, 5.3.112), "*Thrusts his rapier in Ferneze*" (*Malcontent*, 2.5.5), "*In scuffling they change Rapiers*" (Folio *Hamlet*, 3777, 5.2.302), "*They catch one another's Rapiers, and both are wounded*" (Q1 *Hamlet*, I3v, [5.2.302]), "*Walks by, and uses action to his Rapier*" (Quarto *Every Man Out*, 2110), "*In the act-time De Flores hides a naked rapier*" (*Changeling*, 3.1.0); see also *Three Lords of London*, H1r; *Country Girl*, C1v.

raving
see ***mad***

ravished
usually a ***fictional*** rather than a theatrical description, as seen in "*Enter the discontented Lord Antonio, whose wife the Duchess's youngest son ravished; he Discovering the body of her dead to certain Lords*" (*Revenger's Tragedy*, C1v); best known is Lavinia's entrance in *Titus Andronicus* "*her hands cut off, and her tongue cut out, and ravished*" (E2r, 2.4.0); that *ravished* may have carried with it some sense of how to implement the effect onstage is suggested by the *as* [*if*] implicit in "*Enter Merione (as newly ravished)*" (*Queen of Corinth*, 17); for the various figures who appear onstage after a rape the only recurring detail is disheveled ***hair***: "*her garments loose, her hair disheveled*" (*Unnatural Combat*, 5.2.185), "*loose haired, and weeping*" (*Dick of Devonshire*, 687–9), "*her hair about her ears*" (*Swisser*, 4.1.0).

read, reading
widely used (roughly 500 examples) most often as simply *reads*: "*Boyet reads*" (*Love's Labour's Lost*, D3r, 4.1.60), "*Gloucester reads*" (Folio *King Lear*, 382, 1.2.46, also 3059, 5.3.110); for a sampling of the basic direction see *Richard III*, D1r, 929, 1.4.90; *Alphonsus of Germany*, B3v, E1r; *Edmond Ironside*, 741; *Blind Beggar of Bednal Green*, 5, 16; *Charlemagne*, 1769; *Trick to Catch the Old One*, E2r; *Revenge of Bussy*, 5.3.38; *Cymbeline*, 617, 1.6.22; *Amends for Ladies*, 3.1.41; *Widow*, G3r; *Women Beware Women*, 5.2.33; *Believe as You List*, 276, 280; *Launching of the Mary*, 1219; *Messalina*, 1670; *Cardinal*, 2.2.43, 2.3.37; while typically the object being read is indicated in dialogue, certain properties are sometimes specified, most often a ***letter***: "*Enter Hotspur solus reading a Letter*" (*1 Henry IV*, C4v, 2.3.0), "*Enter Octavius reading a Letter*" (*Antony and Cleopatra*, 428, 1.4.0), "*Enter the King reading of a letter at one door, the Knights meet him*" (*Pericles*, D3r, 2.5.0), "*Enter Gaveston reading on a letter that was brought him from the king*" (*Edward II*, 0, also 1721), "*seems to read the letters, but glances on Mistress Shore in his reading*" (*1 Edward IV*, 61), "*Enter a Page, delivering a letter to Sophonisba which she privately reads*" (*Sophonisba*, 3.1.60), "*reads the letter, frowns and stamps*" (*King Leir*, 1172), "*laughs having read the letter*" (Folio *Every Man In*, 1.3.56), "*reads the letter to himself*" (*Cruel Brother*, 121); for similar signals see Quarto *2 Henry VI*, F4v, 4.4.0; Folio *3 Henry VI*, 1911, 3.3.166; *Alphonsus of Germany*, E1r; *Love's Labour's Lost*, F1r, 4.3.193; Quarto *Merry Wives*, B4r, 2.1.0; *Two Angry Women*, 1117; Folio *Hamlet*, 2985, 4.6.13; *Fair Maid of the Exchange*, 59; *Your Five Gallants*, E1r; Folio *King Lear*, 2715, 4.6.262; *Amends for Ladies*, 2.3.1–2; *Henry VIII*, 1027, 2.2.0; *Changes*, F2r; *Launching of the Mary*, 2024; a ***book*** is also frequently specified: "*Enter Hamlet reading on a Book*" (Folio *Hamlet*, 1203, 2.2.167), "*Enter Matilda, in mourning veil, reading on a book*" (*Death of Huntingdon*, 961–2), "*Enter Doctor Shaw, pensively reading on his book*" (*2 Edward IV*, 162), "*Enter in his chamber out of his study, Master Penitent Brothel, a book in his hand, reading*" (*Mad World*, 4.1.0); see also *Selimus*, 1074; *'Tis Pity*, 2.2.0; *Fatal Contract*, C4v; *Messalina*, 238; elsewhere figures read a *posy* (*Arraignment of Paris*, 364), *sonnet* (*Love's Labour's Lost*, E3v, 4.3.98, also E3r, 4.3.57), *roundelay* (*Orlando Furioso*, 647), *schedule* (*Henry VIII*, 1963, 3.2.104), ***proclamation*** (Quarto *Othello*, E3r, 2.2.0; see also *Queen*, 2340), ***bill*** (*May Day*, 2.4.206; see also *Old Fortunatus*, 3.1.389), *note* (*Alphonsus of Germany*, B1v), *patent* (*Malcontent*, 3.2.0), *supplication* (*What You Will*, B1v), *epitaph* (*Timon of*

Athens, 2591, 5.4.70), **petition** (*Cobbler's Prophecy*, 884), "*a long scroll*" (*If This Be Not a Good Play*, 2.2.34; see also *Soddered Citizen*, 2376), "*Palmerin of England*" (*Knight of the Burning Pestle*, 172), "*the Oracle*" (*Thracian Wonder*, E3v), **papers** (*Antipodes*, 280).

Signals indicative of the range of stage business linked to *reading* include "*Here do the Ceremonies belonging, and make the Circle, Bullingbrooke or Southwell reads, Conjuro te, etc.*" (Folio 2 *Henry VI*, 643–5, 1.4.22), "*plucks it out of his bosom and reads it*" (*Richard II*, H4v, 5.2.71), "*as in his study reading*" (*Greene's Tu Quoque*, B4v), "*Let him write a little and then read*" (*Locrine*, 341, 344), "*reads to himself*" (*Love's Sacrifice*, 875), "*Breaks it open, and reads*" (*Very Woman*, 5.2.4), "*While he reads the Antiquary falls asleep*" (*Antiquary*, 496), "*reads aside*" (*Jovial Crew*, 421), "*Antonius disguised like Timon, reading*" (*Cleopatra*, C7v), "*sits down having a candle by her, and reads*" (*Hoffman*, 1728–9); for more see *Edward I*, 2323; *Soliman and Perseda*, I1v; *Warning for Fair Women*, H3r; *Histriomastix*, B1v, C1r; *Malcontent*, 1.6.73; *Welsh Ambassador*, 1183; *Sophy*, 3.157; *Lost Lady*, 556.

ready

occurs in two contexts: (1) in the language of the tiring house *ready* or *be ready* is an advance signal, (2) in the language of stage action *ready* commonly describes a state of dress but also other conditions of readiness; a number of playtexts with book-keeper notations contain anticipatory directions: "*Table ready: and six chairs to set out*," "*the great book of Accompts ready*," "*Gascoine and Hubert below: ready to open the Trapdoor for Mr. Taylor*" (*Believe as You List*, 654–6, 982–4, 1825–31, also 1877–9, 1968–72, 2378–9, 2824–6), "*Ink: paper ready*" and "*Bar ready*" (*Captives*, 1341, 2834, also 1464), "*Bowl of wine ready*" and "*Bawd ready above*" (*Chances*, 210/398, 226/398), "*Musicians come down to make ready for the song at Arras*" (*City Madam*, [5.1.7], also 5.1.95, 5.2.68, 5.3.44), "*Altar ready, tapers and book*" (*Knight of Malta*, 152, also 85/387), "*Chessboard and men set ready*" (*Spanish Curate*, 102/501, also 96/501, 113/501, 117/501, 123/501, 129/501, 132/501), "*Three Hearses ready*" (*Two Noble Kinsmen*, C4v, [1.4.26], also C3v, [1.3.58]); this signal is most extensively used in the annotated quarto of *Two Merry Milkmaids*: "*Act Ready*," "*Ready Flourish*," "*Ready Bed*" (E2r, H1v, K3r, and more); for other anticipatory uses of *ready* see *Edward I*, 2108; *Blind Beggar of Bednal Green*, 88; *Love's Cure*, 205; *Love's Pilgrimage*, 290/417; *Mad Lover*, 69; *Lovesick King*, 289; *Custom of the Country*, 312/455, 313/455, 328/455; *Welsh*

Ambassador, 796–8, 831–3, 1156–7; *Wasp*, 41; rev. *Aglaura*, [5.3.112]; *Distresses*, 301.

To describe a figure's state of dress or undress–also conveyed by **unready**–the locution *make ready* is common: "*comes out making himself ready*" (*Epicœne*, 1.1.0), "*unlace themselves, and unloose their buskins: only Calisto refuseth to make her ready*" (*Golden Age*, 35), "*Tharsalio solus, with a Glass in his hand making ready*" (*Widow's Tears*, 1.1.0); see also *John a Kent*, 583; *Shoemakers' Holiday*, 1.4.0; Folio *Every Man In*, 1.5.71; *Blurt*, 3.2.0; *Cupid's Whirligig*, 4.4.0; *Hog Hath Lost His Pearl*, 689; *Match at Midnight*, 5; *Late Lancashire Witches*, 222; *Tale of a Tub*, 1.1.69; variants include "*half ready, and half unready*" (1 *Henry VI*, 722, 2.1.38; for **half** ready see also *Wise Woman of Hogsdon*, 311; *Woman Is a Weathercock*, 1.1.1–2), "*not full ready*" (1 *Honest Whore*, 2.1.12), "*ready for bed*" (*Sophonisba*, 3.1.169); other uses of *ready* are "*a Priest holding a Taper ready to kindle it*" (*Amyntas*, 2C1r), "*ready for execution*" (*Atheist's Tragedy*, 5.2.238; see also *Blind Beggar of Bednal Green*, 50), "*some ready with a cord to strangle Zenocia*" (*Custom of the Country*, 357), "*the Armies make ready to join battle*" (1 *Iron Age*, 296); see also *Three Ladies of London*, F3r; *James IV*, 409–10; *Sir Thomas More*, 1002; *Thracian Wonder*, C2v; *Sir John Oldcastle*, 876–7; *Malcontent*, 2.5.0; *Herod and Antipater*, F4r; *Fancies Chaste and Noble*, 2396; *'Tis Pity*, 1.2.0; *Lovesick Court*, 162; *Gentleman of Venice*, K3v.

recorder

sometimes called a **pipe** or **flute**, this wooden wind instrument is played from the end rather than along the side, comes in many sizes and tones, and produces **soft music**; directions almost invariably use the plural *recorders*, probably indicating that typically more than one was played; *recorder* can refer to the musician or the instrument, with the **sound** usually from **within**; recorders are linked to (1) **funerals** and other **sad** or quiet occasions, (2) supernatural events; examples of *recorders* accompanying a funeral and/or called for at the entry of a **hearse** are "*Music of recorders; during which enter four bearing Ithocles on a hearse*" (*Broken Heart*, 5.3.0), "*Recorders. Enter Disanius before a hearse*" (*Lovesick Court* 162, also 163); that *recorders* for funerals were conventional is suggested in *Old Law* when at "*Recorders*" the Duke asks "*Hark whence those sounds, what's that?*" and a courtier replies "*Some funeral*" after which two figures enter "*with a hearse*" (D2r); the kind of sound required is indicated in *Chaste Maid*: "*Recorders dolefully playing, enter at one door the Coffin of the Gentleman*

... at the other door, the coffin of the virgin" (5.4.0); see also *Second Maiden's Tragedy*, 2455–6; *Fatal Dowry*, 2.1.45–6; *Wasp*, 474; *recorders* are associated with death in *Sophonisba*, 5.4.36; *Revenge for Honour*, H4r; *Traitor*, 5.3.0; perhaps the convention is invoked in *Queen and Concubine* to create the false appearance of death: "*Recorders. Enter Sforza and Petruccio, bringing Alinda in a Chair, veiled*" (127).

Supernatural or "heavenly" events of various kinds are signaled or accompanied by the sound of the *recorder*; in *Two Noble Ladies* "*Recorders play. The Spirit vanishes,*" then "*Recorders still. Enter an Angel*" (1099, 1101), and a figure asks "whence comes this sound, this heavenly harmony?"; in *Grateful Servant* "*Recorders. Enter again where the Nymphs suddenly leave him*" (I2r) is acknowledged "Vanished like Fairies? Ha what music this? the motion of the Spheres, or am I in Elysium"; for other examples of *recorders* linked to the supernatural see *Maid's Tragedy*, 8; *Lady Mother*, 2488; *Love's Mistress*, 94, 109, 129; *Ladies' Privilege*, 149; *recorders* are linked to death in *Cruel Brother* with the sequence "*She riseth up ... Recorders sadly: ... She dies. Still music above*" (183); for more uses of the instrument see *Sophonisba*, 2.3.113; *Two Noble Kinsmen*, L1v, 5.1.136; *Little French Lawyer*, 417/464, 418; *Hyde Park*, I4v; *Fool Would Be a Favourite*, D4r, F1v, F8v; *Queen and Concubine*, 122; *Landgartha*, B1v, I1r.

recover

used occasionally to mean (1) "to regain possession" of an object or person, (2) "to regain consciousness"; examples of *recover* as regaining possession (all in **fight** scenes) are "*Bowyer hath the wench, rescued by France, recovered by Navarre*" (*Trial of Chivalry*, I2v), "*her Ensign bearer slain: Katherine recovereth the Ensign, and fighteth with it in her hand*" (*Devil's Charter*, I1v), "*recovers a sword, having first used his spade to side with the Englishman*" (*Gentleman of Venice*, D3v); examples of *recovering* from a **faint** include "*recovers a little in voice, and groans*" (*Revenger's Tragedy*, I3v), "*Caelia sounds the Ladies recover her*" and "*She recovers her senses*" (*Tom a Lincoln*, 1706, 2308–10, also 370, 2114, 2292); figures recently tortured enter "*as not yet fully recovered*" (*Double Marriage*, 364); see also *Gentleman of Venice*, K3r; *Fool Would Be a Favourite*, C8r.

red

items described as *red* include a **cap** (*Taming of a Shrew*, C3v), **dragon** (*Birth of Merlin*, F3r, G3v), herring (*Every Man In*, Quarto 3.1.188, Folio 3.4.53), **box** with "*red painting*" (*1 Honest Whore*, 2.1.0), **petticoats**

(*Country Girl*, D3r), "*an overgrown red Beard*" (*Caesar and Pompey*, 2.1.0), **angel's** "*red crosier staff*" (*Two Noble Ladies*, 1103); Fraud appears "*in a blue gown, red cap and red sleeves*" (*Three Lords of London*, I2v), the king's **wounded** soldiers enter "*every man with his red Cross on his coat*" (*Edward I*, 40), a **letter** written in **blood** is signaled by "*Red ink*" (*Spanish Tragedy*, 3.2.25); in *Devil's Charter* a **devil** has "*a red face*" (G1v), and in *No Wit* "*the South Wind has a great red face*" (4.3.143); *Tom a Lincoln* includes "*a garland of Red Roses*" (404), and Octavo *3 Henry VI* provides Lancastrians with "*red Roses in their hats*" and an action in which "*Clarence takes his red Rose out of his hat, and throws it at Warwick*" (A3r, 1.1.49; E2r, 5.1.82); see also Quarto *Merry Wives*, G3r, 5.5.102; *World Tossed at Tennis*, D2r.

reel

typically describes a **drunken** whirling or staggering action: "*Reels and falls*" (*Chaste Maid*, 3.2.164), "*reels in*" (*Royal Master*, D3v), "*sings and reels*" (*Country Captain*, C6v), "*Exit reeling*" (*Two Maids of More-Clacke*, D1r); for similar signals see *Vow Breaker*, 5.1.84; *Knave in Grain*, 1905; *Princess*, E3r; *Conspiracy*, C4v; elsewhere *reel* describes an unsteady movement not linked to drunkenness: a wounded figure "*Reels off*" (*Just Italian*, 264), others "*reel in the dance*" (*Late Lancashire Witches*, 217); see also *King Leir*, 1503; atypical is "*Ubaldo spinning, Ricardo reeling*" (*Picture*, 5.1.40)–or winding thread onto a *reel*.

remain

an alternative to **manet/stay** whereby some figures *exeunt* but others *remain* onstage: "*every one severally depart, Maximilian, Paulo Ferneze, and Angelo remain*" (*Case Is Altered*, 1.9.93), "*Bazulto remains till Hieronimo enters again*" (*Spanish Tragedy*, 3.13.132); see also *Locrine*, 8, 437–8, 1358–9; *Histriomastix*, D1r; *Bride*, 70; *Hannibal and Scipio*, 230, 250; *Unfortunate Mother*, 100, 127; Marston uses the Latin *remanent* (*Fawn*, 1.2.188, 317).

rescue

found regularly in **battle** scenes, usually as a verb but occasionally as a noun: "*Excursions, wherein Talbot's Son is hemmed about, and Talbot rescues him*" (*1 Henry VI*, 2169–71, 4.6.0), enter "*to his rescue*" (*Tom a Lincoln*, 923–4), "*pursues them out in rescue of Martin*" (*Maid in the Mill*, 59; see also *Captives*, 1497); *Cymbeline* provides both "*Cymbeline is taken: Then enter to his rescue, Belarius, Guiderius, and Arviragus*" and "*They Rescue Cymbeline*" (2908–10, 5.2.10;

2915–16, 5.2.13); for figures who are *rescued/rescue* another see *1 Troublesome Reign*, E3r; Octavo *3 Henry VI*, C2v, [2.4.11]; *True Tragedy of Richard III*, 1360–1; *Captain Thomas Stukeley*, 1173; *Death of Huntingdon*, 1748; *Trial of Chivalry*, I2v; *Lust's Dominion*, 4.2.135; *Silver Age*, 160; *2 Iron Age*, 389; *Tom a Lincoln*, 955; *Valiant Welshman*, G4v; *Shoemaker a Gentleman*, 3.4.17; *Rebellion*, 39; variations include "*offer to rescue them*" (*Prophetess*, 363), "*A noise within, crying Rescue, rescue*" (*Rebellion*, 39; *Isle of Gulls*, 243); see also *Three Lords of London*, H1r.

resign

to relinquish formally a right or claim: "*Rises and resigns his chair*" (*Great Duke of Florence*, 4.2.208), "*enter and resign their several Scepters to Peace, sitting in Majesty*" (*Histriomastix*, H3r); see also *World Tossed at Tennis*, F1v.

rest

see *permissive stage directions*

retire

used primarily as a verb to mean either (1) "retreat, withdraw from a fight" or (2) "withdraw to a removed position onstage"; *fight* situations include "*retreat is sounded, the enemies begin to retire*" (*Trial of Chivalry*, I2v), "*Enter two Soldiers retiring, beaten in by three others*" (*Princess*, A3r), "*in the scuffling retire, Montague chaseth them off the Stage*" (*Honest Man's Fortune*, 234), "*draws, and they make him retire*" and "*The Soldiers retire, and go out*" (*Conspiracy*, G2v, K1r), "*Virgilius charges him, he retires, and Virgilius follows him off the Stage*" (*Princess*, H2r); see also *Captain Thomas Stukeley*, 2773; *Jews' Tragedy*, 862; *Goblins*, 2.3.14; examples of *retire* as "withdraw" are more plentiful: "*Retire Heralds with the pages to their places*" (*Three Lords of London*, G4v), after an *embrace* with the king "*Perkin in state retires some few paces back*" (*Perkin Warbeck*, 2.1.39), "*Stukeley draws near toward the king, and having awhile conferred, at last retires to his soldiers*" (*Captain Thomas Stukeley*, 2451–3), "*Wittworth dances an antic mockway, then retires to his chair and sleeps*" (*Soddered Citizen*, 1917–19); an eavesdropper told to "withdraw, take up your stand" "*retires himself*" (*All Fools*, 2.1.37), and "*He kisses her and retires*" is followed by the question "Why do you stand aloof Sir?" (*Antipodes*, 314–15); for other figures who *retire* in this sense see *Bonduca*, 128; *Cleopatra*, C6v; *Late Lancashire Witches*, 245; *Court Beggar*, 260; *Queen and Concubine*, 41; *Court Secret*, F4r; *Sisters*, C8v; *Unfortunate Mother*,

111; for *retire* as a noun: "*Enter Cominius as it were in retire, with soldiers*" (*Coriolanus*, 603, 1.6.0).

retreat

a frequent direction for *sound* (roughly fifty examples) from a *trumpet* or *drum* played *within* to mark a particular stage in *battle*, sometimes called for alone, more often with *alarum* and other sounds; for the basic *retreat* or *retreat sounded* see *1 Henry VI*, 774, 2.2.3; *Edward III*, E3v, G1r, I2v; *Woodstock*, 2924; *Alphonsus of Germany*, I3r; *1 Henry IV*, K4r, 5.4.158; *2 Henry IV*, G4r, 4.3.25; *Thracian Wonder*, G4v; *Troilus and Cressida* plot, 17; *Troilus and Cressida*, B1v, 328, 1.2.174; F1v, 1619, 3.1.147; L4v, 3520, 5.9.0; *Valiant Welshman*, D3r; *1 Iron Age*, 315; *Bonduca*, 124; *Costly Whore*, 270; *Prophetess*, 373; more context is offered in "*The four brethren each of them kill a Pagan King, take off their Crowns, and exeunt: two one way, and two another way. Retreat*" (*Four Prentices*, 247), "*Achilles beats him off, retreat sounded*" (*1 Iron Age*, 327), "*Paris is slain by Pyrrhus. A retreat sounded*" (*2 Iron Age*, 362), "*retreat is sounded, the enemies begin to retire, Roderick chased by Philip: Enter at several doors, after retreat sounded, Pembroke and Ferdinand*" (*Trial of Chivalry*, I2v); *alarum* and *retreat* usually occur in that order: "*Alarum, and Retreat. Enter again Cade, and all his rabblement*" (Folio *2 Henry VI*, 2773–4, 4.8.0), "*Alarum. Retreat. Enter Antony, Octavius, Messala, Lucillius, and the Army*" (*Julius Caesar*, 2699–2700, 5.5.51), "*Alarum and Retreat. Then Enter Leonato, Volternio, Hortensio, and Soldiers in Triumph, at one door*" (*Imposture*, B3v); see also Folio *3 Henry VI*, 1311, 2.6.30; *Alphonsus of Germany*, I1r; *King Lear*, K4r, 2926, 5.2.4; *Travels of Three English Brothers*, 331.

More complex directions with *retreat* include "*Alarum, Enter Richard and Richmond, they fight, Richard is slain then retreat being sounded. Enter Richmond, Derby, bearing the crown*" (Quarto *Richard III*, M3r, 5.5.0), "*Retreat, and Flourish. Enter with Drum and Colors, Malcolm, Seyward, Ross, Thanes, and Soldiers*" (*Macbeth*, 2478–9, 5.9.0), "*Flourish. Alarum. A Retreat is sounded. Enter at one Door Cominius, with the Romans: At another Door Martius, with his Arm in a Scarf*" (*Coriolanus*, 744–7, 1.9.0), "*A Battle struck within: Then a Retreat: Flourish. Then Enter Theseus (victor) the three Queens meet him, and fall on their faces before him*" (*Two Noble Kinsmen*, C4r, 1.4.0), "*A shout within: Enter Crispianus and the rest, driving off the Vandals: he takes Roderick prisoner; a retreat sounded: Enter Dioclesian with victory*" (*Shoemaker a Gentleman*, 3.5.16), "*Alarum Enter Canutus flying Edmond following they fight The Two*

kings parley sound a Retreat and part" (*Edmond Ironside*,
976–8), *"Enter a Drum covered with black, beating a sad
Retreat"* (*Jews' Tragedy*, 3044); see also *1 Henry VI*, 638,
1.5.39; 1551–2, 3.2.109; *King John*, 1297–8, 3.3.0;
Edward II, 1493; *Woodstock*, 2956–7; *Captain Thomas
Stukeley*, 1174–5; *Histriomastix*, G1v; *Devil's Charter*,
I1v; *2 Iron Age*, 368; *Double Marriage*, 404; *Love and
Honour*, 101; atypical is a figure who *"seems to retreat a
little"* (*Platonic Lovers*, 16).

return

(1) usually refers to figures who re-***enter*** or start to
depart and then *return*, but can occasionally mean (2)
"give back," (3) *return* from abroad; typical of
exit/*return* are *"goes off, and returns in his own shape"*
(*Very Woman*, 4.2.165), *"Offers to go and returns"* (*Herod
and Antipater*, F1v), *"Arm her off and return"* (*Country
Girl*, G1v); for some of the twenty-five figures who
simply *return* see *James IV*, 1051; *Edmond Ironside*, 1592;
Looking Glass for London, 523–4; *Hamlet*, Q2 H1v, Folio
1997, 3.2.135; *Cynthia's Revels*, 4.3.364; *Sejanus*, 5.121,
149; *Maid in the Mill*, 59; *Maid's Tragedy*, 71; *Mad Couple*,
22; *Queen and Concubine*, 93; *Soddered Citizen*, 1184;
Duke's Mistress, G2r; *Young Admiral*, K3r; variations
include *returns calmly* (*Fatal Contract*, E2r), ***wounded***
(*2 Passionate Lovers*, I1v), ***hastily*** (*Politician*, A4v;
Princess, C3v), ***presently*** (*What You Will*, B3v; *Whore of
Babylon*, DS before Act 1, 36, 47), *in a* ***fury*** (*Mad World*,
5.2.41), *"returns and listens"* (*Herod and Antipater*, C2r),
"Return as they went" (*Three Lords of London*, I3r); also
common are actions such as *"bring him to the door and
return"* (*1 If You Know Not Me*, 239), *"follows him to the
door, and returns"* (*King Leir*, 2625), *"drive the rest out, and
return"* (*Miseries of Enforced Marriage*, 2296–7); see also
Conspiracy, I2v, L2r, L2v, M4v; *Country Captain*, C12r;
Distresses, 304–5; *Landgartha*, H4v; examples of *return*
as "give back" are *"they return her child"* (*Bloody
Banquet*, 855), *"Returns the Casket"* (*Renegado*, 3.5.48),
"Strike, and the blow returned" (*Atheist's Tragedy*, 3.2.25);
figures enter *"returned from Travel"* (*Faithful Friends*,
3–4), *"as returning from war"* (*Blurt*, 1.1.0; see also *Two
Maids of More-Clacke*, A3r).

revels

twice figures ***enter*** to revels (*Alphonsus of Germany*,
E3r; *Golden Age*, 53), and *Revellers* are cited once
(*Thierry and Theodoret*, 36).

reverence

a visible demonstration of respect or veneration:
figures paying homage to Pope Alexander *"with all

reverence kiss his feet" (*Devil's Charter*, E1r), *"the two
Knights, with low reverence, ascend"* to the chief priest
(*Christian Turned Turk*, F2v); *reverence* is usually
linked to ***kneeling***, ***curtsies***, and ***ceremony***: *"reverences
and kneels"* (*Prisoners*, B5r), *"make reverend Curtsies"*
(*Henry VIII*, 2648–9, 4.2.82), *"conges with great reverence
and ceremony to the Queen"* (*Fatal Contract*, H4r), *"they
set the censer and tapers on Juno's altar with much reverence"* (*Women Beware Women*, 5.2.72); figures sometimes *do reverence*, as when Isabella uncovers her
husband's portrait, *"does three reverences to it, and
kisses it thrice"* (*White Devil*, 2.2.23); see also *Downfall
of Huntingdon*, 44, 61–2.

ribbon

found occasionally in ***ceremonies***: a ***mourning*** figure
"all in white, her hair loose, hung with ribbons"
(*Swetnam*, G2r), a figure at a festival *"with Garlands
upon his Hook, himself dressed with Ribbons and Scarfs"*
(*Thracian Wonder*, C4r); as part of a ***wedding*** night ceremony a groom *"draws a white ribbon forth of the bed, as
from the waist of Sophonisba"* (*Sophonisba*, 1.2.40).

rich, richly

usually describe a figure's ***apparel***/***attire***/
clothes/***habit***: a dead ***body*** in *"a rich robe"* (*Broken
Heart*, 5.3.0), figures *"in rich habits Vizarded"*
(*Cardinal*, 3.2.85), *"in a rich Gown, great farthingale,
great Ruff, Muff, Fan, and Coxcomb on her head"* (*Lover's
Melancholy*, 3.3.48), *"richly attired and decked with
Jewels"* (*Lovesick King*, 1711–12), *"Very Richly Attired In
New fashions"* (*Woodstock*, 1130), *"richly robed and
Crowned with Bays"* (*Queen and Concubine*, 124), *"richly
clothed"* (*Wits*, 130, 179); sometimes the figures
linked to *rich* garments are noteworthy: *"one rich
Citizen"* (*Wit of a Woman*, 395), *"Pomp in rich robes"*
(*Three Lords of London*, B1r), *"many Servitors richly
appareled"* (*Antipodes*, 246), *"the devil in man's habit,
richly attired, his feet and his head horrid"* (*Birth of
Merlin*, D2v), *"devils, giving crowns and rich apparel to
Faustus"* (*Doctor Faustus*, A 525–6, B 472–3); for other
uses of *rich* to describe clothing see *Three Lords of
London*, A4v; *Looking Glass for London*, 1509; *James IV*,
2444; *Summer's Last Will*, 443; *Four Prentices*, 177;
Taming of a Shrew, A3v; *Hoffman*, 1930; *Devil's Charter*,
G4v; *Dumb Knight*, 166; *Michaelmas Term*,
Induction.29; *Whore of Babylon*, 2.2.149; *Shoemaker a
Gentleman*, 5.1.59; *Henry VIII*, 3359, 5.4.0; *Faithful
Friends*, 2481; *Maid of Honour*, 4.4.48; *Women Beware
Women*, 4.3.0; *Game at Chess*, 1577, 1605; *Escapes of
Jupiter*, 930; *Grateful Servant*, I2r; *Just Italian*, 230;

Traitor, 3.2.8, 25; *Guardian*, 3.2.0; *Unfortunate Lovers*, 31; *rich* items of clothing include a **cap** (*Devil's Charter*, A2v; *Double Marrige*, 350), **gown** (*White Devil*, 3.2.3.), **gloves** (*Whore of Babylon*, 4.1.0); also described as *rich* are a **cradle** (*Royal King*, 67), **banquet** (*City Madam*, 5.3.7), **bed** (*Faithful Friends*, 2613), **bowl** (*Devil's Charter*, H1r), **hearse** (*Wasp*, 474), **plate** (*Devil's Charter*, A2r).

ridiculous

used to characterize comic or satiric actions: "*They all make ridiculous conges*" (*Fair Maid of the Inn*, 175), enter "*with a Tablecloth*" and "*spread it ridiculously on the ground*" (*Thracian Wonder*, C4v), an inept **dancer** who "*ridiculously imitates*" another (*Women Beware Women*, 3.3.227; see also *World Tossed at Tennis*, D2r).

riding

used for (1) a *riding* **rod**, **suit** or other item of costume, (2) less commonly figures *riding* upon an animal; figures are directed to **enter** with *riding rods* (*Amends for Ladies*, 4.3.16; *Honest Man's Fortune*, 255; *Wit without Money*, 170), *riding switches* (*Jovial Crew*, 411), "*in a woman's riding habit*" (*Distresses*, 320), "*in a riding suit*" (*Yorkshire Tragedy*, 296; *Picture*, 1.1.0; *Witch of Edmonton*, 1.1.155; *Perkin Warbeck*, 5.1.0), "*in riding clothes*" (*Variety*, C2r); variations include entrances "*with their riding rods, unpinning their masks*" (*1 Edward IV*, 39), "*booted and spurred, a riding wand, and a letter in his hand*" (*King Leir*, 398–9), "*in haste, in her riding cloak and safeguard, with a pardon in her hand*" (*2 Edward IV*, 139); see also **booted, safeguard**; for examples of *riding* upon an animal, entrances include a **devil** who **ascends** "*riding upon a Lion, or dragon*" (*Devil's Charter*, G1v), Bacchus "*riding upon an Ass*" (*Summer's Last Will*, 967), a figure "*riding of a Mule*" (*Soliman and Perseda*, B4r); the latter scene ends with "*getteth up on his Ass, and rideth with him to the door*" (B4v); see also *Thracian Wonder*, H3r.

rifle, rifling

a seldom used term that carries the sense of "rob thoroughly by searching clothing and baggage": "*The Irish man falls to rifle his master*" (*Sir John Oldcastle*, 2315), "*Seize and rifle his Pack*" (*Queen and Concubine*, 34); see also *Four Prentices*, 186; *Duchess of Suffolk*, F1v; *Just Italian*, 259; *Wits*, 161.

ring

either (1) a piece of jewelry or (2) a signal for the **sound** of a **bell**; the small property appears in various contexts: "*the ceremony of the Cardinal's instalment in the habit of a soldier, performed in delivering up his cross, hat, robes and ring*" (*Duchess of Malfi*, 3.4.7), "*Throweth down a ring to him*" (*Dutch Courtesan*, 2.1.56), "*Angelina brings Gerrard and Violanta to the Friar; he joins them hand in hand, takes a Ring from Gerard, puts it on Violanta's finger; blesseth them*" (*Four Plays in One*, 321), "*with Gloves, Ring, Purse, etc.*" (*Wise Woman of Hogsdon*, 286), "*misses her ring*" (*Challenge for Beauty*, 38), "*as the ring is putting on, Cordolente steps in rudely, breaks them off*" (*Match Me in London*, 5.3.0), "*Passing by spies the Ring*" (*Two Merry Milkmaids*, K2v), "*loses her ring in a paper*" (*Fine Companion*, E4v), "*Gives him a Ring*" (*Messalina*, 2059; see also *Charlemagne*, 1819, 1929), "*shows a Ring on his finger and delivers it Sly*" (*Soddered Citizen*, 2784–7; see also *Maid of Honour*, 2.2.161), "*draws off her ring and offers it to him*" (*Wizard*, 1857–8); for other examples see *Warning for Fair Women*, B1v; *Fleer*, 5.2.26; *Insatiate Countess*, 2.2.50; *Atheist's Tragedy*, 1.2.170; *Amends for Ladies*, 5.2.235; *Siege*, 405; *Country Girl*, K4v; *Hyde Park*, B3v; *Bashful Lover*, 2.2.0, 3.3.193; *Princess*, F1r; *Unfortunate Lovers*, 75; *Parson's Wedding*, 417; a figure "*Takes off the ring, and a pane of glass*" in order to scratch a message with the *ring's* stone (*Great Duke of Florence*, 5.1.37), and another appears "*with a Ring in his mouth, a Marigold in his hand, and a fair suit of apparel on his back*" (*Rare Triumphs*, 1373–4); an atypical usage describes six dancing moors with "*their legs also naked, encircled with rings of gold; the like their Arms*" (*Amorous War*, E2v).

Signals to *ring* a bell typically refer to a sound simulating a tower clock or a gate-bell rung **within**: "*The bell rings to matins*" (*Captives*, 869; and book-keeper's "*Bell Rung*," 867), "*The Exchange Bell rings*" (*Englishmen for My Money*, 677), "*The alarm bell rings*" (*Golden Age*, 57), "*A Bell rings as far off*" and "*Bell rings as near at hand*" (*Messalina*, 691, 712); for others see Quarto *Every Man In*, 1.4.146; *Shoemakers' Holiday*, 5.2.176; *Wit of a Woman*, 1527; Quarto *Othello*, F1r, 2.3.160; *Macbeth*, 642, 2.1.61; 836, 2.3.80; *Roaring Girl*, 2.1.354; *Bloody Brother*, 295; *Changeling*, 5.1.73; *Island Princess*, 92, 113; *Novella*, 114, 149, 150, 170; *Launching of the Mary*, 42, 1135; *Bird in a Cage*, F3r; *Arcadia*, E2r; *Cardinal*, 5.3.180; directions for a bell to be rung onstage are few: "*Enter an old Shepherd, with a bell ringing*" (*Faithful Shepherdess*, 387), "*he rings a bell, and draws a curtain*" (*Histriomastix*, B4v; see also *Weeding of Covent Garden*, 33); atypical is "*A great Hubbub and noise, a ringing of basins*" (*Knave in Grain*, 2882).

rise, arise

a signal either (1) for a figure to *rise* from **kneeling**, **sitting** or **lying**, although the originating position is rarely provided in the direction or (2) for an object or figure to *rise* through the **trapdoor** and from certain specific locations that may or may not involve the trap; most common is *rising* from kneeling: "*rise, doing obeisance to the altar*" (*Broken Heart*, 5.3.0), "*Kneels down, holds up his hands speaks a little and riseth*" (*Love's Sacrifice*, 2663–4); for other examples where *rise* is given a context in dialogue see *Alphonsus of Aragon*, 232, 1910; *King Leir*, 2302, 2304, 2319, 2331, 2348, 2353; *Sir Thomas More*, 1251; *Old Fortunatus*, 4.1.153; *Antonio's Revenge*, 3.1.0; *Prophetess*, 363; *Albovine*, 60; *Soddered Citizen*, 2314; *Princess*, B3v; directions for figures to *rise/arise* from sitting include "*rise in a rage from thy chair*" (*Alphonsus of Aragon*, 1051; see also *Cobbler's Prophecy*, 958), "*Catiline sits down, and Cato rises, from him*" (*Catiline*, 4.142), "*King riseth from his State*" (*Henry VIII*, 331, 1.2.8, also 749, 1.4.60; 1363–4, 2.4.12), "*The Lords rise from Table*" (*Timon of Athens*, 490, 1.2.145), "*Rises and resigns his chair*" (*Great Duke of Florence*, 4.2.208), "*The Lady rises from his knee*" (*Woman Hater*, 141), "*all rise, and mingle in the dance*" (*Antipodes*, 338), "*rise and talk privately*" (*Cardinal*, 2.1.34); for more see *Arraignment of Paris*, 1077; *Wounds of Civil War*, 252; *John a Kent*, 1249–51; *Cobbler's Prophecy*, 1589; *Edmond Ironside*, 1518; *Sir John Oldcastle*, 2114; *Malcontent*, 4.2.0; *Devil's Charter*, C1v; *Coriolanus*, 1275, 2.2.66; *Your Five Gallants*, I2v; *Faithful Shepherdess*, 376; *Christian Turned Turk*, B1r; *1 Iron Age*, 305, 340; *Virgin Martyr*, 5.1.5, 36; *Knave in Grain*, 1857–8; *Siege*, 387; *Maid's Revenge*, I3r; *Jews' Tragedy*, 80–1; *Platonic Lovers*, 60; *Queen and Concubine*, 25; *Conspiracy*, D3v; *Landgartha*, F2v; figures also *rise/arise* from lying on the stage or in a **bed**: "*riseth from the bed*" (*Cruel Brother*, 194), "*wake and rise*" (*King Leir*, 1475), "*riseth up from the dead bodies*" (*2 Iron Age*, 427, also 428), "*Rises distractedly*" (*Roman Actor*, 5.1.187); for similar examples see *Guy of Warwick*, B4r; *David and Bethsabe*, 492; Q1 *Romeo and Juliet*, G1r, 3.3.91; K2r, 5.3.147; *Alphonsus of Germany*, B2r, E1v; *Two Lamentable Tragedies*, I2r; *Downfall of Huntingdon*, 1227; Quarto *Merry Wives*, G3r, 5.5.102; *Old Fortunatus*, 3.1.356; *Jack Drum's Entertainment*, D2r; *Atheist's Tragedy*, 3.1.77; *White Devil*, 5.6.149; *Two Noble Kinsmen*, K4v, 5.1.61; *Tom a Lincoln*, 1482–3, 1822; *Siege*, 394; *Bride*, 65; *Prisoners*, C8v; *Princess*, E3r, G1r, I1v; elsewhere a figure *rises* from a **coffin** (*Swisser*, 3.2.123), *hamper* (*King John and Matilda*, 22),

hearse (*Mad Lover*, 72); atypical is a figure who "*riseth up*" **above** (*Cruel Brother*, 183).

Signals to *rise* from **under the stage** include "*rises in disguise*" from a "charnel house" (*Atheist's Tragedy*, 4.3.174), "*rising from the vault*" (*Aglaura*, 5.1.120), "*from under the ground in several places, rise up spirits*" (*If This Be Not a Good Play*, 5.4.0), "*from under the stage, at both ends, arises Water and Earth, two persons*" (*No Wit*, 4.3.40; see also *2 Henry VI*, C1r, 647, 1.4.22), "*riseth like a ghost*" (*Lost Lady*, 595), "*Night rises in mists*" (*Maid's Tragedy*, 8, also 10); for similar actions see *Rare Triumphs*, 2; *Old Wives Tale*, 645; *Whore of Babylon*, 4.1.0; *Faithful Shepherdess*, 409; *Golden Age*, 78; *Silver Age*, 139, 140; properties and effects also *rise* from **below**: "*Hereupon did rise a Tree of gold*" (*Arraignment of Paris*, 456; see also *Looking Glass for London*, 523–5; *Warning for Fair Women*, E3v), "*from one part let a smoke arise*" (*Cobbler's Prophecy*, 1565), "*a flame riseth*" (*Two Noble Ladies*, 1901, also 1860–1); see also *Brazen Age*, 231; *Four Plays in One*, 307, 362; some directions specify *rising out* of **fictional** locations that may or may not be the trap: "*Crackstone riseth out of the Tomb*" (*Fedele and Fortunio*, 598; see also *Valiant Welshman*, A4v; *Love's Sacrifice*, 2763), "*Victoria rises out of the cave, white*" (*Martyred Soldier*, 244; see also *Woman in the Moon*, D4r), "*Out of the altar the ghost of Asdrubal ariseth*" (*Sophonisba*, 5.1.38; see also *Bonduca*, 113).

river

a rare **fictional** term (comparable to **well**) for the **trapdoor** in the main platform of the **stage**; two **dumb shows** provide a figure "*who being pursued of the French, leaps into a River, leaving the child upon the bank*" (*Weakest Goeth*, 5–6), "*A Crocodile sitting on a river's bank, and a little Snake stinging it. Then let both of them fall into the water*" (*Locrine*, 961–4); also in *Locrine* after saying "gentle Aby take my troubled corpse" Humber is directed to "*Fling himself into the river*" (1756); three onstage figures are identified as *rivers*; "*the river Achelous, his weapons borne in by Water Nymphs*" enters to compete with Hercules for Dejanira (*Brazen Age*, 173); the other two *rivers* are directed to **rise** rather than enter: "*The river Arethusa riseth from the stage*" to report that Pluto has abducted Proserpine (*Silver Age*, 140), after Amoret "*flings her into the well*," "*The God of the River riseth with Amoret in his arms*" (*Faithful Shepherdess*, 409).

roar

a **sound** linked to **devils**: "*a roaring Devil*" (*Histriomastix*, C4r), "*the fiends roar and fly back*" and "*the Devils sink roaring*" (*Two Noble Ladies*, 1847, 1860), "*Madge with a Devil's vizard, roaring*" (*Monsieur Thomas*, 138); see also *Friar Bacon*, 2073; *Virgin Martyr*, 4.2.110.

rob

used rarely for a variety of similar actions: "*Here they rob them and bind them*" (*1 Henry IV*, C4r, 2.2.92); see also *Sir John Oldcastle*, 2330; *Wit at Several Weapons*, 94; in *Love's Pilgrimage* the term describes appearance after the event when figures enter "*as robbed*" (262), and in *Phoenix* first in the *entr'acte* "*Toward the close of the music, the Justice's three men prepare for a robbery,*" then soon after "*Enter Phoenix, Fidelio being robbed, Constable, Officers and the Thief Furtivo*" (F3r, F4v).

robe

found mostly in **ceremonies** and other special occasions: "*Jupiter crowned with his Imperial Robes*" (*Golden Age*, 68; see also *If This Be Not a Good Play*, 1.2.0), "*the King puts on his royal robes*" (*1 Edward IV*, 88), the **dead** Ithocles "*in a rich robe*" and the **mourning** "*Calantha in a white robe*" (*Broken Heart*, 5.3.0), a coronation where "*they take off his black habit, and put on him a Scarlet Robe*" (*Conspiracy*, G1r); see also *Christian Turned Turk*, F2v; *Duchess of Malfi*, 3.4.7; MS *Poor Man's Comfort*, 1093–4; *Antipodes*, 313; figures **enter** "*in royal robes*" (*Lust's Dominion*, 5.1.162), "*in Senator's robes*" (MS *Poor Man's Comfort*, 2032), "*in a Robe and Garland*" (*Philaster*, 133), "*with a robe and a crown under his arm*" and later "*with a Robe upon him, and a Crown on his head*" (*Jews' Tragedy*, 2994–5, 3027–8); **white** robes are specified for six personages who appear in a vision (*Henry VIII*, 2644, 4.2.82), a boy who strews **flowers** before a **wedding** (*Two Noble Kinsmen*, B1r, 1.1.0), **masquers** (*Malcontent*, 5.5.66; *'Tis Pity*, 4.1.35), the **spirit** of the martyred Dorothea who enters "*in a white robe, crowns upon her robe, a Crown upon her head*" (*Virgin Martyr*, 5.2.219); other distinctive *robes* include "*Masquing Robes*" (*Woman Is a Weathercock*, 5.1.64–5, 128), "*a conjuring robe*" (*Bussy D'Ambois*, 4.2.7), "*Prospero (in his Magic robes)*" (*Tempest*, 1946, 5.1.0), Truth "*clothed in a robe spotted with Stars*" (*Whore of Babylon*, DS before Act 1, 37–8), "*Ganymede in a blue robe powdered with stars, and Hebe in a white robe with golden stars*" (*Women Beware Women*, 5.2.50), "*puts off the Priest's Weeds, and has a Devil's robe under*" (*Woman Is a Weathercock*, 5.2.70), a "*devil in robes pontifical with a triple Crown on his head*" and another **devil** "*in black robes like a pronotary*" (*Devil's Charter*, A2v); Henslowe's inventory includes "*Dido's robe*" (*Diary*, App. 2, 162), "*one blue robe with sleeves*" (157);

figures are directed to **put** on robes (*Fedele and Fortunio*, 987–8; Q2 *Bussy D'Ambois*, 4.2.51), *put off robes* (*Fatal Contract*, H1r), *disrobe* (*Devil's Charter*, G3r; *Jews' Tragedy*, 1756–7); atypical are "*hides his face with his robe*" (*Caesar and Pompey*, 5.1.266), "*with as many Jewels robes and Gold as he can carry*" (*2 Seven Deadly Sins*, 66–7), masquers with **weapons** concealed "*under their robes*" (*Malcontent*, 5.5.66); see also *Fedele and Fortunio*, 945; *Caesar and Pompey*, 4.4.0; *Mad Lover*, 62; *Fatal Contract*, G4v, H1r.

rock

although Henslowe's inventory includes a *rock* (*Diary*, App. 2, 56) and some directions and dialogue indicate the use of a property, what is meant remains unclear; a large object seems to be required for "*climbs up the Rock*" and "*Enter Zephirus and takes Psyche from the Rock*" (*Love's Mistress*, 100–1), "*Enter Eolus out of a Rock,*" called a "rocky den" (*Maid's Tragedy*, 10), "*sleeping on a Rock*" (*Whore of Babylon*, DS before Act 1, 28), "*casts herself from the rock*" (*Tom a Lincoln*, 2828–30); Folio *Bonduca* has "*Enter Petillius and Junius on the rock*" (158, also 143, 155, 156) which in the manuscript is "*climbing the rock: fight*" (2567–8); in *Brazen Age* Hercules enters "*from a rock above, tearing down trees*" (252) making it unlikely that the *rock* is the upper level; several signals indicate the use of the **trapdoor**, perhaps covered by a *rock*: "*Thunder and Lightning in the Rock*" and "*The Rock encloses him*" (*Birth of Merlin*, G2v), "*the Rock cleaves, she sinks; thunder and lightning*" (*Seven Champions*, C2v), "*Plutus strikes the Rock, and flames fly out*" (*Four Plays in One*, 362, also 307, 363); twice a hand-held property *rock* is called for (*Golden Age*, 78; *1 Iron Age*, 300); atypical is "*Rock and spindle*" (*English Moor*, 67); see also **stone**.

rod

a property linked to (1) supernatural events or figures, (2) **riding**, (3) other actions; when used for **magic**, *rod* is an alternative to **wand**: "*charms him with his rod asleep*" (*Cobbler's Prophecy*, 137, also 91), "*Standing without the circle he waveth his rod to the East*" (*Devil's Charter*, G1v, also A2r), "*The Magi with their rods beat the ground, and from under the same riseth a brave Arbor*" (*Looking Glass for London*, 522–5), "*Throws his charmed rod, and his books under the stage. A flame riseth*" (*Two Noble Ladies*, 1899–1901); for similar stage business see *Rare Triumphs*, 213; *Prophetess*, 363; *Twins*, E1v; a *riding rod* indicates travel in *1 Edward IV*, 39; *Amends for Ladies*, 4.3.16; *Honest Man's Fortune*, 255; *Wit without Money*, 170; elsewhere in a procession are "*some bearing Axes, bundles of rods*" (*Caesar and Pompey*, 1.2.0; see also *Wounds of Civil War*, 5; *Valentinian*, 88); two figures hold a ***white*** rod (*Queen*, 3786–7; *School of Compliment*, L2r); other examples are "*a rod of gold with a dove on it*" (*Friar Bacon*, 2076), "*an Angling rod*" (*Patient Grissil*, 5.1.56), a schoolmaster with "*a rod in his hand, and two or three Boys with their books*" (*How a Man May Choose*, C3r; see also *Fancies Chaste and Noble*, 1783–4).

room

refers to either (1) a ***fictional*** space that is part of the narrative or (2) a designated space in the theatre such as the ***music room*** or (very late in the period) the *tiring room* (*Parson's Wedding*, 494, 506); usually the main ***stage*** is to be imagined as the *room*: "*They kick him, and thrust him out of the room*" (*Parson's Wedding*, 462), two figures "*whispered out of the room*" (*White Devil*, 2.2.37), entrances "*perfuming a room*" (*Wonder of a Kingdom*, 3.1.0; *Launching of the Mary*, 2018–19) and "*at several doors, as hallowing the Room*" (*New Trick*, 296); an offstage *room* is implied by "*Puts them into another room*" (*Bride*, 33); the account of a murder in *Two Lamentable Tragedies* presumably refers to the acting area ***above*** as a fictional *room*: "*Then being in the upper Room Merry sticks him in the head fifteen times*" (B4r).

rope, ropes

cited in a variety of contexts, most notably (1) suicide or ***strangling***, (2) ***climbing***; for the former a *rope* can be an equivalent to a ***halter***/strangling ***cord***, as when figures presenting a ***petition*** enter "*with ropes about their necks, their weapons with the points towards them*" (*Christian Turned Turk*, H1v); *rope/halter* appear to be interchangeable in *Spanish Tragedy* where Hieronimo contemplating suicide enters "*with a poniard in one hand, and a rope in the other*" and subsequently "*flings away the dagger and halter*" (3.12.0, 19) and in *Looking Glass for London* where a suicidal usurer enters "*with a halter in one hand, a dagger in the other*" and then is tempted by being offered "*the knife and rope*" (2041–2, 2064–5); signals linked to climbing include "*He goes up the rope*" (*Christian Turned Turk*, F4r), "*lets down a Rope*" (*City Wit*, 361), enter "*above with a Rope to come down and make his escape*" (*Claracilla*, F12v), "*takes the rope, and offers to climb*" (*Downfall of Huntingdon*, 2435), "*a ladder of ropes*" (*May Day*, 3.3.0); "*a rope's end*" is twice called for as a property (*Comedy of Errors*, 1288, 4.4.7; *Northern Lass*, 33); atypical are "*John tolls the bell, as if he pulled the rope*" (*Two Maids of More-Clacke*, B4v) and "*ropes of pearl*" (*Wonder of a Kingdom*, 4.1.0).

rosemary

Ophelia associates *rosemary* with "remembrance" (*Hamlet*, 4.5.175) but as an onstage property it is linked more specifically to ***weddings***: figures ***enter*** "*with Rosemary, as from a wedding*" (*Woman's Prize*, 2), "*with rosemary as from church*" (*Insatiate Countess*, 1.1.141), "*They pass as to the Wedding with Rosemary*" (*City Wit*, 358); in *Noble Spanish Soldier* a ***faction*** enters "*with Rosemary in their hats*" (5.2.0) with one of them commenting that "*every one asked me who was married today*"; see also *Eastward Ho*, D2r; *Fair Quarrel*, 5.1.36; *Parson's Wedding*, 514; other plays provide "*a basin of rosemary and a great flagon with wine*" (*Match at Midnight*, 81), "*Servants placing Yew, Bays, and Rosemary, etc.*" (*Wedding*, I1r); Q1 *Romeo and Juliet* sets up a complex effect involving wedding, death and remembrance when after lamenting over the supposedly ***dead*** body of Juliet "*They all but the Nurse go forth, casting Rosemary on her and shutting the Curtains*" (I2v, 4.5.95).

roses

sometimes appear singly but more often are found in numbers; calls for *roses* include the entrance of a servant "*with Shoes, Garters and Roses*" (*City Madam*, 1.1.104), "*Garlands of Roses*" in the ***triumph*** of Love (*Four Plays in One*, 334), a ***hearse*** attended by a queen "*bearing in her hand a Garland, composed of Roses and Lilies*" (*King John and Matilda*, 84); *Tom a Lincoln* (where the title figure is known as the Red Rose Knight) includes "*a garland of Red Roses*" and figures "*with Roses in their hats*" (404–5), and Octavo *3 Henry VI* provides Yorkists "*with white Roses in their hats,*" Lancastrians with "*red Roses in their hats,*" an action in which "*Clarence takes his red Rose out of his hat, and throws it at Warwick*" (A2r, 1.1.0; A3r, 1.1.49; E2r, 5.1.82); other single *roses* are "*a white Rose in her bosom*" (*Warning for Fair Women*, I1r), "*Pins up a Rose*" (*Brennoralt*, 2.2.27); atypical is *Two Noble Kinsmen* where a ***silver*** hind is set upon an ***altar*** which is set on ***fire***, "*the Hind vanishes under the Altar: and in the place ascends a Rose Tree, having one Rose upon it,*" and after a distinctive sound "*the Rose falls from the Tree*" (L2r, 5.1.162, 168).

round

typically a ***tune*** and/or ***dance*** in which the performers move in a circle or ring: "*they dance a round*" (*What*

You Will, B3r), "*dance the drunken round*" (*Eastward Ho*, E3r), "*a round of Fairies, or some pretty dance*" (*James IV*, 634), "*all take hands, and dance round*," then pull another "*into the Round*" (*Northern Lass*, 64); see also *James IV*, 1725; in *Court Beggar* a figure "*whistles and Dances Sellenger's round*" (262), a popular old tune/*song*, which in *Late Lancashire Witches* is signaled twice (213, 215); in *Orlando Furioso* a figure "*hangs up the roundelays on the trees*" (572–3, also 640, 647; see also *Woman in the Moon*, A2v); atypical is "*He roundeth with Frescobaldi*" (*Devil's Charter*, E4r); see also *catch*.

rude

a pejorative term that (1) usually means "unmannerly, offensively discourteous" but can also extend to (2) the barbarous behavior of the *rabble*, (3) discordant or raucous *music*; examples of unmannerly behavior include "*as the ring is putting on, Cordolente steps in rudely, breaks them off*" (*Match Me in London*, 5.3.0), "*Enter a Poet rudely, and seeing the Princess, and other Ladies steps back as rudely*" (*Conspiracy*, D3r), "*they rudely Come to him, strike down his Book and Draw their swords upon them*" (*Hengist*, DS before 2.2, 4–5), "*Enter the passionate Cousin, rudely, and carelessly appareled, unbraced, and untrussed*" (*Nice Valour*, 170); related signals call for servants who enter *rudely* (*Soddered Citizen*, 1892), "*A Rabble of rude Fellows*" (*Damoiselle*, 434), "*Enter all the factions of Noblemen, Peasants, and Citizens fighting: the ruder sort drive in the rest and cry a sack, a sack*" (*Histriomastix*, G1r); descriptions of music are "*Fiddling rude tunes*" (*Weeding of Covent Garden*, 33), "*A great noise within of rude Music, Laughing, Singing*" (*Jovial Crew*, 423).

ruff

a stiff circular collar; a *mad* woman afflicted with pride enters "*in a rich gown, great farthingale, great ruff, muff, fan, and coxcomb on her head*" (*Lover's Melancholy*, 3.3.48); see also *Dead Man's Fortune*, 19–20; *Amends for Ladies*, 2.4.2–3; *Siege*, 396.

run, running

of the roughly 260 examples (1) the largest group directs figures to *enter*/*exit* running/in *haste* but also common are (2) *runs in*/*away*/*out*/*off*, (3) *runs at* someone or is *run through* with a *sword*, (4) *runs over*/*about the stage*; of the many entrances *running*, *Tom a Lincoln* provides "*running hastily*," "*amazedly Running and looking on the king*," "*running with her hair about her ears*," "*two ladies with victuals running*" (699,

2105, 2252, 2830, also 379) and *Alarum for London* provides "*two Burgers running*," "*two or three Citizens running*," "*two little children running*," "*two Spaniards running, with their swords drawn*" (212, 269, 1105, 1126); variations include a clown "*running in haste, and laughing to himself*" (*Selimus*, 1877–8), "*Enter Segasto running and Amadine after him, being pursued with a bear*" (*Mucedorus*, A3v); the many signals to *run in*/*out*/*off*/*away* include "*run out diverse ways*" (*Atheist's Tragedy*, 4.3.69), "*run out of the house affrighted*" (*Silver Age*, 122), "*The Lion roars, Thisby runs off*" (Folio *Midsummer Night's Dream*, 2065, 5.1.264), "*seeing the hurly-burly, runs away*" (*Ram Alley*, G1r), "*After the Beadle hath hit him once, he leaps over the Stool, and runs away*" (Folio *2 Henry VI*, 902–3, 2.1.150), "*They all run away, and Falstaff after a blow or two runs away too, leaving the booty behind them*" (*1 Henry IV*, C4v, 2.2.101); examples of *run* linked to *weapons* are "*runs Marcello through*" (*White Devil*, 5.2.14; see also *Wallenstein*, 62), "*They run all at Piero with their rapiers*" (*Antonio's Revenge*, 5.3.112, also 1.2.217, 5.3.105), "*The Moor runs at Iago, Iago kills his wife*" (Quarto *Othello*, M4v, 5.2.235), "*draws his sword, and runs at him when he turns aside*" (*Cupid's Revenge*, 286, also 285); see also *Three Ladies of London*, B1r; *Histriomastix*, F3r; *Traitor*, 5.3.137; figures are directed to *run about*/*over the stage*: "*Here she runs about the stage snatching at every thing she sees*" (*Cobbler's Prophecy*, 107–8; see also *Grim the Collier*, G4v), "*running over the stage in a Nightgown*" (*Woman Killed*, 138), "*Devils run laughing over the stage*" (*Seven Champions*, H1r), "*Enter two or three running over the Stage, from the Murder of Duke Humphrey*" (Folio *2 Henry VI*, 1690–1, 3.2.0); see also *Silver Age*, 159; *Valentinian*, 70; *Jovial Crew*, 431; *Osmond*, A2r; related actions include "*runs up and down laughing*" (*Two Noble Ladies*, 1538, also 1505, 1523), "*The Satyr enters, he runs one way, and she another*" (*Faithful Shepherdess*, 403), "*Enter two devils, and the clown runs up and down crying*" and "*sets squibs at their backs: they run about*" (*Doctor Faustus*, A 412–13, 1012–13); atypical are "*runs to the door and holds it*" (*Weeding of Covent Garden*, 24), "*runs against the Cage and brains herself*" (*1 Tamburlaine*, 2100), "*they all run out in couples*" at the end of a *dance* (*Lover's Melancholy*, 3.3.91), "*She runs lunatic*" and "*runs to hang himself*" (*Spanish Tragedy*, 3.8.5, 4.4.152).

rush, rushes

either (1) a verb used with *in* for *sudden* entrances or (2) the stem of a grass-like plant used as a floor covering or strewn on the ground for processions; for figures who *enter* rushing in see *Downfall of*

Huntingdon, 1624; *Richard II*, K1r, 5.5.104; *Volpone*, 5.4.61; *Turk*, 1446; *Country Girl*, E2v; *Wizard*, 2290; variations include *"suddenly rush in"* (*Christian Turned Turk*, H1v), *"Break open door; rush in"* (*No Wit*, 5.1.150), *"rush in with their swords drawn, and seize upon the Ladies"* (*Conspiracy*, K2v), *"Those in ambush rusheth forth and take him"* (*Dutch Courtesan*, 5.1.49); non-entrances are *"rush upon them"* (*Prophetess*, 363), *"rush from the table"* (*Devil's Charter*, L1v), *"rush at the Tower Gates"* (*1 Henry VI*, 374, 1.3.14); such use of *rushing in* along with the absence of *rustling* in any other direction suggests that *"Enter the Guard rustling in"* (*Antony and Cleopatra*, 3574, 5.2.319) may be an error; references to the floor covering include a signal for *"strewers of rushes"* (*2 Henry IV*, K4r, 5.5.0), a figure who *"sits on the rushes, and takes out a book to read"* (*Fair Favourite*, 251); *Gentleman Usher* provides *"servants with Rushes, and a carpet,"* a *Rush-wench*, a *Rush-maid* (2.1.71, 2.1.153, 2.2.47).

rustici

a seldom used Latin term for peasants/countrymen: *"Enter Rustici, five or six, one after another"* (Quarto *Every Man Out*, 2363); *Guardian* provides *"Exeunt Cario et Rustici"* although the scene had begun with *"Enter Cario and Countrymen"* (4.2.49, 0); similarly, *Queen and Concubine* provides *"Exeunt Rustici with Doctor and Midwife"* and *"Exeunt omnes Rustici"* (90, 55) but elsewhere calls for *"countrymen"* (57, 75, 83, 86, 93); examples of the English equivalent, *rustics*, are *"Diverse country rustics"* (*Late Lancashire Witches*, 234), *"a company of Rustics"* (*Valiant Welshman*, G1v); see also *Lovesick Court*, 144, 158.

rustling

see *rush*

S

sack

either (1) a seldom used alternative to *wine* or (2) a large cloth *bag*; the *drink* is called for in *"The Prince draws it out, and finds it to be a bottle of Sack"* (*1 Henry IV*, K1v, 5.3.54), *"a Bottle of Sack and a Cup"* (*Lady Mother*, 573–4), *"a Silver Can of Sack"* (*Jovial Crew*, 418); see also *Gentleman Usher*, 2.1.0; *Staple of News*, 4.3.8; *Princess*, E1v; the most memorable use of a *sack* for carrying objects is in *Two Lamentable Tragedies* where a body is chopped up so that when a figure takes *"the Sack by the end, one of the legs and head drops out"* (F4v); *Jack*

Drum's Entertainment provides *"Monsieur with a Sack, and Jack Drum in it"* (F4v); see also *1 Henry VI*, 1422–3, 3.2.0; *Old Couple*, 39; *Lovesick King*, 942.

sackbut

a bass *trumpet* corresponding to the modern trombone; although probably often part of a *consort*, the instrument is cited only twice: *"A strange Music. Sackbut and Troupe Music"* (*Little French Lawyer*, 440), *"A Dead March within of Drum and Sackbuts"* (*Mad Lover*, 40); a *sackbut* is listed in Henslowe's inventory (*Diary*, App. 2, 85).

sacrifice

a *ceremony* called for in several plays: *"carrying in their hands several kinds of Sacrifice"* (*Faithful Friends*, 2482–3), *"the solemnity of a sacrifice"* (*Sophonisba*, 3.1.116), *"a sacrificing knife"* (*Amyntas*, 2C1r); more elaborate is *"Enter Busyris with his Guard and Priests to sacrifice; to them two strangers, Busyris takes them and kills them upon the Altar; enter Hercules disguised, Busyris sends his Guard to apprehend him, Hercules discovering himself beats the Guard, Kills Busyris and sacrificeth him upon the Altar, at which there falls a shower of rain"* (*Brazen Age*, 183, also 247); see also *Gallathea*, 5.2.6; *Dido*, 1094; *Looking Glass for London*, 1445.

sad, sadly

used to describe either (1) a figure's appearance and/or actions, often upon entering, or (2) a kind of *music*; figures *enter* *"in a sad posture"* (*City Match*, 212), *"sad, with a Letter in his hand"* (*Cure for a Cuckold*, B3r), *"sadly"* (*1 Honest Whore*, 2.1.117); for more see *Fedele and Fortunio*, 2–3; *Two Lamentable Tragedies*, H1r; *Old Fortunatus*, 1.2.0; *Satiromastix*, 5.1.0; *Two Maids of More-Clacke*, D3v; *Golden Age*, 13; *Brazen Age*, 239; *Second Maiden's Tragedy*, 819–20; *No Wit*, 4.3.0; *Queen*, 2719; *Bride*, 7; *Bloody Banquet*, 492; other *sad* behavior includes *"Walks sadly"* (*Bashful Lover*, 1.1.60; see also *David and Bethsabe*, 601; *Jovial Crew*, 445), *"sits sadly"* (*David and Bethsabe*, 679), *"stands sadly by"* (*Lust's Dominion*, 1.2.49), *"turns away sad, as not being minded"* (*English Traveller*, 87), *"looks sadly upon him"* (*Princess*, B4v, also D3r, F2r); see also *Witch of Edmonton*, 4.2.69; *Little French Lawyer*, 396; atypical is *"Truth in sad habiliments"* (*Whore of Babylon*, DS before Act 1, 27).

A *sad sound* is usually music, often for a *funeral*: *"a sad Music of Flutes heard"* (*King John and Matilda*, 83), *"Soft sad music"* (*Broken Heart*, 4.3.141), *"there is a sad song in the music room"* (*Chaste Maid*, 5.4.0), *"Recorders: sadly"* (*Cruel Brother*, 183), *"They bear him off with a sad* and funeral march, etc." (2 Iron Age, 414), "Enter a Drum covered with black, beating a sad Retreat" (Jews' Tragedy, 3044); for more see Queen of Corinth, 45; Unnatural Combat, 2.1.263; Roman Actor, 4.2.308; City Madam, 5.3.59; Love's Sacrifice, 2733; Emperor of the East, 5.3.0; Fatal Contract, E3v; in Bonduca "A sad noise within" is not music but "this loud lamentation" (150); see also **solemn**.

safeguard

an outer **skirt** or **petticoat** worn by a woman to protect her skirt when **riding** and therefore (along with **boots**, **spurs**, riding **wands**, riding **cloaks**) an indicator that a figure has recently completed a journey or is about to undertake one: "the men booted, the gentlewomen in cloaks and safeguards" (Merry Devil of Edmonton, B1r); like other items of riding costume the safeguard can be linked to **haste** or weariness: "Jane in haste, in her riding cloak and safeguard, with a pardon in her hand" (2 Edward IV, 139); see also Roaring Girl, 2.1.154.

salutation

see **salute**

salute

widely used (fifty-six examples) (1) usually to denote male–male exchanges that involve some combination of **bows**, **hand** gestures, and doffing of **hats** but (2) occasionally to denote a **kiss**; most often salute is found as a verb with no further details; for a representative sampling see Case Is Altered, 1.4.0; Quarto Every Man Out, 2055; Patient Grissil, 2.1.140; Puritan, F2v; Caesar and Pompey, 2.3.72; 2 Iron Age, 406; Hengist, 4.2.0; Jews' Tragedy, 1501–2; Witch of Edmonton, 1.2.109; Perkin Warbeck, 2.1.39; New Academy, 63–4; Antipodes, 338; Rebellion, 16; Wedding, F4r; Example, H2v; Distresses, 344, 363; an example of a male–male salute clearly linked to **gestures** is "Enter two Citizens at both doors, saluting afar off" (Double Marriage, 360) with an observer commenting "How they duck! / This senseless, silent courtesy methinks, / Shows like two Turks, saluting one another, / Upon two French Porters' backs"; other salutes that involve some distance between the two parties include the **masquers** in Henry VIII who "pass directly before the Cardinal, and gracefully salute him" (755–6, 1.4.63), "salutes, and stands to the bar" (Tragedy of Byron, 5.2.42), "saluting the Company as a stranger, walks off" (1 Honest Whore, 2.1.117); salutes are linked to **wedding** parties (Great Duke of Florence, 2.1.77; Fatal

Dowry, 2.2.310), the military and royalty: "Salutes the Brides" (Mad Couple, 98), "(A Song) whilst they salute" (Fair Maid of the Inn, 212), "meet embrace, salute the Generals" (Appius and Virginia, H3v), "both salute the Emperor" (Doctor Faustus, B 1297), after a coronation "the rest stand before, and salute him saying, the gods preserve the King" (Conspiracy, G1r).

For examples of the salute as a kiss, in New Way to Pay after Lord Lovell and Margaret "salute" (3.2.180, also 246, 262) Overreach comments "That kiss, / Came twanging off," in Distresses Orgemon brings Claramante "to Basilonte and Amiana, who salute her" with Basilonte commenting upon "that comfortable kiss" (363), in Wits Younger Palatine tells Lady Ample that his friend Pert deserves a kiss so "if you please, / For my humble sake, unto your lip too" and "Pert salutes her" (168); for other male–female salutes (that may or may not involve a kiss) see Antipodes, 335; Money Is an Ass, F2r; Swaggering Damsel, D3r; Lost Lady, 572; News from Plymouth, 148.

More elaborate salutes include a pair who "salute with silence at the door," then two more "salute each other with silence at the door, then are saluted by" others (Humorous Courtier, I2v–I3r), "The Duke and Abbot meet and salute, Bianca and the rest salute, and are saluted" (Love's Sacrifice, 1818–19); variations include "salute and whisper" (Politician, F4v), "salute and confer" (Queen's Exchange, 530), "salutes them humbly" (Sejanus, 5.311), "salute with ceremony" (Soddered Citizen, 1610), "with Courtly Compliments salute and part" (Noble Spanish Soldier, 1.1.0), "salutes Crostill, and puts by Bellamy" (Mad Couple, 65), "salute as they meet in the walk" (Quarto Every Man Out, 2033–4), "Ariola seems to retreat a little at Phylomont's salute" (Platonic Lovers, 16); examples of the less common salutation are "kind salutations" (Sir Thomas More, 1532), "Salutations ended, cease music" at the end of a **ceremony** (Perkin Warbeck, 2.1.39), the "gentle actions of salutations" provided by the "several strange shapes" (Tempest, 1536–7, 3.3.19) who bring in the **banquet** to the courtiers.

satin

two figures in **disguise** enter "like wealthy citizens in satin suits" (Michaelmas Term, 3.4.176; see also Your Five Gallants, F2r), a figure "throws off his Gown, discovering his doublet with a satin forepart and a Canvas back" (Hengist, 5.1.286–9), six Moors enter "from the waist, to their knees covered with bases of blue Satin, edged with a deep silver fringe" (Amorous War, E2v); although seldom cited in directions, satin is well represented in Henslowe's inventory which includes "one ash color satin doublet, laid with gold lace" (*Diary*, App. 2, 97), "one peach color satin doublet" (98), "one old white satin doublet" (99), "one black satin coat" (103), "one black satin suit" (134), "one black satin doublet, laid thick with black and gold lace" (147), "Harry the fifth satin doublet, laid with gold lace" (177).

scaffold

a large property that is "*thrust forth*" (*Virgin Martyr*, 4.3.4) or "*put out*" (*Barnavelt*, 2852–3) onto the **stage** for **executions** and other special events; *Knight of Malta* provides "*The Scaffold set out, and the stairs*" (109) for spectators to a single **combat**, but most of the relevant signals are linked to executions and often include headsmen/executioners: "*Hillus, Officers with the Scaffold, and the Executioner*" (*Herod and Antipater*, L2v), "*Don Sago guarded, Executioner, scaffold*" (*Insatiate Countess*, 5.1.0), "*Enter Headsman with Scaffold and a Guard*" (*Messalina*, 2562); also signaled are **ascents/descents**: "*goes up the Scaffold*" (*Queen*, 3187), "*ascends the scaffold*" (*Insatiate Countess*, 5.1.128), "*Leaps up the scaffold*" and "*staggers off the scaffold*" (*Atheist's Tragedy*, 5.2.130, 241), "*She mounts the Scaffold, submits her head to the block, and suddenly rising up leaps down, Snatcheth Evodius's Sword and wounds herself*" (*Messalina*, 2592–6); the bookkeeper adds "*Scaffold*" to the manuscript of *Barnavelt* (2851); see also *Dumb Knight*, 152.

scale, scaling, scalado

the **climbing** of **walls** on a **ladder** is variously signaled: "*Alarm, and they scale the walls*" (2 *Tamburlaine*, 4174; see also *Selimus*, 1200; *Humour out of Breath*, 479), "*Scaling Ladders at Harflew*" (Folio *Henry V*, 1082, 3.1.0; see also 1 *Henry VI*, 683–4, 2.1.7), "*entereth by scalado*" (*Devil's Charter*, I1v).

scarf

used for (1) **wounded** figures, (2) **disguise**, (3) other stage business; a wounded figure may **enter** "*with his arm in a scarf*" (*Humorous Day's Mirth*, 4.3.0; *Coriolanus*, 746–7, 1.9.0; *Lovers' Progress*, 85; *Sparagus Garden*, 192), "*with his hand in a scarf, halting*" (*Edmond Ironside*, 1631–2), "*with his Arm in a scarf, a nightcap on his head*" (*Widow's Tears*, 4.1.0); a disguised figure can enter "*with a scarf before his face*" (*Orlando Furioso*, 1350–1, 1475), "*with a Scarf on her face*" (*Trial of Chivalry*, K1v), and a group of robbers appears "*in Scarfs*" (*Wit at Several Weapons*, 94); to shed such a disguise a figure "*lets fall her Scarf*" (*Wit at Several Weapons*, 102), "*Takes off the Scarf*" (*Bondman*, 4.3.76); a *scarf* can be used as a love token (*Old Couple*, 36), a badge of rank, a restraint for a **prisoner**, or a signal: "*with his scarf like a Captain*" (*Hoffman*, 1126), "*her arms in a scarf pinioned*" (*Love and Honour*, 103), "*takes his scarf and ties it about his arm*" (*Hieronimo*, 11.163), "*Enter the Bandit dragging Evadne by the hair: she drops a scarf*" (*Rebellion*, 60); "*Ribbons and Scarfs*" are worn in a pastoral festival (*Thracian Wonder*, C4r), and an entertainment calls for "*many School Boys with Scarfs and Nosegays, etc.*" (*Queen and Concubine*, 124); in *Whore of Babylon* Dekker apparently equates *scarfs* and **veils** so that initially a group has "*scarfs before their eyes*" until Truth and Time pull "*the veils from the Councillors' eyes*" (DS before Act 1, 33, 38–9).

scarlet

a distinctive color associated with high office and **ceremonies**: "*Tamburlaine all in scarlet*" (1 *Tamburlaine*, 1638), a *scarlet* **robe** for a coronation (*Conspiracy*, G1r), a chancellor and other officials "*in scarlet gowns*" (*Tragedy of Byron*, 5.2.0), "*the Lady Mayoress in Scarlet*" (*Sir Thomas More*, 955), "*the Lord Mayor, in his scarlet gown, with a gilded rapier by his side*" (1 *Edward IV*, 57).

scene

either (1) a segment of a play or (2) the tiring-house wall; references to the action are "*This Scene is acted at two windows*" (*Devil Is an Ass*, 2.6.37), "*Having discovered part of the past scene, above*" (*Epicœne*, 4.6.0), "*The Plot of a Scene of Mirth, to conclude this fourth Act*" (*Faithful Friends*, 2815–16), "*Narcisso stepping in before in the Scene, Enters here*" (*If This Be Not a Good Play*, 1.2.158); see also *John of Bordeaux*, 1058; *Parson's Wedding*, 494; *Landgartha*, K1r; part of the performance space is referred to in "*He opens the Scene; the Beggars are discovered in their postures; then they issue forth*" (*Jovial Crew*, 365), "*The scene adorned with Pictures*" (*Gentleman of Venice*, F2r); atypical directions in *Covent Garden* designate the **door** through which figures come or go as "*the right Scene,*" "*the left Scene,*" "*the middle Scene*" (7, 25, and throughout).

scepter

a **staff** associated with a sovereign: "*Enter six Saxon Kings' ghosts crowned, with Scepters in their hands, etc.*" (*Queen's Exchange*, 505); the *scepter* is called for in various **ceremonies** where it is combined with a **purse** (*Downfall of Huntingdon*, 42, 60), **sword** (*Downfall of Huntingdon*, 2699), most commonly a

crown (*Friar Bacon*, 2077; *2 Tamburlaine*, 3110; *Look about You*, 2821–2; *Golden Age*, 78; *Four Plays in One*, 311; *Constant Maid*, H1r); *1 If You Know Not Me* provides "*Sussex bearing the Crown, Howard bearing the Scepter, the Constable the Mace, Tame the Purse, Shandoyse the Sword*" (239, also 195, 244); variations include five figures who "*enter and resign their several Scepters to Peace, sitting in Majesty*" (*Histriomastix*, H3r), Fortune followed by "*four Kings with broken Crowns and Scepters*" (*Old Fortunatus*, 1.1.63); Henslowe's inventory includes "one globe and one golden scepter" (*Diary*, App. 2, 61).

sconce
a *lantern* (carried by a handle rather than suspended from a chain) mentioned once: "*Enter Mendoza with a sconce, to observe Ferneze's entrance*" (*Malcontent*, 2.1.0).

scrape
to *bow* or otherwise show respect in obsequious fashion, as in enter "*legging and scraping*" (*Swaggering Damsel*, F2v).

scroll
a rarely cited property: "*reading a long Scroll of Parchment*" (*Soddered Citizen*, 2376; see also *If This Be Not a Good Play*, 2.2.34), "*takes the scroll and peruses it*" (*Court Beggar*, 191); see also *City Wit*, 280; *Renegado*, 5.7.5.

scuffle
a confused *fight* in which something unexpected and usually fatal occurs, as in Folio *Hamlet* when "*In scuffling they change Rapiers*" and Laertes is poisoned by his own *weapon* (3777, 5.2.302) and in *Duchess of Malfi* when Ferdinand "*wounds the Cardinal, and in the scuffle gives Bosola his death-wound*" (5.5.53); other examples include "*in the scuffling retire*" (*Honest Man's Fortune*, 234), "*tripped up his heels in scuffle and sits on him*" (*Fatal Contract*, H4v); see also *Amends for Ladies*, 3.4.130–1; *2 Iron Age*, 427; *Sparagus Garden*, 164.

scutcheon
an ornamental *shield* associated with *funerals* and other *ceremonies*: "*a Funeral, a Coronet lying on the Hearse, Scutcheons and Garlands hanging on the sides*" (*1 Honest Whore*, 1.1.0), "*Enter Funeral. Body borne by four Captains and Soldiers. Mourners. Scutcheons, and very good order*" (*Fatal Dowry*, 2.1.47), a *chariot* in a *triumph* "*on the top, in an antique Scutcheon, is written Honor*" (*Four Plays in One*, 311); *Four Prentices* calls for a group

to enter "*with their Shields and Scutcheons*" (229), and *Spanish Tragedy* provides "*three Knights, each his scutcheon*" and "*He takes the scutcheon and gives it to the King*" (1.4.137, 140).

scythe
linked twice to allegorical figures: Time appears in *black* with "*all his properties (as Scythe, Hourglass and Wings)*" (*Whore of Babylon*, DS before Act 1, 29–30), and Harvest enters "*with a scythe on his neck, and all his reapers with sickles*" (*Summer's Last Will*, 803).

sea, sea gown, sea fight
references to the *sea* are mostly linked to (1) personnel, (2) distinctive costumes, (3) *sound* effects for an offstage *battle*; personnel include a Sea pirate (*Very Woman*, 5.1.0), Sea captains (*World Tossed at Tennis*, E2r; *Unnatural Combat*, 2.1.0, 192, 216), "*Enter Bess like a Sea-captain*" (*1 Fair Maid of the West*, 313); calls for costumes include a sea *gown* (*Antonio and Mellida*, 4.1.0), "*two Mariners, in sea gowns and sea caps*" (*King Leir*, 1991–2; see also *Antipodes*, 263), "*Fustigo in some fantastic Sea suit*" (*1 Honest Whore*, 1.2.0); *sea* battles linked to offstage sounds include "*A Sea fight within, alarm*" (*Knight of Malta*, 94), "*Alarum. Fight at Sea. Ordnance goes off*" (Folio *2 Henry VI*, 2168, 4.1.0), "*the noise of a Sea fight. Alarum*" and "*Alarum afar off, as at a Sea fight*" (*Antony and Cleopatra*, 1975–6, 3.10.0; 2752, 4.12.3), "*Alarms within, and the chambers be discharged, like as it were a fight at sea*" (Quarto *2 Henry VI*, F1v, 4.1.0); the most extensive *sea* battle is in *Fortune by Land and Sea* and is keyed to personnel, sound effects and figures who enter "*all furnished with Sea devices fitting for a fight*" (416); figures who enter *wet* are sometimes linked to the *sea*: "*the Master of the ship, some Sailors, wet from sea*" (*Looking Glass for London*, 1368–9), "*all wet as newly shipwrecked and escaped the fury of the Seas*" (*Captives*, 653–4); atypical are "*Exeunt, fall as into the sea*" (*2 Passionate Lovers*, L5r) and *Golden Age* where after the gods draw *lots* "*Neptune draws the Sea, is mounted upon a seahorse*" (78); the difficulty of bringing *sea* scenes onstage is noted by the *chorus* in *1 Fair Maid of the West*: "*Our Stage so lamely can express a Sea, / That we are forced by Chorus to discourse / What should have been in action*" (319); see also *ship*.

search
used primarily as a verb, most commonly for *searching* a *pocket*: "*searcheth his pocket, and findeth certain papers*" (*1 Henry IV*, E4r, 2.4.531), "*searches first one,*"

then the other Pocket" (*Witch of Edmonton*, 4.2.69), "*searches the queen's pockets, hands, neck Bosom and Hair*" (*Charlemagne*, 1094–6); see also *Bride*, 65; *Brennoralt*, 1.2.11; *Wits*, 166; related are "*searches his scrip*" for food (*Bashful Lover*, 3.1.34), "*The Surgeon searcheth*" the king's **wound** (*Massacre at Paris*, 1206; see also *English Moor*, 8); for the *searching of him/them* see *Mucedorus*, D3v, F1r; *Alarum for London*, 738; *Conspiracy*, B4r, C1v; *Just Italian*, 268; examples of *search* as a noun are "*He goes out in Search, and returns again*" (*Conspiracy*, I2v), "*two Searchers*" (*Looking Glass for London*, 2258).

secret, secretly

the ten examples offer a variety of uses: "*Edricus talketh with Edmond secretly*" (*Edmond Ironside*, 1383; see also *Jews' Tragedy*, 353), "*Here the Lord Warden, and Cromer uncover to the Bishop, and secretly whispers with him*" (*Sir John Oldcastle*, 1878–9), "*speaketh this secretly at one end of the stage*" (*Fair Em*, 235), "*Secretly gives her a Letter*" (*Maid's Revenge*, D4v; see also *Women Pleased*, 299), "*gives Adriana his purse secretly*" (*Ram Alley*, D1v), "*placing them in secret*" (*Spanish Tragedy*, 2.2.6; see also *Satiromastix*, 4.3.68), "*eating secretly*" (*Patient Grissil*, 2.1.76).

sedan

a portable **chair** or closed vehicle borne on poles by bearers and mentioned in three directions from the 1630s: "*Enter the Sedan, Hoyden in it, in woman's clothes*" (*Sparagus Garden*, 208), "*Enter Sedan-man*" (*Antipodes*, 305), enter "*with a Sedan*" (*Wit in a Constable*, 228); in the latter a figure refers to "this carriage" or "close conveyance" as "the cunningest wooden bawdy house" carried by "blue coat man-mules."

seek

used rarely to describe entering figures: "*a soldier in the Woods, seeking Timon*" (*Timon of Athens*, 2496, 5.3.0), "*Amoret, seeking her love*" (*Faithful Shepherdess*, 418), "*a devil to seek Miles*" (*Friar Bacon*, 2010); see also *Atheist's Tragedy*, 4.3.204; *Goblins*, 3.4.9; more detailed is "*seeks up and down for a place to hide*" (*Weakest Goeth*, 261–2; see also *Locrine*, 1649).

seem, seeming

used widely (roughly eighty examples) (1) most often for events in **dumb shows** and other pantomimed actions but also (2) as an equivalent to **counterfeit, feign**, pretend; examples of *seem* as pretend include "*seeming to put the keys under his bolster con-*

veyeth them into her pocket" (*Hog Hath Lost His Pearl*, 1568–9), "*seems to read the letters, but glances on Mistress Shore in his reading*" (*1 Edward IV*, 61), "*Mendoza bestrides the wounded body of Ferneze and seems to save him*" (*Malcontent*, 2.5.9); more common are a wide range of locutions wherein the *seeming* action is usually (but not always) true, not feigned: "*seems to foot the tune*" (*Mad World*, 2.1.143), "*in a rage, seeming to break off the ceremony*" (*Women Beware Women*, 4.3.0), "*seeming to complain of being sick*" (*City Wit*, 358), "*Some seem to applaud the King, some pity Eulalia*" (*Queen and Concubine*, 22); figures *seem* **angry** (*Noble Spanish Soldier*, 1.1.0), harsh (Q2 *Hamlet*, H1v, 3.2.135), **amazed** (*Blurt*, 4.2.0; *Birth of Merlin*, C3r; *Antipodes*, 335), **fearful/affrighted** (*Family of Love*, D1r; *Lust's Dominion*, 3.2.0; *Wisdom of Doctor Dodypoll*, 1615), distrustful (*Your Five Gallants*, I3r), troubled (*Maid of Honor*, 3.3.200), "loath and unwilling" (Folio *Hamlet*, 2001, 3.2.135), "greatly discontented" (*1 Edward IV*, 67), "unwilling to dance" (*Woman Is a Weathercock*, 5.2.8–9); for examples of actions, figures *seem* to chide (*Four Plays in One*, 321), **sleep** (*Bondman*, 2.2.125), **sound** (Q2 *Bussy D'Ambois*, 4.1.146), **pray** (*Four Plays in One*, 321; *Roman Actor*, 5.1.180), entreat (*Spanish Tragedy*, 3.1.101), **smell** (*Captain*, 309), **drink** (*Night Walker*, 359), **poison** (*Malcontent*, 5.3.35), **conjure** (MS *Humorous Lieutenant*, 2328), comfort (*Brazen Age*, 239; *Jovial Crew*, 445), condole (*Antonio's Revenge*, 5.3.92; Q2 *Hamlet*, H1v, 3.2.135), **lament** (Folio *Hamlet*, 1999, 3.2.129), **stay** (*Henry VIII*, 2877, 5.1.86), **overhear** (*Dutch Courtesan*, 1.2.161), **lock/open** a **door** (*Death of Huntingdon*, 1921; *Love's Cruelty*, G2v; *Platonic Lovers*, 47), "weep and mourn" (*Chaste Maid*, 5.4.0).

Seeming is used to describe **compliments** (*Antonio and Mellida*, 1.1.115), **passion** (*Antonio's Revenge*, 1.2.254), a **letter** (*Antonio and Mellida*, 3.2.92), a figure "*seeming dead*" (*Humour out of Breath*, 452); one dumb show in *Four Plays in One* provides "*seems to restrain him . . . they seem sorry . . . seem to crave justice . . . she seems to expostulate . . . beckons Ferdinand to him (with much seeming passion)*" (326, also 333), and another in *Antonio's Revenge* provides "*seemeth to send out Strotzo; . . . talks with her with seeming amorousness; she seemeth to reject his suit . . . they go to her, seeming to solicit his suit*" (3.1.0); for comparable examples in dumb shows see *Warning for Fair Women*, G3r; *Thracian Wonder*, B4v; *Devil's Charter*, A2v; *Travels of Three English Brothers*, 404; *Christian Turned Turk*, H1v; *Valiant Welshman*, C4v; *Herod and Antipater*, F3v; *Hengist*, DS before 2.2, 11–12; *Changeling*, 4.1.0; *Grateful Servant*, I2r; variations include "*seemeth lasciviously to her*" (*Revenger's*

Tragedy, H1v), "*Subtle seems come to himself*" (*Alchemist*, 4.5.77), "*seems here near his end*" (*White Devil*, 5.3.129); see also **make as though**, **make signs**.

seize

primarily signals capture, often by a guard: "*The Guard seizeth Zanthia*" (*Sophonisba*, 4.1.86), "*Enter a Guard, Bufo with them seize Petruchi*" (*Queen*, 2176–7), "*Enter Guard and Servants, they seize upon Rutilio and bind him*" (*Custom of the Country*, 381), "*They seize upon him, bind his arms and feet, and blind him with a bag*" (*Gentleman of Venice*, D4v), "*a Captain, and Soldiers, rush in with their swords drawn, and seize upon the Ladies*" (*Conspiracy*, K2v); for more see *Malcontent*, 5.5.124; *Prophetess*, 363; *Two Noble Ladies*, 1168, 2031; *Spanish Gypsy*, B1v; rev. *Aglaura*, 5.1.25; *Prisoners*, A10v; *Princess*, B4v; *Claracilla*, E5v, F10v, F11v; *Wit in a Constable*, 235; *2 Passionate Lovers*, K8r; *Fair Favourite*, 258; *Unfortunate Lovers*, 41; *Arcadia*, G1r; elsewhere a property is *seized*: "*Horatio has Prince Balthazar down; then enter Lorenzo and seizes his weapons*" (*Hieronimo*, 11.126), Jupiter "*beats away Saturn, seizeth his crown, and swears all the Lords of Crete to his obeisance*" (*Golden Age*, 53), "*Seize and rifle his Pack*" (*Queen and Concubine*, 34); atypical are "*He seizeth on his face*" (*Devil's Charter*, M1v), "*Jupiter seizeth the room* [crown?] *of Lycaon*" (*Golden Age*, 23).

sennet

a fanfare played **within** on a **trumpet** or **cornet** when important figures **enter**/**exit**; the signal, usually simply *sennet* or **sound** *a sennet*, occurs about sixty times in half as many plays, frequently in the Shakespeare canon (Folio *2 Henry VI*, 487, 1.3.100; Folio *Richard III*, 1735, 3.1.150; Folio *Henry V*, 3366, 5.2.374; *Julius Caesar*, 115, 1.2.24; Folio *Troilus and Cressida*, 454, 1.3.0; *Macbeth*, 992, 3.1.10; *King Lear*, B1v, 37–8, 1.1.33; *Coriolanus*, 1059, 2.1.161); stage plots and playhouse manuscripts with directions for a *sennet* include *Battle of Alcazar* plot, 4–5, 17–18, 45–46; *2 Seven Deadly Sins*, 14; *1 Tamar Cham*, 5; *John of Bordeaux*, 448, 1265; *Woodstock*, 350; *Second Maiden's Tragedy*, 5; see also the annotated *Two Merry Milkmaids*, I2v, I3r, K1v; for other instances of the basic *sennet* see *Hieronimo*, 1.0; *Doctor Faustus*, B 1235; *1 If You Know Not Me*, 244; *King and No King*, 152; MS *Poor Man's Comfort*, 1093, Quarto G4v; *Rape of Lucrece*, 173; the few more specific signals include "*The cornets sound a Sennet*" (*Antonio and Mellida*, 1.1.34, 2.1.292; see also *Antonio's Revenge*, 5.3.32), "*The still flutes sound a mournful Sennet*" (*Antonio and Mellida*,

5.2.208), "*A Sennet while the Banquet is brought in*" (*Doctor Faustus*, B 1012), "*Trumpets sound a flourish, and then a sennet*" (*Satiromastix*, 3.1.166), "*A Sennet with Trumpets*" (*Valentinian*, 88).

serpent

a rarely cited supernatural creature; in the annotated *Looking Glass for London* the bookkeeper wrote "*Sun*," "*Vine*," "*Serpent*" just before the direction "*A Serpent devoureth the vine*" (H4r, 2190), and in *Valiant Welshman* "*Enter the Serpent*" (F1v) occurs twice, as well as "*Enter the Serpent. Caradoc shows the herb. The Serpent flies into the Temple. Caradoc runs after. It thunders*" (G1r); see also **dragon**, **snake**.

service

(1) most commonly used for **banquets** and the presentation of food but also linked to (2) military action, (3) a religious **ceremony**, (4) the offering of dutiful *service*; usually *service* is associated with the **dishes**/utensils for serving a meal: "*services carried covered over the stage*" (*Wonder of a Kingdom*, 5.2.0), "*A service as for dinner, pass over the stage, borne by many Servitors, richly appareled*" (*Antipodes*, 246), "*A banquet brought in, with limbs of a Man in the service*" (*Golden Age*, 21); *service* is linked to a **sewer**, an attendant who oversees a banquet: "*Enter an armed Sewer, after him the service of a Banquet*" (*Satiromastix*, 5.2.0), "*Enter a Sewer, and diverse Servants with Dishes and Service over the Stage*" (*Macbeth*, 473–4, 1.7.0); see also *Case Is Altered*, 1.3.0, 1.4.0; *Histriomastix*, C2v; for an example of military action, "*Here is a very fierce assault on all sides, wherein the prentices do great service*" (*1 Edward IV*, 20); for religion, "*After a solemn service, enter from the widow's house a service*" (*James IV*, 2051–2); for duty, **dancing** figures enter "*offering service to Anthropos*" (*Four Plays in One*, 363).

sessions

see **trial**

set, set out, set forth

widely used to mean (1) "put, place, or placed" and as part of various locutions, (2) most commonly *set forth*/*out* properties on the stage but also (3) *set upon*/"attack," (4) *set*/*set down* for "sit, seated"; for examples of *set* as "put, place," **garlands**/*a* **crown** are *set* on **heads** (*Amends for Ladies*, 5.2.298–9; *Alphonsus of Aragon*, 794, 835–6), and **coffins**/**biers**/**hearses** are brought onstage and *set down* (*Titus Andronicus*, A4v, 1.1.69; *Antonio's Revenge*, 2.1.0; *Chaste Maid*, 5.4.0;

Fatal Contract, E3v; *Lovesick Court*, 163) as are
lights/*cards*/a *censer* (*Woman Killed*, 121; *Bloody
Banquet*, 1073–4; *Women Beware Women*, 5.2.72); *meat*
(*Old Wives Tale*, 734; *Patient Grissil*, 4.3.11) and *bags*
(*Captain Thomas Stukeley*, 2273) are *set* on a *table*,
tables are *set* (*All Fools*, 5.2.0; *Devil's Charter*, L3r), a
"*chair is set under a Canopy*" (*Satiromastix*, 5.2.22), a
prophet is "*set down over the Stage in a Throne*" (*Looking
Glass for London*, 159–60); other locutions include "*set
back to back*" (*Amends for Ladies*, 5.2.183–4), "*lists set up*"
(*Devil's Law Case*, 5.6.0), "*set up the gibbet*" (*Sir Thomas
More*, 584), "*Let there be a brazen Head set in the middle of
the place behind the Stage*" (*Alphonsus of Aragon*, 1246–7;
see also *Death of Huntingdon*, 2912–13).

Regularly *set forth*/*out* are large properties such as a
scaffold (*Knight of Malta*, 109), *altar* (*2 Iron Age*, 426;
Match Me in London, 5.3.0; *Faithful Friends*, 2822), *bar*
(*Lovers' Progress*, 144; *Spanish Curate*, 98; *Parliament of
Love*, 5.1.32; *City Nightcap*, 119, 133; *Dick of Devonshire*,
1626; *Arcadia*, H4r), *tomb* (*Second Maiden's Tragedy*,
1726–7), *banquet* (*Satiromastix*, 4.1.0; *Westward Ho*,
4.2.52; *Bloody Brother*, 306; *Custom of the Country*, 334;
Love's Mistress, 101, 149; *Thierry and Theodoret*, 24;
Faithful Friends, 2485; *Duke of Milan*, 1.3.0; *Great Duke
of Florence*, 4.2.153; *Unnatural Combat*, 3.2.136; *Noble
Spanish Soldier*, 5.4.0; *Obstinate Lady*, H3v; *Rebellion*,
65), some combination of a table/*chairs*/*stools*/
lights; for a sampling of the thirty-five items in the
latter category see *1 Honest Whore*, 4.1.0; *If This Be Not a
Good Play*, 2.2.0, 4.4.0; *Fortune by Land and Sea*, 420;
1 Fair Maid of the West, 307; *Lovers' Progress*, 104; *Love's
Pilgrimage*, 265; *Spanish Curate*, 133; *Devil's Law Case*,
3.3.0; *Noble Spanish Soldier*, 1.2.0; *Renegado*, 2.4.0;
Believe as You List, 654–6, 1794–5; *Welsh Ambassador*,
1934–5; *Bloody Banquet*, 1051; *Antipodes*, 324; *City Wit*,
279; *Wedding*, I1r; *Doubtful Heir*, D7r, E5r; *Variety*, B7r,
D6v, D12r; typical is "*A Table, Count book, Standish,
Chair and stools set out*" (*City Madam*, 1.2.143); occasionally a banquet/bar/stools are merely *set* (*Sir Thomas
More*, 878; *Jews' Tragedy*, 356; *Soddered Citizen*, 1802).

For *set upon* as attack see *Battle of Alcazar*, 1384–5;
Blurt, 2.1.85; Folio *3 Henry VI*, 2253–5, 4.3.27; *Miseries
of Enforced Marriage*, 1350; *Captain Thomas Stukeley*,
2812; for *set* as "sit, seated" see *Three Ladies of London*,
F2r; *Grim the Collier*, G2v; *Sir John Oldcastle*, 2086–7;
Widow's Tears, 3.2.106; *Devil's Charter*, E1r; *Inconstant
Lady*, 2.4.48; typical are "*As they are sharing, the Prince
and Poins set upon them*" (*1 Henry IV*, C4v, 2.2.101), "*They
set them down on two low stools and sew*" (*Coriolanus*,
361, 1.3.0); in Quarto *Othello* set could mean either *sit*
or *placed*: "*Enter Duke and Senators, set at a Table with
lights and Attendants*" (C1r, 1.3.0).

several, severally

widely used terms (roughly 250 examples) (1) found
primarily when figures *enter*/*exit* but also linked
regularly to (2) figures, (3) objects, (4) actions; most
commonly *several* is used to describe *doors* and
denotes "two": "*Enter at two several doors*" (*Four
Prentices*, 234), "*Enter at several doors Mizaldus with
Claridiana; Guido with Rogero at another door*" (*Insatiate
Countess*, 1.1.288), enter two figures "*at several doors
opposite*" (*Malcontent*, 5.1.0); atypical are enter "*at
three several doors*" (*Maid's Metamorphosis*, D4v), enter
two figures "*at several doors*" and a third "*in the midst*"
(*Patient Grissil*, 3.2.0); for a sampling of over fifty
entrances *at several doors* see *Woodstock*, 2; Folio
Richard III, 2213, 3.7.0; *Twelfth Night*, 656, 2.2.0; *Trial
of Chivalry*, I2v; *Antonio's Revenge*, 5.2.19; *Eastward Ho*,
A2r; *Insatiate Countess*, 2.2.0, 2.4.0, 3.3.0; Quarto *King
Lear*, F3r, 3.1.0; *Coriolanus*, 723, 1.8.0; *Woman's Prize*,
20, 29; *Love's Cure*, 198; *Maid of Honour*, 4.5.0;
Shoemaker a Gentleman, 5.1.0; *Lady's Trial*, 80; *Late
Lancashire Witches*, 218, 244; *Imposture*, B1r; for
"*Exeunt at several doors*" see *Antonio's Revenge*, 2.1.182;
Andromana, 207; figures also enter "*at several places*"
(*Wise Woman of Hogsdon*, 308), "*at two several places*"
(*Devil's Charter*, A3r), "*in several places, Sextus and
Valerius above*" (*Rape of Lucrece*, 243), at two doors and
"*stand at several ends of the Stage*" (*Queen*, 2507–8);
also common are directions to "*Enter several ways*"
(*1 Henry VI*, 720–1, 2.1.38; *Sir Thomas More*, 1675;
2 Seven Deadly Sins, 31; *2 Edward IV*, 98; *May Day*, 2.1.0;
Cruel Brother, 190), "*Exeunt several ways*" (*Doctor
Faustus*, B 742; *Philaster*, 95; *King and No King*, 213;
1 Iron Age, 287; *Queen of Aragon*, 342, 365; *Cruel Brother*,
164, 170; *Distresses*, 334; *Platonic Lovers*, 36; *News from
Plymouth*, 137, 181), "*go forth two several ways*" (*Devil's
Charter*, K4r), "*part several ways*" (*Timon of Athens*,
1579, 4.2.29; *Brazen Age*, 239), "*go off several ways*"
(*New Way to Pay*, 2.2.33); variations include "*Enter
three several ways the three Brothers*" (*Travels of Three
English Brothers*, 404), "*Enter at four several corners the
four winds*" (*Golden Age*, 78; see also *No Wit*, 4.3.148).

Also widely used for entrances/exits is *severally* to
mean "separately, not together" with the term often
indistinguishable from *at several doors*/*several ways*;
for a sampling of *enter severally* see *2 Seven Deadly Sins*,
36; *Sir Thomas More*, 1158–9; *Taming of the Shrew*, 1811,
4.1.178; *King John*, 2550, 5.6.0; *Thracian Wonder*, C1r,
C3r; *Hoffman*, 1918; *Four Prentices*, 223; Folio *King Lear*,
927, 2.1.0; 1075, 2.2.0; 1615, 3.1.0; *Sea Voyage*, 27, 58,
61; *Island Princess*, 116; *Late Lancashire Witches*, 187;
Match at Midnight, 75; for a sampling of *exeunt severally* see *Sir Thomas More*, 565, 583; *Thracian Wonder*,

D3v; *Fleer*, 5.2.32; *Philaster*, 120; *Little French Lawyer*, 403, 423; *Humorous Lieutenant*, 352, 353; *Herod and Antipater*, C2v; *Northern Lass*, 73; *Court Beggar*, 260; *Doubtful Heir*, D4v, D6v; *Politician*, K1r; variations include "*Exeunt all severally*" (*Four Plays in One*, 321), "*Enter severally at several doors*" (*Lust's Dominion*, 3.1.20), "*Enter Ancient, crying Brooms, and after him severally, four Soldiers, crying other things*" (*Loyal Subject*, 128), "*descend severally*" (*Four Plays in One*, 359), pass "*over the stage severally*" (*White Devil*, 3.1.64).

When applied to figures or objects, *several* can function as a *permissive* term wherein the exact number is not specified: "*Enter several strange shapes*" (*Tempest*, 1536, 3.3.19), "*a Masquerado of several shapes, and Dances*" (*Women Pleased*, 308), "*several branches of poppy*" (*Sejanus*, 5.177), "*several kinds of Sacrifice*" (*Faithful Friends*, 2483); objects include several **books** (*Jovial Crew*, 357), **papers** (*Fair Maid of the Inn*, 175; *Conspiracy*, D3v), **dishes** (*White Devil*, 4.3.19), **patches** (*Amends for Ladies*, 3.4.2–3), **trumpets** (*Devil's Law Case*, 5.6.2), **fireworks** (*Silver Age*, 159), **scepters** (*Histriomastix*, H3r), **trees** (*Gentlemen of Venice*, I1r), "*several pots of colors*" (*Two Merry Milkmaids*, L4r), "*several suit of clothes*" (*Goblins*, 3.7.58), enter "*stealing to several stands*" (*Broken Heart*, 3.2.16); atypical is "*Enter Theodosia and Phillipo on several Beds*" (*Double Marriage*, 246); actions include "*bow several ways*" (*Two Noble Kinsmen*, H1v, 3.6.93), "*severally stab him*" (*Roman Actor*, 5.2.74), "*fight their several Combats*" (*Seven Champions*, L1r), "*Kisses them severally*" (*New Way to Pay*, 2.2.11), **dance**/enter "*in several postures*" (*Fair Maid of the Inn*, 175; *City Madam*, 1.1.46), "*dancing severally by turns*" (*World Tossed at Tennis*, E3r), "*seat themselves at a Table severally*" (*Thracian Wonder*, C2r), "*trying several ways to wear his cloak and hat*" (*Twins*, E1v), "*The Ghosts use several gestures*" (*Unnatural Combat*, 5.2.278); see also *Dido*, 995; *2 If You Know Not Me*, 317; *Four Prentices*, 234; *Bonduca*, 118.

sewer

an attendant who superintends a **banquet** or the **service** for a meal: "*Enter an armed sewer, after him a company with covered dishes*" (*Wonder of a Kingdom*, 3.1.148), "*Enter an armed Sewer, after him the service of a Banquet*" (*Satiromastix*, 5.2.0), "*Enter a Sewer, and diverse Servants with Dishes and Service over the Stage*" (*Macbeth*, 473–4, 1.7.0); in *Epicœne* when a figure "*enters like a sewer*" (3.3.100) another comments that "Sir Amorous has his towel on already"; see also *Case Is Altered*, 1.3.0, 1.4.0; *Histriomastix*, C2v; *Bloody Brother*, 267.

sewing

an activity that (along with the presence of children and household servants) can establish the "place" as domestic, inside the **house**; typically women **enter** "*with their sewing works*" (*Sir Giles Goosecap*, 2.1.16), "*with work sewing a purse*" (*Woman Is a Weathercock*, 4.3.1–2), "*with needlework*" (*Atheist's Tragedy*, 4.1.0), and then "*set them down on two low stools and sew*" (*Coriolanus*, 361, 1.3.0); in *All Fools* Gazetta enters "*sewing*" and "*sits and sings sewing*" (2.1.221, 229), and in *1 Edward IV* Jane Shore enters "*with her work in her hand*" and "*sits sewing in her shop*" (63–4); see also *James IV*, 724–5; *Eastward Ho*, A4r; *Law Tricks*, 163; a man *sewing* is found in *Weakest Goeth* where a botcher "*hangs three or four pair of hose upon a stick, and falls to sewing one hose heel*" (227–8); see also **work**.

shackles

a restraint for **prisoners** comparable to **chains**, **fetters**, **gyves**, **irons**, **manacles**: "*in shackles, nightcap, plasters on his face*" (*Dick of Devonshire*, 941, also 1447, 1541), "*Enter Palemon as out of a Bush, with his Shackles*" (*Two Noble Kinsmen*, F2v, 3.1.30); those seeking to capture a rogue "*appear with Cords and Shackles*" (*English Traveller*, 81); atypical is "*like Amazon Captives, shackled with Golden Fetters, and pinioned with silken cords*" (*Amorous War*, C2v).

shake

used in a variety of actions; most common is *shaking* of the **head**: "*answers with shaking his head*" (Folio *Every Man In*, 4.2.50), "*Exit shaking his head, and shoulders*" (*Example*, G1r); see also *1 Henry VI*, 2448, 5.3.19; *Royal King*, 51; *Queen and Concubine*, 36; *Country Girl*, G2v; figures also *shake* **hands** (*Locrine*, 1208; *Princess*, H3r), *shake* in **fear** (*Bondman*, 3.2.51; *Launching of the Mary*, 2130), *shake* someone else (*Famous Victories*, D4v; *City Wit*, 363); other actions are "*Shakes his legs*" (*Inconstant Lady*, 3.4.4), "*shake their whips*" (*Bondman*, 4.2.128), "*Shakes the Ladder*" (*Duchess of Suffolk*, C4r), "*Shakes a purse*" (*Royal King*, 47; *Princess*, A4r), "*draws the naked Dagger from his girdle and shakes it*" (*Twins*, E2v); a **sound** effect calls for "*Shake Irons within*" (*Pilgrim*, 208, also 213) followed by the entrance of madmen; see also *Antipodes*, 279; *Money Is an Ass*, B3v; *Parson's Wedding*, 500.

shape

an equivalent to "form, guise" that can refer to (1) unusual figures or costumes, (2) **disguise**, and (3) the discarding of a disguise when a figure re-**enters** in his/her own *shape*; unusual *shapes* include "*in a fantas-*

tical shape" (*Antipodes*, 316), "*in the shape of a Dragon*" (*Brazen Age*, 175), **dancers** "*in odd shapes*" (*Love's Sacrifice*, 1847), "*a Masquerade of several shapes*" (*Women Pleased*, 308), "*four Boys shaped like Frogs*" (*Fair Maid of the Inn*, 201), "*diverse Spirits in shape of Dogs and Hounds*" (*Tempest*, 1929–30, 4.1.254, also 1536, 3.3.17; 1617, 3.3.82), and **devils** "*in a fearful shape*" (*Virgin Martyr*, 5.1.122), "*in a frightful shape*" (*If This Be Not a Good Play*, 4.4.38), "*in most ugly shape*" (*Devil's Charter*, A2v); disguises include "*second Luce in her boy's shape*" (*Wise Woman of Hogsdon*, 332) and devils in the *shape* of women: "*Erictho in the shape of Sophonisba, her face veiled*" (*Sophonisba*, 4.1.213), "*Spirit in shape of Katherine, vizarded*" (*Witch of Edmonton*, 3.1.70); see also *Mad World*, 4.1.29; *Silver Age* provides "*Ganymede shaped like Socia,*" "*Jupiter shaped like Amphitrio,*" "*Juno in the shape of old Beroe*" (98, 100, 148); for examples of reappearances *in his/her own shape*, a doctor enters "*like a Philosopher,*" exits, "*and returns in his own shape*" (*Very Woman*, 4.2.165), and Amaryllis first appears "*in the shape of Amoret,*" then reappears "*in her own shape*" (*Faithful Shepherdess*, 406, 408); see also *Doctor Faustus*, B 1013; *Mad World*, 5.2.177; *Fawn*, 5.469; *Fair Maid of Bristow*, D3r; *Two Merry Milkmaids*, H1r; *Broken Heart*, 3.1.0; *City Wit*, 363; *Telltale*, 1493–4; *Parson's Wedding*, 482; alternative locutions include re-entrances "*in his true attire*" (*Satiromastix*, 2.2.0), "*like himself*" (*2 Honest Whore*, 4.1.28), "*in her own apparel*" (*Night Walker*, 380); atypical is "*an Angel shaped like a patriarch*" (*Two Noble Ladies*, 1101).

shave

the tormentors of Edward II "*wash him with puddle water, and shave his beard away*" (*Edward II*, 2301), a **prisoner** appears "*his head shaved in the habit of a slave*" (*Believe as You List*, 2322–3), a **disguised** figure enters "*shaven in shepherd's habiliments*" (*Two Lamentable Tragedies*, H4r).

shawm

a wind instrument commonly called a **hoboy** that appears in two Brome directions: "*A Flourish of Shawms*" (*Jovial Crew*, 443; *Queen and Concubine*, 123); see also **waits**.

sheet

usually a **winding sheet** for a **corpse**: "*carrying Feliche's trunk in a winding sheet*" (*Antonio's Revenge*, 4.2.23), "*two winding sheets stuck with flowers*" (*Devil's Law Case*, 5.4.125); see also *Two Maids of More-Clacke*, F4r; *Love's Sacrifice*, 2763–4; in *Atheist's Tragedy* the **disguise** for a fake **ghost** is "*a sheet, a hair, and a beard*" (4.3.55); a

white sheet can be part of public penance so that Jane Shore enters "*in a white sheet barefooted with her hair about her ears, and in her hand a wax taper*" (*2 Edward IV*, 165), Dame Elinor "*barefoot, and a white sheet about her, with a wax candle in her hand*" (Quarto *2 Henry VI*, D2r, 2.4.16, also Folio 1188–9).

shield

a piece of protective **armor**, larger than a **buckler** or **target**, that served to ward off enemy blows and often bore an insignia or crest of the bearer's allegiance; a *shield* is linked to **battle** in "*armed with shields and swords*" (*Martyred Soldier*, 250), "*in this combat both having lost their swords and Shields*" (*1 Iron Age*, 300), "*his sword drawn, his body wounded, his shield struck full of darts*" (*Sophonisba*, 1.2.61, also 2.2.0, 5.2.32); see also *Antonio and Mellida*, 1.1.34; *Four Prentices*, 222, 224; more often the *shield* appears in a **ceremonial** context: "*deliver the shields to their several mistresses*" (*Insatiate Countess*, 2.1.48), "*investing him with sword, helmet, shield and spurs*" (*Duchess of Malfi*, 3.4.7); see also *Your Five Gallants*, I2v; *Faithful Friends*, 1049, 2824; the heraldic decoration is sometimes specified: "*Oswald bearing the Standard, Toclio the Shield, with the Red Dragon pictured in them*" and "*a King in Armor, his Shield quartered with thirteen Crowns*" (*Birth of Merlin*, G3v, G4r), "*Godfrey's Shield, having a Maidenhead with a Crown in it. Charles his Shield the Haberdasher's Arms*" (*Four Prentices*, 229, also 234), "*shields pictured with Neptune riding upon the Waves*" (*Thracian Wonder*, H3r); Henslowe's inventory lists "*one shield with three lions*" (*Diary*, App. 2, 80); see also *Three Lords of London*, B1r, G1v, and more; *Two Noble Ladies*, 1082.

shift

used as a verb to mean "exchange, change, transfer"; for an exchange of clothing two figures "*shift apparel*" (*Edmond Ironside*, 1226; *May Day*, 4.3.53), "*shift cloaks*" (*Fine Companion*, G3r); for a change of costume, in *Just Italian* a wooer is accompanied by friends "*shifted like his servants*" (230), in *Antipodes* "Now cast your Sea weeds off, and don fresh garments" is followed by "*Shift*" (264), in *Whore of Babylon* Time initially is dressed in **black** but after Truth awakens is "*shifted into light Colors*" (DS before Act 1, 36); for examples of *shift* not linked to clothing, a figure "*shifts folds and turns the paper*" to conceal what he has written (*Soddered Citizen*, 972–3) and Altofront speaks in his own **voice** to Celso but when Bilioso enters resumes his Malevole disguise and "*shifteth his speech*"

(*Malcontent*, 1.4.43); when the senators learn
Sejanus is out of favor they "*shift their places*"
(*Sejanus*, 5.609), and when Redcap "*Offers to strike*"
Gloster (who is disguised as a hermit), the latter
"*shifts Skink*" (also disguised as a hermit) "*into his
place*" (*Look about You*, 2630–1); Folio *Every Man Out*
sets up four pairs of figures, then "*Here they shift*"
(3.4.82) so as to change the pairings; see also Folio
Midsummer Night's Dream, 1460, [3.2.416].

ship

usually linked to personnel: "*the Master of the ship,
some Sailors, wet from sea*" (*Looking Glass for London*,
1368–9); for examples of *Master of a ship/Shipmaster/
Captain of a ship* see Quarto *2 Henry VI*, F1v, 4.1.0;
Captain Thomas Stukeley, 1994; *Caesar and Pompey*,
2.5.38; *Tempest*, 3, 1.1.0; *Love's Pilgrimage*, 265; *Fortune
by Land and Sea*, 413; *Dick of Devonshire*, 434; only in
Pericles does a figure enter "*a Shipboard*" (E1v, 3.1.0); in
Sea Voyage a call that a ship is departing is followed
by "*goes up to see the Ship*" (14); the results of a *shipwreck* can be displayed by an **as from** effect so that
figures enter "*all wet, looking about for shelter as shipwrecked*" (*Thracian Wonder*, B4v), "*all wet as newly shipwrecked and escaped the fury of the Seas*" (*Captives*,
653–4); see also **sea**.

shirt

widely used like the **nightgown** to indicate that a
male figure is **unready**, surprised, or vulnerable: "*in
his shirt, as started from bed*" (*Amends for Ladies*, 4.1.2),
"*The French leap over the walls in their shirts*" (*1 Henry VI*,
720, 2.1.38), "*six Citizens in their Shirts, barefoot, with
halters about their necks*" (*Edward III*, I3v); occasionally
figures enter with "*shirts nightcaps and Halters*" (*Wasp*,
534–5), "*in his nightgown and his shirt*" (*Alphonsus of
Germany*, B1r, F2r, G1r; *Humorous Day's Mirth*, 1.1.0;
Insatiate Countess, 3.1.121; *Parson's Wedding*, 500), but
more common are variations on *in his shirt*: "*bareheaded in his shirt: a pair of Pantoffles on*" (*Blurt*, 4.2.0),
"*in their shirts, as from Torments*" (*Shoemaker a
Gentleman*, 4.2.0), "*in their shirts, and without Hats*"
(*Thomas Lord Cromwell*, C2r); see also *Spanish Tragedy*,
2.5.0; *Old Wives Tale*, 587; *Two Lamentable Tragedies*,
C4r; *Hieronimo*, 11.85; *Ram Alley*, H3v; *Dumb Knight*,
165, 168; *Widow*, E4r; *Picture*, 4.2.130; *Vow Breaker*,
2.4.0, 41, 5.2.81; *Constant Maid*, E3v; *Example*, E3v;
Maid's Revenge, F4v; *News from Plymouth*, 193; for
examples of gender distinctions, in *Lust's Dominion* a
man enters "*in his shirt*" but the queen "*in her night
attire*" (2.3.87, 90, 91), and *Herod and Antipater* signals
"*at one door Alexandra in her petticoat; at another,*

Aristobulus the high Priest in his waistcoat or shirt" (B1r);
less common are *shirts* as murderous devices (*Brazen
Age*, 247–8; *Herod and Antipater*, C3r), materials for
sewing (*Woodstock*, 1015), "*a shirt of mail*" (*Sir Thomas
More*, 410–11; *Captain Thomas Stukeley*, 1114); see also
More Dissemblers, B8v; *Bloody Banquet*, 1142; actions
include "*showeth his shirt all bloody*" (*Woman in the
Moon*, B4v), "*strip themselves into their shirts, as to
vault*" (*White Devil*, 2.2.37), "*thrusts his dagger betwixt
Alphonso's doublet and shirt*" (*Twins*, D3r); Henslowe's
inventory includes five *shirts* (*Diary*, App. 2, 42).

shoot, shot

(1) as a verb, used for the onstage and offstage *shooting* of **pistols**, **muskets**, occasionally **arrows**, (2) as a
noun, a signal for a **sound** from **within**; with a few
exceptions (*Bonduca*, 156; *Women Beware Women*,
5.2.138) the *shooting* of arrows is threatened rather
than carried out: "*Enter one like a Cupid, offering to
shoot at him*" (*Nice Valour*, 156), "*Zenocia with Bow and
Quiver, an Arrow bent*" (*Custom of the Country*, 315);
usually the playgoer sees not the *shooting* of the
arrow but the results: "*Hercules shoots, and goes in:
Enter Nessus with an arrow through him, and Dejanira*"
(*Brazen Age*, 181); firearms are more likely to be *shot*
or **discharged** onstage: "*They shoot and run to him and
tread upon him*" (*White Devil*, 5.6.118); see also
Spanish Tragedy, 3.3.32; *2 Tamburlaine*, 4263, 4268;
Massacre at Paris, 823; *Alarum for London*, 203, 1078;
Devil's Charter, K4r; *Bloody Banquet*, 1522; for figures
who **offer** to shoot pistols see *2 If You Know Not Me*,
325–6; *Satiromastix*, 4.2.25; sometimes a pistol is
shot offstage: "*A Pistol shot within*" (*Lovers' Progress*,
109; Q2 *Bussy D'Ambois*, 5.4.72; *Rebellion*, 66;
1 Arviragus and Philicia, A10r), the anticipatory
warning "*John Bacon ready to shoot off a Pistol*" (*Love's
Pilgrimage*, 290/417); atypical are "*Shot with a
Thunderbolt*" (*Messalina*, 2187), "*the dragon shooting
fire*" (*Friar Bacon*, 1197).

As a noun, *shot* signals an offstage **sound**, with the
source sometimes specified as **chambers** (*Revenge of
Bussy*, 4.1.10; *World Tossed at Tennis*, E2r; *Renegado*,
5.8.16) or **ordnance** (*Massacre at Paris*, 338; Folio
Hamlet, 3906, 5.2.403); elsewhere the direction is "*a
peal of shot*" (*Antonio and Mellida*, 1.1.139; *2 If You Know
Not Me*, 338), "*small shot*" (*Devil's Charter*, D1r), or
simply *shot* (*Edward III*, E3r; Folio *Hamlet*, 3751,
5.2.283; Quarto *Othello*, D3v, 2.1.55; *1 Fair Maid of the
West*, 296, 316; *Love's Pilgrimage*, 292; *Double Marriage*,
343), as when a victory at **sea** is indicated by "*A great
Alarum and shot*" (*Fortune by Land and Sea*, 410); the
effects of an offstage *shot* can be acted out onstage:

"As they march upon the stage, the Lord Scales is struck down, and two Soldiers slain outright, with great shot from the town" (*2 Edward IV*, 101).

shop

used primarily for figures who (1) are **discovered** *in a shop*, (2) **enter** *in a shop*, (3) *sit*/at **work** *in*/*as* [*if*] *in a shop*; to discover a *shop* is to draw a **curtain** so as to reveal a tableau, sometimes with a figure **walking** by: *"Juniper a Cobbler is discovered, sitting at work in his shop and singing"* (*Case Is Altered*, 1.1.0), *"A Mercer's Shop discovered, Gartred working in it, Spendall walking by the Shop"* (*Greene's Tu Quoque*, B1r; see also *Renegado*, 1.3.0), *"They draw the Curtains from before Nature's shop, where stands an Image"* (*Woman in the Moon*, A2v), *"At the middle door, Enter Golding discovering a Goldsmith's shop, and walking short turns before it"* (*Eastward Ho*, A2r); for comparable discoveries see *Chaste Maid*, 1.1.0; *Anything for a Quiet Life*, C3r; *Shoemaker a Gentleman*, 1.2.0; *Mad Couple*, 55; occasionally signaled is *"A shop opened"* (*Match Me in London*, 2.1.0), and figures then enter; most elaborate is *Roaring Girl* where *"The three shops open in a rank: the first a Pothecary's shop, the next a Feather shop: the third a Seamster's shop: Mistress Gallipot in the first, Mistress Tiltyard in the next, Master Openwork and his wife in the third"* and then follow a series of signals for customers to be *"At the Feather shop now," "At the Seamster's shop now"* (2.1.0, 127, 137, 151, and more).

Most common is the locution *enter* **in** *the shop* that can be read either as a discovery or possibly as *enter* [*as if*] *in the shop* wherein the *shop* is **set forth** on the main **stage**: *"Enter Signior Alunio the Apothecary in his shop with wares about him"* (*Fleer*, 4.2.0), *"Enter Luce in a Seamster's shop, at work upon a laced Handkerchief, and Joseph a Prentice"* (*Wise Woman of Hogsdon*, 284), *"Enter in the shop two of Hobson's folks, and opening the shop"* (*2 If You Know Not Me*, 283), *"Enter Jane in a Seamster's shop working, and Hammond muffled at another door, he stands aloof"* (*Shoemakers' Holiday*, 3.4.0); see also *Case Is Altered*, 4.5.0; *Fair Maid of the Exchange*, 64; *1 Honest Whore*, 1.5.0, 3.1.0, 4.3.0; *Knight of the Burning Pestle*, 172; variations include *"Candido and his wife appear in the Shop"* (*2 Honest Whore*, 3.3.0), *"Enter two prentices, preparing the Goldsmith's Shop with plate"* (*1 Edward IV*, 63), *"Enter Boy in a Shop, cutting up square parchments"* (*Fair Maid of the Exchange*, 40); figures *in a shop* are directed to *sit*/*work*: *"Sit and work in the shop"* (*Fair Maid of the Exchange*, 41), *"Enter Hodge at his shop board"* with others *"at work"* (*Shoemakers' Holiday*, 4.1.0); after Mistress Shore enters *"with her work in her*

hand," "The boy departs, and she sits sewing in her shop" (*1 Edward IV*, 63–4); *Two Lamentable Tragedies* provides *"Sit in his shop," "Then Merry must pass to Beech's shop, who must sit in his shop," "the boy goeth into the shop," "coming to Beech's shop finds the boy murdered"* (A3v, B3v, C4r, G3v); other actions include *"runs to her shop"* (*Bartholomew Fair*, 3.4.98), *"Seldome having fetched a candle, walks off at the other end of the shop"* (*Amends for Ladies*, 2.1.71–2); an explicit *as* [*if*] signal is found in *Amends for Ladies*: *"Enter Seldome and Grace working as in their shop"* (2.1.1); atypical is *"Enter Lyon-rash to Fourchier sitting in his study: at one end of the stage: At the other end enter Vourcher to Velure in his shop"* (*Histriomastix*, F4r); see also *Eastward Ho*, A2v.

short

describes (1) offstage **music** or other **sound**, (2) actions or properties; four plays in the Shakespeare canon signal a *short* **alarum** with little apparent reason for the distinction (*1 Henry VI*, 608, 622, 1.5.14, 26; Folio *3 Henry VI*, 479, 1.4.21; Folio *Henry V*, 2463, 4.5.5; *All's Well*, 2007, 4.1.88); see also *Rape of Lucrece*, 250; elsewhere a *short* **flourish** comes usually at an entrance or exit (*Sophonisba*, 5.4.59; *Turk*, 286; *Two Noble Kinsmen*, E4v, 2.5.0; *Bonduca*, 127; *Faithful Friends*, 775; *Roman Actor*, 3.2.148); various one-off locutions suggest that *short* denotes a token effect or other brief actions, as found several times in the Marston canon: *"a short strain"* (*Antonio's Revenge*, 1.2.64), *"some short song"* (*Insatiate Countess*, 3.4.82; *Sophonisba*, 4.1.210), *"a short silence"* (*Sophonisba*, 2.1.103); other examples are *"short dance"* (*If This Be Not a Good Play*, 4.4.7; *Women Beware Women*, 5.2.50), *"short nimble antic"* (*Landgartha*, E4v), *"Short Curtsies"* (*Two Merry Milkmaids*, C4r), *"a short Thunder as the burst of a Battle"* (*Two Noble Kinsmen*, K4v, 5.1.61)–a pleased response from Mars; *short* limits onstage action with *"He is going out, but turns short"* (*Andromana*, 250), *"They seem to make some short discourse"* (*Antipodes*, 335); occasionally *short* describes properties: *"short swords under their robes"* (*Malcontent*, 5.5.66; see also *Eastward Ho*, A2r), *"short silver wands"* (*Henry VIII*, 1333, 2.4.0), and altogether unique *"suits of green moss, representing short grass"* (*Summer's Last Will*, 160).

shot
see **shoot**

shoulder, shoulders
found in a variety of locutions; **hair** can be *"hanging over his shoulders"* (*Locrine*, 1573–4), *"about her*

shoulders" (*Two Noble Kinsmen*, L1v, 5.1.136); for a surreptitious look "*One of the Guard peeps over his shoulder*" (*Brennoralt*, 2.1.36), "*They peruse the papers, Orco looking over their shoulders*" (*Distresses*, 358), "*They advance. Look over their shoulders*" (*Jews' Tragedy*, 1391–2); entrances *as from* an offstage meal include a *napkin* "*on his shoulder*" (*Roaring Girl*, 1.1.0; *Downfall of Huntingdon*, 166–8; *Humorous Day's Mirth*, 3.1.0; *Shoemakers' Holiday*, 5.4.0); *shoulders* can be linked to *carrying*: "*the body of the King, lying on four men's shoulders*" (*Massacre at Paris*, 1263), "*The boy comes in on Minos's shoulders*" (*Poetaster*, 3.4.345), "*Boy sings upon Bartello's Shoulder*" (*Women Pleased*, 294); to take someone into custody the figure in authority "*Takes him by the shoulder*" (*Bird in the Cage*, E3v), more often *claps* the individual "*on the shoulder*" (*2 Edward IV*, 123; *Great Duke of Florence*, 4.1.43; *Lady Mother*, 1302), with a *devil* sometimes doing the clapping (*Mad World*, 4.1.29; *New Trick*, 270); to show special favor a monarch enters "*leaning on the Cardinal's shoulder*" (*Henry VIII*, 317–18, 1.2.0), "*leaning on his shoulder and giving much grace unto him*" (*Two Merry Milkmaids*, H1v; see also *Summer's Last Will*, 104; *Captain Thomas Stukeley*, 2044–5); other actions include two sons "*bringing out their Mother one by one shoulder, and the other by the other*" (*Revenger's Tragedy*, H1v), "*stabs him into the arms and shoulders*" (*Edward I*, 894), "*Exit shaking his head, and shoulders*" (*Example*, G1r); atypical are "*a shoulder of mutton on a spit*" (*Friar Bacon*, 293–4), an *angel* described as having "*on his shoulders large wings*" (*Two Noble Ladies*, 1103).

shout

the roughly 130 examples almost always signal a *sound* from *within*: "*Shout within, they all start up*" (*Midsummer Night's Dream*, F4v, 4.1.138), "*After a triumphant shout within*" (*Alarum for London*, 799), "*A shout in the prison*" (*Eastward Ho*, H3v), "*After great shouts, enter Venus*" (*Brazen Age*, 192), "*A shout within, and enter a messenger*" (*Jews' Tragedy*, 113–16); for the basic *shout* or *shout within* see *As You Like It*, 376, 1.2.215; *Sejanus*, 5.736; *Antony and Cleopatra*, 2532, 4.4.23; *Coriolanus*, 47, 1.1.46; 3624, 5.4.51; *Hengist*, 1.1.0, 60; *False One*, 370; *Two Noble Ladies*, 61, 96, 798–9; *Appius and Virginia*, D1v, I2r; *Swisser*, 5.3.147; *Bashful Lover*, 4.3.33; *Amorous War*, D3v; *Antipodes*, 312; *Fair Favourite*, 234; *Lady Mother*, 2457–8; *Andromana*, 230; typically *shout* occurs in the context of *battle* together with other offstage sounds such as *flourish* (*Julius Caesar*, 174, 1.2.78, also 230, 1.2.131), *alarum* (*Shoemaker a Gentleman*, 3.5.0), *retreat* (Folio *Troilus*

and *Cressida*, 3520, 5.9.0), *trumpet* (*Two Noble Ladies*, 1226), *charges* (*White Devil*, 5.3.0); more elaborate directions include "*Drums and Trumpets sounds, with great shouts of the people*" (*Coriolanus*, 3705–6, 5.6.48), "*This short flourish of Cornets and Shouts within*" (*Two Noble Kinsmen*, E4v, 2.5.0, also M1v, M2r, 5.3.71, 77, 92), "*a great shout and noise*" (*Sir Thomas More*, 689); see also *Sir Thomas Wyatt*, 2.2.53; *Rape of Lucrece*, 240, 245; *Revenge of Bussy*, 4.1.10; *Silver Age*, 94, 126; *Faithful Friends*, 632–3; *Seven Champions*, E3v; other *shouts* with related sounds include "*After a noise of horns and shoutings, enter certain Huntsmen*" (*James IV*, 1548–9), "*A shout within, the Music, sound the Bells*" (*Queen's Exchange*, 478), "*Confused noise of betting within, after that a shout*" (*Hyde Park*, G4r); see also *Woodstock*, 2095; *More Dissemblers*, B7v; *Launching of the Mary*, 2798; sometimes the words *shouted* are given: "*Shout within, A Lancaster, A Lancaster*" (Folio *3 Henry VI*, 2653, 4.8.50), "*A loud shout within crying Ajax, Ajax*" (*1 Iron Age*, 338, also 340), "*Enter (after a shout crying Antonio)*" (*Rebellion*, 28), "*Shout within, Victory*" (*Queen and Concubine*, 4), "*Loud Music. Shouts within: Heaven preserve the Emperor, Heaven bless the Empress*" (*Emperor of the East*, 3.2.0); see also *Swetnam*, F1r, F2r; *Lovesick Court*, 100; occasionally the *shout* is produced onstage: "*The soldiers shout et exeunt*" (*Edmond Ironside*, 1036–8; see also *Andromana*, 220), "*with a shout carry him away*" (*Four Prentices*, 246), "*the Soldiers lift up Euphanes, and shout*" (*Queen of Corinth*, 60); see also *cry*.

show

used widely to signal (1) a *showing* of a property by one figure to another, (2) a *discovery* or other revelation, (3) a display of emotion, (4) other actions; the most common properties to *show* are something with *writing* such as a *paper* (Quarto *Richard III*, M2v, 5.3.302; *Night Walker*, 381; *Wasp*, 38, 1675; *Conspiracy*, D2v), *parchment* (*Cruel Brother*, 159), *petition* (*1 If You Know Not Me*, 216), *book* (*Spanish Tragedy*, 4.1.79; *King Leir*, 1511), *challenge* (*Island Princess*, 144), *bills* (Quarto *Every Man Out*, 1972), "*the confirmation of the marriage*" (*Messalina*, 1656–7), and most commonly a *letter*: "*Pericles shows the Letter to Cleon*" (*Pericles*, C1v, 2.Chorus.16; E1r, 3.Chorus.14; see also *John a Kent*, 30–1; *King Leir*, 1641; *Herod and Antipater*, I4v; *Fatal Contract*, E3r, F3v, G1r; *Politician*, F2v); elsewhere a figure "*writes and sometimes shows her*" (*Court Beggar*, 260); various *weapons* shown, usually as a threat, include a *poniard* (*Duchess of Malfi*, 3.2.71; *Fair Maid of the Inn*, 208; *Traitor*, 3.3.76), *dagger* (*Massacre at Paris*,

355; *Whore of Babylon*, 5.2.157), **pistol** (*White Devil*, 5.6.104; *Rule a Wife*, 228; *City Nightcap*, 179; *Duke's Mistress*, H4v), **piece** (*Staple of News*, 2.4.107), **halter** (*Epicœne*, 2.2.27), "*a Knife hanging by her side*" (*Woman Is a Weathercock*, 5.1.13), "*a keen knife which he pulls out of his sleeve*" (*Fatal Contract*, H4v), "*hot Pincers*" (*Edward I*, 897); also frequently *shown* is a **ring** (*Charlemagne*, 2762; *Maid of Honour*, 2.2.161; *Fine Companion*, H1r; *Hyde Park*, B3v; *Soddered Citizen*, 2784–6; *Princess*, F1r); other items *shown* include a **cabinet** (*Gentleman of Venice*, G1r), **picture** (*Fawn*, 1.2.108), **arm** (*Travels of Three English Brothers*, 362), **purse** (*Bartholomew Fair*, 3.5.36, 115, 137; *King Leir*, 1521), **skull** (*White Devil*, 5.4.135), **gold** (*Mad Couple*, 31), "*bag of money*" (*King Leir*, 1683; see also *Locrine*, 616), **key** and "*the dead*" (*Charlemagne*, 2270, 2729–30), "*her work*" (*Launching of the Mary*, 2393; *Queen and Concubine*, 110), **jewels** (*Valentinian*, 31; *Soddered Citizen*, 1230–1); a figure in **disguise** "*Pulls the coats up, and shows the breeches*" (*City Wit*, 371), and clothing is also the focus when figures *show* "*a swaddled leg*" (*Damoiselle*, 457), "*the habit, the cord, etc.*" (*Novella*, 155), "*his shirt all bloody*" (*Woman in the Moon*, B4v).

Less often *show* indicates a figure or object being revealed or discovered: "*draws the curtains and shows Duke Humphrey in his bed*" (Quarto *2 Henry VI*, E3r, [3.2.146]), "*Shows his dead son*" (*Spanish Tragedy*, 4.4.88), "*Draw the curtain and show the picture*" (*Fatal Contract*, B3v, also I4r), "*shows himself to be Antifront*" (*Fleer*, 5.5.104); see also *Old Wives Tale*, 424; *Pericles*, G3r, 4.Chorus.22; elsewhere *show* signals the appearance of previously hidden figures: "*stamps with his foot, and the Soldiers show themselves*" (Folio *3 Henry VI*, 189–90, 1.1.169), "*Musicians show themselves above*" (*Late Lancashire Witches*, 216), "*leads him to the door, and shows him a Guard*" (*Aglaura*, 1.6.46); for more see *Rare Triumphs*, 1739; MS *Bonduca*, 1048–9; *Match at Midnight*, 45; *King John and Matilda*, 77; atypical is "*some show of wonder*" (*Night Walker*, 380); *show* signals the expression of emotion with "*in show frighted*" (*Amorous War*, G4r), "*Stops his ears, shows he is troubled with the Music*" (*Captain*, 297), "*showing very sad countenance*" (*Fedele and Fortunio*, 3), "*shows several humors and moods*" (*Your Five Gallants*, C1r), "*shows signs of joy*" (*Conspiracy*, H4r), "*shows his tongue*" (*Edmond Ironside*, 512–13); other notable uses include "*Alonzo's ghost appears to De Flores in the midst of his smile, startles him, showing him the hand whose finger he had cut off*" (*Changeling*, 4.1.0), "*shows him his son's breast*" (*Antonio's Revenge*, 4.2.68), "*shows her his Arms besmeared with blood*" (*Just Italian*, 255); see also *Battle*

of *Alcazar*, 26; *Alphonsus of Aragon*, 475–6, 492; *Valiant Welshman*, G1r; *Welsh Ambassador*, 820; see also **dumb show**.

shut

figures are directed to *shut* a **door** (*Thomas Lord Cromwell*, C4r; Quarto *Every Man Out*, 3825–6; *Amends for Ladies*, 5.2.130), **tomb** (*Widow's Tears*, 4.2.178, 4.3.77, 5.3.60, 177), **lantern** (*Distresses*, 293), **curtains** (Q1 *Romeo and Juliet*, I2v, 4.5.95; *Downfall of Huntingdon*, 56; *Parson's Wedding*, 407), and be *shut in* (*Lust's Dominion*, 1.1.145; *Messalina*, 754), *shut out* (*David and Bethsabe*, 319); variations include "*follows them to gates, and is shut in*" (*Coriolanus*, 538–9, 1.4.46), "*Enter one and opens the door, in which Lamira and Anabel were shut, they in all fear*" (*Little French Lawyer*, 440); atypical is an **armed** figure with his "*beaver shut*" (*Sophonisba*, 5.3.6).

sick

of the many ill, **wounded** or dying figures fewer than thirty are actually specified as *sick*; most of the signals are for figures to **enter** so that they are **led** in *sick* often accompanied by appropriate figures and properties: "*two leading the Pursuivant sick*" (*Look about You*, 1615), "*Katherine Dowager, sick, led between Griffith, her Gentleman Usher, and Patience her Woman*" (*Henry VIII*, 2548–50, 4.2.0), "*Frank sick, Physicians, and an Apothecary*" (*Monsieur Thomas*, 120), "*Isabella sick Picentio as a doctor with her water*" (*Telltale*, 1381–2), "*discovered sick, Queen, Doctors*" (*Politician*, H1v); *sick* figures often appear in/on a **bed/couch**: "*A bed thrust out, Antoninus upon it sick, with Physicians about him*" (*Virgin Martyr*, 4.1.0); see also *Two Lamentable Tragedies*, B1r; *Martyred Soldier*, 175; *Wits*, 183; *Princess*, E1r; equally common are entrances *sick* in a **chair**: "*Bedford brought in sick in a Chair*" (*1 Henry VI*, 1469–70, 3.2.40); see also *Valentinian*, 76; *Herod and Antipater*, H3r; *Wonder of a Kingdom*, 2.1.0; for other figures identified as *sick* see Folio *Richard III*, 1121, 2.1.0; *Richard II*, C3r, 2.1.0; *Grim the Collier*, I5r; *Atheist's Tragedy*, 1.2.191, 3.4.54; occasionally figures get *sick* onstage: "*is sick on the sudden*" (*Mad Lover*, 55), "*then enters Death and strikes him, he growing sick*" (*Birth of Merlin*, G4r), "*She takes leave of her Mother, seeming to complain of being sick*" (*City Wit*, 358); atypical are "*Enter Fredeline, creeping in, as he were sick*" (*Platonic Lovers*, 100), a figure pretending to be poisoned who "*Counterfeits a sick voice, sitting*" (*Albovine*, 102); for *sick* figures identified by means of costume see **gown**, **nightcap**.

side

the roughly eighty-five examples are (1) found mostly in entrances, *exits*, and the positioning of figures in relation to an object or another figure in locutions such as *one side, other side, each side, both sides* but occasionally as (2) a verb (to *side with*) or the related noun ("faction, cause"), (3) a *weapon* at one's *side*; most common are versions (usually when figures *enter*) of *one side/another side* where *side* is an equivalent to *door/way/end*: "*Enter all the Greeks on one side, all the Trojans on the other*" (1 *Iron Age*, 302); see also *Edward I*, 101; Folio 2 *Henry VI*, 3–6, 1.1.0; 2 *Edward IV*, 130, 183; *Histriomastix*, F2v; *Lust's Dominion*, 4.2.116; *Look about You*, 76; *Escapes of Jupiter*, 1442–3; *Four Prentices*, 176; *Faithful Shepherdess*, 437; 1 *Fair Maid of the West*, 298; *Faithful Friends*, 2486–7; *Witch of Edmonton*, 4.2.69; *Broken Heart*, 4.4.0; *Duchess of Suffolk*, H3r; *Lovesick Court*, 163; *Rebellion*, 53; *Noble Stranger*, B1r, I2r; related locutions are *both sides* (*Edward I*, 1822; Quarto 2 *Henry VI*, B3r, [1.3.100]; *Lust's Dominion*, 4.2.116; *Hieronimo*, 10.32; *Escapes of Jupiter*, 122; 1 *Iron Age*, 299; *Unnatural Combat*, 2.1.114), *either side* (*Honest Lawyer*, F4r; *Rape of Lucrece*, 187; *Swetnam*, G2r; *Perkin Warbeck*, 4.3.0; *Queen*, 1029), *the other side* (*Sir Giles Goosecap*, 4.2.141; *Monsieur D'Olive*, 5.2.9; *New Academy*, 77), *each side* (*Battle of Alcazar* plot, 18, 86; *Henry VIII*, 890–1, 2.1.53; 1346–7, 2.4.0; 3040, 5.2.35; *Knight of Malta*, 161); detailed examples include "*place him on one side of the altar*" (*Broken Heart*, 5.3.0; see also *Chabot*, 3.2.0), "*on his right side*" (*Henry VIII*, 319–20, 1.2.0), "*kneeling on the left side of the Chair*" (*King John and Matilda*, 29), "*sitting on either side of the stall*" (*Eastward Ho*, B2r), "*the Pope taketh his place, three Cardinals on one side and captains on the other*" (*Devil's Charter*, L1r), "*his father and his wife on each side*" (*Chabot*, 3.1.0), "*four stand on one side, and four on the other*" (Folio 3 *Henry VI*, 2027–8, 4.1.6), "*with trailing the Colors on both sides depart*" (1 *Iron Age*, 345); occasionally an implicit *of the stage* is made explicit: "*at one side of the stage*" (*Locrine*, 1461; *No Wit*, 4.3.40), "*at another side of the Stage*" (*Caesar and Pompey*, 5.2.161), "*sit on the two sides of the stage, confronting each other*" (*New Inn*, 3.2.0).

For examples of the verb to *side with* see *English Moor*, 8; *Gentleman of Venice*, D3v; a *side* can be a faction: "*They fight, and Momford's side wins*" (*Blind Beggar of Bednal Green*, 109); see also *Hoffman*, 1187; *Lust's Dominion*, 4.2.135; *Aglaura*, 3.1.18; *by/at one's side* can be a person (*Four Plays in One*, 311) but usually a weapon such as a *pistol/dagger* (*Satiromastix*, 4.2.0;

Woman Is a Weathercock, 5.1.13; *Unnatural Combat*, 3.3.36; *Seven Champions*, D3v; *Twins*, E1v), most commonly a *sword/rapier* (*Wounds of Civil War*, 253; *Death of Huntingdon*, 925–6; 1 *Edward IV*, 57; *Your Five Gallants*, I3r; *Roaring Girl*, 2.1.217; *Albovine*, 105); related are "*an arrow in his side*" (*Gentleman Usher*, 4.1.10), "*Beats his fingers against his sides*" (*Duchess of Suffolk*, C3v); other usages include "*side by side*" (*Henry VIII*, 1342, 2.4.0), *bed's side* (*Alphonsus of Germany*, B2r; *Witch of Edmonton*, 4.2.69; *Love's Sacrifice*, 1271), a *side* of *paper* (*Soddered Citizen*, 961–3), "*Scutcheons and Garlands hanging on the sides*" of a *hearse* (1 *Honest Whore*, 1.1.0), "*set a ladder to the side of the litter*" (*Edward I*, 1015), "*casting one side of his cloak under his arm*" (*Warning for Fair Women*, D2v); see also *Arraignment of Paris*, 827; *Histriomastix*, C2v; *Blurt*, 5.3.0; *Princess*, H3r.

sigh

a rarely used signal, usually simply *sigh* (*Humorous Day's Mirth*, 2.1.136; *Blind Beggar of Bednal Green*, 42; *Honest Man's Fortune*, 237; *Jovial Crew*, 419; *Goblins*, 1.3.23, 42); the few more detailed directions are "*weeps and sighs*" (*Brennoralt*, 1.4.33, also 36), "*looks on the Queen, sighs, and goes in again*" (*Queen of Aragon*, 393).

sign

(1) usually part of a signal for a mimed action but can refer to (2) the *signs* of the Zodiac, (3) a *sign* that identifies a place; directions for actions/*gestures* include "*gives a sign*" (*Prophetess*, 363), "*threatens him by signs*" (*Death of Huntingdon*, 1351, also 928), "*Answered still by signs*" (*Unnatural Combat*, 5.2.297), "*in dumb signs, Courts him*" (*Westward Ho*, 4.2.52), "*expressing all signs of joy*" (*Bloody Banquet*, 851–2); see also *Warning for Fair Women*, E3v; *Whore of Babylon*, DS before Act 1, 51; *Conspiracy*, H4r, I4v, K4r; most common especially in *dumb shows* is the locution *make signs*: "*makes signs of consent*" (*Four Prentices*, 178), "*takes their hands and makes signs to marry them*" (*Maidenhead Well Lost*, 144, also 152), "*makes signs for a knife to mend his pen*" (*Spanish Tragedy*, 4.4.198); for an example of the Zodiac, figures in a *masque* enter "*with the twelve signs, made like banqueting-stuff*" (*No Wit*, 2.1.89); for an example of a *sign* that marks a specific place, "*Richard kills him under the sign of the Castle in Saint Albans*" (Quarto 2 *Henry VI*, H2r, 5.2.65; see also *Bartholomew Fair*, 3.2.57); Henslowe's inventory includes "*one sign for Mother Redcap*" (*Diary*, App. 2, 79).

silent, silence

although *silences* of various kinds are integral to performance, these specific terms are found in only ten
plays; most notable is the climactic moment in
Coriolanus where after Volumnia's pleas in behalf of
Rome, Coriolanus *"Holds her by the hand silent"* (3539,
5.3.182); in *Second Maiden's Tragedy* after the Lady's
body is brought in the Tyrant *"stands silent awhile
letting the Music play"* (2227–8); figures are directed
to *enter* *"silent all"* for a surprise attack (Folio *3 Henry
VI*, 2246–7, 4.3.22), *"silentus"* (MS *Poor Man's Comfort*,
2222), and, after entering, a pair *"salute with silence at
the door"* (*Humorous Courtier*, I2v, also I3r); for an *exit*
"Soliman dies, and they carry him forth with silence"
(*Soliman and Perseda*, I2r); other usages include *"Silent
actions of passions, kiss her hand"* (*2 Arviragus and
Philicia*, F11v), *"present Sophonisba with a paper, which
she having perused, after a short silence, speaks"*
(*Sophonisba*, 2.1.103), *"silent congratulation"* between
two groups during which a figure enters *above*
(*Messalina*, 2229–30); in *Winter's Tale* "Silence" is set
forth as an apparent direction but is often changed
by editors to a word spoken by the officer to quiet
the crowd (1185, 3.2.10); this *silence* could be directed
at Hermione who is not to respond verbally to the
order to "appear in person here in court," as may be
indicated by a comparable moment in *Henry VIII*
where, in response to "Katherine Queen of
England, / Come into the Court" she *"makes no
answer"* but *"rises out of her Chair, goes about the Court,
comes to the King, and kneels at his Feet. Then speaks"*
(1363–5, 2.4.12).

silk

a rarely cited fabric; figures are directed to *"tear the
Silks out of the shops"* (*Histriomastix*, G1r), and a late
Caroline play provides an entrance *"like Amazon
Captives, shackled with Golden Fetters, and pinioned with
silken cords"* (*Amorous War*, C2v).

silver

specified in a variety of contexts, often for *ceremonies* and other special effects; a royal entrance
includes *"two Vergers, with short silver wands," "two
Priests, bearing each a Silver Cross," "a Sergeant at Arms,
bearing a Silver Mace: Then two Gentlemen bearing two
great Silver Pillars"* (*Henry VIII*, 1333, 1338–42, 2.4.0);
Two Noble Ladies provides *"two Tritons with silver
trumpets"* and an *angel* with *"a blue table full of silver
letters"* (1166–7, 1102), and in *Old Fortunatus* kings
"chained in silver Gyves" follow Fortune, and Vice

wears a *garment* *"painted before with silver half
moons"* (1.1.63, 1.3.0); a *silver* hind is used for a
sacrifice (*Two Noble Kinsmen*, L1v, 5.1.136), a silver *rod*
is used for *magic* (*Devil's Charter*, A2r; *Twins*, E1v), a
silver oar is associated with ceremonies linked to
the *sea* (*2 Edward IV*, 136; *Fortune by Land and Sea*,
427); *silver* is associated with containers for *drink*: a
silver *goblet* (*Doctor Faustus*, A 985), *bowl* (*Swaggering
Damsel*, B1r), *"Silver Can of Sack"* (*Jovial Crew*, 418),
"silver Can and Napkin" (*New Academy*, 19); see also
Whore of Babylon, DS before Act 1, 37; *Golden Age*, 11;
Amorous War, E2v.

sing, singing

widely used stage business (roughly 320 signals)
with lyrics for the *song* sometimes given; the typical
direction simply says that a figure *sings* (*Looking
Glass for London*, 1687; *Downfall of Huntingdon*, 1582;
Midsummer Night's Dream, C3r, 2.2.8; *Twelfth Night*,
738, 2.3.46; Q2 *Hamlet*, K4r, 4.5.23; *All Fools*, 2.1.407;
Revenge of Bussy, 1.2.24; *2 Honest Whore*, 5.2.298;
Epicœne, 1.1.22; *Two Noble Kinsmen*, I3r, 4.1.152;
Martyred Soldier, 241; *Changeling*, 3.3.88; *Maid's
Revenge*, I3r; *Soddered Citizen*, 1582; '*Tis Pity*, 4.3.59;
Money Is an Ass, C2r; *English Moor*, 13; *Damoiselle*, 380;
Jovial Crew, 445; *Goblins*, 3.2.71); another basic signal
is for figures to *enter* singing: *"all the Friars to sing the
Dirge"* (*Doctor Faustus*, A 914), *"the harvest men singing,
with women in their hands"* (*Old Wives Tale*, 532),
"Enchanter, with spirits singing" (*Gentleman Usher*,
1.2.47), *"Citizens carrying boughs, boys singing after
them"* (*Island Princess*, 121), *"Calis and her Train with
lights, singing"* (*Mad Lover*, 59), *"like a Sowgelder,
singing"* (*Beggar's Bush*, 234); for more see *Arraignment
of Paris*, 709; *Gallathea*, 4.2.0; *Sir Thomas More*, 1080;
Measure for Measure, 1769, 4.1.0; *Fair Maid of the
Exchange*, 32; *Malcontent*, 5.1.0; *Winter's Tale*, 1668,
4.3.0; *Two Noble Kinsmen*, B1r, 1.1.0; *More Dissemblers*,
B7v; occasionally figures *exit* singing: *"The fifth Act
being done, let the Consort sound a cheerful Galliard, and
every one take hands together, depart singing"* (*Fedele and
Fortunio*, 1807–9), *"they rank themselves and go out the
Choir singing"* (*Love's Sacrifice*, 1819–20); see also *Loyal
Subject*, 130; elsewhere figures *dance* and *sing*: *"Here
enter a company of shepherds, and dance and sing"* (*David
and Bethsabe*, 753), *"The Morris sing and dance"* (*Jack
Drum's Entertainment*, A4r), *"a troupe of Indians, singing
and dancing wildly about him"* (*Four Plays in One*, 360),
"capers and sings" (*Fair Maid of the Exchange*, 71), *"sings
and reels"* (*Country Captain*, C6v); see also *John a Kent*,
781; *Summer's Last Will*, 211; *Maid's Metamorphosis*, B3v,

C4r, F1r; *Widow's Tears*, 5.1.31; *Country Girl*, D1r;
Bride, 51.

More detailed signals to *sing* include an instrument: "*Ophelia playing on a Lute, and her hair down singing*" (Q1 *Hamlet*, G4v, 4.5.20), "*Ariel, invisible playing and singing*" (*Tempest*, 519, 1.2.374), "*while Œnone singeth, he pipeth*" (*Arraignment of Paris*, 287); see also *Fedele and Fortunio*, 192–3; *Midas*, 4.1.108; *Cobbler's Prophecy*, 999–1000; *Dutch Courtesan*, 1.2.145; other directions call for accompanying **music**: "*Music suddenly plays, and Birds sing*" (*Blurt*, 4.2.0), "*A noise of still music; and Enter the high Priest with attendants, Guards, and Choristers: they sing*" (*Jews' Tragedy*, 2147–8, also 2215–17); see also *Golden Age*, 27; elsewhere details about the song are given: "*Here the lady sings a Welsh song*" (1 *Henry IV*, F3v, 3.1.244; see also *John a Kent*, 572–3), "*singeth an old song called the wooing of Colman*" and "*the enamored shepherd singeth his passion of love*" (*Arraignment of Paris*, 721, 536), "*sing to the tune of Who list to lead a Soldier's life*" (*Edward I*, 455), "*Here they sing the three men's Song*" (1 *Edward IV*, 52), "*Music sounds a while; and they sing, Boire a le Fountaine*" (*Wisdom of Doctor Dodypoll*, 463–4, 471, 477, 480), "*Sings part of the old Song*" (*Court Beggar*, 247), "*Monks and Friars, singing their Procession*" (*Doctor Faustus*, B 892; see also *Hengist*, 1.1.28), "*Sings a Catch*" (*Goblins*, 3.2.27; see also *Wits*, 209), "*sing this following Song in four or five parts, to a pleasing Tune*" (*Landgartha*, F1r); see also *Old Wives Tale*, 534; *Histriomastix*, C1r; *Maid's Metamorphosis*, F2v; 1 *Honest Whore*, 2.1.0; *Bartholomew Fair*, 3.5.94; *Claracilla*, F12v; *Distresses*, 305; *singing* is several times linked to **work**: "*a Cobbler is discovered, sitting at work in his shop and singing*" (*Case Is Altered*, 1.1.0; see also *Locrine*, 569–70; *Cobbler's Prophecy*, 52–3), "*with their sewing works and sing*" (*Sir Giles Goosecap*, 2.1.16), "*sits and sings sewing*" (*All Fools*, 2.1.229); other directions include "*sings drunkenly*" (*Tempest*, 1223, 2.2.177), "*singing fantastically*" (*Antonio and Mellida*, 2.1.61), "*The nightingales sing*" (*Dutch Courtesan*, 2.1.68; see also *Jovial Crew*, 358, 361), "*they bring him singing unto Victoria's window*" (*Fedele and Fortunio*, 1409–13), "*Corporal and Watch above singing*" (*Knight of Malta*, 116), "*An Angel ascends from the cave, singing*" (*Martyred Soldier*, 241), "*Nuns Discovered singing*" (*Imposture*, C3r), "*A confused noise within of laughing and singing, and one crying out*" (*Jovial Crew*, 386); see also *Love's Metamorphosis*, E2r, E2v; Q1 *Romeo and Juliet*, E2v, 2.4.133; Quarto *Merry Wives*, G2r, 5.5.36; G3r, 5.5.102; *Tempest*, 1003, 2.1.299; *Second Maiden's Tragedy*, 1894; *Constant Maid*, H1v; *Court Beggar*, 247; *Variety*, D9r.

sink

examples are divided evenly between figures who (1) **descend** through the **trapdoor**, (2) **fall** in a **swoon** or **dead**; figures *sink* through the trap, frequently to **hell**: "*The Devils sink roaring*" (*Two Noble Ladies*, 1860); see also *Arraignment of Paris*, 462 (here a **tree** sinks); *Alphonsus of Aragon*, 970; Quarto 2 *Henry VI*, C1r, 1.4.40; *If This Be Not a Good Play*, 5.3.150; *Silver Age*, 139; *Brazen Age*, 176, 231; *Virgin Martyr*, 5.1.152, 5.2.238; *Messalina*, 2191; *Seven Champions*, C2v; figures also *sink* to the stage in a **faint** (*Birth of Merlin*, B4v; *English Traveller*, 91; *Just Italian*, 277; *Sparagus Garden*, 130, 217; *Lovesick Court*, 106, 116); a variant is "*She sinks in his arms*" (*Downfall of Huntingdon*, 213); in *Sophonisba* first "*She sinks into Massinissa's arms*" in joy, then again later, dead (5.3.34, 106); dying figures also *sink* to the stage (*Warning for Fair Women*, H1v; *Brazen Age*, 254; *Virgin Martyr*, 4.3.181; *Queen's Exchange*, 487, 493).

sit

of the roughly 185 examples (1) most specify only *sit/sit down/sitting* but others link *sitting* to (2) **work**, (3) places such as **shop** and **study**, (4) **chairs** and **tables**, (5) activities such as **sleeping** and **reading**; in addition to simple *sit/sit down* figures are directed to *sit up/upright* (*Death of Huntingdon*, 687, 963; *Two Maids of More-Clacke*, G2r; *Witch of Edmonton*, 4.2.69), **together** (*Devil's Charter*, L4r), **close** (*David and Bethsabe*, 1826, 1842; *Herod and Antipater*, F3v), **still** (*Arraignment of Paris*, 621), **sadly** (*David and Bethsabe*, 679), *by another* (*Amends for Ladies*, 2.1.72; *Devil's Law Case*, 3.3.0); women and tradesmen *sit at/to work* (*James IV*, 725; *Monsieur D'Olive*, 2.2.0; *Launching of the Mary*, 2398), "*in his shop*" (*Two Lamentable Tragedies*, B3v, G3v), "*on his stool*" (*Cobbler's Prophecy*, 52–3), "*at his desk*" (*Dumb Knight*, 158); more detailed are "*sitting at work in his shop*" (*Case Is Altered*, 1.1.0), "*sitting on either side of the stall*" (*Eastward Ho*, B2r), "*sits sewing in her shop*" (1 *Edward IV*, 64), "*sits working on a piece of Cushion work*" (*Wisdom of Doctor Dodypoll*, 3–4, also 1311), "*a Shoemaker sitting upon the stage at work*" (*George a Greene*, 971–2), merchant's men who "*sit down to write Tickets*" (*If This Be Not a Good Play*, 2.2.0); related locutions are "*sit in council*" (*Rebellion*, 29), "*sitting at his master's door*" (*Two Lamentable Tragedies*, C4r; see also *Warning for Fair Women*, B2v), "*sit in state*" (*Staple of News*, 2.5.44; see also *Histriomastix*, H3r).

For *sitting* linked to a specific place, figures are directed to *sit in a* **tent** (*Edward I*, 1932; Folio *Richard*

III, 3685–6, 5.3.222), *arbor* (Q1 *Hamlet*, F3r, [3.2.135]), *study* (*Thomas Lord Cromwell*, D1r; *Histriomastix*, F4r; *Satiromastix*, 1.2.0), *closet* (*Rebellion*, 51), *cabin* (*Faithful Shepherdess*, 437), *chariot* (*Four Plays in One*, 334, 363) and sit "*to the banquet*" (*Spanish Tragedy*, 1.4.127), to/at/about a *table* (*Warning for Fair Women*, D1r; *Edmond Ironside*, 4; *Insatiate Countess*, 1.1.0; *Faithful Friends*, 2486–7; *Staple of News*, 5.4.0; *Rebellion*, 84), "*under her Canopy*" (*Humorous Courtier*, I3r), "*under a tree together*" (*Arraignment of Paris*, 249), "*behind a Curtain*" (*Lovers' Progress*, 104; see also *Sir Giles Goosecap*, 5.2.132); *sitting* is linked to a *bed* (*Antonio's Revenge*, 3.2.72; *What You Will*, B3v; *Princess*, E1v), most commonly a *chair* (*Alphonsus of Aragon*, 501; Folio *3 Henry VI*, 2258, 4.3.27; *Amends for Ladies*, 2.3.1, 5.2.84; *Lust's Dominion*, 1.1.0; *Trial of Chivalry*, D1r; *Woman Is a Weathercock*, 3.2.69; *Devil's Charter*, C2r; *Match Me in London*, 5.3.0; *Fatal Dowry*, 4.1.0; *'Tis Pity*, 3.6.0); *sitting* figures can be *sleeping* (*Old Wives Tale*, 843; *2 Tamburlaine*, 3673; *Doctor Faustus*, B 1551; *Death of Huntingdon*, 925; *Herod and Antipater*, L1r), *reading/writing* (*Edmond Ironside*, 1159; *What You Will*, C4r; *If This Be Not a Good Play*, 4.4.0; *Henry VIII*, 1101, 2.2.61; *Fair Favourite*, 251; *Love and Honour*, 143), "*weeping and praying*" (*2 Edward IV*, 167; see also *Messalina*, 2520); other actions include: "*sit and whisper*" (*Histriomastix*, F4v), "*sits on his knee*" (*Woman Hater*, 141), "*tripped up his heels in scuffle and sits on him*" (*Fatal Contract*, H4v), "*The maids sit down at her feet mourning*" (*Broken Heart*, 4.4.0; see also *Alphonsus of Aragon*, 935), "*sit to hear*" a *prologue* (*Histriomastix*, C1r), David "*sits above viewing*" Bethsabe (*David and Bethsabe*, 23); atypical are Jupiter "*sitting upon an Eagle*" (*Cymbeline*, 3126–7, 5.4.92), Pope Alexander discovering "*the devil sitting in his pontificals*" (*Devil's Charter*, L3v), "*A Crocodile sitting on a river's bank*" (*Locrine*, 961–2), Banquo's ghost who "*sits in Macbeth's place*" (*Macbeth*, 1299, 3.4.36), a Court of Love where two figures "*sit on the two sides of the stage, confronting each the other*" (*New Inn*, 3.2.0).

skirmish

an onstage *fight* between two or more representatives of opposing sides in a conflict; like the more frequently used *excursions* this term is given little explanation or dialogue description: "*Then enter again in Skirmish Iachimo and Posthumus; he vanquisheth and disarmeth Iachimo, and then leaves him*" (*Cymbeline*, 2896–7, 5.2.0); in *1 Henry VI* "*Mayor of London, and his Officers*" is followed by "*Here they skirmish again*" (425–7, 1.3.56; 441, 1.3.69, also 629, 1.5.32), and later

in this play three servingmen "*Enter in skirmish with bloody Pates*" (1298, 3.1.85, also 1305, 3.1.91); elsewhere the phrasing and punctuation make it difficult to know if a signal refers to the *skirmish* itself or subsequent action: "*Pyrocles fights with them, Basilius comes in with a two handed sword, after some skirmish Enter Philonax and Calander with a guard; the Rebels beaten off*" (*Arcadia*, E2r), "*Skirmish: Queen taken, Matilda rescued*" (*Death of Huntingdon*, 1748); Peele twice specifies duration probably to indicate a particularly fierce *battle*: "*A long Skirmish, and then enter his brother*" (*Battle of Alcazar*, 1336–7), "*Alarum, a charge, after long skirmish, assault, flourish. Enter King Edward with his train and Baliol prisoner*" (*Edward I*, 2207); for other examples of the basic *skirmish* see *Hengist*, 2.3.0; *Vow Breaker*, 1.3.128, 4.1.24; the phrasing of a direction in *Devil's Charter* suggests offstage effects: "*Alexander with his company off the walls, ordnance going off (after a little skirmish within) he summons from the Castle with a trumpet*" (D3v).

skirt

specified only twice with neither example a woman's *garment*; in *Goblins* a figure "*pulls one of the Fiddlers by the skirt*" (4.1.96), and in *Yorkshire Tragedy* a father "*takes up the child by the skirts of his long coat in one hand and draws his dagger with the other*" (506–8).

skull

each use of this property–elsewhere a *death's head*– has symbolic implications: "*a servant setting out a Table, on which he places a skull, a picture, a book and a Taper*" (*1 Honest Whore*, 4.1.0), "*Vindice, with the skull of his love dressed up in Tires*" (*Revenger's Tragedy*, F1r), "*Ghost, in his leather cassock and breeches, boots, a cowl, a pot of lily-flowers with a skull in it*" and "*The Ghost throws earth upon him and shows him the skull*" (*White Devil*, 5.4.123, 135), figures with "*the flesh with a skull all bloody*" (*Bloody Banquet*, 1921), "*a skull, made into a drinking bowl*" (*Albovine*, 38).

sleep, asleep, sleeping

widely used (roughly 140 examples) most commonly in the signal simply to *sleep*; for a sampling see *Taming of a Shrew*, F3r; *Famous Victories*, C3v; Folio *Richard III*, 3560, 5.3.117; Folio *Midsummer Night's Dream*, 676, 2.2.26; 718, 2.2.65; 1484, 3.2.436; *Warning for Fair Women*, D1v; *Sir John Oldcastle*, 2448; Folio *Hamlet*, 2095, 3.2.227; *Hoffman*, 884; Quarto *King Lear*, E3r, 2.2.173; *Cymbeline*, 916, 2.2.10; *Atheist's Tragedy*, 2.6.19; *Silver Age*, 121; *1 Iron Age*, 282; *Roman*

Actor, 5.1.159; *Guardian*, 5.2.9, 10, 57; *Lovesick Court*, 128; *Bloody Banquet*, 1429; also common is **fall** *asleep*; for a sampling see *Endymion*, D3r, G3r; *Friar Bacon*, 1601; *Taming of a Shrew*, A2r, F2r; *Taming of the Shrew*, 17, Induction.1.15; *King Leir*, 1452; *Old Fortunatus*, 2.2.328; *Devil's Charter*, I3r; *Tom a Lincoln*, 1466; *Love's Mistress*, 152; *All's Lost by Lust*, 3.1.78; *Queen and Concubine*, 45; variations include "*sits to sleep*" (*Doctor Faustus*, B 1551, also A 1174), "*sits in a chair and falls asleep*" (*Amends for Ladies*, 5.2.84), "*nods and sleeps*" (*News from Plymouth*, 148), *lies/lies down to sleep* (*Old Fortunatus*, 1.1.63, 4.1.111; *Grim the Collier*, G2v; *Escapes of Jupiter*, 2354; *Fair Maid of Bristow*, D2r; *2 Fair Maid of the West*, 410), "*They sleep all the Act*" and "*Sleepers lie still*" (Folio *Midsummer Night's Dream*, 1507, [3.2.463]; 1620, [4.1.101]); signals for pretended *sleep* include "*seems to sleep*" (*Bondman*, 2.2.125), "*Feigns sleeping*" (*Country Captain*, B10r), "*counterfeits sleep*" (*2 Fair Maid of the West*, 350).

Figures already *asleep* can be **discovered** *sleeping*; for a sampling see *Old Wives Tale*, 843; *Dido*, 0; *Downfall of Huntingdon*, 1490; *Death of Huntingdon*, 925; *Old Fortunatus*, 3.1.356; *Atheist's Tragedy*, 5.1.0; *Brazen Age*, 217; *Tom a Lincoln*, 150–1; *Two Noble Ladies*, 1752; *Love's Mistress*, 121; *Love's Sacrifice*, 1269–70; *Lover's Melancholy*, 2.2.10; typical are "*Discover her sitting in a chair asleep*" (*Trial of Chivalry*, D1r), "*discovered sleeping in the lap of Evadne*" (*Rebellion*, 67); related are **enter/appear** *sleeping* (*Two Lamentable Tragedies*, C4r; *Whore of Babylon*, DS before Act 1, 28; *Bonduca*, 143), *in sleep* (*Faithful Shepherdess*, 399), *asleep* (*Dido*, 810; *2 Tamburlaine*, 3673; *2 Seven Deadly Sins*, 2; *Wars of Cyrus*, D2r; *Alphonsus of Germany*, B1v; *Country Captain*, D1r); typical is "*Enter a maid with a child in her arms, the mother by her asleep*" (*Yorkshire Tragedy*, 527–8); figures are "*brought forth asleep in a chair*" (*Roman Actor*, 2.1.287; *Taming of a Shrew*, A3v; *Rebellion*, 65; *Tottenham Court*, 163), **thrust** *out sleeping in a **bed*** (*Fatal Contract*, G1r), "*drawn out upon a Bed as sleeping*" (*Messalina*, 1100), "*A Bed thrust out: Lodovico sleeping in his clothes*" (*City Nightcap*, 111); atypical is "*Exeunt with Anthynus asleep*" (*Queen's Exchange*, 507); figures are put to *sleep* by **magic** (*Orlando Furioso*, 1252–3; *Love's Mistress*, 152), as seen in "*charms him with his rod asleep*" (*Cobbler's Prophecy*, 137); as [**if**] signals include an entrance "*as newly waked from sleep*" (*English Traveller*, 33; see also *Andromana*, 238), a discovery of two bound figures "*both as asleep*" (*Fatal Contract*, H3r), "*Error at his foot as asleep*" (*Game at Chess*, 13–14), "*holds his head down as fast asleep*" (*If This Be Not a Good Play*, 4.4.16); actions include "*talks in his*

sleep" (*Tom a Lincoln*, 1474; *Devil's Charter*, I3v; *Twins*, G2r), "*starts from his sleep*" (*Guy of Warwick*, D2v), "*stirs, and sleeps again*" (*Two Noble Ladies*, 1774), "*in sleep, maketh signs to avoid*" (*Death of Huntingdon*, 928), "*makes (in her sleep) signs of rejoicing*" (*Henry VIII*, 2654–5, 4.2.82), "*in his sleep troubled, seems to pray to the Image*" (*Roman Actor*, 5.1.180), **ghosts** who "*circle Posthumus round as he lies sleeping*" (*Cymbeline*, 3071, 5.4.29).

sleeve

cited in a variety of actions and contexts; most common is for one figure to **pull**/*take* another *by the sleeve*: "*pulls Turkillus by the sleeve, as he is going and stays him*" (*Edmond Ironside*, 219–20); see also *Dido*, 598; *Two Lamentable Tragedies*, E1v; *2 Edward IV*, 147; *Woman Is a Weathercock*, 1.2.156; *Wedding*, H3v; figures enter "*hanging upon Martia's sleeve*" (*Humorous Day's Mirth*, 1.5.0), "*with a Napkin on his sleeve*" (*Swaggering Damsel*, B1r), "*with his sleeves stripped up to the Elbows*" (*Jews' Tragedy*, 2658); specific *sleeves* are occasionally required: a servant "*in white sleeves and apron*" (*Two Maids of More-Clacke*, H1v), "*Fraud in a blue gown, red cap and red sleeves*" (*Three Lords of London*, I2v), country wenches wearing "*all red Petticoats, white stitched Bodies, in their Smock-sleeves*" (*Country Girl*, D3r); Henslowe's inventory includes "one pair of yellow cotton sleeves" (*Diary*, App. 2, 37), "one blue robe with sleeves" (157); actions include "*shows a keen knife which he pulls out of his sleeve*" (*Fatal Contract*, H4v), the drawing of blood by a devil who "*strippeth up Alexander's sleeve*" (*Devil's Charter*, A2v); atypical is "*a sleeveless shirt*" used to murder Agamemnon (*Herod and Antipater*, C3r).

slip

used (1) most often as "move surreptitiously," but also occasionally as (2) *slip off* clothing, (3) "slide unexpectedly," (4) *slip in/insert* smoothly; for examples of surreptitious movement, figures are directed to *slip aside* (*Three Lords of London*, H3r; *Herod and Antipater*, C3r), *slip away* (*Three Lords of London*, H1r, H3r, I3v; *Jovial Crew*, 431; *English Moor*, 77; *Witty Fair One*, H3r; *Goblins*, 4.6.0); variations include "*slips behind the Arras*" (*Philaster*, 93/405), a **devil** that "*slips into the ground*" (*Sophonisba*, 5.1.21), "*She runs in and presently slips out*" (*Witty Fair One*, H2v); examples of other usages are "*Slips off his Devil's weeds*" (*Woman Is a Weathercock*, 5.2.78), "*he takes hold of a death's head; it slips and staggers him*" (*Atheist's Tragedy*, 4.3.77), "*He guards himself, and puts by with his hat, slips, the other*

running falls over him, and Forrest kills him" (Fortune by
Land and Sea, 386), "As they open the stocks, Wasp puts his
shoe on his hand, and slips it in for his leg" (Bartholomew
Fair, 4.6.77).

slippers, pantoffles

slippers are occasionally specified along with the
widely used **nightgown**: "*Enter Priam in his nightgown
and slippers*" (2 Iron Age, 385); see also *Captain*, 296; *2 If
You Know Not Me*, 302, 309; *Parson's Wedding*, 500;
comparable is an entrance "*bareheaded in his shirt: a
pair of Pantoffles on*" (Blurt, 4.2.0); other examples of
pantoffles are not linked to the nightgown/**unreadiness** but to some special effect or stage business; in
Renegado as an act of devotion a Turk takes off his
yellow pantoffles (1.2.58, 63), in *Humour out of Breath*
"*The Page puts his pantoffle to his lips; he kisses it*" (464),
a **dumb show** includes "*let Omphale turn about, and
taking off her pantoffle, strike Hercules on the head*"
(Locrine, 1356–8); see also *What You Will*, E4r.

slow

surprisingly, this term appears in only one signal:
"*Enter Sabinus Arminius and others with Olive Branches
in their hands, Colours wrapped up, and slow march*"
(Faithful Friends, 2098–100).

small

describes either (1) size or (2) the volume of **sounds**;
small properties include a **table** (Henry VIII, 661–2,
1.4.0; *Bloody Banquet*, 1901–2), **book** (Maid of Honour,
4.3.0), **money** (Knave in Grain, 2969), **desks** (If This Be
Not a Good Play, 2.2.0), "*small shot*" (Devil's Charter,
D1r), "*small banquet*" (Launching of the Mary, 244); calls
for sound are "*Trumpets small above*" (Four Plays in
One, 359), "*A small voice*" (Cobbler's Prophecy, 628);
atypical are "*some small distance*" (Henry VIII, 1336–7,
2.4.0), "*after a small respite of time all taken away*"
(Launching of the Mary, 245–6).

smell

an action rarely called for: "*seem to smell*" (Captain,
309), "*smells to him*" (Princess, H3r); related is "*Busy
scents after it like a Hound*" (Bartholomew Fair, 3.2.80).

smile

the signal for this silent action in a few late plays is
simply *smiles* (Jews' Tragedy, 1439; *Country Girl*, G2v;
Goblins, 3.2.95; *Brennoralt*, 4.7.25, 35; *Parson's
Wedding*, 468); more detailed are "*as she passeth by, he
smiles*" (Death of Huntingdon, 963–4), "*the Nobles

throng after him smiling, and whispering*" (Henry VIII,
2080–1, 3.2.203), "*Alonzo's ghost appears to De Flores in
the midst of his smile*" (Changeling, 4.1.0), "*The
Hangmen torment them, they still smiling*" (Roman Actor,
3.2.74), "*reads and smiles*" (Duchess of Suffolk, A3r; see
also *Fair Maid of the Exchange*, 59); for other examples
see *Night Walker*, 381; *Lady of Pleasure*, 3.3.332;
Landgartha, H1r.

smock

a woman's shift or undergarment: "*in her smock and a
tattered petticoat*" (Soddered Citizen, 1268), "*the maid in
her smock*" and "*Mistress Frankford in her smock,
Nightgown, and night attire*" (Woman Killed, 138, 139); in
Country Girl country wenches enter in "*all red
Petticoats, white stitched Bodies, in their Smock-sleeves*"
(D3r).

smoke

a rarely called for effect linked to supernatural
events; twice *smoke* comes from **under the stage**,
probably through the **trapdoor**: "*compass the stage,
from one part let a smoke arise: at which place they all stay*"
(Cobbler's Prophecy, 1565–6), "*exhalations of lightning
and sulphurous smoke in midst whereof a devil in most
ugly shape*" (Devil's Charter, A2v); "*A smoke from the
Altar*" shows the gods' displeasure (Bonduca, 112).

smother, stifle

to **strangle** a figure is common, but to *smother/stifle* is
rare; in *Battle of Alcazar* murderers "*smother the young
princes in the bed*" (37–8), and in Quarto *2 Henry VI*
"*Duke Humphrey is discovered in his bed, and two men
lying on his breast and smothering him in his bed*" (E2r,
[3.2.0]); for the murder of Desdemona in *Othello*
(5.2.83) the Folio directs "*Smothers her*" (3342) and
the Quarto "*he stifles her*" (M2r).

snake, asp, crocodile

specified for four different situations; a **dumb show**
calls for "*A Crocodile sitting on a river's bank, and a little
Snake stinging it. Then let both of them fall into the water*"
(Locrine, 961–4); a **devil** in **hell** enters with "*a handful
of Snakes*" (If This Be Not a Good Play, 5.4.34) and torments the damned with "*Art hungry, eat this adder:
dry? Suck this Snake*"; Iris and Juno bring in "*two
snakes*" to "*young Hercules in his Cradle*" and "*Hercules
strangles them*" (Silver Age, 126); for the murder of two
boys Pope Alexander "*draweth out of his boxes aspics*,"
"*putteth to either of their breasts an Aspic*," "*taketh off the
Aspics and putteth them up in his box*" (Devil's Charter,

I4r); Henslowe's inventory includes "one snake" (*Diary*, App. 2, 74).

snatch
used in a variety of actions (roughly forty examples) often with *at/off*: "*As they lift up the Cake, the Spirit snatches it, and pours down bran*" (*Late Lancashire Witches*, 205), "*Here she runs about the stage snatching at every thing she sees*" (*Cobbler's Prophecy*, 107–8), "*Snatches off his hat and makes legs to him*" (*Revenger's Tragedy*, G3r); often *snatched* are **weapons**, most commonly a **sword** (*Elder Brother*, 41; *Bashful Lover*, 3.3.84; *Fatal Contract*, I4r; *Messalina*, 1282, 2595; *Lovesick Court*, 157; *Albovine*, 105) but also a **hatchet** (*Alphonsus of Germany*, E1v), **dagger** (*Cobbler's Prophecy*, 1328–9), **staff** (*Locrine*, 639, 1176–7), **halberd** (*Match Me in London*, 4.3.76), **spear** (*Woman in the Moon*, B4v), **knife** (*Sophonisba*, 4.1.51), "*some weapon*" (*Whore of Babylon*, 2.2.185); more detailed are "*all snatch out their swords*" (*Bloody Banquet*, 55), "*snatches at his sword which hung by his Bed side*" (*Alphonsus of Germany*, B2r), "*offers to stab himself, and Nurse snatches the dagger away*" (Q1 *Romeo and Juliet*, G1v, 3.3.108); other objects *snatched* are a strangling **cord** (*Antonio's Revenge*, 4.1.195), **picture** (*Conspiracy of Byron*, 3.2.138), **dish** (*Doctor Faustus*, A 887), **pestle** (*Knight of the Burning Pestle*, 187), **crow** (*Widow's Tears*, 5.5.68), **scarf** (*Albovine*, 97), most commonly a **letter** (*Fair Em*, 577; Folio *Richard II*, 2442, [5.2.71]; *Fair Maid of the Exchange*, 59; *Conspiracy*, H4r); see also *Maidenhead Well Lost*, 152; *Conspiracy*, D4r; *snatch* can be linked to **tear**: "*Gloster offers to put up a Bill: Winchester snatches it, tears it*" (1 *Henry VI*, 1203–4, 3.1.0; see also *King Leir*, 2586); occasionally figures *snatch* another figure (*Two Maids of More-Clacke*, B3v; *Court Beggar*, 234; *Just Italian*, 260).

sneaking
surreptitious activity signaled only once: "*Enter Harpax sneaking*" (*Virgin Martyr*, 4.2.104).

soft, softly
the roughly eighty-five examples of this common modifier are linked primarily to **music** (1) to mark the sadness of death and **mourning**, (2) to enhance supernatural or strange events, (3) to induce or accompany **sleep**, (4) to set the mood for a **banquet**/ entertainment or as general background, and in related fashion (5) to call for the modulation of music or **sound** or to create the impression of distance, (6) to indicate that an action is to be performed quietly/silently; when *soft* describes sound

the effect is usually created **within** and when specified the instruments are the relatively quiet **lute**, **viol**, **recorder** or muted **drum**; for a **funeral** procession "*Soft Music. Enter Angelina with the bodies of Ferdinand and Violanta on a bier*" (*Four Plays in One*, 333; see also *Bonduca*, 143); "*A sad sound of soft music*" begins a **dumb show** of mourning (*Love's Sacrifice*, 2733), "*Soft sad music. A song*" foreshadows the appearance of the dead Penthea (*Broken Heart*, 4.3.141, also 5.3.0); for other examples see *Antonio's Revenge*, 1.2.317; *Fawn*, 4.408; *Shoemaker a Gentleman*, 1.3.0; *Devil's Law Case*, 5.4.134; supernatural or otherwise **strange** business is sometimes accompanied by *soft music*, as in *Tempest* when the "shapes" enter and when Prospero's masque begins (1616, 3.3.82; 1716–17, 4.1.59), in *Chances* when the conjurer sings "Raise these forms from under ground / With a soft and happy sound" (236), in *Martyred Soldier* at the appearance of an angel (209), and in *Seven Champions* when a ghost appears (C1v); in the manuscript of *Two Noble Ladies* the bookkeeper crossed out a scribal "*Soft music*" and specified "*Recorders. Enter the patriarch-like Angel*" (1856); in *Sophonisba* "*Infernal music plays softly*" to accompany the entrances of the underworld spirit Erictho (4.1.101, also 190), then "*A treble Viol and a base Lute play softly*" and "*soft Music*" is signaled again (4.1.200, 210, 5.3.31); in *Fatal Contract* figures sleep "*whilst the waits play softly*" (H3r); *soft music* is also linked to sleeping in *Charlemagne*, 1071; *Soddered Citizen*, 1916–19; *Northern Lass*, 87; *Broken Heart*, 3.2.0; *Lady Mother*, 738; *Rebellion*, 52; **banquets** and similar occasions sometimes call for mood-setting music: "*Soft Music. Enter the Tyrant with the Queen, her hair loose, she makes a Curtsy to the Table. Sertorio brings in the flesh with a skull all bloody*" (*Bloody Banquet*, 1919–21, also 1051–2, 1141–2); see also *Seven Champions*, G4r; *Faithful Friends*, 2485–6; *Antipodes*, 313; *Constant Maid*, E2r; for other examples of *soft music* see *Satiromastix*, 5.2.22; *When You See Me*, 2073; *Woman Is a Weathercock*, 5.2.13; *Thierry and Theodoret*, 37; *Wit at Several Weapons*, 126; *Prophetess*, 336; *Just Italian*, 280; *Queen and Concubine*, 109; *Bride*, 17; *Imposture*, C3r.

When used to call for the effect of sounds **afar off** or **low**, *soft* is typically linked to **drums**/soldiers and often acknowledged with "hark"; in *Four Prentices* "*Sound a Drum within softly*" and "*soft march*" (173, 192) elicit "But hark, I hear our enemies' Drums do brawl" roughly twelve lines before the drum and soldiers enter; in *Rape of Lucrece* "*Soft March*" (203) is explained "The host is now / Upon their March," then six soldiers enter (similarly at 247); in *Thracian Wonder* a "*Soft charge*" (G3r) is acknowledged with "hark, they charge" and "*Soft Alarum*" (G3v) with "Hark, the fight renews"; in *Doubtful Heir* at "*soft alarm*" (F3r) Ferdinand asks "what clamor's that? the frightful noise increases" which makes more sense if *soft* means "distant" rather than "quiet"; this usage perhaps explains a seemingly out of place direction in *Dick of Devonshire*: "*Alarum. As the soft music begins, a peal of ordnance goes off; then Cornets sound a Battle*" (433–5); see also *Bonduca*, 96; the use of sound to create the impression of offstage events is also apparent in *Birth of Merlin* when "*Soft Music*" (D3v) "sounds the Marriage" which is not shown.

Soft also describes stealthy actions: "*enter again softly, stealing to several stands, and listen*" (*Broken Heart*, 3.2.16); in *2 Iron Age* "*Agamemnon, Menelaus, Ulysses, with soldiers in a soft march, without noise*" (378) is elaborated "Soft, soft, and let your stillness suit with night," then "*They march softly in at one door, and presently in at another. Enter Synon with a stealing pace*" (379) and "Now with a soft march enter at this breach"; in *Captain Thomas Stukeley* figures enter "*softly as by night*" (924–5); for similar examples see *Antonio's Revenge*, 5.1.0; *Mad Lover*, 62; *Jews' Tragedy*, 1016, 1338–9; *Distresses*, 338; *Andromana*, 209; other locutions are "*She speaks softly*" (*Epicœne*, 2.5.35; see also *English Moor*, 68; *English Traveller*, 80; "*holdeth up his hands wringing and softly crying*" (*Devil's Charter*, M1r); in *Princess* "*speaks softly to him*" (G1r) is followed by "*Aloud*" indicating that here the meaning is *aside*; action to be performed slowly and solemnly is implied with "*Pass softly over the stage*" (*Swetnam*, G2r), "*walk gravely afore all softly on*" (*Woman Is a Weathercock*, 2.1.119–20), "*a soft dance to the solemn music*" (*Warning for Fair Women*, D1r); atypical are "*pulling her back softly by the arm*" (*Warning for Fair Women*, D1r) and a supernatural *dog* "*pawing softly at Frank*" (*Witch of Edmonton*, 4.2.109).

sola

see *solus*

solemn, solemnly

the roughly thirty-five uses of this modifier are divided between descriptions of (1) *music* and (2) actions; calls for *solemn music* are often linked to a *funeral* or death: "*Solemn Music, to a funeral song the Hearse borne over the stage*" (*Law Tricks*, 67); see also *David and Bethsabe*, 716; *Cymbeline*, 2482, 4.2.186; 3065–71, 5.4.29; *Duchess of Malfi*, 3.4.7; *Fatal Dowry*,

2.1.47; *Renegado*, 4.2.70; *Emperor of the East*, 1.1.82; some signals indicate that *recorders* produced the required *solemn* effect: "*A solemn lesson upon the Recorders*" (*Antipodes*, 335), "*a sweet solemn Music of Recorders is heard*" (*Landgartha*, I1r); see also *Second Maiden's Tragedy*, 2454–5; *Wasp*, 473–4; comparable directions for other *solemn* occasions are "*Solemn and strange Music: and Prosper on the top (invisible)*" (*Tempest*, 1535, 3.3.17, also 2008, 5.1.57), "*some strange solemn music like bells is heard within*" (*Warning for Fair Women*, D1r), "*a solemn flourish of Trumpets*" (*Devil's Charter*, E1r, also L1r), "*solemn Music plays during his speech*" (*Messalina*, 1510–12, also 2207); for more *solemn sounds* see *Fedele and Fortunio*, 1096; *Four Plays in One*, 295, 307; *Pilgrim*, 225; *Fatal Contract*, E3v; various actions or events are *solemn*: "*Recorders dolefully playing, enter at one door the coffin of the Gentleman, solemnly decked*" (*Chaste Maid*, 5.4.0), "*all bow as the Pope marcheth solemnly through*" (*Devil's Charter*, E1r), "*solemnly draws the Canopy*" (*Fatal Contract*, H3r), "*a solemn service*" (*James IV*, 2051), "*a solemn measure with changes*" (*Soddered Citizen*, 1917), "*the solemn show of the marriage*" (*Two Maids of More-Clacke*, A1v, also A3r); for comparable uses see *Sophonisba*, 3.1.116; *Turk*, 588, 644; *White Devil*, 2.2.23; *Henry VIII*, 2643, 4.2.82; 2369, 4.2.80; *Two Noble Kinsmen*, C4v, 1.5.0; *Bonduca*, 111; *Changeling*, 4.1.0; *Landgartha*, B2r; see also *sad*.

solus, sola

roughly 150 figures are directed to *enter solus* (for women *sola*) with another 100 entering *alone*; in most of these scenes an actor enters onto an empty stage to deliver a speech, sometimes a weighty utterance: York before his capture (Octavo *3 Henry VI*, A8v, [1.4.0; not in Riv.]), Henry VI on the molehill (Octavo *3 Henry VI*, C2v, [2.5.0; not in Riv.]; Folio, *alone*, 1134), Proteus for forty-three lines (*Two Gentlemen of Verona*, 929, 2.6.0), Richard of Gloucester to begin *Richard III* (A2r, 2, 1.1.0), Edmund for his speech on bastardy (Quarto *King Lear*, C1r, 1.2.0); the speech delivered by a *solus* figure can also be comic/satiric and in prose (Thersites in *Troilus and Cressida*, D4v, 1205, 2.3.0; Falstaff in *1 Henry IV*, K1r, 5.3.29), nor need he/she be a central figure (Thaliard in *Pericles*, B3r, 1.3.0); sometimes a *solus* figure is not alone for very long: Oberon is joined by Puck within a few lines (Folio *Midsummer Night's Dream*, 1021, 3.2.0), Sebastian enters *solus*, has three lines, and "*Enter Sir Alexander and listens to him*" (*Roaring Girl*, 2.2.0, 3, also 4.1.0); for plays with multiple examples of entrances *solus* see *Mucedorus*, A4v,

C3r, D1r, D2r, D3r, E3v; *King Leir*, 743, 925, 1061, 1157, 1294, 1790, 2356; *Devil's Charter*, F1v, F4r, I3v, L3r; *Guy of Warwick*, C2v, E1r, E2v, E4r, F1r; *Looking Glass for London*, 951, 1092, 2041, 2151, 2237; *Nero*, 27, 44, 58, 69, 90; *Obstinate Lady*, C2v, D1v, D4v, E2v, E4r, F2v, H1r, H3r; *solus* can be linked to *exits* as well as entrances: "*Manet Pericles solus*" (*Pericles*, A4r, 1.1.120; see also *Hieronimo*, 1.96), "*solus stays behind*" (*Aglaura*, 1.3.50); see also *Maid's Metamorphosis*, B4v; *Cure for a Cuckold*, D2v; *Heir*, 535; *Nero*, 21, 36, 43.

As with *alone*, *solus* does not always signify "alone on stage," for occasionally the entering figure joins others already present; examples are Rossacler who enters *solus* (*John of Bordeaux,* 1102) and eventually sees John of Bordeaux ("but stay what aged man lies here"), and a disguised Byron who enters *solus* (*Conspiracy of Byron*, 3.3.19), delivers a seventeen-line speech, then addresses La Brosse who is already onstage; in *Wisdom of Doctor Dodypoll* with Haunce already onstage Cornelia enters "*sola, looking upon the picture of Alberdure in a little Jewel, and singing. Enter the Doctor and the Merchant following, and hearkening to her*" (85–7); of interest is the high percentage of speeches and situations *not* designated *solus/alone*, including many famous soliloquies (no speech in any of the three texts of *Hamlet* is so designated, and in *Macbeth* only Lady Macbeth's entrance at 348, 1.5.0 is *alone*); the links between *solus/alone* and today's sense of *soliloquy* (a term not found in directions) are therefore suggestive but tenuous.

song

occurs as a direction or heading roughly 380 times, often with lyrics; usually the signal is merely *song*, but a call to **sing** and detailed contexts are sometimes given, as well as many directions for the timing of a *song* relative to other action; for instances of the basic term without accompanying lyrics see *Rare Triumphs*, 612; Folio *Love's Labour's Lost*, 771, 3.1.2; *When You See Me*, 2081; *White Devil*, 5.4.65; *Laws of Candy*, 272; *Faithful Friends*, 1491; *Barnavelt*, 2144, 2783; *Prophetess*, 343; *Weeding of Covent Garden*, 10; *Fancies Chaste and Noble*, 815; *English Moor*, 56; for a *song* with the lyrics given see *Looking Glass for London*, 1537; *As You Like It*, 890, 2.5.0; *Old Fortunatus*, 1.1.63; Q2 *Hamlet*, K4r, K4v, L2r, 4.5.29, 38, 48, 165, 190; M2r, M2v, 5.1.62, 71, 94; *Volpone*, 2.2.120, 3.7.165; *Antony and Cleopatra*, 1465, 2.7.113; *Faithful Shepherdess*, 376; *Epicæne*, 1.1.90; *Cymbeline*, 2576, 4.2.257; *Winter's Tale*, 1791, 4.3.122; *Roaring Girl*,

4.1.100; *More Dissemblers*, B1r, B7v; *Hengist*, 1.1.29; *Two Merry Milkmaids*, P3r; *Spanish Gypsy*, E1r; *Cruel Brother*, 179; *Northern Lass*, 77, 79; *Hyde Park*, G2r; *Broken Heart*, 3.2.0; *Inconstant Lady*, 2.4.48; *Antipodes*, 314.

More detailed directions include "*Song above*" (*Antiquary*, 437; see also *Tragedy of Byron*, 2.2), "*A song within*" (*All's Lost by Lust*, 3.1.78; see also *Blurt*, 4.2.0; *Cardinal*, 5.3.99), "*Song and Dance*" (*Argalus and Parthenia*, 47), "*Music and a Song. Black Spirits, etc.*" (*Macbeth*, 1572, 4.1.43), "*Music and Welsh song*" and "*there is a sad song in the music room*" (*Chaste Maid*, 4.1.151, 5.4.0; see also *Custom of the Country*, 312/455; *Country Girl*, K4v), "*Harry Willson and Boy ready for the song at the Arras*" and "*the Lute strikes and then the Song*" (*Believe as You List*, 1968–71, 2022–3; see also *City Madam*, 5.1.7), "*A song to the organs*" (*Mad World*, 2.1.155), "*The Song with the Viols*" (*Jack Drum's Entertainment*, G4v), "*a Song of the Bride's loss*" (*John a Kent*, 581–2), "*Song of John Dorrie*" (*Chances*, 214), "*singeth an old song called the wooing of Colman*" (*Arraignment of Paris*, 721), "*The Players' Song*" and "*The harvest folk's Song*" (*Histriomastix*, A4v, B3r), "*A Charm Song: about a Vessel*" (*Witch*, 1998), "*The Song in parts*" (*King John and Matilda*, 84; see also *Swetnam*, G2r), "*Enter the masque and the Song*" (*Every Woman In*, H2v), "*The Fairies dance, and with a song pinch him*" (*Endymion*, G3r), "*Music an Altar discovered and Statues, with a Song*" (*Game at Chess*, 2038–9), "*Solemn Music, to a funeral song the Hearse borne over the stage*" (*Law Tricks*, 183), "*Here, by a Madman, this song is sung, to a dismal kind of music*" (*Duchess of Malfi*, 4.2.60), "*The second Song, sung by two Priests, holding two marriage Tapers*" (*Amorous War*, L3r), "*Song in untunable notes*" (*Antipodes*, 337), "*A Song, during which, she washes*" (*Challenge for Beauty*, 37), "*Loud music as they pass, a song in the praise of war*" (*Picture*, 2.2.122), "*They go out, with a Song*" (*New Inn*, 5.5.156); for more of the numerous directions for a *song* see *Midas*, 4.1.89; *Old Wives Tale*, 249, 534; *Your Five Gallants*, C1r; *Tempest*, 999, 2.1.296; *World Tossed at Tennis*, C4r, D4r, E3r; *Women Beware Women*, 1.3.101; *Beggar's Bush*, 238; *Faithful Friends*, 2831–3; *Court Beggar*, 247; *Emperor of the East*, 5.3.0; *Messalina*, 2521; *Claracilla*, F12v; *Queen and Concubine*, 127; *Unfortunate Lovers*, 78; *Distresses*, 305.

The timing of a *song* in relation to other events is frequently indicated; action occurs while a *song* is sung: "*A Song the whilst Bassanio comments on the caskets to himself*" (*Merchant of Venice*, E4r, 3.2.62), "*The song to the cornets, which playing, the masque enters*"

(*Malcontent*, 5.5.66), "*(A Song) whilst they salute*" (*Fair Maid of the Inn*, 212), "*as the Song is singing, ascends up the Altar*" (*Knight of Malta*, 161), "*Dance and Song together. In time of which the Boy speaks*" (*Late Lancashire Witches*, 221), "*During these Songs, Andrugio peruses a Letter*" (*More Dissemblers*, B8r); see also *What You Will*, C3r; *Westward Ho*, 4.2.52; *Martyred Soldier*, 209; *Queen of Aragon*, 357; *Soddered Citizen*, 432–3; elsewhere action begins at the *end* of a *song*: "*Enter Malevole after the song*" (*Malcontent*, 1.3.0), "*The song ended, the cornets sound a sennet*" (*Antonio's Revenge*, 5.3.32), "*the song ended, the Hearse is set down between both companies*" (*Fatal Contract*, E3v), "*Music, a Song, at the end of it enter Montague, fainting, his Sword drawn*" (*Honest Man's Fortune*, 239), "*Before the Dance, Constance sings this Song*" (*Northern Lass*, 41); see also *Arraignment of Paris*, 313; *Edward I*, 1246; *Woman in the Moon*, B1r; Quarto *Merry Wives*, G2r, 5.5.36; *Sir Giles Goosecap*, 2.1.16; *Sophonisba*, 3.1.116; *Insatiate Countess*, 3.4.82; *Valiant Welshman*, C2v; *Love's Cruelty*, E4v; *Very Woman*, 4.2.165; *Country Girl*, K4v; *Lovesick Court*, 163; *Imposture*, C3r; *Queen of Aragon*, 378; less often a *song* follows other action: "*Exeunt, ere the wench fall into a Welsh song*" (*Edward I*, 630), "*exeunt Pallas and Achilles. After which the Nymphs of Mount Ida sing this following Song in four or five parts, to a pleasing Tune*" (*Landgartha*, F1r); see also **ballad, catch, ditty, tune**.

sound

occurs in over 450 directions typically as a verb to signal *sound* produced **within** (1) mostly for military signals, (2) sometimes for **music**; the basic direction for *sound* appears in playhouse plots and manuscripts (*Battle of Alcazar* plot, 4, 14, 16, 17, and more; *1 Tamar Cham*, 4, 9, and more; *John of Bordeaux*, 183, 408, 1266; *Woodstock*, 1238, 1995; *Tom a Lincoln*, 600, 1029, 1251); for a sampling of similar uses of *sound* in printed texts see *1 Henry VI*, 2570, 5.3.130; Folio *3 Henry VI*, 2580, 4.7.70; Folio *Richard III*, 2592, 4.2.3; *Love's Labour's Lost*, G3v, 5.2.156; *When You See Me*, 2860, 2863, 2882, and more; *Royal King*, 25, 40; *Golden Age*, 73; *Hollander*, 139; a common signal especially in the Shakespeare canon is *sound* **trumpet**: "*Sound Trumpets, and lay the Coffin in the Tomb*" (*Titus Andronicus*, B1v, 1.1.149), "*Trumpet sounds, and shot goes off*" (Folio *Hamlet*, 3751, [5.2.283]), "*Sound Trumpets. Enter King, Queen, and Somerset on the Tarras*" (Folio *2 Henry VI*, 2848–9, 4.9.0), "*Trumpets sound. Enter Alcibiades with his Powers before Athens*" (*Timon of Athens*, 2507–8, 5.4.0); for more see *Battle of Alcazar*, 375, 389; *Taming of the*

Shrew, 78, Induction.1.73; *Edward III*, I3r; *1 Henry IV*, I1v, 5.1.8; *Weakest Goeth*, 1794; Folio *King Lear*, 3058, 5.3.109; *Devil's Charter*, L1r; *Antony and Cleopatra*, 1619, 3.2.67; *Epicœne*, 4.2.70; *Queen*, 3427–8, 3431; other signals are *sound* **cornet** and *sound* **drum**: "*The cornets sound a battle within*" (*Antonio and Mellida*, 1.1.0; see also *Dick of Devonshire*, 434–5), "*Cornets sound a march*" (*Sophonisba*, Prologue.0), "*The Cornets sound a Lavolta*" (*Blurt*, 2.2.239), "*Drum sounds afar off*" (*1 Henry VI*, 1614, 3.3.28; see also *Valiant Welshman*, B2r; *Edmond Ironside*, 963–4), "*Sound drums within*" (*Alphonsus of Aragon*, 1558; see also *Four Prentices*, 173), "*Sound drums. Exeunt omnes*" (*Cobbler's Prophecy*, 1485); sometimes both drum and trumpet are specified: "*Sound Drums and Trumpets, and then enter two of Titus's sons, then two men bearing a Coffin covered with black*" (*Titus Andronicus*, A4r, 1.1.69), "*Drums and Trumpets sounds, with great shouts of the people*" (*Coriolanus*, 3705–6, 5.6.48); see also *Famous Victories*, F2v; *Alphonsus of Aragon*, 505, 791; *Amorous War*, A2r.

Other terms linked to *sound* are **flourish** (*1 Henry VI*, 192, 1.2.0; Folio *2 Henry VI*, 1168, 2.3.105; *Woodstock*, 2095; Folio *Hamlet*, 1945, 3.2.89; *Satiromastix*, 3.1.166), **alarum** (*James IV*, 2442; *Edward I*, 830; *Locrine*, 801, 821, 832; *Troilus and Cressida*, A3r, 122, 1.1.88; *Landgartha*, H4r), **sennet** (*John of Bordeaux*, 448; *Woodstock*, 350; Folio *2 Henry VI*, 487, 1.3.100; *Macbeth*, 992, 3.1.10; *Antony and Cleopatra*, 1351, 2.7.16), **parley** (*1 Henry VI*, 1624, 3.3.35; *1 Henry IV*, H4r, 4.3.29; *Four Prentices*, 230; *Timon of Athens*, 2511, 5.4.2; *Coriolanus*, 499, 1.4.12; *Double Marriage*, 403), **retreat** (*Edward III*, I2v; *Woodstock*, 2924; Quarto *Richard III*, M3r, 5.5.0; *1 Henry IV*, K4r, 5.4.158; *Troilus and Cressida*, B1v, 328, 1.2.174; *Coriolanus*, 744, 1.9.0); less common are *sound* **tucket** (*Timon of Athens*, 455, 1.2.114; *Case Is Altered*, 1.9.93) and **hoboys** (*Whore of Babylon*, 1.2.81; *King John and Matilda*, 83); elsewhere *sound* is the action of a herald: "*Enter a herald sounding a trumpet*" (*Queen*, 3514, also 3433), "*The Herald departeth from the king to the walls sounding his trumpet*" (*Edmond Ironside*, 872–3); see also *Whore of Babylon*, 4.3.25; occasionally *sound* is linked to a duel or tilting: "*Enter Edgar at the third sound, a trumpet before him*" (Quarto *King Lear*, L1v, 5.3.117), "*Trumpets sound as to a charge*" (*Two Noble Kinsmen*, M1r, 5.3.55), "*sound within to the first course*" and "*Sound to the second course*" (*Soliman and Perseda*, B2v).

Sometimes *sound* is linked to **music**: "*Music sound, Mephostophilis brings in Helen, she passeth over the stage*" (*Doctor Faustus*, B 1802–3), "*Then sounding Music. A fur-*

nished Table is brought forth" (*Revenger's Tragedy*, I2v), "*Music sounds a short strain*" (*Antonio's Revenge*, 1.2.64), "*A dreadful Music sounding*" (*Roman Actor*, 5.1.180), "*Sound of Music*" (*Love's Sacrifice*, 1808, also 2733), "*Music sounds within*" (Folio *Troilus and Cressida*, 1477, 3.1.0; see also *Lust's Dominion*, 1.1.0), "*Sound Music, and enter a Dumb Show*" (*Jews' Tragedy*, 1102), "*Sound loud music*" (*Devil's Charter*, L1r), "*Music sounds ceremoniously*" (*Wizard*, 1818); for more see *Fedele and Fortunio*, 387–8; *Alphonsus of Aragon*, 922; *Sophonisba*, 2.1.0; *Valiant Welshman*, C2r; *World Tossed at Tennis*, D3r; *Challenge for Beauty*, 56; some atypical uses of *sound* are "*Trumpets sound a dead march*" (*Spanish Tragedy*, 4.4.217), "*Sound victory*" (*1 Troublesome Reign*, E3r), "*Sound Instruments within*" (*Alphonsus of Aragon*, 980, 994), "*Sound drum answer a trumpet*" (*Devil's Charter*, D1v), "*New sound within*" (*Little French Lawyer*, 441), "*Sound a health*" (*Opportunity*, E3v), "*funeral sound*" (*Charlemagne*, 2721); Jonson twice uses the term to refer to the practice of having trumpets announce the start of a play: "*After the second sounding*" and "*The third sounding*" (*Cynthia's Revels*, Induction.0, Prologue.0, also *Poetaster*, Induction.0, Prologue.0); see also *swoon*, of which *sound* is a variant spelling.

sowgelder's horn

presumably a *horn* with a distinctive *sound*, specified in three directions; in *English Moor* "*A sowgelder's horn blown*" is acknowledged with "What hideous noise is this?" (14); *Picture* provides "*A sowgelder's horn blown. A Post*" (2.1.82); see also *Court Beggar*, 243.

spade

a rarely cited digging tool: "*with Lantern, Crown* [i.e. Crow], *and Spade*" (Q2 *Romeo and Juliet*, L3v, 5.3.120), "*with spades digging*" (*Old Wives Tale*, 587), "*with pickax and spades, as on the sands*" (*Two Maids of More-Clacke*, F4r, also G1r); see also *2 If You Know Not Me*, 302; *Isle of Gulls*, 294; *If This Be Not a Good Play*, 2.3.0; *Gentleman of Venice*, D3v.

spaniel

in two plays groups enter "*with water Spaniels and a duck*" (*Roaring Girl*, 2.1.361; *Histriomastix*, C2r) with a figure in the former anticipating "the bravest sport at Parlous pond" and one in the latter saying "Let's Duck it with our Dogs to make us sport"; in *Charlemagne* a figure enters "*leading in*" a spaniel (2639–40) described as "my faithful trusty spaniel / The very type and truth of true affection"; see also *dog*, *greyhound*.

Spanish pavin

a slow and stately *dance* (also spelled *pavane*): "*Fulgoso whistles the Spanish Pavin*" (*Lady's Trial*, 767–9); see also *Blurt*, 4.2.29, 32.

spear

a *weapon* with a long wooden shaft and pointed metal end: "*Lluellen's head on a spear*" (*Edward I*, 2361), "*Achilles with his Spear and Falchion*" (*Birth of Merlin*, C3r), "*horns about their necks and boarspears in their hands*" (*Woodstock*, 2120); see also *Woman in the Moon*, B4v; *Tom a Lincoln*, 798; Henslowe's inventory lists "one gilt spear" (*Diary*, App. 2, 82); see also *pole*.

spin, spindle

occasionally cited with reference to women *sewing* or at *work*: "*Enter discovered in a Shop, a Shoemaker, his Wife Spinning*" (*Shoemaker a Gentleman*, 1.2.0), a figure "*in his bed, Audry spinning by*" (*Trick to Catch the Old One*, G3r); examples of male *spinners* are "*Ubaldo spinning, Ricardo reeling*" (*Picture*, 5.1.40), "*He sings and dances and spins with a Rock and spindle*" (*English Moor*, 67, also 69), "*Hercules attired like a woman, with a distaff and a spindle*" (*Brazen Age*, 241).

spirit

a figure in the same general category as a *devil* or *fury*, typically associated with the underworld and supernatural events; frequently *spirits* are linked to a *magician*/*conjurer*/*enchanter*/*witch*: "*Here do the Ceremonies belonging, and make the Circle, Bullingbrooke or Southwell reads, Conjuro te, etc. It Thunders and Lightens terribly: then the Spirit riseth*" (Folio *2 Henry VI*, 643–7, 1.4.22), "*diverse Spirits in shape of Dogs and Hounds, hunting them about, Prospero and Ariel setting them on*" (*Tempest*, 1929–31, 4.1.254), "*the Enchanter Ormandine with some selected friends that live with him in his Magic Arts, with his spirits*" (*Seven Champions*, G1r, also C2r, G3r, G3v, H3v, H4r), "*she Conjures: and Enter a Cat (playing on a Fiddle) and Spirits (with Meat)*" and "*A Spirit like a Cat descends*" (*Witch*, 437–40, 1345–6); see also *Wisdom of Doctor Dodypoll*, 951–3, 1063–4; *Gentleman Usher*, 1.2.47; *Birth of Merlin*, C3r, E2v, G2v; some *spirits* appear with named demonic figures: "*Ascendit Behemoth, with Cartophylax and other spirits*" (*Bussy D'Ambois*, 4.2.40), "*Lurchall and another Spirit comes up*" and "*Shacklesoul with a burning torch, and a long knife, Lurchall with a handful of Snakes, A third spirit with a ladle full of molten gold*" (*If This Be Not a Good Play*, 1.1.53, 5.4.34, also 4.4.38, 5.4.0); *invisible* spirits play tricks: "*As they lift up the Cake, the Spirit snatches* it, and pours down bran" (*Late Lancashire Witches*, 205, also 187, 196, 204, and more); several times a *spirit* is specifically a **ghost**: "*The Spirit of Susan his second Wife comes to the Bed's side*" (*Witch of Edmonton* 4.2.69, also 3.1.70; see also *Second Maiden's Tragedy*, 2446–50); for more see *Friar Bacon*, 1280; *1 Tamar Cham*, 25–30, 33, 80–1, 86; *Doctor Faustus*, B 96; *Merry Devil of Edmonton*, A3v; *Two Merry Milkmaids*, I1v, O3r; *Two Noble Ladies*, 1079, 1081, 1099, 1796; *Prophetess*, 385; *Messalina*, 2518; only in *Michaelmas Term* are these figures merely "human": "*Quomodo with his two spirits, Shortyard and Falselight*" (1.1.73, 4.1.0) – although they clearly function as familiars.

spit

appears (1) as a noun meaning "a pointed rod on which meat is impaled for cooking," (2) as a verb; uses of the noun include "*a spit in her hand*" (*Fedele and Fortunio*, 1615–16), "*spits and dripping-pans*" (*Orlando Furioso*, 949–50), "*spits and logs, and Baskets*" (*Q2 Romeo and Juliet*, K1v, 4.4.13), "*a shoulder of mutton on a spit*" (*Friar Bacon*, 293–4); for examples of the verb, in *Richard III* Lady Anne *spits* at Richard to reject his wooing (B2r, 334, 1.2.144) as do women in *All's Lost by Lust*, 3.1.16; *Fair Quarrel*, 3.2.117; Christians rejecting a Roman god "*spit at the Image, throw it down, and spurn it*" (*Virgin Martyr*, 3.2.53); other instances where figures *spit/spit at* someone include *Dutch Courtesan*, 2.2.252; *May Day*, 4.3.51, 52; *Osmond*, B8r; *City Wit*, 343; *1 Passionate Lovers*, E6v; variations are "*Cough and spit*" (*City Wit*, 310; *Sparagus Garden*, 149), "*Drinks and spits*" (*Brennoralt*, 2.2.44), "*Spits in the dog's mouth*" (*Roaring Girl*, 2.1.371).

spurs, spurred

found mostly in (1) **ceremonies**, (2) the locution **booted** and spurred; to turn a cardinal into a warrior involves "*investing him with a sword, helmet, shield and spurs*" (*Duchess of Malfi*, 3.4.7), and a group **mourning** at a **hearse** includes "*two Heralds with gilt spurs and Gauntlet*" (*Wasp*, 474); see also *Hieronimo*, 1.0; *Knight of Malta*, 155; to **enter** booted and spurred is to indicate a recently completed journey or one about to be undertaken (and by extension weariness or **haste**), as in *Friar Bacon* where the gentlemen arrive "*booted and spurred*" (1935) with Lacy announcing "we have hied and posted all this night to Fressingfield"; see also *When You See Me*, 198–9; *Tale of a Tub*, 2.2.0; variations include "*booted and spurred, a riding wand*" (*King Leir*, 398–9, 408–9), a servant who enters "*with boots and spurs*" (*Woman Killed*, 133); atypical is "*a pair of*

long-necked big-rolled Spurs on her heels" (*Landgartha*, E3r, also H4r).

spurn

visibly reject or scorn, as when the husband in *Yorkshire Tragedy* twice *spurns* his wife (178–9, 347); for other *spurning* of individuals see *Match Me in London*, 3.3.32; MS *Poor Man's Comfort*, 1045; *Nero*, 76; the term can also be used in a religious context: two Christians "*both spit at the Image, throw it down, and spurn it*" (*Virgin Martyr*, 3.2.53), a Christian renouncing his religion is offered "*a cup of wine by the hands of a Christian: He spurns at him, and throws away the Cup*" (*Christian Turned Turk*, F2v).

squib

a small exploding firecracker, cited once: "*Enter Mephostophilis: sets squibs at their backs: they run about*" (*Doctor Faustus*, A 1012–13); see also **fireworks**.

stab

a large number of figures are directed to *stab* others or be *stabbed*; *Devil's Charter* alone provides *stabbeth* (C3r, L2r), "*stab him*" (F4r), "*three stabs together*" (C3r), "*offers to stab herself*" (C4r), "*the ghost of Candie stabbed*" (M2r), "*the Ghost of Candie ghastly haunted by Caesar pursuing and stabbing it*" (G2r); for a sampling of roughly forty figures who simply *stab* see *Spanish Tragedy*, 2.4.55, 4.4.52, 66; *Friar Bacon*, 1856; *2 Tamburlaine*, 3794; *Massacre at Paris*, 306, 347, 1013; *Titus Andronicus*, K3r, 5.3.63; Folio *3 Henry VI*, 3014, 3016, 3018, 5.5.38, 39, 40; Quarto *Richard III*, D3v, 1.4.269; *Julius Caesar*, 1287, 3.1.76; *Alarum for London*, 1081, 1180, 1182, 1183; *Antonio's Revenge*, 5.3.109; *Satiromastix*, 4.3.129; *Yorkshire Tragedy*, 519; *Bussy D'Ambois*, 4.2.116; *Thierry and Theodoret*, 38; *Faithful Friends*, 2161; *Hengist*, 5.2.140, 179; *Roman Actor*, 5.2.74; *Valiant Scot*, K3v; *Rebellion*, 85; *Maid's Revenge*, I3r; figures regularly *stab* themselves (*Spanish Tragedy*, 4.2.37, 4.4.67; *Wars of Cyrus*, G3r; Q1 *Romeo and Juliet*, K2v, 5.3.169; Quarto *Othello*, N2r, 5.2.356; *Love's Sacrifice*, 2829; **offer** to stab (Q1 *Romeo and Juliet*, G1v, 3.3.108; *Jack Drum's Entertainment*, F1r; *Antonio's Revenge*, 3.1.139; *Insatiate Countess*, 3.2.91; *Philaster*, 145; *Tom a Lincoln*, 38–9; *Match Me in London*, 5.3.0; *Herod and Antipater*, B4v; *Two Merry Milkmaids*, G2v; *Love's Sacrifice*, 2651; *Sparagus Garden*, 164; *Obstinate Lady*, H2v; *Claracilla*, E6r); sometimes the place to be stabbed is specified: the **arm** (*Fair Maid of Bristow*, D2v), "*in the left arm*" (*Amends for Ladies*, 4.4.73–4), "*into the arms and shoulders*" (*Edward I*, 894); sometimes a **knife/poniard** is called for: *"draws his poniard and stabs her"* (*Love's Sacrifice*, 2544–5), *"with a knife stabs the Duke and himself"* (*Spanish Tragedy*, 4.4.201); see also *Massacre at Paris*, 1185; *Cupid's Revenge*, 288; *Messalina*, 752–3; actions include *"draw to stab them"* (*King Leir*, 2495), *"suddenly fall upon him, and stab him"* (*Love's Sacrifice*, 1853–4), *"Pretending a violent stab he flings away the Poniard"* (*Messalina*, 1181–2), *"she stabs at herself but misseth by falling"* (*Tom a Lincoln*, 2280, also 2673); atypical are a body *"stabbed thick with wounds"* (*Antonio's Revenge*, 1.2.207), *"Sound drums within and cry stab stab"* (*Mucedorus*, A2v).

staff, staves

the singular and plural terms for a long stick or **rod**: *"a broken staff"* (*Look about You*, 2583), *"Bills and staves"* (*Nobody and Somebody*, H3v), *"burning staves"* (*1 Iron Age*, 314), *"his Staff, with a Sandbag fastened to it"* (Folio *2 Henry VI*, 1117–18, 2.3.58), *"two of the Rebels with long staves"* (Quarto *2 Henry VI*, F3r, 4.2.0, 30), *"a Company of Mutinous Citizens, with Staves, Clubs, and other weapons"* (*Coriolanus*, 2–3, 1.1.0); actions include *"strikes his staff on London stone"* (Folio *2 Henry VI*, 2613–14, 4.6.0; Quarto *"sword,"* G1v), *"writes his name with his staff and guides it with feet and mouth"* and *"takes the staff in her mouth, and guides it with her stumps and writes"* (*Titus Andronicus*, F4v, 4.1.68; G1r, 4.1.76), a figure pretending blindness who *"Goes knocking with his staff"* (*Downfall of Huntingdon*, 1498); for other *staff/staves* see *George a Greene*, 1107; *Jack Straw*, 797; *Locrine*, 639, 1176–7; *Thracian Wonder*, E1r; *Lust's Dominion*, 2.1.33; *What You Will*, D3r; *Shoemaker a Gentleman*, 5.1.42; *Lover's Melancholy*, 5.2.63; *Wasp*, 1686, 1888; often the *staff/staves* are a specific kind, as when indicating office/rank in *"Duke of Norfolk with his Marshall's Staff"* (*Henry VIII*, 3355–6, 5.4.0; see also *Alphonsus of Germany*, E3r; *Royal King*, 25), *"Constable's staff"* (*Night Walker*, 357); elsewhere an episcopal or **crosier** staff is cited: *"Saint Dunstan with his Beads, Book, and Crosier staff"* (*Grim the Collier*, G2r, also G4v), *"the patriarch-like Angel with his crosier staff"* (*Two Noble Ladies*, 1855–6, also 1103), *"Images, Crosier staves"* (*Whore of Babylon*, DS before Act 1, 48–9) and see Henslowe's inventory (*Diary*, App. 2, 69); a *staff* with a tip or cap of metal is carried as a sign of office: *"Hodge very fine with a Tipstaff"* (*Thomas Lord Cromwell*, E1v), or the term can conflate the property and figure carrying it: *"Enter Buckingham from his Arraignment, Tipstaves before him"* (*Henry VIII*, 889, 2.1.53; see also *Queen and Concubine*, 1150); a *staff* carried by a commanding officer is called for with

"shows Penda with a Leading staff, Voltimar at his back" (*Welsh Ambassador*, 820–1), *"the Lord Mayor, Master Shore, Master Josselin, in their velvet coats and gorgets, and leading staves"* (*1 Edward IV*, 11), *"King Henry, his gorget on, his sword, plume of feathers, leading staff"* (*Perkin Warbeck*, 3.1.0); twice a ceremonial *"white staff"* is cited (*Perkin Warbeck*, 2.2.112; *Sisters*, B6v); see also **pole**.

stag

cited obliquely twice: *"a Stag's head"* (*Death of Huntingdon*, 333–4), **masquers** as *"a Stag, a Ram, a Bull and a Goat"* (*City Nightcap*, 156).

stage

a theatrical term in roughly 225 directions (1) with more than half for the action of figures crossing *over the stage* (to **enter** by one **door** and **exit** by another; see also **pass** over); other phrases include (2) *about the stage*, (3) *on/upon the stage*, (4) **end** *of the stage*; basic signals to go *over the stage* frequently imply subsequent "events" offstage: *"Canidius Marcheth with his Land Army one way over the stage, and Taurus the Lieutenant of Caesar the other way; After their going in, is heard the noise of a Sea fight"* (*Antony and Cleopatra*, 1973–5, 3.10.0), *"Jockey is led to whipping over the stage"* (*2 Edward IV*, 180), *"the Prologue leads Massinissa's troops over the stage, and departs; Syphax's troops only stay"* (*Sophonisba*, Prologue.29), *"Enter Borachio warily and hastily over the stage, with a stone in either hand"* (*Atheist's Tragedy*, 2.4.0), *"Spaniards and Moors with drums and colors fly over the stage, pursued by Philip, Cardinal, King of Portugal, And others"* (*Lust's Dominion*, 4.2.135), *"Enter Prophilus, Bassanes, Penthea, Grausis, passing over the stage; Bassanes and Grausis enter again softly, stealing to several stands, and listen"* (*Broken Heart*, 3.2.16), *"Phebe passes over the stage in night attire, Careless follows her as in the dark"* (*Mad Couple*, 76); sometimes figures go *over the stage* in the context of other onstage action: *"Enter Warwick, Somerset, and the rest, bringing the King out in his Gown, sitting in a Chair; Richard and Hastings fly over the Stage"* (Folio *3 Henry VI*, 2257–9, 4.3.27), *"A Mercer's Shop discovered, Gartred working in it, Spendall walking by the Shop: Master Ballance walking over the Stage: after him Longfield and Geraldine"* (*Greene's Tu Quoque*, B1r), *"Enter over the Stage all the Grecian Princes, courting and applauding Ulysses, not minding Ajax"* (*1 Iron Age*, 343); see also *Antiquary*, 487; a formal event or a procession is often established by the action of going *over the stage*: *"Trumpets sound, and the King, and his train* *pass over the stage"* (2 *Henry IV*, K4r, 5.5.4), *"Exeunt, first passing over the Stage in Order and State"* (*Henry VIII*, 2444, 4.1.36), *"Alarum. Enter the powers of France over the stage, Cordelia with her father in her hand"* (Quarto *King Lear*, K3v, 5.2.0), *"The organs play, and covered dishes march over the stage"* (*Mad World*, 2.1.151), *"to a funeral song the Hearse borne over the stage"* (*Law Tricks*, 183), *"A service as for dinner, pass over the stage, borne by many Servitors, richly appareled"* (*Antipodes*, 246), masked figures enter *"between every couple a torch carried, they march over the Stage, and Exeunt"* (*Changes*, K2v); for comparable processions see *Hieronimo*, 1.0; *Shoemakers' Holiday*, 5.3.0; *Revenge of Bussy*, 3.1.0; *Tom a Lincoln*, 2699; *Coriolanus*, 3639–40, 5.5.0; *Birth of Merlin*, C1r; *Revenger's Tragedy*, A2r; *Brazen Age*, 247; *Swetnam*, G2r; *Faithful Friends*, 2476–84; *Wonder of a Kingdom*, 5.2.0; *Queen and Concubine*, 124; *Messalina*, 1859–60; *Amyntas*, Z1v; *over the stage* can mean *in haste*, as when directions specify *running*: *"Enter two or three running over the Stage, from the Murder of Duke Humphrey"* (Folio 2 *Henry VI*, 1690–1, 3.2.0), *"Thunder and Lightning, Devils run laughing over the stage"* (*Seven Champions*, H1r), *"After an Alarum, and people running over the Stage, Enter Osmond, a Tartar with his Sword bloody"* (*Osmond*, A2r); see also *Wounds of Civil War*, 333–4; *Woman Killed*, 138; *Caesar and Pompey*, 2.1.89; *Two Maids of More-Clacke*, H1v; *Valentinian*, 70; *Lover's Melancholy*, 1.2.101; *Jovial Crew*, 431; other locutions include *"go softly over the Stage"* (*Antonio's Revenge*, 5.1.0), *"driven over the Stage"* (*Caesar and Pompey*, 4.2.0), *"Excursions over the Stage"* (*Revenge of Bussy*, 4.1.0), *"as from Church over the Stage"* (*Spanish Gypsy*, H3v), *"walks over the stage"* (Folio *Every Man In*, 4.7.107; *Faithful Friends*, 2837–9), *"carrying Placentia over the Stage"* (*Magnetic Lady*, 3.3.0), *"dancing over the Stage"* (*Thracian Wonder*, E4r); a variant is *along the stage*: *"march along the stage one an other"* (*Edmond Ironside*, 1785–6), *"stealing along the stage"* (*May Day*, 3.3.156), *"she draws one of the ladies by the hair of the head along the stage"* (*Tom a Lincoln*, 2620–1); unique is *"cross the stage"* (*Histriomastix*, G1r).

Although directions are not specific, dialogue frequently indicates that figures crossing *over the stage* (or *passing over*) are watched and commented on by others already onstage, as in *Second Maiden's Tragedy* where at *"Enter Bellarius passing over the Stage"* Votarius says "ha, what's he? / 'Tis Bellarius my rank enemy" (928–30); for comparable examples see Q2 *Hamlet*, K3r, 4.4.0; *Patient Grissil*, 2.1.220; *Sejanus*, 1.176; *Rape of Lucrece*, 203; *Puritan*, B2v; *Dumb Knight*, 140; *Match Me in London*, 2.4.35; *Monsieur Thomas*, 115;

Mad Lover, 62; *Loyal Subject*, 136; *Little French Lawyer*, 416, 441; *Changeling*, 5.2.8; *Doubtful Heir*, D5r; *Damoiselle*, 437; *Cardinal*, 4.1.33.

Figures also move *about the stage*: *"beats them about the stage"* and *"they fight again Edmond drives Canute back about the Stage"* (*Edmond Ironside*, 562–4, 1996–7), *"the Devils go forth; Dunstan rising, runneth about the Stage, laying about him with his Staff"* (*Grim the Collier*, G4v), *"runs about the stage snatching at every thing she sees"* (*Cobbler's Prophecy*, 107–8), *"Sennet about the Stage in order"* (1 *If You Know Not Me*, 246), *"flying about the stage"* (*Edward II*, 1777), *"trips about the stage"* (*Eastward Ho*, A4v), *"march about the Stage"* (Q2 *Romeo and Juliet*, C2v, 1.5.0; see also *Three Lords of London*, G1v; 2 *Edward IV*, 108; 2 *If You Know Not Me*, 342); less common are the generally synonymous *on/upon the stage*: *"meet on the stage"* (2 *Edward IV*, 142; see also *Cobbler's Prophecy*, 3–4), *"a Tomb, placed conveniently on the Stage"* (*James IV*, 3), *"fall asleep on the Stage"* (*Histriomastix*, E1v), *"sit a good while on the Stage"* (*What You Will*, A2r), *"A bed thrust out upon the stage, Allwit's Wife in it"* (*Chaste Maid*, 3.2.0), *"place him in a chair upon the stage"* (*Devil's Charter*, L3r, also C1r, G1r, I3v), *"Enter a Shoemaker sitting upon the stage at work"* (*George a Greene*, 971–2); see also *Three Lords of London*, D1v; *Fedele and Fortunio*, 1368; 2 *Seven Deadly Sins*, 1; *Looking Glass for London*, 1460–1; *Summer's Last Will*, 116; 2 *Edward IV*, 101; *Malcontent*, 4.2.0; *Valiant Welshman*, H4r; atypical is *"They throw all the bottles in at a hole upon the Stage"* (*Princess*, G4r); various other phrases focus on the *stage*: *"pass round the stage"* (*Sir Thomas Wyatt*, 1.2.58), *"compass the stage"* (*Cobbler's Prophecy*, 1565), *"keep the Stage"* (1 *Iron Age*, 277), *"possess the Stage"* (2 *Iron Age*, 408); signals for an exit include *"depart the stage"* (*Warning for Fair Women*, G3r), *"forsake the stage"* (*Antonio's Revenge*, 5.1.0), *"quits the Stage"* (*Prisoners*, B7r), *"vanish off the Stage"* (*Histriomastix*, D1r), *"chaseth them off the Stage"* (*Honest Man's Fortune*, 234), *"follows him off the Stage"* and *"pulls him by the heels off the Stage"* (*Princess*, H2r, H3v), *"they go off the Stage grappling together"* (*Twins*, D2v).

The phrase *end of the stage* can denote a *side* of the stage or a door in the tiring-house wall; references to an onstage location include *"they sit at the other end of the stage"* (*Antipodes*, 264), *"speaketh this secretly at one end of the stage"* (*Fair Em*, 235), *"a chair is placed at either end of the Stage"* (1 *Iron Age*, 335), *"standing at several ends of the Stage gazing"* (*Love's Sacrifice*, 1851; see also *Queen*, 2507–8); signals to enter are *"at one end of the stage"* and *"at the other end of the stage"* (2 *If You Know*

Not Me, 309; *Histriomastix*, F4r; *Fair Maid of the Exchange*, 41; *Dumb Knight*, 128, 129; *Witch of Edmonton*, 4.2.109), "*from one end of the Stage*" and "*from the other end of the Stage*" (*John a Kent*, 780, 798), "*at the further end of the stage*" (*Captain Thomas Stukeley*, 260–1, also 2575); there is one reference to the "*top of the Stage*" (*Alphonsus of Aragon*, 2–3).

stagekeeper

referred to by the bookkeeper of the *Captives* manuscript, first with two actors "*Gib: Stage: Taylor*" (1492), then "*Stagekeeper as a guard*" (2805); see also **keeper**.

stagger

figures *stagger* in a variety of contexts: "*takes hold of a death's head; it slips and staggers him*" and "*strikes out his own brains, staggers off the scaffold*" (*Atheist's Tragedy*, 4.3.77, 5.2.241, also 4.5.60), "*staggers on, and then falls down*" (*Insatiate Countess*, 3.1.84), "*staggers with faintness*" (*Fatal Contract*, H4v), "*stabs himself then staggers and speaks*" (*Tom a Lincoln*, 2673–4); see also *Eastward Ho*, B3v; *Duchess of Suffolk*, F2v; *Princess*, I1r.

stairs

each use of the term may denote something different: "*As he is going up the stairs, enters the Earls of Surrey and Shrewsbury*" (*Sir Thomas More*, 1920), "*The Scaffold set out, and the stairs*" (*Knight of Malta*, 109), "*Run down the stairs*" (*Weeding of Covent Garden*, 33); Henslowe's inventory lists "*one pair of stairs for Phaeton*" (*Diary*, App. 2, 58).

stall

a booth, stand or counter that forms part of a **shop** called for once: "*Touchstone, Quicksilver, Golding, and Mildred, sitting on either side of the stall*" (*Eastward Ho*, B2r).

stamp

to *stamp* the **foot** is (1) usually to show **anger** but less commonly (2) to give a signal, (3) to *stamp on* someone or something; examples of anger include "*Gives them the letters and they stamp and storm*" (*Fair Maid of the Exchange*, 70), "*stamps and goes out vexed*" (*Widow's Tears*, 1.3.118), "*reads the letter, frowns and stamps*" (*King Leir*, 1172), "*chafing and stamping*" (*Swaggering Damsel*, G1v), "*she stamps, and seems to be angry at the first*" (*Queen of Corinth*, 60); for *stamping* as a signal: "*He stamps with his foot, and the Soldiers show themselves*" (Folio 3 *Henry VI*, 189–90, 1.1.169), "*Plutus stamps. Labor rises*" (*Four Plays in One*, 362), "*stamps*

with his foot: to him a Servant*" (*Amends for Ladies*, 2.3.2), "*she stamps: the chair and dog descend*" (*Rebellion*, 66); examples of *stamping on* are the revengers "*stamping on*" the old duke (*Revenger's Tragedy*, F2v), Bajazet who "*stamps upon*" offered food (1 *Tamburlaine*, 1679); for other examples (mostly of anger) see *John a Kent*, 1300–1; *Guy of Warwick*, C4r; *Your Five Gallants*, I3r; *Mad World*, 4.1.72; *Four Plays in One*, 326; *Roman Actor*, 1.2.73; *Bashful Lover*, 4.2.106; *Witch of Edmonton*, 2.1.227; *Seven Champions*, L1r; *Osmond*, C7r; *Dick of Devonshire*, 1714–15; *Country Girl*, B1v, B2v.

stand

used regularly as a verb for onstage positioning and movement, often attached to an adverb or adverbial phrase; figures separated from the main action *stand* **private** (*Little French Lawyer*, 416; *Swaggering Damsel*, G1v), *stand* **off/afar off** (*Thomas Lord Cromwell*, E1v; *Tom a Lincoln*, 167; *Fair Maid of the Inn*, 175; *Double Marriage*, 366), "*Stand at distance*" (*News from Plymouth*, 193), *stand* **by** (*Taming of the Shrew*, 349, 1.1.47; *Two Lamentable Tragedies*, B3v; 2 *Edward IV*, 180; *Sejanus*, 5.424; *Lust's Dominion*, 1.2.49; *Miseries of Enforced Marriage*, 1351; *Fair Maid of the Inn*, 178; *Knave in Grain*, 2927), *stand* **aloof** (Folio 3 *Henry VI*, 1847, 3.3.111; 2 *Edward IV*, 173; *Lust's Dominion*, 4.3.48; *Satiromastix*, 2.1.156; *Whore of Babylon*, 2.1.24, 4.1.0; *Two Noble Kinsmen*, L1v, 5.1.136; *Witch of Edmonton*, 5.1.76; *English Moor*, 76); typical is "*Enter Jane in a Seamster's shop working, and Hammond muffled at another door, he stands aloof*" (*Shoemakers' Holiday*, 3.4.0); most common is for an eavesdropper or observer to *stand* **aside**: "*Enter second Luce, and stands aside*" (*Wise Woman of Hogsdon*, 292), "*Parthenius goes off, the rest stand aside*" (*Roman Actor*, 5.2.19); see also *Locrine*, 2021; *Alphonsus of Aragon*, 57, 1910; *Love's Labour's Lost*, E2v, 4.3.20; *Patient Grissil*, 4.1.111; 2 *Edward IV*, 171; *Histriomastix*, F3v; *Wily Beguiled*, 1003; *Alarum for London*, 359; *Lust's Dominion*, 5.1.7; *Ram Alley*, F4v; *Thracian Wonder*, E4r; *Turk*, 369; *Faithful Friends*, 1223; *King John and Matilda*, 76; *Damoiselle*, 420; *Weeding of Covent Garden*, 21; surreptitious figures also *stand* **close** (*May Day*, 3.3.199; *Revenge of Bussy*, 5.1.32; *Mad Lover*, 47; *Claracilla*, F1ov), enter "*standing out of sight*" (*Antonio and Mellida*, 4.1.131), "*stand unseen*" (*Escapes of Jupiter*, 1583; *Widow*, C4v), "*steals in, and stands in some by place*" (*Match Me in London*, 5.3.0), "*stands behind the post*" (*Devil's Charter*, F3v).

Figures who are not hiding *stand* **bare** when showing respect (*Coriolanus*, 796, 1.9.40; *Shoemaker a*

Gentleman, 4.1.240; *Conspiracy*, F4v), and others *stand still* (*Antonio and Mellida*, 1.1.98; *Sophonisba*, Prologue.0; *Aglaura*, 4.4.150; *Platonic Lovers*, 12), *musing* (*Aglaura*, 4.3.53), *amazed* (*Cobbler's Prophecy*, 1335; *1 Henry IV*, D2v, 2.4.79; *Henry VIII*, 2273, 3.2.372; *Faithful Shepherdess*, 373; *No Wit*, 4.3.148; *Renegado*, 2.4.9; *Fatal Contract*, F1r, K1r; *Court Beggar*, 264; *Late Lancashire Witches*, 221; *Rebellion*, 37; *Launching of the Mary*, 1233; *Bloody Banquet*, 56), "*staring and quaking*" (*Death of Huntingdon*, 2607, 2612); the guard under a magical spell "*stands fixed, their eyes rolling*" and "*stands fixed in a posture of running at him with his sword*" (*Two Noble Ladies*, 480–1, 488–9); *stand* can be used for onstage positioning: "*four stand on one side, and four on the other*" (Folio *3 Henry VI*, 2027–8, 4.1.6), "*stand in convenient order about the Stage*" (*Henry VIII*, 1348–9, 2.4.0), "*stand at several ends of the Stage*" (*Queen*, 2507–8), "*One stands at one end, and one at tother*" (*Thomas Lord Cromwell*, C2v); other usages include "*stands on him*" (*Coriolanus*, 3806, 5.6.130), "*stands to the bar*" (*Tragedy of Byron*, 5.2.42), "*standing in their torments*" (*If This Be Not a Good Play*, 5.4.0), "*stand in their tent*" (Quarto *Troilus and Cressida*, F4v, 3.3.37), "*stand in rank for the measure*" (*Antonio's Revenge*, 5.3.36), "*stand in Council*" (*Death of Huntingdon*, 2971); for *stand up* see *David and Bethsabe*, 1623; *If This Be Not a Good Play*, 4.2.74; *Albovine*, 35; for *stand* as a noun see **make a stand**.

standard

an *ensign* or *flag* bearing an identifying insignia used occasionally in *battle* scenes; in *Valiant Welshman* "*the Roman Standard-bearer of the Eagle*" enters, then after a fight "*Constantine winneth the Eagle, and waveth it about*" (I3r); see also *Four Prentices of London*, 233, 234; *2 If You Know Not Me*, 337; *Birth of Merlin*, G3v.

standish

a stand containing *ink* and *pens* that is introduced for onstage *writing*: "*A Bar, Tablebook, two Chairs, and Paper, standish set out*" for a court scene (*Spanish Curate*, 98), "*One bearing light, a standish and paper, which sets a Table*" when Tamyra is forced to write a *letter* (*Bussy D'Ambois*, 5.1.0), the entrance of a would-be poet "*in his Nightcap, with leaves in his hand, his man after him with lights, Standish and Paper*" (*Northward Ho*, 4.1.0); the *standish* is linked to the writing of a will (*Spanish Curate*, 117) and the conducting of business (*City Madam*, 1.2.143); see also *Widow*, B1r; *Cardinal*, 2.1.50.

star

see **blazing star**

stare

the few uses imply a disturbed state: "*raving and staring as if he were mad*" (Quarto *2 Henry VI*, F1v, 3.3.0), "*stands staring and quaking*" (*Death of Huntingdon*, 2607, also 2612); see also *Spanish Tragedy*, 3.13.132; *Merry Devil of Edmonton*, A3v; *Witch of Edmonton*, 4.2.69; *Cardinal*, 4.2.202.

start

used in roughly sixty signals for a sudden involuntary movement linked to surprise or awakening from *sleep*: two figures "*look one upon another, and start to see each other there*" (*King Leir*, 420–1) and four lovers awakened by the huntsmen's *horns* "*all start up*" (*Midsummer Night's Dream*, F4v, 4.1.138); the reaction can be linked to a supernatural visitation or specifically to fear: "*The Spirits come about him with a dreadful noise; he starts*" (*Late Lancashire Witches*, 245), "*starting as something affright*" (*David and Bethsabe*, 93), "*affrightedly starts up*" (*Lovesick Court*, 129), "*Starts up and quakes*" (*Bashful Lover*, 3.3.194); *Atheist's Tragedy* provides "*starts up*," "*starts and wakes*," "*starts at the sight of a death's head*" (5.1.31, 2.6.23, 4.3.210); in *Maid of Honour* "*Adorni starts and seems troubled*" (3.3.200) so that Camiola says "Why change you color?"; with Paris pretending to sleep "*Exeunt all, but Paris and Helen, at which he starts up from his Chair and takes her by the hand*" (*1 Iron Age*, 282); other links to sleep include "*starts from his sleep*" (*Guy of Warwick*, D2v), "*half unready, as newly started from their Beds*" (*2 Iron Age*, 413; see also *Amends for Ladies*, 4.1.1–2), "*He offers to Kiss and she starts, wakes, and falls on her knees*" (*Two Noble Ladies*, 1793–4); in *2 Fair Maid of the West* Mullisheg first "*counterfeits sleep*," then "*starts out of his chair as from a dream*" and later another figure "*lies to sleep*" and "*starts*" (350–1, 410–11).

Elsewhere figures *start back* (*Spanish Tragedy*, 2.1.78; *Your Five Gallants*, A2r; *Jews' Tragedy*, 1435; *Antipodes*, 313; *Unfortunate Lovers*, 35; *Andromana*, 225), *start up* (*Woman in the Moon*, B1r; *John a Kent*, 1167; *Locrine*, 1648; *James IV*, 3–4; *Warning for Fair Women*, D2r, G3r; *Antonio's Revenge*, 4.2.76; *Revenge of Bussy*, 5.5.29; *Fair Maid of Bristow*, D2v; *Guardian*, 5.2.103; *Court Beggar*, 208), most commonly simply *start* (Quarto *2 Henry VI*, F2r, [4.1.32]; Folio *Richard III*, 1205–6, 2.1.80; Quarto *Merry Wives*, G3r, 5.5.88; *Two Lamentable Tragedies*, D1r; *Death of Huntingdon*, 963, 965; *1 Edward IV*, 62; *Sophonisba*, 2.2.41; *Devil's Charter*,

C3r, L3v, M2v; *Tempest*, 1807, 4.1.138; *Captain*, 297; *Wonder of a Kingdom*, 3.1.67; *English Traveller*, 72; *Bondman*, 3.2.16, 81; *Two Noble Ladies*, 1504–5, 1537–8, 1793–4; *Lovesick Court*, 142; *Lost Lady*, 563; *Conspiracy*, L3r, M3r; *Andromana*, 209, 242); that usages are anything but consistent can be seen in two signals in *Richard III* where the Folio Richard "*starts out of his dream*" and the Quarto Richard "*starteth up out of a dream*" (3638, L4v, 5.3.176).

state

(1) royal or noble figures ***enter*** in state–in a procession with ***pomp*** and solemnity, (2) such figures are also seated in a ***chair*** of state on a dais with a ***canopy***, (3) the canopy itself is sometimes called a *state*; examples of entrances are "*in State, Cymbeline, Queen, Cloten, and Lords*" (*Cymbeline*, 1374–5, 3.1.0), "*in great state the Duke and Bianca richly attired, with Lords, Cardinals, Ladies, and other attendants; they pass solemnly over*" (*Women Beware Women*, 4.3.0, also 5.2.0), "*in full state, triumphal ornaments carried before him*" (*Sophonisba*, 5.4.0); for less detailed signals see *Woodstock*, 350–1; *David and Bethsabe*, 1106; *Fawn*, 4.408, 587; *When You See Me*, 1–2; *Nobody and Somebody*, H3r; *Travels of Three English Brothers*, 348; *Christian Turned Turk*, H1v; *White Devil*, 4.3.58; *Golden Age*, 62; *1 Iron Age*, 286; *Valentinian*, 88; *More Dissemblers*, B7v; *Changeling*, 4.1.0; *Noble Spanish Soldier*, 1.1.0; *Two Noble Ladies*, 1240–1; *Duchess of Suffolk*, I2v; *Escapes of Jupiter*, 1154–5; *Roman Actor*, 2.1.246; *Soddered Citizen*, 1609; *Valiant Scot*, K3v; *Emperor of the East*, 3.2.0; *Messalina*, 1508–10, 1858–9; *Doubtful Heir*, F2v; *Sisters*, B7v; for ***exits*** in state see *Antonio and Mellida*, 2.1.292; *Antonio's Revenge*, 3.1.0; *Coriolanus*, 1121, 2.1.204; *Queen's Exchange*, 530; *Antipodes*, 315.

Signals for a raised *chair of state* are "*The state being in place*" for Queen Elizabeth (*Arraignment of Paris*, 1207), "*King riseth from his state*" and "*Enter Cardinal Wolsey, and takes his State*" (*Henry VIII*, 331, 1.2.8; 710, 1.4.34), "*coming near the chair of state, Ferdinand Ascends*" (*Hoffman*, 483–4), "*ascends his Chair of state*" (*Jews' Tragedy*, 7); for similar directions see *Doctor Faustus*, B 1297; *Antonio and Mellida*, 2.1.183; *Fawn*, 5.122, 139; *1 If You Know Not Me*, 244; *Devil's Charter*, E1r; *Thierry and Theodoret*, 38; *World Tossed at Tennis*, D3r; *Cleopatra*, E1v; *Bondman*, 1.3.159; *Julia Agrippina*, 4.683; MS *Poor Man's Comfort*, 1270; *Great Duke of Florence*, 5.2.107, 157; *King John and Matilda*, 29; *Queen*, 640–1; *Coronation*, 264; rev. *Aglaura*, 5.1.0.

State means *canopy* twice in *Henry VIII* (only two

other Shakespeare plays use *state* in a direction; this play has six examples): "*The King takes place under the Cloth of State*" and "*A small Table under a State for the Cardinal* (1343–4, 2.4.0; 661, 1.4.0, also 3035–6, 5.1.35; 2444, 4.1.36); other unique locutions are "*a banquet in state*" (*1 Iron Age*, 302), "*They possess the Stage in all State*" (*2 Iron Age*, 408), "*Zenocrate lies in her bed of state*" (*2 Tamburlaine*, 2968), "*Perkin in state retires some few paces back*" (*Perkin Warbeck*, 2.1.39), "*in state under a Canopy*" (*Picture*, 1.2.128), "*sits in state*" (*Staple of News*, 2.5.44); in *Soddered Citizen* the context suggests both "manner" and "pomp": "*Carried in an Antic state, with Ceremony*" (995); see also ***throne***.

statue

see ***image***

stay

(1) most commonly "***remain*** when others ***depart***" but also (2) "***prevent*** from departing," (3) "prevent from completing an action"; *Love's Sacrifice* provides examples of all three usages: "*D'avolos only stays*," "*Exeunt. D'avolos stays Fernando*," "*Offers to stab himself, and is stayed by Fernando*" (1820, 291–3, 2651–3); typical of *stay* as *remains* ***behind*** is "*Thersites only stays behind*" (*1 Iron Age*, 345); for a sampling of roughly forty examples see *Cobbler's Prophecy*, 1566; *Fair Em*, 291; *Old Fortunatus*, 4.2.28; *Thracian Wonder*, B2r; *Lust's Dominion*, 4.2.56; *Blurt*, 3.3.186; *All's Well*, 1089, 2.3.183; *Caesar and Pompey*, 1.2.0; *Dutch Courtesan*, 4.1.22; *Rape of Lucrece*, 173; *Noble Spanish Soldier*, 1.1.0; *Two Noble Ladies*, 1549; *Unnatural Combat*, 4.2.25; *Valiant Scot*, H2r; *Lover's Melancholy*, 2.1.272; *Grateful Servant*, F2r; for figures prevented from exiting see *Fedele and Fortunio*, 246–7; *Edmond Ironside*, 219–20; Quarto *2 Henry VI*, A3r, 1.1.74; *Humour out of Breath*, 448; *Mad Lover*, 14; *Spanish Gypsy*, G1v, H3v; *Four Plays in One*, 321; *Guardian*, 1.1.138; *Broken Heart*, 4.3.97; *Wits*, 145; typical is "*As they are going out, Antonio stays Mellida*" (*Antonio and Mellida*, 2.1.292); the interrupted actions are usually intended violence with versions of *stays his* ***hand*** most common: "*offers to strike and Jack stays him*" (*Old Wives Tale*, 903), "*after him with his sword drawn, the maid in her smock stays his hand*" (*Woman Killed*, 138), "*offers to run at Piero: but Maria holds his arm and stays him*" (*Antonio's Revenge*, 1.2.217), "*snatches away her knife, and sets it to his own breast, she stays his hand*" (*Fair Maid of the Inn*, 215); see also *Cobbler's Prophecy*, 958; *Doctor Faustus*, B 1300; *Weakest Goeth*, 1349; *Escapes of Jupiter*, 2218; *Brazen Age*, 247; *Fair Maid of the Exchange*,

40; *King John and Matilda*, 62; *Andromana*, 260; *Love and Honour*, 109.

steal

(1) usually "move stealthily" but can also mean (2) "rob, take away"; to indicate stealth, *steal* is combined with *away* (*Selimus*, 2079–80; *2 Edward IV*, 101; *Epicœne*, 2.2.88; *Tottenham Court*, 166; *Lost Lady*, 589), *forward* (*Look about You*, 663), **out** (*Lover's Melancholy*, 2.1.125), *after* (*Woman Is a Weathercock*, 2.2.1; *Twins*, D4r), **behind** (*Woman's Prize*, 85), **off** (*Fair Maid of the Inn*, 178); typical are "*Here they all steal away from Wyatt and leave him alone*" (*Sir Thomas Wyatt*, 4.3.51), "*muffled in a cloak steals off the Stage*" (*Maid's Revenge*, F1v); variations include enter *stealing/stealingly* (*Patient Grissil*, 4.1.90; *Woman Is a Weathercock*, 4.3.26), "*stealing along the stage*" (*May Day*, 3.3.156), "*comes out in his gown stealing*" (*Sir John Oldcastle*, 2210), "*with a stealing pace*" (*2 Iron Age*, 379), "*enter again softly, stealing to several stands, and listen*" (*Broken Heart*, 3.2.16), "*steals nearer and nearer*" (*Twins*, D2v), "*steals near him and shoots him*" (*MS Bonduca*, 2502–3), "*steals in, and stands in some by place*" (*Match Me in London*, 5.3.0); see also *Just Italian*, 255; atypical are murderers who "*steal out their swords*" (*Revenger's Tragedy*, I3v); examples of robbery include "*steals the bottle*" (*Bashful Lover*, 3.1.73), "*steals away the Bride*" (*Alphonsus of Germany*, F1v), "*steal away their cloaks*" (*New Wonder*, 124); after a page picks up a letter "*Hercules steals it out of his pocket*" (*Fawn*, 4.57), and at the climax of Quarto *Merry Wives* Caius "*steals away a boy in red*" and Slender "*takes a boy in green: And Fenton steals mistress Anne, being in white*" (G3r, 5.5.102).

stick

two directions for this property imply small pieces of *wood*: "*gathering sticks*" (*Witch of Edmonton*, 2.1.0), "*with dry sticks and straw, beating two flints*" (*Valiant Scot*, G3r), two require a longer *stick* or a *staff*: "*hangs three or four pair of hose upon a stick*" (*Weakest Goeth*, 227), "*drawing the curtains with a white stick*" (*Friar Bacon*, 1561), and one refers to equipment for a *game*: "*a trap-stick*" (*Women Beware Women*, 1.2.87).

stifle

see *smother*

stiletto

a short *dagger* with a thick blade; figures in two plays *draw* a stiletto (*Just Italian*, 224, 238; *Novella*, 120).

still

of the roughly sixty-five uses (1) most are calls for *sound* or action to continue, others (2) describe stasis or (3) are a synonym for *soft* to describe instrumental sound; examples of *still* for sound *within* to continue are "*Alarum continues still afar off*" and "*Sound still with the Shouts*" (*Coriolanus*, 573, 1.5.3; 3632, 5.4.57), "*Skirmish still*" (*Battle of Alcazar*, 1302), "*Music still playing*" (*English Moor*, 67), "*Thunder still*" (*Julius Caesar*, 540, 1.3.99, also 2674, 5.5.29), "*Storm still*" (Folio *King Lear*, 1615, 3.1.0; 1655, 3.2.0; 1780, 3.4.3; 1843, 3.4.62; 1880, 3.4.100; 1942, 3.4.162), "*Noise still*" (*Spanish Curate*, 124); see also Quarto *2 Henry VI*, H3v [5.2.71; not in Riv.]; Octavo *3 Henry VI*, C2v, [2.5.0]; Folio *Midsummer Night's Dream*, 1600, 4.1.83; *Death of Huntingdon*, 1943; *Old Fortunatus*, 3.1.356, 389; *Revenge of Bussy*, 4.1.6, 10; *If This Be Not a Good Play*, 5.1.76; *Two Noble Ladies*, 66, 1101, 1212; elsewhere *still* can signal continuation of an action: "*She kisses and flatters him along still*" (*Catiline*, 2.351), "*Contempt still turns from Venus*" (*Cobbler's Prophecy*, 1500, also 1025), "*Still he stands staring*" (*Death of Huntingdon*, 2612), "*still reads on*" (*Fatal Contract*, D1r), "*fight still*" (*Honest Lawyer*, B2r), "*Still runs*" (*Look about You*, 401), "*still striving to hold each other's sword*" (*Lovesick Court*, 142); other directions for continuing stage business are *still* **disguised** (*Malcontent*, 4.4.0; see also *Two Maids of More-Clacke*, I1v), **following** (*2 Seven Deadly Sins*, 38), **sitting** (*Arraignment of Paris*, 621), **sleeping** (*Tom a Lincoln*, 155), **smiling** (*Roman Actor*, 3.2.74), **pulls** (*Parson's Wedding*, 411; see also *Princess*, A3v), **whispers** (*Queen's Exchange*, 528); for more see *2 Edward IV*, 173; *Poetaster*, 2.1.107; *Trial of Chivalry*, I3r; *Two Maids of More-Clacke*, G4v, H2r; *Epicœne*, 2.1.10; *Unnatural Combat*, 5.2.297; *Great Duke of Florence*, 2.1.39; *Princess*, F4v; *still* means "unmoving" in *stand still* (*Antonio and Mellida*, 1.1.98; *Sophonisba*, Prologue.0; *Platonic Lovers*, 12; *Aglaura*, 4.4.150); either meaning is possible for "*sleepers lie still*" (Folio *Midsummer Night's Dream*, 1620, [4.1.101]).

Still signals quiet or soft *music* in "*Loud Music, and still Music*" (*Love's Mistress*, 108), "*Still Music of Records*" (*Two Noble Kinsmen*, L1v, 5.1.136), "*A noise of still music; and Enter the high Priest*" (*Jews' Tragedy*, 2147); "*She dies. Still music above*" elicits "the spheres do welcome her / With their own music" (*Cruel Brother*, 183); see also *As You Like It*, 2682, 5.4.107; *Little French Lawyer*, 431; *Double Marriage*, 331; atypical is *still* **march** (*King Leir*, 2464; *Alarum for London*, 319, 322).

stir

signals movement after passivity, usually the result of unconsciousness or *sleep*: "*Ferneze stirs, and Malevole helps him up and conveys him away*" (*Malcontent*, 3.1.160), "*stirs in the bed*" (*Fatal Contract*, G2r), "*stirs, and sleeps again*" (*Two Noble Ladies*, 1774), "*left wounded, and for dead, stirs and creeps*" (*Warning for Fair Women*, F1v); see also *Death of Huntingdon*, 673; *Satiromastix*, 5.1.0; *Devil's Charter*, I3v, I4r; *Bride*, 65; *Prisoners*, C8v; *Landgartha*, I1v; atypical is "*Plangus stirs behind the hangings. Rinatus draws, and runs at him*" (*Andromana*, 261).

stocks

an instrument of punishment in which the individual was placed in a sitting posture with his ankles confined between two planks furnished with holes to receive them; Folio *King Lear* provides "*Stocks brought out*" (1217, 2.2.139), and *Perkin Warbeck* calls for "*A pair of stocks*" at the beginning of a scene (5.3.0); two directions mention *stocks* at the end of an action: "*Exeunt, having left Mulligrub in the stocks*" (*Dutch Courtesan*, 4.5.70), "*Exit Jailer leaving Sir Thomas in the stocks*" (*Travels of Three English Brothers*, 391); three signals are part of an extended action in *Bartholomew Fair*: "*They put him in the stocks*," "*As they open the stocks, Wasp puts his shoe on his hand, and slips it in for his leg*," "*they leave open the stocks*" (4.1.34, 4.6.77, 163).

stone

small *stones* are needed for "*Throw stones*" and "*Another stone*" (*Alarum for London*, 1329, 1330, also 1332–4), "*Borachio warily and hastily over the stage, with a stone in either hand*" (*Atheist's Tragedy*, 2.4.0), "*Sir Thomas being weaponless defends himself with stones*" (*Travels of Three English Brothers*, 360); probably fake, light-weight *stones* were used, especially when "*A stone falls and kills Proximus*" (*Birth of Merlin*, F2v), "*Caratach kills Judas with a stone from the rock*" (*Bonduca*, 156), "*they beat him down with a stone*" (*Jews' Tragedy*, 2762); in *Martyred Soldier* "*They bind him to a stake, and fetch stones in baskets*" (222) but they are "*soft as sponges*"; in *Captives* "*Either strikes him with a staff or Casts a stone*" (2432–4) is followed by dialogue indicating a *stone* was used; a larger property seems required for "*Enter Sorrow and the three Ladies, he sets them on three stones on the stage*" (*Three Lords of London*, D1v, also I1r), "*the Tombstone flies open*" (*Second Maiden's Tragedy*, 1927); but the *stone* is *fictional* when Jack Cade "*strikes his staff on London stone*" (Folio *2 Henry VI*, 2613–14, 4.6.0); see also *rock*.

stool

a basic item of stage furniture though not cited as often as *chairs*, *tables*, and *beds*; in the roughly forty examples many are *set*/*set out*: "*Servingmen setting stools*" (*Sir Thomas More*, 878), "*A Table set out, and stools*" (*1 Fair Maid of the West*, 307; *English Traveller*, 66); *stools* are regularly linked to tables (*Spanish Curate*, 117, 133; *Lovers' Progress*, 113; *Knight of Malta*, 129; *Imposture*, E5r; *Launching of the Mary*, 1926; *Platonic Lovers*, 81; *Rebellion*, 83; *Variety*, D6v) and chairs (*Woman Is a Weathercock*, 5.2.1; *Two Noble Kinsmen*, G2v, [3.5.64]; *Country Girl*, K1v); detailed examples are "*bringing in a table, with chairs and stools placed above it*" (*1 Iron Age*, 334), "*Gismond sitteth down in a Chair, Lucretia on a stool beside him*" (*Devil's Charter*, C2r), "*A Council Table brought in with Chairs and Stools*" (*Henry VIII*, 3035, 5.2.35); figures *enter* with "*a Banquet and stools*" (*Deserving Favourite*, D3v), "*with Bar, Table, Stools*" for a *trial* (*Doubtful Heir*, C2v), "*with Cards, Carpet, stools, and other necessaries*" (*Woman Killed*, 121), "*with napkins in their hands, followed by pages with stools and meat*" (*Fawn*, 2.0); see also *Malcontent*, Induction.0; *1 Honest Whore*, 2.1.0; *2 Honest Whore*, 4.1.186; *City Madam*, 1.2.143; *stools* can be associated with *work*: "*set them down on two low stools and sew*" (*Coriolanus*, 361, 1.3.0), "*Cobbler with his stool, his implements and shoes, and sitting on his stool, falls to sing*" (*Cobbler's Prophecy*, 52–3); several directions call for "*low stools*" (*Sir Thomas More*, 1413), "*three footed stools*" (*Launching of the Mary*, 77); actions include "*leaps over the stool*" (*2 Henry VI*, C3r, 902–4, 2.1.150), "*drinks and falls over the stool*" (*Look about You*, 1503), "*Stands upon a stool*" (*Wily Beguiled*, 2021), "*Ralph Cobbler creeps under the stool*" (*Cobbler's Prophecy*, 75), "*A confused fray with stools, cups and bowls*" (*Silver Age*, 142), "*Draw and fight, throw pots and stools*" (*Amends for Ladies*, 3.4.133–4).

stoop

the few examples are an old man "*stooping to gather*" sticks and straws (*Old Wives Tale*, 140), "*Friar stoops and looks on the blood and weapons*" (Q1 *Romeo and Juliet*, K2r, 5.3.139), "*The Sophy gives Sir Anthony his hand as he offers to stoop to his foot*" (*Travels of Three English Brothers*, 322).

stop

found mostly in (1) *stop* someone's *mouth*, (2) the threat or prevention of onstage violence; to *stop* a figure's *mouth* is to *silence* him: "*The Guard lead off Lamia stopping his mouth*" (*Roman Actor*, 2.1.239); see also *Grim the Collier*, H1or; *Hieronimo*, 8.55; *Devil's Charter*, C2v; "*the people within stops*" (*Cupid's Revenge*, 277) signals the cessation of an offstage *sound*; threatened violence includes "*with his drawn sword stops them*" (*Captain Thomas Stukeley*, 2446–7), enter "*running with a rapier, his Brother stops him*" (*Revenger's Tragedy*, H1v), "*They offer to run all at Piero, and on a sudden stop*" (*Antonio's Revenge*, 5.3.105); see also *Nobody and Somebody*, F4r; *Princess*, E2r, E4v.

storm

a synonym for either (1) *rage* or (2) a *tempest*; examples of *anger* are "*Sforza storms*" (*Queen and Concubine*, 9), "*they stamp and storm*" (*Fair Maid of the Exchange*, 70), "*Queen and Malateste storms*" (*Noble Spanish Soldier*, 5.4.57); see also *1 If You Know Not Me*, 216; *Late Lancashire Witches*, 258; more frequently *storm* describes bad weather and probably calls for a special effect: "*Storm and Tempest*" and "*Storm still*" (Folio *King Lear*, 1584, 2.4.284; 1615, 3.1.0, and more), "*The storm being past of thunder and lightning*" (*Arraignment of Paris*, 355), "*A Storm. Enter Boreas*" (*Love's Mistress*, 123, 127); in the manuscript of *Captives* "*a great Tempestuous storm*" (456) is followed by the bookkeeper's "*Storm continued*" (651); see also *Dido*, 995; *Thracian Wonder*, B4v; *2 If You Know Not Me*, 268; *Unnatural Combat*, 5.2.259; *Prisoners*, C1v, C2r, C3v.

strain

a segment of a piece of *music* or simply a melody or tune, usually also denoting a *change* or figure of a *dance*: "*Here they dance the first strain*," "*The first strain ends*," "*In this strain Mariana came to Philocles*" (*Dumb Knight*, 176–7)–prompting the pun "this strain contained a pretty change"; signals to dance several *strains* also occur in *Cynthia's Revels*, 5.10.41, 94, 110; *Timon of Athens*, 492–3, 1.2.145; *Woman Is a Weathercock*, 5.2.8, 28–9, 31; couples *dance a strain* (*Blurt*, 1.1.158; *Satiromastix*, 2.1.131); for more examples see *Mad World*, 2.1.143; *Nice Valour*, 188, and more; *World Tossed at Tennis*, D2r; *New Trick*, 250–1; *Late Lancashire Witches*, 238; for a *masque* in *Messalina* figures "*during the first strain of Music played four times over, enter by two at a time*" (2203–5); sometimes *strain* refers only to a short tune: "*Music sounds a short strain*" (*Antonio's Revenge*, 1.2.64), "*after one strain of music they fall asleep*" (*Devil's Charter*, I3r); in *Emperor of the East* figures enter "*after a strain of music*" (1.1.89); see also *Antipodes*, 338; *Lovesick Court*, 128.

strange

variously describes *music*/*sounds*, actions, and *clothing*; most often the implication is "unusual, mysterious" but with little or no indication of the particular effect or how it is to be achieved; this adjective occurs three times in *Tempest* directions but not elsewhere in the Shakespeare canon: "*strange Music*," "*strange shapes*," "*a strange, hollow and confused noise*" (1535–6, 3.3.17, 19; 1807–8, 4.1.138); similar usages appear in *Brazen Age*: "*A strange confused fray*" and "*Medea with strange fiery-works, hangs above in the Air in the strange habit of a Conjuress*" (196, 217); signals for *strange music* or other sounds also occur in *Warning for Fair Women*, D1r; *Double Marriage*, 348; *Little French Lawyer*, 440; *Unfortunate Lovers*, 78; various actions are similarly described: "*strange faces*" (*Fair Maid of the Inn*, 201), "*strange Conges*" (*Silver Age*, 116), "*strange gestures*" (*Mad Lover*, 14), "*a strange wild fashioned dance*" (*More Dissemblers*, E5r), "*strange posture*" (*Witch of Edmonton*, 2.1.93), "*strange pauses*" (*Cunning Lovers*, I2v); atypical is "*women in strange habits*" (*Wonder of a Kingdom*, 4.1.0); see also *odd*.

strangle

a fairly common signal (as opposed to the rare *smother*/*stifle*); in most instances no further details are provided; see *Massacre at Paris*, 1115; *Soliman and Perseda*, H1v; *Selimus*, 1240, 2311; *Captives*, 1812; *Duchess of Malfi*, 4.2.237 (also "*shows the Children strangled*," 4.2.257); *White Devil*, 5.3.175; *Herod and Antipater*, G4v; two figures are directed to *strangle* themselves (*Sir Thomas Wyatt*, 2.3.84; *2 Iron Age*, 430), and the infant Hercules *strangles* two *snakes* (*Silver Age*, 126); atypical is "*He strangles her with her own hair*" (*Turk*, 2106–7); the instrument usually specified for this action is a *strangling cord*, as in "*some ready with a cord to strangle Zenocia*" (*Custom of the Country*, 357); in *Antonio's Revenge* Strotzo enters with "*a cord about his neck*," then "*Piero comes from his chair, snatcheth the cord's end, and Castilio aideth him; both strangle Strotzo*" (4.1.162, 195).

strew

to scatter *flowers*: "*Paris strews the Tomb with flowers*" (Q1 *Romeo and Juliet*, I4v, 5.3.11), "*Enter a maid strewing flowers, and a servingman perfuming the door*" (*Two Maids of More-Clacke*, A1r), "*Curtains open, Robin Hood sleeps on a green bank, and Marian strewing flowers on him*" (*Downfall of Huntingdon*, 1490–1); the *strewing* can be part of a *ceremony*: "*Enter in solemnity the Druids singing, the second Daughter strewing flowers*"

(*Bonduca*, Folio 111, MS 1206–7), "*Enter Hymen with a Torch burning: a Boy, in a white Robe before singing, and strewing Flowers*" (*Two Noble Kinsmen*, B1r, 1.1.0, also B1v, 1.1.14); see also *Death of Huntingdon*, 483; Quarto *Every Man Out*, 1406; *Satiromastix*, 1.1.0, 58; atypical are "*strewing herbs*" (*Ram Alley*, H4r), a procession preceded by "*strewers of rushes*" (*2 Henry IV*, K4r, 5.5.0).

strike, struck

of the roughly 200 signals (1) most are simply *strikes* or *strikes him/her*, generally meaning to **hit** with the hand; but there are also a number of more detailed directions and several recurring phrases and contexts of usage, the most common being (2) **offers to** *strike*, (3) *strike up* **heels**, and references to (4) beheadings, (5) a **thunderbolt** and other supernatural events, (6) *striking* an object and, rather different, (7) a call for **sound**; for uses of the basic term to signal violence see Quarto *2 Henry VI*, B4r, 1.3.138; *George a Greene*, 528; *Mucedorus*, D2v; *Woodstock*, 2608; *King Leir*, 1966–7; *Taming of the Shrew*, 1096, 2.1.219; Folio *Henry V*, 2927, 5.1.29; *Sejanus*, 1.565; *Widow's Tears*, 2.2.29; *Trick to Catch the Old One*, B3r; *Yorkshire Tragedy*, 512; *Antony and Cleopatra*, 1102, 2.5.62; *Insatiate Countess*, 4.2.116; *Bondman*, 2.2.25; *Deserving Favourite*, D2r; *Bashful Lover*, 4.1.37; *Brennoralt*, 5.2.9; *Cardinal*, 5.3.173; more detailed directions indicate related actions: "*strikes him down*" (*Richard II*, K1r, 5.5.107), "*Strike him a box on the ear*" (*Friar Bacon*, 575; see also *James IV*, 327), "*Strikes, and they scuffle*" (*Amends for Ladies*, 3.4.130–1), "*Alva steps to defend him and they strike at him*" (*Alarum for London*, 701), "*Strikes them both down with his club*" (*Locrine*, 1294), "*Strike him soundly, and kick him*" (*Northward Ho*, 4.3.180), "*Strike, and the blow returned*" (*Atheist's Tragedy*, 3.2.25), "*Strikes his breast*" (*Two Merry Milkmaids*, H4r), "*Julia meets her and strikes her, then speaks*" (*Maidenhead Well Lost*, 107), "*offers to kiss her, she strikes him*" (*English Moor*, 32), "*he strikes she falls*" (*Arcadia*, E4r), "*They fight, and she strikes him down*" (*Landgartha*, C1v); for more see *2 Edward IV*, 101; *Lust's Dominion*, 4.2.135; *Thracian Wonder*, F2r; *Miseries of Enforced Marriage*, 1521; *Virgin Martyr*, 4.2.85; *Bashful Lover*, 2.8.141.

Elsewhere a figure *offers to strike* (*Alarum for London*, 882; *Look about You*, 2630; *Dumb Knight*, 156; *Valiant Welshman*, E2v; *2 Passionate Lovers*, G8r; *Swaggering Damsel*, G4v) or more elaborately "*offers to strike and Jack stays him*" (*Old Wives Tale*, 903), "*She offers to strike him with the lute*" (*Taming of a Shrew*, C2r), "*Belinus*

offers to strike off Albinius's head" (*Alphonsus of Aragon*, 622), "*offers to strike, and his sword falls*" (*Lovesick King*, 232–3), "*Orestes offers to strike her with his Rapier, and is stayed by Phylander*" (*Maid's Metamorphosis*, A4r); for versions of *strikes up his heels* see *Poetaster*, 3.4.18; *Warning for Fair Women*, F1r; *Wit of a Woman*, 1024; *Little French Lawyer*, 396; *Tale of a Tub*, 4.2.37; *Hollander*, 141; *Fool Would Be a Favourite*, C7v; *strike* is used in the context of an **execution**, more particularly a beheading: "*the Executioner strikes, and Herod dies*" (*Herod and Antipater*, L4r), "*Her head struck off*" (*Virgin Martyr*, 4.3.179; see also *Insatiate Countess*, 5.2.226), and elsewhere the action causes death: "*strikes out his own brains*" (*Atheist's Tragedy*, 5.2.241), "*strikes him in the head fifteen times*" (*Two Lamentable Tragedies*, B4r, also C4r).

Strike is also used of a **thunderbolt**: "*Jupiter above strikes him with a thunderbolt*" (*Brazen Age*, 254; see also *Looking Glass for London*, 529–30, 552–3; *Martyred Soldier*, 249; *Seven Champions*, H3r); a related usage is linked to the supernatural or **magic**: "*Faustus strikes the door, and enter a devil playing on a Drum*" (*Doctor Faustus*, B 1485), "*Plutus strikes the Rock, and flames fly out*" (*Four Plays in One*, 362), "*Oberon strikes Guy with his Wand, he awakes and speaks*" (*Guy of Warwick*, B4r; see also *Rare Triumphs*, 213; *Orlando Furioso*, 1257; *Birth of Merlin*, F3r, G1v, G4r; *Fair Maid of the Inn*, 201), "*Enter the Conjurer, and strike Corebus blind*" (*Old Wives Tale*, 559), "*Death strikes three times at Antonio*" (*Rebellion*, 53; see also *Birth of Merlin*, G4r); for similar examples see *Antonio's Revenge*, 4.2.87; *Whore of Babylon*, 4.1.0; a number of directions are to *strike* an object rather than a person: "*strikes the dish with a knife*" (Folio *Titus Andronicus*, 1504, 3.2.51), "*strikes his sword upon London stone*" (*2 Henry VI*, G1v, 2613–14, 4.6.0), "*strikes the Sack out of his hand*" (*Staple of News*, 4.3.9), "*strikes down her book*" (*Antipodes*, 295; see also *Hengist*, DS before 2.2, 4–5), "*She strikes off Eustace's hat*" (*Elder Brother*, 41), "*striking off crumbs from their shirts*" (*Fair Favourite*, 250), "*strikes ope a curtain where appears a body*" (*Hoffman*, 8–10).

Strike is linked to several kinds of sound, most often to represent a bell-tower **clock** during mysterious or dangerous nighttime events: "*Clock strikes*" (*Cymbeline*, 958, 2.2.50), "*The Watch strikes*" (*Doctor Faustus*, B 2065, also 2035, 2083), "*The clock strikes twelve*" (*Atheist's Tragedy*, 4.3.0); see also *Looking Glass for London*, 337; *Richard III*, M2r, 3743, 5.3.275; *Twelfth Night*, 1344, 3.1.129; *Julius Caesar*, 826, 2.1.191; *Devil's Charter*, F3v; *Christian Turned Turk*, F3v; *Roaring Girl*, 3.1.27; *Changeling*, 5.1.0, 11, 67; similar signals for

music or other sounds include "*Drums strike up*"
(*1 Henry VI*, 902, 2.3.60; *Costly Whore*, 256), "*Strike up
alarum*" (*Alphonsus of Aragon*, 373, 392, 622), "*the Lute
strikes*" (*Believe as You List*, 2022), "*soft Music Strikes*"
(*Faithful Friends*, 2485–6); see also *Rare Triumphs*,
554–5, 968; *Famous Victories*, F1r; *May Day*, 4.1.18; *Two
Noble Kinsmen*, C4r, 1.4.0; *Beggar's Bush*, 224; *World
Tossed at Tennis*, D2r; *Lovers' Progress*, 114.

strip

to remove clothing, most commonly the *sleeve*: "*his
arms stripped up to the elbows all bloody*" (*Appius and
Virginia*, H1r), "*strippeth up Alexander's sleeve and letteth
his arm blood in a saucer*" (*Devil's Charter*, A2v); see also
King Leir, 2125; *Jews' Tragedy*, 2658; other *strippings*
include "*He strips himself*" (*Valiant Welshman*, D4v),
"*They begin to strip her*" (*Alarum for London*, 748;
Princess, H3r), "*Enter Alvaro, soldiers stripping off his
corslet*" (*Love and Honour*, 106), "*strip themselves into
their shirts, as to vault*" (*White Devil*, 2.2.37).

strive, striving

(1) usually "physically *struggle*" but can also mean (2)
"compete, argue," with or without physical contact;
examples of actual struggling include "*Enter three or
four, and offer to bind him: He strives*" (*Comedy of Errors*,
1394–5, 4.4.105), "*strives with the Watch*" (*Spanish
Tragedy*, 3.3.36), "*They struggle, and both fall down, still
striving to hold each other's sword, etc.*" (*Lovesick Court*,
142), "*strives to go from Phormio; he holds her*" (*Lost Lady*,
592); Follywit brings in the courtesan "*striving from
him*" and later she re-enters "*strivingly*" (*Mad World*,
4.5.0, 64); for other figures who *strive* in this fashion
see *Alarum for London*, 719–21; *Blurt*, 4.3.58; *Yorkshire
Tragedy*, 537–8; *Northern Lass*, 64; a more general
sense of competition is conveyed by "*striving for pri-
ority*" (*Devil's Charter*, B3r), "*striving about attire*"
(*Patient Grissil*, 5.2.157), "*They strive which should lead
Bride*" (*Bride*, 59), "*espy the child and strive for it*" (*Bloody
Banquet*, 850–1); occasionally *strive* can mean "try":
"*the king striving to comfort*" a weeping woman (*Tom a
Lincoln*, 170–1), "*strives to rise but cannot*" (*Claracilla*,
E10v).

struggle

a seldom used alternative to *fight*: "*runs upon
Montague, and struggling yields him his Sword*" (*Honest
Man's Fortune*, 234), "*They struggle, and both fall down,
still striving to hold each other's sword*" (*Lovesick Court*,
142); see also *Claracilla*, E10v; *Prisoners*, A9v; *Princess*,
G1r, I1v.

study

(1) usually a male preserve associated with *reading*
and *writing* where a figure *enters* or is *discovered
in/as in* or comes *out* of his study, (2) less commonly a
verb meaning "think, consider"; some signals call
for a figure to be discovered *in his study* by the
parting of a *curtain*: "*Horace sitting in a study behind a
Curtain, a candle by him burning, books lying confusedly*"
(*Satiromastix*, 1.2.0), "*A curtain drawn by Dash (his clerk)
Trifle discovered in his study. Papers, taper, seal and wax
before him, bell*" (*News From Plymouth*, 167), "*draweth
the Curtain of his study where he discovereth the devil
sitting in his pontificals*" (*Devil's Charter*, L3v); for other
figures discovered in their *studies* see *Law Tricks*, 180,
194; *Catiline*, 1.15; *Staple of News*, 2.5.0, 44; related is
"*discovered at his book*" (*Two Noble Ladies*, 83); sometimes a figure is directed to start a scene *in his study*
behind a curtain and then move forward onto the
main platform; an example is *Devil's Charter* where
Pope Alexander is first seen "*unbraced betwixt two
Cardinals in his study looking upon a book, whilst a groom
draweth the Curtain*" and then after one speech "*They
place him in a chair upon the stage, a groom setteth a Table
before him*" (L3r); comparable movements *into/out
of/to a study* are "*Bacon and Edward goes into the study*"
(*Friar Bacon*, 633), "*Thunder and lightning: Enter devils
with covered dishes; Mephostophilis leads them into
Faustus's Study*" (*Doctor Faustus*, B 1775–6), "*Enter
Throte the Lawyer from his study, books and bags of money
on a Table, a chair and cushion*" (*Ram Alley*, B3v), "*Enter
in his chamber out of his study, Master Penitent Brothel, a
book in his hand, reading*" (*Mad World*, 4.1.0), "*Enter
Clinton to the Earl Chester in his study*" (*Royal King*, 74;
see also *Captain Thomas Stukeley*, 250); in
Histriomastix a signal has four figures enter and
"*Chrisoganus in his study*" followed by "*all go to
Chrisoganus's study, where they find him reading*" (B1v);
Devil's Charter (which atypically has ten directions
that call for a *study*) provides "*in his study beholding a
Magical glass with other observations*" (F4v, also B2v),
"*cometh upon the Stage out of his study with a book in his
hand*" (G1r, also I2r), exit "*into the study*" (G2v, I2v),
"*Alexander to his study*" (L2r), "*Bernardo knocketh at the
study*" (I3r).

Most common is the locution *enter in his study*;
when the actor is surrounded by *books* and other
objects a discovery seems likely: "*Enter Bernard in his
Study, Candle and Books about him*" (*Two Merry
Milkmaids*, B1r; see also *Virgin Martyr*, 5.1.0), "*Enter
Guadagni in his Study. A Taper, Bags, Books, etc.*" (*Novella*,
110), "*Cromwell in his study with bags of money before him*

casting of account" (*Thomas Lord Cromwell*, B1v), "*Enter the Friar in his study, sitting in a chair … a table before them and wax lights*" (*'Tis Pity*, 3.6.0); an occasional signal provides considerable detail: "*Sharkino in his study furnished with glasses, vials, pictures of wax characters, wands, conjuring habit, Powders paintings*" (*Maid's Revenge*, E3v); more common is the simple *in his study* formula (*Doctor Faustus*, A 30, 437, B 29, 389, 569; *Massacre at Paris*, 364; *Old Wives Tale*, 334; *Thomas Lord Cromwell*, E4v; *Barnavelt*, 1883; *Two Merry Milkmaids*, I1v), sometimes linked to an activity: "*Enter Soranzo in his study, reading a book*" (*'Tis Pity*, 2.2.0), "*in his study writing*" (*Welsh Ambassador*, 1962); some of these directions may therefore be understood as "*enter [as if] in his study*," a locution made explicit in "*as in his Study*" (*Fair Maid of the Inn*, 193; *Aglaura*, 1.2.6), "*as in his study reading*" (*Greene's Tu Quoque*, B4v), "*As out of his Study*" (*Goblins*, 4.1.32), "*Tutor in his gown as from his study*" (*Witty Fair One*, E1v); a figure may at times have brought his *study* onto the *stage* with him rather than being discovered *in* it, as specified in "*Two Servants bring in a table with books. Arioldus follows*" (*Swisser*, 1.2.0); in some instances *in his study* may have meant "in his study of a book" (as distinct from "in a designated space within his house"), as suggested by "*Lucio being at his study*" (*Woman Hater*, 128); after Frankford enters "*in a study*" (*Woman Killed*, 102) he expresses satisfaction with his education: "How happy am I … I am studied in all Arts"; atypical are "*Hodge sits in the study, and Cromwell calls in the States*" (*Thomas Lord Cromwell*, D1r), Tamora and her sons who "*knock and Titus opens his study door*" (*Titus Andronicus*, I3r, 5.2.8), "*Enter Harpax in a fearful shape, fire flashing out of the study*" (*Virgin Martyr*, 5.1.122), "*Enter Lyon-rash to Fourchier sitting in his study: at one end of the stage: At the other end enter Vourcher to Velure in his shop*" (*Histriomastix*, F4r); examples of the verb can be simply *studies* (*Brennoralt*, 1.4.65, 2.4.15, 36, 3.4.95; *Aglaura*, 5.3.63); more detailed are "*Studies and scratches his head*" and "*stands still and studies*" (*Aglaura*, 1.3.55, 4.4.150), "*This spoke as if she studied an evasion*" (*Great Duke of Florence*, 4.1.106); in *Gentleman Usher* "*he studies*" (4.2.73) follows "I'll devise a speech."

stump

used to signal a missing limb or limbs; in *Titus Andronicus* the term is invoked for the armless Lavinia who to reveal her attackers "*takes the staff in her mouth, and guides it with her stumps and writes*" (G1r, 4.1.76); other examples are the appearance of a *lame*

soldier back from the wars: "*Wallace, like a halting Soldier on wooden stumps, with Mountford dumb, and Glascot blind*" and "*Beaumont with a wooden stump*" (*Valiant Scot*, E1v, F1r); an alternative is "*Enter three soldiers: one without an arm*" (*Maidenhead Well Lost*, 114).

sudden, suddenly

found in over fifty directions: "*Offers to go out, and suddenly draws back*" (*Dutch Courtesan*, 2.1.145), enter "*as if he were suddenly raised from dinner*" (*Downfall of Huntingdon*, 167–8), "*a sudden twang of Instruments*" (*Two Noble Kinsmen*, L2r, 5.1.168), "*sick on the sudden*" (*Mad Lover*, 55), "*on a sudden breaks off*" from a *dance* (*Blurt*, 1.1.169); figures *enter* suddenly (*Blurt*, 2.2.239; *Lust's Dominion*, 3.2.89; *Tragedy of Byron*, 4.2.164; *Love's Sacrifice*, 1846–7), "*enter suddenly and in fear*" (*Blurt*, 3.2.0), "*suddenly rush in*" (*Christian Turned Turk*, H1v), and suddenly *depart* (*Three Lords of London*, G4v; *Four Prentices*, 222), *slip* away (*Three Lords of London*, H1r), *leave* (*Grateful Servant*, I2r), *go* off (*Lady of Pleasure*, 4.1.0), *descend* (*Maid of Honour*, 4.4.58), *rise* from a *tomb* (*James IV*, 3–4), *start*/start off (*John a Kent*, 1257, 1265, 1271; *Tempest*, 1807, 4.1.138; *Lovesick Court*, 129), *awaken* (*Whore of Babylon*, DS before Act 1, 34); sound effects are "*Music suddenly plays*" (*Blurt*, 4.2.0), "*A tumult within and sudden noise*" (*Captives*, 1496), "*suddenly the Hoboys cease*" (*King John and Matilda*, 83), "*a sudden Thunderclap*" (*Captain Thomas Stukeley*, 2456–7; see also *Catiline*, 3.836); actions include "*suddenly is slain*" (*James IV*, 701), "*suddenly draws the curtain*" (*Lust's Dominion*, 1.1.0; *Unnatural Combat*, 5.2.238), "*gives him a box on the ear suddenly*" (*Captain*, 310), "*offer to run all at Piero, and on a sudden stop*" (*Antonio's Revenge*, 5.3.105), "*On a sudden in a kind of Noise like a Wind, the doors clattering, the Tombstone flies open*" (*Second Maiden's Tragedy*, 1926–7), "*suddenly riseth up a great tree between them, whereat amazedly they step back*" (*Warning for Fair Women*, E3v; see also *Cobbler's Prophecy*, 1335); for other examples see *Edward I*, 2607; *Doctor Faustus*, B 1300; *Death of Huntingdon*, 965–6; *Grim the Collier*, G2v; *What You Will*, A2r; *Whore of Babylon*, 4.1.0, 5.2.139; *Catiline*, 4.491; *Fair Maid of the Inn*, 157; *Messalina*, 2593–4; *Fool Would Be a Favourite*, C8r.

suis

found in the locution *cum suis* (literally "with his own"), Latin for "with his *followers*/men/*train*/ attendants," and used regularly when figures *enter* and *exit*; typical are "*Descendit cum suis*" and "*Surgit*

Spiritus cum suis" (*Bussy D'Ambois*, 4.2.138, 5.2.51); for examples see *Death of Huntingdon*, 1449; *Bussy D'Ambois*, 5.2.67; *Conspiracy of Byron*, 2.1.52, 3.2.284, 5.1.155; *Monsieur D'Olive*, 4.2.150; *Rape of Lucrece*, 245; *Bashful Lover*, 2.8.118; *Maid of Honour*, 3.1.198; *Believe as You List*, 487; *Love's Sacrifice*, 785; *Perkin Warbeck*, [3.4.54]; *Messalina*, 534; *Bloody Banquet*, 143; *Rebellion*, 49.

suit

(1) usually refers to a man's *suit* of ***clothes*** but (2) occasionally means "entreaty, petition"; figures appear "*in a masquing suit with a vizard in his hand*" (*Mad World*, 2.4.1), "*in a suit of gray, Velvet gown, Cap, Chain*" (*Wonder of a Kingdom*, 1.4.0), with "*a fair suit of apparel on his back*" (*Rare Triumphs*, 1374); distinctive *suits* include Edward I "*in his suit of Glass*" (*Edward I*, 630), "*a Canvas suit*" (*Jews' Tragedy*, 1998), "*some fantastic Sea suit*" (*1 Honest Whore*, 1.2.0), "*a suit of Leather close to his body*" (*Grim the Collier*, I2r), "*like wealthy citizens in satin suits*" (*Michaelmas Term*, 3.4.176; see also *Your Five Gallants*, F2r), "*Ver with his train, overlaid with suits of green moss, representing short grass*" (*Summer's Last Will*, 160); Henslowe's inventory lists many *suits* that include "one blue taffeta suit" (*Diary*, App. 2, 5), "one black satin suit" (134), "one ghost's suit" (37), "one Phaeton's suit" (141), "Longshank's suit" (7, 175), "one suit for Neptune" (17), "four knaves' suits" (21), "Will Summer's suit" (25), "Robin Hood's suit" (142); as with enter ***booted***, a journey about to be undertaken or just completed is indicated by "*in a riding suit*" (*Yorkshire Tragedy*, 296; *Picture*, 1.1.0; *Witch of Edmonton*, 1.1.155; *Perkin Warbeck*, 5.1.0); figures sometimes appear in an identifiable *suit*: "*in her page's suit*" (*Antonio and Mellida*, 4.1.131), "*Fungoso in Brisk's suit*" (Quarto *Every Man Out*, 1585; see also *Picture*, 4.2.154), "*Allwit in one of Sir Walter's suits*" (*Chaste Maid*, 2.3.0); reclothed figures enter "*freshly suited*" (*Fawn*, 2.29; *Fancies Chaste and Noble*, 407), "*in a new suit*" (Quarto *Every Man Out*, 1636; *Fleer*, 2.1.0), "*in another suit*" (*Looking Glass for London*, 522–3); see also *Goblins*, 3.7.58; examples of entreaties are "*seemeth to reject his suit*" (*Antonio's Revenge*, 3.1.0), "*lays a Suit and Letter at the door*" (*Wit without Money*, 180); see also *Golden Age*, 72; *Staple of News*, 1.2.16.

summon

used occasionally in a ***sound*** signal: "*he summons from the Castle with a trumpet*" (*Devil's Charter*, D3v), "*Summon the battle*" (*2 Tamburlaine*, 3362); see also *1 Troublesome Reign*, C3v, C4v; *Jews' Tragedy*, 798.

sundry

a ***permissive*** term comparable to ***several*** or ***diverse***: "*sundry disguises*" (*Wounds of Civil War*, 1076), "*Cornets in sundry places*" (*Two Noble Kinsmen*, F2r, 3.1.0), an entrance "*at two sundry doors*" (*Fair Em*, 813), "*Exeunt sundry ways*" and "*they dance together sundry changes*" (*Love's Sacrifice*, 1241, 1849), the Muses "*playing all upon sundry Instruments*" (*Alphonsus of Aragon*, 44–5).

supposed

used seldom for "believed" or "mistakenly believed": "*Eurymine, to be supposed Morpheus*" (*Maid's Metamorphosis*, C2v), "*supposed to go*" (*Puritan*, G3r), "*give their supposed King's hand to the Cardinal*" (*Queen's Exchange*, 530); *suppose* appears once as an imperative verb to set up an ***as*** [***if***] situation: "*Suppose the Temple of Mahomet*" (*Selimus*, 2021).

surround

see ***encompass***

swear

the *swearing* of an oath can be done on a ***dagger*** (*Soliman and Perseda*, B2v) but more commonly *on/upon/by* a ***sword***: "*swears them both to secrecy upon his Sword*" (*Maidenhead Well Lost*, 127); see also *Christian Turned Turk*, H1v; *Herod and Antipater*, I4v; *Jews' Tragedy*, 985; as part of a conversion the Mufty "*girds his sword: then swears him on the Mahomet's head, ungirds his sword*" (*Christian Turned Turk*, F2v); when *swords* are not called for, figures *swear* "*performance and secrecy*" (*Hengist*, DS before 4.3, 6–7), "*to secrecy*" (*Golden Age*, 20), "*to his obeisance*" (*Golden Age*, 53; *Silver Age*, 97), and *swear him/them* (*Four Plays in One*, 326; *Hengist*, DS before 2.2, 2–3, DS before 4.3, 12), simply *swear* (*2 Troublesome Reign*, C3v, C4r; *Valiant Scot*, K3v).

sweating

used occasionally to indicate ***haste*** and/or exertion: "*Enter Falselight, like a porter, sweating*" (*Michaelmas Term*, 2.3.314); see also *Humorous Day's Mirth*, 3.1.97; *Sir Thomas Wyatt*, 2.3.8; *Shoemaker a Gentleman*, 4.1.109; *Maid's Revenge*, H2r.

sweet

occasionally describes ***music*** linked to supernatural events with positive or pleasant implications; *Landgartha* gives the instrument likely appropriate: "*They sleep, and a sweet solemn Music of Recorders is heard, then enter an Angel*" (I1r), and an awakening figure says "Methought I heard a most heavenly music"; in MS *Humorous Lieutenant* "*He seems to Conjure; sweet Music is heard, and an Antic of little Fairies enter*" (2328–31); in *Seven Champions* "*The day clears, enchantments cease: Sweet Music*" (G4r); see also *soft*.

switch

refers to either a whip or an action: "*Enter Robin with a switch and a Currycomb*" (*Late Lancashire Witches*, 239, also 196), "*Gives him a touch with his switch*" (*Nice Valour*, 159), "*With riding Switches*" (*Jovial Crew*, 411), "*They switch, and draw*" (*Hyde Park*, F1v); see also *Queen and Concubine*, 9.

swoon, sound

to *faint*; *swoon* and the variant spelling *sound* each occur about a dozen times, often combined with *fall*: "*Falls in a swoon*" (*Atheist's Tragedy*, 3.1.73), "*Falls down in a feigned swoon*" (*Michaelmas Term*, 4.4.55), "*The King falls in a sound*" (Quarto *2 Henry VI*, E2v; Folio "*King sounds,*" 1729, 3.2.32), "*she falls and sounds*" (*Edward I*, 41), "*Runs at her and falls by the way in a Sound*" (*Second Maiden's Tragedy*, 1339–41); for other examples see *1 Edward IV*, 88; *Grim the Collier*, K1r; *1 If You Know Not Me*, 239; *Lovers' Progress*, 127; *Queen*, 3505; typical is simply *swoons/sounds* (*Fair Maid of the Exchange*, 83; *Dutch Courtesan*, 5.2.46; *Devil's Charter*, C4r; *Cupid's Revenge*, 286; *Tom a Lincoln*, 2110; *Old Law*, K2v; MS *Humorous Lieutenant*, 2392; *2 Arviragus and Philicia*, F11r; *Brennoralt*, 2.3.84; *Lovesick Court*, 100); some signals are more elaborate: "*bear out Mellida, as being swooned*" (*Antonio's Revenge*, 4.1.230), "*falls down as in a swoon*" (*Alchemist*, 4.5.62), "*knock him down, hurry him away in a sound*" (*Valiant Scot*, K1r), "*She seems to sound*" (Q2 *Bussy D'Ambois*, 4.1.147), "*Make as if she swoons*" (*Cobbler's Prophecy*, 970), "*She swoons, and he supports her in his arms*" (*2 Edward IV*, 182; see also *Bloody Banquet*, 558), "*Kicks her, she swoons*" (*City Nightcap*, 109), "*Aglaura swoons: rubs her*" and "*Brings up the body, she swoons and dies*" (*Aglaura*, 5.1.145, 184); see also *sink*.

sword

of the many (roughly 375) examples (1) most common are entrances *with a sword drawn* and directions to *draw* a sword, but also found are (2) *swords* linked to *cloaks*, *bucklers*, and other *weapons*, (3) *swords* as part of *ceremonies*, (4) a wide variety of actions and effects; for a sampling of the fifty figures who *enter* with sword drawn see *James IV*, 1808;

Lust's Dominion, 2.3.35, 87, 90; *Woman Killed*, 138; *Amends for Ladies*, 3.2.2; *Malcontent*, 1.7.0, 2.5.0; *Sophonisba*, 1.2.62, 2.2.25, 58; Q2 *Bussy D'Ambois*, 5.1.154; *King and No King*, 222; *Atheist's Tragedy*, 4.3.69; *Bartholomew Fair*, 4.3.0; *Honest Man's Fortune*, 226, 227, 239; *Valiant Welshman*, H3v; *Two Noble Ladies*, 99–100, 768, 1198, 1213; *Unnatural Combat*, 4.2.25; *Love's Sacrifice*, 2380; *City Nightcap*, 169; *Court Beggar*, 233; *Antipodes*, 266; *Imposture*, C5r; variations include "*a sword in her hand*" and "*looking on his sword and bending it*" (*Amends for Ladies*, 4.1.1, 4.4.1, also 5.2.180–1), "*with a sword drawn and a bear's head in his hand*" (*Mucedorus*, A3v), "*wounded, leaning upon his Sword*" (*Jews' Tragedy*, 881), "*with a broken sword*" (*Lust's Dominion*, 4.2.70); for a sampling of roughly forty examples of *draw* a *sword* see *Spanish Tragedy*, 2.1.67, 3.14.141; *Alphonsus of Aragon*, 1651; *Edward III*, A4v; *Warning for Fair Women*, D2r, E3v; *Coriolanus*, 1939, 3.1.222; *Silver Age*, 96; *Prophetess*, 363; *Captain*, 299, 310; *Cure for a Cuckold*, C2v; *Fair Quarrel*, 5.1.91; *City Madam*, 3.1.46; *Two Noble Ladies*, 1523, 2018, 2020; *Welsh Ambassador*, 2221; *Weeding of Covent Garden*, 55; *Bird in a Cage*, I4r; *Love and Honour*, 109, 175; variations include "*all snatch out their swords*" (*Bloody Banquet*, 55), "*Whips forth his Sword*" (*Herod and Antipater*, K2r), "*draws his sword, and runs at him when he turns aside*" (*Cupid's Revenge*, 286), "*Draws his sword and knights them*" (*1 Edward IV*, 32), "*draw their swords: menace each other*" (*Lovesick Court*, 129), "*draws his Sword from under his Gown. Crasy closes with, and disarms him*" (*City Wit*, 360).

Directions call for a *long* sword (Folio *Every Man In*, 5.3.35; *Faithful Friends*, 1047–8; *Fine Companion*, I1v), a *two-handed* sword (*Old Wives Tale*, 253; *Noble Gentleman*, 234), *bloody* swords (*Locrine*, 3–4; *Roman Actor*, 5.1.180; *Fair Favourite*, 256; *Osmond*, A2v); Henslowe's inventory includes "*one long sword*" (*Diary*, App. 2, 44); *swords* are linked to *bucklers* (*Three Ladies of London*, A3r; Q2 *Romeo and Juliet*, A3r, 1.1.0; *Sir Thomas More*, 412; *Histriomastix*, D2v; *Satiromastix*, 4.2.0; *Jews' Tragedy*, 1996) and are found in combination with *cloaks*: "*his sword in his hand, a Cloak on his Arm*" (*Dick of Devonshire*, 715), "*throws his cloak on the other's point; gets within him and takes away his sword*" (*Bride*, 36); see also *Knight of Malta*, 155; *Court Beggar*, 245; *Mad Couple*, 38; *Country Captain*, C5v; *Parson's Wedding*, 495; for a *disguise* a woman appears "*in man's habit, sword and pistol*" (*English Moor*, 75); *swords* are linked to *executions* (*Dead Man's Fortune*, 50–1; *Fatal Contract*, E4r), *funerals* (*Antonio's Revenge*, 2.1.0; *Chaste Maid*, 5.4.0; *Wasp*, 474–5), ceremonies (*Duchess of*

Malfi, 3.4.7), most commonly coronations, processions, and other royal events in some combination with **mace**, **purse**, **scepter**: "*the Mace and Sword laid on the Table*" (*Antipodes*, 287), "*bearing a sword and a Globe*" (*Look about You*, 2823), "*Emperor with a pointless sword, next the King of Castile, carrying a sword with a point*" (*Friar Bacon*, 2074–5), "*Sussex bearing the Crown, Howard bearing the Scepter, the Constable the Mace, Tame the Purse, Shandoyse the Sword*" (*1 If You Know Not Me*, 239, also 195, 244); see also *2 Tamburlaine*, 3110; *Downfall of Huntingdon*, 2699; *If This Be Not a Good Play*, 1.2.0; *Henry VIII*, 1343, 2.4.0; *Birth of Merlin*, C1r; *Believe as You List* calls for swords to be **ready** (2378–80, also 2716–18, 2722–3).

For examples of actions, *swords* can be *fallen upon* (*Caesar and Pompey*, 5.2.161; *Nero*, 97; *Unfortunate Lovers*, 70), **put** up (*All Fools*, 2.1.296; *Jovial Crew*, 400; *News from Plymouth*, 194), *let **fall*** (*Richard III*, B2v, 376, 1.2.182; *Thierry and Theodoret*, 47; *Wizard*, 2112), **thrown/cast** away (*Fair Maid of the Inn*, 217; *Bloody Brother*, 257; *Love's Sacrifice*, 2534–5; *Cruel Brother*, 189), **snatched** away (*Elder Brother*, 41; *Lovesick Court*, 157), **kissed** (*Famous Victories*, G2r; *Jews' Tragedy*, 940; *Love's Sacrifice*, 2644), **waved/flourished** (Folio *Every Man In*, 5.3.35; *Coriolanus*, 695, 1.6.75; *New Way to Pay*, 5.1.360; *Court Beggar*, 233), **offered** at someone (Folio *Richard III*, 371, 1.2.178; *Alarum for London*, 716; *Look about You*, 2518; *Bloody Brother*, 253); figures use *swords* to **swear** oaths (*Christian Turned Turk*, H1v; *Maidenhead Well Lost*, 127; *Herod and Antipater*, I4v; *Jews' Tragedy*, 985), threaten suicide (*Spanish Tragedy*, 2.5.67; *Hengist*, DS before 4.3, 7–8); other actions/effects include "*Claps his Sword over the Table*" (*Amends for Ladies*, 3.4.54–5), "*a sword, as thrust through his face*" (*Caesar and Pompey*, 4.3.0), "*takes a dead man's head upon his sword's point holding it up [to] Edmond's soldiers they fly*" (*Edmond Ironside*, 989–91; see also *Travels of Three English Brothers*, 323), "*runs upon Montague, and struggling yields him his Sword*" (*Honest Man's Fortune*, 234), "*loses his sword, La-writ treads on it*" (*Little French Lawyer*, 396), "*They struggle, and both fall down, still striving to hold each other's sword*" (*Lovesick Court*, 142); see also *Wounds of Civil War*, 252–3; *Battle of Alcazar*, 582–3; *Locrine*, 2110; *Tom a Lincoln*, 2231–2; offstage sounds include "*Within Clashing swords*" (*Love's Cure*, 174; see also *1 Passionate Lovers*, D2r; *Amorous War*, G4v), "*Clashing swords. A cry within, down with their swords*" (*Rule a Wife*, 224; see also *Honest Man's Fortune*, 259); atypical are "*A hand from out a cloud, threateneth a burning sword*" (*Looking Glass for London*, 1636), revengers

with "*pistolets and short swords under their robes*" (*Malcontent*, 5.5.66).

T

table

(1) widely cited (roughly 200 examples) in a variety of contexts, most commonly for meals or **banquets**, (2) occasionally a *tablet* to **write** upon; *tables* are often linked specifically to the serving of food: "*Enter two with a table and a banquet on it*" (*Taming of a Shrew*, A3v), "*They bring forth a table, and serve in the banquet*" (*1 Edward IV*, 58); see also *1 Iron Age*, 302; *Revenger's Tragedy*, I2v; *Faithful Friends*, 2485–8; *English Traveller*, 66; some annotated playbooks call for *tables*: "*be ready Carintha at a Table*" (*Welsh Ambassador*, 1156–7; see also *Barnavelt*, 1184, 1611, 2159; *Two Merry Milkmaids*, I2v, I3r); *tables* are regularly linked to other items of stage furniture such as **chairs** and especially **stools**: "*A Table set out, and stools*" (*1 Fair Maid of the West*, 307; *Spanish Curate*, 133; *Knight of Malta*, 129; *Imposture*, E5r), "*a table, with chairs and stools placed above it*" (*1 Iron Age*, 334); see also *Spanish Curate*, 117; *Lovers' Progress*, 113; *Launching of the Mary*, 1926; *Rebellion*, 83; *Variety*, D6v; *Platonic Lovers*, 81; figures **bring/set** tables **forth/out**: "*A Table, Count book, Standish, Chair and stools set out*" (*City Madam*, 1.2.143; for a sampling see *2 Fortune's Tennis*, 30; *1 Honest Whore*, 4.1.0; *If This Be Not a Good Play*, 2.2.0, 4.4.0; *Fortune by Land and Sea*, 420; *Devil's Law Case*, 3.3.0; *Noble Spanish Soldier*, 1.2.0; *Welsh Ambassador*, 1934–5; *Bondman*, 2.3.0; *Renegado*, 2.4.0; *Bloody Banquet*, 1051; *Antipodes*, 324; *City Wit*, 279; *Doubtful Heir*, D7r, E5r; a few signals call for the removal of *tables*: "*All rise, and Tables removed*" (*Henry VIII*, 749, 1.4.60; see also *Tempest*, 1618, 3.3.82); several figures *enter at a table*: "*Enter Carintha at a Table reading*" (*Welsh Ambassador*, 1183); see also Folio *Richard III*, 1966, 3.4.0; *Women Pleased*, 242; MS *Poor Man's Comfort*, 1647; *tables* are set (*All Fools*, 5.2.0; *Devil's Charter*, L3r), **prepared** (Q2 *Hamlet*, N3v, 5.2.224; *Rape of Lucrece*, 187; *Gentleman of Venice*, H4v), most commonly **covered** (*1 Edward IV*, 50) with **treasure** (*Antipodes*, 324), "*a green Carpet*" (*Sir Thomas More*, 735), **black** (*Noble Spanish Soldier*, 1.2.0; *Rape of Lucrece*, 234); detailed examples include "*cover a Table, two bottles of wine, Dishes of Sugar, and a dish of Sparagus*" (*Sparagus Garden*, 158), "*A Table ready covered with Cloth Napkins Salt Trenchers and Bread*" (*Spanish Curate*, 129/501), "*a table covered with black, on which stands two black tapers lighted, she in mourning*"

(*Insatiate Countess*, 1.1.0); other items set or **placed** on a *table* include **bags** (*Captain Thomas Stukeley*, 2273), **meat** (*Old Wives Tale*, 734; Folio *Titus Andronicus*, 2525–6, 5.3.25; *Patient Grissil*, 4.3.11), writing implements: "*One bearing light, a standish and paper, which sets a Table*" (*Bussy D'Ambois*, 5.1.0); *tables* can be **furnished** (*Revenger's Tragedy*, I2v; *Sea Voyage*, 56; *Wasp*, 2185) or provided with "*furniture for the table*" (*Dutch Courtesan*, 3.3.60).

Sometimes *table* can refer to the people at a *table* or to the act of eating: "*she makes a Curtsy to the Table*" (*Bloody Banquet*, 1920), enter "*with a napkin on his shoulder, and a trencher in his hand as from table*" (*Roaring Girl*, 1.1.0); specific *tables* include a **council** table (*Sir Thomas Wyatt*, 1.6.0; *Henry VIII*, 3035, 5.2.35; 3055, 5.2.42), a **long** table (*1 Iron Age*, 302), a **small** table: "*A banquet brought in, and by it a small Table for the Queen*" (*Bloody Banquet*, 1901–2), "*A small Table under a State for the Cardinal, a longer Table for the Guests*" (*Henry VIII*, 661–2, 1.4.0); a trick *table* (that may be relevant to the **vanishing** banquet in *Tempest*, 3.3) is signaled in *Wasp* where "*the table turns and such things appear*" and "*Table turns*" (2220–1, 2324); actions include "*rise from a Table*" (*Timon of Athens*, 490, 1.2.145; *Christian Turned Turk*, B1r), "*rush from the table*" (*Devil's Charter*, L1v), "*starts from the table*" (*1 Edward IV*, 62), "*Looks out under the Table*" (Quarto *Every Man Out*, 4075), "*rises and throws down the table*" (*Knave in Grain*, 1857–8); a sequence in *Rebellion* provides "*Goes under the table,*" "*sit about the table,*" "*Overthrows the table*" (83, 84, 87); occasionally figures **hide** under a *table* (*Two Noble Ladies*, 98–9), so that *Variety* provides "*creeps under the Table*" and "*peeps from under the Table*" (D10r, D11r).

Table can also refer to a writing *table* (*John of Bordeaux*, 1028; *Nice Valour*, 188; *Christian Turned Turk*, F2v; *Court Beggar*, 260, 261; *Sparagus Garden*, 195), **table**book (*Spanish Curate*, 98; *Maidenhead Well Lost*, 142; *Roman Actor*, 5.1.94; *News from Plymouth*, 132), and *tablet* (*Lover's Melancholy*, 5.2.71); actions include "*Draw out his Tablebook*" (*Love's Labour's Lost*, F4r, 5.1.15), "*draws out his writing tables and writes*" (*Antonio's Revenge*, 1.2.92), "*Cupid enters with a Table written, hung about his neck*" (*Tragedy of Byron*, 2.2); atypical is "*upon his breast a blue table full of silver letters*" (*Two Noble Ladies*, 1102); for *table***cloth** see *Woman Killed*, 117, 132; *Thracian Wonder*, C4v.

tabor

a small **drum** with a skin cover at both ends, suspended from the wrist and played by that hand; the *tabor* is always paired with the **pipe** and sometimes both are played by one figure, as in the titlepage woodcuts of Will Kemp and Richard Tarlton; this "poor man's orchestra" accompanied singing and dancing; although numerous references to the *tabor* and *pipe* occur in dialogue, only a few directions cite them, all in the context of the common people: "*Jack Drum, and Timothy Tweedle, with a Tabor and a Pipe*" and "*The Tabor and Pipe strike up a Morris*" (*Jack Drum's Entertainment*, A2v, A3v), "*A noise within of a Tabor and a Pipe*" followed by "*shoemakers in a morris*" (*Shoemakers' Holiday*, 3.3.47, 51), "*Ariel plays the tune on a Tabor and Pipe*" (*Tempest*, 1481, 3.2.124); see also **fife**, **morris**.

take for

see **mistake**

talk, talking

most of the eighty-five examples direct figures to (1) **enter** *talking*, (2) talk **aside** or **privately**, 3) simply *talk to* or *with* another; for enter *talking* see *John a Kent*, 856; *Edward II*, 2217; *Patient Grissil*, 2.1.76; *1 Edward IV*, 31; *Puritan*, H2v; *What You Will*, E1r; *Antonio's Revenge*, 2.1.0, 3.1.0, 4.1.70, 5.1.0; *Tragedy of Byron*, 4.2.85; *Pericles*, C1v, 2.Chorus.16; MS *Humorous Lieutenant*, 2121; *Coxcomb*, 310; *Dick of Devonshire*, 1555; *Mad Couple*, 44; *1 Passionate Lovers*, D8r; *Faithful Friends*, 774, 2479; variations include entrances "*talking in secret*" (*Jews' Tragedy*, 353), "*as in talk with him*" (*Conspiracy*, N1r), "*walking and talking*" (*How a Man May Choose*, A2v), "*talking at the door*" (*Lost Lady*, 587) and "*People talking without*" (*Parson's Wedding*, 393), exit talking (*Brennoralt*, 3.2.13), "*the rest stand talking*" (*Blurt*, 1.1.169, also 3.1.31), "*they sit a good while on the Stage before the Candles are lighted, talking together*" (*What You Will*, A2r); for talk aside see *Fatal Contract*, C2v; *City Wit*, 307; *Jovial Crew*, 446; *New Academy*, 18, 101; *Novella*, 173; *Queen's Exchange*, 464; variations include enter "*aside talking*" (*Wizard*, 1827), "*takes Memnon aside and talks with him*" (*Mad Lover*, 4), "*Talk in private*" (*Fair Maid of the Exchange*, 68, 69; *Knave in Grain*, 2769–70; *Lost Lady*, Folio 592, MS 1656–7), "*talk privately*" (*Two Merry Milkmaids*, E3r; *Lovesick Court*, 93; *Imposture*, E7v; *Cardinal*, 2.1.35), "*talketh with Edmond secretly*" (*Edmond Ironside*, 1383); for figures who are directed to *talk with/to* another or **together** see *Edmond Ironside*, 1105, 1934, 1958; Quarto *Merry Wives*, C2r, 2.1.205; *Jack Drum's Entertainment*, C1r; *Amends for Ladies*, 1.1.190; *Four Prentices*, 178; *Lust's Dominion*, 5.1.81, 113; *Maidenhead Well Lost*, 133;

Inconstant Lady, 1.2.79; *Parson's Wedding*, 394; variations include "*talks in his sleep*" (*Tom a Lincoln*, 1474; *Twins*, G2r), "*goes to the king, does his duty, and talks with him*" (*Death of Huntingdon*, 3019–20; see also *Fair Favourite*, 252), "*Here they two talk and rail what they list*" (*Greene's Tu Quoque*, I1r), "*talks, and takes tobacco between*" (Folio *Every Man Out*, 3.9.65); see also *Alphonsus of Aragon*, 1833–4, 1910–11; *Gentleman Usher*, 3.2.276; some actions are signaled *as/while* a figure is *talking*: "*Give her the letter as she talks*" (*Two Maids of More-Clacke*, D1r), "*stealing forward, Prince and Lady talking*" (*Look about You*, 663–4), "*as he is talking, Hercules steals it* [a letter] *out of his pocket*" (*Fawn*, 4.57), "*Enter Nobs and cut away the Goose while he talketh, and leave the head behind him*" (*Jack Straw*, 487–8); *talk* occasionally appears as a noun: "*in talk*" (*Sir John Oldcastle*, 215; *Michaelmas Term*, 5.3.0), "*overhears their talk*" (*Hieronimo*, 3.38), "*break off their private talk*" (*Lost Lady*, Folio 592, MS 1677), "*While master Sanders and he are in busy talk one to the other, Browne steps to a corner*" (*Warning for Fair Women*, D2v).

taper

a slender **candle** that (1) like other **lights** by convention can indicate **night**/darkness on a stage with no variable lighting, and is found in (2) **mourning**, devotional, and penitential scenes, (3) the **setting** of **tables** for **banquets**, the **study**, **reading** and **writing**; *tapers*/candles are linked to scenes located indoors, as opposed to **torches**/**links** that usually indicate outdoor locales; an exception is for women doing public penance, so that Dame Elinor appears "*in a white Sheet, and a Taper burning in her hand*" (Folio *2 Henry VI*, 1188–9, 2.4.16) and Jane Shore "*in a white sheet barefooted with her hair about her ears, and in her hand a wax taper*" (*2 Edward IV*, 165; for another "*wax taper*" see *Fatal Contract*, C4v); entrances that involve a *taper*/*tapers*, whether to denote darkness or a *ceremony*, include *Much Ado*, I2v, 5.3.0; *Julius Caesar*, 2148, 4.3.157; *Macbeth*, 2111, 5.1.18; *Sophonisba*, 1.2.0; *Monsieur D'Olive*, 2.1.0; Q2 *Bussy D'Ambois*, 5.3.0; *Elder Brother*, 38; *Lovers' Progress*, 104, 108; *Rule a Wife*, 228; *Maid in the Mill*, 11, 57; *Four Plays in One*, 347; *Guardian*, 3.6.0, 204; *Jews' Tragedy*, 1360–1; *Maid's Revenge*, F4v; *Arcadia*, E4v; *Platonic Lovers*, 28, 33; typical is an entrance "*in her night gown, with a prayer Book and a Taper*" (*Twins*, F2v); *tapers* can be linked to pages (*Antonio's Revenge*, 3.1.0; *Turk*, 1184), "*four old Beldams*" who "*place four tapers at the four corners*" of Danae's **bed** (*Golden Age*, 67), "*two Furies, with black Tapers*" (*Night Walker*, 364); directions call for "*tapers* burning" (*Hoffman*, 1413) but more commonly *lighted tapers* (*Fedele and Fortunio*, 493; *Virgin Martyr*, 2.1.86; *Women Beware Women*, 5.2.72; *Messalina*, 677); for "*Puts out the taper*" see *Insatiate Countess*, 1.1.101; for an anticipatory "*Tapers ready*" see *Custom of the Country*, 326/455.

As to religion, *tapers* can be linked to priests/**altars**; examples are "*Apollo's Priests, with Tapers*" (*Rape of Lucrece*, 184), "*An Altar discovered, with Tapers, and a Book on it*" (*Knight of Malta*, 161, also 152), "*they set the censer and tapers on Juno's altar with much reverence*" (*Women Beware Women*, 5.2.72; see also *Jews' Tragedy*, 2148, *Lovesick King*, 165–6); *tapers* linked to mourning include "*a table covered with black, on which stands two black tapers lighted*" (*Insatiate Countess*, 1.1.0), "*A table set forth with two tapers, a death's head, a book. Jolenta in mourning*" (*Devil's Law Case*, 3.3.0); see also *Death of Huntingdon*, 2984; *1 Honest Whore*, 4.1.0; *Noble Spanish Soldier*, 1.2.0; *tapers* are found in banquets and in the study; examples are "*a rich banquet, and tapers*" (*Guardian*, 3.6.0; see also *Late Lancashire Witches*, 237), "*in his Study. A Taper, Bags, Books, etc.*" (*Novella*, 110; see also *News from Plymouth*, 167); most common is for a *taper* to be included in the setting of a table, sometimes with a specific purpose in mind: "*A Table prepared, two tapers*" (*Two Gentlemen of Venice*, H4v), "*Taper: pen and ink Table*" (*Barnavelt*, 1610–11), "*Table, Chessboard, and Tapers*" (Q2 *Bussy D'Ambois*, 1.2.0); see also *Thracian Wonder*, D1v; *Lovers' Progress*, 113; *Court Secret*, F2r; *Doubtful Heir*, E5r; *Wedding*, I1r; distinctive actions include "*They put Tapers to his fingers, and he starts*" (*Merry Wives*, G3r, 5.5.88), "*takes the taper and finds him not the same*" (*Wizard*, 2286).

target

a light round **shield** or **buckler** used in **battle**, usually cited with a **sword** or **javelin**: "*Guy with his shield, and a Page brings his sword and Target*" (*Four Prentices*, 222), "*combat with javelins first, after with swords and targets*" (*Golden Age*, 51), "*a fierce fight with sword and target*" (*Rape of Lucrece*, 252, also 243), "*Pages with targets and javelins*" (*Sophonisba*, Prologue.0, also 1.2.185, 5.2.0, 5.3.6); see also *Edward II*, 1786; *Locrine*, 434; *Birth of Merlin*, C3r; MS *Poor Man's Comfort*, 2220; *Coronation*, 262; Henslowe's inventory lists "nine iron targets," "one copper target," "four wooden targets" (*Diary*, App. 2, 76, 77, 78).

tarras

or "terrace," a rarely used term for the playing space **above**: "*Enter King, Queen, and Somerset on the Tarras*"

(Folio *2 Henry VI*, 2848–9, 4.9.0), "*Cardinal on the terrace*" (*White Devil*, 4.3.40).

tavern

occasionally cited in directions although several of the most elaborate scenes (*1 Henry IV*, 2.4; *1 Fair Maid of the West*, Act 1) provide no specific signals; groups are directed to enter "*in the tavern*" (*Match at Midnight*, 40), "*in the Tavern with a Drawer*" (*Eastward Ho*, E1r, also E4r); also specified are Mistress Quickly as "*Hostess of the Tavern*" (*2 Henry IV*, C1r, 2.1.0), "*Tavern Boys, etc.*" (*Captain*, 283); three Caroline plays provide **as from**/**as in** signals so that figures are directed to enter "*as coming from a Tavern*" (*Example*, E4v), "*as in a Tavern*" (*Wit in a Constable*, 231), "*as in a Tavern. Drawers*" (*Gamester*, C3r); atypical is a signal for "*The Tavern Scene*" (*Knave in Grain*, 1400–1); see also **cup**, **drawer**, **glass**, **towel**, **wine**.

tawny

a light brown color usually associated with **followers**, servants, and tradesmen; examples are Winchester's men "*in Tawny Coats*" (*1 Henry VI*, 392, 1.3.28, also 1281–2, 3.1.73), a physician with "*his man in a Tawny coat*" (*Grim the Collier*, G5v), "*in a tawny coat like a tinker*" (*Two Maids of More-Clacke*, C3v); in *2 If You Know Not Me* the figure who initially enters as "*Peddler, with tawny coat*" (258) is subsequently referred to as *Tawnycoat*; atypical are a figure "dead in his melancholy" who enters "*in Tawny*" (*Woman Is a Weathercock*, 2.1.25), the description of Morocco as "*a tawny Moor all in white*" (*Merchant of Venice*, B4v, 2.1.0).

tear

of the roughly twenty examples (1) most involve the *ripping*/*ripping off* of items of clothing, **trees**, most commonly **letters** and other **papers**, (2) two are nouns linked to **weeping**; *tearing* of clothing includes "*tears open his breast*" (*Antonio's Revenge*, 3.1.0), "*They tear off his jacket*" (*City Match*, 219), "*tears off his doublet*" (*Fair Maid of the Inn*, 201); other examples of *tearings* are Ajax who "*tears a young Tree up by the roots, and assails Hector*" (*1 Iron Age*, 300; see also *Brazen Age*, 252), "*tearing her hair*" (*Jack Drum's Entertainment*, D3v); for the *tearing* of letters and other papers see *George a Greene*, 134; Quarto *2 Henry VI*, B2v, 1.3.39; *Fair Em*, 589; *Jack Drum's Entertainment*, F3r; *Roaring Girl*, 3.2.73; *Launching of the Mary*, 2031; *English Moor*, 35; *tear* can be linked to **snatch**: "*snatches them and tears them*" (*King Leir*, 2586),

"*Gloster offers to put up a Bill: Winchester snatches it, tears it*" (*1 Henry VI*, 1203–4, 3.1.0); see also *Histriomastix*, G1r; *Aglaura*, 5.3.174; figures who shed *tears* are **mourners** who "*wet their handkerchiefs with their tears, kiss them, and lay them on the hearse*" (*Antonio's Revenge*, 2.1.0), Chastity in a **dumb show** who "*wringing her hands, in tears departs*" (*Warning for Fair Women*, E3v).

tempest

a seldom used synonym for **storm** calling for **sound** and other effects: "*Storm and Tempest*" (Folio *King Lear*, 1584, 2.4.284), "*Sound, Thunder and Tempest*" (*Golden Age*, 78), "*A Tempest, Thunder and Lightning. Enter Master and two Sailors*" (*Sea Voyage*, 2); in *Captives* the bookkeeper wrote "*Tempest*" (901) just before dialogue reference to one.

tent

Elizabethan players did at times set up *tents* onstage, particularly for effects of some importance or duration; examples are the plot of *2 Seven Deadly Sins* which begins "*A tent being placed on the stage for Henry the sixth, he in it Asleep*" (1–2), a **dumb show** where bribes are represented by "*a Tent, where a Table is furnished with diverse bags of money*" and "*another Tent*" that contains "*a great quantity of rich Plate*" (*Devil's Charter*, A2r); at the other extreme are signals likely **fictional** such as "*Alarms again, and then enter three or four, bearing the Duke of Buckingham wounded to his Tent*" (Quarto *2 Henry VI*, H3v, [5.2.65]), "*Enter three Watchmen to guard the King's Tent*" (*3 Henry VI*, 2220, 4.3.0), for in neither scene does the *tent* play a significant role in the staging (and Buckingham's fate in battle is not even included in Folio *2 Henry VI*).

Most of the other *tent* scenes fall between such extremes; *Edward I* provides the most examples: "*the Queen's Tent opens, she is discovered in her bed,*" "*They close the Tent,*" "*The Queen's Tent opens,*" "*The Nurse closeth the Tent,*" "*Enter the Novice and his company to give the Queen Music at her Tent,*" "*Then all pass in their order to the king's pavilion, the king sits in his Tent with his pages about him*" (1453, 1517, 1587, 1686, 1715, 1932); here the number of scenes involved, along with the reference to "*the king's pavilion,*" makes likely the presence of some onstage property that may have remained in place throughout the performance; however, comparable scenes that involve **discoveries** or entrances *from a tent* could be staged in terms of **as in**/**as from**; examples are the entrance of Tamburlaine's two sons "*from the tent where Caliphas* *sits asleep*" (*2 Tamburlaine*, 3673), "*Achilles discovered in his Tent, about him his bleeding Myrmidons, himself wounded*" and later enter "*from his Tent*" (*1 Iron Age*, 324, 328); an *as in* approach is spelled out in a Caroline play where twice figures are directed to enter "*as in their Tent*" (*Conspiracy*, H3r, I3r).

The actual presence of property *tents* is therefore hard to determine; *Richard III*, 5.3 starts with two dialogue references to Richard's *tent*, and Richmond and his followers after his invitation "*withdraw into the tent*" (Folio 3484, 5.3.46); two subsequent directions then cite Richmond's *tent* ("*Enter Derby to Richmond in his Tent*," L3r, 3520, 5.3.78; "*Enter the Lords to Richmond sitting in his Tent*," Folio 3685–6, 5.3.222), but none refers to Richard's nor are there any signals for the pitching of *tents* onstage (only to be found at the opening of the plot of *2 Seven Deadly Sins* where presumably Henry VI was to remain onstage for the entire performance); a long demanding scene such as *Richard III*, 5.3 would justify the pitching of two *tents* onstage but less clear is the situation in *Troilus and Cressida* where at 3.3.37 Achilles and Patroclus are to "*stand in their tent*" (Quarto, F4v) or enter "*in their Tent*" (Folio, 1888); in both Quarto and Folio Ulysses comments that "Achilles stands i'th' entrance of his tent" but an *as in* approach could be generated not by a property introduced for this scene but by a **curtain** or a **door**, Ulysses's line, and the playgoer's imagination; relevant too is *Rape of Lucrece* where various dialogue references to *tents* (e.g., "Command lights and torches in our tents") are accompanied by "*A Table and Lights in the tent*" (245–7); see also *Devil's Charter* where Borgia threatens Countess Katherine by having her two sons brought forth "*from Caesar's Tent*" and then when she thinks her sons are dead surprises her when "*He discovereth his Tent where her two sons were at Cards*" (H4r, I1v), and the *Troilus and Cressida* plot fragment: "*Enter Diomede to Achilles's Tent to them Menelaus, to them Ulysses to them Achilles in his Tent to them Ajax with Patroclus on his back. Exeunt*" (33–7).

terrace
see **tarras**

throat
cited occasionally, mostly for onstage violence: "*cuts their throats*" (*Titus Andronicus*, K1v, 5.2.203), "*catches at her throat*" (*Widow's Tears*, 5.5.69); as part of a trick to get a would-be lover to kill her, Olympia "*anoints*

her throat" (*2 Tamburlaine*, 3959); other examples are "*stretches his Throat in the Tune*" (*Court Beggar*, 261), a **devil** "*with the face, wings, and tail of a Dragon; a skin coat all speckled on the throat*" (*Caesar and Pompey*, 2.1.24).

throne, chair of state
cited less often (roughly forty examples) than it is used; the only *throne* specified in the Shakespeare canon is at Richard III's coronation where he "*ascendeth the throne*" (Quarto *Richard III*, H4v, 4.2.3); one locution calls for the **placing**/**setting**/seating of a figure in a *throne*/*chair of state* (usually simply **chair**): "*placing him in a chair*" (*Broken Heart*, 4.3.0), "*they seat him in the throne and Crown him King*" (*Hengist*, DS before 4.3, 2), "*set down over the Stage in a Throne*" (*Looking Glass for London*, 159–60), "*he raises Herod and sets him in his Chair, makes Alexander and Aristobulus kiss his feet*" (*Herod and Antipater*, F4r, also I4v); see also *Alphonsus of Aragon*, 501; *Conspiracy*, G1r; **ascending** to a *throne*/*chair of state* can be a highly significant bit of stage business: Tamburlaine uses Bajazet as a footstool and "*gets up upon him to his chair*" (*1 Tamburlaine*, 1473), "*Fortune takes her Chair, the Kings lying at her feet, she treading on them as she goes up*" (*Old Fortunatus*, 1.1.63), "*when they come unto the Throne, the Tyrant of Cilicia puts by the old King, and ascends alone*" (*Bloody Banquet*, 53–5); for other figures who *ascend*/**mount** to *thrones*/*chairs* see *Downfall of Huntingdon*, 71; *Escapes of Jupiter*, 1423; *Histriomastix*, H2v; *Jews' Tragedy*, 7, 118; a few signals call for **descents**: "*Descends his throne*" (*Jews' Tragedy*, 3253–4), "*Rises and resigns his chair*" (*Great Duke of Florence*, 4.2.208); in Folio *3 Henry VI* the signal for York and his group to take the *throne* is "*They go up*" and later "*Here they come down*" (38, 1.1.32; 233, 1.1.205); the presence of one or more figures on a raised platform adjacent to a *throne* is sometimes specified: "*coming near the chair of state, Ferdinand Ascends, places Hoffman at his feet, sets a Coronet on his head*" (*Hoffman*, 483–5); see also *Edward I*, 101; *Jews' Tragedy*, 354–5; in *Henry VIII* Wolsey "*places himself under the King's feet on his right side*" and when the queen enters Henry "*riseth from his State, takes her up, kisses and placeth her by him*" (319–20, 331–3, 1.2.0, 8); for other *thrones*/*chairs of state* see *Histriomastix*, B3v; *Sophonisba*, 5.2.49; *Great Duke of Florence*, 5.2.107; *Perkin Warbeck*, 1.1.0; *Doubtful Heir*, F2v; atypical is an entrance "*in a Throne drawn by Dragons*" (*Prophetess*, 341, also 346).

Our sense of how *thrones* were brought onstage has been influenced by Jonson's mocking of the "creaking throne" that "comes down the boys to please" (Folio *Every Man In*, Prologue.16) and by several directions: "*Exit Venus. Or if you can conveniently, let a chair come down from the top of the stage, and draw her up*" (*Alphonsus of Aragon*, 2109–10), "*Music while the Throne descends*" (*Doctor Faustus*, B 2006), "*Throne descends*" and "*A Song in the Throne*" (*Variety*, D11r); the *music* that accompanied such descents (with two of the *thrones* supernatural rather than regal) likely was not designed to cover the "creaking" but, given available theatre technology, to compensate for the slowness of the process; elsewhere signals call for large properties such as *beds* and *scaffolds* to be *thrust* onto the *stage*, so that most *thrones* may have been brought on in the same manner or *discovered* rather than dropped from *above*; a late example is "*A Chair of state discovered*" (*King John and Matilda*, 29).

throw

used roughly eighty-five times in a variety of contexts: (1) *throwing* of properties, (2) the *throwing* off of a disguise, (3) the *throwing* down of one figure by another, (4) other distinctive stage business; a common signal is for the *throwing* of a *weapon*: "*throws away one of the swords*" (*Cardinal*, 4.3.78), "*Throws off his weapon*" (*Country Girl*, H2r), "*Throw away his dags*" (*Court Beggar*, 248), "*throws his Sword at the King*" (*Prisoners*, B7r, also B9r); see also *Massacre at Paris*, 1063; *Bondman*, 4.2.128; *Fair Maid of the Inn*, 217; *Goblins*, 2.3.18; *Brennoralt*, 2.1.41; *Unfortunate Mother*, 149, 150; other items *thrown* include a *book* (*Maid of Honour*, 4.3.20), *cup* (*Christian Turned Turk*, F2v), *purse* (Folio *Richard III*, 1910, 3.2.106; *2 Edward IV*, 169; *Guardian*, 5.4.96; *Lady's Trial*, 1253), *money* (*Thomas Lord Cromwell*, A2v; *Distresses*, 305), *bags* (*Guardian*, 5.4.110), *stones* (*Alarum for London*, 1329), and *wine*: "*Throws the wine in the Drawer's face*" (*Miseries of Enforced Marriage*, 1076–7; see also *Politician*, F4r; *Imposture*, E8r; *Variety*, D11v); other properties and usages include "*Clarence takes his red Rose out of his hat, and throws it at Warwick*" (Octavo *3 Henry VI*, E2r, 5.1.83), "*throws down the broth on the ground*" (*Arden of Faversham*, 380–1), "*Throws down his Gauntlet*" (Folio *3 Henry VI*, 2585, 4.7.75), "*throws up a shovel*" (Q1 *Hamlet*, H4r, 5.1.74), "*shout, and throw up their Caps*" (*Coriolanus*, 2425, 3.3.137), "*throws a Thunderbolt*" (*Cymbeline*, 3127, 5.4.92), "*rises and throws down the table*" (*Knave in Grain*, 1857–8), "*throws up a ladder of cords*" (*Insatiate Countess*, 3.1.42), "*Throws meal in his face, takes his purse, etc.*" (*Hengist*, 5.1.319), "*both spit at*

the Image, throw it down, and spurn it*" (*Virgin Martyr*, 3.2.53), "*tears and throws the paper to him*" (*English Moor*, 35), "*writes a little, throws down the paper and departs*" (*Law Tricks*, 204), "*Draw and fight, throw pots and stools*" (*Amends for Ladies*, 3.4.133–4); see also *Taming of a Shrew*, C2v; *David and Bethsabe*, 1332, 1353; *1 Henry IV*, K1v, 5.3.54; *Two Lamentable Tragedies*, I2r; *Wise Woman of Hogsdon*, 281; *Woman Is a Weathercock*, 3.3.1; *Devil's Charter*, D4r; *Match Me in London*, 3.2.18; *No Wit*, 2.3.165; *White Devil*, 5.4.135; *Bartholomew Fair*, 4.2.73; *'Tis Pity*, 5.1.45; *Challenge for Beauty*, 26; *Wits*, 161; *Lovesick Court*, 114; several directions call for the *throwing* of an item from *above*: "*Throweth down a ring to him*" (*Dutch Courtesan*, 2.1.56), "*comes to the window, and throws out a letter*" (*Fedele and Fortunio*, 435), "*Celia at the window throws down her handkerchief*" (*Volpone*, 2.2.220); see also *Jew of Malta*, 686; *Thracian Wonder*, D1v; *Great Duke of Florence*, 5.1.47; other signals imply use of the *trapdoor*: "*Throws his charmed rod, and his books under the stage*" (*Two Noble Ladies*, 1899–1901), "*throw all the bottles in at a hole upon the Stage*" (*Princess*, G4r); for more see *Fedele and Fortunio*, 590–1; *George a Greene*, 795; see also *cast, toss*.

Various directions have one figure *throw* another: "*Darius is thrown down, Alexander kills him*" (*Doctor Faustus*, B 1294), "*throws him down, and discovers his Breeches*" (*Bird in a Cage*, E4r), "*throws him from him*" (*Captain*, 310), "*Throws her and takes her Knife*" (*Little French Lawyer*, 437), "*throwing down the dead body*" (*Aglaura*, 5.3.72); for more see *Humour out of Breath*, 467; *Yorkshire Tragedy*, 541; *Valiant Welshman*, G1v; *Sparagus Garden*, 164; *Seven Champions*, E3r; *Brennoralt*, 1.2.0; see also *overthrow*; occasionally a figure *throws off clothing*, often in the *discovery* of a *disguise*: "*throw off their disguises*" (*Aglaura*, 3.1.22), "*Throws off his cloak and doublet*" (*Renegado*, 3.5.50); see also *Staple of News*, 1.1.15; *Gentleman of Venice*, K1r; *Wasp*, 1072–3; atypical signals are "*throws his cloak on the other's point; gets within him and takes away his sword*" (*Bride*, 36), "*Throws off the Dog*" (Quarto *Every Man Out*, 3551), "*throws herself upon a bed*" (*White Devil*, 4.2.128), "*Enter Husband as being thrown off his horse, And falls*" (*Yorkshire Tragedy*, 632).

thrust

a verb linked to (1) *weapons* or *fights*, (2) the introduction of actors or large properties onto the *stage*, (3) stage business that involves shoving; weapon *thrusts* include an entrance with "*a sword, as thrust through his face*" (*Caesar and Pompey*, 4.3.0), "*Offers a thrust at him*" (*Jews' Tragedy*, 956), "*Thrust himself through with his sword" (*Locrine*, 2110, also 901), "*Tybalt under Romeo's arm thrusts Mercutio in and flies*" (Q1 *Romeo and Juliet*, F1v, 3.1.90), "*Alphonso makes a thrust at Carolo, he wards it with his dagger, and gets within him, thrusts his dagger betwixt Alphonso's doublet and shirt, he with conceit falls down*" (*Twins*, D3r); see also *Malcontent*, 2.5.5; *Wonder of a Kingdom*, 1.3.21; *Young Admiral*, K2v; *1 Passionate Lovers*, E7r; for examples of the *thrusting* of large properties, a *scaffold* can be "*thrust forth*" (*Virgin Martyr* 4.3.4) but more common are *beds* that are *thrust out/on/forth* (*Escapes of Jupiter*, 1368; *Two Merry Milkmaids*, M2v; *Witch of Edmonton*, 4.2.0; *Virgin Martyr*, 4.1.0; *Late Lancashire Witches*, 249; *Fatal Contract*, G1r; *Lost Lady*, 606; *City Nightcap*, 111; *Faithful Friends*, 2613–14); typical is "*A bed thrust out upon the stage, Allwit's Wife in it*" (*Chaste Maid*, 3.2.0); for a sampling of figures who are *thrust* on or *off* the stage see *David and Bethsabe*, 306; *James IV*, 702; *Looking Glass for London*, 587; *Taming of a Shrew*, G1r; *Amends for Ladies*, 4.4.83; *Four Plays in One*, 326; *Match Me in London*, 5.3.0; *New Way to Pay*, 3.2.218; *Unnatural Combat*, 5.2.185; *Country Girl*, E3r; *Court Beggar*, 268; *New Academy*, 10; *Cardinal*, Epilogue.2; *Parson's Wedding*, 462; stage business includes figures who are *thrust away* (*2 Seven Deadly Sins*, 23; *Warning for Fair Women*, D1r; *Albovine*, 33), *thrust back* (*Caesar and Pompey*, 5.2.175; *Wits*, 146); variations include "*thrusts Em upon her father*" (*Fair Em*, 926), "*thrusts her hands in her pocket*" (*Woman in the Moon*, B1r), "*thrusts him down into the gravel pit*" (*Atheist's Tragedy*, 2.4.13), "*the devils thrust him down and go Triumphing*" (*Devil's Charter*, M2v), "*Soldiers thrust up Lysander from the Tomb*" (*Widow's Tears*, 5.5.126), "*A hand is thrust out between the Arras*" (*Albovine*, 63), "*Pucell on the top, thrusting out a Torch burning*" (*1 Henry VI*, 1451–2, 3.2.25).

thumb

cited only twice: "*exit, biting his thumbs*" (*Dick of Devonshire*, 1714–15), "*gives her a ring, and she puts it on her thumb*" (*Amends for Ladies*, 5.2.235).

thunder

this term – like the more usual combination *thunder and lightning* – is linked to the supernatural, as in *Macbeth* where "*Thunder*" accompanies both the entrance of the *witches* (97, 1.3.0; 1429, 3.5.0; 1527, 4.1.0) and appearance of the *apparitions* (1603, 1615, 1627, 4.1.68, 76, 86); in *1 Henry VI* Joan calls on *spirits* and *thunder* sounds (2429, 5.3.4) and in *Tempest* Caliban enters carrying wood to "*a noise of*

Thunder heard"–a reminder of Prospero's *storm*–and later Ariel "*vanishes in Thunder*" (1038–9, 2.2.0; 1616, 3.3.82); *Julius Caesar* has "*Thunder, and Lightning*" and "*Thunder still*" (431, 1.3.0; 540, 1.3.99, also 981, 2.1.334; 983, 2.2.0); like other *sounds* thunder received the attention of the bookkeeper as shown in the annotated manuscripts of *Two Noble Ladies* (1075, 1081, 1164) and *Captives* (456, 469, 903); *thunder* frequently accompanies the entrance of figures from the underworld (and probably masked the sound of machinery used to raise or lower them): "*Thunder. Ascendit Behemoth, with Cartophylax and other spirits*" (Q2 *Bussy D'Ambois*, 4.2.60, also 5.3.6, 53, 68, 5.4.0), "*Thunder. Enter Lucifer and four devils*" (*Doctor Faustus*, B 225, also 242, 1894, 2088); for comparable examples see *Woodstock*, 2459; *1 Tamar Cham*, 25; *Caesar and Pompey*, 2.1.24, 2.5.0; *Puritan*, G2v; *Silver Age*, 135; *Valiant Welshman*, F1v, G1r; *New Trick*, 282; similarly *thunder* is several times interpreted as the voice of the gods, as in *Wounds of Civil War* where at "*Thunder*" (887) Antonius says "Hark how the heavens our follies hath controlled"; see also *Two Noble Kinsmen*, K4v, 5.1.61; *Golden Age*, 78; *Mad Lover*, 61; *Faithful Friends*, 2833; elsewhere *thunder* accompanies the entrance of heavenly figures when the gods are angry: "*Thunder. Enter Angel, three murdered Dames with revenge threatening*" (*Messalina*, 2170–1; see also *Martyred Soldier*, 188); the sound can be demonic, as in *Birth of Merlin* where at "*Thunder, then Music*" Joan says to a *devil* "not thy loud throated thunder, not thy adulterate infernal Music, shall e're bewitch me more" (G2r, also C3r, E1r, F3r); see also *King Leir*, 1739; *Revenger's Tragedy*, I3v; *All's Lost by Lust*, 5.1.32; twice *thunder* denotes what is elsewhere a *thunderbolt*: "*Thunder strikes him*" (*Seven Champions*, H3r), "*draws the Curtains and finds her struck with Thunder, black*" (*Looking Glass for London*, 552–3); in *Jews' Tragedy* the sound comes when supernatural business is conflated with a *storm* (1318, 1327, 1336, 1342, 2990, 2994); only once is the effect for weather only: "*It snows, and rains, thunders*" (*Duchess of Suffolk*, F2v).

thunder and lightning

usually occur together (but not always – see also *thunder* and *lightning*) and frequency indicates a popular theatrical device; most often the effects are linked to a supernatural figure such as a *devil*, *spirit*, *ghost*, *witch*, *magician*, or god and accompany *descents* through the *trapdoor* into the underworld; on the few occasions when *thunder and lightning* signals a *storm*, divine or satanic agency is usually assumed; one result of these effects would have been to mask the sounds of machinery for lowering or raising figures or objects, but *thunder and lightning* is signaled more often than **ascents** or descents from **above** or into the stage; uses of *thunder and lightning* in the Shakespeare canon are representative: in Folio *2 Henry VI* when Bolingbroke **conjures** "*It Thunders and Lightens terribly: then the Spirit riseth*" (645–7, 1.4.22); more famously *Macbeth* has "*Thunder and Lightning. Enter three Witches*" (2, 1.1.0) asking "*When shall we three meet again? / In thunder, lightning, or in rain?*"; in *Cymbeline* "*Jupiter descends in Thunder and Lightning*" (3126, 5.4.92), and in *1 Henry VI* just before the arrival of Joan "a holy prophetess" is "*an Alarum, and it Thunders and Lightens*" (569, 1.4.97), possibly in acknowledgment of her powers; similarly in *Julius Caesar* "*Thunder and Lightning*" (431, 1.3.0; 983, 2.2.0) is taken as a sign that heaven is angry, and Caesar later says "Nor heaven nor earth have been at peace tonight," and in *Tempest* "*A tempestuous noise of Thunder and Lightning heard*" is succeeded by "*Thunder and Lightning. Enter Ariel (like a Harpy)*" (2–3, 1.1.0; 1583, 3.3.52); other examples are "*Thunder and Lightning, two Dragons appear*" (*Birth of Merlin*, F3r, also E1r), "*Thunder and lightning: Enter devils with covered dishes; Mephostophilis leads them into Faustus's study*" (*Doctor Faustus*, B 1775–6), "*It thunders and lighteneth; enter Pluto, Minos, Aeacus, Rhadamanthus, with Furies bringing in Malbecco's ghost*" (*Grim the Collier*, K1v, also G2v, G4v, K3r); in the annotated manuscript of *John of Bordeaux* at the entrance of "hellish spirits" the bookkeeper wrote "*Thunder lightning*" (1133–4), and in the annotated quarto of *Looking Glass for London* the bookkeeper added "*thunder*" at the printed "*Lightning and thunder wherewith Remilia is struck*" (C1r, 529–30); *Seven Champions* has the most directions for these effects, always accompanying occult events (B1r, B2r, C1r, C1v, C2r, C2v, G3r, H1r, H4r); several directions for *thunder and lightning* are found in the Peele canon (*Arraignment of Paris*, 355; *Battle of Alcazar*, 1263; *Edward I*, 2175; *Old Wives Tale*, 415, 645); for more examples see *King Leir*, 1634; *Woodstock*, 2439; *Guy of Warwick*, B3v, B4v; *Locrine*, 2, 1989–90; *Devil's Charter*, A2v, G1v, G2r, M2v; *Catiline*, 3.836; *If This Be Not a Good Play*, 4.2.33; *Match Me in London*, 5.3.0; *Silver Age*, 98, 122; *Atheist's Tragedy*, 2.4.140, 2.6.5; *Witch of Edmonton*, 2.1.142; *All's Lost by Lust*, 5.2.0; *Prophetess*, 345, 388; *Messalina*, 2149–51; *Rebellion*, 61; *Bloody Banquet*, 1859; for the few instances where the effects are simply signs of bad weather see *Caesar and Pompey*, 2.4.147; *Thracian*

Wonder, B4v; *Hoffman*, 13; MS *Poor Man's Comfort*, 617; *Sea Voyage*, 2.

thunderbolt
as the term implies this **weapon** of the gods is more accurately a "lightning bolt" although never so named; in *Cymbeline* "*Jupiter descends*" and "*throws a Thunderbolt*" (3126–7, 5.4.92); in the Heywood canon "*Jupiter draws heaven: at which Iris descends and presents him with the Eagle, Crown and Scepter, and his thunderbolt*" (*Golden Age*, 78), "*Jupiter descends in his majesty, his Thunderbolt burning*" (*Silver Age*, 154), "*Jupiter above strikes him with a thunderbolt*" (*Brazen Age*, 254); in *Martyred Soldier* "*A Thunderbolt strikes*" (249) a figure, and in *Messalina* one is "*Shot with a Thunderbolt*" (2187); the term is occasionally abbreviated: "*A hand with a Bolt appears above*" (*Prophetess*, 388) and "*lightning and bolt*" from a bookkeeper (annotated *Looking Glass for London*, E2v); see also **lightning**.

thunderclap
a rarely called for special effect: "*with a sudden Thunderclap the sky is one* [or *on?*] *fire*" (*Captain Thomas Stukeley*, 2456–7), "*a clap of Thunder*" (*Faithful Friends*, 2833); see also **thunder**.

tire, tires, headtire
linked to (1) coverings for the **head** though (2) *tire* can denote **attire**, **clothing**, costume (as in *tiring house*); examples of *tires* for the head are an entrance "*with a tire upon his head*" (*Queen*, 3754–5), "*Plucks off his headtire*" when a supposed woman reveals herself to be a man (*Amends for Ladies*, 3.2.41–3), two female servants "*in their petticoats, cloaks over them, with hats over their headtires*" (*Gentleman Usher*, 2.1.153); Vindice's entrance "*with the skull of his love dressed up in Tires*" (*Revenger's Tragedy*, F1r) may be an exception if these *tires* include a **gown**; occasionally *attire* is used for *tire*, headdress: "*Gertrude in a French head attire*" (*Eastward Ho*, A4r), "*Robin Hood in the Lady Falconbridge's gown, night attire on his head*" (*Look about You*, 1747–8); Henslowe's inventory includes "six headtires" (*Diary*, App. 2, 43).

to him, to her, to them
widely used (roughly 250 examples) to signal that a figure **enters** to join and usually interact with one or more figures already onstage; examples are "*Enter a Shoemaker sitting upon the stage at work, Jenkin to him*" (*George a Greene*, 971–2), "*Enter Anne Drewry, and Trusty Roger her man, to them Browne*" (*Warning for Fair*

Women, B3v), "They draw, to them enters Tybalt, they
fight, to them the Prince, old Montague, and his wife, old
Capulet and his wife, and other Citizens and part them"
(Q1 Romeo and Juliet, A4v, [1.1.72]); these locutions are
common in playhouse manuscripts and plots; see
Frederick and Basilea, 3, 6, 9, 12, and more; Captives
1586, 1759, 2850; 2 Seven Deadly Sins, 4, 10, 27, 31, 40,
43, and more; Dead Man's Fortune, 4, 6–7, 9, 14, 17, 20,
23, and more; representative is "Enter Diomede to
Achilles's Tent to them Menelaus, to them Ulysses to them
Achilles in his Tent to them Ajax with Patroclus on his
back" (Troilus and Cressida plot, 33–7).

to himself, to herself

an alternative to speak aside, apart, privately: "speaks
to himself" (Folio Richard III, 792, 1.3.317), "gives the
letter to Mustaffa, and speaks the rest to himself" (Selimus,
973–4), "A Song the whilst Bassanio comments on the
caskets to himself" (Merchant of Venice, E4r, 3.2.62); in
King Leir servants have speeches "to himself" not
heard by their masters (404–5, 414–15) and Gonorill
"Speaks to herself" (1425–6, also 1393); for other
speeches to himself/herself see Locrine, 1565; Selimus,
2002; Death of Huntingdon, 1034, 1134; Satiromastix,
1.2.0; All Fools, 3.1.74; King John and Matilda, 67;
Aglaura, 2.1.41; Brennoralt, 1.4.10; attached to to
himself/herself are speak (Famous Victories, F3v; Wily
Beguiled, 770, 1881; Maidenhead Well Lost, 140), private
(Four Prentices, 179), apart (Four Prentices, 187;
Maidenhead Well Lost, 145), read (Three Ladies of London,
E3r; Devil's Charter, K2v; Love's Sacrifice, 875; Old
Couple, 80; Cruel Brother, 121; Deserving Favourite, K2r;
Sophy, 3.157; Conspiracy, M3r); atypical are "pondering
to himself" (Sir Thomas More, 1575), an entrance
"running in haste, and laughing to himself" (Selimus,
1877–8).

tobacco

the property is actually tobacco in a pipe, sometimes
called for in tavern scenes; in Amends for Ladies a page
enters "with a pipe of Tobacco" for a lord who then
"Takes Tobacco" (2.1.69, 77, also 3.4.36); in Folio Every
Man Out Fastidius "talks, and takes tobacco between"
(3.9.65); Roaring Girl requires a "Tobacco shop" where
Laxton "blows tobacco in their faces" (2.1.151, 66); for
more tobacco/pipes see Cynthia's Revels,
Induction.121; Lust's Dominion, 1.1.0; Blurt, 4.2.0;
Satiromastix, 1.2.191; What You Will, B3r; Law Tricks,
133; 1 Honest Whore, 2.1.155; Fleer, 2.1.39; Woman Is a
Weathercock, 3.2.5; Fair Quarrel, 4.1.115; Siege, 426;
Soddered Citizen, 994; Weeding of Covent Garden, 13.

together

used regularly for joint or group actions: "both sing
this together" (Maid's Metamorphosis, F2v), "Witches
charm together" (Late Lancashire Witches, 256), "Arm in
arm together" (No Wit, 4.3.0), "In council together"
(Captain Thomas Stukeley, 2688), "run together and
embrace" (Warning for Fair Women, E3v), "every one
taking hands together, depart" (Fedele and Fortunio,
1808); verbs linked to together include enter (Fedele
and Fortunio, 1148; 2 Tamburlaine, 2696; Two
Lamentable Tragedies, D4v; Tottenham Court, 101), talk
(Antonio's Revenge, 4.1.70; What You Will, A2r;
Gentleman Usher, 3.2.276), speak (Two Lamentable
Tragedies, D4v; Antony and Cleopatra, 2495, 4.3.18;
Alchemist, 4.5.25; Bartholomew Fair, 2.6.146), whisper
(Three Lords of London, H2v; 1 Henry VI, 1495, 3.2.59;
Octavo 3 Henry VI, E2r, 5.1.79; King Leir, 1119;
Prophetess, 363; Tom a Lincoln, 152; 1 Arviragus and
Philicia, C12v; Bloody Banquet, 854; Unfortunate Lovers,
16), sit (Arraignment of Paris, 249; Wit of a Woman, 1684;
Devil's Charter, L4r), stand (Widow's Tears, 5.5.282),
kneel (Massacre at Paris, 532), walk (Quarto Every Man
Out, 1850; Fair Maid of the Exchange, 67), march
(Faithful Friends, 2159), dance (Love's Sacrifice, 1849;
Muses' Looking Glass, M2r; Late Lancashire Witches, 221;
Grateful Servant, I2r); participants in a fight can be
"together by the ears" (Mucedorus, D3v; Atheist's Tragedy,
2.2.28; Bartholomew Fair, 5.4.335); for other usages
see David and Bethsabe, 716; Old Fortunatus, 1.3.0;
Antonio and Mellida, 4.2.0; Antonio's Revenge, 5.2.97;
Lust's Dominion, 4.3.49; Devil's Charter, C3r; Swisser,
5.2.117; Twins, D2v; Parson's Wedding, 531; Princess, I1v;
uses of altogether are rare: "Song. Altogether here" (As
You Like It, 926, 2.5.37), "Trumpets, Hoboys, Drums beat,
altogether" (Coriolanus, 3621, 5.4.48); see also Jovial
Crew, 409.

toll

linked twice to the sound of a bell: "ordnance being
shot off, the bell tolls" (Massacre at Paris, 338), "A Bell tolls
within" (Weakest Goeth, 1774); see also ring.

tomb

the roughly forty examples include (1) tombs that are
discovered, (2) figures that rise in/from a tomb, (3)
kneeling and mourning at a tomb, (4) the opening and
shutting of a tomb; for tombs that are discovered see
Widow's Tears, 4.2.0; Knight of Malta, 138/388, also 145;
Love's Sacrifice, 2734; Lost Lady, Folio 549, MS 240;
directions include "diverse Monks, Alphonso going to the
Tomb" and "discover the Tomb and a Chair" (Wife for a

Month, 26), "*Enter the Tyrant again at a farther door, which opened, brings him to the Tomb where the Lady lies buried; The Tomb here discovered richly set forth*" (*Second Maiden's Tragedy*, 1725–7); less clear are signals that do not specify a discovery such as "*Countess in the Tomb*" (*Law Tricks*, 206), "*Mistress Arthur in the Tomb*" (*How a Man May Choose*, H2r) with the latter asking "How come I then in this Coffin buried?"; for figures who *rise in/from a tomb* see *Turk*, 807; *Valiant Welshman*, A4v; an early comedy provides "*lifts up his head out of the Tomb, and ducks down again*," "*they throw their candles into the Tomb where Crackstone lieth*," "*Crackstone riseth out of the Tomb with one candle in his mouth, and in each hand one*" (*Fedele and Fortunio*, 494–5, 590–1, 598–9); mourning at a *tomb* includes "*kneels to the Tomb*" (*Lost Lady*, Folio 553, MS 383), "*kneels at the Tomb wondrous passionately*" (*Second Maiden's Tragedy*, 1891–3), "*Paris strews the Tomb with flowers*" (Q1 *Romeo and Juliet*, I4v, 5.3.11), "*she seemeth to reject his suit, flies to the tomb, kneels and kisseth it*" (*Antonio's Revenge*, 3.1.0), "*Cleon shows Pericles the tomb, whereat Pericles makes lamentation, puts on sackcloth, and in a mighty passion departs*" (*Pericles*, G3r, 4.4.22), "*Coming near the Tomb they all kneel, making show of Ceremony. The Duke goes to the Tomb, lays his hand on it*" (*Love's Sacrifice*, 2738–40); examples of opening a *tomb* include "*Romeo opens the tomb*" (Q1 *Romeo and Juliet*, K1r, 5.3.48), "*One goes to open the Tomb, out of which ariseth Fernando in his winding sheet, only his face discovered*" (*Love's Sacrifice*, 2763–4); *Titus Andronicus* provides "*They open the Tomb*," "*Sound Trumpets, and lay the Coffin in the Tomb*," "*they put him in the tomb*" (A4v, 1.1.89; B1v, 1.1.149; C1r, 1.1.386); atypically elaborate is "*On a sudden in a kind of Noise like a Wind, the doors clattering, the Tombstone flies open, and a great light appears in the midst of the Tomb; His Lady as went out, standing just before him all in white, Stuck with Jewels and a great crucifix on her breast*" (*Second Maiden's Tragedy*, 1926–31); by far the most extensive *tomb* sequence is found in the final two acts of *Widow's Tears* where first Lysander "*discovers the Tomb, looks in and wonders*" (4.2.0, also 5.1.22), the next scene begins "*Cynthia, Ero, the Tomb opening*" (4.3.0, also 5.2.0), and much opening and shutting follows (5.3.60, 177, 5.5.18) including "*Tomb opens, and Lysander within lies along, Cynthia and Ero*" (5.3.0), "*Ero opens, and he sees her head laid on the coffin*" (5.3.137), so that finally "*Soldiers thrust up Lysander from the Tomb*" (5.5.126); Henslowe's inventory lists three *tombs*, two of them linked to specific plays: "one tomb of Guido, one tomb of Dido" (*Diary*, App. 2, 56–7).

tongue

three of the five examples are linked to violence in revenge tragedies: in *Spanish Tragedy* Hieronimo "*bites out his tongue*" (4.4.191), in *Titus Andronicus* Lavinia is brought in "*her hands cut off, and her tongue cut out, and ravished*" (E2r, 2.4.0), in *Antonio's Revenge* "*The conspirators bind Piero, pluck out his tongue, and triumph over him*" (5.3.62); for non-violent examples, Rumor enters "*painted full of Tongues*" (2 *Henry IV*, A2r, Induction.0), and in response to the question "wants he tongue?" Stich replies "No sir, I have tongue enough if that be good" and "*shows his tongue*" (*Edmond Ironside*, 512–13).

top

used seldom for a location where one figure appears *above* the main platform and possibly above the upper playing level, as when having breached the walls of Rouen, Pucell enters "*on the top*" (1 *Henry VI*, 1451, 3.2.25) and "in yonder turret," then appears "on the walls," which perhaps differentiates the two locations; in *Tempest* Prospero watches "*on the top (invisible)*" (1535–6, 3.3.17), in *Double Marriage* a "*Boy a top*" on a supposed ship's mast cries "a Sail, a Sail" (342), in *Alphonsus of Aragon* Venus is "*let down from the top of the Stage*" (2–3).

torch

the most often cited property *light* that by convention can indicate night or darkness on a stage with no variable lighting; typical are "*in his nightgown, and his shirt, and a torch in his hand*" (*Alphonsus of Germany*, B1r), "*with a Torch, a Nightcap, and his Doublet open*" (*Fleer*, 5.3.0), "*with a torch, a mattock, and a crow of iron*" (Q1 *Romeo and Juliet*, I4v, 5.3.21); *torches*/**links** usually indicate outdoor locales as opposed to *tapers*/**candles** which denote scenes located indoors; for a sampling of the sixty figures who enter *carrying*/*bearing*, most commonly *with a torch/torches* see *Humorous Day's Mirth*, 5.2.128; *Antonio's Revenge*, 2.1.0, 3.2.0, 86, 5.1.0, 5.3.0; Folio *Hamlet*, 1944, 3.2.89; *Blurt*, 5.3.0; *Othello*, B3r, 175, 1.1.159; B3v, 203, 1.2.0; B4r, 233, 1.2.28; 269, 1.2.54; *Sophonisba*, Prologue.0, 1.2.185, 4.1.42; *Widow's Tears*, 3.2.78; Folio *Troilus and Cressida*, 2168–70, 4.1.0; Folio *King Lear*, 970, 2.1.36; 1890, 3.4.113; *Macbeth*, 583, 2.1.9; 1237, 3.3.14; *Devil's Charter*, F3v; 2 *Iron Age*, 379; *Rape of Lucrece*, 245; *Wit without Money*, 198, 199, 201, 205, 206; *Bashful Lover*, 2.8.0; *Birth of Merlin*, C3r; *Fatal Contract*, C1r; *Love's Sacrifice*, 1815, 2735; *Bloody Banquet*, 1551; *Maid's Revenge*, F4v; *Wits*, 203.

Often the *torch* is borne *before* a figure by a page or attendant (*Warning for Fair Women*, D2v; *What You Will*, A4r; *London Prodigal*, F4r; *Second Maiden's Tragedy*, 1878; *Macbeth*, 569–70, 2.1.0; *Henry VIII*, 2769–70, 5.1.0); for entrances that involve a *torch* and a *weapon* see *Locrine*, 3–4; *Lust's Dominion*, 3.2.151; *Woman Is a Weathercock*, 5.1.48–9; *If This Be Not a Good Play*, 5.4.34; *Aglaura*, 5.1.99; detailed examples are "*their weapons drawn and torches*" (*2 Iron Age*, 381), "*unbraced, his arms bare, smeared in blood, a poniard in one hand, bloody, and a torch in the other*" (*Antonio's Revenge*, 1.1.0, also 3.2.86); directions call for *torchbearers*, especially for *masques*, sometimes with the placement specified: "*between every two a torchbearer*" (*Cardinal*, 3.2.85), "*between every couple a torch carried*" (*Changes*, K2v), "*A torchbearer, a shieldboy, then a masquer, so throughout*" (*Your Five Gallants*, I2v); see also Q2 *Romeo and Juliet*, C1r, 1.4.0; *Antonio's Revenge*, 5.3.32; *Tragedy of Byron*, 2.2; *Insatiate Countess*, 2.1.48; *King John and Matilda*, 51.

Occasionally (as with *halberds*, *drums*, *trumpets*) *torches* denote "figures carrying torches": "*Enter four torches*" (*1 If You Know Not Me*, 234, also 239), "*Hoboys and Torches*" (*Macbeth*, 431, 1.6.0; 472, 1.7.0; see also *City Wit*, 358); *exits* include "*every one with torches ushered to their several chambers*" (*2 Iron Age*, 411), and when one of a group of *spirits* "*holding torches*" *departs* "*a torch removes*" (*Bussy D'Ambois*, 4.2.40, 66); occasionally *torches* are described as *lighted* (*Sir Thomas More*, 956; *2 Edward IV*, 162), *burning* (*Two Noble Kinsmen*, B1r, 1.1.0; *Messalina*, 2252–3), and figures are "*lighted in with Torches*" (*Escapes of Jupiter*, 1699–70), provided with *torchlight* (*Revenger's Tragedy*, A2r; *Double Marriage*, 352); for the *putting* out of *torches* see *Devil's Charter*, F3v; *Miseries of Enforced Marriage*, 1480; *Faithful Friends*, 2621; two signals call for *torches* *ready* (*Love's Cure*, 205; *Distresses*, 301); actions include "*tossing his torch about his head in triumph*" (*Antonio's Revenge*, 5.1.0), "*two Servants, drunk, fighting with their torches*" (*Atheist's Tragedy*, 2.4.2), "*on the top, thrusting out a Torch burning*" (*1 Henry VI*, 1451–2, 3.2.25), *ghosts* who "*surround her with their Torches*" (*Messalina*, 2546).

torment

signals onstage or offstage torture (with onstage *torment* likely acted out by means of a *rack*); figures enter "*in their shirts, as from Torments*" (*Shoemaker a Gentleman*, 4.2.0), and devils discover four damned souls "*standing in their torments*" (*If This Be Not a Good Play*, 5.4.0); *torment* can appear as a verb: "*The*

Hangmen torment them, they still smiling" (*Roman Actor*, 3.2.74; see also *Virgin Martyr*, 5.2.206); for a more general sense of "distress": "*Here Alexander is in extreme torment and groaneth whilst the devil laugheth at him*" (*Devil's Charter*, M1v).

toss

occurs in three directions: "*toss their pikes*" (*Four Prentices*, 203), "*tosseth him about his head and kills him*" (*2 Iron Age*, 393), "*tosses off her Bowl, falls back, and is carried out*" (*Jovial Crew*, 391).

toward

used for a wide variety of actions; verbs combined with *toward* include *make* (*Soddered Citizen*, 1287–8), *move* (*Court Beggar*, 261), *turn* (*Edmond Ironside*, 1082), *point* (*Alphonsus of Aragon*, 328), *walk* (*Match at Midnight*, 10), *look* (*King John and Matilda*, 74), *come* (*Alphonsus of Aragon*, 192; Quarto *Every Man Out*, 1217; *Roaring Girl*, 3.1.155; *Soddered Citizen*, 1609), most commonly *go* (*Three Lords of London*, G1v; *Alphonsus of Aragon*, 337, 354, 483, 1919, 1939; *Silver Age*, 96; *Night Walker*, 380; *Aglaura*, 5.3.112; *Goblins*, 1.1.36; *Claracilla*, F1v); variations include "*As Aymwell comes towards Violetta she turns and Exit*" (*Witty Fair One*, C2r), "*going with Drum and Trumpet toward Cominius*" (*Coriolanus*, 710–11, 1.7.0), "*The Armies make towards one another*" (*Edmond Ironside*, 1860), "*Exeunt towards the Temple*" (*Two Noble Kinsmen*, B4v, 1.1.218), "*dancing (and Masked) towards the Rock*" (*Four Plays in One*, 363), "*Cupid's Bow bent all the way towards them*" (*Nice Valour*, 157), "*turn him thrice about, set his face towards the contrary post, at which he runs*" (*Three Lords of London*, I3v); see also *Captain Thomas Stukeley*, 2452; *2 Edward IV*, 173; *Hengist*, DS before 2.2, 13–15; those under sentence of death may have the *edge* or *point* of a *weapon* *toward* them; an example is "*the Ax with the edge towards him*" (*Henry VIII*, 890, 2.1.53; see also *Christian Turned Turk*, H1v); timing signals for *music*/a *dance* *toward* the end of which an action is to take place include "*Toward the close of the music, the Justice's three men prepare for a robbery*" (*Phoenix*, F3r; see also *World Tossed at Tennis*, C4r), "*a graceful dance, towards the end whereof, Prospero starts suddenly and speaks*" (*Tempest*, 1806–7, 4.1.138); atypical is a speech to be delivered *aside* designated as *toward* a figure (*Wit at Several Weapons*, 87).

towel

one of the properties that typically identify a *drawer*, thus a *tavern* setting; a *drawer* enters "*with a* towel" (*Bride*, 27; *Imposture*, E5r), "*with cup, towel, and wine*" (*Hoffman*, 1527; see also *May Day*, 3.3.188), "*a table and towel and stools*" (*Launching of the Mary*, 1926); a *towel* appears in other contexts: "*Enter Robin Hood, a cup, a towel*" (*Death of Huntingdon*, 518), "*Quicksilver unlaced, a towel about his neck, in his flat Cap, drunk*" (*Eastward Ho*, B3r), "*Secco, his apron on, Basin of water, Scissors, Comb, Towels, Razor, etc.*" (*Fancies Chaste and Noble*, 2372–3); see also *What You Will*, B3v.

tower

used occasionally to designate the platform **above** the main level of the stage: "*Assault, and they win the Tower, and Joab speaks above*" (*David and Bethsabe*, 212), "*Enter Lord Scales upon the Tower walking. Then enters two or three Citizens below*" (*2 Henry VI*, G1r, 2598–9, 4.5.0); possibly **fictional** are "*Enter Gloster to King Henry in the Tower*" (Octavo *3 Henry VI*, E5v, 5.6.0), "*Then the marshall bears them to the tower top*" (*Soliman and Perseda*, H2r); see also **walls**.

train

widely used (roughly 140 examples) to denote either (1) the retinue that accompanies an important figure or (2) the extended part of a **gown** that trails **behind**; of the more than 100 examples of *train* as **followers** or retinue, *2 Tamburlaine* provides nine (2325, 2402, 2680, 2794, 2857, 3348, 3444, 3502, 3649), and other plays offer four or more: *Battle of Alcazar*, 896, 979, 1303, 1505; *Thomas Lord Cromwell*, F2v–F3r; *Merchant of Venice*, B4v, 2.1.0; D2v, 2.7.0; D4v, 2.9.3; H4v, 4.1.407; *Antony and Cleopatra*, 15–16, 1.1.10; 69, 1.1.55; 428–9, 1.4.0; 1792, 3.6.38; 3334–5, 5.2.110; 3424, 5.2.190; 3595, 5.2.332; *Emperor of the East*, 1.1.100, 1.2.89, 1.2.119, 3.2.38; as with comparable collective nouns (*others, attendants, men, women, the rest*, **cum suis**) *train* can serve as a **permissive** term that leaves open the number of actors involved; typical examples from the Shakespeare canon are "*Enter the King of Fairies at one door with his Train, and the Queen at another with hers*" (*Midsummer Night's Dream*, B3v, 2.1.59, also C3r, 2.2.0; F4r, 4.1.102; H4r, 5.1.390), "*the King, and his train pass over the stage*" (*2 Henry IV*, K4r, 5.5.4, also K4v, 5.5.40).

For examples of *train* as **garment**, occasionally a figure is *holding up* the *train* (*Two Noble Kinsmen*, B1r, 1.1.0; L1r, 5.1.136; *Fatal Contract*, E3v), but usually it is *borne up* (*Picture*, 1.2.128; *Renegado*, 4.2.70; *Faithful Friends*, 2481–2) or attendants are **bearing**/*bearing up* the *train* (*Malcontent*, 1.6.0; *Gentleman Usher*, 2.2.0; *Sophonisba*, Prologue.0, 5.3.0; *Widow's Tears*, 1.2.32;

1 If You Know Not Me, 244; *Bondman*, 3.3.0; *Duchess of Suffolk*, A3r; *Queen's Exchange*, 530); typical is "*her train with all state borne up by Julia, Cenis, and Domitilla*" (*Roman Actor*, 2.1.246); for both senses of *train* in the same play, *Henry VIII* provides "*Cardinal, and his Train*" (187, 1.1.119), "*Duke and Train*" (983, 2.1.136), "*Train borne by a Lady*" (3360, 5.4.0); see also *Two Noble Kinsmen*, B1r, 1.1.0; L1v, 5.1.136 versus G3r, 3.5.94; H2v, 3.6.131; K3v, 5.1.17; and *Emperor of the East*, 3.2.0 versus the four examples listed above; atypical is *train* as a trail of gunpowder to set an explosion so that an offstage **sound** is signaled by "*The Train takes*" (*Island Princess*, 113; see also 120, 121).

trample

an offstage **sound** usually linked to **horses**: "*A trampling of horses heard*" (*Insatiate Countess*, 2.4.0), "*Trampling above*" (*Chances*, 229); in *Captives* the bookkeeper wrote "*Trample*" (2723), then "*Trampling noise*" at the direction "*A Noise within Trampling of Horses*" (2744–5, 2743–4).

trapdoor

the opening in the main platform through which figures **ascend**/**rise** or **descend**/**sink**; used rarely, *trapdoor* (or *trap*) occurs in the bookkeeper-annotated *Believe as You List*: "*Gascoine and Hubert below: ready to open the Trapdoor for Mr Taylor*" (1825–31) and in *Fatal Contract*: "*Enter Lamot at the trapdoor*" (H1r); in *Queen's Exchange* a cryptic "*opens*" (536) is explained "here is the trap door, the mouth of the rich mine"; usually references are not to a *trapdoor* but to the space **beneath**/**below**/**under the stage** in fictional terms such as **cave, gulf, vault, well**.

traverse

a rarely used synonym for **curtain** or **arras**: "*peeps from behind a traverse*" (*Volpone*, 5.3.9), "*Here is discovered, behind a traverse, the artificial figures of Antonio and his children, appearing as if they were dead*" (*Duchess of Malfi*, 4.1.55).

tread

either (1) "to walk or dance" or (2) "to step upon, trample"; examples of the former are "*takes a Lady to tread a measure*" (*Malcontent*, 4.2.0), "*tread a solemn measure with changes*" (*Soddered Citizen*, 1916–17), "*nine knights in armor, treading a warlike Almaine, by drum and fife*" (*Arraignment of Paris*, 478); examples of *tread* as "step upon" are "*treads on her Father*" (*Rape of Lucrece*,

173), "*Beaupre loses his sword. La-writ treads on it*" (*Little French Lawyer*, 396), "*They shoot and run to him and tread upon him*" (*White Devil*, 5.6.118), "*Fortune takes her Chair, the Kings lying at her feet, she treading on them as she goes up*" (*Old Fortunatus*, 1.1.63).

treasure
a generic term for a visible display of wealth; *Antipodes* provides "*a table set forth, covered with trea- sure*" (324), and in *False One* after "*Treasure brought in*" (340) Caesar responds "What rich Service! / What mines of treasure!"; *treasure* can be linked to the spoils of conquest or theft so that figures enter "*with treasure*" (*Battle of Alcazar*, 213; *Sea Voyage*, 38), "*laden with treasure*" (*1 Tamburlaine*, 196).

treble
the smallest and highest toned *viol*; in *Country Girl* "*A Treble plays within*" (D1r, D3r) for dancing and singing; but "*the Treble Violin and Lute*" (*Messalina*, 2518–19) and "*A treble viol and a base Lute*" (*Sophonisba*, 4.1.200, 218) are linked to the appearance of *spirits*.

tree
cited (1) for *dumb shows* and special effects, (2) in what appear to be *fictional* situations but (3) rarely in scenes that take place in the *woods*/forest; that *trees* were available as stage properties is clear in Henslowe's inventory which includes "one bay tree," "one tree of golden apples," "Tantalus's tree" (*Diary*, App. 2, 63, 75–6); special effects include "*a Child Crowned, with a Tree in his hand*" (*Macbeth*, 1628, 4.1.86), "*Hereupon did rise a Tree of gold laden with Diadems and Crowns of gold*" and "*The Tree sinketh*" (*Arraignment of Paris*, 456, 462), "*Here the Hind vanishes under the Altar: and in the place ascends a Rose Tree, having one Rose upon it*" (*Two Noble Kinsmen*, L2r, 5.1.162), "*Here Bungay conjures and the tree appears with the dragon shooting fire*," "*Here he begins to break the branches*," "*Exit the spirit with Vandermast and the Tree*" (*Friar Bacon*, 1197–8, 1214, 1280); in *Old Fortunatus* Vice is directed to "*bring out a fair tree of Gold with apples on it*" and Virtue "*a tree with green and withered leaves mingled together, and little fruit on it*," and onstage figures "*set the trees into the earth*" (1.3.0, 19); see also *Warning for Fair Women*, E3v.

Trees are regularly cited in the dialogue (as when figures are tied to a *tree*) where a stage *post* may have been used, so that "*They bind him to a Tree*" (*Distresses*, 322) should be compared to "*Bind him to the post*" (*Greene's Tu Quoque*, L1v); the few specific signals include "*They sit under a tree together*"

(*Arraignment of Paris*, 249), "*hangs the crowns upon a tree*" (*Battle of Alcazar*, 1268–9), "*The fourth out of a tree, if possible it may be*" and "*Enter Shrimp leading Oswen and Amery about the tree*" (*John a Kent*, 836, 1393); most common are directions for figures to *climb* a *tree* (where the scaling of a stage post seems likely); examples are "*The Clown climbs up a tree*" (*Thracian Wonder*, D1r), "*Onion gets up into a tree*" (*Case Is Altered*, 4.8.1), "*Enter Benjamin, Robin, Thirsty; Thirsty climbing up into a tree. Robin into a bush*" (*Honest Lawyer*, I2r), "*Whilst the act is a-playing, Hercules and Tiberio enter; Tiberio climbs the tree, and is received above by Dulcimel*" (*Fawn*, 5.0); in *If This Be Not a Good Play* Scumbroth climbs the black *tree*, Lucifer "*Sits under the tree, all about him*," eventually "*Scumbroth falls*" (4.2.53, 125); see also *arbor*.

trencher
a plate or platter used with other properties to set a scene: "*a cloth and trenchers and salt*" (*Friar Bacon*, 1325), "*a Tablecloth, Bread, Trenchers, and salt*" (*Woman Killed*, 132; see also *Spanish Curate*, 129/501), "*a Trencher, with broken meat and a Napkin*" (*Wise Woman of Hogsdon*, 335), "*a napkin on his shoulder, and a trencher in his hand as from table*" (*Roaring Girl*, 1.1.0); see also *bread*, *dish*, *napkin*, *plate*, *table*.

trial, court
the staging of a *trial*/courtroom apparently involved a *bar*, a *table*, *chairs* and placement for the judges, and distinctive costumes for judges, sheriffs, advo- cates, and other court personnel, as suggested when a figure takes on a *disguise* "*like a Court Messenger*" and "*in his Court habit*" (*City Wit*, 320, 324); most of the many courtroom scenes provide no signals other than an *enter* and a list of personae (typical are *Merchant of Venice*, 4.1; *Revenger's Tragedy*, 1.2); occa- sionally a generic signal leaves the implementation to the players; an example is Hermione's entrance "*as to her Trial*" (*Winter's Tale*, 1174–5, 3.2.0); in *Sir Thomas More* a *curtain* is drawn to reveal a *court* configuration already in place: "*An Arras is drawn, and behind it (as in Sessions) sit the Lord Mayor, Justice Suresby, and other Justices, Sheriff More and the other Sheriff sitting by, Smart is the Plaintiff, Lifter the prisoner at the bar*" (104–6), but the more common procedure is to bring the courtroom onstage; the property regularly asso- ciated with such scenes is the bar; typical are *Barnavelt* where the order "Let him be sent for presently" is accompanied by both a direction ("*A Bar brought in*") and a bookkeeper's marginal annota- tion ("*Bar*" and "*Table*," 2159–60) and *Two Merry*

Milkmaids where a bookkeeper has added *"A Table A Bar"* at the quarto's *"the form of a court"* (I3r); in addition to the bar other properties are sometimes specified: *"A Bar, Tablebook, two Chairs and Paper, standish set out"* (*Spanish Curate*, 98); occasionally the emphasis is not upon the bar or the *prisoner* but upon the seating of the judges: *"Enter Officers preparing seats for the judges"* (*Devil's Law Case*, 4.2.0), *"Enter some to prepare the judgment seat to the Lord Mayor, Lord Justice, and the four Lords, and one Clerk, and a Sheriff, who being set, command Browne to be brought forth"* (*Warning for Fair Women*, H3v); *Chabot* provides two unusually elaborate directions: *"Enter Officers before the Chancellor, Judges, the Proctor general, whispering with the Chancellor; they take their places. To them enter Treasurer and Secretary who take their places prepared on one side of the Court. To them the Captain of the Guard, the Admiral following, who is placed at the bar,"* *"Enter Officers before, Treasurer, Secretary, and Judges, attended by Petitioners, the Advocate also with many papers in his hand; they take their places. The Chancellor with a guard, and placed at the Bar"* (3.2.0, 5.2.0); also elaborate are the Court of Love scene in *New Inn* (3.2.0) and the trial of Queen Katherine in *Henry VIII* where an unusually long direction concludes *"The King takes place under the Cloth of State. The two Cardinals sit under him as Judges. The Queen takes place some distance from the King. The Bishops place themselves on each side the Court in manner of a Consistory: Below them the Scribes. The Lords sit next the Bishops. The rest of the Attendants stand in convenient order about the Stage"* (1343–9, 2.4.0).

trip

either (1) to cause to stumble/*fall* or (2) to move nimbly with light rapid steps in a *dance* or dance-like movement; a figure can *trip* another (*Two Angry Women*, 995) but more common is *"trips up his heels"* (*Look about You*, 2630; *Roaring Girl*, 2.1.331; *Devil's Charter*, F4r; *Sisters*, B6r); variations include *"trips up his heels and holds him"* (*Eastward Ho*, A3v), *"tripped up his heels in scuffle and sits on him"* (*Fatal Contract*, H4v), *"disarms and trips him down"* (*Dick of Devonshire*, 1711–12); movements include *"The boy trips round about Oswen and Amery"* (*John a Kent*, 1145), personages in a vision who *"Enter solemnly tripping one after another"* (*Henry VIII*, 2643, 4.2.82), *"She trips about the stage"* in *"the court-Amble"* (*Eastward Ho*, A4v); see also *Sir John Oldcastle*, 1495.

triumph

stage business to indicate *victory* and celebration though the specific implementation is unclear;

figures typically *enter in triumph*: *"Enter in triumph with drum and ensign"* (*David and Bethsabe*, 1561), *"tossing his torch about his head in triumph"* (*Antonio's Revenge*, 5.1.0), *"Enter Ventidius as it were in triumph"* (*Antony and Cleopatra*, 1494, 3.1.0), *"The Arms borne in triumph before Ulysses"* (*1 Iron Age*, 341); see also Folio *3 Henry VI*, 2855, 5.3.0; *2 Seven Deadly Sins*, 69; *Alarum for London*, 1609; *Four Plays in One*, 293; *Herod and Antipater*, C3r; *Prophetess*, 374; *Hyde Park*, H1r; *Imposture*, B3v; examples of *triumphant* and other variants include *"Augustus triumphant with his Romans"* (*Herod and Antipater*, I4v), *"After a triumphant shout within"* (*Alarum for London*, 799), *"in triumph in his chair triumphant of gold"* (*Wounds of Civil War*, 1070), *"in full state, triumphal ornaments carried before him"* (*Sophonisba*, 5.4.0), *"in his Triumphant Chariot"* (*Roman Actor*, 1.4.13); sometimes a *triumph* is signaled: *"The Show of Honor's Triumph"* (*Four Plays in One*, 311; a heading, *The Triumph*, and a description at 334, 355, also 363), *"Fortune's Triumph"* (*Rare Triumphs*, 1523, also 554, 968); a signal in *James IV* gives several possibilities: *"musical songs of marriages, or a masque, or what pretty triumph you list"* (2052–3); atypical is *"the devils thrust him down and go Triumphing"* (*Devil's Charter*, M2v); see also *garland*, *wreath*.

trumpet

an instrument and/or musician widely used (roughly 250 examples) in a number of locutions, most often occurring when important figures *enter* and/or for military business; Henslowe's inventory lists "three trumpets" (*Diary*, App. 2, 39); *sound trumpet* occurs frequently in the Shakespeare canon: *"Sound Trumpets. Enter the King and State, with Guard, to banish the Duchess"* (Folio *2 Henry VI*, 1051–2, 2.3.0, also 1706–8, 3.2.14), *"The trumpets sound and the King enters with his nobles,"* *"The trumpets sound. Enter Duke of Hereford appellant in armor,"* *"The trumpets sound, Richard appeareth on the walls"* (*Richard II*, B2r, 1.3.6, 25; F4v, 3.3.61), *"the trumpets sound, the king entereth with his power"* (*1 Henry IV*, K1r, 5.3.0, also H4r, 4.3.29; I1v, 5.2.8; K4r, 5.5.0), *"Sound Trumpets, and lay the Coffin in the Tomb"* (*Titus Andronicus*, B1v, 1.1.149), *"Trumpets sound, and shot goes off"* (Folio *Hamlet*, 3751, 5.2.283), *"Trumpets sound. Enter Lord Timon, addressing himself courteously to every Suitor"* (*Timon of Athens*, 117–19, 1.1.94, also 286, 1.1.239; 2507–8, 5.4.0); for other instances in Shakespeare see Quarto *Richard III*, H4v, 4.2.0; *Taming of the Shrew*, 78, Induction.1.73; *2 Henry IV*, K4r, 5.5.39; *Troilus and Cressida*, C2v, 723, 1.3.259; Folio *King Lear*, 3058,

5.3.109; *Antony and Cleopatra*, 1619, 3.2.66; *Coriolanus*, 1059, 2.1.161; examples of *sound trumpet* elsewhere are "*The Trumpets sound, the chambers are discharged*" (*Battle of Alcazar*, 977), "*The trumpets sound a dead march*" (*Spanish Tragedy*, 4.4.217), "*Sound trumpets solemnly, enter a table spread*" (*Devil's Charter*, L1r), "*The Trumpet sounds, enter the Prologue*" (*Sir Thomas More*, 1028), "*The Herald departeth from the king to the walls sounding his trumpet*" (*Edmond Ironside*, 872–3), "*Morose speaks from above: the trumpets sounding*" (*Epicœne*, 4.2.70); see also 1 *Tamburlaine*, 705; *Edward I*, 40, 2070; *Downfall of Huntingdon*, 41; *Blind Beggar of Bednal Green*, 103; *Satiromastix*, 2.1.83; *Queen*, 3514; probably synonymous and also very common is *flourish* trumpet: "*Flourish of Trumpets: Then Hoboys*" (Folio 2 *Henry VI*, 2, 1.1.0), "*Exeunt, first passing over the Stage in Order and State, and then, A great Flourish of Trumpets*" (*Henry VIII*, 2444–5, 4.1.36), "*Enter Caesar after a flourish of trumpets*" (*Devil's Charter*, K1r); see also Q2 *Hamlet*, D1r, 1.4.6; *Thracian Wonder*, G4v; *Satiromastix*, 3.1.166; 2 *If You Know Not Me*, 338; *Antony and Cleopatra*, 2533, 4.4.23; *Birth of Merlin*, F4r; *Swetnam*, A2v; *Double Marriage*, 344–5; *Two Noble Ladies*, 1226; a few signals are simply *trumpet* (Quarto *Othello*, K1v, 4.1.213; *Perkin Warbeck*, 4.1.17; *Picture*, 2.2.38; *Prophetess*, 371; *Vow Breaker*, 1.3.50).

While most calls for *trumpet* imply sound produced offstage, only a few specify *within*: "*Trumpets within. Enter Othello and Attendants*" (Quarto *Othello*, E1r–v, 2.1.177), "*Trumpet answers within*" (Folio *King Lear*, 3066, 5.3.117), "*Sound Trumpets within, and then all cry vive le Roi two or three times*" (*Massacre at Paris*, 592), "*A Trumpet within Enter herald sounding*" (*Queen*, 3432–3, also 3427–8; see also *Jews' Tragedy*, 1971–3); for more see *Revenge of Bussy*, 3.1.58; *Valiant Welshman*, F3v; *Unnatural Combat*, 1.1.341; several signals are for *trumpets afar off* (2 *If You Know Not Me*, 316; *Look about You*, 1002; *Tom a Lincoln*, 801–3; *Virgin Martyr*, 1.1.108).

Often the *trumpet* is accompanied by a *drum*: "*Enter the Duke of Florence, Rossillion, drum and trumpets, soldiers, Parolles*" (*All's Well*, 1539–40, 3.3.0), "*Alarum, Drums and Trumpets*" (*Antony and Cleopatra*, 2621, 4.7.0), "*Trumpets sound, and Drums*" (*Coriolanus*, 822, 1.9.66, also 3705–6, 5.6.48), "*A table prepared, Trumpets, Drums and officers with Cushions, King, Queen, and all the state*" (Q2 *Hamlet*, N3v, 5.2.224, also G4v, 3.2.89); for more see *Alphonsus of Aragon*, 791, 799; *Edmond Ironside*, 383; 2 *Tamburlaine*, 2325, 2402, 2569, 2680, 4333; Folio 3 *Henry VI*, 870–2, 2.2.0; 2256, 4.3.27; *Devil's Charter*, D1v; *Antipodes*, 313; sometimes

the musician playing the *trumpet* is specified: "*Enter Edgar at the third sound, a trumpet before him*" (Quarto *King Lear*, L1v, 5.3.117), "*Enter Trumpet and Herald*" (*Humorous Lieutenant*, 329), "*Enter Martius, and Titus with a Trumpet*" (*Coriolanus*, 574, 1.5.3), "*Enter York with a Trumpet, and many Soldiers*" (1 *Henry VI*, 2008–9, 4.3.0); see also *King John*, 608–9, 2.1.299; 622, 2.1.311; 1 *Troublesome Reign*, C4v; *Birth of Merlin*, C3r; *Shoemaker a Gentleman*, 3.2.0; *Swetnam*, E2v, E3v; *Herod and Antipater*, C3r; atypical are "*Sound drum answer a trumpet*" (*Devil's Charter*, D1v, D2r, H3r), "*Charge Trumpets and shot within*" (*Double Marriage*, 343), "*a noise of Trumpets sounding cheerfully*" and "*Trumpets small above*" (*Four Plays in One*, 311, 359); see also **horn**.

truncheon

a *club*/*cudgel* linked to a *fight*/*battle*: "*The prince marching, and Falstaff meets him, playing upon his truncheon like a fife*" (1 *Henry IV*, G3r, 3.3.87), "*Durham armed, a truncheon in his hand*" (*Perkin Warbeck*, 3.4.3), "*The passionate man enters in fury with a Truncheon*" (*Nice Valour*, 173); see also *Three Lords of London*, I2v; *Edward II*, 1337; *What You Will*, E4r; *City Wit*, 347.

trunk

usually a large *chest* or container: "*the chest or trunk to be brought forth*" (*Dead Man's Fortune*, 66), "*two Watermen, bearing his trunks*" (1 *Edward IV*, 81), "*sitting on his bed appareling himself, his trunk of apparel standing by him*" (*What You Will*, B3v); most of the examples are found in scenes in which a figure is concealed in the *trunk*: "*Iachimo from the Trunk*" (*Cymbeline*, 917, 2.2.10), "*Here they break open the trunks, and find Alexandra, and Aristobulus*" (*Herod and Antipater*, B3v), "*Enter two sailors with a trunk, wherein is Mistress Mary in her winding sheet*" and "*They break the Trunk open, and she sits up*" (*Two Maids of More-Clacke*, F4r, G2r); see also *Tottenham Court*, 167, 173; a sequence in *Family of Love* includes "*Enter Maria over the Trunk*," "*Gerardine rising out of the Trunk*," "*Gerardine out of the Trunk*" (C4v, D1r, E3r); for other trunks see *Your Five Gallants*, A2v; *Loyal Subject*, 115; *Valiant Scot*, F1v, F4r; *trunk* is an alternative to *body* when three figures enter "*carrying Feliche's trunk in a winding sheet, and lay it thwart Antonio's breast*" (*Antonio's Revenge*, 4.2.23).

trussing, untrussed

the process of tying the strings and laces (*points*) on a man's clothing, so that *enter trussing* signals "enter dressing, not fully **dressed**, **unready**"; figures are directed to enter with an attendant "*trussing his points*" (*Hieronimo*, 6.0; *Merry Devil of Edmonton*, F2r; *Hog Hath Lost His Pearl*, 457), "*trussing him*" (*Your Five Gallants*, F2v; *Woman Is a Weathercock*, 1.2.1; *Chaste Maid*, 2.3.0), or enter "*untrussed*" (*Phoenix*, F3v; *2 Edward IV*, 153); more detailed signals include "*trussing their points as new up*" (*Merry Devil of Edmonton*, E4r), "*in his nightcap trussing himself*" (*Westward Ho*, 2.1.0), "*untrussed in his Nightcap, tying his points*" (*Devil's Charter*, C1v), "*rudely, and carelessly appareled, unbraced, and untrussed*" (*Nice Valour*, 170); atypical is "*untrusses and capers*" (*All Fools*, 2.1.398); a special instance is "*Enter Friar Tuck in his truss, without his weed*" (*Downfall of Huntingdon*, 2490) and a related item in Henslowe's inventory: "the friar's truss in *Robin Hood*" (*Diary*, App. 2, 165).

tucket

a fanfare played on a **trumpet** usually when nobility **enter**, each nobleman having his own call; of the roughly twenty signals for a *tucket* many are in the Shakespeare canon; in Folio *Merchant of Venice* when "*A Tucket sounds*" (2541, 5.1.121) Lorenzo tells Portia "Your husband is at hand; I hear his trumpet," and in Folio *King Lear* "*Tucket within*" is acknowledged "Hark, the Duke's trumpets" (1014, 2.1.78, also 1466, 2.4.182); see also Folio *Troilus and Cressida*, 672, 1.3.212; Folio *Henry V*, 1562, 3.6.113; 2342, 4.3.78; for more see *Four Prentices*, 211; *Case Is Altered*, 1.9.93; *Troilus and Cressida* plot, 9–10; *Hieronimo*, 8.79; a *tucket* also announces the appearance of rival duelists: "*Tucket. Enter Hereford and Herald*" (Folio *Richard II*, 322; Quarto "*Trumpets sound*," B2r, 1.3.25); in the annotated manuscript of *John of Bordeaux* at "*trumpets sound*" is the bookkeeper's "*A tucket*" (1247), and in *Two Noble Ladies* the bookkeeper wrote "*Tucket*" in both margins at "*flourish. Enter Herald with Lysander in armor*" (1938, 1943, 1945–6, also 1969); the direction is precise in *Devil's Law Case*: "*Two tuckets by several trumpets*" (5.6.2); see also MS *Poor Man's Comfort*, 2189, 2202, 2222; atypical are "*A Tucket afar off*" (*All's Well*, 1602, 3.5.0) marking the departure of the French and "*Sound Tucket. Enter the Masquers of Amazons*" (*Timon of Athens*, 455, 1.2.114); see also *Thracian Wonder*, G1r.

tug

an infrequently used alternative to **pull**: "*Exit Hamlet tugging in Polonius*" (Folio *Hamlet*, 2585, 3.4.217), "*They tug him, and make him kneel*" (*Parson's*

Wedding, 460), Hercules "*tugs with the Bull, and plucks off one of his horns*" (*Brazen Age*, 176).

tumult

either a **noise**, usually **within**, or an onstage disturbance, with most examples in the Heywood canon: "*A noise of tumult within*" (*Golden Age*, 7), "*a tumult within*" (*Captives*, 1496), "*In the tumult enter Acrisius to pacify them*" (*Silver Age*, 96), "*Into this Tumult Enter Calisto as affrighted*" (*Escapes of Jupiter*, 109); see also *Malcontent*, 2.5.1; *Valentinian*, 22; *Conspiracy*, K2v.

tune

typically refers to a **song** and/or the **music** for it: "*Ariel plays the tune on a Tabor and Pipe*" (*Tempest*, 1481, 3.2.124), "*Enter the Harper, and sing to the tune of Who list to lead a Soldier's life*" (*Edward I*, 455), "*A strain played by the consort, Sir Bounteous makes a Courtly honor to that lord and seems to foot the tune*" (*Mad World*, 2.1.143), "*The Doctor stretches his Throat in the Tune*" (*Court Beggar*, 261), "*sing this following Song in four or five parts, to a pleasing Tune*" (*Landgartha*, F1r); for more see *Soddered Citizen*, 333–5; *Weeding of Covent Garden*, 33; *Late Lancashire Witches*, 215; *Messalina*, 2205; *Seven Champions*, G4r; *Unfortunate Lovers*, 78; *Distresses*, 305; other locutions are "*a Boy sings to the tuned Music*" (*Woman Is a Weathercock*, 2.1.120–1), "*The vilest out-of-tune music being heard*" (*Malcontent*, 1.1.0), "*Fiddlers below tuning*" (*Weeding of Covent Garden*, 33), "*Lady and Lucy dance. Monsieur singing, and correcting them in tune*" (*Variety*, C7r; see also *Staple of News*, 1.3.11).

turn

widely used (over ninety examples) usually as a verb linked to onstage action: "*Nurse offers to go in and turns again*" (Q1 *Romeo and Juliet*, G2r, 3.3.162), "*As Aimwell comes towards Violetta she turns and Exit*" (*Witty Fair One*, C2r), "*He looks towards the Garden door, and whilst she turns herself that way, he changes the Glove, and gives her the other poisoned*" (*King John and Matilda*, 74); the verb is found in a variety of locutions, most commonly *turns to*; typical are "*turns to Em, and offers to take her by the hand*" (*Fair Em*, 468), "*First turns to the Monk, then to the Abbess*" (*Death of Huntingdon*, 2508); see also *Doctor Faustus*, A 617; *Locrine*, 223; Q1 *Romeo and Juliet*, E3r, 2.4.154; *Downfall of Huntingdon*, 2702; *Warning for Fair Women*, D1v; Quarto *Every Man Out*, 1406; *Sejanus*, 1.259, 4.354; *Great Duke of Florence*, 2.3.141; *Conspiracy*, H1v; *Parson's Wedding*, 479; *Prisoners*, A10r; other locutions include *turns away*

(*Edmond Ironside*, 1934, 1957; *Prophetess*, 363; *English Traveller*, 87; *Parson's Wedding*, 415; *Claracilla*, D5r), *turns from* (*Cobbler's Prophecy*, 1500; 1 *Iron Age*, 277; *Late Lancashire Witches*, 211; *Lost Lady*, 602; *Conspiracy*, D3r; *Princess*, E4v), *turns suddenly* (*Catiline*, 4.491; *Fool Would Be a Favourite*, C8r), *turns back* (*Lust's Dominion*, 4.4.0, 5.1.239; *Trick to Catch the Old One*, H2v; *Fair Maid of the Exchange*, 68), *turns his back* (*Famous Victories*, F2v; *Hengist*, DS before 2.2, 8), *turns aside* (*Taming of a Shrew*, B3r; *Cupid's Revenge*, 286), "*turneth his face*" (*Devil's Charter*, A2v); *turn* can be linked to pages/*paper*: "*turns over a Book*" (MS *Humorous Lieutenant*, 787–8, 836–7), "*turns over the leaves and reads*" (*Conspiracy*, D3v), "*he shifts folds and turns the paper*" (*Soddered Citizen*, 972–3); less common examples include a traitor "*with his coat turned*" (*David and Bethsabe*, 1083), "*turns a key*" (*Bussy D'Ambois*, 5.1.40), "*Capers and turns*" (*Queen and Concubine*, 56), "*turns him off*" the *ladder* for an *execution* (*Spanish Tragedy*, 3.6.104), "*the table turns*" for a stage trick involving a *banquet* (*Wasp*, 2220–1, 2324), after a *shipwreck* "*the Clown turning the child up and down, and wringing the Clouts*" (*Thracian Wonder*, B4v); examples of *turn* as a noun include "*walking short turns*" (*Eastward Ho*, A2r), "*makes a turn or two*" (*Parson's Wedding*, 469), "*With a turn both ways*" (*Edward I*, 463), "*kiss his hand by turns*" (*Humorous Courtier*, K1v), "*dancing severally by turns*" (*World Tossed at Tennis*, E3r).

turrets

an alternative to *walls* used once: "*Enter Salisbury and Talbot on the Turrets, with others*" (1 *Henry VI*, 487–8, 1.4.22).

U

umbra

Latin for *ghost*, used only by Chapman: "*Intrat Umbra Comolet*" and "*Intrat Umbra Friar*" (*Bussy D'Ambois*, 5.3.56), "*Ascendit Umbra Bussi*" (*Revenge of Bussy*, 5.1.0).

unbeard

see *beard, undisguise*

unbraced

describes a man's entrance with his clothes unfastened, hence *unready*, in *haste*, or disturbed; for figures who *enter* unbraced see *Bussy D'Ambois*, 5.1.0; *Devil's Charter*, L3r; *Dumb Knight*, 163; *'Tis Pity*, 4.3.0;

more detailed is "*Enter the passionate Cousin, rudely, and carelessly appareled, unbraced, and untrussed*" (*Nice Valour*, 170); Marston's plays include figures "*walking unbraced*" (*Antonio and Mellida*, 3.2.0), "*unbraced and careless dressed*" (*What You Will*, A4r), "*unbraced, his arms bare, smeared in blood*" and "*in his nightgown and a nightcap, unbraced*" (*Antonio's Revenge*, 1.1.0, 3.1.0); in *Malcontent* Ferneze heading to Aurelia's *bed* enters "*unbraced*" and re-enters "*in his shirt*" (2.1.0, 2.5.2); atypical is a king who enters "*his Drum unbraced, Ensigns folded up*" (*Thracian Wonder*, E1r).

under the stage

the usual theatrical term for the space *below/beneath* the main platform, sometimes given such *fictional* designations as *cave, grave, gulf, pit, vault*, or *well* and from which *sounds* emanate and figures or properties *ascend/rise* or *descend/sink*; signals and dialogue for such business indicate that access was gained through a *trapdoor* in the main platform; sometimes the space has supernatural or underworld connotations: "*Ghost cries under the Stage*" (Q2 *Hamlet*, D4v, 1.5.148), "*Music of the Hoboys is under the Stage*" (*Antony and Cleopatra*, 2482, 4.3.12); *Antonio's Revenge* provides "*From under the stage a groan*" (3.1.195) from a *ghost*, and "*Balurdo from under the stage*" (5.2.0) calling for help from a *prison*; similarly in *Renegado* a jailer speaks to a prisoner "*under the Stage*" (4.3.4); in *Fatal Contract* a figure pretending to be his father's *ghost* enters "*from under the Stage with his Father's Gown and Robes on*" (G4v), in *John a Kent* figures enter from several locations including "*from under the Stage the third Antic*" (819), in the annotated manuscript of *Believe as You List* the bookkeeper provides "*Antiochus–ready: under the stage*" (1877–9); for other examples of the phrase see *Silver Age*, 139; *No Wit*, 4.3.40; *Valiant Welshman*, D4v; *Two Noble Ladies*, 1900–1; see also *earth, ground*.

undisguise

to reveal one's true identity, as when Altofront "*undisguiseth himself*" (*Malcontent*, 4.5.147); *undisguise* occurs five times in *City Match* (265, 313–14, 316), "*undisguises himself*" occurs three times in *Wizard* (483, 2556, 2636), a figure enters *undisguised* in *Fatal Contract* (H1v); in related usages figures are directed to *unbeard* another in *Lovesick Court* (143) and *unvizard* a *body* in *Cardinal* (3.2.94); more common are variations on *discover* wherein a *beard*, false *hair, mask, patch, peruke, scarf, veil, vizard* is taken off.

unready

a large category that includes in various combinations entrances in a *nightgown, nightcap, shirt, slippers*, or *trussing, unbraced, half naked*; figures are directed to *enter* unready (*Rape of Lucrece*, 226; *Coxcomb*, 323; *Lady of Pleasure*, 3.1.0), "*all unready*" (*2 Iron Age*, 381; *Match Me in London*, 1.3.0), "*half ready*" (*Woman Is a Weathercock* 1.1.1–2; *Wise Woman of Hogsdon*, 311), "*half unready*" (*Fedele and Fortunio*, 1614; *Captives*, 2464, 2512), "*making him ready*" (*Hog Hath Lost His Pearl*, 689), "*not full ready*" (*1 Honest Whore*, 2.1.12); to join Danae in *bed* "*Jupiter puts out the lights and makes unready*" (*Golden Age*, 69); many unready situations result from interrupted *sleep*, so that various items of night *attire*, especially the nightgown, are regularly specified; examples include "*half unready, as newly started from their Beds*" (*2 Iron Age*, 413), "*in a nightgown unready*" (*Platonic Lovers*, 86), "*unready, in his nightcap, garterless*" (*Two Maids of More-Clacke*, E3v).

unseen

denotes figures who *enter/place* themselves so as not to be noticed by others onstage (comparable to *aloof, apart*); figures can enter unseen (*Aglaura*, 2.3.74), "*as unseen*" (*Unnatural Combat*, 3.4.19), "*following unseen*" (*Conspiracy of Byron*, 3.1.0, 5.2.0) or can "*stand unseen*" (*Escapes of Jupiter*, 1583; *Widow*, C4v); with two figures above "*Leopold places himself unseen below*" (*Custom of the Country*, 355), whereas *Court Beggar* provides "*Unseen Above*" and "*Above unseen*" (233); alternatives are "*Enter Mellida, standing out of sight, in her page's suit*" (*Antonio and Mellida*, 4.1.131), enter two with "*Cosmo behind to observe*" (*Telltale*, 368–9); in *Woman's Prize* the manuscript provides "*Enter Livia, and Moroso (as unseen by her)*" but the printed version has "*Enter Livia at one door, and Moroso at another, hearkening*" (22).

untrussed

see *trussing*

unveil

see *veil*

upper stage

the level *above* the main platform cited twice when figures appear "*on the upper stage*" (*Humour out of Breath*, 465; *World Tossed at Tennis*, C4r); one direction refers to "*the upper Room*" (*Two Lamentable Tragedies*, B4r).

urinal

a receptacle for a patient's urine or "water," usually introduced onstage (1) for comic business, (2) to indicate that a figure is *sick*; for examples of comedy see *Fair Em* where the clownish Trotter enters "*with a kerchief on his head, and an Urinal in his hand*" (350–1) and *Wife for a Month* where the fool enters "*with Urinal*" to cast *water* (16); in *Telltale* "*Isabella sick*" is juxtaposed with "*Picentio as a doctor with her water*" (1381–2); in *Wise Woman of Hogsdon* the wise woman's "*clients*" include "*a Countryman with an Urinal*" (291); see also *Monsieur Thomas*, 116; *Wit of a Woman*, 581; *Maid's Revenge*, F1v; *City Wit*, 309.

usher

(1) as a verb, "to lead on or off the stage, usually in ceremonial fashion," (2) as a noun, a distinctive figure to be found as an attendant at court; as a verb, *usher* is widely used, although the many directions provide few details other than the coded term; the participial form is found regularly in the Heywood canon; *Royal King* provides "*Enter the servant ushering in Chester*," "*Enter one ushering the Ladies*," "*Enter the servant ushering Chester and the Queen*" (34, 35, 56); for typical use of this participle see *2 Fair Maid of the West*, 361, 399; *Wise Woman of Hogsdon*, 320, 344; *Captives*, 2168; *Malcontent*, 1.6.0; *2 Honest Whore*, 4.3.33; *Great Duke of Florence*, 4.2.153; *Costly Whore*, 262; *King John and Matilda*, 83 (here a *hearse* rather than a person is *ushered*); *Broken Heart*, 1.2.50; *New Academy*, 34; for *usher/ushered* sometimes combined with *in/by* see *Wise Woman of Hogsdon*, 346; *Histriomastix*, H2v; *Antonio and Mellida*, 2.1.183; *Malcontent*, 4.2.0; *Atheist's Tragedy*, 2.1.0; *Henry VIII*, 329–30, 1.2.8; 753–4, 1.4.63; *New Inn*, 3.2.0; occasionally the verb is used for an *exit*, as when a large group, "*after some compliment*," exits "*with torches ushered to their several chambers*" (*2 Iron Age*, 411); *usher/ushering* can be linked to *state*: "*Enter Zoya, supported by a gentleman usher, followed by Herod and Nymphadoro with much state*" (*Fawn*, 4.408), "*A Banquet, to it Montanus is ushered in state by Saufellus and others, who placing him depart*" (*Messalina*, 1508–10), "*Enter Domitia, ushered in by Aretinus, her train with all state borne up by Julia, Cenis, and Domitilla*" (*Roman Actor*, 2.1.246); alternatives to *usher* include "*He mans her away*" (*How a Man May Choose*, G4r) and a female figure who is "*armed in by Master William*" (*Country Girl*, C1r); see also *bring in, lead*.

Figures designated as *ushers* (such as the title

figure in *Gentleman Usher*) are sometimes *bare*/bare-headed and can be linked to specific duties: "*Enter Argus barehead, with whom another Usher Lycus joins*" (*Widow's Tears*, 1.2.32), "*Enter an Usher bare, perfuming a room*" (*Wonder of a Kingdom*, 3.1.0); ushers often appear *before* high-ranking figures: "*Sound, enter with two Gentlemen-ushers before them, the Queen crowned, her sister to attend her as her waiting-maid, with a train*" (*Royal King*, 65), "*Loud Music, and Enter Ushers before, the Secretary, Treasurer, Chancellor, Admiral, Constable hand in hand, the King following, others attend*" (*Chabot*, 1.1.115).

ut antea
see *as before*

V

vanish
the roughly twenty examples involve either (1) a sudden disappearance by means of a stage trick or (2) a *fictional* situation where a disappearance is important for the narrative but the playgoer actually sees one or more figures *exit*; when an object rather than an actor *vanishes* a stage trick is likely; examples are *Two Noble Kinsmen* where a *silver* hind is set upon an *altar* which is set on *fire* and "*the Hind vanishes under the Altar: and in the place ascends a Rose Tree, having one Rose upon it*" (L2r, 5.1.162), and *Tempest* where "*Ariel (like a Harpy) claps his wings upon the Table, and with a quaint device the Banquet vanishes*" (1583–5, 3.3.52) with the harpy's wings presumably concealing the mechanism (in a comparable scene a trick *table* is signaled in *Wasp*, 2220–1, 2324); *vanishings* of a single actor may also have involved a theatrical trick (such as a sudden departure through a *trapdoor*), as when Ariel "*vanishes in Thunder*" (*Tempest*, 1616, 3.3.82); other single figures who *vanish* include a *ghost* (*2 Iron Age*, 423), *angel* (*Looking Glass for London*, 985; *Virgin Martyr*, 5.1.56; *Martyred Soldier*, 209), *spirit* (*Four Plays in One*, 352; *Two Noble Ladies*, 1099); unusually detailed is the signal in *Witch of Edmonton* where a figure in *bed* "*lies on one side: the Spirit of Susan his second Wife comes to the Bed's side. He stares at it; and turning to the other side, it's there too. In the mean time, Winnifride as a Page comes in, stands at his Bed's feet sadly: he frighted, sits upright. The Spirit vanishes*" (4.2.69).

Less likely to involve stage trickery are situations involving two or more figures; in *Late Lancashire*

Witches at the end of a wedding *dance* "*Mal vanishes, and the piper*" (217) followed by the comment "Vanished, she and the Piper both vanished, nobody knows how," and in *Devil's Charter* two groups cross the stage and *vanish* with the direction for the first suggesting an *exeunt*, not a trick disappearance: "*He goeth to one door of the stage, from whence he bringeth the Ghost of Candie ghastly haunted by Caesar pursuing and stabbing it, these vanish in at another door*" (G2r); in *Macbeth* directions twice call for the three *witches* to *vanish* (179, 1.3.78; 1680, 4.1.132), in *Tempest* after Prospero's reaction "*to a strange, hollow, and confused noise*" the group of nymphs and reapers "*heavily vanish*" (1807–8, 4.1.138), in *Cymbeline* the father, mother, and two brothers of Posthumus "*Vanish*" (3159, 5.4.122), in *Henry VIII* the six "personages" who appear in the queen's vision "*in their Dancing vanish, carrying the Garland with them*" (2655–6, 4.2.82); groups also are directed to *vanish* in *2 Seven Deadly Sins*, 83–4; *Histriomastix*, D1r, H2r.

vault
a seldom used *fictional* term for the *trapdoor* and the space under the main platform through which figures *ascend* or *descend*: "*rising from the vault*" (*Aglaura*, 5.1.120, also 3.2.158), "*Descends through the vault*" (*Sophonisba*, 3.1.205); for more ascents see *Sophonisba*, 4.1.42; *Revenge of Bussy*, 5.3.18; *Arcadia*, F4r; for another descent see Q2 *Bussy D'Ambois*, 5.1.193.

veil, veiled, unveil
widely used for a variety of situations or effects that include (1) *disguise*, (2) *mourning*, (3) other ceremonial occasions, (4) situations involving propriety, modesty, confidentiality; occasionally a man is *led* in "*veiled*" (*Welsh Ambassador*, 1645), but more typical is the distinction in *Changes* when each of the male *masquers* discovers himself but each of the women *unveils* (K2v) or in *English Moor* where a man enters "*in his false beard*" leading in a woman *veiled* (76); for examples of disguise, in *Sophonisba* the devil Erictho enters "*in the shape of Sophonisba, her face veiled*" (4.1.213), and for a comparable effect "*Brusor hides*" Perseda's face "*with a Lawn*" so that Soliman will not be swayed by her beauty (*Soliman and Perseda*, F4r); mourning figures *enter* "*veiled in mourning*" (*Young Admiral*, C1r), "*in Black, with veils stained*" (*Two Noble Kinsmen*, B1v, 1.1.24); in *Love and Honour* Melora enters "*in mourning*" and then *unveils* (152); *Country*

Girl provides both "*Enter the Lady Mosely in mourning, veiled*" and for a disguise "*Enter Master William and Barbary, as his Lady veiled*" (B3r, I2v); figures who enter or are **brought** in *veiled* include the dead Penthea (*Broken Heart*, 4.4.0), Lavinia in the final scene of *Titus Andronicus* (K2r, 5.3.25), Mistress Sanders led in by Lust and rejecting Chastity (*Warning for Fair Women*, D1r); for a sampling of the many other women who enter *veiled/with a veil* see *1 Fair Maid of the West*, 321; *Captain*, 272; *Mad Lover*, 68; *Knight of Malta*, 158; *Costly Whore*, 288; *Prophetess*, 360; *Rule a Wife*, 171; *Thierry and Theodoret*, 44; *Renegado*, 1.3.97; *Queen and Concubine*, 127; *Gentleman of Venice*, I1r; *Wizard*, 2410; *Distresses*, 307, 316, 361; *Hannibal and Scipio* provides "*Ladies all in white, and veiled*" who enter, **dance**, then "*discover themselves in order*" (220–1); for other figures who *unveil*, are *unveiled*, *pull off/put off* their *veils* see *Mad Lover*, 68; *Thierry and Theodoret*, 47; *Renegado*, 1.3.142; *Welsh Ambassador*, 1671; *English Moor*, 77; *Queen and Concubine*, 127; *King John and Matilda*, 85; *Traitor*, 5.1.134; *Osmond*, A4r, A5v; *Gentleman of Venice*, I1r; *Unfortunate Lovers*, 39; for the onstage **putting** on of *veils* see *Queen and Concubine*, 129; *Cruel Brother*, 139; **black** *veils* are specified in *Warning for Fair Women*, D1r; *Devil's Law Case*, 4.2.52; *Welsh Ambassador*, 774; *Shoemaker a Gentleman*, 1.3.0; in *Whore of Babylon* Dekker apparently equates **scarfs** and *veils*, so that initially a group has "*scarfs before their eyes*" until Truth and Time pull "*the veils from the Councillors' eyes*" (DS before Act 1, 33, 38–9); in *Swaggering Damsel* a female figure enters "*veiled*" and then "*unpins her mask*" (I2v); the many *veils* not specified in directions include those worn by Olivia (*Twelfth Night*, 1.5) and Cressida (*Troilus and Cressida*, 3.2).

velvet

occasionally specified for (1) important citizens, (2) figures seeking to be stylish; examples of rank are the Mayor and citizens "*in their velvet coats*" (*1 Edward IV*, 11), "*a velvet coat, and an Alderman's gown*" for Simon Eyre (*Shoemakers' Holiday*, 2.3.93); figures seeking to impress enter "*in a black velvet cap, and a white feather*" (*Lover's Melancholy*, 3.1.0), "*in a suit of gray, Velvet gown, Cap, Chain*" (*Wonder of a Kingdom*, 1.4.0); a *velvet* **patch** is used as a disguise in *Edmond Ironside* (1313), and the Tyrant in *Second Maiden's Tragedy* brings out the dead Lady "*dressed up in black velvet which sets out the paleness of the hands and face*" (2225–6); Henslowe's inventory includes "*one long black velvet cloak*" (*Diary*, App. 2, 133, also 135),

"*Harry the fifth's velvet gown*" (11), "*Tamburlaine's breeches of crimson velvet*" (139).

vial

a small container for liquids, usually **poison** (Q1 *Hamlet*, F3r, 3.2.135; *Devil's Charter*, G4v; *Wife for a Month*, 39; *Love's Sacrifice*, 2798); the link to poison is implied in "*A Halter, a Knife, a Vial*" (*Novella*, 146); other examples are "*Vial of Water*" (*Noble Stranger*, G4v) and "*a vial with white color in it*" (*1 Honest Whore*, 2.1.0); a *vial* is also found in a sickroom (*Mad World*, 3.2.0) and in the **study** of a **conjurer** (*Maid's Revenge*, E3v).

victory

usage suggests that *with victory* is equivalent to *in* **triumph**: "*Jupiter kills Enceladus, and enters with victory*" (*Golden Age*, 51; see also *Silver Age*, 143; *Brazen Age*, 224), "*takes Roderick prisoner; a retreat sounded: Enter Dioclesian with victory*" (*Shoemaker a Gentleman*, 3.5.16), "*Enter with victory … The Spaniards Prisoners*" (*1 Fair Maid of the West*, 317); for more see *Woodstock*, 2956; *Captain Thomas Stukeley*, 2889; *Travels of Three English Brothers*, 360; see also **garland**, **wreath**.

viol

a bowed string instrument in several sizes, the base *viol* being the most popular; the **music** of a *viol* almost always accompanies a **song**; the instrument is specified most often in the Marston canon (*Antonio's Revenge*, 3.2.18; *Jack Drum's Entertainment*, G4v; *Sophonisba*, 3.2.84, 4.1.200, 218); see also *Rare Triumphs*, 968; Quarto *Every Man Out*, 2537; *Sir Giles Goosecap*, 1.4.16; *Roaring Girl*, 2.2.18; *Love's Mistress*, 137; *Arcadia*, F1r; Henslowe's inventory lists "*one bass viol*" (*Diary*, App. 2, 39).

violently, with violence

used occasionally as intensifiers; typical are entrances "*dragging the old Earl violently*" (*Four Prentices*, 186), "*throwing open the doors violently*" (*Guardian*, 3.6.142), "*break with violence into the Chamber*" (*Alphonsus of Germany*, F4v); *King John and Matilda* provides "*Offers violence*" (9, 62; see also *Osmond*, A8r), "*pulls her violently*" (52); other actions performed *violently* include holding (*Launching of the Mary*, 1258–9), **knocking** on a **door** (*Wizard*, 2233, 2511–12), "*breaks violently from them*" (*Noble Stranger*, G4r), "*Pretending a violent stab*" (*Messalina*, 1181); "*Violent Thunder*" is signaled in *Escapes of Jupiter* (1395–6; see also *Catiline*, 3.836).

violin

a four-stringed instrument similar to the modern one, cited less often than the *fiddle*: "*Two Spirits dreadfully enter and (to the Treble Violin and Lute) sing a song of despair*" (*Messalina*, 2518–19), "*They dance to music of Cornets and Violins*" (*English Moor*, 16), "*enter six Satyrs and dance a short nimble antic to no Music, or at most to a single Violin*" (*Landgartha*, E4v).

visor

see *vizard*

vizard

a *mask* or visor used for *disguise* or as part of a *masque* or comparable event; *vizards* are usually worn by men rather than women as indicated by the entrance of "*Boyster vizarded, and Luce masked*" (*Wise Woman of Hogsdon*, 308); occasionally the term *disguised* is independent of the *vizard*: "*Enter Chartley disguised, and in a Vizard*" (*Wise Woman of Hogsdon*, 308), "*Enter Androlio disguised, and others in vizards*" (*Distresses*, 322); more common is for figures to *enter* with vizards (*Queen of Corinth*, 18; *Duchess of Malfi*, 3.5.95; *Picture*, 3.3.0), in vizards (*Cruel Brother*, 176), vizarded (*Mad World*, 2.4.6; *Cardinal*, 3.2.85; *Picture*, 3.5.0; *Sisters*, B5v; *Wasp*, 1407); sometimes the *putting* on (*Sisters*, B2v) or taking off of *vizards* is signaled: "*Columbo points to the body, they unvizard it, and find Alvarez bleeding*" (*Cardinal*, 3.2.94), "*pulls off his vizard and discovers himself to be Altamont*" (*Just Italian*, 277); *vizards* are often linked specifically to masques, as when Follywit enters "*in a masquing suit with a vizard in his hand*" (*Mad World*, 2.4.1) or when a masquer "*Pulls off his Vizard*" (*King John and Matilda*, 52); *vizards* can also be linked to allegorical, supernatural, and other special effects; examples are the entrances of Love "*with a vizard behind*" (*Three Ladies of London*, F1v), the six personages in Queen Katherine's vision with "*golden Vizards on their faces*" (*Henry VIII*, 2645, 4.2.82), a *spirit* "*in shape of Katherine, vizarded, and takes it off*" (*Witch of Edmonton*, 3.1.70) announcing "Thus throw I off mine own essential horror, / And take the shape of a sweet lovely Maid"; in *Old Fortunatus* Vice and her attendants appear with "*gilded vizards, and attired like devils*" (1.3.0); for a comic effect in *Monsieur Thomas* "*Madge with a Devil's vizard roaring, offers to kiss him, and he falls down*" (138); Henslowe's inventory includes eight *vizards* (*Diary*, App. 2, 71); atypical is "*Enter Scudmore like a Vizard-maker*" (*Woman Is a Weathercock*, 5.1.93);

visor as an alternative to *vizard* is found only once: "*pulls off the visors*" (*Aglaura*, 3.1.34).

voices

typically refers to **sound** from **within**: "*Voices are heard within, Treason, Treason, save the Prince, Treason*" (*Conspiracy*, G3r), "*A song within in Voices*" (*Second Maiden's Tragedy*, 2230); for more see *Cobbler's Prophecy*, 628, 632, 641, 662; *Phoenix*, G3v; *Mad World*, 2.6.0; *If This Be Not a Good Play*, 3.2.166; *Unnatural Combat*, 4.2.25; other directions for *voices* are "*Counterfeits a sick voice*" (*Albovine*, 102; see also *Witty Fair One*, E1r), "*A voice and flame of fire*" (*Old Wives Tale*, 555); see also *Locrine*, 1648; three directions in *Sophonisba* use the term: "*organ, and voices: Io to Hymen!*," "*Organs, viols, and voices play for this Act*," "*Organ and recorders play to a single voice*" (1.2.42, 3.2.84, 5.4.36).

W

waistcoat

a vest or undergarment cited occasionally; male figures *enter* "*in a plain Waistcoat*" (*Soddered Citizen*, 1667), "*in their waistcoats with rackets*" (*Devil's Charter*, I2v); see also *Staple of News*, 1.1.0; *Parson's Wedding*, 494; *Herod and Antipater* distinguishes the female *petticoat* from the male *waistcoat* by having Alexandra enter "*in her petticoat*" and Aristobulus "*in his waistcoat or shirt, both amazedly*" (B1r), but elsewhere a woman can appear in a *waistcoat* (*Fair Maid of Bristow*, C3r); more detailed is an entrance "*in a petticoat waistcoat. With her work in her hand*" (*Launching of the Mary*, 2376–7).

waits

the name for certain musicians; *waits* were watchmen in London from the thirteenth century when they called the hours of night for the change of guard with an ox-horn; by the fifteenth century they were also City musicians, typically playing *hoboys* at functions both royal and civic; they are also known to have hired themselves out to the public theatres, perhaps explaining use of the term in three plays although the usage could as easily be *fictional*: "*The waits plays, Enters Lord Mayor*" (*Sir Thomas More*, 954), "*Enter the Eunuch, whilst the waits play softly*" (*Fatal Contract*, H3r); in *2 If You Know Not Me* the musicians also act as supernumeraries: "*the Waits in Sergeants' gowns*" (297).

wake, awake

figures regularly (1) *wake/awake* and less commonly (2) *wake* another; for a sampling of roughly twenty-five examples of the former see *Old Wives Tale*, 478; *Wounds of Civil War*, 1037; *Orlando Furioso*, 1213–14, 1259; *2 Seven Deadly Sins*, 10; Folio *Midsummer Night's Dream*, 1661, [4.1.138]; 1727, 4.1.200; *Old Fortunatus*, 1.1.146; *Yorkshire Tragedy*, 545; *1 If You Know Not Me*, 228; *Lust's Dominion*, 3.2.116; *Cymbeline*, 2612, 4.2.291; *Twins*, E2r, G2r; *Bloody Banquet*, 1468; *Brennoralt*, 3.4.28; variations include "*amazedly awake*" (*Silver Age*, 122), "*wake and rise*" (*King Leir*, 1475), "*starts and wakes*" (*Atheist's Tragedy*, 2.6.23; see also *Guardian*, 5.2.103), "*stretches himself, and wakes*" (*Cobbler's Prophecy*, 166), "*He offers to Kiss and she starts, wakes, and falls on her knees*" (*Two Noble Ladies*, 1793–4); figures enter "*new waked*" (*Golden Age*, 70), "*as newly awaked*" (*Swaggering Damsel*, H2v), "*as newly waked from sleep*" (*English Traveller*, 33); see also *Whore of Babylon*, DS before Act 1, 30, 34; *Tom a Lincoln*, 170; *Valiant Welshman*, A4r; *Parson's Wedding*, 506; for figures who *wake* another see *Warning for Fair Women*, G3r; *If This Be Not a Good Play*, 4.4.34; *Tom a Lincoln*, 1589–90; *Valiant Welshman*, H4r; *Launching of the Mary*, 2012; *Landgartha*, I1v; more detailed is "*rise up as it were in a fury, wake Amurack*" (*Alphonsus of Aragon*, 1027).

walk, walking

figures are regularly directed to *walk/enter walking* (*Satiromastix*, 3.1.38; *Monsieur D'Olive*, 1.1.0; *Bashful Lover*, 1.1.270), often with an adverb or adverbial phrase attached; typical are *walk about, off, apart, aside* (*Albovine*, 26; *Love and Honour*, 167), *up and down* (*Old Wives Tale*, 734; *Alphonsus of Aragon*, 1386; *Satiromastix*, 3.1.62; *Look about You*, 80–1; *Humorous Courtier*, C1r; *Parson's Wedding*, 430); variations include "*walking apart with a Book*" (*Bussy D'Ambois*, 2.2.0), "*walks aside full of strange gestures*" (*Mad Lover*, 14), "*walks up and down musing*" (*Lust's Dominion*, 4.3.92), "*seems amazed, and walks so up and down*" (*Blurt*, 4.2.0), "*walks ere he speak once or twice about cracking Nuts*" (*Old Fortunatus*, 1.1.0); also common are directions to *walk by* (*Greene's Tu Quoque*, B1r; *1 Honest Whore*, 3.1.0; *Maid of Honour*, 3.1.113; *Emperor of the East*, 2.1.123, 3.4.9; *Renegado*, 1.3.0), *walk off* (*Bloody Banquet*, 472); more specific are "*walks by, reading*" (*Broken Heart*, 1.3.50), "*walking by musing*" (*Maid of Honour*, 4.4.133; *New Way to Pay*, 2.3.60; see also *Old Fortunatus*, 3.1.195), "*walking by carelessly*" (*Bloody Banquet*, 850), "*walking by, and practising his postures*" (*Maid of Honour*, 1.2.7), "*walks off, meditating*" (Quarto

Every Man Out, 3544), "*saluting the Company as a stranger, walks off*" (*1 Honest Whore*, 2.1.117), "*walks off at the other end of the shop*" (*Amends for Ladies*, 2.1.71–2), "*She espies her husband, walking aloof off, and takes him for another Suitor*" (*1 Edward IV*, 83); figures are directed to *walk **passionately*** (*Devil's Charter*, C1v), ***fearfully*** (*Woman in the Moon*, A3r), ***sadly*** (*Bashful Lover*, 1.1.60; *David and Bethsabe*, 601), ***fantastically*** (*Maid of Honour*, 1.2.0); more detailed are "*walking discontentedly weeping to the Crucifix*" (*Noble Spanish Soldier*, 1.2.0), "*walks sadly, beats his breast, etc.*" (*Jovial Crew*, 445); other variations include "*walking reading to himself*" (*Devil's Charter*, K3r), "*walks in meditation, seeming to pray*" (*Four Plays in One*, 321), "*walking before the gate*" (*English Traveller*, 62), "*walking short turns before*" a ***door*** (*Eastward Ho*, A2r), "*upon the Tower walls walking*" (*2 Henry VI*, G1r, 2598, 4.5.0), enter "*walking to Tottenham Court*" (*Tottenham Court*, 116), "*walks over the stage*" (Folio *Every Man In*, 4.7.107; *Patient Grissil*, 2.1.220; *Greene's Tu Quoque*, B1r; *Mad Lover*, 62; *Faithful Friends*, 2838–9); *as [if]* signals include entrances "*as walking*" (*Sir Thomas More*, 1282), "*as from Walking*" (*English Traveller*, 44); *walk* can be combined with another verb: "*walk and talk*" (*How a Man May Choose*, A2v), "*Walks and Whispers*" (*Henry VIII*, 1171, 2.2.120), "*Walk and confer*" (*Challenge for Beauty*, 23), "*John walks and stalks by Skink, never a word between them*" (*Look about You*, 847–8).

walls

although strictly speaking a ***fictional*** designation for the level ***above*** the main platform, *walls* had virtually become a technical term, usually used in the context of ***battle***; in the roughly forty signals figures typically are or ***enter** on/upon the walls*: "*Enter Reignier on the Walls*" (*1 Henry VI*, 2570, 5.3.130, also 639, 1.6.0; 1472, 3.2.40), "*the Lord Scales upon the Tower walls walking*" (Quarto *2 Henry VI*, G1r, 4.5.0), "*The trumpets sound, Richard appeareth on the walls*" (*Richard II*, F4v, 3.3.61), "*two Senators with others on the Walls of Corioles*" (*Coriolanus*, 499–500, 1.4.12), "*Enter above upon the walls*" (*1 Iron Age*, 298), "*make the proclamation upon the walls*" (*Edward I*, 2070, also 830), "*to them on the walls*" (*Troilus and Cressida* plot, 15–16, 47, 50); for more see *2 Tamburlaine*, 4112; *John a Kent*, 900, 918, 1448; *3 Henry VI*, Folio 2511, 4.7.16; 3073, 5.6.0; E1r, 2673, 5.1.0; *George a Greene*, 299; *King John*, 505, 2.1.200; 1996, 4.3.0; *1 Troublesome Reign*, C3v; *2 Troublesome Reign*, A3r; *Orlando Furioso*, 394; *Soliman and Perseda*, F1v, H4r; *Selimus*, 1165–6; *Guy of Warwick*, C2r; *David and Bethsabe*, 186; *Alphonsus of Germany*, H3r; *Blind*

Beggar of Alexandria, 2.0; *Death of Huntingdon*, 2123, 2702; *1 Edward IV*, 19; *Four Prentices*, 230; *Captain Thomas Stukeley*, 1176; *Sir Thomas Wyatt*, 4.3.12; *Devil's Charter*, D1v, D2r, D3v, H3r; *Timon of Athens*, 2512, 5.4.2; *Maid's Tragedy*, 65; *Brazen Age*, 206, 223; *Hengist*, 5.2.7–9; *Barnavelt*, 888; *Vow Breaker*, 2.1.113, 5.1.0; *Jews' Tragedy*, 799, 2732; *Politician*, G3v; other references to *walls* as battlements include "*The French leap over the walls*" (*1 Henry VI*, 720, 2.1.38), "*mounts the walls*" (*Brazen Age*, 224; see also *Four Prentices*, 234), "*assail the walls*" (*Edmond Ironside*, 914, also 872), "*As they are scaling the walls*" (*Humour out of Breath*, 479; see also *Selimus*, 1200; *2 Tamburlaine*, 4174), "*Exeunt from the walls*" (*King John and Matilda*, 83; see also *1 Henry VI*, 1510, 3.2.74; *1 Iron Age*, 320); only a few directions use *wall* in another sense: "*Canby takes the Wall, and justles Strowd*" (*Blind Beggar of Bednal Green*, 36), "*brings her to her husband's picture hanging on the wall*" (*Warning for Fair Women*, E3v), "*hangs his Harp on the wall*" (*Grim the Collier*, G7r, also G8r).

wand

a property either (1) linked to supernatural events or figures or (2) used as a synonym for *rod*; examples of a *wand* for *magic* are "*Merlin strikes his wand. Thunder and Lightning, two Dragons appear*" (*Birth of Merlin*, F3r, also G1v), "*Oberon strikes Guy with his Wand, he wakes and speaks*" (*Guy of Warwick*, B4r), "*Melissa striketh with her wand, and the Satyrs enter*" (*Orlando Furioso*, 1257–8, also 1252–3); for similar examples see *Three Ladies of London*, A3r; *Fair Maid of the Inn*, 201; *Maid's Revenge*, E3v; *Seven Champions*, G4r; context indicates that *wand* is synonymous with *rod* in "*short silver wands*" (*Henry VIII*, 1333, 2.4.0), "*a golden Wand*" (*Queen and Concubine*, 22), "*with riding wands in their hands, as if they had been new lighted*" (*Look about You*, 2–3; see also *King Leir*, 309, 409); for more see *Patient Grissil*, 5.2.13; *Roaring Girl*, 5.1.241.

wanton

a seldom used term for "amorous, lascivious": "*Courting Paris wantonly*" (*Roman Actor*, 4.2.108), "*Exeunt, wanton Music played before them*" (*City Madam*, 3.1.98), "*depart in a little whisper and wanton action*" (*Your Five Gallants*, A2r).

warrant

a specific and probably *fictional* designation for a *paper* property; only one of the five examples is from relatively early in the period: "*Tears the warrant*" (*Lust's Dominion*, 4.4.95); those from later are "*a warrant sealed*" (*Aglaura*, 4.3.0; *Fair Favourite*, 223), "*gives a Warrant and Signet to Petruccio*" (*Queen and Concubine*, 46), "*delivers the warrant*" (*Parson's Wedding*, 478).

water

specified for a wide variety of situations; signals for entrances include "*water, wine, and oil, Music, and a banquet*" (*David and Bethsabe*, 712), "*Water and a Towel*" (*What You Will*, B3v), "*his apron on, Basin of water, Scissors, Comb, Towels, Razor, etc.*" (*Fancies Chaste and Noble*, 2372–3), "*to the well for water*" (*Old Wives Tale*, 768); in *Believe as You List* a jailer enters "*with brown bread, and a wooden dish of water*" for his **prisoner**, and the bookkeeper notes in the margin "*with bread and water*" (1985–90); *water* is contained in a **glass** (*Atheist's Tragedy*, 5.2.209; *Love's Pilgrimage*, 235), **vial** (*Noble Stranger*, G4v), porringer (*John a Kent*, 370), **dish** (*Bashful Lover*, 3.3.200); actions include enter "*with water*" and "*Throws it on her face*" (*Renegado*, 5.3.110, 115), **disguised** figures **dancing** and "*sprinkling water on her face*" (*Queen of Corinth*, 18), "*a Friar with a holy water-pot casting water*" (*Devil's Charter*, E1r), "*They wash him with puddle water, and shave his beard away*" (*Edward II*, 2301), "*a wench with a pail of water*" who "*Pours the water into the tub*" (*Tottenham Court*, 143–4); see also *Taming of the Shrew*, 1778, 4.1.149; *Humorous Lieutenant*, 345; atypical are a **dumb show** with "*A Crocodile sitting on a river's bank, and a little Snake stinging it. Then let both of them fall into the water*" (*Locrine*, 961–4), entrances "*with water Spaniels and a duck*" (*Roaring Girl*, 2.1.361; *Histriomastix*, C2r); examples of perfumed **sweet** water are the "*flowers and sweet water*" Paris brings to Juliet's **tomb** (Q1 *Romeo and Juliet*, I4v, 5.3.0), "*a casting-bottle of sweet water in his hand, sprinkling himself*" (*Antonio and Mellida*, 3.2.24); *Telltale* signals water as urine: "*Isabella sick Picentio as a doctor with her water*" (1381–2).

wave

to *flourish* or brandish a **sword**, **rod** or other object; examples include "*waving a Torch*" (*Herod and Antipater*, L3v), "*They all shout and wave their swords, take him up in their Arms, and cast up their Caps*" (*Coriolanus*, 695–6, 1.6.75; see also *Roman Actor*, 5.1.180), "*They fight, and Constantine winneth the Eagle, and waveth it about*" (*Valiant Welshman*, I3r), "*Standing without the circle he waveth his rod to the East*" (*Devil's Charter*, G1v; see also *Twins*, E1v); atypical are "*shields pictured with Neptune riding upon the Waves*" (*Thracian Wonder*, H3r).

way

found primarily in directions for figures to **enter** and **exit**, usually variations on **several** ways, *one way/another way*; of the roughly 100 examples most common are signals to "*Enter several ways*" (*1 Henry VI*, 720–1, 2.1.38; *Sir Thomas More*, 1675; *2 Seven Deadly Sins*, 31; *2 Edward IV*, 98; *May Day*, 2.1.0; *Honest Lawyer*, F4r; *Cruel Brother*, 190), "*Exeunt several ways*" (*Doctor Faustus*, B 742; *1 Iron Age*, 287; *Philaster*, 95; *King and No King*, 213; *City Match*, 239; *Sophy*, 4.310; *Bloody Banquet*, 857; *Queen of Aragon*, 342, 365; *Cruel Brother*, 164, 170; *Distresses*, 334; *Platonic Lovers*, 36; *News from Plymouth*, 137, 181; *Unfortunate Lovers*, 65); variations include **diverse** ways (*Golden Age*, 71; *1 Iron Age*, 309; *Atheist's Tragedy*, 4.3.69; *Royal King*, 74; *Brennoralt*, 4.3.13), "*contrary ways*" (*Queen*, 2669), "*sundry ways*" (*Love's Sacrifice*, 1242), "*at several ways*" (*Jews' Tragedy*, 1993), "*go forth two several ways*" (*Devil's Charter*, K4r), "*part several ways*" (*Brazen Age*, 239; *Timon of Athens*, 1579, 4.2.29), "*go off several ways*" (*New Way to Pay*, 2.2.33; *Unnatural Combat*, 2.3.130), "*Exeunt with Trumpets two ways*" (*Look about You*, 464–5), "*he runs one way, and she another*" (*Faithful Shepherdess*, 403), "*Flies into the woods several ways*" (*Goblins*, 1.1.84), "*Enter three several ways the three Brothers*" (*Travels of Three English Brothers*, 404).

Entrances and exits *one way/the other way* are a variation of the more common *at one* **door**/*at another door* (less commonly **side/end**); see *James IV*, 937–8, 1186, 1549–50, 1558, 1821–3; *2 Seven Deadly Sins*, 27; Quarto *Merry Wives*, G3r, 5.5.102; *Captain Thomas Stukeley*, 2441; *Thracian Wonder*, G4v; *Golden Age*, 20; *Silver Age*, 123; *Fleer*, 3.3.0, 4.1.0, 5.1.0; *Rape of Lucrece*, 168, 235; *Noble Spanish Soldier*, 2.2.0; *Money Is an Ass*, B4v; *Fair Favourite*, 255; *Parson's Wedding*, 477; variations include exeunt "*two one way, and two another way*" (*Four Prentices*, 247), "*at one door, another way*" (*White Devil*, 5.4.0), one army **marching** "*one way over the stage*" and a second "*the other way*" (*Antony and Cleopatra*, 1973–4, 3.10.0), "*Exeunt three ways*" wherein one group goes "*one way*," a second "*down to hell*," others "*ascend to heaven*" (*Silver Age*, 164); see also *Arraignment of Paris*, 819; *Edward III*, E2r; *Monsieur D'Olive*, 1.1.0; *Widow's Tears*, 5.4.3; *1 Fair Maid of the West*, 275; *Cruel Brother*, 195.

Other locutions include *gives way/***retreats** (*Caesar and Pompey*, 4.3.0), **leading** the way (*Arraignment of Paris*, 180), "*goes her way*" (*Old Wives Tale*, 624; *Captain*, 310), "*makes way through them wounded, and escapes*" (*Jews' Tragedy*, 2070–1); a **permissive** signal for the duration of an action calls for "*Shrimp playing on some*

instrument, a pretty way" (*John a Kent*, 1098; see also *Gentleman Usher*, 3.2.276); actions can be performed *several ways* and *half way*: "*bow several ways*" (*Two Noble Kinsmen*, H1v, 3.6.93), "*trying several ways to wear his cloak and hat*" (*Twins*, E1v; see also *Four Prentices*, 234), "*draws his sword out half way*" (*Twins*, D2v), "*Love descends half way, then speaks*" (*Rebellion*, 52); other actions include "*courts her in a gentle way*" (*Jovial Crew*, 426), "*Cupid's bow bent all the way towards them*" (*Nice Valour*, 157), "*Runs at her and falls by the way in a Swoon*" (*Second Maiden's Tragedy*, 1339–41), "*the Drawer stands amazed not knowing which way to go*" (*1 Henry IV*, D2v, 2.4.79); see also *Edward I*, 463; *Hieronimo*, 6.3; *Valiant Welshman*, C4v; *King John and Matilda*, 74.

weapon, weapons

the more than sixty directions using these terms show that *weapon* virtually always denotes **sword** while *weapons* designates various items; frequently dialogue, context, and the implication of "*drawing a weapon*" indicate that it is a sword: "*with his weapon drawn*" (*Titus Andronicus*, E3v, 3.1.22; see also *2 Henry VI*, E3v, 1944–5, 3.2.236), "*with lights and weapons*" (Quarto *Othello*, B4v, 1.2.54), "*stoops and looks on the blood and weapons*" (Q1 *Romeo and Juliet*, K2r, 5.3.139); for other uses of *weapon(s)* **drawn** see *2 Seven Deadly Sins*, 22; *Histriomastix*, F2v; *Shoemaker a Gentleman*, 5.1.36; *Fortune by Land and Sea*, 388; *Golden Age*, 24; *If This Be Not a Good Play*, 5.1.0; *2 Iron Age*, 381–2, 427; *Maid in the Mill*, 59; *Jews' Tragedy*, 945–7; *Messalina*, 2319; for more examples where *weapon* almost certainly means sword see *Fedele and Fortunio*, 1616, 1633; *Mucedorus*, B3r; *1 Edward IV*, 33; *Antonio and Mellida*, 3.2.248; *Your Five Gallants*, I3r; *Hengist*, DS before 4.3, 16–17; *Love's Sacrifice*, 2609; *Goblins*, 2.3.18; *Lovesick Court*, 144; *Country Captain*, C11r; *Cardinal*, 4.3.75; when *weapons* are not swords the dialogue sometimes clarifies but often merely echoes the unspecific direction; examples where the term likely denotes items other than a sword are "*a Company of Mutinous Citizens, with Staves, Clubs, and other weapons*" (*Coriolanus*, 2–3, 1.1.0), "*Pluto with a club of fire … Proserpine, the Judges, the Fates, and a guard of Devils, all with burning weapons*" (*Silver Age*, 159), "*Mechanics with Weapons*" (*Jews' Tragedy*, 1372); other signals offer a range of locutions and possibilites: "*the river Achelous, his weapons borne in by Water Nymphs*" (*Brazen Age*, 173), "*a devil playing on a Drum, after him another bearing an Ensign, and diverse with weapons*" (*Doctor Faustus*, B 1485–6), "*Flings down his weapons*" (*Lust's Dominion*, 4.4.85), "*march out with the* body of the King … with a dead march, drawing weapons on the ground" (Massacre at Paris, 1263), "snatcheth at some weapon to kill himself" (Whore of Babylon, 2.2.185), "manage their weapons to begin the Fight" (Birth of Merlin, C3r), "all cast down their weapons at his feet" (Herod and Antipater, F4r); figures *enter* "weaponed" in Three Lords of London, F4v; Downfall of Huntingdon, 1571; Blurt, 5.1.0; Honest Lawyer, A3r.

wedding, marriage
usually cited when figures *enter/exit*, often *as from/as to* the *ceremony* (with figures carrying *rosemary*); explicit *as [if]* directions include "*as newly come from the Wedding*" (Fortune by Land and Sea, 371), "*in solemnity as to marriage; and pass over*" (Four Plays in One, 338), "*with Rosemary, as from a wedding*" (Woman's Prize, 2), "*They pass as to the Wedding with Rosemary*" (City Wit, 358); other signals may include an implicit *as [if]*: "*Enter all to the Wedding*" (London Prodigal, D4r), enter "*going to be Married*" (Scornful Lady, 281), "*Music, and a Bride Cake to the wedding*" (Old Law, K3r); other entrances include "*Enter the solemn show of the marriage*" (Two Maids of More-Clacke, A1v), "*Here a passage over the Stage, while the Act is playing, for the Marriage of Charalois with Beaumelle, etc.*" (Fatal Dowry, 2.2.359), simply "*Enter Wedding*" (Goblins, 4.3.33); see also James IV, 2051–2; Messalina, 1656–7; Aglaura, 1.4.51; the *wedding* ceremony is usually to be imagined offstage, as when a group enters "*After the Christening and marriage done*" (Edward I, 1927), but in a *dumb show* in Maidenhead Well Lost "*the Bishop takes their hands and makes signs to marry them*" (144); *fictional* signals include "*Enter Quomodo's wife, married to Easy*" (Michaelmas Term, 5.1.13), "*Enter the new-married widow*" (No Wit, 4.3.0), "*Parolles and Lafew stay behind, commenting of this wedding*" (All's Well, 1089–90, 2.3.183), enter two figures "*who were present at the marriage*" (Swaggering Damsel, I2v) and one "*married now*" (Trick to Catch the Old One, E4r); atypical is "*She plays with the wedding ring upon her finger*" (Parson's Wedding, 417).

weed, weeds
an alternative to *apparel*, *attire*, *clothes*, *garment*, *habit* with most examples linked to *disguise*; typical are entrances "*in Friar's weed*" (Edward I, 2431; Insatiate Countess, 5.1.149), "*in Shepherd's weeds*" (School of Compliment, E2r), "*with the Beggar's weed*" (Fedele and Fortunio, 1511), a woman "*putting on the weed of a Sailor's boy*" (Christian Turned Turk, B2v); in Lust's Dominion two friars enter followed by "*the*

Cardinal in one of their weeds, and Philip putting on the other" (2.3.0); Woman Is a Weathercock provides "*puts off the Priest's Weeds, and has a Devil's robe under*" and "*Slips off his Devil's weeds*" (5.2.70, 78); weeds not part of a disguise are entrances "*in his hunting weeds*" (Insatiate Countess, 3.4.34, 116), "*Friar Tuck in his truss, without his weed*" (Downfall of Huntingdon, 2490).

weep
over 100 directions call for a figure to *weep* or presumably to simulate *weeping*, sometimes with happiness, more often in fear, entreaty, or sorrow; usually the figure is a woman, and often either she or another calls attention to the *weeping* which the audience is unlikely actually to see; the basic signal to *weep* is common (Famous Victories, C2r, C2v; Guy of Warwick, D4r; Great Duke of Florence, 4.2.4; Deserving Favourite, G2r; Bashful Lover, 3.1.100; Bride, 18; Antipodes, 242; Damoiselle, 465; Cardinal, 1.2.124); more detailed are "*she sits weeping and praying*" (2 Edward IV, 167), "*while all the company seem to weep and mourn, there is a sad song in the music room*" (Chaste Maid, 5.4.0), "*she kneels, sues, weeps*" (Match Me in London, 5.3.0), "*Both speak weeping*" (City Madam, 2.2.208), "*loose haired, and weeping*" (Dick of Devonshire, 687–9), "*weeps, and wrings her hands*" ('Tis Pity, 3.6.0), "*Kicks her and Exit. She weeps*" (City Nightcap, 96), "*He feigns to weep*" (City Match, 263), "*Offers to weep*" (2 Passionate Lovers, I4r), "*rises up weeping, and hanging down her head*" (Aglaura, 5.3.108), "*She weeps and sighs*" (Brennoralt, 1.4.33, 36), "*She leans on him and weeps*" (Claracilla, D5r), "*Unveils Amaranta who weeps*" (Unfortunate Lovers, 39); for more see Sir Thomas More, 1551; Greene's Tu Quoque, I1r; Hog Hath Lost His Pearl, 930; Tom a Lincoln, 170, 1703, 2863; Night Walker, 380; Four Plays in One, 321, 326; Hengist, DS before 1.2, 9; Fatal Dowry, 2.1.47; Martyred Soldier, 211; Witch of Edmonton, 5.3.0; Noble Spanish Soldier, 1.2.0; Herod and Antipater, C1v; Jews' Tragedy, 1762, 2242, 2252, 3132; Duchess of Suffolk, C2r; Love's Sacrifice, 1387, 2055; Messalina, 2520; Landgartha, B1v; see also *lament*.

well
a rare *fictional* term for the *trapdoor* in the main platform: "*Angel ascends out of the Well, and after descends again*" (Shoemaker a Gentleman, 1.3.101), "*flings her into the well*" (Faithful Shepherdess, 409); see also Old Wives Tale, 634, 768; Prophetess, 385.

wet

used to describe figures who enter *as from* a ship-wreck or other immersion in *water*; the link is sometimes spelled out: *"wet from sea"* (*Looking Glass for London*, 1369), *"all wet as newly shipwrecked and escaped the fury of the Seas"* (*Captives*, 653–4), *"all wet, looking about for shelter as shipwrecked"* (*Thracian Wonder*, B4v); more common are directions for figures to *enter* *"all wet"* (*Doctor Faustus*, A 1175; *Tempest*, 1869, 4.1.193; *Four Prentices*, 177), *"wet on his legs"* (*Merry Devil of Edmonton*, E3r), simply *wet* (*Doctor Faustus*, B 1552; *Pericles*, C1v, 2.1.0; *Tempest*, 59, 1.1.50; *Witch of Edmonton*, 3.1.91; *Lady of Pleasure*, 5.2.57); an acting out of wetness has a baby rescued from a shipwreck and *"the Clown turning the child up and down, and wringing the Clouts"* (*Thracian Wonder*, B4v); atypical is *wet* as a verb when *mourning* figures *"wet their handkerchiefs with their tears"* (*Antonio's Revenge*, 2.1.0).

while, a pretty while, a good while

a sub-category of *permissive* directions wherein the duration of an action is left indeterminate: *"A noise heard about the house, a pretty while, then enter the Constable"* (*Sir John Oldcastle*, 2222–3), *"they sit a good while on the Stage before the Candles are lighted, talking together"* (*What You Will*, A2r); the locution can be linked to *fights* and *alarums*: *"They fight a good while and then breathe"* (*Orlando Furioso*, 1536), *"they fight a while and pause"* (*Birth of Merlin*, F3r; see also *Brennoralt*, 5.3.233; *Unfortunate Lovers*, 68), *"strike up alarum a while"* (*Alphonsus of Aragon*, 373, 1354; see also *Landgartha*, C1r, H3v); most common are signals linked to *music*: *"Sound Instruments a while within"* (*Alphonsus of Aragon*, 994, 1007, 1020), *"Loud music a while"* (*No Wit*, 4.3.40), *"The Music plays on a while"* (*Your Five Gallants*, F2v), *"Music awhile, and then cease"* (*Old Fortunatus*, 4.1.114, also 1.1.146, 4.1.111); entrances are signaled after figures already onstage *"consult a little while"* (*Valiant Welshman*, C4v), *"have Danced a while"* (*Court Beggar*, 266), *"hath a while made some dumb show"* (*Rare Triumphs*, 1375); other usages include *"pauses for a while"* (*Woman Killed*, 138), *"whisper a while"* (*Lovesick Court*, 129), *"goes to his pavilion, and sits close a while"* (*David and Bethsabe*, 1826), *"look ghostly awhile at one another"* (*Just Italian*, 254), *"stands silent awhile letting the Music play"* (*Second Maiden's Tragedy*, 2227–8), *"After they have scrambled a while at their Victuals: This Song"* (*Jovial Crew*, 388); see also *Warning for Fair Women*, D1v; *Caesar and Pompey*, 1.2.0; *Wisdom of Doctor Dodypoll*, 463–4; *Jews' Tragedy*, 2215–17.

whip

found most famously in the entrance of *"Tamburlaine drawn in his chariot by Trebizon and Soria with bits in their mouths, reins in his left hand, in his right hand a whip, with which he scourgeth them"* (*2 Tamburlaine*, 3979); twice *whips* are linked to *knives*: *Warning for Fair Women* directs Tragedy to appear *"in her one hand a whip, in the other hand a knife"* (A2r), and the plot of *Battle of Alcazar* provides three *furies* *"one with a whip: another with a bloody torch: and the third with a Chopping knife"* (29–30) along with the marginal note *"a whip brand and Chopping knife"* (27–30); in *Bondman* a group of senators faced with rebellious slaves *"shake their whips, and they throw away their weapons, and run off"* (4.2.128); figures who *enter/exit* with a *whip* include a beadle (Folio *2 Henry VI*, 894, 2.1.143), a carter (*Jews' Tragedy*, 1646), a coachman (*Roaring Girl*, 3.1.22); see also *Family of Love*, C4r, E2r; *Country Girl*, F4v; all that remains of what may have been a comic *scene* in the manuscript of *John of Bordeaux* is *"Enter the scene of the whipper"* (1058); for *whip* as a verb, *Three Ladies of London* provides the entrance of a *prisoner* *"with an Officer to whip him, or two if you can"* and *"Lead him once or twice about, whipping him, and so Exit"* (F1v, F2r); see also *Warning for Fair Women*, A3r; related is *"Jockey is led to whipping over the stage, speaking some words, but of no importance"* (*2 Edward IV*, 180).

whisper

a widely used verb (roughly 300 examples) that usually indicates a speech not heard by the playgoer (in contrast to the *aside*): *"whisper aside"* (*Amends for Ladies*, 5.2.83), *"Whisper in private"* (*Fair Maid of the Exchange*, 71), *"secretly whispers"* (*Sir John Oldcastle*, 1879), *"sit and whisper whilst the other two speak"* (*Histriomastix*, F4v), *"whisper together in council"* (*1 Henry VI*, 1495, 3.2.59), *"Exit King, frowning upon the Cardinal, the Nobles throng after him smiling, and whispering"* (*Henry VIII*, 2080–1, 3.2.203), *"Juno and Ceres whisper, and send Iris on employment"* (*Tempest*, 1792, 4.1.124); spoken words to be *whispered* include *"This they whisper, that Overdo hears it not"* (*Bartholomew Fair*, 2.4.37), Lorenzo *"whispereth in her ear"* words not to be overheard by Balthasar (*Spanish Tragedy*, 3.10.77); most of the signals provide only *whisper/whispering*, with ten examples in *Country Girl* (D2v, E4v, F3v, G2v, G3r, G3v, I2v, I4r) and nine in *Herod and Antipater* (B3v, C1r, C3r, D1v, E4r, F4r, F4v, G2v), but roughly a dozen figures are directed to *whisper in* someone's *ear* (*Woman in the Moon*, D1v; *Three Lords of London*, B1v; *Friar Bacon*, 391; *George a Greene*, 1243;

Edmond Ironside, 96; 1 *Troublesome Reign*, A4r; Quarto *Richard III*, F4v, 3.2.111; I1v, 4.2.79; Q1 *Romeo and Juliet*, C4r, 1.5.122; *Antony and Cleopatra*, 1378, 2.7.38; *Grim the Collier*, H9r; *Monsieur D'Olive*, 5.2.9; *Chabot*, 3.1.0; *Appius and Virginia*, B3r); variations include "*She hangs about his neck whispering*" (*Albovine*, 66), "*Whispers, and uses vehement actions*" (*Renegado*, 2.1.68), "*Marcello and two more whispered out of the room*" (*White Devil*, 2.2.37), "*kiss these three wenches, and depart in a little whisper and wanton action*" (*Your Five Gallants*, A2r).

whistle

the action of blowing either through the lips or the instrument, although the limited evidence indicates that usually the **sound** rather than the instrument is meant: "*Boy whistles and calls*" (Q1 *Romeo and Juliet*, I4v; Q2 "*Whistle Boy*," L2r, 5.3.17); see also *Fedele and Fortunio*, 434, 1501; 1 *Henry IV*, C3v, 2.2.28; 1 *Honest Whore*, 2.1.0; *Bartholomew Fair*, 4.2.22; *Little French Lawyer*, 419; *Picture*, 3.6.63; *Antipodes*, 283; *Goblins*, 3.4.9; *Claracilla*, F9v; *Sisters*, D1r; several carters whistle (*Jews' Tragedy*, 1646, 1762–3; *Woman Killed*, 152); sometimes a certain tune is required, as in *Woodstock* where a figure "*a whistling*" (1706) "whistles treason"–probably a ballad known to the audience; in *Lady's Trial* "*Fulgoso whistles the Spanish Pavin*" (767–9, also 742), and in *Court Beggar* a figure "*whistles and Dances Sellenger's round, or the like*" (262); the instrument is specifically referred to in *Sparagus Garden* where at "pray use this whistle for me" "*Cautious whistles*" (190); when the sound is linked to mariners a specific instrument or set of notes may be implied: "*the whistling of the Boatswains*" (*Launching of the Mary*, 2672; also 2731, 2734, 2739); "*Whistles within*" (*Very Woman*, 2.1.74) is acknowledged "the Boatswain whistles you aboard," and *Prisoners* has a signal for the master to *whistle* an alarm at a shipwreck (C5v).

white

the roughly seventy examples include a wide range of objects and **clothing**; a few signals refer to *white* coloring or makeup: "*his face whited*" (*Lover's Melancholy*, 3.3.19), "*white-faced*" and "*white*" (*English Moor*, 63, 82), a "*White moor*" (*Thracian Wonder*, H2r), a **spirit** that "*rises out of the cave, white*" (*Martyred Soldier*, 244); Bellafront's cosmetics include "*a vial with white color in it, and two boxes, one with white, another red painting*" (1 *Honest Whore*, 2.1.0); *white* can be associated with age: "*white head and beard*" (*Captain*, 296),

"*with a long white hair and beard*" (*Picture*, 2.1.85; *Thracian Wonder*, C4v); as to clothing, figures are often directed to enter *in white/all in white*, less commonly *clothed in white*; see *Three Lords of London*, E4v; *Merchant of Venice*, B4v, 2.1.0; *Merry Wives*, G3r, 5.5.102; *Warning for Fair Women*, D1r; *Old Fortunatus*, 1.3.0; *Two Noble Kinsmen*, L1v, 5.1.136; *Queen of Corinth*, 72; *Hannibal and Scipio*, 220; *Unfortunate Lovers*, 24; *Fair Favourite*, 252; examples are "*a funeral in white, and bearers in white*" (*Turk*, 585–6; see also *Swetnam*, G2r), a **hearse** accompanied by "*two Nuns in white*" and "*two little boys in white*" (*Fatal Contract*, E3v); **ghosts** or **spirits** can appear *in white* (*Second Maiden's Tragedy*, 1930; *Jews' Tragedy*, 2722), as when the martyred Dorothea enters "*in a white robe, crowns upon her robe, a Crown upon her head*" with others **following** "*all in white, but less glorious*" (*Virgin Martyr*, 5.2.219); *white* **robes** are also specified for six personages who appear in a vision (*Henry VIII*, 2644, 4.2.82), a boy who strews **flowers** before a marriage (*Two Noble Kinsmen*, B1r, 1.1.0), **masquers** (*Malcontent*, 5.5.66; '*Tis Pity*, 4.1.35), Calantha with the **body** of Ithocles (*Broken Heart*, 5.3.0), "*Hebe in a white robe with golden stars*" (*Women Beware Women*, 5.2.50); other items of *white* clothing include a **veil** (*Cruel Brother*, 139), **cloak** (*Michaelmas Term*, Induction.0), **ribbon** (*Sophonisba*, 1.2.40), surplice (*Alphonsus of Aragon*, 951), **apron** (*Death of Huntingdon*, 457), "*white sleeves and apron*" (*Two Maids of More-Clacke*, H1v), country wenches in "*all red Petticoats, white stitched Bodies*" (*Country Girl*, D3r), "*three white-coat Soldiers*" (1 *If You Know Not Me*, 209); *white* is associated with penance or disgrace: the *white* **sheets** worn by Dame Elinor and Jane Shore (2 *Henry VI*, D2r, 1188, 2.4.16; 2 *Edward IV*, 165), "*her hair loose, a white rod in her hand*" (*Queen*, 3786–7), "*a Wreath of Cypress, and a white Wand*" (*Queen and Concubine*, 22); other *white* objects include a **pendant** (*Death of Huntingdon*, 2909–10), **hourglass** (*Summer's Last Will*, 360), **banneret** (*Four Plays in One*, 311), **stick** (*Friar Bacon*, 1561), **flag** (*Jews' Tragedy*, 797), **feather** (*Lover's Melancholy*, 3.1.0), **cross** (*Maid of Honour*, 5.2.289), **staff** (*Perkin Warbeck*, 2.2.112; *Sisters*, B6v), **tapers** (*Death of Huntingdon*, 2984), **roses** (Octavo 3 *Henry VI*, A2r, 1.1.0; *Warning for Fair Women*, I1r); occasionally an object such as an **altar** (*Broken Heart*, 5.3.0) or **bed** (*Vow Breaker*, 4.2.0) is **covered** in white; see also *No Wit*, 4.3.148; *World Tossed at Tennis*, D2r; *Birth of Merlin*, F3r.

wig

see **periwig**

wind

to *blow* a *horn*, usually *within*, a *sound* linked to *hunting*: "*Here a cry of Hounds, and wind horns in a peal*" (Quarto *Titus Andronicus*, D1r, 2.2.10, also Folio 1082–3, 2.4.10), "*Wind horns. Enter a Lord from hunting*" (*Taming of the Shrew*, 18, Induction.1.15), "*Wind horns. Enter with Javelins, and in green*" and "*The fall of the Boar being winded*" (*Brazen Age*, 187, 194), "*Horns winded, a great noise of hunting*" (*Golden Age*, 32); for similar examples see *Woodstock*, 2095; *Downfall of Huntingdon*, 1258–61; *Death of Huntingdon*, 331–4; *Midsummer Night's Dream*, F4r, 4.1.102; F4v, 4.1.138; *Royal King*, 9, 12; *Two Noble Kinsmen*, G3r, 3.5.92; *Woman Killed*, 98; *Silver Age*, 130; *Thierry and Theodoret*, 19, 21; *Maidenhead Well Lost*, 122; elsewhere *winding* a horn marks the arrival of a messenger: "*One winds a horn without*" (*Epicœne*, 2.1.38); see also *1 Tamar Cham*, 51–2; *Queen's Exchange*, 529; *Sophy*, [1.2.56]; sometimes a figure *winds* a horn onstage: "*she windeth a horn in Vulcan's ear and runneth out*" (*Arraignment of Paris*, 813), "*The Devil windeth his horn in* [Alexander's] *ear*" (*Devil's Charter*, M2v); see also *John a Kent*, 469; *Old Wives Tale*, 838, 872; *English Traveller*, 82; *Princess*, H2r; a few signals refer not to a horn but to a *cornet*: "*The Cornet is winded*" (*What You Will*, G4v; see also *Wit at Several Weapons*, 134), "*One winds a cornet within*" (*Antonio's Revenge*, 1.2.193); in *Two Noble Kinsmen* editions sometimes change the Quarto's "*Wind horns of Cornets*" to "*Wind horns* [*off*]. *Cornets*" (F3v, 3.1.96).

winding sheet

the *sheet* in which a *corpse* is wrapped: "*Feliche's trunk in a winding sheet*" (*Antonio's Revenge*, 4.2.23), "*Enter two sailors with a trunk, wherein is Mistress Mary in her winding sheet*" (*Two Maids of More-Clacke*, F4r), "*Leonora, with two coffins borne by her servants, and two winding sheets stuck with flowers*" (*Devil's Law Case*, 5.4.125), "*One goes to open the Tomb, out of which riseth Fernando in his winding sheet, only his face discovered*" (*Love's Sacrifice*, 2763–4); related are ladies "*winding Marcello's corpse*" (*White Devil*, 5.4.65).

window

cited in the directions of roughly thirty-five plays, almost always to designate a location *above/aloft*; with no reliable external evidence of actual *windows* on the upper level this is best considered a *fictional* term for a dialogue-created location or perhaps an implicit *as* [*if*] situation, as made explicit in "*appeareth above, as at her chamber window*" (*Poetaster*, 4.9.0); Q1 *Romeo and Juliet* directs the lovers to *enter*

"*at the window*" (G3r) as opposed to Q2's "*aloft*" (H2v, 3.5.0), and later in Q1 Juliet "*goeth down from the window*" (G3v, 3.5.67), and similarly Quarto *Othello* directs "*Brabantio at a window*" (B2r) as opposed to the Folio's "*above*" (89, 1.1.81); often both terms are used: "*the King, and Butts, at a Window above*" (*Henry VIII*, 3014–15, 5.2.19), "*Benvolio above at a window*" (*Doctor Faustus*, B 1205); see also *Christian Turned Turk*, F3v; *Widow*, B2r, E3v; *Devil's Law Case*, 5.5.0; *Wizard*, 2143; *Princess*, C3v; other examples are "*throws up a ladder of cords, which she makes fast to some part of the window; he ascends, and at top falls*" (*Insatiate Countess*, 3.1.42), "*At the Window. He comes down in his nightgown*" (*Tale of a Tub*, 1.1.22), "*Celia at the window throws down her handkerchief*" (*Volpone*, 2.2.220), "*She lets the Cabinet fall out of the Window*" (*Novella*, 151); wooing scenes or related actions often have the woman symbolically above at a *window*: "*Bel-imperia at a window*" (*Spanish Tragedy*, 3.9.0), "*Victoria comes to the window, and throws out a letter, which Fedele taketh up*" (*Fedele and Fortunio*, 435–6, also 1388–90, 1409–13), "*Maria beckons him in the window*" (*Hog Hath Lost His Pearl*, 256–7); see also *Two Angry Women*, 1495; *Jack Drum's Entertainment*, D3r; *Family of Love*, A3v; *Heir*, 525; *Knave in Grain*, 313; *Just Italian*, 259, 260; figures also observe from a *window* above: "*look down from the window*" (*Lost Lady*, 590), "*looking out at a window*" (*Parson's Wedding*, 402); see also *Woman Hater*, 123; *Captain*, 259; probably "*Pedant looks out of the window*" from above in *Taming of the Shrew* (2397, 5.1.15) but neither dialogue nor direction confirms this; in *Jews' Tragedy* a figure above "*draws her window curtain*" (2225, 2941–2); for more *window* scenes on the upper level see *Two Lamentable Tragedies*, C4r; Quarto *Every Man Out*, 1018, 1122; *Devil Is an Ass*, 2.6.37, 2.7.8; *Vow Breaker*, 2.2.42–3; *Hannibal and Scipio*, 199; *Distresses*, 302; atypical are a figure who "*Looks in at the window*" on the main stage level (*Amends for Ladies*, 5.2.163–5), "*lets he down his window, and it breaks Black Will's head*" (*Arden of Faversham*, 839–40)—referring to the pentice of a shop stall on the main level.

wine

the most common item in *tavern* or *banquet* scenes or at other times when figures *drink* (roughly sixty-five examples); *wine* is usually brought on by a *drawer*, sometimes by a vintner or other servant, rarely by the drinkers themselves; a drawer who *enters* with *wine* and certain other properties frequently establishes a tavern setting: "*with Wine,*

Plate, and Tobacco" (Amends for Ladies, 3.4.36), "with wine and Sugar" (Look about You, 1497), "with Wine and a Cup" (All Fools, 5.2.53), "with four quarts of wine" (Coxcomb, 318), "Vintner with a quart of Wine" (Histriomastix, C1r), "A Table, Stools, Bottles of wine, and Glasses, set out by two Drawers" (Variety, D6v); for similar signals see May Day, 3.3.188; 1 Fair Maid of the West, 267; Miseries of Enforced Marriage, 1076–7; Greene's Tu Quoque, D2r; Captain, 281, 283; Scornful Lady, 248; Love's Pilgrimage, 242; Queen of Corinth, 27; 2 Fair Maid of the West, 397; Launching of the Mary, 1935–7, 1958–9; Weeding of Covent Garden, 60, 67, 70; Bride, 31, 49; wine also helps to create scenes of hospitality, as when servants enter "with Wine" (Timon of Athens, 946, 3.1.29), or of celebration: "with Foils, and Gauntlets, a Table and Flagons of Wine on it" (Folio Hamlet, 3675–6, 5.2.224), with "flagons of Wine" and "bring in water, wine, and oil, Music, and a banquet" (David and Bethsabe, 491, 712); for similar scenes using wine see Downfall of Huntingdon, 1516; 1 Edward IV, 61; Wily Beguiled, 351–2, 354–5; 2 Fortune's Tennis, 19; Yorkshire Tragedy, 442–3, 445; MS Bonduca, 963–4; Chaste Maid, 3.2.48; Fair Quarrel, 4.1.115; Woman's Prize, 4; Chances, 186, 213; Lovers' Progress, 114; English Traveller, 66; Siege, 385–6; Late Lancashire Witches, 237; Messalina, 2205–6; wine is a popular means of administering poison, but no other signal is as explicit as "She poisons the wine" (Bloody Banquet, 1826, also 410, 1120, 1124, 1822); signals for wine to poison–as in Hamlet already cited–are Satiromastix, 5.1.0; Hoffman, 1527; How a Man May Choose, G3v; Sophonisba, 5.3.88; Hannibal and Scipio, 235; Fatal Contract, H4r; Lovesick Court, 155–6; Cardinal, 5.3.234; because wine is sometimes called for by a figure onstage and brought on by another it was a special concern of the tiring house, as is apparent in the manuscript of Barnavelt where the bookkeeper's "R.T. Enter with wine" (2015–17) follows Barnavelt's call for it, and in the annotated quarto of Two Merry Milkmaids where the bookkeeper twice added "wine" when it is needed (D3r, E1r); several other plays, especially in the Fletcher canon, have similar calls for wine to be ready: "Bowl of wine ready" (Chances, 210/398; Custom of the Country, 313/455; see also Little French Lawyer, 417/464; Spanish Curate, 113/501, 117/501), "A cup of Wine ready" (Lovesick King, 289), "The Banquet ready. One Chair, and Wine" (City Madam, 5.1.95); for other signals for wine see Julius Caesar, 2148, 4.3.157; Patient Grissil, 2.2.135; Westward Ho, 2.3.17; Fawn, 5.152; Devil's Charter, I2v, I3r, L1v; If This Be Not a Good Play, 2.2.170, 174; Atheist's Tragedy,

5.2.200; Humorous Lieutenant, 325; New Trick, 230, 279; Queen, 1563; City Wit, 367; Novella, 120; Conspiracy, I4r; Princess, E1v; see also sack.

wings

required for several supernatural or allegorical figures: an angel "on his shoulders large wings" (Two Noble Ladies, 1103), a devil "with the face, wings, and tail of a Dragon; a skin coat all speckled on the throat" (Caesar and Pompey, 2.1.24), Time "in black, and all his properties (as Scythe, Hourglass and Wings) of the same Color" (Whore of Babylon, DS before Act 1, 29–30), four masquers "like the four winds, with wings, etc." (No Wit, 4.3.148); in Tempest Ariel enters "(like a Harpy) claps his wings upon the Table, and with a quaint device the Banquet vanishes" (1583–5, 3.3.52), so that presumably the wings conceal or enhance the stage trick; Henslowe's inventory includes "Mercury's wings" (Diary, App. 2, 80).

witch

a figure linked to supernatural events or effects: "Thunder and Lightning. Enter three Witches" and "The Witches Dance, and vanish" (Macbeth, 2, 1.1.0; 1680, 4.1.132, and more), "Witches charm together" (Late Lancashire Witches, 256, also 187, 218, 244, 256), "Witch, Tarpax, with other spirits armed ... Thundering and Lightning" (Seven Champions, C2r, also B1r); sometimes a witch is named: "Enter Hecate: and other witches: (with Properties and Habits fitting)" (Witch, 181–2, also 2022–4; see also Macbeth, 1566, 4.1.38); for more see Folio 2 Henry VI, 619, 1.4.0; Valiant Welshman, E4r, G1v; Witch of Edmonton, 4.1.20; 1 Arviragus and Philicia, D7v; 2 Arviragus and Philicia, E8v.

with child

the most common locution to denote "pregnant"; see Pericles, E1r, 3.Chorus.14; Blind Beggar of Alexandria, 10.30, 10.99; Four Plays in One, 313; Shoemaker a Gentleman, 4.1.0; Witch of Edmonton, 1.1.0; Landgartha, F4v; a few signals imply that pregnancy meant padding: "big with Child" (When You See Me, 135–6), "great with child" (Birth of Merlin, B3r), "big-bellied" (Lover's Melancholy, 3.3.74), "great-bellied" (Devil's Law Case, 5.1.0; Antipodes, 269); in Golden Age Diana and her nymphs "unlace themselves, and unloose their buskins: only Calisto refuseth to make her ready. Diana sends Atlanta to her, who perforce unlacing her, finds her great belly, and shows it to Diana, who turns her out of her society, and leaves her" (35); for a fake pregnancy, early in *Heir* Luce appears "*gravida*" but is later revealed to be "yet an untouched virgin" so that Franklin says "Cushion, come forth; here, Signior Shallow, take your child unto you" and "*flings the cushion at him*" (521, 575); see also **cushion**.

withdraw

to **draw** back, **retreat**, **retire**: "*Antonio offers to come near and stab; Piero presently withdraws*" (*Antonio's Revenge*, 3.1.139), "*They withdraw into the Tent*" (Folio *Richard III*, 3484, 5.3.46); in four instances the verb is linked specifically to parts of the stage, so that figures are directed to *withdraw* "*behind the Arras*" (*English Traveller*, 79), "*behind the hangings*" (*Traitor*, 3.3.8; *Northern Lass*, 75), and to be observers "*at the other part of the stage*" (Quarto *Every Man Out*, 1121); for figures who are directed simply to *withdraw* see *Cobbler's Prophecy*, 1086; *Death of Huntingdon*, 2006; *Poetaster*, 3.4.269; *Thierry and Theodoret*, 37; *City Wit*, 319; *Unfortunate Lovers*, 34; *Changes*, G2r; *Witty Fair One*, H2v; *Obstinate Lady*, C1v.

within

widely used (roughly 800 examples) to indicate the location of a **sound** or the presence of a figure *within* the tiring house and therefore offstage out of sight of the playgoer; most of the examples (1) anticipate an entrance so that a **voice**, **knocking**, or other offstage sound is followed by the appearance of a figure/figures or (2) suggest by means of sound an **unseen** action/event; the majority of examples call for a voice/knocking offstage followed by an entrance; typical is "*Knocks within*" (*Woman Is a Weathercock*, 1.1.38) followed by "Who's there: Come in" and an entrance; comparable **noises** other than knocking include "*A noise within of a Tabor and a Pipe*" followed by the entrance of shoemakers "*in a morris*" (*Shoemakers' Holiday*, 3.3.47, 51), "*A noise of uproar within*" followed by the entrance of figures "*as newly started from their Beds*" (*2 Iron Age*, 413); for representative examples from the Shakespeare canon see *Comedy of Errors*, 1657, 1665, 5.1.183, 189; *Measure for Measure*, 2101, 2114, 4.3.28, 36; 2191, 2198, 4.3.106, 111; Folio *Troilus and Cressida*, 2279, 2280, 4.2.19, 20; 2435, 2488, 2490, 2499, 4.4.49, 98, 99, 108; *Macbeth*, 127, 136, 1.3.29, 37; 1229, 1237, 3.3.9, 14; *Coriolanus*, 1988, 1993, 3.1.259, 262; 3366, 3369, 5.3.19, 21; *Tempest*, 451, 458, 1.2.314, 320; *Virgin Martyr* provides an unusually complex effect when the **devil** Harpax is first heard "*within*" **laughing** twice, then "Louder," "At one end," "At the other end," "At the middle,"

"*Within*," and finally enters "*in a fearful shape, fire flashing out of the study*" (5.1.81, 86, 93–4, 97, 100, 119, 122); occasionally a figure heard *within*, such as "*Malvolio within*" in his madhouse (*Twelfth Night*, 2005, 4.2.20), does not enter.

The hundreds of sounds designated *within* include **thunder** (*Birth of Merlin*, C3r), "*A Pistol shot*" (*Lovers' Progress*, 109), "*Knocking and calling*" (*Hoffman*, 548), "*Music and healthing*" (*2 Iron Age*, 409), "*strange cries, horrid noise, Trumpets*" (*Double Marriage*, 348), "*A Bell tolls within*" (*Weakest Goeth*, 1774), "*Sound Trumpets and Drums within*" (*Alphonsus of Aragon*, 505), "*The cornets sound a battle within*" (*Antonio and Mellida*, 1.1.0); also common are spoken words *within*: "*A cry within, Brave Master Welborne*" (*New Way to Pay*, 4.2.31), "*Sound drums within and cry stab stab*" (*Mucedorus*, A2v), "*Cry within follow, follow*" (*Bloody Banquet*, 240), "*A shout, and a general cry within, whores, whores*" (*Maid of Honour*, 4.1.23); sounds *within* can be presented *as [if]*: "*A noise within, as the fall of a Horse*" (*Guardian*, 4.1.0), "*Noise within as of a coach*" (*New Way to Pay*, 3.2.241).

without

used sporadically, usually as a synonym for the more familiar and widely used **within** but occasionally as its opposite; in various late Jacobean or Caroline plays *without* is linked to an offstage **horn** (*Sophy*, [3.153]; *Andromana*, 230), **noise** (*Aglaura*, 3.2.65), **knocking** (*Emperor of the East*, 3.4.39; *Inconstant Lady*, 4.2.4), **voices** (*Parson's Wedding*, 393), **shouts** (*Goblins*, 5.5.185); see also *Conspiracy*, K2v; Jonson in particular uses *without* rather than *within* for knocking (*Volpone*, 1.2.82, 3.8.15, 5.4.47; *Alchemist* 1.2.162, 3.2.159), and other offstage **sounds** (*Epicœne*, 2.1.38; *Catiline*, 1.185); examples of *without* as the opposite of *within* (and therefore comparable to today's distinction between *onstage* and *offstage*) are rare; in *Caesar and Pompey* "The Consuls enter the Degrees" with "Caesar staying a while without with Metellus" (1.2.0) for the opening speeches of the scene; a clear distinction between *within* and *without* is most likely when both terms are used in the same signal: "*The song. A choir within and without*" (*Arraignment of Paris*, 166), "*Enter Talbot and Burgundy without: within, Pucelle, Charles, Bastard, and Regnier on the Walls*" (*1 Henry VI*, 1471–2, 3.2.40), "*Parley without, and answer within*" (Folio *Richard II*, 1646, 3.3.61).

wonder

seldom used (as opposed to the widely used **amazed**); as a noun *wonder* signals some corresponding action: "*Enter Gentlemen, Vermandero meeting them with action of wonderment at the flight of Piracquo*" (*Changeling*, 4.1.0), "*after some show of wonder, he goes towards her*" (*Night Walker*, 380); such **actions**/**shows** presumably apply as well to *wonder* as a verb: "*The Boy goes to Maria, and gives her a paper; she wonders, and smiles upon Hartlove, he amazed, approaches her*" (*Night Walker*, 381), "*Sertorio brings in the flesh with a skull all bloody, they all wonder*" (*Bloody Banquet*, 1920–2); see also *White Devil*, 2.2.37; *Widow's Tears*, 4.2.0.

woo, court

seldom used verbs; *woo* is found only in three **dumb shows**: "*a fair lass wooeth him. He crabbedly refuseth her*" (*Arraignment of Paris*, 721), "*the Poisoner Woos the Queen with Gifts, she seems loath and unwilling awhile, but in the end, accepts his love*" (*Hamlet*, Q2 H1v, Folio 2000–2, 3.2.135); see also *Silver Age*, 146; *court* is found only in *Fair Maid of the Exchange*: "*Go to Phillis and court her to themselves*" and "*courts her again in private*" (68, 69).

wood, woods

used for (1) *wooden* objects, (2) a *woodman* or *wood nymph*, (3) *the woods*; objects are "*a wooden Bowl of Drink*" (*Jovial Crew*, 390), "*a Voider and a wooden Knife*" to clear away a meal (*Woman Killed*, 117), "*brown bread, and a wooden dish of water*" for a **prisoner** (*Believe as You List*, 1987–90), "*a halting Soldier on wooden stumps*" (*Valiant Scot*, E1v, also F1r); Henslowe's inventory includes "Kent's wooden leg" (*Diary*, App. 2, 69); figures are directed to **enter** "*with wood*" (*Patient Grissil*, 5.2.51), "*with a burden of Wood*" (*Tempest*, 1038, 2.2.0); entrances are signaled in "*woodman's habit*" (*Twins*, C2v), "*like a woodman*" (*Isle of Gulls*, 232; *Silver Age*, 150), "*like a woodman in green*" (*Silver Age*, 146), and "*Sylvanus's woodman*" carries "*an oaken bow laden with acorns*" (*Arraignment of Paris*, 29); see also *Maid's Metamorphosis*, B3v; *Philaster*, 118, 120; *wood nymphs* appear in *Summer's Last Will*, 104, 1871; *Twins*, E1v; references to *the woods* include entrances "*in the woods*" (*Timon of Athens*, 1602, 4.3.0; 2496, 5.3.0; *Hog Hath Lost His Pearl*, 1177), "*lies down in the Wood*" (*Princess*, H2v), "*Song in the Wood*" (*Little French Lawyer*, 430), "*Flies into the woods several ways pursued by Thieves in Devil's habits*" (*Goblins*, 1.1.84); since directions for *woods*/forest scenes do not call for **trees**, *in the woods* may be **fictional** or may contain an implicit **as [if]** made explicit in "*Andrugio, as out of the woods, with Bow and Arrows, and a Cony at his girdle*" (*Promos and Cassandra*, K4r).

work

working/*at work*/*with work* are found in both domestic and commercial contexts; these locutions are regularly linked to women in their homes or at court who enter **sewing**, "*as at work*" (*Henry VIII*, 1615, 3.1.0), "*with needlework*" (*Atheist's Tragedy*, 4.1.0), "*with their work in their hands*" (*Knack to Know an Honest Man*, 660–1; *1 Edward IV*, 63; *Queen and Concubine*, 110; *Launching of the Mary*, 2376–7); sewing/needlework are associated with **sitting**: "*sitting at work*" (*James IV*, 725), "*sit down to work*" (*Monsieur Olive*, 2.2.0; *Launching of the Mary*, 2398), "*sits working on a piece of Cushion work*" (*Wisdom of Doctor Dodypoll*, 2–4); the three Destinies who follow Fortune are to be "*working*" (*Old Fortunatus*, 2.2.213); see also *Sir Giles Goosecap*, 2.1.16; *Woman Is a Weathercock*, 4.3.1–2; shoemakers and seamsters are directed to **enter** "*sitting at work in his shop*" (*Case Is Altered*, 1.1.0), "*sitting upon the stage at work*" (*George a Greene*, 971–2), "*in a Seamster's shop, at work upon a laced Handkerchief*" (*Wise Woman of Hogsdon*, 284), "*in a Seamster's shop working*" (*Shoemakers' Holiday*, 3.4.0), "*working as in their shop*" (*Amends for Ladies*, 2.1.1), simply "*at work*" (*Shoemakers' Holiday*, 4.1.0; *Fair Maid of the Exchange*, 44); see also *Greene's Tu Quoque*, B1r; *Fair Maid of the Exchange*, 41; for less familiar forms of *work* additional details are sometimes supplied, as when a tiler enters "*going to work with a tray of Tiles and a Ladder*" (*Duchess of Suffolk*, C3r); in *Patient Grissil* a **basket**-maker enters "*with his work*" but other signals specify "*two baskets begun to be wrought*," "*burdens of Osiers*," "*a bundle of Osiers*" (1.2.74, 0, 4.2.0, 20).

wound, wounded

wound as both verb and noun and *wounded* are widely used: "*wounded in several places*" (*Lovers' Progress*, 86), "*is wounded, and falls to the ground*" (*Sir John Oldcastle*, 55), "*They survey his wounds*" (*Two Lamentable Tragedies*, D3v), "*wounds the Cardinal, and in the scuffle gives Bosola his death-wound*" (*Duchess of Malfi*, 5.5.53), "*the body of Feliche, stabbed thick with wounds, appears hung up*" (*Antonio's Revenge*, 1.2.207); for a sampling of the roughly forty figures who **enter** *wounded* see *Locrine*, 835; *1 Tamburlaine*, 851, 2184; *Sir Thomas Wyatt*, 4.4.23; Folio *3 Henry VI*, 1281, 2.6.0; *King John*, 2466, 5.4.6; *Thracian Wonder*, F4r, G4v; *Antony and Cleopatra*, 2627, 4.7.3; *Trial of Chivalry*, I3r; *1 Iron Age*, 312, 313; *Maid of Honour*, 2.5.0, 3.3.16; *Shoemaker a Gentleman*, 1.1.0; *Two Noble Ladies*, 1198; *Valiant Welshman*, B3r; *Gamester*, A4v; such entering figures are often **led** or otherwise assisted onto the stage: "*wounded and led*" (*Love and Honour*, 112), "*wounded, led by his son and Lester*" (*Death of Huntingdon*, 1749–50), "*supporting Doron deadly wounded*" (*Two Noble Ladies*, 222), "*bringing forth Warwick wounded*" (Folio 3 *Henry VI*, 2799–2800, 5.2.0); see also Quarto 2 *Henry VI*, H3v, [5.2.65]; *Imposture*, B3v; *Princess*, H2v; details for entrances include "*his face wounded*" (*Dick of Devonshire*, 865), "*wounded, with an arrow in his neck*" (Octavo 3 *Henry VI*, C3v, 2.6.0), "*wounded in the Leg with an Arrow*" and "*wounded, leaning upon his Sword*" (*Jews' Tragedy*, 862–3, 881), "*his sword drawn, his body wounded, his shield struck full of darts*" (*Sophonisba*, 1.2.61).

For a sampling of figures who *wound* another/themselves see *Trial of Chivalry*, E2v; *Philaster*, 127; 2 *Iron Age*, 412, 423, 427; *Witch of Edmonton*, 3.3.68; *Dick of Devonshire*, 798; *Messalina*, 2349; *Brennoralt*, 5.3.42; *Duke's Mistress*, K3r; *Politician*, H1v, I2r; *Cardinal*, 4.3.78; *Traitor*, 3.3.95, 5.1.133, 5.3.52, 65; *Albovine*, 105; *Princess*, H2r; actions include "*They catch one another's Rapiers, and both are wounded*" (Q1 *Hamlet*, I3v, [5.2.302]), "*chaseth them off the Stage, himself wounded*" (*Honest Man's Fortune*, 234), "*is wounded, and put to flight*" (*Weakest Goeth*, 592–3), "*left wounded, and for dead, stirs and creeps*" (*Warning for Fair Women*, F1v), "*Hector lies slain by the Myrmidons, then Achilles wounds him with his Lance*" (1 *Iron Age*, 322), "*They espy one another draw, and pass at each other, instantly both spread their arms to receive the wound*" (*Lovesick Court*, 141), "*fight with single swords, and being deadly wounded and panting for breath, making a stroke at each other with their gauntlets they fall*" (*Rape of Lucrece*, 252); *ghosts* who exhibit their *wounds* are the "*Ghost of Agamemnon, pointing unto his wounds*" (2 *Iron Age*, 423; see also *Woman in the Moon*, B4v; *Fatal Contract*, E1r), "*with wounds as they died in the wars*" (*Cymbeline*, 3070, 5.4.29); see also *Devil's Charter*, G2r; *Unnatural Combat*, 5.2.271.

wreath

a widely used property linked to a variety of occasions; a *wreath* can denote **victory** in war ("*Enter King of Naples, on his head a wreath of Bays, as from Conquest,*" *Noble Stranger*, B1r), or at the other extreme, disgrace ("*The Bishops take her Crown and Wand, give her a Wreath of Cypress, and a white Wand,*" *Queen and Concubine*, 22); figures are **crowned** with *wreaths*, usually of **laurel** (*Bashful Lover*, 4.3.68; *Jews' Tragedy*, 6) but sometimes unspecified (*Valentinian*, 88), and the climactic **masque** of *Malcontent* includes "*dukes' crowns upon laurel wreaths*" (5.5.66); "*a wreath of nettles*" awaits

Horace at the end of *Satiromastix* (5.2.158), "*a wheaten wreath*" is part of a religious **ceremony** (*Two Noble Kinsmen*, L1v, 5.1.136), "*a wreath of poplar*" is worn by the forsaken Œnone (*Arraignment of Paris*, 578), a *wreath* is wrested from the head of the **conjurer** Sacrapant (*Old Wives Tale*, 808).

wreathed arms

see *arm in arm*

wringing her hands

linked to **mourning** or **weeping** women; most usages involve only a formulaic *wrings/wringing her hands* (*Cobbler's Prophecy*, 2–3; *Death of Huntingdon*, 961; *Warning for Fair Women*, E3v; *Bondman*, 3.2.25; *Emperor of the East*, 4.4.221; *Herod and Antipater*, F1r); more detailed are "*she weeps, and wrings her hands*" ('*Tis Pity*, 3.6.0), "*she looks for her Babe and finding it gone, wrings her hands*" (*Bloody Banquet*, 852–3), "*Lepida with her hair disheveled wringing her hands*" (*Messalina*, 1860–1), "*The Widow wringing her hands, and bursting out into passion, as newly come from the Burial of her husband*" (*Puritan*, A3r); occasionally the figure is a man, as when Pope Alexander faced with a **devil** "*holdeth up his hands wringing and softly crying*" (*Devil's Charter*, M1r); the locution is found twice in Q1 *Romeo and Juliet*: "*Enter Nurse wringing her hands, with the ladder of cords in her lap*" and "*All at once cry out and wring their hands*" (F3r, 3.2.31; I2r, [4.5.51]); examples of the verb *wring* in other locutions are "*wrings him by the nose*" (*Woman's Prize*, 23), "*the Clown turning the child up and down, and wringing the Clouts*" (*Thracian Wonder*, B4v) after a baby is rescued from a shipwreck.

write, writing

of the roughly ninety signals for this action many are simply *writes* (*Massacre at Paris*, 671; *Jew of Malta*, 1788; *Sir Thomas More*, 1270; Quarto *Merry Wives*, B4r, 1.4.88; *Sir John Oldcastle*, 880; 1 *If You Know Not Me*, 228; Q2 *Bussy D'Ambois*, 5.1.177; 1 *Honest Whore*, 3.3.9; *Whore of Babylon*, 4.2.34; *White Devil*, 4.1.122, 5.6.10; *Woman Is a Weathercock*, 3.3.23, 26, 30, 31, 35; *Captives*, 1363; *Jews' Tragedy*, 718; *Roman Actor*, 5.1.96; *Sparagus Garden*, 143; *Brennoralt*, 2.1.30; *Country Captain*, A3r, D1v); more detailed directions include "*takes the staff in her mouth, and guides it with her stumps and writes*" (*Titus Andronicus*, G1r, 4.1.76, also F4v, 4.1.68), "*draws out his writing tables and writes*" (*Antonio's Revenge*, 1.2.92), "*He writes and she dictates*" (*Sir Giles Goosecap*, 4.1.150), "*Let him write a little and *then read*" (*Locrine*, 341), "*As he is writing an Angel comes and stands before him*" (*Martyred Soldier*, 209), "*writeth and blotteth*" (*Edmond Ironside*, 1159, 1178), "*writes and sometimes shows her*" (*Court Beggar*, 260), "*Writes and Seals it*" (*Northern Lass*, 66), "*writes two lots*" (*Lovesick Court*, 154); see also *Three Ladies of London*, B4v; *John of Bordeaux*, 1028; *Thomas Lord Cromwell*, F3r; *Thracian Wonder*, C2r; *Two Maids of More-Clacke*, A2v; *Humorous Lieutenant*, 300, MS 772; *Welsh Ambassador*, 1962; *Soddered Citizen*, 962–3, 971; *Platonic Lovers*, 92.

Occasionally figures enter with a *writing* (something written): "*Celia with a writing*" (*As You Like It*, 1321, 3.2.122), "*Shortyard with writings, having cozened Sim Quomodo*" (*Michaelmas Term*, 5.1.0), "*Usurer and Scrivener, with writings*" (*New Trick*, 217), "*with a parchment writing, and pocket inkhorn*" (*Platonic Lovers*, 90); for other instances of *writing* as a noun see Quarto 2

Henry VI, B2r, [1.3.5]; *Sophonisba*, 2.1.0; *Devil's Charter*, A2r; *Hog Hath Lost His Pearl*, 1232–3; *Scornful Lady*, 240; *Widow*, H4r; *Fatal Dowry*, 3.1.214; *Believe as You List*, 1; *Brennoralt*, 1.4.82.

Y

yellow
occasionally cited for special properties or effects: "*yellow Pantoffles*" (*Renegado*, 1.2.58), "*Hymen in yellow*" (*Women Beware Women*, 5.2.50), a **blue** headdress "*guarded with yellow*" for a prostitute (*2 Honest Whore*, 5.2.366), a pageant that includes "*one dressed like a Moor, with a Tun painted with yellow ocher*" (*John a Kent*, 369–70), a figure in a **masque** "*with yellow hair and beard, intermingled with streaks like wild flames*" (*No Wit*, 4.3.40); see also *World Tossed at Tennis*, D2r.

Terms by category

These alphabetical lists provide an overview of entry terms roughly categorized. All terms are listed at least once but many will be found several times, although the lists are not necessarily exhaustive.

Actions

ambush
appear
ascend
aside
assail
assault
bastinado
bear
beat
beckon
bind
bite
blow
bounce
bow
break
breath, breathe
bring, brought
bustle
caper
carry
cast
catch
cease
cense
chafe
change
charm
chase
clap
climb
close
combat
come
compliment
conceal
conduct
confer

conge
conjure
consult
continue
court
creep
cross
crown
cudgel
curtsy
cut
dance
deliver
depart
descend
dies
dig
disarm
discharge
disclose
discover
disguise
disperse
displayed
dog
drag
draw
dress
drink
drive
drop
drown
embrace
encompass, compass
encounter
enter
entertain
exit, extent
exiturus
faint

fall
feel
feign
fetch
fiddle
fight
find
fire
fling
flourish
fly
follow
foot
gaze
gesture
glance
go
going
groan
halloo
hammer
hang
heave
hide
honor
hug
hurry
intrat
join
justle
keep
kick
kill
kiss
kneel
knock
knock down
lament
laugh
lead

leap
leave
let
lift
listen
lock
look
make a lane
make a leg
make a stand
make as though
make signs
manet
march
measure
meditating
meet
menace
mistake, take for
mock
moritur
mount
musing
obeisance
observe
offer
open
overcome
overhear
overthrow
pass
pause
peep
perfume
peruse
pick
pinch
pipe
place
play

pledge
pluck
point
poison
pray
prepare
prevent
proffer
pull
pursue
put
rage
raise
read
recover
reel
remain
rescue
resign
retire
return
rise
roar
rob
run
rush
salute
scale
scrape
scuffle
search
seek
seem
seize
set, set out, set forth
shake
shave
shift
shoot
shout
show
shut
sigh
sign
sing
sink
sit
sleep
slip
smell
smile

smoke
smother
snatch
spin
spit
spurn
stab
stagger
stamp
stand
stare
start
stay
steal
stir
stoop
stop
storm
strangle
strew
strike
strip
strive
struggle
study
summon
swear
switch
swoon, sound
talk
tear
throw
thrust
toss
trample
tread
trip
trussing
tug
turn
undisguise
usher
vanish
wake
walk
wave
weep
whip
whisper
whistle
wind

withdraw
wonder
woo
work
wound
wringing her hands
write

Animals

ass, mule
bear
bull
cat
cock
dog
duck
goat
greyhound
horse
lion
monkey
serpent
snake, asp, crocodile
spaniel
stag

Appearance

affrighted
amazed
angry
antic, antique
apparel
armed
as before
as from
attire, attired
bare, bareheaded
barefoot
beard
blindfold
bloody, bleeding
booted
brave
button, unbutton
carelessly
chafing
confused
cover
coxcomb

deformed
discontented
disguised
dressed
drunk
dying
fantastic
fearful
feign
for (disguised as)
frown
gallant
garment
habiliment
habit
hoodwinked
hunting
invisible
lame
laughing
like
little
malcontented
manner
masked
mean
meditating
melancholy
mourning
muffled
musing
naked
odd
painted
panting
passion
pinioned
poor, poorly
posture
raging
rags, ragged
ravished
reading
rich, richly
ridiculous
sad, sadly
seem
shape
short
sick
small

smile
solemn
spurred
stump
sweating
trussing
unbraced
undisguise
unready
veiled
wanton
with child
wounded
wringing her hands

Blocking/Staging

abed
above
action
afar off
aloft
alone
aloof
ambo
apart
arm in arm
as at
as from
as [if]
as in
as to
aside
before, afore
behind
below
beneath
between, betwixt
bring, brought
carry
chase
circle
clear
climb
come
confer
consult
cum
degrees
descend
disclose

discover
disperse
displayed
down
encompass, compass
end
enter
excursions
exit, exeunt
exiturus
fall
follow
forth
go
going
guarded
haste
helter skelter
here
hide
hurly-burly
hurry
in
intrat
issue
join
lead
leave
listen
make a lane
make a stand
manet
meet
midst, middle
mount
observe
off
offer
open
order
out
part
pass
praeter
private
proffer
pursue
raise
rank
remain
retire

return
rise
round
scale
secret
set, set out, set forth
side
sink
sit
skirmish
sleep
solus
spurn
stairs
stand
start
state
stay
steal
still
stop
throw
thrust
to him/her/them
to him/herself
together
top
toss
toward
triumph
turn
undisguise
unseen
vanish
victory
violently
walk
walls
way
whisper
withdraw

Body parts

arm
beard
body
bosom
brains
breast
cheek

chest
corpse
ear
eyes
face
finger
foot
hair
hand
head
heart
heels
knee
lap
leg
limbs
mouth
neck
nose
shoulder
side
skull
throat
thumb
tongue

Ceremonies/
Formal events

altar
banquet
bar
bare, bareheaded
bearing
bier
bow
branches, boughs
candle
canopy
cense
ceremony
chair
chariot
coffin
colors
compliment
conge
coronet
council, parliament
court
crosier

crucifix
curtsy
cushion
dance, dancing
dead march
dish
doleful
dumb show
entertain
flourish
flowers
funeral
garland
goblet
halberd
health
hearse
hoboy
honor
image, statue
join
kiss
kneel
laurel
mace
make a lane
make a leg
march
masque
measure
mourning
music
oar
obeisance
oration
pledge
pomp
prologue
revels
reverence
ring
rosemary
sacrifice
sad, sadly
salute
scarlet
scutcheon
sennet
service
solemn
swear

throne
train
trial, court
triumph
tucket
usher
victory
water
wedding
wine

Clothing, etc.

apparel
apparition
apron
armed
armor
attire
bare, bareheaded
beaver
booted
bosom
buckler
button
canvas
cap
cloak
clothes
coat
disguise
doublet
fan
fetters
furnished
garland
gauntlet
glove
gorget
gown
habiliment
habit
handkerchief, kerchief
hat
headpiece
helmet
hood, hoodwinked
hose
jewel
laurel
leaf, leaves

manacles
mask
meal
mean
muffled
nightcap
nightgown
patch
pendant
periwig
peruke
petticoat
pocket
point
poor, poorly
purse
rags, ragged
ribbon
rich, richly
robe
ruff
safeguard
satin
scarf
sea gown
sheet
shirt
silk
skirt
sleeve
slippers, pantoffles
smock
suit
tire, tires, headtire
unbraced
unready
veil
velvet
waistcoat
weeds
winding sheet
wings

Colors

black
blue
gold
green
red
scarlet

silver
tawny
white
yellow

Dancing

caper
change
coranto
dance
galliard
jig
lavolta
measure
morris
reel
Spanish pavin
strain
trip

Deception/ Disguise

alias
as before
aside
beard
blind, blindfold
conceal
counterfeit
disclose
discover
disguise
feign
for (disguised as)
habit
headpiece
hide
hood, hoodwinked
invisible
like
mask
muffled
patch
periwig
peruke
pull
scarf
secret
seem

sneaking
steal
supposed
tire, headtire
undisguise
unseen
veil
vizard

Discoveries

bed
curtain
disclose
discover
disguise
displayed
find
invisible
shop
show
study
tent
tomb
undisguise

Eating and Drinking

banquet
beer, ale
bottle
bowl
bread
can
cover
cup
dish
drawer
drink
flagon
goblet
jack, blackjack
meat
napkin
pitcher
plate
pot
sack
service
sewer

table
tavern
trencher
water
wine

Emotions

affrighted
amazed
anger
chafe
confused
discontented
fearful
frown
fury
lament
laugh
mad
malcontented
mourning
passion
rage
reverence
sad
sigh
silent
smile
solemn
stamp
swoon, sound
tear
torment
weep
wringing her hands

Fictional terms

as at
as from
as [if]
as in
as to
bower
cabin
casement
castle
cave
chamber
city

closet
council, parliament
dark
earth
field
garden
gate
grave
gulf
hell
house
keyhole
make as though
night
pit
prison
river
room
sea, sea fight
ship
shop
study
tavern
tomb
tower
turrets
vault
walls
well
window
woods

Figures

angel
antic
apparition
army
astringer
captive
choir
chorus
conjurer
devil
drawer
drum
enchanter
ensign
executioner
fairy
fiddler

fiend
fury
gallant
ghost
halberd
harper
keeper
magician
milkmaid
multitudes
music
musketeer
nun
omnes
people
post
power
presenter
prisoner
prologue
rabble
rustici
sewer
spirit
stagekeeper
trumpet
usher
waits
witch

Latin

abscondit se
alias
aliis
ambo
caeteri
cantat, cantant
cum
exit, exeunt
exiturus
intrat, intrant
manet, manent
moritur
nisi
omnes
praeter
rustici
solus
suis
umbra

Military

armor
arms
army
battle
beaver
buckler
colors
combat
discharge
drum
ensign
excursions
fife
flag
flourish
gauntlet
gorget
halberd
helmet
lance
linstock
march
musket
ordnance
parley
power
retreat
scalado
shield
shoot, shot
spear
standard
summon
sword
tabor
target
tent
triumph
trumpet
truncheon
tucket
victory
weapon
walls

Modifiers

affrighted
alone
aloof
amazed
antique
apart
appareled
arm in arm
armed
as before
bloody, bleeding
blue
booted
brave
burning
busy
captive
carelessly
confused
counterfeit
crying
dancing
dark
dead
deformed
discontented
disguised
diverse
doleful
dreadful
drinking
drunk
earnest
fantastic
fearful
for (disguised as)
furnished
gallant
gold
great
green
guarded
half
hanging
hastily
hellish
helter skelter
hideous
hoodwinked
horrid
hurt
infernal
little
long
looking
loud
low
mad
malcontented
marching
masked
meditating
melancholy
mourning
muffled
musing
mute
naked
odd
painted
panting
posting
privately
quaint
raging
ravished
reading
ready
ridiculous
riding
round
rude
running
sad
secretly
seem, seeming
several
sewing
sick
silent
sleeping
slow
small
sneaking
soft, softly
solemn
spurred
strange
suddenly
sundry
supposed
sweating
sweet
tawny
together
trussing
unbraced
unready
unseen
veiled
violently
wanton
wet
white
with child
within
without
wounded
wringing her hands
writing
yellow

Musical instruments

bell
chime
cornet
crowd
drum
fiddle
fife
flute
harp
hoboy
horn
instrument
lute
organ
pipe
recorder
sackbut
shawm
sowgelder's horn
tabor
treble
trumpet
viol
violin
waits

Offstage events/sounds

afar off
alarm
answer
bell

betting
bird
bounce
call
cantat
chambers
charge
chime
clamor
clap
cry
dead march
discharge
drum
echo
fight
flourish
groan
halloo
heard
hurly-burly
infernal [music]
knock
music
noise
ordnance
parley
peal
pewter
pot birds
retreat
roar
sennet
shoot, shot
shout
sing
skirmish
song
sound
storm
strike
summon
tempest
thunder
thunder and lightning
thunderclap
toll
trample
tucket
tumult
voices
whistle

Permissive terms

aliis
army
belonging
caeteri
certain
convenient
diverse
during
followers
multitudes
omnes
or
power
pretty
proper
rustici
several
still
suis
sundry
train
while

Places/Settings

above
aloft
altar
arbor
bush
cabin
casement
castle
cave
chamber
city
closet
cloud
corner
council, parliament
curtain
degrees
door
garden
gate
gibbet, gallows
grate
grave
ground
gulf

hangings
hell
hole
house
monument
music room
pavilion
pit
river
rock
room
scaffold
sea
ship
shop
stall
state
stocks
study
tarras
tavern
tent
tower
traverse
trial, court
turrets
under the stage
upper stage
vault
walls
well
window
within
without
woods

Properties – large/part of set

altar
arbor
bank
banquet
bar
bed
bier
bower
bush
canopy
chair
chariot
couch

degrees
engine
gibbet, gallows
hearse
ladder
litter
monument
pavilion
pillar
post
rack
rock
rushes
scaffold
sedan
stairs
stall
state
stocks
stone
table
tent
throne
tomb
tree

Properties – small/hand held

apricock
ax, battleax
bag
ball
banner
basin
basket
battledore
beer, ale
bell
bill
block
book, tablebook
bottle
bowl
box
branches, boughs
brand
buckler
cabinet
can
candle
cards

carpet
casket
chain
chair
chess, chessboard
chest
cloth
coals
coffin
cord
coronet
cradle
crosier
cross
crow
crown
crucifix
cudgel
cup
cushion
dag
dagger
death's head
dice
dish
distaff
drum
ensign
fan
feather
fetters
fiddle
flag
flowers
flute
furniture
garland
glass, looking glass
globe
goblet
gold
gyves
halberd
halter
hammer
handkerchief, kerchief
harp
hat
hatchet
hood
horn
hourglass

image, statue
indenture
ink
instrument
irons
jack, blackjack
javelin
jewel
keys
knife
lamp
lance
lantern
laurel
letter
light
link
linstock
logs
lute
mace
manacles
map
mattock
meal
milk
money
napkin
net
nosegay
note
oar
paper
parchment
pearl
pen
pendant
petition
pickax
picture
piece
pike
pipe
pistol
pitchfork
plate
plot
pole
poleax
poniard
pot
powder

proclamation
property
purse
rackets
rapier
recorder
ring
rock
rod
rope
rosemary
roses
sack
sackbut
scepter
sconce
scroll
scutcheon
scythe
shackles
shield
skull
sowgelder's horn
spade
spit
staff, staves
standard
standish
stick
stiletto
stone
stool
switch
sword
tabor
taper
target
tobacco
torch
towel
treasure
trumpet
truncheon
trunk
urinal
vial
viol
violin
wand
warrant
water
weapon

whip
wine
wreath
writing

Reading and Writing

bill
bonds
book, tablebook
indenture
ink
leaf, leaves
letter
note
paper
parchment
pen
peruse
petition
proclamation
read
scroll
warrant
write

Sounds and Music

afar off
alarm
answer
ballad
bell
bolt
bounce
cantat
catch
chambers
clamor
clock
consort
coranto
cry
dead march
discharge
ditty
dreadful
fray
galliard
great

halloo
hellish
hideous
horrid
hunt
infernal
knock
laugh
lavolta
lesson
levet
loud
measure
morris
music
music room
noise
parley
parts
peal
pewter
play
pot birds
ring
roar
sad
sea fight
sennet
shoot, shot
short
shout
sigh
sing
skirmish
soft
solemn
song
sound
Spanish pavin
stamp
still
strain
summon
sweet
tempest
thunder
thunder and lightning
thunderclap
toll
trample
tune
voices

waits
whistle

Special effects

blazing star
burn
conjure
fire
fireball
fireworks
flame
flash
lightning
magic
mist, fog
rain
rise
sink
smoke
squib
storm
tempest
thunder
thunder and lightning
thunderbolt
thunderclap

Stage location

above
aloft
arras
balcony
below
beneath
corner
curtain
door
end
gallery
heavens
in
lower stage
midst, middle
music room
off
out
post
side
stage
stairs

tarras
top
trapdoor
traverse
under the stage
upper stage
walls
window
within
without

Supernatural

angel
apparition
appear
ascend
blazing star
charm
chime
circle
conjure, conjurer
devil
dragon
enchanter,
    enchantments
fairy
fiend
fire
fireball
fireworks
flame
flash
fury
ghost
invisible
lightning
magic
rise
rod
spirit
squib
thunder
thunder and
    lightning
thunderbolt
thunderclap
umbra
under the stage
vanish
wand
witch

Technical terms

act
chorus
clear
prologue
ready
scene
stagekeeper

Timing related

again
begin
behind
cease
clear
continue
done
during
end
here
now
pause
presently
still
stop
sudden, suddenly
while

Violence

ambush
arrow
assail
assault
ax
bastinado
battle
beat
bind
bite
bloody, bleeding
bodkin
brains
break
buffet
bustle
club
combat
cudgel
cut
dag

dagger
dart
dies
disarm
drag
draw
ear
encounter
engine
excursions
execution
fall
fight
fling
foil
fray
groan
hale
halter
hammer
helter skelter
hurly-burly
hurt
javelin
justle
kick
kill
knife
knock
knock down
moritur
musket

overcome
overthrow
pickax
piece
pike
pinioned
pistol
poison
poniard
rack
rapier
ravished
rifle
rock
scepter
scuffle
scythe
seize
shake
shoot, shot
skirmish
smother
spear
stab
stiletto
stocks
strangle
strike
struggle
sword
tear
thrust

thunderbolt
torment
trample
tumult
violently
whip
wound

Visual business

action
appear
dance
discover
disguise
dumb show
excursions
fight
make as though/as if
make signs, make show
masque
seem, seeming
show
sign
triumph
undisguise
victory

Weapons

arrow
ax

bill
bodkin
club
cudgel
dag
dagger
engine
foil
hammer
hatchet
javelin
knife
lance
linstock
musket
pickax
piece
pistol
point
poleax
poniard
rapier
rock
scepter
scythe
spear
stiletto
stone
sword
truncheon
weapon
whip

Plays and editions cited

Compiled by PETER W. M. BLAYNEY

Within the entries, each play is identified either by its title or by an easily recognized short-title. As explained in the Introduction, reference within each play is determined by the nature of the edition cited, and may be by line, through-line, act–scene–line, page, or signature. The following list identifies the edition(s) of each play used and cited.

Titles are usually given in the form used in the third edition of Alfred Harbage's *Annals of English Drama, 975–1700* (revised by S. Schoenbaum, further revised by Sylvia Stoler Wagonheim, 1989) unless the edition cited uses a materially different form. Where appropriate, a cross-reference is provided under the *Annals* version of the title.

Each title is followed, in brackets, by the date assigned to it by the *Annals* – usually the known or conjectured date of first performance. Plays cited from a playwright's collected works are assumed to be by that playwright unless otherwise indicated. Elsewhere, when the *Annals* offers a confident attribution, the playwright's name precedes the bracketed date. A plausibly conjectured attribution likewise precedes the date, but *inside* the bracket. If, however, the *Annals* offers a choice between rival conjectures, both are ignored. It should be noted that the authors have taken these dates and attributions from the *Annals* only for the sake of standard reference and do not necessarily agree with them.

When a play is cited from a modern edition (e.g., *Alphonsus, King of Aragon*), that edition is identified as concisely as possible by editor, place (or series), and date. Abbreviations (listed below) are used for the most frequently cited series, such as the Malone Society Reprints, the Revels Plays, etc.

When a play is cited from a modern collected edition (*Aglaura*), the cited collection will usually be found listed under the playwright's surname. The only exceptions are the two multi-author collections listed among the abbreviations below as "Bullen" and "Dodsley." When a play (*All Fools*) was edited by someone other than the general editor of the collection, the editor is also identified in the primary listing.

Shakespeare's plays have been cited either from *The Norton Facsimile* (abbreviated "First Folio") or from the 1981 volume of quarto facsimiles ("Quartos") or both. Plays whose texts are substantially the same in both a quarto and the Folio edition are listed only once (though with both editions cited); otherwise each substantive text is separately listed.

When no modern edition has been found suitable for citation, the original printed edition is identified by either STC or Wing number (*The Amorous War* and *Amyntas*) with the date of publication in parentheses. When what the authors usually consulted was a published facsimile likely to be easily accessible, that facsimile has also been cited, either individually (*Alphonsus,*

Emperor of Germany) or by series (*The Birth of Merlin*). Obviously, though, any published facsimile ought to be equally serviceable—and in most university libraries the early editions can be consulted on either microfilm or microfiche.

Abbreviations

Bullen	*A Collection of Old English Plays*. Ed. A. H. Bullen. 4 vols. London, 1882–5.
Dodsley	*A Select Collection of Old English Plays. Originally Published by Robert Dodsley in the Year 1744*. 4th edition, ed. W. Carew Hazlitt. 15 vols. London, 1874–6.
First Folio	*The Norton Facsimile: The First Folio of Shakespeare*. Ed. Charlton Hinman. New York and London, 1968. Reprinted 1996.
MSR	The Malone Society Reprints. London.
Materialien	Materialien zur Kunde des älteren Englischen Dramas. Louvain and London.
Materials	Materials for the Study of the Old English Drama, Being the Completion and Continuation of the Materialien zur Kunde des älteren Englischen Dramas. Louvain.
Quartos	*Shakespeare's Plays in Quarto*. Ed. Michael J. B. Allen and Kenneth Muir. Berkeley, 1981.
Revels	The Revels Plays. Manchester and Baltimore.
RRD	Regents Renaissance Drama Series. Lincoln, Nebraska.
STC	Alfred W. Pollard and G. R. Redgrave. *A Short-Title Catalogue of Books Printed in England, Scotland, and Ireland, and of English Books Printed Abroad, 1475–1640*. 2nd edition, rev. W. A. Jackson, F. S. Ferguson, and Katharine F. Pantzer. 3 vols. London, 1976–91.
TFT	The Tudor Facsimile Texts. Ed. John S. Farmer. London and Edinburgh, 1907–9; [Amersham], 1910–14.
Wing	Donald Wing, *Short-Title Catalogue of Books Printed in England, Scotland, Ireland, Wales, and British America, and of English Books Printed in Other Countries, 1641–1700*. 2nd edition, rev. Timothy J. Crist, John J. Morrison, Carolyn W. Nelson, and others. 3 vols. New York, 1982–94.

Aglaura [1637]: Suckling, *Plays*, 33–119
Alarum for London [1599], see *A Larum for London*
Albertus Wallenstein [1634]: Glapthorne, *Plays*, II: 3–80
Albovine, King of the Lombards [1628]: Davenant, *Works*, I: 1–107
The Alchemist [1610]: Ben Jonson, V: 273–408
All Fools [1601], ed. G. Blakemore Evans: Chapman, *Comedies*, 227–309
All's Lost by Lust [1619], ed. Charles Wharton Stork: *William Rowley: His All's Lost by Lust, and A Shoe-Maker a Gentleman* (Philadelphia, 1910), 68a–155

All's Well That Ends Well [1603]: First Folio, 248–72

Alphonsus, Emperor of Germany [George Peele? 1594], Wing C 1952 (1654): facsimile ed. Herbert F. Schwarz (New York and London, 1913)

Alphonsus, King of Aragon, Robert Greene [1587], ed. W. W. Greg (MSR 1926)

Amends for Ladies [1611]: Field, *Plays*, 141–235

The Amorous War, Jasper Mayne [1638], Wing M 1463 (1648)

Amyntas, Thomas Randolph [1630], STC 20694 (1638), ^{2}N1r–Dd4v

Andromana, or The Merchant's Wife, J. S. [1642]: Dodsley, XIV: 193–271

The Antipodes [1638]: Brome, *Works*, III: 225–339

The Antiquary, Shackerly Marmion [1635]: Dodsley, XIII: 411–523

Antonio and Mellida, [1599]: Marston, *Plays*, 1–91

Antonio's Revenge [1600]: Marston, *Plays*, 93–185

Antony and Cleopatra [1607]: First Folio, 848–76

Anything for a Quiet Life, Thomas Middleton and John Webster [1621], Wing M 1979 (1662)

Appius and Virginia, John Webster [1624], Wing W 1215 (1654)

The Arcadia, James Shirley [1640], STC 22453 (1640)

Arden of Faversham [Thomas Kyd? 1591], ed. Hugh MacDonald (MSR 1947)

Argalus and Parthenia [1638]: Glapthorne, *Plays*, I: 1–66

Armin, Robert, *The Collected Works of Robert Armin*, ed. J. P. Feather, 2 vols. (New York and London, 1972)

The Arraignment of Paris [1581], ed. R. Mark Benbow: Peele, *Works*, III: 1–131

1, 2 Arviragus and Philicia, Lodowick Carlell [1636], STC 4627 (1639)

As You Like It [1599]; First Folio, 203–25

The Atheist's Tragedy, Cyril Tourneur [1611], ed. Irving Ribner (Revels 1964)

The Ball, James Shirley [and George Chapman? 1632], STC 4995 (1639)

Barnavelt [1619], see *Sir John van Olden Barnavelt*

Bartholomew Fair [1614]: *Ben Jonson*, VI: 1–141

The Bashful Lover [1636]: Massinger, *Plays*, IV: 291–385

The Battle of Alacazar [1589], ed. W. W. Greg (MSR 1907)
[plot]: Greg, *Dramatic Documents*, II: no. VI

Beaumont and Fletcher, *The Works of Francis Beaumont and John Fletcher*, ed. Arnold Glover and A. R. Waller, 10 vols. (Cambridge, 1905–12)

Beggars' Bush [Fletcher, 1622]: Beaumont and Fletcher, *Works*, II: 208–80

Believe as You List, Philip Massinger [1631], ed. Charles J. Sisson (MSR 1927)

The Bird in a Cage, James Shirley [1633], STC 22436 (1633)

The Birth of Merlin, William Rowley [1608], Wing R 2096 (1662: TFT 1910)

The Blind Beggar of Alexandria [1596], ed. Lloyd E. Berry: Chapman, *Comedies*, 7–58

The Blind Beggar of Bednal Green [Day and Henry Chettle, 1600]: Day, *Works*, no. 7

The Bloody Banquet, T. D. [1639], ed. S. Schoenbaum (MSR 1962)

The Bloody Brother [Fletcher and Philip Massinger, 1617]: Beaumont and Fletcher, *Works*, IV: 246–313

Blurt, Master Constable [Thomas Dekker? 1601], ed. Thomas Leland Berger
(Salzburg, 1979)

The Bondman [1623]: Massinger, *Plays*, I: 301–95

Bonduca [Fletcher, 1613]: Beaumont and Fletcher, *Works*, VI: 79–159
[manuscript], ed. Walter Wilson Greg (MSR 1951)

The Brazen Age [1611]: Heywood, *Works*, III: 165–256

Brennoralt [1639]: Suckling, *Plays*, 183–244

The Bride [1638]: Nabbes, *Works*, II: 1–81

The Broken Heart, John Ford [1630], ed. T. J. B. Spencer (Revels 1980)

Brome, Richard, *The Dramatic Works of Richard Brome*, 3 vols. (London, 1873)

The Brothers, James Shirley [1641], Wing S 3460 (1652)

Bussy D'Ambois [1604], ed. John H. Smith: Chapman, *Tragedies*, 7–263

Caesar and Pompey [1605], ed. Thomas L. Berger and Dennis G. Donovan:
Chapman, *Tragedies*, 529–615

Campaspe [1583], ed. G. K. Hunter: *John Lyly: Campaspe, Sappho and Phao*
(Revels 1991), 1–139

The Captain [Fletcher, 1612]: Beaumont and Fletcher, *Works*, V: 230–319

Captain Thomas Stukeley [1596], ed. Judith C. Levinson (MSR 1975)

The Captives, Thomas Heywood [1624], ed. Arthur Brown (MSR 1953)

The Cardinal, James Shirley [1641], ed. E. M. Yearling (Revels 1986)

The Case Is Altered [1597]: *Ben Jonson*, III: 93–190

Catiline His Conspiracy [1611]: *Ben Jonson*, V: 409–550

Chabot, Admiral of France [1612], ed. G. Blakemore Evans: Chapman, *Tragedies*,
617–710

A Challenge for Beauty [1635]: Heywood, *Works*, V: 1–79

The Chances [Fletcher, 1617]: Beaumont and Fletcher, *Works*, IV: 174–245

The Changeling, Thomas Middleton and William Rowley [1622], ed. N. F.
Bawcutt (Revels 1958)

Changes, James Shirley [1632], STC 22437 (1632)

Chapman, George, *The Plays of George Chapman: The Comedies*, ed. Allan
Holaday (Urbana, 1970)

The Plays of George Chapman: The Tragedies with "Sir Gyles Goosecappe," ed.
Allan Holaday (Cambridge, 1987)

Charlemagne, or The Distracted Emperor [George Chapman? 1604], ed. John
Henry Walter (MSR 1938)

A Chaste Maid in Cheapside, Thomas Middleton [1613], ed. R. B. Parker (Revels
1969)

A Christian Turned Turk, Robert Daborne [1610], STC 6184 (1612)

1 The Cid, Joseph Rutter [1637], STC 5770 (1637)

2 The Cid, Joseph Rutter [1638], STC 5771 (1640)

The City Madam [1632]: Massinger, *Plays*, IV: 1–99

The City Match, Jasper Mayne [1637]: Dodsley, XIII: 199–320

The City Nightcap [1624]: Davenport, *Works*, 89–185

The City Wit [1630]: Brome, *Works*, I: 273–374

Claracilla, Thomas Killigrew [1636], Wing K 452 [= STC 14959] (1641), C12r–F12v

Cleopatra, Queen of Egypt, Thomas May [1626], STC 17717 (1639)

The Cobbler's Prophecy, Robert Wilson [1590], ed. A. C. Wood (MSR 1914)

The Comedy of Errors [1592]: First Folio, 103–18

The Conspiracy, Henry Killigrew [1635], STC 14958 (1638)

The Conspiracy and Tragedy of Charles, Duke of Byron [1608], ed. John B. Gabel: Chapman, *Tragedies*, 265–422

The Constant Maid, James Shirley [1638], STC 22438 (1640)

Coriolanus [1608]: First Folio, 617–46

The Coronation [James Shirley, 1635]: Beaumont and Fletcher, *Works*, VIII: 240–307

The Costly Whore [1620]: Bullen, IV: 219–98

The Country Captain, William Cavendish [and James Shirley? 1640], Wing N 877 (1649), A1r–D12r

The Country Girl, T. B. [1632], Wing B 4425 (1647)

The Court Beggar [1640]: Brome, *Works*, I: 181–272

The Court Secret, James Shirley [1642], Wing S 3463 (1653)

Covent Garden [1633]: Nabbes, *Works*, I: 1–91

The Coxcomb [1609]: Beaumont and Fletcher, *Works*, VIII: 308–78

The Cruel Brother [1627]: Davenant, *Works*, I: 109–97

The Cunning Lovers, Alexander Brome [1638], Wing B 4850 (1654)

Cupid's Revenge [1608]: Beaumont and Fletcher, *Works*, IX: 220–89

Cupid's Whirligig [1607]: Sharpham, *Works*, 347–578

A Cure for a Cuckold, John Webster and William Rowley [1625], Wing W 1220 (1661)

The Custom of the Country [Fletcher and Philip Massinger, 1620]: Beaumont and Fletcher, *Works*, I: 302–88

Cymbeline [1609]: First Folio, 877–907

Cynthia's Revels [1600]: *Ben Jonson*, IV: 1–184

The Damoiselle [1638]: Brome, *Works*, I: 375–468

Davenant, Sir William, *The Dramatic Works of William Davenant*, ed. James Maidment and W. H. Logan, 5 vols. (Edinburgh and London, 1872–4)

Davenport, Robert, *The Works of Robert Davenport*, ed. A. H. Bullen, *Old English Plays*, new series, III (London, 1890)

David and Bethsabe [1594], ed. Elmer Blistein: Peele, *Works*, III: 133–295

Day, John, *The Works of John Day*, ed. A. H. Bullen (London, 1881)

The Dead Man's Fortune [1590, plot]: Greg, *Dramatic Documents*, II: no. I

The Death of Robert, Earl of Huntingdon, Henry Chettle and Anthony Munday [1598], ed. John C. Meagher (MSR 1967)

Dekker, Thomas, *The Dramatic Works of Thomas Dekker*, ed. Fredson Bowers, 4 vols. (Cambridge, 1953–61)

Demetrius and Enanthe, John Fletcher [manuscript version of *The Humorous Lieutenant*, 1619], ed. Margaret McLaren Cook (MSR 1951)

The Deserving Favourite, Lodowick Carlell [1629], STC 4628 (1629)

The Devil Is an Ass [1616]: *Ben Jonson*, VI: 143–270

The Devil's Charter, Barnabe Barnes [1606], STC 1466 (1607: TFT 1913)

The Devil's Law Case, John Webster [1619], ed. Frances R. Shirley (RRD 1972)

Dick of Devonshire [1626], ed. James G. and Mary R. McManaway (MSR 1955)

Dido, Queen of Carthage [Marlowe and Thomas Nashe, 1586]: Marlowe, *Works*, 387–439

The Distresses [1639]: Davenant, *Works*, IV: 281–363

Doctor Faustus, Christopher Marlowe [1592]: parallel texts of 1604 and 1616 ed. W. W. Greg (Oxford, 1950)

The Double Marriage [Fletcher and Philip Massinger, 1620]: Beaumont and Fletcher, *Works*, VI: 321–407

The Doubtful Heir, James Shirley [1638], Wing W 3466 (1652)

The Downfall of Robert, Earl of Huntingdon, Henry Chettle and Anthony Munday [1598], ed. John C. Meagher (MSR 1965)

The Duchess of Malfi, John Webster [1614], ed. John Russell Brown (Revels 1964)

The Duchess of Suffolk, Thomas Drue [1624], STC 7242 (1631)

The Duke of Milan [1621]: Massinger, *Plays*, I: 199–300

The Duke's Mistress, James Shirley [1636], STC 22441 (1638)

The Dumb Knight, Gervase Markham and Lewis Machin [1608]: Dodsley, X: 107–200

The Dutch Courtesan [1605]: Marston, *Plays*, 289–393

Eastward Ho [Ben Jonson, George Chapman, and John Marston, 1605], STC 4970 (1605: TFT 1914)

Edmond Ironside [1595], ed. Eleanore Boswell (MSR 1927)

Edward I [1591], ed. Frank S. Hook: Peele, *Works*, II: vii–212

Edward II [1592]: Marlowe, *Works*, 307–85

Edward III [1590], STC 7501 (1596: TFT 1910)

1, 2 Edward IV [1599]: Heywood, *Works*, I: 1–90, 91–187

The Elder Brother [Fletcher, 1625]: Beaumont and Fletcher, *Works*, II: 1–59

The Emperor of the East [1631]: Massinger, *Plays*, III: 391–488

Endymion, the Man in the Moon, John Lyly [1588], STC 17050 (1591)

The English Moor [1637]: Brome, *Works*, II: no. 1 (1–86)

The English Traveller [1627]: Heywood, *Works*, IV: 1–95

Englishmen for My Money, William Haughton [1598], ed. W. W. Greg (MSR 1912)

Epicœne [1609]: *Ben Jonson*, V: 139–272

The Escapes of Jupiter, Thomas Heywood [1625], ed. Henry D. Janzen (MSR 1978)

Every Man in His Humour (F1) [1598]: *Ben Jonson*, III: 291–403 (Q1): *Ben Jonson*, III: 191–289

Every Man out of His Humour (F1) [1599]: *Ben Jonson*, III: 405–604 (Q1), ed. F. P. Wilson and W. W. Greg (MSR 1920)

Every Woman in Her Humour [1607], STC 25948 (1609: TFT 1913)

The Example, James Shirley [1634], STC 22442 (1637)

Fair Em, the Miller's Daughter of Manchester [Robert Wilson? 1590], ed. W. W.
    Greg (MSR 1927)

The Fair Favourite [1638]: Davenant, *Works*, IV: 201–80

The Fair Maid of Bristow [1604], STC 3794 (1605: TFT 1912)

The Fair Maid of the Exchange [Heywood? 1602]: Heywood, *Works*, II: 1–87

The Fair Maid of the Inn [Fletcher, 1626]: Beaumont and Fletcher, *Works*, IX:
    143–219

1 The Fair Maid of the West [1604]: Heywood, *Works*, II: 255–331

2 The Fair Maid of the West [1631]: Heywood, *Works*, II: 333–424

A Fair Quarrel, Thomas Middleton and William Rowley [1617], ed. George R.
    Price (RRD 1976)

The Faithful Friends [1621], ed. G. M. Pinciss and G. R. Proudfoot (MSR 1975)

The Faithful Shepherdess [Fletcher, 1608]: Beaumont and Fletcher, *Works*, II:
    372–448

The False One [Fletcher and Philip Massinger, 1620]: Beaumont and Fletcher,
    Works, III: 300–72

The Family of Love, Thomas Middleton [1603], STC 17879 (1608)

The Famous Victories of Henry V [1586], STC 13072 (1598: TFT 1912)

The Fancies Chaste and Noble [1635]: Ford, *Works*, 243–327

The Fatal Contract, William Hemming [1639], Wing H 1422 (1653)

The Fatal Dowry [Massinger and Nathan Field, 1619]: Massinger, *Plays*, I:
    1–103

The Fawn [1604], see *Parasitaster, or The Fawn*

Fedele and Fortunio, Anthony Munday [1584], ed. Percy Simpson (MSR 1909)

Field, Nathan, *The Plays of Nathan Field*, ed. William Peery (Austin, 1950)

A Fine Companion, Shackerly Marmion [1633], STC 17442 (1633)

The Fleer [1606]: Sharpham, *Works*, 183–344

The Fool Would Be a Favourite, Lodowick Carlell [1637], Wing C 580 (1657),
    A3r–G4v

John Ford's Dramatic Works, ed. Henry de Vocht (Materials 1927)

Fortune by Land and Sea [Heywood and William Rowley, 1609]: Heywood,
    Works, V: 359–435

2 Fortune's Tennis [1602, plot]: Greg, *Dramatic Documents*, II: no. IV

Four Plays or Moral Representations in One [Fletcher and Nathan Field, 1613]:
    Beaumont and Fletcher, *Works*, X: 287–364

The Four Prentices of London [1594]: Heywood, *Works*, II: 159–254

Frederick and Basilea [1597, plot]: Greg, *Dramatic Documents*, II: no. III

Friar Bacon and Friar Bungay, Robert Greene [1589], ed. W. W. Greg (MSR 1926)

Gallathea, John Lyly [1585]: *Gallathea and Midas*, ed. Anne Begor Lancashire
    (RRD 1969), 1–74

A Game at Chess, Thomas Middleton [1624], ed. T. H. Howard-Hill (MSR 1990)

The Gamester, James Shirley [1633], STC 22443 (1637)

The Gentleman of Venice, James Shirley [1639], Wing S 3468 (1655)

The Gentleman Usher [1602], ed. Robert Ornstein: Chapman, *Comedies*, 131–225

George a Greene [Robert Greene? 1590], ed. F. W. Clarke (MSR 1911)

Glapthorne, Henry, *The Plays and Poems of Henry Glapthorne*, ed. John Pearson, 2 vols. (London, 1874)

The Goblins [1638]: Suckling, *Plays*, 121–82

The Golden Age [1610]: Heywood, *Works*, III: 1–79

The Grateful Servant, James Shirley [1629], STC 22444 (1630)

The Great Duke of Florence [1627]: Massinger, *Plays*, III: 95–180

Greg, W. W., *Dramatic Documents from the Elizabethan Playhouses*, 2 vols. (Oxford, 1931)

Greene's Tu Quoque, J. Cooke [1611], STC 5673 (1614: TFT 1911)

Grim the Collier of Croydon, William Haughton [1600]: *Gratiae Theatrales* (1662: Wing G 1580), G1r–K3r (TFT 1912)

The Guardian [1633]: Massinger, *Plays*, IV: 107–200

Guy, Earl of Warwick, B. J. [1593], Wing J 5 (1661)

Hamlet (F1) [1601]: First Folio, 760–90

  (Q1): Quartos, 579–611

  (Q2): Quartos, 612–62

Hannibal and Scipio [1635]: Nabbes, *Works*, I: 185–270

The Heir, Thomas May [1620]: Dodsley, XI: 501–84

Hengist King of Kent, Thomas Middleton [1618], ed. R. C. Bald (New York and London, 1938)

1 Henry IV [1597]: Quartos, 331–71; First Folio, 368–93

2 Henry IV (F1) [1597]: First Folio, 394–422

  (Q1): Quartos, 372–415

Henry V (F1) [1599]: First Folio, 423–49

  (Q1): Quartos, 524–50

1 Henry VI [1590]: First Folio, 450–73

2 Henry VI (F1) [1590]: First Folio, 474–500

  (Q1): Quartos, 43–74

3 Henry VI (F1) [1591]: First Folio, 501–26

  (O1): Quartos, 77–116

Henry VIII [Shakespeare and John Fletcher? 1613]: First Folio, 559–86

Herod and Antipater, Gervase Markham and William Sampson [1622], STC 17401 (1622)

Heywood, Thomas, *The Dramatic Works of Thomas Heywood*, ed. R. H. Shepherd, 6 vols. (London, 1874)

1 Hieronimo [1604], ed. Andrew S. Cairncross: *Thomas Kyd: The First Part of Hieronimo and The Spanish Tragedy* (RRD 1967), 1–54

Histriomastix [John Marston? 1599], STC 13529 (1610: TFT 1912)

Hoffman, Henry Chettle [1602], ed. Harold Jenkins (MSR 1951)

The Hog Hath Lost His Pearl, Robert Tailor [1613], ed. D. F. McKenzie (MSR 1972)

Holland's Leaguer, Shackerly Marmion [1631], STC 17443 (1632)

The Hollander [1636]: Glapthorne, *Plays*, I: 67–157

The Honest Lawyer, S. S. [1615], STC 21519 (1616: TFT 1914)

The Honest Man's Fortune [Fletcher and Nathan Field, 1613]: Beaumont and Fletcher, *Works*, X: 202–80

[manuscript], ed. Dr. J. Gerritsen (Groningen, 1952)

1 The Honest Whore [Dekker and Thomas Middleton, 1604]: Dekker, *Works*, II: 1–130

2 The Honest Whore [1605]: Dekker, *Works*, II: 131–227

How a Man May Choose a Good Wife from a Bad [Thomas Heywood? 1602], STC 5594 (1602: TFT 1912)

The Humorous Courtier, James Shirley [1631], STC 22447 (1640)

An Humorous Day's Mirth [1597]: Chapman, *Comedies*, 59–130

The Humorous Lieutenant [Fletcher, 1619]: Beaumont and Fletcher, *Works*, II: 281–371

[manuscript], see *Demetrius and Enanthe*

Humour out of Breath [1608]: Day, *Works*, no. 4

Hyde Park, James Shirley [1632], STC 22446 (1637)

If This Be Not a Good Play, the Devil Is in It [1611]: Dekker, *Works*, III: 113–223

1 If You Know Not Me You Know Nobody [1604]: Heywood, *Works*, I: 189–247

2 If You Know Not Me You Know Nobody [1605]: Heywood, *Works*, I: 249–351

The Imposture, James Shirley [1640], Wing S 3476 (1652)

The Inconstant Lady, Arthur Wilson [1630], ed. Linda V. Itzoe (New York and London, 1980)

The Insatiate Countess, John Marston and William Barkstead [1607], ed. Giorgio Melchiori (Revels 1984)

1, 2 The Iron Age [1612]: Heywood, *Works*, III: 257–345, 347–431

The Island Princess [Fletcher, 1621]: Beaumont and Fletcher, *Works*, VIII: 91–170

The Isle of Gulls [1606]: Day, *Works*, no. 3

Jack Drum's Entertainment, John Marston [1600], STC 7243 (1601: TFT 1912)

Jack Straw [1591], ed. Kenneth Muir (MSR 1957)

James IV, Robert Greene [1590], ed. A. E. H. Swaen (MSR 1921)

The Jew of Malta [1589]: Marlowe, *Works*, 230–306

The Jews' Tragedy, William Hemming [1626], ed. Heinrich A. Cohn (Materialien 1913)

John a Kent and John a Cumber, Anthony Munday [1589], ed. Muriel St. Clair Byrne (MSR 1923)

John of Bordeaux, Henry Chettle [and Robert Greene? 1592], ed. William Lindsay Renwick (MSR 1936)

Ben Jonson, ed. C. H. Herford and Percy and Evelyn Simpson, 11 vols. (Oxford, 1925–52)

A Jovial Crew [1641]: Brome, *Works*, III: 341–452

Julia Agrippina, Thomas May [1628], ed. F. Ernst Schmid (Materialien 1914)
Julius Caesar [1599]: First Folio, 717–38
The Just Italian [1629]: Davenant, *Works*, I: 199–280

A King and No King [1611]: Beaumont and Fletcher, *Works*, I: 149–230
King John [1591]: First Folio, 323–44
King John and Matilda [1628]: Davenport, *Works*, 1–88
King Lear (F1) [1605]: First Folio, 791–817
   (Q1): Quartos, 663–703
King Leir [1590], ed. W. W. Greg (MSR 1907)
A Knack to Know a Knave [1592], ed. G. R. Proudfoot (MSR 1964)
A Knack to Know an Honest Man [1594], ed. H. De Vocht (MSR 1910)
The Knave in Grain, J. D. [1625], ed. R. C. Bald (MSR 1961)
The Knight of Malta [Fletcher, Nathan Field, and Philip Massinger, 1618]:
   Beaumont and Fletcher, *Works*, VII: 78–163
The Knight of the Burning Pestle [Beaumont, 1607]: Beaumont and Fletcher,
   Works, VI: 160–231

The Ladies' Privilege [1637]: Glapthorne, *Plays*, II: 81–160
The Lady Mother, Henry Glapthorne [1635], ed. Arthur Brown (MSR 1959)
The Lady of Pleasure, James Shirley [1635], ed. Ronald Huebert (Revels 1986)
The Lady's Trial [1638]: Ford, *Works*, 329–408
Landgartha, Henry Burnell [1640], Wing B 5751 (1641)
A Larum for London [1599], ed. W. W. Greg (MSR 1913)
The Late Lancashire Witches [Heywood and Richard Brome, 1634]: Heywood,
   Works, IV: 167–262
The Launching of the Mary, Walter Mountfort [1633], ed. John Henry Walter
   (MSR 1933)
Law Tricks [1604]: Day, *Works*, no. 5
The Laws of Candy [John Ford, 1619]: Beaumont and Fletcher, *Works*, III:
   236–99
Like Will to Like, Ulpian Fulwell [1568], STC 11473 (1568: TFT 1914)
The Little French Lawyer [Fletcher and Philip Massinger, 1619]: Beaumont and
   Fletcher, *Works*, III: 373–454
Locrine, W. S. [1594], ed. Ronald B. McKerrow (MSR 1908)
The London Prodigal [1604], STC 22333 (1605: TFT 1910)
Look about You [1599], ed. W. W. Greg (MSR 1913)
A Looking Glass for London, Robert Greene and Thomas Lodge [1588], ed. W. W.
   Greg (MSR 1932)
   [manuscript annotations], see C. R. Baskervill, "A Prompt Copy of *A*
     Looking Glasse for London and England," *Modern Philology* 30 (1932): 29–51
The Lost Lady, William Berkeley [1637]: Dodsley, XII: 537–627
   [manuscript], ed. D. F. Rowan (MSR 1987)
Love and Honour [1634]: Davenant, *Works*, III: 91–192
Love's Cruelty, James Shirley [1631], STC 22449 (1640)

Love's Cure [1606]: Beaumont and Fletcher, *Works*, VII: 164–236

Love's Labour's Lost [1595]: Quartos, 292–330; First Folio, 140–62

Love's Metamorphosis, John Lyly [1590], STC 17082 (1601)

Love's Mistress [1634]: Heywood, *Works*, V: 81–160

Love's Pilgrimage [Fletcher, 1616]: Beaumont and Fletcher, *Works*, VI: 232–320

Love's Sacrifice [1632]: *John Fordes Dramatische Werke*, ed. W. Bang (Materialien 1908), 91–174

The Lover's Melancholy, John Ford [1628], ed. R. F. Hill (Revels 1985)

The Lovers' Progress [Fletcher, 1623]: Beaumont and Fletcher, *Works*, V: 74–152

The Lovesick Court [1639]: Brome, *Works*, II: no. 2 (87–171)

The Lovesick King, Anthony Brewer [1617], ed. A. E. H. Swaen (Materialien 1907)

The Loyal Subject [Fletcher, 1618]: Beaumont and Fletcher, *Works*, III: 76–169

Lust's Dominion [Dekker, John Day, and William Haughton? 1600]: Dekker, *Works*, IV: 115–230

Macbeth [1606]: First Folio, 739–59

A Mad Couple Well Matched [1639]: Brome, *Works*, I: 1–99

The Mad Lover [Fletcher, 1617]: Beaumont and Fletcher, *Works*, III: 1–75

A Mad World My Masters, Thomas Middleton [1606], ed. Standish Henning (RRD 1965)

The Magnetic Lady [1632]: *Ben Jonson*, VI: 499–597

The Maid in the Mill [Fletcher and William Rowley, 1623]: Beaumont and Fletcher, *Works*, VII: 1–77

The Maid of Honour [1621]: Massinger, *Plays*, I: 105–97

The Maid's Metamorphosis [1600], STC 17188 (1600: TFT 1908)

The Maid's Revenge, James Shirley [1626], STC 22450 (1639)

The Maid's Tragedy [1610]: Beaumont and Fletcher, *Works*, I: 1–74

A Maidenhead Well Lost [1633]: Heywood, *Works*, IV: 97–165

The Malcontent [1604]: Marston, *Plays*, 187–287

Marlowe, Christopher, *The Works of Christopher Marlowe*, ed. C. F. Tucker Brooke (Oxford, 1910)

Marston, John, *The Selected Plays of John Marston*, ed. MacDonald P. Jackson and Michael Neill (Cambridge, 1986)

The Martyred Soldier, Henry Shirley [1618]: Bullen, I: 165–256

The Massacre at Paris [1593]: Marlowe, *Works*, 440–84

Massinger, Philip, *The Plays and Poems of Philip Massinger*, ed. Philip Edwards and Colin Gibson, 5 vols. (Oxford, 1976)

A Match at Midnight, William Rowley [1622]: Dodsley, XIII: 1–98

Match Me in London [1611]: Dekker, *Works*, III: 251–363

May Day [1602], ed. Robert F. Welsh: Chapman, *Comedies*, 311–96

Measure for Measure [1604]: First Folio, 79–102

The Merchant of Venice [1596]: Quartos, 449–86; First Folio, 181–202

The Merry Devil of Edmonton [Thomas Dekker? 1602], STC 7493 (1608: TFT 1911)

The Merry Wives of Windsor (F1) [1597]: First Folio, 57–78
    (Q1): Quartos, 551–78
Messalina, Nathaniel Richards [1635], ed. A. R. Skemp (Materialien 1910)
Michaelmas Term, Thomas Middleton [1606], ed. Richard Levin (RRD 1966)
Midas, John Lyly [1589]: *Gallathea and Midas*, ed. Anne Begor Lancashire
    (RRD 1969), 75–161
A Midsummer Night's Dream [1596]: Quartos, 416–48; First Folio, 163–80
The Miseries of Enforced Marriage, George Wilkins [1606], ed. Glenn H. Blayney
    (MSR 1964)
Money Is an Ass, Thomas Jordan [1635], Wing J 1047 (1668)
Monsieur D'Olive [1605]: Chapman, *Comedies*, 397–471
Monsieur Thomas [Fletcher, 1615]: Beaumont and Fletcher, *Works*, IV: 93–173
More Dissemblers Besides Women, Thomas Middleton [1615], Wing M 1989
    (1657), A2r–G2r
Mother Bombie, John Lyly [1591], ed. Kathleen M. Lea (MSR 1948)
Mucedorus [1590], STC 18230 (1598: TFT 1910)
Much Ado about Nothing [1598]: Quartos, 487–523; First Folio, 119–139
The Muses' Looking Glass, Thomas Randolph [1630], STC 20694 (1638),
    ²A1r–M4r

Nabbes, Thomas, *The Works of Thomas Nabbes*, ed. A. H. Bullen, 2 vols., Old
    English Plays, new series, I–II (London, 1887)
Nero [1619]: Bullen, I: 3–98
The New Academy [1635]: Brome, *Works*, II: no. 4
The New Inn [1629]: Ben Jonson, VI: 383–498
A New Trick to Cheat the Devil [1625]: Davenport, *Works*, 187–299
A New Way to Pay Old Debts [1625]: Massinger, *Plays*, II: 273–377
A New Wonder, a Woman Never Vexed, William Rowley [1611]: Dodsley, XII:
    85–202
News from Plymouth [1635]: Davenant, *Works*, IV: 105–99
The Nice Valour [Fletcher? and Thomas Middleton, 1616]: Beaumont and
    Fletcher, *Works*, X: 143–98
The Night Walker [Fletcher, 1611]: Beaumont and Fletcher, *Works*, VII: 311–83
No Wit, No Help Like a Woman's, Thomas Middleton [1611], ed. Lowell E.
    Johnson (RRD 1976)
The Noble Gentleman [Fletcher, 1606]: Beaumont and Fletcher, *Works*, VIII:
    171–240
The Noble Spanish Soldier [1622]: Dekker, *Works*, IV: 231–300
The Noble Stranger, Lewis Sharpe [1639], STC 22377 (1640)
Nobody and Somebody [1605], STC 18597 (1606: TFT 1911)
The Northern Lass [1629]: Brome, *Works*, III: 1–107
Northward Ho [Dekker and John Webster, 1605]: Dekker, *Works*, II: 405–90
The Novella [1632]: Brome, *Works*, I: 101–79

The Obstinate Lady, Aston Cokain [1639], Wing C 4896 (1657)
The Old Couple, Thomas May [1636]: Dodsley, XII: 1–83

Old Fortunatus [1599]: Dekker, *Works*, I: 105–205

The Old Law, Thomas Middleton and William Rowley [1618], Wing M 1048
     (1656)

The Old Wives Tale [1590], ed. Frank S. Hook: Peele, *Works*, III: 297–443

The Opportunity, James Shirley [1634], STC 22451 (1640)

Orlando Furioso, Robert Greene [1591], ed. W. W. Greg (MSR 1907)

Osmond the Great Turk, Lodowick Carlell [1637], Wing C 579 (1657)

Othello (F1) [1604]: First Folio, 818–47

     (Q1): Quartos, 787–834

Parasitaster, or The Fawn, John Marston [1604], ed. David A. Blostein (Revels
     1978)

The Parliament of Love [1624]: Massinger, *Plays*, II: 97–179

The Parson's Wedding, Thomas Killigrew [1641]: Dodsley, XIV: 369–535

1, 2 The Passionate Lovers, Lodowick Carlell [1638], Wing C 581 (1655)

Patient Grissil [Dekker, Henry Chettle, and William Haughton, 1600]:
     Dekker, *Works*, I: 207–98

Peele, George, *The Life and Works of George Peele*, ed. Charles Tyler Prouty, 3
     vols. (New Haven and London, 1952–70)

Pericles [1608]: Quartos, 751–86

Perkin Warbeck, John Ford [1633], ed. Peter Ure (Revels 1968)

Philaster [1609]: Beaumont and Fletcher, *Works*, I: 75–148

Philotas, Samuel Daniel [1604], STC 6239 (1605), ²A3r–F6v

The Phoenix, Thomas Middleton [1604], STC 17892 (1607)

The Picture [1629]: Massinger, *Plays*, III: 181–292

The Pilgrim [Fletcher, 1621]: Beaumont and Fletcher, *Works*, V: 153–229

The Platonic Lovers [1635]: Davenant, *Works*, II: 1–105

Poetaster [1601]: *Ben Jonson*, IV: 185–325

The Politician, James Shirley [1639], Wing S 3482 (1655)

The Poor Man's Comfort, Robert Daborne [1617], Wing D 101 (1655)
     [manuscript], ed. Kenneth Palmer (MSR 1955)

The Princess, Thomas Killigrew [1636], Wing K 450 (1664), A1r–I2r

The Prisoners, Thomas Killigrew [1635], STC 14959 [= Wing K 452] (1640),
     A3r–C11r

1, 2 Promos and Cassandra, George Whetstone [1578], STC 25347 (1578: TFT
     1910)

The Prophetess [Fletcher and Philip Massinger, 1622]: Beaumont and
     Fletcher, *Works*, V: 320–89

The Puritan [Thomas Middleton? 1606], STC 21531 (1607: TFT 1911)

The Queen, John Ford [1628], ed. W. Bang (Materialien 1906)

The Queen and Concubine [1635]: Brome, *Works*, II: no. 5

The Queen of Aragon, William Habington [1640]: Dodsley, XIII: 321–409

The Queen of Corinth [Fletcher, 1617]: Beaumont and Fletcher, *Works*,
     VI: 1–78

The Queen's Exchange [1631]: Brome, *Works*, III: 453–550

Ram Alley, Lording Barry [1608], STC 1502 (1611: TFT 1913)

The Rape of Lucrece [1607]: Heywood, *Works*, V: 161–257

The Rare Triumphs of Love and Fortune [1582], ed. W. W. Greg (MSR 1930)

The Rebellion, Thomas Rawlins [1638]: Dodsley, XIV: 1–92

The Renegado [1624]: Massinger, *Plays*, II: 1–96

Revenge for Honour [Henry Glapthorne? 1640], Wing C 1948 (1654)

The Revenge of Bussy D'Ambois [1610], ed. Robert J. Lordi: Chapman, *Tragedies*, 423–527

The Revenger's Tragedy [Thomas Middleton? 1606], STC 24149 (1607): facsimile ed. MacD. P. Jackson (London and Toronto, 1983)

1 Richard II, or Thomas of Woodstock [1592], ed. Wilhelmina P. Frijlinck (MSR 1929)

Richard II [1595]: Quartos, 202–39; First Folio, 345–67

Richard III (F1) [1592]: First Folio, 527–58

   (Q1): Quartos, 244–91

The Roaring Girl [Dekker and Thomas Middleton, 1611]: Dekker, *Works*, III: 1–112

The Roman Actor [1626]: Massinger, *Plays*, III: 1–93

Romeo and Juliet (F1) [1596]: First Folio, 669–93

   (Q1): Quartos, 117–55

   (Q2): Quartos, 156–201

The Royal King and the Loyal Subject [1602]: Heywood, *Works*, VI: 1–84

The Royal Master, James Shirley [1637], STC 22454 (1638)

Rule a Wife and Have a Wife [Fletcher, 1624]: Beaumont and Fletcher, *Works*, III: 170–235

Sappho and Phao [1583], ed. David Bevington: *John Lyly: Campaspe, Sappho and Phao* (Revels 1991), 141–300

Satiromastix [1601]: Dekker, *Works*, I: 299–395

The School of Compliment, James Shirley [1625], STC 22456 (1631)

The Scornful Lady [1613]: Beaumont and Fletcher, *Works*, I: 231–301

The Sea Voyage [Fletcher and Philip Massinger, 1622]: Beaumont and Fletcher, *Works*, IX: 1–65

The Second Maiden's Tragedy, Thomas Middleton [1611], ed. W. W. Greg (MSR 1909)

Sejanus His Fall [1603]: *Ben Jonson*, IV: 327–486

1 Selimus [Robert Greene? 1592], ed. W. Bang (MSR 1908)

The Seven Champions of Christendom, John Kirke [1635], STC 15014 (1638)

2 The Seven Deadly Sins [Richard Tarlton? 1590, plot]: Greg, *Dramatic Documents*, II: no. II

Shakespeare, William, *The Riverside Shakespeare*, ed. G. Blakemore Evans (Boston, 1974)

Sharpham, Edward, *A Critical Old Spelling Edition of the Works of Edward Sharpham*, ed. Christopher Gordon Petter (New York and London, 1986)

The Shepherds' Holiday, Joseph Rutter [1634], Dodsley, XII: 361–444

A Shoemaker a Gentleman [1608], ed. Charles Wharton Stork: *William Rowley: His All's Lost by Lust, and A Shoe-Maker a Gentleman* (Philadelphia, 1910), 157–260

The Shoemakers' Holiday [1599]: Dekker, *Works*, I: 7–104

The Siege [1629]: Davenant, *Works*, IV: 365–437

The Silver Age [1611]: Heywood, *Works*, III: 81–164

Sir Giles Goosecap [1602], ed. John F. Hennedy: Chapman, *Tragedies*, 711–802

1 Sir John Oldcastle, Michael Drayton, Richard Hathway, Anthony Munday, and Robert Wilson [1599], ed. Percy Simpson (MSR 1908)

Sir John van Olden Barnavelt, John Fletcher and Philip Massinger [1619], ed. T. H. Howard-Hill (MSR 1980)

Sir Thomas More, Anthony Munday, Henry Chettle, Thomas Dekker [Thomas Heywood? and William Shakespeare? 1595], ed. W. W. Greg (MSR 1911)

Sir Thomas Wyatt [Dekker and John Webster, 1602]: Dekker, *Works*, I: 397–469

The Sisters, James Shirley [1642], Wing S 3485 (1653)

The Soddered Citizen, John Clavell [1629], ed. John Henry Pyle Pafford (MSR 1936)

Soliman and Perseda [Thomas Kyd? 1592], STC 22894 (1592)

Sophonisba [1605]: Marston, *Plays*, 395–481

The Sophy [1641], ed. Theodore Howard Banks: *The Poetical Works of Sir John Denham* (New Haven, 1928), 232–309

The Spanish Curate [Fletcher and Philip Massinger, 1622]: Beaumont and Fletcher, *Works*, II: 60–145

The Spanish Gypsy, Thomas Dekker and John Ford [1623], Wing M 1986 (1653)

The Spanish Tragedy, Thomas Kyd [1587], ed. Philip Edwards (Revels 1959)

The Sparagus Garden [1635]: Brome, *Works*, III: 109–223

The Staple of News [1626]: *Ben Jonson*, VI: 271–382

Suckling, Sir John, *The Works of Sir John Suckling: The Plays*, ed. L. A. Beaurline (Oxford, 1971)

Summer's Last Will and Testament [1592]: *The Works of Thomas Nashe*, ed. Ronald B. McKerrow (Oxford, 1904–10), III: 227–95

The Swaggering Damsel, Robert Chamberlain [1640], STC 4946 (1640)

Swetnam the Woman Hater Arraigned by Women [1618], STC 23544 (1620: TFT 1914)

The Swisser, Arthur Wilson [1631], ed. Linda V. Itzoe (New York and London, 1984)

A Tale of a Tub [1633]: *Ben Jonson*, III: 1–92

1 Tamar Cham [1596, plot]: Greg, *Dramatic Documents*, II: no. VII

1 Tamburlaine [1587]: Marlowe, *Works*, 1–70

2 Tamburlaine [1588]: Marlowe, *Works*, 73–138

The Taming of a Shrew [1592], STC 23667 (1594: TFT 1912)

The Taming of the Shrew [1592]: First Folio, 226–47

The Telltale [1639], ed. R. A. Foakes and J. C. Gibson (MSR 1960)

The Tempest [1611]: First Folio, 19–37

Thierry and Theodoret [Fletcher and Philip Massinger, 1617]: Beaumont and Fletcher, *Works*, X: 1–70

Thomas Lord Cromwell, W. S. [1600], STC 21532 (1602: TFT 1911)

The Thracian Wonder [1599], Wing T 1078A (1661)

The Three Ladies of London, Robert Wilson [1581], STC 25784 (1584: TFT 1911)

The Three Lords and Three Ladies of London, Robert Wilson [1588], STC 25783 (1590: TFT 1912)

Timon of Athens [1607]: First Folio, 694–715

'Tis Pity She's a Whore, John Ford [1632], ed. Derek Roper (Revels 1975)

Titus Andronicus [1594]: Quartos, 3–42; First Folio, 647–68

Tom a Lincoln [1615], ed. G. R. Proudfoot (MSR 1992)

Tottenham Court [1634]: Nabbes, *Works*, I: 93–184

The Tragedy of Byron [1608], see *The Conspiracy and Tragedy of Charles, Duke of Byron*

The Traitor, James Shirley [1631], ed. John Stewart Carter (RRD 1965)

The Travels of the Three English Brothers [Day, William Rowley, and George Wilkins, 1607]: Day, *Works*, no. 6

The Trial of Chivalry [1601], STC 13527 (1605: TFT 1912)

A Trick to Catch the Old One, Thomas Middleton [1605], STC 17896 (1608: Scolar Press facsimile 1970)

Troilus and Cressida, Henry Chettle and Thomas Dekker [1599, plot]: Greg, *Dramatic Documents*, II: no. V

Troilus and Cressida (F1) [1602]: First Folio, 587–615
(Q1): Quartos, 704–50

1, 2 The Troublesome Reign of King John [1591], STC 14644 (1591: TFT 1911, 2 vols.)

The True Tragedy of Richard III [1591], ed. W. W. Greg (MSR 1929)

The Turk, John Mason [1607], ed. Joseph Q. Adams, Jr. (Materialien 1913)

Twelfth Night [1601]: First Folio, 273–93

The Twins, William Rider [1635], Wing R 1446 (1655)

1 The Two Angry Women of Abingdon, Henry Porter [1598], ed. W. W. Greg (MSR 1912)

The Two Gentlemen of Verona [1593]: First Folio, 38–56

Two Lamentable Tragedies, Robert Yarington [1594], STC 26076 (1601: TFT 1913)

The Two Maids of More-Clacke [1606], STC 773 (1609: TFT 1913); Armin, Works, II: no. 2

The Two Merry Milkmaids, J. C. [1619], STC 4281 (1620: TFT 1914)
[manuscript annotations], see Leslie Thomson, "A Quarto 'Marked for Performance': Evidence of What?" *Medieval and Renaissance Drama in England* 8 (1996): 176–210

The Two Noble Kinsmen, John Fletcher and William Shakespeare [1613]: Quartos, 836–81

The Two Noble Ladies [1622], ed. Rebecca G. Rhoads (MSR 1930)

The Unfortunate Lovers [1638]: Davenant, *Works*, III: 1–90
The Unfortunate Mother [1639]: Nabbes, *Works*, I: 83–157
The Unnatural Combat [1624]: Massinger, *Plays*, II: 181–272

Valentinian [Fletcher, 1614]: Beaumont and Fletcher, *Works*, IV: 1–92
The Valiant Scot, J. W. [1626], STC 24910 (1637)
The Valiant Welshman [1612], STC 16 (1615: TFT 1913); Armin, *Works*, II: no. 3
The Variety, William Cavendish [1641], Wing N 877 (1649), ²A1r–E8r
A Very Woman [1634]: Massinger, *Plays*, IV: 201–89
The Virgin Martyr [Dekker and Philip Massinger, 1620]: Dekker, *Works*, III: 365–480
Volpone [1606]: *Ben Jonson*, V: 1–137
The Vow Breaker, William Sampson [1625], ed. Hans Wallrath (Materialien 1914)

Wallenstein [1634], see *Albertus Wallenstein*
A Warning for Fair Women [Thomas Heywood? 1599], STC 25089 (1599: TFT 1912)
The Wars of Cyrus [1588], STC 6160 (1594: TFT 1911)
The Wasp [1638], ed. J. W. Lever (MSR 1976)
The Weakest Goeth to the Wall [1600], ed. W. W. Greg (MSR 1912)
The Wedding, James Shirley [1626], STC 22460 (1629)
The Weeding of the Covent Garden [1632]: Brome, *Works*, II: no. 3
The Welsh Ambassador, Thomas Dekker and John Ford [1623], ed. H. Littledale and W. W. Greg (MSR 1920)
Westward Ho [Dekker and John Webster, 1604]: Dekker, *Works*, II: 311–403
What You Will, John Marston [1601], STC 17487 (1607)
When You See Me You Know Me, Samuel Rowley [1604], ed. F. P. Wilson (MSR 1952)
The White Devil, John Webster [1612], ed. John Russell Brown (Revels 1960)
The Whore of Babylon [1606]: Dekker, *Works*, II: 491–592
The Widow, Thomas Middleton [1616], Wing J 1015 (1652)
The Widow's Tears [1604], ed. Robert Ornstein: Chapman, *Comedies*, 473–556
A Wife for a Month [Fletcher, 1624]: Beaumont and Fletcher, *Works*, V: 1–73
The Wild Goose Chase [Fletcher, 1621]: Beaumont and Fletcher, *Works*, IV: 314–90
Wily Beguiled [Samuel Rowley? 1602], ed. W. W. Greg (MSR 1912)
The Winter's Tale [1610]: First Folio, 295–321
The Wisdom of Doctor Dodypoll [1600], ed. M. N. Matson (MSR 1965)
The Wise Woman of Hogsdon [1604]: Heywood, *Works*, V: 275–354
Wit at Several Weapons [Thomas Middleton and William Rowley, 1613]: Beaumont and Fletcher, *Works*, IX: 66–142
Wit in a Constable [1638]: Glapthorne, *Plays*, I: 159–241
The Wit of a Woman [1604], ed. W. W. Greg (MSR 1913)

Wit without Money [Fletcher, 1614]: Beaumont and Fletcher, *Works*, II: 146–207

The Witch, Thomas Middleton [1613], ed. W. W. Greg and F. P. Wilson (MSR 1950)

The Witch of Edmonton [1621]: Dekker, *Works*, III: 481–568

The Wits [1634]: Davenant, *Works*, II: 107–244

The Witty Fair One, James Shirley [1628], STC 22462 (1633)

The Wizard, Simon Baylie [1638], ed. Henry de Vocht (Materials 1930)

The Woman Hater [Beaumont, 1606]: Beaumont and Fletcher, *Works*, X: 71–142

The Woman in the Moon, John Lyly [1593], STC 17090 (1597)

A Woman Is a Weathercock [1609]: Field, *Plays*, 55–139

A Woman Killed with Kindness [1603]: Heywood, *Works*, II: 89–158

The Woman's Prize [Fletcher, 1611]: Beaumont and Fletcher, *Works*, VIII: 1–90 [manuscript]: Folger Shakespeare Library, MS J. b. 3

Women Beware Women, Thomas Middleton [1621], ed. J. R. Mulryne (Revels 1975)

Women Pleased [Fletcher, 1620]: Beaumont and Fletcher, *Works*, VII: 237–310

The Wonder of a Kingdom [1631]: Dekker, *Works*, III: 569–649

Woodstock [1592], see *1 Richard II, or Thomas of Woodstock*

The World Tossed at Tennis, Thomas Middleton and William Rowley [1620], STC 17909 (1620)

The Wounds of Civil War, Thomas Lodge [1588], ed. J. Dover Wilson (MSR 1910)

A Yorkshire Tragedy [Thomas Middleton? 1606], ed. Sylvia D. Feldman (MSR 1973)

The Young Admiral, James Shirley [1633], STC 22463 (1637)

Your Five Gallants, Thomas Middleton [1607], STC 17907 (1608)

Select bibliography

Annals of English Drama 975–1700. Alfred Harbage, rev. S. Schoenbaum. 3rd edition rev. Sylvia Stoler Wagonheim. London, 1989.

Astington, John H. "Descent Machinery in the Playhouses." *Medieval and Renaissance Drama in England* 2 (1985): 119–33.

"Gallows Scenes on the Elizabethan Stage." *Theatre Notebook* 37 (1983): 3–9.

"Malvolio and the Dark House." *Shakespeare Survey* 41 (1988): 55–62.

Baskervill, C. R. *The Elizabethan Jig and Related Song Drama*. Chicago, 1929.

Beckerman, Bernard. *Shakespeare at the Globe, 1599–1609*. New York, 1962.

"Theatrical Plots and Elizabethan Stage Practice." In *Shakespeare and Dramatic Tradition: Essays in Honor of S. F. Johnson*, ed. W. R. Elton and William B. Long, 109–24. Newark, Delaware, 1989.

"The Use and Management of the Elizabethan Stage." In *The Third Globe: Symposium for the Reconstruction of the Globe Playhouse*, ed. C. Walter Hodges, S. Schoenbaum, and Leonard Leone, 151–63. Detroit, 1981.

Bentley, Gerald Eades. *The Profession of Player in Shakespeare's Time, 1590–1642*. Princeton, 1984.

Shakespeare and His Theatre. Lincoln, Nebraska, 1984.

Berger, Thomas L., Sydney L. Sondergard and William C. Bradford, Jr. *An Index of Characters in Early Modern English Drama: Printed Plays, 1500–1660*. Rev. edition. Cambridge, 1998.

Bevington, David. *Action is Eloquence: Shakespeare's Language of Gesture*. Cambridge, Massachusetts, 1984.

Bradbrook, Muriel. *Elizabethan Stage Conditions*. Cambridge, 1932.

Themes and Conventions of Elizabethan Tragedy. Cambridge, 1935.

Bradley, David. *From Text to Performance in the Elizabethan Theatre: Preparing the Play for the Stage*. Cambridge, 1992.

Brissenden, Alan. *Shakespeare and the Dance*. Atlantic Heights, New Jersey, 1981.

Carson, Neil. *A Companion to Henslowe's Diary*. Cambridge, 1988.

Coghill, Nevill. *Shakespeare's Professional Skills*. Cambridge, 1964.

Cook, Ann Jennalie. *The Privileged Playgoers of Shakespeare's London, 1576–1642*. Princeton, 1981.

Cowling, G. H. *Music on the Shakespearian Stage*. Cambridge, 1913.

Craik, T. W. "The Reconstruction of Stage Action from Early Dramatic Texts." In *The Elizabethan Theatre V*, ed. G. R. Hibbard, 76–91. Hamden, Connecticut, 1975.

Dessen, Alan C. *Elizabethan Drama and the Viewer's Eye*. Chapel Hill, 1977.

Elizabethan Stage Conventions and Modern Interpreters. Cambridge, 1984.

Recovering Shakespeare's Theatrical Vocabulary. Cambridge, 1995.

Diehl, Huston. "The Iconography of Violence in English Renaissance Tragedy." *Renaissance Drama* 11 (1980): 27–44.

Edelman, Charles. *Brawl Ridiculous: Swordfighting in Shakespeare's Plays.* Manchester, 1992.

Fleischer, Martha Hester. *The Iconography of the English History Play.* Salzburg, 1974.

Foakes, R. A. *Illustrations of the English Stage 1580–1642.* Stanford, 1985.

Galpin, Francis, W. *Old English Instruments of Music.* 4th edition, rev. with supplementary notes by Thurston Dart. London, 1965.

Graves, R. B. "*The Duchess of Malfi* at the Globe and Blackfriars." *Renaissance Drama* 9 (1978): 193–209.

"Elizabethan Lighting Effects and the Conventions of Indoor and Outdoor Theatrical Illumination." *Renaissance Drama* 12 (1981): 51–69.

"Shakespeare's Outdoor Stage Lighting." *Shakespeare Studies* 13 (1980): 235–50.

Greg, W. W. *Dramatic Documents from the Elizabethan Playhouses.* 2 vols. Oxford, 1931.

Gurr, Andrew. *Playgoing in Shakespeare's London.* Cambridge, 1987.

The Shakespearean Stage 1574–1642. 3rd edition. Cambridge, 1991.

"The 'State' of Shakespeare's Audiences." In *Shakespeare and the Sense of Performance: Essays in the Tradition of Performance Criticism*, ed. Marvin and Ruth Thompson, 162–79. Newark, Delaware, 1989.

Habicht, Werner. "Tree Properties and Tree Scenes in Elizabethan Theater." *Renaissance Drama* 4 (1971): 69–92.

Hammond, Antony. "Encounters of the Third Kind in Stage Directions in Elizabethan and Jacobean Drama." *Studies in Philology* 89 (1992): 71–99.

Henslowe's Diary. Ed. R. A. Foakes and R. T. Rickert. Cambridge, 1961.

Honigmann, E. A. J. "Re-Enter the Stage Direction: Shakespeare and Some Contemporaries." *Shakespeare Survey* 29 (1976): 117–25.

Hapgood, Robert. *Shakespeare's Theatre Poetry.* Oxford, 1988.

Hosley, Richard. "The Discovery-Space in Shakespeare's Globe." *Shakespeare Survey* 12 (1959): 35–46.

"The Gallery Over the Stage in the Public Playhouse of Shakespeare's Time." *Shakespeare Quarterly* 8 (1957): 15–31.

"The Playhouses." In *The Revels History of Drama in English: Volume III, 1576–1613*, ed. J. Leeds Barroll, Alexander Leggatt, Richard Hosley, and Alvin Kernan, 121–235. London, 1975.

"Shakespearian Stage Curtains: Then and Now." *College English* 25 (1964): 488–92.

"The Staging of Desdemona's Bed." *Shakespeare Quarterly* 14 (1963): 57–65.

"Was There a Music-Room in Shakespeare's Globe?" *Shakespeare Survey* 13 (1960): 113–23.

Howard, Jean E. *Shakespeare's Art of Orchestration: Stage Technique and Audience Response.* Urbana, 1984.

Hunter, G. K. "Flatcaps and Bluecoats: Visual Signals on the Elizabethan Stage." *Essays and Studies* 33 (1980): 16–47.

Jorgensen, Paul A. *Shakespeare's Military World*. Berkeley and Los Angeles, 1956.

Jowett, John. "New Created Creatures: Ralph Crane and the Stage Directions in *The Tempest*." *Shakespeare Survey* 36 (1983): 107–20.

King, T. J. *Shakespearean Staging, 1599–1642*. Cambridge, Massachusetts, 1971.

Lawrence, William J. *The Elizabethan Playhouse and other Studies*. Stratford-upon-Avon, 1912.

   Pre-Restoration Stage Studies. Cambridge, Massachusetts, 1927.

   Those Nut-Cracking Elizabethans: Studies of the Early Theatre and Drama. London, 1935.

Linthicum, M. Channing. *Costume in the Drama of Shakespeare and His Contemporaries*. Oxford, 1936.

Long, John H. *Shakespeare's Use of Music*. 3 vols. Gainsville, 1955–71.

Long, William B. "'A bed / for woodstock': a Warning for the Unwary." *Medieval and Renaissance Drama in England* 2 (1985): 91–118.

   "*John a Kent and John a Cumber*: an Elizabethan Playbook and Its Implications." In *Shakespeare and Dramatic Tradition: Essays in Honor of S. F. Johnson*, ed. W. R. Elton and William B. Long, 125–43. Newark, Delaware, 1989.

   "Stage Directions: a Misinterpreted Factor in Determining Textual Provenance." *Text* 2 (1985): 121–37.

MacIntyre, Jean. "Conventions of Costume Change in Elizabethan Plays." *Explorations in Renaissance Culture* 12 (1986): 105–14.

   Costumes and Scripts in the Elizabethan Theatres. Edmonton, 1992.

   "Shakespeare and the Battlefield." *Theatre Survey* 23 (1982): 31–44.

McGuire, Philip C. *Speechless Dialect: Shakespeare's Open Silences*. Berkeley, 1985.

McMillin, Scott. *The Elizabethan Theatre and "The Book of Sir Thomas More."* Ithaca and London, 1987.

   "The Rose and the Swan." In *The Development of Shakespeare's Theater*, ed. John H. Astington, 159–83. New York, 1992.

Manifold, J. S. *The Music in English Drama*. London, 1956.

Mehl, Dieter. *The Elizabethan Dumb Show*. Cambridge, Massachusetts, 1966.

Mitchell, Lee. "Shakespeare's Lighting Effects." *Speech Monographs* 15 (1948): 72–84.

Moore, John Robert. "Theater Songs at Shakespeare's Time." *The Journal of English and Germanic Philology* 28 (1929): 166–202.

Morsberger, Robert E. *Swordplay and the Elizabethan and Jacobean Stage*. Salzburg, 1974.

New Issues in the Reconstruction of Shakespeare's Theatre. Ed. Frank J. Hildy. New York, 1990.

Newton, Stella Mary. *Renaissance Theatre Costume and the Sense of the Heroic Past*. London, 1975.

Nicoll, Allardyce. " 'Passing Over the Stage'." *Shakespeare Survey* 12 (1959): 47–55.

Powell, Jocelyn. "Marlowe's Spectacle." *Tulane Drama Review* 8 (1964): 195–210.

Reynolds, G. F. *The Staging of Elizabethan Plays at the Red Bull Theater, 1605–25.* New York, 1940.

Rhodes, Ernest. *Henslowe's Rose: The Stage and Staging.* Lexington, Kentucky, 1976.

Rowan, D. F. "The Staging of the *Spanish Tragedy*." In *The Elizabethan Theatre V*, ed. G. R. Hibbard, 112–23. Hamden, Connecticut, 1975.

Saunders, J. W. "Staging at the Globe, 1599–1613." *Shakespeare Quarterly* 11 (1960): 401–25.

"Vaulting the Rails." *Shakespeare Survey* 7 (1954): 69–81.

Shapiro, Michael. "Annotated Bibliography on Original Staging in Shakespeare's Plays." *Research Opportunities in Renaissance Drama* 24 (1981): 23–49.

Shirley, Frances Ann. *Shakespeare's Use of Off-Stage Sounds.* Lincoln, Nebraska, 1963.

Slater, Ann Pasternak. *Shakespeare the Director.* Brighton, 1982.

Smith, Hal H. "Some Principles of Elizabethan Stage Costume." *Journal of the Warburg and Courtald Institutes* 25 (1962): 240–57.

Southern, Richard. *The Staging of Plays before Shakespeare.* London, 1973.

Sternfeld, F. W. *Music in Shakespearean Tragedy.* London, 1963.

Styan, J. L. *Shakespeare's Stagecraft.* Cambridge, 1967.

Taylor, Gary. "General Introduction." In *William Shakespeare: A Textual Companion*, ed. Stanley Wells and Gary Taylor, 1–68. Oxford, 1987.

Teague, Frances. *Shakespeare's Speaking Properties.* Lewisburg, 1991.

Thomson, Leslie. "*Antony and Cleopatra*, Act 4 Scene 16: 'A Heavy Sight'." *Shakespeare Survey* 41 (1988): 77–90.

"Broken Brackets and 'Mended Texts: Stage Directions in the Oxford Shakespeare." *Renaissance Drama* 19 (1988): 175–93.

"*Enter Above*: the Staging of *Women Beware Women*." *Studies in English Literature* 26 (1986): 331–43.

" 'On ye walls': the Staging of *Hengist, King of Kent*, V.ii." *Medieval and Renaissance Drama in England* 3 (1986): 165–76.

"A Quarto 'Marked for Performance': Evidence of What?" *Medieval and Renaissance Drama in England* 8 (1996): 176–210.

"Window Scenes in Renaissance Plays: a Survey and Some Conclusions." *Medieval and Renaissance Drama in England* 5 (1990): 225–43.

Thomson, Peter. *Shakespeare's Theatre.* London, 1983.

Ward, John M. "Points of Departure." *Harvard Library Bulletin* new series 2 (1991): 9–16.

Wickham, Glynne. *Early English Stages 1300–1660.* Vol. 2. *1576 to 1660.* 2 parts. New York, 1963–72.

" 'Heavens,' Machinery, and Pillars in the Theatre and Other Early

Playhouses." In *The First Public Playhouse: The Theatre in Shoreditch, 1576–1598*, ed. Herbert Berry, 1–15. Montreal, 1979.

Shakespeare's Dramatic Heritage. New York, 1969.

Wright, Peter M. "Jonson's Revision of the Stage Directions for the 1616 Folio *Workes*." *Medieval and Renaissance Drama in England* 5 (1991): 257–85.

Zitner, S. P. "Four Feet in the Grave: Some Stage Directions in *Hamlet*, V.1." *Text* 2 (1985): 139–48.